THE MONGO MYSTERIES

The Beasts of Valhalla

COMING SOON FROM DELL

An Affair of Sorcerers
City of Whispering Stone
Shadow of a Broken Man
Two Songs This Archangel Sings

The Beasts of Valhalla

George C. Chesbro

A DELL BOOK

Published by
Dell Publishing Co., Inc.
1 Dag Hammarskjold Plaza
New York, New York 10017

Dell ® TM 681510, Dell Publishing Co., Inc.

ISBN: 0-440-10484-X

Reprinted by arrangement with Atheneum Publishers, a division of Macmillan Publishing Company

Printed in the United States of America

November 1987

10 9 8 7 6 5 4 3 2 1

KRI

The Beasts of Valhalla

BOOK I

Game of Beasts

An August Sunday, so hot you couldn't tell sweat from tears. It was an expensive funeral, costing more than I suspected my sister and her husband could easily afford, in a bargain basement family plot inside a rummage sale cemetery. Somebody had sold my sister the Deluxe Package, silk-lined mahogany casket and an acre or two of flowers that served only to magnify the decrepitude of the small village cemetery. The rusting backhoe that had dug and would refill the grave was visible a hundred yards away, parked beside a rotting maintenance shack. The backhoe's unshaven operator was sitting in its cab, chewing the stub of yesterday's cigar and reading last month's magazine.

"Amen," the young, fresh-faced minister intoned as he finished a prayer. He sprinkled a handful of dirt over the lowered casket, wiped his hands.

"Shit," Garth murmured. We were standing a few yards apart from the rest of the family—our mother and father, Janet and her husband, assorted cousins, nieces and nephews, uncles and aunts. There were a lot of Fredericksons in Peru County, Nebraska.

"Yeah."

"How are you holding up?"

The sun was directly behind my brother's hand, forming a shimmering penumbra around thinning, wheat-colored hair that waved like a shredded, sad banner in the gentle, hot breeze that blew through this wasteland of weeds and pitted grave markers. "Why ask me? Tommy was your nephew, too."

"You know what I mean. We've been here two days now, and I thought you might be feeling the effects."

"I'm all right."

It wasn't true. Although I loved my parents dearly, wrote regularly, and had, over the years, managed to coax members of my immediate family into visiting me in New York City, home for me represented nothing so much as a long nightmare that had taken a lot of time and shrink money to kick into submission. I hadn't been back to Peru County in seventeen years, and the fragility of the scars remaining on my psyche amazed me. I felt porous, like something filled with stale air that was compacting under pressure of memory so fierce it was threatening to squeeze away and pop my center. Only something like the

death of a favorite nephew could have brought me back to Peru.
I knew it was a silly and unbecoming way to feel in the face of
the awesome peace Tommy Dernhelm had found, but people
preoccupied with questions of self-worth are easily smothered
by the trivial. The *me* that had been constructed and nurtured
far from this place was gasping for breath, desperate for escape.

It was finished. We all gathered around Janet and stood in
silence for a few moments, as though sheer numbers were a
poultice that could absorb some of her pain. Then we started
slowly back along the dusty path leading out of the cemetery.
Unconsciously, like a marionette still controlled by rotten
strings implanted in its soft center a long time ago, I found
myself walking apart from the other members of the family, as
if I were something disgusting that could only add to the shame
surrounding Tommy's death. Garth, as he had always done,
walked with me.

Growing up a dwarf is a real pain in the mind; you're always
a foot or two, and a lot of poundage, behind the inevitable
tormenters. Also, in fairness to the fun group that had tossed
me around like a medicine ball in an alley behind the local
movie theater one night, I wasn't exactly the mellowest kid in
the neighborhood; I'd never suffered anybody, much less loud-
mouthed fools, gladly. My brain had always been quick enough,
and I'd been able to out-insult any gang of ten in the school.
The problem, as I'd quickly learned, was that a sharp tongue
was no defense against a punch in the mouth. The fact that
Garth always thumped on the people who thumped on me
wasn't enough. I hadn't needed an avatar so much as I'd needed
to find my own means of self-defense and feelings of self-worth
in a world of bigger things and bigger people where I'd always
felt in imminent danger of being crushed, physically and spiritually.

The love of my family, combined with Garth's muscle, had
carried me through childhood and adolescence; I'd known that
I was going to have to make it as a whole, if undersized, adult
on my own.

I'd escaped from Peru County by means of an academic
scholarship to New York University. In New York, a state of
mind as well as a geographical location where just about all
things great and small would be considered freaky by Peru

County standards, I'd immediately felt at home, and had begun to escape from the terrible, debilitating preoccupation with my dwarfism. I'd majored in criminology, probably out of a perverse fascination with freaks of a different dimension, graduated with honors, an invitation to graduate school, and the offer of a post as a research assistant.

I'd succeeded in school—but then, I'd always succeeded in school. I had other, more pressing, hungers—other things to prove. Nature, in her infinite irony, had made me a dwarf, but with maturation I discovered that I had also been endowed with considerable, if improbable, physical skills—excellent reflexes, coordination, and speed. Being a somewhat unusual dwarf—a redundancy, if ever there was one—in need of a means of livelihood, I pursued the only logical course of action: I joined the circus, in this case one owned by a gentleman named Phil Statler—the ugliest and kindest human being I've ever known.

With the exception of my parents and Garth, Statler would become the most nurturing influence in my life. He'd seen in me possibilities as a performer that no one else, most particularly me, would ever have thought of. I'd eventually become a star attraction with the Statler Brothers Circus, a headliner as a kind of funky gymnast and aerialist bouncing and flying his way through a succession of visually spectacular stunts involving fire and ice.

I parlayed my developing physical skills into a black belt in karate, and used the money I earned to finance my doctorate in criminology. With my advanced degree in hand, I retired from the circus and took up a post as an associate professor at NYU.

By this time Garth had joined me in the city, where his own considerable talents had led to his rapid advancement in the NYPD. As for me, I'd left the circus when I was on top and was settling into a career in academia . . . and I still wanted more. I wasn't certain what I wanted more of, but it seemed I needed constantly to test myself against new challenges. Garth called it overcompensation, and I couldn't argue with him.

I acquired a private investigator's license, well aware that no sane person was likely to hire a dwarf as a private detective and that I'd probably never earn a penny in this particular corner of the marketplace. Surprise. I didn't get a lot of business, but the business I did get was certainly challenging; like some kind of ·

bent, psychic lightning rod, I seemed to attract only the most bizarre cases. No matter how simple or straightforward an investigation might appear at the beginning, it almost inevitably ended up with people shooting at me, or worse. By now I'd achieved a certain degree of notoriety, a state of celebrity which NYU looked upon with distinct disapproval. However, I was still teaching—and I was still investigating, whenever a case came my way. The dual careers had kept me busy, reasonably satisfied, and reasonably happy.

Until now.

Now it was all escaping from me. All my successes, my very sense of self, was imploding under the pressure of memory. I was losing my center, feeling like a frightened, angry defiant— and worthless—dwarf child again.

My brother grunted softly, a kind of warning. I looked up from the ground and saw the gaunt figure standing on the hillside, partially eclipsing the sun. His features were blacked out, but the shape of the boy had grown into the shape of the man. I would have known him anywhere.

"Coop Lugmor." The name in my mouth tasted like sickness. "The man's got a great sense of timing. I wonder what the hell he wants here?"

"I'm afraid we're about to find out."

Lugmor was over six feet, almost as tall as my brother. He was lanky, with arms too long for his torso and hands too small for his arms. His greasy black hair was long for Nebraska, and hung in strings around his long, pinched face. The smell of rotgut whiskey hovered about him like poison gas. I could feel tension spring from the group behind me, almost as palpable as a prod in the back.

Lugmor nodded sheepishly in the direction of my family, then fell into step beside me. His eyes darted nervously, slyly, all around, as if searching for hidden enemies, but never quite met my gaze. "Hello, Robby. Garth."

Garth and I said nothing.

"I sure am awful sorry about what happened."

We kept walking.

"Robby, can I talk to you?"

"Call my office for an appointment the next time you're in New York, Coop. My number's in the Manhattan directory."

A hand jerked into the air like a broken bird; grimy fingers with black nails gripped my shoulder. "Robby, I *gotta* talk to you!"

Lugmor's hand on my shoulder had much the same effect as a steep shot of liquor on an empty stomach; heat flashed across my face. I had a sudden, immensely gratifying vision of the man writhing on the ground with a broken kneecap. Then I remembered my mother and father walking behind me, my sister and brother-in-law with their grief, Tommy's corpse in the ground. I said quietly: "If you don't take your hand off me, Coop, I'll break something in you."

Lugmore laughed nervously and quickly snatched his hand away. "From what I hear tell about you, I actually think you could."

"Believe it," Garth said evenly.

"Robby? Please?"

He wasn't going to leave, and the palpable force of discomfort pushing on my back was growing stronger; I decided that the least I could do was remove Coop Lugmor from the immediate vicinity. I nodded toward a nearby copse of ragged fir trees and stepped off the path.

"Mongo . . . ?"

"It's all right, Garth, I'll handle it."

"I'll wait for you in the car," Garth replied as he slowed his pace in order to walk with the rest of the family.

"They really do call you 'Mongo,' " Lugmor said nervously as we reached the chiaroscuro shade of the trees. "Just like it says in the papers and newsmagazines."

"Some of my friends call me that," I said pointedly. "Not you."

Lugmor slipped his hands into the torn pockets of his baggy overalls and looked down at the tops of his stained rubber boots. "You're still mad at me even after all these years, aren't you, Robby?"

"For heaven's sake, Coop, whatever gave you that impression?"

He winced as if my words had been a physical blow, stared at me with brown, bloodshot eyes. "We were just kids, Robby, and you were the only dwarf anyone around here had ever seen outside the county fair freak show."

My first instinct was to hit him, my second to laugh. I laughed. Coop Lugmor, one of the two great monsters caged in my memory, was beginning to seem a very small and pathetic beastie indeed. It made me wonder how much I had distorted all the other memories; it occurred to me that, if I stayed around Peru County long enough, I might find all the monsters rolling belly-up in the surf like Lugmor, and I would go back to New York a paragon of mental health. "You always had such a way with words, Coop," I said evenly.

"I'm trying to say I'm sorry."

"Why don't you try saying why you want to talk to me?"

Lugmor slowly drew his hands out of his overalls. He balled one hand into a fist, punched his opposite palm. "Your nephew and my little brother weren't having any fag love affair, Robby, and they didn't have any suicide agreement."

"How do you know?"

Lugmor stared hard at me, frowned. "Because Rod wasn't a fag."

"Tommy was?"

"I don't know, Robby," Lugmor said evasively. "I'm not accusing Tommy of anything; I'm just saying Rod wasn't a fag."

"Coop," I sighed, suddenly very tired and very sad, "what difference does it make?"

He flushed, thrust out his lower lip. "It makes a *difference!*"

"They're dead, Coop. How they felt about, and what they did with, each other isn't important."

Lugmor shook his head like a dog trying to rid itself of fleas. "Don't you *care* that people are saying they were fags and that they had a suicide agreement?"

"No."

"Well, *I* do! Rod was my *brother!*"

"That's your problem."

He smacked his lips in frustration, worked his mouth about, finally forced some words out. "Robby, I'm telling you Rod wasn't a fag; if he wasn't a fag, then he and Tommy weren't having a love affair; if they weren't having a love affair, then Rod didn't shoot Tommy and then kill himself."

"The county sheriff and coroner say he did."

Lugmor hawked and spat; that made me wince. "The coroner ain't no doctor, and he's a bigger drunk than me. Jake Bolesh may be county sheriff, but he's on the take. He does and says whatever that big Goddamn company wants him to."

"I thought Jake Bolesh was a friend of yours. I seem to remember the two of you as being inseparable, especially when you were beating up on me."

"He's no friend of mind anymore, Robby. I tell you he's lying!"

"As far as I know, nobody else thinks so."

"Horseshit! What does anyone around here know?! They're a bunch of farmers who'll believe anything a guy with a badge and a uniform tells them to! This ain't New York City, Robby. We don't have many murders around these parts."

"Or homosexuals?"

"Everybody just wants to forget about it as quick as possible, Robby! They want to forget it for personal reasons, and they want to forget it because the company wants them to! Nobody *cares!*"

"There were letters."

"Phony letters! That was a lot of crap they printed in the newspapers. Those letters were typed, and there were no signatures!"

"They were typed on your brother's typewriter."

"No!" It was an anguished howl.

"Coop, you think somebody else killed them?"

"Yes!"

"Who would want to kill two fourteen-year-old boys?"

He shrugged, shuffled his feet.

"Why would anyone want to kill them?"

Another shrug, and then he mumbled something I couldn't quite catch. I asked him to repeat it.

Lugmor swallowed hard. "I said, that's what I'd like you to find out."

"Me?"

"Yeah!" Now his words came quickly, bumping into each other. "There's always a lot about you in the local newspaper, Robby. You may not be interested in us, but we're sure as hell interested in you; you're the hometown boy made good. I know all about you being an important college professor who's some kind of doctor, and I know all about you being a private detective. I want to hire you. I don't have much money right now, but—"

"To do what?"

"To find out the *truth!*"

"As far as I can see, you're the only person who doesn't believe we already know the truth. Let me tell you something straight, Coop; I loved my nephew very much, but he was nuttier than one of Jesse Braxton's fruitcakes. Sometimes that goes with the territory when you're a very bright kid. Maybe he would have grown out of it, maybe not; we'll never know. My sister accepts the fact that Tommy and most of his friends were a little crazy. Why can't you?"

"Because Rod was no fag!"

"Oh," I said quietly. "Coop, you know how muddled a dwarf can get, so let's see if I have a line on where you're coming from. You'd like me to root around, keep the dust and *my* family unsettled, and probably end up looking like the village idiot you always thought I was, on the off chance I might be able to prove that someone in *your* family wasn't a homosexual. Have I got it?"

"Robby, I—"

"I thought so," I said, starting to walk away.

"Robby, please! Wait a second!"

Wheeling around, I placed my stiffened index and middle fingers squarely over the center of Coop Lugmor's solar plexus, pressed slightly. "Stay!" I snapped, and he did.

2.

We finished the lunch my mother had insisted on making. My parents, Garth, Janet, and I sat in silence at the table, staring into our empty coffee cups. Sparkling motes of dust floated in beams of golden sunlight, and the muffled laughter of a horde of young nieces and nephews could be heard outside in the yard. John Dernhelm, Janet's husband, emerged from the kitchen, wiped his eyes, then went out the door. Two burly uncles sat in a corner of the adjacent living room, talking in low voices, discussing weather and corn prices. Their wives sat at opposite ends of a worn sofa, crocheting.

My father disappeared for a few moments, then returned with a jug of corn liquor, surprising me, since I had never seen him or my mother drink so much as a glass of wine. He poured small glasses half full for everyone. My second surprise came when I drank the potion and came to an instant, complete understanding of why such stuff is called white lightning. My father offered me a second helping, and I covered my glass with a hand that already felt numb.

"To everything there is a season," my mother said softly, daintily touching a linen napkin to her thin, trembling lips.

"Amen," my father added in a voice that rumbled out of his chest like distant thunder but was also, always, gentle.

"To everything there is a season," Janet repeated in a small voice. "This, too, shall pass."

It meant that a kind of unofficial mourning period had passed, following Tommy into the ground. Now we could speak of other things. Farmers don't have a lot of time for things like grief or self-pity; there are always animals to be cared for, crops to be tended. Fences to be mended.

"I would like to say something," my mother said in a voice so low it could barely be heard. She paused, pushed back a stray, gossamer strand of silver hair with a frail, liver-spotted hand. She turned, looked at me with her faded, violet eyes, and a smile wreathed her face. She reached across Garth and took my hand in hers. "It's so good to have Garth and Robby with us. I'm sorry it has to be such a sad occasion that brings you here, Robby, but it's wonderful to have you home after so many, many years."

"I'm sorry, Mom," I mumbled at the tablecloth.

"Your mother wasn't looking for an apology, son," my father said. "All of us understand. Nobody's ever written more letters than you, and you've brought us to New York many times. She's just saying that we love you, and we're very proud of you."

Garth, sensing that I was close to tears, came to my rescue. "Poor Mongo's just a social cripple," he said, somberly shaking his head and winking at Janet.

"Stop that, Garth!" my mother said, whacking my brother on

a broad shoulder. "And what is this 'Mongo' business? Robby is Robby. You, of all people, shouldn't talk like that about your brother. You love him more than anybody, if that's possible."

That embarrassed everyone but my mother, and for a few moments we lapsed back into awkward silence. It was Janet who finally spoke. Her voice was low, quavering.

"Robby? What did Coop Lugmor want?"

Garth and I exchanged glances. I looked down at the table, shrugged. "Nothing. He was just drunk and feeling sorry for himself."

Janet sat trembling for a few seconds, then stifled a sob as she abruptly rose and rushed into a small sewing room. I went after her, closed the door. I sat down beside her on the small sofa, took her hands away from her face and kissed them. Gradually she stopped sobbing.

"Thank you for coming, Robby."

"Please don't thank me, Janet."

"I know how it hurts you. You haven't been here in seventeen years."

"It hasn't been as bad as I thought it would be."

"Still."

"Tommy was very special to me. You know that."

Janet nodded. Tears welled again in her eyes, but she didn't sob. "And you were certainly special to him." She pressed my hand to her wet cheek. Long, fine hair the texture and color of corn silk fell across my wrist. "We've never been close, Robby, have we?"

"I feel close to you now."

"It was my fault. I was a snot-nosed kid, and as lousy a sister as Garth was good a brother. You embarrassed me, Robby."

"That's all right—I embarrassed me, too." She glanced at me quickly, her face clenched in hurt. Janet wasn't used to my brand of humor. I smiled, added: "What's past is past, Janet."

She leaned forward and kissed me on the lips. "What I just said has been sticking in my throat for a long, long time, Robby. I wanted to get it behind me, and I just did. I love you."

"And I love you."

She kissed me again, then quickly looked away—but not before I had glimpsed something dark, perhaps a question, moving in her eyes. I cleared my throat, said softly: "Lugmor was bellyaching about the way Jake Bolesh handled the investigation. He doesn't think Jake did a very good job, and he doesn't agree with the findings." I paused, touched Janet's wrist. "What do you think?"

It seemed to me that Janet considered her answer very carefully. "I haven't had much time to think about anything but the fact that my son is dead," she said after some time.

"Of course," I sighed, sorry I had brought up the subject.

"Besides," she said with a shudder. "What's to think about? Why *shouldn't* Jake do a good job? They've said such terrible things about Tommy and Rodney. Why would Jake lie about something like that?"

"You'd have to answer that," I said carefully. "I don't live here. *Can* you think of any reason for Jake to lie?"

"Not really."

"Not really?"

"No. It's just that everything happened so *fast*. Tommy disappears for a week, and the next thing you know they find both him and Rodney Lugmor shot to death near the creek on Coop Lugmor's farm. Then they printed that . . . *stuff* . . . in the newspaper, and Jake was giving press conferences. Why would Jake and the reporters say such horrible things if they weren't true?" She covered her face with her hands, but her voice came through clear and bitter. "They couldn't even wait until those boys were in the ground."

I squeezed my sister's hand, but Janet no longer needed my solace; she was angry now, not grief-stricken; in some corner of her mind that wasn't flooded with tears, she *had* obviously been doing a lot of thinking. "Did you ever find out where Tommy had been for that week, or why he'd gone?"

Janet shook her head. "He called me once, just to say he was all right and not to worry. He said there were things he had to sort out in his mind before he made a decision."

"Do you have any idea what he was talking about?"

"No." She got to her feet and began to pace. The starched black material of her dress crackled like flames from a combustible mixture of rage, confusion, and grief. She abruptly stopped pacing and turned to me. I thought she would burst into tears again, but she didn't. "Robby," she said hoarsely, "you know

how to find out about things. Would it be possible for you
. . . ?" Maybe . . . ?"

"Janet, please sit down." She did. I stroked her back, continued: "Let me tell you what a private detective does; he runs up
a big phone bill and he spends a lot of money for good shoes to
walk around in. All the time he's talking to people he knows,
contacts in important places like the police department, Motor
Vehicle, the telephone company, and a dozen different licensing
agencies. Private detectives need friends; if not friends, people
who think they may be paid back someday in bits and pieces of
information. You can move almost anything—certainly nations,
and probably the planet itself—if you have a strong enough
lever of information."

"You really believe that, Robby?"

"I've learned it. I know a secret that nations would sacrifice
tens of thousands of men in order to share."

"What—?"

"What I'm saying is that I don't even have a license to operate here, and if I did it wouldn't be worth the match it would
take to burn it. I don't have any contacts here, Janet, and the
county sheriff isn't exactly an old boyhood chum. Do you understand? In Peru County I was, and always will be, a freak.
When I'm here, I think of *myself* as a freak. I wouldn't exactly
be taken seriously. I think you know I'd do anything for you
and Tommy, but this is a situation where anything I might try
to do would be counter productive. I don't mind these people
laughing at me, but I wouldn't want them laughing at you and
the rest of the family."

"They're already laughing, Robby; snickering behind their
hands. When school starts in September, don't you think it's
going to be hell for the other kids?"

Having nothing to say, I folded my hands in my lap and
stared at them. I felt shriveled inside, but I knew I was right;
the situation was far too delicate and serious to tolerate token
gestures.

"They take you pretty seriously in New York," Janet persisted.

"That's because in New York you can't tell the freaks from
the straights without a very detailed score card."

Janet looked at me for a long time. "Robby, I don't think I like your sense of humor," she said at last.

"You'll get used to it," I said with a smile. "I intend to see a lot more of you after this." I waited for a response. Janet, stony-faced, simply continued to stare at me. "I'll tell you what can be done," I continued quietly. "You have serious questions about the scope of Jake Bolesh's investigation, and that's what I'm gong to tell the State Police. I'm going to find you a good lawyer. He or she will know a competent P.I. who knows the territory and can work here."

Janet slowly, sadly, shook her head. "I can do that myself, and I don't want to bring in strangers until I've had more time to think about it. I have to talk it over with John."

"Of course," I said, feeling like a trapped animal gnawing on its own leg. No matter how hard I chewed, I knew I wasn't going to get free; if I went back to New York, I would just be carrying the trap with me.

"Are you and Garth leaving soon?"

"In an hour or so," I said, glancing at my watch. "We have to catch a six-o'clock flight, and it's a three-hour drive to the airport." Janet said nothing, and it didn't take me too long to realize what I was going to do. "Janet, if you're certain it's what you want, I'll stick around for a few days and see what I can find out."

Janet slowly raised her head. Tears filled her eyes, rolled down her cheeks. She smiled wanly, nodded.

"Mongo, you sure you don't want me to stay?"

I shook my head, leaned back on the car fender, and crossed my arms over my chest. "There's no sense in both of us wasting our time, and I know you're anxious to get back on the Madden case. Besides, Jake Bolesh has your old job. He'll remember me as the dwarf he pounded on, but he'll remember *you* as the dwarf's big brother who pounded on *him*. He's a good man for you to stay away from."

"He's a good man for *you* to stay away from."

"Oh, I don't know," I replied with a shrug. "If Ben's Country Kitchen still caters for the county jail, how bad can the food be?"

"I'm not concerned about Bolesh putting you in jail,

Mongo," Garth said seriously, "I'm worried that you'll kill the son-of-a-bitch if he hassles you. The kid he used to beat up didn't have a black belt in karate."

"Your concern is touching."

"Don't forget, Robby," Garth said, pinching my cheek, "I'm the one who loves you most."

"Kiss my ass, Garth."

My brother laughed. "Very good. I'd say you're in the right frame of mind to do battle."

"You think there's going to be a battle?"

"Not really," Garth said evenly. "If I thought so, I'd stick around. I'm glad you're staying, though. It will make Janet feel better."

"You think Jake handled this properly?"

Garth took some time to consider his answer. "Like it or not, I think you have to give Bolesh the benefit of the doubt. I've been back here a few times, and you haven't. You were born here, but you're a New Yorker through and through; for you, Peru County might as well be a foreign country. These are good people, Mongo. They keep on reelecting Bolesh, so he must be doing something right."

"What about the speed of the investigation?"

Garth shrugged. "Here things like that tend to go the way the county sheriff wants them to. As much as it twists my guts to say so, Bolesh may have been doing the family a favor. It was a messy scene out there, Mongo, and Bolesh had enough sensitivity to keep the news photographers away. Tommy took a shotgun slug through the chest; the Lugmor kid put the barrel in his mouth and pulled the trigger."

"A *shotgun?!*"

"Guns—sometimes even shotguns—are as common with the kids out here as peashooters in New York. The gunstock had Rodney Lugmor's prints all over it, and there were the letters. It looks like the kids had something hot and heavy going, and they couldn't handle it. It had gotten completely out of hand. They were both afraid people were going to find out. At the end they got together to try and figure out what to do, and they decided that the answer was to die together. It's a bitch, Mongo, but it looks like the straight dope."

"You seem to know a hell of a lot."

"I made some phone calls, Mongo. Naturally, I had some questions of my own."

"Thanks for telling me."

"I spent maybe forty-five minutes on the phone yesterday afternoon, talking to people I trust. I didn't have a chance to get you alone, and I couldn't see the sense in stirring up any more emotion by questioning the investigation. I didn't know Janet had doubts."

"Coop Lugmor has doubts."

"Lugmor's a heavy drunk, Mongo, an alcoholic. He's been going downhill for a decade—just not fast enough to finally put himself out of his misery. The guy had nothing to begin with, and now he's gone out of his head worrying about people calling his dead brother queer. Our merry memories aside, I think Bolesh may have simply wanted to get it all out in the open fast so it could be done with."

Annoyed, I pushed off the car and kicked at a clod of dirt. "You knew what Janet and I had talked about earlier. Why didn't you tell *her* you were satisfied with the investigation? It would have put her mind at ease, and I'd be flying my ass out of Peru County."

Garth stared at me for some time before he finally answered. "Janet came to *you* and I think that's significant. It's not going to hurt you to spend a few extra days around here, Mongo. You've got a lot of relatives you haven't seen or spoken to since you were a kid. They're very interested in you, but they're also very sensitive about your feelings. You have to make the first move, show them you're not as crazy or arrogant or whatever as everyone thinks you are."

"Is this what the NYPD calls 'sensitive social management'?"

"Classes at the university don't start for a month, and I know you don't have any big business pending because you've been goofing off for the past three weeks. Spend some time here. Ask some questions, satisfy *yourself* that everything's been done that can be done. *You* put Janet's mind at ease. While you're at it, you'll spend a lot of good time with Mom and Dad and get to know the rest of your family. They're part of you, brother. Fill in your empty spaces."

It should have been time for me to come up with something appropriately sarcastic. Instead, I said: "Okay."

"Anything you want me to do for you when I get back to the city?"

"Yeah. Check with my answering service. If I've got any important calls, touch base for me. Tell them I'll be back in a week."

"Will do." Garth smiled, tapped me on the shoulder with a big, meaty fist. "This is going to be good for you, Mongo. Now I'm going to sit with Mom and Dad for a few minutes."

3.

A quote from Edward Teller was typed on a card taped to the door.

<u>Science is a fable which has been made consistent.</u>

Tommy Dernhelm's "room" was half of a spacious farmhouse basement, and he'd used every inch of it. The walls were papered with fantasy posters and artwork from what looked like every *Lord of the Rings* calendar ever published. There were multiple copies of everything J. R. R. Tolkien had ever written. The three volumes of the *Rings* trilogy and *The Hobbit* stacked next to a Radio Shack TR4100 computer terminal looked worn to a point just this side of dust. Attached to the computer terminal were a display screen, printer, and banks of arcane computer components.

"Expensive hobby," I said.

Janet walked across the room to the computer terminal, caressed the back of the rickety swivel chair sitting in front of it. "He was *so* bright, Robby. He never wanted to spend money on the things other kids do, so John and I wanted to help him get everything he did want. Tommy did little odd jobs for neighbors to earn money, and for the past couple of years we've had extra money from the test plantings. We believed Tommy would be a great scientist one day."

"What 'test plantings'?"

"The Volsung Corporation," Janet replied absently. "It's a

private company that's trying to develop new disease-resistant strains of wheat, sorghum, corn, and soybeans. When they first started building they mailed out a brochure to everyone in the county. explaining what they were doing, but I didn't understand a lot of it. It talked about DNA, gene splicing, enzymes, things like that. They had a name for what they were doing, but I don't recall what it was."

"Agrigenetics?"

"That sounds like it. Anyway, they lease a certain amount of acreage from just about every farmer in the county, and they use the plots for test plantings. I must say they pay very well for the privilege—much more than we would have asked for if they'd asked what we wanted for the land instead of making an offer straight out."

"Interesting. Where is this Volsung Corporation?"

"About twenty miles west of Duck Pond, out on the prairie. Why?"

"Just curious. What did the cops take out of here?"

"Nothing," Janet said, a look of surprise on her face. "They never even looked down here."

If Janet was surprised at the question, I was even more surprised at the answer; it was a little tidbit Garth obviously hadn't picked up during the course of his phone conversations. "You're sure they didn't even *look* down here?"

My sister nodded. Her fair hair, drained of its usual brightness by fatigue and tension, bounced listlessly on her shoulders. "Jake came to tell me the bad news, but he never really asked me any questions." She quickly put a hand to her mouth and stifled a sob. "I suppose he felt he'd found all the answers he needed out at Coop's place."

"Uh-huh."

"Everything here is just the way it was when Tommy ran away. As you can see, he was very good about keeping his room clean, and he didn't like anyone to touch anything. He stored a lot of books and magazines in a shed out back, but I think it would take you a year to go through it all."

A year was a conservative estimate. Three-quarters of the shed was stacked to the ceiling with taped cartons. I opened a couple, found textbooks, magazines, computer journals, some science fiction novels and a lot more fantasy novels and comic books. There were two editions of the fantasy game Dungeons and Dragons, with half a dozen accompanying worn manuals. I thought I could safely presume that anything that might be connected with Tommy's death was back in his room, and we returned there.

John Dernhelm was waiting for us. Janet's husband was in his mid-forties and, like most farmers, in good shape from clean air and hard, clean work. I'd met him for the first time three days before, and it hadn't taken me long to see that we weren't going to find many interests in common. Still, in light of the fact that Janet had seen fit to marry him, I assumed he had something going for him. He was a nice enough fellow, but I had a strong feeling that my dwarfism, combined with Tommy's eerie, incandescent brilliance, had confirmed his suspicion that he'd married into a family with more funny genes that the Volsung Corporation.

He was carrying a large glass tumbler filled to the brim with a delicious-looking amber fluid and lots of ice; Dernhelm was looking better and better to me.

"Janet told me you like Scotch," Dernhelm said with a thin smile, "so I went out and bought some. I meant to offer you a drink before dinner, but I forgot. I thought you might like one now."

"Thanks," I said, reaching for the glass like a drowning man clutching at a life preserver, downing a quick swallow. It was good Scotch, smooth and mellow but with just enough bite to remind you that it wasn't iced tea. My throat was still raw from the firewater my father had given me in the afternoon. I took a second sip, looked at him. He was staring at me with an expression on his face that was very difficult to read. "John, I understand you lease out some land to the Volsung Corporation?"

Dernhelm shot a quick, irritated look at his wife. His dark brown eyes flashed, and some of the color went out of his sunscorched flesh. "I guess that's so, Robby," he said, obviously annoyed. "Just about every farmer in the county leases out acreage. They tell me there are differences in the soil throughout the county, and they like to check every variable."

"Does each farmer tend the crop that's planted on his land?"

Dernhelm's jaw muscles clenched; he was a man who didn't like answering questions, personal or otherwise. "No," he said at last. "We sign a contract that says we won't interfere with the crops in any way. We're not even allowed to look at them. They're all important scientists connected with the place, and I guess they have their own way of doing things."

"Do you mind my asking how much they pay you to lease the land?"

He flushed, jammed his hands into his pockets. "What does this have to do with Tommy's death?"

"Probably nothing," I replied evenly.

"Then I guess I do mind, Robby," he said tightly.

"Okay, John. I didn't mean to pry."

"If you don't mean to pry, how come you ask so many questions about my business?"

I considered telling him what Coop Lugmor had said about Jake Bolesh's financial connection with Volsung, but decided it wasn't the time to repeat what, at the moment, amounted to nothing more than mere gossip from the lips of a frenzied alcoholic—especially when that gossip involved an old enemy I was probably going to have to deal with eventually. "I apologize, John," I said quietly.

Janet came across the room, touched her husband's arm. "John? Robby didn't mean any harm."

But John Dernhelm was worked up. "I've got something I want to get out of my craw," he said through clenched teeth. "Robby, I know you're supposed to be some hot-shot college professor and private detective; I also know that Janet asked you to poke around. I'm opposed to it, and I've told her so. We know what's happened, and it's better to just let it be. Excuse me. I'm going to watch television."

Dernhelm turned and wearily, like a man carrying a very heavy bag of sorrow, trudged back up the steps. Janet and I stood in silence for a few moments, then Janet said: "I'm sorry, Robby. I'll get you any information you need."

"No, don't go against your husband. I can get the information someplace else. And don't be sorry. John's feelings are perfectly understandable. John's not going to be the only member of our family upset if I continue."

Janet thought about it. Shadows of doubt moved in her eyes as she absently chewed at her lower lip. "I wonder if I'm doing the right thing," she said at last. I waited, suddenly finding it difficult to breathe. "What do you think, Robby?"

"From what I've learned in the past hour, I don't think you could characterize this as a lousy investigation—there hasn't *been* an investigation. Tommy and Rodney Lugmor were found early Wednesday morning; this is Sunday, and it's all over. The cops didn't even look through Tommy's things. The *least* they should have done was to question you, and check out what Tommy put on that computer."

Janet uttered a strange, hollow laugh that was at once tinged with bitterness and burnished with pride. "I suspect they'd have had one heck of a time doing that."

"Why?"

"That computer was Tommy's pride and joy. He built a lot of the components himself. In some ways he was very open and childlike, but he was very secretive in other ways. He used the computer for all sorts of things."

"Like maybe keeping a diary in it?"

Janet stared at me hard. "Yes," she breathed. "It's possible. But I don't know how anyone can get at it. Tommy was fascinated with the problem of computer security—and how to break it. I'm pretty sure he encoded everything, and you'd have to know the code to get into the memory banks. Knowing Tommy, that would be some code." She sighed, glanced toward the steps. "Robby, what should I do?"

"You're Tommy's mother, Janet. Also, you have to live with whatever dirt I may dig up or bitterness I may cause. In a few days I'll be back in New York and just an afterthought to these people."

"You can advise me. What would you do if you were me?"

"I'd want to make sure I wasn't haunted for the rest of my life by doubts or unanswered questions," I replied evenly. "No matter what the cost, I'd want to satisfy myself that I knew as much of the truth as there was to know."

"That's what I want."

There were fourteen memory discs stacked neatly in an open-faced file next to the computer terminal, but there was no way I was going to fool with them. I wasn't even going to turn the computer on, for fear of erasing something. However, there were other things to look at.

I worked my way around the room, systematically checking between and inside the well-worn books for stray scraps of paper. Nothing. I sat down in the swivel chair and carefully leafed through the four volumes of J. R. R. Tolkien—*The Hobbit* and *The Lord of the Rings* trilogy: *The Fellowship of the Ring, The Two Towers,* and *The Return of the King*—that had been placed on the table supporting the computer terminal.

The books had been gone through so many times that the pages were falling out. There were what appeared to be thousands of notations in the volumes—underlined passages, margin notes, notes to check certain sections of his diary, and the word *score!* written in heavy block letters in a number of places.

Pushing the books aside, I opened a drawer in the table. There was a blue plastic card with what looked like strips of magnetic tape on both surfaces and which I assumed fit into one of the many slots in the various computer components. I placed the card on top of the stack of books and turned my attention to the scraps of paper in the drawer. The first one I read startled me.

There are monsters in Mirkwood! Unclean!

"Does the term 'Mirkwood' mean anything to you?"

Janet, who had been studying me from across the room, shrugged wearily. "I think it's some evil forest mentioned in one of the Tolkien books."

"I know that. I've read them. Have you?"

She nodded. "Tommy insisted. I can't say I could really get into them; I like some science fiction, but fantasy doesn't much interest me."

"Fantasy certainly fascinated Tommy."

Janet cocked her head to one side, smiled wryly. "Tommy used to go around reciting passages from *Lord of the Rings* by heart. He said it relaxed him."

"Did 'Mirkwood' have any connection for Tommy outside the books?"

She thought about it, finally shook her head. "Not that I know of. Why?"

I showed her the paper. "That phrase—'There are monsters

in Mirkwood!'—was in the last letter he wrote me. I got it about two weeks ago, which means he must have written it just before he ran away. I didn't think anything of it at the time because he was always dropping odd phrases into his letters—usually out of context; he used them to separate paragraphs. Now I'm wondering if 'Mirkwood' meant something else to him."

"I'm sorry, Robby, I just don't know. Tommy's mind could be like a laser one moment, a scattergun the next. He could be thinking of a dozen things at one time."

I stared at the books, the plastic card, the computer terminal and memory discs—all the strange legacy of a tormented fourteen-year-old genius—and wondered what secrets they held, if any.

"Janet?" I asked softly. "Was Tommy a homosexual?"

The question didn't seem to upset her, as I'd feared it might, but she considered it for a long time. "Robby, I don't really know," she said at last. "You know how physically slight Tommy was; he was all brain, certainly undeveloped physically and socially. He didn't have any girl friends, but that was because he was so absorbed in his schoolwork, his computer, and the game. The friends he did have were brains like he was, other students in the extension program for gifted children sponsored by the university. If you'd ask me that question two weeks ago, I'd have said that Tommy was probably asexual at this point in his life. Now . . ." Her voice trailed off.

"What game?"

Janet raised her eyebrows. "They called it Sorscience. Tommy never mentioned it in his letters?"

"No."

"I really am surprised, Robby. As far as Tommy was concerned, you were a big part of it. I know he used you to score a lot of points."

"Tell me about it."

"I'll tell you what I know, which isn't a lot; I told you Tommy was very secretive. Sorscience was a fantasy game: magic, sword and sorcery, dungeons, dragons, wizards, and monsters—that sort of thing."

"I've heard of Dungeons and Dragons. I saw it with Tommy's things in the shed, and I know it's very popular with college kids. I've never heard of Sorscience."

"Tommy and his friends used to play Dungeons and Dragons, but they all got so good that everyone wanted to be Dungeon Master and they eventually got bored with it. I suppose they could have invited other kids to play with them, but they tended to be very impatient with kids who weren't as bright as they were. The end result was that they made up their own game. The object of Sorscience was to find scientific discoveries, theories, or inventions that duplicated magical situations or feats of sorcery described in *Lord of the Rings*. As you can imagine, they spent hours in the library poring over newspapers and scientific journals. As I understand it, a player would score points for finding a situation or discovery, and even more points if the experiment could be duplicated or physical evidence displayed. That's about all I know."

"What did I have to do with it?"

Janet flushed, laughed. "Can't you guess?"

"I'm afraid to."

"You were Frodo!"

"Frodo was a hobbit with furry feet," I replied drily, "not a dwarf."

Janet, still grinning, shrugged. "Close enough. After all, what's a fantasy novel without a dwarf?" She paused, sighed, and her smile became bittersweet. "Tommy was so *proud* of you, Robby. He was proud that you were a dwarf, so very proud that you were his uncle. He lived for his visits with you in New York. He couldn't wait to grow up and finish his schooling so he could move to New York like you and Garth."

"He scored points in this game because his uncle was a dwarf?"

Janet nodded. "The fact that you were a relative made you his private property, so to speak. He scored simply because you were a dwarf, and thus matched a *Rings* character, but he *kept* scoring if you became involved in a case or did something that he could correlate to action in the books." She walked slowly across the room, put her hand on my shoulder and raised her eyebrows. "You *have* been involved in some bizarre cases, Robby."

"Umm."

"Like that business with the witches' coven."

"Yeah. They were playing the game then?"

"No. The game was a recent invention, but Tommy got a ruling to the effect that, since you were 'his' dwarf, anything you'd ever done counted. You were 'Frodo the Ring Bearer.' For example, he correlated the witches' coven to Tolkien's Orcs. You entered their lair and survived. Points."

"No wonder he was always pressing me for information. I don't understand why he never mentioned it."

"He might have been afraid you'd be angry. Or maybe he just didn't want you to feel self-conscious."

"Was Rodney Lugmor a player?"

"Yes," Janet said, frowning. "Rodney was very bright, as you probably know, and he was also in the university's extension program."

"Janet, I'd like a copy of the rules for this game. Also, a list of all the players."

My sister shook her head, then placed her hand on top of the computer terminal. "I've never seen a rule book or player list, Robby. If they exist, they're probably in here. In code."

"Secrecy is one leg of the so-called Witch's Triangle of Power," I said tightly. "Secrecy may have been part of the game, or a way to score points."

"Robby, I do know of one other player—Bill Jackson. His family has a small farm over on Arrowrun Road. Tommy, Rodney, and Bill used to meet here once in a while to discuss strategy and fine points of the game. I'll call his mother for you, if you want. He's only fifteen, so I suppose the ground should be prepared before you talk to him."

"Do that," I said, rising from the swivel chair and looking at my watch. "Janet, I'd like to fly in someone from New York to help me. I know it will be sticky with John, but I'd like this guy to be able to stay here in Tommy's room. Believe me, you'll never see him—and he'll starve to death if you don't bring him food from time to time. Can you manage it?"

"I'll manage it."

"May I use your car?"

"Of course," Janet said, slightly puzzled. "The keys are in the ignition. You can keep it as long as you like; we have the pickup. Where are you going?"

"Coop Lugmor's place. How do I get there?"

She wrote down the directions. I put the paper in my pocket, headed for the stairs.

"Call Mom for me, will you?" I asked. "Tell her I've got my key, and not to wait up for me."

"People around here to to bed pretty early!" Janet called after me. "Coop may be asleep!"

"I hope so," I said over my shoulder. "It'll be a pleasure to wake him up."

4.

Coop Lugmor wasn't asleep, only drunk. He smelled of bad booze and filth; his unshaven face and wasted, haunted eyes were like a microcosm of the crumbling, weather-bombed farmhouse where he lived. Chest-high sawgrass and weeds were a moat around the house, and I literally had to beat a path up to the front door where Lugmor, alerted by the sound of the car's engine, was waiting for me.

"Robby?" he mumbled. "That you?"

"The ghost of Christmas past, Coop." Garth had sounded as if he were feeling sorry for Lugmor; but then, Garth had never been a dwarf. Lugmor had helped to make my childhood miserable, and I was feeling mean. "You still interested in hiring me?"

He licked his lips. Some of the drunkenness seemed to go out of him, chased by grief—or hope. "Sure am, Robby. Uh, I don't have much—"

"This is what it will cost you to have me find out things for you. You're an old boyhood acquaintance, so you get a very special rate; it's a thousand dollars a day, plus expenses."

At first I wasn't sure he'd heard me. He continued to stare down at me in the bright moonlight, his mouth half open. "A thou—?"

"A thousand dollars a day, Coop, plus expenses. And I don't guarantee I'll find out a thing you don't already know. What I'll do is poke around and ask a few questions. You hire me, you'll be wired to any answers I get."

"Robby," Lugmor rasped, "things haven't been too good for

me the last few years. I haven't got anywhere near that kind of money."

"Tough shit, Coop." I turned and headed down off the porch into the jungle that was his front yard. "Ask your own fucking questions."

Now I knew I was being really ornery, and I knew that neither my mother, father, nor my brother would have been very proud of me at the moment. Yet, I couldn't stop myself; it was as if there were a cruel stranger growing inside me, taking over. Coop Lugmor had thumped me good, and now I was thumping back in the worst way possible—I was kicking his mind.

There was a cry like the bark of a sick dog, then a thump of flesh and crash of pottery. I spun around and crouched, thinking that Lugmor might be trying to attack me. The man was sprawled on the ground; rushing after me, he'd fallen off the porch and broken his jug. He sat up and sobbed; his right hand was bleeding, and tears ran down his face collecting dirt. Feeling slightly nauseated, I walked back to him. I'd have stooped to help almost any other creature in his position, but I couldn't bring myself to touch the horrible memory that was Coop Lugmor.

"There are awful bad things going on in this county, Robby!" Lugmor said. "That's God's truth! Nobody cares! My brother and your nephew get killed and all they do is tell lies! Somebody's got to show them we're not all robots! Somebody's got to *do* something!"

"I said I'd ask questions. You want to hear the answers, you pay my price."

Lugmor flapped his bleeding hand at me. I grimaced, took a step back. "I haven't got it!" he wailed.

"You've got land, which means you get money from the Volsung Corporation."

"They cut me off last year. I've got *nothing,* Robby! I've been living off the vegetables I grow."

"You've got the farm," the cruel stranger in me said coldly and evenly.

"You want me to sell my *farm?*"

"Frankly, I don't give a shit what you do. You came to me. I might suggest you get a mortgage. You've got a house, a barn, and a few hundred acres. It ought to be worth something."

"Holy Jesus," Lugmor moaned. "How would I pay off the loan? They'd take the farm, Robby, and I don't want to live like some animal in the woods."

"Think about it. If you change your mind, you can call me at my folks' place."

"Wait!" He struggled to his feet, swayed. "I'll do it, Robby! I'll get a mortgage, pay you what you want!"

"Splendid."

"It'll take time!"

"I'll take a note to the effect of our agreement. Now, Coop."

Lugmor led the way into his house, a hovel that would make any woods I'd ever seen look like the Ritz in comparison. Apparently the man really was existing on nothing but vegetables, because there were scraps of rotting greens scattered about what I assumed to be the living room. A single kerosene lamp was burning something that wasn't kerosene, and Lugmor lit two others. Dirt was everywhere.

Standing in the center of the room as far away from any piece of furniture as I could get, I waited while Lugmor rummaged around for pencil and paper. He wrote something down, handed me the slip. I put it in my pocket without looking at it; it would be illegible. It was also worthless, but Coop Lugmor wouldn't know that. I wanted him crawling around in the woods; I wanted him hurt and broken the way he had hurt and tried to break me.

Now I wasn't too proud of myself. I was growing myself a monster, I thought, and the stranger was beginning to make my insides decidedly uncomfortable. He was crowding out my soul, making it hard to breathe. My heart hurt.

And there wasn't even any satisfaction.

Lugmor had wrapped his bleeding hand in a filthy rag. He blew his nose with an equally filthy rag he carried in a pocket of his overalls, then dried his eyes with the back of his hand. "Thanks, Robby," he said in a trembling voice. "I appreciate your being a friend to me. You'll find out I'm telling the truth. Rod was no fag, and he didn't kill himself and your nephew. You want a drink?"

"No."

"Why don't you sit down?"

"You sit, I'll stand. I want to ask you some questions."

"Shoot," he said, grinning nervously as he eased himself down on the arm of a broken chair and leaned forward eagerly. "God, Robby, I can't tell you how much I appreciate this."

"At the cemetery you mentioned that Jake Bolesh was working for a company. You meant the Volsung Corporation, didn't you?"

"You got it, Robby. The Volsung Corporation. This county hasn't been the same since they built that place."

"Does Jake own land?"

"Nah. He sold his place when he was first elected sheriff. He lives in a house in Peru City."

"How do you know Jake is taking money from Volsung?"

"*Everybody* knows it, Robby. He's got a fancy car, fancy clothes, and he takes vacations in Hawaii. The reason nobody cares is because just about everyone around here gets money from Volsung one way or another. They get cash in the pocket if they lease land, and they get lower property taxes because of all the taxes Volsung pays. Also, Volsung donated a big park over by Polliwallow; it's got a swimming pool and everything. Folks around here think it's really something for a big company like Volsung to set up right in the middle of Peru County. Nobody wants to rock the boat."

"You think the Volsung Corporation had something to do with the boys' deaths?"

"Nah, I'm not saying that. I'm saying that everybody wants to keep things *quiet* because that's the way Volsung wants it; they're pretty secretive about what they do down there. Murders attract attention. It's like this great big building filled with gold plopped down on the prairie one night, and nobody wants to blink or talk too loud for fear they'll wake up and Volsung will be gone."

"Why did Volsung cut you off?"

Lugmor flushed, ground the stumps of his teeth together. "Jake caught me checking out one of the plots they planted on my land; you're not supposed to do that. He reported me. The next day the plot was plowed under and I was off the payroll. Jake also made sure the word got around so that nobody else would make the same mistake." He paused, stared at me with his bloodshot, rheumy eyes. "I'll tell you something, Robby. You see a drunk in front of you, but there was a time when I was a pretty damn good farmer. I know plain old ordinary field corn when I see it."

"Field corn?"

"Yeah. If I'd had pigs or cows, I could've fed it to 'em, or I could've ground it up for silage. No good for anything else. There's nothing experimental about plain old field corn; it'll grow anywhere—which is a good thing, since most of those plots are half-filled with weeds."

"Experiments need controls. How do you know your plot wasn't a control?"

Lugmor scowled. "I know what field corn looks like; I don't know anything about experiments or controls."

"How long has the Volsung Corporation been here?"

"A little over three years. They put the place up fast—matter of months. One minute there's nothing but prairie out there, the next thing you know there's this big building."

"Did Rod ever mention a place called 'Mirkwood' to you?"

"No, can't say that he did."

"What do you think Jake Bolesh does for Volsung?"

His eyes suddenly came to life, glittering with fear. "You're not gonna' tell Jake I've been talking about him, are you?"

"No."

"Okay. The way I figure it, Jake provides them Volsung guys with extra security. He's got patrol cars cruising around there all the time. He makes sure the farmers stay off the lands they've leased out, and he keeps an eye out for strangers nosing around—things like that. Like I said, I think he's paid to keep things nice and quiet."

"If what you say about the Volsung people being big taxpayers is true, they might figure they're entitled to a little extra security. And, considering what everyone in the county gets out of the company, I can understand why no one would object. They'd probably vote Bolesh out of office if he *didn't* give them extra service."

Lugmor scowled again. I wasn't making him happy, but I had to make an effort to see things from the points of view of the Volsung Corporation and the people of Peru County.

"For a thousand bucks a day, Robby, I'd think you'd be on my side."

"You're paying me to try and get a fix on things, Coop, to try to find out what really happened. It may be that things are just the way Bolesh says they are. Now, who in the county actually works inside the building?"

"Nobody."

"Nobody?"

"That's what I said." Lugmor was grinning now, as if he'd finally scored a point in some mysterious game we were playing. "There's maybe a half dozen young guys paid to run a weeder through the plots now and then, but that's it."

"What bars and restaurants do the Volsung people go to when they come into town?"

Another grin, another score. This one he savored, smacking his lips. "They never come to town," he said at last.

"Their people never come out of the *building?*"

Lugmor nodded. "I told you it was a funny place. Oh, the shifts change every few weeks. They bring in people, supplies, and equipment in little airplanes. They got a landing strip out there. You can see the planes coming in real low over Peru City, and I saw them unloading once."

"There must be *somebody* there who handles the local contacts."

"Not that I know of; if anyone knows, it would be Jake. He's the one who tells the local boys with the weeders what to do."

"How much do they pay for the land they lease?"

"Five hundred dollars a month per acre."

"Someone must have contacted you at the beginning about leasing acreage."

"Guy never gave me his name. It was a phone call, and the guy just said he worked for the Volsung Corporation. Contract came in the mail, same as the checks."

"What was the return address on the envelopes?"

Lugmor raised his hand and cocked a thumb toward the southwest, Duck Pond and the prairie beyond.

"No other corporate address in New York? Chicago?"

"Uh-uh."

"Who signed the contract and the checks?"

"I never looked."

"You have a telephone book?"

"I haven't had a telephone for better'n two years, Robby. If it's a listing for Volsung you're looking for, I'll bet everything I've ever owned that it isn't in there."

"Coop, according to the newspaper stories I read, you found the bodies. Is that right?"

Lugmor opened his mouth to speak, but only managed to produce a gagging sound.

"Coop," I prodded, "it's important."

"Just a minute," he mumbled. He rose, picked up a flickering lamp and shuffled through a door. I heard the sound of a cabinet door being opened, and I went after him. I caught his arm just as he was raising a jug to his mouth; obviously, Coop Lugmor still managed to distill alcohol. This batch smelled raw.

"I need this bad, Robby." His eyes were wide and pleading.

"In a minute," I said, wrestling away the jug. "I have to know exactly what happened, and what the scene looked like when you got there."

He leaned forward on the greasy countertop where he had placed the lamp, bowed his head, and moaned softly as I stepped back, holding the jug with both hands like a football Coop Lugmor wasn't going to take away until I'd found out what I wanted to know. There was almost a minute of silence. When he finally spoke, his voice was whiskey-hoarse, climbing up and down a ragged scale.

"I don't sleep too good," he whispered. "Hardly at all. It must've been two or three in the morning. It was clear, full moon like tonight; I could hear neighbors' dogs barking from three, four farms away. Then I heard the shots. Two shotgun blasts, real loud. I got my own gun, went out. I . . . I . . . I found them down by the creek."

"How far away is that?"

"I dunno, maybe a half, three-quarters of a mile straight out back of the barn. They were under a big willow. They . . . they . . . I found them . . ."

"Come on, Coop. Tell me *exactly* what you saw. I need to know everything in detail; I know it's hard, but I have to know. Pretend you're a camera looking back there; tell me what you see."

"They . . . they . . ."

"Goddamn it, Coop, *tell* me!"

"Tommy . . . his chest and stomach and guts . . . Rodney

. . . all of his head from his jawbone up was gone. Brains and bone were splashed . . . *gagh! Gagh!*"

Overcoming my revulsion, I stepped forward, gripped his elbow and turned him around, shoved the jug into his hands. I counted three heavy gulps before I managed to pull the jug away again.

"They're dead, Coop," I said quietly.

"You're a pretty cold fish, Robby," he said in a strained, accusing voice. "You oughtta' be ashamed of yourself."

I was ashamed of myself, but not for forcing him to tell me what he had seen. I was ashamed of the stranger inside me, and ashamed of the things he'd said and done. There were enough rotten people in Peru County, I thought, and I saw no reason to add myself to the number. The stranger was just going to have to go back to whatever dark place in my heart he had come from.

But Coop Lugmor was still going to have to tell me what had happened.

"From the way you describe it, the boys died instantly, without any physical suffering. Think about that, not what they looked like afterward; you'll feel better. Now, I want you to draw me a diagram on paper showing everything—"

"I can't, Robby." Lugmor held up his hands; they were vibrating like bass tuning forks.

"Then you have to tell me what you saw, in detail. You said there was a willow tree. How were the bodies positioned?"

He wiped his mouth with the back of his hand, looked hungrily at the jug. I retreated into my end zone. "It looked like your nephew had been blown down next to the stream; he was half in, half out of the water. There were . . . crawfish at him."

"Where was your brother?"

"Leaning against the tree."

"The gun? You said it was a shotgun?"

He swallowed, nodded. "Remington 1100. Belonged to our pop."

"How long is that gun from the trigger to the end of the barrels?"

He showed me with his flapping hands.

"Where was it?"

Lugmor screwed his eyes shut. "They didn't suffer?"

"I don't think so, Coop. No."

"Rod was holding it."

"*How,* Coop?" I looked around, saw a broken broom lying on the floor in a corner. I grabbed it, handed it to him. "Get down on the floor and show me exactly how Rod was holding it. Pretend the bristles are the butt end."

My stomach tightened as I watched Lugmor slump down on the floor and angle into position against the broken door of a cabinet. I sighed as I saw him put his finger on the "trigger" and, with eyes popping from his head like great red moons, slide the other end into his mouth. The "gun" was short enough. I shoved the broom out of his mouth and hands, helped him to his feet.

"Coop," I said gently, "so far you haven't told me anything that wouldn't jibe with the newspaper accounts and what I've heard."

"What they say isn't true."

"We come back to the letters Bolesh is supposed to have found in Tommy's pocket."

"Not signed!"

"Written on Rodney's typewriter."

"Bolesh says! Nobody around here would know one typewriter from another!"

"The police certainly would, Coop. It's a simple thing to check; it's as if typewriters have fingerprints."

He clenched his fists and shook his head.

"Just for the sake of argument, let's assume that the letters were written on that typewriter. Could anyone else have gotten to that typewriter without someone in the family knowing it?"

"That week they couldn've. Rod was staying there by himself, and he was probably out of the house a lot. Our folks were away at a Grange convention."

"I want to talk to them tomorrow, Coop, and they may not be too happy to see one of Tommy's relatives coming up the driveway. I want you to come over with me."

"Can't, Robby. They both went away Saturday morning, right after Rod's funeral. Took it real hard, said they couldn't stand knowing that the whole county's talking about us."

"When will they be back?"

"Dunno. They're paying a couple of neighbors to look after the place."

"Coop, I asked you this before and I'm going to ask you again; this time I want you to think very hard before you answer. Who might want to kill your brother and my nephew?"

"I don't *know!*" he wailed. "That's what *you're* supposed to find out!"

"The only thing you're really certain about is that your brother wasn't homosexual, right?"

"Yes! Barney Mason, a friend of mine who works in the drugstore in Peru City, told me he saw Rod in there one day sneaking peeks in some of those dirty magazines. Those magazines have pictures of naked *women* in them, Robby!"

"Great." I handed him the jug. As I watched him suck at its contents, I took the paper he had given me out of my pocket, tore it up, dropped the pieces on the floor. "My regular fee is two hundred a day, Coop. That's what you'll pay, along with expenses. And you *will* pay it. The first expense is the biggest. I'm flying in a hacker from New York."

"What's a hacker?"

"Never mind. You can't even take care of your own business, so don't start worrying about mine. I sure as hell don't want this farm, or any money out of it, which means that you're going to have to haul your ass out and go to work someplace so you can pay me. Maybe I'll talk to some of my relatives, see if one of them will take you on as a hired hand—which means that the nasty dwarf you 'heard tell' about will *personally* break your ass into little pieces if you drink on the job or otherwise fuck up."

"Robby, I—"

"I've been known to carry client accounts for a time, so I may not bill you until you've got a job and saved some money. The *first* thing you do in the morning is take a bath, shave, find some clean clothes, and hitch a ride into Peru City. Go to the welfare agency. Don't tell them about me, *do* tell them you need help. Drag somebody out here; once they see this place, they'll fall all over themselves giving you emergency assistance."

He drew himself up straight, stumbled, braced himself on the cabinet shelf. "I'm not taking any charity."

"You'll do exactly as I say, Coop!" I snapped, picking my

way through the garbage and heading for the door. "Otherwise, you can start thinking about mortgaging your farm. And you can be damn sure I'll check to make sure you go there."

5.

Cockadoodledoo.

My father had retired five years ago, sold the animals, and leased out most of his acreage. Nevertheless, he and my mother still rose at dawn; consequently, I found my parents, along with a big breakfast of ham, eggs, and potatoes, waiting for me when I went downstairs early the next morning. We made small talk in an atmosphere that was at once warm but oddly strained. I couldn't tell whether their discomfort arose from the fact that they weren't accustomed to the idea of their son the private detective tilling home soil, or anxiety in the face of all the emotions I was bound to keep stirred up. I finished quickly, went into the living room, and checked the telephone directory.

There was no listing for the Volsung Corporation, and Information couldn't even tell me if they had an unlisted number. Volsung, obviously, thought money was all the public relations they needed, and they were probably right. I borrowed a map of the county from my father and was out of the house before seven.

My first stop was Coop Lugmor's farm. Not a creature was stirring in the house, so I parked my sister's car in the driveway and hiked back of the barn in the general direction Lugmor had indicated the night before. I had no trouble finding the creek, or the area where the killings had taken place; there was only one willow tree, and there were still bloodstains on its trunk. But that was all I found. It had rained hard, twice, since the killings, and not even the depression in the bank where Tommy had fallen was left. If there had been footprints, they had been washed away. Just for form I searched around in the grass and poked with a stick in the mud, but found nothing.

Here, by myself, I sat down on a log for a few minutes and, tasting the salt of my own sorrow, honored the memory of a slight, beaming boy with boundless energy who had looked

upon New York City as a vast amusement park and thought of
death merely as something his uncle always seemed to be involved with.

Lugmor still wasn't up by the time I came back. I pounded on
the door until I heard him shuffling around inside, then shouted
something through the door to the effect that I'd castrate him if
he wasn't cleaned up and on his way to welfare in Peru City
within the hour.

I got into the car, checked the map, then drove southwest on
the highway toward the small town of Duck Pond and the
prairie beyond. There was no indication on the map, but the
Volsung Corporation turned out to be just about where my
sister had said it would be, about twenty miles west of the town.

Somebody went in and out of Volsung on land; on a barely
discernible dirt road cutting off the main highway there were
tire tracks and crushed weeds. I drove up the road three-quarters of a mile, came over a rise, braked hard, and backed up. I
turned off the engine, got out of the car and walked slowly to
the crest of the rise.

Below me, perhaps three hundred yards away, was one of the
strangest sights I had ever seen. The building housing the Volsung Corporation appeared to be a single windowless cube covering at least a half dozen acres and painted the color of the
prairie. There were no signs, no company logo, just the brown-
ish-green structure. To the east, I could just make out a section
of a concrete landing strip, inside a double fence.

There were no guards, only the whistling of the prairie wind
to challenge me as I walked down the dirt road to a mammoth
steel gate that rose perhaps fifteen feet into the air. The gate was
very strong, very solid; where there should have been a bolt
plate or keyhole there was only a single rectangular notch.

A fifteen-minute walk in either direction convinced me that
the Volsung Corporation was impregnable to anything on legs
with the possible exception of a monster kangaroo. The entire
complex was surrounded by an electrified fence. There were
signs, in English, every twenty yards or so warning of danger,
along with skulls and crossbones for the benefit of the illiterate.
There was a second fence inside the first, also electrified, topped
with barbed wire. What looked like small car antennas sticking

up from the ground at random intervals inside the no-man's-land between the fences made me strongly suspect that the area was laced with sensory devices. It was all very neat, very simple, very effective, and—I assumed—astronomically expensive.

I walked back to the car and drove to Peru City, the county seat. After a brief stop at what passed for the local deli, I headed for the county sheriff's office. Jake Bolesh was in.

"Hello, Robby," Bolesh said, rising from the padded swivel chair behind his desk and extending his hand. "I heard you were in town."

I hadn't really expected to see all of my old enemies brought low in the fashion of Coop Lugmor, but I couldn't help but be slightly disappointed at seeing how *good* Jake Bolesh looked. But then, I reminded myself, Bolesh had always been smarter than Lugmor. This man was not the beady-eyed, club-fisted creature that had lurked for so many years in my memories. Bolesh had lost a lot of weight since elementary and high school; he looked tough and trim in his tailored uniform. The only remnant of the sixties in his appearance was his hair; he had kept most of it, and he still wore it in a large, wavy, out-of-date pompadour held in place with greasy pomade that gave off a slightly sweet odor. Good genes, lousy sensibility. The loss of weight made his coal-black eyes seem larger than I remembered. He still had a scar high on his right cheekbone where Garth had hit him with a two-by-four after Bolesh had worked me over in a bathroom.

"Hello, Jake," I replied, taking his hand. Bolesh was Power in Peru County, the man who probably had the answers to all my questions. There was absolutely no percentage in not accepting his gesture of truce. "It's been a time."

"Better than seventeen years, as I reckon it. I'm glad you stopped in. Sorry about your nephew."

"Okay. Thanks."

"Where's Garth?"

"He had to get back to New York." I opened the paper bag I was carrying, took out two containers of coffee, handed one to Bolesh. "Research has shown that it's impossible to remain in police work without becoming addicted to coffee. I thought you might like a fix."

Bolesh smiled thinly. opened the container. "Thanks, Robby."

"You take cream or sugar?"

Bolesh shook his head, then absently patted the sides of his head as though the motion might have messed his hair. "I like it black. Sit down, Robby."

I sat, opened my container, sipped my coffee. "You're looking good, Jake."

"You too. You've done pretty well for yourself since you left Peru County. From here to college on a scholarship, then on to star in the Statler Brothers' Circus. I saw you perform once. Did you know that?"

I shook my head.

"It was in Chicago. I was at a police convention, and your show was in town. You had a great· act—especially that stunt with the rings of fire. You always were a fast little critter."

"Not always fast enough," I said in what I hoped was a neutral tone.

Bolesh shrugged. "Sorry about that. I sure was one mean son-of-a-bitch as a kid. Anyway, Garth always gave me as good as I gave you." He paused, stared at me over the rim of his coffee container. It struck me how his eyes, viewed by themselves, glowed with a strange, muted light, as though the thoughts moving behind them had nothing to do with the chit-chat coming out of his mouth. It occurred to me that, for some reason, I had Jake Bolesh worried.

" 'Mongo the Magnificent,' " Bolesh continued. "That was your billing, right?"

"Right. You seem to know a lot about me, Jake."

"Every time the local paper needs to fill up space, it runs a piece on the famous dwarf from Peru County. Also, I've seen you written up in *Time* and *Newsweek*. You earned your PhD while you were with the circus. Now you're a college professor. Criminology. Also, of course, you hire out as a private detective."

"You have my dossier up to date."

"Do I? It occurs to me to ask what you might be investigating at the moment."

Again I reached down into the bag at my feet, drew out a jar of honey and placed it on the desk in front of Bolesh.

"First coffee, now honey," Bolesh said with a sharp, brittle laugh. "Cute."

"I thought you'd see the point."

"Sharpen it for me."

"My family still has a few questions about Tommy's death. I'm sure you understand."

"Not really. Why didn't John or Janet come to me?"

"Maybe they would have eventually. Things have happened pretty quickly. The funeral was just yesterday, and they're still pretty much in shock."

"But you're not."

"It seems to me that it would be in everyone's interest to get some of the fine points cleared up quickly so the whole matter can be laid to rest for good."

Bolesh unscrewed the cap on the honey jar, sniffed its contents. "You carrying a gun?"

"No. Why do you ask?"

"Because it seems to me that you're doing a private detective number, even if it's unofficial, and you're not licensed in this state. Your handgun license is no good, either, unless it's registered with me. You want to register a handgun?"

"Do you think I need a gun?"

"No. I'm just laying things out, Rob, so we both know where we stand. What would you like to know?"

"I'd like to see your raw file on the case and the coroner's report, if there is one."

"No."

"Why not?"

"It would be unprofessional."

"I'm a professional."

"You have no standing in this county. It would set a bad precedent. If I let you see things like that, who knows who'd be in to second-guess me next week?"

"Who would know that you let me see the files?"

"I would. I happen to take my job very seriously. I can tell you that it's an open and shut case of murder-suicide."

"Will there be a grand jury hearing or coroner's inquest?"

"Why should there be? There's no one to accuse, and we're satisfied that all the facts are known."

"It seems to me that you closed up shop pretty quickly."

"Did I? You weren't at the scene. There wasn't much to investigate. The kids were queer, Rob, as I'm sure you've heard."

"What would I have seen if I'd been there?"

"A mess. The Lugmor kid shot out your nephew's chest, then blew his own head off. My deputies and I went over that scene on our hands and knees, Robby; the only footprints there belonged to the two boys. Besides, no one else would have a motive. Things were just the way I reported, and if I had any doubts I'd still be investigating. I'm afraid you'll just have to take my word for that. We're not hicks here, Rob, despite what New Yorkers may think. The people in this county have seen fit to keep me in this office for twelve years; they must think I know my business."

"Aren't you interested in where Tommy might have been the week before he was killed?"

"I know where he was."

Surprise. "Where?"

"Shacked up with Rod Lugmor. Lugmor's folks were away."

"How do you know Tommy was with Rodney Lugmor?"

"We found his toilet kit and a bag full of his clothes in the Lugmor kid's room."

"Why didn't you tell my sister?"

"You tell her. Under the circumstances, I didn't feel Janet and John would be too anxious to find out that those two kids were alone with each other for a week, buggering—"

"It may be true that Tommy was with Rodney Lugmor. What you think they were doing is just your opinion."

"Have it your way. People are close to each other in this county, Rob, and we try to respect each other's feelings. Have any other questions?"

Not at the moment, and not for Bolesh. "I guess not. You've been very helpful, Jake. I appreciate it, and I know my family will appreciate it."

"Okay, then let me ask you one. What was Coop Lugmor whispering in your ear yesterday at the cemetery?"

"Who told you about Lugmor?"

"A source. I've extended courtesy to you, and now I'd appreciate a little from you."

"He was just saying he was sorry for what had happened."

Bolesh stared at me for some time. Again, I had the definite impression that he was worried—and growing angry. I certainly didn't want Bolesh angry at me, because he could easily and quickly close me down with nothing more than a trumped-up traffic ticket. I was a long way from home, and I wanted to keep my fingers clear of the light socket that was the county sheriff—at least until I'd cut his wires.

"I don't think I believe you, Rob," Bolesh said at last, "but I'll let it pass. For now. In any case, if you've seen Coop you know he's pissed his life away. He's bitter, he's crazy, and he'll say anything just to stir up trouble. I'd hate to see him use you to try and settle some of his personal grudges."

"I'll try to keep from being used."

"Let me be straight with you, Robby. You're an old acquaintance, a private citizen with family here, and you haven't broken any laws—yet. You've got as much right to be here as anybody else."

"Thanks, Jake," I said evenly.

If he noted any sarcasm, he ignored it. "Go ahead and ask around, but I'll take it as a personal kindness if you'd be very discreet about who you talk to, what questions you ask, and how loud you ask them. This is a quiet county. Outsiders—and you *are* an outsider—could easily upset things."

"What things?"

"Something very good has happened to this county, Rob, and everybody benefits. I'm not going to go into detail because it has nothing to do with your nephew's death, and it isn't any of your business. Even your own brother-in-law, Tommy's father, will tell you that it's better if things remain nice and quiet. The point is that you're quite a famous dwarf, Robby; if it becomes widely known that you're roaming around Peru County and investigating something sensational, it's going to attract attention from a lot of vultures in the media. It's very important that that doesn't happen here; I don't want to come to work some morning and find Mike Wallace and a camera crew camped outside my office. Understand, I'm not trying to pressure you. I'm just asking that you satisfy yourself and your family that all the facts are known, and then go back to New York. You'll be doing everybody a favor, including your relatives and yourself."

"Why myself?"

"Because a lot of people will be very pissed if you mess things up for them."

"This sounds like 'Cinderella.' Is there a golden coach parked somewhere that will turn into a pumpkin if I step into it?"

"There are a lot of guns in this county, Rob, and I can't be everywhere."

"I hear you, Jake," I said, rising to my feet.

"One more thing, Robby," Bolesh said, rising with me and staring at me hard. "We could be friends. I admire and respect you, and I'd like some respect in return. I've read your articles in *Criminology* and the *Journal of Criminology,* and I'm impressed. I wouldn't try to put anything over on you, and I'd appreciate it if you don't try to put anything over on me."

"Okay, Jake," I said, heading for the door.

"Because—" The tone was sharp, meant to stop and turn me around. It did. He continued in a softer tone: "Because I'm responsible for the well-being of the people in this county. If I think you're disturbing the peace in any way, I'm going to come down hard on you. It won't be like it used to be, Rob; now I'm the law."

"A heavy threat, Jake."

"It was meant to be. I just want to make things clear now, so there won't be any misunderstanding later."

"See you, Jake."

6.

Janet had called Bill Jackson's mother to make arrangements and negotiate certain ground rules for my visit with her fifteen-year-old son. I went to see him after lunch. The red and white farmhouse was close to the road, surrounded by a quaint, whitewashed picket fence. Mrs. Jackson, with her son standing slightly behind her, answered the door. She was a handsome woman, with sculpted features and alabaster skin highlighted by freckles. Her eyes were clouded with concern, but her son's were wide with excitement. Bill Jackson was a stocky, raw-boned boy with reddish-blond hair and dark blue eyes that glittered with intelligence and good humor. I immediately liked him.

"Hey, you're Mongo!"

"Dr. Frederickson," Bill Jackson's mother said sternly, correcting her son.

" 'Mongo' is fine, Mrs. Jackson."

"We'll compromise," the woman said, shooting her son a sharp glance. "You can call Dr. Frederickson 'Mr. Mongo.' And don't get too excited; you talk too much when you get excited." She took a deep breath, looked back at me. "Janet told you what we agreed on, Dr. Frederickson?"

"Yes, ma'am."

"Aw, Mom," the boy said. "I know all about what happened. Mr. Mongo's not going to upset me."

"I'll decide what's going to upset you, Bill," the woman replied, stepping back and holding the door open for me. I stepped into the spacious house, redolent with the scent of flowers and other growing things.

Mrs. Jackson brought me a tall, cool glass of lemonade, and I went off with her son to his room which, like Tommy's, was decorated with fantasy posters and *Lord of the Rings* memorabilia. Bill closed the door, turned to me. His eyes were filled with tears.

"What happened to Tommy and Rodney was so terrible, Mr. Mongo."

Mrs. Jackson had known what she was talking about, I thought as I squeezed the boy's shoulder. "Thank you, Bill. Let's not discuss that, okay?"

"Okay." He wiped his eyes, brightened. "Boy, Mr. Mongo, it's really something to meet you. It's like meeting Frodo."

"I understand Tommy used me to score a lot of points."

"Yeah; that's because you're always getting involved with weird things. You know about Sorscience?"

"A little. I'd like you to tell me all about it. You scored points by matching real scientific phenomena with places and events in *Lord of the Rings,* right?"

"That's the basic idea, yes."

"Can you give me an example of how you'd score?"

He thought about it, shrugged. "Sure. Take Water Gel, for example. It's a clear paste that won't burn or transfer heat. If you cover yourself with it, you can walk through fire. Firemen are starting to use it."

"The correlation would be Frodo going inside Mount Doom to return the ring?"

"Right! Actually, there are a number of correlations, but that would probably be the best. Hey, you've read *Lord of the Rings?*"

"Where do you think I get my inspiration?" I asked with a wry smile.

Bill Jackson laughed. "I like you, sir."

"And I like you. What are some other examples?"

"Oh, changing lead into gold. Physicists have been able to do that in atomic reactors for years, but the process costs more than the gold is worth."

"Ah, yes, elementary wizardry; something Gandalf might do as a limbering up exercise before breakfast."

That earned another chuckle. "Yeah," the boy said, "but knowledge of the process isn't worth many points. First, none of us could duplicate it; second, Gandalf never actually changed lead into gold. You could score a couple of points by arguing that he *could* have done it if he'd wanted to." He paused, snapped his fingers excitedly. "Here! Let me show you something! I just charged up this stuff this morning."

He opened a deep drawer in a desk and took out a capped cylinder full of what looked like water but which smelled vaguely like a dentist's office when he took off the lid. He went across the room and took a fat gerbil out of its cage. Holding the wriggling animal by its tail, he came back to the desk and unceremoniously plopped the gerbil into the solution; the animal paddled around, its pink nose sniffing the air. I started to protest when Bill pushed it under and screwed the cap on.

"It's okay, Mr. Mongo, I'm not going to hurt him. As a matter of fact, he likes this. Watch."

Sure enough, the gerbil seemed to like it. I gaped in astonishment as the animal, obviously having undergone the experience before, didn't even bother trying to come back up to the sealed-off surface; it paddled about in the depths of the liquid, to all appearances as content and adjusted as your average trout. At first I thought that Bill had somehow taught the gerbil to hold its breath, but when I looked closer I could see its rib cage moving as if it were breathing. Since that was obviously impossible, I examined the surface of the desk, the wall behind it, and even the ceiling, for mirrors. There weren't any.

"That's one hell of a trick," I said. "How's it done?"

"No trick," Bill said, beaming with pleasure. "It's Fluosol-DA, an oxygenated perfluorochemical; PFC, for short. As a matter of fact, it's a distant cousin of Teflon. The Japanese have been making the stuff for years. It's used as artificial hemoglobin, and the FDA has approved its use for blood transfusions in certain circumstances, like with Jehovah's Witnesses. It exchanges oxygen and carbon dioxide, just like blood. As you can see, lab animals can actually 'breathe' the stuff, if it's been oxygenated."

"What purpose does that serve?"

"None. It's just an interesting phenomenon associated with Fluosol-DA."

The boy seemed to be immensely enjoying my stunned silence as he opened the cannister, plucked the gerbil from the fluid, and returned it to its cage, where it began plodding happily on its running wheel.

"How many points is that worth?"

Bill shrugged. "I think Obie was awarded twenty-eight out of a possible hundred for that. It's spectacular, and he had physical possession, but the correlations are weak. Nobody actually breathes underwater in *Lord of the Rings*. He matched it to the slaying of the Seeker in the lake. The Seeker *could* have been air-breathing, and the slayer had to hold his breath for a long time."

"Obie is another player?"

"Yes, sir. Obie—Auberlich—Loge. His father was the official scorer and arbitrator. In fact, Dr. Loge invented Sorscience."

The name Loge, Richard Wagner's God of Fire, rang a big, Nobel Prize–winning bell. Loge was certainly not a common name, and the Dr. Loge I knew of had earned doctorates in virtually every one of the life sciences. He'd won two Nobels—one for the invention of his Triage Parabola, a statistical model used for predicting the survival rates of various endangered species. But Siegmund Loge was into animals, not plants; he certainly didn't grow corn. Indeed, Siegmund Loge didn't do much of anything any longer, except make a fool of himself. At the age of seventy-four he'd gone instant bonkers, resigned all his positions, abandoned his research projects, and when last heard of was roaming around the country as "Father," a new brand of mystical messiah preaching Armageddon and Resurrection to people in the wilderness communes he had set up around the world. At last membership estimate, he'd passed the Rosicrucians and was breathing hard on the neck of the Reverend Moon. Some people will insist on believing anything.

"Do you know this Dr. Loge's first name, Bill?"

"Siegfried, Mr. Mongo. Like in the opera."

It had to be the son, I thought. Siegmund, Siegfried, and Auberlich; it sounded like an invitation list to a cast party for Wagner's *Der Ring dès Nibelungen*. Rings within Rings. I made a mental note to myself to drop Garth a cryptical postcard saying that the doings in Peru County were more fun than a three-ring circus. "What does Dr. Loge do?"

"He heads the Volsung Corporation. That's all I know about his work."

"Have you ever met him?"

The boy shook his head. "No, sir. The scientists never come out of there. They're flown in and out."

"Obviously, Obie must have come out."

"Yes, sir. He was going to school here, at the university."

"The extension program?"

"No. He was a regular student. He must be nineteen or twenty. He hung around with us because we were all interested in fantasy."

"Obie boards at the university?"

"Right. But he'd visit his father on weekends. Someone would pick him up in a car, take him back and forth. That's where he got the Fluosol-DA. He brought it out to demonstrate for us so he could get a big score, and he gave it to me. It's not like there's anything secret about it; I told you they discovered twenty years ago that lab animals could breathe the stuff."

"What else can it be used for besides blood transfusions?"

"Nothing, at least nothing that I know of."

"What would a bunch of plant geneticists want with artificial hemoglobin?"

"I have no idea, Mr. Mongo." He suddenly grinned mischievously. "Hey! Maybe they're all 'pod people' in there, like *Invasion of the Body Snatchers!*"

For some reason, I didn't find the notion overwhelmingly amusing. "Did Obie ever talk about what went on in there?"

"Never—except to tell us what we already knew; the Volsung Corporation was involved with plant genetics, gene splicing, recombinant DNA." He took a deep breath, got slightly red in the face. "Recombinant DNA research is the key to the future, sir. We'll have all disease-free crops that will grow anywhere, and even manufacture their own fertilizer. They already have bacteria that produce insulin, other bacteria that eat up oil spills."

Also bacteria that could produce human growth hormone, I thought. Unfortunately, the scientists had pieced together the little fellows too late to be of any help to me.

"We have super-wheat and super-corn," Bill Jackson continued in a voice that was steadily climbing in pitch. "It's going to revolutionize agriculture around the world! We'll be able to feed everybody! No one need ever go hungry again! They—" He abruptly stopped speaking, bit his lower lip, flushed. "I'm sorry, sir. I *do* talk too much when I get excited."

"It's all right, Bill. I'm interested in everything you have to say. Obie never even hinted at what specific projects Volsung might be working on?"

"No, sir. He never talked about specifics, and we all understood. There's a lot of top secret stuff in that industry, you know. They're always worried about industrial espionage."

Or some other kind of espionage, judging from the camouflage coloring of their building. Since General Foods wasn't likely to order up a bombing run, I assumed Volsung had to be concerned about someone—something—else spotting them from the air. Like a spy satellite.

"Bill, I'd very much like to talk to Obie Loge. Is he boarding at the university this summer?"

"No way. He was taking summer courses, but he was yanked out and flown home right after . . . after . . ."

"Take it easy, Bill," I said, gently patting his shoulder. "You want to take a lemonade break?"

He shook his head, wiped his eyes. Bill Jackson was a very sensitive, gentle, and kind young man.

"Where does Obie live?"

"Actually, I don't know. I guess I must have asked him, but he couldn't even tell me that." He cocked his head to one side, grimaced. "Of course, I never really cared. I wouldn't have wanted to visit him anyway."

"Why not?"

The boy shrugged. "Well, first of all he's a lot older than I am, and the only thing we really had in common was an interest in fantasy. He could really be a mean—excuse me—sucker when he wanted to be. A *real* sore loser. It's probably why he liked to hang around with us; he could push us around when he felt like it, and nobody his own age would put up with him."

"Bill, does 'Mirkwood' mean anything to you?"

He grinned, laughed. "Sure! You've got to be kidding, Mr. Mongo. Mirkwood's the evil forest that the Company passes through on their Quest. Don't you remember those giant spiders?"

"But does it mean anything to you in another context? Did it mean anything else to Tommy?"

He thought a long time about it, obviously anxious to please me, but ended up shaking his head. "No, sir. It doesn't mean anything else to me, and I never heard Tommy mention it outside the context of Tolkien and Sorscience."

"Bill, did Sheriff Bolesh or any of his deputies ask you questions like these?"

"No, sir."

"Did—?"

"Someone else did, though."

"Who?"

"I don't know his name."

"Would your mother?"

"I doubt it. He came up to me at the university. He didn't give me his name, but I knew he worked at the Volsung Corporation. I'd seen him around town once or twice."

"I thought you said—"

"The scientists never come out. This guy's like a chauffeur and handyman. He drives into town to pick up odds and ends, and he used to chauffeur Obie on weekends." Bill Jackson frowned, shook his head. "Spooky guy."

"How so?"

"He's kind of hard to describe. He wasn't spooky-crazy or spooky-mean; otherwise, I wouldn't have talked to him. He was just . . . *spooky*. He had these big brown eyes that kind of looked right through you, and you just knew he could tell if you were lying or telling the truth. He never smiled, and he was completely bald—like Yul Brynner. I'm positive he was pretty old, but I can't tell you why I think that. It was hard to tell his age."

Bill Jackson's words startled me. His description could have fit one of the two men with whom I shared the terrible secret I had mentioned to Janet, a secret that would die with me. But the man I was thinking of wouldn't be holed up in a windowless blockhouse in Peru County doing odd jobs and chauffeuring kids. Not likely.

"Bill, as far as you know, did anyone in the county work on the construction of that building?"

"I don't think so, sir. They brought in truckloads of construction workers, and they set up tents for them out on the prairie. When the building was finished, the workers were taken away."

My watch read four thirty. "Bill, thank you for answering my questions."

"Oh, any time, Mr. Mongo."

"You've been very helpful. I have to pick up someone at the bus station. May I come back if I have any more questions about Sorscience or Obie Loge?"

"Gee, I hope you do come back, Mr. Mongo. Listen, I think there's something else you should know. Tommy was real upset about something just before he took off."

"Bill," I said quietly, "I know that, and I don't think you and I should discuss it. I promised your mother I'd only ask questions about Sorscience."

"But this *does* have to do with Sorscience. I'm sure Tommy was mad because of something that had to do with Obie Loge. They had a big argument. Rodney told me. Obie was sore because Tommy had questioned something Obie wanted to use for a score."

"What?" I asked, feeling a chill run up and down my spine.

"I don't know. Rodney was in a hurry to get someplace. He

just said that Obie was full of—excuse me—shit because nothing like what Obie was describing could ever exist in real life."

Zeke Cohen got off the bus, blinked and sniffed in the late afternoon sunlight like some lost night creature searching for New York's night air. His black hair was wrapped in a crimson bandana, worn low across his forehead. A wide-brimmed leather hat sat on top of his head; buckskin, fringed vest over red silk shirt, jeans, boots; about a pound of gold chains hanging around his neck, one small gold earring in his ear. It was a perfect disguise for traveling unnoticed around Peru County, Nebraska. Zeke was a graduate student in criminology, studying for his doctorate in laboratory sciences. He enjoyed a reputation as the fastest computer gun in the East, West, North, or South. He taught a new undergraduate class in computer sciences, and his students called him Wyatt.

"You're not carrying, are you, Zeke?" I asked as we drove across the flat farmland that stretched to the horizon in all directions. "Coke here is something that gives you cavities instead of holes in the nose, and grass is a soft green growth they cut with a machine called a lawn mower. They'll bust your ass good if they catch you with any shit."

"Huh? Oh, no. Not even a joint."

"Also, no cruising—in case you're feeling horny. There's nothing to cruise. 'Gay' here means ho-ho."

Zeke had been staring out the window; now he slowly turned his glittering black eyes on me. "Hey, Doc, what *is* that stuff out there?"

"It's called wheat, Zeke," I replied drily.

"So that's what it looks like when it's in the ground, huh?"

"You got it. You stop bullshitting me, and I'll stop bullshitting you."

He laughed loudly. "Man, I've never seen so much open space!"

"It's 'the heartland,' Zeke, m'boy."

"It looks kind of weird, you know?" He paused, glanced at me again. "You look funny here, Doc. Out of place."

"You mean, like a dwarf?"

"Yeah," he said thoughtfully. "Here you look like a dwarf." He laughed quickly, self-consciously. "Sorry, Doc. I didn't mean anything personal. I must be suffering from culture shock."

"No offense taken," I said evenly. "Here, I feel like a dwarf. But don't be too smug; you don't exactly blend into the landscape, either. Did you make those calls I asked you to?"

"Yeah. There's no Volsung Corporation listed on any of the stock exchanges, so maybe it really is a privately held and capitalized company. Just to make sure, I checked with a friend of mine in business administration who's a stock market maven. Genetic engineering is the hottest thing going, witness Genentech. If there were a new genetic sciences company that had gone public, or was about to, she'd know about it."

"Thanks, Zeke. You're already earning your money. I'll give you an advance when we get to my sister's place."

"Hey, Doc, I really appreciate this gig. Summer sessions are out, I'm tired of research, and New York is boring in August. Besides, I can use the money. Just what is it I'm supposed to do? You were a little vague on the phone."

"My nephew was big on computers; he's got a roomful of stuff. The basic unit is a Radio Shack TR4100, but don't let that fool you—and don't get careless. He's added on all sorts of goodies that he built himself, and he knew what he was doing. Basically, I want to know everything that's on the memory discs stacked next to the terminal. It's probably all encoded. You into fantasy?"

"You mean sword and sorcery stuff? Not really." He looked at me, leered. "I like detective novels. Somebody should write a huge detective saga, like one of those four-volume fantasy mothers."

"You'll just have to wait for my memoirs, Zeke. I hope you brought your glasses, because Tommy—my nephew—was up to his eyeballs in fantasy. He was particularly into the *Lord of the Rings,* which you'll find on the table by the terminal. It's almost certain that Tommy built codes from those books, so you'll have to read them. Take your time; the important thing is to make sure you don't erase anything."

"Got it."

"You'll be staying at my sister's home, in Tommy's room, so you can set your own schedule. You'll love the food. Anything you want, she or I will get for you. I'll check in with you at least once a day, and probably more. I'll give you my parents' number; that's where I'm staying. I want to know the minute you find out anything."

"Sounds like fun."

"I'd like you to stay put in the house. If you get restless, take a cow for a walk. In Peru County, you're a walking one-man band of minority groups, and a lot of people here won't like your music. I don't want anyone to know you're here."

Another leer. "Why? You think the good folks of Peru County would hang a gay black Jew?"

"No," I said without smiling. "I'm afraid they'll hang a dwarf and his sister."

7.

It was all I could do to stay away from Janet's home the next morning, but I knew that it wouldn't do any good to stand over Zeke and drool down his neck while he was working. I certainly wanted quick results, but pressuring Zeke would be counter productive.

I spent the morning in the Peru City library reading everything I could find on DNA research and genetic engineering. I assumed I was slightly better informed than the average layman because of my long-standing interest in human growth hormone, but I wanted to dig deeper.

It struck me how far and fast the field had expanded since the time, only a few years ago, when gene splicing had been viewed as a sure road to self-destruction, a doomsday device impossible to defuse and just waiting to swallow up, or deform, all life on earth. Many scientists had urged that all research into genetic engineering be banned, for fear of creating diseases that could not be defended against. Indeed, although a total ban was never seriously considered, DNA research was virtually the only human endeavor every scientist on the face of the earth had agreed must be carefully controlled, with strict international safeguards. Protocols had been signed.

First individual cells had been cloned, then frogs. There'd been a report of the cloning of a human, but it had been universally dismissed as ridiculous and the "clone" had never been produced; genetic research and gene splicing with higher forms of life had proved far more difficult, and was still considered highly dangerous, if not unethical.

However, the scientists had shown that some gene splicing could be conducted safely, and gradually the controls in certain specific areas had been relaxed. A great deal of genetic research was still taboo, but work with bacteria and plants had already yielded the wondrous results Bill Jackson had alluded to. In the fields of bacteriology and botany, nothing less than new species of life were being created virtually every day. Universities with genetic research programs had toyed with the idea of setting up their own profit-making companies, and the first gene-splicing concern to go public, Genentech, had sold all its stock within minutes of its initial offering on Wall Street.

Perceptions had changed dramatically; the end of human disease and deformity was being confidently forecast; the doomsday device had become, in the view of many, the key to the Gates of Eden.

There was absolutely no reason for an outfit like Volsung to have set up shop in secret, in the middle of a midwestern prairie, behind a death fence. Not if they were doing what they said they were doing. Which, of course, I damn well knew they weren't.

Tense and nervous with growing anxiety over just how big a beast I had stumbled on, I still managed to put on a happy face for my parents while we had lunch. Exhausted, more from tension than any exertion, I lay down afterward. I'd just fallen asleep when my father came to wake me up. Janet had called and asked that I come over right away.

Flying in Zeke had certainly brought quick results, but they weren't exactly what I'd hoped or looked for.

Jake Bolesh was standing on my sister's porch, gripping Zeke's elbow. Zeke's hands were cuffed behind his back. Two of Bolesh's deputies were going in and out of the house, lugging Tommy's computer components, book collection, and taped cartons, loading everything into a police van. Janet, looking sullen and angry, was standing at the end of the driveway, arms folded defiantly across her chest. John Dernhelm stood at the far end of the porch, looking sheepish and unsure of himself; it told me who had informed Bolesh about my conversation with Coop Lugmor, and how Bolesh had found out about Zeke. It occurred to me that most of the people in Peru County probably acted as informers for the county sheriff.

"Robby, I'm sorry," Janet said tersely as I got out of the car. "John got frightened and did a stupid thing."

"It's all right, Janet," I said, patting her on the arm as I walked past her. "I'll take care of it."

"I couldn't help it, Doc," Zeke began as I approached the porch, stopped on the first step. "This cracker barged in here half an hour ago and—"

"Shut up, nigger!" Bolesh snapped.

Like a poisonous chameleon, the old Jake Bolesh I'd known and loved had changed back to his true colors. In an odd way, I found that comforting; as a mean-spirited, cruel, and dangerous son-of-a-bitch, he was easier to see and to defend against. The fencing, the dainty little gavotte that had begun the day before in his office, was ended. Perhaps, I thought, it was just as well.

I found it a bit unsettling to realize how much I enjoyed nursing the near lifelong grudge that was Jake Bolesh; more than anything else, I wanted to nail him for something. Anything. A character defect.

"You're in trouble, Frederickson."

"Oh? Why is that, Jake?"

"Aiding and abetting a felony, after the fact."

"Terrific charge. I love it. What's the felony? Hiring someone to index my nephew's effects?"

"How about conspiring to withhold evidence?"

I glanced at Zeke, who gave a slight shake of his head. He hadn't found out anything. I was just about to turn my eyes away when I saw him roll his eyes in an exaggerated manner, then look down at his chest and close his left eye. He had something for me in his left shirt pocket.

"What evidence?" I asked, turning my attention back to Bolesh. "You said the investigation was over."

"A murder investigation is never officially closed, Frederickson. You're a hot-shot criminologist; you should know that. If you had reason to believe there was something important in that computer, you should have told me; you broke the law when you *didn't* tell me, and I warned you what would happen if you broke the law here."

"Jake, my man, I haven't the vaguest notion what's in that computer. I had no reason to tell you anything, and I don't even know what the hell you're talking about. I wasn't investigating any murder-suicide. I was interested in my nephew's frame of mind, looking for some clue to what could have gotten him in the mess he did. It's strictly personal family business. Isn't that what you told him, Zeke?"

"Doc, that is precisely what I told him," Zeke answered in a carefully measured tone. "No more, no less."

"I told you to shut up!" Jake shouted, yanking on Zeke's handcuffs so hard that I winced. "Don't play word games with me, Frederickson! You believe there's something in that computer or those books that could have a bearing on this case! You should have told me about them!"

"Arguable. Look, Jake, if you want to arrest and charge me, be my guest. I can't wait for the trial; I guarantee you I'll hire the loudest lawyer in the country. You have a warrant to take this stuff out?"

"Damn right. In any case, I have the permission of the dead boy's father."

"Robby?" John Dernhelm said in a small voice. "What you're trying to do hasn't been right from the beginning. Tommy should be allowed to rest in peace."

"Are you arresting this man?" I asked Bolesh, ignoring my brother-in-law. "He was just doing a job for me."

"I should arrest him for conspiracy, but I'm going to give him a break."

"Then why don't you take the cuffs off?"

"When I put him on the bus to the airport."

"I'll take him to the airport."

"The hell you will. I figure you'll be too busy, starting right now, making your own travel arrangements."

"You throwing me out of town, Jake? Don't I get until sundown?"

"You figure out where you'd rather be, Frederickson; home with all the other weirdos in New York City, or in the Peru County jail facing those charges I mentioned."

"I'll give it some thought."

We glared at each other in silence for a few moments before
Bolesh clumped down the steps, brushed me aside, and went to
inspect the van. Zeke picked that opportune moment to suffer a
severe coughing fit. Careful not to appear that I was in a hurry,
I climbed up on the porch and patted him on the back as he
doubled over. At the same time I slipped my hand into his shirt
pocket, felt the plastic card I'd found earlier in Tommy's table
drawer.

"It doesn't go with the computer," Zeke whispered. "It's a
magnetic pass card. You find the right game, and that'll open
it."

8.

Ah, yes, my commando costume: black seaman's cap found in
the attic, black shoes, denim shirt and jeans, charcoal-blacked
face and hands. I'd have happily traded the whole outfit for my
snub nose, but that wasn't possible. It was time to check out
what I was now certain was Tommy's "Mirkwood."

I didn't want Janet vulnerable to a valid conspiracy charge if
I were caught, so I parked her car in some tall weeds off the
main highway and hiked down the dirt road leading to the
building housing the Volsung Corporation. The moon was
bright, but it was occasionally hidden by passing clouds.

The plastic, tape-striped card fit neatly into the notch in the
steel gate. There was a soft click, and the gate popped open
about two inches. I pushed on the edge of the gate; the massive
steel barrier swung open easily and without a sound. The road
between the two gates was hard-packed, apparently free of sensing devices. I couldn't tell if there were silent alarms wired into
the gate; since there wasn't anything I could do about it if there
were, I dismissed the problem from my mind.

After repeating the procedure with the inner gate, I was inside the compound. I ran low and fast down the remaining
quarter mile of road to the building itself, pressed back hard
against what seemed to be a garage door. I stayed that way for
long minutes, breathing hard and listening. I could hear no
alarms, no signs of activity inside; there was only the chirping

of crickets, the bellowing of a horny bullfrog, the faint rustle of insects and reptiles in the grass.

Nothing happened when I put the magnetic pass card into the notch on the garage door. I wiggled the card, and still nothing happened; there was no soft click, no small jump of the door, and for a moment I feared I'd reached the end of the blue plastic and black tape road. Then I thought to push on the door. It moved in slightly, and then there was the soft whir of an electric motor. The garage door lifted. I stepped inside, leaving the door open.

I was inside Mirkwood.

There was an initial flickering when I pressed a light switch on the wall, and then soft fluorescent light flooded the spacious garage. Parked inside were a brown Toyota pickup, a red Chevrolet van, a black, late-model Cadillac.

There was a narrow stairway to my right. I went up it, pressed another glowing plate on the wall, stood and stared. The open space before me was massive, perhaps three-quarters the size of a football field, more if you counted the dozens of rooms radiating off the outer wall. The floor was all off-white tile, soothing to the eyes under the same type of fluorescent lighting installed in the garage.

It looked like some scientist's idea of heaven. There were six separate computer banks, all still now, their black tape spools staring at me like reproving eyes out of faces of glass and stainless steel. Long, rectangular, marble-topped work tables, spaced a few yards apart, marched like silent soldiers down the center of the space; the surfaces of the tables were covered with Bunsen burners, test tube racks, pipettes, microsurgery equipment, state-of-the-art microscopes, including no less than four huge, portable electron scanners.

A number of theater-size speakers, high-fidelity Bose models, hung in pairs from the ceiling, but I could not see any television monitors or electronic eyes.

There were cages, empty now but irrevocably *there* just the same. Since I'd never seen a corn stalk that required a cage, it meant they were experimenting on animals—some of them large. A scientific no-no.

When five minutes passed and no welcoming committee arrived to greet me, I took an exploratory stroll around the perimeter of the space. At the far end a moving walkway—now still —disappeared into darkness down a long, narrow corridor. I assumed it led to the scientists' sleeping and recreation quarters, and I didn't bother going down it.

Three-quarters of the way around the circuit, on the inside wall, I found something I certainly would have gone through if I'd been able. It was a red door with a notch configuration different from that on the outer gates and the garage door. I tried the card, but it fit loosely in the slot; the door would not move, no matter how hard I pushed, pounded, and kicked. I leaned my head against the cool metal, fought against a sudden, unexpected welling of tears.

As hangar-large as this workspace was, it formed only a small part of the huge complex I'd viewed from outside. There was more, much more, on the other side of the red door.

Tommy, I was certain, had been through the red door. He and Rodney Lugmor, escorted by Obie Loge, had been into the inner sanctum; although it seemed beyond belief, the son of Volsung's director, in order to score some points in a bizarre fantasy game, had somehow been able to bypass a few million dollars' worth of security and show his two friends the "monsters in Mirkwood." It had to have happened.

My fourteen-year-old nephew had been bright and sophisticated enough to recognize the grave danger in what he saw, decent enough to be profoundly disturbed by it. Fourteen years old, torn between a natural desire not to betray a "friend" who had trusted him and a need to shout that there was evil growing in the county—evil that could conceivably be let loose, or escape, into the land. The pressures on him had been enormous.

Tommy and Rodney Lugmor had not known what to do. They had spent a week together debating what course of action to take, wrestling with an awesome conflict that would have brought most adults to their knees. I was immensely proud of my nephew, and of Rodney Lugmor.

But it had been too late to do anything. Whether alerted by a nervous Obie Loge who had begun to have doubts, or whether the breach had been independently discovered, the darker—obviously more efficient—arm of Volsung's security operation had gone into action. The price of the tour through Mirkwood had been death.

Somebody had cold-bloodedly blown up two gentle teenagers with a shotgun; there could be nothing more twisted or monstrous beyond the red door.

For a few seconds I considered the pleasant, simple expedient of trashing the place, but realized that such as exercise would accomplish nothing except to get me very sweaty and very dead. The equipment was only money, and the Volsung Corporation obviously had all of that they needed, and more. I kept moving.

The first room I entered looked like an office-lab that was being renovated or repaired. Part of the wall had been torn out, and the steel, cast-iron, and zinc components of a slop sink were sitting in an open case by the hole, waiting to be assembled.

The second room was a spacious office, well-furnished and elegant. There was a large desk and file cabinet against one wall, a small computer terminal on a hardwood stand. There were more file cabinets against another wall, as well as an enormous, thousand-gallon aquarium, empty now of fish, attached to complex compression and filtration equipment. A six-foot-high working model of the DNA double helix stood against another wall, looming over me like some knobby, multicolored skeleton creature unearthed on some very distant planet; in fact, the construct represented the fundamental basis of life on our own.

Although the files seemed to be arranged in the normal alphabetical indexing system, there was but a single label at the top of each file cabinet.

THE VALHALLA PROJECT

It had a logo—four thick, interconnecting rings forming a larger ring. It didn't surprise me.

Starting with the file cabinet next to the desk, I slid open the top drawer, stuck my hand in—and froze. The hairs on the back of my neck prickled, stood up. I hadn't heard anything, but suddenly I felt another presence in the room with me. I turned and found myself face to face with a gorilla.

He was a big mountain gorilla, three hundred to three hundred and fifty pounds, a male silverback. He was sitting on his ample haunches, filling the doorway, staring at me with beady bloodshot eyes under a jutting black brow that ran across his low, sloping forehead like a cliff edge. He wore what looked like an upside-down electronic typewriter with display screen strapped to his chest. The expression on his face was almost human; at the moment he seemed bemused, perhaps by my size, more likely because he wasn't quite sure what to do with me.

Normally, mountain gorillas are the gentlest beasts imaginable, dangerous only if provoked or cornered. However, I had a strong suspicion that this fellow was an exception; he was a "watch-gorilla," and he had me cornered.

"Uh, down boy?" I flashed a great smile and made little kissing noises.

The gorilla looked down at the machine on his chest, then slowly and deliberately punched a few color-coded buttons. When he'd finished he glanced up at me and—I was absolutely certain—arched what would pass for gorilla eyebrows while I read the message on the display screen.

?
THE WHO FUCK YOU SMALL SONBITCH

Cute as a button, I thought, the creation of an animal behaviorist with immense patience, a lot of time, a few tons of bananas, and a bent sense of humor. He'd been trained to respond to a password—or the lack of it.

"Valhalla," I said quickly, taking pains to clearly enunciate each syllable. "Wotan? *Götterdämmerung? Rheingold?*"

He just wasn't into opera. I was still rummaging around in my very limited Wagnerian vocabulary when he came for me. As big as he was, he was quick. I managed to sidestep his rush a couple of times, but he cut me off at the pass each time, blocking my route to the door while he lurched after me like some great hairy express train.

After five minutes of this, he decided to take a rest break. He sat in the doorway, pointing and glowering at me. I stood against the opposite wall, panting and glowering back at him.

"Valkyrie? Fafner?"

A message.

LITTLE SONBITCH QUICK QUICK

"Volsung? Siegfried? Bayreuth?"

FUCK ALL OUT TIRE

A conversationalist, smarter than the average gorilla. "Me, too. Let's you and I go find a nice quiet bar, have a few drinks, and talk this over."

?
STOP RUN

"Polly want a banana?"

BIG NOW PISSOFF

he flashed, signaling that halftime was over.

Finally he got hold of an ankle and reeled me in with what I could have sworn was a rumbling grunt of satisfaction. I flailed at him, but I knew I had as much chance of hurting him as of unhinging a heavy punching bag. I expected him to start picking me apart like a fried chicken, but he wasn't going to do anything that gross or messy. Instead he casually lifted me off the floor by the seat of my pants, grabbed the back of my neck, and plunged my head under the water in the aquarium. And he held me there.

Real panic, I discovered, was colored silver, despair brown; those were the colors of the dots that swirled in front of my eyes as I held my breath. My lungs felt ready to explode as I used up still more oxygen futilely struggling against the black leather fingers that held me in a grip as tight and final as death.

Hope, on the other hand, smelled like a dentist's office. That was the faint odor I'd detected just before the gorilla had dunked me in the "aquarium"; the "water" I was under wasn't water.

With absolutely nothing to lose, I released the pressure from my lungs. The breath exploded from my mouth and nose in great silver bubbles. Then I played gerbil, sucking in the fluid just as if it were nothing more than good old only-slightly-polluted New York City air.

Air it wasn't. In connection with my coven of witches, I'd undergone a series of rabies shots. They'd been exquisitely painful, given directly in the belly. The sensation I'd experienced then was a feeling of swelling in my stomach and chest, of being pumped full of some viscous liquid, like silicone. The feeling of swelling now was essentially the same, without the searing pain. There was a bubbling, tickling sensation in my sinuses, as if I'd drunk warm soda too quickly, a bitter licorice taste; then the taste and sensation were gone and I was—breathing.

There was an unexpected side effect of immersion that could explain why the gerbil I had seen paddling around in Bill Jackson's jar of Fluosol-DA had seemed so content with his lot; I was getting high.

It occurred to me that this particular gorilla was going to be looking for something a bit more dramatic than a submerged, giggling dwarf. I sucked in a huge lungful of the solution, held my breath for a few seconds, then executed what I hoped was a very convincing performance of twitches, shudders, and kicks. Then I went limp and waited.

And waited.

It looked as if I were going to have to start "breathing" again, but just as I was about to exhale my hairy attacker pulled me up out of the tank. I opened my eyes to slits and watched as the gorilla dangled me in the air by the back of my shirt and peered quizzically up into my face. I hated to hurt him, would have much preferred a long session with his trainer, but I didn't have too many options. I despised cruelty to dwarfs even more than cruelty to animals, so I poked him in the right eye with my index finger. The force of the stab wasn't hard enough to puncture his eyeball, just sufficient to produce an unpleasant diversion.

The gorilla bellowed in pain and dropped me to the floor as he reflexively let go of my shirt in order to alternately swipe at his eye and thump his chest. I jumped to my feet—and immediately ran into a problem. The gerbil had obviously had lots of practice clearing fluid out of its lungs; I wasn't so fortunate, and the transition from breathing Fluosol-DA to breathing air wasn't a problem I'd given a lot of thought to. Consequently, I began coughing and choking as the fluid spurted out of my lungs through my mouth and nose. By the time I recovered, my companion was in full, lumbering gait, heading in my direction, trailing multicolored wires from the smashed machine on his chest.

At the last moment I tumbled out of his way, and he smashed into a file cabinet. By the time he turned, I was out the door and running; I could hear the rhythmic padding of him on all fours right behind me. I didn't know whether he could catch me over a short course, but I didn't want to risk a foot race I might lose. I sprinted fifteen yards, cut sharply to my left into the unfinished office-laboratory. I felt a leathery paw slap against my shoulder, slip off as the gorilla's momentum carried him past the entrance. He recovered, came scampering through the door.

"Me the fuck Mongo, *you* sonbitch," I said as I bounced a length of stainless-steel pipe off his forehead.

It was an immense relief to find that it was possible to knock a gorilla unconscious. Every instinct urged me to get out of Volsung as quickly as possible, rush home and do something sensible—like crawl under the bed. But if I left empty-handed, the evening's expedition would have been for nothing. Worse than nothing; unless I somehow managed to cover my tracks, Jake Bolesh and his masters in Volsung would know there had been a break-in. Bolesh would have no problem knowing who to come looking for.

What, I asked myself, do you do with an unconscious gorilla? The answer came: frame him, try to make it look as though he'd been playing house with the equipment and had hurt himself.

I went out of the office, hurried to the far end, and peered down the darkened corridor leading to the scientists' quarters. Either the scientists were very sound sleepers or their quarters were soundproofed, because the lights remained out and the walkway remained still.

The huge electron microscopes were on rollers, obviously designed to be moved about the complex. I pushed one into the office-laboratory and used a pipe as a lever to topple it over on the floor next to the gorilla; the half-million-dollar piece of equipment smashed to the tile with a resounding crash, which spelled the beginning of the end to my evening of fun and games.

I'd hoped to be able to sort through the files at my leisure, try to understand some part of what was in them, make some copies on the Xerox machine in another office, replace the files and steal safely away into the night. I should have done it before tipping over the electron microscope, but the reassuring silence that had returned after the cacophonous bellowing of the gorilla had made me feel secure. Cocky.

Stupid.

Just as I was digging into the first open filing cabinet, I heard a distant clicking sound, then a whir. The walkway. I grabbed three files that were thin enough so that I hoped they wouldn't be missed right away. I closed the file cabinet, then raced like hell to the stairway leading to the garage, slapping light switches on the way.

9.

"Robby?" my mother whispered through the half-open door.

"I'm awake, Mom. Come on in."

My mother, slippers on her feet and quilted robe cinched loosely about her waist, came quietly into my room and sat down on the edge of the bed. The promise of dawn shone in her silver hair and softly spotlighted her face. She looked very old, very tired, very worried. She still seemed incredibly beautiful to me, as lovely as she had been in reality when she was young. Only her eyes were absolutely unchanged; even beneath a veil of anxiety, they shone like beacons.

"Coop Lugmor called twice during the night," she said softly. "Said he was calling from some phone out on the highway. He wants you to go over there as soon as possible. He sounded very strange."

"I'll bet he did," I said wryly. Jake Bolesh had undoubtedly paid him a visit.

"He said he had something important to tell you."

That surprised me; I'd assumed he was simply in a big hurry to cut any ties. "Okay, Mom, I'll take care of it later. I'm sorry he woke you up."

"He didn't wake me. I heard you get up, looked out the window later, and saw you leave in that funny outfit. I've been so worried about you."

I sat up in bed, took her right hand and pressed it against my lips. "You shouldn't worry," I said, kissing the translucent, parchmentlike flesh of her hand.

"Robby, there's a strange odor about you. Did you have an upset stomach?"

The Fluosol-DA I'd absorbed was still transpiring out of my system through my lungs and skin. "No, Mom. I'm all right."

"Where did you go, son?"

"Out drinking and womanizing," I said with a large grin, again kissing the back of her hand.

"Please, son."

"Mom," I replied seriously, "I've never lied to you or Dad, and I don't want to have to start now. I can't tell you where I went. It's not that I don't want to, but that I can't. I have to ask you to trust me and believe that I wouldn't intentionally do anything wrong."

"Oh, I know that, Robby, and it goes without saying that I trust you."

"I wouldn't intentionally do anything to hurt you and Dad, or any member of our family."

"You wouldn't intentionally hurt anyone."

"I'm going to ask you not to mention to anyone that I went out last night. That's important. It's not for me."

"What you're doing is very dangerous, isn't it?"

"Yes," I said after a pause.

"I heard you come in and clean up, and then I heard you moving around down in the root cellar. Did you leave something down there?"

"Yes, but it won't be there for long. I just have to figure out what to do with it."

"I won't ask you what it is, Robby. I know you're thinking of me and your father; if you don't want us to know something, it's for a good reason."

"Did Dad hear me go out or come in?"

"I don't think so. He won't tell you, but he hasn't been feeling well at all. He stays active during the day because he wants to put on a good show for you, but he's exhausted at night."

"When this is over, the three of us will go away someplace and be together. Okay?"

My mother gently stroked my hair with both her hands, and I was startled to see tears in her eyes. "I've always loved you so much, Robby," she murmured in a choked voice. "You were God's special gift to me—so clever, so good. I've always been so proud. Every day since you were born I've thanked God for you, and for giving me Garth to protect you when you were a boy."

"Thank you, Mom. I love you very much."

Tears were flowing freely now, but she still managed to smile. I reached out to brush away her tears, but she grabbed both my hands and clasped them to her breast. "You want to hear something strange, Robby? Even with all this crazy and dangerous business you've gotten into as a private detective, I've never really worried about you. I know you've almost been killed a number of times—but I still didn't really worry about you. I believed that you were also very special in the eyes of God, and that God wouldn't let any harm come to you. There's something different happening now."

"God's a very busy woman, Mom, and I imagine I'm hard to keep track of under the best of circumstances."

"Don't be blasphemous, Robert," my mother said sternly, unsmiling.

"I didn't mean to be, Mom," I said quickly, thoroughly chastened. "Just trying to lighten up the conversation."

"I've had a recurring dream every night since you and Garth came here," she said distantly. My mother was still weeping, still deadly serious. "It's a dream of death and destruction, the same each time. Somehow you, Garth, and a man I've never seen before are at the center of it all. There are strange creatures no one has ever seen before. God weeps over the whole earth as He holds you and Garth in His arms. In this dream both my sons are dead, Robby, and the earth is changed forever."

I pulled my hands from her grasp, cradled my mother's face, kissed her eyes. "Believe me, sweetheart, it's just something you ate."

"Robby," she sobbed, "please don't make fun of me."

"I'm not, Mom. Nothing is that serious, and none of it is worth a single one of your tears. Garth isn't even here—and I don't *want* him here."

My mother stopped crying, sighed heavily, stared hard at me. There was still love in her eyes, but there was also a hard glint, like sun on snow. "Rodney Lugmor didn't shoot Tommy, did he?"

"No," I said quietly, transfixed by her eyes and her unexpected strength. "They were both murdered—probably drugged or beaten unconscious someplace else, then taken to the stream on Coop Lugmor's farm and shot. Also, there's absolutely no evidence that they had a homosexual relationship. That doesn't mean a whole lot to me, but it may to you and Dad."

"It will mean something to Janet and John."

"Well, they can't know. I'm sorry, Mom. I'm only telling you this because you're old; I don't think even these men will lean on you *unless* they believe I've shared information with you. I won't ask you to keep secrets from Dad, but neither of you can repeat *anything* I've said tonight to *anyone;* not even to Janet, and especially not to John."

"Do you know who did this thing?"

"I know who pulled the trigger. I know where to find the men responsible, but only one of their names."

"What are you going to do about it, Robby?"

"Probably nothing." The words tasted bitter and sharp, but they rang true. As the sun had come up, so had answers and realizations dark and cold enough to eclipse the dawn, at least for me.

"I don't understand, son," my mother said quietly.

"Mom, ever since I got home I've been lying here, thinking, trying to decide what I *can* do. I keep getting an image of a single man trying to harvest the Great Plains with a scythe."

"If these men are murderers, and you can prove it, there must be a way to bring them to justice."

"You're wrong, Mom. You see, I might manage to cut down a half acre or so; I could . . . punish . . . the man who shot Tommy and Rodney, but he's nothing more than a small, very rotten potato who was taking care of other people's business and erasing their mistakes. Knowing that, maybe I get frustrated and start shouting at the sky, telling things I know. You know what happens? A great wind comes up across all those millions of acres I haven't managed to touch. That wind howls like nothing you've ever heard before; it's colder than any winter, and it keeps gaining velocity. It immediately drowns out my shouts and blows me away forever, but it doesn't stop there; it keeps blowing. It comes here, into this home and Janet's home, into the homes of all our relatives. People who've had any contact with me in Peru County could catch cold, Mom. Some of them could die. Do you understand what I'm saying?"

"Nothing that evil or powerful could exist here. This is America."

"It certainly is. God bless America."

"Yes," my mother said with a frown, obviously puzzled by my tone. "God bless America." She paused and patted my head, just like a mother. "You thought my dream was exaggerated, Robby. Well, I think your story about a wind on the Great Plains is exaggerated."

"It isn't, Mom. Believe me, it can happen if I make the wrong move. In this case, any move at all would be a wrong move."

"We have laws here. Justice."

"I can't do something that may harm the people I love, Mom. I should've got smart quicker, gone home sooner."

My mother slapped me across the face, hard. In the thirty-six years of my existence, it was the first time either of my parents had hit me. I was so stunned by her action that I didn't even feel the blow. Shocked and numb, I simply sat and stared at her as she reared back to hit me again, then thought better of it.

"That's the first time I've ever hit you, Robby, because this is the first time you've ever made me angry and ashamed of you!" Her voice, usually so soft and gentle, was trembling with fury. "First I hear you tell me you know that your nephew and another boy were murdered, and in the next breath you tell me that you're not going to do anything about it. You won't even tell me who did it. How terribly, terribly *arrogant* of you, Robert! You're not God!"

"Mom—"

"If you've become a coward so quickly, tell *me* what you know and I'll *damn* well do something about it!"

The first time I'd ever heard her swear; it was turning into a week of firsts. I continued to sit with my lower jaw hanging open.

"Oh, Robby, Robby," she continued, whispering in my ear as she caressed the spot on my cheek where she'd slapped me. "I'm sorry I hurt you, but you can't worry about me or your dad, or about anyone else. You have to decide and do what's *right:* you have to relearn something I thought I'd taught you a long time ago. You see, God put both good and evil in the world in equal amounts in order to make us free, and to enable us to test ourselves so that we could grow and become strong as spiritual beings. At the beginning, good and evil were equally balanced. People have no control over evil, but good is different.

Every time someone does something for somebody else, it creates a little piece of goodness that wasn't there before. But if a just person sees evil and chooses to do nothing about it, a little good leaks out of the world. That hurts everyone, everywhere. Don't you cause any good to leak away, son. That would make the tragedy of Tommy's death even worse."

I put my arms around my mother and kissed her. Then, resting my head on her shoulder, I heaved a deep sigh. "Reverend Blackwood tell you that?"

"My heart tells me that."

"Is Dad up yet?"

"By now, yes. He's probably shaving."

"Well, you go up and talk to him for a half hour or so. I'm going to make a phone call I don't want either one of you to hear."

Information gave me the number I wanted. I wrote it down, then sat and stared at the telephone. I had a real dilemma; the federal government rearing up in front of me, my mother behind me, and I wasn't sure whom, which, I feared most.

I'd been a little slow on the uptake. It should have occurred to me much earlier that there was only one group not included in the Fortune 500 that could afford to piss away the kind of money the Volsung Corporation represented, and that was the merry pranksters of the Pentagon. The nation's military establishment was engaged in illegal gene-splicing experiments, secure in its belief that it was safe from discovery in paid-off Peru County, Nowhere, U.S.A. I didn't know what they were up to, didn't want to; putting a stop to Pentagon hanky-panky would be out of my league even if most of my relatives weren't living on Volsung's doorstep. I might whisper something in Ralph Nader's ear if I ever got the chance, but the best I could hope for was to get a pass to kill Jake Bolesh personally, and assurances that the scalps of the men who had authorized Volsung's "enforcer" to kill two boys would be lifted.

How to accomplish that without bringing the roof down on everybody was the problem. The trick was to get this great, often myopic, meat eater to take a little nip out of itself and leave everyone else alone.

Finally I picked up the receiver again and dialed the number in Omaha, two hundred and thirty-five miles away. The phone was answered on the second ring.

"Federal Bureau of Investigation. Agent Randall speaking."

"Agent Randall, my name is Dr. Robert Frederickson. I'm a professor of criminology, as well as a private investigator licensed by the state and city of New York. If you don't mind, I'll wait while you check my credentials on that National Registry I know you gentlemen keep. You'll find out I'm a straight arrow. My P.I. license number is J A 044—"

"I've heard of you, Dr. Frederickson," the agent replied drily. "What can I do for you?"

"I'm calling from Peru County. I'd like you and two or three other agents to load up and pay me a visit. I need your help to nail a very crooked county sheriff who just happens to be a murderer. It's important that you get here as quickly as possible, because right now he could be in the process of destroying vital evidence."

There was a prolonged silence, then: "It sounds like a problem for the State Police."

"Uh-uh. I'm not sure how far the corruption has spread; we're talking very big payoffs here. You're the only people I can trust, and you can slip in with a violation of civil liberties wedge."

What I didn't mention was that I feared the State Police might be plugged in to whatever Volsung really was, but there was a good chance, however strange or ironic, that the F.B.I. wasn't. The Defense Intelligence Agency, like the Central Intelligence Agency, didn't think too much of the F.B.I., and the respective agencies shared information only at the point of a cannon.

"You'll have to give me more details, Frederickson. Tell me exactly what the problem is."

I gave him a good version, some of it truth, some of it fiction, all of it designed to make the agent on the other end of the line believe I had a great deal more hard evidence than I actually did. I carefully avoided any mention of the Volsung Corporation. The F.B.I. might be temporarily ignorant of the secret government research facility, but that didn't mean Randall might not do some checking and find out if I even hinted at its existence. In my present position, I was finished if it were even suspected that I'd been inside the Volsung Corporation complex. Bolesh would kill me on sight if he found out, and the F.B.I. would probably deliver me to Bolesh if Randall ever put all the pieces together. The information I had on Volsung and the Valhalla Project, whatever that might be, had to be meted out in very small bits, if at all, only when absolutely necessary, and only in the right company and situation. Those cards were the only hand I had, or was likely to get. Played right, they could get me what I wanted; one card laid down at the wrong time, or in the wrong sequence, could get me dead. I was balanced on a taut high wire, and the green felt was a long way down.

Randall was silent for a long time after I'd finished. "Okay, Frederickson," he said at last. "I'll look into it."

"You'll *come* here and look into it?"

"Right."

"Now? I told you he's probably destroying—"

"I'll get there as soon as I can."

"Do you have a plane or helicopter?"

That produced an irritated sigh, and I knew I was pushing too hard.

"I drive a 'seventy-five Pontiac that hasn't been tuned in fifteen months."

"We can meet at my parents' farm," I said, and gave him the address and directions.

"I'll be there in a few hours."

"Please step on it, Agent Randall. And bring some serious firepower."

10.

From body temperature, swelling of the ankles, odor, and state of rigor mortis, I made a very rough estimate that Coop Lugmor had been dead at least twelve hours, and probably more. He'd never made the phone calls to my parents' home during the night. If I'd been home, and if I'd believed it was Lugmor and had come over, I'd probably be dead too.

It was a thought that prompted me to run back out the door,

crouch down on the porch, and look around. There was no one outside or on the highway. I pulled Janet's car into the barn, closed the door, then went back into the house to examine the body some more.

Bolesh had, I assumed, come here and killed Lugmor right after he'd cleaned out Tommy's room and put Zeke on the bus to the airport. *How* Lugmor had been killed was another question, and the murder weapon certainly wasn't the butcher knife sticking out of his gut. There was hardly any blood around the site of the wound, none at all coming from his mouth. Lugmor's heart had stopped beating for at least a minute before Bolesh had found the knife and stuck it into the dead meat of the corpse just for the sake of appearances.

It looked to me like Coop Lugmor had been frightened to death.

He was slumped in a seated position, legs splayed at a forty-five-degree angle, against a wall in the garbage-strewn living room. As it sometimes does, rigor mortis must have set in almost immediately. Lugmor's toothless mouth gaped open in a huge O of a scream. His eyes were as open as eyes ever get, almost literally popping from his head. His arms were half raised, the fingers of the hands curled into claws as if he were clutching at something on his chest that was no longer there; the hands were at least a foot above the shaft of the knife.

I stepped closer, knelt down close to the body, and took rapid, shallow breaths as a defense against the ripeness of the dead flesh. There were small marks—some like scratches, others like pimples—on his face. Up close, I could see tiny, white crystals trapped in the stubble of his beard. There were more of the crystals on the front of his shirt, surrounded by what looked like dried water stains. There were other water stains on the peeling, faded wallpaper above his head, more crystals.

I licked my finger, lifted one of the crystals off the wall and tasted it. Salt.

When I bent back Lugmor's stiff fingers and examined them, I found little pieces of dried gray matter sitting on top of the grease and dirt beneath the nails. I stood up and shuddered. Water stains; salt crystals; terror. It was as if something had risen from the sea—or the depths of Volsung—to strike Coop Lugmor dead.

But now I had another "monster from Mirkwood" to contend with. I heard this one walk on its two legs through the door at the front, enter the living room, stop. I slowly turned to face Jake Bolesh and his leveled shotgun. He'd been waiting around a while, probably in the woods to the southwest; he was unshaven, and his eyes were bloodshot and black-rimmed; binoculars hung from a strap around his neck. His voice, when he spoke, was curiously flat.

"Old grudges die hard, don't they, Robby?"

"Hey, Jake," I said as Bolesh slammed the cell door shut on me, "have you seen the old B movie where the innocent victim tells the bad guy he won't get away with it?"

Bolesh turned and stared at me. His expression was strangely blank, his eyes dull; the gorilla had looked more human than Bolesh did at the moment. The liveliest part of him now was his hair; every strand of the pompadour was neatly combed into place, greased and gleaming.

"You're no innocent victim, Frederickson," he said at last.

"What did you use to kill Coop?"

"I didn't kill Lugmor; you did. You came back home here a hotshot hero from New York City. You always thought you were better than anybody else. Now you were upset about your nephew's death, and you decided to use the occasion to even up some old scores while you were here. I know that, because you threatened me at least three times."

"You think Mike Wallace is going to believe that?"

"I seriously doubt that Mike Wallace is going to show up in Peru County."

"Come on, Jake, use your head. I may be a lot smaller than Coop, but you'll find I won't disappear anywhere near as easily."

"No? We'll see."

"How about a phone call? I want to speak to my girl friend."

"The phone's out of order."

"People will come looking for me."

"Will they?"

"Garth, for one. You know that."

He shrugged, touched the gun in the holster at his side.

"Jake, I really feel we should discuss this problem with a third party."

"There isn't any problem."

"I think we should negotiate what we're going to do with me."

He stepped up to the bars, stared down at me. Now, studying him, I realized I'd made a mistake in thinking that his face and eyes were blank; I'd merely been looking at the surface of a black sea. Now I could see below the surface where great tides of rage and hatred swelled.

"What do you have to negotiate with, Frederickson?"

When things get bad, a moderate amount of worry is in order; when things get *really* bad, a person might as well laugh as cry. I managed a weak chuckle. "I'll make you an offer, Jake. You give yourself up and sign a full confession, and I promise I'll appear at your trial as a character witness."

Bolesh wasn't amused. "You've got balls, Frederickson; I'll say that for you. Just like your parents."

The laughter turned hot and choking in my throat. "What about my parents?" I asked in a tone of voice just short of a plea.

"They're tough," Bolesh said, a thin, cruel smile spreading like a skin disease across his face. "I needed four men—one to grab hold of your mother, another to hold a gun on your father, and two to help me—to search their house. I'm afraid we made a mess of things. It's a shame we had to tear up the home of a nice old couple like that just because their dwarf son is a retard with a big nose who ignores good advice when he hears it."

"Seriously, Jake," I said, struggling to control a surging rage that was pumping my blood pressure up to the top of the graph, making everything around Bolesh seem red, "you're a real shit. Leave my parents alone, for Christ's sake. Even you can't be dumb enough to think there's anything to gain in hurting them."

"We found the papers you took from Volsung, Frederickson."

"Ah." My situation did not look good; it had dropped from really bad to near hopeless. "Did you read them?"

"I destroyed them."

An interesting admission, which wasn't likely to do me any

good. It was time to swing down from the high wire, belly up to the green felt, and play. I squeezed up my first card, slapped it down on the table.

"Tell your people in Volsung that I want to see Mr. Lippitt."

"Who's Lippitt?"

"He's an operative for the Defense Intelligence Agency, and he's probably in charge of the silly joke they call security out there."

"Never heard of him."

"It's possible you don't know his name, but he's there. Your bosses will sure as hell know who he is."

Silence. A second card.

"Tell Lippitt I want to discuss the Valhalla Project. I may have put other files in other places; maybe I wrote some letters."

Silence. A dangerous, razor-edged joker from high up in my sleeve.

"Tell your bosses to remind Lippitt that he owes me. If he doesn't show up here, I'm going to start shouting at the top of my lungs about a certain talented mutual friend of ours we're both interested in. Tell him there may be a lot of unmarked graves in Peru County, but the Russians and Chinese have big ears. They'll hear about our friend. You repeat every word I just said, Jake. I guarantee it will get a response, and the people at Volsung will thank you for it."

"You're full of shit, Frederickson," Bolesh said, and abruptly walked out of the cell block.

Lacking a lock pick and having absolutely nothing better to do, I lay down on the hard jail cot and proceeded to catch up on some of the sleep I'd lost the night before. I had a strong suspicion that, very soon, I was going to need all the strength and clear thinking I could muster.

I woke up to the sound of shouting. The voices were muffled by the thick wall between the cell block and the outer office, but one of the voices sounded wondrously familiar all the same.

"Goddamn it, Bolesh, I know he's in there! I want to see him now! You open that door or you're going to have more fucking lawyers in Peru City than you can fit into the town hall!"

My initial surge of relief immediately hardened into a sharp blade of anxiety that pressed against my heart. There was no way Bolesh and the Volsung Corporation were going to allow the loose cannon that was my brother to roll around Peru County.

"Garth!" I shouted, leaping off the cot and banging on the bars. "Garth, run! Get the hell out of here! Don't let them take you!"

Garth had quick reflexes, and he was good with a gun. I hoped my warning shout would allow him to get the drop on Bolesh and any of the deputies who might be in the office. There were more muffled shouts, but no gunfire. There were the sounds of scuffling, large pieces of furniture being broken or overturned; the soft, thudding *phonk* of knuckles on flesh. Curses. Whatever was happening, Garth was giving as good as he got; if the outcome were still in doubt, at least it meant that my bull of a brother still had a chance.

"Come on, Garth!" I screamed. *"Do it, baby! Heeyai!"*

There was another thump; deep, resonant. Ominous. Then I heard a heavy body fall to the floor. A few seconds later the door to the cell block opened and Jake Bolesh staggered through. His pomaded hair was thoroughly messed; it also looked slightly askew, as if Garth had pulled Bolesh's scalp down over his left ear. A toupee; very expensive, expertly fitted, but a rug just the same. Bolesh was bleeding from the mouth, and as he grimaced I thought I saw a large gap where a few front teeth were missing. His shirt was torn and flapping; all of the buttons were missing. He was carrying a fat, ugly truncheon wrapped in black leather and stained with blood.

He stood for a few moments, glaring at me, then abruptly swung the truncheon at the brick wall behind him.

Thunk! Thunk!

"Bastards!" he panted in a hoarse, sibilant whisper, the breath whistling in the spaces where his front teeth had been. "Sons-of-bitches!"

He lunged and swung at the bars, and I just managed to snatch my fingers away in time to keep them from being crushed.

Clong!

"Something upsetting you, Jake? Having a bad day at the office?"

Clong! Clong!

"God!" Bolesh, white-faced and shuddering, hunched his shoulders and writhed, as if he were burning up from some unquenchable, white-hot fire blazing deep in whatever was left of his soul. "How I *hate* the two of you! *I hate you!*"

"Now, Jake, it's nothing more than a slight personality conflict. Why don't you calm down?"

Thunk! Thunk!

"Shut up, you little dwarf shit! You *fuck!* You're a *diseased* thing, Frederickson! You're *crooked!* Wait until you see what I've got waiting for the two of you!".

The last words were almost, if not quite, enough to make me want to kiss him. It meant he hadn't beaten Garth to death, and wasn't planning to—at least not in the short run. The steel fist that had been clenched around my heart relaxed slightly.

"Put the sapper away, Jake," I said evenly. "Come on in here and we'll go one on one. You're not afraid of a little old diseased, crooked dwarf, are you?"

Clong! Clong! Clong!

"You always thought you were so Goddamn smart! Robby, the smart freak! Robby, the all-A's freak!"

Thunk!

"—and Garth the protector!"

Clong!

"—do you understand, dwarf?! *God didn't make you right!*"

My old buddy Jake had gone right over the edge, fallen a long way, landed on his head and bounced a few times. Always the optimist, I kept glancing down the corridor and hoping that someone would come running in with a bucket of cold water. Nope. If there were deputies in the office outside, they were too smart to get in the way of the rabid animal who was their boss. It didn't bode well.

Thunk! Clong!

"They're going to be looking for my brother too, Jake," I said quickly, deciding that it was time for some serious discussion. I was making an effort to sound calm, but I was forced to shout in order to be heard over his ranting. "You know how big the Volsung Corporation is! You may hate Garth and me, but you have to be afraid of them! You're running amok, and they're not going to like it!"

"Shut *up,* you diseased dwarf fuck! I don't need their per-
emission to do what I'm going to do to you! Wait! Just *wait!*"

Clong! Thunk! Clong!

"This has become too big for you, Jake! Give yourself a
break! Ask for some help, some guidance! Put in that call to
Lippitt!"

"You bastard! You shit bastard! You've ruined everything!"

"Jake," I sighed wearily, realizing that I would have had a
better chance of communicating with a shark in a feeding
frenzy, "you were always the once-and-future asshole. At least
fix your wig. Seeing you with your hair hanging off really makes
me want to throw up."

He went bone white, gaped at me for a few seconds, then
clawed at his hair with his free hand. The toupee came off in his
fingers, leaving strands of tacky hair glue clinging like cobwebs
to his furry scalp.

"Brenner!" the county sheriff bawled. "Peters! Get in here!"

Now they came. Two pasty-faced deputies ran into the cell
block, winced when they saw the snit their boss was in, stopped
in front of him and stiffened.

Bolesh threw the greasy mat that was his hair into a corner,
then took a key ring out of his pocket and unlocked the door to
my cell. He had stopped ranting, but his hands were trembling
and he was taking in great, gulping breaths, as if he could not
get enough air. It was, I thought, a terrific time for him to suffer
a heart attack.

He pushed open the cell door, swung the truncheon.

Clong!

"Keep your guns on him," Bolesh said to his deputies. "If he
tries to fight back or get away, shoot him in the legs."

There wasn't going to be any heart attack. My initial fear was
that he'd come forward and try to smash out my brains summarily, which meant that I'd have to make some kind of move;
I'd be shot, but I'd damn well try to kill Bolesh before I went
down.

I sat down on the edge of the cot, planted both feet flat on the
floor, and tried to look terrified—a feat that wasn't at all difficult. I stiffened the fingers of my right hand and concentrated
all my attention on the spot on his thorax just below the rib
cage, the gateway to his solar plexus; a blow delivered there at

the right angle and with sufficient force could burst his heart. I would have only one chance, and I'd spend it if I didn't like the angle his first blow was coming from.

The deputies were in the cell now, flanking me; each was steadying his gun with both hands and aiming at my kneecaps.

The initial blow was angled away from my head, toward the soft flesh on my right side, below the rib cage. Bolesh didn't seem to be interested in beating me to death either—just close to it. I relaxed my fingers, exhaled loudly, and leaned slightly to my left in an effort to absorb some of the blow's force and pain.

There was nothing to do now but take the beating. It wouldn't be the first time Jake Bolesh had made me piss blood, but I swore it would be the last. I vowed that I would survive anything Bolesh did to me, and then—some way—I would kill him. Planning what I was going to do to *him* served as a kind of anesthetic while he worked me over. Finally he made a mistake, hit me just a bit too hard, and I passed out.

11.

Dreams of dragons and dungeons, tunnels and trolls, marched through my head; Orcs, elves, hobbits, and dwarfs. Magic swords and sashes. There were magnificent, sentient horses, brave Companies on heroic Quests battling against impossible odds with the salvation of the Earth hanging in the balance. There were vast treasure hordes, savage winds capable of stripping flesh from bone, poisonous spiders as big as boxcars, giant slinking beasts. There were Heroes and—of course—an abominable Prince of Evil so powerful it seemed nothing could stop his inexorable advance toward the conquest of the planet and the enslavement, forever, of its peoples. Only the Hero, usually frail and hopelessly outnumbered, could save the world; but time was running out, and the hoary legions of the Prince of Evil were closing in . . .

Whoopee.

And, of course, there was usually a Wizard with a magical staff around to bail the Hero out of *really* tacky situations. This particular Wizard looked like a Ku Klux Klansman in drag, but I knew he was a Wizard because his flowing black satin robe was ornately decorated with magical symbols woven out of sparkling gold and silver thread. He wore a peaked cap of black satin, and a black leather flap in which eyeholes had been cut out covered his face.

This Wizard was really Gandalf-on-the-spot, because he happened to be in my cell, bending over me and expertly probing my body for broken bones or torn ligaments and muscles. However, I had mixed feelings about the fact that the Wizard appeared to be a mere apprentice, despite his sartorial splendor; instead of a magic staff he carried a gun.

I tried to get up, intending to jab my fingers into his windpipe. I got about two inches off the mattress, uttered an earsplitting yowl as pain washed over and through me like a tidal wave of boiling water; the scalding liquid sloshed around my ankles, swept up through my ribs, scorched my skull. I bent double, but somehow managed to sidle over on the cot and swing my feet to the floor.

The yell had frightened me more than it had the Wizard; also, in my present condition, he was a bit too fast for me. He'd calmly stepped back and was now standing across the cell, beside an unconscious deputy who was sprawled on the floor. My little show of aggression had obviously pissed off the Wizard, because he raised his gun and shot me in the chest.

I woke up to find that my tongue had grown a fur coat and I'd acquired a drug-induced hangover to go with all my other miseries. The dart had penetrated my right pectoral muscle, and the residual pain there was like an irritating bee sting sitting on the great swollen bruise that was the rest of my body. I grunted, tried to sit up, banged my forehead on something; a steering wheel. I grabbed it, pulled myself up into a sitting position.

The car I was in was a battered Ford sitting in the shade twenty-five yards or so off a major state highway. Cars whizzed by, their tires singing in the heat. I recognized the highway; I was at least halfway to the airport, perhaps an hour out of Peru County. In the woods to the right, a pair of jays were severely criticizing me for invading their territory. There was a note taped to the inside of the windshield. I peeled it off, waited for my eyes to focus, read it.

Peru County is no place for Hobbits; you're a dead man if you come back. Find a hole and hide in it. Nothing you can do in PC except get buried.

First I drained half the water in the canteen my savior had so thoughtfully provided. Then, holding my breath and tensing against all the aches and stabbing pains in me, I forced myself to get out of the car in order to test my moving parts. After grunting my way through a few very slow laps around the car, I was satisfied that Bolesh hadn't broken anything. Eventually I began to move a little better, and my head cleared some—although it continued to pound like a drunk beating a full set of out-of-tune tympani. I reversed direction, kept hobbling and groaning and stretching and trying to think.

The Wizard knew what he was talking about. The problem was that his magic spell had only managed to whisk me out of Peru County. Bolesh still had Garth in his possession, not to mention a county full of Fredericksons in assorted sizes waiting to be snatched off the shelf. Somehow, the people at Volsung had found out I'd been inside their complex and had seen things. I knew of the existence of the Valhalla Project, if not its objective, and there was no way they could give me a pass now. I could take the Wizard's advice and hide. I could even go back to New York, make some noise—and then wait for the fingers, toes, and maybe an ear or two, to start arriving in the mail. Indeed, an odd digit could well be waiting to greet me when I got back.

The car keys were in the ignition. I pulled the car back onto the highway, rumbled across the grass divider strip, and headed back toward Peru County. I stopped at the first pay phone on the highway.

With all the incredible luck I'd had so far, it was only natural that I continue my great roll; I found forty-three cents in the dirt and dustballs under the front seat. I used a greasy quarter to place a collect call to Omaha.

"Federal Bureau of Investigation. Agent Calder speaking."

A woman. "This is Dr. Robert Frederickson. I—"

"Just a moment, Dr. Frederickson!" the woman said excitedly. "We've been waiting for your call! I'll patch you through to Agent Randall. Just hang on. Don't hang up, all right?"

Agent Calder was making me very nervous—and I wasn't exactly the picture of calm to begin with. Calling the F.B.I. earlier hadn't given me great joy; it was simply the only option I'd been able to come up with. I trusted the federal agency even less now, but still couldn't think of anything else to do; one unarmed, busted-up dwarf wasn't going to be much of a match for Bolesh and his deputies, not to mention whoever—or whatever—else might be waiting to jump out at me from some closet.

"Dr. Frederickson . . . ?"

"Mmmm."

"You're still there?"

"Mmmm."

"You'll hold on?"

"Until the bough breaks. Go ahead and do what you have to do, lady. I'm not going anywhere."

There was a series of whirs, whines, and clicks, and then Randall came on the line.

"Frederickson! I went to your parents' farm, but you never showed up! Where are you?"

"Just kind of floating around in a holding pattern. Where are you?"

"Sitting in Sheriff Jake Bolesh's broken swivel chair talking to you."

Randall sounded positively jovial. I said nothing, waited.

"Frederickson?"

"Mmmm."

"You don't sound anywhere near as happy as I thought you would."

"I've got a bruised smiler, and I'm a tough audience to begin with. Keep trying."

"It's over, Dr. Frederickson. I've got Bolesh and his deputies locked up in their own jail. Your nephew's computer equipment hasn't been damaged, and my agents are at this moment loading it all into a confiscated van. I've been sitting here for hours, drinking too many Cokes and waiting for you to call."

"If you're telling the truth, I'll pay all your dental bills."

"Why should I lie?" Randall asked, sounding genuinely puzzled. "We got here and found Bolesh and his deputies unconscious on the floor. I still don't know the details of what happened, but Bolesh woke up and started babbling like a baby. After a few minutes of listening to him, I locked up the whole crew."

"Where's my brother?"

"Sorry, Frederickson," the agent said quietly. "Fractured skull. He's in the hospital, in a coma. He'll live, but he needs surgery. He'll be out of things for a while. Now, come on in. I know you'll want to be at the hospital when they operate on your brother, but I want to get you to Omaha as soon as possible. I've got an awful lot of questions, and you're the only one with the answers."

"Let me tell you something up front, Randall," I said slowly. "I need you, and you know I need you. But I'm not sure I can trust you. If you're bullshitting me and trying to close a trap, it's a big mistake. Too much has happened in Peru County for it to be hushed up for long, no matter how many powerful people are putting their fingers to their lips."

"You're telling me! Frederickson, listen—"

"Taking out Garth and me can't be sanctioned, Randall. If you're running a game on me, think about it some more."

"Frederickson," Randall said, exasperation creeping into his tone. "I guess you have a right to be paranoid. You've been beat up, and maybe that's why you're not making any sense. I really don't understand what you're talking about."

"If you're lying to me, someday—somehow—people will find out about it. You'll find yourself sweating under television lights while you're taken apart by a congressional committee. Remember Watergate? I've written letters."

Randall laughed, long and hard. *"Good!* Come *in,* Frederickson! It's *over!"*

"I'll be there in an hour or so."

The moment I saw Randall's face I knew I'd lost the gamble, crapped out; but it was too late to turn around and walk out. As soon as the office door closed behind me, Bolesh and his two deputies marched out of the cell block, riot guns aimed at me.

Randall had, at least, been telling the truth when he'd told me he was sitting in Bolesh's chair. He was still sitting there—a boyish-looking man in his late twenties or early thirties, brown hair cut very short, tan suit and matching vest. I couldn't tell the color of his eyes, because he wouldn't look at me.

"Where's Garth?"

Randall wouldn't answer. The F.B.I. agent looked ashen, but Bolesh was grinning. The county sheriff's hair was glued back in place, carefully combed and pomaded.

"For Christ's sake, Randall," I continued. "This man killed two kids, and he's going to kill Garth and me—if he hasn't already killed Garth. You don't want to be a part of this. Help me."

This time Randall squirmed a bit, but he still wouldn't answer.

"Listen to me, Randall; you lied your ass off to me, but I was telling the truth when I said I wrote letters. I can appreciate what top secret means, and Garth and I know how to keep our mouths shut. We're not interested in passing secrets, or in screwing the government in any other way. All I'm asking for is the right to take care of this crazy bastard, Bolesh, myself, and for you people to punish the men at Volsung who let him off his leash. It's not much, and it's fair. Give me those things, and our problem ends right here in this office. Tell Bolesh and his men to leave; he's not about to kill an F.B.I. agent. I'll make sure you get those letters back, unopened. We can deal, Randall."

Finally he spoke. His voice was tortured, and I could see the cords moving in his neck. "No. You didn't write any letters. You are a straight arrow; even if you'd had time to write letters, you'd have been concerned about who might have to pay the return postage." He rose, turned his head in Bolesh's direction. "Remember what you were told; I haven't been here."

The agent gave me a fleeting glance just before he walked out the door. His eyes were brown.

Bolesh pulled down the shade, took out his sap.

12.

"Hey."

The word reverberated like a gong in the great empty cathedral that was located just behind my eyes. Sharp metal was biting into my wrists, holding my arms back around a square wooden object that was rough with splinters. Unable to move my hands or arms, I tried my head.

"Hey. Mongo."

My head worked; at least it moved. I tried my eyes. I panicked for a few moments when I couldn't see anything, but then relaxed when I caught sight of a shaft of moonlight. It was night. Gradually my eyes became accustomed to the dim glow of moonlight, and I could see that I was sitting on matted, filthy straw, chained to a support post inside what looked like Coop Lugmor's barn. Garth was chained to a second post, about twenty feet to my right.

"Hey, Mongo. You all right?"

"Of course I'm all right. I'm just sitting here filling in my empty spaces."

"Oh, I love it. That's good."

"And wondering why Bolesh hasn't added a few more. As long as you're up, signal the beach boy, will you? I can use a drink."

"Goddamn it, *you're* all right. How about asking if *I'm* all right?!"

"Are you all right?"

"No, I am *not* all right. I *hurt.* I cracked a knuckle on Bolesh's front teeth, and with all the stomping they did on me I do believe they managed to crack a couple of ribs and break a foot. I'll survive, but it was a shocking example of police brutality."

"What the hell's the matter with you? Didn't you realize you were supposed to beat the shit out of Bolesh and his deputies and rescue me?"

"I'm tired of rescuing you; it gets boring after a few years. I figured this time I'd let the villains keep you, just to see how it turns out."

"Well, you certainly have a front-floor seat."

"Yeah. I can't wait for the next reel."

"Seriously; from past experience, I've learned to view these little setbacks as character-building, consciousness-raising events."

Garth chuckled softly. When he spoke again, his deep voice was resonant with emotion. "It's good to see you, Mongo."

"It's good to see you, brother. Do you hurt bad?"

"No. I've got a very hard head, and the foot's numb. You?"

"No. Seeing you alive is the only painkiller I needed."

"Okay."

"Okay. Mom and Dad . . . ?"

"They were all right the last time I saw them, aside from being worried out of their minds about you. Bolesh and his crew really trashed the house, but all the relatives are over there helping to put it back together again."

"By the way, what the hell are you doing here?"

"Janet called me after Bolesh snatched Tommy's computer. She thought you might need some help."

"You're a big help. You were afraid I might get lonesome in the afterlife, right?"

"I forgive you for that thoughtless remark, the same as I forgive you for being absolutely, congenitally unable to keep your dwarf ass out of the most fucking *outrageous* situations." He paused, and I could hear him breathing heavily. When he spoke again, his tone had changed and taken on a jagged edge of real anger. "I'll tell you what I won't forgive you for, Mongo; I won't forgive you for not calling me the second you knew things here weren't right, and you realized you were in trouble. I *could* have helped then. Forget the stupidity; I'm used to you doing stupid things. I know why you didn't want me here, but you had no *right* to try to protect me. Tommy was *my* nephew, too; *my* family lives here, and you just happen to be my brother. Reverse our positions and tell me how you'd feel. It was a bad insult, Mongo."

"You're right," I replied quietly. "I'm sorry, Garth."

"Your apology is accepted." The anger was gone as quickly as it had come, the boil lanced and drained. "You don't even look like the Lone Ranger."

"Other people have commented on that."

"What would you suggest we do?"

"Aw, hell, you were right about letting the villains keep me; this is kind of exciting. Why don't we just hang around, breathe the good country air, and wait to see what happens?"

"Why not? While we're waiting, why don't you tell me what the hell's been going on?"

"Sure. How do you feel about dragon stories? I mean, what's your general attitude?"

"About the same as toward stories about giant alligators in New York's sewers."

"Mad scientists?"

"I like shaggy dog stories. Get on with it, Mongo."

"You're going to love this one."

Bolesh showed up about an hour later. He snapped a wall switch, and a single naked light bulb hanging just above our heads came on. A pigeon in the loft, startled by the light, swooped down, brushing against the electric cord. The bulb jerked, then swung back and forth, casting shifting, chiaroscuro shadows, patterns of light and dark, across Bolesh's grim face. He was carrying a black leather satchel, and I was afraid I was about to find out what had killed Coop Lugmor.

"Hi, shithead," Garth said brightly. "How's your mouth?"

In our present position, it didn't seem like a good idea to talk like that to Bolesh; I tensed in anticipation of the terrible beating I was certain Garth was going to get.

Bolesh didn't even blanch. He smiled slowly—which made me even more nervous. Then he opened the satchel, took out a pint bottle full of an amber-colored liquid. Next came a hypodermic syringe. He punched the needle through the rubber sheeting covering the mouth of the bottle, depressed the plunger, filled the tube of the hypodermic. Then he came for me, angling around toward my back so I couldn't kick at him.

"I told you God didn't make you right, dwarf," Bolesh said in a fluttering voice that bubbled with unfinished, insane laughter. His upper lip kept catching on the edges of his broken teeth, giving him a very wet lisp. "Now I'm going to fix you and your brother up good."

I winced and screwed my eyes shut as the needle sliced into the soft flesh of my left shoulder—reacting not to pain, but in terror of just what might be in the solution Bolesh was injecting into me, and what its effect would be; I had a gnawing suspicion it would make my memories of the rabies shots seem like morphine dreams.

Bolesh refilled the syringe, repeated the procedure with Garth. Then he went across the barn, sat down on the dirty

straw about fifteen yards from us, and leaned back against another support pillar. Rolling the hypodermic like a cigar in his
fingers, he drew his knees up to his chest, rested his forearms on
them and stared at us with a childlike grin of anticipation on his
face.

Garth and I stared back at him.

After a half hour or so Bolesh began to look unhappy. After
another half hour he gave each of us a second shot. He'd emptied almost a quarter of the bottle into our veins.

More staring. Garth began to snore loudly, although I suspected he wasn't really asleep.

Finally, around what my stomach told me was lunchtime,
Bolesh got up. He cursed, spat at us, then picked up his phar-
maceutical outfit and stalked out of the barn.

"Hi, shithead," Garth announced in a determinedly cheerful
tone as Bolesh and bag entered the barn in the afternoon.
"Good to see you, Jake. We've really missed you. How about
another shot of that happy juice? That's good stuff."

Bolesh's jaw muscles clenched tightly, and his eyes narrowed
to slits. He didn't seem to be able to believe what he was seeing
—or wasn't seeing. He set the bag down, came over and, still
being careful to stay out of kicking range, tore off our shirts and
examined the flesh of our necks and torsos. He looked like he
wanted to take our pants off but was afraid of what we might be
able to do with our feet.

Then he obliged Garth, gave us both another injection. This
time he gave the shots directly in a vein in the neck, as if he
wanted to make certain the fluid was entering our bloodstreams. Then he sat down against his pillar and stared.

We stared back.

This time it took him until dusk to get impatient. He gave us
both still another shot, paced around until it got dark, left.

Bolesh brought us water, but no food. It was just as well; with
nothing solid going in, nothing solid came out. Our keeper obviously wasn't worried about surprise visits from state health in-
spectors. "It's gone, you fuckers, all gone!" Bolesh shouted as
he entered the barn on the morning of the next day.

"Come on, shithead," Garth replied. "Stop teasing us. I can

see the bottle right there in your hand; there's lots of that good stuff left. Be a sport and give us another shot."

He did.

By late afternoon, something was starting to happen.

Garth had begun to suffer occasional muscle spasms which rippled up and down his body in undulating waves, causing his knees to knock and teeth to chatter. However, each time the spasms passed after two or three minutes and Garth assured me that he was all right, insisting there was nothing wrong with him that three steaks and a gallon of whiskey sours wouldn't cure.

I wasn't certain I believed him. His vicious and insistent defiance of Bolesh was no mere act of wasted macho or false bravado; it was, I knew, part of a ritual. Like a samurai, Garth was preparing to die, and refusal to give Bolesh the slightest bit of satisfaction was part of his death song.

My own symptoms were more subtle, but no less real. Although the sun was starting to go down, I noticed that I was squinting against the twilight. I realized I had been squinting all day and had suffered a hammering headache until an hour or so before, when it had begun to grow darker and cooler.

My eyes were becoming intensely photosensitive.

The symptoms were uncomfortable and distressing, but—even if Bolesh had been aware of them—I was certain they weren't what he seemed so anxious to write home about; our host was looking for something a lot more dramatic, and he was very annoyed by the fact that he wasn't getting it.

"It's gotta' work," Bolesh mumbled thickly as he injected the last of the solution into our veins. "I've seen it work."

Finding out what would happen when the stuff "worked" was not high on my list of priorities. I was no samurai.

The next morning it was clear that Bolesh was all out of patience. He arrived with a shotgun.

"Hi, shithead," Garth said. "If you've run out of happy juice, why don't you get the hell out of here so we won't have to look at your ugly face?"

"Yeah," I said wearily. "Jake, why don't you just unlock our handcuffs and go away?" I couldn't work up much enthusiasm for Garth's ritual, or hope to match his fanciful, New York City–detective type sense of humor. I had the most absurd yet insistent urge to take a bath, smell a rose, eat three eggs boiled for exactly three minutes, and drink one cup of coffee. Not necessarily in that order.

Bolesh propped up his shotgun by the door, came over to examine us once more. No sale. He cursed, kicked at us, stalked back toward his shotgun.

Fortunately, we had a visitor. A trim but solidly built man dressed in combat boots, khaki slacks, and matching tank top stepped silent as a flesh-colored shadow into the barn. He was totally bald, with large, almost soulful, brown eyes. There had been a time when he hadn't been able to walk around in the summer without a coat—a psychological malady caused by repeated dousings in Nazi ice baths. Our "mutual friend" had cured that. The man had to be pushing seventy, but you certainly couldn't tell by looking at his flat stomach, his toned, rippling muscles, or his eyes.

He could have used Bolesh's gun, but preferred to wield his own—a Remington 870 with modified choke and combat barrel designed to tighten the focus of a buckshot pattern. He shot from the hip. The charge caught Bolesh in the neck just below the jaw, permanently fixing his teeth as it blew his head off.

Garth's astonished shout pierced the deafening echo of the blast. *"Lippitt!"*

"Oh, yeah," I breathed, staring transfixed at Bolesh's decapitated body and the shiny mop of greasy, blood-stained hair that had somehow managed to land on a wall peg fifteen yards away. I would dearly have loved to kill Bolesh myself, but I decided I was willing to settle for the status quo. "I forgot to tell you about him. He's been playing chauffeur for the Volsung Corporation."

"Jesus," Garth gasped. *"Jesus!"* He had expected to die, had prepared himself for it from the moment he had found himself handcuffed to the post. Now, like me, he wasn't quite sure what to make of the fact that he was going to live.

"Where the hell have you been, Lippitt?" I said, still unable to take my eyes off Bolesh's twitching corpse. "You took your sweet time getting here. We've been sitting here pissing our pants in anticipation."

Lippitt stared at me hard, a single question in his eyes; he wanted to know if I had broken our pact, with Garth or anyone else. I shook my head slightly. He grunted softly, put his Remington aside, and searched through Bolesh's pockets until he found the keys to the handcuffs. He came around behind us, unlocked the cuffs.

"It took me a while to find you. You two threw Bolesh off his feed; he's been holed-up in the farmhouse."

"Where's your wizard costume, Lippitt?" I asked. "I rather liked that. Nice touch."

"Being currently unemployed, I don't need a disguise any longer."

Our handcuffs off, Garth and I slowly got up, stretched to the accompaniment of cracking joints, rubbed our raw wrists.

"Mongo's told me half the story," Garth said softly to Lippitt, a slight threatening edge to his voice. After an afternoon of smoke and gunfire a few years before on a New York dock, Garth had never much cared for Lippitt. "Why don't you give us the punch line?"

"Later," Lippitt replied evenly as he walked to a corner where Bolesh had thrown the valise, empty bottle, and syringe. He knelt down and tore the rubber sheeting off the top of the bottle. He sniffed at the inside of the bottle, rubbed his index finger around the rim, put the tip of his finger on his tongue. He spat, bowed his head, sighed. "How much of this stuff did he give you?"

"The whole Goddamn bottle," I said. "Half in me, half in Garth. I lost track of the number of shots."

"Over how long a period of time?"

"He started Thursday. This must be"—I paused to think about it—"Sunday. Three days."

Lippitt, obviously very concerned, straightened up, looked over at us and frowned. "And?"

"And what?"

"How do you feel?"

"Like shit."

"Come on, Frederickson!" Lippitt snapped. "Tell me precisely how you feel!"

"I thought I did. My eyes have become very photosensitive. You've got a halo around you—as unlikely as that may seem.

Everything seems very bright, and this amount of light hurts my eyes. Garth has been having intermittent muscle spasms for about a day and a half."

"They're painful," Garth said in a flat voice. "What was that shit, Lippitt?"

Lippitt nodded toward Garth's left foot, which was raised slightly in the air. "Bad?"

Garth shrugged. "Broken metatarsal. I can hop."

"Anything else broken?"

"Cracked ribs on the right. You haven't answered—"

"Come on," Lippitt said as he abruptly walked up to Garth. The Defense Intelligence Agency operative put his arm around Garth's waist, planted his shoulder in my brother's left armpit.

I took the side with the cracked ribs, supporting Garth as best I could by his belt. Together we formed a six-legged beast that hobbled uncertainly out of the barn into bright morning sunlight that hit my eyes and burned me like golden acid.

Lippitt had the black Cadillac from Volsung, and we drove in silence. Lippitt seemed deep in thought, and Garth and I were —for the time—content not to speak; we were intoxicated with the sensation of being alive, the feel of the wind from the open window whipping our hair and caressing our faces, the song of churchbells in the distance.

Lippitt knew exactly where he wanted to go. The ride took forty-five minutes, and we ended up in Sagemoon, the county seat of Ogden County, where there was a large and sophisticated medical laboratory complex serving doctors and hospitals in a three-county area.

Lippitt parked the Cadillac in back of the complex, opened a rear entrance with a lock pick. We went inside, walked up a flight of stairs, through a waiting room, and into a receptionist's office. Lippitt stepped behind a desk and began thumbing rapidly through a Rolodex file.

"You two go inside and get cleaned up," the agent said as he tore three cards out of the file, put them in his pocket. "There must be some clean lab smocks around here someplace that you can put on. Drink all the water you want, but don't take anything else. Rip out all the telephones; make sure you don't miss any."

"Lippitt!" I croaked. "What's wrong with us?"

"Don't call *anyone*. I'll be back as soon as I can."

"What's wrong with us?"

"That's what I'm going to try and find out," he said, heading for the stairs.

13.

Lippitt returned fifty minutes later with three frightened-looking medical technicians, a man and two women, in tow, and a box full of new clothes which he tossed onto a chair in the waiting room. One of the women turned out to be a doctor, and the first item on the agenda was to patch up Garth. His broken foot was placed in a walking cast, his ribs and the knuckles of his right hand taped. That done, we proceeded to the serious business of the day.

From the length of the list of tests Lippitt pulled from his pocket, it looked like Garth and I were going to be padding around nude for some time. Lippitt obviously knew what he was doing; he briefed the medical personnel on exactly what tests he wanted. Then he sat down in a secretary's chair, placed a revolver on top of a pile of papers where the three people could see it, and leaned back and put his feet up on the desk.

One of the technicians began the festivities by drawing samples of our blood. Lots of blood.

"Illegal gene-splicing experiments," I said as I watched the plastic tube at the end of the needle sticking out of my forearm fill up with blood.

" 'Illegal' is a matter of interpretation," Lippitt replied flatly as he stared up at the ceiling.

"Attempts at genetic engineering with mammals."

"Right."

"Large mammals."

"Right. Let's be a bit discreet, Frederickson. We're not alone."

"Looking for applications to humans?"

No answer.

"You're unemployed now, remember? You don't owe them your loyalty any longer."

"Really? How do you know who 'them' are? I'm not sure myself."

"You've got to be kidding. What are you, a salesman for Saks Fifth Avenue?"

"It may not be as simple as you think it is."

"So? Who *is* 'them'?"

No answer.

"You think I'm an idiot?"

"No. But I've had more time to think about it."

Mucous smears; nose, throat, rectum.

"Project Valhalla. *Jesus,* Lippitt! Some kind of biobomb?"

No answer.

X-rays. *Whir, clickety-clunk, whir.*

"What killed Coop Lugmor?"

"A star wasp. It's a jellyfish that lives in the surf off the coast of Australia. Its toxin is lethal, but most useful as a molecular probe. I suppose you'll want to know what a molecular probe is?"

"It's a chemical used to trace the passage of substances through cell walls."

"Correct. Would you care to discuss osmosis?"

"I think not. A pineapple like Jake Bolesh shouldn't have been able to get security clearance to piss on a tree within five miles of the Pentagon, what's more connect up with a top secret research facility. How the hell did he get to work for Volsung?"

"Siegfried Loge hired him. Bolesh was just what Loge was looking for."

"Somehow, Jake always struck me as being a bit crude."

That almost got a smile out of Lippitt, who was standing across the room, wearing a lead apron. "You should meet Loge. He and Bolesh didn't have much in common academically, but they were blood brothers in every other respect. If you were fond of Jake Bolesh, you'd fall in love with Siegfried Loge."

"I'd like very much to meet him," I said evenly.

"You won't."

"Why not?"
No answer.

Sonar tests; lungs and stomach.

"Where did Bolesh get the star wasp and the stuff he shot into us?"

"The star wasp was probably given to him by Loge."

"The director of Volsung gave him a thing like that to kill a man?"

Lippitt nodded. "I told you; Loge is a prince."

"The serum?"

"Lot Fifty-Six. Loge certainly wouldn't have given that to Bolesh. I don't know where Bolesh got it, but my guess would be from Rodney Lugmor's room. You're aware that that stupid prick Obie Loge took your nephew and Rodney Lugmor into the complex?"

"I guessed. They were playing a game, and Obie Loge was looking to score some heavy points."

"That I didn't know; I never could figure out why Obie Loge would take two friends in there. A *game?*"

"A fantasy game."

Lippitt thought about it, made a sound of disgust in his throat. "It figures."

"Whatever Tommy and Rodney saw in there scared the shit out of them—enough so that they thought they might want to tell somebody else about it. Rodney may have smuggled the serum out, the same as my nephew snuck out a pass card. Rodney's parents were away, so Tommy took off to stay with his friend and talk about what they should do."

"Your nephew—and Lugmor; pretty gutsy kids."

"Damn right," I said, feeling a lump rise in my throat. "I'd never realized how gutsy. Tommy wasn't exactly your Superman type." I swallowed, choked back tears, cleared my throat. "Anyway, after a few days Obie Loge knew he was up to his ass in alligators; either he told his father what he'd done, or his father found out about it."

Lippitt nodded.

"Jake Bolesh, Volsung's happy warrior in charge of doings on the outside, was told to take care of them."

"Correct."

"Did you give that order, Lippitt?"

"No."

"I didn't think so. Killing kids—or having someone else do it for you—isn't your style. What's behind the red door?"

No answer.

"*You* didn't much like what you saw either, did you? That's why you're 'unemployed.' They're hunting you, aren't they?"

No answer.

Urinalysis. Tinkle-splash, fill the bottle. Wait. Fill another bottle. They wanted stool specimens, but Garth and I just laughed at them.

"I want to take time out to call our folks," Garth said in a deep voice still resonant with anger. "They'll be worried out of their minds about us."

"No."

"You're not my commanding officer, Lippitt!"

"It really isn't a good idea."

The doctor had Garth and me lying on twin examination tables while she listened, poked and probed and punched, then listened some more. Lippitt was standing between the tables, checking off items on the list he had made for himself.

"How long were you down there?"

"Too long."

"How did you come to be there?"

No answer.

"You seem to have picked up some medical expertise."

"Some." A long pause, then: "I used to be a medical doctor, Frederickson. It was a long time ago."

"How did they find out so fast that I'd been inside Volsung and had taken files on the Valhalla Project?"

"Careful, Frederickson. Ears."

"Ears, bullshit; she's working on my gall bladder. You don't care what we're talking about, do you, Doc?"

The doctor, a handsome brunette in her mid-thirties, seemed to be taking a liking to me. She gave me a slow wink, but said nothing as she continued her prolonged voyage over my abbreviated body.

"Lippitt? How did they find out I was in the unmentionable building and took the unmentionable files?"

Lippitt looked up from his sheets, smiled faintly. "Why, Frederickson, you disappoint me. I'd have thought you'd have figured that out a long time ago."

"I've been slow this week. Bad biorhythms. Give me a clue."

"The gorilla snitched on you."

It occurred to me that Lippitt had gone a little mad.

Anal and genital examinations. Sperm samples.

"Garth and I are a mite hungry, Lippitt. We haven't eaten in half a week."

"I know that, Mongo," Lippitt said quietly. "You can't eat until I'm sure we have all the blood and urine samples we need. I'm sorry."

"Not even a Twinkie?"

"Not even a Twinkie."

The idea of having catheters threaded into our hearts didn't hold great appeal to me.

"Angiograms are dangerous," I said, gripping the technician's wrist.

Lippitt just stared at me.

"Yes," I sighed at last, relaxing my grip and leaning back. "I see your point."

The spinal taps and bone marrow tests hurt. A lot.

"Where—ouch!—*did* you get the wizard outfit? *Ouch!*"

"Siegfried Loge's collection of fantasy memorabilia; Loge is obsessed with fantasy literature and 'heroic' music. I'd just heard what had happened to you, and I was in a hurry to get to the jail before Bolesh found some excuse to kill you. I was still working at Volsung, so I couldn't let Bolesh—or you—see my face. I grabbed the first thing I could find, which happened to be in Loge's closet."

"You putting me on?"

"On the contrary," the D.I.A. agent said easily. "I told you you'd love Loge. He's indisputably a genius, but he's also mad as a hatter and cruel as . . . a Nazi." He paused, smiled wryly. "The whole damn place was a madhouse. You get a bunch of superscientists together, give them any piece of equipment they ask for and carte blanche to do with it what they want, and you find out they're like children loose in a toy store after all the adults have gone home. At least this crew was like that."

Lippitt, most uncharacteristically, seemed to be feeling positively chatty, and I didn't want to break his mood. I flashed a broad grin. "Sounds like a great place to work."

Lippitt grunted. "He used to play Wagner's *Ring* constantly —all sixteen hours of it at a stretch. He'd let a few hours go by, then start it all over again. He had everybody else wearing earplugs."

"I saw the speakers. I thought they were part of a PA system."

"Oh, they were that all right. You know how many times I've listened to *Das Rheingold, Die Walküre, Siegfried,* and *Götterdämmerung?* I know the scores by heart. I feel eminently qualified to conduct at Bayreuth."

"You know something, Lippitt? I actually think you're mellowing with age. That was funny."

His smile disappeared. "There's nothing funny about Siegfried Loge."

"Like father—*ouch,* Goddamnit!—like son, huh?"

Lippitt studied me for a long time. Something dark and dangerous moved in his limpid brown eyes, and suddenly I felt very uncomfortable.

"What do you know about Father?"

At first I didn't understand the question, and then I realized that Lippitt had misunderstood me. I'd been talking about Siegfried and Auberlich, just making small talk and trying to sidle up on Lippitt. He thought I'd been referring to "Father"— Siegmund Loge. The subject didn't seem to be Lippitt's idea of small talk, and my heart began to beat a little faster.

"Just what's common knowledge," I said, trying to sound casual while I watched him and tried to read his reaction. "Double Nobel winner. He got one for his work with enzymes. The second was for his design of the Triage Parabola, a complex mathematical model used to rate endangered species in order to focus the most effort and resources toward those it's still possible to save. Some called him the smartest man in the world— until his cracker barrel tipped over. Now he thinks he's God, and a few thousand hyped-up kids agree with him. What do *you* know about him?"

No answer.

"Is *Siegmund* Loge involved with Volsung and the Valhalla Project?"

No answer.

Eye tests; for me, excruciatingly painful. I could only tolerate the bright lights for a few seconds at a time, and so—with Lippitt's permission—the doctor and technicians turned their attention to Garth.

"What does Father have to do with all this, Lippitt?"

No answer.

Treadmill. Gasp, wheeze, pant.

"Getting information out of you is like trying to mine diamonds with a toothpick, Lippitt."

"Later, I'd like to try again with the eye tests. We'll use a little more anesthetic."

"I'd love to know the whole story before these tests kill me. For that matter, even *you're* not going to live forever."

"What is evil lives forever," Lippitt said in a distant, cryptic tone.

"Oh, good. A—*wheeze*—riddle. Let's see . . . we're talking about—*wheeze*—DNA research, genetic engineering. The cell lives forever." *Ahuh, ahuh ahuh. Wheeze.* "In a very real sense, the cell is immortal; it keeps passing on bits of itself in the form of genetic information from generation to generation, and it's been that way since we all crawled out of the slime. Every once in a while there's a missed signal, and that's what evolution is all about. So, what's evil about a cell?"

Gasp, pant, wheeze.

"Just a Spanish fable," Lippitt said quietly.

Galvanic skin reaction tests.

"Is Father more than foolish? Is Father evil?"

"As a matter of fact, he's one of the kindest, gentlest men I've ever met. And, as you may have suspected from all the names, a devotee of Richard Wagner."

"How do you know him?"

No answer.

"What does Father have to do with the Valhalla Project?"

No answer.

"Why can't you just tell us all of it, Lippitt?"

"Maybe I will," Lippitt said softly, after a long pause.

"Why *maybe?* Don't you think Garth and I have a right to know?"

"I'm still thinking about it."

"Exactly *what* are you thinking about?"

No answer.

Lippitt was becoming increasingly distracted as the tests progressed. For some reason I couldn't pinpoint—a vague tension in my empty stomach—I found that ominous.

Reflexes. Bangety-bang, twitch.

"What do you owe these people?"

"It's our country, Frederickson. There are a lot of things to be considered."

"Our country, my ass! Our beloved country killed my nephew."

"No."

"And now they're hunting you."

"No."

"Bullshit, Lippitt! *Bullshit!*"

"I don't believe these people represent the country, Frederickson. Not in the sense that you mean."

"The government is damn well responsible!"

Lippitt sighed. "The government of the United States isn't the all-powerful, omniscient bureaucracy you like to think it is, Frederickson."

"No? Well, I've had some bad experiences. So have you."

He shot me a quick, sharp warning glance. I shrugged, let the tag line alone.

"The proof of what I'm saying is the fact that the Volsung Corporation was built in Peru County in the first place." Lippitt paused, smiled wryly. "If the 'government' you keep referring to had had the faintest inkling that *you* were associated with Peru County in *any* way, they wouldn't have come within five hundred miles of the place."

"I'll take that as a compliment, Lippitt."

"Sure."

My turn to sigh. *"Why* can't you tell us everything?"

"I'm thinking about it."

My stomach flopped and tightened again. "You're making me nervous, Lippitt."

"I don't mean to."

"What's your connection with Father?"

No answer.

More blood tests. Incredible. They were draining us dry.

"Volsung had the most piss-poor security operation I've ever seen or heard of."

"You noticed," Lippitt replied drily.

"Kids wander in and out, material is taken out."

"I told you; the place was a madhouse, and the inmates were in charge."

"You were supposed to be in charge of security."

"Was I?"

"But then, you're pretty old, aren't you?" I said, watching him carefully. "They should have retired you a long time ago."

"Operatives who've done what I've done and know what I know don't retire, they just fade away."

"Clever use of the cliché."

"No cliché. 'Fading' is the term we use to describe the placing of an older or burnt-out agent into a cushy job."

"You were 'faded' into Volsung?"

"No. I was buried in Volsung. I had no real authority, and I had almost as much trouble finding out what was really going on in there as you did. In a very real sense, I was a prisoner; I was put in Volsung because I knew too much. If I'd moved around too much, asked too many questions, or made too many complaints, I'm sure Jake Bolesh would have been ordered to kill me, too. Meanwhile, it was Siegfried Loge who was really in charge of security—which was exactly the way he wanted it. Loge figured that the fences, the support of the community, the 'growing' program, and Jake Bolesh were all the security he needed."

"And Loge gave his smart-ass son the run of the place?"

Lippitt nodded. "These people had the most unbelievable contempt for people they considered less bright than they were.

They thought they could take care of any problem. It was a security disaster."

"I'll grant you that it doesn't sound like the way the Pentagon likes to do things."

"Precisely. Those people cared about nothing but their work; when they got involved in something, Barnum and Bailey could have marched through there and they wouldn't have known the difference."

"But the funds—and your orders—had to come through the Pentagon."

No answer.

"Volsung isn't a box of paper clips; a very big budget item and continued flow of funds had to be approved by *somebody* in Washington, and it would have to show up in budget reports."

No answer.

"Who cooked up the Volsung Corporation and the Valhalla Project?"

No answer.

"You accepted your 'prisoner' status, not to mention all the shit going on around you, passively—at least for a time. That doesn't sound like the Lippitt I used to know."

His brown eyes searched mine. "I wasn't the Lippitt you used to know," he said at last. "First, it took me some time—too much time—to appreciate the fact that I was a prisoner. Then I realized I'd been manipulated, co-opted, by . . . whoever. I was feeling tired, depressed, defeated. Old. Then I got wind of this crazy dwarf who was tearing up Peru County, giving Jake Bolesh—and, incidentally, Siegfried Loge—fits. That's when I decided it was time to get off my ancient ass and do something." He paused and smiled in a way I had never seen before; it was a warm smile, lighting his eyes, softening his face. "I must say, Frederickson, you're an inspiration to an old man."

"What's behind the red door, Lippitt?"

"I'm thinking about it." The Ice Age that was the more familiar Lippitt had returned.

"You said you were 'buried' at Volsung because you knew too much. About what?"

No answer. The brown eyes were still bright, but the fire there was now cold. Dangerous.

"What does Father have to do with the Valhalla Project?"

"Let's eat."

14.

Garth and I kept an eye on the medical personnel while Lippitt went out to his car, returned with a large ice chest filled with fruit and juices. There were thin vanilla milk shakes for dessert. I wasn't exactly overjoyed, and Garth wasn't too happy, either.

"Lippitt, you're a real prick," my brother growled, his voice ringing with utter sincerity.

"You should eat lightly at first," Lippitt replied evenly. "Otherwise, you'll get sick. I'll buy you a good dinner later."

"What does Father have to do with the Valhalla Project?" I asked through a mouth filled with the most delicious banana that had ever been grown.

Lippitt sipped at a container of apple juice, stared at the floor.

"If the government isn't behind Volsung and the Valhalla Project, who is?"

"Eat, Frederickson. There are still things I'm trying to sort out."

Up to this point Garth had been content to watch, listen, and evaluate while I did the interrogating. I'd been stalking the elusive Lippitt all day, but it was Garth who now fired the silver bullet.

"Lippitt," Garth said casually, picking a piece of apple skin from between his teeth, "why are you afraid of us?"

It struck him in the heart, and he started. He recovered quickly, but I had seen the unmistakable reaction in his eyes, the twitch of the muscles in his jaw and throat. A puddle of apple juice shimmered on the floor like a silent, liquid witness.

"I'm afraid for you," Lippitt said tightly.

"Yes," I responded quickly. "But Garth is right. You're also afraid *of* us! It's why you won't answer the most important questions. Why are you afraid of us?"

"The ring," Lippitt whispered.

"What are you talking about?" I asked, not liking the look on Lippitt's face. "What fucking ring?"

Lippitt's response was to rise from his chair and walk quickly from the room, slamming the door behind him.

Electrocardiogram.

"What's your connection with Father?"

"Don't talk; you'll disrupt the test." The Ice Man returneth.

"Then you talk to me. Do it, Lippitt. You came close before. Just think of me as your friendly neighborhood priest, and remember that confession is good for the soul. Enthrall me with the whole truth."

Lippitt stared at me intently for a few moments, then gave a curt nod to the technician who was operating the machine. The technician went into the other room where Garth, who had finished the test, was sitting. Lippitt quietly closed the door, then took over the controls of the machine himself. He had obviously made some kind of decision.

"I was faded to a place I believe you're familiar with," Lippitt said quietly, making delicate adjustments to two knobs, leaning closer to study the inky squiggles left behind by the needles. "The Institute for the Study of Human Potential."

That piece of information must have caused quite a jolt in my personal magnetism. It was, as far as I could see, a four-knobber; Lippitt looked like he was trying to control a ship at sea.

"Relax, Frederickson."

I lay back on the cold black vinyl, took a series of deep breaths.

The Institute for the Study of Human Potential was, indeed, familiar to me. It had been founded by a friend of mine, Jonathan Pilgrim. Pilgrim, an ex-astronaut who had walked on the moon, had "died"—suffered clinical death, inasmuch as his heart had stopped for almost three minutes—as the result of a crash in an experimental plane. The doctors had brought him back, and he'd been profoundly changed by the experience. He'd resigned his commission in the Air Force, then used his name to raise money to found the Institute, located on a mountain in northern California, near Crescent city.

"Pilgrim wouldn't let a government agent set foot on his place. Not knowingly."

"You're wrong. In order to establish a research facility of the size and scope that he has, he was forced to make some compromises."

"Jonathan takes government money?"

Lippitt nodded. "In exchange for allowing the D.I.A. to monitor his experiments. The Institute studies unusual human phenomena and exhaustively tests people with very special talents from all over the world, from musicians to Indian fire walkers"—he paused, chuckled—"to gifted dwarfs who defy all the odds to become star circus gymnasts and karate experts. Every once in a while someone with a special talent or talents comes along whom we feel warrants our attention. I was the agency's monitor."

"Father accepted an invitation to go to the Institute to be tested. He certainly 'warranted your attention,' didn't he?"

"It was two and a half years ago. He wasn't 'Father' then—just Dr. Siegmund Loge. He was there to take special, computer-generated intelligence tests. Incidentally, he went right off the charts on everything; he was—is—just about the smartest man in the world. He was a pioneer in DNA research, work with basic enzymes, and an expert in all the life sciences. Naturally, I recommended that he be interviewed by our people. He was, and he agreed to work for us in certain research areas."

"But he's been out in the wilderness walking on water for almost *two* years now. He must have had his breakdown right after he went to work for the Pentagon."

"It would seem that way," Lippitt replied in an oddly distant tone.

"Meanwhile, you were thrown out of Pilgrim's Institute and 'buried' at Volsung. How did you fall into the shithouse?"

"Very sensitive, top secret human genetic data was stolen from the Institute, along with a collection of sperm samples taken from a variety of very unusual individuals. The data was 'leached' out of computer banks that were equipped with the latest in supposedly unbreakable lock codes."

"You were responsible for security on those items, so they held you responsible for their theft. Get thee to Volsung?"

"Right."

"There's a certain irony in the fact that you helped recruit Siegmund Loge, then ended up working for his screwball son and chauffeuring his grandson."

"You think so, Frederickson? I don't. Given enough time and support, I'm sure I could have traced the theft of the material and nailed the people responsible."

"Ah."

"I was sent to Volsung because that was the best place to contain and keep an eye on me."

"Why should the D.I.A. want to contain and keep an eye on you? You *work* for them."

"It wasn't the D.I.A. that was responsible—at least not my immediate superiors. I've had a lot of time to think about it, and I'm convinced there's a small group of very powerful men —a cabal, if you will, made up of people in all phases of government—who are responsible for Volsung and the work conducted there. They've got the bit between their teeth, and they're up to . . . something." He hissed, clenched his fists; for Lippitt, one more absolutely incredible display of emotion. "They're mad, Frederickson. Mad!"

"*Who*, Lippitt?"

"The people who helped Siegmund Loge steal genetic data and sperm samples from Pilgrim's Institute."

Garth, Lippitt, and I stood in the darkened room, silently staring at the large X-ray negatives on the fluorescent display screen in front of us. They were pictures of my spine and Garth's. In both X-rays there were small gray blotches—shadows with small, radiating fingers, like tentacles—in the spinal fluid, just below the base of the skull.

"What are they?" I asked softly.

Lippitt slowly shook his head. "I don't know. Nothing shows up in the spinal fluid itself; only in the X-rays, under fluorescent light. Whatever is causing those shadows must have been incorporated into your genetic material at the most fundamental level. It's part of your DNA. Something might show up on an electron scanner, but frankly I doubt it. My guess is that we're looking at something caused by viroids—tiny organisms that can transform genetic material; they're much smaller than viruses, and even viruses are difficult to see."

"After all the tests we've been through, *that's* all you can say?"

"Oh, we've determined that the rods and cones on your retina have multiplied three- or four-fold."

"Does that mean I can give up eating carrots?"

It wasn't funny, and nobody so much as smiled.

"You'll notice that your night vision is dramatically improved, Frederickson," Lippitt said grimly. "Also, you'll probably be able to see further into both the infrared and ultraviolet bands of the spectrum than other people. The problem is that you'll be virtually blind—or in great pain—during the day, unless you wear very dark glasses."

"What about me?" Garth asked quietly.

"There's an alteration in the way your acetylcholine activates the nerve impulses that fire across your nerve synapses. We don't have basal tests for comparison, but I'd guess that your reflexes are now two or three times as fast as they were before Bolesh got hold of you."

My hand trembled as I raised it, touched the shadows in our spinal columns. *"That's* causing it?"

"We have to assume so," Lippitt replied in the same soft voice. "We can identify some of the symptoms, but not the precise causal effect."

"What the hell is in Lot Fifty-Six?"

"I don't know. It would take a team of biochemists to try and answer that, and I'm not at all sure they'd be able to do a final analysis."

"Father knows, doesn't he?"

Lippitt nodded once, very slowly. "I believe so. Also, perhaps, Siegfried Loge and the other scientists working on the Valhalla Project."

"Then we'll have to pay them a visit, won't we?" I asked tightly.

Lippitt just grunted.

"Lippitt, what's wrong with us?"

Lippitt thought about it, said: "As dramatic and disturbing as your symptoms may seem to you, it's what's *not* wrong with you that's important."

"Maybe to *you.* I know there's still more to this. What 'ring' were you talking about before?"

There was no response, but now Lippitt seemed not so much evasive as very distant and distracted.

"What the hell is Father up to?"

No answer.

Now Garth spoke, and there was menace in his voice. "Lippitt, I'm giving serious thought to doing something to *your* spine. After all the good times Mongo and I have had over the past few days, don't you think we have a right to know everything?"

"I'm sorry," Lippitt said in a voice so low Garth and I could hardly hear him. "I'm still thinking about it."

15.

We stood on the crest of the rise and stared down at the enormous black stain on the prairie. "Mirkwood" was gone; the entire Volsung Corporation complex had been expertly and efficiently destroyed, probably with hundreds of strategically placed incendiary grenades.

Despite the fact that I was wearing dark glasses, the light of day hurt my eyes and had given me a headache. Garth was having muscle spasms with increasing frequency; he would clench his fists, throw his head back and stiffen his body until they passed.

"You knew it was gone, didn't you?" I asked quietly.

Lippitt nodded absently.

"And you weren't kidding about the gorilla snitching on me, were you?"

"I have to find Siegmund Loge and kill him," Lippitt said distantly. "I'm responsible for him."

"What difference would that make?" Garth asked, using a handkerchief to mop sweat from his face as yet another spasm passed. "You'd still have all those other scientists working merrily away someplace else. How can you even be sure Siegmund Loge is involved with Project Valhalla?"

"Every once in a while they'd run into problems at Volsung," Lippitt replied. "I wasn't supposed to know, but I've been in the finding-out business for a long time. They'd struggle with the problem for a week or so before a call would go out, in code. A day or so later a call would come back, and the problem would be solved."

"Father was feeding them information, guiding the research?"

"I'm sure of it. Without him, they'll eventually run into a problem they can't solve and work will stop."

"*What* work?" I asked. "Just what is it you think Siegmund Loge is trying to do?"

No answer.

Garth closed his eyes and clenched his fists as a new series of spasms seized him.

"What do we do now, Lippitt?"

"You and your brother must run, Frederickson, and you must keep running. Don't go near any member of your family; don't contact anyone you've ever known; don't go anyplace you've ever been. Sooner or later—probably sooner—men will be hunting you."

"What will you do?"

"Hunt Siegmund Loge."

"Where?"

"I don't know."

"Well, we're sure as hell going with you."

"No," Lippitt said in a flat voice. "Mongo, my friend, you're just a bit conspicuous. Also, the shadows in your spines are growing. I don't know what's going to happen to you, or what form the symptoms may take."

"Fuck that," Garth said, his voice trembling with rage as he came out of his seizure. "We sure as hell are not going to just run around. You say you don't know what's finally going to happen to us. Men will be after us. You're the only link we have to what's happened. You think we're just going to wave goodbye to you?"

"I'm sorry, Garth," Lippitt said evenly. "I don't have any other advice. You can't come with me for the reasons I already gave you. I'll be far more effective traveling alone. I don't know what else you can do but run. You could see some doctors, but I strongly doubt that anyone is going to be able to help you."

"Father—or his son—may be able to help us," I said. "At

least they know what's wrong with us. Given that information, we may be able to stop it—find a cure."

Lippitt abruptly turned and walked back to the car. There was nothing for Garth and me to do but follow. We sat in the back and waited for Lippitt to start the engine. He didn't. He simply sat stiffly behind the wheel, staring intently through the windshield. He sat like that for close to ten minutes before his curt voice cut through the silence.

"Get out."

Garth and I got out, walked around to meet Lippitt at the front of the Cadillac."

"You've finished thinking," I said. It wasn't a question.

"Yes."

"What is it you've been thinking about?"

"I've been trying to decide whether or not I should kill the two of you."

Garth and I instinctively stepped back and apart, ready to attack Lippitt from two sides if it looked as if he were going to reach for a gun. The D.I.A. agent gave no indication that he'd even noticed our sudden, sharp movement.

"Mongo and I are thinking that's not such a good idea," Garth said quietly. "Maybe you should think about it some more."

"I've decided not to kill you, but in a short time one or both of you may wish I had."

"Oh, hell," I said. "We'll risk it."

Lippitt stared at me for a long time, finally said: "What if I told you that your deaths—voluntary or otherwise—might benefit every human being, perhaps every living creature, on the face of the planet?"

"I suspect I'd ask for a few details."

"Then you shall have them."

Lippitt opened the trunk of the car, took out a metal canister the size of a water pail. He unscrewed the top, and the sharp smell of formaldehyde cut through the air, causing my eyes to tear. Lippitt reached into the canister with his bare hands, withdrew two lumpy things, and perfunctorily tossed them onto the fender. They landed on the metal with a slurpy, ominous *plop*.

Garth and I stepped closer in order to see what the things were; we both cried out, lurched back. I could feel bile rising in my throat, and I fought back the urge to vomit at the sight of those monsters from Mirkwood.

"Project Valhalla seems to be about devolution," Lippitt said tersely.

One of the dead beasts was a large bird that had been a reptile—or vice versa. It had wings, a beaked head; the rest of it was a long, tubular, scale-covered body that ended in tiny webbed feet and a feathered tail.

The second creature was a rabbit with large purple gill slits on both sides of its throat.

Garth was making a desperate effort to speak, but he was caught in the throes of another seizure and could make only choked, strangling noises. Tears streamed from his eyes as he fought to control the spasms.

I wasn't suffering a seizure, but it felt as if my vocal cords were paralyzed. I could only stand and stare in horror at the dead, pathetically deformed creatures.

"As you pointed out, Mongo, the cell is immortal," Lippitt said in a hollow voice. "Each cell of every species carries within its genetic material not only directions for replicating itself the way it is, but also a complete genetic record of its evolutionary history. We're nothing more than sentient mammals, and we carry a long evolutionary history. It's why we have so many vestigial organs—the appendix is a legacy from birds, hair is fur that has not completely disappeared yet, newborn infants have a strong gripping reflex in hands and feet that comes from lower primates. Human fetuses go through a stage of development in the womb when they actually have gills. We—"

Mercifully, Lippitt stopped when I held up my hand.

"Are . . . we going to end up like . . . that?"

"I have no idea. By rights, the two of you should have been dead and looking something like that within an hour after Bolesh gave you the first injection. The stuff is incredibly fast-acting. It just tears apart the cellular structure and re-forms it, virtually before your eyes. It seems to act by magnifying the genetic information of the evolutionary past, throwing all the biological controls out of whack and commanding the cells to try to do everything at once. Naturally, the organism quickly dies as a result of the . . . molecular insult. I tried it on these specimens myself, I'm sorry to say, but I had to observe exactly what happened. There were many more—things—like this behind the red door in Volsung, all in various stages of dying."

"Maybe it works differently in humans," I said, my voice quavering as I squinted through a nimbus of light at Garth. My brother hobbled over to me and put his arm around my shoulders.

Lippitt slowly shook his head "I'm sure there's been human experimentation."

"Bolesh couldn't understand why it wasn't working," Garth said, his voice a deep rumble. "He said he'd seen it work."

"Yes," Lippitt replied. "I think we can safely assume that there's a shallow, unmarked grave by a roadside somewhere in Peru County where a hobo or hitchhiker is buried." He paused, looked somewhere over our heads. "And Father continues to organize his communes around the world."

It took a moment for the full impact of his words to strike me, and then the sweat began to slide from my pores. "But most of the communes are *here*, Lippitt, in the United States!"

"Now you begin to see the depth of *my* particular nightmare," he said, focusing his eyes on my face. "Remember; I'm responsible for him."

"If you hadn't recruited him, somebody else would have."

"Somebody else didn't recruit him; I did."

"Loge may or may not be crazy, but—"

"He knows exactly what he's doing," Lippitt said in a clipped voice. "I'm certain of it."

"Why don't you *show* these specimens to people, tell them your story?"

Lippitt smiled thinly. "Show and tell to whom? The editors of *The New York Times* or the *Washington Post?*"

"You're Goddamn right!" Garth snapped. "For openers!"

"The story might or might not be believed; I think not. Freaks like this do occasionally occur spontaneously in nature. In any case, the government—or the men I spoke of—will come back with a heavy story people are much more likely to believe. There's my age, after all, and you see what's happened to Volsung. The same thing would happen to me. There's no other evidence."

"You have *us!*"

"So, what's wrong with you? You've developed eye problems, and your brother's become an epileptic."

"It's a bit more than that, Lippitt."

"I suspect both of you would be killed—or worse, kidnapped—within an hour after you checked into any medical center large enough to conduct the proper tests."

I glanced at Garth, then back at Lippitt. "Euthanasia aside, what would be the point in your killing us? Frankly, I'd rather be kidnapped."

"That's because you still don't understand."

"Then explain it to us!"

It was some time before Lippitt answered. Finally, he asked: "Have you read Tolkien's *Lord of the Rings?*"

"Jesus *Christ!*" I exploded. "I'm getting tired of that question! What dwarf hasn't? Is *that* the ring you were talking about? What the hell does a fantasy trilogy have to do with saving the world by killing us? I think *you've* gone crazy, Lippitt!"

"In this instance, the work is instructive as an analogy," Lippitt replied evenly, fixing me with his gaze. "In the novels there are seven magical rings of great power. The Dark Lord has all of them—save for the one in Frodo's possession. If the Dark Lord gains possession of the last ring, he will rule the world forever. All that is good will be vanquished."

Suddenly, with a pang that clenched my heart, I recalled my mother's dream. And Jake Bolesh's words came back to me, screaming like an icy wind through the back doors of my mind.

God didn't make you right!

And I understood what Lippitt was talking about. "Garth and I are the last ring," I whispered hoarsely.

"Precisely. Let's assume that the object of the Valhalla Project is to develop a capacity to bring about rapid devolution in adult humans and their offspring in selected populations. Not kill; bombs and bullets can do that, and everybody has all of those that are needed. And, of course, there's no point in simply deforming. The process of devolution must be controlled—subtle, and virtually undetectable. Let's say a prototype serum is needed that will generate devolution just to the point where you have stupid, manageable humans—who wouldn't really be human at all. For the sake of argument, let's call it a population of

human-*like* creatures somewhere on the evolutionary cusp between Neanderthal and Cro-Magnon."

"What's to prevent this 'capacity' from accidentally escaping
into the rest of the earth's ecosystem?" Garth asked.

"To ask the question is to understand the potential horror,"
Lippitt replied. "Even to attempt such a thing is insane—and
yet someone is doing it. Obviously, developing a serum that will
give a controlled reaction is enormously difficult. It seems to me
that the two of you are now the laboratories where the final
answer Siegmund Loge is looking for can be found. You've become human Petrie dishes, and indescribable evil is growing in
you."

God didn't make you right!

"Perhaps it's because you're a dwarf, Mongo," Lippitt added
in a flat voice.

"Garth isn't a dwarf."

"No, but he's your brother. His genetic pattern must be very
close to yours; although he isn't a dwarf, he certainly must
carry the recessive gene for dwarfism. The pattern is close
enough so that he too becomes a kind of living laboratory. If
Father gets hold of either one of you, he may finally have the
key that will enable him to produce Lot Fifty-Seven—the serum
that will be effective for every human."

"Why couldn't any of my blood relatives do? Or any dwarf,
for that matter?"

"It's possible they would do, but I suspect not. There can be
enormous differences, even within families. The three generations of Loges are a good example; Siegmund Loge is as kind
and gentle as Siegfried and Auberlich are savage. Who is to say
such differences aren't at least partially genetically induced?"

"If the old man is so nice, what's he doing creating monsters?"

"A very good question. Perhaps I'll be able to find the answer
before I kill him." He paused, sighed. "In any case, I don't
know what all the genetic factors may be. That's another reason
I decided not to kill you; they might just find somebody else."

"Thanks a lot, Lippitt. That's very thoughtful of you."

Lippitt shrugged, almost smiled. "Besides, I'm rather fond of
the two of you. Frederickson, you know that's true."

Garth grunted in disgust.

"I believe this nightmare will end if I can kill Father," Lippitt continued seriously. "But you *do* see why I want the two of you to hide; you may be the only people in the world who can help Loge develop Lot Fifty-Seven—*if* he finds you, and if he discovers exactly what's happened to you. His people *will* be looking for you, because you're both loose ends; it's important for them not to find you. After a time, they may simply assume you're dead."

"We're lousy hiders!" Garth snapped, and immediately began to shudder.

"Frodo returned the ring to Mount Doom, where it was forged," I said. "He destroyed it."

"Frodo made his journey at the risk of letting the ring fall into the hands of the Dark Lord. Since *you* are the ring in this case, the usefulness of the analogy ends."

"Not for us," Garth said through clenched teeth. *"We'll* kill the son-of-a-bitch, after he fixes whatever is wrong with us."

"You'll risk delivering to Siegmund Loge exactly what he may need to bring the Valhalla Project to completion."

"Garth and I just want to get straight," I said wearily. "We're not into saving the world."

"Aren't you, Mongo?" Lippitt said quietly. "Think about it. Things could actually come down to that."

"If this group of men behind Loge is as powerful as you say it is, Loge's people are bound to find us eventually anyway. When they do, they'll realize what's happened. Better to take the offensive. Garth and I will hunt Loge in our own way."

Lippitt thought about it, shrugged. "Why not? Maybe it's just as well. That way, if they stop me, you may still have a shot at Loge."

"A Company," I whispered.

Lippitt laughed loudly. In the past I'd rarely seen him smile, much less laugh. "On a Quest!" Lippitt said at last, and then laughed some more. Garth and I exchanged an uneasy glance.

Finally the laughter tapered off, and Lippitt shook his head. "You realize it's hopeless, don't you?" the D.I.A. agent continued. "It's going to happen. Siegmund Loge is going to pull off the Valhalla Project, and God only knows what this planet is going to look like in two or three generations."

"You say it's hopeless, Lippitt."

"Well, maybe there's a million-in-one chance of finding Loge, getting through *his* security, and then nailing him before one hell of a lot of forces combine to capture or kill us. An old man, an epileptic policeman, and a half-blind dwarf who can barely tolerate sunlight. So, why do I feel like laughing?"

"Because you've set aside lifelong loyalties and given up everything in order to come down on the right side. 'Freedom's just another word for nothing left to lose,' Lippitt: Kris Kristofferson."

Lippitt walked up to Garth and extended his hand; after a long hesitation, Garth took it. Not being inclined toward theatrics or emotionalism, I held back. Then, almost without realizing it, I found myself stepping forward, reaching out and clasping my hands around theirs.

16.

Lippitt had given us a lot of cash and left the car with us, after changing the plates. Suspicious of motels so close to Peru County, we slept in the car that night.

In the morning I found a cool, swift-moving stream and took a bath. We stopped at a diner and I ate three eggs boiled for exactly three minutes, drank one cup of coffee. There was a single rose growing outside the diner, and I smelled it.

We headed north toward Wisconsin and a place where one of Father's communes was rumored to be located. Garth, with his unpredictable seizures, couldn't drive, and so I had to. Even with dark glasses the sun was hurting my eyes, so I stopped at a medical supply house for glasses with smoked lenses. When I came out, Garth was suffering a seizure. In his fury or frustration or desperation, Garth grabbed the edge of the door and yanked. The door tore off its hinges.

BOOK II

Pieces for Death and Silence

17.

There are a lot of cows and trees in Wisconsin, and it took the better part of three months and most of our liberated Pentagon money to find Father's commune in northern Bayfield County, near Lake Superior.

The good news was that no one seemed to be on our trail, which could mean that Garth and I were presumed dead, and any loose guns belonging to Father or the Pentagon were off somewhere chasing after an ancient, wily Defense Intelligence Agency operative. The rest was all red ink. Whatever had been injected into our bloodstreams had been absorbed into every cell in our bodies, where it was merrily cooking away in the chromosomes, canceling controls in the DNA, finding and randomly transcribing tiny, forgotten genetic messages which had been discarded in an evolutionary wastebasket hundreds of millions of years deep, sending those messages back into our flesh First Class, Special Delivery. It had been almost two days since Garth had suffered a nervous seizure, but my right foot—the one with the scaly membrane growing between the big and second toes—itched all the time.

Naturally, it was Halloween.

We switched places a mile or so down the highway from the commune-operated fruit and dairy stand we had spotted on the first pass; Garth slid behind the wheel, and I climbed in the back. I rested my hand on the stock of the Colt automatic Lippitt had given us and pulled a blanket up over my lap; if word had been sent to Father's worldwide ring of communes to be on the lookout for the "keys to Valhalla," some unfortunate acolyte was going to find out that this particular set of keys could do a lot more than unlock genetic secrets.

Garth drove slowly up the highway, then pulled into a small parking lot and stopped close enough to the stand so that I could see without being seen, hear the conversation, and cover him. I felt vaguely ridiculous; the stand, framed by cheerful and intricately carved jack-o'-lanterns, was staffed by two young men and a woman, all of whom I judged to be in their early or mid twenties. Except for a common unisex uniform comprised of pale green overalls and matching turtleneck sweater, the three young people could have stepped off the pages of a Norman Rockwell calendar; in Nebraska they would have been described as clean-cut and fresh-faced. The men wore their hair cut very short, and the girl wore hers in a style that nicely framed a face that was every parent's—and lover's—dream. With her firm body, sensual mouth, and flashing brown eyes, she looked like the Ultimate Cheerleader, promising paradise to some lucky member of the right team.

Here, if the information given to us by a real estate agent was accurate, the team consisted of stone fundamentalists—although the woman had not been sure exactly what it was they considered fundamental. Their theology and politics were reportedly somewhere to the right of a Philadelphia television evangelist's. They were Born-Again Christians with a few twists nobody in the region had been able to describe with any accuracy.

The three smiled in unison as Garth stepped out of the car.

"Father love you," the girl said brightly. "May we serve you, sir?"

"Father love you," Garth replied easily.

Suddenly a shudder ran through Garth's body, and he staggered backward, came up hard against the car. I tensed, put my fingers on the door handle. It seemed a poor time for a seizure; if Garth did his Hulk number, the entire stand as well as the small warming hut behind it were likely to disappear, and I didn't feel this would start us off on the right foot with the commune. But the tremors passed, and I sank back down into the seat with a sigh of relief.

One of the young men started to come around from behind the stand. "Are you all right, sir?"

"Just a dizzy spell," Garth said as he pushed off the car and walked over to the stand. "Everything you have here looks absolutely beautiful."

The Ultimate Cheerleader beamed. "And everything is delicious, sir. We make all the cheeses ourselves, and the fruit pies were baked only a few hours ago. Also, you get a free jack-o'-lantern with anything you buy."

"It isn't food for my body that I need," Garth said. Nice. "I'd like to join your community."

The three young people exchanged uncertain glances. It was the girl who spoke.

"Do you have anything to say to us?"

Shit, I thought with something approaching religious fervor. If sounded like an invitation to play Password.

"I seek Father's peace." That only brought more uncertain, uneasy glances. Garth folded his hands in front of him, bowed his head. I had to strain to hear his voice. "Please. I've been so troubled—and I've come so far. There were words, but in my fear that you'd reject me I've forgotten them. Please allow me to serve Jesus and Father."

The girl came around from behind the stand, walked up to Garth and tentatively touched his hand. "You're one of the hundred and forty-four thousand?"

A beat. "Yes," Garth said.

A dozen beats. "I believe you," the girl said at last. Then she wrapped her arms around Garth's waist and pressed her cheek against his chest. "I hear the words in your heart," she continued as she put her head up and covered my brother's mouth with her own. The two young men gave little yelps of joy, ran around from behind the stand and began to dance in a circle around Garth, patting him on the head, back, and shoulders as the girl continued to kiss him.

That would have been enough to give me a seizure. However, when the girl removed her mouth from his, he turned his head slightly in my direction—winked.

Even my choked-off laugh felt good; it had been some time since Garth and I had even smiled.

The mood didn't last long. Garth was beginning to untangle himself, and I assumed he was getting ready to introduce me. Then the girl unwrapped herself from around his waist, whispered something in his ear, and skipped off into the warming hut behind the stand. Garth made a small warning gesture with his hand behind his back, and I stayed put.

The girl returned from the hut, and the four of them engaged in conversation conducted in voices too low for me to hear. After about five minutes something with a broken muffler could be heard approaching on the dirt road that ran through the apple orchards behind the stand; a trail of dust rose over a sea of trees with leaves the color of blood.

A battered, brown Willys Jeep roared out of the orchards, skidded into a turn that took it all the way around the stand,

and stopped with its nose almost touching our car's. The driver got out, and I released the safety catch on my gun.

The man was as tall as my brother, a little over six feet, and burly, with a fair complexion and a shock of sand-colored hair visible under a brown beret. His matching brown jumpsuit was definitely paramilitary in style, with the cuffs stuck into shiny black leather boots. He wore black leather gloves. On one sleeve of the jumpsuit was a shoulder patch with what looked like an anemic Olympic symbol—four interlocking black rings, stacked two on two, on a gold background; it was virtually identical to the logo I had seen inside the Volsung Corporation building. He also wore a shoulder holster filled to overflowing with a .38. The man had not come to kiss and dance.

The man moved off a few yards with the three young people, and I had to shift position slightly to keep track of what was going on. I didn't like what I saw. The man in the jumpsuit listened in silence as the three spoke, didn't change expression when Garth meekly approached and said something to him. Suddenly he turned his head slightly and looked at the car. I sank back into the seat, heart pounding, and stared straight ahead through my smoked glasses.

In the middle of something Garth was saying, the man abruptly turned and marched toward the car. Garth, his face impassive, followed behind. The man studied me from outside the car, but I waited for a rap on the window before rolling it down.

"This is my brother, Boris," Garth said quietly. "As I told you, he's blind."

"Who are the hundred and forty-four thousand, Brother Boris?" the man snapped at me.

Now I turned toward him, cocked my head at an angle, and smiled benignly. His eyes, cold and appraising as he gazed at me, were set wide apart on either side of a nose that looked as if it had been broken at least once, and he had a lantern jaw that was too big for the rest of his features. "Father love you, brother. We seek Father's peace."

"Who sent you? Who's your sponsor?"

"Father's spirit is our guide."

The muscles in the man's lantern jaw clenched and his eyes narrowed to slits as he stared at me. Then he appeared to reach a decision. "Follow me," he said curtly to Garth, then turned and walked quickly to the Willys.

Garth started up the car, followed the Willys around the stand and up the dirt road through the orchards. "We seem to be missing a password," I said.

"Yeah. Incidentally, we're the Jamisons—I'm Billy, you're Boris."

"I heard. I really don't feel like a Boris, Billy."

"Well, Billy's already said you're Boris, so Boris you shall be."

I leaned on the back of the front seat, looked at my brother. The pale, late-afternoon light did not flatter his profile; in the three months that we had been searching for this commune, his nose had inexorably broadened and flattened. "It looks like we go to Plan B," I said.

Garth shook his head. "Not yet."

"I'm going to shoot Captain Midnight the first chance I get."

"No," Garth said firmly. The Willys had disappeared around a bend fifty yards ahead of us. Garth had to grip the wheel firmly to maintain control on the deeply rutted road, and now he accelerated in an attempt to catch up with the speeding Jeep. "This commune is our only link to Siegmund Loge, and we may never find another—not in time, anyway."

"You think that's news to me, Garth?" I asked irritably.

"Just a reminder."

"I don't need a reminder."

"Plan B will never work. We have no idea now big this place is. We don't know how many members there are, and we don't even know what we're looking for. Shooting this guy isn't going to solve the problem. They have to let us in."

"There's no way we're going to bullshit our way past this guy, and you know it. He's Goddamn well taking us back here so that he can shoot us."

"I think there's still a chance we can pull this off, Mongo. This is my hand; let me play it out."

"What the hell do you know that I don't? What were all of you talking about back there?"

"This big joker's more than just a guard; he's a member of the commune. He shares their beliefs."

"What the hell difference does that make?"

"There's no time to explain now. Just keep that Colt hidden, and let me do all the talking."

We came around the blind turn and Garth had to slam on the brakes to avoid smashing into the Willys, which was blocking the road. The uniformed man was standing next to the Willys, beret pulled down low over his forehead, gloved hands folded across his chest.

"Leave the gun, Mongo," Garth whispered.

I left the gun—in my belt, next to my spine, under my shirt. As far as I was concerned, Lot 56 had softened Garth's brain. I didn't plan on letting the uniformed man bury Garth and me in a Wisconsin apple orchard, and I didn't want us to end up looking like the squishy things we had seen splashed over the Caddy's fender. I was in no mood to horse around with anyone —or to waste time. In a way, I preferred Plan B. I was certain that, as night fell, I could infiltrate the commune, find some clue to the whereabouts of Siegmund Loge, and get out again. Garth might not be able to see in the dark, but I could. It was daylight I couldn't handle.

"Stay cool, brother," Garth continued as the man walked up to the side of the car and motioned for Garth to roll down the window.

"Get out," the man said.

Garth opened the door, stepped out onto the dirt road. I opened my door, waited for Garth to take my arm and help me out. I let him guide me around to the front of the car, where we stood like soldiers awaiting inspection.

The man raised a gloved hand, rested his index finger on the center of Garth's chest. "You're a liar."

"No," Garth replied simply.

"Who sent you here?"

"Fa—"

"You private detectives? Parents? Reporters?"

"We're pilgrims."

"You're a liar."

"No."

"Who are the hundred and forty-four thousand?"

"I told you—"

"Who's your sponsor?"

"Father."

"Have you brought an offering?"

"We have some money—"

"If you had any business being here, you'd know I wasn't talking about money."

"I've tried to explain to you—"

"You say your brother's blind. Where's his cane?"

"I'm his cane."

The man laughed harshly. "You're not only a liar, you're an idiot. No sponsor would ever send us a dwarf, what's more a blind dwarf."

Without warning the man's hand shot toward my face. Somehow, I managed to limit my reaction to screwing my eyes shut. Nothing happened. I'd expected my glasses to be torn off. They weren't, and when I opened my eyes I was amazed to find that Garth's reflexes had been quick enough to enable him to reach out and grip the man's wrist, stopping the hand in midair. I was impressed.

Rather than reach for his gun, the man brought his other gloved hand back, cocked it with the fingers straight, the edge on a direct line with Garth's temple. Garth continued to grip the other wrist, but otherwise made no move to defend himself.

I was content to wait and watch—for the moment; if the man couldn't control his itch to strike Garth, I was going to scratch his brains with a bullet.

"Boris mustn't be hurt," Garth said evenly. "He's holy."

My brother's fingers remained locked around the man's left wrist; the man's right hand remained cocked in the air. I just remained.

"I wasn't going to hurt him," the uniformed man said at last. His tone had become slightly uncertain. "I just wanted to look at his eyes."

"That will hurt him. His affliction was cast upon him by Father personally. It's special—as is mine. Light burns Boris."

Now it was the man who seemed impressed. Slowly, the gloved hand came down. Garth released his grip on the other wrist.

Since there had been no claim of my being mute, I decided it might be a good time to do a little downfield blocking for my brother. I cleared my throat, spoke in my sweetest voice. "If this man wishes to gaze upon Father's mark, Billy, let him. My pain will be a small price to pay if it will enable us to be admitted into Father's larger family."

Garth nodded, stepped aside. The uniformed man stepped closer, reached out with both hands and—tentatively—removed my smoked glasses.

I knew what was going to happen, and every instinct screamed for me to close my eyes—but I had to leave them open long enough for our interrogator to see the lack of iris and the huge pupils that extended vertically, like knife wounds, across the eyeballs. I managed—and paid the price. The raw sunlight poured through the pupils and smashed into my optic nerve like a bullet. Then I did go blind as the inside of my head went nova in an explosion of crimson. I bit back a scream as tears flooded my eyes and rolled down my cheeks. My hands flew to my face a split second later, but the man had seen my eyes—and the sight had apparently produced the desired effect. I heard a gasp, and then a click as the glasses dropped to the frozen, hard-packed dirt at my feet; I winced inwardly, but there was no sound of breaking glass.

I felt Garth's arms wrap around me, realized that he had gone down on his hands and knees. "Hurts, huh?" he whispered in my ear.

"Like a son-of-a-bitch," I whispered back, nuzzling my face in his shoulder and allowing him to pat the back of my head. "Speaking of sons-of-bitches—"

"Shh. If you can continue to refrain from making smart-ass remarks, I think I'm going to be able to pull this off."

"How do you know?"

"I can smell it."

That sounded pretty much like a smart-ass remark to me, but I didn't have time to reply as Garth unwrapped himself from around my neck, wiped the tears from my face, and repositioned the smoked glasses on the bridge of my nose.

Slowly, I opened my eyes. Everything was surrounded by an aura, as if I'd spent too much time in a heavily chlorinated pool. However, the pain was beginning to ebb, and I could at least see once again. It also made me feel considerably better to see that my snake eyes had given the uniformed man a pretty good case of the shakes; even through the smoked glasses I could see that his face was ashen, and he was breathing very rapidly.

Garth stayed on his hands and knees. He shuffled around in the dirt until he was facing the other man, then clasped his hands in front of him and bowed his head. "It happened when the vision came to us," he said in a hoarse, dramatic stage whisper that would have made Laurence Olivier proud—at the delivery, if not the content. "The vision asked if each of us would accept an affliction upon our bodies if that would assure our admission into the family of Father's Children. We accepted, of course. Our afflictions were visited upon us, and we were told to come here. We were not told anything else."

It was the most outrageous line of bullshit I'd ever heard, but what was even more outrageous was the fact that it actually seemed to have an effect on the uniformed man. His Adam's apple bobbed up and down as he swallowed nervously, and he appeared uncertain of what to do next.

"You've seen Boris's eyes," Garth continued quietly, raising his head and looking directly at the man. "We accepted our afflictions as a test of our faith. Now it seems that we have become a test of *your* faith."

The man wiped off a glistening sheet of perspiration that had suddenly appeared on his face with the back of a gloved hand. "What's your affliction?" he asked Garth.

It had occurred to me that Garth had gone a bit too far in claiming afflictions for both of us, and now it was crunch time. His broad, flat nose was ugly enough, but it couldn't very well be described as an affliction. Unless he intended to ask the man to wait around until he had a nervous tic that would enable him to tear the car apart, I didn't understand what he planned to do.

What he did was to rise to his feet, take off his parka and throw it to the ground. Then he took off his shirt, stood half-naked in the frozen afternoon.

The uniformed man uttered a startled cry and stepped back two paces. I lowered my head and swallowed a low, tortured moan that had begun somewhere at the bottom of my soul. I wanted to weep and shout my rage at the sky—not out of revulsion, but for the brother I loved so dearly. It had not occurred to me until then that Garth had not undressed or bathed in front of me for close to a month and a half, and now I understood why.

A sleek, glistening mat of blue-black fur girdled his torso, starting at a point just below his nipples and disappearing down into his slacks.

"The vision was of Father," Garth said evenly as he slipped back into his shirt, picked up the parka and draped it across his broad shoulders. "Father said that we would find peace here. He said to trust in the faith and wisdom of the man in uniform who would meet us. Please allow us to join you."

"Wait here," the man said in a voice that cracked. "Please."

"Oh, Garth," I moaned through clenched teeth as the man walked ahead to the Willys, opened the trunk and began to rummage around inside. "Oh, Jesus Christ."

"Shut up," Garth said flatly. "You're not in such great shape yourself, and this isn't exactly the time for an extended conversation on our mutual woes. Besides, I don't want to talk about it."

Garth and I stood side by side in awkward, embarrassed silence while the man continued to rummage. I've experienced a few bad moments in my life, but this time—being forced to battle raging emotions and play a passive role when all I wanted to do was reach out and take my brother's hand—was perhaps the worst.

Finally the man emerged from the trunk and came back to us. He was carrying two heavy, pale-green robes and two pairs of sandals. Neither of the robes looked as if it would fit me, but the man had obviously made an effort to find my size.

"I'm Mike Leviticus," the man said, extending his hand to Garth.

"An unusual name," Garth replied as he took the hand.

"We all assume biblical names—first or last—when we're accepted as Father's Children," Leviticus said, then turned to me. The gloved hand he rested on my shoulder somehow felt strange, but I wasn't sure why. "Forgive me, Brother Boris, for causing you pain. It's not easy to find this place, yet some do. Most of those who come here uninvited mean to cause trouble. That's why I'm here. I hope you understand."

"I do understand, Brother Mike, and there's nothing to forgive. Uh, do some of the people who decide to leave the family tell others about it?"

Leviticus shook his head. "Nobody ever leaves. What Father's Children find here is what we've been searching for all our lives."

"Mmm."

"I realize that you've been given no instructions, so I'll give them to you now. At this point you leave behind everything from your old lives. All of your personal possessions will be sold, and the proceeds will go to the commune. Your clothes, which you'll leave here in your car, will be burned in a ritual ceremony. You'll don these robes and sandals while I wait, and then walk the rest of the way to the commune—a symbolic journey signifying that you join Father's Children with nothing, and are ready to be reborn. Even though it's cold, I think you'll find the walk invigorating and spiritually cleansing."

"Are you going to walk with us?" Garth asked.

"No. I've already taken the walk; this is for the two of you. I'll stay behind and check out your car. From the looks of it, we may be better off stripping it down and selling the parts."

Garth seemed tense, and I knew why; he thought the gun was in the car. He didn't know how big a problem we had. Fortunately, Garth was large enough to cover a lot of sins.

Sidling closer to and slightly behind him, I reached behind my back and took the Colt out of my belt. I pressed it against his spine so that he'd know what it was. Leviticus glanced away for a moment; Garth coughed loudly, and I flipped the gun into some brush at the side of the road.

Because of the cold, Mike Leviticus suggested that we change in the car. However, Garth—as if in defiance of his discomfort —proceeded to strip in the middle of the road. I did the same. We donned the heavy robes and sandals, looked at Leviticus.

"The commune is two miles down the road," the man said, beaming. "I'll drive back to the stand and call ahead. Reverend Ezra and the others will be waiting for you. Welcome, and the peace of Father be with you."

18.

"That was the most incredible performance I've ever seen," I said, hitching up the hem of my overly roomy robe as we rounded a sharp bend in the dirt road. "I was ready to shoot the big dumb bast—"

"Mongo, help me," Garth slurred as he suddenly began to stagger.

I felt short of breath, panicky. Garth was about to suffer another seizure, and each time he was in the grip of the terrible electrical and chemical storm taking place inside his body, I feared he was going to die or break his own bones with the uncontrollable, incredibly powerful contractions of his muscles.

Garth swayed, and his entire body began to twitch spasmodically. I put my shoulder against his hip and shoved as hard as I could, pushing him off the road into the orchard; in our time on the road, we had learned that a seizure would pass more quickly if he had some object against which to exert the force.

"Garth, there's a branch over your head!" I shouted, hoping he could hear me through whatever thick mists shrouded his mind whenever he had an attack. "Grab it!"

He didn't respond. As always, he was resisting the attack; his head was thrown back, his teeth were clenched, and low, guttural sounds escaped from deep in his chest and throat. The storm was upon him—every muscle in his body had gone rigid and was twitching. I slapped his right elbow, trying to get it up. The arm jerked and flopped, almost hitting me in the head—then shot up. The other arm whirred like a broken pinwheel until it was stopped by the palm hitting the overhead branch. The fingers of both hands curled over the branch—and stayed there.

There was nothing more I could do except stay out of Garth's way, and I went back out on the road to see if the noises Garth had been making had attracted any attention. The road was empty. Suddenly I heard an explosive crack, then the sound of something heavy falling to the ground. I ran back into the orchard.

Garth was just coming out of the brief period of unconsciousness that always followed his most severe seizures. He was sprawled on the ground, face covered with sweat despite the cool, moist breeze blowing through the trees. Both palms were scraped and bleeding, but there was no sign that the limb, perhaps six inches in diameter, had fallen on him.

"Hey, Godzilla," I said, kneeling beside him and wiping his face and palms with the edge of my robe. "You all right?"

Garth blinked rapidly, then slowly nodded. He rolled away the huge, broken limb, then eased himself up into a sitting position and leaned back against the trunk of the tree. "Sit down a minute, Mongo," he said with a sigh.

"Garth, I'm freezing my ass off and you're going to catch pneumonia. Also, our new friends are waiting for us down the road. I know you're weak now, and I don't want to rush you, but I don't think this is a good time for a chat. We've got to get moving."

"I want you to sit down, Mongo," Garth said evenly. "This is important."

Stepping forward, I grabbed his right wrist with both hands and pulled. The notion that I could pull Garth to his feet against his will was ludicrous, but I was looking to make a point. "Garth, I can't believe you got us this far. They weren't looking for us, which is the break of our lives. That kind of luck isn't going to last. For one thing, we're carrying a whole library on genetics and evolution in the trunk of the car. Leviticus and the others are going to want to know why we're interested in such unholy things—and the answer could come with a phone call at any moment. We have to get in, find the information we're after, and get our asses out of here fast. We may need the minutes we're wasting here."

Garth twisted his wrist free, grabbed my wrist. "We can't outrace a phone call, Mongo. What with all this 'visions of Father' bullshit, Leviticus or somebody else in the commune may already have called the people we're looking for—in which case, an unwelcoming committee is already forming and these minutes won't matter. They matter to me now, because I need to get straight with you."

Not understanding what he meant but responding to the emotion in his voice, I shrugged and sat down on the tree limb.

"I could tell you that I didn't mention the fur growing on my body because I didn't want you to worry," Garth continued in a flat tone as he released my wrist. "That would be a lie. The fact is that I was ashamed and disgusted, and *that's* why I didn't show you. I was wrong not to tell you. If there's any hope at all of us surviving this Goddamn horror show, there can't be any walls between us. I won't keep secrets from you again."

My response was to slip my right foot out of the sandal. I raised my foot, spread my toes and wiggled my web at him. "Speaking of shameful and disgusting secrets, welcome to the club."

Garth looked at the web, then suddenly burst into laughter. He pushed my foot away from his face, leaned over and put both his hands on my shoulders. "Well, our friend Jake never promised a rose garden when he shot us full of that shit, did he?"

"Now that you mention it, I don't recall that he did."

Garth rose to his feet, grabbed the collar of my robe, and pulled me to mine. "Come on, Brother Boris. It's time to work some more miracles."

The cusps of day—dusk, and the aura just before sunrise—were the most dangerous times for me, periods of a half hour to forty-five minutes when I was almost totally blind; there was enough sunlight to inflict pain on my uncovered eyes, but not enough to penetrate the smoked glasses. Now it was dusk, and I was content to close my eyes and traipse along on Garth's arm.

"Slowly turning into a beastie is a bitch, isn't it?" Garth said drily.

"What the hell are you complaining about? At least you seem to be staying with the mammals. I seem to be slipping off to join the reptiles."

"It's your sneaky, slimy nature, Mongo."

"Another crack like that and I'll pull your fucking fur."

"How's your nose?"

"One hell of a lot prettier than yours."

"Seriously. Do you notice anything different about your sense of smell?"

"No. Do you?"

"I've got another flash for you. Besides providing me with a built-in fur coat, that shit Bolesh gave us has been working overtime on my olfactory nerve. With this new schnoz, I'll go one-on-one with any bloodhound. It turns out that the world is really a pretty smelly place. Right now I can smell apples on the trees, as well as those rotting on the ground. I can smell leaves, wood, dirt."

I stopped walking, pushed the smoked glasses down on the bridge of my nose, and squinted up at the red-haloed figure of my brother. "Back there, you said you knew Leviticus was going to let us in because—"

"I could smell it," Garth interrupted, pushing the glasses back up on my nose and pulling me along. "Don't do that again. You're supposed to be blind, remember?"

"Jesus, you were serious, weren't you?"

"Yep. No joke. I seem to be able to smell emotions—at least I have to believe they're emotions; the odors come and go quickly, and I've noticed a correspondence with people's behavior."

"Pheromones?"

"Must be. Different emotions, it seems, smell differently."

"What the hell did you smell on Leviticus?"

"Religious ecstasy."

"How would you know what religious ecstasy smells like?"

"Certainly not from sniffing around you," Garth replied drily. "Your problem is that you don't understand religion, or religious people. Deep down, you think that people who say they believe in a deity, or miracles, are just funning you. They're not. You let me handle these people, Mongo."

"I am letting you handle them. You didn't answer my question."

"I picked up the scent from the two boys and the girl when I first told them that we'd come to join the commune; at the time I didn't know what it was. At first, Leviticus just smelled of suspicion and hostility—until I told him about the vision of Father. Then he smelled like the others. These people believe in magic; they believe that it will literally rain cats and dogs if God, or Father, wants it to. They were looking for a miracle, so I gave them one. As you see, a miracle is as good as a password any day."

"What does religious ecstasy smell like?"

Garth thought about it. "Turnips," he said at last.

"I'm sorry I asked."

"They believe that Father sent us here for some purpose."

"What purpose?"

Garth laughed. "How the hell should I know? You think I talk to Father?"

"That's great material, Garth; I love it. I can't wait to see what miracle you conjure up to stop a bullet."

"This miracle comes with a strictly limited guarantee; one phone call to or from either of the Loges, and it's canceled."

"Meaning we're canceled. With some luck, we may have a few hours. I'll go out tonight and poke around. All we need is one clue to the whereabouts of the Loges, and we'll be gone before dawn."

"We also have to get our clothes and the car back. I doubt we'll get very far on foot, dressed in sandals and green robes."

"I wonder where the hell Lippitt is?"

"He's probably dead," Garth said distantly. "Regardless of the reasons he gave for taking off on his own, he took the heat off us—and he knew what he was doing. As you know, Lippitt was never one of my favorite people—but the man had guts."

"He also saved our lives. I'm not so sure he's dead."

"He's an old man, Mongo. How long can he keep running and dodging? The Loges and the Pentagon probably have half the world looking for him."

"You saw what he can do with a shotgun. He's a *tough* old man."

"No question about that. You know, half the world's going to be looking for *us* if we manage to pull off this little commune caper. We're going to be up to our asses in alligators."

"Gee whiz, Garth, I'd hate to think we could be in any serious difficulty."

"I wish we could call Mom and Dad, at least let them know we're alive."

"No way. If there's a tap on their phone, it would only cause grief for them and us. Right now, a poll of any reasonable group of men and women would guarantee that we're dead. Let's keep it that way."

"Always the eternal optimist. Listen, brother, I'm counting

on my close proximity to you to pull me through this. You've got more lives than a litter of cats."

"The problem is that I'm feeling distinctly reptilian of late."

"I guess there'd be no point in getting in touch with the folks, anyway. I mean, what would we say? Hi, Mom and Dad, we're alive, but we can't come home because we have to catch a crazy before his crazies catch us. Any day now we're likely to turn into a couple of slimy blobs, but not to worry. Oh, and by the way, do you know of anything that will remove fur and webs between the toes?"

That set us both to laughing—but it was the laughter of desperate men, or semi-men, trying to fend off despair and tearing memories of a family in Nebraska, people who loved us and whom we might never see or speak to again.

Suddenly Garth stopped laughing and poked me gently in the shoulder. "All right, Brother Boris," he continued, "button up. The wind's blowing in our direction, and the schnoz smells people."

I buttoned up, moved closer to Garth and gripped his arm more tightly. I was at once thankful and regretful that the time for casual conversation and symptom sharing had passed. In fact, I had one secret left, a symptom I hadn't told Garth about, a feeling that filled me with such terror and a sense of revulsion that I could barely stand to think, much less talk, about it. Images of what I could become, or what I was becoming, constantly threatened to drown me in a sea of horror and disgust.

Three days before, I had awoke in the morning to find that the glands on both sides of my neck had grown painfully swollen. They had remained so, and now each time I swallowed, my saliva left behind the taste of burnt, bittersweet chocolate and produced a numbing, prickly sensation in the tip of my nose.

19.

"Can you see yet?"

"A little."

"Just don't get caught peering over the top of your glasses."

"I won't."

The last rays of the setting sun were glancing off the surface of Lake Superior, the relative darkness triggering the infrared receptors in my altered retinas, bathing everything in a shimmering glow that ranged from pale violet to crimson. It was like watching life through a tinted X-ray negative; although I'd been seeing like this for months, I still wasn't used to it. It was positively otherworldly.

But then, I was becoming positively otherwordly.

The site of the commune, which we now approached as we trudged down a long slope, was in a large, grass-covered clearing flanked by orchards and forest on three sides, and Lake Superior to the west. To the north was another large clearing which could have been a cow pasture, but was now empty. In the main clearing were a myriad of garden plots set out in a checkerboard pattern. There were perhaps a dozen buildings constructed of wood and sheets of corrugated steel.

At the end of the road and mouth of the clearing was a large wooden shack, and waiting outside the shack was a reception committee of one. I'd been expecting something a bit more festive, assuming Garth's story had stuck—or disastrous, if it hadn't. I found it a rather murky omen, and it seemed to mean that the others had either not been told about us, or had been instructed to stay away.

The man waiting for us was older than Leviticus, and had thick, dark hair that seemed to explode out of his head in unruly ringlets. His face was gaunt, his eyes haunted, his manner dark and brooding. He wore overalls like the three young people out at the stand, but in addition he wore a gold cross around his neck that looked big enough to ward off a tribe of vampires —which, judging by the uncertain expression on his face as we approached, he may have been expecting.

It had to be Reverend Ezra.

"Father love you, Reverend," Garth boomed cheerfully as he pulled me to a stop in front of the man. "I'm Billy Jamison, and this is my brother, Boris."

The Reverend nervously cleared his throat, tentatively extended a thin, bony hand to Garth; in the light cast by two spotlights over the entrance to the shack, viewed through my smoked glasses, the hand looked skeletal. "Father love you,

Brother Billy and Brother Boris. I'm Reverend Ezra. Uh . . . welcome."

"You can't imagine how happy we are to be here," Garth said as he pumped the other man's hand. "Boris and I have been on a very long spiritual journey, and this is the end of the trail."

"So I've heard," the Reverend said, obviously uncomfortable. He retrieved his hand from Garth's grasp, glanced at his watch. "Would you come with me, please? I'd like to see that you're comfortable, and we don't have time to talk now. I'm expecting an important phone call."

Oh-oh. Suddenly I didn't much care for Garth's description of the commune as the end of the trail.

"Of course," Garth said easily.

We followed the Reverend along a path to a building that resembled a large quonset hut. Two burly men wearing overalls and uncertain expressions on their faces flanked the entrance. "Father love you," Garth said to the two men as we passed between them.

It was a spacious, neatly appointed office with a long, heavy oak desk as the centerpiece. The only items on the desk were a telephone and a large, well-worn Bible. There was a sofa and three straight-backed chairs in addition to the swivel chair behind the desk, two more doors—both closed. Above each door hung a framed painting, one of Jesus, the other of Siegmund Loge. Father.

"I think you'll be warmer here," the Reverend mumbled, not looking at us. He gestured toward the sofa. "Please sit down. This shouldn't take long."

Garth led me over to the sofa, and we both sat down. The Reverend eased himself down into the swivel chair behind the desk, then stared off into space and absently drummed his fingers on the oak. Obviously, we were to wait with him until he got his phone call. I sorely missed the Colt; punching out Reverend Ezra wasn't going to get us past the two men at the door, and it wasn't going to help us find Siegmund Loge.

It was Garth who finally broke the silence. "Reverend? Is something wrong?"

For a time I wasn't sure he was going to answer. He cast a longing look at the telephone, stared up at the ceiling for almost a minute, then finally looked at us. "Frankly, I'm not sure what to do," he said at last.

"Billy?" I said, tugging anxiously at Garth's sleeve. "Is something the matter? Father said everything would be all right."

"We did have a vision, Reverend," Garth intoned ominously. "Was Father wrong in telling us to come here?"

"Mike told me about your vision and your afflictions," the Reverend answered in a distinctly nervous tone of voice. "Would you describe them to me, please?"

He was stalling for time, I thought, waiting for the phone to ring.

Garth launched into his vision patter, embellishing it with a few rhetorical flourishes that included descriptions of flashes of lightning and claps of thunder when Father spoke. Reverend Ezra seemed quite impressed with it all.

He was even more impressed when Garth capped off his performance by opening his robe to the waist.

"The mark of the beast!" the man cried, leaping up out of his chair and making the sign of the cross.

"The mark of Father," Garth replied evenly as he closed his robe.

"How can I be sure?"

"Who else could wield such power?"

" 'And I saw the beast, and the kings of the earth and their armies, gathered together to make war against Him that sat on the Throne, and against His army.' " The Reverend swallowed hard, sank back down into the chair. The blood had drained from his face. "The two of you have received the mark of the beast," he added in a barely audible whisper.

His words had triggered long-buried memories; I was a child again, smaller than other children, more frightened than other children. As she did every night, my mother was reading to me from the Bible. I'd always liked Revelations; the apocalyptic visions that spilled forth from the pages had jibed with my childhood anger and sense of injustice, had given me hope that, maybe, one day things would be all right, that one morning I might wake up and find I was no longer a dwarf.

Suddenly I knew who the hundred and forty-four thousand were. "Wrong beast, Reverend," I said. "We are two of the four."

Garth glanced at me quickly, a confused expression on his face. I continued, " 'And I looked, and, lo, a Lamb stood on the Mount Sion, and with Him a hundred and forty-four thousand, having his Father's name written in their foreheads.' Billy and I don't have the mark on our foreheads, Reverend, because we *are* the forehead—Father's forehead."

"Mike said you didn't know about the hundred and forty-four thousand!"

"Obviously, we do."

" 'And I heard a voice from heaven,' " Garth intoned as his own memories were stirred, " 'as the voice of many waters, and as the voice of a great thunder.' "

"Why were you sent here?"

"That was not revealed to us, Reverend," I said, then quoted some more Scripture. " 'And they sung a new song before the throne, and before the four beasts and the elders, and no man could learn that song but the hundred and forty-four thousand, which were redeemed from the earth.' We're two of the four beasts, Reverend; we represent Father's truth. You have been chosen to receive us. Will you hear our lesson, or is Father to send us somewhere else?"

"What is your lesson?"

"We must wait until it is revealed to us; or Father may wish us to discover it for ourselves. I think we should reason together. Don't you agree, Billy?"

"I certainly do, Boris," Garth said, giving me a pat of encouragement on the leg. "Reverend, you'd do well to listen to my brother. I think you should take that phone off the hook so there'll be no interruptions, and then we should try to work this out."

Reverend Ezra slumped forward in his chair, rested his head in his hands, and kneaded his temples with the ends of his long, bony fingers. He didn't take the phone off the hook. "It doesn't make sense," he said at last.

"What doesn't make sense?" Garth asked.

The Reverend slowly put his hands down on the desk, fixed his gaze on me. "That Father should mark two men to send us a lesson, and that one of those men would be a dwarf."

"What the he—uh, what do you have against dwarfs?"

"The choice of a dwarf would seem to mock everything Father has promised and taught us. The Great Time is very near at hand. Satan knows this, and it is to be expected that his armies are on the march. How can I be certain that the two of you weren't sent here by Satan?"

"Father would prevent it," Garth said with a broad gesture of dismissal. "If we were servants of Satan, Father would strike us dead."

Reverend Ezra thought about it, shook his head. "Father may have marked your bodies to show that you serve Satan, then sent you to us as a challenge to see if we are worthy of His trust and teachings. If that's true, and we accept you into our family, none of us will live to see the Great Time. I need guidance."

"Who gives you guidance?" I asked. "Father?"

"Of course," the Reverend answered in a somewhat distant tone. "But Father is not always of this world. Now I must rely on the son . . . and the son is not Father."

Beside me, I felt Garth tense with excitement. I sat up straighter, concentrated on keeping my face impassive and my voice even. The Reverend's words seemed to suggest that it would be Siegfried Loge, not Siegmund, who would be on the other end of the line if the phone rang. If so, it would confirm a link between Project Valhalla and the communes of Siegmund Loge—a link that, up to now, only Lippitt had been absolutely convinced of.

"Where is the son?" I ventured.

The question seemed to echo in the prolonged silence that followed. One question. If the Reverend answered it, he could stop worrying about his phone call; he'd be taking a nap while Garth and I were taking our leave.

"Don't you know?" Reverend Ezra was no longer making much of an effort to hide his suspicion.

"It was Father who appeared to us," I replied, "not the son."

Suddenly the telephone rang, startling all three of us. The Reverend snatched up the receiver.

"Yes?" Reverend Ezra said, his voice nervous and high-pitched.

Garth, with disarming casualness, inched forward to the edge of the sofa and planted both feet firmly on the floor; at the first sign of distress on the part of the Reverend, the man would be even more distressed to find Garth's hands wrapped around his throat. Out of the corner of my eye I watched the front door, which had been left partially ajar. Given the element of surprise, I was confident that I could take out one of the big guards quickly and silently; taking out both of them, without raising a ruckus that could summon Mike Leviticus and his gun, was a problem of considerably greater magnitude.

Fortunately, the problem appeared to become academic when the Reverend hung up the phone and did nothing more than absently stare at the receiver. His expression displayed no signs of fear or alarm—only disappointment.

"So, what does Siegfried Loge have to say?" Garth asked in a flat tone as he leaned back in the sofa and crossed his legs.

"He's unavailable," the Reverend mumbled with obvious distaste.

"For how long?"

"They won't say."

"Why is he unavailable?"

"I don't like to even imagine. There are rumors about that place—" Suddenly the Reverend's head came up, and he looked startled. "How do you know of Dr. Loge, Brother Billy?"

"The vision," Brother Boris answered. Garth had always been the more patient of the two of us, and Brother Boris was starting to get pissed. Somewhere under Reverend Ezra's frizzy curls was an address or a telephone number that could save Garth's and my life, and I had a growing urge to start banging the man's head on the desk top, or against a wall behind one of the two closed doors, to see what answers might drop out. "Father told us *who* the son is, but not *where* he is. That's what you're supposed to tell us."

"If Father didn't tell you, I don't think I should."

"Father forgot. He's got a lot of things on his mind these days, and everybody knows how distracting appearing to people in visions can be."

"Father never forgets anything," Garth interrupted quickly. "It's Brother Boris whose mind occasionally gets muddled these days; it's the remembered ecstasy of the vision. However, Father did say that you would tell us anything we wanted to know, Reverend."

Again, there was a prolonged silence while the Reverend

pondered whatever it was he was pondering. Now fear moved across his face—but I somehow sensed that it was not fear of us. "I don't understand why you want to know about Dr. Loge," he said at last. "He's not a member of our family. He is of . . . them."

"Who?" Garth asked carefully.

"Warriors of Father. Dr. Loge leads them."

"Men like Mike Leviticus?"

Reverend Ezra nodded. "Mike is a Warrior, but he is also a member of our family. That's why he was assigned to guard us."

"If Siegfried Loge doesn't have anything to do with your—our—family, why do you have to check with him?"

"Dr. Loge is our . . . supervisor. Father has told us that we must follow His son's instructions."

"Father marked us, Reverend," I said softly. "We are Father's emissaries, so you have nothing to hide from us. Where did that telephone call come from?"

"I . . . I just can't tell you, Brother Boris. Not without permission."

"Really? In that case, maybe it's time for Brother Billy and myself to do some marking of our—"

Instantly, Garth was on his feet and pulling me to mine by the collar of my robe. "Don't pay any attention to Brother Boris, Reverend; he hasn't had his supper, and he gets cranky. Uh, would it be possible for us to meet some of the others while you wait for your phone call? We're anxious to meet the people who will be our companions in the Great Time."

The Reverend thought about it as he fiddled with the telephone receiver, then finally nodded his head. "There's a Halloween party in the commons building, and I guess there's no harm in your waiting there. Brother Amos and Brother Joshua will show you the way."

"Maybe we should have jumped him, Mongo," Garth said in a low, uncertain voice as we followed the two hulking Children of Father along a narrow path on the edge of a cliff overlooking Lake Superior. "I'm starting to have second thoughts."

"Don't. You were right. With these two waiting outside, it

would have been too risky. I wonder why he's letting us mingle with the others?"

"You call this mingling? Observe that these guys' instructions don't include being too chummy with us. We make the good Reverend decidedly uncomfortable, so he figured he'd let the others keep an eye on us for a while."

"Well, we'll hang out at the party until one of us gets a chance to slip away and go back for a serious discussion with the Reverend."

Garth nodded. His mouth was set in a grim line. "We'd best be quick about it—and careful."

"What did you smell on the Reverend?"

"Doubt."

20.

With his gloves off, Mike Leviticus could peel an apple with the side of his hand. He was too far away, and the light in the commons building meeting hall too dim, for me to see precisely how he did it, but it was a neat trick.

Standing off in a corner, feeling warm enough but rather silly in my robe and slippers, I watched as the girl from the fruit and dairy stand came into my field of vision. With her was a tall, very thin young man who, like most of the others, looked to be in his early twenties. The girl said something to him, then pointed to me. He shook his head. She grabbed his hand, pulled him across the room to me. Even with her mouse ears and pasted-on whiskers, she looked just as gorgeous as when I'd seen her earlier. I hoped I was in for some hugging and kissing.

"Everyone's afraid of you," the girl said to me in a bright, clear voice.

Pretending to react to unexpectedly hearing a voice in my face, I started slightly, then cocked my head and fixed my gaze on a spot just between the two of them. "Obviously, you're not. Father love you."

"And Father love you," she replied with a broad smile that revealed the predictable white, even teeth. She took my right hand in both of hers, squeezed it gently. She had a nice touch.

"Can I get you something, Brother Boris? A cold drink? An apple?"

"No, thank you."

"I think it's terrible the way everyone's been avoiding you. I'm Sister Esther. Brother Luke is with me. Luke just joined our family two days ago."

The man reached out to shake my hand. When I didn't react, he flushed with embarrassment and patted me tentatively on the shoulder. "Hi," he said tightly.

"Hi."

"Where's Brother Billy?" the girl asked.

Off—I hoped—pounding on the Reverend, looking for an answer, our car, and our clothes. "I think he's in one of the other rooms, trying to circulate."

"He shouldn't have left you alone."

"I don't mind."

"You two have created quite a stir around here, the way you just popped up. We know something happened on the road when Mike was bringing you back here, but Brother Mike won't say what it was—and we've been instructed not to ask. There's talk that a miracle occurred."

"I thought miracles were what this place was all about," I said, studying Brother Luke. He looked decidedly uncomfortable, as if he wanted to bolt and run.

"Oh, that's right," the girl replied cheerfully. "For sure."

"Well, why not think of Billy and me as just two of your average, run-of-the-mill mira—" I cut myself off in mid-sentence; without Garth around to edit me with a poke in the ribs or a pull on my robe, I was going to have to watch my mouth. Garth was absolutely right; I didn't understand these people at all. "Then why should Father's Children be afraid of us?"

Sister Esther shrugged her magnificent shoulders. "I guess knowing that miracles happen and having one occur in your own backyard are two different things. Also, Reverend Ezra and Brother Mike are obviously nervous—and that makes everybody nervous. I'm not afraid because I sense you and Brother Billy have good hearts. Maybe it doesn't make any difference that you're a dwarf."

"Why should a dwarf make you nervous?" I'd lost track of Mike Leviticus, and that made me nervous.

"You don't know?"

I shook my head.

"Dwarfism is an infirmity," Brother Luke said, speaking for the first time. "There won't be any illness or people with infirmities in Great Time, the same as there won't be any niggers, kikes, spicks, chinks, japs, or Catholics—no people like that. No communists, either."

Without moving my head, I swept my gaze around the room; I hadn't taken notice before, but now that Brother Luke had raised my consciousness, it struck me that everyone in the commune was white and WASPish-looking. "No kidding?" I said.

The girl nodded agreeably. "In the beginning, Father—Who is God made flesh—created many different kinds of people. All were given a chance to accept Jesus as their Savior. Not everyone did. Father has been very patient, but now his wrath will descend on all nonbelievers. Armageddon is upon us. After Armageddon will come Great Time, in which Father and Jesus will reign supreme. Only one hundred and forty-four thousand of us will be left to enjoy it."

"All white and Christian?"

"No Catholics," Brother Luke mumbled. "They worship the Pope."

"Uh, what about nonwhite Christians?"

"Only whites can truly be Christians," the tall, thin young man explained to me. "Other races just don't have the moral strength."

"It says this in the Bible?"

"Father revealed it to us," the girl said. She hugged herself, shivered with ecstasy. "The whole world will be brand-new, and it will belong just to us. Won't it be *wonderful?!*"

"It'll certainly do wonders for rush-hour traffic." The couple exchanged somewhat startled glances, and I quickly added: "Maybe Father has sent me here to tell you that he's having second thoughts."

"No," Sister Esther declared emphatically. "It has all been promised."

"Have you actually heard Father tell you these things?"

"Not in person. Other Children of Father—leaders like Reverend Ezra—bring us the teachings. Only a very few people have actually seen Father since He revealed that He was God."

"That must be very frustrating for you," I said in a neutral tone, glancing around the room. The girl no longer seemed quite so attractive to me, and I didn't need Garth's nose to smell her companion's paranoia. I was getting tired of these loonies, and was anxious to get on with the hunt for the Chief Loony; but there was still no sign of Garth—or of Mike Leviticus.

"Oh, it is," the girl said with a solemn nod. "What were you before you came here, Brother Boris?"

"A dwarf, Sister Esther. What were you?"

"An X-ray technician," she answered hesitantly, after a pause. I could see that I was beginning to make her nervous, too, but I didn't really care. "One of Father's Children found me, looked into my heart, and saw my need. I was invited to come here, and it changed my life. Now I know there are others who believe as I do, and we were right all the time."

"That must be a great comfort. So, now all of you are just kind of hanging around here and waiting to have a Great Time?"

That was pushing it. Sister Esther frowned, glanced uncertainly at her companion, then looked back at me. "You seem to have a strange attitude for someone who claims to have been sent here by Father, Brother Boris," she said softly.

"Sorry. It's just my manner of speaking. Dwarfism does that to some people."

"Well, we certainly haven't simply been 'hangng around,' " the girl said, a touch of pique in her tone. "Since our founding less than two years ago, we've had seven marriages. Those marriages have produced five babies, who are now with Father."

"They're *where?*"

"With Father. Our babies don't have time to make the necessary choices, and so Father personally molds their souls in preparation for Great Time."

"You send your babies off to this—to Father?"

"Of course," Sister Esther said, obviously taken aback by my open astonishment. "It is the only way our babies can be saved. In the meantime, we wait for Father's Treasure."

"Father's Treasure?"

"I don't think I should discuss that," the girl said softly.

No discussion was necessary. No matter what these people

believed, "Father's Treasure" had to be Lot 57—the next generation of genetic juice that was tearing up Garth and me. If Lippitt's information was correct, Siegmund Loge had dozens of communes like this one, ringing the world, providing him not only with infants for direct human experimentation, but with a huge test population when Lot 57 was ready. Loge was going to show these people a great time, all right, but I knew that trying to warn them of the danger would have about as much chance of success as trying to convince them that Siegmund Loge wasn't really God. Garth and I had wandered into what amounted to no more than a breeding pen for test animals, and the realization made me nauseous.

Where was Garth?

"What did you do before you came here, Brother Luke?" I asked, quite content to change the subject.

"I was a metallurgist," the young man replied tersely.

"Oh, you're being very modest, Brother Luke," Sister Esther said, smiling coquettishly at him. "He was an exceptionally gifted metallurgist, Brother Boris, a member of an elite society of knifemakers called the Anvil Ring. In fact," she added proudly, "he was the youngest person ever invited to join."

"That's nice." I was becoming increasingly distracted and wished the two Children of Father would just go away. If Garth didn't show up in another ten minutes, I was going to go looking for him.

But Brother Luke's accomplishments were obviously a subject Sister Esther enjoyed talking about. "Tell Brother Boris about Whisper," she continued. "Tell him how it was made."

Brother Luke frowned. "It's a secret, Sister Esther."

"Oh, come on!" the girl said, pinching his cheek playfully. "You're with Father now, so there's no need for secrets like that. Share your triumph." She turned to me. "Whisper is one of the most remarkable achievements in the history of personal arms," she said primly.

"The members of our society collaborated over a period of years to create her," the young man said reluctantly.

"This 'Whisper,' I take it, is a knife?" I asked.

Brother Luke nodded. "Yes—named for the sound she makes when she's unsheathed. Whisper's made of Damascus steel, and there's no other blade like her—hasn't been for centuries. Do you know anything about knives or steelmaking, Brother Boris?"

"Not really." Five minutes. If Sister Esther and Brother Luke weren't going to go away, I was going to have to figure out a way to get rid of them.

Now Brother Luke was warming to his subject, and his eyes had taken on a strange glow. "Damascus steel was made by a secret process thought lost forever in the Middle Ages, and it's a formula I will share with Father, if he so desires. Alexander the Great had swords of Damascus steel, and the finest samurai swords were made of it. A blade made of Damascus steel can split a feather in midair, yet cut through hardwood for hours without losing its edge. Damascus steel is at once incredibly flexible and incredibly strong. Anyway, members of my group rediscovered the secret process, and Whisper is the result. When I was invited to become one of Father's Children, I knew I had to bring Whisper as my offering to Father."

"You mean you stole it."

Brother Luke didn't much care for that. "Everything belongs to Father," he said, scowling.

"It's just that a knife seems like a strange gift to bring to Father. After all, who'll need weapons in the Great Time?"

Brother Luke flushed, turned to the girl. "He doesn't understand," he said tightly, then wheeled and walked stiffly away.

One down, one to go.

Where was Garth?

"There's no need to be rude, Brother Boris," the girl said reprovingly. "The offerings are only symbolic."

"Of what?"

"Our love. It's suggested that new Children bring certain kinds of offerings, tokens of affection and commitment. The practice is said to please Father and members of His earth family greatly."

"It wouldn't surprise me." Whatever happened to the rest of the world in Great Time, I thought, the Loges would be going into it with quite a collection of loot, some of it, undoubtedly, of considerable value.

"Brother Luke's offering has created a lot of excitement around here. It's so perfect."

I started to ask why it was so perfect, but the words stuck in my throat.

"You look very strange, Brother Boris," the girl said. "Are you all right?"

No, I was most definitely not all right—and, as I watched Garth stagger through a door and fall to his knees in a bright circle of light at the opposite end of the hall, it occurred to me that neither my brother nor I might ever again know what it felt like to be all right. The left side of Garth's face looked to be swollen to about twice its normal size, and he was bleeding from his mouth and nose. Every instinct cried out for me to go to him, but I somehow managed to stay where I was, staring stupidly off into space as Sister Esther gasped and backed away to join the other Children, who had retreated to stand against the walls.

Suddenly the hall was silent as—well, a grave.

Mike Leviticus, Reverend Ezra, Brothers Amos and Joshua came into the hall, took up positions in a semicircle around Garth, who was struggling to get to his feet. Reverend Ezra's frizzy locks were plastered to his forehead with nervous sweat. Leviticus's gloves were off, and in the bright light it appeared as if the sides of both hands were sheathed with blades of polished, bare bone that was actually growing out of the flesh.

Which, of course, was impossible.

Leviticus pulled Garth to his feet, shoved him toward me. Garth staggered, then recovered his balance and walked fairly steadily the rest of the way.

"Well done, Mongo," Garth said in a low, thick voice as he stopped in front of me. "They still don't know that you can see."

"How badly are you hurt, Garth?"

"It probably looks worse than it is. I lost a couple of teeth in the back, but the jaw doesn't seem to be broken. Brother Mike has a curious set of hands, and he definitely knows how to use them. We're in the shithouse, brother. We're now officially certified as servants of Satan."

"That much I surmised. Did you find out anything?"

"Nope. I no sooner let myself out a window than I ran into the side of one of Leviticus's hands. It took me this long to wake up."

"Satan isn't going to like this," I said in a loud voice. "I have a good mind to turn everybody black."

An alarmed murmur rose from the Children ringing the hall, and Garth grinned through his swollen lips. "I was sent to get you. Should we go quietly, or make a *beau geste* and let them beat the shit out of us?"

"Do you think they mean to kill us when they get us outside?"

"There's always that possibility, but I tend to doubt it. After all, Siegfried Loge finally got back to the Reverend, and I wasn't killed outright. No matter what other avenues of research those crazy fuckers are pursuing, it seems the two live Frederickson brothers are still considered the keys to Valhalla."

"Then let's save our energy," I said, reaching out for Garth's arm.

21.

"Shit," Garth said when the others had finished nailing some kind of barricade over the door of our improvised holding pen and left.

"My sentiments exactly," I replied, removing my smoked glasses and looking around.

"Where the hell are we?"

"Your marvelous nose doesn't tell you?"

"A supermarket deli section?"

"Close. A cheese-processing shed."

Although it would be pitch dark to Garth, I could see quite well by the faint moonlight spilling in through vents left open under the corrugated steel eaves of the shed. There was a space heater. I plugged it in, and Garth, shivering, came over and squatted down next to the warming cherry glow.

"You want me to turn on the lights?" I asked.

"What's to see?"

"Three stainless-steel curdling vats and a lot of rubber hosing."

"It sounds depressing; you look at it."

"For now, it seems we're still the apples of Father's eye," I said as I began slowly making a circuit of the area, looking for a ladder—anything—that could get me up to one of the vents that looked to be at least eighteen feet overhead. "That situation may not last much longer. The Loges have got themselves some raw breeding stock; these people—and, presumably, the other communes, as well—send their babies to Father."

"Oh, Jesus," Garth murmured. "The sons-of-bitches are experimenting directly on humans."

"Yeah," I replied, completing my search of the shed and coming back to squat next to Garth. I'd found nothing. "How's your face?"

"It smarts. The edge of that big prick's hand is as hard as bone."

"It is bone," I said. Now that I'd had time to think about it, I knew what I'd seen. "It's collagen."

"Collagen?"

"A while back some researchers at Harvard Medical School came up with a technique for growing bone, without rejection, virtually anywhere in the body."

"A bone graft?"

"It's not really a graft. They extract collagen from any bone, mix it with a few other nonorganic materials into a paste, then spread it over an area where they want new bone to grow. The paste has the effect of stimulating the surrounding cells into producing bone tissue. Siegfried Loge must give his Warriors' hands the collagen treatment when they complete their training. I'm sure it impresses the hell out of them."

"It impressed the hell out of my face. It sounds like Loge is still playing Sorscience."

"Yep. He's a real gamester, that one."

"You think Leviticus was told the real reason the Loges want us?"

"No. Leviticus is here because he's a member of the belief system, and they wouldn't tell him anything that would conflict with his beliefs. This place is sealed off. The only information they get is over the phone, and Siegfried Loge is on the other end of the line."

"Other Warriors will be coming to get us."

"Sure."

"You think it would do any good to try and reason with Leviticus, tell him what's really happening?"

"You tell me, Garth. You're the one who said he smelled of religious ecstasy. You think he's going to listen to two servants of Satan?"

"Sorry. Getting hit by bone-hand must have knocked my brains loose. Incidentally, I really hated to lose those back teeth; I just had a root canal job on that side."

"Feel like having a seizure? You can bang the door open."

"Hey, I wish I could. Unfortunately, I don't have any control over the damn things. We could be paste ourselves, smears under a Loge microscope, before I have another one."

"That's what I call a really comforting thought. How about if I tickle your feet?"

Garth laughed. "That would probably get me pissed at you, but it wouldn't bring on a seizure. Sorry, Mongo." He paused, looked down as I stuffed my glasses deep into the pocket in his robe. "What are you doing?"

"Putting my glasses in a safe place. I'm splitting."

"You walk through walls?"

I pulled Garth to his feet, guided him across the concrete floor to a position against one of the corrugated steel walls. "Look up."

"The vent? You've got to be kidding. Have you got suckers on your fingertips to go with your snake eyes?"

"I've got a strong brother. You're going to toss me up there."

Garth lowered his gaze, shook his head. "The hell I am. You're fucking crazy."

"You like the idea of ending up paste?"

"You'll end up paste now if you miss and fall back on this concrete. I can't see to catch you. Even if you do get up and through, it's still a twenty-foot drop to the ground."

"You seem to forget that you're talking to none other than Mongo the Magnificent. I used to do tougher shit than this for a living."

"Those were your circus days, and they were a long time ago."

"Squat, and cup your hands between your knees. I'll get a running start to work up a head of steam. You'll hear me coming. When you feel my foot hit your hands, it's launch time. Don't hold back on the horsepower."

"No. We'll bide our time, wait until we're picked up. There'll be other chances to make a break. This stunt's too dangerous."

"Come on, Garth," I said, pacing to the opposite side of the shed. "We're wasting time."

Garth sighed in resignation. "Mongo," he said quietly, "if you do get out of here, I want you to keep going. You can't get me out; they've got the door nailed shut."

"Thanks, Garth. That's what I was going to do, anyway. I'm glad you'll understand."

"I'm serious, Mongo. You have to take your glasses."

"I'm serious, Garth; *squat!"*

He did so, and I lit out across the shed. "Now!" I shouted as I leaped off the floor and planted my right foot in the pocket of his cupped hands.

Garth didn't hold back in the muscle department. Up, up, and away I went—as if I'd been shot out of a cannon. A split second after Garth threw me I knew that making the eighteen feet to the vent was not going to be a problem; catching hold of the edge of the wall on the way down after I'd banged into the roof was the problem. I twisted in the air, absorbed the force of impact against the tin roof with my right shoulder and hip. I bounced with a mighty clang that I hoped couldn't be heard too far away, stretched. My fingers caught the sharp edge of the wall, and I squeezed. My grip held, and my body banged into the corrugated steel.

"Mongo?!"

"Uh, just a tad too much exuberance there, brother," I managed to say as I gasped for breath.

"Mongo, I'm sorry! I was afraid—"

"I'm all right, Garth," I said quickly, looking down. Garth, stricken, was squinting up into the darkness, silver tears running down his cheeks. "Really; I'm not hurt. However, I think it only fair to warn you that the next time there's something like this to be done, you're the one who gets thrown."

"Anybody outside?" Garth asked as he wiped away the tears and shook his head with relief.

"I don't know; I haven't looked yet. Let's hope not."

"Look, you little smart-ass bastard," Garth said, looking up at me and shaking his fist, "you'd damn well better find a good way of getting down from there, because if you fall—or you get caught—I'm going to be very pissed. You hear me?"

"Yeah, yeah, yeah. I've got no more time to hang around here, brother. I'll drop in later to see how you're doing. *Ciao.*"

Sucking in a deep breath, I flexed my shoulder muscles and pulled, at the same time swinging my right leg up. The heel caught, and I scrambled up and over the wall, hung down on the other side. At the moment the moon was obscured by clouds, making the green-robed dwarf hanging off the side of the commune's cheese-processing shed a bit less conspicuous; that was good. The raw metal edge was cutting through my palms, making them bleed and hurt like hell; that was bad.

For a few moments I considered taking the fast way down, dropping eighteen feet and taking my chances on a good break-roll. I thought better of it. Garth was right; the circus had been a long time ago, and there was a definite risk that I'd break more than I'd roll. Hanging first from one hand, then the other, I grabbed the hem of my spacious robe, used the material to cushion my palms. That took care of the pain and bleeding problems, but it made my grip on the edge considerably more tentative. The act was going to have to be speeded up.

Overhanging eaves prevented me from climbing up on the roof, which left me a choice of going to my left or right. I went right, swinging and sliding in the direction of another building which looked to have been built very close to the shed.

The muscles in my hands, arms, and shoulders were burning by the time I'd covered the twenty or so yards, but the trip had been worth it; in the narrow alleyway between the two buildings, the walls were no more than three feet apart. I went around the corner, crossed one hand over the other and flipped around so that I was hanging with my back against the corrugated steel wall of the cheese-processing shed.

I'd already lost one sandal; now I kicked off the other, stretched out my leg and planted one foot against the wall of the opposite building. Pressing hard with my shoulders against the shed wall, I firmly planted my other foot, then released my grip. With my body braced between the two walls, I easily "walked" down the narrow shaft to the ground.

22.

The door to Reverend Ezra's office was open, and there was nobody home. The first thing I did after closing the door behind me was to hop up on a windowsill, huddle in my robe, and plant my thoroughly frozen feet directly on the metal shield of a radiator. I'd grown seriously concerned about frostbite, but after about five minutes sensation returned to the toes. I rewarded myself for good behavior by letting my feet toast for another minute or so, then got down and began to search the office.

There was nothing in the Reverend's desk drawer but two well-worn Bibles, dozens of bizarre religious tracts which looked like they'd been run off on a mimeograph machine, and two sticks of Juicy Fruit gum. It was all very depressing; there were no letters, no letterheads, and no address book. So far, all Garth and I had managed to accomplish by infiltrating the commune was to get caught; even if we escaped now, our enemies had been alerted to the fact that we were alive. There were going to be a lot of men in brown uniforms with bony hands scouring this part of the country, hunting for us. We desperately needed to mount some kind of an attack, and to do that we needed an address.

It didn't help my mood to find a toilet behind the door under Siegmund Loge's portrait. I tried the door under Jesus, and barely suppressed a whoop of delight. It looked like the Big Bingo—a room used for the temporary storage of "offerings" brought for Father by new commune members. In the center of the room was a table apparently used for sorting and repacking; on it were a number of battered boxes and bags, and a variety of articles. There was a built-in shelf running along one wall; packing boxes, strapping tape, and a postal scale. Above the scale, taped to the wall, was a large card with neat, block-printed letters.

> RAMDOR
> RFD RTE. 113
> CENTRALIA PA

Somewhere, I'd heard or read something strange about Centralia, Pennsylvania, but I couldn't recall what it was. I didn't care; having the address was all that mattered, and I was doubly pleased to find our clothes piled on the shelf, next to the postal scale. I discarded my robe, quickly dressed, then walked across the room, went up on my toes and looked out the window.

Parked behind the building were our car and the Willys.

I allowed myself the luxury of humming a few bars of the Hallelujah Chorus.

All that remained was to spring Garth, and to do that I needed a claw hammer or a crowbar.

Fat chance.

I might have been able to find something in one of the cars, but, having come this far, I was unwilling to risk recapture by being in the open any longer than I had to be. Instead, I began to rummage through the items on the table, looking for anything that might be used to pry loose the boards that had been nailed across the door to the cheese-processing shed.

Under a pile of Styrofoam blocks used for packing, I found a long, heavy case covered with fine-grain, beautifully tooled cordovan leather. I snapped open the case, found a huge knife in a leather-and-chrome scabbard inside. I lifted the knife out of the case, pulled it from its scabbard.

Shhh.

Whisper.

The Anvil Ring had delivered themselves of a beautiful piece of work, all right. The blade itself, almost half the size of a broadsword, was in the shape of a Bowie model. The color of the steel was an odd, very pale gray and, when viewed from a certain angle, displayed a rippling pattern of parallel lines; at first I thought the lines had been engraved into the steel, but when I ran my finger across the flat face of the blade I found that they were a part of the metal itself.

The handle was extremely heavy—black stone, probably onyx or obsidian, reinforced with steel bands, decorated at both ends with rings of diamond chips.

It was a hell of a thing to have to use for prying boards loose —Damascus steel or no, I wondered how much pressure the blade could take. However, it was the only thing on the table or

in the room that looked even remotely useful, and so it was
going to have to do. I slipped the knife back into its scabbard,
slipped myself back out into the night after picking up Garth's
clothes.

"Hey," I said, rapping lightly on the door with my knuckles.
"Did you wait there like I told you?"

"Mongo?" Garth's anxious whisper was clearly audible; he'd
been waiting by the door.

"You guessed."

"Did you get an address?"

"Sure did. I wish I could tell you it was in Florida, but it's
not. We're going to Centralia, Pennsylvania. It looks like one of
the Loges—maybe both of them—is holed up there."

Shhh.

"What's that?"

"Something I snitched from the collection plate."

"What?"

"Never mind; you'll see for yourself. Give me a chance to
work on these boards."

There were two heavy planks nailed in a crisscross pattern
over the door, anchored to a doorframe of paired two-by-fours.
The wood was heavy and gnarled, and looked as if it would
present a respectable workout for a chainsaw. I still intended to
use the knife to pry the boards loose, but—out of curiosity, and
as a kind of test of the blade I undoubtedly was about to snap—
I took a casual whack at the edge of one of the planks.

Whisper didn't so much bite into the wood as kiss and seduce
it; although I'd virtually done little more than let the blade fall
of its own weight, the razor edge slid more than an inch
through the wood. The resulting *thwuck* was solid, resonant,
satisfying, and somehow—confident.

Whisper was a supremely self-confident knife, and to prove
her prowess she effortlessly lifted out a sizable triangular plug
of knotted wood when I raised her and—applying only slightly
more force—slashed into the plank at an angle to the first cut.

Removing my parka and draping it over my head and shoulders to muffle noise, I squatted down on the frozen ground and
began—with growing excitement and not a little reverential awe
—whacking away at the planks. In less than ten minutes I'd

whittled through both of them, and hadn't even worked up a
sweat. I sheathed Whisper, stuck the scabbard into my belt,
pulled open the door. A shivering but much relieved-looking
Garth stood grinning in a box of moonlight.

"Don't spend too much time in the dressing room, brother,"
I said as I tossed him his clothes. "It's time to take our leave of
these sweet, gentle people. Our car awaits us down the block."

Garth handed me my smoked glasses, pointed to the scabbard in my belt. "Is that what you were hacking with out
here?"

"As a matter of fact, yes. This is Whisper. Observe."

Shhh.

I barely brushed Whisper against the edge of the doorframe,
and a yard-long sliver of wood dropped to the floor.

Garth raised his eyebrows slightly, grunted. "Impressive," he
said as he began to dress.

"That she is."

"She?"

"She has a sexy feel to her."

Garth laughed. "You've been too long in the wilderness,
brother. You've always tended to anthropomorphize, but this is
ridiculous."

Garth finished dressing. We closed the shed door, repositioned the planks across it as best we could, then moved around
the building, keeping low and in the moon shadows.

"How much money have you got in your pockets?" I asked.

"Change."

"What about the cash in the car, assuming it's still there?"

"About forty dollars."

"We need money, or goods to barter. Whisper's too specialized an item, and she's the only weapon we have at the moment.
There's more stuff where she came from—a room behind the
Reverend's office. Maybe I should go back in there and look for
something we can sell."

"Agreed," Garth replied tersely. "Make it fast."

"You want to wait outside?"

"No. We'll stick together."

We circled around the building with the Reverend's office,
still saw nobody. We went to the front, quickly entered, closed
the door behind us. I led Garth through the darkness, posi-

tioned him in the second doorway while I went to rummage around in the items on the table.

Most of the stuff was junk, nothing to even begin to compare to Whisper, and would undoubtedly be discarded when it reached Ramdor—whatever that was. However, one item was of more than passing interest—a leather pouch filled with gold coins which must have weighed upwards of five pounds. I put the gold in the pocket of my parka along with the hard plastic case containing my glasses, then turned toward Garth.

The beam of a powerful flashlight hit me squarely in the eyes. "Hold it right there, dwarf!" Mike Leviticus commanded.

It felt as though someone had poured molten metal into my eye sockets; I shrieked, clapped my hands to my face and slowly crumpled to my knees as white-hot rivers of neon flashed around inside my head with kaleidoscopic, searing fury.

There was a soft coughing sound, like the pop of an air gun, and something whistled through the air over my head and pinged into the wall behind me.

Intent on sneaking up on me in the darkness, Leviticus had apparently missed Garth altogether—until now. There was the thud of a fist hitting flesh, then a crash as the flashlight fell to the floor. Scuffling, muttered curses, then the sharp, ominous sound of wood breaking—that would be Leviticus swinging with the bony side of his hand at Garth's head, missing and hitting a wall.

Leviticus, I assumed, would be a heavy hitter in karate. Garth was not. The popping sound I'd heard had to be a tranquilizer gun, which meant that a Loge or Loges placed a high premium on keeping us alive. However, now that he was being pressed, Leviticus might well feel that he could afford to kill Garth. Garth's body could be preserved . . . and they still had me.

Me was going to have to get rolling.

The sounds of struggle continued as Garth and Leviticus flailed blindly at each other in the darkness. Somebody fell across the table just above my head. The table collapsed, and I rolled away as various "offerings" rained down on me.

My eyes still burned with acid-heat, but I took my hands away from them and tried a tentative squint just as I heard another soft cough.

The flashlight, unbroken, had rolled across the room, and its strong beam was now focused on a small area in a corner, beneath the window. Garth, blood running from a cut on his forehead and with his left arm hanging uselessly at his side, was a few feet away, struggling to get to his feet amid a pile of junk, cardboard boxes, and blocks of Styrofoam.

Leviticus was by the door, reaching for the light switch.

I picked up a broken table leg and threw it at the bare, overhead bulb just as Leviticus threw the switch. The bulb exploded with a flash which I managed to avoid by closing my eyes and turning my head away. The movement cost me a half second. When I opened my eyes again, Garth had only managed to work his way to his knees, and Leviticus was striding purposefully toward the flashlight.

I leaped to my feet, kicked a section of broken table to the side, and sprinted across the room. I launched myself into the air and landed on the Warrior's back just as he was bending down for the flashlight, knocking him off balance. Instantly I wrapped my left arm around his throat while I searched for his eyes with the fingers of my right hand.

Leviticus knocked my hand away, half turned and lunged backward, banging me into the wall—once, twice. The third time did it. Stunned, the wind knocked out of me, I lost my grip on his neck and ignominiously fell to the floor.

Struggling not to lose consciousness, I groped in my pocket for my glasses, found them, ripped them out of their case and put them on.

With the glasses on, I could only see the beam of light and the things it touched; it touched the tranquilizer gun, then swung around into my face and approached like an attacking sun. Desperately, I struggled with fingers that wouldn't work properly at the zipper of my parka, which seemed to be stuck.

"You two have given me enough trouble," Leviticus said in a dry, almost bored voice as I gave up on the zipper and reached under the edge of my parka. "Now I'm—"

Shhh.

Lunging forward, I swung the huge blade of Damascus steel in an arc, aiming at a point behind the light, and felt only a slight tug on the handle as Whisper cut through the flesh and bone of Mike Leviticus's wrist. Blood splattered over my face.

Leviticus's initial grunt of surprise was drawn out to a soul-deep, sorrowful moan as his hand and the flashlight flew across the room and landed against the wall with sufficient force to break the flashlight. Then I heard the Warrior sit down hard on the floor.

I rolled away, sprang to my feet and whipped off my glasses, preparing to strike again. It wasn't necessary. Leviticus had apparently felt he needed only his hands and the tranquilizer gun to handle us, because his shoulder holster was empty. He was slumped against the wall, staring in my direction with eyes that were rapidly glazing over with pain and shock. The fingers of his right hand were wrapped around the stump of his left wrist as he tried to stanch the flow of blood. He wasn't having much success; the blade of bone that made his hand such a formidable weapon also made it more difficult for him to close his fingers tightly. Blood oozed—and occasionally pulsed—out of the stump. The tranquilizer gun had fallen, skidded out of his reach. I turned my attention to Garth.

Garth had never made it out of the pile of debris in the middle of the room. He was sitting with his head lolling back and forth, as if he were asleep. There was a steel dart with narrow green stablizers sticking out of his left shoulder. I replaced Whisper in her scabbard, kicked the tranquilizer gun even farther across the room, then hurried over to him.

The cut on his forehead had stopped bleeding and looked to be minor. I pulled the dart out of his shoulder, then pulled back his parka and shirt and looked at his shoulder. There was a thin trickle of blood, but it was obvious that the thickness of the parka had prevented him from getting a full dose of the drug in the hypodermic mechanism that was part of the dart. But he'd gotten enough to pose a problem.

"Garth!"

"Mmmmmm."

"Wake up!" I shook him.

". . . sleepy . . ."

"Yeah, well this is no time to take a fucking nap! I Goddamn well can't carry you! The bad guys are after us, remember?"

"Guy . . . packs one . . . hell . . . of a punch."

I slapped him hard, twice. All he did was grin stupidly. I

stood up and kicked him in the stomach—just hard enough to get his attention.

Garth's eyes opened, searched for me in the darkness. "You do that again, I'll tear off your head and hand it to you," he said in a clear voice.

I did it again. Then I grabbed two handfuls of parka and struggled to pull him up. "Get up, Garth!" I pleaded. "You have to stay awake just a little longer! Too much noise! Others will be coming!"

Garth grunted, grabbed hold of my forearms and managed to pull himself to his knees. "Yeah. I . . . know. Sorry about this, Mongo . . ."

Stepping around behind him, I draped one heavy arm over my shoulder, anchored my forehead in his armpit and shoved with all my might. Slowly, Garth rose to his feet. I shoved him in the direction of the door, and he wobbled forward. I followed him into the Reverend's office, then abruptly grabbed hold of his parka, stopping him.

"Wait here," I said, shoving him back against the wall. His head banged against the plaster, then rolled around on his shoulders—but he stayed on his feet. I went back into the other room. I knew I was probably being incredibly stupid, considering the racket Garth and Leviticus had made, but there was some business I felt I had to attend to.

I took some heavy wrapping twine off the shelf, picked up a shard of wood off the floor, then went over to Leviticus. The Warrior was just barely conscious; in another five minutes, or less, he'd have bled to death.

"Listen to me," I said quietly as I knelt down beside him, pushed his hand away from the bleeding stump and started to fashion a tourniquet. "As my mother would say, some people will believe anything. You people have yourselves one cock-amamy religion here, but I'm not going to argue theology—except to tell you that everything you believe about Siegmund Loge is bullshit. Garth and I aren't servants of Satan—even Satan can't get good help these days. The old man you believe is God heads up a project that would have made the Nazis drool with envy, and rumor has it that he's not as crazy as his son, or as mean as his grandson; these are people you and the others here think dance with angels. Can you hold this stick?"

Leviticus nodded weakly, put his hand over the stick controlling the tension of the tourniquet.

"Let go of it and you'll die," I continued, rising to my feet. "So stay awake, and think about what I said."

I hurried back into the office, tore the phone out of the wall, grabbed Garth's parka and slung him in the general direction of the door, which Leviticus had left open. Garth staggered out, and almost knocked over a startled Reverend Ezra.

Shhh.

"Uh, Father love you," Reverend Ezra said tightly as he craned his neck, went up on his toes and stared down at Whisper, which was nestled in his crotch.

"Fuck him and you, Reverend." Lights were coming on all over the place, and I had to squint. My eyes were beginning to burn. "You got a medical kit in this place?"

"Yes, but—"

"Well, I hope it's a good one. Mike Leviticus is inside, and he's hurt badly. Go get the kit. *Run,* you silly jerk-off!"

Reverend Ezra ran. I grabbed the front of Garth's parka and pulled him around to the rear of the building. The ignition keys were still in our car. I pushed Garth into the rear seat, paused to slash the front tires of the Willys, then jumped behind the wheel of our car and turned the keys in the ignition.

The car wouldn't start.

Garth had begun to snore.

Holding my breath, I turned off the ignition. I pumped the gas pedal, waited three beats, then tried it again.

Grind.

Snore.

The engine finally turned over on the third try. I gunned the motor, popped the clutch and spun around in a power slide, narrowly missing Brothers Amos and Joshua. I straightened the car out, shot up the dirt road leading out to the main highway. The car banged over frozen ridges, crashed into potholes. The door Garth had torn off, and which we'd roped back on, flew off. I hit the ceiling a couple of times, barely managing to keep my grip on the steering wheel, and Garth rolled on the floor with a loud *clunk.*

"Huh . . . ?" Mongo?"

"Go back to sleep," I said through clenched teeth.

Problem. Dozens of flashlight beams were dancing in the orchards to my right, and they were ahead of me; Children of Father were running through the trees, and they obviously intended to cut off the servants of Satan at the pass. I managed to dig my glasses out of my pocket, put them on. I turned on the car's high beams and floored the accelerator. I fishtailed around a sharp bend to find half a dozen Children standing in the middle of the road, arms linked, eyes closed, faces wreathed in ecstasy. More Children poured out of the orchards, lined up behind them.

Convinced they were going to pop up from the dead in Great Time, the Children of Father were obviously perfectly willing to temporarily check out of this not-so-great-time as martyrs; I wasn't willing to oblige them. I slammed on the brakes, managed to bring the car to a halt an inch or two from the closest of the Children, a teenage girl with a bad case of acne. Garth rolled around in the back. Bodies clambered up on the hood. A rock came out of the darkness, shattering the window and just missing my head, spraying glass over the back of my neck.

"Garth, upsy-daisy!" I shouted, slamming the gears into reverse and flooring the accelerator again. "Nap time is over! Wake up!"

"Yeah," Garth said groggily, pulling himself up on the back of the seat. "Where are—"

We hit a rut, silencing Garth and removing half the bodies from the hood. A pothole took care of the rest of the bodies, but behind me, flashlights jumping in their hands, more Children were running up the road.

"Hang on, Garth! When we stop, you've got to get out and run! Do you understand?!"

Garth made a sound which I hoped was a "yes" grunt. I reached over, opened the glove compartment and groped through its contents as I suddenly whipped the steering to the left. The rear of the car veered sharply, hit the frozen shoulder and took off. We soared through the air, crashing through tinder-dry brush in the raw forest on this side of the road. I kept the accelerator to the floor; the car landed, the tires bit, and we continued to shoot backwards, crashing through underbrush and knocking over small trees until we finally hit one large enough to stop us.

It felt as if my teeth were shaking loose and my brains being scrambled, but I had somehow managed to keep one hand on the steering wheel and the other in the glove compartment; now the tips of my fingers touched what I had been desperately hoping to find—a book of matches.

The air was suddenly filled with the acrid odor of gasoline.

My door had sprung open. I leaped out, ran around the car, and was relieved to see that Garth was at least halfway out—the pocket of his parka had caught on the door handle, and he was still too groggy to release it. I unhooked the pocket, helped him stand, then turned him in the general direction of the woods and pushed as hard as I could. Garth wobbled and swayed, but he managed to stay on his feet—and he was walking away.

The lights were closing, converging on us from two directions.

I waited until Garth was perhaps fifteen yards away, then turned back to the car, squinted over the top of my glasses, and lit a match. It went out. I lit another, used it to light the matchbook; when it flared in my hand, I tossed it toward the ruptured gas tank, turned back and sprinted after Garth.

The car's gas tank had been close to three-quarters full, and when it went the concussion of the blast hit me in the small of the back like a giant fist, slamming me to the ground. Flaming pieces of metal and upholstery whistled through the air over my head, rained down to start dozens of little fires in the dry brush that surrounded us. I pushed myself to my feet, pulled the hood of my parka up over my head and ran on.

I found Garth sitting on the ground, legs splayed out in front of him, back braced against the trunk of a tree. His eyes were still glassy and half-closed, but at least he was conscious. I squatted down beside him, turned back and squinted through my smoked glasses at the conflagration I had started.

The car was a roaring inferno of orange-white flame that was rapidly spreading through the dry brush and leafless trees on either side to form a wall of fire between us and the Children of Father. The wind was blowing from our backs, carrying the fire toward the Children, who were beginning to beat a fairly hasty retreat, and the orchards on the other side of the road. It looked like the beginnings of a fairly decent forest fire which could well reach and destroy the buildings of the commune itself.

"Hooee," Garth mumbled in a slurred voice.

"You took the word right out of my mind. Does this utterance indicate that you've decided to stay awake for a while?"

"I'm positively bright-eyed and bushy-tailed," Garth said as he tried to rise and promptly slid down the tree trunk. He made it on the second try. "Nice work, brother—whatever you did. I wish I'd been around to see it. The last thing I remember was feeling this prick in my shoulder."

"Oh, I was brilliant. Actually, losing the car may be for the best; we probably wouldn't have gotten far in it, anyway. Maybe the bad guys will think we burned up in it."

"Sure. Besides, who needs a car? How long a walk is it to Pennsylvania?"

"Oh, probably fifteen hundred miles or so, as the crow flies."

"That's good," Garth mumbled, pushing off the tree and starting to walk southeast. "I was afraid it might be farther."

As we walked through the night forest, Garth gradually became more alert. After a couple of miles I realized that he was softly whistling; when I recognized the tune as "We're Off to See the Wizard," I lunged sideways and drove my shoulder into his hip, pushing him into a bramble bush.

23.

We rode the rails for almost three weeks, two weeks longer than necessary, in order, as it were, to let things cool down and encourage any speculation that we might have died in the car explosion. We ate in hobo jungles, paying for our meals with a few of the gold coins I had taken from the commune. For the most part the other "bos" were friendly, and only once did Whisper have to dissuade potential thieves. During this time our symptoms did not become better; on the other hand, they didn't grow worse—and we were willing to settle for that. It gave us faint hope that the shadows in our spinal fluid were not growing larger.

We abandoned our made of transportation when we reached

Scranton, walked from the yards into the center of the city, where we found a coin dealer who was willing to put up with our smell long enough to examine our treasure with no questions asked. The coins turned out to be, literally, worth more than their weight in gold, since they were quite rare. We sold three-quarters of the bag's contents for twenty thousand dollars. We bought clothes and a few items we thought we might need for our assault on Ramdor. Then we checked into a hotel to clean up and change.

Happy time was over. With the dirt off me, I could see scales growing on the backs of my hands and feet; there were gossamer webs between all my toes, the beginnings of one between the thumb and forefinger on my left hand. We immediately checked out, bought a used van and headed for Centralia.

Viewed from the turnpike, there appeared to be a gray cloud, in an otherwise azure sky, hanging over the section of the state where Ramdor was located. It jogged my memory, and I recalled reading how Centralia, along with a large area surrounding it, was situated over hundreds of miles of coal mines and raw seams that, almost two decades before, had somehow caught fire. The underground fire still raged, eating through the black, bituminous veins and arteries of the earth like cancer. Occasionally the fire would gnaw through the skin of the earth in and around Centralia, bursting out with blast-furnace heat approaching two thousand degrees, spewing sulphur and other poisonous gases into the air; whole houses had disappeared into sinkholes that suddenly opened overnight. It was a perfectly hellish place, and we were sure the Loges felt right at home.

A few discreet inquiries around town told us that Siegfried Loge had been able to buy up hundreds of acres north of Centralia—ostensibly for a dairy farm—some three years before, at what could only be described as fire sale prices. If the owner of Ramdor occasionally lost a dairy cow or two to the natural barbecue pits riddling his property, he did not seem overly concerned. His neighbors did not care at all; their only concern was with somehow finding a buyer for *their* property so that they could move out.

Loge had picked up a lot of cheap real estate, but reports were that he'd sunk a lot of money—probably the Pentagon's—into it. A lot of blasting and building had been going on, and this spooked the other residents, who could not understand why anyone would want to build anything around Centralia. Also, it was said, some very strange people worked there.

We had no difficulty finding the place. A dirt road snaked off the main highway into a thick, slightly singed forest. In the distance was what looked to be an escarpment, and at the top of the escarpment, situated at the very lip, was a windowless building that gleamed in the sunlight like stainless steel. There was a heavy gate across the entrance to the dirt road, and at the gate was a brown-uniformed, black-gloved sentry. We kept going, driving around the perimeter.

A flimsy rail fence surrounded the property, and there was no sign of more guards, Warriors of the Father or otherwise. Although we passed a few meadows where, in spring and summer, diligent cows might be able to scare up a snack, Ramdor certainly did not look like a dairy farm; what it looked like was something Dante had thought up and then rejected in an early draft as too depressing. Although this part of Pennsylvania was in a heavy snow belt, there was no snow on the ground here; the earth was obviously too hot. There were numerous fissures, surrounded by wasted earth where escaping fire and poison gas had scoured away all the vegetation. In some places fire leaped out of the ground and licked like the tongue of a blowtorch at the sky; the air was filled with the smell of rotten eggs—hydrogen sulfide.

We parked the van in a ravine off the highway, some three miles from the main entrance. We prepared some food over a portable butane stove, prepared backpacks, then got some much needed sleep. Some time after midnight we stepped over the rail fence onto the grounds of Ramdor, headed toward the escarpment.

Our plan, out of stark necessity, was starkly simple; snatch somebody. If Siegmund Loge turned out to be at Ramdor, we'd grab him and use a little gentle persuasion to force him to administer an antidote to Lot 56, if an antidote existed—or cook one up in a hurry, if it didn't. If Father wasn't there, we'd grab Siegfried or Auberlich for use as a bargaining chip, breakable, until the elder Loge was sufficiently inspired to halt the death working in us. Then, regardless of what Siegmund Loge did or didn't do, somebody was going to pay for Tommy's and Rodney Lugmor's deaths.

That was all there was to it.

Dawn found us in a copse of scrub evergreens on a knoll overlooking the main buildings of Ramdor. Considering his surroundings, Siegfried Loge had chosen the site well; it was a valley of black stone, which protected the wood-frame buildings from the fire beneath. The black-stone cliff rose from the valley floor like a periscope from hell, and at the top, inaccessible by any route we could see, was the windowless metal building we had glimpsed from the road. At the base of the cliff, built into it, was a ranch house, its stone front yard decorated with potted plants. A hundred yards to the left of the ranch house was a barn, and beyond that a smaller building which could have been a bunk house. To the east was the forest; to the west, at the end of the valley, were green and brown patches of meadow.

If not for the owner, and if not for the ominous building—a new, or backup, Volsung—on top of the escarpment, it might all have seemed rather quaint.

"I'm really glad we have a plan," Garth said wryly as he peered down at the complex through his binoculars. Two brown-uniformed Warriors on horseback clattered past the ranch house, waved to a third Warrior standing guard at a gate. All three men wore what appeared to be machine pistols in shoulder holsters, standard dairy farmer issue.

"Of course," I replied as I adjusted the focus on my own binoculars. "Where would we be if we didn't have a plan?"

"About where we are right now, I'd say." There was anger in Garth's voice, but I knew that it was directed at the situation, not me. "Our plan is no plan. We don't even know what Siegfried Loge and his kid look like, what's more where to find them, what's more how to get past those men down there with guns, what's more—"

"You're a barrel of laughs this morning."

"We're not even certain any of the Loges are here."

"True."

"I think we should give some more thought to this."

"Fine. You can groom your new fur coat while you're thinking, and I'll tend to my webs and scales. This is the only place we have left to look. We need at least one Loge as a hostage, and I say that ranch house is the logical place to look first; after that, the building upstairs. They're not going to come to us, Garth; we have to go to them. What else is there to say?"

"Nothing," Garth sighed.

"We'll go tonight. With luck, we'll get some cloud cover. I'll still be able to see."

"I won't."

"Neither will the guards. In the meantime, we'll sit tight and keep checking things out. Maybe one of the Loges will come out wearing a sign around his neck."

"Now *that's* a good plan."

"The place is staffed by freaks—if you'll pardon the expression," Garth observed around noon.

He was right. True to Siegfried Loge's sense of humor, or to his bizarre obsession with fantasy, the "dairy farm" was worked by genetic outtakes like myself; dwarves, fat ladies, midgets, and a variety of other men and women with congenital defects moved about the valley, in and out of the barn, performing various chores. I wondered if any of these people staffed the building on top of the cliff, thought not; there was nothing whimsical about what went on in the windowless building, and it was staffed by technicians of death. The dairy farm itself was literally just a sideshow.

"Yeah," I said. "As a matter of fact, I know the giant. His name's Hugo Fasolt. He was with the Statler Brothers' Circus. Not a particularly good omen. Hugo's not exactly the smartest giant you've ever met. He's also congenitally grumpy, and more than a little self-pitying."

"What giant?"

"The one on the tractor with the gorilla. They're just coming out of the woods."

Garth aligned his binoculars with mine, looked toward the east where the tractor and its odd riders were hauling a wagon loaded with firewood. "A big son-of-a-bitch," Garth said.

"Eight feet, three inches, four hundred and forty-four pounds when he was with Statler Brothers. And he was always on a diet."

"The gorilla the same one that doused you?"

"No. That one was a big silverback. This one's smaller, probably female."

"This one's wearing the same kind of screen and typewriter keyboard that you told me about, and she's flashing signals at the big guy. He's talking to her. You think the gorilla understands what he's saying?"

For some reason, the notion of talking gorillas bothered me far beyond the fact that one had almost killed me. I grunted noncommittally.

"The giant acts like she does," Garth persisted.

"All things considered," I said tightly, "the one that grabbed me was pretty articulate—and Lippitt as much as told me that it was the gorilla that told Loge I'd been inside the Volsung complex. But Lippitt has a jet-black sense of humor. Maybe a gorilla can be trained and conditioned to indicate simple responses, but I don't believe even the Loges can make one sentient, or teach it to communicate on a level approaching human language."

"Why not? They're doing a pretty good job of nudging you and me in the opposite direction."

"Hugo always talked to himself a lot," I replied, letting the binoculars drop around my neck and looking away.

"Damned if it doesn't look like the gorilla is carrying a portable cassette player."

"Yeah. Hugo always liked rock and roll."

It all reminded me too much of my mother's dream.

"Hey, pal. I'm down here."

The Warrior who had been standing at the gate outside the ranch house started, then glanced down at about the same time that I punched him in the groin. The breath exploded from his lungs as he crumpled to his knees, hands clasped between his legs. I spun clockwise to gain momentum, cracked him in the jaw with my elbow. I had a little bone on me, too.

Garth appeared beside me, carrying the length of rope I had retrieved during a premidnight reconnaissance of the barn. I relieved the Warrior of his machine pistol, checked the magazine; it was full. We tied the man up, and Garth dragged him back to the barn. He returned five minutes later.

"I gave him another rap on the jaw for insurance, Mongo. That one will stay put. Any others?"

"We have to assume there are always two by the gate out on the highway, but they're stationary. I've seen one night rider; he'll be back around in another twenty minutes or so."

Garth glanced nervously around him. "There doesn't seem to be much security."

"There's probably a battalion of these jokers in the building up on the cliff, and they all may eat and sleep there. That's where the action is. This whole operation is just a little show for the benefit of the neighbors. What I am worried about is an alarm system in the ranch house."

"That seems like a reasonable concern."

"You're the cop. How do we defeat it?"

Garth thought about it, shook his head. "We probably can't —not in the time we have. If this guy does have an alarm system, it'll be state-of-the-art. On the other hand, with the armed guards, he may not have felt the need for an alarm system in the house."

"What do you suggest?"

Garth shrugged, pushed through the gate. "Let's go. We'll find out soon enough if there's an alarm."

Garth, moving slowly and deliberately to avoid creaking steps, went up on the porch and began running his fingertips around the doorjamb. I stayed behind for a few moments to dig a hole next to one of the potted plants, buried Whisper. Then I joined my brother on the porch. Garth was on his knees, probing the keyhole with the lock pick he always carried in his wallet.

"Can you see?" I asked.

"I don't need to see to do this. What were you up to?"

"I planted Whisper in one of the pots. We've got this cannon, and I figure it's always a good idea to have some insurance against a rainy day."

"I'm glad to see you haven't lost your rather kinky sense of humor, brother. If it rains on us any harder than it is now, we'll drown."

There was a soft click. Garth rose to his feet, sucked in a deep breath, turned the knob. The door opened. There was no sound from inside, and moonlight falling through the windows provided sufficient illumination for me to see that the huge living room was empty. I gripped Garth's hand and started to go inside.

Garth pulled me back outside, closed the door. "I know what the alarm system is," he said tightly, touching his broad nose.

"What?"

"A state-of-the-art gorilla. It washes with shampoo and uses cologne, but it's still a fucking gorilla."

"How do you know what a gorilla smells like?"

"I know what it doesn't smell like. Whatever's roaming around in there ain't no doggy, and it ain't no pussycat."

"Shit," I said with heartfelt sincerity. It was beginning to look like Volsung all over again. I debated whether or not to retrieve Whisper, decided against it. I still wanted that backup insurance, and I didn't plan on letting the gorilla get close enough for me to stick a knife in it. I took the machine pistol out of my belt, turned the knob and pushed the door open. "Let's go. Grab a handful of my parka and stay close."

"There's going to be a hell of a racket when you shoot that gorilla—which is what I assume you're going to do."

"If it comes to that, I'll hit the light switch; I've got my glasses in my pocket. We storm the barricades, and I blow away anything that doesn't look crazy enough to be a Loge."

"Go," Garth said, resting a hand on my shoulder.

With the gun in my right hand and the glasses in my left, I slowly moved into the living room. After going a few feet, I stopped and looked around, peering into red-tinted shadows of blue and gray. There was no sign of any gorilla, and I proceeded toward a wide, winding staircase at the opposite end of the room.

Garth sniffed, and his hand suddenly tightened on my shoulder. "Behind you, brother," he said, and whirled me around.

I dropped to one knee and thrust the gun out in front of me. A large ball of black fur darted across the room, disappeared behind a sofa. A few seconds later a head poked out and two bloodshot eyes stared at me; the head quickly ducked back.

"What's happening?" Garth whispered tersely.

"She knows we're here. At the moment, she's lying low behind a sofa."

"She must have good night vision, too, because I think she

knows you have a gun. She must know what it can do, because there's a strong smell of fear."

"Good," I said, keeping the gun leveled on the spot where the head had appeared. "I don't want to wake up Loge, and I don't want to shoot the animal unless I have to."

"Go?"

"Go." Without taking my eyes off the sofa, I reached behind me and grabbed hold of Garth's parka. "The staircase is about four steps behind you. Take it slow and easy. I'll keep my eye on the gorilla."

Garth started to back up, pulling me after him—and then suddenly his parka jerked from my hand. There was a loud crash as he fell into the banister, a guttural, strangled cry. I wheeled around, saw my brother writhing on the floor. He'd torn loose a piece of the banister, and now the wood snapped in his hands like a matchstick. Saliva frothed on his lips as his body twitched, jerked, and banged around on the floor.

"Garth!"

Lights came on, blinding me and burning my eyes. I whipped on my glasses, spun around and fell on my back as I heard a muffled *paddy-pad-pad* coming up behind me. I had no choice now, and I squeezed off three shots between my upraised knees —aiming at a spot I estimated would be just above the animal's head. Then I lowered the gun a foot and waited; the instant I felt hot breath or a paw on me, the gorilla was dead.

My vision cleared in time for me to see the beast beating a hasty retreat back behind the sofa.

Getting to my feet, keeping the gun aimed in the general direction of the sofa, I turned my attention back to Garth. There was nothing I could do except grind my teeth in frustration, nothing I could do to bring him out of the seizure or ease the pain of his horribly cramped muscles; if he got hold of me in this state, he could snap me like he'd snapped the banister.

I watched as Garth struggled to get to his feet. His eyes rolled and he fell down again, flopping like some broken thing, tearing at his clothes.

Paddy-pad-pad.

Spinning around, I aimed the gun directly at the gorilla's chest. This time I had her—and she knew it; there was no time or place to retreat. She came to an abrupt halt a few paces away, and we stared at each other. A chill ran through me as I looked into the eyes; they were yellowish and bloodshot, but they were also eerily human—or near human. We stayed like that for a few seconds, and then she reached a leathery hand up to the keyboard-screen device strapped to her chest.

NO FUCKING KILL PLEASE

It seemed this gorilla studied from the same vocabulary list as the one I'd run into at Volsung. "Then get out of my fucking face!" I snapped. "Back off and I won't shoot."

FUCKING THANKS

She backed away across the room, meekly squatted down in a corner.

Suddenly the ceiling above my head shook with heavy footsteps; someone very large was running toward the stairs. I turned, went down on one knee, and used both hands to aim the gun at the top of the stairs. I might have qualms about killing dumb—or even not-so-dumb—animals, but I had no qualms whatever about killing dumb humans who were trying to kill me.

With some exceptions.

"Mongo!"

"Drop the shotgun, Hugo," I said in a flat voice, trying hard to ignore the fact that both barrels were lined up on my chest. "You and I were friends once, and I hope we still are. The man on the floor is my brother, and we're in trouble. We could use your help. I haven't got time for explanations, except to say that you're mixed up in some bad business here. I will kill you if you force me to. Don't."

The giant shook his head angrily, and his long, brown hair rippled across his shoulders. His brown eyes narrowed, and his lips drew back from his teeth. "I should be the one saying those things to you, Mongo," Hugo Fasolt said in his deep, rumbling voice. "This is a shotgun I've got on you."

"If you pull the trigger, we both die. I'm a good shot."

Paddy-pad-pad.

There'd been one gorilla too many for me to keep track of, and now long, hairy, powerful arms wrapped themselves around me, squeezing my arms to my sides. The gorilla with fur whacked the gun out of my hand. Then she lifted me in the air, turned me over, and casually dropped me on my head.

24.

Gradually, I struggled up through what felt like a sea of foul-smelling cotton to consciousness. I was lying on my back on stone, felt cold, clammy, and sleepy. Also, my head and neck hurt like hell. I opened my eyes to slits, immediately closed them again when light lanced into them.

"Garth?"

"Here, Mongo." Garth's voice came to me from somewhere just behind and above my head. His large hand felt very warm as it touched my forehead. "You all right?"

"Yeah, except that I can't see in this light. Any sign of my glasses?"

"No. What happened to you? You've got a bump on your head the size of a coconut."

"That damn gorilla dropped me on it. I should have shot her when I had the chance."

"I had a seizure, didn't I?"

"A seizure and a half. You okay?"

"Yes." He was quiet for some time, then added: "That was the worst one yet. I'm sorry, Mongo. I guess I'm responsible for us being here."

"That's ridiculous," I said, pushing his hand aside and sitting up. Pain flashed through my skull, but my head stayed on my shoulders, so I assumed nothing was broken. "It was just a lousy plan. Where's 'here'?"

Garth pulled me to my feet, then began to chuckle. "Take a guess."

"Come on, Garth. Damn it, I'm really not in the mood."

He chuckled again. "Oh, be a sport. This is Ramdor, right? We're the guests of the Loges, those masters of fun and fantasy, right? Now, give it some thought and tell me where we are."

"A dungeon," I answered with a sigh.

"There, now; I knew you'd get the answer. It comes complete

with stone walls, floor, and ceiling; the cells have genuine rust-ing iron bars, and it's dank and gloomy. There are blazing torches on the wall, although they may have fudged a bit there because I think they're gas-burning. There's no sign of any rats, but I haven't given up hope. It's really neat."

"Yeah. It sounds like a real sight for sore eyes."

"There are two other cells like ours, empty at the moment. There's a narrow stone corridor outside that ends at a heavy wooden door about twenty yards to our left. At the other end of the corridor is a room with walls of polished black stone that looks like marble; there's a television monitor and floodlight mounted in the ceiling, an unlit torch and short sword mounted in brackets on the wall."

"They should have put us there."

"I'm not sure what it's supposed to be. There's a knobless door cut into the rear wall, but it's open on this end. I don't like the look of it."

I turned my head to the left at the sound of the wooden door opening; it creaked quite nicely. Three sets of footsteps approached. "Company?"

"Yep. A fat, mean-looking kid who probably thinks he's a bad-ass because he wears a machine pistol in a holster; he's got a pimple on the end of his nose, and he doesn't like the fact that I just told you. There's a solid, tall guy in a Warrior uniform, and he probably is a bad-ass. The third guy is about my height, angular, hawk nose, and pale eyes. He's wearing a Bayreuth Eight-three T-shirt and a Mets baseball cap. Good morning, motherfuckers. Kill any kids today?"

"I'm Siegfried Loge—"

"The Mets cap," Garth interjected.

"The kid killer."

Epithets didn't seem to have much effect on Siegfried Loge. "Why are you keeping your eyes closed, Dr. Frederickson?" he asked calmly. His voice was slightly nasal, airy.

"I'm trying to take a nap."

"Your eyes are very photosensitive, aren't they, Dr. Frederickson?"

"Yes," Garth answered. I slapped his arm, and he put his hand on my shoulder. "They'll find out anyway, Mongo."

"Indeed, we will," Siegfried Loge said.

"My brother needs the glasses he was wearing, Loge. He can't see without them."

"Give him the glasses, Obie."

"Fuck him, Dad." Dear, sweet Auberlich. "Let him be blind."

"All right, Obie," the elder Loge replied casually. "And you can lead him wherever he has to go."

There was a silence that lasted a few seconds, then Garth squeezed my shoulder. "Put out your hand, Mongo."

I did, and felt the smoked glasses drop into my palm. I put them on, looked around. The "dungeon," including the sinister-looking black cell and the pimple on the end of Obie Loge's nose, was as Garth had described it to me.

The Warrior standing next to Loge was staring at me impassively. He had a distinctly military bearing exuding quiet self-confidence, and he looked rock solid. Like the other Warriors, he wore black gloves, and I assumed he had bone-blades on the sides of his hands. His dark hair was cropped very short, and his eyes glinted with intelligence. He held his head high, his broad shoulders back; he would easily have blended into the scenery at West Point.

Siegfried Loge, in his sneakers, jeans, T-shirt, and baseball cap, looked more like the third-string pitcher on a local saloon softball team than the scion of an ultrabrilliant scientific family, and Auberlich Loge looked like what he was—a fat teenage thug. Both Loges had the kind of pale hooded eyes that I cross the street to avoid.

Siegfried Loge absently fingered the medallion around his neck, a gold wire sculpture of the four-ring symbol the Warriors had emblazoned on their shoulder patches. "Do you know where Lippitt is?" he asked me.

"Damn," I said, patting my pockets. "I seem to have misplaced him."

The man with the close-set, pale eyes smiled wanly. "What's the most terrible thing that comes into your mind when you hear the word 'torture,' Dr. Frederickson?"

"Being forced to sit through *Götterdämmerung*."

"They don't know," the Warrior said in a flat voice as he continued to study Garth and me. "Even if they made a joint decision to split up, Lippitt wouldn't tell these two where he was going, or what he planned to do." He paused, added softly: "A very dangerous man."

"What do you think of them, Stryder?"

"I don't know what you mean, sir," the Warrior replied without looking at Loge.

"You wouldn't think one dwarf and his big brother could wreak so much havoc or be so elusive, would you? I guess it's a good thing they decided to come to us, or we'd never had found them."

"I take full responsibility for the failure of my men," the Warrior replied evenly, still not looking at Loge.

"Good," Loge said curtly. "That's what I wanted to hear. On occasion, you can be rather arrogant. I wanted to hear you admit failure." He paused, addressed Garth and me. "This is Stryder London, gentlemen. He's been described as the 'ultimate warrior,' and he leads our security forces. I find it rather amusing that the ultimate warrior and all his merry men couldn't stop you two from wrecking a multimillion dollar operation in Nebraska and burning down half the state of Wisconsin. We've got a great security force, all right; it took a half-crazy giant and a gorilla to finally catch you as you were on the way up to my bedroom."

"I wouldn't stand too close to the cell, sir," Stryder London said drily.

Loge ignored him as he glanced back and forth between Garth and me. "It's amazing that it should come down to the two of you. Jake Bolesh should be around to see what an incredible contribution he made when he tried to kill you with those injections. You may be the only two people in the world who could have survived this long, and we have to find out what it is in your genetic makeup that allows for a controlled reaction. That's the breakthrough. There are the answers to a lot of questions in your bodies."

"What are you trying to do, Loge?" I asked. "Is it a biological weapon for the Pentagon? Spell it out. What's the point?"

"Point?" Siegfried Loge removed his baseball cap and ran his fingers through a tangle of thick, wavy black hair. Then he began to laugh; the laughter began as a chuckle, but quickly built up to a kind of nasal bray that grated against my senses like fingernails scraping a blackboard. Obie Loge glanced uncertainly at his father, then also began to laugh—but nervously. Stryder London's face revealed nothing, and he continued to stare straight ahead.

"Why does there have to be a point?" Loge continued when he had finally managed to bring his laughter under control. "Why can't science just be *fun?*"

Now Garth decided to take matters—in this instance, Siegfried Loge's neck—in hand. In a blur of motion, his right arm shot through the bars and his fingers closed around Siegfried Loge's neck. The scientist's eyes went wide and his face started to turn blue as Garth, smiling grimly, squeezed his windpipe.

Stryder London reacted almost instantaneoulsy, stepping forward and jabbing stiff fingers up into Garth's exposed armpit, attacking the nerve cluster there that controlled the arm and hand. Obie Loge was shouting obscenities as he engaged in the futile exercise of trying to pry loose Garth's fingers from around his father's neck.

Grabbing the bars for support, I kicked Obie Loge in the groin with sufficient force to ruin his sex life for at least a week. He dropped like a stone, mewling in a high whine as he rolled around on the floor and clutched at his testicles. I started to go for London, but the Warrior had already managed to break Garth's grip and had stepped back, out of reach. Loge had collapsed to the floor next to his groaning son and was holding his throat with both hands.

"Nice work, brother," I said.

"Likewise, brother," Garth replied as he shook and rubbed his arm to restore feeling.

Loge swallowed hard, with obvious difficulty, then took a hand away from his throat and pointed a trembling finger at Garth. "Blind him," he rasped. "Do it right now!"

The basic Siegfried Loge: gone was the soft-spoken gentility, and the nasal laughter was just an echo in the bizarre in-house prison he had built. All that was left was the mad, naked cruelty of a man who tortured animals and men, and ordered children murdered. I stepped closer to Garth.

"London, did you hear me!" Loge continued. "I want to see and hear that man's eyeballs pop! Get in there and do it now!"

"No," Stryder London said evenly.

Ignoring his stricken son, Loge struggled to his feet. His face was livid as he confronted the Warrior, and his hoarse voice cracked. "You do what I tell you to do, damn it! What's the matter?! You afraid to go in there?"

"No, sir," London replied calmly, his voice very soft. "I'm a soldier, not a torturer. I did warn you about standing too close to the cell."

"I'm giving you a fucking order!"

"I don't take orders from you, sir. Your father is my commander, and I won't do anything I feel is against his wishes or interests. If he ordered me to step into the black cell, I would; in the meantime, I must carry out my duties as I see them. I think you forget the value of these men."

"Why don't *you* step in here, kid killer?" I said to Loge. "I'll kick *your* balls up far enough to open your throat."

Loge stood trembling with fury, and for a moment I thought he was going to attack Stryder London; I would have liked to see that. Instead, he abruptly began to laugh. "Some bodyguard you are, London," he said contemptuously as he hauled his son to his feet, pushed the teenager toward the door. "Let's get out of here, super-soldier."

"In a minute, sir," London said as he studied Garth. "I have to find out something." He stepped up to the bars, motioned to my brother. "Come here, please."

"You want to talk to me at close range, London, get rid of your gun and step in here. That will put us on a little more equal footing."

"I won't hurt you, Frederickson. If that were my intention, I'd have done it while you were choking Dr. Loge. I could have maimed or killed you in seconds, and you know it."

"Yeah, but you didn't know then how cranky this fruitcake was going to get. He said science should be fun; I wanted to run an experiment to find out how long a fruitcake can go without breathing."

"What I want is for you to try to blind me. If you can do it, it's done. There'll be no retaliation."

Garth and I exchanged glances. There was silence; even Obie Loge had stopped groaning, and was staring, shocked, at the Warrior. Stryder London was serious.

"Why?" Garth asked quietly.

"Your reflexes appear to be extraordinary. You must be kept

alive, and as long as you're alive you pose a threat to the personnel here at Ramdor. It's my job to protect these people, and —as you noticed—scientists are not always as cautious as they should be. I need to test your combat skills, and in exchange for your cooperation I'm offering you the opportunity to blind me."

Garth shook his head. "You go play your games with somebody else. I've got nothing against you, pal. I'll save my energies for those people I do have something against."

London stared at Garth for some time in silence. When he did finally speak, his tone was curt, edged with anger. "People like you are a big part of what's gone wrong with this country, Frederickson. Both of you; neither of you thinks straight, and so you make the wrong decisions for the wrong reasons—usually out of sheer sentimentality. Your dwarf brother, for whatever reason, couldn't bring himself to kill a gorilla; he couldn't even bring himself to kill a man who had a shotgun leveled on his chest, simply because that man had once been a friend. If he had been able to do these killings, Dr. Loge and his son might now be your captives—instead of the other way around. Do you see my point?"

"Uh, an ounce of prevention is worth a pound of cure? Do unto others as you would have them do unto you?"

"You're a fool."

"I'm sorry; I'm trying as hard as I can to understand your point. A stitch in time saves nine? When in Ramdor, kill, kill, kill?"

"I am your enemy."

"Be what you want to be. What I said was that I have nothing against you."

"You have an opportunity now to neutralize an enemy, without risk. It's only simple logic that you take the opportunity. If you need emotion to make you act in a logical manner, consider that *I* would have killed your nephew and his friend without a second thought, if my first thought had been that the act was necessary."

"That does it, London; I'm not going to invite you to any of my parties." Garth nodded in the direction of the father and son standing by the open wooden door at the end of the corridor. "If you want to see what effect the shit Jake Bolesh put into me has had on my nervous system, send those two in here."

London shook his head, then abruptly turned and walked quickly out of the dungeon. The Loges followed, slamming the heavy door shut behind them.

"He seems impressed with your speed," I said as we both stared at the closed door. "Me, too."

Garth turned to me, a haunted expression on his face. "It doesn't stop. We're still changing, aren't we?"

I sighed, nodded as I absently scratched the scales on the back of my right hand.

The Loges found a way to get in their licks without fatally damaging the goods.

They returned an hour later, by themselves. The tranquilizer darts they shot us with contained a little extra something— probably scopolamine, to enhance the effects of the electronic choke collars we found around our necks when we woke up. The collars were made of leather laced with wires and radio-controlled electronic components that caused the wires to contract in varying degrees in response to the movement of a joy-stick on a black metal control box; the farther back the joystick was pulled, the tighter the collar grew.

For an hour the Loges had at us, occasionally trading control boxes, choking us into unconsciousness a half dozen times. Finally they got tired of it and went away.

The experience, as my mother would say, took a lot of the starch out of us.

25.

Déjà vu.

X-rays. clickety-click-click.

For some reason, Garth and I had been separated for the biological testing. Each of us had been assigned a keeper with a control box; Garth had drawn the gorilla.

"Hugo, what's a friendly giant like you doing in a place like this?"

Too big to fit in any of the chairs in the small examination room, the eight-foot giant was seated cross-legged on the floor, his back against the wall and the black box in his lap. His head was bowed slightly, and he wouldn't look at me. "I don't feel like joking, Mongo," he rumbled. "I don't like having to guard you like this."

"Who the fuck is joking?" I snapped. I was rapidly losing patience with Siegfried Loge and his minions. I managed to twist my arm around under the leather straps that held me to the table, held up the back of my hand; the scales glistened in the fluorescent light. "You think this is a *joke,* Hugo? You think what's happened to my eyes is a *joke?* Those crazy Loges are going to kill Garth and me when this is finished. You were my friend. Why should you help them harm the two of us?"

Hugo raised his head, brushed his long hair away from his eyes, and looked at me. "They said you'd say strange things, Mongo. It won't do you any good. We've all been briefed."

"What?"

"I know what happened."

I glanced around at the X-ray technician, who was putting another plate in the machine suspended over my head. Except for her full beard, she was an attractive woman with a pleasant manner. "Do you know what he's talking about?" I asked.

"Please hold still, Dr. Frederickson," she said, smiling sweetly. "We understand, and we don't hold anything against you. Your brother should have known better, though."

"Uh, Hugo; refresh my memory. What happened?"

"Why do you want me to tell you what you already know?"

"Humor me. It helps to pass the time."

Hugo shrugged resignedly. "You were at Dr. Loge's first clinic, in New York City—"

"What?"

"You asked me to tell you what happened."

"Yeah; sorry. Go ahead. What was I doing in this New York clinic?"

"The clinic was for people like you and me with congenital birth defects. They did the same things there as they do here at Ramdor."

"Jesus Christ, Hugo, you think Ramdor is a *clinic?*"

"It is a clinic. The research Dr. Loge does is incredibly important."

"Research. Tell me, Hugo, are tests like this run on you people, too?"

"Of course. All the time."

"Shit," I mumbled to myself. "Loge is trying to bring Lot Fifty-Seven in through the back door."

"What?"

"Nothing. What's Garth's congenital birth defect?"

"He doesn't have one. He became accidentally infected when he tried to help you inject yourself with the experimental serum you'd stolen."

"The experimental serum I'd stolen. Oh, yeah."

"I'm surprised at you, Mongo. You were told that the serum wasn't anywhere near ready for human experimentation, and you were warned that it could have very dangerous side effects. But you got impatient—as if being a dwarf is any worse than the defects the rest of us suffer from. You stole the serum and, with your brother's help, tried to treat yourself. Now it turns out that the condition you and your brother are in may be contagious. That's why we have to run these tests, even against your will. We can't run the risk that you and your brother will infect innocent people."

"Aren't you and the others here afraid that you'll catch something?"

It was some time before Hugo answered. When he spoke, his bass voice was soft, sad. "For most of us here, our lives were over the moment we were born. Suffering in hospitals, or being forced to earn a living by allowing ourselves to be gawked at in freak shows and roadside carnivals, can't really be called living. We have nothing to lose. The least we can do is make sure that innocent children don't end up like us because of something you and your brother are carrying."

"Hugo, my friend, it's all bullshit; everything you and the others here have been told is bullshit. The truth has been turned on its head, and you're all looking down the ass end. The truth is that the Loges are trying to make the whole world into one big freak show."

"Dr. Loge said you'd lie."

Blood tests. Ouch.

"Hugo, are you still a religious man?"

"Yes," the giant replied, apparently puzzled by the question. "Why shouldn't I be?"

"You used to be a Catholic."

"I'm still a Catholic."

"You are?"

"Of course."

"You used to believe in the Trinity—Father, Son, and Holy Ghost."

"Right," Hugo replied impatiently. "What are you getting at, Mongo? Why do you want to argue about religion?"

"I don't want to argue about your religion," I said, wincing as the technician, a fat lady who'd give Hugo a run for his money on the scales, slipped a needle into a vein for what seemed the fiftieth time; I had to be running out of blood. "I want to find out more about it. I want to know when the Trinity became a Quadrangle. There are two Fathers now, right?"

Hugo's eyes glinted dangerously. "You've changed, Mongo. You never used to make fun of people's religion."

"Siegmund Loge: don't you believe he's a god, or a new messiah?"

"Who's Siegmund Loge?"

PET—positron emission test—scan. Whirrrr.

"How long have you been here, Hugo?"

"A little over two years."

"Don't you ever read a newspaper, or watch the news on television?"

"I'm not interested in what goes on in the rest of the world."

"What goes on here?"

"Research that, one day, will eliminate giantism, dwarfism, mental retardation, and dozens of other genetic defects. You know that, Mongo. You're just trying to fool with me."

"You ever see a tall, elderly guy with long, wavy white hair walking around here?"

"No."

"That's Siegmund Loge—this Loge's father, the grandfather of the kid."

Hugo's response was a disinterested shrug.

"What about Siegfried Loge? Do you think *he's* some kind of god or messiah?"

Hugo snorted; it was a most impressive sound. "Of course not. That would be ridiculous—and blasphemous."

"Hugo, what if I told you that Garth and I just came from a religious commune where they worship Siegmund Loge as God?"

"I'm not sure I'd believe you. Even if it's true, what difference would it make? Dr. Loge can't be responsible for what his father does, or for what some people believe about him."

"They have a solution for congenital defects, too. They believe Siegmund Loge is going to wipe out everyone in the world who isn't genetically perfect. Oh, and while he's at it, he's also going to eliminate everyone who isn't white and fundamentalist Christian."

"So what? They're obviously crazy; there are a lot of crazy people in the world. That's their problem."

"No, my friend, it's also our problem; your problem. There's a direct link between that commune and Ramdor. It was guarded by a man wearing the same kind of uniform as the guards around this place. Stryder London is their commander; they're called Warriors of Father. London answers to Siegmund Loge—and only to Siegmund Loge."

That got me an even louder snort. "Stop it, Mongo. You think I'm stupid? Stryder is just the head of security at Ramdor."

"Why does a clinic need armed security guards?"

"To discourage people from coming around and gawking at us. Also, there's a lot of expensive equipment here. That machine you've got your head in is worth more than a million dollars."

"Where does the money come from to buy the equipment?"

"Who cares? I'm just glad they have the equipment."

"What they're doing here is developing a biochemical weapon such as the world has never seen, Hugo. What's happening to Garth and me is what Siegfried Loge *wants* to happen to other people who are targeted. You're helping him and his father find out why it works so well in us, without turning us into instant jelly. International covenants are being broken, Hugo. This kind of research, this kind of weapon, is banned in this country, and in every civilized nation in the world. *That's* what you're involved in, my friend, and that's as simply as I can put it."

Hugo leaned forward. His face was flushed as he waggled a huge finger in my face. "I'm tired of this, Mongo. I don't want to hear any more."

"I'll tell you another connection between the commune and this place, Hugo. The members bring in items—some of them extremely valuable—to contribute to Siegfried Loge, who must have quite a collection of loot by now. They think they're bringing offerings to Siegmund Loge, and they view it as a kind of religious rite. Garth and I got the address for this place off a big poster taped to a wall in a room where they pack and ship the stuff here. Did you know that?"

"It's a lie!"

"It's the truth! Look around you, Hugo. *Look* at this place; look at *you* and the others around here! He's using you for genetic research, but you and the surroundings also keep him and his kid highly amused; you feed their obsessions. Ramdor is right out of Wagner or Tolkien."

"No *more*, Mongo!" His voice was so loud that it echoed inside the steel cylinder around my head. "I don't want to hear it! You're upsetting me!"

I winced when I saw him reach for the black box, sighed with relief when he took his hand away. "Would you choke me just because you don't want to hear what I have to say?" I asked quietly.

Hugo lowered his head. "I'm sorry, Mongo. I don't want to hurt you, but I don't want to listen to any more crazy talk. Dr. Loge warned me; the serum you took has affected your mind."

"All right, Hugo. Have it your way." Hugo was hopeless. "Is Garth all right?"

"Yes."

"Have you seen him?"

"Yes."

"Why did they split us up?"

"Just to save time with the testing. You're too suspicious, Mongo. We're just trying to help you. You'll thank Dr. Loge and the rest of us when you get better and you're not crazy anymore."

* * *

Urine and stool specimens.

Silence.

"Hugo, nothing's happening. It must be anxiety."

"We're in no hurry, Mongo," Hugo replied from the other side of the thin partition. "We'll just wait until something does happen."

"We're in the building on top of the cliff, right?"

"Right."

"You have the run of the whole place?"

"No, only these test laboratories. I work on the dairy farm. Why?"

"Because I'm certain that if you could see everything that goes on in this place, you'd believe my story."

"Mongo, I thought we agreed that you weren't going to talk crazy anymore."

"Okay, okay. What's with the gorilla?"

"Gollum?"

"That's her name?"

"Yes."

"Gollum's the name of a particularly loathsome creature out of J. R. R. Tolkien. Doesn't that pique your curiosity?"

"Not really." Hugo sounded bored.

"Can she really understand what people say?"

"Of course," the giant replied, sounding surprised at the question. "And she can talk back with her word screen. She's really quite smart; sometimes I think she's as smart as I am."

That, I wasn't going to touch. "Who made her that way?"

"Dr. Loge."

"How?"

"I don't really know. Drugs, I suppose. It's the result of his research into cures for mental retardation. If he can do that with a gorilla, can you imagine what he'll be able to do with humans?"

"Oh, it boggles the mind; it would boggle anyone's mind, which leads me to ask why nobody—nobody at all—in the rest of the world scientific community seems to know a single thing about what's going on here. Do you find that strange, Hugo?"

"What do I know about these things?"

He had a point. "Okay, Hugo, forget everything else I said

about the Loges. Just consider what Loge has done with this gorilla, and with the other one I met—"

"There are no other gorillas like Gollum, Mongo. Don't start."

"Fine. Just consider Gollum. Twenty-four hours after Siegfried Loge took that gorilla for a walk out of here, he'd be nominated for every scientific prize there is. He'd be hailed as one of the greatest scientists who ever lived—"

"He is one of the greatest scientists who ever lived."

"True. But, on the strength only of what he's accomplished with the gorilla, he'd be famous, and he'd be rich. They'd probably turn Harvard over to him for his research; he certainly wouldn't have to hang out over a bunch of burning coal mines, or have you people leading around a few scraggly cows. Now, why hasn't a word about that gorilla appeared in any scientific journal? Why doesn't Loge take the gorilla out of here and show the world what he's been able to accomplish, Hugo?"

"I don't know, and I don't care. Dr. Loge isn't trying to help gorillas; he's trying to help people like you and me. What's your point? What does Gollum have to do with anything?"

"Jesus Christ, Hugo! I'm trying to reason with you!"

"You don't have to shout, Mongo. And please don't curse. Have you moved your bowels yet?"

"I'm telling you that teaching a fucking gorilla to communicate like that is one of the greatest scientific achievements in the history of humankind, and Siegfried Loge treats her like a toy! He doesn't *give* a damn about the gorilla, Hugo, because he and his father are cooking up some juice that could fuck up the entire human race! Are you *listening* to me, Hugo?!"

"Mongo, aren't you finished in there yet?"

Galvanic skin reaction tests.

Zap-twitch.

"Hugo, my friend, they've got all of you here by the emotional balls, but they're also shoveling out enough bullshit to cover the planet. Do you know what evolution is?"

"No. I just know it's something I'm not supposed to believe in."

"Evolution is what's made all of us—normal or not—people, and that process has taken place over millions of years. We've gone through many stages, and there are traces of those stages still left in our genes—our DNA."

"I told you I'm not supposed to believe in evolution."

"The Loges are trying to find a way to *unmake* us, Hugo. Can you understand, Hugo? Siegfried Loge isn't searching for a cure to genetic defects, he wants to find a way to inflict massive genetic damage. What he's doing endangers every animal and plant on the face of the earth. *That's* why everything is being kept such a big secret!"

"Enough, Mongo!" Hugo snapped. "I've had enough! I won't listen to any more of your crazy stories!"

Sonograms.

Beep-beep.

"What's a friendly gorilla like you doing in a place like this?"

FUCKING WATCHING YOU

"A narrow interpretation of my question, to say the least. Can you really understand what I'm saying?"

FUCKING YES

"You know, you're a very foul-mouthed gorilla."

?

" 'Fucking' isn't a nice word. It's unladylike."

MUST ALWAYS USE FUCKING WORD

"Why?"

MAKES MASTER FUCKING LAUGH

"Master is Siegfried Loge?"

FUCKING YES

"That figures. How did Loge teach you? What did he do to make you so smart?"

That got an unexpected reaction. Up to that point, primarily because of the bright expressiveness of the animal's yellow eyes and her facility with the screen-keyboard, talking to Gollum had seemed almost like talking to a human in a gorilla costume. Not any longer. For a fleeting instant the light in her eyes faded as if someone had turned a dimmer switch. She cowered, bared her teeth, and a rumbling snarl worked its way out of her chest.

Fearful that the gorilla might hit the joystick on the control box and strangle me by accident, I arched under the restraining straps and looked back at the technician—the fat lady. The woman shot me a hostile glance, then carefully stepped away from the controls of the machine and approached the gorilla. She reached out her hand, tentatively stroking the animal's shoulder. For a moment I was afraid Gollum was going to bite the technician, or literally knock her head off—but the animal gradually began to calm down.

Finally Gollum snorted, reached into a canvas shoulder bag she carried with her and took out a portable cassette player. Refusing even to look at me, she put the earphones over her head and turned on the machine.

"You upset her," the fat lady said to me accusingly.

"What can I do to upset you, lady? All of you here seem happy as clams, but that's because you don't have the slightest idea of what's going on. Can I tell you?"

"You can't tell me anything, Dr. Frederickson," the woman snapped, the eyes in the great folds of flesh that was her face glinting with annoyance. "I'm not deaf; I heard the conversations between you and Hugo, and I thought Hugo was very patient with you. Paranoids can really get to you after a time, the way they keep pestering you with their stupid fantasies."

"Is that what I am? Paranoid?"

"It's the drug you stole and injected yourself with. I understand that, and it's a good thing. If it weren't for my psychiatric training, I'd have slapped you in the face for what you said about Siegmund Loge."

"You've met Siegmund Loge?!" That got a good spike out of the microphone monitoring my heart.

"Yes. A number of times."

"He comes here?"

"Yes—to this facility. Hugo's just a farmhand, and Siegmund Loge doesn't bother himself with that part of the operation. That's just to keep the patients occupied."

" 'Patients.' I love it. What do you do here?"

"What you see me doing. I run tests on the patients—myself included. As you can see, I have a glandular problem."

"Have you been all through this building?"

"No, and don't you start with me. Siegfried Loge and that creepy kid of his may be no great shakes in the personality department, but Siegmund Loge is an absolute wonder. He could *never* be involved in anything that was wrong or hurtful to anyone. He's the kindest, warmest, gentlest human being I've ever met. With people and things in the world the way they are today, it's no wonder some young people think he's holy."

Eye tests.

Howl.

There was no way my eyes could be examined without shining lights in them. It didn't kill me, despite a profound desire, but I must have done a lot of screeching, and I kept passing out.

The fourth time I woke up, the testing was over and I was apparently being allowed a rest period. There were no technicians around, and I was still strapped into the chair where they'd conducted the eye exam. The gorilla was leaning back against the wall, the cassette player cradled in her lap and the earphones over her head. She had a contented expression on her face, and occasionally she would waggle a leathery finger in time—I presumed—to whatever she was hearing.

"What are you listening to?" I asked loudly.

The question got no response on her keyboard—but she did glance at me out of the corners of her eyes. I motioned for her to remove the earphones. After some hesitation and a loud, impatient smacking of her lips, she did so.

?

WHAT DO YOU FUCKING WANT

"What are you listening to, Gollum?"

FUCKING MOZART

"Mozart!"

I SAID FUCKING MOZART

"You like fu . . . you like Mozart?"

MUCH FUCKING YES

"So do I. May I listen with you?"

She thought about it, finally heaved her chest in what I assumed was an indulgent gorilla sigh. She unplugged the earphone jack, and the strains of *The Magic Flute* filled the air.

"What else do you like besides Mozart?" I asked after a few minutes.

JUST LIKE FUCKING MOZART

"Why?"

MAKE GOLLUM NOT FUCKING SAD

"You mean Mozart makes you happy?"

MEAN MOZART MAKE GOLLUM NOT FUCKING SAD

"You're sad when you don't listen to Mozart?"

FUCKING YES

"Why?"

FUCKING WRONG

"It's wrong to feel sad, or wrong to listen to Mozart?"

GOLLUM FUCKING WRONG

"I don't understand."

She stared at me hard, and suddenly her yellow eyes were filled with—a profound sadness. Her thick lips trembled, and I had the distinct impression that she was debating whether or not, or how, to reply. Suddenly the fingers of both hands flew over the keyboard.

I stared at the screen in disbelief, a lump rising in my throat, tears welling in my eyes.

    GOLLUM MADE FUCKING WRONG
    GOLLUM HAVE FUCKING PERSON FEELINGS
    GOLLUM NOT A FUCKING PERSON
    GOLLUM NOT A FUCKING GORILLA
    GOLLUM FUCKING WRONG

"Oh, my God," I whispered in a choked voice. "You understand that?"

GOLLUM FUCKING WRONG
GOLLUM NOT FUCKING STUPID

And she put her earphones back on.

CAT Scan.

Mmmmmmm.

Whatever else they were finding in my body, the machines would have blown out if they'd been able to measure rage. I was getting seriously pissed.

"Loge hurt you very badly when he made you wrong, didn't he?" I asked quietly.

Gollum studied me for a long time from beneath her thick, bony brows. Finally the answer came.

FUCKING YES

"I'm sorry I upset you before. I didn't mean to."

FUCKING OKAY

"I'm also sorry Loge hurt you."

?

FUCKING WHY
MASTER NOT FUCKING HURT YOU

"He has hurt me, and he is hurting me and my brother, but that isn't the point. I'm saying that I'm sorry he hurt you. You didn't deserve it. Neither do Garth and I deserve to be hurt."

?

WHY MASTER HURT GOLLUM AND FUCKING
PEOPLE

"Because Loge is a bad man."

?

MASTER IS FUCKING WRONG

"Loge is bad—he's evil. He likes to hurt. That's much worse than being wrong." I glanced over my shoulder, saw that the technician—a surly midget—was sitting by the controls across the room, thoroughly absorbed in an issue of *Hustler*. I turned back to Gollum, lowered my voice, "Will you let me go so that these people can't hurt me any more?"

She tensed, quickly reached for the keyboard.

> FUCKING NO
> FUCKING CHOKE

"Why not, since you know they're making me wrong and hurting me?"

> HURT FUCKING GOLLUM MORE
> MASTER KILL FUCKING GOLLUM

"Okay."

> GOLLUM SORRY YOU MADE FUCKING WRONG
> GOLLUM SORRY MASTER FUCKING HURT YOU
> GOLLUM SORRY SHE DROP YOU ON FUCKING
> HEAD

I smiled at her, shrugged. "It's fucking okay."

GI series: Injections of irradiated barium, more X-rays. Clickety-click.

"I'm not going to call you Gollum any longer," I announced to my watch-gorilla after a particularly nasty spasm of nausea had passed. "The kid named you that, didn't he?"

> FUCKING YES

"That's a bad name, and you're a good gorilla. I'm going to call you Golly. Okay?"

> FUCKING OKAY
> FUCKING SPEAK SPELL PLEASE

I said the name slowly, and Golly tried out a series of spellings. When she hit the right one, I nodded my head.

> ?
> HOW FUCKING GOLLY CALL YOU

"Mongo," I said, and spelled it for her. The gorilla did some fast fingering on her keyboard, assigned me a symbol.

> MONGO FUCKING OKAY

Rest time.

Figuring that a watch-gorilla and my choke collar were sufficient to make me stay put, my last technician had not bothered to strap me into the leather recliner while he'd gone off for a smoke.

Golly was slumped in another recliner in the small lounge. She had her earphones on, and her eyes were closed. She appeared to be asleep.

Moving very slowly, I eased myself out of the recliner and tiptoed across the room. I would have liked to try and snatch the control box for my choke collar, but that was in Golly's lap and it seemed best to let sleeping gorillas lie. I tiptoed past her, out of the lounge. I turned right and sprinted as fast as I could down a narrow, white corridor toward a swinging door. I didn't know the range of the control box, but it couldn't be limitless; if I could only get beyond it, I'd find a way to get the collar off and get down to serious business.

Halfway down the corridor, I felt the leather collar snap tight around my neck and begin to squeeze. I held my breath and kept running toward the door. My only hope was to get beyond range, or get behind something that was shielded with lead.

Anybody who wants to learn the hard way about oxygen debt should try sprinting while holding his breath and while a leather collar is threatening to squeeze his head off. Anyway, I kept running, legs and arms pumping, trying to reach the door. At least I thought I was running. Everything was beginning to look hazy through my smoked glasses, and a giant fist was pounding my chest. My head felt ready to explode.

Still, I was somehow convinced that I was making progress, that I might still escape. I kept feeling that way right up to the point where, clawing at the leather band around my neck, I collapsed to my knees, then fell forward on my face.

26.

I'd expected that Garth and I would be killed after our biosamples were taken and safely stored away. Instead, it seemed to be game time; we were getting a tour of Ramdor, personally conducted by Siegfried Loge and his son.

"You two don't seen to be entering into the spirit of things," the hawk-nosed, pale-eyed scientist said as he paused in the middle of a long land bridge that had been constructed over an area of earth that actually glowed with the furnace heat beneath it.

"Fuck you, creep," Garth said, and yawned.

"Garth never liked to go on outings, even as a kid," I added. "Besides, when you've seen one dairy farm you've seen them all."

Loge took a piece of paper from his pocket, crumpled it into a ball and dropped it over the railing; the paper burst into flames even before it hit the ground. "It's better than a thousand degrees Fahrenheit down there on the surface. There are a number of areas like this around Ramdor. You two are lucky you weren't fried on your way in."

It occurred to me that it might have been better for millions of people if we had been fried, or if Lippitt had killed us back in Nebraska. We'd accomplished nothing by chasing after the Loges, except to supply them with what they wanted and needed. It was precisely what Lippitt had feared would happen.

I remembered my mother's dream.

"This place is a regular Disneyland," I said, glancing around to look at Golly, who trailed behind us and held both control boxes. The gorilla had been in a snit ever since I'd tried to run off on her, refusing even to look at me. Throughout the tour she'd been off with Mozart, the thin cables to her earphones snaking out of her canvas shoulder bag. However, on more than one occasion her thumb, as if by accident, had brushed against the joystick on my control box; the tugs of the collar around my neck caused only minor discomfort, but Golly had made it clear that she felt hurt and betrayed. "Where's Hugo?"

"Hugo has chores to do," the scientist said in a tone that sounded evasive. "Gollum can easily handle the two of you in this situation."

"Let's show them the Treasure Room," Obie Loge said to his father. The teenager's face was flushed with excitement.

"Whoopee. How about showing us the exit?"

"Hey, creep," Garth said to Loge. "You've got what you wanted. Why haven't you killed us?"

It was a question to which I'd given some thought, and I thought I knew the answer. "It's because Gramps has to check the results to make certain everything's all right. That's it, isn't it, Loge?"

"Of course," Loge replied evenly. "Also, it would be senseless to dispose of you while the reaction continues in your bodies. We'll simply continue to monitor you."

"Where is the old man?"

"You'll enjoy seeing the Treasure Room. As long as I have absolute power over you, why not relax and enjoy my hospitality? Both of you are intelligent, and there aren't a great many people I can share all of Ramdon's wonders and secrets with."

"I believe that."

"Hey, Loge," Garth said quietly. "What would you think of another fun experiment in which we see if I can break your neck before this collar chokes me to death?"

"I wouldn't do that!" Loge snapped, wheeling on my brother. "Don't even think about it!"

"Why not?" Garth asked in a mild tone that caused me to wince; committing suicide didn't seem to make much sense. "You don't think that would be as much fun as ordering the murder of two boys who'd befriended your fat, ugly son? On second thought, it might be even more fun to throw the two of you over the railing and watch you sizzle."

"Hey, fucking Gollum!" Loge shouted.

Golly jumped, snatched the earphones from her head. Her eyes glittered with terror, and her hand trembled as she fumbled at the keyboard.

?
FUCKING WHAT

"Show them the kill button."

Using the thumbs of both hands, Golly flipped open the tops on the cases of the boxes to reveal bright blue buttons.

"It's true that we want to keep you alive," Loge continued as he glanced back and forth at Garth and me, "but not to the extent of allowing you to attack either Obie or me. There'll be no repetition of what happened in the dungeon. If one of you does attack my son or me, I absolutely guarantee that the button on your box will be pushed; then it's your brains that will sizzle. Do I make myself clear?"

"You're a real spoilsport," Garth said.

"Enough unnecessary unpleasantness," Loge said, turning away. "Come. Obie wants you to see the Treasure Room and Mount Doom."

We went back to the ranch house, walked through it to the rear. Loge opened the door to what I thought was a closet; it turned out to be the entrance to a long, unlighted tunnel that had been carved out of the rock. He removed two gasoline-soaked torches from brackets on the wall, lit them with a cigarette lighter, handed one to his son. Then they led us down the tunnel, with Golly bringing up the rear.

At the end of the tunnel was a door with its edges set flush to the rock; like the door in the black cell, there was no keyhole.

Loge, his eyes glassy in the torchlight, turned to face us. "Behold," he intoned as he removed the ring medallion from around his neck and slowly passed it back and forth over the flame.

The metal of the medallion slowly changed its configuration to the shape of a key. Garth yawned loudly.

His spirits undampened, Loge turned and passed the flame across the surface of the door; a section of metal appeared to melt and flow apart to form a keyhole. Garth yawned again.

Loge turned the key in the lock, pushed open the door. Instantly, the air was filled with the music of Siegfried's Funeral March, from *Götterdämmerung,* and the darkness beyond the door began to glow like sunrise. The torches were extinguished and cast aside as the light came up, and we followed the Loges into the room.

This time Garth didn't yawn.

The Treasure Room, bathed in soft blue fluorescent light, was a huge circular chamber blasted out of the rock. On the wall opposite the door was an enormous, Cinerama-size panel of some material on which was projected a photomural of scenes from Wagner's *Ring*. The chamber was filled with an astonishing array of Wagnerian memorabilia. There was gold, of course, but even more impressive were other artifacts—special, undoubtedly rare, musical instruments, bejeweled swords and daggers, antique costumes, opera posters with Richard Wagner's distinctive signature scrawled across them.

"This is from a practice room at Bayreuth," Loge announced proudly as he walked across the room and sat down at an old, scarred upright piano. "Wagner himself played on it. The page on the stand here is from the original manuscript of *Das Rheingold*. Here; listen."

And he began to play. He was actually quite good, and I might have enjoyed it if not for the fact that the recital was being given by the man responsible for the fact that Garth and I were standing around there dying. Impulsively, I marched across the room and slammed my fists down on the keys. The collar around my neck tightened, but did not choke.

"You don't like my playing," Loge continued sardonically as he smiled at me. "I'm told I have some talent."

"Save it for somebody else, Loge."

"You understand, of course, why there aren't too many people I can bring in here."

"Oh, I understand perfectly." It struck me that the medallion, which he had replaced around his neck, had returned to its original shape.

"You and your brother should feel honored that Obie and I choose to share it with you."

"Once, everything in this room was rare, intriguing and beautiful; in your hands, they're just pieces for death and silence."

"I understand that you have one of my pieces," Loge said as he rose from the piano stool. "I'm told it's an exquisite knife—which, incidentally, you used to lop off the hand of one of Stryder's men."

"It was lost in the car crash and fire."

"Too bad. I understand it was made of Damascus steel; truly

one of a kind. It would have made a nice addition to my collection."

"Hey, pimple nose," Garth said to Obie Loge. "What do you play with in here? This is all Wagner. No Tolkien?"

The boy flushed angrily, but Siegfried Loge just laughed. "Relax, Obie. Remember what they say about sticks and stones. Show the gentlemen Mount Doom. It will make you feel better."

The boy hesitated, then shrugged and walked over to a panel of switches that appeared to be part of a console controlling lights, a videotape machine, and a bank of six large television monitors. Obie Loge flipped a switch. The lights dimmed, and for a few moments my eyes had trouble making the transition. I started to remove my smoked glasses, then saw a reddish glow building where the photomural had been. Garth, sensing my difficulty, put his hand on my shoulder and guided me toward the red glow.

"Behold Mount Doom," Obie Loge said, and he sounded almost as spooky as his father until he ruined it all with a giggle.

With the lights out, the projected photomural had disappeared, leaving a huge, transparent panel of what was probably Plexiglas. Standing next to Garth in front of the panel, I found myself staring out over what looked like a miniature Grand Canyon which wasn't so miniature. It was a great, stone-bounded cathedral or amphitheater with dimensions I could only guess at. The reddish glow emanated from fire somewhere far below the Treasure Room, and was swallowed up by darkness far above. On the great stone wall across the chasm, perhaps two hundred yards away, three different series of steps running in different directions from a central point high to the right had been carved out of the stone, which was pockmarked with caves. There were bones—bare, polished bones—and scraps of clothing strewn over the steps at three different sites. Even at that distance and without the evidence of the clothes, I'd have been able to tell that the skulls were unmistakably human.

"How quaint," I muttered. "I don't know why you don't show this to Hugo. He's really into clinics."

"What the hell is that?!" Garth said, shying as something big and brown flapped down out of the darkness, banged against the Plexiglas by his head, then soared on hot air currents up out of sight.

The Loges looked at each other, laughed. "We don't know," the elder Loge said. "We haven't been able to figure out a way to capture one."

I turned to look at the scientist. "You don't know what it *is?*"

"No," Loge said, grinning. "As a matter of fact, there are a great many curious things in Mount Doom. Obie likes to put things in there to see what happens. The results, as you see, have been totally unexpected; serendipity in science. What's become of the things he drops in there isn't a question that's likely to be answered soon. We've never known a man to go in there and come out again."

Wheeling around, I fixed my gaze on the apex of the three sets of steps; I could just barely make out the outlines of a door cut into the rock. "The black cell," I whispered in horror as two more of the things swooped past; the flying things were leathery, looked something like bloated pterodactyls with hair and teeth.

"Right," Obie Loge said with obvious satisfaction. "Man, you should see those fuckers attack."

"Totally unexpected," Siegfried Loge repeated in a somewhat distant tone. "There was no way to predict . . . I really should have paid more attention to what you threw in there, Obie."

"Aw, shit," Garth drawled. "This is really a bummer. What you need in there is a dragon. What's a Mount Doom without a dragon?"

Once again the Loges looked at each other and tittered; this time, I thought I detected more than a hint of nervousness in their looks and laughter.

"Where did they come from originally?" I asked, watching one of the leathery beasts drop down out of sight toward the furnace glow below.

"You'll see on the exit leg of the tour," Siegfried Loge replied. "Right now, I'm sure Obie wants to show your wisecracking big brother a dragon."

Obie Loge nodded enthusiastically, turned on the videotape machine. One of the monitors on the wall came alive with fast-moving, fuzzy images. The images slowed, became what looked like a large metal pipe suspended over a mound of bones.

"You'll have to excuse the somewhat blurred picture," Loge continued. "The cameras we sunk down there are state-of-the-art and highly heat-resistant, but they've never really worked properly. What you're looking at is the bottom of a waste chute extending up through the escarpment to the laboratories above. Obie, let the tape run."

The younger Loge released the pause button on the machine; something blurred and unrecognizable plummeted out of the chute, fell onto the mound of bones. Instantly, dozens of dark shapes darted from the surrounding darkness, converging on the hapless creature that had fallen down the chute, swarming over it, tearing it apart.

"Too bad the microphones down there don't work," Obie Loge said to his father. "I'll bet we'd really hear some crunching and munching."

"As you see," Siegfried Lodge said to Garth and me, "some things have survived. Now, it's the survival of the fittest down there. Nothing Obie threw down there was ever more than barely alive, yet something in Mount Doom not only arrested the process of their dying, but changed them into creatures that probably exist nowhere else. Most interesting. It's too bad we don't have the time or resources to investigate what's happening." He paused, turned to his son. "Obie, that's enough of this crunchy-munchy shit. Skip ahead to six-eighty-nine."

Keeping his eye on the machine's tape counter, Obie Loge pushed the fast-forward control, held it down for a half minute, released it.

On the monitor, two large, black spots floated in toward the camera, hit it; the screen went blank.

Garth yawned.

"That's it?" I asked. "Some fucking dragon. Frankly, I was more impressed with your key trick."

For a time, I wasn't sure Loge was going to answer. When he did, his voice was distant. "There's something very big down there," he said, gazing out toward the chasm. "That camera was sunk into a mine some distance from here, to the south. It was suspended from the ceiling, and as far as we could tell it was at least five feet off the ground, with a lighting system that was sensor-activated. Whatever passed in front of that camera broke it. Nothing even approaching that size was ever thrown down the chute; it grew to that size while it was down there. It's mutated into something huge, and—from what we know about that section of the mines—it chooses to live in total darkness. I wouldn't care to run into it."

"Oh, I don't know; I think I'd take a dragon over the Loges any time."

Loge continued to stare out over the chasm, as if in a trance, for more than a minute. Then he abruptly turned and walked across the Treasure Room to what appeared to be the door to an elevator. "Come," he said tersely. He seemed distracted now, oddly subdued, as if his bizarre personality were suddenly shifting gears in him. "Next stop on the tour, and I think it will interest you. However, if you don't wish to see it, Gollum will take you back to the dungeon. Suit yourselves."

Garth and I exchanged glances. "We'll see it all," Garth said.

"Fine. Then let's go; I have other work to do today."

"Dad?"

"Be quiet, Obie. I'm all right." Loge pressed the button, and the elevator door sighed open. Loge pushed his son past him to the back of the elevator. "Let's go, fucking Gollum."

The gorilla was hanging back; her shoulders were slumped, and she was holding her cassette player cradled against her chest like a baby.

"Leave her alone," I said to Loge. "She's been upset all through this tour of yours, and she's obviously very upset by whatever you've got upstairs. Let her go. You and your kid can handle us with the boxes easily enough."

"Fucking Gollum!"

Golly scampered across the room, fairly leaped into the elevator, and cringed in a corner. Garth and I followed, but Loge kept the door propped open with his hand. He was staring at me, and his eyes seemed slightly out of focus.

"Gollum impresses the hell out of you, doesn't she, Frederickson?" Loge continued.

"Yeah, she does."

"Then I'll let you and your brother in on a little secret; most of it's a trick, computer-enhanced communications using random-sorting circuit boards you can buy off the shelf in any good hobby store. Oh, I've worked on her cognitive brain centers, to be sure, and she sure as hell is smarter than the average gorilla, but she has nowhere near the capacities for thought, communication, and feeling that you think she does. Most of the work is done by the computer behind the keyboard."

"You're wrong," I said flatly. "Christ, look at her."

Loge smiled thinly. "You stick to criminology, Professor, and leave the hard science to me. Artificially enhanced intelligence, yes, but she's still basically just a clever tame gorilla. I'm telling you this because I thought you'd be interested; it's part of the tour."

"I still say you're wrong."

"I know what Gollum is; I made her, and Obie designed the computer."

"I think she's your most remarkable creation, Loge."

"No. That distinction belongs to you and your brother."

"Your old man had to a lot to do with making us."

Loge shrugged. "Of course."

"What'd you do to enhance her intelligence?"

"There's less than a one-percent difference between the DNA structures of man and great apes; lay slides of the structures next to each other, and you need a very powerful microscope to discern the difference. That tiny percentage accounts for all the differences between apes and us. My father and I were able to isolate a gene chain that's responsible for much of primate cognitive intelligence. There are also enzyme pairs involved, and those chains and enzyme pairs can be stimulated and reorganized if you find the right catalyst. I used massive doses of ionizing radiation on the appropriate brain centers, specifically on what passes for a cerebral cortex in a gorilla."

Obie Loge laughed. "If you want to see something really funny, you should see a puking gorilla without fur."

I had a sudden vision of Golly with radiation sickness, naked and cold, her mind lost and whirling in a foggy world of torment between beast and something else. I badly wanted to cripple Loge, but knew that if I hit the scientist the animal he'd hurt so badly would choke—and perhaps kill—me.

". . . and pain," Loge was saying.

"Huh? What?"

"Operant conditioning. Reorganizing the gene chains was

one thing, but you might say that we also had to get her attention in order to teach her—as well as the one you ran across in Nebraska—what to do with this new sense of awareness."

"Torture."

"I got her attention, and I must say that she performs quite nicely. But it's still basically tricks, totally beside the point. You and your brother are the point."

There was absolutely nothing I could think of to say. I was astonished, dumbfounded, by Loge's apparently total blindness to what had happened with Golly. The man had penetrated the most mysterious of all worlds, the spiritual, had ignited the flame of a soul in a beast, and didn't know it. He wouldn't—or couldn't—see it. Nothing seemed to exist for him outside the narrow, intense focus of his interests; he was a man who could casually order up the murder of two teenagers, then appear vaguely distressed when the uncles of one of them appeared less than enthused with his work and hobbies. He was enough to make an institutionalized sociopath look like an emotional overachiever.

Loge stepped back. The door closed, and the elevator began to rise. The shaft had been sunk through both solid rock and burnt-out mines, some of which were populated by the strange creatures which, like Garth and me, suffered chaos in their genes. The walls of the elevator were transparent; although the trip to the building at the top of the escarpment lasted less than a minute, it became a protracted, nightmare journey through black rock and backlit mines where things skittered away as we passed. It was worse than anything dreamed up by Hieronymus Bosch.

I had a pretty good idea of what we were going to see when the door opened, but that still didn't prepare me for the panorama of agony—unidentifiable creatures in various stages of devolution, all lined up in rows inside glassed-in, soundproofed cages atop steel pedestals inside a large laboratory that was all gleaming white tile. Wires from monitoring devices inside the cages snaked to the ceiling, were bundled into cables that ran along the ceiling to a central monitoring and control panel that filled half of one wall to the left of the elevator. Garth, a tough New York City cop, was green, and I turned away as I felt my stomach turn.

What was in the cages were all variations of the things Lippitt had splashed over a fender to show us what we were up
against, and why we might want him to kill us; Loge's laboratory was Lippitt's horror show multiplied a hundredfold. All of
the creatures, to various extents, were "melting" into bizarre
combinations of fur and feathers, fangs and beaks, claws and
flippers, hide and scales.

Every living thing in the room, except for the two Loges, was
dying like that.

"This is a terrible thing" was all I could think of to say, and I
delivered the line rather feebly.

"So are nuclear weapons," Loge declared flatly as he stared
at the cages where the creatures mewled, coughed, barked, and
screamed in—to us—silent agony.

"Then it is a weapon you're developing."

"Don't be stupid, Frederickson," Loge said in the same odd,
flat tone of voice. "It's unbecoming. Did you think we were
making cheesecake."

"I wanted to hear you admit it."

"This is a unique weapon. When we learn from your bodies
how to control the reaction, it will be only a minor step to
tailoring it so that it can be targeted against specific populations
based upon membership in gene pools."

"Races?"

"Oh, it can be targeted to race, certainly. More important, it
can be targeted against nationality, as long as the gene pool is
sufficiently discrete."

"It would work better against, say, Icelander or Georgian
Russians than against Americans."

"Correct, Frederickson."

"You need to control the reaction so that you can mask
what's happening to the people, slow it down, make its source
untraceable. The victims might not even know they'd been attacked, much less know what kind of weapon had been used
against them."

"Correct, Frederickson."

"That makes it an offensive weapon."

"Right again."

Obie Loge was checking cages. When he found a dead animal, he would open a side of the cage, don elbow-length rubber

gloves, then remove the animal and carry it to our end of the lab where the waste chute was located. He would pull open the large lid, drop the creature down the chute, close the lid. Then he would watch the show down below on a television monitor to the left of the waste chute.

Garth nudged me. I looked up into the profound sadness of his face and eyes, knew instantly what he wanted to do. I winked, nudged him back. Garth yawned, thrust his hands into his pockets and, under the watchful eye of Golly, began to stroll in and out of the rows of cages.

"It's illegal."

"Naiveté doesn't become you either, Frederickson. Every nation stockpiles illegal antipersonnel weapons, from mustard gas, to anthrax bombs, to binary nerve gas. Besides, it's arguable whether this research is actually illegal. The United States isn't a signatory to the Geneva protocols outlawing this kind of weaponry."

"For Christ's sake, Loge, forget what's legal or illegal; forget the question of morality. What if this—whatever it is you're cooking up in here—gets loose into the environment before you have a handle on it? It could change the face of the planet."

"Trust us."

"Dad?" Obie Loge called from where he was standing in front of the television monitor. "It's pretty quiet down there now. Can I use live ones to feed the kitty?"

Siegfried Loge nodded, held up three fingers.

"You and your father are fucking lunatics, Loge. No; you're beyond lunacy. I don't know what to call you."

"If we're lunatics, I don't know what that makes all those nice people in Washington who run this country," Loge replied mildly as he watched his son select something that quivered, carry it back and drop it down the chute. "Government people came to my father on this matter, not the other way around. You think we could throw around money like this, or enjoy the protection we do, without government backing?"

"Where is your father? I would think he'd be anxious to meet his two prize specimens." The cries of the animal Obie Loge had carried across the laboratory still echoed in my mind.

"He is anxious to meet you, and he will. He's a busy man."

"He's carrying on direct human experimentation somewhere, isn't he?"

"He's a busy man."

"Maybe he's a dead man. Lippitt had him targeted from the beginning. You're a fairly bright man for a lunatic, but you don't have the mind of your old man. Without him, Project Valhalla will never be completed. Lippitt always understood that."

Loge shook his head. "Mr. Lippitt will never find my father. It's Lippitt who will die—if he's not dead already."

The next animal spewed fluid all over the floor, screamed as Obie Loge brought it to the chute, dropped it down.

"Specifically, what's happening to us?" Garth asked in a casual tone as he leaned against one of the pedestals near the waste chute.

"Your brother, if his cells don't suddenly explode, will become a creature closely resembling a snake," Loge answered matter-of-factly. "Your changes are less dramatic, but in a way more interesting. You seem to be following a very direct evolutionary line back through the humanoids. If you don't explode, I think we'll actually be able to see what the precursor of Neanderthal and Cro-Magnon looked like. I really hope you make it; anthropology is a minor interest of mine."

"I think it might be a good idea for you to tell your boy to call it a day on the live animal thing," I said as I watched Obie Loge looking for another animal, then glanced at Garth.

Loge shrugged, smiled thinly. "He has to keep Mount Doom populated. Why should I tell him to stop?"

"I think you should tell him to stop because Garth is getting aggravated."

Obie Loge yelped as Garth's fingers closed around his throat; the boy went up on his toes, and his tongue started to protrude from his mouth.

"Wait!" I shouted, wheeling on Golly and extending both my arms. "He won't kill! Don't you! Just wait!" I tensed, holding my breath. Golly had immediately flipped open the tops on both control boxes, and her thumbs hovered near the blue kill buttons. She looked uncertainly at me, then at Loge.

"Kill the animals in the cages," I continued as I slowly

turned around to face Loge. "Kill them all. Then Garth will release your son."

Loge had cocked his head to one side and was staring at me intently. "If I nod to that gorilla, your brother dies instantly from electrical shock. You know that."

"Not quite instantly, Loge. You've seen his reflexes and you know how strong he is; at the instant you're burning his brain, he'll be snapping your kid's neck. Then I go after you, and Golly will have to kill me."

"What the hell do you think you're doing?" He seemed more interested in the answer than he was in whether or not Garth killed his son. Obie Loge's face was turning blue, and Garth was grinning. "I won't let you escape. You try to escape, you die."

"You're not listening. We have a simple request; put these animals out of their misery. Do it now. Then Garth will let your kid go. We're not trying to escape."

"What's the point? I'll have a new shipment of test animals trucked in."

"We'll take whatever victories we can find in small doses, one day at a time. You have a simple choice, Loge; kill the animals, or have your boy die and be forced to kill your two prize specimens."

"This is insane, Frederickson. You and your brother risk your lives just to make a silly, token gesture? It doesn't make sense."

"It's like you told Hugo; the shit in us has affected our minds. Do it, Loge. Then your boy can start breathing again, and Garth and I can get back to our nice, cozy dungeon."

Loge shrugged, turned and walked to the control panel on the wall. He snapped back a protective plate, began pushing a series of small brown buttons. Electric grids in the bottoms of the cages sparked; one by one, the tormented creatures in the cages stiffened and were still.

When Loge was finished, Garth pushed Obie Loge away from him.

"Choke them," Siegfried Loge said casually to Golly, and Golly did.

27.

Chore time. Garth was put to work shoveling manure, and I got to milk cows. It was lousy busy work, but it beat sitting around in the dungeon.

Golly, who still seemed upset, had refused even to look at me for two days. On the morning of the third day I felt a leathery hand touch my shoulder. I turned on my milking stool to find Golly standing by me, her earphones draped around her neck.

MASTER ALMOST MADE FUCKING GOLLY KILL
YOU

"We understand that you have to do what Loge tells you. Don't worry about it."

GOLLY DON'T WANT TO FUCKING KILL YOU

"I know."

WHY MAKE MASTER KILL FUCKING ANIMALS

"The animals were suffering a lot of pain."

PLEASE KILL FUCKING GOLLY

"Why?" I asked, frowning. "I know Loge hurt you before, but are you in pain now?"

FUCKING NO
GOLLY FUCKING WRONG

I shook my head. "If you know you're wrong, you're not that wrong."

GOOD THAT YOU KILL FUCKING ANIMALS

"That's what Garth and I thought."

MONGO AND GARTH FUCKING GOOD

"Thank you."

MONGO AND GARTH FUCKING STUPID

I laughed. "Loge thinks that it's the machine on your chest that makes you seem so smart. What do you think?"

GOLLY FUCKING WRONG

"I'm tired of milking cows, sweetheart," I said, stretching and arching my back. "How about letting me do some gardening for a change of pace?"

?

"Gardening; I want to work on those plants by the house."

PLANTS FUCKING DEAD

"No. They're like that because it's cold now, but things should be done so that they'll grow when it's warm again. I like digging around in the dirt. Okay?"

FUCKING OKAY

Whisper was where I'd left her.

Since I'd been such a well-behaved specimen, Loge granted my request for a changing of the guard. Golly was hurt, and Hugo was surprised.

After a morning spent watching me milk cows, even Hugo seemed bored. After lunch, he accepted my suggestion that we go for a walk in the woods. We strolled, chatting amiably about the difficulties of dwarves and giants, while I kept my fingers looped in the shoulder straps of my baggy green overalls.

"Hugo," I said as we stopped to examine the tracks of some animal in the thin cover of snow, "there's something I want to show you."

The eight-foot giant peered down at me, his large limpid eyes aglow with curiosity. "What is it, Mongo?"

"Look at that tree over there."

Hugo turned to his right. "What—?"

Zip.

Shhh.

Thunk.

Hugo jumped—and a jumping giant is a sight to see. He stared, transfixed, at Whisper as she quivered in the tree trunk a few feet away. "Holy shit," he said. It was the first time I'd ever heard him curse.

"Do I have your attention, Hugo?" Still staring at Whisper, he grunted. "Go get the knife."

Hugo walked stiffly to the tree, removed Whisper from the trunk, turned the knife over in his hands.

"That wasn't a nice thing to do, Mongo," the giant rumbled, looking at me and frowning. Hugo was recovering from his initial shock, and now looked a mite peeved. "I heard this thing go past; you could have slicked off my ear."

"It's a nice knife, isn't it?"

"Where'd you get it?"

"From the religious commune I was telling you about. I told you that's how Garth and I got the address of this place."

"Mongo!"

"Shut up, Hugo. Forget your ear; I could have sliced off your head. I could easily have killed you just now, but I didn't. After killing you, I could have strolled back to the manure pile and killed the gorilla. Garth and I could probably even have killed the Loges, and then just walked off. Escaping isn't enough anymore. Loge took things from Garth and me, and we have to get them back and destroy them; if the things aren't here, we have to find out where they were sent. To do that, we need somebody on the inside—you. The fact that you're holding my knife instead of your head in your hands would seem to give me the right to hold forth for a minute or two without you interrupting to tell me how crazy I am."

Hugo narrowed his eyes. "What things?"

"Body fluids and tissue; blood, urine, bone marrow, skin tissue, muscle tissue, feces, sperm. All of it has to be found and destroyed, along with the results of all the tests that were conducted."

"Why?"

"You're not ready for that yet. Let's take a small step first. When I think that you may be beginning to trust and believe me, I'll tell you the answer to that question. The first thing is to show you that Loge is a liar. Then, maybe you'll consider the possibility that I'm not, and that all of you are being used for purposes exactly the opposite of what you think they are."

"How are you going to do that?"

"I want to show you the room where Loge keeps all the things that are sent to him by commune members; I want to show you a place where the bones of men the Loges have killed have been left lying out in the open; I want to show you a room where animals are tortured in a way beyond anything you can imagine."

Hugo was silent for a long time, and we stared into each other's eyes. "Show me," he said at last.

"I'd like my knife back."

"First show me these things."

"If I don't show them to you, then you can take it back. You know that I have it; it's enough. You have the choke collar, and you're just a tad bigger than I am."

Hugo thought about it, flipped Whisper in his hand and held her out. I took the handle, but Hugo maintained his grip on the blade. "When are you going to show me?"

"Tonight. And I'll need your help for that, too."

"What do you want me to do?"

"It's dangerous, Hugo. I have to tell you that you could be killed."

"You claim that Dr. Loge is trying to hurt, not help, people like us?"

"It's worse than that, Hugo. Much worse."

"Mongo, if this turns out to be just crazy talk, I swear I'll be so upset that I don't think I'll be able to keep myself from hurting you real bad."

"I'll take my chances."

Hugo released his grip on Whisper, and I replaced her in the sheath in my belt, inside my overalls.

"What do you want me to do, Mongo?"

"First, you mustn't tell Golly about this conversation, or have her find out what you're doing."

"All right."

"You and Golly live in the house, guard it at night?"

"Yes."

"With those big feet of yours, do you think you can sneak into Loge's room while he's sleeping without waking him or having Golly hear you?"

"Maybe," Hugo said after some hesitation. "Why do you want me to do that?"

"The thing he wears around his neck all the time is a key to the room I want to show you. Bring it to Garth and me tonight, along with the keys to our cell."

"Mongo, you remember that I warned you what could happen if this turns out to be crazy talk."

"I'll remember. You remember what I said about this being dangerous. Is there any way I can get you to help us get the biosamples and test results back without showing you these things?"

"No."

"Don't get caught, Hugo. If the nice people who run this place that you think is a friendly neighborhood clinic catch you at this, they'll probably kill you on the spot. I'd hate to have you learn the truth the hard way, while a bullet's ripping through your brain."

Garth, holding a torch, led Hugo and me down the long stone corridor leading to the Treasure Room. Two floors above, according to Hugo, Siegfried and Obie Loge were sleeping, and Golly was watching "The Late, Late Show" on television while she listened to Mozart, earphones on her head; tiptoeing through the house, Garth hadn't smelled the gorilla, and we assumed she hadn't smelled us.

"Hey, Mongo," Garth whispered, "I really *was* impressed with Loge's magic key trick. As I recall, you have difficulty cutting a deck of cards."

"Behold," I said as we reached the door at the end of the corridor and I took the torch from Garth's hand. I passed the medallion back and forth over the flame, and the four rings began to curl and twist into the shape of a key. I touched the flame to the door, and the keyhole appeared. "No trick; just a little Sorscience from that sociopathic delinquent. This is made of a substance called anitol molten alloy—it's metal with a memory. The area of the keyhole is the same thing. The molecules will return to the same configuration they were in when the metal was shaped at a certain temperature. This anitol was formed into the shape of a key when it was heated to flame-temperature, then twisted into the rings after it had cooled. Heat it, and it goes back to its original shape. It's used in the newer thermostats and thermocouplings."

I twisted the key in the lock and pushed open the door. The sound and light show began. Hugo, who'd looked rather dazed when we'd entered the corridor and lit the torches, looked even more dazed as he roughly pushed between Garth and me, ducked through the doorway and entered the Treasure Room. Garth and I followed.

We let the giant browse around for a couple of minutes, and then Garth went to the control panel and dimmed the lights. The photo-mural disappeared, and Hugo's gasp was audible. He stumbled slightly as he went across the room and stood before the clear Plexiglas shield, staring out over Mount Doom.

"Those are human bones over there," Hugo whispered hoarsely as Garth and I came over and joined him.

"As advertised, Hugo," I said.

"Don't bother asking what those flying things are," Garth said drily as two of the leathery flappers swooped across our field of vision. "Nobody seems to know. Now we'll show you—"

"You won't show anything to anybody," Siegfried Loge said.

Pfft.

Pfft.

I reached for the dart in my left shoulder, never got my arm up; a powerful, fast-acting paralytic had almost instantly erased all sensation in my body, and nothing worked. I started to collapse, was grabbed under the arms and turned around by a burly Warrior. Garth, in the same condition and supported by another Warrior, found himself helpless and unable to do anything more than stare at the Loges, Golly, and a third Warrior who were standing by the entrance.

Golly must have grown bored with "The Late, Late Show."

Siegfried Loge lowered his dart gun, and the third Warrior slowly advanced across the room, his machine pistol aimed directly at the center of Hugo's forehead. Golly followed and, looking about as shamefaced as a gorilla is ever likely to look, took the control boxes from the giant's hand. Hugo, the bore of the gun pressed against his spine, was ushered out of the Treasure Room, and Garth and I were turned around again to look out over the chasm of Mount Doom.

"I figured I'd use synthetic curare instead of PCP in the darts this time," Siegfried Loge said as he and his son came over to stand beside us at the shield. "I didn't want to let you do anything to get yourselves killed, but I didn't want you to sleep through this show."

Out of the corner of my eye, I could see Golly growing increasingly agitated.

PLEASE NO KILL FUCKING HUGO
PLEASE NO KILL FUCKING HUGO

"Obie, turn on the monitor and bring me the microphone."

The younger Loge, still in his bathrobe and slippers and looking rather sleep-eyed, flopped across the room and turned on one of the television monitors; it showed the inside of the black cell. He took a hand microphone on a long extension cable out of a small recess, brought it back to his father.

A few moments later the monitor showed Hugo being shoved into the black cell. A door slammed down out of the ceiling, trapping him. The giant shaded his eyes and squinted into the floodlight and television camera, which were on a level with his head.

"Take the torch off the wall, Hugo," Loge said into the microphone. "It will light automatically when you take it out of the bracket."

Hugo pulled the torch out of the bracket, and it instantly burst into flame. Loge pressed a button on the side of the microphone; across the chasm, at the apex of the three sets of steps, a door opened in the rock. I could see Hugo in the opening, and he was shielding his face with one hand as his long hair whipped around his head. It was very hot in the chasm, with a lot of swirling air currents.

"Ohhhh . . . ahhhhh . . . my . . . faawwlt. Doohhnt . . . kill . . . him."

Loge ignored my rather pathetic, probably unintelligible, attempt at speech.

"The door behind you won't open again, Hugo," the scientist said. "You can wait there until you rot, or you can take your chances in Mount Doom. Choose a set of steps, try to make it to one of the caves. Who knows? You might be the first one to find your way out of there. Lots of luck, you oversize idiot."

Loge grunted and draped the microphone cord around his neck as Hugo, his torch held aloft and his body bathed in a red glow, stepped through the opening. He chose the middle set of steps, which appeared to be the widest.

He'd gone about twenty yards before the flying things hit him.

Hugo draped one arm over his head and flailed blindly with his torch, but the brown things kept drooping clumsily but accurately from the darkness above; they bit at him with their teeth, pounded his body with the appendages that served as wings, swarmed over him like huge, murderous bats. His clothes torn and bloody, Hugo staggered to the edge of a step, slipped, and fell out of sight toward the furnace glow below.

The curare hadn't paralyzed my tear glands.

28.

Stunned by the death of Hugo, racked by guilt, I sat in a corner of our dungeon cell and mourned in silence. Garth understood and left me alone.

After dinner we had a visitor—Stryder London. The head of Siegmund Loge's private army was out of uniform; he wore a pin-striped suit under a camel's hair topcoat—they were his traveling clothes, I decided, his "real people" disguise. In each hand he carried a cylindrical metal canister.

"What the fuck do you want?" Garth growled.

"I came to say good-bye," the man with the close-cropped hair and hard eyes replied evenly. "You both have great courage. I have considerable respect for the Frederickson brothers, and I'm sorry things are the way they are."

"That's touching, London." Garth turned to me. "Mongo, don't be rude. Come on over here and say bye-bye to the nice man."

I got to my feet, walked to the front of the cell. I pointed to the canisters. "You've got Garth and me in there, right?"

"Yes," London answered simply.

"You're taking the biosamples to Siegmund Loge."

London did not reply.

"Where is he, London? Where does Siegmund Loge hang out?" When he remained silent, I shook my head impatiently.

"For Christ's sake, London, Garth and I are probably going to be dead soon. What difference does it make what you tell us?"

"It makes a difference to me. It's a matter of security which is unrelated to the question of your survival."

"You're a pisser, London—as well as a traitor."

Stryder London stiffened. "Does it make you feel better to insult me, Frederickson? I'm not responsible for what's happened to you."

"You work for the people who are responsible. It makes me feel better to state the truth when everybody else is telling lies, even to themselves. There are no good Nazis; it's not enough to say that you're following orders."

"I am following orders, but I'm following them because I choose to. I take full responsibility for my actions."

"You *choose* to work for these homicidal maniacs? You want to take responsibility for what goes on in Ramdor?"

"My responsibility is to Siegmund Loge, and his goals may be different from what you think they are. You shouldn't take anything anybody around here says too seriously. They're unbalanced, as I'm sure you've noticed."

That got a hoot of laughter from Garth and me.

"I knew it!" Garth said. "They *are* making cheesecake!"

London frowned. "What does that mean?"

"Forget it," Garth said with a derisive gesture of dismissal.

"What are Siegmund Loge's goals?" I asked.

Silence.

"It doesn't make any difference, London. You're still a traitor."

"You're wrong, Frederickson," the Warrior said in a low voice that trembled just slightly. "If I were free to tell you certain things, you'd understand—and might even approve of what Siegmund Loge will accomplish. It's for the good of America—the America we used to know, and the America that will exist once again."

"Oh, yeah; *that* good old America—the one that sneaks up on its enemies and turns them all—man, woman, and child—into monsters."

London shook his head. "No. That's not what Project Valhalla is about."

"Your security has already been breached, London. The demented delinquent upstairs—the one with the baseball cap—already admitted as much to us."

"Dr. Siegfried Loge is a brilliant scientist, Frederickson; the work at Ramdor must be done, no matter how unattractive it may appear to you. However, Dr. Loge often has difficulty separating reality from his own personal fantasies. When it comes to his father's ultimate goals, he doesn't know what's he's talking about."

"Huh?"

"There will be no monsters created—except for the two of you, and that was an accident; a fortuitous accident, but still an accident."

"Accident, bullshit. Jake Bolesh was plugged into the command network of Project Valhalla, just as you are."

"You purposely miss my point, Frederickson. What Siegmund Loge is doing is for the benefit of all mankind."

"You and Hugo must have hit it off real good."

"Order, Frederickson," Stryder London said quietly. "That's what the Valhalla Project is about."

The statement wafted about in the dungeon air, went in one of my ears and out the other, then came back in and squatted; it was cold. "Genetic control of behavior," I said.

"Yes," London said evenly. "Everything that's been done, and is being done, is part of a search for the specific genes that control behavior."

"You may be hunting a ghost. How can you put a net around what makes us individuals?"

"No, Frederickson; the hunt is for those genes which bind us to the group and which compel us to work for the common good under the command of leaders."

"What leaders?"

"Those men who are fit to lead."

"I note that you don't say 'elected' to lead."

"Don't play that silly patriotic game with me, Frederickson; we're both too sophisticated. Democracy is a farce. You're a criminologist, and you know it's a farce. Only fools, phonies, or idiots ever go into politics, and so only fools, phonies, or idiots are ever elected to office. Our society falls apart, and thus the world falls apart."

"Because our society should lead the world?"

"Of course. I'm a man of peace, Frederickson, and soon we will have peace; we'll have peace because we'll have order."

"Because everyone will do what the government tells them to do."

"Yes. The entire world will be a place of peace and order."

"Under the control of Siegmund Loge, your *fuehrer.*"

"Under the control of Siegmund Loge, my leader, and the one man best suited to bring our species back from the brink of destruction where it finds itself."

"Is there a religious angle to any of this?"

"Not really. In an ordered, peaceful society free of stress and delusion, all men will naturally gravitate toward Christ, since Christ is God's Son, and mankind's Savior. However, Jesus taught us that it is right to render unto Caesar what is Caesar's, and unto God what is God's. We are Caesar; with us in command, Christianity will naturally flourish."

"I think I prefer the version Father feeds his flock," Garth said drily. "It has more meat to it."

"He's getting ready to experiment on those people, isn't he, London?" I asked.

The Warrior shrugged. "Eventually, yes. Since some initial experimentation will be needed, who better to use than those who will submit joyfully?"

"He already controls their behavior."

London smiled thinly. "You'd be surprised how many different types of communes there are, Dr. Frederickson."

"Nothing about any of you people or Project Valhalla would surprise me anymore. On the other hand, there may be a surprise in store for you."

"What would that be?"

"You keep forgetting Mr. Lippitt. I'm betting our old man blows away your old man, and that'll be all she wrote on Project Valhalla."

"I'm sorry to take away your last hope," London said with apparent sincerity. "There's no longer any chance of that happening. I also came to tell you that I regret what's about to take place. I don't believe in unnecessary killing, or in torture, but certain things at Ramdor are outside my areas of responsibility and control." He paused, nodded in the direction of the great wooden door. The door banged open, and two Warriors dragged a bleeding, feebly struggling, semiconscious bald man down the corridor.

"Lippitt!"

"Frederickson," Mr. Lippitt gasped as he turned his head toward me. "You must—"

That was all he was able to say before the Warriors threw him into the black cell and the steel door crashed down from the ceiling.

"Let us talk to him!" I said to London.

Stryder London slowly shook his head.

"Why the hell not?" Garth snapped.

"Security."

"Fuck security," Garth said. "He's our friend, and he's about to be killed. You're not an evil man; now try being a kind man. Let Mongo and me talk to him before he's murdered."

"I'm sorry," London said, turning toward the door. "Goodbye." Flanked by the other two Warriors, London walked out of the dungeon, and the door closed behind them.

"Lippitt!" I shouted. "Lippitt, can you hear me?!"

There was nothing but silence; either the black cell was sound-proofed, or Lippitt had lapsed into unconsciousness. In the Treasure Room, Siegfried Loge and his son would be waiting to cast Mr. Lippitt into Mount Doom.

"Mongo, we owe that bald-headed son-of-a-bitch," Garth said in a low, tense voice. "Besides that, he's our only link to whatever else is going on outside here. We don't have any idea where London is headed; Lippitt may. I suggest we make a move."

"Yep."

"Where the hell is the panic button in this cell?"

Hidden under my overalls, inside my belt.

Shhh.

I slipped Whisper up between Garth's neck and his choke collar, pulled; the blade of Damascus steel sliced through the leather and wire constraint as if it were no more than a band of silk. I cut away my own collar, threw it away into a corner, then handed the blade to Garth. "You're better at picking locks than I am; see what you can do with the tip of this."

Holding Whisper like a pen, Garth knelt down before the large, rusty lock and probed the keyhole with the blade's tip. He worked at it for more than a minute, paused to wipe sweat from his brow, then went at it again.

"Uh, I don't want to hurry you, Garth, but one could say that time is of the essence."

Garth nodded, continued to work. I could hear Whisper grating against steel, but there was no clicking of tumblers; her blade was too wide to gain the necessary penetration.

"This isn't going to work," Garth said tensely, leaning back and resting on his knees.

"Garth, it *has* to work! Our only chance is to get to Loge before he forces Lippitt out onto the face of that rock wall! Try jamming the knife and twisting!"

"That'll only make matters worse," Garth said as he flipped Whisper over in his hand, handed her back to me. He slumped forward, bowed his head as if in prayer, and planted his palms flat on the floor on either side of him. He murmured, "I'm going to try something."

"Garth . . . ?"

"There's an aura that precedes each seizure," he said in a voice so low I could hardly hear him. "Just before I get hit with one, I feel like I can take off and fly; there's a high whine in my head, and a cold feeling in the pit of my stomach. If I can concentrate . . . try to touch those sounds and feelings . . . maybe I can . . ."

"You're going to try and *induce* an attack? Garth, I don't know. We're in pretty close quarters here; you're liable to kill us both."

His spine stiffened, and both arms started to twitch. I was afraid.

"Garth, wait! What am I supposed to—?!"

"You . . . go," Garth mumbled through tightly clenched jaws. I watched in terror and awe as Garth, his entire body twitching, struggled to his feet. His eyes bulged, and the cords in his neck stood out like steel cables. Spittle dribbled from the corners of his mouth.

"Garth!"

"Leave . . . me. Kill . . . fucking . . . Loges."

Then he hit the door with his shoulder; the bars shook, and the bolt securing the door clanged in its socket. Garth hit the lock with his hip, spun around and grabbed the bars of the doors with both hands. Animal moans of agony and rage escaped from his froth-flecked lips as he shook the bars, banged against them with his shoulders, hit the rusty plate of the lock with his hips. He spun around, staggered to the rear of the cell, then turned and charged the door. At the last moment he lowered his shoulder and banged it against the plate.

The bolt snapped, the door crashed open, and Garth fell into the corridor.

Ignoring the possibility that he would snap me next, I rushed to him, rolled him over on his back and wiped the froth off his mouth. His arms were flapping around, and I lay across his chest, trying to pin him; it was a ridiculous gesture, his dwarf brother trying to pin two-hundred-and-twenty pounds of rock-hard Garth when he was in the midst of a seizure, but it was the only thing I could think of. I didn't want him to die, and I wasn't going to leave him behind.

The flapping stopped. Somewhat amazed that I was all in one piece, I slowly eased myself off him, looked into his face. Sweat was pouring off him, and his eyes were filled with—terror. He was trembling now, but not from the seizure.

"Garth?"

"Mongo, I'm afraid. It's like . . . white-hot wires inside my head. I think I broke something in my mind."

"No! I'll take care of you, Garth. You'll be all right." I got to my feet, struggled to pull Garth to his. "Come on! We have to move!"

Garth struggled to his feet and, with me pulling at his sleeve, we ran down the corridor. The two Warriors who had thrown Mr. Lippitt into the black cell came through the door. Garth literally ran over one, hitting him under the chin with his elbow and knocking him very cold. I slammed the other one in the solar plexus with Whisper's handle, followed up with a kick to the groin and a rabbit punch. He joined his colleague on the dank stone floor, and Garth and I raced along the narrow, slightly curving corridor that we knew led to a short flight of stairs that led to a door opening into the ranch house, close to the corridor that led to the Treasure Room.

I didn't much care for the sounds Garth was making in his throat.

We went up the steps, through the door, and into the house.

The door in the house had been left open, and we sprinted down the stone corridor. The door at the far end was closed; without slowing, Garth smashed into it, taking the force of impact on his right shoulder. The door crashed open, and we stepped into the red glow of the Treasure Room.

Siegfried and Obie Loge spun around, saw us, and scrambled off in opposite directions. Garth hit Siegfried Loge across the back with a forearm, sending him somersaulting through the air and crashing into a wall—but not before he had pushed another button on the microphone. The lights in the Treasure Room began to flash, and somewhere a siren wailed.

Obie Loge, screeching with panic, ran around me. I had no time to bother with him, and so I let him go. I had other things on my mind, for I could see that we were too late to save Mr. Lippitt from Mount Doom. Through the Plexiglas shield, I could see the old man teetering on the edge of a ledge as he flailed with his torch at the leathery flying things that flapped all around him. He was very close to the mouth of a small cave, and could make it there if he wasn't blinded or knocked off the steps.

Garth was huddled on the floor, trembling, his arms wrapped around his body. "Mongo, I'm sorry," he said in a voice that quavered with fear. "I . . . can't seem to . . ."

"It's all right!" I shouted as I picked up a piece of sculpture and hurled it at the shield. "You're doing fine! Just hang on!"

The sculpture bounced off the shield. I picked up the piano stool by two legs, spun around a couple of times and hurled that; it bounced back and almost took my head off.

Shhh.

Holding Whisper above my head with both hands, I charged forward, stabbed at the Plexiglas; Whisper's point penetrated the shield, and her blade slid down as easily as if I'd been slicing cheese. I cut out a window, which blew back over my head as the superheated air inside Mount Doom immediately rushed toward the cooler air and lower pressure of the Treasure Room. Instantly, my nostrils were filled with the odor of death and heat.

"South!" I screamed at Lippitt through the opening, holding on to the edges of the window with both hands to keep from being blown backward. *"Head south!"*

He couldn't hear me, of course, but I'd created enough of a commotion to distract the flappers—which were now riding the rushing air currents directly toward the window.

"South!" I screamed again, accentuating the movement of my mouth in the hope that he could read my lips. *"South! South!"*

Then I ducked as one of the flying things, lidless eyes wide and toothed jaws agape, crashed through the opening—and into the face of Siegfried Loge, who had struggled to his feet and was coming up behind me. He screamed, reeled around, and clawed at the thing that was clawing at his face.

"Mongo, fire!" Garth shouted. He had risen to his feet and was holding his head with both hands. "Fire! It's coming up! I can smell it! We have to get out of here!"

Cutting out the window had instantly transformed the Treasure Room, the open corridor and the ranch house beyond into a kind of superchimney. There was about to be one dandy of a chimney fire, and it did seem a good idea to absent ourselves; the problem was that I could hear a lot of running footsteps in the corridor.

"The elevator!" I shouted, ducking and running toward Garth as a blast of flame, smoke, and a roasted flapper shot over my head. "Hit the elevator button!"

Although he was still shaking with terror, Garth managed to press the button next to the elevator. The door opened with gratifying quickness; I grabbed Garth's shirt with both hands, dragged him in after me, punched the single button inside. The door sighed shut on a Treasure Room rapidly filling with flame, smoke, poison gas, blown-in dead flappers, and screaming Warriors.

Now that I'd transformed the neighborhood into a fairly serious inferno, it remained to be seen whether the elevator, which had to pass through that neighborhood, was going to work. Nothing was happening; there was only one button, and on our previous trip I'd noticed that the door opened when the button was pressed a second time. That didn't seem like a good idea.

In frustration, I kicked a wall. The elevator jerked up a few feet, stopped. I kicked the wall again. Twice. Once again the elevator jerked upward—but this time it kept going, through a kaleidoscope of stone and fire, all the way to the top. I pushed the button to open the door. Nothing happened. I kicked the wall; nothing happened.

Shhh.

I jammed Whisper between the edge of the door and the jamb, jimmied her back and forth. The door opened and we stepped out into the animal laboratory, where the glass cages had already been restocked. We started toward the entrance at the far end, came to an abrupt halt when the door opened and Obie Loge and Golly came in.

Obie Loge wasn't going to fool with any tranquilizer guns; he saw us, drew his machine pistol from his holster, aimed and fired off a burst as Garth and I dove behind one of the steel columns that supported the glass enclosures.

Another burst. Bullets ricocheted crazily back and forth between the steel columns, but somehow managed to miss Garth and me. Glass shattered, and suddenly the cool air was filled with terrible smells and terrible screams; fluids sprayed over us, tormented creatures flopped to the floor all around, quivered, crawled, rolled.

Garth wrapped his handkerchief around his hand, picked up a long, jagged shard of glass, looked at me and made a circling motion with his hand; there was still fear in his face, but it was tempered now with determination, dampened by my brother's incredible courage. I nodded to him, then darted across open space to the next row of cages, crouched, and waited as more bullets ricocheted around.

The understanding between Garth and me was unspoken, but clear; whoever got the first shot at the kid and the gorilla would go for them, sacrificing his life if need be. One of us had to survive and escape Ramdor.

Project Valhalla had to be stopped.

Suddenly the firing stopped. There was the sound of something metallic falling to the floor, then another scream—this one human.

A few seconds later Golly came strolling down between the rows with a screaming, struggling Obie Loge draped over her shoulder. Garth and I straightened up, glanced at each other, then watched Golly open the waste chute and casually dump Obie Loge down it. His screams were abruptly cut off as the cover slammed shut.

If there is such a thing as a gorilla grin, that's what Golly was wearing.

GOLLY WASTE FUCKING OBIE

Yes, indeedy. And suddenly I knew how I was going to get to Mr. Lippitt, who, if he had made it into a cave in time to escape the holocaust in the chasm, could probably use a little help, as well as provide some very helpful information.

"You are the most beautiful gorilla in the whole world," I said as I went up to Golly, wrapped my arms around her neck and planted a very wet kiss on her wrinkled brow. Then I turned to Garth. "Go back to the van and wait for me. I'll see you later."

Garth smiled tentatively. "You will, huh? Where the hell are you going?"

"Garth, I *will* see you," I said as I closed my eyes, took off my glasses and put them in their case in a pocket in my overalls. I reached out, found the handle on the waste chute cover. "You just get your ass out of here and back to the van. Don't worry; I know what I'm doing."

"Mongo, *no!!*"

"Don't worry," I repeated as I pulled open the cover and executed a rather neat little hop and roll into the waste chute. *"Ciao."*

It was a fast track down, made even faster by slicks on the metal left by decomposing or devolving animals. I landed hard on the pile of bones, scattering them, and immediately started slashing with Whisper. But Whisper wasn't needed, at least not at the moment. The little critters who fed at the bottom of the waste chute were occupied elsewhere; there were indeed a lot of crunching and munching sounds down there, and they were all coming from a writhing mound of black hair, teeth and tentacles to my right, at the base of the bone pile. If he hadn't been at the bottom of the mound, Obie Loge probably would have immensely enjoyed the spectacle.

I rolled to my left, just in time to avoid being squashed by Garth as he came crashing into the pile of bones.

"Mongo!" he cried, groping in the darkness until he found me, then squeezing my arms so hard I thought they'd break. "Are you all right? I can't see a damn thing!"

"I'm all right, I can see, and what the fuck are you doing here?—not necessarily in that order."

He didn't have time to answer as the next tourist landed and bowled us both over. I just managed to grab her hand and pull her back as she started to slide down toward the writhing mound—which was now starting to move in our direction.

GOLLY FUCKING HELP

"Let's get out of here," I said, grabbing Garth's hand and sliding down the pile of bones.

Golly, who could apparently also see by the faint, cold, chemical luminescence given off by fungus growing on the walls of the burnt-out mine tunnel, followed. Keeping a tight grip on Garth's hand, I ran down the tunnel, turned into the first one branching to the right. Golly loped up beside me, and I slowed to a fast walk.

"How's the head?" I asked Garth.

"I'm scared out of my fucking mind, Mongo, and it's a good thing for you I am. If I weren't, I'd probably break your back for coming down here."

"We'll get out—but I don't think Lippitt can without my help. I love you both very much for coming down to help me. I know what it cost you, climbing into that chute blind, and realize how very much you love me. Thank you both."

"Fuck you, Mongo. If we ever get out of here, and I most certainly do *not* share your boundless optimism, I may still break your back."

"Excellent. I'm glad to see you're feeling better."

GOLLY FUCKING AFRAID TOO

"That makes three of us, sweetheart."

I pulled Garth to a halt, and Golly edged closer to me as dozens of eyes belonging to dozens of nasty-looking, bow-legged, chattering things skittered toward us. I pushed Garth back against the wall, gripped Whisper in both hands, and braced for the onslaught.

FUCK YOU

The chattering, skittering mob stopped.

FUCK YOU
FUCK YOU
FUCK YOU

Apparently thoroughly frightened by the flashing green lights on Golly's display screen, the things turned and scurried away.

"Good girl," I said, giving Golly a hug.

"What the hell was that all about?" Garth asked as I again took his hand and started off down the tunnel.

"Don't ask."

"Bad company, huh?"

"Nobody promised you a rose garden when you came down that chute, brother."

"Ho-ho-ho. You told Lippitt to head south. Why?"

"Because that's where the dragon is, silly."

"What?"

"The Loges' dragon is a fucking cow—a Guernsey, to be exact. I should know; I milked enough of them to recognize the hide markings when I see them. Our dear, departed hosts were always oblivious to everything around them except for what they were doing or dreaming about. With all this fantasy shit, they managed to spook their own brains away. If a cow managed to wander into these mines somewhere to the south, then we can wander out somewhere to the south."

"You're pretty fucking clever for a dwarf."

MONGO FUCKING SMART DWARF

"Thanks, guys. I really wish you'd both waited in the van."

"Next question: How do you know which way is south?"

"I know which way is north."

"I knew before I got down here, but now I can just about handle left and . . . what?"

"I said I know which way is north."

"How?"

"You ready for this?"

"Damn. Another symptom?"

"There must be some homing pigeon mixed in with all my reptile—although some amphibians share the characteristic. I seem to be wired into the earth's magnetic field. For the past two or three weeks, there's been something like a soft breeze blowing through my head; it always blows from south to north."

"No shit?"

"You'd better hope it's no shit. For some reason, I'm already tired of this place."

29.

Problems in Mount Doom.

"Gas," Garth said as I led the way up a ladder in a shaft leading to a network of mines on another level.

"What?"

"Gas," he repeated, grabbing my ankle and holding me steady. "There's poison gas somewhere up there; I can smell it. We can't go this way."

"We have to go this way. We've wasted too much time already."

"We haven't 'wasted' anything, Mongo. You can only see in the tunnels where the fungus grows, and none of us can walk through fire. We'll find another way up."

"Which could take another two hours. Lippitt's torch will be out by now, and he can't last long in the dark. We have to get to him."

"Mongo, why the hell am I arguing with you? I'm telling you there's poison gas up there. We have to find another way."

"I think you've still got a case of nerves," I said as I pulled my ankle free and started climbing again. "You and I live in New York City; we breathe poison gas all the—"

Something green and black exploded inside my head at the same time as a wrecking ball smashed into my chest, blowing my breath away along with my strength. I choked and coughed, and my fingers slipped from the rough wooden rung above my head. My knees collapsed, and I plummeted.

Fortunately I didn't plummet very far, because fortunately Garth had lunged upward at the last moment and grabbed my ankle again. I dangled in Garth's strong grip, hacking and gasping for breath, until Golly reached out and hauled me in. Grabbing a handful of overall, she turned me upright and planted me firmly on the ladder between her and Garth.

"Okay, guys," I said when I could breathe again. "I'm all right now."

"You sure?"

"Yeah. I think I'm glad the two of you decided to come along."

"Why, Mongo, that's a terribly sweet and generous thing for you to say."

"Think nothing of it."

"Now, O Great Leader, would you care to reconsider your previous decision?"

"Yeah. After thinking things over, I feel it might be better if we searched for an alternate route."

GOOD FUCKING IDEA

There was nothing in the tunnels ahead of us but fire. Unable to go ahead or up, where I was pretty certain Lippitt would be, we went down to another level, then circled back along a route that took us, I believed, beneath the Treasure Room and in the general direction of the chasm. Hot air was blowing at a pretty good speed, and there was enough of a glow in some of the branching tunnels for Garth and Golly to see by. I put on my smoked glasses, turned into a tunnel to my left, and almost tripped over Hugo.

The giant, asleep or unconscious, lay beside a puddle of brackish water that had formed from water dripping from the ceiling. He was covered with blood, scrapes, and bruises, but I saw no deep wounds, and no twisted limbs that would indicate broken bones. The worst damage seemed to be to his legs just below both knees, which were discolored and blistered with second- or third-degree burns. The soles of his shoes had been burned away.

All things considered, I thought as I knelt down beside a head that had a circumference almost as large as my hips, giants must not cook as well as they bounce.

"Hugo?"

The giant's eyelids flickered; he opened his eyes, peered up at me. "Mongo!"

"And friends."

HELLO FUCKING HUGO
GOLLY HAPPY TO SEE FUCKING HUGO
GOLLY FUCKING SORRY SHE TOLD MASTER

"Dream," Hugo sighed, and closed his eyes.

"It's no dream, Hugo."

Again, Hugo opened his eyes; now there were tears in them. "Did Loge throw you in here?"

"No. Actually, we dropped in here on our own—and we're all going to get out after we find another man who's down here someplace. How the hell did *you* survive?"

Hugo sat up, moaned with pain. He cupped handfuls of water, splashed them on his legs. "I landed on a ledge. It knocked me unconscious. When I woke up, I was . . . burning. I managed to crawl in here, by the water."

"Anything broken?" I asked as I scooped water, dribbled it over his burns.

"No. At least I don't think so."

"I know these burns hurt like hell. Do you think you can walk?"

With Golly lending him her not inconsiderable support, Hugo struggled to his feet. Leaning on Golly, he took a few tentative steps, then nodded. "I can walk."

"Good. See if you can walk and shout at the same time. Lippitt is the name of the man we're looking for."

"Mongo, Garth . . . I'm sorry I was so incredibly fucking stupid. I don't know what else to say."

"You don't have to say anything, Hugo. We all have our deep psychological needs, dreams and fantasies; sometimes they're all we can see."

One hour, three levels, and four tunnels later we found Mr. Lippitt. He was seated with his back against a wall, his profile sharply outlined by the fiery tunnel behind him, casually swatting with his extinguished torch at the occasional creature that scuttled out of the darkness at him.

"It's about time you got here, Frederickson," Lippitt announced gruffly as Golly chased the creatures with a few obscenities. "I've been hearing the booming voice of your friend there for the last forty-five minutes. I shouted myself hoarse.

There are some hungry little things around here. What the hell took you so long?"

"Meet Mr. Lippitt," I said to Hugo and Golly. "When you get to his advanced age, little things tend to upset you. I'd like to say that he isn't always this crotchety, but it wouldn't be the truth."

"Hello, Garth," Lippitt said, rising to his feet and taking my brother's hand in both of his. "Thanks for coming along on the rescue party."

"You're welcome, Lippitt."

"This is Hugo and Golly," I said. "Golly's the pretty one, and don't you forget it. She's very sensitive."

HELLO MISTER FUCKING LIPPITT

"Hello, fucking Golly," Lippitt said as he affectionately patted the gorilla's head. He shook Hugo's hand, grimaced when he noticed the burns on the giant's legs. "You've got some pain, Hugo. We should wrap those burns."

"If you don't mind," Hugo replied, "I'd just as soon wait until we get out of here."

Lippitt looked at me. "Are we going to get out of here, Frederickson?"

"Hey, are you joking? Are there dragons in Mount Doom?"

"This is just about what I'd expect to find in this loony bin," Mr. Lippitt mumbled. "One dwarf, one giant, a foul-mouthed gorilla, and a New York City police detective rapidly going to seed."

Lippitt's tone was gruff, but his physician's touch was exceedingly gentle as the Defense Intelligence Agency operative knelt beside another brackish puddle and wrapped Hugo's burns with strips of cloth I'd cut from my overalls.

Although we were "camped" less than a dozen yards from a thick column of fire that shot up through an elevator shaft, the flame sucked air past us and, like so many other areas in the mines, it was quite cold. By my reckoning, it was almost dawn in the outside world. I longed to see the sun again, wondered if we ever would.

"How are we doing, Mongo?" Hugo asked tentatively.

"We're okay. We have to hang a left the next chance we get.

That'll put us back on track to the south. Don't worry. There's plenty of fresh air in these mines, and it has to come from someplace."

Lippitt had asked Garth and me to describe in detail what had happened to us since we'd parted company in Nebraska. We'd complied. Now, when he had finished wrapping Hugo's legs, he asked us both to undress. We stripped, and by the light cast by the column of fire, he carefully examined our bodies; his face was impassive as he ran his fingers through Garth's fur and stroked my scales, and he made no comment.

Next, he interrogated Hugo on the Ramdor operation, and then Golly. Not surprisingly, Golly was able to provide the most useful information on the overall operation, and if Lippitt felt at all strange chatting up a gorilla, nothing in his tone or manner betrayed it; the man would ask questions in a flat voice, and the gorilla would flash the answers on her computer display screen.

"How do Garth and I look to you?" I asked Lippitt when he had finished talking to to Golly.

"You look like you're still alive."

"So are the things down here."

"That hasn't escaped my attention, Frederickson. Obviously, more changes have taken place in these animals—but their general deterioration was arrested. Not only have they survived, but they've reproduced. Interesting. I wish I had a dissection kit."

"Sorry we neglected to bring one along. Let's get back to Garth and me. How close are we to cellular explosion?"

"I have no way of predicting that. What I can tell you is that Garth seems to be devolving along a fairly straightforward humanoid and ape line."

"Loge told us that."

"You, Mongo, are a mess."

"For Christ's sake, Lippitt!" Garth snapped.

"It's all right, Garth," I said. "He knew I wanted it straight. Lippitt, make an educated guess. How long can I last?"

"A pessimist would say that you could explode at any moment. An optimist might give you a couple of weeks—a month at the very most. Then, even if you don't explode, you're not going to make very good company."

"I hear what you're saying, Lippitt, and I thank you for laying it out like that. I consider you my friend. If I get too, uh, snaky, I want you to look out for me."

"I will, Mongo," Lippitt said quietly. "And I promise you there'll be no pain."

"You'll do shit unless *I* say so," Garth said angrily. *"I'll* make any final decision about killing him."

"That goes without saying," Lippitt replied evenly.

PLEASE NO KILL FUCKING MONGO

"It's all right, Golly. Nobody's talking about doing anything I wouldn't want them to do."

"What about your mental faculties?" Lippitt asked.

Garth and I looked at each other. "No changes at all, as far as we can tell," I answered. "I don't think we're any loonier than we've ever been. Just seriously pissed."

"I agree there's been no apparent intellectual or psychological change in either of you," Lippitt said in a somewhat distant tone. "That's also interesting."

"And now I'm really glad we didn't bring you a dissection kit. How did you find this place, Lippitt?"

"I didn't find it; a team of Warriors found me."

"Then you haven't killed Siegmund Loge?"

"Not yet," Lippitt said tersely.

"Good," Garth said. "If we can get to him, there's still a chance for Mongo and me."

"It's possible Loge knows of, or can cook up, an antidote. But one thing must be clearly understood: If we can find an antidote for your condition, that's wonderful, but nothing is more important then putting Siegmund Loge out of commission for good, because that's the only way of ensuring that the Valhalla Project will never be completed. No life, obviously including my own, matters more than stopping whatever it is Loge is up to."

"We know what he's up to. He's trying to develop a biochemical agent that will enable him to control behavior genetically—everyone's behavior. He's set himself the modest task of ruling the world."

Lippitt's reaction was somewhat unexpected; he threw back his head and laughed. "Who the hell told you that?"

"Stryder London. He's—"

"I know who he is. Stryder London is full of shit."

"Funny; that's how London described Siegfried Loge when we told him that Loge believed the Valhalla Project was a straightforward, bomb-the-enemy-into-beasties, biological weapon being funded by your friendly ex-employees in the Pentagon."

"They're both full of shit," Lippitt said casually. "Neither man knows what he's talking about. Siegmund Loge has absolutely no interest in power, nor in ruling anyone. Also, he has nothing but contempt for the way governments perceive and treat each other as enemies."

"Then what is he up to?"

"What difference does it make? What he's doing is a threat to all life on this planet."

"It has to be funded by the Pentagon, Lippitt. Why do you have so much trouble with that?"

"The trouble is that you don't know what you're talking about, and you have an antigovernment attitude. I've spent my life working for this country, and I know something about authorized research projects. I know something about the development of biological and chemical weapons. The government authorizes research into some pretty hairy areas; it has to, because it must assume that other countries are doing the same thing. The point is not what Loge is doing—it's *how* he's doing it. The Pentagon would *never* allow this kind of cockamamy, strewn-all-over-the-landscape kind of operation. Siegmund Loge is a loose cannon, and he's a loose cannon because the people who fund him can't control him."

"Who do you think funds him?"

"My best guess is a secret cabal of politicians, businessmen, and military men. A lot of government money is being siphoned off, yes, but I'm convinced that no official committee in the military or in government has ever heard of Project Valhalla. The money men behind Loge are extremely powerful, and they probably believe that what they're doing is in the best interests of the country, but they're renegades and traitors."

"London seems to be pretty close to Siegmund Loge," Garth said quietly.

"Oh? Closer than Loge's own son and grandson?"

"You have a point," Garth replied with a shrug.

"Let me tell you a few things about Lieutenant General Stryder London. For openers, he's listed as AWOL from the U.S. Army."

"It wouldn't be the first time the military faked a desertion, or falsified a classification, in order to put a man on a secret operation."

Lippitt dismissed my comment with an impatient wave of his hand. "London was at the Institute for the Study of Human Potential the same time that Loge and I were there. He's what the military thinks of as the model for the future fighting man, and they'd contracted with the Institute to do a complete physical and psychological workup on him. London is an awesome combat soldier—but he's also a raving fascist who has a lot of problems with people who don't share his views on what this country should be and do. What he told you about the genetic control of behavior is his fantasy."

"Loge must have told him *something*," Garth said.

"Of course Loge told him something," Lippitt answered tersely. "Loge gave him the fantasy. Loge tells a lot of different people a lot of different things, and even his funders may not know what he's really up to. He has personal presence and charisma you can't believe until you meet and talk with him. He mesmerizes people. You visited a commune of lunatic Christians. I infiltrated three communes—one of murderous Moslems into whipping themselves with chains, another of Jewish Defense League types, and a third of Zoroastrians. Each commune was isolated. Each thought Loge was God or a messiah, and each thought Loge had come to fulfill their particular religious vision. The only person who knows what Siegmund Loge really wants may be Siegmund Loge."

"Do you have any idea where Stryder London's taking our biosamples?"

Lippitt slowly nodded. "If my information is correct, Loge has control of the Institute for the Study of Human Potential— the best-equipped facility in the world for extracting the kind of genetic data he needs from your biosamples. If you two are the keys to Valhalla, and I believe you are, Loge may now have all he needs to open the lock. Obviously, Loge thinks you're the keys."

"The Institute," I said. "That's where it all started for you—when you tried to find out who was leaching data from the computer banks."

Again, Lippitt nodded. "It's hard for me to believe that Jonathan Pilgrim is involved in this; I would have trusted the man with my life. Loge must have found the right button of his to push, too."

For some time there was silence, broken only by the hissing of the fire column. Fire, one of humankind's oldest allies and enemies, can soothe the soul at a very deep level; everyone seemed reluctant to leave it and go back into the darkness around us, a night with claws and teeth.

"We're never going to get out of here, are we, Mongo?" Hugo said in his deep, rumbling voice.

"Wrong."

HUGO FUCKING RIGHT

"Wrong."

Lippitt laughed. "You and Hugo worry too much, Golly. Frederickson said he was going to get us out of here. If you knew Frederickson as well as I do, you'd know that he usually manages to do what he says he's going to do. He's going to take us out of here. Right, Frederickson?"

"Right." I nodded in the direction of a tunnel to my left. "Let's go find us a dragon."

30.

The dragon was dead and decomposing—a condition that enabled Garth, following his nose, to lead us on the last leg of our journey out of Mount Doom. The way out of the final labyrinth of mine tunnels and caves was marked by a beacon of strong, fresh breezes blowing in our faces, rushing past us to feed the ravenous, fiery beast at our backs and beneath our feet.

Now we stood at the far end of the valley of black stone, watching the final destruction of Ramdor. The ranch house and barn were gone, leaving black, smoldering holes in the face of the escarpment. Somehow—probably through the elevator shaft

—fire had gotten into the laboratory building at the brink of the escarpment; black, foul-smelling smoke leaked from the seams of the windowless building, staining the morning, blocking out the sun.

Then, suddenly, it exploded.

"Jesus!" I said, startled as flaming debris rained on and scattered the odd asortment of people gathered in the valley below. "What the hell was that?"

"Probably incendiary bombs," Lippitt answered. "The same as at Volsung, in Nebraska. The people involved in this wanted to ensure there was no evidence left lying around when they finished. The easiest way to get rid of something is to blow or burn it up."

"They put incendiary bombs in a building that sits on top of burning coal mines?!"

Lippitt shrugged, smiled thinly. "How could they know you'd be along to light a match to the whole escarpment?"

I felt a tug at my sleeve, turned to look at Golly.

FUCKING THANKS FOR SAVING US

"Thank *you* for coming down to help me. If it hadn't been for you, we'd have probably been eaten."

?
GOLLY STAY WITH FUCKING MONGO

"You have to stay with me, sweetheart. Who else would put up with a foul-mouthed gorilla?"

FUCKING THANKS

"Thank you, Hugo, for believing in me and taking the chance you did," I said to the giant. "I'm sorry you were burned. The medics in the ambulance down there will treat you. I'm sure your friends will be glad to see you. One more favor: Please don't tell anyone what really happened. We'd just as soon that the people we're going to visit next didn't expect to see us."

Hugo refused to shake my hand, and he scowled a very serious giant scowl. "I want to come with you. These people used and made a fool of me."

"Being a fool is one thing, my friend; being dead is quite

another. We keep right on truckin', but the chances for our survival aren't very good."

"What difference does it make?" Hugo said, his face still set in a scowl. "I heard you and Mr. Lippitt talking; if these people aren't stopped, there may not be a decent world left for anyone to live in—or we may all be dead. Let me help."

FUCKING HUGO WANTS TO COME
GOOD FUCKING IDEA TO HAVE A GIANT

"The lovely lady is right," Lippitt said, ending the debate. "Your offer of asistance is accepted, Hugo, and we thank you. Now we have to figure out a way to get some money."

"Mongo and I still have almost half a bag of gold coins stashed in the van," Garth said. "If nobody found and took the van, there's easily enough there to get us to California."

Lippitt stood looking down the valley for a long time, thinking. "We should split up," he said at last. "Garth, you take Hugo and Golly with you in the van to the Institute. Do what you can to size up the situation, play it by ear. I understand that you want to wring an antidote out of Loge, but I know that you also understand it's even more important to stop the Valhalla Project."

"Where are you and Mongo going?"

"Washington."

"Why?"

"With Hugo and Golly, the only safe way to travel is in the van. It will take at least four days of hard driving for you to get to the Institute. London's plane has probably already landed, and Siegmund Loge may be working on your biosamples right now. We're running out of time. Mongo is walking proof of the danger we're all up against; with him, I should be able to get the right people to listen to me. Then we'll have heavy help."

Garth shoved his hands in his pockets, shook his head uncertainly. "That's assuming the 'right people' you want to talk to haven't been behind this thing from the beginning."

"Right."

"That's a big assumption, Lippitt," I said.

"It's a correct one. In any case, it's the only logical move at this time. Alone, we're still up against impossible odds. This way, we at least have a chance to turn everything around. I might even be able to expose the cabal I believe exists. We can't all go, because then we risk total defeat if we're captured or killed before we sort out the good guys from the bad guys. This way, each group will have a backup in the event the other fails. Garth, Hugo and Golly attack the brain of the operation while you and I, Mongo, attack the heart."

Garth and I looked at each other, nodded in agreement.

"There's one more reason we have to split up," Lippitt continued. "Mongo and I have to see someone in New York before we go to Washington. If this man agrees to help us in Washington, it will narrow the odds against Mongo and me considerably."

Feeling the hair on the back of my neck rise, I looked at Lippitt to see if he meant the man I thought he meant. He did.

"Who?" Garth asked.

"I'm sorry, Frederickson, but we can't tell you without his permission. I told you what I did just now because I believe there's hope we can not only succeed, but survive; I wanted to share that hope with you."

Garth looked at me, hurt in his eyes. "Mongo?"

"He's right, Garth," I said, feeling an ache in my belly. "We can't tell you—not now. But it's the best reason of all for splitting. Lippitt and I have to go to New York alone."

Garth stared at me for some time. When he did speak, the hurt had moved to his voice. "This has something to do with what happened in New York years ago—the killings, the torture, the gun fight and explosion on the waterfront. Right?"

"Yes," I replied softly.

"That's the bond between you and Lippitt—this secret you share."

"Right," Lippitt said tersely. "And don't blame Mongo for not sharing it with you; he was doing you a favor. The secret is a compact which can't be broken without the consent of all three parties—Mongo, this man, and myself. The man has lived up to his bargain; Mongo and I must continue to live up to ours." Lippitt paused, gazed hard at Garth. "This man could start World War Three. In a way, he controls a power that's as awesome as what Loge threatens to unleash."

Now Garth seemed impressed. "And you think he'll help us nail Siegmund Loge?"

"All Mongo and I can do is ask him."

Garth shrugged, smiled thinly. "Tell your man he'll be join-ing a pretty strange Company."

"Oh, I will. And I'll tell him we're on a pretty strange Quest." On the very rare occasions when he chose to display it, Lippitt had a rather pleasant smile.

"Where do you want us to drop you off?"

"We'll cruise the airport. If there aren't any black gloves there, maybe Mongo and I will see if we can get on a plane."

GOLLY NOT TELL FUCKING SECRET
GOLLY GO WITH FUCKING MONGO

"No, Golly," I said, patting the gorilla's shoulder. "You go with Garth and Hugo. They need a beautiful lady to keep their minds off their troubles."

Walking across the sulphurous, burning landscape back toward where Garth and I had left the van, I caught Lippitt's eye, indicated that he should join me behind the others. He fell into step beside me as I slowed my pace even further.

"What is it, Frederickson?" Lippitt asked in a low voice.

"I've got a problem, and I don't want Garth to know about it —there's nothing he can do, and he has enough to worry about."

"What's the problem?"

"After they drop us off, do you think you can rig a battery pack and heating elements inside my parka and clothing? It has to be unobstrusive; we can't afford to have me looking like an astronaut, but I have to keep my body temperature elevated."

Lippitt touched my cheek with the back of his hand. "You're going cold-blooded, aren't you?"

"Right, I'm okay now, but I'll get sleepy the moment we hit the cold."

"How long?"

"It's a fairly recent symptom—a couple of days. But it's de-veloping quickly. I had a real problem with the cold areas in the mines. If I fall asleep and get really chilled, I'm not going to wake up again. I want to be around to see how this all comes out."

BOOK III

Warriors

31.

New York, New York. Home—at least it had been my home in the distant past, in the time when I had been human. Now, having traveled for months in rather unusual social circles and traipsing around Ramdor and inside Mount Doom, I knew how Dorothy and Toto must have felt when they returned to Kansas.

It was also depressing, after surviving being entertained by two generations of loony Loges, to see how much the looniest Loge of all had been able to accomplish in my absence. Posters of Siegmund Loge, looking like a Norman Rockwell rendering of God, were everywhere, along with announcements of rallies and prayer meetings. Outside the isolated communes, where the members believed they possessed secret knowledge of Father's real intentions, Father's message, as proclaimed in ubiquitous radio, television, and print ads, was nothing if not general, benign, and banal; everybody would kind of make nice with each other after April 1, when Father would deliver his "Treasure."

Not if we could help it.

"It doesn't make any sense," I said to Lippitt as we drove in our stolen car over the George Washington Bridge into Manhattan. "When's the last time anybody publicly announced the delivery of a weapons system that could turn out to be a doomsday device?"

"You're assuming 'Father's Treasure' is a weapons system. How's your heating unit working?"

"It's working fine; if I suddenly fall asleep, check it out fast. I'm not assuming that everything about the Valhalla Project has been kept secret. In fact, you're convinced it's a renegade operation."

"I am."

"You agree that 'Father's Treasure' has to be Lot Fifty-Seven—the juice that's finally going to do whatever Siegmund Loge wants it to do?"

"Yes."

"Then why announce it to the world, for Christ's sake? Are they preparing to issue an ultimatum, or are they looking for public acceptance?"

"I don't know."

"A psychological ploy for recruiting hard-core commune

members to experiment on? Come April first, Loge may deliver
a lovely homily to the rest of the world while Warriors are
shooting up commune members with Lot Fifty-Seven."

"I don't know, Frederickson," the D.I.A. operative said with
uncharacteristic weariness in his voice. "You have to remember
that everyone believes what he or she wants to about Siegmund
Loge. This is February; if we don't get to him soon, it won't
make any difference what he's planning to do in April. He'll
have solved all the major problems, and other people will be
able to carry on for him. Let's just hope Victor Rafferty is
where he's supposed to be."

All Victor Rafferty did was read minds like other people read
newspapers, and the existence of a bona fide telepath—only one,
and an American at that—tended to create delicate problems
and a crushing dilemma in all the world's espionage agencies.

Good intelligence wins wars—hot, cold, and lukewarm wars;
declared and undeclared wars; military, political, and economic
wars; idealogical wars. All wars. Brain damage almost always
debilitates; in Rafferty's case, it had somehow transformed the
neurological circuitry in his brain to enable him to pick up
other's thoughts, and the fact that this facility, when used, cost
Rafferty dearly in terms of psychic and physical pain mattered
not at all to the various intelligence agencies which viewed him
as a kind of ultimate weapon, a human vacuum cleaner of the
mind who, after plastic surgery and with a new identity, could
assume various diplomatic posts, attend various cocktail parties, chat up various generals, ambassadors and politicians, and
emerge in an hour with more ultrasensitive information than
ten teams of conventional agents could gather in a year at considerable risk to their lives.

As he was recovering from an automobile accident, a bewildered and frightened Rafferty had shared the discovery of his
growing powers with his surgeon, who had in turn brought in a
psychologist. The psychologist had felt it her patriotic duty to
inform certain government officials of the existence of this "perfect telepath." The information had leaked, and before long
every intelligence agency that knew the secret had assigned people to carry out a single mission: enlist the services of Victor
Rafferty. Recruit him at any cost—through money or promises

of power, if possible; through threats or torture, if necessary—
or kill him, to prevent him from being recruited by anybody
else.

Mr. Lippitt, from the Defense Intelligence Agency, had been
America's man on the job.

Victor Rafferty had wanted simply to be free. He had won
that freedom, finally, by giving up everything—his wife, his career as a very successful architect, his identity; everything. He'd
faked his own death in a manner that was sufficiently spectacular to convince his pursuers—including Mr. Lippitt—that he
was no longer available, or a threat, to anyone. Then, after the
necessary surgery and with a new identity, he had gone to work
for an old and trusted friend—the Secretary-General of the
United Nations.

International diplomacy had never been the same since.

Enter a certain dwarf private detective. Working on a case
involving the question of who had really designed a certain
building in New York City, I started uncovering certain curious
facts and questions concerning a dead architect by the name of
Victor Rafferty—who might not be so dead. I picked up Rafferty's scent, and other people started picking up my scent. Very
heavy people started dropping in on me. One of these people
had been Lippitt, who had assured me that Rafferty was very
dead, and that people would be hurt and killed if I kept running
around asking questions that suggested otherwise. I was, he'd
said, acting as a kind of siren whose wail could be heard around
the world. I must, Lippitt had insisted, stop my investigation.

I did not stop my investigation. People were hurt. People
were killed. I was tortured to a point where I didn't want to live
any longer, even after my physical wounds had healed. Rafferty, whom by this time I had flushed, had healed me—as he
had earlier healed a curious but devastating psychological malady from which the D.I.A. operative had suffered most of his
life. Both of us owed more than we could ever repay to the
telepath, and when both Lippitt and I caught Rafferty trying to
stage a second, even more spectacular, death on New York's
waterfront, I had managed to broker an agreement. Lippitt certainly did not want to kill Rafferty or me. On the other hand,
since Rafferty was still adamant in his refusal to work for the
government, Lippitt considered it his duty to make certain that

Rafferty wasn't running around loose; if Rafferty were loose, then Lippitt also had to worry about *me,* since I would be in a position to sell Rafferty to the highest bidder. All of this had led to a certain atmosphere of tension in the smoky, bullet-riddled boathouse where the three of us had ended up.

I'd offered a simple suggestion; since the three of us rather liked each other, why not try trusting each other? A pact of secrecy would never be broken by anyone without the consent of the other two; Victor Rafferty would, as "Ronald Tal," continue his work at the U.N., and would always be where Lippitt could reach and check on him. Years had passed, and the agreement had held. Now we needed the telepath's help.

Victor Rafferty was, indeed, a man who could tell the good guys from the bad guys. In Washington or anywhere else.

Except for streaks of gray in his otherwise jet black hair, Rafferty hadn't changed very much since I'd last seen him. He still looked exceptionally fit, his black eyes still glinted with intelligence, and his somewhat brooding appearance was offset by a friendly and casual manner.

"Gentlemen," Rafferty said, swinging around in his leather swivel chair as Lippett and I entered the office suite of Ronald Tal, Special Assistant to the Secretary-General. "I've been expecting you."

"Can we be overheard?" Lippett asked in a low voice as he closed the door behind us.

"No," Rafferty said as he rose and shook my hand warmly. "The walls are soundproofed, and the offices are electronically swept every morning. We can talk here."

"You've been expecting us?"

"Yes, my friend," Rafferty said to me as he motioned for Lippett and me to sit on the divan beside his desk. "You know I don't use my—talent—just to invade people's privacy; for one thing, it hurts too much. When I do scan, it's to serve some useful purpose. One gentleman I scan regularly is a certain diplomat from South Africa. By international agreement, only two facilities on earth are authorized to store live smallpox virus; one is operated by the U.N. in Geneva, and the other is the Disease Control Center in Atlanta. South Africa keeps live smallpox virus, and it isn't too hard to figure out why they keep it. I figure it behooves the millions of blacks in South Africa for me to know how nervous their white rulers are at any given moment. Anyway, a couple of months ago I scanned this joker and plugged into quite a fantasy—except that, to him, it wasn't a fantasy. He was smugly congratulating himself and his government for secretly funding our latest media guru, Siegmund Loge, in work to produce a biochemical agent that will render all so-called colored peoples happy with their lot, totally docile, and totally content to be ruled by the white peoples of the world, no questions asked. This agent would be released into the atmosphere at some point in the future—which, I assume by reading the papers, is now April first. Within days, 'colored' people would know and accept their 'place,' and South Africa's racial policies would, at long last, be vindicated. Interesting?"

"Interesting," Lippitt said.

"Interesting," I said.

"Either of you want something? Coffee? A drink?"

Lippitt and I shook our heads.

"I would have written off the thoughts as a bad daydream, except for the matter of government funding; that wasn't a daydream. This man considered himself to be Siegmund Loge's most trusted confidant, the only person to whom Loge unburdened himself and shared all his secrets."

"There are a lot of people around here with that fantasy, aren't there?" I asked.

Rafferty nodded. "Not a lot—but quite a few. There's a Russian, a West German, a Pole, and a few others—including, of course, an American. With the exception of the American, each believes that *his* government is the sole, secret source of funds for Siegmund Loge, and that Loge's work will serve the particular interests of that country."

"Why is the American the exception?" Lippett asked in a flat voice.

"Oh, the American has his own fantasy—total domination of the world by the United States. The difference is that his group is nonofficial. Funding Loge isn't an official policy of the government. Some money comes from businessmen, and the rest is siphoned off from legitimate government funds. In their view, the biggest threat in this country is the press; they're afraid that anything official would eventually be discovered."

Lippitt looked at me. He had the grace not to say anything; he didn't even smile. Still, the look told me that as far as he was concerned, I'd been put in my place.

"You're being hunted by a great many people," Rafferty continued, glancing back and forth between Lippitt and me. "They don't know *why* you're so important, only that you're important and should be captured—alive, if at all possible. It's why I was expecting you; I was hoping you'd come to me for help. Mongo, where's Garth?"

I touched my head. "Don't you know?"

"I haven't scanned you or Mr. Lippitt; I wouldn't do that without your permission. I only know what I'm able to scan from the people around here."

"Garth's on his way to California. We think Siegmund Loge may be at the Institute for the Study of Human Potential, in northern California. He's traveling in a van with, believe it or not, a giant and a gorilla."

Rafferty frowned. "Something's wrong."

"What?" I breathed as I edged forward on the divan.

"It's bad news I picked up this morning—I was waiting until we had the other things out of the way. The van was captured a few hours ago. Garth wasn't in it. There was only a giant, a gorilla, and some other animal that nobody—at least not the man I was scanning—seemed able to identify. It was wearing clothes, but it definitely wasn't a man."

I must have made a noise—a sigh, a moan, a shout, a scream. Then I must have fainted, because the next thing I knew I was on the floor with Rafferty hovering over me and Lippitt cradling my head in his arms. I remembered about the animal wearing clothes, and I opened my mouth to make another noise.

"You've got to hold it together, Frederickson," Lippitt said in a voice that was as firm as his touch was gentle. "If Garth is past help, that's it; if not, we'll move as quickly as possible to help him. Your falling apart won't solve anything, and it will create problems. You're needed—for yourself, and to help Rafferty and me. To help all of us."

"I'm all right now," I said tersely as I got to my feet and pushed Lippitt away from me. I looked up into the concerned, brooding face of Victor Rafferty. "You know we're being hunted, but you don't know why Loge wants Garth and me, do you?"

Rafferty shook his head. "The men I've been scanning don't know."

"You'd better look," I said as I again touched my head, then removed my parka. "It will explain the smoked glasses and the battery-pack around my waist."

"Scan me, too," Lippitt said.

A sensation like the tickling of a psychic feather joined the magnetic wind inside my mind as I rolled up my sleeves to bare my scales, held up my hands and spread the fingers; I'd cut away the webs three days before, but they were already growing back.

It took Rafferty less than a minute to extract Lippitt's story and mine from our minds. During that time, shadows moved in his eyes and across his face—pain, horror, pity, shock, outrage, rage, determination. Then the tickling stopped. "God," he said in a near whisper as he stepped forward and put both his hands on my shoulders.

"We want you to come with us to Washington," Lippitt said to the telepath. "You'll be able to tell us who it's safe to talk to."

"It's too late for that, Lippitt," Rafferty replied.

"Why? We need to put a stop to this, and fast. To do that, we need some big political and military guns."

"Those guns could end up aimed at us."

"But you said—"

"I said the government wasn't involved—but it might as well be. There's a large conspiracy, and many of the people involved control the levers of power, both political and military. I can find somebody for you to talk to safely, but I can't scan over the telephone; I can't scan the people that man will talk to—or, in turn, the people *those* people will talk to. At the moment there are only these Warriors after you. Go to Washington, and you're likely to have the F.B.I., the military, and every local police department after you as well. Orders will go out."

It was my turn to look at Lippitt. He looked away.

"We have to go to California right away," I said.

"No!" Lippitt snapped. His face was uncharacteristically flushed. "That's not the way! It's a miracle we've gotten this far, and sooner or later our luck is going to run out! We can't keep bucking the odds, Frederickson; now that there's an alternative, we have no right not to exercise it. Too much depends on us. We need help. We have to go to Washington."

"You go wherever you want," I said as I brushed past the D.I.A. operative and headed for the door. "I'm going after my brother."

"No!" Lippitt shouted, reaching out and grabbing my arm, pulling me back. "You're my proof, you dumb little dwarf bast—" Lippitt abruptly released my arm, flushed again and turned away. "I'm sorry, Frederickson; truly sorry. But I need you. Without your symptoms and story to back me up, they'll just lock me away."

"Mongo's absolutely right, Lippitt," Rafferty said quietly. "Siegmund Loge has accomplished what he has through the uncanny ability to play on and manipulate people's mind-sets and fantasies. You've fallen into the same trap with your mind-set, except that you've trapped yourself. You can't believe that a country which you love so much, and to which you've devoted your life, could be involved in something like the Valhalla Project. Well, it's not, so you can take comfort in that; however, a lot of powerful people who work for that country *are* very deeply involved, so you needn't be a fool and risk playing into their hands. *Your* fantasy is that everything is going to turn out all right if you can get the right people, your people, in government involved. The chance of our succeeding alone may be hopelessly slim, but it's the only chance. You don't want to go to Washington because you think it's the best, or only, move; you want to go to validate your belief in the United States of America."

"I want to make a phone call," Lippitt said in a strangled voice.

"Lippitt, that's a really dumb idea," I said.

"One phone call—to a onetime friend who now sits on the Joint Chiefs of Staff. His name is General Baggins. We served together in World War Two, and I'd trust the man with my life."

"You'll be trusting him with a hell of a lot more than just *your* life, my friend. It's a dumb idea."

"One phone call," Lippitt said. "I'll tell him everything that's happened, try to convince him of the need for speed. He has the juice to have a battalion of Marines circling the Institute an hour after I hang up. Then it would be over: Project Valhalla would be stopped, and there might even be time left over to help Garth. Isn't that worth the risk?"

"Lippitt may be right," I said to Rafferty. "Maybe you and I are being too paranoid. There must be *somebody* in the military structure who can help, and Lippitt's general may be the person."

Rafferty shrugged, then went behind his desk, opened a drawer and took out a green telephone. "Go ahead and make your call, Mr. Lippitt—but do it on this telephone; the call can't be traced. Also, I might suggest that you don't tell him we're up here. If he insists on knowing where you are, tell him you and Mongo are at a pay phone on Roosevelt Island."

Rafferty went to a window looking out over the East River, and I sat down on the edge of the desk as Lippitt picked up the receiver and dialed a number. He got the general himself after ten minutes, and then spent almost a half hour talking to him. During that half hour I watched relief and joy spread across his face like a gentle fire of mercy, burning away a thick detritus of horror and hopelessness, fear and frustration, making him seem almost young again.

When Lippitt had finished, I spent fifteen minutes on the phone with the general, telling the same story but providing additional details when I remembered them. The general seemed sufficiently impressed with it all, supportive, grateful, and anxious to assure me that he believed our story. He assured me that a large armed force would be at the Institute within a very short time, and that every effort would be made to guarantee Garth's safety and force Siegmund Loge to prepare an antidote to whatever was poisoning our systems. When I hung up, I was almost happy.

Neither Rafferty nor Lippitt seemed happy. Lippitt had joined Rafferty at the window. Their backs were to me, but there was something in the stiffness of their stances and the tense angle of their shoulders and necks that I didn't like.

"Lippitt, Rafferty? What's the matter?"

Neither man answered, and so I hopped off the desk and went across the room to join them. As they stepped apart to

make room for me by the window, an olive-drab helicopter
swooped past and rushed to join a force of a few of its brothers
and sisters around Roosevelt Island, in the middle of the East
River, a half mile or so to the north.

We didn't need binoculars to see what was going on.

Power boats of every description—including a couple with
Coast Guard and Navy markings—were converging on the island from both north and south. Military and NYPD helicopters hovered over the island, occasionally descending to dis-
gorge soldiers and black-gloved Warriors in civilian clothes.
Residents of the apartment buildings on the island came out
and stared in awe as teams of armed men raced around the
island, in and out of buildings, searching for a certain dwarf
with smoked glasses and an old, bald-headed Defense Intelligence Agency operative.

"I'm sorry, Lippitt," I said sincerely.

"Yeah," Lippitt answered with a kind of grunt. "Me, too."

Rafferty opened a wall safe, took out a .45-caliber automatic
and a box of shells. He loaded the gun, put it and the box of
shells in the pocket of a tweed overcoat, which he'd taken out of
a closet. Lippitt and I were still staring out the window, our
energy drained by entropy, our hope eaten away by despair.

"Gentlemen," Rafferty said as he stood by the door of the
private elevator in his office, "it's time to go."

32.

We descended in the elevator to the underground VIP parking
garage, hurried to Rafferty's sleek black limousine. Lippitt and
I got in the back, lay down across the seat.

"I have a private plane at Flushing Airport," Rafferty said as
he got behind the wheel and turned on the engine. "Nobody in
official circles knows about it, and, for obvious reasons, I keep it
serviced and ready to go at all times. It's only a two-seater, but
I think we can manage to squeeze Mongo in."

"At this point, I don't much care if you strap me to the
wing."

"You're leaving?" Lippitt said to Rafferty. "Just like that?"

Rafferty laughed. "What would you suggest I say in my letter of resignation, Lippitt?"

That got a grudging smile out of the old man. "Right," he mumbled. " 'Gone to save the world' might seem a bit grandiose."

We came up out of the garage, turned left on Forty-ninth Street, then south on Second Avenue. Suddenly Rafferty braked to a stop. "Roadblock," the telepath said, leaning back over the seat. "Police and Warriors; they're looking in all the cars."

"That's it," Lippitt said, opening the door on his side as I opened the door on mine. "Rafferty, we'll meet you at Flushing Airport."

"Wait!" Rafferty said, turning off the engine and starting to open his door. "I'll come with you! You may need my help!"

"No!" Lippitt snapped. "We don't need a mind reader to know what's going to happen if they catch Mongo and me in your car, or you with us. If the two of us are caught, you're the last person left on earth who can stop Project Valhalla. Stay with the car and get out to the airport."

"It's an isolated hangar on the north side of the airport!" Rafferty shouted as Lippitt and I rolled out into the street from opposite sides of the car, slammed our doors shut. "Good luck!"

Keeping low, using the stopped cars as cover, Lippitt and I sprinted across the avenue and up Forty-ninth Street.

"There's a subway station at Third Avenue and Fifty-third!" I gasped as I sprinted, pumping my arms.

"Right!" Lippitt shouted. "That's where we go!"

By the time we'd gone three blocks, we'd picked up three pursuers—Warriors. They were fast, but we were damn well motivated; we made it to the subway entrance, spun around on the metal railing and leaped down the stone stairs.

"Stop, or we'll shoot!"

With Garth in their hands, my life insurance policy had run out.

Lippitt and I bounded down the steps, knocking over two businessmen, three black-jacketed members of the Stinking Skulls, and one nodding junkie. We reached the platform just as a train was starting up, raced beside the accelerating train toward the black mouth of the tunnel, fifty to sixty yards ahead of us. A shot rang out, sharp as the crack of a giant whip in the stone and steel chamber, and something tugged at the left side of my parka. More shots rang out, whizzing over our heads and skipping off the platform around our feet.

We reached the mouth of the tunnel barely a few yards ahead of the train; now it was either stop and get punctured with bullets, or jump into the path of the onrushing train. Naturally, we jumped. I landed on the gravel with my legs pumping, stumbled, but managed to keep going, darting to my left and hugging the cold stone wall as the train roared past. I'd heard Lippitt land on the gravel just behind me, but now I was alone. I kept moving down the tunnel, sidestepping along and hugging the wall, as steel whirred past a few inches from my back.

Then the train was past, sucking sound and air with it, leaving me with a roar in my ears and a large steel wrecking ball in my chest where my heart should be. I wheeled around, took off my glasses and saw a familiar figure hugging the wall almost directly across the tracks.

"Lippitt!"

"Mongo!" The D.I.A. operative turned from the wall, held out his arms. "I can't see a fucking thing down here."

"Stay where you are! Move around too much and you're likely to get fried!"

Taking care to avoid the electrified third rail, I went across the tracks and gripped his arm. Leading the old man by the hand, staying close to the wall, I jogged down the tracks, turned into what appeared to be a maintenance access tunnel, kept running as flashlight beams bobbed past the entrance behind us. We kept running until there were no more lights, no sounds, behind us. I stopped to allow us to catch our breath, leaned wearily against the wall.

"Shit," Lippitt said with genuine passion.

"That about says it all. I think we've got a problem. It's a long way to Flushing Airport, and we've got a river to cross. The streets of New York just aren't safe for citizens who happen to be bald-headed or slight in stature."

Lippitt stared off into space for some time, his jaw muscles clenched. "Fuck this," he said at last, pushing off the wall. "I've had enough of dark, underground places; one Mount Doom in a lifetime is enough. Let's get the hell out of here."

"Jolly good idea. It probably isn't that far to the next station, or to a manhole. But what good will it do to go up into the streets? There are a hell of a lot of people up there looking for us."

"How's that creepy internal guidance system of yours working?"

"It's still creepy, and it's still working."

"Which way is the East River?"

I pointed to the rock wall on my left.

"That's where we're going as soon as we can get out of here."

"Christ, Lippitt, this is no time to go senile on me. The last time I looked, there were a lot of bad guys floating around in the East River."

"You let me worry about the bad guys, Frederickson. Go."

I stayed put. "What do you have in mind?"

"Cutting through all this bullshit. Find us a manhole. We're going uptown."

"Why? What's up there?"

"The heliport."

"Ah."

Nervous time as we came up out of a manhole into the middle of a street, darted across, and padded down the sidewalk toward the river. We stopped at the end of the block, pressed back against the side of a building and peered across the East River Drive at the heliport on the river where an Army Jet Ranger was parked. The pilot was casually leaning against a wooden railing, talking with a burly man who wore black leather gloves.

There was no way we were going to get across the narrow access bridge without the men seeing us.

Lippitt picked up a sharp-edged piece of broken pavement, put it in his pocket. "Walk fast," he said, stepping directly in front of me. "Stay in step, and try to stay hidden. I'm going to kill the first man who makes a move for his gun."

Off we went, with me feeling like second banana in an old vaudeville act as I tried to stay out of sight behind Lippitt's flowing overcoat.

"We're going to make it," Lippitt said in a low voice as we reached the point on the bridge directly over the center divider on the East Side Drive. "They don't quite know what to make of me, and at the moment they're just staring. I'll take the Warrior. You see what you can do with the pilot, on your left."

What I did with the pilot, as Lippitt cracked the Warrior across the jaw with the piece of pavement, was jump out at him from the folds of the overcoat, shout, then kick him in the groin. He crumpled to his knees, then went down as Lippitt turned and finished my job with a hard, straight right to the Army captain's temple. Lippitt grabbed the men's guns, sprinted toward the helicopter, ducked under the idling rotors and leaped up into the cockpit. I ran around to the other side and just managed to climb up and close the door before Lippitt opened the throttle, pulled back on the joystick and set us shooting into the air.

Lippitt, it seemed, was an expert helicopter pilot—at least he impressed the hell out of me as he effortlessly swooped us around, then started down the East River Drive, toward Roosevelt Island; as far as I could tell, we were flying no more than five of six feet above the roofs of the cars below us, and I hated even to think about the heart attacks and collisions we were leaving in our wake.

"See if you can spot Rafferty's Lincoln anywhere down there," Lippitt said as he hopped us gently over an elevated walkway. "If nobody saw or reported us rolling out of his car, he could be halfway to Flushing by now. If not—"

"Not," I said as we swept past Forty-seventh Street and I spotted his car pulled up onto the long, brick plaza there.

"Where?" Lippitt asked, pulling back on the joystick and sending us soaring aloft.

I told him. Lippitt made a lazy circle, eased back on the throttle, and virtually putt-putted us over the tops of a couple of buildings, then descended directly down toward the plaza. Keeping back, peering over the edge of the door, I could see a lot of upturned faces. One of the faces belonged to Victor Rafferty; he was spread-eagled across the trunk of his car, and was surrounded by police and Warriors. One of the Warriors held a familiar-looking .45 and box of shells.

As Lippitt hovered at treetop level just over the Lincoln, I rolled out of my seat back into the cargo bay, kicked open the bay door, and threw out the helicopter's rope ladder.

Lippitt threw the switch that activated the craft's PA system.

"All right, gentlemen," he said in an affected, electronic southern drawl that must have carried all the way to Central Park. "Thank you very much for your assistance. We'll take custody of this man now."

Southern drawl or not, Rafferty knew the sound of the cavalry when he heard it. While police and Warriors looked at each other, Rafferty looked up and saw me. He pushed away a Warrior, leaped into the air and grabbed hold of the bottom rung of the ladder.

"Go!" I shouted, but Lippitt had felt the tug and already yanked back on the joystick. We shot up, headed back toward the river.

The sudden movement of the helicopter had thrown me to the floor. Keeping a firm grip on an anchor line strung through pins in the ceiling, I inched forward, looking down. Rafferty was still on the ladder; exhibiting incredible upper-body strength, Rafferty had managed to haul himself up and was clambering up toward us. The problem was that someone else had exhibited great legs and incredible upper-body strength; there was a Warrior on the ladder right behind Rafferty.

Rafferty reached the top. I grabbed the back of his coat, hauled him in just ahead of the Warrior, who was now trying to brace himself against the wind drag at the same time as he aimed a pistol up at me.

Shhh.

I cut through both support strands of the ladder with one swipe of Whisper; Warrior and rope ladder entwined as both fell down toward the river.

Two NYPD helicopters, searchlights blazing in the darkening sky, swooped down behind us. Lippitt made a tight turn, headed across the river. He dipped down behind a huge Pepsi-Cola sign, turned back. He flew under the pursuing helicopters, back across the river; he kept going, flying straight down the narrow corridor of Fiftieth Street as he entered the concrete and steel jungle of Manhattan. The two helicopters behind us, piloted by men who were obviously a lot saner than Lippitt, abruptly pulled up and soared over the tops of the skyscrapers.

Flying with his lights out just above the rush hour traffic, Lippitt hung a right on Fifth Avenue, sliced off the tops of three trees, and headed uptown. Fifth Avenue was wide enough for sane men to fly on, and the two helicopters dropped down out of the sky and resumed the pursuit. We could see another Jet Ranger approaching us. Maneuvering in an ascending semicircle across Central Park to get a proper angle, Lippitt turned left on Eighty-first. He kept going, shooting over the Henry Hudson Parkway and out over the Hudson, seemingly on a collision course with the cliffs on the other side. At the last moment he veered to the north and went upriver, the tips of his rotors just inches from the New Jersey Palisades, his landing skids just feet above the water, so as to avoid radar.

Behind us, the lights of the pursuing helicopters swooped and circled in confused patterns. Lippitt flew under the central span of the George Washington Bridge, swooped up, circled, then brought us down to a soft landing in Fort Tyron Park, near The Cloisters.

We were quite alone.

"Not bad, Lippitt," I squeaked when I could finally make my vocal cords work.

"Yes, Mr. Lippitt," Victor Rafferty added drily. "That piece of flying was almost outstanding."

Lippitt turned around in his seat. "You got any cash, Rafferty?"

"Yes. About two hundred dollars."

"Good. Mongo and I are down to change and a few gold coins, which I'd hate to have to give away for cab fare. You're dressed like a diplomat; you should be able to hail us a taxi down on Riverside Drive. I think that's safest."

"Right," Rafferty replied easily, a smile playing around the corners of his mouth. "That really was a nice piece of flying, Mr. Lippitt. Thank you for leading the rescue party."

"I've got two things I want to say. First, I'm sorry for the mess I got us into." He paused, glanced sharply at me. "Second, I trust I'll hear no more talk from you about me being senile."

"Not a peep."

33.

Flying at low altitudes to avoid radar, stopping only at remote airports to refuel, it took us three days to reach the northern tip of California, where Jonathan Pilgrim's Institute for the Study of Human Potential was located.

A former astronaut who had experienced a profound shifting of consciousness while walking on the moon, Pilgrim, a retired Air Force colonel, had spent almost a decade seeking to fund and shape an institute that would provide the cutting edge in all the social, psychological, and physical sciences relating to humankind. He had succeeded. The Institute's sports medicine research program was second only to East Germany's, and its myriad other programs were second to none. Leading scientists from all over the world came to "Pilgrim's Mountain" to lecture and continue their own research with the Institute's state-of-the-art equipment and massive computer files on human types ranging from New Guinea pygmies to African Watusi. Research volunteers ranged from geniuses to idiot savants, prodigies in chess, music and mathematics, world record holders in virtually every organized sport and not a few unorganized ones, smart people and stupid people, altruists and sociopaths, heroes and mass murderers. Pilgrim had even done a workup on a certain dwarf who'd used his rather remarkable athletic abilities to become a circus headliner, but I'd been there long before Siegmund Loge, Stryder London, and Mr. Lippitt.

A huge sign on the highway at the foot of the mountain bore Siegmund Loge's likeness, and the logo: FATHER IS THE AN- SWER. We left the clunker we'd stolen in a plowed parking area off the main highway and, after checking my battery pack, hiked up the mountain through snow and forest, moving parallel to the Institute's access road.

Because of the many celebrities, talented and powerful people who might be at the Institute at any given time, there had always been tight security; there was still tight security, but now it appeared to be provided exclusively by Warriors. From our position in a culvert across the road from one of the entrance gates, we watched for almost an hour; the gate, guarded by two Warriors, was open, but nobody came or went.

"Can you do anything about those guards?" Lippitt asked Rafferty.

"I'm not sure," the telepath replied after some hesitation. "It's been a long time since I've done any probing and manipulation."

"I know the layout of this place very well. If we can find a way of getting in through this entrance, we'll be close to a good hiding place we can use as a base of operations."

Rafferty nodded. "You two wait here. I'm going to talk to the guards. When you see me motion for you to come, just walk across the road and through the gate. Walk at a normal pace, and act normal. Don't speak to me or the guards. I'll follow you."

Keeping low, hiding behind the banks of snow at the side of the road, Rafferty moved off to his left, disappeared from sight around a bend in the road. Ten minutes later we saw him coming down the highway on the Institute side, walking with a pronounced limp. The Warriors watched him approach, but showed no signs of nervousness. Rafferty stopped by the gate and began talking to the men; from his gestures, he appeared to be describing an automobile accident farther up the road. Then the Warriors began talking to each other; their conversation grew increasingly animated, until finally they seemed to be engaged in a heated argument, virtually ignoring Rafferty.

Then the hand signal came.

Lippitt and I looked at each other uncertainly. Both of us had very good reason to be in awe of Victor Rafferty's powers, but it was still unnerving to think that we were now expected to leave our cover and try to stroll past two fully conscious Warriors.

But Rafferty's instructions had been explicit.

"Let's do it," I said, clambering up over the snowbank and sliding down the other side.

Lippitt followed. Keeping his hand on the gun inside the pocket of his overcoat, he walked behind me at an unhurried pace across the road, around Rafferty and the two Warriors, and through the open gate.

The Warriors were arguing with each other over which of

several service stations provided the best towing service. Rafferty's face was clenched with the strain of maintaining the illusion he had placed in the men's minds; blood ran bright crimson from both nostrils, staining his lips, dripping off his chin.

I followed Lippitt down a narrow road between low-roofed buildings which looked as if they were used for storage. We ducked into an alleyway, waited. Rafferty joined us a few minutes later.

"Are you all right?" I asked anxiously.

"Yes," Rafferty answered evenly. Blood was smeared on his face where he had wiped it off with a handkerchief, but it was no longer running from his nose. I could tell by his eyes that he was still in pain.

"Did you find out anything?"

Rafferty shook his head. "I can't do the sort of thing I just did and scan at the same time."

I went to the opposite end of the alley, looked around in the dusk, saw nobody.

"Where the hell is everybody?" Lippitt said as I reported back to him.

"They're getting ready to close the place down," Rafferty answered. "That much I picked up when I first went into their minds. There's just a skeleton crew of Warriors, technicians, and a couple of researchers left."

"Working over Garth," I said through jaws that suddenly ached with tension. "Now that Loge has the biosamples, and Garth himself, he figures he's ready to go from research into production. Lippitt, let's go catch us somebody who knows where Garth is."

Lippitt glanced at his watch. "I'll do the catching—in another hour or so, when it's dark." He removed the machine pistol and three clips of ammunition from his pocket, handed them to Rafferty.

"Aren't you going to need this?" the telepath asked.

Lippitt shook his head. "I'll get another one from where that came from—I hope. I can't afford to fire a gun out there, anyway. Mongo has his own gun. If they catch me, it may all come down to how much heavy killing the two of you can do."

* * *

A half hour after Lippitt went out into the night a brown-
uniformed Warrior with mud on his chest and blood on his
mouth came crashing through the door of the near empty building where Rafferty and I were holed up. The man staggered
around in a circle, at which point Lippitt entered and whacked
him in the chest with the butt of the Warrior's captured machine pistol. The Warrior sat down hard.

I was definitely never, ever, again going to suggest to Mr.
Lippitt that he was senile; the D.I.A. agent was one tough old
man.

"Stay, you son-of-a-bitch!" Lippitt snapped at the dazed Warrior. "Just sit there and answer our questions. Try to get up,
and I'll kill you."

"Where's Siegmund Loge?" I asked the man.

The Warrior, a husky blond Nordic type, shook his head,
looked at me. "Fuck you, dwarf," he said as his eyes came into
focus.

"Now, now," Lippitt said, tapping the Warrior on top of the
head with the barrel of the machine pistol. "There's no need to
be rude. If you want me to kill you and go get one of your
buddies, just keep it up. The gentleman of slight stature just
asked you a question."

"I don't know where Siegmund Loge is," the Warrior said
sullenly. "If I did know, I wouldn't tell you."

"Where are the passengers in the van you stopped?"

"What van?"

"Is Father's Treasure almost ready?" Lippitt asked.

Silence.

"Is Stryder London here?"

Silence.

Lippitt and I kept peppering the Warrior with questions.
Considering his refusal to speak, we could understand his growing bewilderment at our somewhat casual persistence; what he
couldn't understand was that it was necessary only for him to
hear a question and register the answer in his mind.

After about ten minutes of this I glanced across the room at
Rafferty, who was standing in a dark corner, behind the Warrior. Rafferty stepped quietly out of the shadows and nodded to

me. I nodded to Lippitt, who clipped the Warrior hard across the jaw, knocking him out.

"The Institute was taken over by Loge's people, with unofficial government backing, some ten months ago," the telepath said in a low voice as he slowly walked toward us, rubbing his temples. "All of the genetic computer data has been electronically leached and transmitted somewhere, but this man doesn't know where. He trained here, and believes he's a member of an elite security force of Warriors who will police the world after Father's Treasure is administered to most of the world's population. He doesn't know where Loge is, doesn't know what Loge is doing—he simply believes that whatever it is will enable him to exercise control over a great many people. Stryder London is here. If we can capture and interrogate him, then we may be able to find out where Loge is. You'll both be happy to know that Jonathan Pilgrim fought this from the beginning; they have him and a large part of the staff locked away in some southern military installation."

"What about Garth, Hugo, and Golly?" I asked anxiously.

Rafferty bent over the unconscious Warrior, removed a set of keys from his pocket. "Hugo and your hairy friend are locked up in a room three buildings away. They're continuing to run tests on Garth in a laboratory in the winter sports complex."

"I know where it is," Lippitt said tersely.

I swallowed hard. "Is Garth . . . is he . . . ?"

Rafferty avoided my eyes. "Garth is still alive, Mongo. Hold on to that. You won't recognize him. I don't know about his mind, and I don't know whether he'll be able to understand anything you say. He definitely won't be able to speak to you." Now Rafferty looked at me, his dark, brooding eyes filled with sorrow. "He's not human anymore, Mongo."

"There isn't much human left in me, either," I said, turning toward the door to hide my tears, stoking my anger to displace what would otherwise be panic, "and he's still my brother."

The two prisoners down the block, after they'd recovered from their initial shock, seemed rather pleased to see us.

> HELLO FUCKING MONGO
> HELLO FUCKING MISTER LIPPITT
> HELLO FUCKING MAN

"Hello, fucking gorilla," Rafferty answered without hesitation, smiling at her. After all, he'd already met Golly in my mind.

"Mongo!" Hugo shouted, and I quickly closed the door to cover his booming voice. I was too far away to grab, and so it was a somewhat perplexed Mr. Lippitt who was forced to suffer, feet dangling a good six inches off the floor, a very serious giant hug.

Finally Lippitt managed to extricate himself. Taking deep breaths, he rubbed his chest for a few moments, then nodded toward a bemused Rafferty. "This is Ronald Tal," Lippitt said in a hoarse voice. "He's a friend of ours from the U.N."

Hugo flung his arms out to his sides, and Lippitt quickly stepped back, almost knocking me over. "The U.N.!" Hugo said. "Does that mean—?"

"No, it doesn't," Lippitt replied. "There's just Tal. But he's been a big help so far. We might not be standing here with you right now if it weren't for him."

Rafferty and Hugo shook hands, and I felt a smooth, leathery hand grip mine.

GOLLY LOVE FUCKING MONGO

"Yeah, babe. I love you, too."

"Mongo, they caught us—"

"Later, Hugo. First we get Garth, and then we hunt up Stryder London. I have a real urge to hit that man."

"Mongo," Hugo said, his voice breaking as he reached out with a trembling hand and gently touched my shoulder, "your brother . . . It was no more than an hour or two after you left . . ."

"I know about it, Hugo," I said, patting his hand reassuringly. "I'll handle it. As long as he's alive, there's still a chance Loge may have something that can reverse the process."

I had to believe that, I thought, as, with Lippitt in the lead, we slipped out into the night and walked quickly through a series of narrow alleyways in the warren of storage buildings. Without hope, there was . . . nothing. If Siegmund Loge couldn't heal and make us human again, then we would die. And the world would probably die with us.

And my mother's dream would come true.

GOLLY KILL FUCKING STRYDER LONDON

"No, sweetheart. At least not until we're finished with him."

FUCKING OKAY

"That's the winter sports lab," Lippitt said, pointing across a snow-covered open area to where a blue and white building sat near the lip of a deep bowl used for skiing and jumping.

Rafferty nodded. "It's the building that was in the man's mind. Garth is in a room at the far end."

"Let's go get him," I said, stepping away from the side of the building where we were pressed.

Lippitt put a hand on my chest, pushed me back into the shadows. "I don't like it," he said in a low voice. "I found the one that's tied up back there easily enough. Now there's nobody around. I know there's only a skeleton crew here, but it's still too quiet. It doesn't feel right."

"Maybe they feel there's nothing left to guard. They may be having dinner."

"It may be a trap."

"Garth's in there, Lippitt, and that's where I have to go. I'll go alone. If you hear shooting, you'll know it's a trap and you can get out of here."

Lippitt shook his head. "Unless we can find out where Loge has his main base of operations, there's no place to go, and we have no way of communicating if we separate. I think we have no choice but to go in together and take our chances." He paused, turned to the giant. "Except for you, Hugo. You stay here and act as lookout."

Hugo scowled. "I want to go in with you. You may need me."

"We do need you—and we need you here. Do you know how to use one of these pistols?"

"No," Hugo answered grudgingly.

"Right," Lippitt said evenly. "Even if you did know how to use one, we don't have an extra one to give you. Your voice will carry as far as a gunshot. If you spot trouble after we go in there, give a warning shout—and then get lost. That's the best help you can give us."

"All right," Hugo said softly, bowing his head in resignation.

Lippitt turned to Golly, smiled kindly. "You stay with Hugo, lovely lady."

PLEASE FUCKING NO
PLEASE GOLLY GO WITH FUCKING MONGO

The D.I.A. operative gently stroked the gorilla's jaw with the back of his hand. "If this is a trap, Golly, you'll be killed. You have no way of defending yourself against guns."

GOLLY FUCKING WRONG
GOLLY LOST WITHOUT FUCKING FRIENDS

"She has a point, Lippitt," I said. "There's nothing she can do out here, so she may as well come with us."

Lippitt nodded, then stepped out from the side of the building. Keeping low and spreading out to present more difficult targets, three men and an ape ran across the open area to the blue and white laboratory on the lip of the snow bowl. There was no gunfire, no warning shots.

Motioning for us to stay back, Lippitt gripped the knob of the door, then flung it open and went down into a crouch, gun aimed into the lighted interior. There was no one inside.

Victor Rafferty took the lead as we entered the building, running down a wide corridor toward a closed green metal door at the end.

"There," Rafferty said, pointing at the door.

I pushed Lippitt and Rafferty aside and, with Golly close by my side, opened the door and stepped into the large, fluorescently lit laboratory. I abruptly stopped and probably would have fallen if Golly hadn't grabbed me and held me up. Horror wrapped its arms around me and squeezed the breath from my body, the hope from my soul.

Except for a bank of monitoring machines hooked up to a crude cage erected in the center of the room, the laboratory had been virtually stripped. Next to the cage was a stainless steel operating table covered with gleaming surgical instruments; somebody was getting ready to do a dissection.

Although he wasn't around to enjoy it, Jake Bolesh had finally gotten at least a part of what he'd wanted.

Inside the cage, rearing on its haunches on a bed of filthy

straw littered with waste and food scraps as it tore at the wires attached to its shrunken, hairy body, was the bawling thing that had been my brother.

34.

"His mind isn't damaged," Rafferty said quickly as he came up beside me. "That part of Garth which makes him your brother is still there. He's been drugged, but he knows we're here."

It was true, I thought as I forced myself to walk across the room, up to the cage. My expression, whatever it was, felt frozen, pasted on, and I shrugged to keep it that way; Garth had enough of his own horror to contend with without seeing more reflected on my face. Although the cage did not allow him to stand, I estimated that he was now no more than three-quarters of his former height. He was covered with glossy black fur, except for his face and hands, which had turned the color of shoe leather. He had a jutting brow, a flat nose with extremely broad nostrils, and a massive, protruding jaw structure, which made it impossible for him to do anything but bawl, roar, bark, and scream.

But the eyes were those of my brother. At the moment they reflected horror, disgust and terror, which was to be expected, but they also reflected love. And hope.

"Shut up," I said, unable any longer to hold back tears as I reached through the bars of the cage and gripped his hairy, sinewy shoulder. "You always talked too much anyway. Also, this settles once and for all which one of us has more animal in him."

Lippitt took a key on a large ring off its peg on the wall, came over and opened the cage. Garth, trying and failing to walk upright, slouched out of the cage, and we held each other.

"Garth," I continued in a whisper, "neither of us is finished yet. I swear to you I'm going to get our bodies back, and when I do you're going to owe me all the Scotch I can drink for the rest of my life." I paused, turned to Rafferty. "Can he understand?"

The telepath nodded. "Oh, yes. He just can't speak."

I shook my head in bewilderment, squinted at Garth through my tears. "How can that be possible? Look at him."

Rafferty shrugged. "Look at you. You've also gone through all kinds of rapid and progressive physical changes, but your mental capacities seem to be intact. Obviously, something in the body—or, perhaps, the mind itself—forms a barricade to protect the brain. At least up to a point. Neither of you has reached that point yet."

It was true, I thought. I'd had so many things on my mind that it hadn't even occurred to me to be properly grateful for the fact that I still had a mind at all. I wondered what Siegmund Loge thought about this little kink in his project—if he thought about it at all. Or if it was a kink.

Rafferty was staring hard at my brother, and I could tell by the wonder moving in Garth's eyes that Rafferty was scanning his mind—and letting Garth know that he was doing it.

"Garth wants you to know that he'd really like you to get his body back," the telepath continued, turning to me, "but a case of gin should be sufficient payment. He also wants to know if we brought aspirin; he says he's feeling just a bit under the weather."

Garth made a barking sound of laughter and astonishment, saluted Rafferty.

"Pretty good trick, huh?" I said to Garth. "You probably remember him being introduced to you as Ronald Tal, but his real name is Victor Rafferty. He's—"

"He already knows the story," Rafferty interrupted softly. "I just told him. I can also transfer my own thoughts."

"Yeah, well; what he does is the secret Lippitt and I have shared all these years. When we sic Rafferty on Loge's head, we're going to know everything there is in there—including a cure to what ails us, if there is one."

"That's it," Rafferty said suddenly, glancing up in alarm. "They're here."

There was a chugging sound in the night outside, and a large gray canister smashed through the window; the canister exploded in the air over our heads, releasing a weighted net that abruptly began to descend. Golly grabbed Garth's arm and pulled him beyond the perimeter of the falling net, but it was too late for the rest of us.

Shhh.

Whisper shredded the net as easily as if the thick rope strands had been made of bailing twine, and in moments I had freed Lippitt, Rafferty, and myself. It was wasted effort; Stryder London and five Warriors had rushed into the room, and were aiming their machine pistols at us.

Lippitt, Rafferty, and I aimed back. It was a Mexican standoff—of sorts; the problem was that their side had twice as many armed Mexicans as our side. But then, a machine pistol can do a lot of damage, even when it's only the twitch of a dead man's finger that pulls the trigger.

"Drop your guns," London said evenly. He had his free arm wrapped around Garth's throat, and was using my brother's shrunken body as a shield; Garth, drugged and dazed, was powerless to resist. Golly was to one side of the room, crouched between two filing cabinets. Both her long arms were crossed over her head, but her head was up and her gaze was intense, darting back and forth between the Warriors and us, as she sat in silent witness.

"You drop yours," I replied.

"Why die when you don't have to?"

"We die, you die." I had my gun aimed directly at London's forehead.

"In hindsight, I guess it was a mistake for Siegfried Loge to give you back your glasses, Frederickson. You've become a real pain in the ass."

"Fuck you, General. I have nothing to lose, which makes me a very dangerous man. I'm probably going to die anyway, and it would give me great pleasure to take as many of you with me as I can. You'd better let go of Garth and back off while I'm still in a good mood."

London rested the bore of his gun in Garth's ear. "Maybe I'll just blow his brains out."

"I don't think so. Loge doesn't have it quite right yet, does he, London? He doesn't have all his answers; he still needs Garth and me, and he'd prefer us alive. If that weren't the case, you wouldn't have bothered with the net business; you'd have killed us outright."

"I'll take him your bodies."

"Somebody may, London, but it won't be you; once the first

shot is fired, the chances are that everyone in this room will die."

"Where is Siegmund Loge?" Rafferty asked in a flat voice that was almost a monotone.

London's eyes narrowed as he slowly leveled his gun on Rafferty. "Who's your friend, Frederickson?"

"My name is Ronald Tal," the telepath said without taking his eyes off the two Warriors in front of him. His machine pistol was aimed at a point equidistant between them.

"What do you do, Tal? Frederickson has some strange friends, and I suspect you're one of them."

"I ask strange questions. All of the computer data, including the information you've been extracting from Garth's body, is instantly transformed into telemetric signals and sent to some other place, via satellite relay. What are—"

"How the hell do you know that?!" The blood had drained from London's face.

"I'm a veritable mind reader," Rafferty answered drily. "What are the coordinates of the receiving site?"

"I don't think he's going to tell us that, Tal," I said, "but I do believe he's giving some thought to declaring this a draw. What do you say, London? Nobody dies today. Release Garth. You and your men take a walk, and come after us another day."

"No, Frederickson. I—"

A deep, burbling sound from the doorway behind him caused London to start, then half turn in that direction; only his soldier's discipline saved him, for if his gun had wavered I'd have put a bullet in his head.

The Warrior directly in front of me moved aside and turned slightly, enabling me to see the huge form of Hugo slumped in the doorway. Somebody had slit the giant's throat, and the last of his life was dribbling out through the fingers of both hands, which he'd wrapped tightly around his neck in an effort to keep it in. Hugo's eyes were glazing, but he had managed to stagger this far—and he was still on his feet. Now those huge feet started to move.

Blood spurted and pulsed when Hugo took his hands away from his throat. Throwing his arms wide, he uttered a bubbling roar and charged. Two of the Warriors spun around and pumped Hugo's body full of bullets a split second before Raf-

ferty cut them down. London and the other three Warriors dove
in opposite directions to the floor while both Lippitt and I fell
on our backs and went for the lights. Instantly, the laboratory
was plunged into darkness that was complete except for a shaft
of moonlight falling in through the broken window. I rolled to
my left under a shower of falling glass and a hail of bullets, kept
rolling until I came up hard against the wall. Rolling up into a
ball to make as small a target as possible, I took off my smoked
glasses and looked around.

Golly was still huddled between the two filing cabinets, face
down, eyes closed and arms tightly wrapped over her head.
Lippitt was crouched behind one of the filing cabinets, spraying
bursts of fire down the length of the laboratory. Rafferty lay flat
on the floor a few yards away, partially protected by the bars
and base of the steel cage, returning the fire of the three Warriors, who were concealed behind heavy packing crates and another filing cabinet. Bullets flew everywhere, many ricocheting
off the steel bars of the cage and striking sparks that hurt my
eyes almost as much as the sharp, bright flashes from the muz-
zles of the machine pistols.

I did not see Stryder London—or Garth.

What I did see was a band of blue-black suddenly appear on
the wall opposite me. The silhouette of a tall man carrying
something over his shoulder appeared for an instant, and then
the door slammed shut.

There was no way for me to make it across the room to the
door without risk of being torn apart in the thundering, murderous gunfire. The nearest exit was the broken window, and
that's where I headed at a dead run.

Lippitt must have caught my movement in the moonlight out
of the corner of his eye. "Don't do it, Frederickson!" he yelled,
his voice punctuated by gunfire. "London will kill you! Your
brother's already a dead man!"

I left my feet, ducked and crossed my arms over my face,
sailed through the broken window and did a shoulder roll as I
landed outside in the snow. Rafferty's shout from inside just
reached me.

"Greenland, Mongo! Look for the ring!"

I came up on my knees with my gun in firing position.
Stryder London, with Garth slung over his shoulder, was

clearly silhouetted against the night sky as he ran along the rim of the snow bowl, almost directly in front of me, thirty yards away. I braced, aiming the machine pistol with both hands, and fired off a short, low burst, aiming at his knees. My aim was too low, and bullets kicked up little showers of snow around his feet. The Warrior hurled Garth down the slope, then dove over the rim himself, disappearing from sight.

Rising to my feet, I ran forward, then slowed, dropped on my belly and crawled the last few yards to the rim; once I looked over, it would be my head that was silhouetted, and there was no doubt in my mind that this "super soldier" would have little difficulty putting a bullet through it if he had a clear shot.

I was too cautious, had waited too long; suddenly there was a roar, and I got to the rim in time to see London on a snowmobile shoot out from an observation shelter used by both the Institute's researchers and its resident ski patrol and rescue team. Garth, apparently knocked unconscious, was crammed into a narrow space just behind London, and his hairy, naked body flopped dangerously over the side as London raced at an angle down the face of the bowl. There was no way I could fire at the Warrior without the risk of killing Garth.

Flinging myself over the rim of the bowl, I slid, rolled, and ran through the snow toward the shelter, desperately hoping there would be a second snowmobile there.

There was, and London hadn't even bothered to take the simple precaution of removing the key from the ignition—a "lapse" that I strongly suspected had been intentional. I jumped on the seat, reached for the key, and was almost bounced out on the snow when something very heavy and furry landed on the rear of the snowmobile, rolled into the cockpit with me.

GOLLY HELP FUCKING MONGO

I didn't know what I was going to do with a gorilla, except not try to push her out. London had already reached the bottom of the slope, and I expected him to race toward the throat of the bowl, a half mile away; instead, he began climbing the opposite face. I turned on the ignition of my snowmobile and, with Golly hugging me around the waist, shot out over the snow, taking a dangerously precipitous angle in an attempt to cut the distance between the Warrior and myself.

London had already slipped over the rim of the bowl by the time I got to the bottom and started up the face. I was almost to the top when the thought came to me that it was highly arguable who was playing cat and who was playing mouse in this chase. I turned the snowmobile at an angle where its treads would hold it on the slope, shut off the engine and listened.

Except for the distant, snow-muffled chatter of the firefight still in progress at the laboratory across the bowl, there was silence: London was waiting for me somewhere over the rim.

"Go back, Golly," I whispered as I got out of the snowmobile and snapped a fresh magazine into my machine pistol. "There's nothing you can do, and it's too cold out here for you. I don't know how long this is going to take."

FRIEND HUGO FUCKING DEAD

"I know, sweetheart. I'm sorry. There's no reason for you to die, too. Go back and find someplace warm where you can hide."

GOLLY FUCKING WRONG
NO PLACE FOR FUCKING GOLLY TO GO
NO ONE TO LOVE FUCKING GOLLY

"I love you," I replied, and as soon as I'd said it knew that I'd just lost a debating point to a gorilla.

FUCKING RIGHT
GOLLY STAY WITH FUCKING MONGO

"All right," I said, starting up the slope. "But you stay put right there."

I crawled the last ten yards, slowly raised my head and peered over the rim. London might be able to pick up my silhouette, and he might be able to see shapes fairly well in the reflected glow of moonlight on snow—but I could see one hell of a lot better. What I saw was London crouched next to a tree in the middle of a cross-country ski trail, slowly tracking his machine pistol back and forth across the rim. His snowmobile, with Garth still slouched unconscious over the side, was parked behind the tree.

I flung my shoulders over the rim, aimed and fired off a burst;

snow kicked up around his feet and bark flew off the tree—too
close to Garth. I stopped firing.

London fired in my general direction, but he knew that he
was at a deadly disadvantage in this situation; he spun around
behind the tree, jumped into the snowmobile. An instant later
the engine roared to life and he shot off heading west.

?
LONDON FUCKING DEAD

"Not yet, babe," I said, leaping into the snowmobile and
gunning the engine to life. "I'm still working on it."

I shot over the rim. The snowmobile landed hard, bounced,
and I almost lost control. I straightened it out, raced down past
the tree and settled into London's tracks. I doubted that I carried any more total weight than he did, but the problem was
that I had to stop frequently, turn off the engine, and listen to
make certain that he had not stopped and set up an ambush.

Each time I stopped I continued to hear his engine—growing
farther and farther distant. He seemed to be heading in a
straight direction, away from the Institute, which suggested to
me that he had a plan, a specific destination, in mind. Yet there
was nothing ahead of him but wilderness—the "steppes," a savage morass of swamps in summer and bleak, frozen desert in
winter, where the Institute conducted survival clinics and research, on government contracts. London would know the
steppes well.

"Shit," I said, then turned when I felt a shivering, leathery
hand touch my shoulder.

?
WHAT FUCKING SHIT

"We've got problems, babe," I said, shouting in order to be
heard over the roar of the engine. Not the least of our problems
was that the cells in my battery pack had to be changed fairly
frequently, and I knew that the intense cold had to be draining
them rapidly; keeping my body temperature at a minimum of
eighty degrees in zero weather required a lot of battery power.
And I wondered how long Golly, still a jungle animal despite
her fur coat, could last.

I wondered how long Garth could last. I wondered if my

brother was already dead, from further cellular explosion or from exposure. I had to find out, and in any case had to prevent Stryder London from getting Garth—dead or alive—to Siegmund Loge.

Twenty minutes later I emerged from a copse of trees. I turned off the engine, stood up and looked out over the beginning of the six-hundred-acre steppes; before me was nothing but a vast, windswept ocean of snow—angry now, tossing from the gelid breath of what I feared was an approaching storm. Somewhere out in that frozen ocean were my brother and his captor; the difference was that the captain of that ship knew where harbors, if there were any, could be found.

Golly patted my shoulder, and I turned to look at her; she was shivering, and her yellow eyes were clouded with misery. Her hands were trembling so violently that she could barely manage to work the keyboard of her computer display screen.

GOLLY FUCKING COLD

"I know, sweetheart. Me too. I'm sorry, but I'm afraid we're going to get even colder. Just hang in there. I'll try to find a place where I can build a fire."

MONGO FUCKING BRAVE

"You're fucking brave, too."

GOLLY LOVE FUCKING MONGO

"The feeling is mutual, babe."

GOLLY FEEL FUCKING FUNNY

"You mean you're cold?"

GOLLY FUCKING COLD
GOLLY ALSO FEEL FUCKING FUNNY

"You mean 'wrong'?"

GOLLY FUCKING WRONG
GOLLY ALSO FEEL FUCKING FUNNY

I still didn't understand what she meant, but it didn't really make a difference. What was important was how I felt—and I felt cold. Dangerously cold. My batteries were starting to fail.

I was growing sleepy.

Shhh.

Sometimes gestures, even empty ones, are important; I slowly turned back to face the steppes, held Whisper aloft and in front of me like a talisman of defiance.

One fucking cold and funny-feeling gorrilla and one dwarf in imminent peril of falling into permanent hibernation were up against a super-soldier operating in his own neighborhood.

I swallowed hard, grimaced at the sudden numbness in the tip of my nose and the bitter aftertaste of burnt chocolate in my mouth. Then I turned on the engine and, with Golly hugging me for mutual warmth, slowly headed out into the steppes.

BOOK IV

Wall of Tears, Curtains of Ice

35.

At dawn, I knew I was in a lot of trouble.

The wind had died down, but as the sun rose the field of snow before me became a blinding glare of luminescence that leaked into my eyes around the edges of my smoked glasses, causing me considerable pain and just about blinding me. I was very cold, and it was a constant battle to keep my eyes open and absorbing the pain. I shut off the snowmobile, turned to Golly.

The gorilla was a picture of wretchedness as she shivered and huddled against me, and I knew just how she felt.

"I'm sorry, Golly," I said through chattering teeth. "If it's any consolation to you, Stryder London has to be just as cold as we are. We have to keep going as long as Stryder London; if we don't, I'm afraid we may never find him."

If I hadn't lost him already—which seemed a pretty good possibility.

GUFLLY CKIN C LD

"What?"

I Y FUGHKCG C?DL

My first thought was that the computer, even with its atomic battery, was malfunctioning in the cold. I reached out to touch Golly's face—and almost lost a finger when she snapped at my hand. I pulled back my hand and stared into the yellow eyes—which now seemed murky, their light dim. Her lips curled back from her yellow teeth, and a low snarl came rumbling up from deep in her chest.

Golly was feeling funny all right, I thought, and a rogue gorilla suddenly gone stupid and nasty wasn't exactly what I needed at the moment; I certainly wasn't going to mess with her.

Cursing softly to myself, I slowly turned around and started up the engine. I was almost glad to see that the wind had risen again, for in the gusts I could see better—or, at least, without pain—than I could against the glare.

I'd gone about fifteen yards when I bumped into the back of London's snowmobile.

Shhh.

With Whisper in one hand and my machine pistol in the

other, I leaped out of my snowmobile and waded forward through the snow, ready to put a bullet through the first thing that didn't have hair and moved.

Half frozen, disoriented in the swirling snow and very much afraid, I ducked down and looked around me, half expecting at any moment to see Stryder London emerge from the gusts to put me out of my misery.

A dark shape went past me, but it wasn't Stryder London. Golly, growling and slapping at the snow on the ground and in the air, was wallowing away from the snowmobile.

"*Golly!*" I shouted, struggling after her. "Don't go away! We have to stick together! If I can find something to burn, I'll start a fire!"

I managed to reach her, wrapped my fingers in her fur—and ducked just in time to avoid having my head torn off my shoulders as her arm swung around. I sat down hard, couldn't have escaped if I wanted to as she hovered over me, eyes bloody with rage. Then she shivered, turned around, and disappeared in the swirling snow.

Golly—who had saved Garth and me by throwing Obie Loge down the waste chute into Mount Doom and had then come down to help me—was going to freeze to death in a very short time unless I could get her back with me and start a fire.

Dangerous or not, I had to try and save her.

Fighting against the desire simply to lie down and go to sleep, I struggled forward toward the spot where Golly had disappeared, swinging my shoulders back and forth to gain momentum, pumping my knees up and down, thinking that being a dwarf in a snowstorm is a real pain in the ass.

Then, suddenly, it was as if I were looking through a window in the storm, and what I saw through the window, twenty yards ahead, were the bare, skeletal shapes of trees—lots of them; Golly, whatever her mental state, had known where she was going. Whimpering with both cold and delight, I half ran, half swam through the drifts and fell on my face inside the shelter of the trees.

Protected by the natural windbreak of the forest, I could see. Lying still on my belly, hugging the frozen loam of the forest floor, I looked around; there was no sign of Stryder London. Already I felt warmer.

"Golly!" I shouted as I got to my feet. "Come here! I'm going to start a fire!"

Nothing.

I ran around for a while, shouting her name, making a lot of noise. I knew that I might attract London as well as Golly, but that was the point of the exercise. Even if I hadn't been dependent for my life on a battery pack that was rapidly draining, I knew now that I could never hope to track down Stryder London. I suspected—desperately hoped—that I had one last, secret weapon in my arsenal, one that had apparently gone unnoticed even during the extensive biotesting; if anyone had detected what I considered to be my most horrible symptom, it had never been mentioned to me. To use it against Stryder London, I had to be in physical contact, and if I couldn't find the Warrior leader, then he would have to find me.

Shhh.

Whisper made short work of cutting up deadwood on the ground into a collection of wood shavings, twigs, and a good-sized pile of logs. I gathered together a mound of wood shavings and dead leaves, stuck the muzzle of the machine pistol into it and emptied the gun. The flame discharge from the barrel ignited the leaves, and within minutes I had a roaring fire to warm me and save my batteries. I placed the empty machine pistol and Whisper on the ground near the fire where they could be seen, then sat cross-legged by the flames and waited.

I didn't have long to wait. I heard nothing and was just comfortably dozing off when I felt a circle of very cold steel touch my ear.

"Hello, General," I said. "Please don't tell me to freeze. I've already done that number."

"What the hell is this all about, Frederickson?"

"What's what about? Take that gun out of my ear, will you? It's cold."

"The shots and this fire; you must have known I'd find you."

"That was the idea, dumbie."

Keeping his machine pistol leveled on my chest, London moved around me. He picked up Whisper, lifted up the edge of his parka and stuck her in his belt. He examined the empty machine pistol, threw it away into the forest behind him. Then he studied me through narrowed lids. "What do you think you have up your sleeve, Frederickson?" he asked at last.

"Nothing but arms."

"Show me."

I stood, unzipped my parka and spread it to show that I had no more weapons.

"What's with the battery pack?"

"I've gone cold-blooded, and I need a heating unit to keep me alive. You can check it out if you want to, but there's no trick. The game's over. One way or another, I'm going to die soon. I want to die with my brother."

"I don't believe you, Frederickson," London answered without hesitation. "You're not a quitter. I've known a lot of very good fighting men, but I've never met a man who keeps coming, no matter what the odds, the way you do. You're quite mad, you know."

"Now you sound like Garth," I replied as I zipped up my parka. "Would you take me to him, please?"

"You have no chance of defeating me or the purpose of Siegmund Loge, Frederickson. Absolutely none. You never did."

"I thought I just said that."

London used Whisper to slice narrow strips of bark from a tree, and he used the strips to tie my hands behind my back. Then, using a long strip as a choke tether, he led me off through the trees to the northwest. We traversed a gully, went over a couple of small hills, finally came to his camp. He'd built a solid lean-to on the lee side of a small cliff, and there was a steady hardwood fire that was virtually smokeless. Garth, his hands and feet bound by rope, was lying on the ground close to the fire. A rope around his neck snaked away and was anchored to the trunk of a tree close to the lean-to.

Garth glanced up at our approach, and by the light of the fire I watched his human eyes fill with inconsolable grief and a sense of loss. I shrugged, managed a very thin smile.

"What now?" I asked as I sat down next to Garth.

London tied my neck tether to a tree. "I take you to Dr. Loge," he answered as he tied my ankles together with a length of rope he'd taken from the lean-to.

"He's somewhere in Greenland, isn't he? Inside a ring."

London looked up, obviously startled. "Who told you that?! How could you know?!!"

"I do know. What kind of a ring is it? *Where* is it?"

London straightened up. "You'll find out where Dr. Loge is when I take you to him."

"He's going to dissect Garth and me, you know. That's what you're taking us to."

London removed Whisper from his belt, turned her over in his hands. "My job is to deliver you," he said as he hefted Whisper, then flicked his wrist and sent her flying through the air. The blade stuck in a log, quivered, the Damascus steel glinting in the firelight. "What's done with you isn't my concern. You know I have my regrets, but I have my duty."

"What's done with us may not be your concern, but it's still your reponsibility."

"I'm sorry."

"When do we go?"

London looked up at the sky, which had grown very dark. "There's a storm coming—a bad one. We'll wait it out here, and by tomorrow morn—"

Suddenly Golly came flying off the edge of the cliff above the lean-to. She hit the ground, rolled, and came up charging at London. The Warrior clawed for his gun and had it halfway out of his holster when Golly hit him. The Warrior flew backward through the air and almost landed in my lap. Golly started to charge again, abruptly stopped when she saw the gun swinging around toward her, turned to her left and headed around the fire for the trees. London leaned over me, took careful aim on Golly's back and was about to pull the trigger when I leaned forward and sank my teeth into his right cheek.

London's burst of fire went over Golly's head, and she disappeared from sight as London cursed and flailed at me. I hung on to his cheek, chewing the raw flesh and working saliva into the wound. Finally he tore free, and I spat out the chunk of flesh he'd left in my mouth.

Holding one hand to his bleeding cheek, London raised his machine pistol to club me, then thought better of it. "You're not the class act I thought you were, Frederickson," he said, as if that were the best insult he could think of. Then he turned and walked away into the woods, apparently looking for Golly.

London looked more than a litle peaked when he returned about five minutes later. In fact, he didn't look well at all. His face had gone gray and seemed to grow even darker before my eyes as he staggered, caroming off the naked trees. He fell on his back in front of the lean-to, got up on his knees, crawled toward us.

Somehow, he'd managed to hang on to his machine pistol.

Garth and I looked at each other, and I could see in his eyes that he understood what was happening.

London also understood what was happening, and I could see by the look in *his* eyes that he didn't appreciate the irony of it all.

"You . . . poisoned me," Lieutenant General Stryder London, AWOL from the U.S. Army, whispered hoarsely as he flopped on the ground in front of me. "Kill . . . you . . . too."

Garth and I watched with more than passing interest as the hand with the machine pistol lifted off the ground; it was trembling violently, but it was moving. Toward us. Then it stopped, collapsed to the ground.

"Now *that's* a class act," I said as London twitched and died.

Garth threw back his head and uttered a long, drawn-out howl of triumph and joy.

"Don't get too excited yet, brother," I said as I tested the strength of the tether around my neck and only managed to tighten it. "There's a blizzard on the way, the fire's going out, and London hog-tied us pretty good. Can you work yourself up into one of your mighty snits?"

Garth slowly shook his head. I glanced at Whisper, stuck in the log twenty feet away; she might as well have been twenty miles away.

"Golly!"

There was no response, no gorilla—only the rising wind whistling through the swaying trees. The flames of the campfire were starting to gutter and die, and I was growing cold and sleepy. I fumbled at the knot around my wrists with my gloved fingers, got nowhere.

"Golly?! Golly! Hey, babe, we could really use a little help here!"

Inspired by desperation, I began belting out arias from *The*

Magic Flute like show tunes, shouting them out at the top of my lungs, hoping I could be heard above the wind. Finally I stopped, looked around.

Nothing.

Act Two. More arias, complete with a la-la-la orchestral accompaniment. I could feel my voice going when I suddenly felt a tap on my shoulder. I yelped, looked around to see Golly standing behind me.

GO Y LOV ?UPQINGM ZART

"Right, babe. I love Mozart too, remember? Listen to me carefully, Golly. I want you to take the knife out of that log over there and bring it here. I want you to cut us free. Do you understand?"

?

More Mozart. This time I hummed a cheerful, soothing étude. Golly inclined her head, half closed her eyes, and seemed to be swaying tentatively in time to the music.

"Golly, please try to concentrate and understand," I said softly. "I understand now what you meant when you told me you felt funny; you're losing your wrongness. But you have to stay like people just a while longer. Understand?"

FUCKING TRY

"If you can't, sweetheart, Garth and I will die. You have to take the knife out of the log and bring it here."

Golly slowly ambled over to Whisper. She cocked her head and stared at the blade for a few moments, then pulled it free. She shuffled around the campfire three times, then responded to more Mozart and coaxing, and came over to me. Half an aria, another instruction, and she cut the bark strips around my wrist.

Not knowing how she would respond, and not caring, I wrapped my arms around her neck and kissed her brow. Then I took Whisper from her hand, cut the rope around my ankles, and cut Garth free. I immediately rushed to throw more logs on the fire, and the three of us huddled around the leaping, life-giving flames.

"Listen, guys," I said, "I've got a problem. London's plan

was the best; wait here in the shelter of the cliff, by the fire, until the storm blows over. I can't do that. I've gone cold-blooded, and the only thing keeping me alive in this cold is a battery-operated heating unit. The batteries are going dead. I have to make a run for it now, hope that I can find the snowmobile, and hope there's enough gas to get me back to the Institute—if I can find it in the—"

Garth didn't wait to hear any more. He straightened up, came over and pushed me in the direction from which we had come. I resisted, clutched both his naked, hairy forearms.

"Garth, I don't know what's going to happen out there. I've lost my sense of direction; even without the storm, I'm not sure I can find my way back before I run out of gas. If you and Golly stay here, at least you have a fire, and maybe there's a chance—"

Now Garth actually growled at me, and anger flared in his eyes as he motioned for me to lead the way. I grabbed one of Golly's hands, Garth grabbed the other, and together we hurried back through a forest that had grown ominously still. Heavy snowflakes had begun to fall.

36.

A half hour after we'd dug one of the snowmobiles out of a drift and started off, I knew we were hopelessly lost. The sense of direction that had guided me so unerringly through Mount Doom had disappeared. By now the storm was hitting us in full fury, and we were wallowing in a howling, wind- and snow-blasted world of freezing cold that had no horizon.

Even with Garth and Golly huddling around me, I kept nodding off at the controls, and it was only Garth's persistent shaking and slapping that kept me even semiconscious.

Then we ran out of gas.

My mother's dream . . .

Bad decision to allow Garth and Golly to come with me into the blizzard; maybe they could have made it out on their own, in the morning.

Maybe other Warriors from the Institute would have

mounted a rescue party, found them; at least Garth would have been alive.

Maybe Garth's cells would have stopped exploding.

Despite his prehuman form, maybe Garth could have found Siegmund Loge on his own and stopped Project Valhalla.

While there's life, there's hope. Ho, ho, ho.

Maybe Loge, or even some other scientist, could have cured Garth.

Maybe.

April Fool's Day.

Bad decision.

My mother's dream . . .

Suddenly I realized that I had been asleep, and Garth's sharp pinch on my cheek had awakened me. I was in his arms, and he was on foot, struggling through snow that was thigh-deep, refusing to give up until his last strength was gone.

My mother's dream . . .

All the world . . .

Then Garth could go on no longer. Swaying, he held me very close, kissed me good-bye, then toppled sideways with me into the snow.

Something furry and very heavy fell on top of me, driving me even farther down into the snow. I wriggled, pushed at Golly, and she raised herself just enough so that I could see her display screen.

GOLLY LOVE MONGO
GOLLY KEEP MONGO WARM

While there's life, there really is hope. No ho, ho, ho.

Alive, Golly and her sacrifice might keep me alive for a few more minutes, at most.

Dead, her sacrifice might keep both Garth and me alive for a considerably longer time.

Shhh.

"I love you, Golly. Thank you for your life."

I sliced open her throat, killing her instantly. Hot blood gushed forth into my face, momentarily clearing my senses, melting down the snow around my head. I wriggled the upper part of my body free, wiped the blood off my glasses, then buried Whisper in the base of Golly's throat and ripped down through bone and flesh, spilling her steaming guts into the snow.

Garth saw and understood what I was trying to do, and he helped me stretch and break open Golly's rib cage. Covered with warm, life-sustaining gore, we squeezed together into more gore, huddled together with our bodies wrapped around one another inside Golly's carcass.

Dripping blood and strands of gut hanging from the ripped rib cage almost immediately began to freeze, forming a bloody, intricate, lacelike barrier of strange and unlikely beauty between us and the storm outside.

Gestures, even empty ones, can mean something. Now there was absolutely nothing left to do. But we had fought to the best of our ability to the very end, and I believed that our mother and father would be proud of our struggle, no matter what kind of world they ended living in.

Garth and I, two beasts of Valhalla, lay inside the body of another, waiting to die behind a wall of tears and curtains of ice.

37.

Knock-knock.

Who's that tapping at my door?

Knock-knock.

Only death and nothing more?

The knocking continued, and as I opened my eyes and squinted I could see booted feet moving in clear sunlight outside the curtain of frozen blood.

Somebody was chopping away at Golly's frozen carcass, trying to get at us.

I tried to grope for Whisper, but everything around me seemed frozen solid, and I couldn't move. I could feel Garth's bulk next to mine, but he seemed so very still; I tried to speak, couldn't.

Then the prison of frozen flesh around us cracked open, and I found myself looking up into the faces of three Warriors, the fur around the hoods of their parkas being whipped about by the wash of helicopter rotors.

Thwop-thwop-thwop.

A fourth Warrior came into my field of vision, bent down over me. He was a big man, and his left sleeve was empty. His eyes were set wide apart, and he had a lantern jaw.

"They're alive!" Mike Leviticus shouted.

They're alive. Garth was alive. If there had been any tears left in me, I would have cried once again.

By helicopter, it was only a five-minute ride to the Institute, where we were taken. I could still barely stay awake, much less speak, so I didn't bother to try.

My initial elation at our surviving the storm had been dampened somewhat by my memory of the steel table and surgical instruments that had been set up beside Garth's cage.

It occurred to me that we were being thawed out simply so that the scalpels wouldn't break when they dissected us.

We weren't dissected.

Groggy most of the time, I existed in a kind of dopy torpor as teams of men and women in white coats ministered to us. I had completely lost track of any sense of time; minutes, days, or weeks could have gone by, and I wouldn't have known the difference.

Once, in one of my more alert periods, I lifted my head off my pillow and saw Garth, asleep, lying in another bed.

He appeared strange to me.

Or didn't appear strange.

I wasn't sure which.

Mike Leviticus never spoke, but he did a lot of staring at me; there was a strange look in his eyes which I found impossible to read. Often, he absently touched the stump of his left wrist.

If, finally, Garth and I were to be killed, I strongly suspected that Mike Leviticus would be highly pleased to be chosen as our executioner.

* * *

More time passed, still impossible to measure, and I continued to float groggily through it all. Now I suspected that Garth and I were being tranquilized, but I wasn't sure.

Except for mealtimes, when we were assisted by nurses, we were allowed simply to rest. There were no needles, no X-rays, no sonograms, no biosamples taken.

There was no cutting.

Garth continued to appear strange to me.

Or not strange.

An airplane. Now I was convinced that Garth and I were being doped up, for I continued to segue in and out of sleep, soothed by the engines' steady drone.

Garth, also asleep, was in a seat across the aisle, accompanied by a Warrior guard. My guard was Mike Leviticus, who kept staring at me and touching his stump.

Once, when I woke up and glanced out the window, I saw water. Lots of water. An ocean.

The next time I woke up we were over a vast, barren land mass, which I assumed was Greenland.

Greenland, I thought, was a perfect site for Siegmund Loge's main base of operations. It was a vast land, thinly populated, midway between Russia and the United States, and beneath a nexus of dozens of communications satellites. When the time came to deliver "Father's Treasure" to the test subjects in the ring of communes around the world, cargo planes, flying at low levels, could fly in and out with minimal risk of detection.

Another feature of the continent had also enabled Loge, using what I assumed was the latest "burnout" technology—massive steel conduits lined with reflective brick and sunk directly into a volcano's underground magma pool—to solve the problem of finding a source of energy, in this case heat transfer.

Loge certainly had plenty of power, I thought as the plane descended toward his headquarters, of which only a huge, transparent, sunlight-collecting dome was visible aboveground. He was situated on a vast, barren plain inside a massive ring of volcanoes which I estimated to be at least ten miles in diameter.

The plane landed on the tundra, taxied toward a spot where a massive, radio-operated panel was sliding back to reveal an equally massive elevator platform.

It was only after the plane stopped on the platform and the elevator began to descend that it struck me that I had been seeing in sunlight, without pain, without my glasses—and had been ever since the Warriors had taken us out of the steppes. The smoked glasses, like Whisper, had been lost inside Golly's frozen carcass.

38.

For three days we were kept in obviously impromptu but effective confinement inside a locked and reinforced storeroom with an adjoining toilet. We had no contact with anyone, and our meals were delivered to us through a narrow opening cut out at the bottom of the door.

On the evening of the third day we got a special surprise for dinner, a hose instead of food trays. We were gassed.

We awoke in separate beds, in a rather cheerful and tastefully decorated bedroom illuminated by recessed lights.

"Shit, I'm shedding again," Garth said as he rose, stripped, then shook out his pajamas and brushed hair off his sheets and pillow. As his body continued its rapid transmutation back to normal size and appearance, his fur kept falling off in thick, matted chunks.

My own pajamas even fit me, which attested to the fact that someone—presumably Siegmund Loge—had gone to a lot of trouble to see that we were comfortable. On dressers next to each of our beds had been laid out several changes of underwear, three pale blue overalls which looked appropriately sized, fine leather boots, and Adidas sneakers.

I grunted. "It always amazes me how you find exactly the right thing to say in any given situation. Here we wake up in a Louis the Fourteenth bedroom, original Picassos on the walls, and the first thing you worry about is grooming. This is the Magic Kingdom, m'boy."

"What can I tell you? I'm anal-compulsive." Garth pulled a

handful of fur off his buttocks, dropped it into the large metal wastebasket next to his bed. "Sorry I'm messing up the place. Let's hope our host has provided us with a vacuum cleaner."

There wasn't a vacuum cleaner, but we weren't missing too many other things. There was a large bathroom with separate tub and shower stall—most welcome, since we were a bit gamy after sitting around in the storeroom for three days—and two sets of toilet articles. The refrigerator in the kitchen was well stocked, and there was a freezer filled with meat and frozen fresh vegetables. There was even a wet bar in the living room, also well stocked; it sat next to a Plexiglas shield, similar to the one in Siegfried Loge's Treasure Room, which cut us off from what appeared to be a very expensively equipped media room and a rather long, narrow corridor with a door at the end.

What we didn't have in our section of the apartment, besides a vacuum cleaner, was an exit.

The man standing on the other side of the shield was two or three inches taller than Garth. He was gangling and rawboned, had large, gentle-looking hands, and appeared remarkably fit for someone who had to be in his mid-eighties. His full head of snow-white hair was longer than in his pictures or on his posters, and fell across his shoulders. His face was full, free of wrinkles, and he had eyes of the deepest blue I had ever seen; the eyes were limpid, swimming with compassion and glinting with intelligence. He was wearing a loosely belted white cardigan sweater over a blue silk shirt, finely tailored charcoal slacks, and looked like a physically fit Santa Claus, or a Sunday school God, out of costume, smoking a pipe. Simply standing still and silent, his personal magnetism was enormous; he was a man who'd successfully lied to tens of millions of people, yet I knew he was a man whose words I would trust instinctively. If I didn't know better.

"I'm Siegmund Loge," the scientist said, removing his pipe from his mouth and stepping closer to the shield. His voice, slightly amplified through hidden speakers in the apartment, was deep, rich and resonant, slightly hypnotic, the kind of voice a person can listen to for long periods of time without growing tired. "I'm most pleased to meet you at last, Garth and Dr. Robert Frederickson."

Garth and Dr. Robert Frederickson would have been most

pleased to meet Dr. Siegmund Loge on more intimate terms, and we both hurled our bodies at the Plexiglas, again and again. The shield was remarkably resilient, and all we did was manage to bruise our shoulders. I sorely missed Whisper.

"Please don't," Loge said, looking genuinely concerned as Garth and I, panting, sat down on the thick carpet for a breather. "You'll hurt yourselves."

The thought that Siegmund Loge should be so solicitous of our health gave both Garth and me a good chuckle, and caused us to redouble our efforts to get at him. This time all we managed to do was break up most of the living room furniture, and snap three steak knives from the kitchen.

Loge had waited patiently through our little tantrum. Now, as we stood and glared at him, he relit his pipe, puffed on it thoughtfully as he stared back at us, then sighed and shook his head. "This is very disturbing," he said in his sonorous voice.

Garth and I looked at each other, puzzled. It took a while, but I finally realized that Loge was referring to our recovery. "You didn't know the process could be reversed, did you?" I asked.

Loge grunted his affirmation. "Apparently severe trauma will do precisely that, which may mean that even less severe trauma could arrest the process. I believe the problem can be solved, but I should have anticipated it."

Severe trauma, indeed, I thought—like almost freezing to death. "Don't feel bad," I said. "All the clues were right under the noses of your crazy son and grandson, in their Mount Doom, but they were too busy jerking off with their toys, games, and fantasies to see the implications of the fact that many of the animals they threw into that heat and cold not only survived, but multiplied. Is there a chemical antidote?"

Loge slowly blinked, shook his head. "What would be the point of having an antidote?"

"What's the point of the Valhalla Project?"

Loge simply stared at us. Once he removed his pipe from his mouth and seemed about to speak, then thought better of it; he put his pipe back in his mouth and puffed.

Garth tapped on the Plexiglas in front of Loge's nose. "Mongo wants to know why a nice senior citizen like yourself wants to risk destroying the world."

Loge just continued to puff and stare; he seemed lost in thought.

"I'd say it doesn't make any difference, Loge," I said. "The whole thing looks like a bust to me. You may do a lot of damage and cause a lot of suffering, but doctors and scientists will certainly discover the temperature factor before too long. The shit you want to make may not even work anywhere outside the temperate zones, which excludes most of Russia. What do you say we all go home and forget this thing? You gave it the old college try."

Loge grunted, took a pencil and small note pad out of the pocket of his sweater, and began doodling; before our eyes, he was apparently solving the problem. "No," he mumbled. "The problem can be solved. It's in the reverse transcriptase."

"Just where I thought it was," I said, and looked at my Chief Researcher.

"It's a genetic substance that can read RNA into DNA," Garth said. "You can inject new material into genetic programs, cause those programs to run backwards along evolutionary lines. Controlling the reaction from the reverse transcriptase is the key to this thing."

"I'm sorry I asked," I replied, and turned back to Loge. "Where are Mike Leviticus and the other Warriors who brought us here?"

Loge finished a series of equations, gave a smile of satisfaction which I found maddening, put the pencil and pad back in his pocket. "They were sent back after they wired your apartment for sound and constructed this shield."

"You didn't want us to talk to them, did you?"

"No," Loge answered simply.

"Because what we had to say might contradict some of the things they believe about you and Project Valhalla. In fact, each one of them may believe something different. No wonder you kept us drugged. Warriors are trained to be close-mouthed, even with each other. You certainly didn't want us to start them debating with each other."

"Correct. The two of you happen to be the most dangerous men on the face of the earth; yet, you may still end as the saviors of humankind."

"Oh, you're just saying that because you like us—you're going to give us delusions of grandeur. I assume you're referring to our reaction to the shit Jake Bolesh put in us?"

"Of course. Without the two of you, and your unique reaction to that particular formulation, I might never have found the correct formulation."

"You have it now?" Garth asked quietly.

"Yes," Loge answered with a saintly smile of gratitude. "It is done, thanks to the information I was able to gain from your bodies. Also—thanks to your remarkable wills to survive, your resourcefulness and resilience—I discovered, and was able to correct, this problem of reversal outside certain temperature parameters. You are, or were, the most dangerous men on the planet because you would not stop coming at me, and I must confess that on a number of occasions I was afraid that you might actually be able to stop me from completing the project. That would have been a tragedy with dimensions you can't imagine—yet."

"Oh, woe. When do we get to know what you're really up to, so that we can try to imagine the dimensions of the tragedy we would have caused if we'd been able to stop you? Garth and I are really into tragedy."

"Soon. Not yet. When you do understand the reason for Project Valhalla, Dr. Frederickson, I don't believe you'll find things so amusing."

"Listen, Dr. Loge, Garth and I aren't exactly splitting our sides now; a lot of people find our sense of humor somewhat bizarre." To my mind, Project Valhalla, whatever it really was, still had one major flaw. But I couldn't recall ever winning a single Nobel Prize, and I wasn't about to argue with a double laureate. Also, after watching him casually doodle through the problem of reversal with a pencil and paper, I wasn't about to stimulate him with any hints. "Who else is here?" I asked.

"Nobody. We're alone."

"Bullshit."

Loge simply shrugged. "Why should I lie about something like that? It's true; we are alone."

"No security?"

"Security against what? The only threat against us in this place would be from a Greenland or NATO force, and my Warriors couldn't defend against that. Illusion and isolation remain my principal weapons of security, as they have always been. Next week, of course, things will be different. Hundreds of people will begin arriving to prepare for manufacture and distribution."

"What about the babies who were sent to you?" Garth asked in a low, menacing tone.

"They were sent back to their parents some time ago—and I would like you to believe that, while they were here, they were expertly cared for by a trained staff. No infant suffered because of its stay here."

"They weren't . . . tampered with?"

"No, Garth. After I learned of your reactions to the last formulation, I knew there was no need for the work I had planned to do with the infants; you two were the work, the human experimental subjects, the living laboratories in which the solution to a correct formulation could be found. Indeed, it's arguable whether I could have produced that reaction in any other humans on earth. You were indispensable in bringing the Valhalla Project to fruition. I believe Mr. Lippitt understood this danger from the beginning. Considering his mind set, I'm surprised he didn't kill the both of you. An unpredictable man, that one."

"What happened to Mr. Lippitt and the man who was with him at the Institute?" I asked carefully, almost afraid to hear the answer.

"They're both dead. I'm sorry."

The news hit both Garth and me like bullets in the stomach. We were alone, without allies, imprisoned and at the mercy of Siegmund Loge while the clock of the world ran down.

Seeing our reaction, Loge stepped closer to the shield. Tears actually glistened in his sea-blue eyes. "I really *am* sorry," he said. "I know they were your friends, and I understand your grief. But remember that I've lost a son and a grandson. Believe me, it doesn't make a difference. All of the death and suffering for which you hold me responsible is insignificant compared to . . . what would have been, and can now be prevented."

"What's it about, Loge?" I asked through clenched teeth. "Which of the dozen different versions of Project Valhalla we've heard is the right one?"

"None."

Garth and I looked at each other, then at Loge. The old man had both his hands placed on the shield, almost as if he wanted to reach through and touch us. For a brief moment, grief and loneliness swam in his eyes. Then it was gone. He stepped back, seemed to be making an effort to compose himself as he refilled his pipe from a pouch in his pocket, lit it.

I asked, "Besides yourself, who else knows what the Valhalla Project is really supposed to do?"

"Nobody," Loge answered in a voice that trembled slightly.

Garth punched the shield with his fist. "Damn it, don't you think we have the right to know?!"

"Yes," Loge murmured in a voice that was almost inaudible. "And I want you to know."

"So *tell* us, already!" I said, thoroughly exasperated.

"Soon."

"Why not now?"

"First, there's something you must see. I believe it will explain many things—my need for the isolation in which you find me, the things I think about in that isolation. Then you will understand Project Valhalla."

Again, Garth punched the shield. His face was flushed a deep, brick red. "Let's get one thing straight between us, you fucking screwball. You don't need us any longer, do you?"

"For experimentation and knowledge, no," Loge replied evenly.

"Then for what?" I asked quickly.

"Soon, Dr. Frederickson."

Garth stepped back from the shield, took a deep breath, and slowly relaxed his fists. "If you don't need us, why are we still alive? Why bother bringing us here in the first place?"

"All your questions will be answered soon, Garth. I promise you."

"Go to hell, you fucking Nazi," Garth said, and spat at the glass. "Shit, even the rest of the Nazis couldn't have thought this one up—it took the biggest Nazi of all."

Loge's face, distorted by Garth's spittle on the Plexiglas, contorted in pain; Garth's words had cut him deeply. He wiped tears from his eyes, looked down at me. "You like people, don't you?"

"Yes," I answered softly. "But I like them the way they are."

Loge nodded absently, then turned and slowly walked away down the long corridor.

We didn't see Loge for the rest of the day, and he didn't come in the morning. We tried shouting into the intercom in the living room, but it seemed to be dead. We tried shouting at the walls, where we assumed microphones must be hidden, but got no response and no Loge. We even tried shouting up at the recessed television cameras in all the rooms, but there was still no response.

We were just sitting down to a lunch Garth had prepared when the lights in the apartment went out. A few moments later we heard the haunting, E-flat opening chords of *Das Rheingold;* the sound filled the apartment and seemed to be coming from everywhere at once, vibrating in our bones as well as our ears.

Suddenly there was a glow, then a flicker at the entrance to the living room. We rose, walked into the other room—and came to a dead stop.

Standing, we didn't move for close to three hours.

Like the shield in the Treasure Room, the Plexiglas sealing off the living room could reflect images, which in this case were being rear-projected from the media room beyond. What we were watching was a series of slides and short film clips, a visual presentation precisely edited in rhythms that matched the music in the introductory opera in Wagner's *Ring* cycle.

One brief series of slides showed a soldier snatching an infant from its mother's arms, then bashing the baby's head against a brick wall.

Another series showed a soldier disemboweling a pregnant woman.

These images passed before our eyes even before the thirty-six E-flat opening bars of *Das Rheingold* were over, and were followed by other, similar images throughout the length of the opera. As horrible as were these opening sequences, the ones that followed were just as horrible, and had the same emotional impact. Although each sequence was brief, some images consisting only of the flash of a single slide, not a single image or sequence of images was ever repeated in the three hours.

None had to be. The record of human cruelty, even when

presented in snippets, was easily long enough to stretch through *Das Rheingold.*

And beyond.

Each day for the next three days, beginning at precisely one o'clock in the afternoon, another opera in the cycle was presented, each with its own accompanying slide and film show. During this time I—and Garth, too, I believed—came to understand what heretofore had been only a vaguely bemusing puzzlement when practiced or described by other people: religion and religious experience.

Siegmund Loge was our high priest, and he was baptizing us in an ocean of feeling inside ourselves deeper than we had ever imagined.

After *Die Walküre* we began to fast. And we continued our fast.

Also, we were silent for these four days . . . not only during each opera and its accompanying visual presentation, but afterwards, like monks in retreat.

Tens, hundreds of thousands of slides and film clips flashed through the seventeen-and-a-half-hour length of the *Ring* cycle. Loge, the Nobel laureate, was also revealed to us now as a consummate artist as well as an ultrabrilliant scientist. By precisely matching these images of unspeakable and indiscribable horror to Wagner's masterpiece, the vast opus of a Nazi sympathizer, Loge had found a way to speak of the unspeakable and describe the indescribable; what he had done was to construct a kind of spiritual submersible, comprised of music and light, that took us to the very bottom of the ocean of evil that stains the shores of the human heart.

The onslaught of horror was so terrible that finally, with music as a catalyst, it transcended horror; it created in us a feeling of profound sadness that I realized, with a suddenness that literally took my breath away, was a reflection, the tender and merciful grace, of my own goodness, the air supply that kept me from drowning in what I was seeing.

So our decency, too, Loge showed us, though the horror of the images never stopped. Whatever feelings Garth and I had ever felt stir in us were nothing, mere breezes on the skin of the soul, compared to what we were feeling now; Siegmund Loge was working on our souls' skin with a tattooer's needle of notes and colors.

How Siegmund Loge had lived for more than eighty years with this pain weighing on his soul without being crushed by it, I couldn't imagine, and I realized, with shame, what a very shallow human being I was compared to this very great and very sad and very compassionate old man. I believed that Garth felt the same.

Mr. Lippitt had told me I'd be impressed by Siegmund Loge. I was impressed. And I knew that whatever happened next, a sea change had taken place in my soul by the time the last sweet and haunting notes of *Götterdämmerung* had faded away.

Garth and I would never forget what we had experienced in this room, and we would never be the same.

39.

At precisely one o'clock in the afternoon on the day after *Götterdämmerung,* Siegmund Loge came to us. His eyes were red-rimmed, as if he had been crying recently, but his voice was steady, if soft, when he spoke.

"I've spent almost my entire lifetime compiling that—since I was seventeen. It was completed, the last pictures matched to the last bars of the music, only recently—in the morning of the day you were found. This is the first time *I've* experienced it as a whole, and so it's an experience we've shared together." He took a deep breath, and his voice trembled slightly when he continued. "Please tell me what you think."

"I couldn't find any fucking popcorn in the kitchen, Loge," Garth said evenly. "What good are movies without popcorn?"

Loge's face was stony as he stared intently at Garth. The muscles in his jaw began to twitch, and emotions—clear as the images in the vast montage he had assembled—passed across his eyes: bewilderment, shock, hurt, grief—rage. "How *dare* you make such a remark?!" he shouted at Garth, pounding the shield with his fist. "You have no right to do what you're doing! I've been watching you for the past four days, and I've seen your reactions! I know how my work affected you! I've seen you both sobbing, and I've seen you sitting in silence, lost in grief! I've watched the two of you tossing in your sleep! *The three of us have felt the same!* Don't you *dare* deny your pain to me! *It's our common bond!*"

Garth reached inside his overalls as if to scratch, pulled out a tuft of fur and casually tossed it into the air. The glossy black hair drifted to the floor.

"That's my brother's way of telling you we'll share nothing with you that we don't have to," I said, scratching at the residual scales on the back of my forearm. "You've taken everything else from us from shit to toenail clippings, but you can't have our emotions. In addition to everything else, it turns out you're a nasty old voyeur. Why did you show that to us, anyway? Do we look like art critics?"

Loge swallowed hard, then stepped back from the shield. He seemed stunned, as if he had made some simple miscalculation and couldn't find his mistake. "It's my explanation," he said hoarsely.

"Your *explanation?!*" I snapped. "Do you really think you can justify or explain the murder of our nephew and his friend by giving Garth and me an emotional root canal job?! Do you think art can justify all the death and suffering you've caused?! You're part of the problem! Man, right now you *are* the problem! *You're killing the world!*"

Loge screwed his eyes shut, tilted his head back and clenched his fists. When he spoke, his voice was like a long moan. "I had hoped that you and your brother would understand, Dr. Frederickson, but you still don't. It's not a question of emotion or justification, not a matter of good or evil. It is mathematics. Our world, the world humans dominate and rule, is dying. But I'm not killing it; I'm trying to save it."

Then, suddenly, I understood—and wished I hadn't. "My God," I said in a voice I didn't recognize as my own. "It's the Triage Parabola."

Loge emitted a sigh, lowered his head, opened his eyes, unclenched his fists. "Yes, Dr. Frederickson. I do think you now understand."

"Mongo," Garth said, gripping my arm, "what the hell are you two talking—?"

I quickly put my fingers to his lips, then pointed to Loge,

who had begun to pace back and forth in front of the shield, nervously running his long fingers through his long silver hair.

"As you know," Loge said in the tone of voice some professors use when lecturing students, "the Triage Parabola has proved useful in helping to predict which of several endangered species will most benefit from human intervention, thus enabling us to focus our attention and resources where they will do the most good. To apply the formulas of the Triage Parabola to human beings is almost impossibly complex, because the number of variables in human behavior—economic, political, social, psychological—approaches infinity. However, almost a decade ago I was able to apply the formulas, using a Cray computer and a mathematics system of my own invention. I kept my findings secret; I saw nothing to be gained in revealing them, since there was absolutely nothing that could be done to alter what seemed to be inevitable—or so I thought, until I was approached at the Institute for the Study of Human Potential by certain representatives of the Pentagon."

"Mongo," Garth murmured, "tell me what this banana is talking about."

"He's saying humanity is an endangered species, that we're on the verge of extinction."

"From what? Nuclear war?"

"Maybe, maybe not," I said, recalling that in the entire visual montage accompanying the *Ring*, only two sequences, each lasting less than twenty seconds, had been devoted to the melting flesh of Hiroshima and Nagasaki. "I think what Loge is saying is even worse than that."

The scientist, who had heard me, nodded in affirmation, then resumed his pacing. "Correct, Dr. Frederickson. Thermonuclear war may destroy human life—indeed, all life—over the planet, but not necessarily so. In fact, the solutions to the equations indicate that the outside parameters for our existence may be as much as three or four hundred years. But no more. The *means* by which we destroy ourselves cannot be predicted mathematically—and are, in any case, irrelevant. It is of no value to look around for the catastrophe that will come; in an evolutionary sense, we *are* the catastrophe, a unique species of self-aware, intelligent creatures that are, as an entire species, quite insane. We are, as the Triage Parabola makes quite clear, simply an evolutionary dead end. Nature, as is well-known from even the most casual observation, is unforgiving and implacable in erasing her mistakes. On an evolutionary scale, we rose with lightning speed; we shall disappear with lightning speed. In four hundred years, or maybe only four hundred months or weeks or days or hours or seconds, there will not be a single human being left on the face of the earth. In four thousand years—a snap of the fingers in evolutionary time—there will probably not even be a trace left of our existence."

"What's going to replace us?" I asked.

"If nothing is done to alter our course?" Loge shrugged. "Who knows? The Triage Parabola is an extremely powerful mathematical tool, but it's not a crystal ball. Data to predict the end of our existence is available; that necessary to predict what sort of sentient creature, if any, will replace us is not. The only thing that's certain is that we will be gone."

"No, it's not certain," I said, knowing I sounded slightly foolish and petulant, and not caring; I couldn't think of anything else to say. "There is also love in the world."

"It is certain, Dr. Frederickson. You have not learned the lessons of your odyssey, as I had hoped you would. First, love is ephemeral; it vanishes at the torturer's first pass. Yes, there is love, and it is responsible for much that we have accomplished that is beautiful, good, and true. But love cannot triumph over evil because, for most people, only their evil transcends tribal boundaries, not their love. The young men and women in the commune you visited *loved*—each other. They were looking forward, with ecstasy, to the death of virtually everyone else. Stryder London loved—his country, which is to say his tribe, and was perfectly willing to countenance a weapon of terrible evil as long as it would subjugate the wills of all tribes to which he did not belong. Tribes, Dr. Frederickson. Tribes. National tribes; religious tribes; ethnic tribes; family tribes; sexual tribes; cultural tribes. By swinging down from the trees, by emerging from the caves, we only ensured our own eventual destruction. We are an evolutionary dead end precisely because we were able to replace sticks and stones with nerve gas and thermonuclear weapons without ever evolving, intellectually and morally, beyond the ridiculous, childish superstitions and primitive, tribal mind-sets that necessitated the use of the comparatively harmless sticks and stones in the first place. Once we poisoned the wells of neighboring tribes; now we poison oceans. The Triage Parabola provided me with a mathematical demonstration of our species' demise; I have given the world a practical demonstration. Of all people on earth, the Frederickson brothers have experienced the greatest overall view of that demonstration. By accident, my work touched your bodies; by design, I touched your souls. Yet you react to me as if I were some kind of mad scientist."

Garth and I looked at each other. "Perish the thought," I said quickly. "You're planning to send us *all* back in evolutionary time to see if we can't get it right the second time, aren't you? *That's* what the Valhalla Project is about, right?"

Loge slowly nodded. "Yes. Once I have tested the formulation in an initial trial run in my communes, any necessary corrections will be made, and then a second batch of 'Father's Treasure' will be delivered. This formulation will be highly infectious. Then the commune members will all be sent out into the world to await what the members of the commune you visited think of as the 'Good Time.' That time will come quickly. We will be rendered comparatively harmless to each other, at least on a global scale, and can only hope that we will evolve in a more appropriate manner if given this second chance. It is the ultimate, most humane, use of the Triage Parabola, gentlemen, and it is humankind's only hope for long-term survival."

"Uh, Loge . . ." I swallowed, found my mouth was just a bit dry. "Dr. Loge, before you go ahead and do anything we all may regret in the morning, why don't you recheck your figures?"

Loge shook his head sadly, looked at me with profound sadness in his eyes. "I have rechecked them, Dr. Frederickson; I've rechecked them hundreds of times. I know you're not a scientist or a mathematician, so it may be difficult for you to understand. Without the intervention represented by the Valhalla Project, our extinction is a *certainty.*"

"You mentioned that no one else had tried to apply the Triage Parabola to humans because it was almost impossible. Maybe it *is* impossible. Now, you're a fairly bright man, but you're not a god, despite what a lot of folks think. Even you could be wrong."

"No, I'm not a god," Loge said simply. "There are no gods, of course. I'm just a man, one representative of a species that, quite possibly, may be the only one in the entire universe which has such a high degree of self-awareness and intelligence. No other species anywhere may have the potential to travel to the stars to find out. Unless someone intervenes to save us from ourselves, it is doubtful we will even have time to accomplish the relatively simple task of traveling to another planet and colonizing it. I am not a god; I can be wrong, and often have been in the past. This is not such a time. I am not wrong. The figures are correct. Someone had to take the responsibility for altering our course, and I have done it; the Valhalla Project is the only solution I could think of. I feel I've come to know the two of you quite well, through the reports that came to me of the havoc you've been wreaking. Once, I thought perhaps the two of you could appreciate my burden and understand my terrible loneliness. Now I believe I was mistaken. The Triage Parabola is correct about the imminent extinction of humankind; I was wrong about you."

"Jesus Christ," Garth said with a snort of disgust. "You don't think *you're* insane?!"

Loge said nothing. He continued to stare at us with his sad eyes.

"Damn it, Loge," I said, "don't do it. Even if you're right, there must be some answer besides the Valhalla Project."

"No," Loge replied softly. "There is no other answer."

"You didn't need us anymore," Garth said. "You still haven't explained why we were thawed out and brought here. If you consider us so dangerous, why didn't you just let us die?"

Loge sighed, shrugged his shoulders. "But I have explained. I've explained everything, only to you. I wanted to meet you. I *needed* to explain to someone, and I needed someone to understand. I'd have entertained the hope that the two of you would help me."

"Help you do what?" I asked. "Manufacture and distribute 'Father's Treasure'?"

"No. I have hundreds of people to do that. The first of the manufacturing technicians will begin arriving tomorrow."

"Then what?"

"I wanted you to help me bear witness," Loge said softly. "I believe the two of you are now immune to the formulation; you are the only two people on the planet who will not change. I can take steps to protect myself against infection, and I will. I'd hoped that until our natural deaths, the three of us could travel over the face of the earth, safeguarding treasures when we can, but primarily bearing witness, as the last humans, to the goodness and beauty that was in our genes. Our existence, and our passage among the beasts, would serve as a kind of prayer for human salvation in the future."

"It sounds like a good idea to me," I said as Garth and I exchanged quick glances. "My brother and I are honored by your invitation, and we accept."

Loge didn't speak for some time, and I didn't like the look of the shadows that moved in his eyes. "You mock me, Dr. Frederickson," he said at last. "You *do* believe I am nothing more than a mad scientist, perhaps a paranoid schizophrenic, like my son —or simply morally corrupt, like my grandson. Do you believe I haven't seen into your hearts? You are both transparent. You believe that you can trick me into releasing you, so that you can stop the Valhalla Project—perhaps by killing me. Incredibly— despite all you have seen, and all I have told you—you still have hope. That is *your* insanity."

Loge abruptly moved to one side of the shield, disappeared from sight. There was a soft *click,* and then an even more ominous sound in the apartment.

hisssssssss

"I've taken great care in preparing this gas," Loge said kindly as he stepped back into view. "It is a gentle death; indeed, I think you will find it delightful. The two of you have suffered enough, and now I hope to give you considerable pleasure as you die. It's the least I can do."

hisssssssss

The sound seemed to be coming from everywhere inside the apartment, and there was the strong smell of lilacs.

My mother's dream.

"Loge, shut off the gas," I said, making a desperate effort to keep my voice even. "We have to talk to you. You still need us, because there's still one drawback to your plan, which you don't seem to understand. The rest of the body changes, but the brain cells don't. Somehow, the brain protects itself—like in the infant diving reflex, when the brain in a drowning person conserves its own oxygen. Your stuff won't work, because the membrane of the brain filters it out. Memory, self-awareness, instinct, prejudice, love, hate—all remain. You may have a planet filled with monkey people, but their human consciousness will remain the same. You'll accomplish nothing—*nothing*, Loge, except to inflict unimaginable suffering on the species you profess to love so much. You still need us if you hope to solve that problem. Shut off the gas."

Loge smiled gently, brushed a lock of silver hair away from his face. "I'm aware of what you just told me, Dr. Frederickson. I discovered this phenomenon when Garth was examined for the last time at the Institute. The adjustment in the formulation has already been made. All of the things you mentioned will be erased. Humankind will be able to start anew on its evolutionary path with a clean slate."

Oh-oh.

hissssssssss

My mother's dream!

"Loge, you have no right to decide alone what's best for four billion people!"

"Of course not," Siegmund Loge replied evenly. "I hope you don't think I would be so presumptuous as to take on such an awesome responsibility alone, without guidance."

"But you said nobody else knows what you're doing."

"God knows."

Loge's eyes teared, shimmered with gentleness and love.

"What?"

"I must confess that I haven't been totally forthcoming with the two of you," the old man said in a voice that was suddenly vibrant with ecstasy. "I said there were no gods, but there is God—the God of the universe, the God of us all. He first spoke to me when I was twelve years old, told me to begin collecting the pictures and film clips you saw. He has been speaking to me on a regular basis ever since, guiding me in my work. It was God who gave me the mathematical system I needed to apply the Triage Parabola to humankind, God who urged me to take responsibility for developing the Valhalla Project. I am doing

God's will. You see, gentlemen, I *am* the Messiah. Good-bye, now."

Stunned, Garth and I watched Siegmund Loge turn and walk away down the long corridor to the door, which he closed quietly behind him.

Then Garth and I really got serious about trying to break through the shield.

hisssssssssss

MY MOTHER'S DREAM!!

More broken furniture; muscles and bones near to breaking as we hurled ourselves against the Plexiglas, bounced off.

hissssssssss

MY MOTHER'S DREAM!!

. . . the end of the world, all hope gone . . .

MY MOTHER'S DREAM!!

hisssssssssss

It seemed an appropriate time to panic, so we did—at least to the extent that Loge's happy death gas allowed us, which wasn't much. Actually, we were kind of laughing, singing and prancing around the living room when Mike Leviticus, submachine gun crooked in his one whole arm, yanked open the door at the end of the corridor and sprinted toward us. It was the funniest thing we'd ever seen, and Garth and I stood with our noses pressed against the Plexiglas and howled with laughter. We wouldn't move, even when Leviticus frantically motioned with his stump for us to get down, so he finally fired just over our heads. The shield didn't so much shatter as disintegrate, showering powder, slivers, and shards over us.

"Fly away home, Mike, m'boy," I cackled. "Poison gas. Get out of here."

Garth, even though he was in the middle of the Toreador Song from *Carmen,* nevertheless had the presence of mind to stumble over the rubble of the shield, find the switch and shut off the gas. Leviticus, his face red from the strain of holding his breath, used his machine gun—none too gently, beating the butt and barrel on our backs—to herd the giggling Fredericksons down the corridor and out the door, which he slammed shut behind him. He managed to whack us along another corridor, steered us to the left, and plopped us down on the floor directly beneath a huge ventilator shaft. After twenty minutes, our howls of laughter had dribbled off to an occasional, high-pitched giggle; another twenty minutes, and we managed to hold it down to spasmodic grins.

"Mongo?"

"I think I'm all right, Garth. You?"

"Me, too."

"Mike," I said, grinning foolishly up at the Warrior, "how can we thank you?"

Leviticus, his lantern jaw set firmly, shook his head. "I'm the one who has to thank you, Frederickson. If it weren't for you, my soul would have been doomed to eternal damnation."

"Huh?"

Leviticus held out his naked stump. "This is a sign, a warning —God at once punishing me for, and trying to rescue me from, my own stupidity. It's taken me all this time to realize it; thank God I realized it in time. I helped install the gas system, so I knew what Satan—when I understood a few hours ago that Loge was Satan—had planned for you."

"Good thinking," Garth said drily, then hiccuped with laughter.

"I know what the two of you have been through," Leviticus said, first staring at me intently, then at Garth.

"Yeah," Garth said with a dreamy smile, "it's been kind of a bummer."

"I saw what the two of you looked like when you were brought to the Institute . . . and I watched you both heal before my eyes. Only God could have done that; only God could have helped you survive all your trials, and only God's wonderful Grace could have healed you. Satan made you into beasts, but God made you human again. It was a miracle. That's when I began thinking."

"Ah," Garth said as we both began giggling again. "And not a moment too soon, dear boy."

"I realized then that I must be God's Warrior, not Satan's, at peril to my soul. It was up to me to rescue you from Satan. I picked up this machine gun, stole the plane, and came here as fast as I could." The Warrior paused, bowed his head low to us. "Please, please forgive me for my part in your suffering, and for taking so long to understand your true mission, to stop Satan."

"Right," I said as Garth and I got to our feet, dragged Leviticus to his. "Before we split, we have to figure out a way to blow up this place. Do you know anything about vulcan technology and heat transfer?"

"No, but I think I'd recognize the main power control source, if that's what you're asking."

"Right. All of the huge pipes you see running across the ceilings carry magma to someplace where it's converted into steam to run turbines. Look for a wall filled with pressure gauges. We'll separate to save time, and maintain communications through the intercom system. If you stumble across Satan in your travels, bring him along. If he puts up a fuss, shoot the fucker in the knees and carry him. We need him alive to give us all the details of the Valhalla Project and tell us everyone who's involved."

Leviticus held out his machine gun. "You want this?"

Garth and I shook our heads. "With Loge," I said, "all we'll need is a butterfly net."

40.

"Come out, come out, wherever you are!"

"Ally-ally-in-free!"

Loge had always done things, or gotten others to do things, in a big way, and the underground complex in Greenland was no exception. We had no idea how many levels there were, and after forty-five minutes Garth and I had not even finished exploring the level we were on, which contained apartments of varying sizes which we assumed were for the technical and manufacturing personnel scheduled to come in.

"Do you suppose he knows we're looking for him?" Garth asked.

"Sure. He must have been watching the whole show on television."

An intercom in the corridor we were passing through buzzed, and a button marked "General" lit. Garth pressed the button. "Yeah, Leviticus?"

"I found the guts of this place. I'm down on the fourth level, in the Pressure Control Room. I'm going to bust it up."

"Wait, Mike! Don't do anything until we—!"

But the intercom had gone dead and the light had winked out. A few seconds later we heard and felt the *ratta-tatta-tatta* of machine gun fire, the vibrations carrying clearly through the massive steel magma-flow pipes overhead and the ventilating shafts.

"Shit!" I said as we raced down the corridor and stepped into the first elevator we came to. Garth hit the button marked 4, the elevator doors closed, and we descended.

On the fourth level, the doors opened and we sprinted down the corridor to our left, toward the sound of machine gun fire. We almost ran over Siegmund Loge, who was just stepping out of an office. He was holding an open cardboard carton in his hands; in the carton was a gallon container of some amber-colored fluid. Garth grabbed the scientist by the front of his sweater, while I took the carton from his hands and gently set it on the floor.

"It's my work!" Loge cried. "It must be saved!"

The magma-flow pipes overhead were starting to make funny noises, and the temperature in the corridor was definitely rising. "Garth, take the banana back and wait by the elevator!" I shouted as I sprinted ahead down the corridor. "I'll see how much damage Leviticus has done!"

"You have to hurry!" Loge called after me. "That man has done something he shouldn't have done!"

Mike Leviticus had indeed done something he shouldn't have done; he'd shot off most of the pressure gauges from the control pipes. One steam pipe had ruptured while he was about it, and when I found him I wished I hadn't. He'd taken a blast of live, superheated steam full in the face and was now lying on the floor of the Pressure Control Room, very done and very dead.

rrrrrrrrr

The walls of the room began to shake. I made a hasty departure from the Pressure Control Room and sprinted back along the corridor toward the elevator at the far end. The pipes overhead had begun to glow cherry red and were doing some serious banging. What I suspected had happened was that, with the pressure control valves on the pipes suddenly blown away, the giant main conduits, stretching perhaps as much as half a mile underground directly into the magma pools of the surrounding ring of volcanoes, were acting as monstrous siphons, out of control, sucking hundreds of tons of magma—here. In a very short time, the entire underground complex was going to be just one more pool of molten rock.

That was for openers. With all the displacement that was going on, there was one hell of a lot of geography moving beneath my fast-running feet.

rrrrruummmmm

Blurp.

The seam of a pipe twenty feet ahead of me ruptured, and a great bubble of steaming, flaming magma began to ooze out. I dove and rolled, feeling the flames singe my hair and burn my back, heard the mass plop behind me. Sulphur gas burned my eyes and clogged my lungs. Coughing, gasping for breath, I grabbed Garth's outstretched hand and let him yank me into the elevator. The doors sighed shut and we began to ascend— much too slowly, as far as I was concerned. I had a distinctly unpleasant sense of having been here before.

Rrrrrruuummmmmmmmble.

"Loge!" I gasped as fumes began to fill the elevator. "What's the fastest fucking way out of here?!"

"I already got that out of him," Garth said, brushing ashes and shreds of burned fabric off my back. "You've got a pretty good burn there, brother."

"You ain't seen nothin' yet unless we get out of here! I mean, like ten minutes ago! This place is *gone!*"

"There's an access tunnel a hundred yards to our left," Garth said, stopping the elevator on the second level. Garth slapped Loge—hard. "Is that right, you son-of-a-bitch?"

Loge, blood dripping from the corner of his mouth, nodded, swallowed hard. "It's twenty degrees below zero up on the surface. We'll freeze to death without coats."

"*Go,* jerk-off!" I said, goosing Loge as the door opened and Garth sprinted off down the corridor. I wasn't about to let our resident mad scientist entertain any suicidal thoughts; he was too important to our future—assuming we had one.

We reached the huge mouth of a tunnel of corrugated steel sloping upwards. Garth slapped a button on the wall, and a door slid back far up at the opposite end to reveal a square of pale, ice-blue sky. A blast of frigid air blew into our faces, a rather unpleasant complement to the burning at our backs. I felt I knew what a minute steak feels like just before it's dropped on the grill.

"You know how to fly a plane?!" Garth shouted at me as we ran up the tunnel.

"Nope! You?!"

"Nope! Loge?!"

The old man, staggering along in Garth's firm grasp, merely shook his head.

"Garth, does this mean we're going to have to wing it?!"

"Mongo, that's the *worst* joke you've ever laid on me, and I'm never going to let you forget it!"

"What fucking joke?!"

It didn't make any difference that none of us could fly a plane, because nobody was going to be winging it anywhere in Mike Leviticus's plane.

GGGrrruuuuuMMMBLE.

The force of the tremor knocked us to the ground. We got up, stumbled out of the mouth of the tunnel into the freezing air just in time to see the jet lazily topple over and disappear into a quarter-mile-long fissure that had opened in the ground.

Flaming magma was bubbling up in the tunnel behind us, and the huge glass dome was beginning to glow.

"What now?" Garth asked. "You want to stay here and cook, or move out and freeze?"

"I'm not sure it makes a difference. I've got a feeling that one or more of the volcanoes around us is going to blow. If that happens, we could be in serious trouble."

"They will all erupt," Loge said distantly. "My estimate is that we have less than fifteen minutes. We are dead men."

"Garth," I said, "I'm going to see if I can reach Leviticus's plane. There may be some survival gear in it."

I was twenty yards out over the trembling, frozen tundra when Garth's shout stopped me. I turned, then looked toward the west, where his finger was pointing. Just above the horizon, something silver glinted in the sunlight. The plane was flying low and fast, heading directly toward us.

Ah. Rescue.

GGGrrruuuuuMMMBLE.

The problem was that the pilot couldn't land; if he did, the chances were very good that the same thing would happen to his plane that had happened to Leviticus's. The entire area inside the circle of volcanoes was shaking, cracking like glass. The glass dome had burst, and magma was flowing out in uneven, smoking rivers on all sides.

Rescue would have been very nice, I thought, but it made no sense at all to feed one more body into the outraged earth. I staggered across the shaking ground, frantically trying to wave the plane off.

The pilot not only ignored me, but almost decapitated me as he swooped in over my head. Just before I sprawled on the ice, I caught a glimpse in the cockpit of a grimly smiling face that looked familiar.

Getting up unsteadily, shivering, I turned in time to see the plane land, skid, spin around in a couple of circles, then straighten around and taxi toward us. I walked back to Garth and Loge, stood and watched in amazement as the plane stopped and Mr. Lippitt, carrying a huge BAR machine gun over his shoulder, stepped out, hopped over a rivulet of hissing lava that was flowing beneath the training jet, then casually strolled toward us.

"Why did you lie to us about Lippitt?" I asked Loge.

Loge stared at me, his eyes filled with sadness. "I was certain he was going to be dead soon, anyway," the scientist said. "It was only a matter of time. I badly wanted the two of you to commit to me and join me in bearing witness. I knew you wouldn't do that if you maintained any hope of rescue, and so I wanted to destroy that hope."

"What about the other man?"

Loge shrugged sadly. "He escaped too."

RRRRRUUUUUmmmmmmmmmmm.

It was one of the volcanoes to the west erupting, throwing flame, smoke and lava a mile into the sky. The earth shook, throwing us all to the ground. Lippitt's plane turned, one of the wings fell off, and it crashed over on its side. Lippitt didn't even bother to look back.

"I think you just lost something," I said as the Defense Intelligence Agency operative came up.

"I see the Fredericksons have everything under control," Lippitt said, dropping the BAR to the ground and hooking his thumbs in the ammunition belts that crossed his chest. "It figures."

"What?!" Garth and I exclaimed in unison.

"Don't worry about the plane; there are others where that came from. There's a U.N. task force on the way, and they have helicopters. Thanks to our mutual friend, Mongo, I was finally able to talk to some good guys . . . and our friend did a little of his mental nudging. He'd picked up the coordinates for this place from Stryder London, of course."

The horizon was growing dark with smoke and ash, and there were no planes in sight.

"Uh, Lippitt . . ."

"Not to worry, Mongo. They'll be here. By the way, you two are looking considerably better than you were the last time I saw you. Garth, you seem to have lost a little hair."

"Yeah," Garth said, looking nervously up at the sky.

"Any hostiles around?"

"No," I said tersely. "There's just us chickens—and I don't have to tell you what kind of chickens we're going to be if your people don't get here fast. What are *you* doing here?"

"You mean before the others? I took that particular plane because it was the fastest one on the base. I figured you might need a little help. Of course, I was wrong. I'm glad I didn't get here any sooner; I'd probably only have gotten in your way."

RRRRRUUUUUUMMMBLE.

"How'd you know we were here?"

"You can't be serious. This is where the action is, right? This is where the evil wizard himself hangs out, right? Where else would Mongo and Garth Frederickson be?"

"You're fucking crazy, Lippitt," Garth said as we stepped aside to avoid a thick stream of lava that flowed past us, to our right. It joined the stream that was flowing to our left, encircling us in a ring of fire. "What if this place had been full of Warriors? Did you think you were going to shoot your way in, blow everybody away, and take us out all by yourself?"

Lippitt smiled thinly. "Hanging around with the Fredericksons must have made me a little soft in the head."

GGGRRROOOOOOOOOOORRRRR.

"Lippitt," I said through lips that already felt half-cooked, "you don't seem to be much worried about all this, but that was another volcano that just went."

"Hell, I'm not worried because I'm with you. I've decided that you and your brother are indestructible; you wouldn't die if somebody threw you out of an airplane. As long as I'm with you two, I'm convinced everything is going to turn out just fine." He paused, glanced at his watch, continued seriously: "Don't worry, Mongo; they'll get here. Five minutes."

"Damn it, Lippitt, I'm not worried about them getting here! I'm worried about us *being* here when they get here!"

"Mr. Lippitt," Siegmund Loge said, speaking for the first time since the D.I.A. operative had arrived, "we *must* be rescued. My work can be reconstructed if I'm alive, and that work must be done. When I explain, you'll see why this is so. You can't imagine the danger humanity faces."

Lippitt took a .45-caliber automatic from the pocket of his parka, put the gun to Siegmund Loge's head and shot him through the brain.

EPILOGUE

Rafferty, on horseback, waved to us from the hilltop where Hugo and Golly were buried. We waved back.

"You still feel lousy?" Garth asked as he tugged at his fishing line, which had become tangled on an underwater log in the stream that ran through our parents' farm.

"Yeah." Something was nibbling on my hook, but I didn't tug on the line. I didn't feel like killing anything.

"Me, too."

"Well, we spent a lot of time with lousy people, so I guess it's going to take some time for us to stop feeling lousy."

"That's not the reason we feel lousy, and you know it. What if he was right?"

"Shut up, Garth," I said, meaning it.

"He may have been stone fucking crazy, but that doesn't mean he wasn't right. If he was right, and the Valhalla Project was the only way to save the human race, do you know what that makes us?"

"It doesn't make us anything. Even if he was right, he didn't have the right to do what he was doing. Our only responsibility is to live our own lives in the best, most honorable, way possible. Now, I don't want to talk about it anymore."

"We have to talk about it sometime, Mongo."

"Not today."

"Okay. How long have we all been holed up here?"

"Going on four months."

"When do you want to go back to New York?"

"Not today."

"I'll drink to that."

"You drink too much now, Garth. So do I."

"As long as the government is willing to pay for a ring of guards around this place to keep people away from us, we may as well just sit here and wait until we get our heads straight."

"Booze doesn't help."

"So we'll start drying out. Today."

"Today."

"You talk to your people at the university?"

"Once a week. They want me back, but they're not pressing. What about the NYPD?"

"They want me back, but they're not pressing. There are one hell of a lot of people waiting to ask us questions, Mongo."

"What are you going to tell them?"

"I'm not going to tell a damn, fucking thing to anybody. I'm not going to make up stories about where we've been, or what happened. I'm just not going to say anything."

"Agreed. We'll let Lippitt take the responsibility for deciding who should be told what."

"I wonder what the hell is happening in the outside world?"

"I don't know, and I don't give a shit."

"Mongo, we should really start reading newspapers and watching television again."

"Not today."

Our parents and Lippitt, on their daily walk, emerged from the apple orchard across the stream. Their arms linked, they ambled slowly in our direction along the opposite bank. Garth and I might have felt a tad depressed, but our mother and father certainly didn't; they hadn't stopped grinning since the day, four months before, when Lippitt, driving a sleek government limousine, had pulled into their driveway. And they never seemed to tire of Lippitt's company, nor he of theirs. My mother looked radiant, my father looked ten years younger. Lippitt looked . . . like Lippitt.

"Mongo, just for the sake of argument, let's assume he was right. Maybe, if we told people, it could change the outcome."

"Loge said no. Let Lippitt decide; he's the one with the direct phone lines to the White House, Congress, and the Pentagon. Maybe he's already told them."

"No," Garth said. "He may have told them everything else, and he's probably directing the cleanup operation . . . but he hasn't told them what the Valhalla Project was really all about. I'm certain of it. He's still mulling it over, trying to decide what to do next. The same with Rafferty. If either had made that decision, there'd be no reason for them to stay holed up here with us. Lippitt talks only on the telephone; he's no more ready to go back than we are."

"Hey, you two fishermen!" my mother called, waving to us from across the stream. "Come on back now and wash up. Lunch is in half an hour, and you're getting your favorite dessert."

"Okay, Mom," I said, starting to reel in my line.

"Xavier just *never* seems to run out of stories about the two of you." She paused, put on a mock frown. "But he says you curse a great deal."

Garth and I looked at each other, and we both started howling with laughter.

"Xavier?!"

Lippitt's frown was genuine as he stepped to the bank, put his arm gently around my mother's waist and pointed a very menacing forefinger in our direction. "I'll always be Mr. Lippitt to the two of you, and don't you ever forget it!"

"Come on," I said, rising to my feet as our parents and a stiff-backed Lippitt continued on down the bank, toward the house. "Xavier will be cranky if we're late for lunch."

"Okay," Garth said, still chuckling. "Just give me a minute to get this line free."

"The hell with the line."

Shhh.

Praise for
CAESAR'S WOMEN

"AN EXQUISITELY RESEARCHED
AND RICHLY IMAGINATIVE EPIC."
The Hollywood Reporter

"WONDERFUL...
COLLEEN McCULLOUGH RETAINS
HER GREAT SKILL AS A STORYTELLER...
The great names of ancient Rome
are the richly drawn characters
of this novel...McCullough's words give them
flesh and bones and speech and sight."
Newark Star-Ledger

"CRAMMED WITH PAINSTAKING DETAIL.
ITS SWEEP IS PANORAMIC"
Philadelphia Inquirer

"EPIC...
Marvelously researched and detailed...
With great brio...McCullough captures
the driven, passionate soul of ancient Rome."
Publishers Weekly

"DELIGHTFUL...
Rich in detail and well-plotted."
Chattanooga Times

"A PLEASURE...
A muscular, convincing re-creation
of Rome's political arena—
and some legendary combatants."
Kirkus Reviews

Other Avon Books by
Colleen McCullough

THE FIRST MAN IN ROME
FORTUNE'S FAVORITES
THE GRASS CROWN

THE LADIES OF MISSALONGHI
A CREED FOR THE THIRD MILLENNIUM
AN INDECENT OBSESSION
THE THORN BIRDS
TIM

COLLEEN
McCULLOUGH

CAESAR'S WOMEN

AVON BOOKS ◆ NEW YORK

For Selwa Anthony Dennis
Wisewoman, witch, warm and wonderful

AVON BOOKS
A division of
The Hearst Corporation
1350 Avenue of the Americas
New York, New York 10019

Copyright © 1996 by Colleen McCullough
Inside cover author photo by Anthony Browell
Published by arrangement with the author
Library of Congress Catalog Card Number: 95-34498
ISBN: 0-380-71084-6

Published in hardcover by William Morrow and Company, Inc.; for information address Permissions Department, William Morrow and Company, Inc., 1350 Avenue of the Americas, New York, New York 10019.

First Avon Books Printing: February 1997

AVON TRADEMARK REG. U.S. PAT. OFF. AND IN OTHER COUNTRIES, MARCA
REGISTRADA, HECHO EN U.S.A.

Printed in the U.S.A.

OPM 10 9 8 7 6 5 4 3

LIST OF MAPS
AND ILLUSTRATIONS

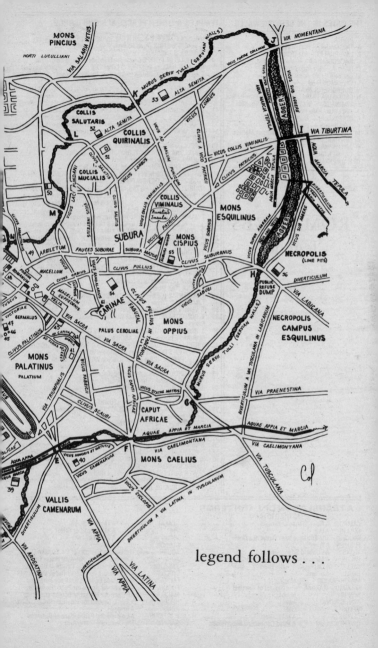

legend follows . . .

THE GATES IN THE SERVIAN WALLS

PORTA
A TRIGEMINA — Port of Rome
B LAVERNALIS — Via Ostiensis
C RAUDUSCULANA — Via Ostiensis
D NAEVIA — Via Ardeatina
E CAPENA — Via Appia & Via Latina
F CAELIMONTANA — Via Tusculana
G QUERQUETULANA — Via Praenestina
H ESQUILINA — Via Labicana & Via Praenestina
I VIMINALIS — Via Collatina & Via Tiburtina
J COLLINA — Via Nomentana
K QUIRINALIS — Via Salaria Vetus
L SALUTARIS — Via Flaminia
M SANQUALIS — Via Lata & Campus Martius
N FONTINALIS — Campus Martius
O TRIUMPHALIS — Triumphal Parades Only
P CARMENTALIS — Circus Flaminius
Q FLUMENTANA — Circus Flaminius

ROMA URBS
legend

TEMPLES & OTHER PLACES of SIGNIFICANCE

1 MAUSOLEUM OF THE JULII CAESARES (Hypothetically Sited)
2 T. VENUS VICTRIX (Atop Pompey's Auditorium)
3 POMPEY'S THEATER
4 PORTICUS OF POMPEY, with the Hundred-Pillared Colonnade
5 MEETING HALL OF POMPEY'S COMPLEX (Site of Caesar's Murder)
6 T. HERCULIS MUSARUM (Hercules & the Nine Muses)
7 FOUR TEMPLES   ? Juno Curitis (Juno of Meetings)
8 ADJACENT TO   ? Fortunae Huiusce Diei (Today's Luck)
9 POMPEY'S   ? FERONIA (Freedom For Slaves)
10 THEATER COMPLEX   ? Lares Permarini (Lares of the Seafarer)
11 OLD PORTICUS MINUCIA IN THE CIRCUS FLAMINIUS
12 TEMPLES   Vulcan (Fire, Earthquakes, Smiths)
13 OF THE CIRCUS   Hercules Custos (Guardian of the Circus)
14 FLAMINIUS   Mars Invictus (Undefeated Mars)
15 PORTICUS of the METELLI
16 T. APOLLO SOSIANUS (Medicine & Healing)
17 T. BELLONA & "ENEMY TERRITORY" (Foreign War)
18 T. JUNO REGINA (Juno the Ruler)
19 T. JUPITER STATOR (Stayer of Soldiers in Retreat)
20a POSSIBLE SITE OF NEW PORTICUS MINUCIA — OR POMPEY'S VILLA?
20b POSSIBLE SITE OF NEW PORTICUS MINUCIA — T. DIANA
21 FOUR TEMPLES — PIETAS, JANUS, SPES (Hope), JUNO SOSPITA
22 TWO TEMPLES   T. FORTUNA (Chastity & Virginity)
23 OF ALLIED CULTS   T. MATER MATUTA (Childbearing)
24 T. PORTUNUS (Ports & Port Trades)
25 T. JANUS (Doorways, Both In & Out, Beginnings & Ends)
26 THREE CENTERS   HERCULES OLIVARIUS (Oil Merchants)
27 FOR THE WORSHIP   ARA MAXIMA HERCULIS (Great Altar)
28 OF HERCULES   HERCULES INVICTUS (Undefeated Hercules)
29 T. CERES (Bounty) — Headquarters of the Plebeian Aediles
30 T. FLORA (Vegetation)
31 TWO TEMPLES FOR ALLIED   JUNO REGINA FOR WOMEN
32 CULTS OF THE FREE CITIZEN   JUPITER LIBERTAS for MEN
33 SACRED PRECINCT of the ARMILUSTRIUM (Mars, the Army, the Salii)
34 T. DIANA (Protectress of Slaves)
35 T. LUNA (The Moon)
36 T. JUVENTAS (Coming of Age for Roman Citizen Males)
37 T. MERCURY (Trade) — Headquarters of Guild of Merchants
38 T. VENUS OBSEQUENS (Protectress of Prostitutes & Adulterers)
39 T. BONA DEA (Protectress of Women) & SAXUM SACRUM (Sacred Rock)
40 T. HONOS ET VIRTUS (A Cult for Military Commanders)
41 CURIAE VETERES — THE ANCIENT MEETING HALLS
42 BIRTHPLACE of GAIUS OCTAVIUS, LATER AUGUSTUS (Hypothetical)
43 T. JUPITER STATOR (Stayer of Soldiers in Retreat)
44 THE LUPERCAL (Cave of the Suckling Wolf of Romulus)
45 THE ROUND HUT OF ROMULUS (Carefully Preserved)
46 THE MUNDUS (A Vent of the Underworld)
47 T. MATER MAGNA (The Asian Great Goddess)
48 BASILICA JULIA (Replaced Basilicae Sempronia & Opimia)
49 FORUM JULIUM
50 T. SEMO SANCUS DIUS FIDIUS (Oaths & Treaties)
51 HOUSE OF TITUS POMPONIUS ATTICUS (Hypothetical)
52 T. SALUS (Good Health)
53 T. QUIRINUS (The Roman Citizen)
54 T. TELLUS (The Roman Earth Goddess)
55 T. JUNO LUCINA (Registry of Roman Citizen Births)
56 T. VENUS LIBITINA (Registry of Roman Citizen Deaths)—Hypothetical
57 T. AESCULAPIUS (Medicine) & SHIP of the PRECINCT ON THE INSULA
58 SEWER OUTLET FOR QUIRINAL & CAMPUS MARTIUS (R. Petronia)
59 CLOACA MAXIMA — SEWER OUTLET FOR SUBURA, Etc. (R. Spinon)
60 SEWER OUTLET FOR ESQUILINE, CIRCUS, Etc. (R. Nodinus)
61 TIGILLUM (Yoke), SHRINES of JUNO SORORIA (Puberty of Girls) & JANUS CURIATUS (Puberty of Boys) — Site Hypothetical

A TRANSLATION OF LATIN TERMS
(AS USED HEREIN)

CAMPUS	A Flat Expanse of Ground		SCALAE	A Flight of Steps
COLLIS	A Hill		VIA	A Main Road or Street
FAUCES	The Entrance to or Outlet of a Defile		VICUS	A Street or Lane
FLUMEN	A River		CLOACA	A Sewer
MONS	An Upland Spur or Ridge		AGGER	The Double Rampart of the Esquiline
PALUS	A Marshy Area with Many Springs		AQUA	A Water Channel, Above or Below Ground
VALLIS	A Depression in the Ground		BASILICA	Clerestory-Lit Hall for Courts or Business
HORTI	Gardens		CIRCUS	An Enclosure for Chariot Races and Games
MAIOR-MAJOR	Major		EMPORIUM	A Dockside Building for Trade Purposes
MAXIMUS-MAXIMA	The Biggest or Greatest		FORUM	An Open-Air Space for Public Business
MINOR	Minor		MACELLUM	An Open-Air Market of Booths and Stalls
NOVUS-NOVA	New		NECROPOLIS	A Burial Ground for Inhumation/Cremation
VETUS	Old		PONS	A Bridge
CLIVUS	A Hilly Street		PORTICUS	A Colonnaded Public Place of Business
DIVERTICULUM	A Road Connecting Main Roads		SAEPTA	The Centurate Voting Area

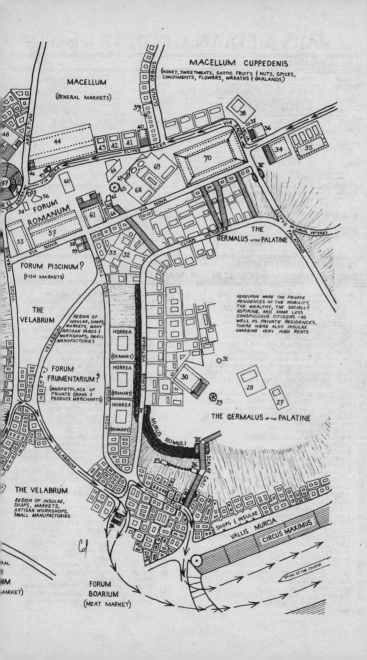

MACELLUM CUPPEDENIS
(HONEY, SWEETMEATS, EXOTIC FRUITS & NUTS, SPICES,
CONDIMENTS, FLOWERS, WREATHS & GARLANDS)

MACELLUM
(GENERAL MARKETS)

CLIVUS ORBIUS

39

38
37
36

VIA SACRA

40
43 42 41

CLIVUS SACER

44

48

35
34

70

VIA SACRA

47

46 45

VIA SACRA

60

66
69

VIA NOVA

68

65

FORUM
ROMANUM

56
54

61

62
64

VIA NOVA

53
57

CLIVUS VICTORIAE

THE
GERMALUS of the PALATINE

CLIVUS AD CURIAS VETERES

59
58

33
32

FORUM PISCINUM?
(FISH MARKETS)

THE
VELABRUM

REGION OF INSULAE, SHOPS,
MARKETS, MANY
ARTISAN YARDS &
WORKSHOPS, SMALL
MANUFACTORIES

VICUS TUSCUS

HEREUPON WERE THE PRIVATE
RESIDENCES OF THE NOBILITY,
THE WEALTHY, THE SOCIALLY
ASPIRING, AND SOME LESS
CONSPICUOUS CITIZENS —AS
WELL AS PRIVATE RESIDENCES,
THERE WERE ALSO INSULAE
CHARGING VERY HIGH RENTS

VICUS TUSCUS

HORREA
(GRANARY)

CLIVUS VICTORIAE

VELABRUM

FORUM
FRUMENTARIUM?
(MARKETPLACE OF
PRIVATE GRAIN &
PRODUCE MERCHANTS)

HORREA
(GRANARY)

31

30

28

29

27

HORREA
(GRANARY)

THE GERMALUS of the PALATINE

MURUS ROMULI

SCALAE CACI

THE VELABRUM

REGION OF INSULAE,
SHOPS, MARKETS,
ARTISAN WORKSHOPS,
SMALL MANUFACTORIES

25

26

VICUS TUSCUS

SHOPS & INSULAE

VELABRUM

Col

VALLIS MURCIA   CIRCUS MAXIMUS

AL

M
MARKET)

FORUM
BOARIUM
(MEAT MARKET)

SPINA OF THE COURSE

PARS MEDIANA ROMAE legend

A TRANSLATION of LATIN TERMS

ASYLUM	A SACRED PLACE or REFUGE	PORTA	A GATE IN A DEFENSIVE WALL
BASILICA	A CLERESTORY-LIT HALL FOR STATE BUSINESS & COMMERCE	PORTICUS	A COLONNADED PLACE FOR PUBLIC BUSINESS & COMMERCE
CAMPUS	A FLAT EXPANSE OF GROUND	SCALAE	A FLIGHT OF STEPS
CIRCUS	AN ENCLOSURE FOR CHARIOT RACES & GAMES	VALLIS	A DEPRESSION IN THE GROUND
		VIA	A MAIN STREET or ROAD
CLIVUS	A HILLY STREET	VICUS	A MINOR STREET or LANE
DOMUS	A ONE-FAMILY CITY HOUSE (of One to Four Storeys)	VILLA	A LARGE COUNTRY HOUSE
DOMUS PUBLICUS	A STATE-OWNED DWELLING INHABITED BY A MAJOR PONTIFEX or FLAMEN		. . . IN THE SENSE USED HEREIN
FORUM	AN OPEN-AIR GATHERING-PLACE FOR STATE BUSINESS OR PRIVATE COMMERCE		
HORREA	A WAREHOUSE, also A GRANARY		
INSULA	A BUILDING for MULTIPLE OCCUPANCY (Between Three & Twelve Storeys High)		**GATES**
MACELLUM	AN OPEN-AIR MARKET of STALLS & BOOTHS		
MURUS	A DEFENSIVE WALL		
PODIUM	A HIGH PLATFORM ELEVATING A TEMPLE, CONTAINING USABLE SPACE WITHIN IT		

GATES

I	CARMENTALIS	}	IN THE SERVIAN WALLS
II	TRIUMPHALIS	}	
III	FONTINALIS		
IV	MUGONIA	}	IN THE ANCIENT WALLS OF THE PALATINE CITY OF ROMULUS
V	ROMULANA	}	
VI	CACANA		

TEMPLES, OTHER PLACES AND BUILDINGS of INTEREST IN THE HEART OF ROME

1 HOUSE OF GAIUS MARIUS (Exact Site Unknown)
2 T. JUNO MONETA (Giver of Timely Warnings) THE MINT LAY BENEATH, INSIDE ITS PODIUM
3 T. VENUS ERUCINA (Protectress of Prostitutes)
4 T. MENS (Goddess of Proper Roman Thinking)
5 THE LAUTUMIAE PRISON
6 TULLIANUM or CARCER
7 T. CONCORD (Amicable Co-existence of Classes)
8 SENACULUM (Ambassadorial Reception Hall)
9 TABULARIUM (Repository of Records & Laws)
10 T. VEDIOVIS (Young Jupiter, God of Disappointments)
11 PORTICUS DEORUM CONSENTIUM (The Twelve Gods)
12 T. JUPITER FERETRIUS (Treaties & Armaments)
13 T. JUPITER OPTIMUS MAXIMUS
14 T. FORTUNA PRIMIGENIA (Protectress of First Born)
15 T. HONOS ET VIRTUS (Cult for Military Commanders)
16 T. OPS (Plenty) AN EMERGENCY FUND OF SILVER BULLION WAS STORED INSIDE ITS PODIUM
17 THE TARPEIAN ROCK
18 T. FIDES (Good Faith)
19 T. BELLONA (War with Foreign Powers)
20 "ENEMY TERRITORY"
21 T. APOLLO SOSIANUS (Medicine & Healing)
22 T. MATER MATUTA (Mothers & Childbearing)
23 T. FORTUNA (Virgins & Prepubescent Girls)
24 T. JANUS (Doorways, Beginnings & Ends)
25 SHRINE of the GENIUS LOCI (Procreative Power)
26 CAVE of the LUPERCAL (The Suckling She-Wolf)
27 HOUSE of LUCIUS SERGIUS CATILINA (Exact Site Unknown)
28 HOUSE of QUINTUS HORTENSIUS HORTALUS (Site Known)
29 THE ROUND HUT of ROMULUS
30 T. MAGNA MATER (The Asian Great Goddess)
31 THE MUNDUS (A Vent of the Underworld)
32 HOUSE of ① MARCUS LIVIUS DRUSUS ② MARCUS LICINIUS CRASSUS ③ MARCUS TULLIUS CICERO— EXACT SITE IS HYPOTHETICAL
33 HOUSE of ① GNAEUS ② LUCIUS DOMITIUS AHENOBARBUS — SITE IS COMPLETELY IMAGINARY
34 T. JUPITER STATOR (Stayer of Army Retreats)
35 BATHS (Privately Owned) ? Senian Baths
36 T. PENATES (The Public Penates)
37 EQUESTRIAN STATUE of CLOELIA
38 DOMUS PUBLICUS of the REX SACRORUM— "THE KING'S HOUSE" (Site Approximate)
39 INN

40 T. LARES PRAESTITES (The Public Lares)
41 } THE DOMI PUBLICI of the THREE MAJOR
42 } FLAMINES — FLAMEN DIALIS, FLAMEN
43 MARTIALIS, FLAMEN QUIRINALIS (Sites Are Purely Imaginary)
44 BASILICA AEMILIA (Business & Commercial Premises, Some Public Activities, Shops) Also Known as the Basilica Fulvia
45 T. VENUS CLOACINA (Purification of the Waters)
46 T. JANUS (Doorways, Beginnings & Ends)
47 THE WELL OF THE COMITIA & Its Inclusions ⓐ LAPIS NIGER ⓑ ROSTRA
48 OFFICES ATTACHED to the SENATE HOUSE
49 CURIA HOSTILIA (Senate House)
50 BASILICA PORCIA (Business & Commercial Premises, Particularly Banking — College of Tribunes of Plebs Headquartered Here)
51 T. SATURN (Unchanging Prosperity of the Roman State) THE TREASURY (Aerarium) LAY BENEATH, INSIDE THE PODIUM
52 ALTAR of the VOLCANAL (Vulcan Earthshaker)
53 BASILICA OPIMIA (Shops, Business, Courts)
54 TRIBUNAL of VARIOUS MAGISTRATES
55 SACRED TREES & STATUE of SATYR MARSYAS
56 LACUS CURTIUS (Pool of Curtius)
57 BASILICA SEMPRONIA (Shops, Courts, Business)
58 SHRINE of VOLUPIA & STATUE of DIVA ANGERONA
59 TOMB (Shrine) of LARENTIA
60 TRIBUNAL of the PRAETOR URBANUS — MAGISTRATES' STATION
61 T. CASTOR & POLLUX (Standard Weights & Measures Housed Within Podium, Also a Second Base for Tribunes of the Plebs)
62 FONS JUTURNA (Sacred Well of Juturna)
63 CULT SHRINE & STATUE of JUTURNA
64 ROOMS FOR USE OF PILGRIMS to JUTURNA
65 T. VESTA (Hearthfire of the State)
66 THE REGIA (Offices of PONTIFEX MAXIMUS)
67 CULT SHRINE & STATUE of VESTA
68 ATRIUM VESTAE of the DOMUS PUBLICUS (Home of the Vestal Virgins)
69 DOMUS PUBLICUS of the PONTIFEX MAXIMUS
70 PORTICUS MARGARITARIA (Jewelers, Pearl Vendors, Perfumiers, Luxury Shops & Stalls)

CAESAR'S WOMEN

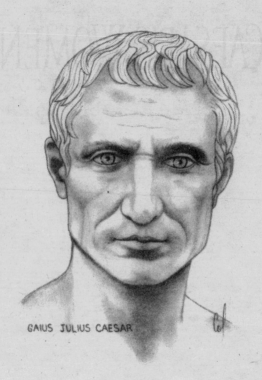

GAIUS JULIUS CAESAR

PART I

---

from JUNE of 68 B.C.
until MARCH of 66 B.C.

SERVILIA

YOUNG BRUTUS

"Brutus, I don't like the look of your skin. Come here to the light, please."

The fifteen-year-old made no sign that he had heard, simply remained hunched over a single sheet of Fannian paper with his reed pen, its ink long since dried, poised in midair.

"Come here, Brutus. At once," said his mother placidly.

He knew her, so down went the pen; though he wasn't *mortally* afraid of her, he wasn't about to court her displeasure. One summons might be safely ignored, but a second summons meant she expected to be obeyed, even by him. Rising, he walked across to where Servilia stood by the window, its shutters wide because Rome was sweltering in an unseasonably early heatwave.

Though she was short and Brutus had recently begun to grow into what she hoped was going to be tallness, his head was not very far above hers; she put up one hand to clutch his chin, and peered closely at several angry red lumps welling under the skin around his mouth. Her hand released him, moved to push the loose dark curls away from his brow: more eruptions!

"How I wish you'd keep your hair cut!" she said, tugging at a lock which threatened to obscure his sight— and tugging hard enough to make his eyes water.

"Mama, short hair is unintellectual," he protested.

"Short hair is practical. It stays off your face and doesn't irritate your skin. Oh, Brutus, what a trial you're becoming!"

"If you wanted a crop-skulled warrior son, Mama, you should have had more boys with Silanus instead of a couple of girls."

"One son is affordable. Two sons stretch the money further than it wants to go. Besides, if I'd given Silanus a son, you wouldn't be his heir as well as your father's." She strode across to the desk where he had been working and stirred the various scrolls upon it with impatient fingers. "Look at this mess! No wonder your shoulders are round and you're swaybacked. Get out onto the Campus Martius with Cassius and the other boys from school, don't waste your time trying to condense the whole of Thucydides onto one sheet of paper.''

"I happen to write the best epitomes in Rome," said her son, his tone lofty.

Servilia eyed him ironically. "Thucydides," she said, "was no profligate with words, yet it took him many books to tell the story of the conflict between Athens and Sparta. What advantage is there in destroying his beautiful Greek so that lazy Romans can crib a bare outline, then congratulate themselves that they know all about the Peloponnesian War?"

"Literature," Brutus persevered, "is becoming too vast for any man to encompass without resorting to summaries."

"Your skin is breaking down," said Servilia, returning to what really interested her.

"That's common enough in boys my age."

"But not in my plans for you."

"And may the Gods help anyone or anything not in your plans for me!" he shouted, suddenly angry.

"Get dressed, we're going out" was all she answered, and left the room.

When he entered the atrium of Silanus's commodious house, Brutus was wearing the purple-bordered toga of childhood, for he would not officially become a man until December and the feast of Juventas arrived. His mother was already waiting, and watched him critically as he came toward her.

Yes, he definitely was round-shouldered, swaybacked. Such a lovely little boy he had been! Lovely even last January, when she had commissioned a bust of him from Antenor, the best portrait sculptor in all Italia. But now puberty was asserting itself more aggressively, his early beauty was fading, even to her prejudiced gaze. His eyes were still large and dark and dreamy, interestingly heavy-lidded, but his nose wasn't growing into the imposing Roman edifice she had hoped for, remaining stubbornly short and bulb-tipped like her own. And the

skin which had been so exquisitely olive-colored, smooth
and flawless, now filled her with dread—what if he was
going to be one of the horribly unlucky ones and produced
such noxious pustules that he scarred? Fifteen was too
soon! Fifteen meant a protracted infestation. Pimples! How
disgusting and mundane. Well, beginning tomorrow she
would make enquiries among the physicians and herbal-
ists—and whether he liked it or not, he was going to the
Campus Martius every day for proper exercise and tutor-
ing in the martial skills he would need when he turned
seventeen and had to enrol in Rome's legions. As a *contubernalis,* of course, not as a mere ranker soldier; he
would be a cadet on the personal staff of some consular
commander who would ask for him by name. His birth
and status assured it.

The steward let them out into the narrow Palatine
street; Servilia turned toward the Forum and began to walk
briskly, her son hurrying to keep up.

"Where are we going?" he asked, still chafing because she had dragged him away from epitomizing Thucydides.

"To Aurelia's."

Had his mind not been wrestling with the problem of
how to pack a mine of information into a single sentence—and had the day been more clement—his heart
would have leaped joyously; instead he groaned. "Oh, not
up into the slums today!"

"Yes."

"It's such a long way, and such a dismal address!"

"The address may be dismal, my son, but the lady
herself is impeccably connected. Everyone will be there."
She paused, her eyes sliding slyly sideways. "Everyone,
Brutus, everyone."

To which he answered not a word.

Her progress rendered easier by two ushering slaves,
Servilia clattered down the Ringmakers' Steps into the
pandemonium of the Forum Romanum, where all the
world adored to gather, listen, watch, wander, rub shoulders with the Mighty. Neither Senate nor one of the Assemblies was meeting today and the courts were on a short

vacation, but some of the Mighty were out and about nonetheless, distinguished by the bobbing red-thonged bundles of rods their lictors carried shoulder-high to proclaim their imperium.

"It's so hilly, Mama! Can't you slow down?" panted Brutus as his mother marched up the Clivus Orbius on the far side of the Forum; he was sweating profusely.

"If you exercised more, you wouldn't need to complain," said Servilia, unimpressed.

Nauseating smells of foetor and decay assailed Brutus's nostrils as the towering tenements of the Subura pressed in and shut out the light of the sun; peeling walls oozed slime, the gutters guided dark and syrupy trickles into gratings, tiny unlit caverns that were shops passed by unnumbered. At least the dank shade made it cooler, but this was a side of Rome young Brutus could happily have done without, "everyone" notwithstanding.

Eventually they arrived outside a quite presentable door of seasoned oak, well carved into panels and owning a brightly polished *orichalcum* knocker in the form of a lion's head with gaping jaws. One of Servilia's attendants plied it vigorously, and the door opened at once. There stood an elderly, rather plump Greek freedman, bowing deeply as he let them in.

It was a gathering of women, of course; had Brutus only been old enough to put on his plain white *toga virilis,* graduate into the ranks of men, he would not have been allowed to accompany his mother. That thought provoked panic—Mama must succeed in her petition, he must be able to continue to see his darling love after December and manhood! But betraying none of this, he abandoned Servilia's skirts the moment the gushing greetings began and slunk off into a quiet corner of the squeal-filled room, there to do his best to blend into the unpretentious decor.

"Brutus, *ave,*" said a light yet husky voice.

He turned his head, looked down, felt his chest cave in. *"Ave, Julia."*

"Here, sit with me," the daughter of the house commanded, leading him to a pair of small chairs right in the corner. She settled in one while he lowered himself awkwardly into the other, herself as graceful and composed as a nesting swan.

Only eight years old—how could she already be so beautiful? wondered the dazzled Brutus, who knew her well because his mother was a great friend of her grandmother's. Fair like ice and snow, chin pointed, cheekbones arched, faintly pink lips as delicious as a strawberry, a pair of widely opened blue eyes that gazed with gentle liveliness on all that they beheld; if Brutus had dipped into the poetry of love, it was because of her whom he had loved for—oh, years! Not truly understanding that it was love until quite recently, when she had turned her gaze on him with such a sweet smile that realization had dawned with the shock of a thunderclap.

He had gone to his mother that very evening, and informed her that he wished to marry Julia when she grew up.

Servilia had stared, astonished. "My dear Brutus, she's a mere child! You'd have to wait nine or ten years for her."

"She'll be betrothed long before she's old enough to marry," he had answered, his anguish plain. "Please, Mama, as soon as her father returns home, petition for her hand in marriage!"

"You may well change your mind."

"Never, never!"

"Her dowry is minute."

"But her birth is everything you could want in my wife."

"True." The black eyes which could grow so hard rested on his face not unsympathetically; Servilia appreciated the strength of that argument. So she had turned it over in her mind for a moment, then nodded. "Very well, Brutus, when her father is next in Rome, I'll ask. You don't need a rich bride, but it is essential that her birth match your own, and a Julia would be ideal. Especially this Julia. Patrician on both sides."

And so they had left it to wait until Julia's father returned from his post as quaestor in Further Spain. The most junior of the important magistracies, quaestor. But trust Servilia to know that Julia's father had filled it extremely well. Odd that she had never met him, considering how small a group the true aristocrats of Rome were. She was one; he was another. But, feminine rumor had it, he was something of an outsider among his own kind, too busy for the social round most of his peers cultivated whenever they were in Rome. It would have been easier to sue for his daughter's hand on Brutus's behalf did she know him already, though she had little doubt what his answer would be. Brutus was highly eligible, even in the eyes of a Julian.

Aurelia's reception room could not compare to a Palatine atrium, but it was quite large enough comfortably to hold the dozen or so women who had invaded it. Open shutters looked out onto what was commonly regarded as a lovely garden, thanks to Gaius Matius in the other ground-floor apartment; his was the hand had found roses able to bloom in the shade, coaxed grapevines into scaling the twelve storeys of latticed walls and balconies, trimmed box bushes into perfect globes, and rigged a cunning gravity feed to the chaste marble pool that allowed a rearing two-tailed dolphin to spout water from its fearsome mouth.

The walls of the reception room were well kept up and painted in the red style, the floor of cheap terrazzo had been burnished to an appealing reddish-pink glow, and the ceiling had been painted to simulate a cloud-fluffed noon sky, though it could claim no expensive gilding. Not the residence of one of the Mighty, but adequate for a junior senator, Brutus supposed as he sat watching Julia, watching the women; Julia caught him, so he looked too.

His mother had seated herself next to Aurelia on a couch, where she managed to display herself to good advantage despite the fact that her hostess was, even at the age of fifty-five, still held one of Rome's great beauties. Aurelia's figure was elegantly slim and it suited her to be in repose, for one didn't notice then that when she moved it was too briskly for grace. No hint of grey marred her ice-brown hair, and her skin was smooth, creamy. It was she who had recommended Brutus's school to Servilia, for she was Servilia's chief confidante.

From that thought Brutus's mind skipped to school, a typical digression for a mind which did tend to wander. His mother had not wished to send Brutus to school, afraid her little boy would be exposed to children of inferior rank and wealth, and worried that his studious nature would be laughed at. Better that Brutus have his own tutor at home. But then Brutus's stepfather had insisted that this only son needed the stimulus and competition of a school. "Some healthy activity and ordinary playmates" was how Silanus had put it, not precisely jealous of the first place Brutus held in Servilia's heart, more concerned that when Brutus matured he should at least have learned to associate with various kinds of people. Naturally the school Aurelia recommended was an exclusive one, but pedagogues who ran schools had a distressingly independent turn of mind that led them to accept bright boys from less rarefied backgrounds than a Marcus Junius Brutus, not to mention two or three bright girls.

With Servilia for mother, it was inevitable that Brutus should hate school, though Gaius Cassius Longinus, the fellow pupil of whom Servilia approved most, was from quite as good a family as a Junius Brutus. Brutus, however, tolerated Cassius only because to do so kept his mother happy. What had he in common with a loud and turbulent boy like Cassius, enamored of war, strife, deeds of great daring? Only the fact that he had quickly become teacher's pet had managed to reconcile Brutus to the awful ordeal of school. And fellows like Cassius.

Unfortunately the person Brutus most yearned to call friend was his Uncle Cato; but Servilia refused to hear of his establishing any kind of intimacy with her despised half brother. Uncle Cato was descended, she never tired of reminding her son, from a Tusculan peasant and a Celtiberian slave, whereas in Brutus were united two separate lines of exalted antiquity, one from Lucius Junius Brutus, the founder of the Republic (who had deposed the last King of Rome, Tarquinius Superbus), and the other from Gaius Servilius Ahala (who had killed Maelius when Maelius had attempted to make himself King of Rome some decades into the new Republic). Therefore a Junius Brutus who was through his mother also a patrician Servilius could not possibly associate with upstart trash like Uncle Cato.

"But your mother married Uncle Cato's father and had two children by him, Aunt Porcia and Uncle Cato!" Brutus had protested on one occasion.

"And thereby disgraced herself forever!" snarled Servilia. "I do not acknowledge either that union or its progeny—and neither, my lad, will you!"

End of discussion. And the end of all hope that he might be allowed to see Uncle Cato any more frequently than family decency indicated. What a wonderful fellow Uncle Cato was! A true Stoic, enamored of Rome's old austere ways, averse to splash and show, quick to criticize the pretensions to potentatic grandeur of men like Pompey. Pompey the Great. Another upstart dismally lacking in the right ancestors. Pompey who had murdered Brutus's father, made a widow of his mother, enabled a lightweight like sickly Silanus to climb into her bed and sire two bubble-headed girls Brutus grudgingly called sisters—

"What are you thinking, Brutus?" asked Julia, smiling.

"Oh, nothing much," he answered vaguely.

"That's an evasion. I want the truth!"

"I was thinking what a terrific fellow my Uncle Cato is."

Her wide brow crinkled. "Uncle Cato?"

"You wouldn't know him, because he's not old enough to be in the Senate yet. In fact, he's almost as close to my age as he is to Mama's."

"Is he the one who wouldn't permit the tribunes of the plebs to pull down an obstructing column inside the Basilica Porcia?"

"That's my Uncle Cato!" said Brutus proudly.

Julia shrugged. "My father said it was stupid of him. If the column had been demolished, the tribunes of the plebs would have enjoyed more comfortable headquarters."

"Uncle Cato was in the right. Cato the Censor put the column there when he built Rome's first basilica, and there it belongs according to the *mos maiorum*. Cato the Censor allowed the tribunes of the plebs to use his building as their headquarters because he understood their plight—because they are magistrates elected by the Plebs alone, they don't represent the whole People, and can't use a temple as their headquarters. But he didn't give them the building, only the use of a part of it. They were grateful enough *then*. Now they want to alter what Cato the Censor paid to build. Uncle Cato won't condone the defacement of his great-grandfather's landmark and namesake."

Since Julia was by nature a peacemaker and disliked argument, she smiled again and rested her hand on Brutus's arm, squeezing it affectionately. He was such a spoiled baby, Brutus, so stuffy and full of self-importance, yet she had known him for a long time, and—though she didn't quite know why—felt very sorry for him. Perhaps it was because his mother was such a—a *snaky* person?

"Well, that happened before my Aunt Julia and my mother died, so I daresay no one will ever demolish the column now," she said.

"Your father's due home," said Brutus, mind veering to marriage.

"Any day." Julia wriggled happily. "Oh, I do miss him!"

"They say he's stirring up trouble in Italian Gaul on the far side of the river Padus," said Brutus, unconsciously echoing the subject becoming a lively debate among the group of women around Aurelia and Servilia.

"Why should he do that?" Aurelia was asking, straight dark brows knitted. The famous purple eyes were glowering. "Truly, there are times when Rome and Roman noblemen disgust me! Why is it *my* son they always single out for criticism and political gossip?"

"Because he's too tall, too handsome, too successful with the women, and too arrogant by far," said Cicero's wife, Terentia, as direct as she was sour. "Besides," added she who was married to a famous wordsmith and orator, "he has such a wonderful way with both the spoken and the written word."

"Those qualities are innate, none of them merits the slanders of some I could mention by name!" snapped Aurelia.

"Lucullus, you mean?" asked Pompey's wife, Mucia Tertia.

"No, he at least can't be blamed for it," Terentia said. "I imagine King Tigranes and Armenia are occupying *him* to the exclusion of anything in Rome save the knights who can't make enough out of gathering the taxes in his provinces."

"Bibulus is who you mean, now he's back in Rome," said a majestic figure seated in the best chair. Alone among a colorful band, she was clad from head to foot in white, so draped that it concealed whatever feminine charms she might have owned. Upon her regal head there reared a crown made of seven layered sausages rolled out of virgin wool; the thin veil draped upon it floated as she swung to look directly at the two women on the couch. Perpennia, chief of the Vestal Virgins, snorted with suppressed laughter. "Oh, poor Bibulus! He never can hide the nakedness of his animosity."

"Which goes back to what I said, Aurelia," from Terentia. "If your tall, handsome son will make enemies of tiny little fellows like Bibulus, he only has himself to blame when he's slandered. It is the height of folly to make a fool of a man in front of his peers by nicknaming him the Flea. Bibulus is an enemy for life."

"What ridiculous nonsense! It happened ten years ago, when both of them were mere youths," said Aurelia.

"Come now, you're well aware how sensitive tiny little men are to canards based on their size," said Terentia. "You're from an old political family, Aurelia. Politics is all about a man's public image. Your son injured Bibulus's public image. People still call him the Flea. He'll never forgive or forget."

"Not to mention," said Servilia tartly, "that Bibulus has an avid audience for his slurs in creatures like Cato."

"What precisely is Bibulus saying?" Aurelia asked, lips set.

"Oh, that instead of returning directly from Spain to Rome, your son has preferred to foment rebellion among the people in Italian Gaul who don't have the Roman citizenship," said Terentia.

"That," said Servilia, "is absolute nonsense!"

"And why," asked a man's deep voice, "is it nonsense, lady?"

The room fell still until little Julia erupted out of her corner and flew to leap at the newcomer. "*Tata!* Oh, *tata!*"

Caesar lifted her off the ground, kissed her lips and her cheek, hugged her, smoothed her frosty hair tenderly. "How is my girl?" he asked, smiling for her alone.

But "Oh, *tata!*" was all Julia could find to say, tucking her head into her father's shoulder.

"Why is it nonsense, lady?" Caesar repeated, swinging the child comfortably into the crook of his right arm, the smile now that he gazed upon Servilia gone even from his eyes, which looked into hers in a way acknowledging her sex, yet dismissing it as unimportant.

"Caesar, this is Servilia, wife of Decimus Junius Silanus," said Aurelia, apparently not at all offended that her son had so far found no time to greet her.

"Why, Servilia?" he asked again, nodding at the name.

She kept her voice cool and level, measured out her words like a jeweler his gold. "There's no logic in a rumor like that. Why should you bother to foment rebellion in Italian Gaul? If you went among those who don't have the citizenship and promised them that you would work on their behalf to get the franchise for them, it would be fitting conduct for a Roman nobleman who aspires to the consulship. You would simply be enlisting clients, which is proper and admirable for a man climbing the political ladder. I was married to a man who did foment rebellion in Italian Gaul, so I am in a position to know how desperate an alternative it is. Lepidus and my husband Brutus deemed it intolerable to live in Sulla's Rome. Their careers had foundered, whereas yours is just beginning. Ergo, what could you hope to gain by fomenting rebellion anywhere?''

"Very true," he said, a trace of amusement creeping into the eyes she had judged a little cold until that spark came.

"Certainly true," she answered. "Your career to date—at least insofar as I know it—suggests to me that if you did tour Italian Gaul talking to non-citizens, you were gathering clients."

His head went back, he laughed, looked magnificent—and, she thought, knew very well that he looked magnificent. This man would do nothing without first calculating its effect on his audience, though the instinct telling her that was purely that, an instinct; he gave not a vestige of his calculation away. "It is true that I gathered clients."

"There you are then," said Servilia, producing a smile of her own at the left corner of her small and secretive mouth. "No one can reproach you for that, Caesar." After which she added grandly, and in the most condescending tone, "Don't worry, I'll make sure the correct version of the incident is circulated."

But that was going too far. Caesar was not about to be patronized by a Servilian, patrician branch of the clan or no; his eyes left her with a contemptuous flick, then rested on Mucia Tertia among the women, who had all listened enthralled to this exchange. He put little Julia down and went to clasp both Mucia Tertia's hands warmly.

"How are you, wife of Pompeius?" he asked.

She looked confused, muttered something inaudible. Soon he passed to Cornelia Sulla, who was Sulla's daughter and his own first cousin. One by one he worked his way around the group, all of whom he knew save for Servilia. Who watched his progress with great admiration once she had coped with the shock of his cutting her. Even Perpennia succumbed to the charm, and as for Terentia—that redoubtable matron positively simpered! But then remained only his mother, to whom he came last.

"Mater, you look well."

"I am well. And you," she said in that dryly prosaic deep voice of hers, "look healed."

A remark which wounded him in some way, thought Servilia, startled. Aha! There are undercurrents here!

"I am fully healed," he said calmly as he sat down on the couch next to her, but on the far side of her from Servilia. "Is this party for any reason?" he asked.

"It's our club. We meet once every eight days at someone's house. Today is my turn."

At which he rose, excusing himself on grounds of travel stains, though Servilia privately thought she had never seen a more immaculate traveler. But before he could leave the room Julia came up to him leading Brutus by the hand.

"*Tata,* this is my friend Marcus Junius Brutus."

The smile and the greeting were expansive; Brutus was clearly impressed (as no doubt he was meant to be impressed, thought Servilia, still smarting). "Your son?" asked Caesar over Brutus's shoulder.

"Yes."

"And do you have any by Silanus?" he asked.

"No, just two daughters."

One brow flew up; Caesar grinned. Then he was gone.

And somehow after that the rest of the party was— not quite an ordeal, more an insipid affair. It broke up well before the dinner hour, with Servilia a deliberate last to leave.

"I have a certain matter I wish to discuss with Caesar," she said to Aurelia at the door, with Brutus hanging behind her making sheep's eyes at Julia. "It wouldn't be seemly for me to come with his clients, so I was wondering if you would arrange that I see him in private. Fairly soon."

"Certainly," said Aurelia. "I'll send a message."

No probing from Aurelia, nor even evidence of curiosity. That was a woman strictly minded her own business, thought the mother of Brutus with some gratitude, and departed.

* * *

Was it good to be home? Over fifteen months away. Not the first time nor the longest time, but this time had been official, and that made a difference. Because Governor Antistius Vetus had not taken a legate to Further Spain with him, Caesar had been the second most important Roman in the province—assizes, finances, administration. A lonely life, galloping from one end of Further Spain to the other at his usual headlong pace; no time to form real friendships with other Romans. Typical perhaps that the one man he had warmed to was not a Roman; typical too that Antistius Vetus the governor had not warmed to his second-in-command, though they got on well enough together and shared an occasional, rather business-filled conversation over dinner whenever they happened to be in the same city. If there was one difficulty about being a patrician of the Julii Caesares, it was that all his seniors to date were only too aware how much greater and more august his ancestry was than theirs. To a Roman of any kind, illustrious ancestors mattered more than anything else. And he always reminded his seniors of Sulla. The lineage, the obvious brilliance and efficiency, the striking physical appearance, the icy eyes . . .

So was it good to be home? Caesar stared at the beautiful tidiness of his study, every surface dusted, every scroll in its bucket or pigeonhole, the pattern of elaborate leaves and flowers in the marquetry of his desk top on full display, only a ram's horn inkstand and a clay cup of pens to obscure it.

At least the initial entry into his home had been more bearable than he had anticipated. When Eutychus had opened the door upon a scene of chattering women, his first impulse had been to run, but then he realized this was an excellent beginning; the emptiness of a home without his darling Cinnilla there would remain internal, need not be spoken. Sooner or later little Julia would bring it up, but not in those first moments, not until his eyes had grown accustomed to Cinnilla's absence, and would not fill with tears. He hardly remembered this apartment without her, who had lived as his sister before she was old enough to be wife, a part of his childhood as well as his manhood. Dear lady she had been, who now was ashes in a cold dark tomb.

His mother walked in, composed and aloof as always.

"Who's been spreading rumors about my visit to Italian Gaul?" he asked, drawing up a chair for her close to his own.

"Bibulus."

"I see." He sat down, sighing. "Well, that was only to be expected, I suppose. One can't insult a flea like Bibulus the way I insulted him and not become his enemy for the rest of one's days. How I disliked him!"

"How he continues to dislike you."

"There are twenty quaestors, and I had luck. The lots gave me a post far from Bibulus. But he's almost exactly two years older than me, which means we'll always be in office together as we rise up the *cursus honorum.*"

"So you intend to take advantage of Sulla's dispensation for patricians, and stand for curule office two years earlier than plebeians like Bibulus," said Aurelia, making it a statement.

"I'd be a fool not to, and a fool I am not, Mater," said her son. "If I run for election as a praetor in my thirty-seventh year, I will have been in the Senate for sixteen of those years without counting the *flamen Dialis* years. That is quite long enough for any man to wait."

"But still six years off. In the meantime, what?"

He twisted restlessly. "Oh, I can feel the walls of Rome hemming me in already, though I passed through them only hours ago! Give me a life abroad any day."

"There are bound to be plenty of court cases. You're a famous advocate, quite up there with Cicero and Hortensius. You'll be offered some juicy ones."

"But inside Rome, always inside Rome. Spain," said Caesar, leaning forward eagerly, "was a revelation to me. Antistius Vetus proved a lethargic governor who was happy to give me as much work as I was willing to take on, despite my lowly status. So I did all the assizes throughout the province, as well as managed the governor's funds."

"Now the latter duty," said his mother dryly, "must have been a trial to you. Money doesn't fascinate you."

"Oddly enough, I found it did when it was Rome's money. I took some lessons in accounting from the most remarkable fellow—a Gadetanian banker of Punic origin named Lucius Cornelius Balbus Major. He has a nephew almost as old as he is, Balbus Minor, who is his partner. They did a lot of work for Pompeius Magnus when he was in Spain, and now they seem to own most of Gades. What the elder Balbus doesn't know about banking and other things fiscal doesn't matter. It goes without saying that the public purse was a shambles. But thanks to Balbus Major, I tidied it up splendidly. I liked him, Mater." Caesar shrugged, looked wry. "In fact, he was the only true friend I made out there."

"Friendship," said Aurelia, "goes both ways. You know more individuals than the rest of noble Rome put together, but you let no Roman of your own class draw too close to you. That's why the few true friends you make are always foreigners or Romans of the lower classes."

Caesar grinned. "Rubbish! I get on better with foreigners because I grew up in your apartment block surrounded by Jews, Syrians, Gauls, Greeks, and the Gods know what else."

"Blame it on me," she said flatly.

He chose to ignore this. "Marcus Crassus is my friend, and you can't call him anything but a Roman as noble as I am myself."

She riposted with "Did you make any money at all in Spain?"

"A little here and there, thanks to Balbus. Unfortunately the province was peaceful for a change, so there were no nice little border wars to fight with the Lusitani. Had there been, I suspect Antistius Vetus would have fought them himself anyway. But rest easy, Mater. My piratical nest egg is undisturbed, I have enough laid by to stand for the senior magistracies."

"Including curule aedile?" she asked, tone foreboding.

"Since I'm a patrician and therefore can't make a

reputation as a tribune of the plebs, I don't have much choice,'' he said, and took one of the pens from its cup to place it straight on the desk; he never fiddled, but sometimes it was necessary to have something other than his mother's eyes to look at. Odd. He had forgotten how unnerving she could be.

''Even with your piratical nest egg in reserve, Caesar, curule aedile is ruinously expensive. I know you! You won't be content to give moderately good games. You'll insist on giving the best games anyone can remember.''

''Probably. I'll worry about that when I come to it in three or four years,'' he said tranquilly. ''In the meantime, I intend to stand at next month's elections for the post of curator of the Via Appia. No Claudius wants the job.''

''Another ruinously expensive enterprise! The Treasury will grant you one sestertius per hundred miles, and you'll spend a hundred denarii on every mile.''

He was tired of the conversation; she was, as she always had been whenever they exchanged more than a few sentences, beginning to harp on money and his disregard for it. ''You know,'' he said, picking up the pen and putting it back in the cup, ''nothing ever alters. I had forgotten that. While I was away I had started to think of you as every man dreams his mother must be. Now here is the reality. A perpetual sermon on my tendency to extravagance. Give it up, Mater! What matters to you does not matter to me.''

Her lips thinned, but she stayed silent for a few moments; then as she rose to her feet she said, ''Servilia wishes to have a private interview with you as soon as possible.''

''What on earth for?'' he asked.

''No doubt she'll tell you when you see her.''

''Do you know?''

''I ask no questions of anyone save you, Caesar. That way, I am told no lies.''

''You acquit me of lying, then.''

''Naturally.''

He had begun to get up, but sank back into his chair and plucked another pen from the cup, frowning. ''She's interesting, that one." His head went to one side. "Her assessment of the Bibulus rumor was astonishingly accurate."

"If you remember, several years ago I told you she was the most politically astute woman of my acquaintance. But you weren't impressed enough by what I said to want to meet her."

"Well, now I have met her. And I'm impressed—though not by her arrogance. She actually presumed to patronize *me*."

Something in his voice arrested Aurelia's progress to the door; she swung round to stare at Caesar intently. "Silanus is not your enemy," she said stiffly.

That provoked a laugh, but it died quickly. "I do sometimes fancy a woman who is not the wife of an enemy, Mater! And I think I fancy her just a little. Certainly I must find out what she wants. Who knows? Maybe it's me."

"With Servilia, impossible to tell. She's enigmatic."

"I was reminded a trifle of Cinnilla."

"Do not be misled by romantic sentiment, Caesar. There is no likeness whatsoever between Servilia and your late wife." Her eyes misted. "Cinnilla was the sweetest girl. At thirty-six, Servilia is no girl, and she's far from sweet. In fact, I'd call her as cold and hard as a slab of marble."

"You don't like her?"

"I like her very well. But for what she is." This time Aurelia reached the door before turning. "Dinner will be ready shortly. Are you eating here?"

His face softened. "How could I disappoint Julia by going anywhere today?" He thought of something else, and said, "An odd boy, Brutus. Like oil on the surface, but I suspect that somewhere inside is a very peculiar sort of iron. Julia seemed rather proprietary about him. I wouldn't have thought he'd appeal to her."

"I doubt he does. But they're old friends." This time it was her face softened. "Your daughter is extraordinarily kind. In which respect she takes after her mother. There's no one else from whom she could have inherited *that* characteristic.''

As it was impossible for Servilia to walk slowly, she went home at her usual brisk pace, Brutus still toiling to keep up, but without voicing a complaint; the worst of the heat had gone out of the sun, and he was, besides, once more immersed in hapless Thucydides. Julia was temporarily forgotten. So was Uncle Cato.

Normally Servilia would have spoken to him occasionally, but today he may as well not have been with her for all the notice she took of him. Her mind was fixed on Gaius Julius Caesar. She had sat with a thousand worms crawling through her jaw the moment she saw him, stunned, blasted, unable to move. How was it that she had never seen him before? The smallness of their circle ought to have guaranteed that they met. But she had never even set eyes on him! Oh, heard about him—what Roman noblewoman hadn't? For most, the description of him sent them running to find any ploy which might introduce him to them, but Servilia was not a woman of that kind. She had simply dismissed him as another Memmius or Catilina, someone who slew women with a smile and traded on that fact. One look at Caesar was enough to tell her he was no Memmius, no Catilina. Oh, he slew with a smile and traded on that fact—no argument there! But in him was much more. Remote, aloof, unattainable. Easier now to understand why the women he indulged with a brief affair pined away afterward, and wept, and despaired. He gave them what he didn't value, but he never gave them *himself*.

Owning a quality of detachment, Servilia passed then to analysis of her reaction to him. Why him, when for thirty-six years no man had really meant more to her than security, social status? Of course she did have a penchant for fair men. Brutus had been chosen for her; she met him first on her wedding day. That he was very dark had been as big a disappointment as the rest of him turned out to be. Silanus, a fair and strikingly handsome man, had been her own choice. One which continued to satisfy her on a visual level, though in every other respect he too had proven a sad disappointment. Not a strong man, from his health to his intellect to his backbone. No wonder he hadn't managed to sire any sons on her! Servilia believed wholeheartedly that the sex of her offspring was entirely up to her, and her first night in Silanus's arms had made her resolve that Brutus would remain an only son. That way, what was already a very considerable fortune would be augmented by Silanus's very considerable fortune too.

A pity that it was beyond her power to secure a third and far greater fortune for Brutus! Caesar forgotten because her son had intruded, Servilia's mind dwelled with relish upon those fifteen thousand talents of gold her grandfather Caepio the Consul had succeeded in stealing from a convoy in Narbonese Gaul some thirty-seven years ago. More gold than the Roman Treasury held had passed into Servilius Caepio's keeping, though it had long ago ceased to be actual gold bullion. Instead it had been converted into property of all kinds: industrial towns in Italian Gaul, vast wheatlands in Sicily and Africa Province, apartment buildings from one end of the Italian Peninsula to the other, and sleeping partnerships in the business ventures senatorial rank forbade. When Caepio the Consul died it all went to Servilia's father, and when he was killed during the Italian War it went to her brother, the third to bear the name Quintus Servilius Caepio during her lifetime. Oh yes, it had all gone to her brother Caepio! Her Uncle Drusus had made sure he inherited, though Uncle Drusus had known the truth. And what was the truth? That Servilia's brother Caepio was only her half brother: in reality he was the first child her mother had borne to that upstart Cato Salonianus, though at the time she had still been married to Servilia's father. Who found himself with a cuckoo in the Servilius Caepio nest, a tall, long-necked, red-haired cuckoo with a nose which proclaimed to all of Rome whose child he was. Now that Caepio was a man of thirty, his true origins were known to everyone in Rome who mattered. What a laugh! And what justice! The Gold of Tolosa had passed in the end to a cuckoo in the Servilius Caepio nest.

Brutus winced, wrenched out of his preoccupation; his mother had ground her teeth as she strode along, a hideous sound which caused all who heard it to blanch and flee. But Brutus couldn't flee. All he could hope was that she ground her teeth for some reason unconnected with him. So too hoped the slaves who preceded her, rolling terrified eyes at each other as their hearts pattered and the sweat suddenly poured off them.

None of this did Servilia so much as notice, her short and sturdy legs opening and closing like the shears of Atropos as she stormed along. Wretched Caepio! Well, it was too late for Brutus to inherit now. Caepio had married the daughter of Hortensius the advocate, of one of Rome's oldest and most illustrious plebeian families, and Hortensia was healthily pregnant with their first child. There would be many more children; Caepio's fortune was so vast even a dozen sons couldn't dent it. As for Caepio himself, he was as fit and strong as were all the Cato breed of that ludicrous and disgraceful second marriage Cato the Censor had contracted in his late seventies, to the daughter of his slave, Salonius. It had happened a hundred years ago, and Rome at the time had fallen down laughing, then proceeded to forgive the disgusting old lecher and admit his slave-offspring into the ranks of the Famous Families. Of course Caepio might die in an accident, as his blood father, Cato Salonianus, had done. Came the sound of Servilia's teeth again: faint hope! Caepio had survived several wars unscathed, though he was a brave man. No, it was bye-bye to the Gold of Tolosa. Brutus would never inherit the things it had purchased. And that just wasn't fair! At least Brutus was a genuine Servilius Caepio on his mother's side! Oh, if only Brutus could inherit that third fortune, he would be richer than Pompeius Magnus and Marcus Crassus combined!

Some few feet short of the Silanus front door both slaves bolted for it, pounded on it, vanished the moment they scrambled inside. So that by the time Servilia and her son were admitted, the atrium was deserted; the household knew Servilia had ground her teeth. She therefore received no warning as to who waited for her in her sitting room,

just erupted through its entrance still fulminating about
Brutus's ill luck in the matter of the Gold of Tolosa. Her
outraged eyes fell upon none other than her half brother,
Marcus Porcius Cato. Brutus's much-beloved Uncle Cato.

He had adopted a new conceit, taken to wearing no
tunic under his toga because in the early days of the Republic no one had worn a tunic under his toga. And, had
Servilia's eyes been less filled with loathing of him, she
might have admitted that this startling and extraordinary
fashion (which he could prevail on no one to emulate)
suited him. At twenty-five years of age he was at the peak
of his health and fitness, had lived hard and sparingly as
an ordinary ranker soldier during the war against Spartacus, and ate nothing rich, drank nothing save water.
Though his short and waving hair was a red-tinged chestnut and his eyes were large and a light grey, his skin was
smooth and tanned, so he contrived to look wonderful in
exposing all of the right side of his trunk from shoulder
to hip. A lean and hard and nicely hairless man, he had
well-developed pectoral muscles, a flat belly, and a right
arm which produced sinewy bulges in the proper places.
The head on top of a very long neck was beautifully
shaped, and the mouth was distractingly lovely. In fact,
had it not been for his amazing nose, he might have rivaled
Caesar or Memmius or Catilina for spectacular good looks.
But the nose reduced everything else to sheer insignificance, so enormous, thin, sharp and beaked was it. A nose
with a life of its own, so people said, awed into worship.

"I was just about to go," Cato announced in a loud,
harsh, unmusical voice.

"A pity you hadn't," said Servilia through her teeth
(which she did not grind, though she wanted to).

"Where's Marcus Junius? They said you took him
with you."

"Brutus! Call him Brutus, like everyone else!"

"I do not approve of the change this past decade has
brought to our names," he said, growing louder. "A man
may have one or two or even three nicknames, but tradition demands that he be referred to by his first and family
names alone, not by a nickname."

"Well, I for one am profoundly glad of the change, *Cato*! As for *Brutus,* he isn't available to you."

"You think I'll give up," ·he went on, his tone now achieving its habitual hectoring mode, "but I never will, Servilia. While there is life in me, I'll never give up on anything. Your son is my blood nephew, and there is no man in his world. Whether you like it or not, I intend to fulfill my duty to him."

"His stepfather is the *paterfamilias,* not you."

Cato laughed, a shrill whinny. "Decimus Junius is a poor puking ninny, no more fit than a dying duck to have supervision of your boy!"

Few chinks in his enormously thick hide though Cato had, Servilia knew where every one of them was. Aemilia Lepida, for example. How Cato had loved her when he was eighteen! As silly as a Greek over a young boy. But all Aemilia Lepida had been doing was using Cato to make Metellus Scipio come crawling.

Servilia said, apropos of nothing, "I saw Aemilia Lepida at Aurelia's today. How well she looks! A real little wife and mother. She says she's more in love with Metellus Scipio than ever."

The barb visibly lodged; Cato went white. "She used me as bait to get him back," he said bitterly. "A typical woman—sly, deceitful, unprincipled."

"Is that how you think of your own wife?" asked Servilia with a broad smile, eyes dancing.

"Atilia *is* my wife. If Aemilia Lepida had honored her promise and married me, she would soon have found out that I tolerate no woman's tricks. Atilia does as she's told and lives an exemplary life. I will permit nothing less than perfect behavior."

"Poor Atilia! Would you order her killed if you smelled wine on her breath? The Twelve Tables allow you to do so, and you're an ardent supporter of antique laws."

"I am an ardent supporter of the old ways, the customs and traditions of Rome's *mos maiorum,*" he blared, the nose squeezing its nostrils until they looked like blisters on either side of it. "My son, my daughter, she and I eat food she has personally seen prepared, live in rooms she has personally seen tended, and wear clothing she has personally spun, woven and sewn.''

"Is that why you're so bare? What a drudge she must be!''

"Atilia lives an exemplary life,'' he repeated. "I do not condone farming the children out to servants and nannies, so she has the full responsibility for a three-year-old girl and a one-year-old boy. Atilia is fully occupied.''

"As I said, she's a drudge. You can afford enough servants, Cato, and she knows that. Instead, you pinch your purse and make her a servant. She won't thank you.'' The thick white eyelids lifted, Servilia's ironic black gaze traveled from his toes to his head. "One day, Cato, you might come home early and discover that she's seeking a little extramarital solace. Who could blame her? You'd look so pretty wearing horns on your head!''

But that shaft went wide; Cato simply looked smug. "Oh, no chance of that,'' he said confidently. "Even in these inflated times I may not exceed my great-grandfather's top price for a slave, but I assure you that I choose people who fear me. I am scrupulously just—no servant worth his salt suffers under my care!—but every servant belongs to me, and knows it.''

"An idyllic domestic arrangement,'' said Servilia, smiling. "I must remember to tell Aemilia Lepida what she's missing.'' She turned her shoulder, looking bored. "Go away, Cato, do! You'll get Brutus over my dead body. We may not share the same father—I thank the Gods for that mercy!—but we do share the same kind of steel. And I, Cato, am far more intelligent than you.'' She managed to produce a sound reminiscent of a cat's purr. "In fact, I am more intelligent by far than either of my half brothers.''

This third barb pierced him to the marrow. Cato stiffened, his beautiful hands clenched into fists. "I can tolerate your malice when it's aimed at me, Servilia, but not when your target is Caepio!'' he roared. "That is an undeserved slur! Caepio is *your* full brother, not *my* full brother! Oh, I wish he was my full brother! I love him more than anyone else in the world! But I will not permit that slur, especially coming from you!''

"Look in your mirror, Cato. All of Rome knows the truth.''

"Our mother was part Rutilian—Caepio inherited his coloring from that side of her family!''

"Rubbish! The Rutilians are sandy-fair, on the short side, and quite lacking the nose of a Cato Salonianus.'' Servilia snorted contemptuously. "Like to like, Cato. From the time of your birth, Caepio gave himself to you. You're peas from the same pod, and you've stayed as thick as pea soup all your lives. Won't be parted, never argue— Caepio is your full brother, not mine!''

Cato got up. "You're a wicked woman, Servilia.''

She yawned ostentatiously. "You just lost the battle, Cato. Goodbye, and good riddance.''

He flung his final word behind him as he left the room: "I will win in the end! I always win!''

"Over my dead body you'll win! But you'll be dead before me.''

After which she had to deal with another of the men in her life: her husband, Decimus Junius Silanus, whom she had to admit Cato had summed up neatly as a puking ninny. Whatever was the matter with his gut, he did have a tendency to vomit, and he was inarguably a shy, resigned, rather characterless man. All of his goods, she thought to herself as she watched him pick his way through dinner, are on his countertop. He's just a pretty face, there's nothing behind. Yet that is so obviously not true of another pretty face, the one belonging to Gaius Julius Caesar. Caesar . . . I am fascinated with him, by him. For a moment there I thought I was fascinating him too, but then I let my tongue run away with me, and offended him. Why did I forget he's a Julian? Even a patrician Servilian like me doesn't presume to arrange the life or the affairs of a Julian. . . .

The two girls she had borne Silanus were at dinner, tormenting Brutus as usual (they deemed Brutus a weed). Junia was a little younger than Caesar's Julia, seven, and Junilla was almost six. Both were medium brown in coloring, and extremely attractive; no fear they would displease their husbands! Very good looks and fat dowries were an irresistible combination. They were, however, already formally betrothed to the heirs of two great houses. Only Brutus was uncommitted, though he had made his own choice very clear. Little Julia. How odd he was, to have fallen in love with a child! Though she did not usually admit it to herself, this evening she was in a mood for truth, and acknowledged that Brutus was sometimes a puzzle to her. Why for instance did he persist in fancying himself an intellectual? If he didn't pull himself out of that particular slough, his public career would not prosper; unless like Caesar they also had tremendous reputations as brave soldiers, or like Cicero had tremendous reputations in the law courts, intellectuals were despised. Brutus wasn't vigorous and swift and outgoing like either Caesar or Cicero. A good thing perhaps that he would become Caesar's son-in-law. Some of that magical energy and charm would rub off, had to rub off. Caesar . . .

Who sent her a message the following day that he would be pleased to see her privately in his rooms on the lower Vicus Patricii, two floors up in the apartment building between the Fabricius dye works and the Suburan Baths. At the fourth hour of day on the morrow, one Lucius Decimius would be waiting in the ground-floor passage to conduct her upstairs.

Though Antistius Vetus's term as governor of Further Spain had been extended, Caesar had not been honor-bound to remain there with him; Caesar had not bothered to secure a personal appointment, just taken his chances of a province in the lots. In one way it might have been enjoyable to linger in Further Spain, but the post of quaestor was too junior to serve as the basis for a great Forum reputation. Caesar was well aware that the next few years of his life must be spent as much as possible in Rome: Rome must constantly see his face, Rome must constantly hear his voice.

Because he had won the Civic Crown for outstanding valor at the age of twenty, he had been admitted to the

Senate ten years before the customary age of thirty, and was allowed to speak inside that chamber from the very beginning instead of existing under the law of silence until he was elected a magistrate of higher rank than quaestor. Not that he had abused this extraordinary privilege; Caesar was too shrewd to make himself a bore by adding himself to a list of speakers already far too long. He didn't have to use oratory as a means of attracting attention, as he carried a visible reminder of his near-unique position on his person. Sulla's law stipulated that whenever he appeared on public business, he must wear the Civic Crown of oak leaves upon his head. And everyone at sight of him was obliged to rise and applaud him, even the most venerable consulars and censors. It set him apart and above, two states of being he liked very much. Others might cultivate as many influential intimates as they could; Caesar preferred to walk alone. Oh, a man had to have hordes of clients, be known as a patron of tremendous distinction. But rising to the top—he was determined he would!—by bonding himself to a clique was not a part of Caesar's plans. Cliques controlled their members.

There were the *boni,* for example: the "good men." Of all the many factions in the Senate, they had the most clout. They could often dominate the elections, staff the major courts, cry loudest in the Assemblies. Yet the *boni* stood for nothing! The most one could say about them was that the only thing they had in common with each other was a rooted dislike of change. Whereas Caesar approved of change. There were so many things screaming out for alteration, amendment, abolition! Indeed, if service in Further Spain had shown Caesar anything, it was that change had to come. Gubernatorial corruption and rapacity would kill the empire unless they were curbed; and that was only one change among the many he wanted to see. Wanted to implement. Every aspect of Rome desperately needed attention, regulation. Yet the *boni* traditionally and adamantly opposed change of the most minor kind. Not Caesar's sort of people. Nor was Caesar popular with them; their exquisitely sensitive noses had sniffed out the radical in Caesar a long time ago.

In fact, there was only one sure road to where Caesar was going: the road of military command. Yet before he could legally general one of Rome's armies he would have to rise at least as high as praetor, and to secure election as one of these eight men who supervised the courts and system of justice required that the next six years be spent inside the city. Canvassing, electioneering, struggling to cope with the chaotic political scene. Keeping his person at the forefront of his world, gathering influence, power, clients, knight supporters from the commercial sphere, followers of all sorts. As himself and solely for himself, not as one of the *boni* or any other group which insisted its members think alike—or preferably not bother to think at all.

Though Caesar's ambition extended beyond leading his own faction; he wanted to become an institution called the First Man in Rome. *Primus inter pares,* the first among his equals, all things to all men, owning the most *auctoritas,* the most *dignitas;* the First Man in Rome was clout personified. Whatever he said was listened to, and no one could pull him down because he was neither King nor Dictator; he held his position by sheer personal power, was what he was through no office, no army at his back. Old Gaius Marius had done it the hard way, by conquering the Germans, for he had owned no ancestors to tell men he deserved to be the First Man in Rome. Sulla had the ancestors, but did not earn the title because he made himself Dictator. Simply, he was Sulla—great aristocrat, autocrat, winner of the awesome Grass Crown, undefeated general. A military legend hatched in the political arena, that was the First Man in Rome.

Therefore the man who would be the First Man in Rome could not belong to a faction; he had to create a faction, stand forth in the Forum Romanum as no one's minion, yet a most fearsome ally. In this Rome of today, being a patrician made it easier, and Caesar was a patrician. His remote ancestors had been members of the Senate when it had consisted of a mere hundred men who advised the King of Rome. Before Rome so much as existed, his ancestors had been kings themselves, of Alba

Longa on the Alban Mount. And before that, his thirty-nine times great-grandmother was the Goddess Venus herself; she had borne Aeneas, King of Dardania, who had sailed to Latin Italia and set up a new kingdom in what would one day be the home domain of Rome. To come from such stellar stock predisposed people to look to a man as leader of their faction; Romans liked men with ancestors, and the more august the ancestors were, the better a man's chances to create his own faction.

Thus it was that Caesar understood what he had to do between now and the consulship, nine years away. He had to predispose men to look upon him as worthy to become the First Man in Rome. Which didn't mean conciliating his peers; it meant dominating those who were not his peers. His peers would fear him and hate him, as they did all who aspired to be called the First Man in Rome. His peers would fight his ambition tooth and nail, stop at nothing to bring him down before he was too powerful ever to bring down. That was why they loathed Pompey the Great, who fancied himself the present First Man in Rome. Well, he wouldn't last. The title belonged to Caesar, and nothing, animate or inanimate, would stop his taking it. He knew that because he knew himself.

At dawn on the day after he arrived home, it was gratifying to discover that a tidy little band of clients had presented themselves to pay him their compliments; his reception room was full of them, and Eutychus the steward was beaming all over his fat face at sight of them. So too was old Lucius Decumius beaming, chirpy and angular as a cricket, hopping eagerly from foot to foot when Caesar emerged from his private rooms.

A kiss on the mouth for Lucius Decumius, much to the awe of many who witnessed their meeting.

"I missed you more than anyone except Julia, dad," said Caesar, enfolding Lucius Decumius in a huge hug.

"Rome are not the same without you either, Pavo!" was the reply, and using the old nickname of Peacock he had given Caesar when Caesar had been a toddler.

"You never seem to get any older, dad."

That was true. No one really knew what age Lucius Decumius actually owned, though it had to be closer to seventy than sixty. He would probably live forever. Of the Fourth Class only and the urban tribe Suburana, he would never be important enough to have a vote which counted in any Assembly, yet Lucius Decumius was a man of great influence and power in certain circles. He was the custodian of the crossroads college which had its headquarters in Aurelia's insula, and every man who lived in the neighborhood, no matter how high his Class, was obliged to pay his respects at least from time to time inside what was as much a tavern as a religious meeting place. As custodian of his college, Lucius Decumius wielded authority; he had also managed to accumulate considerable wealth due to many nefarious activities, and was not averse to lending it at very reasonable rates of interest to those who might one day be able to serve Lucius Decumius's ends— or the ends of his patron, Caesar. Caesar whom he loved more than either of his two stout sons, Caesar who had shared some of his questionable adventures when a boy, Caesar, Caesar . . .

"Got your rooms down the road all ready for you," said the old man, grinning broadly. "New bed—very nice."

The rather icy pale-blue eyes lit up; Caesar returned the grin together with a wink. "I'll sample it before I pass my personal verdict on that, dad. Which reminds me— would you take a message to the wife of Decimus Junius Silanus?"

Lucius Decumius frowned. "Servilia?"

"I see the lady is famous."

"Couldn't not be. She's a hard woman on her slaves."

"How do you know that? I imagine her slaves frequent a crossroads college on the Palatine."

"Word gets round, word gets round! She's not above ordering crucifixion when she thinks they needs a lesson. Has it done in the garden under all eyes. Mind you, she do have 'em flogged first, so they don't last long once they're tied up on a cross."

"That's thoughtful of her," said Caesar, and proceeded to relay the message for Servilia. He did not make the mistake of thinking that Lucius Decumius was trying to warn him against getting involved with her, nor had the presumption to criticize his taste; Lucius Decumius was simply doing his duty and passing on relevant information.

Food mattered little to Caesar—no gourmet, and certainly not of the Epicurean persuasion—so as he passed from client to client he chewed absently on a bread roll crisp and fresh from Aurelia's baker down the road, and drank a beaker of water. Aware of Caesar's open-handedness, his steward had already gone the rounds with platters of the same rolls, watered wine for those who preferred it to plain water, little bowls of oil or honey for dipping. How splendid to see Caesar's clientele increasing!

Some had come for no other reason than to show him they were his to command, but others had come for a specific purpose: a reference for a job they wanted, a position for a properly schooled son in some Treasury or Archives slot, or what did Caesar think of this offer for a daughter, or that offer for a piece of land? A few were there to ask for money, and they too were obliged with ready cheerfulness, as if Caesar's purse was as deep as Marcus Crassus's when in actual fact it was extremely shallow.

Most of the clients departed once the courtesies had been exchanged and some conversation had passed. Those who remained needed a few lines of writing from him, and waited while he sat at his desk dispensing papers. With the result that more than four of the lengthening spring hours had passed before the last of the visitors left, and the rest of the day belonged to Caesar. They had not gone far, of course; when he came out of his apartment an hour later, having dealt with his more pressing correspondence, they attached themselves to him to escort him wherever his business might lead him. A man with clients had to show them off publicly!

Unfortunately no one of significance was present in the Forum Romanum when Caesar and his retinue arrived at the bottom of the Argiletum and walked between the

Basilica Aemilia and the steps of the Curia Hostilia. And there it lay, the absolute center of the entire Roman world: the lower Forum Romanum, a space liberally sprinkled with objects of reverence or antiquity or utility. Some fifteen months since he had seen it. Not that it had changed. It never did.

The Well of the Comitia yawned in front of him, a deceptively small circular tier of broad steps leading down below ground level, the structure in which both Plebeian and Popular Assemblies met. When jam-packed it could hold about three thousand men. In its back wall, facing the side of the Curia Hostilia steps, was the rostra, from which the politicians addressed the crowd clustered in the Well below. And there was the venerably ancient Curia Hostilia itself, home of the Senate through all the centuries since King Tullus Hostilius had built it, too tiny for Sulla's larger enrollment, looking shabby despite the wonderful mural on its side. The Pool of Curtius, the sacred trees, Scipio Africanus atop his tall column, the beaks of captured ships mounted on more columns, statues galore on imposing plinths glaring furiously like old Appius Claudius the Blind or looking smugly serene like wily and brilliant old Scaurus Princeps Senatus. The flagstones of the Sacra Via were more worn than the travertine paving around it (Sulla had replaced the paving, but the *mos maiorum* forbade any improvement in the road). On the far side of the open space cluttered by two or three tribunals stood the two dowdy basilicae Opimia and Sempronia, with the glorious temple of Castor and Pollux to their left. How meetings and courts and Assemblies managed to occur between so many groups of impedimenta was a mystery, but they did—always had, always would.

To the north there reared the bulk of the Capitol, one hump higher than its twin, an absolute confusion of temples with gaudily painted pillars, pediments, gilded statues atop orange-tiled roofs. Jupiter Optimus Maximus's new home (the old one had burned down some years earlier) was still a-building, Caesar noted with a frown; Catulus was definitely a tardy custodian of the process, never in enough of a hurry. But Sulla's enormous Tabularium was

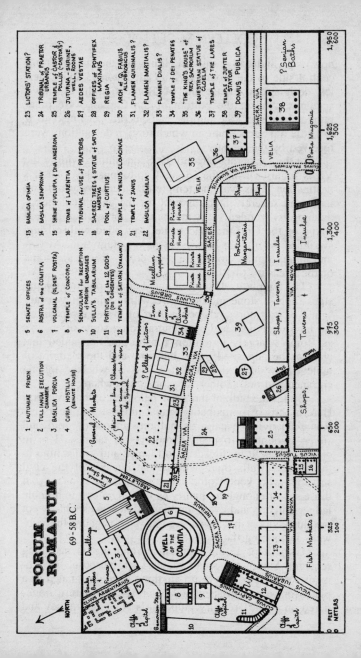

FORUM ROMANUM
69–58 B.C.

NORTH

1 LAUTUMIAE PRISON
2 TULLIANUM EXECUTION CHAMBER
3 BASILICA PORCIA
4 CURIA HOSTILIA (SENATE HOUSE)
5 SENATE OFFICES
6 ROSTRA of the COMITIA
7 VOLCANAL (OLDEST ROSTRA)
8 TEMPLE of CONCORD
9 SENACULUM, for RECEPTION of FOREIGN EMBASSAGES
10 SULLA'S TABULARIUM
11 PORTICUS of the 12 GODS (DII CONSENTES)
12 TEMPLE of SATURN (TREASURY)

13 BASILICA OPIMIA
14 BASILICA SEMPRONIA
15 SHRINE of VOLUPIA & DIVA ANGERONA
16 TOMB of LARENTIA
17 TRIBUNAL for USE of PRAETORS
18 SACRED TREES & STATUE of SATYR MARSYAS
19 POOL of CURTIUS
20 TEMPLE of VENUS CLOACINAE
21 TEMPLE of JANUS
22 BASILICA AEMILIA

23 LICTORS' STATION ?
24 TRIBUNAL of PRAETOR URBANUS
25 TEMPLE of CASTOR (& POLLUX ("CASTOR'S")
26 JUTURNA – SHRINE, WELL, ROOMS
27 AEDES VESTAE
28 OFFICES of PONTIFEX MAXIMUS
29 REGIA
30 ARCH of Q. FABIUS ALLOBROGICUS
31 FLAMEN QUIRINALIS ?
32 FLAMEN MARTIALIS ?
33 FLAMEN DIALIS ?
34 TEMPLE of DEI PENATES
35 "THE KING'S HOUSE" of REX SACRORUM
36 EQUESTRIAN STATUE of CLOELIA
37 TEMPLE of THE LARES
38 TEMPLE of JUPITER STATOR
39 DOMUS PUBLICA

FEET
METRES
0   525   650   975   1,300   1,625   1,950
0   100   200   300   400   500   600

now well and truly finished, filling in the whole front-central side of the mount with arcaded storeys and galleries designed to house all of Rome's archives, laws, accounts. And at the bottom of the Capitol were other public premises—the temple of Concord, and next to it the little old Senaculum, in which foreign delegations were received by the Senate.

In the far corner beyond the Senaculum, dividing the Vicus Iugarius from the Clivus Capitolinus, lay Caesar's destination. This was the temple of Saturn, very old and large and severely Doric except for the garish colors be-daubing its wooden walls and pillars, home of an ancient statue of the God that had to be kept filled with oil and swaddled with cloth to prevent its disintegration. Also—and more germane to Caesar's purpose—it was the home of the Treasury of Rome.

The temple itself was mounted atop a podium twenty steps high, a stone infrastructure within which lay a labyrinth of corridors and rooms. Part of it was a repository for laws once they had been engraved on stone or bronze, as Rome's largely unwritten constitution demanded that all laws be deposited there; but time and the plethora of tablets now dictated that a new law be whisked in one entrance and out another for storage elsewhere.

By far the bulk of the space belonged to the Treasury. Here in strong rooms behind great internal iron doors lay Rome's tangible wealth as bullion—ingots of gold and silver amounting to many thousands of talents. Here in dingy offices lit by flickering oil lamps and grilles high in the outside walls there worked the nucleus of the civil servants who kept Rome's public account books, from those senior enough to qualify as *tribuni aerarii* to humble ledger-enterers and even humbler public slaves who swept the dusty floors but usually contrived to ignore the cob-webs festooning the walls.

Growth of Rome's provinces and profits had long rendered Saturn too small for its fiscal purpose, but Romans were loath to give up anything once designated as a place for some governmental enterprise, so Saturn floundered on as the Treasury. Subhoards of coined money and bullion had been relegated to other vaults beneath other temples, the accounts belonging to years other than the current one had been banished to Sulla's Tabularium, and as a consequence Treasury officials and underlings had proliferated. Another Roman anathema, civil servants, but the Treasury was, after all, the Treasury; the public moneys had to be properly planted, cultivated and harvested, even if that did mean abhorrently big numbers of public employees.

While his entourage hung back to watch bright-eyed and proud, Caesar strolled up to the great carved door in the side wall of Saturn's podium. He was clad in spotless white toga with the broad purple stripe of the senator on the right shoulder of his tunic, and he wore a chaplet of oak leaves around his head because this was a public occasion and he had to wear his Civic Crown on all public occasions. Whereas another man might have gestured to an attendant to ply the knocker, Caesar did that himself, then waited until the door opened cautiously and a head appeared around it.

"Gaius Julius Caesar, quaestor of the province of Further Spain under the governorship of Gaius Antistius Vetus, wishes to present the accounts of his province, as law and custom demand," said Caesar in a level voice.

He was admitted, and the door closed behind him; all the clients remained outside in the fresh air.

"I believe you only got in yesterday, is that right?" asked Marcus Vibius, Treasury chief, when Caesar was conducted into his gloomy office.

"Yes."

"There isn't any hurry about these things, you know."

"As far as I'm concerned there is. My duty as quaestor is not ended until I have presented my accounts."

Vibius blinked. "Then by all means present them!"

Out from the sinus of Caesar's toga came seven scrolls, each one sealed twice, once with Caesar's ring and once with Antistius Vetus's ring. When Vibius went to break the seals on the first scroll, Caesar stopped him.

"What is it, Gaius Julius?"

"There are no witnesses present."

Vibius blinked again. "Oh well, we don't usually worry too much about trifles like that," he said easily, and picked up the scroll with a wry smile.

Caesar's hand came out, wrapped itself around Vibius's wrist. "I suggest you commence to worry about trifles like that," said Caesar pleasantly. "These are the official accounts of my quaestorship in Further Spain, and I require witnesses throughout my presentation. If the time isn't convenient to produce witnesses, then give me a time which is convenient, and I will come back."

The atmosphere inside the room changed, became frostier. "Of course, Gaius Julius."

But the first four witnesses were not to Caesar's taste, and it was only after some twelve had been inspected that four were found who did suit Caesar's taste. The interview then proceeded with a speed and cleverness which had Marcus Vibius gasping, for he was not used to quaestors with a grasp of accounting, nor to a memory so good it enabled its owner to reel off whole screeds of data without consultation of written material. And by the time that Caesar was done, Vibius was sweating.

"I can honestly say that I have rarely, if ever, seen a quaestor present his accounts so well," Vibius admitted, and wiped his brow. "All is in order, Gaius Julius. In fact, Further Spain ought to give you a vote of thanks for sorting out so many messes." This was said with a conciliatory smile; Vibius was beginning to understand that this haughty fellow intended to be consul, so it behooved him to flatter.

"If all is in order, I will have an official paper from you to say so. Witnessed."

"I was about to do it."

"Excellent!" said Caesar heartily.

"And when will the moneys arrive?" asked Vibius as he ushered his uncomfortable visitor out.

Caesar shrugged. "That is not in my province to control. I imagine the governor will wait to bring all the moneys with him at the end of his term."

A tinge of bitterness crept into Vibius's face. "And

isn't that typical?" he exclaimed rhetorically. "What ought to be Rome's this year will remain Antistius Vetus's for long enough for him to have turned it over as an investment in his name, and profited from it."

"That is quite legal, and not my business to criticize," said Caesar gently, screwing up his eyes as he emerged into bright Forum sunshine.

"*Ave,* Gaius Julius!" snapped Vibius, and shut the door.

During the hour that this interview had consumed, the lower Forum had filled up a little, people scurrying about to complete their tasks before midafternoon and dinnertime arrived. And among the fresh faces, noted Caesar with an inward sigh, was that belonging to Marcus Calpurnius Bibulus, whom he had once lifted effortlessly and put on top of a lofty cupboard in front of six of his peers. Then apostrophized as a flea. Not without reason! They had taken but one look at each other and detested each other; it did happen that way from time to time. Bibulus had offered him the kind of insult which called for physical retaliation, secure because his diminutive size prevented Caesar's hitting him. He had implied that Caesar obtained a magnificent fleet from old King Nicomedes of Bithynia by prostituting himself to the King. In other circumstances Caesar might not have let his temper slip, but it had happened almost immediately after the general Lucullus had implied the same thing. Twice was once too many; up went Bibulus onto the cupboard, with some pungent words accompanying him. And that had been the start of almost a year living in the same quarters as Bibulus while Rome in the person of Lucullus showed the city of Mitylene in Lesbos that it could not defy its suzerain. The lines had been divided. Bibulus was an enemy.

He hadn't changed in the ten years which had elapsed since then, thought Caesar as the new group approached, Bibulus in its forefront. The other branch of the Famous Family Calpurnius, cognominated Piso, was filled with some of Rome's tallest fellows; yet the branch cognominated Bibulus (it meant spongelike, in the sense of soaking up wine) was physically opposite. No member of the

Roman nobility would have had any difficulty in deciding which Famous Family branch Bibulus belonged to. He wasn't merely small, he was tiny, and possessed of a face so fair it was bleak—jutting cheekbones, colorless hair, invisible brows, a pair of silver-grey eyes. Not unattractive, but daunting.

Clients excluded, Bibulus was not alone; he was walking side by side with an extraordinary man who wore no tunic under his toga. Young Cato, from the coloring and the nose. Well, that friendship made sense. Bibulus was married to a Domitia who was the first cousin of Cato's brother-in-law, Lucius Domitius Ahenobarbus. Odd how all the obnoxious ones stuck together, even in marriage. And as Bibulus was a member of the *boni,* no doubt that meant Cato was too.

"In search of a little shade, Bibulus?" asked Caesar sweetly as they met, his eyes traveling from his old enemy to his very tall companion, who thanks to the position of the sun and the group did actually cast his shadow across Bibulus.

"Cato will put all of us in the shade before he's done" was the reply, uttered coldly.

"The nose will be a help in that respect," said Caesar.

Cato patted his most prominent feature affectionately, not at all put out, but not amused either; wit escaped him. "No one will ever mistake my statues for anyone else's," he said.

"That is true." Caesar looked at Bibulus. "Planning to run for any office this year?" he asked.

"Not I!"

"And you, Marcus Cato?"

"Tribune of the soldiers," said Cato tersely.

"You'll do well. I hear that you won a large collection of decorations as a soldier in Poplicola's army against Spartacus."

"That's right, he did!" snapped Bibulus. "Not everyone in Poplicola's army was a coward!"

Caesar's fair brows lifted. "I didn't say that."

"You didn't have to. *You* chose Crassus to campaign with."

"I had no choice in the matter, any more than Marcus Cato will have a choice when he's elected a tribune of the soldiers. As military magistrates, we go where Romulus sends us."

Whereupon the conversation foundered and would have ceased except for the arrival of another pair far more congenial to Caesar at least: Appius Claudius Pulcher and Marcus Tullius Cicero.

"Barely here, I see, Cato!" said Cicero merrily.

Bibulus had had enough, and took himself and Cato off.

"Remarkable," said Caesar, watching the diminishing Cato. "Why no tunic?"

"He says it's part of the *mos maiorum,* and he's trying to persuade all of us to go back to the old ways," said Appius Claudius, a typical member of his family, being a dark and medium-sized man of considerable good looks. He patted Cicero's midriff and grinned. "All right for fellows like himself and Caesar, but I can't think exposure of your hide would impress a jury," he said to Cicero.

"Pure affectation," said Cicero. "He'll grow out of it." The dark, immensely intelligent eyes rested on Caesar and danced. "Mind you, I remember when your sartorial affectations upset a few of the *boni,* Caesar. Those purple borders on your long sleeves?"

Caesar laughed. "I was bored, and it seemed like something bound to irritate Catulus at the time."

"It did, it did! As leader of the *boni,* Catulus fancies himself the custodian of Rome's customs and traditions."

"Speaking of Catulus, when does he plan to finish Jupiter Optimus Maximus? I can't see any progress at all."

"Oh, it was dedicated a year ago," said Cicero. "As to when it can be used—who knows? Sulla did leave the poor fellow in severe financial difficulties over the job, you know that. Most of the money he has to find out of his own purse."

"He can afford it, he sat comfortably in Rome making money out of Cinna and Carbo while Sulla was in exile. Giving Catulus the job of rebuilding Jupiter Optimus Maximus was Sulla's revenge.''

"Ah, yes! Sulla's revenges are still famous, though he's been dead ten years."

"He was the First Man in Rome," said Caesar.

"And now we have Pompeius Magnus claiming the title," said Appius Claudius, his contempt showing.

What Caesar might have said in answer to this was not said, for Cicero spoke.

"I'm glad you're back in Rome, Caesar. Hortensius is getting a bit long in the tooth, hasn't been quite the same since I beat him in the Verres case, so I can do with some decent competition in the courts."

"Long in the tooth at forty-seven?" asked Caesar.

"He lives high," said Appius Claudius.

"So do they all in that circle."

"I wouldn't call Lucullus a high liver at the moment."

"That's right, you're not long back from service with him in the East," said Caesar, preparing to depart by inclining his head toward his retinue.

"And glad to be out of it," said Appius Claudius with feeling. He snorted a chuckle. "However, I sent Lucullus a replacement!"

"A replacement?"

"My little brother, Publius Clodius."

"Oh, that will please him!" said Caesar, laughing too.

And so Caesar left the Forum somewhat more comfortable with the thought that the next few years would be spent here in Rome. It wouldn't be easy, and that pleased him. Catulus, Bibulus and the rest of the *boni* would make sure he suffered. But there were friends too; Appius Claudius wasn't tied to a faction, and as a patrician he would favor a fellow patrician.

But what about Cicero? Since his brilliance and innovation had sent Gaius Verres into permanent exile, everyone knew Cicero, who labored under the extreme disadvantage of having no ancestors worth speaking of. A *homo novus,* a New Man. The first of his respectable rural family to sit in the Senate. He came from the same district as Marius had, and was related to him; but some flaw in his nature had blinded him to the fact that outside of the Senate, most of Rome still worshiped the memory of Gaius Marius. So Cicero refused to trade on that relationship, shunned all mention of his origins in Arpinum, and spent his days trying to pretend that he was a Roman of the Romans. He even had the wax masks of many ancestors in his atrium, but they belonged to the family of his wife, Terentia; like Gaius Marius, he had married into the highest nobility and counted on Terentia's connections to ease him into the consulship.

The best way to describe him was as a social climber, something his relative Gaius Marius had never been. Marius had married the older sister of Caesar's father, Caesar's beloved Aunt Julia, and for the same reasons Cicero had married his ugly Terentia. Yet to Marius the consulship had been a way to secure a great military command, nothing else. Whereas Cicero saw the consulship itself as the height of his ambitions. Marius had wanted to be the First Man in Rome. Cicero just wanted to belong by right to the highest nobility in the land. Oh, he would succeed! In the law courts he had no peer, which meant he had built up a formidable group of grateful villains who wielded colossal influence in the Senate. Not to mention that he was Rome's greatest orator, which meant he was sought after by other men of colossal influence to speak on their behalf.

No snob, Caesar was happy to accept Cicero for his own merits, and hoped to woo him into that Caesar faction. The trouble was that Cicero was an incurable vacillator; that immense mind saw so many potential hazards that in the end he was likely to let timidity make his decisions for him. And to a man like Caesar, who had never let fear conquer his instincts, timidity was the worst of all masters. Having Cicero on his side would make political life easier for Caesar. But would Cicero see the advantages allegiance would bring him? That was on the lap of the Gods.

Cicero was besides a poor man, and Caesar didn't have the money to buy him. His only source of income aside from his family lands in Arpinum was his wife; Terentia was extremely wealthy. Unfortunately she also controlled her own funds, and refused to indulge Cicero's taste for artworks and country villas. Oh, for money! It removed so many difficulties, especially for a man who wanted to be the First Man in Rome. Look at Pompey the Great, master of untold wealth. He bought adherents. Whereas Caesar for all his illustrious ancestry did not have the money to buy adherents or votes. In that respect, he and Cicero were two of a kind. Money. If anything could defeat him, thought Caesar, it was lack of money.

On the following morning Caesar dismissed his clients after the dawn ritual and walked alone down the Vicus Patricii to the suite of rooms he rented in a tall insula located between the Fabricius dye works and the Suburan Baths. This had become his bolt-hole after he returned from the war against Spartacus, when the living presence of mother and wife and daughter within his own home had sometimes rendered it so overpoweringly feminine that it proved intolerable. Everyone in Rome was used to noise, even those who dwelled in spacious houses upon the Palatine and Carinae—slaves shouted, sang, laughed and squabbled as they went about their work, and babies howled, small children screamed, womenfolk chattered incessantly when they weren't intruding to nag or complain. Such a normal situation that it scarcely impinged upon most men at the head of a household. But in that respect Caesar chafed, for in him resided a genuine liking for solitude as well as little patience for what he regarded as trivia. Being a true Roman, he had not attempted to reorganize his domestic environment by forbidding noise and feminine intrusions, but rather avoided them by giving himself a bolt-hole.

He liked beautiful objects, so the three rooms he rented on the second floor of this insula belied their location. His only real friend, Marcus Licinius Crassus, was an incurable acquisitor of estates and properties, and for once Crassus had succumbed to a generous impulse, sold Caesar very cheaply sufficient mosaic flooring to cover the two rooms Caesar himself used. When he had bought the house of Marcus Livius Drusus, Crassus had rather despised the floor's antiquity; but Caesar's taste was unerring, he knew nothing so good had been produced in fifty years. Similarly, Crassus had been pleased to use Caesar's apartment as practice for the squads of unskilled slaves he (very profitably) trained in prized and costly trades like plastering walls, picking out moldings and pilasters with gilt, and painting frescoes.

Thus when Caesar entered this apartment he heaved a sigh of sheer satisfaction as he gazed around the perfections of study-cum-reception-room and bedroom. Good, good! Lucius Decumius had followed his instructions to the letter and arranged several new items of furniture exactly where Caesar had wanted. They had been found in Further Spain and shipped to Rome ahead of time: a glossy console table carved out of reddish marble with lion's feet legs, a gilded couch covered in Tyrian purple tapestry, two splendid chairs. There, he noted with amusement, was the new bed Lucius Decumius had mentioned, a commodious structure in ebony and gilt with a Tyrian purple spread. Who could guess, looking at Lucius Decumius, that his taste was quite up there with Caesar's?

The owner of this establishment didn't bother checking the third room, which was really a section of the balcony rimming the interior light well. Either end of it had been walled off for privacy from the neighbors, and the light well itself was heavily shuttered, allowing air but forbidding prying eyes any sight of its interior. Herein the service arrangements were located, from a man-sized bronze bath to a cistern storing water to a chamber pot. There were no cooking facilities and Caesar did not employ a servant who lived in the apartment. Cleaning was in the care of Aurelia's servants, whom Eutychus sent down regularly to empty the bath water and keep the cistern filled, the chamber pot sweet, the linen washed, the floors swept, and every other surface dusted.

Lucius Decumius was already there, perched on the

couch, his legs swinging clear of the exquisitely colored merman on the floor, his eyes upon a scroll he held between his hands.

"Making sure the College accounts are in order for the urban praetor's audit?" asked Caesar, closing the door.

"Something like that," Lucius Decumius answered, letting the scroll fly shut with a snap.

Caesar crossed to consult the cylinder of a water clock. "According to this little beast, it's time to go downstairs, dad. Perhaps she won't be punctual, especially if Silanus has no love of chronometers, but somehow the lady didn't strike me as a person who ignores the passage of time."

"You won't want me here, Pavo, so I'll just shove her in the door and go home," said Lucius Decumius, exiting promptly.

Caesar seated himself at his desk to write a letter to Queen Oradaltis in Bithynia, but though he wrote as expeditiously as he did everything else, he had not done more than put paper in front of him when the door opened and Servilia entered. His assessment was right: she was not a lady who ignored time.

Rising, he went round the desk to greet her, intrigued when she extended her hand the way a man would. He shook it with exactly the courteous pressure such small bones demanded, but as he would have shaken a man's hand. There was a chair ready at his desk, though before she arrived he had not been sure whether to conduct this interview across a desk or more cozily ensconced in closer proximity. His mother had been right: Servilia was not easy to read. So he ushered her to the chair opposite, then returned to his own. Hands clasped loosely on the desk in front of him, he looked at her solemnly.

Well preserved if she was nearing thirty-seven years of age, he decided, and elegantly dressed in a vermilion robe whose color skated perilously close to the flame of a prostitute's toga and yet contrived to appear unimpeachably respectable. Yes, she was clever! Thick and so black its highlights shone more blue than red, her hair was pulled back from a center parting to meet a separate wing covering the upper tip of each ear, the whole then knotted into a bun on the nape of her neck. Unusual, but again respectable. A small, somewhat pursed mouth, good clear white skin, heavily lidded black eyes fringed with long and curling black lashes, brows he suspected she plucked heavily, and—most interesting of all—a slight sagging in the muscles of her right cheek that he had also noticed in the son, Brutus.

Time to break the silence, since it appeared she was not about to do so. "How may I help you, *domina*?" he asked formally.

"Decimus Silanus is our *paterfamilias,* Gaius Julius, but there are certain things pertaining to the affairs of my late first husband, Marcus Junius Brutus, that I prefer to deal with myself. My present husband is not a well man, so I try to spare him extra burdens. It is important that you do not misunderstand my actions, which may seem on the surface to usurp duties more normally in the sphere of the *paterfamilias,*" she said with even greater formality.

The expression of aloof interest his face had displayed since he sat down did not change; Caesar merely leaned back a little in his chair. "I will not misunderstand," he said.

Impossible to say she relaxed at that, for she had not seemed from the moment of her entry to be anything other than relaxed. Yet a more assured tinge crept into her wariness; it looked at him out of her eyes. "You met my son, Marcus Junius Brutus, the day before yesterday," she said.

"A nice boy."

"I think so, yes."

"Still technically a child."

"For some few months yet. This matter concerns him, and he insists it will not wait." A faint smile touched the left corner of her mouth, which seemed from watching her speak to be more mobile than the right corner. "Youth is impetuous."

"He didn't seem impetuous to me," said Caesar.

"Nor is he in most things."

"So I am to gather that your errand is on behalf of something young Marcus Junius Brutus wants?"

"That is correct."

"Well," said Caesar, exhaling deeply, "having established the proper protocol, perhaps you'll tell me what he wants."

"He wishes to espouse your daughter, Julia."

Masterly self-control! applauded Servilia, unable to detect any reaction in eyes, face, body.

"She's only eight," said Caesar.

"And he not yet officially a man. However, he wishes it."

"He may change his mind."

"So I told him. But he assures me he will not, and he ended in convincing me of his sincerity."

"I'm not sure I want to betroth Julia yet."

"Whyever not? My own daughters are both contracted already, and they are younger than Julia."

"Julia's dowry is very small."

"No news to me, Gaius Julius. However, my son's fortune is large. He doesn't need a wealthy bride. His own father left him extremely well provided for, and he is Silanus's heir too."

"You may yet have a son to Silanus."

"Possibly."

"But not probably, eh?"

"Silanus throws daughters."

Caesar leaned forward again, still appearing detached. "Tell me why I should agree to the match, Servilia."

Her brows rose. "I should have thought that was self-evident! How could Julia look higher for a husband? On my side Brutus is a patrician Servilius, on his father's side he goes back to Lucius Junius Brutus, the founder of the Republic. All of which you know. His fortune is splendid, his political career will certainly carry him to the consulship, and he may well end in being censor now that the censorship is restored. There is a blood relationship through the Rutilii as well as through both the Servilii Caepiones and the Livii Drusi. There is also *amicitia* through Brutus's grandfather's devotion to your uncle by marriage, Gaius Marius. I am aware that you are closely related to Sulla's family, but neither my own family nor my husband had any quarrel with Sulla. Your own dichotomy between Marius and Sulla is more pronounced than any Brutus can lay claim to.''

"Oh, you argue like an advocate!" said Caesar appreciatively, and finally smiled.

"I will take that as a compliment."

"You should."

Caesar got up and walked round the desk, held out his hand to help her rise.

"Am I to have no answer, Gaius Julius?"

"You will have an answer, but not today."

"When, then?" she asked, walking to the door.

A faint but alluring perfume came stealing from her as she preceded Caesar, who was about to tell her he would give her his answer after the elections when he suddenly noticed something that fascinated him into wanting to see her again sooner than that. Though she was irreproachably covered up as her class and status demanded, the back of her robe had sagged to expose the skin over neck and spine to the middle of her shoulder blades, and there like a finely feathered track a central growth of black fuzz traveled down from her head to disappear into the depths of her clothing. It looked silky rather than coarse and lay flat against her white skin, but it was not lying as it was intended to lie because whoever had dried her back after her bath hadn't cared enough to smooth it carefully into a crest along the well-padded knobs of her spine. How it cried out for that small attention!

"Come back tomorrow, if that is convenient," said Caesar, reaching past her to open the door.

No attendant waited on the minute stair landing, so he walked her down two flights to the vestibule. But when he would have taken her outside, she stopped him.

"Thank you, Gaius Julius, this far will do," she said.

"You're sure? It's not the best neighborhood."

"I have an escort. Until tomorrow, then."

Back up the stairs to the last lingering tendrils of that subtle perfume and a feeling that somehow the room was emptier than it had ever been. Servilia . . . She was deep and every layer was differently hard, iron and marble and basalt and *adamas*. Not at all nice. Not feminine, either, despite those large and shapely breasts. It might prove disastrous to turn one's back on her, for in his fancy she had two faces like Janus, one to see where she was going and one to see who followed behind. A total monster. Little wonder everyone said Silanus looked sicker and sicker. No *paterfamilias* would intercede for Brutus; she hadn't needed to explain that to him. Clearly Servilia managed her own affairs, including her son, no matter what the law said. So was betrothal to Julia her idea, or did it indeed stem from Brutus? Aurelia might know. He would go home and ask her.

And home he went, still thinking about Servilia, what it would be like to regulate and discipline that thin line of black fuzz down her back.

"Mater," he said, erupting into her office, "I need an urgent consultation, so stop what you're doing and come into my study!"

Down went Aurelia's pen; she stared at Caesar in amazement. "It's rent day," she said.

"I don't care if it's quarter day."

He was gone before he had quite finished that short sentence, leaving Aurelia to abandon her accounts in a state of shock. Not like Caesar! What had gotten into him?

"Well?" she asked, stalking into his *tablinum* to find him standing with his hands behind his back and rocking from heels to toes and back again. His toga lay in a massive heap on the floor, so she bent to pick it up, then tossed it out the door into the dining room before shutting herself in.

For a moment he acted as if she hadn't yet arrived, then started, glanced at her in mingled amusement and—exhilaration? before moving to seat her in the chair she always used.

"My dear Caesar, can't you stay still, even if you can't sit down? You look like an alley cat with the wind in its tail."

That struck him as exquisitely funny; he roared with

laughter. "I probably feel like an alley cat with the wind in its tail!"

Rent day disappeared; Aurelia realized from what interview with whom Caesar must just have emerged. "Oho! Servilia!"

"Servilia," he echoed, and sat down, suddenly recovering from that fizzing state of exaltation.

"In love, are we?" asked the mother clinically.

He considered that, shook his head. "I doubt it. In lust, perhaps, though I'm not even sure of that. I dislike her, I think."

"A promising beginning. You're bored."

"True. Certainly bored with all these women who gaze adoringly and lie down to let me wipe my feet on them."

"She won't do that for you, Caesar."

"I know, I know."

"What did she want to see you for? To start an affair?"

"Oh, we haven't progressed anywhere as far along as that, Mater. In fact, I have no idea whether my lust is reciprocated. It may well not be, because it only really began when she turned her back on me to go."

"I grow more curious by the moment. What did she want?"

"Guess," he said, grinning.

"Don't play games with me!"

"You won't guess?"

"I'll do more than refuse to guess, Caesar, if you don't stop acting like a ten-year-old. I shall leave."

"No, no, stay there, Mater, I'll behave. It just feels so good to be faced with a challenge, a little bit of *terra incognita*."

"Yes, I do understand that," she said, and smiled. "Tell me."

"She came on young Brutus's behalf. To ask that I consent to a betrothal between young Brutus and Julia."

That obviously came as a surprise; Aurelia blinked several times. "How extraordinary!"

"The thing is, Mater, whose idea is it? Hers or Brutus's?"

Aurelia put her head on one side and thought. Finally she nodded and said, "Brutus's, I would think. When one's dearly loved granddaughter is a mere child, one doesn't expect things like that to happen, but upon reflection there have been signs. He does tend to look at her like a particularly dense sheep."

"You're full of the most remarkable animal metaphors today, Mater! From alley cats to sheep."

"Stop being facetious, even if you are in lust for the boy's mother. Julia's future is too important."

He sobered instantly. "Yes, of course. Considered in the crudest light, it is a wonderful offer, even for a Julia."

"I agree, especially at this time, before your own political career is anywhere near its zenith. Betrothal to a Junius Brutus whose mother is a Servilius Caepio would gather you immense support among the *boni,* Caesar. All the Junii, both the patrician and the plebeian Servilii, Hortensius, some of the Domitii, quite a few of the Caecilii Metelli—even Catulus would have to pause."

"Tempting," said Caesar.

"Very tempting if the boy is serious."

"His mother assures me he is."

"I believe he is too. Nor does he strike me as the kind to blow hot and cold. A very sober and cautious boy, Brutus."

"Would Julia like it?" asked Caesar, frowning.

Aurelia's brows rose. "That's an odd question coming from you. You're her father, her marital fate is entirely in your hands, and you've never given me any reason to suppose you would consider letting her marry for love. She's too important, she's your only child. Besides, Julia will do as she's told. I've brought her up to understand that things like marriage are not hers to dictate."

"But I would like her to like the idea."

"You are not usually a prey to sentiment, Caesar. Is it that you don't care much for the boy yourself?" she asked shrewdly.

He sighed. "Partly, perhaps. Oh, I didn't dislike him

the way I dislike his mother. But he seemed a dull dog.''

"Animal metaphors!"

That made him laugh, but briefly. "She's such a sweet little thing, and so lively. Her mother and I were so happy that I'd like to see her happy in her marriage."

"Dull dogs make good husbands," said Aurelia.

"You're in favor of the match."

"I am. If we let it go, another half as good may not come Julia's way. His sisters have snared young Lepidus and Vatia Isauricus's eldest son, so there are two very eligible matches gone already. Would you rather give her to a Claudius Pulcher or a Caecilius Metellus? Or Pompeius Magnus's son?"

He shuddered, flinched. "You're absolutely right, Mater. Better a dull dog than ravening wolf or mangy cur! I was rather hoping for one of Crassus's sons."

Aurelia snorted. "Crassus is a good friend to you, Caesar, but you know perfectly well he'll not let either of his boys marry a girl with no dowry to speak of."

"Right again, Mater." He slapped his hands on his knees, a sign that he had made up his mind. "Marcus Junius Brutus let it be, then! Who knows? He might turn out as irresistibly handsome as Paris once he's over the pimple stage."

"I do wish you didn't have a tendency to levity, Caesar!" said his mother, rising to go back to her books. "It will hamper your career in the Forum, just as it does Cicero's from time to time. The poor boy will never be handsome. Or dashing."

"In which case," said Caesar with complete seriousness, "he is lucky. They never trust fellows who are too handsome."

"If women could vote," said Aurelia slyly, "that would soon change. Every Memmius would be King of Rome."

"Not to mention every Caesar, eh? Thank you, Mater, but I prefer things the way they are."

Servilia did not mention her interview with Caesar when she returned home, either to Brutus or Silanus. Nor did she mention that on the morrow she was going to see him again. In most households the news would have leaked through the servants, but not in Servilia's domain. The two Greeks whom she employed as escorts whenever she ventured out were old retainers, and knew her better than to gossip, even among their compatriots. The tale of the nursemaid she had seen flogged and crucified for dropping baby Brutus had followed her from Brutus's house to Silanus's, and no one made the mistake of deeming Silanus strong enough to cope with his wife's temperament or temper. No other crucifixion had happened since, but of floggings there were sufficient to ensure instant obedience and permanently still tongues. Nor was it a household wherein slaves were manumitted, could don the Cap of Liberty and call themselves freedmen or freedwomen. Once you were sold into Servilia's keeping, you stayed a slave forever.

Thus when the two Greeks accompanied her to the bottom end of the Vicus Patricii the following morning, they made no attempt to see what lay inside the building, nor dreamed of creeping up the stairs a little later to listen at doors, peer through keyholes. Not that they suspected a liaison with some man; Servilia was too well known to be above reproach in that respect. She was a snob, and it was generally held by her entire world from peers to servants that she would deem Jupiter Optimus Maximus beneath her.

Perhaps she would have, had the Great God accosted her, but a liaison with Gaius Julius Caesar certainly occupied her mind most attractively as she trod up the stairs alone, finding it significant that this morning the peculiar and rather noisome little man of yesterday was not in evidence. The conviction that something other than a betrothal would come of her interview with Caesar had not occurred until, as he had ushered her to the door, she sensed a change in him quite palpable enough to trigger hope—nay, anticipation. Of course she knew what all of Rome knew, that he was fastidious to a fault about the condition of his women, that they had to be scrupulously clean. So she had bathed with extreme care and limited her perfume to a trace incapable of disguising natural odors underneath; luckily she didn't sweat beyond a modicum, and never wore a robe more than once between launderings. Yesterday she had worn vermilion: today she chose a rich deep amber, put amber pendants in her ears and amber beads around her neck. I am tricked out for a seduction, she thought, and knocked upon the door.

He answered it himself, saw her to the chair, sat behind his desk just as he had yesterday. But he didn't look at her as he had yesterday; today the eyes were not detached, not cold. They held something she had never seen in a man's eyes before, a spark of intimacy and ownership that did not set her back up or make her dismiss him as lewd or crude. Why did she think that spark honored her, distinguished her from all her fellow women?

"What have you decided, Gaius Julius?" she asked.

"To accept young Brutus's offer."

That pleased her; she smiled broadly for the first time in his acquaintance with her, and revealed that the right corner of her mouth was definitely less strong than the left. "Excellent!" she said, and sighed through a smaller, shyer smile.

"Your son means a great deal to you."

"He means everything to me," she said simply.

There was a sheet of paper on his desk; he glanced down at it. "I've drawn up a proper legal agreement to the betrothal of your son and my daughter," he said, "but if you prefer, we can keep the matter more informal for a while, at least until Brutus is further into his manhood. He may change his mind."

"He won't, and I won't," answered Servilia. "Let us conclude the business here and now."

"If you wish, but I should warn you that once an agreement is signed, both parties and their guardians at law are fully liable at law for breach-of-promise suits and compensation equal to the amount of the dowry."

"What is Julia's dowry?" Servilia asked.

"I've put it down at one hundred talents."

That provoked a gasp. "You don't have a hundred talents to dower her, Caesar!"

"At the moment, no. But Julia won't reach marriageable age until after I'm consul, for I have no intention of allowing her to marry before her eighteenth birthday. By the time that day arrives, I will have the hundred talents for her dowry."

"I believe you will," said Servilia slowly. "However, it means that should my son change his mind, he'll be a hundred talents poorer."

"Not so sure of his constancy now?" asked Caesar, grinning.

"Quite as sure," she said. "Let us conclude the business."

"Are you empowered to sign on Brutus's behalf, Servilia? It did not escape me that yesterday you called Silanus the boy's *paterfamilias*."

She wet her lips. "*I* am Brutus's legal guardian, Caesar, not Silanus. Yesterday I was concerned that you should think no worse of me for approaching you myself rather than sending my husband. We live in Silanus's house, of which he is indeed the *paterfamilias*. But Uncle Mamercus was the executor of my late husband's will, and of my own very large dowry. Before I married Silanus, Uncle Mamercus and I tidied up my affairs, which included my late husband's estates. Silanus was happy to agree that I should retain control of what is mine, and act as Brutus's guardian. The arrangement has worked well, and Silanus doesn't interfere."

"Never?" asked Caesar, eyes twinkling.

"Well, only once," Servilia admitted. "He insisted I should send Brutus to school rather than keep him at home to be tutored privately. I saw the force of his argument, and agreed to try it. Much to my surprise, school turned out to be good for Brutus. He has a natural tendency toward what he calls intellectualism, and his own pedagogue inside his own house would have reinforced it."

"Yes, one's own pedagogue does tend to do that," said Caesar gravely. "He's still at school, of course."

"Until the end of the year. Next year he'll go to the Forum and a *grammaticus*. Under the care of Uncle Mamercus."

"A splendid choice and a splendid future. Mamercus is a relation of mine too. Might I hope that you allow me to participate in Brutus's rhetorical education? After all, I am destined to be his father-in-law," said Caesar, getting up.

"That would delight me," said Servilia, conscious of a vast and unsettling disappointment. Nothing was going to happen! Her instincts had been terribly, dreadfully, horribly wrong!

He went round behind her chair, she thought to assist her departure, but somehow her legs refused to work; she had to continue to sit like a statue and feel ghastly.

"Do you know," came his voice—or *a* voice, so different and throaty was it—"that you have the most delicious little ridge of hair as far down your backbone as I can see? But no one tends it properly, it's rumpled and lies every which way. That is a shame, I thought so yesterday."

He touched the nape of her neck just below the great coil of her hair, and she thought at first it was his fingertips, sleek and languorous. But his head was immediately behind hers, and both his hands came round to cup her breasts. His breath cooled her neck like a breeze on wet skin, and it was then she understood what he was doing. Licking that growth of superfluous hair she hated so much, that her mother had despised and derided until the day she died. Licking it first on one side and then the other, always toward the ridge of her spine, working slowly down, down. And all Servilia could do was to sit a prey to sensations she had not imagined existed, burned and drenched in a storm of feeling.

Married though she had been for eighteen years to two very different men, in all her life she had never known anything like this fiery and piercing explosion of the senses reaching outward from the focus of his tongue, diving inward to invade breasts and belly and core. At some stage she did manage to get up, not to help him untie the girdle below her breasts nor to ease the layers of her clothing off her shoulders and eventually to the floor—those he did for himself—but to stand while he followed the

line of hair with his tongue until it dwindled to invisibility
where the crease of her buttocks began. And if he produced a knife and plunged it to the hilt in my heart, she
thought, I could not move an inch to stop him, would not
even want to stop him. Nothing mattered save the ongoing
gratification of a side of herself she had never dreamed
she owned.

His own clothing, both toga and tunic, remained in
place until he reached the end of his tongue's voyage,
when she felt him step back from her, but could not turn
to face him because if she let go the back of the chair she
would fall.

"Oh, that's better," she heard him say. "That's how
it must be, always. Perfect."

He came back to her and turned her round, pulling
her arms to circle his waist, and she felt his skin at last,
put up her face for the kiss he had not yet given her. But
instead he lifted her up and carried her to the bedroom,
set her down effortlessly on the sheets he had already
turned down in readiness. Her eyes were closed, she could
only sense him looming over her, but they opened when
he put his nose to her navel and inhaled deeply.

"Sweet," he said, and moved down to mons veneris.
"Plump, sweet and juicy," he said, laughing.

How could he laugh? But laugh he did; then as her
eyes widened at the sight of his erection, he gathered her
against him and kissed her mouth at last. Not like Brutus,
who had stuck his tongue in so far and so wetly it had
revolted her. Not like Silanus, whose kisses were reverent
to the point of chasteness. This was perfect, something to
revel in, join in, linger at. One hand stroked her back from
buttocks to shoulders; the fingers of the other gently explored between the lips of her vulva and set her to shivering and shuddering. Oh, the luxury of it! The absolute
glory of not caring what kind of impression she was making, whether she was being too forward or too backward,
what he was thinking of her! Servilia didn't care, didn't
care, didn't care. This was for herself. So she rolled on
top of him and put both her hands around his erection to
guide it home, then sat on it and ground her hips until she

screamed her ecstasy aloud, as transfixed and pinioned as a woodland creature on a huntsman's spear. Then she fell forward and lay against his chest as limp and finished as that woodland creature killed.

Not that he was finished with her. The lovemaking continued for what seemed hours, though she had no idea when he attained his own orgasm or whether there were several or just the one, for he made no sound and remained erect until suddenly he ceased.

"It really is very big," she said, lifting his penis and letting it drop against his belly.

"It really is very sticky," he said, uncoiled lithely and disappeared from the room.

When he returned her sight had come back sufficiently to perceive that he was hairless like the statue of a god, and put together with the care of a Praxiteles Apollo.

"You are so beautiful," she said, staring.

"Think it if you must, but don't say it" was his answer.

"How can you like me when you have no hair yourself?"

"Because you're sweet and plump and juicy, and that line of black down ravishes me." He sat upon the edge of the bed and gave her a smile that made her heart beat faster. "Besides which, you enjoyed yourself. That's at least half the fun of it as far as I'm concerned."

"Is it time to go?" she asked, sensitive to the fact that he made no move to lie down again.

"Yes, it's time to go." He laughed. "I wonder if technically this counts as incest? Our children are engaged to be married."

But she lacked his sense of the ridiculous, and frowned. "Of course not!"

"A joke, Servilia, a joke," he said gently, and got up. "I hope what you wore doesn't crease. Everything is still on the floor in the other room."

While she dressed, he began filling his bath from the cistern by dipping a leather bucket into it and tossing the water out from the bucket into the bath tirelessly. Nor did he stop when she came to watch.

"When can we meet again?" she asked.

"Not too often, otherwise it will pall, and I'd rather it didn't," he said, still ladling water.

Though she was not aware of it, this was one of his tests; if the recipient of his lovemaking proceeded with tears or many protestations to show him how much she cared, his interest waned.

"I agree with you," she said.

The bucket stopped in mid-progress; Caesar gazed at her, arrested. "Do you really?"

"Absolutely," she said, making sure her amber earrings were properly hooked into place. "Do you have any other women?"

"Not at the moment, but it can change any day." This was the second test, more rigorous than the first.

"Yes, you do have a reputation to maintain, I can see that."

"Can you really?"

"Of course." Though her sense of humor was vestigial, she smiled a little and said, "I understand what they all say about you now, you see. I'll be stiff and sore for days."

"Then let's meet again the day after the Popular Assembly elections. I'm standing for curator of the Via Appia."

"And my brother Caepio for quaestor. Silanus of course will stand for praetor in the Centuries before that."

"And your other brother, Cato, will no doubt be elected a tribune of the soldiers."

Her face squeezed in, mouth hard, eyes like stone. "Cato is not my brother, he's my half brother," she said.

"They say that of Caepio too. Same mare, same stallion."

She drew a breath, looked at Caesar levelly. "I am aware of what they say, and I believe it to be true. But Caepio bears my own family's name, and since he does, I acknowledge him."

"That's very sensible of you," said Caesar, and returned to emptying his bucket.

Whereupon Servilia, assured that she looked passable if not as unruffled as she had some hours before, took her departure.

Caesar entered the bath, his face thoughtful. That was an unusual woman. A plague upon seductive feathers of black down! Such a silly thing to bring about his downfall. Down fall. A good pun, if inadvertent. He wasn't sure he liked her any better now they were lovers, yet he knew he was not about to give her her congé. For one thing, she was a rarity in other ways than in character. Women of his own class who could behave between the sheets without inhibition were as scarce as cowards in a Crassus army. Even his darling Cinnilla had preserved modesty and decorum. Well, that was the way they were brought up, poor things. And, since he had fallen into the habit of being honest with himself, he had to admit that he would make no move to have Julia brought up in any other way. Oh, there were trollops among his own class, women who were as famous for their sexual tricks as any whore from the late great Colubra to the ageing Praecia. But when Caesar wanted an uninhibited sexual frolic, he preferred to seek it among the honest and open, earthy and decent women of the Subura. Until today and Servilia. Who would ever have guessed it? She wouldn't gossip about her fling, either. He rolled over in the bath and reached for his pumice stone; no use working with a *strigilis* in cold water, a man needed to sweat in order to scrape.

"And how much," he asked the drab little bit of pumice, "do I tell my mother about this? Odd! She's so detached I usually find no difficulty in talking to her about women. But I think I shall don the solid-purple toga of a censor when I mention Servilia."

The elections were held on time that year, the Centuriate to return consuls and praetors first, then the full gamut of patricians and plebeians in the Popular Assembly to return the more minor magistrates, and finally the tribes in the Plebeian Assembly, which restricted its activities to the election of plebeian aediles and tribunes of the plebs.

Though it was Quinctilis by the calendar and therefore ought to have been high summer, the seasons were dragging behind because Metellus Pius Pontifex Maximus had not been prone to insert those extra twenty days each second February for many years. Perhaps not so surprising then that Gnaeus Pompeius Magnus—Pompey the Great—was moved to visit Rome to behold the due process of electoral law in the Plebeian Assembly, since the weather was springish and halcyon.

Despite his claim that he was the First Man in Rome, Pompey detested the city, and preferred to live upon his absolutely vast estates in northern Picenum. There he was a virtual king; in Rome he was uncomfortably aware that most of the Senate detested him even more than he did Rome. Among the knights who ran Rome's business world he was extremely popular and had a large following, but that fact couldn't soothe his sensitive and vulnerable image of himself when certain senatorial members of the *boni* and other aristocratic cliques made it clear that they thought him no more than a presumptuous upstart, a non-Roman interloper.

His ancestry was mediocre, but by no means nonexistent, for his grandfather had been a member of the Senate and married into an impeccably Roman family, the Lucilii, and his father had been the famous Pompey Strabo, consul, victorious general of the Italian War, protector of the conservative elements in the Senate when Rome had been threatened by Marius and Cinna. But Marius and Cinna had won, and Pompey Strabo died of disease in camp outside the city. Blaming Pompey Strabo for the epidemic of enteric fever which had ravaged besieged Rome, the inhabitants of the Quirinal and Viminal had dragged his naked body through the streets tied behind an ass. To the young Pompey, an outrage he had never forgiven.

His chance had come when Sulla returned from exile and invaded the Italian Peninsula; only twenty-two years old, Pompey had enlisted three legions of his dead father's veterans and marched them to join Sulla in Campania. Well aware that Pompey had blackmailed him into a joint command, the crafty Sulla had used him for some of his more dubious enterprises as he maneuvered toward the dictatorship, then held it. Even after Sulla retired and died, he looked after this ambitious, cocksure sprig by introducing a law which allowed a man not in the Senate to be given command of Rome's armies. For Pompey had taken against the Senate, and refused to belong to it. There had followed the six years of Pompey's war against the rebel Quintus Sertorius in Spain, six years during which Pompey was obliged to reassess his military ability; he had gone to Spain utterly confident that he would beat Sertorius in no time flat, only to find himself pitted against one of the best generals in the history of Rome. In the end he simply wore Sertorius down. So the Pompey who returned to Italia was a much changed person: cunning, unscrupulous, bent on showing the Senate (which had kept him shockingly short of money and reinforcements in Spain) that he, who did not belong to it, could grind its face in the dust.

Pompey had proceeded to do so, with the connivance of two other men—Marcus Crassus, victor against Spartacus, and none other than Caesar. With the twenty-nine-year-old Caesar pulling their strings, Pompey and Crassus used the existence of their two armies to force the Senate into allowing them to stand for the consulship. No man had ever been elected to this most senior of all magistracies before he had been at the very least a member of the Senate, but Pompey became senior consul, Crassus his colleague. Thus this extraordinary, underaged man from Picenum attained his objective in the most unconstitutional way, though it had been Caesar, six years his junior, who showed him how to do it.

To compound the Senate's misery, the joint consulship of Pompey the Great and Marcus Crassus had been a triumph, a year of feasts, circuses, merriment and prosperity. And when it was over, both men declined to take provinces; instead, they retired into private life. The only significant law they had passed restored full powers to the tribunes of the plebs, whom Sulla had legislated into virtual impotence.

Now Pompey was in town to see next year's tribunes of the plebs elected, and that intrigued Caesar, who encountered him and his multitudes of clients at the corner of the Sacra Via and the Clivus Orbius, just entering the lower Forum.

"I didn't expect to see you in Rome," said Caesar as they joined forces. He surveyed Pompey from head to foot openly, and grinned. "You're looking well, and very fit besides," he said. "Keeping your figure into middle age, I see."

"Middle age?" asked Pompey indignantly. "Just because I've already been consul doesn't mean I'm in my dotage! I won't turn thirty-eight until the end of September!"

"Whereas I," said Caesar smugly, "have very recently turned thirty-two—at which, Pompeius Magnus, you were not consul either."

"Oh, you're pulling my leg," said Pompey, calming down. "You're like Cicero, you'll joke your way onto the pyre."

"That witty I wish I was. But you haven't answered my serious question, Magnus. What are you doing in Rome for no better reason than to see the tribunes of the plebs elected? I wouldn't have thought you'd need to employ tribunes of the plebs these days."

"A man always needs a tribune of the plebs or two, Caesar."

"Does he now? What are you up to, Magnus?"

The vivid blue eyes opened wide, and the glance Pompey gave Caesar was guileless. "I'm not up to anything."

"Oh! Look!" cried Caesar, pointing at the sky. "Did you see it, Magnus?"

"See what?" asked Pompey, scanning the clouds.

"That bright pink pig flying like an eagle."

"You don't believe me."

"Correct, I don't believe you. Why not make a clean breast of it? I'm not your enemy, as you well know. In fact, I've been of enormous help to you in the past, and there's no reason why I oughtn't help your career along in the future. I'm not a bad orator, you have to admit that.''

''Well . . .'' began Pompey, then fell silent.

''Well what?''

Pompey stopped, glanced behind at the crowd of clients who followed in their wake, shook his head, and detoured slightly to lean against one of the pretty marble columns which propped up the arcade outside the Basilica Aemilia's main chamber. Understanding that this was Pompey's way of avoiding eavesdroppers, Caesar ranged himself alongside the Great Man to listen while the horde of clients remained, eyes glistening and dying of curiosity, too far away to hear a word.

''What if one of them can read our lips?'' asked Caesar.

''You're joking again!''

''Not really. But we could always turn our backs on them and pretend we're pissing into Aemilia's front passage.''

That was too much; Pompey cried with laughter. However, when he sobered, noted Caesar, he did turn sufficiently away from their audience to present his profile to it, and moved his lips as furtively as a Forum vendor of pornography.

''As a matter of fact,'' muttered Pompey, ''I do have one good fellow among the candidates this year.''

''Aulus Gabinius?''

''How did you guess that?''

''He hails from Picenum, and he was one of your personal staff in Spain. Besides, he's a good friend of mine. We were junior military tribunes together at the siege of Mitylene.'' Caesar pulled a wry face. ''Gabinius didn't like Bibulus either, and the years haven't made him any fonder of the *boni*.''

''Gabinius is the best of good fellows,'' said Pompey.

''And remarkably capable.''

''That too.''

''What's he going to legislate for you? Strip Lucullus's command off him and hand it to you on a golden salver?''

"No, no!" snapped Pompey. "It's too soon for *that*! First I need a short campaign to warm my muscles up."

"The pirates," said Caesar instantly.

"Right this time! The pirates it is."

Caesar bent his right knee to tuck its leg against his column and looked as if nothing more was going on than a nice chat about old times. "I applaud you, Magnus. That's not only very clever, it's also very necessary."

"You're not impressed with Metellus Little Goat in Crete?"

"The man's a pigheaded fool, and venal into the bargain. He wasn't brother-in-law to Verres for nothing—in more ways than one. With three good legions, he barely managed to win a land battle against twenty-four thousand motley and untrained Cretans who were led by sailors rather than soldiers."

"Terrible," said Pompey, shaking his head gloomily. "I ask you, Caesar, what's the point in fighting land battles when the pirates operate at sea? All very well to say that it's their land bases you need to eradicate, but unless you catch them at sea you can't destroy their livelihood— their ships. Modern naval warfare isn't like Troy, you can't burn their ships drawn up on the shore. While most of them are holding you off, the rest form skeleton crews and row the fleet elsewhere."

"Yes," said Caesar, nodding, "that's where everyone has made his mistake so far, from both Antonii to Vatia Isauricus. Burning villages and sacking towns. The task needs a man with a true talent for organization."

"Exactly!" cried Pompey. "And I am that man, I promise you! If my self-inflicted inertia of the last couple of years has been good for nothing else, it has given me time to think. In Spain I just lowered my horns and charged blindly into the fray. What I ought to have done was work out how to win the war before I set one foot out of Mutina. I should have investigated everything beforehand, not merely how to blaze a new route across the Alps. Then I would have known how many legions I needed, how many horse troopers, how much money in my war chest—and I would have learned to understand my enemy. Quintus Sertorius was a brilliant tactician. But, Caesar, you don't win wars on tactics. Strategy is the thing, strategy!''

"So you've been doing your homework on the pirates, Magnus?''

"Indeed I have. Exhaustively. Every single aspect, from the largest to the smallest. Maps, spies, ships, money, men. I know how to do the job,'' said Pompey, displaying a different kind of confidence than he used to own. Spain had been Kid Butcher's last campaign. In future he would be no butcher of any sort.

Thus Caesar watched the ten tribunes of the plebs elected with great interest. Aulus Gabinius was a certainty, and indeed came in at the top of the poll, which meant he would be president of the new College of Tribunes of the Plebs which would enter office on the tenth day of this coming December.

Because the tribunes of the plebs enacted most new laws and were traditionally the only legislators who liked to see change, every powerful faction in the Senate needed to ''own'' at least one tribune of the plebs. Including the *boni,* who used their men to block all new legislation; the most powerful weapon a tribune of the plebs had was the veto, which he could exercise against his fellows, against all other magistrates, and even against the Senate. That meant the tribunes of the plebs who belonged to the *boni* would not enact new laws, they would veto them. And of course the *boni* succeeded in having three men elected— Globulus, Trebellius and Otho. None was a brilliant man, but then a *boni* tribune of the plebs didn't need to be brilliant; he simply needed to be able to articulate the word ''Veto!''

Pompey had two excellent men in the new College to pursue his ends. Aulus Gabinius might be relatively ancestorless and a poor man, but he would go far; Caesar had known that as far back as the siege of Mitylene. Naturally Pompey's other man was also from Picenum: a Gaius Cornelius who was not a patrician any more than he was a member of the venerable *gens Cornelia.* Perhaps he was not as tied to Pompey as Gabinius was, but he certainly would not veto any plebiscite Gabinius might propose to the Plebs.

Interesting though all of this was for Caesar, the one man elected who worried him the most was tied neither to the *boni* nor to Pompey the Great. He was Gaius Papirius Carbo, a radical sort of man with his own axe to grind. For some time he had been heard to say in the Forum that he intended to prosecute Caesar's uncle, Marcus Aurelius Cotta, for the illegal retention of booty taken from Heracleia during Marcus Cotta's campaign in Bithynia against Rome's old enemy, King Mithridates. Marcus Cotta had returned in triumph toward the end of that famous joint consulship of Pompey and Crassus, and no one had questioned his integrity then. Now this Carbo was busy muddying old waters, and as a tribune of the fully restored Plebs he would be empowered to try Marcus Cotta in a specially convened Plebeian Assembly court. Because Caesar loved and admired his Uncle Marcus, Carbo's election was a big worry.

The last ballot tile counted, the ten victorious men stood on the rostra acknowledging the cheers; Caesar turned away and plodded home. He was tired: too little sleep, too much Servilia. They had not met again until the day after the elections in the Popular Assembly some six days earlier, and, as predicted, both had something to celebrate. Caesar was curator of the Via Appia ("What on earth possessed you to take that job on?" Appius Claudius Pulcher had demanded, astonished. "It's *my* ancestor's road, but that big a fool I am not! You'll be poor in a year"), and Servilia's so-called full brother Caepio had been elected one of twenty quaestors. The lots had given him duty inside Rome as urban quaestor, which meant he didn't have to serve in a province.

So they had met in a mood of satisfaction as well as mutual anticipation, and had found their day in bed together so immensely pleasurable that neither of them was willing to postpone another. They met every day for a feast of lips, tongues, skin, and every day found something new to do, something fresh to explore. Until today, when more elections rendered a meeting impossible. Nor would they find time again until perhaps the Kalends of September, for Silanus was taking Servilia, Brutus and the girls to the seaside resort of Cumae, where he had a villa. Silanus too had been successful in this year's elections; he was to be urban praetor next year. That very important magistracy would raise Servilia's public profile too; among other things, she was hoping that her house would be chosen for the women-only rites of Bona Dea, when Rome's most illustrious matrons put the Good Goddess to sleep for the winter.

And it was time too that he told Julia that he had arranged her marriage. The formal ceremony of betrothal would not take place until after Brutus donned his *toga virilis* in December, but the legalities were done, Julia's fate was sealed. Why he had put the task off when such was never his custom niggled at the back of his mind; he had asked Aurelia to break the news, but Aurelia, a stickler for domestic protocol, had refused. He was the *paterfamilias;* he must do it. Women! Why did there have to be so many women in his life, and why did he think the future held even more of them? Not to mention more trouble because of them?

Julia had been playing with Matia, the daughter of his dear friend Gaius Matius, who occupied the other ground-floor apartment in Aurelia's insula. However, she came home sufficiently ahead of the dinner hour for him to find no further excuse for not telling her, dancing across the light-well garden like a young nymph, draperies floating around her immature figure in a mist of lavender blue. Aurelia always dressed her in soft pale blues or greens, and she was right to do so. How beautiful she will be, he thought, watching her; perhaps not the equal of Aurelia for Grecian purity of bones, but she had that magical Julia quality which Aurelia, so pragmatic and sensible and Cottan, did not. They always said of the Julias that they made their men happy, and he could believe that every time he saw his daughter. The adage was not infallible; his younger aunt (who had been Sulla's first wife) had committed suicide after a long affair with the wine flagon, and his cousin Julia Antonia was on her second ghastly husband amid increasing bouts of depression and hysterics. Yet Rome continued to say it, and he was not about to contradict it; every nobleman with sufficient wealth not to need a rich bride thought first of a Julia.

When she saw her father leaning on the sill of the dining room window her face lit up; she came flying across to him and managed to make her scramble up and over the wall into his arms a graceful exercise.

"How's my girl?" he asked, carrying her across to one of the three dining couches, and putting her down beside him.

"I've had a lovely day, *tata*. Did all the right people get in as tribunes of the plebs?"

The outer corners of his eyes pleated into fans of creases as he smiled; though his skin was naturally very pale, many years of an outdoor life in forums and courts and fields of military endeavor had browned its exposed surfaces, except in the depths of those creases at his eyes, where it remained very white. This contrast fascinated Julia, who liked him best when he wasn't in the midst of a smile or a squint, and displayed his fans of white stripes like warpaint on a barbarian. So she got up on her knees and kissed first one fan and then the other, while he leaned his head toward her lips and melted inside as he never had for any other female, even Cinnilla.

"You know very well," he answered her, the ritual over, "that all the right people never get in as tribunes of the plebs. The new College is the usual mixture of good, bad, indifferent, ominous and intriguing. But I do think they'll be more active than this year's lot, so the Forum will be busy around the New Year."

She was well versed in political matters, of course, since both father and grandmother were from great political families, but living in the Subura meant her playmates (even Matia next door) were not of the same kind, had scant interest in the machinations and permutations of Senate, Assemblies, courts. For that reason Aurelia had sent her to Marcus Antonius Gnipho's school when she turned six; Gnipho had been Caesar's private tutor, but when Caesar donned the *laena* and *apex* of the *flamen Dialis* on arrival of his official manhood, Gnipho had returned to conducting a school with a noble clientele. Julia had proven a very bright and willing pupil, with the same love of literature her father owned, though in mathematics and geography her ability was less marked. Nor did she have Caesar's astonishing memory. A good thing, all who loved her had concluded wisely; quick and clever girls were excellent, but intellectual and brilliant girls were a handicap, not least to themselves.

"Why are we in here, *tata*?" she asked, a little puzzled.

"I have some news for you that I'd like to tell you in a quiet place," said Caesar, not lost for how to do it now that he had made up his mind to do it.

"Good news?"

"I don't quite know, Julia. I hope so, but I don't live inside your skin, only you do that. Perhaps it won't be such good news, but I think after you get used to it you won't find it intolerable."

Because she was quick and clever, even if she wasn't a born scholar, she understood immediately. "You've arranged a husband for me," she said.

"I have. Does that please you?"

"Very much, *tata*. Junia is betrothed, and lords it over all of us who aren't. Who is it?"

"Junia's brother, Marcus Junius Brutus."

He was looking into her eyes, so he caught the swift flash of a creature stricken before she turned her head away and gazed straight ahead. Her throat worked, she swallowed.

"Doesn't that please you?" he asked, heart sinking.

"It's a surprise, that's all," said Aurelia's granddaughter, who had been reared from her cradle to accept every lot Fate cast her way, from husbands to the very real hazards of childbearing. Her head came round, the wide blue eyes were smiling now. "I'm very pleased. Brutus is nice."

"You're sure?"

"Oh, *tata*, of course I'm sure!" she said, so sincerely that her voice shook. "Truly, *tata*, it's good news. Brutus will love me and take care of me, I know that.''

The weight of his heart eased, he sighed, smiled, took her little hand and kissed it lightly before enfolding her in a hug. It never occurred to him to ask her if she could learn to love Brutus, for love was not an emotion Caesar enjoyed, even the love he had known for Cinnilla and for this exquisite sprite. To feel it left him vulnerable, and he hated that.

Then she skipped off the couch and was gone; he could hear her calling in the distance as she sped to Aurelia's office.

"*Avia, avia,* I am to marry my friend Brutus! Isn't that splendid? Isn't that good news?''

Then came the long-drawn-out moan that heralded a bout of tears. Caesar listened to his daughter weep as if her heart was broken, and knew not whether joy or sorrow provoked it. He came out into the reception room as Aurelia ushered the child toward her sleeping cubicle, face buried in Aurelia's side.

His mother's face was unperturbed. ''I do wish,'' she said in his direction, ''that female creatures laughed when they're happy! Instead, a good half of them cry. Including Julia.''

Fortune certainly continued to favor Gnaeus Pompeius Magnus, reflected Caesar early in December, smiling to himself. The Great Man had indicated a wish to eradicate the pirate menace, and Fortune obediently connived to gratify him when the Sicilian grain harvest arrived in Ostia, Rome's port facility at the mouth of the Tiber River. Here the deep-drafted freighters unloaded their precious cargo into barges for the final leg of the grain journey up the Tiber to the silo facilities of the Port of Rome itself. Here was absolute security, home at last.

Several hundred ships converged on Ostia to discover no barges waiting; the quaestor for Ostia had mistimed things so badly that he had allowed the barges an extra trip upstream to Tuder and Ocriculum, where the Tiber Valley harvest was demanding transportation downstream to Rome. So while captains and grain tycoons fulminated and the hapless quaestor ran in ever-decreasing circles, an irate Senate directed the sole consul, Quintus Marcius Rex, to rectify matters forthwith.

It had been a miserable year for Marcius Rex, whose consular colleague had died soon after entering office. The Senate had immediately appointed a suffect consul to take his place, but he too died, and too quickly even to insert his posterior into his curule chair. A hurried consultation of the Sacred Books indicated that no further measures ought to be taken, which left Marcius Rex to govern alone. This had utterly ruined his plan to proceed during his consulship to his province, Cilicia, bestowed on him when hordes of lobbying knight businessmen had succeeded in having it taken off Lucullus.

Now, just when Marcius Rex was hoping to leave for Cilicia at last, came the grain shambles in Ostia. Red with temper, he detached two praetors from their law courts in Rome and sent them posthaste to Ostia to sort things out. Each preceded by six lictors in red tunics bearing the axes in their *fasces,* Lucius Bellienus and Marcus Sextilius bore down on Ostia from the direction of Rome. And at precisely the same moment, a pirate fleet numbering over one hundred sleek war galleys bore down on Ostia from the Tuscan Sea.

The two praetors arrived to find half the town burning, and pirates busily forcing the crews of laden grain ships to row their vessels back onto the sea lanes. The audacity of this raid—whoever could have dreamed that pirates would invade a place scant miles from mighty Rome?—had taken everyone by surprise. No troops were closer than Capua, Ostia's militia was too concerned with putting out fires on shore to think of marshaling resistance, and no one had even had the sense to send an urgent message for help to Rome.

Neither praetor was a man of decision, so both stood stunned and disorientated amid the turmoil on the docks. There a group of pirates discovered them, took them and

their lictors prisoner, loaded them on board a galley, and
sailed merrily off in the wake of the disappearing grain
fleet. The capture of two praetors—one no less than the
uncle of the great patrician nobleman Catilina—together
with their lictors and *fasces* would mean at least two hundred talents in ransom!

The effect of the raid inside Rome was as predictable
as it was inevitable: grain prices soared immediately;
crowds of furious merchants, millers, bakers and consum-
ers descended upon the lower Forum to demonstrate
against governmental incompetence; and the Senate went
into a huddle with the Curia doors shut so that no one
outside would hear how dismal the debate within was
bound to be. And dismal it was. No one even wanted to
open it.

When Quintus Marcius Rex had called several times
to no avail for speakers, there finally rose—it seemed with
enormous reluctance—the tribune of the plebs–elect Aulus
Gabinius, who looked, thought Caesar, even more the
Gaul in that dim, filtered light. That was the trouble with
all the men from Picenum—the Gaul in them showed
more than the Roman. Including Pompey. It wasn't so
much the red or gold hair many of them sported, nor the
blue or green eyes; plenty of impeccably Roman Romans
were very fair. Including Caesar. The fault lay in Picentine
bone structure. Full round faces, dented chins, short noses
(Pompey's was even snubbed), thinnish lips. Gaul, not Roman. It put them at a disadvantage, proclaimed to the
whole of their world that they might protest all they liked
that they were descended from Sabine migrants, but the
truth was that they were descended from Gauls who had
settled in Picenum over three hundred years ago.

The reaction among the majority of the senators who
sat on their folding stools was palpable when Gabinius the
Gaul rose to his feet: distaste, disapproval, dismay. Under
normal circumstances his turn to speak would have been
very far down the hierarchy. At this time of year he was
outranked by fourteen incumbent magistrates, fourteen
magistrates-elect, and some twenty consulars—if, of
course, everyone was present. Everyone was not. Every-

one never was. Nonetheless, to have a tribunician magistrate open the debate was almost unprecedented.

"It hasn't been a good year, has it?" Aulus Gabinius asked the House after completing the formalities of addressing those above and below him in the pecking order. "During the past six years we have attempted to wage war against the pirates of Crete alone, though the pirates who have just sacked Ostia and captured the grain fleet—not to mention kidnapped two praetors and their insignia of office—don't hail from anywhere half as far away as Crete, do they? No, they patrol the middle of Our Sea from bases in Sicily, Liguria, Sardinia and Corsica. Led no doubt by Megadates and Pharnaces, who for some years have enjoyed a really delightful little pact with various governors of Sicily like the exiled Gaius Verres, whereby they can go wherever they please in Sicilian waters and harbors. I imagine they rounded up their allies and shadowed this grain fleet all the way from Lilybaeum. Perhaps their original intention was to raid it at sea. Then some enterprising person in their pay at Ostia sent them word that there were no barges at Ostia, nor likely to be for eight or nine days. Well, why settle for capturing a part only of the grain fleet by attempting to raid it at sea? Better to do the job while it lay intact and fully laden in Ostia harbor! I mean, the whole world knows Rome keeps no legions in her home territory of Latium! What was to stop them at Ostia? What did stop them at Ostia? The answer is very short and simple—*nothing*!"

This last word was bellowed; everyone jumped, but no one replied. Gabinius gazed about and wished Pompey was present to hear him. A pity, a great pity. Still, Pompey would love the letter Gabinius intended to send him this night!

"Something has got to be done," Gabinius went on, "and by that I do not mean the usual debacle so exquisitely personified by the campaign our chief Little Goat is still waging in Crete. First he barely manages to defeat some Cretan rabble in a land battle, then he lays siege to Cydonia, which eventually capitulates—but he lets the great pirate admiral Panares go free! So a couple more

towns fall, then he lays siege to Cnossus, within whose
walls the great pirate admiral Lasthenes is skulking. When
the fall of Cnossus looks inevitable, Lasthenes destroys
what treasures he can't carry away with him, and escapes.
An efficient siege operation, eh? But which disaster causes
our chief Little Goat more sorrow? The flight of Lasthenes
or the loss of the treasure trove? Why, the loss of the
treasure trove, of course! Lasthenes is only a pirate, and
pirates don't ransom each other. Pirates expect to be crucified like the slaves they once were!''

Gabinius the Gaul from Picenum paused, grinning
savagely in the way a Gaul could. He drew a deep breath,
then said, ''Something has got to be done!'' And sat down.

No one spoke. No one moved.

Quintus Marcius Rex sighed. ''Has no one anything
to say?'' His eyes roamed from one tier to another on both
sides of the House, and rested nowhere until they encountered a derisive look on Caesar's face. Now why did Caesar stare like that?

''Gaius Julius Caesar, you were once captured by pirates, and you managed to get the better of them. Have
you nothing to say?'' asked Marcius Rex.

Caesar rose from his seat on the second tier. ''Just
one thing, Quintus Marcius. Something has got to be
done.'' And sat down.

The sole consul of the year lifted both hands in the
air as a gesture of defeat, and dismissed the meeting.

''When do you intend to strike?'' asked Caesar of
Gabinius as they left the Curia Hostilia together.

''Not quite yet,'' said Gabinius cheerfully. ''I have a
few other things to do first, so does Gaius Cornelius. I
know it's customary to start one's year as a tribune of the
plebs with the biggest things first, but I consider those bad
tactics. Let our esteemed consuls-elect Gaius Piso and
Manius Acilius Glabrio warm their arses on their curule
chairs first. I want to let them think Cornelius and I have
exhausted our repertoire before I so much as attempt to
reopen today's subject.''

''January or February, then.''

''Certainly not before January,'' said Gabinius.

"So Magnus is fully prepared to take on the pirates."

"Down to the last bolt, nail and skin of water. I can tell you, Caesar, that Rome will never have seen anything like it."

"Then roll on, January." Caesar paused, turned his head to look at Gabinius quizzically. "Magnus will never succeed in getting Gaius Piso on his side, he's too glued to Catulus and the *boni,* but Glabrio is more promising. He's never forgotten what Sulla did to him."

"When Sulla forced him to divorce Aemilia Scaura?"

"Precisely. He's the junior consul next year, but it's handy to have at least one consul in thrall."

Gabinius chuckled. "Pompeius has something in mind for our dear Glabrio."

"Good. If you can divide the consuls of the year, Gabinius, you can go a lot further, a lot faster."

Caesar and Servilia resumed their liaison after she returned from Cumae at the end of October, no less absorbed in it and in each other. Though Aurelia tried to fish from time to time, Caesar confined his information about the progress of the affair to a minimum, and gave his mother no real indication how serious a business it was, nor how intense. He still disliked Servilia, but that couldn't affect their relationship because liking wasn't necessary. Or perhaps, he thought, liking would have taken something vital away from it.

"Do you like me?" he asked Servilia the day before the new tribunes of the plebs assumed office.

She fed him one breast at a time, and delayed her answer until both nipples had popped up and she could feel the heat start to move downward through her belly.

"I like no one," she said then, climbing on top of him. "I love or I hate."

"Is that comfortable?"

Because she lacked a sense of humor, she did not mistake his question for a reference to their present juxtaposition, but went straight to its real meaning. "Far more comfortable than liking, I'd say. I've noticed that when people like each other, they become incapable of acting as they ought. They delay telling each other home truths, for example, it seems out of fear that home truths will wound. Love and hate permit home truths.''

''Would you care to hear a home truth?'' he asked, smiling as he kept absolutely still; that drove her to distraction when her blood was afire and she needed him to move inside her.

''Why don't you just shut up and get on with it, Caesar?''

''Because I want to tell you a home truth.''

''All right, then, tell it!'' she snapped, kneading her own breasts when he would not. ''Oh, how you love to torment!''

''You like being on top a great deal more than being underneath, or sideways, or any other way,'' he said.

''That's true, I do. Now are you happy? Can we get on with it?''

''Not yet. Why do you like being on top best?''

''Because I'm on top, of course,'' she said blankly.

''Aha!'' he said, and rolled her over. ''Now I'm on top.''

''I wish you weren't.''

''I am happy to gratify you, Servilia, but not when it means I also gratify your sense of power.''

''What other outlet do I have to gratify my sense of power?'' she asked, wriggling. ''You're too big and too heavy this way!''

''You're quite right about comfort,'' he said, pinning her down. ''Not liking someone means one is not tempted to relent.''

''Cruel,'' she said, eyes glazing.

''Love and hate are cruel. Only liking is kind.''

But Servilia, who did not like anyone, had her own method of revenge; she raked her carefully tended nails from his left buttock to his left shoulder, and drew five parallel lines with his blood.

Though she wished she hadn't, for he took both her wrists and ground their bones, then made her lie beneath him for what seemed an eternity ramming himself home deeper and deeper, harder and harder; when she cried and screamed at the end, she scarcely knew whether agony or ecstasy provoked her, and for some time was sure her love had turned to hate.

The worst of that encounter did not occur until after Caesar went home. Those five crimson tracks were very sore, and his tunic when he peeled it away showed that he was still bleeding. The cuts and scratches he had sustained in the field from time to time told him that he would have to ask for someone to wash and dress the damage or run the risk of festering. If Burgundus had been in Rome it would have been easy, but these days Burgundus lived in the Caesar villa at Bovillae with Cardixa and their eight sons, caring for the horses and sheep Caesar bred. Lucius Decimius wouldn't do; he was not clean enough. And Eutychus would blab the story to his boyfriend, his boyfriend's boyfriends and half the members of the crossroads college. His mother, then. It would have to be his mother.

Who looked and said, "Ye immortal Gods!"

"I wish I was one, then it wouldn't hurt."

Off she went to bring two bowls, one half-full of water and the other half-full of fortified but sour wine, together with wads of clean Egyptian linen.

"Better linen than wool, wool leaves fluff behind in the depths of the wounds," she said, beginning with the strong wine. Her touch wasn't tender, but it was thorough enough to make his eyes water; he lay on his belly, as much of him covered as her sense of decency dictated, and endured her ministrations without a sound. Anything capable of festering after Aurelia got through with it, he consoled himself, would kill a man from gangrene.

"Servilia?" she asked some time later, finally satisfied that she had got enough wine into the tracks to cow any festering thing lurking there, and beginning afresh with water.

"Servilia."

"What sort of relationship is this?" she demanded.

"Not," he said, and shook with laughter, "a comfortable one."

"So much I see. She might end in murdering you."

"I trust I preserve sufficient vigilance to prevent *that*."

"Bored you're not."

"Definitely not bored, Mater."

"I do not think," she finally pronounced as she patted the water dry, "that this relationship is a healthy one. It might be wise to end it, Caesar. Her son is betrothed to your daughter, which means the two of you will have to preserve the proprieties for many years to come. Please, Caesar, end it."

"I'll end it when I'm ready, not before."

"No, don't get up yet!" Aurelia said sharply. "Let it dry properly first, then put on a clean tunic." She left him and began to hunt through his chest of clothes until she found one which satisfied her sniffing nose. "It's plain to see Cardixa isn't here, the laundry girl isn't doing her job as she ought. I shall have something to say about that tomorrow morning." Back to the bed she came, and tossed the tunic down beside him. "No good will come of this relationship, it isn't healthy," she said.

To which he answered nothing. By the time he had swung his legs off the bed and plunged his arms into the tunic, his mother was gone. And that, he told himself, was a mercy.

On the tenth day of December the new tribunes of the plebs entered office, but it was not Aulus Gabinius who dominated the rostra. That privilege belonged to Lucius Roscius Otho of the *boni,* who told a cheering crowd of senior knights that it was high time they had their old rows at the theater restored for their exclusive use. Until Sulla's dictatorship they had enjoyed sole possession of the fourteen rows just behind the two front rows of seats still reserved for senators. But Sulla, who loathed knights of all kinds, had taken this perquisite away from them together with sixteen hundred knight lives, estates and cash fortunes. Otho's measure was so popular it was carried at once, no surprise to Caesar, watching from the Senate steps. The *boni* were brilliant at currying favor with the knights; it was one of the pillars of their continuing success.

The next meeting of the Plebeian Assembly interested Caesar far more than Otho's equestrian honeycomb: Aulus Gabinius and Gaius Cornelius, Pompey's men, took over. The first order of business was to reduce the consuls of the coming year from two to one, and the way Gabinius did it was deliciously clever. He asked the Plebs to give the junior consul, Glabrio, governance of a new province in the East to be called Bithynia-Pontus, then followed this up by asking the Plebs to send Glabrio out to govern it the day after he was sworn into office. That would leave Gaius Piso on his own to deal with Rome and Italia. Hatred of Lucullus predisposed the knights who dominated the Plebs to favor the bill because it stripped Lucullus of power—and of his four remaining legions. Still commissioned to fight the two kings Mithridates and Tigranes, he now had nothing save an empty title.

Caesar's own feelings about it were ambivalent. Personally he detested Lucullus, who was such a stickler for the correct way to do things that he deliberately elected incompetence in others if the alternative was to ignore proper protocols. Yet the fact remained that he had refused to allow the knights of Rome complete freedom to fleece the local peoples of his provinces. Which of course was why the knights hated him so passionately. And why they were in favor of any law which disadvantaged Lucullus. A pity, thought Caesar, sighing inwardly. That part of himself longing for better conditions for the local peoples of Rome's provinces wanted Lucullus to survive, whereas the monumental injury Lucullus had offered his *dignitas* by implying that he had prostituted himself to King Nicomedes demanded that Lucullus fall.

Gaius Cornelius was not quite as tied to Pompey as Gabinius was; he was one of those occasional tribunes of the plebs who genuinely believed in righting some of Rome's most glaring wrongs, and that Caesar liked. Therefore Caesar found himself silently willing Cornelius not to give up after his first little reform was defeated. What he had asked the Plebs to do was to forbid foreign communities to borrow money from Roman usurers. His reasons were sensible and patriotic. Though the money-lenders were not Roman officials, they employed Roman officials to collect when debts became delinquent. With the result that many foreigners thought the State itself was in the moneylending business. Rome's prestige suffered. But of course desperate or gullible foreign communities were a valuable source of knight income; little wonder Cornelius failed, thought Caesar sadly.

His second measure almost failed, and showed Caesar that this Picentine fellow was capable of compromise, not usual in the breed. Cornelius's intention was to stop the Senate's owning the power to issue decrees exempting an individual from some law. Naturally only the very rich or the very aristocratic were able to procure an exemption, usually granted when the senatorial mouthpiece had a meeting specially convened, then made sure it was filled with his creatures. Always jealous of its prerogatives, the Senate opposed Cornelius so violently that he saw he would lose. So he amended his bill to leave the power to exempt with the Senate—but only on condition that a quo-rum of two hundred senators was present to issue a decree. It passed.

By now Caesar's interest in Gaius Cornelius was growing at a great rate. The praetors earned his attention next. Since Sulla's dictatorship their duties had been con-fined to the law, both civil and criminal. And the law said that when a praetor entered office he had to publish his *edicta,* the rules and regulations whereby he personally would administer justice. The trouble was that the law didn't say a praetor had to abide by his *edicta,* and the moment a friend needed a favor or there was some money to be made, the *edicta* were ignored. Cornelius simply asked the Plebs to stop up the gap, compel praetors to adhere to their *edicta* as published. This time the Plebs saw the sense of the measure as clearly as Caesar did, and voted it into law.

Unfortunately all Caesar could do was watch. No pa-trician might participate in the affairs of the Plebs. So he couldn't stand in the Well of the Comitia, or vote in the

Plebeian Assembly, or speak in it, or form a part of a trial process in it. Or run for election as a tribune of the plebs. Thus Caesar stood with his fellow patricians on the Curia Hostilia steps, as close to the Plebs in session as he was permitted to go.

Cornelius's activities presented an intriguing aspect of Pompey, whom Caesar had never thought the slightest bit interested in righting wrongs. But perhaps after all he was, given Gaius Cornelius's dogged persistence in matters which couldn't affect Pompey's plans either way. More likely, however, Caesar concluded, that Pompey was merely indulging Cornelius in order to throw sand in the eyes of men like Catulus and Hortensius, leaders of the *boni*. For the *boni* were adamantly opposed to special military commands, and Pompey was once again after a special command.

The Great Man's hand was more evident—at least to Caesar—in Cornelius's next proposal. Gaius Piso, doomed to govern alone now that Glabrio was going to the East, was a choleric, mediocre and vindictive man who belonged completely to Catulus and the *boni*. He would rant against any special military command for Pompey until the Senate House rafters shook, with Catulus, Hortensius, Bibulus and the rest of the pack baying behind. Owning little attractive apart from his name, Calpurnius Piso, and his eminently respectable ancestry, Piso had needed to bribe heavily to secure election. Now Cornelius put forward a new bribery law; Piso and the *boni* felt a cold wind blowing on their necks, particularly when the Plebs made its approval plain enough to indicate that it would pass the bill. Of course a *boni* tribune of the plebs could interpose his veto, but Otho, Trebellius and Globulus were not sure enough of their influence to veto. Instead the *boni* shifted themselves mightily to manipulate the Plebs—and Cornelius—into agreeing that Gaius Piso himself should draft the new bribery law. Which, thought Caesar with a sigh, would produce a law endangering no one, least of all Gaius Piso. Poor Cornelius had been outmaneuvered.

When Aulus Gabinius took over, he said not one word about the pirates or a special command for Pompey the Great. He preferred to concentrate on minor matters, for he was far subtler and more intelligent than Cornelius. Less altruistic, certainly. The little plebiscite he succeeded in passing that forbade foreign envoys in Rome to borrow money in Rome was obviously a less sweeping version of Cornelius's measure to forbid the lending of money to foreign communities. But what was Gabinius after when he legislated to compel the Senate to deal with nothing save foreign delegations during the month of February? When Caesar understood, he laughed silently. Clever Pompey! How much the Great Man had changed since he entered the Senate as consul carrying Varro's manual of behavior in his hand so he wouldn't make embarrassing mistakes! For this particular *lex Gabinia* informed Caesar that Pompey planned to be consul a second time, and was ensuring his dominance when that second year arrived. No one would poll more votes, so he would be senior consul. That meant he would have the *fasces*—and the authority—in January. February was the junior consul's turn, and March saw the *fasces* back with the senior consul. April went to the junior consul. But if February saw the Senate confined to foreign affairs, then the junior consul would have no chance to make his presence felt until April. Brilliant!

In the midst of all this pleasurable turbulence, a different tribune of the plebs inserted himself into Caesar's life far less enjoyably. This man was Gaius Papirius Carbo, who presented a bill to the Plebeian Assembly asking that it arraign Caesar's middle uncle, Marcus Aurelius Cotta, on charges of stealing the spoils from the Bithynian city of Heracleia. Unfortunately Marcus Cotta's colleague in the consulship that year had been none other than Lucullus, and they were well known to be friends. Knight hatred of Lucullus inevitably prejudiced the Plebs against any close friend or ally, so the Plebs allowed Carbo to have his way. Caesar's beloved uncle would stand trial for extortion, but not in the excellent standing court Sulla had established. Marcus Cotta's jury would be several thousand men who all hungered to tear Lucullus and his cronies down.

"There was nothing to steal!" Marcus Cotta said to Caesar. "Mithridates had used Heracleia as his base for months, then the place withstood siege for several months more—when I entered it, Caesar, it was as bare as a newborn rat! Which *everybody* knew! What do you think three hundred thousand soldiers and sailors belonging to Mithridates left? They looted Heracleia far more thoroughly than Gaius Verres looted Sicily!"

"You don't need to protest your innocence to me, Uncle," said Caesar, looking grim. "I can't even defend you because it's trial by the Plebs and I'm a patrician."

"That goes without saying. However, Cicero will do it."

"He won't, Uncle. Didn't you hear?"

"Hear what?"

"He's overwhelmed by grief. First his cousin Lucius died, then his father died only the other day. Not to mention that Terentia has some sort of rheumatic trouble which Rome at this season makes worse, and she rules that particular roost! Cicero has fled to Arpinum."

"Then it will have to be Hortensius, my brother Lucius, and Marcus Crassus," said Cotta.

"Not as effective, but it will suffice, Uncle."

"I doubt it, I really do. The Plebs are after my blood."

"Well, anyone who is a known friend of poor Lucullus's is a target for the knights."

Marcus Cotta looked ironically at his nephew. "*Poor* Lucullus?" he asked. "He's no friend of yours!"

"True," said Caesar. "However, Uncle Marcus, I can't help but approve of his financial arrangements in the East. Sulla showed him the way, but Lucullus went even further. Instead of allowing the knight *publicani* to bleed Rome's eastern provinces dry, Lucullus has made sure Rome's taxes and tributes are not only fair, but also popular with the local communities. The old way, with the *publicani* permitted to squeeze mercilessly, might mean bigger profits for the knights, but it also means a great deal of animosity for Rome. I loathe the man, yes. Lucullus not only insulted me unpardonably, he denied me the military credit I was entitled to as well. Yet as an administrator he's superb, and I'm sorry for him.''

''A pity the pair of you didn't get on, Caesar. In many ways you're as like as twins.''

Startled, Caesar stared at his mother's half brother. Most of the time he never saw much of a family resemblance between Aurelia and any of her three half brothers, but that dry remark of Marcus Cotta's was Aurelia! She was there too in Marcus Cotta's large, purplish-grey eyes. Time to go, when Uncle Marcus turned into Mater. Besides, he had an assignation with Servilia to keep.

But that too turned out to be an unhappy business.

If Servilia arrived first, she was always undressed and in the bed waiting for him. But not today. Today she sat on a chair in his study, and wore every layer of clothing.

''I have something to discuss,'' she said.

''Trouble?'' he asked, sitting down opposite her.

''Of the most basic and, thinking about it, inevitable kind. I am pregnant.''

No identifiable emotion entered his cool gaze; Caesar said, ''I see,'' then looked at her searchingly. ''This is a difficulty?''

''In many ways.'' She wet her lips, an indication of nervousness unusual in her. ''How do you feel about it?''

He shrugged. ''You're married, Servilia. That makes it your problem, doesn't it?''

''Yes. What if it's a boy? You have no son.''

''Are you sure it's mine?'' he countered quickly.

''Of that,'' she said emphatically, ''there can be no doubt. I haven't slept in the same bed as Silanus for over two years.''

''In which case, the problem is still yours. I would have to take a chance on its being a boy, because I couldn't acknowledge it as mine unless you divorced Silanus and married me before its birth. Once it's born in wedlock to Silanus, it's his.''

''Would you be prepared to take that chance?'' she asked.

He didn't hesitate. "No. My luck says it's a girl."

"I don't know either. I didn't think of this happening, so I didn't concentrate on making a boy or a girl. It will indeed take its chances as to its sex."

If his own demeanor was detached, so, he admitted with some admiration, was hers. A lady well in control.

"Then the best thing you can do, Servilia, is to hustle Silanus into your bed as soon as you possibly can. Yesterday, I hope?"

Her head moved slowly from side to side, an absolute negative. "I am afraid," she said, "that is out of the question. Silanus is not a well man. We ceased to sleep together not through any fault of mine, I do assure you. Silanus is incapable of sustaining an erection, and the fact distresses him."

To this news Caesar reacted: the breath hissed between his teeth. "So our secret will soon be no secret," he said.

To give her credit, she felt no anger at Caesar's attitude, nor condemned him as selfish, uninterested in her plight. In many ways they were alike, which perhaps was why Caesar could not grow emotionally attached to her: two people whose heads would always rule their hearts— and their passions.

"Not necessarily," she said, and produced a smile. "I shall see Silanus today when he comes home from the Forum. It may be that I will be able to prevail upon him to keep the secret."

"Yes, that would be better, especially with the betrothal of our children. I don't mind taking the blame for my own actions, but I can't feel comfortable with the idea of hurting either Julia or Brutus by having the result of our affair common gossip." He leaned forward to take her hand, kissed it, and smiled into her eyes. "It isn't a common affair, is it?"

"No," said Servilia. "Anything but common." She wet her lips again. "I'm not very far along, so we could continue until May or June. If you want to."

"Oh yes," said Caesar, "I want to, Servilia."

"After that, I'm afraid, we won't be able to meet for seven or eight months."

"I shall miss it. And you."

This time it was she who reached for a hand, though she did not kiss his, just held it and smiled at him. "You could do me a favor during those seven or eight months, Caesar."

"Such as?"

"Seduce Cato's wife, Atilia."

He burst out laughing. "Keep me busy with a woman who stands no chance of supplanting you, eh? Very clever!"

"It's true, I am clever. Oblige me, please! Seduce Atilia!"

Frowning, Caesar turned the idea over in his mind. "Cato isn't a worthy target, Servilia. What is he, twenty-six years old? I agree that in the future he might prove a thorn in my side, but I'd rather wait until he is."

"For me, Caesar, for me! Please! *Please!*"

"Do you hate him so much?"

"Enough to want to see him broken into tiny pieces," she said through her teeth. "Cato doesn't deserve a political career."

"Seducing Atilia won't prevent his having one, as you well know. However, if it means so much to you—all right."

"Oh, wonderful! Thank you!" She huffed happily, then thought of something else. "Why have you never seduced Bibulus's wife, Domitia? Him you certainly owe the pleasure of wearing horns, he is already a dangerous enemy. Besides, his Domitia is my half sister Porcia's husband's cousin. It would hurt Cato too."

"A bit of the bird of prey in me, I suppose. The anticipation of seducing Domitia is so great I keep postponing the actual deed."

"Cato," she said, "is far more important to me."

Bird of prey, nothing, she thought to herself on the way back to the Palatine. Though he may see himself as an eagle, Servilia thought, his conduct over Bibulus's wife is plain feline.

Pregnancy and children were a part of life, and, with the exception of Brutus, just a something which had to be endured with a minimum of inconvenience. Brutus had been hers alone; she had fed him herself, changed his diapers herself, bathed him herself, played with him and amused him herself. But her attitude to her two daughters had been far different. Once she dropped them, she handed them to nursemaids and more or less forgot about them until they grew sufficiently to need a more sternly Roman supervision. This she applied without much interest, and no love. When each of them turned six, she sent them to Marcus Antonius Gnipho's school because Aurelia had recommended it as suitable for girls, and she had not had cause to regret this decision.

Now, seven years later, she was going to have a love child, the fruit of a passion which ruled her life. What she felt for Gaius Julius Caesar was not alien to her nature, that being an intense and powerful one well suited to a great love; no, its chief disadvantage stemmed from him and his nature, which she read correctly as unwilling to be dominated by emotions arising out of personal relationships of any kind. This early and instinctive divination had saved her making the mistakes women commonly made, from putting his feelings to the test, to expecting fidelity and overt demonstrations of interest in anything beyond what happened between them in that discreet Suburan apartment.

Thus she had not gone that afternoon to tell him her news in any anticipation that it would provoke joy or add a proprietary feeling of ownership in him, and she had been right to discipline herself out of hope. He was neither pleased nor displeased; as he had said, this was her business, had nothing to do with him. Had she anywhere, buried deep down, cherished a hope that he would want to claim this child? She didn't think so, didn't walk home conscious of disappointment or depression. As he had no wife of his own, only one union would have needed the legality of divorce—hers to Silanus. But look at how Rome had condemned Sulla for summarily divorcing Aelia. Not that Sulla had cared once the young wife of Scau-

rus was freed by widowhood. Not that Caesar would have
cared. Except that Caesar had a sense of honor Sulla had
not; oh, it wasn't a particularly honorable sense of honor,
it was too bound up in what he thought of himself and
wanted from himself to be that. Caesar had set a standard
of conduct for himself which embraced every aspect of his
life. He didn't bribe his juries, he didn't extort in his province, he was not a hypocrite. All no more and no less than
evidence that he would do everything the hard way; he
would not resort to techniques designed to render political
progress easier. His self-confidence was indestructible; he
never doubted for one moment his ability to get where he
intended to go. But claim this child as his own by asking
her to divorce Silanus so he could marry her before the
child was born? No, that he wouldn't even contemplate
doing. She knew exactly why. For no other reason than
that it would demonstrate to his Forum peers that he was
under the thumb of an inferior—a woman.

She wanted desperately to marry him, of course,
though not to acknowledge the paternity of this coming
child. She wanted to marry him because she loved him
with mind as much as body, because in him she recognized
one of the great Romans, a fitting husband who would
never disappoint her expectations of his political and military performance any more than his ancestry and *dignitas*
could do aught than enhance her own. He was a Publius
Cornelius Scipio Africanus, a Gaius Servilius Ahala, a
Quintus Fabius Maximus Cunctator, a Lucius Aemilius
Paullus. Of the true patrician aristocracy—a quintessential
Roman—possessed of immense intellect, energy, decision
and strength. An ideal husband for a Servilia Caepionis.
An ideal stepfather for her beloved Brutus.

The dinner hour was not far away when she arrived
home, and Decimus Junius Silanus, the steward informed
her, was in his study. What *was* the matter with him? she
wondered as she entered the room to find him writing a
letter. At forty years of age he looked closer to fifty, lines
of physical suffering engraved down either side of his
nose, his prematurely grey hair toning into grey skin.
Though he was striving to acquit himself well as urban

praetor, the demands of that duty were sapping an already fragile vitality. His ailment was mysterious enough to have defeated the diagnostic skills of every physician Rome owned, though the consensus of medical opinion was that its progress was too slow to suggest an underlying malignancy; no one had found a palpable tumor, nor was his liver enlarged. The year after next he would be eligible to stand for the consulship, but Servilia for one now believed he had not the stamina to mount a successful campaign.

"How are you today?" she asked, sitting in the chair in front of his desk.

He had looked up and smiled at her when she entered, and now laid down his pen with some pleasure. His love for her had grown no less with the accumulation of almost ten years of marriage, but his inability to be a husband to her in all respects ate at him more corrosively than his disease. Aware of his innate defects of character, he had thought when the disease clamped down after the birth of Junilla that she would turn on him with reproaches and criticisms; but she never had, even after the pain and burning in his gut during the night hours forced him to move to a separate sleeping cubicle. When every attempt at lovemaking had ended in the ghastly embarrassment of impotence, it had seemed kinder and less mortifying to remove himself physically; though he would have been content to cuddle and kiss, Servilia in the act of love was not cozy and not prone to dalliance.

So he answered her question honestly by saying, "No better and no worse than usual."

"Husband, I want to talk to you," she said.

"Of course, Servilia."

"I am pregnant, and you have good cause to know that the child is not yours."

His color faded from grey to white, he swayed. Servilia leaped to her feet and went to the console table where two carafes and some silver goblets resided, poured unwatered wine into one and stood supporting him while he sipped at it, retching slightly.

"Oh, Servilia!" he exclaimed after the stimulant had done its work and she had returned to her chair.

"If it is any consolation," she said, "this fact has nothing to do with your own illness and disabilities. Were you as virile as Priapus, I would still have gone to this man."

The tears gathered in his eyes, poured faster and faster down his cheeks.

"Use your handkerchief, Silanus!" snapped Servilia.

Out it came, mopped away. "Who is he?" he managed to ask.

"In good time. First I need to know what you intend to do about my situation. The father will not marry me. To do so would diminish his *dignitas,* and that matters more to him than I ever could. I do not blame him, you understand."

"How can you be so rational?" he asked in wonder.

"I can see little point in being anything else! Would you rather I had rushed in squalling and screaming, and made what is still our business everyone's business?"

"I suppose not," he said tiredly, and sighed. The handkerchief was tucked away. "No, of course not. Except that it might have proved you are human. If anything about you worries me, Servilia, it is your lack of humanity, your inability to understand frailty. You bore on like an auger applied to the framework of your life with the skill and drive of a professional craftsman."

"That is a very muddled metaphor," said Servilia.

"Well, it was what I always sensed in you—and perhaps what I envied in you, for I do not have it myself. I admire it enormously. But it isn't comfortable, and it prevents pity."

"Don't waste your pity on me, Silanus. You haven't answered my question yet. What do you intend to do about my situation?"

He got up, supporting himself by holding on to the back of his chair until he was sure his legs would hold him up. Then he paced up and down the room for a moment before looking at her. So calm, so composed, so unaffected by disaster!

"Since you don't intend to marry the man, I think the best thing I can do is move back into our bedroom for enough time to make the child's origin look like my doing,'' he said, going back to his chair.

Oh, why couldn't she at least accord him the gratification of seeing her relax, or look relieved, or happy? No, not Servilia! She simply looked exactly the same, even within her eyes.

"That," she said, "is sensible, Silanus. It is what I would have done in your situation, but one never knows how a man will see what touches his pride."

"It touches my pride, Servilia, but I would rather my pride remained intact, at least in the eyes of our world. No one knows?"

"He knows, but he won't air the truth."

"Are you very far along?"

"No. If you and I resume sleeping together, I doubt anyone will be able to guess from the date of the child's birth that it is anyone's but yours."

"Well, you must have been discreet, for I've heard not one rumor, and there are always plenty of people to let slip rumors like that to the cuckolded husband."

"There will be no rumors."

"Who is he?" Silanus asked again.

"Gaius Julius Caesar, of course. I would not have surrendered my reputation to anyone less."

"No, of course you wouldn't have. His birth is as great as rumor says his procreative equipment is," said Silanus bitterly. "Are you in love with him?"

"Oh, yes."

"I can understand why, for all that I dislike the man. Women do tend to make fools of themselves over him."

"I," said Servilia flatly, "have not made a fool of myself."

"That's true. And do you intend to go on seeing him?"

"Yes. I will never not see him."

"One day it will come out, Servilia."

"Probably, but it suits neither of us to have our affair made public, so we will try to prevent that."

"For which I should be grateful, I suppose. With any luck, I'll be dead before it does."

"I do not wish you dead, husband."

Silanus laughed, but its note was not amused. "For which I ought to be grateful! I wouldn't put it past you to speed my quittance if you thought it might serve your purposes."

"It does not serve my purposes."

"I understand that." His breath caught. "Ye gods, Servilia, your children are formally contracted to be married! How can you hope to keep the affair secret?"

"I fail to see why Brutus and Julia endanger us, Silanus. We do not meet anywhere in their vicinity."

"Or anyone else's vicinity, obviously. As well that the servants are afraid of you."

"Indeed."

He put his head between his hands. "I would like to be alone now, Servilia."

She rose immediately. "Dinner will be ready shortly."

"Not for me today."

"You should eat," she said on the way to the door. "It has not escaped me that your pain lessens for some hours after you eat, especially when you eat well."

"Not today! Now go, Servilia, go!"

Servilia went, well satisfied with this interview, and in better charity with Silanus than she had expected to be.

The Plebeian Assembly convicted Marcus Aurelius Cotta of peculation, fined him more than his fortune was worth, and forbade him fire and water within four hundred miles of Rome.

"Which denies Athens to me," he said to his younger brother, Lucius, and to Caesar, "but the thought of Massilia is revolting. So I think I'll go to Smyrna, and join Uncle Publius Rutilius."

"Better company than Verres," said Lucius Cotta, aghast at the verdict.

"I hear that the Plebs is going to vote Carbo consular insignia as a token of its esteem," said Caesar, lip curling.

"Including lictors and *fasces*?" asked Marcus Cotta, gasping.

"I admit we can do with a second consul now that Glabrio's gone off to govern his new combined province, Uncle Marcus, but though the Plebs may be able to dispense purple-bordered togas and curule chairs, it's news to me that it can bestow imperium!" snapped Caesar, still shaking with anger. "This is all thanks to the Asian *publicani*!"

"Leave it be, Caesar," said Marcus Cotta. "Times change, it is as simple as that. You might call this the last backlash of Sulla's punishment of the Ordo Equester. Lucky for me that we all recognized what might happen, and transferred my lands and money to Lucius here."

"The proceeds will follow you to Smyrna," said Lucius Cotta. "Though it was the knights brought you down, there were elements in the Senate contributed their mite as well. I acquit Catulus and Gaius Piso and the rest of the rump, but Publius Sulla, his minion Autronius and all that lot were assiduous in helping Carbo prosecute. So was Catilina. I shan't forget."

"Nor shall I," said Caesar. He tried to smile. "I love you dearly, Uncle Marcus, you know that. But not even for you will I put horns on Publius Sulla's head by seducing Pompeius's hag of a sister."

That provoked a laugh, and the fresh comfort of each man's reflecting that perhaps Publius Sulla was already reaping a little retribution by being obliged to live with Pompey's sister, neither young nor attractive, and far too fond of the wine flagon.

Aulus Gabinius finally struck toward the end of February. Only he knew how difficult it had been to sit on his hands and delude Rome into thinking he, the president of the College of Tribunes of the Plebs, was a lightweight after all. Though he existed under the odium of being a man from Picenum (and Pompey's creature), Gabinius was not precisely a New Man. His father and his uncle had sat in the Senate before him, and there was plenty of respectable Roman blood in the Gabinii besides. His ambition was to throw off Pompey's yoke and be his own man, though a strong streak of common sense told him that he would never be powerful enough to lead his own faction. Rather, Pompey the Great wasn't great enough. Gabinius hankered to ally himself with a more Roman man, for there were many things about Picenum and the Picentines exasperated him, particularly their attitude toward Rome. Pompey mattered more than Rome did, and Gabinius found that hard to take. Oh, it was natural enough! In Picenum Pompey was a king, and in Rome he wielded immense clout. Most men from a particular place were proud to follow a fellow countryman who had established his ascendancy over people generally considered better.

That Aulus Gabinius, fair of face and form, was dissatisfied with the idea of owning Pompey as master could be laid at no one else's door than Gaius Julius Caesar's. Much of an age, they had met at the siege of Mitylene and liked each other at once. Truly fascinated, Gabinius had watched young Caesar demonstrate a kind of ability and strength that told him he was privileged to be the friend of a man who would one day matter immensely. Other men had the looks, the height, the physique, the charm, even the ancestors; but Caesar had much more. To own an intellect like his yet be the bravest of the brave was distinction enough, for formidably intelligent men usually saw too many risks in valor. It was as if Caesar could shut anything out that threatened the enterprise of the moment. Whatever the enterprise was, he found exactly the right way to utilize only those qualities in himself able to conclude it with maximum effect. And he had a power Pompey would never have, something which poured out of him and bent everything to the shape he wanted. He counted no cost, he had absolutely no fear.

And though in the years since Mitylene they had not seen much of each other, Caesar continued to haunt Gabinius. Who made up his mind that when the day came that Caesar led his own faction, Aulus Gabinius would be one of his staunchest adherents. Though how he was going to wriggle out of his cliental obligations to Pompey, Gabinius didn't know. Pompey was his patron, therefore Gabinius had to work for him as a proper client should. All of which meant that he struck with more intention of impressing the relatively junior and obscure Caesar than Gnaeus Pompeius Magnus, the First Man in Rome. His patron.

He didn't bother going to the Senate first; since the full restoration of the powers of the tribunes of the plebs, that was not mandatory. Better to strike the Senate without warning by informing the Plebs first, and on a day no one could suspect might produce earthshaking changes.

Some five hundred men only were dotted around the Well of the Comitia when Gabinius ascended the rostra to speak; these were the professional Plebs, that nucleus which never missed a meeting and could recite whole memorable speeches by heart, not to mention detail plebiscites of note going back a generation at least.

The Senate House steps were not well populated either; just Caesar, several of Pompey's senatorial clients including Lucius Afranius and Marcus Petreius, and Marcus Tullius Cicero.

"If we had ever needed reminding how serious the pirate problem is to Rome, then the sack of Ostia and the capture of our first consignment of Sicilian grain a mere three months ago ought to have administered a gigantic stimulus!" Gabinius told the Plebs—and the watchers on the Curia Hostilia steps.

"And what have we done to clear Our Sea of this noxious infestation?" he thundered. "What have we done to safeguard the grain supply, to ensure that the citizens of Rome do not suffer famines, or have to pay more than they can afford for bread, their greatest staple? What have we done to protect our merchants and their vessels? What have we done to prevent our daughters' being kidnapped, our praetors' being abducted?

"Very little, members of the Plebs. Very, very little!"

Cicero moved closer to Caesar, touched his arm. "I am intrigued," he said, "but not mystified. Do you know where he's going, Caesar?"

"Oh, yes."

On went Gabinius, enjoying himself highly.

"The very little we have done since Antonius the

Orator attempted his pirate purge over forty years ago started in the aftermath of our Dictator's reign, when his loyal ally and colleague Publius Servilius Vatia went out to govern Cilicia under orders to flush out the pirates. He had a full proconsular imperium, and the authority to raise fleets from every city and state affected by pirates, including Cyprus and Rhodes. He began in Lycia, and dealt with Zenicetes. It took him three years to defeat *one* pirate! And that pirate was based in Lycia, not among the rocks and crags of Pamphylia and Cilicia, where the worst pirates are. The remainder of his time in the governor's palace at Tarsus was devoted to a beautiful small war against a tribe of *inland* Pamphylian soil-scratching peasants, the Isauri. When he defeated them, took their two pathetic little towns captive, our precious Senate told him to tack an extra name onto Publius Servilius Vatia—Isauricus, if you please! Well, Vatia isn't very inspiring, is it? Knock-knees for a cognomen! Can you blame the poor fellow for wanting to go from being Publius of the plebeian family Servilius who has Knock-knees, to Publius Servilius Knock-knees the Conqueror of the Isauri? You must admit that Isauricus adds a trifle more luster to an otherwise dismal name!''

To illustrate his point, Gabinius pulled his toga up to show his shapely legs from midthigh downward, and minced back and forth across the rostra with knees together and feet splayed wide apart; his audience responded by laughing and cheering.

''The next chapter in this saga,'' Gabinius went on, ''happened in and around the island of Crete. For no better reason than that his father the Orator—a far better and abler man who still hadn't managed to do the job!—had been commissioned by the Senate and People of Rome to eliminate piracy in Our Sea, the son Marcus Antonius collared the same commission some seven years ago, though this time the Senate alone issued it, thanks to our Dictator's new rules. In the first year of his campaign Antonius pissed undiluted wine into every sea at the western end of Our Sea and claimed a victory or two, but never did produce tangible evidence like spoils or ship's beaks. Then, filling his sails with burps and farts, Antonius caroused his way to Greece. Here for two years he sallied forth against the pirate admirals of Crete, with what disastrous consequences we all know. Lasthenes and Panares just walloped him! And in the end, a broken Man of Chalk—for that too is what Creticus means!—he took his own life rather than face the Senate of Rome, his commissioner.

"After which came another man with a brilliant nickname—that Quintus Caecilius Metellus who is the grandson of Macedonicus and the son of Billy Goat—Metellus Little Goat. It would seem, however, that Metellus Little Goat aspires to be another Creticus! But will Creticus turn out to mean the Conqueror of the Cretans, or a Man of Chalk? What do you think, fellow plebeians?"

"Man of Chalk! Man of Chalk!" came the answer.

Gabinius finished up conversationally. "And that, dear friends, brings us up to the present moment. It brings us to the debacle at Ostia, the stalemate in Crete, the inviolability of every pirate bolt-hole from Gades in Spain to Gaza in Palestina! Nothing has been done! *Nothing!*"

His toga being a little rumpled from demonstrating how a knock-kneed man walked, Gabinius paused to adjust it.

"What do you suggest we do, Gabinius?" called Cicero from the Senate steps.

"Why hello there, Marcus Cicero!" said Gabinius cheerfully. "And Caesar too! Rome's best pair of orators listening to the humble pratings of a man from Picenum. I am honored, especially since you stand just about alone up there. No Catulus, no Gaius Piso, no Hortensius, no Metellus Pius Pontifex Maximus?"

"Get on with it, man," said Cicero, in high good humor.

"Thank you, I will. What do we do, you ask? The answer is simple, members of the Plebs. We find ourselves a man. One man only. A man who has already been consul, so that there can be no doubt about his constitutional position. A man whose military career has not been fought from the front benches of the Senate like some I could name. We find that man. And by we, fellow plebeians, I

mean we of this assemblage. *Not* the Senate! The Senate
has tried all the way from knock-knees to chalky substances without success, so I say the Senate must abrogate
its power in this matter, which affects all of us. I repeat,
we find ourselves a man, a man who is a consular of established military ability. *We* then give this man a commission to clear Our Sea of piracy from the Pillars of
Hercules to the mouths of Nilus, and to clear the Euxine
Sea as well. *We* give him three years to do this, and within
three years he must have done this—for if he has not,
members of the Plebs, then *we* will prosecute him and
exile him from Rome forever!''

Some of the *boni* had come running from whatever
business engaged them, summoned by clients they put in
the Forum to monitor even the least suspicious Assembly
meeting. Word was spreading that Aulus Gabinius was
speaking about a pirate command, and the *boni*—not to
mention many other factions—knew that meant Gabinius
was going to ask the Plebs to give it to Pompey. Which
could not be allowed to happen. Pompey must never receive another special command, never! It allowed him to
think he was better and greater than his equals.

With the freedom to look around that Gabinius had
not, Caesar noted Bibulus descend to the bottom of the
Well, with Cato, Ahenobarbus and young Brutus behind
him. An interesting quartet. Servilia wouldn't be pleased
if she heard her son was associating with Cato. A fact
Brutus obviously understood; he looked hunted and furtive. Perhaps because of that he didn't seem to listen to
what Gabinius was saying, though Bibulus, Cato and
Ahenobarbus had anger written large in their faces.

Gabinius ploughed on. ''This man must have absolute
autonomy. He must exist under no restrictions whatsoever
from Senate or People once he begins. That of course
means that we endow him with an unlimited imperium—
but not just at sea! His power must extend inward for fifty
miles on *all* coasts, and within that strip of land his powers
must override the imperium of every provincial governor
affected. He must be given at least fifteen legates of propraetorian status and have the freedom to choose and de-

ploy them himself, without hindrance from anyone. If necessary he must be granted the whole contents of the Treasury, and be given the power to levy whatever he needs from money to ships to local militia in every place his imperium encompasses. He must have as many ships, fleets, flotillas as he demands, and as many of Rome's soldiers.''

At which point Gabinius noticed the newcomers, and gave a huge, stagy start of surprise. He looked down into Bibulus's eyes, then grinned delightedly. Neither Catulus nor Hortensius had arrived, but Bibulus, one of the heirs apparent, was enough.

''If we give this special command against the pirates to one man, members of the Plebs,'' cried Gabinius, ''then we may at last see the end of piracy! But if we allow certain elements in the Senate to cow us or prevent us, then we and no other body of Roman men will be directly responsible for whatever disasters follow on our failure to act. Let us get rid of piracy for once and for all! It's time we dispensed with half-measures, compromises, sucking up to the self-importance of families and individuals who insist that the right to protect Rome is theirs alone! It's time to finish with doing nothing! It's time to do the job properly!''

''Aren't you going to say it, Gabinius?'' Bibulus shouted from the bottom of the Well.

Gabinius looked innocent. ''Say what, Bibulus?''

''The name, the name, the name!''

''I have no name, Bibulus, just a solution.''

''Rubbish!'' came the harsh and blaring voice of Cato. ''That is absolute rubbish, Gabinius! You have a name, all right! The name of your boss, your Picentine upstart boss whose chief delight is destroying every tradition and custom Rome owns! You're not up there saying all of this out of patriotism, you're up there serving the interests of your boss, Gnaeus Pompeius Magnus!''

''A name! Cato said a name!'' cried Gabinius, looking overjoyed. ''Marcus Porcius Cato said a name!'' Gabinius leaned forward, bent his knees, got his head as close to Cato below as he could, and said quite softly, ''Weren't you elected a tribune of the soldiers for this year, Cato? Didn't the lots give you service with Marcus Rubrius in Macedonia? And hasn't Marcus Rubrius departed for his province already? Don't you think you should be making a nuisance of yourself with Rubrius in Macedonia, rather than being a nuisance in Rome? But thank you for giving us a name! Until you suggested Gnaeus Pompeius Magnus, I had no idea which man would be best.''

Whereupon he dismissed the meeting before any of the *boni* tribunes of the plebs could arrive.

Bibulus turned away with a curt jerk of his head to the other three, lips set, eyes glacial. When he reached the surface of the lower Forum he put his hand out, clutched Brutus's forearm.

''You can run a message for me, young man,'' he said, ''then go home. Find Quintus Lutatius Catulus, Quintus Hortensius and Gaius Piso the consul. Tell them to meet me at my house now.''

Not very many moments later the three leading members of the *boni* sat in Bibulus's study. Cato was still there, but Ahenobarbus had gone; Bibulus deemed him too much of an intellectual liability in a council containing Gaius Piso, who was quite dense enough without reinforcements.

''It's been too quiet, and Pompeius Magnus has been too quiet,'' said Quintus Lutatius Catulus, a slight and sandy-colored man whose Caesar ancestry showed less in him than his mother's Domitius Ahenobarbus.

Catulus's father, Catulus Caesar, had been a greater man opposing a greater enemy, Gaius Marius, and he had perished in his own way during the hideous slaughter Marius had inflicted on Rome at the beginning of his infamous seventh consulship. The son had been caught in an invidious position after he chose to remain in Rome throughout the years of Sulla's exile, for he had never truly expected Sulla to overcome Cinna and Carbo. So after Sulla became Dictator, Catulus had trodden very warily until he managed to convince the Dictator of his loyalty. It was Sulla had appointed him consul with Lepidus, who rebelled— one more unhappy chance. Though he, Catulus, had defeated Lepidus, it was Pompey who got the job fighting

Sertorius in Spain, a far more important enterprise. Somehow that kind of thing had become the pattern of Catulus's life: never quite enough in the forefront to excel the way his formidable father had.

Embittered and now well into his fifties, he listened to the story Bibulus told without having the faintest idea how to combat what Gabinius was proposing to do beyond the traditional technique of uniting the Senate in opposition to any special commands.

Much younger, and fueled by a greater reservoir of hatred for the pretty fellows who would stand above all others, Bibulus knew too many senators would be inclined to favor the appointment of Pompey if the task was as vital as eradication of the pirates. "It won't work," he said to Catulus flatly.

"It has to work!" Catulus cried, striking his hands together. "We cannot allow that Picentine oaf Pompeius and all his minions to run Rome as a dependency of Picenum! What is Picenum except an outlying Italian state full of so-called Romans who are actually descended from Gauls? Look at Pompeius Magnus—he's a Gaul! Look at Gabinius—he's a Gaul! Yet we genuine Romans are expected to abase ourselves before Pompeius Magnus? Elevate him yet again to a position more prestigious than genuine Romans can condone? *Magnus!* How could a patrician Roman like Sulla have permitted Pompeius to assume a name meaning great?"

"I agree!" snapped Gaius Piso fiercely. "It's intolerable!"

Hortensius sighed. "Sulla needed him, and Sulla would have prostituted himself to Mithridates or Tigranes if that had been the only way back from exile to rule in Rome," he said, shrugging his shoulders.

"There's no point in railing at Sulla," said Bibulus. "We have to keep our heads, or we'll lose this battle. Gabinius has circumstances on his side. The fact remains, Quintus Catulus, that the Senate hasn't dealt with the pirates, and I don't think the good Metellus in Crete will succeed either. The sack of Ostia was all the excuse Gabinius needed to propose this solution."

"Are you saying," asked Cato, "that we won't manage to keep Pompeius out of the command Gabinius is suggesting?"

"Yes, I am."

"Pompeius can't win against the pirates," said Gaius Piso, smiling sourly.

"Exactly," said Bibulus. "It may be that we'll have to watch the Plebs issue that special command, then sit back and bring Pompeius down for good after he fails."

"No," said Hortensius. "There is a way of keeping Pompeius out of the job. Put up another name to the Plebs that it will prefer to Pompeius's."

A small silence fell, broken by the sharp sound of Bibulus's hand cracking down on his desk. "Marcus Licinius Crassus!" he cried. "Brilliant, Hortensius, brilliant! He's quite as good as Pompeius, and he has massive support among the knights of the Plebs. All they really care about is losing money, and the pirates lose them millions upon millions every year. No one in Rome will ever forget how Crassus handled his campaign against Spartacus. The man's a genius at organization, as unstoppable as an avalanche, and as ruthless as old King Mithridates."

"I don't like him or anything he stands for, but he does have the blood," from Gaius Piso, pleased. "Nor are his chances any less than Pompeius's."

"Very well then, we ask Crassus to volunteer for the special command against the pirates," said Hortensius with satisfaction. "Who will put it to him?"

"I will," said Catulus. He looked at Piso sternly. "In the meantime, senior consul, I suggest that your officers summon the Senate into session at dawn tomorrow. Gabinius didn't convoke another meeting of the Plebs, so we'll bring the matter up in the House and secure a *consultum* directing the Plebs to appoint Crassus."

But someone else got in first, as Catulus was to discover when he tracked Crassus down at his home some hours later.

Caesar had left the Senate steps in a hurry, and went straight from the Forum to Crassus's offices in an insula behind the Macellum Cuppedenis, the spice and flower markets which the State had been compelled to auction off into private ownership years before; it had been the only way to fund Sulla's campaigns in the East against Mithridates. A young man at the time, Crassus had not owned the money to buy it; during Sulla's proscriptions it fell at another auction, and by then Crassus was in a position to buy heavily. Thus he now owned a great deal of very choice property behind the eastern fringe of the Forum, including a dozen warehouses wherein merchants stored their precious peppercorns, nard, incenses, cinnamon, balms, perfumes and aromatics.

He was a big man, Crassus, taller than he looked because of his width, and there was no fat on him. Neck, shoulders and trunk were thickset, and that combined with a certain placidity in his face had caused all who knew him to see his resemblance to an ox—an ox which gored. He had married the widow of both his elder brothers, a Sabine lady of fine family by name of Axia who had become known as Tertulla because she had married three brothers; he had two promising sons, though the elder, Publius, was actually Tertulla's son by his brother Publius. Young Publius was ten years from the Senate, while the son of Crassus's loins, Marcus, was some years younger than that. No one could fault Crassus as a family man; his uxoriousness and devotion were famous. But his family was not his abiding passion. Marcus Licinius Crassus had only one passion—money. Some called him the richest man in Rome, though Caesar, treading up the grimy narrow stairs to his lair on the fifth floor of the insula, knew better. The Servilius Caepio fortune was almost infinitely larger, and so too the fortune of the man he went to see Crassus about, Pompey the Great.

That he had chosen to walk up five flights of stairs rather than occupy more commodious premises lower down was typical of Crassus, who understood his rents exquisitely well. The higher the floor, the lower the rent. Why fritter away a few thousands of sesterces by himself using profitable lower floors which could be rented out? Besides, stairs were good exercise. Nor did Crassus bother

with appearances; he sat at a desk in one corner of a room
in permanent turmoil with all his senior staff beneath his
eyes, and cared not a whit if they jostled his elbow or
talked at the tops of their voices.

"Time for a little fresh air!" shouted Caesar, jerking
his head in the direction of the doorway behind him.

Crassus got up immediately to follow Caesar down
and out into a different kind of turmoil, that of the Macellum Cuppedenis.

They were good friends, Caesar and Crassus, had
been since Caesar had served with Crassus during the war
against Spartacus. Many wondered at this peculiar association, for the differences between them blinded observers
to the far greater similarities. Under those two very con-
trasting facades existed the same kind of steel, which they
understood even if their world did not.

Neither man did what most men would have done,
namely to go over to a famous snack bar and buy spiced
minced pork encased in a deliciously light and flaky pastry
made by covering flour dough with cold lard, folding it
and rolling it, then more lard, and repeating the process
many times. Caesar as usual wasn't hungry, and Crassus
deemed eating anywhere outside his own home a waste of
money. Instead, they found a wall to lean on between a
busy school of boys and girls taking their lessons in the
open air and a booth devoted to peppercorns.

"All right, we're well protected against eavesdroppers," said Crassus, scratching his scalp; it had quite suddenly made itself visible after his year as Pompey's junior
consul when most of his hair fell out—a fact Crassus
blamed on the worry of having to earn an extra thousand
talents to replace what he had spent on making sure he
ended up the consul with the best reputation among the
people. That his baldness was more likely due to his age
did not occur to him; he would turn fifty this year. Irrelevant. Marcus Crassus blamed everything on worries
about money.

"I predict," said Caesar, eyes on an adorable little
dark girl in the impromptu classroom, "that you will re-

ceive a visit this evening from none other than our dear Quintus Lutatius Catulus.''

"Oh?" asked Crassus, his gaze fixed on the extortionate price chalked on a wooden card propped up against a glazed ceramic jar of peppercorns from Taprobane. "What's in the wind, Caesar?"

"You should have abandoned your ledgers and come to today's meeting of the Plebeian Assembly," said Caesar.

"Interesting, was it?"

"Fascinating, though not unexpected—by me, at any rate. I had a little conversation with Magnus last year, so I was prepared. I doubt anyone else was save for Afranius and Petreius, who kept me company on the Curia Hostilia steps. I daresay they thought someone might smell which way the wind was blowing if they stood in the Well of the Comitia. Cicero kept me company too, but out of curiosity. He has a wonderful nose for sensing which meetings might be worth attending."

No fool politically either, Crassus withdrew his gaze from the costly peppercorns and stared at Caesar. "Oho! What's our friend Magnus up to?"

"Gabinius proposed to the Plebs that it should legislate to give an unlimited imperium and absolutely unlimited everything else to one man. Naturally he didn't name the man. The object of this unlimited everything is to put an end to the pirates," said Caesar, smiling when the little girl slammed her wax tablet down on the head of the little boy next to her.

"An ideal job for Magnus," said Crassus.

"Of course. I understand, incidentally, that he's been doing his homework for over two years. However, it won't be a popular commission with the Senate, will it?"

"Not among Catulus and his boys."

"Nor among most members of the Senate, I predict. They'll never forgive Magnus for forcing them to legitimize his desire to be consul."

"Nor will I," said Crassus grimly. He drew a breath. "So you think Catulus will ask me to run for the job in opposition to Pompeius, eh?"

"Bound to."

"Tempting," said Crassus, his attention attracted to the school because the little boy was bawling and the pedagogue was trying to avert a free-for-all among his pupils.

"Don't be tempted, Marcus," said Caesar gently.

"Why not?"

"It wouldn't work, Marcus. Believe me, it wouldn't work. If Magnus is as prepared as I think Magnus is, then let him have the job. Your businesses suffer the effects of piracy as much as any businesses do. If you're clever, you'll stay in Rome and reap the rewards of pirate-free waterways. You know Magnus. He'll do the job, and he'll do it properly. But everyone else will wait and see. You can use the however many months this general skepticism will give you to prepare for the good times to come," said Caesar.

That was, as Caesar well knew, the most compelling argument he could have put forward.

Crassus nodded and straightened. "You've convinced me," he said, and glanced up at the sun. "Time to put in a bit more work on those ledgers before I go home to receive Catulus."

The two men picked their way unconcernedly through the chaos which had descended upon the school, with Caesar giving the small cause of it all a companionable grin as he passed her. "Bye-bye, Servilia!" he said to her.

Crassus, about to go the other way, looked startled. "Do you know her?" he asked. "Is she a Servilia?"

"No, I don't know her," called Caesar, already fifteen feet away. "But she does remind me vividly of Julia's prospective mother-in-law!"

Thus it was that when Piso the consul convoked the Senate at dawn the next morning, the leading lights of that body had found no rival general to put up against Pompey; Catulus's interview with Crassus had foundered.

News of what was in the wind had spread from one back tier clear across to the other, of course, and opposition from all sides had hardened, much to the delight of the *boni*. The demise of Sulla was just too recent for most men to forget how he had held the Senate to ransom, despite his favors; and Pompey had been his pet, his executioner. Pompey had killed too many senators of Cinnan and Carboan persuasion, then killed Brutus too, and had forced the Senate to allow him to be elected consul without ever having been a senator. That last crime was the most unforgivable of all. The censors Lentulus Clodianus and Poplicola were still influential in Pompey's favor, but his most powerful employees, Philippus and Cethegus, were gone, the one into retirement as a voluptuary, the other through the offices of death.

Not surprising then that when they entered the Curia Hostilia this morning in their solid-purple censors' togas, Lentulus Clodianus and Poplicola resolved after looking at so many set faces that they would not speak up for Pompey the Great today. Nor would Curio, another Pompeian employee. As for Afranius and old Petreius, their rhetorical skills were so limited that they were under orders not to try. Crassus was absent.

"Isn't Pompeius coming to Rome?" asked Caesar of Gabinius when he realized Pompey himself was not there.

"On his way," said Gabinius, "but he won't appear until his name is mentioned in the Plebs. You know how he hates the Senate."

Once the auguries had been taken and Metellus Pius Pontifex Maximus had conducted the prayers, Piso (who held the *fasces* for February because Glabrio had vanished east) began the meeting.

"I realize," he said from his curule chair on the elevated platform at the far end of the chamber, "that today's meeting is not, under the recent legislation of Aulus Gabinius, tribune of the plebs, germane to February's business. In one way! But in another, as it concerns a foreign command, it definitely is. All of which is beside the point. Nothing in that *lex Gabinia* can prevent this body's meeting to discuss urgent affairs of any kind during the month of February!"

He rose to his feet, a typical Calpurnius Piso, being tall, very dark, and possessed of bushy eyebrows. "This same tribune of the plebs, Aulus Gabinius from Picenum''—he gestured with one hand at the back of Gabinius's head, below him and on the far left end of the tribunician bench—''yesterday, without first notifying this body, convoked the Assembly of the Plebs and told its members—or those few who were present, anyway—how to get rid of piracy. Without consulting us, without consulting anyone! Toss unlimited imperium, money and forces into one single man's lap, he said! Not mentioning any names, but which one of us can doubt that only one name was inside his Picentine head? This Aulus Gabinius and his fellow Picentine tribune of the plebs, Gaius Cornelius of no distinguished family despite his *nomen,* have already given us who have inherited Rome as our responsibility more trouble than enough since they entered office. I, for example, have been forced to draft counterlegislation for bribery at the curule elections. I, for example, have been cunningly deprived of my colleague in this year's consulship. I, for example, have been accused of numberless crimes to do with electoral bribery.

''All of you present here today are aware of the seriousness of this proposed new *lex Gabinia,* and aware too how greatly it infringes every aspect of the *mos maiorum.* But it is not my duty to open this debate, only to guide it. So as it is too early in the year for any magistrates-elect to be present, I will proceed first to this year's praetors, and ask for a spokesman.''

As the debating order had already been worked out, no praetor offered his services, nor did any aedile, curule or plebeian; Gaius Piso passed to the ranks of the consulars in the front rows on either side of the House. That meant the most powerful piece of oratorical artillery would fire first: Quintus Hortensius.

''Honored consul, censors, magistrates, consulars and senators,'' he began, ''it is time once and for all to put paid to these so-called special military commissions! We all know why the Dictator Sulla incorporated that clause in his amended constitution—to purchase the services of one man who did not belong to this august and venerable body—a knight from Picenum who had the presumption to recruit and general troops in Sulla's employ while still in his early twenties, and who, having tasted the sweetness of blatant unconstitutionality, continued to espouse it—though espouse the Senate he would not! When Lepidus revolted he held Italian Gaul, and actually had the temerity to order the execution of a member of one of Rome's oldest and finest families—Marcus Junius Brutus. Whose treason, if treason it really was, this body defined by including Brutus in its decree outlawing Lepidus. A decree which did not give Pompeius the right to have Brutus's head lopped off by a minion in the marketplace at Regium Lepidum! Nor to cremate the head and body, then casually send the ashes to Rome with a short, semiliterate note of explanation!

"After which, Pompeius kept his precious Picentine legions in Mutina until he forced the Senate to commission him—no senator, no magistrate!—with a proconsular imperium to go to Spain, govern the nearer province in the Senate's name and make war on the renegade Quintus Sertorius. When all the time, Conscript Fathers, in the further province we had an eminent man of proper family and background, the good Quintus Caecilius Metellus Pius Pontifex Maximus, already in the field against Sertorius—a man who, I add, did more to defeat Sertorius than this extraordinary and unsenatorial Pompeius ever did! Though it was Pompeius who took the glory, Pompeius who collected the laurels!"

Quite a good-looking man of imposing presence, Hortensius turned slowly in a circle and seemed to look into every pair of eyes, a trick he had used to good effect in law courts for twenty and more years. "Then what does this Picentine nobody Pompeius do when he returns to our beloved country? Against every provision of the constitution, he brings his army across the Rubico and into Italia, where he sits it down and proceeds to blackmail us into allowing him to stand for consul! We had no choice. Pompeius became consul. And even today, Conscript Fathers, I refuse with every fiber of my being to accord him that abominable name of Magnus he awarded himself! For he is *not* great! He is a boil, a carbuncle, a putrid festering sore in Rome's maltreated hide!

"How dare Pompeius assume he can blackmail this body yet again? How dare he put his fellating minion Gabinius up to this? Unlimited imperium and unlimited forces and unlimited money, if you please! When all the time the Senate has an able commander in Crete doing an excellent job! An excellent job, I repeat! An excellent job! Excellent, excellent!" Hortensius's Asianic style of oratory was now in full flight, and the House had settled down (particularly as it was in agreement with every word he said) to listen to one of its all-time great speakers. "I tell you, fellow members of this House, that I will never, never, never consent to this command, no matter whose name might be put up to fill it! Only in our time has Rome ever needed to resort to unlimited imperium, unlimited commands! They are unconstitutional and unconscionable and unacceptable! We will clear Our Sea of pirates, but we will do it the Roman way, not the Picentine way!"

At which point Bibulus began to cheer and drum his feet, and the whole House joined him. Hortensius sat down, flushed with a sweet victory.

Aulus Gabinius had listened impassively, and at the end shrugged his shoulders, lifted his hands. "The Roman way," he said loudly when the cheering died down, "has degenerated to such a point of ineffectuality that it might better be called the Pisidian way! If Picenum is what the job needs, then Picenum it has to be. For what is Picenum, if it is not Rome? You draw geographical boundaries, Quintus Hortensius, which do not exist!"

"Shut up, shut up, shut up!" screamed Piso, leaping to his feet and down off the curule dais to face the tribunician bench beneath it. "You dare to prate of Rome, you Gaul from a nest of Gauls? You dare to lump Gaul with Rome? Beware then, Gabinius the Gaul, that you do not suffer the same fate as Romulus, and never return from your hunting expedition!"

"A threat!" shouted Gabinius, leaping to his feet. "You hear him, Conscript Fathers? He threatens to kill me, for that is what happened to Romulus! Killed by men

who weren't his bootlace, lurking in the Goat Swamps of
the Campus Martius!''

Pandemonium broke out, but Piso and Catulus
quelled it between them, unwilling to see the House dis-
solve before they had had their say. Gabinius had returned
to his perch on the end of the bench where the tribunes of
the plebs sat, and watched bright-eyed as the consul and
the consular went their rounds, soothing, clucking, persuading men to put their behinds back on their stools.

And then, when quiet had more or less returned and
Piso was about to ask Catulus his opinion, Gaius Julius
Caesar rose to his feet. As he wore his *corona civica* and
therefore ranked with any consular in the speaking order,
Piso, who disliked him, threw him a dirty look which in-
vited him to sit down again. Caesar remained standing,
Piso glaring.

''Let him speak, Piso!'' cried Gabinius. ''He's entitled!''

Though he didn't exercise his oratorical privilege
in the House very often, Caesar was acknowledged as
Cicero's only real rival; Hortensius's Asianic style had
fallen out of favor since the advent of Cicero's plainer but
more powerful Athenian style, and Caesar too preferred to
be Attic. If there was one thing every member of the Senate had in common, it was a connoisseur's appreciation
for oratory. Expecting Catulus, they all opted for Caesar.

''As neither Lucius Bellienus nor Marcus Sextilius
has yet been returned to our bosom, I believe I am the
only member of this House present here today who has
actually been captured by pirates,'' he said in that high,
absolutely clear voice he assumed for public speech. ''It
makes me, you might say, an expert on the subject, if
expertise can be conveyed by firsthand experience. I did
not find it an edifying experience, and my aversion began
in the moment I saw those two trim war galleys bearing
down on my poor, plodding merchant vessel. For, Conscript Fathers, I was informed by my captain that to attempt armed resistance was as certain to produce death as
it was bound to be futile. And I, Gaius Julius Caesar, had
to yield my person to a vulgar fellow named Polygonus,

who had been preying upon merchantmen in Lydian, Carian and Lycian waters for over twenty years.

"I learned a lot during the forty days I remained the prisoner of Polygonus," Caesar went on in more conversational tones. "I learned that there is an agreed sliding scale of ransom for all prisoners too valuable to be sent to the slave markets or chained up to wait on these pirates back home in their lairs. For a mere Roman citizen, slavery it is. A mere Roman citizen isn't worth two thousand sesterces, which is the bottom price he could fetch in the slave markets. For a Roman centurion or a Roman about halfway up the hierarchy of the *publicani*, the ransom is half a talent. For a top Roman knight or *publicanus*, the price is one talent. For a Roman nobleman of high family who is not a member of the Senate, the price is two talents. For a Roman senator of *pedarius* status, the ransom is ten talents. For a Roman senator of junior magisterial status— quaestor or aedile or tribune of the plebs—the ransom is twenty talents. For a Roman senator who has held a praetorship or consulship, the ransom is fifty talents. When captured complete with lictors and *fasces,* as in the case of our two latest praetor victims, the price goes up to one hundred talents each, as we have learned only days ago. Censors and consuls of note fetch a hundred talents. Though I am not sure what value pirates put on consuls like our dear Gaius Piso here—perhaps one talent? I wouldn't pay more for him myself, I do assure you. But then, I am not a pirate, though I sometimes wonder about Gaius Piso in that respect!

"One is expected during one's imprisonment," Caesar continued in that same casual manner, "to blanch in fear and fall down with great regularity to beg for one's life. Not something these Julian knees of mine are accustomed to doing—nor did. I spent my time spying out the land, assessing possible resistance to attack, discovering what was guarded and whereabouts. And I also spent my time assuring everyone that when my ransom was found— it was fifty talents—I would return, capture the place, send the women and children to the slave markets, and crucify the men. They thought that a wonderful joke. I would never, never find them, they told me. But I did find them, Conscript Fathers, and I did capture the place, and I did send the women and children to the slave markets, and I did crucify all the men. I could have brought back the beaks of four pirate ships to adorn the rostra, but since I used the Rhodians for my expedition, the beaks stand now on a column in Rhodus next door to the new temple of Aphrodite that I caused to be built by my share of the spoils.

"Now Polygonus was only one of hundreds of pirates at that end of Our Sea, and not even a major pirate, if they are to be graded. Mind you, Polygonus had been having such a lucrative time of it working on his own with a mere four galleys that he saw no point in joining forces with other pirates to form a little navy under a competent admiral like Lasthenes or Panares—or Pharnaces or Megadates, to move a little closer to home. Polygonus was happy to pay five hundred denarii to a spy in Miletus or Priene in return for information as to which ships were worth boarding. And how assiduous his spies were! No fat pickings escaped their attention. Among his hoard were many items of jewelry made in Egypt, which indicates that he raided vessels between Pelusium and Paphos too. So his network of spies must have been enormous. Paid only for information which found him good prey, of course, not routinely paid. Keep men short and their noses keen, and in the end it's cheaper as well as more effective.

"Noxious and of great nuisance value though they are, however, pirates like Polygonus are a minor affair compared to the pirate fleets under their pirate admirals. They don't need to wait for lone ships to come along, or ships in unarmed convoys. They can attack grain fleets escorted by heavily armed galleys. And then they proceed to sell back to Roman middlemen what was Rome's in the first place, already bought and paid for. Little wonder Roman bellies are empty, half of that vacuum from lack of grain, half because what grain there is sells at three and four times what it should, even from the aedile's dole list."

Caesar paused, but no one interrupted, even Piso, face

red at the insult tossed his way as if no moment. "I do not need to labor one point," he said evenly, "because I can see no merit in laboring it. Namely, that there have been provincial governors appointed by this body who have actively connived with pirates to allow them port facilities, food, even vintage wines on stretches of coast that otherwise would have been closed to pirate tenancy. It all came out during the trial of Gaius Verres, and those of you sitting here today who either engaged in this practice or let others engage in it know well who you are. And if the fate of my poor uncle Marcus Aurelius Cotta is anything to go by, be warned that the passage of time is no guarantee that crimes, real or imagined, will not one day be put to your accounts.

"Nor am I about to labor another point so obvious that it is very old, very tired, very threadbare. Namely, that so far Rome—and by Rome I mean both the Senate and the People!—has not even touched the problem of piracy, let alone begun to scotch it. There is absolutely no way one man in one piddling little spot, be that spot Crete or the Baleares or Lycia, can hope to terminate the activities of pirates. Strike at one place, and all that happens is that the pirates pick up their gear and sail off somewhere else. Has Metellus in Crete actually succeeded in cutting off a pirate head? Lasthenes and Panares are but two of the heads this monster Hydra owns, and theirs are still on their shoulders, still sailing the seas around Crete.

"What it needs," cried Caesar, his voice swelling, "is not just the will to succeed, not just the wish to succeed, not just the ambition to succeed! What it needs is an all-out effort in every place at one and the same moment, an operation masterminded by one hand, one mind, one will. And hand and mind and will must belong to a man whose prowess at organization is so well known, so well tested, that we, the Senate as well as the People of Rome, can give the task to him with confidence that for once our money and our manpower and our matériel will not be wasted!"

He drew in a breath. "Aulus Gabinius suggested *a* man. *A* man who is a consular and whose career says that he can do the job as it must be done. But I will go one better than Aulus Gabinius, and name that man! I propose that this body give command against the pirates with unlimited imperium in all respects to Gnaeus Pompeius Magnus!''

''Three cheers for Caesar!'' Gabinius shouted, leaping onto the tribunician bench with both arms above his head. ''I say it too! Give the command in the war against piracy to our greatest general, Gnaeus Pompeius Magnus!''

All outraged attention swung from Caesar to Gabinius, with Piso in the lead; off the curule dais he jumped, grabbed wildly at Gabinius, hauled him down. But Piso's body temporarily gave Gabinius the cover he needed, so he ducked under one flailing fist, tucked his toga around his thighs for the second time in two days, and bolted for the doors with half the Senate in pursuit.

Caesar picked his way between upended stools to where Cicero sat pensively with his chin propped up on one palm; he turned the stool next to Cicero the right way up, and sat down too.

''Masterly,'' said Cicero.

''Nice of Gabinius to divert their wrath from my head to his,'' said Caesar, sighing and stretching his legs out.

''It's harder to lynch you. There's a barrier built into their minds because you're a patrician Julian. As for Gabinius, he's—how did Hortensius put it?—a fellating minion. Add as understood, Picentine and Pompeian. Therefore he may be lynched with impunity. Besides, he was closer to Piso than you, and he didn't win *that*,'' Cicero ended, pointing to the chaplet of oak leaves Caesar wore. ''I think there will be many times when half of Rome may want to lynch you, Caesar, but it would be an interesting group succeeded. Definitely not led by the likes of Piso.''

Sounds of shouting and violence outside rose in volume; the next thing Piso flew back into the chamber with various members of the professional Plebs behind him. Catulus in his wake dodged around the back of one of the open doors, and Hortensius around the other. Piso fell under a tackle and was dragged outside again, head bleeding.

"I say, it looks as if they're in earnest," Cicero observed with clinical interest. "Piso might be lynched."

"I hope he is," said Caesar, not moving.

Cicero giggled. "Well, if you won't stir to help, I fail to see why I should."

"Oh, Gabinius will talk them out of it, that will make him look wonderful. Besides, it's quieter up here."

"Which is why I transferred my carcass up here."

"I take it," said Caesar, "that you're in favor of Magnus's getting this gigantic command?"

"Definitely. He's a good man, even if he isn't one of the *boni*. There's no one else has a hope. Of doing it, I mean."

"There is, you know. But they wouldn't give the job to me anyway, and I really do think Magnus can do it."

"Conceit!" cried Cicero, astonished.

"There is a difference between truth and conceit."

"But do you know it?"

"Of course."

They fell silent for a while, then as the noise began to die away both men rose, descended to the floor of the chamber, and sallied out into the portico.

There it became clear that victory had gone to the Pompeians; Piso sat bleeding on a step being tended by Catulus, but of Quintus Hortensius there was no sign.

"You!" cried Catulus bitterly as Caesar ranged alongside him. "What a traitor to your class you are, Caesar! Just as I told you all those years ago when you came begging to serve in my army against Lepidus! You haven't changed. You'll never change, never! Always on the side of these ill-born demagogues who are determined to destroy the supremacy of the Senate!"

"At your age, Catulus, I would have thought you'd come to see that it's you ultraconservative sticks with your mouths puckered up like a cat's anus will do that," said Caesar dispassionately. "I believe in Rome, and in the Senate. But you do it no good by opposing changes that your own incompetence have made necessary."

"I will defend Rome and the Senate against the likes of Pompeius until the day I die!"

"Which, looking at you, may not be so far off."

Cicero, who had gone to hear what Gabinius on the rostra was saying, returned to the bottom of the steps. "Another meeting of the Plebs the day after tomorrow!" he called, waving farewell.

"There's another one who will destroy us," said Catulus, lip curling contemptuously. "An upstart New Man with the gift of the gab and a head too big to fit through these doors!"

When the Plebeian Assembly met, Pompey was standing on the rostra next to Gabinius, who now proposed his *lex Gabinia de piratis persequendis* with a name attached to the man: Gnaeus Pompeius Magnus. Everybody's choice, so much was clear from all the cheering. Though he was a mediocre speaker, Pompey had something in its way more valuable, which was a fresh and open, honest and engaging look about him, from the wide blue eyes to the wide frank smile. And that quality, reflected Caesar, watching and listening from the Senate steps, I do not have. Though I do not think I covet it. His style, not mine. Mine works equally well with the people.

Today's opposition to the *lex Gabinia de piratis persequendis* was going to be more formal, though possibly no less violent; the three conservative tribunes of the plebs were very much in evidence on the rostra, Trebellius standing a little in front of Roscius Otho and Globulus to proclaim that he was their leader.

But before Gabinius went into the details of his bill, he called upon Pompey to speak, and none of the senatorial rump from Trebellius to Catulus to Piso tried to stop him; the whole crowd was on his side. It was very well done of its kind. Pompey began by protesting that he had been under arms in Rome's service since his boyhood, and he was profoundly weary of being called upon to serve Rome yet again with yet another of these special commands. He went on to enumerate his campaigns (more campaigns than he had years, he sighed wistfully), then explained that the jealousy and hatred increased each time he did it again, saved Rome. And oh, he didn't want yet more jealousy, yet more hatred! Let him be what he most wanted to be—a family man, a country squire, a private gentleman. Find someone else, he beseeched Gabinius and the crowd, both hands outstretched.

Naturally no one took this seriously, though everyone did approve heartily of Pompey's modesty and self-deprecation. Lucius Trebellius asked leave of Gabinius, the College president, to speak, and was refused. When he tried anyway, the crowd drowned his words with boos, jeers, catcalls. So as Gabinius proceeded, he produced the one weapon Gabinius could not ignore.

"I interpose my veto against the *lex Gabinia de piratis persequendis*!" cried Lucius Trebellius in ringing tones.

Silence fell.

"Withdraw your veto, Trebellius," said Gabinius.

"I will not. I veto your boss's law!"

"Don't force me to take measures, Trebellius."

"What measures can you take short of throwing me from the Tarpeian Rock, Gabinius? And that cannot change my veto. I will be dead, but your law will not be passed," said Trebellius.

This was the true test of strength, for the days had gone when meetings could degenerate into violence with impunity for the man convoking the meeting, when an irate Plebs could physically intimidate tribunes into withdrawing their vetoes while the man in charge of the Plebs remained an innocent bystander. Gabinius knew that if a riot broke out during this proper meeting of the Plebs, he would be held accountable at law. Therefore he solved his problem in a constitutional way none could impeach.

"I can ask this Assembly to legislate you out of your office, Trebellius," answered Gabinius. "Withdraw your veto!"

"I refuse to withdraw my veto, Aulus Gabinius."

There were thirty-five tribes of Roman citizen men. All the voting procedures in the Assemblies were arrived at through the tribes, which meant that at the end of sev-

eral thousand men's voting, only thirty-five actual votes
were recorded. In elections all the tribes voted simultaneously, but when passing laws the tribes voted one after
the other, and what Gabinius was seeking was a law to
depose Lucius Trebellius. Therefore Gabinius called the
thirty-five tribes to vote consecutively, and one after the
other they voted to depose Trebellius. Eighteen was the
majority, so eighteen votes were all Gabinius needed. In
solemn quiet and perfect order, the ballot proceeded inexorably: Suburana, Sergia, Palatina, Quirina, Horatia, An-
iensis, Menenia, Oufentina, Maecia, Pomptina, Stellatina,
Clustumina, Tromentina, Voltinia, Papiria, Fabia . . . The
seventeenth tribe to vote was Cornelia, and the vote was
the same. Deposition.

"Well, Lucius Trebellius?" asked Gabinius, turning
to his colleague with a big smile. "Seventeen tribes in
succession have voted against you. Do I call upon the men
of Camilia to make it eighteen and a majority, or will you
withdraw your veto?"

Trebellius licked his lips, looked desperately at Catulus, Hortensius, Piso, then at the remote and aloof Pontifex Maximus, Metellus Pius, who ought to have honored
his membership in the *boni,* but since his return from
Spain four years ago was a changed man—a quiet man—
a resigned man. Despite all of which, it was to Metellus
Pius that Trebellius addressed his appeal.

"Pontifex Maximus, what ought I to do?" he cried.

"The Plebs have shown their wishes in the matter,
Lucius Trebellius," said Metellus Pius in a clear, carrying
voice which did not stammer once. "Withdraw your veto.
The Plebs have instructed you to withdraw your veto."

"I withdraw my veto," Trebellius said, turned on his
heel and retreated to the back of the rostra platform.

But having outlined his bill, Gabinius now seemed in
no hurry to pass it. He asked Catulus to speak, then Hortensius.

"Clever little fellow, isn't he?" asked Cicero, a trifle
put out that no one was asking him to speak. "Listen to
Hortensius! In the Senate the day before yesterday, he said
he'd *die* before any more special commands with unlim-

ited imperium would pass! Today he's still against special commands with unlimited imperium, but if Rome insists on creating this animal, then Pompeius and no one else should have its leash put into his hand. That certainly tells us which way the Forum wind is blowing, doesn't it?''

It certainly did. Pompey concluded the meeting by shedding a few tears and announcing that if Rome insisted, then he supposed he would have to shoulder this new burden, lethal though the exhaustion it produced would be. After which Gabinius dismissed the meeting, the vote as yet untaken. However, the tribune of the plebs Roscius Otho had the last word. Angry, frustrated, longing to kill the whole Plebs, he stepped to the front of the rostra and thrust his clenched right fist upward, then very slowly extended its *medicus* finger to its full length, and waggled it.

"Shove it up your arse, Plebs!" laughed Cicero, appreciating this futile gesture enormously.

"So you're happy to allow the Plebs a day to consider, eh?'' he asked Gabinius when the College came down from the rostra.

"I'll do everything exactly as it ought to be done.''

"How many bills?''

"One general, then one awarding the command to Gnaeus Pompeius, and a third detailing the terms of his command.''

Cicero tucked his arm through Gabinius's and began to walk. "I loved that little bit at the end of Catulus's speech, didn't you? You know, when Catulus asked the Plebs what would happen if Magnus was killed, with whom would the Plebs replace him?''

Gabinius doubled up with laughter. "And they all cried with one voice, 'You, Catulus! You and no one but you!' ''

"Poor Catulus! The veteran of an hour-long rout fought in the shade of the Quirinal.''

"He got the point,'' said Gabinius.

"He got shafted,'' said Cicero. "That's the trouble with being a rump. You contain the posterior fundamental orifice.''

* * *

In the end Pompey got more than Gabinius had originally asked for: his imperium was *maius* on sea and for fifty miles inland from every coast, which meant his authority overrode the authority of every provincial governor and those with special commands like Metellus Little Goat in Crete and Lucullus in his war against the two kings. No one could gainsay him without revocation of the act in the Plebeian Assembly. He was to have five hundred ships at Rome's expense and as many more as he wanted in levies from coastal cities and states; he was to have one hundred and twenty thousand Roman troops and as many more as he considered necessary in levies from the provinces; he was to have five thousand horse troopers; he was to have twenty-four legates with propraetorian status, all of his own choice, and two quaestors; he was to have one hundred and forty-four million sesterces from the Treasury at once, and more when he wanted more. In short, the Plebs awarded him a command the like of which had never been seen.

But, to do him justice, Pompey wasted no time puffing out his chest and rubbing his victory in to people like Catulus and Piso; he was too eager to begin what he had planned down to the last detail. And, if he needed further evidence of the people's faith in his ability to do away with piracy on the high seas once and for all, he could look with pride to the fact that on the day the *leges Gabiniae* were passed, the price of grain in Rome dropped.

Though some wondered at it, he did not choose his two old lieutenants from Spain among his legates—that is, Afranius and Petreius. Instead, he attempted to soothe the fears of the *boni* by picking irreproachable men like Sisenna and Varro, two of the Manlii Torquati, Lentulus Marcellinus and the younger of his wife Mucia Tertia's two half brothers, Metellus Nepos. It was to his tame censors Poplicola and Lentulus Clodianus, however, that he gave the most important commands, Poplicola of the Tuscan Sea and Lentulus Clodianus of the Adriatic Sea. Italy reposed between them, safe and secure.

He divided the Middle Sea into thirteen regions, each

of which he allocated a commander and a second-in-command, fleets, troops, money. And this time there would be no insubordination, no assuming initiative by any of his legates.

"There can be no Arausio," he said sternly in his command tent, his legates assembled before the great enterprise began. "If one of you so much as farts in a direction I have not myself *in person* instructed as the right direction for farting, I will cut out your balls and send you to the eunuch markets in Alexandria," he said, and meant it. "My imperium is *maius,* and that means I can do whatever I like. Every last one of you will have written orders so detailed and complete that you don't have to decide for yourselves what's for dinner the day after tomorrow. You do as you're told. If any man among you isn't prepared to do as he's told, then speak up now. Otherwise it's singing soprano at the court of King Ptolemy, is that understood?"

"He may not be elegant in his phraseology or his metaphors," said Varro to his fellow *literatus,* Sisenna, "but he does have a wonderful way of convincing people that he means what he says."

"I keep visualizing an almighty aristocrat like Lentulus Marcellinus trilling out his tonsils for the delectation of King Ptolemy the Flautist in Alexandria," said Sisenna dreamily.

Which set both of them to laughing.

Though the campaign was not a laughing matter. It proceeded with stunning speed and absolute efficiency in exactly the way Pompey had planned, and not one of his legates dared do aught else than as his written orders dictated. If Pompey's campaign in Africa for Sulla had astonished everyone with its speed and efficiency, this campaign cast that one into permanent shade.

He began at the western end of the Middle Sea, and he used his fleets, his troops, and—above all—his legates to apply a naval and military broom to the waters. Sweeping, sweeping, ever sweeping a confused and helpless heap of pirates ahead of the broom; every time a pirate detachment broke for cover on the African or the Gallic or the

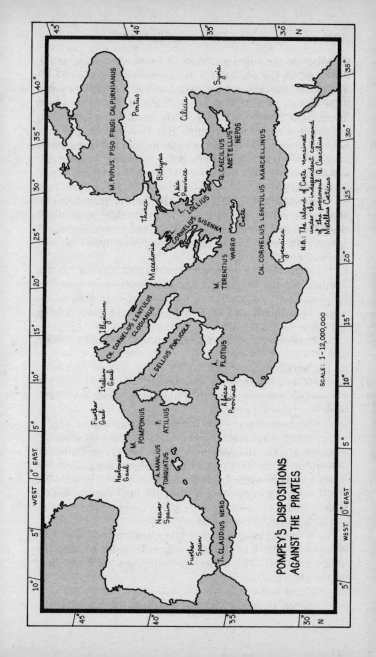

POMPEY'S DISPOSITIONS
AGAINST THE PIRATES

SCALE: 1-12,000,000

N.B.: The island of Crete remained
under the independent command
of the proconsul Q. Caecilius
Metellus Ceticus

M. PUPIUS PISO FRUGI CALPURNIANUS

Pontus

Bithynia

Asia Province

L. CORNELIUS LOLLIUS

CORNELIUS SISENNA

Thrace

Illyricum

Macedonia

CN. CORNELIUS LENTULUS CLODIANUS

Syria

Cilicia

Q. CAECILIUS METELLUS NEPOS

M. TERENTIUS VARRO

Crete

CN. CORNELIUS LENTULUS MARCELLINUS

Cyrenaica

Further Gaul

Italian Gaul

L. GELLIUS POPLICOLA

A. PLOTIUS

Africa Province

Narbonese Gaul

M. POMPONIUS

P. ATILIUS

A. MANLIUS TORQUATUS

Nearer Spain

Further Spain

TI. CLAUDIUS NERO

Spanish or the Ligurian coast, it found no refuge at all, for a legate was waiting for it. Governor-designate of both the Gauls, the consul Piso issued orders that neither province was to provide Pompey with aid of any kind, which meant that Pompey's legate in the area, Pomponius, had to struggle to achieve results. But Piso too bit the dust when Gabinius threatened to legislate him out of his provinces if he didn't desist. His debts mounting with frightening rapidity, Piso needed the Gauls to recoup his losses, so he desisted.

Pompey himself followed the broom from west to east, timing his visit to Rome in the middle to coincide with Gabinius's actions against Piso, and looked more gorgeous than ever when he publicly prevailed upon Gabinius not to be such a cad.

"Oh, what a poseur!" exclaimed Caesar to his mother, but not in any spirit of criticism.

Aurelia, however, was not interested in Forum doings. "I must talk to you, Caesar," she said, ensconced in her chair in his *tablinum*.

Amusement fled; Caesar stifled a sigh. "What about?"

"Servilia."

"There's nothing to say, Mater."

"Did you make a remark to Crassus about Servilia?" was his mother's reply.

Caesar frowned. "To Crassus? No, of course not."

"Then why did Tertulla come to see me on a fishing expedition? She did, yesterday." Aurelia grunted a laugh. "Not one of Rome's more expert fisherwomen, Tertulla! Comes of her Sabine background, I suppose. The hills are not fishing territory for any save the real experts with a willow rod."

"I swear I didn't, Mater."

"Well, Crassus has an inkling, and passed his inkling on to his wife. I take it that you still prefer to keep the union a secret? With a view to resuming it once this child is born?"

"That is my intention."

"Then I suggest you throw a little dust in Crassus's

eyes, Caesar. I don't mind the man, nor do I mind his Sabine wife, but rumors have to start somewhere, and this is a start.''

The frown kept gathering. ''Oh, bother rumors! I'm not particularly concerned about my own part in this, Mater, but I bear poor Silanus no grudges, and it would be far better if our children remained in ignorance of the situation. Paternity of the child isn't likely to be called into doubt, as both Silanus and I are very fair, and Servilia very dark. However the child turns out, it will look as likely to be his as mine, if it does not resemble its mother.''

''True. And I agree with you. Though I do wish, Caesar, that you had chosen some other object than Servilia!''

''I have, now that she's too big to be available.''

''Cato's wife, you mean?''

He groaned. ''Cato's wife. A desperate bore.''

''She'd have to be to survive in *that* household.''

Both his hands came to rest on the desk in front of him; he looked suddenly businesslike. ''Very well, Mater, do you have any suggestions?''

''I think you ought to marry again.''

''I don't want to marry again.''

''I know that! But it is the best way to throw a little dust in everyone's eyes. If a rumor looks likely to spread, create a new rumor which eclipses it.''

''All right, I'll marry again.''

''Have you any particular woman you'd like to marry?''

''Not a one, Mater. I am as clay in your hands.''

That pleased her immensely; she huffed contentedly. ''Good!''

''Name her.''

''Pompeia Sulla.''

''Ye gods, no!'' he cried, appalled. ''Any woman but her!''

''Nonsense. Pompeia Sulla is ideal.''

''Pompeia Sulla's head is so empty you could use it as a dice box,'' said Caesar between his teeth. ''Not to mention that she's expensive, idle, and monumentally silly.''

"An ideal wife," Aurelia contended. "Your dalliances won't worry her, she's too stupid to add one and one together, and she has a fortune of her own adequate enough for all her needs. She is besides your own first cousin once removed, being the daughter of Cornelia Sulla and the granddaughter of Sulla, and the Pompeii Rufi are a more respectable branch of that Picentine family than Magnus's branch. Nor is she in the first flush of youth—I would not give you an inexperienced bride.''

"Nor would I take one," said Caesar grimly. "Has she any children?''

"No, though her marriage to Gaius Servilius Vatia lasted for three years. I don't think, mind you, that Gaius Vatia was a particularly well man. His father—Vatia Isauricus's elder brother, in case you need reminding—died too young to enter the Senate, and about all the political good Rome got from the son was to give him a suffect consulship. That he died before he could assume office was typical of his career. But it does mean Pompeia Sulla is a widow, and therefore more respectable than a divorced woman.''

He was coming around to the idea, she could see that, and sat now without flogging her argument to the death; the notion was planted, and he could tend it for himself. "How old is she now?" he asked slowly.

"Twenty-two, I believe.''

"And Mamercus and Cornelia Sulla would approve? Not to mention Quintus Pompeius Rufus, her half brother, and Quintus Pompeius Rufus, her full brother?''

"Mamercus and Cornelia Sulla asked me if you'd be interested in marrying her, that's how the thought occurred to me,'' said Aurelia. "As for her brothers, the full one is too young to be consulted seriously, and the half one is only afraid that Mamercus will ship her home to him instead of allowing Cornelia Sulla to shelter her.''

Caesar laughed, a wry sound. "I see the family is ganging up on me!" He sobered. "However, Mater, I can't see a young fowl as exotic as Pompeia Sulla consenting to live in a ground-floor apartment right in the middle of the Subura. She might prove a sore trial for you. Cinnilla was as much your child as your daughter-in-law, she would never have disputed your right to rule this particular roost had she lived to be a hundred. Whereas a daughter of Cornelia Sulla might have grander visions.''

''Do not worry about me, Caesar,'' said Aurelia, getting to her feet well satisfied; he was going to do it. ''Pompeia Sulla will do as she's told, and suffer both me and this apartment.''

Thus did Gaius Julius Caesar acquire his second wife, who was the granddaughter of Sulla. The wedding was a quiet one, attended only by the immediate family, and it took place in Mamercus's *domus* on the Palatine amid scenes of great rejoicing, particularly on the part of the bride's half brother, freed from the prospective horror of having to house her.

Pompeia was very beautiful, all of Rome said it, and Caesar (no ardent bridegroom) decided Rome was right. Her hair was dark red and her eyes bright green, some sort of breeding compromise between the red-gold of Sulla's family and the carrot-red of the Pompeii Rufi, Caesar supposed; her face was a classic oval and her bones well structured, her figure good, her height considerable. But no light of intelligence shone out of those grass-colored orbs, and the planes of her face were smooth to the point of highly polished marble. Vacant. House to let, thought Caesar as he carried her amid a reveling band of celebrants all the way from the Palatine to his mother's apartment in the Subura, and making it look far lighter work than it was. Nothing compelled him to carry her, he had to do that only to lift her across the threshold of her new home, but Caesar was ever a creature out to prove he was better than the rest of his world, and that extended to feats of strength his slenderness belied.

Certainly it impressed Pompeia, who giggled and cooed and threw handfuls of rose petals in front of Caesar's feet. But the nuptial coupling was less a feat of strength than the nuptial walk had been; Pompeia belonged to that school of women who believed all they had to do was lie on their backs, spread their legs, and let it happen. Oh, there was some pleasure in lovely breasts and a delightful dark-red thatch of pubic hair—quite a novelty!—but she wasn't *juicy*. She wasn't even grateful, and that, thought Caesar, put even poor Atilia ahead of her, though Atilia was a drab flat-chested creature quite quenched by five years of marriage to the ghastly young Cato.

"Would you like," he asked Pompeia, lifting himself up on an elbow to look at her, "a stick of celery?"

She blinked her preposterously long, dark lashes. "A stick of celery?" she asked vaguely.

"To crunch on while I work," he said. "It would give you something to do, and I'd hear you doing it."

Pompeia giggled because some infatuated youth had once told her it was the most delicious sound, tinkling water over gemstones in the bed of a little brook. "Oh, you are silly!" she said.

Back he flopped, but not on top of her. "You are absolutely right," he said. "I am indeed silly."

And to his mother, in the morning: "Do not expect to see much of me here, Mater."

"Oh dear," said Aurelia placidly. "Like that, is it?"

"I'd rather masturbate!" he said savagely, and left before he could get a tongue-lashing for vulgarity.

Being curator of the Via Appia, he was learning, made far greater demands on his purse than he had expected, despite his mother's warning. The great road connecting Rome with Brundisium cried out for some loving care, as it was never adequately maintained. Though it had to endure the tramp of numberless armies and the wheels of countless baggage trains, it was so old it had become rather taken for granted; beyond Capua especially it suffered.

The Treasury quaestors that year were surprisingly sympathetic, though they included young Caepio, whose relationship to Cato and the *boni* had predisposed Caesar to think he would have to battle ceaselessly for funds. Funds were forthcoming; just never enough. So when the cost of bridge making and resurfacing outran his public funds, Caesar contributed his own. Nothing unusual about that; Rome always expected private donations too.

The work, of course, appealed to him enormously, so he supervised it himself and did all the engineering. After he married Pompeia he hardly visited Rome. Naturally he followed Pompey's progress in that fabulous campaign against the pirates, and had to admit that he could scarcely have bettered it himself. This went as far as applauding Pompey's clemency as the war wound itself up along the Cilician coast, and Pompey dealt with his thousands of captives by resettling them in deserted towns far from the sea. He had, in fact, done everything the right way, from ensuring that his friend and amanuensis Varro was decorated with a Naval Crown to supervising the sharing out of the spoils in such a way that no legate was able to snaffle more than he was entitled to, and the Treasury plumped out considerably. He had taken the soaring citadel of Coracesium the best way, by bribery from within, and when that place fell, no pirate left alive could delude himself that Rome did not now own what had become *Mare Nostrum*, Our Sea. The campaign had extended into the Euxine, and here too Pompey carried all before him. Megadates and his lizardlike twin, Pharnaces, had been executed; the grain supply to Rome was organized and out of future danger.

Only in the matter of Crete had he failed at all, and that was due to Metellus Little Goat, who adamantly refused to honor Pompey's superior imperium, snubbed his legate Lucius Octavius when he arrived to smooth things over, and was generally held to have been the cause of Lucius Cornelius Sisenna's fatal stroke. Though Pompey could have dispossessed him, that would have meant going to war against him, as Metellus made plain. So in the end Pompey did the sensible thing, left Crete to Metellus and thereby tacitly agreed to share a tiny part of the glory with the inflexible grandson of Metellus Macedonicus. For this campaign against the pirates was, as Pompey had said to Caesar, simply a warm-up, a way to stretch his muscles for a greater task.

Thus Pompey made no move to return to Rome; he

lingered in the province of Asia during the winter, and engaged himself in settling it down, reconciling it to a new wave of tax-farmers his own censors had made possible. Of course Pompey had no need to return to Rome, preferred to be elsewhere; he had another trusty tribune of the plebs to replace the retiring Aulus Gabinius—in fact he had two. One, Gaius Memmius, was the son of his sister and her first husband, that Gaius Memmius who had perished in Spain during service with Pompey against Sertorius. The other, Gaius Manilius, was the more able of the pair, and assigned the most difficult task: to obtain for Pompey the command against King Mithridates and King Tigranes.

It was, thought Caesar, feeling it prudent to be in Rome during that December and January, an easier task than Gabinius had faced—simply because Pompey had so decisively trounced his senatorial opposition by routing the pirates in the space of one short summer; at a fraction of the cost his campaign might have incurred; and too quickly to need land grants for troops, bonuses for contributing cities and states, compensation for borrowed fleets. At the end of that year, Rome was prepared to give Pompey anything he wanted.

In contrast, Lucius Licinius Lucullus had endured an atrocious year in the field, suffering defeats, mutinies, disasters. All of which placed him and his agents in Rome in no position to counter Manilius's contention that Bithynia, Pontus and Cilicia should be given to Pompey immediately, and that Lucullus should be stripped of his command completely, ordered back to Rome in disgrace. Glabrio would lose his control of Bithynia and Pontus, but that could not impede Pompey's appointment, as Glabrio had greedily rushed off to govern his province early in his consulship, and done Piso no service thereby. Nor had Quintus Marcius Rex, the governor of Cilicia, accomplished anything of note. The East was targeted for Pompey the Great.

Not that Catulus and Hortensius didn't try. They fought an oratorical battle in Senate and Comitia, still opposing these extraordinary and all-embracing commands.

Manilius was proposing that Pompey be given *imperium maius* again, which would put him above any governor, and also proposing to include a clause which would allow Pompey to make peace and war without needing to ask or consult either Senate or People. This year, however, Caesar did not speak alone in support of Pompey. Now praetor in the Extortion Court, Cicero thundered forth in House and Comitia; so did the censors Poplicola and Lentulus Clodianus, and Gaius Scribonius Curio, and—a real triumph!—the consulars Gaius Cassius Longinus and no less than Publius Servilius Vatia Isauricus himself! How could Senate or People resist? Pompey got his command, and was able to shed a tear or two when he got the news as he toured his dispositions in Cilicia. Oh, the weight of these remorseless special commissions! Oh, how he wanted to go home to a life of peace and tranquillity! Oh, the exhaustion!

Servilia gave birth to her third daughter at the beginning of September, a fair-haired mite whose eyes promised to stay blue. Because Junia and Junilla were so much older and therefore used to their names by now, this Junia would be called Tertia, which meant Third and had a nice sound. The pregnancy had dragged terribly after Caesar had elected not to see her halfway through May, not helped because she was heaviest when the weather was hottest, and Silanus did not deem it wise to leave Rome for the seaside because of her condition at her age. He had continued to be kind and considerate. No one watching them could have suspected all was not well between them. Only Servilia recognized a new look in his eyes, part wounded and part sad, but as compassion was not a part of her nature, she dismissed it as a simple fact of life and did not soften toward him.

Knowing that the gossip grapevine would convey the news of his daughter's arrival to Caesar, Servilia made no attempt to get in touch with him. A hard business anyway, and now compounded by Caesar's new wife. What a shock that had been! Out of the blue, a fireball roaring down from a clear sky to flatten her, kill her, reduce her to a cinder. Jealousy ate at her night and day, for she knew the young lady, of course. No intelligence, no depth—but so beautiful with her off-red hair and vivid green eyes! A granddaughter of Sulla's too. Rich. All the proper connections and a foot in each senatorial camp. How clever of Caesar to gratify his senses as well as enhance his political status! For having no way to ascertain her beloved's frame of mind, Servilia assumed automatically that this was a love match. Well, rot him! How could she live without him? How could she live knowing some other woman meant more to him than she did? How could she live?

Brutus saw Julia regularly, of course. At sixteen and now officially a man, Brutus was revolted by his mother's pregnancy. He, a man, had a mother who was still—was still . . . Ye gods, the embarrassment, the humiliation!

But Julia saw things differently, and told him so. "How nice for her and Silanus," the nine-year-old had said, smiling tenderly. "You mustn't be angry with her, Brutus, truly. What happens if after we've been married for twenty or so years, we should have an extra child? Would you understand your oldest son's anger?"

His skin was worse than it had been a year ago, always in a state of eruption, yellow sores and red sores, sores which itched or burned, needed to be scratched or squeezed or torn at. Self-hate had fueled his hatred of his mother's condition, and was hard to put by now at this reasonable and charitable question. He scowled, growled, but then said reluctantly, "I would understand his anger, yes, because I feel it. But I do see what you mean."

"Then that's a beginning, it will do," said the little sage. "Servilia isn't quite a girl anymore, *avia* explained that to me, and said that she would need lots of help and sympathy."

"I'll try," said Brutus, "for you, Julia." And took himself home to try.

All of which paled into insignificance when Servilia's chance came not two weeks after she had borne Tertia.

Her brother Caepio called to see her with interesting news.

One of the urban quaestors, he had been earmarked earlier in the year to assist Pompey in his campaign against the pirates, a task he had not thought would necessitate his leaving Rome.

"But I've been sent for, Servilia!" he cried, happiness shining in eyes and smile. "Gnaeus Pompeius wants quite a lot of money and accounts brought to him in Pergamum, and I am to make the journey. Isn't that wonderful? I can go overland through Macedonia and visit my brother Cato. I miss him dreadfully!"

"How nice for you," said Servilia listlessly, not in the least interested in Caepio's passion for Cato, as it had been a part of all their lives for twenty-seven years.

"Pompeius doesn't expect me before December, so if I get going immediately I can have quite a long time with Cato before I have to move on," Caepio continued, still in that mood of happy anticipation. "The weather will hold until I leave Macedonia, and I can continue on by road." He shivered. "I hate the sea!"

"Safe from pirates these days, I hear."

"Thank you, I prefer terra firma."

Caepio then proceeded to acquaint himself with baby Tertia, gooing and clucking as much out of genuine affection as out of duty, and comparing his sister's child to his own, also a girl.

"Lovely little thing," he said, preparing to depart. "Most distinguished bones. I wonder where she gets those from?"

Oh, thought Servilia. And here was I deluding myself that I am the only one to see a likeness to Caesar! Still, Porcius Cato though his blood was, Caepio had no malice in him, so his remark had been an innocent one.

Her mind clicked from that thought into an habitual sequel, Caepio's manifest unworthiness to inherit the fruits of the Gold of Tolosa, followed by a burning resentment that her own son, Brutus, could not inherit. Caepio, the cuckoo in her family nest. Cato's full brother, not her full brother.

It had been months since Servilia had been able to

concentrate on anything beyond Caesar's perfidy in marrying that young and delectable nincompoop, but those reflections on the fate of the Gold of Tolosa now flowed into a completely different channel unclouded by Caesar-induced emotions. For she glanced out of her open window and saw Sinon prancing blithely down the colonnade on the far side of the peristyle garden. Servilia loved this slave, though not in any fleshly sense. He had belonged to her husband, but not long after their marriage she had asked Silanus sweetly if he would transfer Sinon's ownership to her. The deed accomplished, she had summoned Sinon and informed him of the change in his status, expecting horror, hoping for something else. She had got that something else, and loved Sinon ever since. For he had greeted her news with joy.

"It takes one to know one," he had remarked impudently.

"If it does, Sinon, bear this in mind: I am your superior, I have the power."

"I understand," he answered, smirking. "That's good, you know. As long as Decimus Junius remained my master, there was always the temptation to take things too far, and that might well have resulted in my downfall. With you as my mistress, I will never forget to watch my step. Very good, very good! But do remember, *domina,* that I am yours to command."

And command him she had from time to time. Cato, she knew from childhood, was afraid of absolutely nothing except large and hairy spiders, which reduced him to gibbering panic. So Sinon was often allowed to prowl out of Rome in search of large and hairy spiders, and was paid extremely well to introduce them into Cato's house, from his bed to his couch to his desk drawers. Not once had he been detected at the business, either. Cato's full sister, Porcia, who was married to Lucius Domitius Ahenobarbus, had an abiding horror of fat beetles. Sinon caught fat beetles and introduced them into that household. Then sometimes Servilia would instruct him to dump thousands of worms or fleas or flies or crickets or roaches into either residence, and send anonymous notes containing worm curses or flea curses or whatever curse was relevant. Until Caesar had entered her life, such activities had kept her amused. But since Caesar had entered her life, those diversions had not been necessary, and Sinon's time had become all his own. He toiled not, save in the procurement of insect pests, as the mantle of the lady Servilia wrapped him round.

"Sinon!" she called.

He stopped, turned, came skipping up the colonnade and round the corner to her sitting room. Quite a pretty fellow, he had a certain grace and insouciance which made him likable to those who did not know him well; Silanus, for instance, still thought highly of him, and so did Brutus. Slight in build, he was a brown person—brown skin, light brown eyes, light brown hair. Pointed ears, pointed chin, pointed fingers. No wonder many of the servants made the sign to ward off the Evil Eye when Sinon appeared. There was a satyr quality to him.

"*Domina?*" he asked, stepping over the sill.

"Close the door, Sinon, then close the shutters."

"Oh, goody, work!" he said, obeying.

"Sit down."

He sat, gazing at her with a mixture of cheek and expectation. Spiders? Roaches? Perhaps she would graduate to snakes?

"How would you like your freedom, Sinon, with a fat purse of gold to go with it?" she asked.

That he did not expect. For a moment the satyr vanished to reveal another quasi-human less appealing underneath, some creature out of a children's nightmare. Then it too disappeared, he merely looked alert and interested.

"I would like that very much, *domina*."

"Have you any idea what I would ask you to do that could earn such a reward?"

"Murder at the very least," he answered without hesitation.

"Quite so," said Servilia. "Are you tempted?"

He shrugged. "Who would not be, in my position?"

"It takes courage to do murder."

"I am aware of that. But I have courage."

"You're a Greek, and Greeks have no sense of honor. By that I mean they do not stay bought."

"I would stay bought, *domina*, if all I had to do was murder and then could disappear with my fat purse of gold."

Servilia was reclining on a couch, and did not alter her position in the slightest through all of this. But having got his answer, she straightened; her eyes grew absolutely cold and still. "I do not trust you because I trust nobody," she said, "yet this is not a murder to be done in Rome, or even in Italia. It will have to be done somewhere between Thessalonica and the Hellespont, an ideal spot from which to disappear. But there are ways I can keep hold of you, Sinon, do not forget that. One is to pay you some of your reward now, and send the rest to a destination in Asia Province."

"Ah, *domina*, but how do I know you will keep your side of the bargain?" Sinon asked softly.

Servilia's nostrils flared, an unconscious hauteur. "I am a patrician Servilius Caepio," she said.

"I appreciate that."

"It is the only guarantee you need that I will keep my side of the bargain."

"What do I have to do?"

"First of all, you have to procure a poison of the best kind. By that I mean a poison which will not fail, and a poison which will not be suspected."

"I can do that."

"My brother Quintus Servilius Caepio leaves for the East in a day or so," said Servilia, level-voiced. "I will ask him if you may accompany him, as I have business for you to do in Asia Province. He will agree to take you, of course. There is no reason why he should not. He will be carrying scrip and accounts for Gnaeus Pompeius Magnus in Pergamum, and he will have no ready money to tempt you. For it is imperative, Sinon, that you do what I require you to do and then go without disturbing one single tiny thing. His brother Cato is a tribune of the soldiers in Macedonia, and his brother Cato is a far different fellow. Suspicious and hard, ruthless when offended. No doubt his brother Cato will go east to arrange my brother Caepio's obsequies, it is in character for him to do so. And when he arrives, Sinon, there must be no suspicion that anything more than illness has put paid to the life of my brother Quintus Servilius Caepio.''

"I understand,'' said Sinon, not moving a muscle.

"Do you?''

"Fully, *domina*.''

"You may have tomorrow to find your tool. Is that possible?''

"That is possible.''

"Good. Then you may run round the corner now to my brother Quintus Servilius Caepio's house, and ask him to visit me today on a matter of some urgency,'' said Servilia.

Sinon left. Servilia lay back on her couch, closed her eyes and smiled.

She was still like that when Caepio returned not long after; their houses were in close proximity.

"What is it, Servilia?'' he asked, concerned. "Your servant seemed most anxious.''

"Dear me, I hope he didn't frighten you!'' said Servilia sharply.

"No, no, I assure you.''

"You didn't take a dislike to him?''

Caepio blinked. "Why should I?''

"I have no idea,'' said Servilia, patting the end of her couch. "Sit down, brother. I have a favor to ask you, and something to make sure you have done.''

"The favor?''

"Sinon is my most trusted servant, and I have some business in Pergamum for him to do. I should have thought of it when you were here earlier, but I didn't, so I do apologize for having to drag you back. Would you mind if Sinon traveled in your party?''

"Of course not!'' cried Caepio sincerely.

"Oh, splendid,'' purred Servilia.

"And what was I supposed to do?''

"Make your will,'' said Servilia.

He laughed. "Is that all? What sensible Roman

doesn't have a will lodged with the Vestals the moment he becomes a man?''

"But is yours current? You have a wife and a baby daughter, but no heir in your own house.''

Caepio sighed. ''Next time, Servilia, next time. Hortensia was disappointed to produce a girl first, but she's a dear little thing, and Hortensia had no trouble in labor. There'll be sons.''

"So you've left it all to Cato,'' said Servilia, making it a statement.

The face so like Cato's registered horror. ''To *Cato*?'' he asked, voice squeaking. ''I can't leave the Servilius Caepio fortune to a Porcius Cato, much and all as I love him! No, no, Servilia! It's left to Brutus because Brutus won't mind being adopted as a Servilius Caepio, won't mind taking the name. But Cato?'' He laughed. ''Can you see our baby brother Cato consenting to bear any other name than his own?''

"No, I can't,'' said Servilia, and laughed a little too. Then her eyes filled, her lips quivered. ''What a morbid conversation! Still, it was one I had to have with you. One never knows.''

"Cato is my executor, however,'' said Caepio, preparing to leave this same room for the second time within an hour. ''He'll make sure Hortensia and baby Servilia Caepionis inherit as much as the *lex Voconia* lets me leave them, and he'll make sure Brutus is properly endowed.''

"What a ridiculous subject this is!'' said Servilia, rising to see him to the door, and surprising him with a kiss. ''Thank you for letting Sinon go with you, and thank you even more for allaying my fears. Futile fears, I know. You'll be back!''

She closed the door behind him and stood for a moment so weak that she swayed. Right, she had been right! Brutus was his heir because Cato would never consent to being adopted into a patrician clan like Servilius Caepio! Oh, what a wonderful day this was! Even Caesar's defection wasn't hurting the way it had a few hours before.

*   *   *

Having Marcus Porcius Cato on one's staff, even if his duties were technically confined to the consuls' legions, was an ordeal the governor of Macedonia could never have imagined until it happened. If the young man had been a personal appointment, home he would have gone no matter if his sponsor had been Jupiter Optimus Maximus; but as the People had appointed him through the medium of the Popular Assembly, there was nothing Governor Marcus Rubrius could do save suffer the continuing presence of Cato.

But how could one deal with a young man who poked and pried, questioned incessantly, wanted to know why this was going there, why that was worth more on the books than in the marketplace, why so-and-so was claiming tax exemptions? Cato never stopped asking why. If he was reminded tactfully that his inquisitions were not relevant to the consuls' legions, Cato would simply answer that everything in Macedonia belonged to Rome, and Roma as personified by Romulus had elected him one of her magistrates. Ergo, everything in Macedonia was legally and morally and ethically his business.

Governor Marcus Rubrius was not alone. His legates and his military tribunes (elected or unelected), his scribes, wardens, bailiffs, *publicani,* mistresses and slaves all detested Marcus Porcius Cato. Who was a fiend for work, couldn't even be gotten rid of by being sent to some outpost of the province, because he'd come back in two or three days at most, his task well done.

A great deal of his conversation—if a loud harangue could be called a conversation—revolved around his great-grandfather, Cato the Censor, whose frugality and old-fashioned ways Cato esteemed immensely. And since Cato was Cato, he actually emulated the Censor in every way save one: he walked everywhere instead of riding, he ate abstemiously and drank nothing but water, his habit of living was no better than that of a ranker soldier, and he kept only one slave to attend to his needs.

So what was that one transgression of his great-grandfather's tenets? Cato the Censor had abhorred Greece, Greeks and things Greek, whereas young Cato admired them, and made no secret of his admiration. This let him in for considerable chaffing from those who had to bear his presence in Grecian Macedonia, all of them dying to pierce his incredibly thick skin. But none of the chaffing so much as made a dent in Cato's integument; when someone twitted him about betraying his great-grandfather's precepts by espousing Greek modes of thought, that person found himself ignored as unimportant. Alas, what Cato did consider important was what drove his superiors, peers and inferiors maddest: living soft, he called it, and was as likely to criticize evidence of living soft in the governor as in a centurion. Since he dwelled in a two-roomed mud brick house on the outskirts of Thessalonica and shared it with his dear friend Titus Munatius Rufus, a fellow tribune of the soldiers, no one could say Cato himself lived soft.

He had arrived in Thessalonica during March, and by the end of May the governor came to the conclusion that if he didn't get rid of Cato somehow, murder would be done. The complaints kept piling up on the gubernatorial desk from tax-farming *publicani,* grain merchants, accountants, centurions, legionaries, legates, and various women Cato had accused of unchastity.

"He even had the gall to tell me that he had kept *himself* chaste until he married!" gasped one lady to Rubrius; she was an intimate friend. "Marcus, he stood me up in the agora in front of a thousand smirking Greeks and lambasted me about the behavior appropriate to a Roman woman living in a province! Get rid of him, or I swear I'll pay someone to assassinate him!"

Luckily for Cato, it was somewhat later on the same day that he happened to pass a remark to Marcus Rubrius about the presence in Pergamum of one Athenodorus Cordylion.

"How I would love to hear him!" barked Cato. "Normally he's located in Antioch and Alexandria; this present tour is unusual."

"Well," said Rubrius, tongue tripping rapidly in the wake of a brilliant idea, "why don't you take a couple of months off and go to Pergamum to hear him?"

"I couldn't do that!" said Cato, shocked. "My duty is here."

"*Every* tribune of the soldiers is entitled to leave, my dear Marcus Cato, and none is more deserving of leave than you. Go, do! I insist upon it. And take Munatius Rufus with you."

So Cato went, accompanied by Munatius Rufus. Thessalonica's Roman contingent went almost mad with joy, for Munatius Rufus so hero-worshiped Cato that he imitated him assiduously. But exactly two months after departing he was back in Thessalonica, the only Roman whom Rubrius had ever known to take a casual suggestion of how long to be away so literally. And with him in his train came none other than Athenodorus Cordylion, Stoic philosopher of some renown, ready to play Panaetius to Cato's Scipio Aemilianus. Being a Stoic, he didn't expect or want the kind of luxuries Scipio Aemilianus had poured upon Panaetius—which was just as well. The only change he made in Cato's way of living was that he, Munatius Rufus and Cato rented a three-roomed mud brick house instead of a two-roomed one, and that there were three slaves in it instead of two. What had prompted this eminent philosopher to join Cato? Simply that in Cato he had seen someone who would one day matter enormously, and to join the Cato household would ensure his own name was remembered. If it hadn't been for Scipio Aemilianus, who would ever remember the name of Panaetius?

The Roman element in Thessalonica had groaned mightily when Cato returned from Pergamum; Rubrius demonstrated that he was not prepared to suffer Cato by declaring that he had urgent business in Athens, and departing in a hurry. No consolation for those he left behind! But then Quintus Servilius Caepio arrived en route to Pergamum in Pompey's service, and Cato forgot about tax-farmers and living soft, so happy was he to see this beloved brother.

The bond between them had been created shortly after Cato's birth, at which time Caepio was only three years old. Ailing, their mother (she was to die within two months) gave baby Cato into toddler Caepio's willing hands. Nothing save duty had parted them since, though even in duty they had usually managed to stay together. Perhaps the bond would naturally have weakened as they grew, had it not been that their Uncle Drusus was stabbed to death in the house they had all shared; when it happened Caepio was six and Cato barely three. That ghastly ordeal forged the bond in fires of horror and tragedy so intense it endured afterward even stronger. Their childhood had been lonely, war torn, unloving, humorless. No close relatives were left, their guardians aloof, and the two oldest of the six children involved, Servilia and Servililla, loathed the two youngest, Cato and his sister Porcia. Not that the battle between oldest and youngest was weighted in favor of the two Servilias! Cato might have been the littlest, but he was also the loudest and the most fearless of all six.

Whenever the child Cato was asked, "Whom do you love?," his answer was the same: "I love my brother." And if he was pressed to qualify this statement by declaring whom else he loved, his answer was always the same: "I love my brother."

In truth he never had loved anybody else except for that awful experience with Uncle Mamercus's daughter, Aemilia Lepida; and if loving Aemilia Lepida had taught Cato nothing else, it taught him to detest and mistrust women—an attitude helped along by a childhood spent with Servilia.

Whereas what he felt for Caepio was totally ineradicable, completely reciprocated, heartfelt, a matter of sinew and blood. Though he never would admit, even to himself, that Caepio was more than half a brother. There are none so blind as those who will not see, and none blinder than Cato when he wanted to be blind.

They journeyed everywhere, saw everything, Cato for once the expert. And if the humble little freedman Sinon who traveled in Caepio's train on Servilia's business had ever been tempted to treat her warning about Cato lightly, one look at Cato made him understand entirely why she had thought Cato worth mentioning as a danger to Sinon's real business. Not that Sinon was drawn to Cato's attention; a member of the Roman nobility did not bother with introductions to inferiors. Sinon looked from behind a crowd of servants and underlings, and made sure he did absolutely nothing to provoke Cato into noticing him.

But all good things must come to an end, so at the beginning of December the brothers parted and Caepio rode on down the Via Egnatia, followed by his retinue. Cato wept unashamedly. So did Caepio, all the harder because Cato walked down the road in their wake for many miles, waving, weeping, calling out to Caepio to take care, take care, take care. . . .

Perhaps he had had a feeling of imminent danger to Caepio; certainly when Caepio's note came a month later, its contents did not surprise him as they ought to have done.

My dearest brother, I have fallen ill in Aenus, and I fear for my life. Whatever is the matter, and none of the local physicians seem to know, I worsen every day.

Please, dear Cato, I beg you to come to Aenus and be with me at my end. It is so lonely, and no one here can comfort me as your presence would. I can ask to hold no hand dearer than yours while I give up my last breath. Come, I beg of you, and come soon. I will try to hang on.

My will is all in order with the Vestals, and as we had discussed, young Brutus will be my heir. You are the executor, and I have left you, as you stipulated, no more than the sum of ten talents. Come soon.

When informed that Cato needed emergency leave immediately, Governor Marcus Rubrius put no obstacles in his path. The only advice he offered was to go by road, as late-autumn storms were lashing the Thracian coast, and there had already been several shipwrecks reported. But Cato refused to listen; by road his journey could not take less than ten days no matter how hard he galloped,

whereas the screaming winds from the northwest would
fill the sails of a ship and speed it along so swiftly he
could hope to reach Aenus in three to five days. And,
having found a ship's captain rash enough to agree to take
him (for a very good fee) from Thessalonica to Aenus, the
feverish and frantic Cato embarked. Athenodorus Cordylion and Munatius Rufus came too, each man accompanied
by only one slave.

The voyage was a nightmare of huge waves, breaking
masts, tattered sails. However, the captain had carried extra masts and sails with him; the little ship ploughed and
wallowed on, afloat and, it seemed to Athenodorus Cordylion and Munatius Rufus, powered in some inscrutable
way out of the mind and will of Cato. Who, when harbor
was reached at Aenus on the fourth day, didn't even wait
for the ship to tie up. He leaped the few feet from ship to
dock and began running madly through the driving rain.
Only once did he pause, to discover from an astonished
and shelterless peddler whereabouts lay the house of the
ethnarch, for there he knew Caepio would be.

He burst into the house and into the room where his
brother lay, an hour too late to hold that hand while Caepio
knew he was holding it. Quintus Servilius Caepio was
dead.

Water pooling around him on the floor, Cato stood
by the bed looking down at the core and solace of his
entire life, a still and dreadful figure bleached of color,
vigor, force. The eyes had been closed and weighted down
with coins, a curved silver edge protruded between the
slightly parted lips; someone else had given Caepio the
price of his ferry ride across the river Styx, thinking Cato
would not come.

Cato opened his mouth and produced a sound which
terrified everyone who heard it, neither wail nor howl nor
screech, but an eldritch fusion of all three, animal, feral,
hideous. All those present in the room recoiled instinctively, shook as Cato threw himself onto the bed, onto
dead Caepio, covered the dreaming face with kisses, the
lifeless body with caresses, while the tears poured until
nose and mouth ran rivers as well, and those dreadful

noises erupted out of him time and time again. And the
paroxysm of grief went on without let, Cato mourning the
passing of the one person in his world who meant everything, had been comfort in an awful childhood, anchor and
rock to boy and man. Caepio it had been who drew his
three-year-old eyes away from Uncle Drusus bleeding and
screaming on the floor, turned those eyes into the warmth
of his body and took the burden of all those ghastly hours
upon his six-year-old shoulders; Caepio it had been who
listened patiently while his dunce of a baby brother learned
every fact the hardest way, by repeating it endlessly; Caepio it had been who reasoned and coaxed and cajoled during the unbearable aftermath of Aemilia Lepida's
desertion, persuaded him to live again; Caepio it had been
who took him on his first campaign, taught him to be a
brave and fearless soldier, beamed when he had received
armillae and *phalerae* for valor on a field more usually
famous for cowardice, for they had belonged to the army
of Clodianus and Poplicola defeated thrice by Spartacus;
Caepio it had always, always been.

Now Caepio was no more. Caepio had died alone and
friendless, with no one to hold his hand. The guilt and
remorse sent Cato quite mad in that room where Caepio
lay dead. When people tried to take him away, he fought.
When people tried to talk him away, he just howled out.
For almost two days he refused to move from where he
lay covering Caepio, and the worst of it was that no one—
no one!—even began to understand the terror of this loss,
the loneliness his life would now forever be. Caepio was
gone, and with Caepio went love, sanity, security.

But finally Athenodorus Cordylion managed to pierce
the madness with words concerning a Stoic's attitudes, the
behavior fitting to one who, like Cato, professed Stoicism.
Cato got up and went to arrange his brother's funeral, still
clad in rough tunic and smelly *sagum,* unshaven, face
smeared and crusted with the dried remains of so many
rivers of grief. The ten talents Caepio had left him in his
will would be spent on this funeral, and when no matter
how he tried to spend all of it with the local undertakers
and spice merchants, all he could procure amounted to one

talent, he spent another talent on a golden box studded with jewels to receive Caepio's ashes, and the other eight on a statue of Caepio to be erected in the agora of Aenus.

"But you won't get the color of his skin or his hair or his eyes right," said Cato in that same hard harsh voice, even harsher from the noises his throat had produced, "and I do not want this statue to look like a living man. I want everyone who sees it to know that he is dead. You will craft it in Thasian marble of solid grey and you will polish it until my brother glitters under the light of the moon. He is a shade, and I want his statue to look like a shade."

The funeral was the most impressive this small Greek colony just to the east of the mouth of the Hebrus had ever seen, with every woman drawn into service as a professional mourner, and every stick of aromatic spice Aenus contained burned upon Caepio's pyre. When the obsequies were over, Cato gathered up the ashes himself and placed them in the exquisite little box, which never left his person from that day until he arrived in Rome a year later and, as was his duty, gave the box to Caepio's widow.

He wrote to Uncle Mamercus in Rome with instructions to act on as much of Caepio's will as was necessary before he himself returned, and was quite surprised to find he didn't need to write to Rubrius in Thessalonica. The *ethnarch* had most correctly notified Rubrius of Caepio's death the day it happened, and Rubrius had seen his chance. So with his letter of condolences to Cato there arrived all Cato's and Munatius Rufus's possessions. It's nearly the end of your year of service, chaps, said the governor's scribe's perfect handwriting, and I wouldn't ask either of you to come back here when the weather's closed in and the Bessi have gone home to the Danubius for the winter! Take a long vacation in the East, get over it the right way, the best way.

"I will do that," said Cato, the box between his hands. "We will journey east, not west."

But he had changed, as both Athenodorus Cordylion and Titus Munatius Rufus saw, both with sadness. Cato had always been a working lighthouse, a strong and steady

beam turning, turning. Now the light had gone out. The
face was the same, the trim and muscular body no more
bowed or cramped than of yore. But now the hectoring
voice had a tonelessness absolutely new, nor did Cato become excited, or enthused, or indignant, or angry. Worst
of all, the passion had vanished.

Only Cato knew how strong he had needed to be to
go on living. Only Cato knew what Cato had resolved:
that never again would he lay himself open to this torture,
this devastation. To love was to lose forever. Therefore to
love was anathema. Cato would never love again. Never.

And while his shabby little band of three free men
and three attendant slaves plodded on foot down the Via
Egnatia toward the Hellespont, a freedman named Sinon
leaned upon the rail of a neat little ship bearing him down
the Aegaean before a brisk but steady winter wind, his
destination Athens. There he would take passage for Pergamum, where he would find the rest of his bag of gold.
Of that last fact he had no doubt. She was too crafty not
to pay up, the great patrician lady Servilia. For a moment
Sinon toyed with the idea of blackmail, then he laughed,
shrugged, tossed an expiatory drachma into the briskly
foaming wake as an offering to Poseidon. Carry me safely,
Father of the Deep! I am not only free, I am rich. The
lioness in Rome is quiet. I will not wake her to seek more
money. Instead, I will increase what is legally mine already.

The lioness in Rome learned of her brother's death
from Uncle Mamercus, who came round to see her the
moment he received Cato's letter. She shed tears, but not
too many; Uncle Mamercus knew how she felt, no one
better. The instructions to the branch of her bankers in
Pergamum had gone not long after Caepio, a risk she had
decided to take before the deed happened. Wise Servilia.
No curious accountant or banker would wonder why after
the death of Caepio his sister sent a large sum of money
to a freedman named Sinon who would pick it up in Pergamum.

And, said Brutus to Julia later that day, "I am to change my name, isn't that amazing?"

"Have you been adopted in someone's will?" she asked, quite aware of the usual manner in which a man's name would change.

"My Uncle Caepio died in Aenus, and I am his heir." The sad brown eyes blinked away a few tears. "He was a nice man, I liked him. Mostly I suppose because Uncle Cato adored him. Poor Uncle Cato was there an hour too late. Now Uncle Cato says he's not coming home for a long time. I shall miss him."

"You already do," said Julia, smiling and squeezing his hand.

He smiled at her and squeezed back. No need to worry about Brutus's conduct toward his betrothed; it was as circumspect as any watchful grandmother could want. Aurelia had given up any kind of chaperonage very soon after the engagement contract was signed. Brutus was a credit to his mother and stepfather.

Not long turned ten (her birthday was in January), Julia was profoundly glad that Brutus was a credit to his mother and stepfather. When Caesar had told her of her marital fate she had been appalled, for though she pitied Brutus, she knew that no amount of time or exposure to him would turn pity into affection of the kind that held marriages together. The best she could say of him was that he was nice. The worst she could say of him was that he was boring. Though her age precluded any romantic dreams, like most little girls of her background she was very much attuned to what her adult life would be, and therefore very much aware of marriage. It had proven hard to go to Gnipho's school and tell her classmates of her betrothal, for all that she had used to think it would give her great satisfaction to put herself on a par with Junia and Junilla, as yet the only betrothed girls there. But Junia's Vatia Isauricus was a delightful fellow, and Junilla's Lepidus dashingly handsome. Whereas what could one say about Brutus? Neither of his half sisters could abide him— at least not to hear them talk at school. Like Julia, they deemed him a pompous bore. Now here she was to marry him! Oh, her friends would tease her unmercifully! And pity her.

"Poor Julia!" said Junia, laughing merrily.

However, there was no point in resenting her fate. She had to marry Brutus, and that was that.

"Did you hear the news, *tata*?" she asked her father when he came home briefly after the dinner hour had ended.

It was awful now that Pompeia lived here. He never came home to sleep, rarely ate with them, passed through. Therefore to have news which might detain him long enough for a word or two was wonderful; Julia seized her chance.

"News?" he asked absently.

"Guess who came to see me today?" she asked gleefully.

Her father's eyes twinkled. "Brutus?"

"Guess again!"

"Jupiter Optimus Maximus?"

"Silly! He doesn't come as a person, only as an idea."

"Who, then?" he asked, beginning to shift about restlessly. Pompeia was home; he could hear her in the *tablinum,* which she had made her own because Caesar never worked there anymore.

"Oh, *tata,* please *please* stay a little while longer!"

The big blue eyes were strained with anxiety; Caesar's heart and conscience smote him. Poor little girl, she suffered from Pompeia more than anyone else because she didn't see much of *tata.*

Sighing, he picked her up and carried her to a chair, sat himself down and put her on his knee. "You're growing quite tall!" he said, surprised.

"I hope so." She began to kiss his white fans.

"Who came to see you today?" he asked, keeping very still.

"Quintus Servilius Caepio."

His head jerked, turned. *"Who?"*

"Quintus Servilius Caepio."

"But he's quaestoring Gnaeus Pompeius!"

"No, he isn't."

"Julia, the only member of that family left alive is not here in Rome!" said Caesar.

"I am afraid," said Julia softly, "that the man you mean is no longer alive. He died in Aenus in January. But there is a new Quintus Servilius Caepio, because the will names him and he must soon be formally adopted."

Caesar gasped. "Brutus?"

"Yes, Brutus. He says he'll now be known as Quintus Servilius Caepio Brutus rather than Caepio Junianus. The Brutus is more important than the Junius."

"Jupiter!"

"*Tata,* you're quite shocked. Why?"

His hand went to his head, he gave his cheek a mock slap. "Well, you wouldn't know." Then he laughed. "Julia, you will marry the richest man in Rome! If Brutus is Caepio's heir, then the third fortune he adds to his inheritance pales the other two into insignificance. You'll be wealthier than a queen."

"Brutus didn't say anything like that."

"He probably doesn't really know. Not a curious young man, your betrothed," said Caesar.

"I think he likes money."

"Doesn't everyone?" asked Caesar rather bitterly. He got to his feet and put Julia in the chair. "I'll be back shortly," he said, dashed through the door into the dining room, and then, so Julia presumed, into his study.

The next thing Pompeia came flying out looking indignant, and stared at Julia in outrage.

"What is it?" asked Julia of her stepmother, with whom she actually got on quite well. Pompeia was good practice for dealing with Brutus, though she acquitted Brutus of Pompeia's stupidity.

"He just threw me out!" said Pompeia.

"Only for a moment, I'm sure."

It was indeed only for a moment. Caesar sat down and wrote a note to Servilia, whom he hadn't seen since May of the preceding year. Of course he had meant to get around to seeing her again before now (it was March), but time got away, he was frying several other fish. How amazing. Young Brutus had fallen heir to the Gold of To-losa!

Definitely it was time to be nice to his mother. This was one betrothal could not be broken for any reason.

PART II

---

from MARCH of 73 B.C.
until QUINCTILIS of 65 B.C.

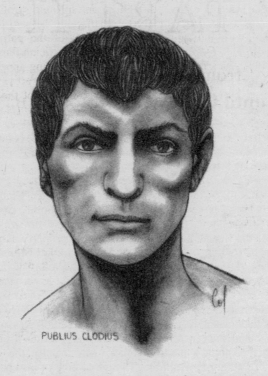

PUBLIUS CLODIUS

The trouble with Publius Clodius was not lack of birth, intellect, ability or money; it was lack of direction, both in the sense of where he wanted to go and in the sense of firm guidance from his elders. Instinct told him he was born to be different, but that was not a novel thought in one springing from the patrician Claudii. If any Roman clan could be said to be stuffed with individualists, it was that of the patrician Claudii. Odd, considering that of all the patrician Famous Families, the Claudian was the youngest, having appeared at about the same time as King Tarquinius Superbus was deposed by Lucius Junius Brutus, and the era of the Republic began. Of course the Claudii were Sabines, and Sabines were fierce, proud, independent, untamable, warlike; they had to be, for they hailed from the Apennines to the north and east of Roman Latium, a cruelly mountainous area whose pockets of kindness were few and far between.

Clodius's father had been that Appius Claudius Pulcher who never managed to recoup his family fortune after his nephew, the censor Philippus, had thrown him out of the Senate and confiscated all his property as punishment for his stubborn loyalty to the exiled Sulla. His mother, the awesomely noble Caecilia Metella Balearica, had died giving birth to him, the sixth child in six years—three boys and three girls. The vicissitudes of war and always managing to be in the wrong place at the wrong time had meant that Appius Claudius Senior was never home, and that in turn had meant that Clodius's oldest brother, Appius Claudius Junior, was usually the only voice of authority available. Though all five of his charges were turbulent, self-willed and full of a desire to wreak havoc, baby Publius was the worst of them. Had he sampled some nonexistent firm discipline, perhaps Publius would have been less subject to the whims which dominated his childhood, but as all five of his elder siblings spoiled him atrociously, he did precisely as he liked, and very early in his life was convinced that of any Claudian who ever lived, he was the most different.

At about the moment that his father died in Macedonia, he told big brother Appius that he would in future spell his name the popular way, Clodius, and would not use the family cognomen of Pulcher. Pulcher meant beautiful, and it was true that most of the Claudii Pulchri were handsome or beautiful; the original owner of the nickname, however, had received it because he owned a singularly unbeautiful character. "What a beauty!" people had said of him, and Pulcher stuck.

Naturally Publius Clodius had been allowed to popularize the spelling of his name; the precedent had been set with his three sisters, the eldest of whom was known as Claudia, the middle as Clodia, and the youngest as Clodilla. Big brother Appius so doted on his charges that he could never resist granting any of them whatever they wanted. For example, if the adolescent Publius Clodius liked to sleep with Clodia and Clodilla because he had nightmares, why not? Poor little things, no mother and no father! Big brother Appius mourned for them. A fact which littlest brother Publius Clodius was well aware of, and used ruthlessly.

At about the time that young Publius Clodius had put on his *toga virilis* and officially become a man, big brother Appius had brilliantly retrieved the tottering family fortune by marrying the spinster lady Servilia Gnaea; she had looked after six other noble orphans, those belonging to the Servilius Caepio, Livius Drusus and Porcius Cato ménage. Her dowry was as immense as her lack of beauty. But they had care of orphans in common and she turned out to suit sentimental big brother Appius, who promptly fell in love with his thirty-two-year-old bride (he was twenty-one), settled down to a life of uxorious content, and bred children at the rate of one a year, thus living up to Claudian tradition.

Big brother Appius had also managed to provide extremely well for his three dowerless sisters: Claudia went to Quintus Marcius Rex, soon to be consul; Clodia went to their first cousin Quintus Caecilius Metellus Celer (who was also the half brother of Pompey's wife, Mucia Tertia); and Clodilla went to the great Lucullus, fully thrice her age. Three enormously wealthy and prestigious men, two of whom were old enough to have already cemented familial power, and Celer not needing to do so because he was the senior grandson of Metellus Balearicus as well as the grandson of the distinguished Crassus Orator. All of which had worked out particularly well for young Publius Clodius, as Rex had not managed to sire a son on Claudia, even after some years of marriage; Publius Clodius therefore confidently expected to be Rex's heir.

At the age of sixteen Publius Clodius went for his *tirocinium fori,* his apprenticeship as legal advocate and aspiring politician in the Forum Romanum, then spent a year on the parade grounds of Capua playing at soldiers, and returned to Forum life aged eighteen. Feeling his oats and aware that the girls thought him swoonable, Clodius looked around for a feminine conquest who fitted in with his ideas of his own specialness, which were growing by leaps and bounds. Thus he conceived a passion for Fabia—who was a Vestal Virgin. To set one's sights on a Vestal was frowned upon, and that was just the sort of amorous adventure Clodius wanted. In every Vestal's chastity resided Rome's luck; most men recoiled in horror from the very thought of seducing a Vestal. But not Publius Clodius.

No one in Rome asked or expected the Vestal Virgins to lead sequestered lives. They were permitted to go out to dinner parties provided the Pontifex Maximus and the Chief Vestal gave approval of the venue and the company, and they attended all the priestly banquets as the equals of priests and augurs. They were permitted to have masculine visitors in the public parts of the Domus Publica, the State-owned house they shared with the Pontifex Maximus, though it was required to be a chaperoned business. Nor were the Vestals impoverished. It was a great thing for a family to have a Vestal in its ranks, so girls not needed to cement alliances by marriage were often given up to the State as Vestals. Most came with excellent dowries; those unprovided for were dowered by the State.

Also aged eighteen, Fabia was beautiful, sweet-natured, merry and just a little stupid. The perfect target for Publius Clodius, who adored to make mischief of the kind which made people stiffen with outraged disapproval. To woo a Vestal would be such a lark! Not that Clodius intended to go as far as actually deflowering Fabia, for that would lead to legal repercussions involving his own much-beloved hide. All he really wanted was to see Fabia pine away from love and want of him.

The trouble began when he discovered that he had a rival for Fabia's affections: Lucius Sergius Catilina, tall, dark, handsome, dashing, charming—and dangerous. Clodius's own charms were considerable, but not in Catilina's league; he lacked the imposing height and physique, for one, nor did he radiate an ominous power. Ah yes, Catilina was a formidable rival. About his person hung many rumors never proven, glamorous and evil rumors. Everyone knew he had made his fortune during Sulla's proscriptions by proscribing not only his brother-in-law (executed) but also his brother (exiled). It was said he had murdered his wife of that moment, though if he had, no one tried to make him answer for the crime. And, worst of all, it was said he had murdered his own son when his present wife, the beauteous and wealthy Orestilla, had refused to marry a man who already had a son. That Catilina's son had died and that Catilina had married Orestilla everyone knew. Yet had he murdered the poor boy? No one could say for certain. Lack of confirmation did not prevent much speculation, however.

There were probably similar motives behind Catilina's siege of Fabia and Clodius's attempted siege. Both men liked making mischief, tweaking Rome's prudish nose, provoking a furor. But between the thirty-four-year-old man of the world Catilina and the eighteen-year-old inexpert Clodius lay the success of the one and the failure of the other. Not that Catilina had laid siege to Fabia's hymen; that reverenced scrap of tissue remained intact, and Fabia therefore technically chaste. Yet the poor girl had fallen desperately in love with Catilina, and yielded everything else. After all, what was the harm in a few kisses, the baring of her breasts for a few more kisses, even the application of a finger or tongue to the deliciously sensitive parts of her pudenda? With Catilina whispering in her ear, it had seemed innocent enough, and the resulting ecstasy something she was to treasure for the rest of her term as a Vestal—and even further than that.

The Chief Vestal was Perpennia, unfortunately not a strict ruler. Nor was the Pontifex Maximus resident in Rome; he of course was Metellus Pius, waging war against Sertorius in Spain. Fonteia was next in seniority, after her the twenty-eight-year-old Licinia, then Fabia at eighteen, followed by Arruntia and Popillia, both aged seventeen. Perpennia and Fonteia were almost the same age, around thirty-two, and looking forward to retirement within the next five years. Therefore the most important thing on the minds of the two senior Vestals was their retirement, the decline in value of the sestertius, and the consequent worry as to whether what had been plump fortunes would run to comfort in old age; neither woman contemplated marriage after her term as a Vestal had finished, though marriage was not forbidden to an ex-Vestal, only thought to be unlucky.

And this was where Licinia came in. Third in age among the six, she was the most comfortably off, and though she was more closely related to Licinius Murena than to Marcus Licinius Crassus, the great plutocrat was nonetheless a cousin and a friend. Licinia called him in as senior consultant in financial matters, and the three senior Vestals spent many a cozy hour huddled together with him discussing business, investments, unhandy fathers when it came to profitably safe dowries.

While all the time right under their noses Catilina was dallying with Fabia, and Clodius was trying. At first Fabia did not understand what the youth was about, for compared to Catilina's smooth expertise, Clodius's advances were clumsily callow. Then when Clodius pounced on her murmuring endearments through little kisses all over her face, she made the mistake of laughing at his absurdity, and sent him away with the sound of her chuckles booming in his ears. That was not the right way to handle Publius Clodius, who was used to getting what he wanted, and had never in his entire life been laughed at. So huge was the insult to his image of himself that he determined on immediate revenge.

He chose a very Roman method of revenge: litigation. But not the relatively harmless kind of litigation Cato, for instance, had elected after Aemilia Lepida had jilted him when he was eighteen. Cato had threatened breach of promise. Publius Clodius laid charges of unchastity, and in a community which on the whole abhorred the death penalty for crimes, even against the State, this was the one crime which still carried an automatic death penalty.

He didn't content himself with revenge upon Fabia. Charges of unchastity were laid against Fabia (with Catilina), Licinia (with Marcus Crassus), and Arruntia and Popillia (both with Catilina). Two courts were set up, one to try the Vestals, with Clodius himself prosecuting the Vestals, and one to try the accused lovers, with Clodius's friend Plotius (he too had popularized his name, from Plautius to Plotius) prosecuting Catilina and Marcus Crassus.

All those charged were acquitted, but the trials caused a great stir, and the ever-present Roman sense of humor was highly tickled when Crassus got off by declaring simply that he had not been after Licinia's virtue, but rather her snug little property in the suburbs. Believable? The jury certainly thought so.

Clodius worked very hard to convict the women, but he faced a particularly able and learned defense counsel in Marcus Pupius Piso, who was assisted by a stunning retinue of junior advocates. Clodius's youth and lack of hard evidence defeated him, particularly after a large panel of Rome's most exalted matrons testified that all three accused Vestals were *virgo intacta*. To compound Clodius's woes, both judge and jury had taken against him; his cockiness and feral aggression, unusual in such a young man, set everyone's back up. Young prosecutors were expected to be brilliant, but a trifle humble, and ''humble'' was not a word in Clodius's vocabulary.

''Give up prosecuting'' was Cicero's advice—kindly meant—after it was all over. Cicero of course had attended as part of Pupius Piso's defense team, for Fabia was his wife's half sister. "Your malice and your prejudices are too naked. They lack the detachment necessary for a successful career as a prosecutor."

That remark did not endear Cicero to Clodius, but Cicero was a very small fish. Clodius itched to make Catilina pay, both for beating him to Fabia and for wriggling out of a death penalty.

To make matters worse, after the trials people who might have been expected to help him shunned Clodius instead. He also had to endure a rare tongue-lashing from big brother Appius, very put out and embarrassed.

"It's seen as sheer spite, little Publius," big brother Appius said, "and I can't change people's minds. You have to understand that nowadays people recoil in horror at the mere thought of a convicted Vestal's fate—buried alive with a jug of water and a loaf of bread? And the fate of the lovers—tied to a forked stake and flogged to death? Awful, just awful! To have secured the conviction of any one of them would have taken a mountain of evidence that couldn't be refuted, whereas you couldn't even produce a small hillock of evidence! All four of those Vestals are connected to powerful families whom you have just antagonized mortally. I can't help you, Publius, but I can help myself by leaving Rome for a few years. I'm going east to Lucullus. I suggest you do the same."

But Clodius was not about to have anyone decide the future course of his life, even big brother Appius. So he sneered, turned his shoulder. And sentenced himself thereby to four years of skulking around a city which snubbed him unmercifully, while big brother Appius in the East accomplished deeds which showed all of Rome that he was a true Claudian when it came to making mischief. But as his mischief contributed greatly to the discomfiture of King Tigranes, Rome admired it—and him—enormously.

Unable to convince anyone that he was capable of prosecuting some villain, and spurned by villains in need of defense counsel, Publius Clodius had a hideous time of it. In others the snubbing might have led to a self-examination bearing positive fruit when it came to reforming character, but in Clodius it merely contributed to his weaknesses. It deprived him of Forum experience and banished him to the company of a small group of young noblemen commonly dismissed as ne'er-do-wells. For four years Clodius did nothing save drink in low taverns, seduce girls from all walks of life, play at dice, and share his dissatisfactions with others who also bore grudges against noble Rome.

In the end it was boredom drove him to do something constructive, for Clodius didn't really have the temperament to be content with a daily round owning no purpose. Thinking himself different, he knew he had to excel at *something*. If he didn't, he would die as he was living, forgotten, despised. That just wasn't good enough. Wasn't grand enough. For Publius Clodius the only acceptable fate was to end up being called the First Man in Rome. How he was going to achieve this he didn't know. Except that one day he woke up, head aching from too much wine, purse empty from too much losing at dice, and decided that the degree of his boredom was too great to bear a moment longer. What he needed was *action*. Therefore he would go where there was action. He would go to the East and join the personal staff of his brother-in-law Lucius Licinius Lucullus. Oh, not to earn himself a reputation as a brave and brilliant soldier! Military endeavors did not appeal to Clodius in the least. But attached to Lucullus's staff, who knew what opportunities might not present themselves? Big brother Appius hadn't earned the admiration of Rome by soldiering, but by stirring up so much trouble for Tigranes in Antioch that the King of Kings had rued his decision to put Appius Claudius Pulcher in his place by making him kick his heels for months waiting for an audience.

Off went Publius Clodius to the East not long before big brother Appius was due to return; it was the beginning of the year immediately after the joint consulship of Pompey and Crassus. The same year Caesar left for his quaestorship in Further Spain.

Carefully choosing a route which would not bring him face-to-face with big brother Appius, Clodius arrived at the Hellespont to find that Lucullus was engaged in pacifying the newly conquered kingdom of King Mithridates, Pontus. Having crossed the narrow strait into Asia, he set off cross-country in pursuit of brother-in-law Lucullus. Whom Clodius thought he knew: an urbane and punctilious aristocrat with a genuine talent for entertaining, immense wealth no doubt now increasing rapidly, and a fabled love of good food, good wine, good company. Just the kind of superior Clodius fancied! Campaigning in Lucullus's personal train was bound to be a luxurious affair.

He found Lucullus in Amisus, a magnificent city on the shores of the Euxine Sea in the heart of Pontus. Amisus had withstood siege and been badly mauled in the process; now Lucullus was busy repairing the damage and reconciling the inhabitants to the rule of Rome rather than the rule of Mithridates.

When Publius Clodius turned up on his doorstep, Lucullus took the pouch of official letters (all of which Clodius had prised open and read with glee) from him, then proceeded to forget he existed. An absent directive to make himself useful to the legate Sornatius was as much time as Lucullus could spare for his youngest brother-in-law before returning to what occupied his thoughts most: his coming invasion of Armenia, the kingdom of Tigranes.

Furious at this offhand dismissal, Clodius hied himself off—but not to make himself useful to anyone, least of all a nobody like Sornatius. Thus while Lucullus got his little army into marching mode, Clodius explored the byways and alleys of Amisus. His Greek of course was fluent, so there was no impediment in the way of his making friends with anyone he met as he drifted around, and he met many intrigued by such an unusual, egalitarian and oddly un-Roman fellow as he purported to be.

He also gathered much information about a side of Lucullus he didn't know at all—about his army, and about his campaigns to date.

King Mithridates had fled two years before to the court of his son-in-law Tigranes when he was unable to

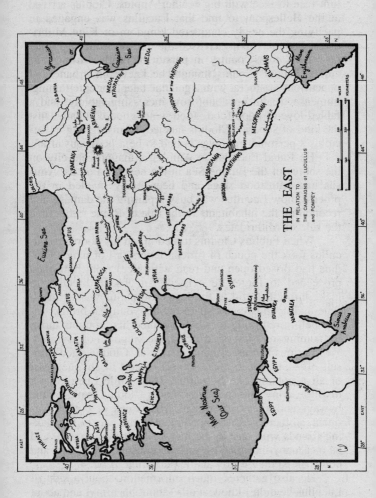

THE EAST

IN RELATION TO

THE CAMPAIGNS OF LUCULLUS
and POMPEY

contend with the Roman remorselessness in war, and feeling the pinch of those quarter-million seasoned troops he had lost in the Caucasus on a pointless punitive expedition against the Albanian savages who had raided Colchis. It had taken Mithridates twenty months to persuade Tigranes to see him, longer still to persuade Tigranes to help him recover his lost lands of Pontus, Cappadocia, Armenia Parva and Galatia.

Naturally Lucullus had his spies, and knew perfectly well that the two kings were reconciled. But rather than wait for them to invade Pontus, Lucullus had decided to go on the offensive and invade Armenia proper, strike at Tigranes and prevent his aiding Mithridates. His original intention had been to leave no sort of garrison in Pontus, trusting to Rome and Roman influence to keep Pontus quiet. For he had just lost his governorship of Asia Province, and now learned from the letters brought by Publius Clodius that the enmity he had stirred in the breasts of the Ordo Equester back in Rome was growing by leaps and bounds. When the letters not only told him that the new governor of Asia Province was a Dolabella, but also that Dolabella was to "supervise" Bithynia too, Lucullus understood much. Obviously the knights of Rome and their tame senators preferred incompetence to success in war. Publius Clodius, concluded Lucullus dourly, was no harbinger of good luck!

The nine commissioners sent from Rome before his power there waned were scattered all over Pontus and Cappadocia, including the man Lucullus loved best in all the world now that Sulla was dead—his younger brother, Varro Lucullus. But commissioners owned no troops, and it seemed from the tone of the letters Publius Clodius carried that they would not last long in the job. Therefore, decided Lucullus, he had no choice other than to leave two of his four legions behind in Pontus to garrison it in case Mithridates tried to win back his kingdom unassisted by Tigranes. The legate he esteemed most was repairing the ravages wreaked upon the isle of Delos, and while he knew Sornatius was a good man, Lucullus wasn't sure enough of his military capabilities to leave him without someone else at his side. The other senior legate, Marcus

Fabius Hadrianus, would have to stay in Pontus too.

Having made up his mind that two of his four legions must remain in Pontus, Lucullus also knew which two legions they would have to be—not a welcome prospect. The legions belonging to the province of Cilicia would stay in Pontus. Leaving him to march south with the two legions of Fimbriani. *Wonderful* troops! He absolutely loathed them. They had been in the East for sixteen years now, and were sentenced never to return to Rome or Italy because their record of mutiny and murder was such that the Senate refused to allow them to go home. Perpetually on the boil, they were dangerous men, but Lucullus, who had used them off and on for many years, dealt with them by flogging them pitilessly during campaigns and indulging their every sensual whim during winter rests. Thus they soldiered for him willingly enough, even grudgingly admired him. Yet they preferred still to nominate themselves as the troops of their first commander, Fimbria, hence the Fimbriani. Lucullus was happy to have it so. Did he want them known as the Liciniani or the Luculliani? Definitely not.

Clodius had fallen so in love with Amisus that he decided he would elect to remain behind in Pontus with the legates Sornatius and Fabius Hadrianus; campaigning had lost its lure for Clodius the moment he heard Lucullus planned a thousand-mile march.

But it was not to be. His orders were to accompany Lucullus in his personal train. Oh well, thought Clodius, at least he would live in relative luxury! Then he discovered Lucullus's idea of campaigning comfort. Namely, that there was none. The sybaritic Epicurean Clodius had known in Rome and Amisus had utterly vanished; Lucullus on the march at the head of the Fimbriani was no better off than any ranker soldier, and if he was no better off, nor was any member of his personal staff. They walked, they didn't ride—the Fimbriani walked, they didn't ride. They ate porridge and hard bread—the Fimbriani ate porridge and hard bread. They slept on the ground with a *sagum* for cover and earth heaped into a pillow—the Fimbriani slept on the ground with a *sagum* for cover and earth heaped into a pillow. They bathed in icicle-fringed streams or else chose to stink—the Fimbriani bathed in icicle-fringed streams or else chose to stink. What was good enough for the Fimbriani was good enough for Lucullus.

But not good enough for Publius Clodius, who not many days out from Amisus took advantage of his relationship with Lucullus and complained bitterly.

The General's pale-grey eyes looked him up and down without expression, as cold as the thawing landscape the army traversed. "If you want comfort, Clodius, go home," he said.

"I don't want to go home, I just want comfort!" said Clodius.

"One or the other. With me, never both," said his brother-in-law, and turned his back contemptuously.

That was the last conversation Clodius had with him. Nor did the dour little band of junior legates and military tribunes who surrounded the General encourage the kind of companionship Clodius now learned he could hardly do without. Friendship, wine, dice, women, and mischief; they were the things Clodius craved as the days turned into what seemed like years and the countryside continued as bleak and inhospitable as Lucullus.

They paused briefly in Eusebeia Mazaca, where Ariobarzanes Philoromaios, the King, donated what he could to the baggage train and wished Lucullus a doleful well. Then it was on into a landscape convulsed by chasms and gorges of every color at the warm end of the rainbow, a tumbled mass of tufa towers and boulders perched precariously on fragile stone necks. Skirting these gorges more than doubled the length of the march, but Lucullus plodded on, insisting that his army cover a minimum of thirty miles a day. That meant they marched from sunup to sundown, pitched camp in semidarkness and pulled camp in semidarkness. And every night a proper camp, dug and fortified against—whom? WHOM? Clodius wanted to shout to the pallid sky floating higher above them than any sky had a right to do. Followed by a WHY? roaring louder than the thunder of endless spring storms.

They came down at last to the Euphrates at Tomisa crossing to find its eerie milky-blue waters a seething mass of melted snows. Clodius heaved a sigh of relief. No choice now! The General would have to rest while he waited for the river to go down. But did he? No. The moment the army halted, the Euphrates began to calm and slow, turn itself into a tractable, navigable waterway. Lucullus and the Fimbriani boated it into Sophene, and the moment the last man was across, back it went to foaming torrent.

"My luck," said Lucullus, pleased. "It is an omen."

The route now passed through slightly kinder country, in that the mountains were somewhat lower, good grass and wild asparagus covered the slopes, and trees grew in small groves where pockets of moisture gave their roots succor. But what did that mean to Lucullus? An order that in easy terrain like this and with asparagus to chomp on, the army could move faster! Clodius had always considered himself as fit and agile as any other Roman, used to walking everywhere. Yet here was Lucullus, almost fifty years of age, walking the twenty-two-year-old Publius Clodius into the ground.

They crossed the Tigris, a minor matter after the Euphrates, for it was neither as broad nor as swift. And then, having marched over a thousand miles in two months, the army of Lucullus came in sight of Tigranocerta.

It had not existed thirty years ago. King Tigranes had built it to cater to his dreams of glory and a far vaster realm: a splendid city of stone with high walls, citadels, towers, squares and courts, hanging gardens, exquisite glazed tiles of aquamarine and acid-yellow and brazen red, immense statues of winged bulls, lions, curly-bearded kings under tall tiaras. The site had been chosen with a view to everything from ease of defense to internal sources of water and a nearby tributary of the Tigris which carried away the contents of the vast sewers Tigranes had constructed in the manner of Pergamum. Whole nations had fallen to fund its construction; wealth proclaimed itself even in the far distance as the Fimbriani came over a ridge and saw it, Tigranocerta. Vast, high, beautiful. Because he craved a Hellenized realm, the King of Kings had started out to build in the Greek fashion, but all those years of Parthian-influenced childhood and young manhood were too strong; when Doric and Ionic perfection palled, he added the gaudy glazed tiles, the winged bulls, the monolithic sovereigns. Then, still dissatisfied with all those low Greek buildings, he added the hanging gardens, the square stone towers, the pylons and the power of his Parthian upbringing.

Not in twenty-five years had anyone dared to bring King Tigranes bad news; no one wanted his head or his hands chopped off, which was the King's reaction to the bearer of bad news. Someone, however, had to inform him that a Roman army was approaching rapidly out of the mountains to the west. Understandably, the military establishment (run by a son of Tigranes named Prince Mithrabarzanes) elected to send a very junior officer with this shockingly bad news. The King of Kings flew into a panic—but not before he had the messenger hanged. Then he fled, so hastily that he left Queen Cleopatra behind together with his other wives, his concubines, his children, his treasures, and a garrison under Mithrabarzanes. Out went the summonses from the shores of the Hyrcanian Sea to the shores of the Middle Sea, anywhere and everywhere Tigranes ruled: send him troops, send him cataphracts, send him desert Bedouins if no other soldiers could be found! For it had never occurred to Tigranes that Rome, so beleaguered, might invade Armenia to knock on the gates of his brand-new capital city.

While his father skulked in the mountains between Tigranocerta and Lake Thospitis, Mithrabarzanes led the available troops to meet the Roman invaders, assisted by some nearby tribes of Bedouins. Lucullus trounced them and sat down before Tigranocerta to besiege it, though his army was far too small to span the length of its walls; he concentrated upon the gates and vigilant patrols. As he was also extremely efficient, very little traffic passed from inside to outside of the city walls, and none the other way. Not, he was sure, that Tigranocerta could not withstand a long siege; what he was counting on was the unwillingness of Tigranocerta to withstand a long siege. The first step was to defeat the King of Kings on a battlefield. That would lead to the second step, the surrender of Tigrano-

certa, a place filled with people who had no love for—
though great terror of—Tigranes. He had populated this
new capital city far from northern Armenia and the old
capital of Artaxata with Greeks imported against their will
from Syria, Cappadocia, eastern Cilicia; it was a vital part
of the program of Hellenization that Tigranes was determined to inflict upon his racially Median peoples. To be
Greek in culture and language was to be civilized. To be
Median in culture and illiterate in Greek was inferior,
primitive. His answer was to kidnap Greeks.

Though the two great kings were reconciled, Mithridates was too cagey to be with Tigranes—instead, he lay
with an army of a mere ten thousand men to the north and
west of where Tigranes had fled; his opinion of Tigranes
as a military man was not high. With him was his best
general, his cousin Taxiles, and when they heard that Lucullus was besieging Tigranocerta and that Tigranes was
gathering an immense force to relieve it, Mithridates sent
his cousin Taxiles to see the King of Kings.

"Do not attack the Romans!" was the Mithridatic
message.

Tigranes was inclined to heed this advice, even after
he had assembled one hundred and twenty thousand infantry from places as far apart as Syria and the Caucasus,
and twenty-five thousand of the awesome cavalry known
as cataphracts, horses and riders clad from head to foot in
chain mail. He lay some fifty miles from his capital in a
cozy valley, but he needed to move. Most of his supplies
were in Tigranocertan granaries and storehouses, so he
knew he must establish fortified contact with the city if
his vast forces were to eat. And that, he reasoned, should
not be too difficult if indeed, as his spies had reported to
him, the Roman army did not have the strength to embrace
the entire perimeter of so great a place as Tigranocerta.

He had not, however, believed the reports which said
the Roman army was minute. Until he himself rode to the
top of a high hill behind his capital and actually saw for
himself what gnat was impudent enough to sting him.

"Too large to be an embassage, but too small to be
an army" was how he put it, and issued orders to attack.

But vast eastern armies were not entities a Marius or a Sulla would have desired for one moment, even had those two Roman generals ever had such military largesse offered to them. Forces must be small, flexible, maneuverable—easily supplied, easily controlled, easily deployed. Lucullus had two legions of superb if disreputable soldiers who knew his tactics as well as he did, plus a very neat contingent of twenty-seven hundred horsemen from Galatia who had been with him for years.

The siege had not been without Roman losses, chiefly because of a mysterious Zoroastrian fire King Tigranes possessed. It was called naphtha by the Greeks, and it came from a Persian fastness somewhere on the southwest of the Hyrcanian Sea. Small light lumps of it lobbed onto the siege towers and shelter sheds roared through the air ablaze and splattered as they landed, flaring up so hot and so incandescent that nothing could extinguish them or the fires which spread from them. They burned and maimed—but worse than that, they terrified. No one had ever experienced anything like them before.

Thus when Tigranes moved his mighty force to attack the gnat, he failed to understand what a difference mood could make to the gnat. Every Roman in that tiny army was fed up—fed up with a monotonous diet, Zoroastrian fire, no women, cataphracts lumbering on their huge Nesaean horses to badger foraging parties, Armenia in general and Tigranocerta in particular. From Lucullus to the Fimbriani to the Galatian cavalry, all of them hungered for a battle. And cheered themselves hoarse when the scouts reported that King Tigranes was in the offing at last.

Promising Mars Invictus a special sacrifice, Lucullus girded his loins for the fray at dawn on the sixth day of Roman October. Siege lines abandoned, the General occupied a hill which intervened between the advancing Armenian giant and the city, and made his dispositions. Though he couldn't know that Mithridates had sent Taxiles to warn the King of Kings not to engage the Romans, Lucullus did know exactly how to tempt Tigranes into an engagement: huddle his little force together and appear to be terrified by the size of the Armenian giant. Since all the eastern kings were convinced an army's strength was in numbers, Tigranes would attack.

Tigranes did attack. What developed was a debacle. No one on the Armenian side, including Taxiles, seemed to comprehend the value of high ground. Nor, so much was clear to Lucullus as the seething host flowed up his hill, had anyone in the Armenian chain of command thought to develop tactics or a strategy. The monster was unleashed; no more was necessary.

Taking his time, Lucullus dealt out frightful punishment from the top of his hill, worried only that the mountains of dead would end in hemming him in, foil a complete victory. But when he put his Galatian cavalry to clearing lines through the Armenian fallen, the Fimbriani spread outward and downward like scythes through a field of wheat. The Armenian front disintegrated, pushing thousands of Syrian and Caucasian foot soldiers into the ranks of the mailed cataphracts until horses and riders fell, or they themselves were crushed. More of the Armenian host died that way than the berserk Fimbriani had the numbers to kill.

Said Lucullus in his report to the Senate in Rome: "Over one hundred thousand Armenian dead, and five Roman dead."

King Tigranes fled a second time, so certain he would be captured that he gave his tiara and diadem to one of his sons to keep, exhorting the princeling to gallop faster because he was younger and lighter. But the youth entrusted tiara and diadem to an obscure-looking slave, with the result that the Armenian symbols of sovereignty came into the possession of Lucullus two days later.

The Greeks forced to live in Tigranocerta opened the gates of the city, so overjoyed that they carried Lucullus shoulder-high. Privation was a thing of the past; the Fimbriani dived with equal glee into soft arms and soft beds, ate and drank, wenched and pillaged. The booty was staggering. Eight thousand talents of gold and silver, thirty million *medimni* of wheat, untold treasures and art works.

And the General became human! Fascinated, Publius Clodius saw the Lucullus he had known in Rome emerge out of the hard-bitten, coldly ruthless man of months past. Manuscripts were piled up for his delectation alongside exquisite children he retained for his own pleasure, never happier than when he could sexually initiate girls just flowering into puberty. Median girls, not Greek! The spoils were divided at a ceremony in the marketplace with Lucullan fairness: each of the fifteen thousand men received at least thirty thousand sesterces in money, though of course it would not be paid over until the loot had been converted into cold, hard Roman cash. The wheat fetched twelve thousand talents; canny Lucullus sold the bulk of it to King Phraates of the Parthians.

Publius Clodius was not about to forgive Lucullus for those months of footslogging and living hard, even when his own share of the booty came in at a hundred thousand sesterces. Somewhere between Eusebeia Mazaca and the crossing at Tomisa he added his brother-in-law's name to the list he kept of those who would pay for offending him. Catilina. Cicero the small fish. Fabia. And now Lucullus. Having seen the gold and silver piled in the vaults—indeed, having assisted in counting it—Clodius concentrated at first upon working out how Lucullus had managed to cheat everyone when the spoils were divided. A mere thirty thousand for each legionary, each cavalryman? Ridiculous! Until his abacus told him that eight thousand talents divided by fifteen thousand men yielded only thirteen thousand sesterces each—so where had the other seventeen thousand come from? Sale of the wheat, said the General laconically when Clodius applied to him for elucidation.

This wasted exercise in arithmetic did give Clodius an idea, however. If he had assumed Lucullus was cheating his men, what would *they* think if someone sowed a seed or two of discontent?

Until Tigranocerta had been occupied, Clodius had been given no chance to cultivate the acquaintance of anyone outside the small and untalkative group of legates and tribunes around the General. Lucullus was a stickler for protocol, disapproved of fraternization between ranker soldiers and his staff. But now, with winter setting in and this new Lucullus prepared to give all who served him the time of their lives, supervision ceased. Oh, there were jobs to do: Lucullus ordered every actor and dancer rounded up, for example, and forced them to perform for his army. A circus holiday far from home for men who would never see home again. Entertainments were plentiful. So was wine.

The leader of the Fimbriani was a *primus pilus* centurion who headed the senior of the two Fimbriani legions. His name was Marcus Silius, and like the rest he had marched, an ordinary legionary not yet old enough to shave, east across Macedonia with Flaccus and Fimbria seventeen years before. When Fimbria won the struggle for supremacy, Marcus Silius had applauded the murder of Flaccus at Byzantium. He had crossed into Asia, fought against King Mithridates, been handed over to Sulla when Fimbria fell from power and suicided, and fought for Sulla, for Murena, and then for Lucullus. With the others he had gone to besiege Mitylene, by which time his rank was *pilus prior,* very high in the tortuous gradations of centurions. Year had succeeded year; fight had succeeded fight. They had all been mere striplings when they left Italy, for Italy by then was exhausted of seasoned troops; now in Tigranocerta they had been under the eagles for half of the years they had lived, and petition after petition for an honorable discharge had been denied them. Marcus Silius, their leader, was a bitter man of thirty-four who just wanted to go home.

It hadn't been necessary for Clodius to ascertain this information now; even legates as sour as Sextilius did speak from time to time, and usually about Silius or the *primus pilus* centurion of the other Fimbriani legion, Lucius Cornificius, who was not of the rising family with that name.

Nor was it hard to find Silius's lair inside Tigranocerta; he and Cornificius had commandeered a minor palace which had belonged to a Tigranic son, and moved in together with some very delectable women and enough slaves to serve a cohort.

Publius Clodius, patrician member of an august clan,

went visiting, and like the Greeks before Troy, he bore gifts. Oh, not the size of wooden horses! Clodius brought a little bag of mushrooms Lucullus (who liked to experiment with such substances) had given him, and a flagon of superlative wine so large it took three servants to manhandle it.

His reception was wary. Both the centurions knew well enough who he was; what relationship he bore to Lucullus; how he had done on the march, in the camp before the city, during the battle. None of which impressed them any more than the person of Clodius did, for he was of no more than average size and far too mediocre of physique to stand out in any crowd. What they did admire was his gall: he barged in as if he owned the place, ensconced himself chattily on a big tapestry cushion between the couches where each man lay wrapped around his woman of the moment, produced his bag of mushrooms and proceeded to tell them what was going to happen when they partook of this unusual fare.

"Amazing stuff!" said Clodius, mobile brows flying up and down in a comical manner. "Do have some, but chew it very slowly and don't expect anything to happen for quite a long time."

Silius made no attempt to avail himself of this invitation; nor, he was quick to note, did Clodius set an example by chewing one of the shrunken little caps, slowly or otherwise.

"What do you want?" he asked curtly.

"To talk," said Clodius, and smiled for the first time.

That was always a shock for those who had never seen the smiling Publius Clodius; it transformed what was otherwise a rather tense and anxious face into something suddenly so likable, so appealing, that smiles tended to break out all around. As smiles did in the moment Clodius triggered his, from Silius, Cornificius, both the women.

But a Fimbrianus was not to be caught so easily. Clodius was the Enemy, a far more serious enemy than any Armenian or Syrian or Caucasian. So after his smile died, Silius maintained his independence of mind, remained skeptical of Clodius's motives.

All of which Clodius half expected, had planned for. It had come to his notice during those four humiliating years he had slunk around Rome that anyone highborn was going to be viewed with extreme suspicion by those beneath him, and that on the whole those beneath him could find absolutely no reasonable reason why someone highborn would *want* to slum it. Rudderless, ostracized by his peers, and desperate for something to do, Clodius set out to remove mistrust among his inferiors. The thrill of victory when he succeeded was warming, but he had also found a genuine pleasure in low company; he liked being better educated and more intelligent than anyone else in the room, it gave him an advantage he would never have among his peers. He felt a giant. And he transmitted a message to his inferiors that here was a highborn chap who really did care, who really was attracted to simpler people, simpler circumstances. He learned to wriggle in and make himself at home. He basked in a new kind of adulation.

His technique consisted in talk. No big words, no inadvertent allusions to obscure Greek dramatists or poets, not one indication that his company or his drink or his surroundings did not please him tremendously. And while he talked, he plied his audience with wine and pretended to consume huge amounts of it himself—yet made sure that at the end he was the soberest man in the room. Not that he looked it; he was adept at collapsing under the table, falling off his stool, bolting outside to vomit. The first time he worked on his chosen quarry they preserved a measure of skepticism, but he'd be back to try again, then be back a third and a fourth time, until eventually even the wariest man present had to admit that Publius Clodius was a truly wonderful fellow, someone ordinary who had been unfortunate enough to be born into the wrong sphere. After trust was established, he discovered he could manipulate everyone to his heart's content provided that he never betrayed his inner thoughts and feelings. The lowly he courted, he soon decided, were urban hayseeds, uncouth, ignorant, unread—desperately eager to be esteemed by their betters, longing for approval. And just waiting to be shaped.

Marcus Silius and Lucius Cornificius were no different from any tavernload of Roman urban lowly, even if they had left Italy at seventeen. Hard they were, cruel they were, ruthless they were. But to Publius Clodius the two centurions seemed as malleable as clay in the hands of a master sculptor. Easy game. Easy . . .

Once Silius and Cornificius admitted to themselves that they liked him, that he amused them, then Clodius began to defer to them, to ask their opinions on this and that—always choosing things they knew, could feel authoritative about. And after that he let them see that he admired them—their toughness, their stamina in their job, which was soldiering, and therefore of paramount importance to Rome. Finally he became their equal as well as their friend, one of the boys, a light in the darkness; he was one of Them, but as one of Us he was in a position to bring every plight he saw to the attention of Them in Senate and Comitia, on Palatine and Carinae. Oh, he was young, still a bit of a boy! But boys grew up, and when he turned thirty Publius Clodius would enter the hallowed portals of the Senate; he would ascend the *cursus honorum* as smoothly as water flowing over polished marble. After all, he was a Claudian, a member of a clan which had never skipped the consulship through all the many generations of the Republic. One of Them. Yet one of Us.

It was not until his fifth visit that Clodius got around to the subject of booty and Lucullus's division of the spoils.

"Miserable skinflint!" said Clodius, slurring his words.

"Eh?" asked Silius, pricking up his ears.

"My esteemed brother-in-law Lucullus. Palming off troops like your chaps with a pittance. Thirty thousand sesterces each when there were *eight thousand talents* in Tigranocerta!"

"Did he palm us off?" asked Cornificius, astonished. "He has always said he preferred to divide the spoils on the field instead of after his triumph because the Treasury couldn't cheat us!"

"That's what he intends you to think," said Clodius,

his cup of wine slopping drunkenly. "Can you do sums?"

"Sums?"

"You know, add and subtract and multiply and divide."

"Oh. A bit," said Silius, not wanting to seem untutored.

"Well, one of the advantages of having your own pedagogue when you're young is that you have to do sum after sum after sum after sum. Flogged raw if you don't!" Clodius giggled. "So I sat down and did a few sums, like multiplying talents into good old Roman sesterces, then dividing by fifteen thousand. And I can tell you, Marcus Silius, that the men in your two legions should have got ten times thirty thousand sesterces each! That supercilious, haughty *mentula* of a brother-in-law of mine went out into that marketplace looking generous and proceeded to shove his fist right up every Fimbrianus arse!" Clodius smacked his right fist into his left palm. "Hear that? Well, that's soft compared to Lucullus's fist up your arses!"

They believed him not only because they wanted to believe him, but also because he spoke with such absolute authority, then proceeded to reel off one set of figures after another as quickly as he could blink, a litany of Lucullus's peculations since he had come east six years before to take command of the Fimbriani yet again. How could anyone who knew so much be wrong? And what was in it for him to lie? Silius and Cornificius believed him.

After that it was easy. While the Fimbriani roistered their way through winter in Tigranocerta, Publius Clodius whispered in the ears of their centurions, and their centurions whispered in the ears of the rankers, and the rankers whispered in the ears of the Galatian troopers. Some of the men had left women behind in Amisus, and when the two Cilician legions under Sornatius and Fabius Hadrianus marched from Amisus to Zela, the women trailed behind as soldiers' women always do. Hardly anyone could write, and yet the word spread all the way from Tigranocerta to Pontus that Lucullus had consistently cheated the army of its proper share in the booty. Nor did anyone bother to check Clodius's arithmetic. It was pref-

erable to believe they had been cheated when the reward
for thinking so was ten times what Lucullus said they were
to get. Besides which, Clodius was so brilliant! He was
incapable of making an arithmetical or statistical mistake!
What Clodius said was sure to be right! Clever Clodius.
He had learned the secret of demagoguery: tell people
what they want most to hear, never tell them what they
don't want to hear.

In the meantime Lucullus had not been idle, despite
voyages into rare manuscripts and underaged girls. He had
made quick trips to Syria, and sent all the displaced Greeks
back to their homes. The southern empire of Tigranes was
disintegrating, and Lucullus intended to be sure that Rome
inherited. For there was a third eastern king who represented a threat to Rome, King Phraates of the Parthians.
Sulla had concluded a treaty with his father giving everything west of the Euphrates to Rome, and everything east
of the Euphrates to the Kingdom of the Parthians.

When Lucullus sold the thirty million *medimni* of
wheat he found in Tigranocerta to the Parthians, he had
done so to prevent its filling Armenian bellies. But as
barge after barge sped down the Tigris toward Mesopotamia and the Kingdom of the Parthians, King Phraates
sent him a message asking for a fresh treaty with Rome
along the same lines: everything west of the Euphrates to
be Rome's, everything east to belong to King Phraates.
Then Lucullus learned that Phraates was also treating with
the refugee Tigranes, who was promising to hand back
those seventy valleys in Media Atropatene in return for
Parthian aid against Rome. They were devious, these eastern kings, and never to be trusted; they owned eastern
values, and eastern values shifted about like sand.

At which point visions of wealth beyond any Roman
dream suddenly popped into Lucullus's mind. *Imagine*
what would be found in Seleuceia-on-Tigris, in Ctesiphon,
in Babylonia, in Susa! If two Roman legions and fewer
than three thousand Galatian cavalrymen could virtually
eliminate an Armenian grand army, four Roman legions
and the Galatian horse could conquer all the way down

Mesopotamia to the Mare Erythraeum! What could the Parthians offer by way of resistance that Tigranes had not? From cataphracts to Zoroastrian fire, the army of Lucullus had dealt with everything. All he needed to do was fetch the two Cilician legions from Pontus.

Lucullus made up his mind within moments. In the spring he would invade Mesopotamia and crush the Kingdom of the Parthians. What a shock that would be for the knights of the Ordo Equester and their senatorial partisans! Lucius Licinius Lucullus would show them. And show the entire world.

Off went a summons to Sornatius in Zela: bring the Cilician legions to Tigranocerta immediately. We march for Babylonia and Elymais. We will be immortal. We will drag the whole of the East into the province of Rome and eliminate the last of her enemies.

Naturally Publius Clodius heard all about these plans when he visited the wing of the main palace wherein Lucullus had set up his residence. In fact, Lucullus was feeling more kindly disposed toward his young brother-in-law these days, for Clodius had kept out of his way and hadn't tried to make mischief among the junior military tribunes, a habit he had fallen into on the march from Pontus the year before.

"I'll make Rome richer than she's ever been," said Lucullus happily, his long face softer these days. "Marcus Crassus prates on about the wealth to be had for the taking in Egypt, but the Kingdom of the Parthians makes Egypt look impoverished. From the Indus to the Euphrates, King Phraates exacts tribute. But after I'm done with Phraates, all that tribute will flow into our dear Rome. We'll have to build a new Treasury to hold it!"

Clodius hastened to see Silius and Cornificius.

"What do you think of his idea?" asked Clodius prettily.

The two centurions thought very little of it, as they made clear through Silius.

"You don't know the plains," he said to Clodius, "but we do. We've been everywhere. A summer campaign working down the Tigris all the way to Elymais? In that kind of heat and humidity? Parthians grow up in heat and humidity. Whereas we'll die.''

Clodius's mind had been on plunder, not climate, but he thought of climate now. A march into sunstroke and sweat cramps under Lucullus? Worse than anything he had endured so far!

"All right," he said briskly, "then we had better make sure the campaign never happens.''

"The Cilician legions!" said Silius instantly. "Without them we can't march into country as flat as a board. Lucullus knows that. Four legions to form a perfect defensive square."

"He's sent off to Sornatius already," said Clodius, frowning.

"His messenger will travel like the wind, but Sornatius won't muster for a march in under a month," said Cornificius confidently. "He's on his own in Zela, Fabius Hadrianus went off to Pergamum."

"How do you know that?" asked Clodius, curious.

"We got our sources," said Silius grinning. "What we have to do is send someone of our own to Zela."

"To do what?"

"To tell the Cilicians to stay where they are. Once they hear where the army's going, they'll down tools and refuse to budge. If Lucullus was there he'd manage to shift them, but Sornatius don't have the clout or the gumption to deal with mutiny."

Clodius pretended to look horrified. "Mutiny?" he squeaked.

"Not really *proper* mutiny," soothed Silius. "Those chaps will be happy to fight for Rome—provided they does it in Pontus. So how can it be classified as a proper mutiny?"

"True," said Clodius, appearing relieved. "Whom can you send to Zela?" he asked.

"My own batman," said Cornificius, rising to his feet. "No time to waste, I'll get him started now."

Which left Clodius and Silius alone.

"You've been a terrific help to us," said Silius gratefully. "We're real glad to know you, Publius Clodius."

"Not as glad as I am to know you, Marcus Silius."

"Knew another young patrician real well once," said Silius, reflectively turning his golden goblet between his hands.

"Did you?" asked Clodius, genuinely interested; one never knew where such conversations led, what might emerge to become grist in a Clodian mill. "Who? When?"

"Mitylene, a good eleven or twelve years ago." Silius spat on the marble floor. "Another Lucullus campaign! Never seem to get rid of him. We was herded together into one cohort, the chaps Lucullus decided were too dangerous to be reliable—we still thought a lot about Fimbria in those days. So Lucullus decided to throw us to the arrows, and put this pretty baby in command. Twenty, I think he was. Gaius Julius Caesar."

"Caesar?" Clodius sat up alertly. "I know him— well, I know *of* him, anyway. Lucullus hates him."

"Did then too. That's why he was thrown to the arrows along with us. But it didn't work out that way. Talk about cool! He was like ice. And fight? Jupiter, he could fight! Never stopped thinking, that was what made him so good. Saved my life in that battle, not to mention everyone else's. But mine was personal. Still don't know how he managed to do it. I thought I was ashes on the fire, Publius Clodius, ashes on the fire."

"He won a Civic Crown," said Clodius. "That's how I remember him so well. There aren't too many advocates appear in a court wearing a crown of oak leaves on their heads. Sulla's nephew."

"And Gaius Marius's nephew," said Silius. "Told us that at the start of the battle."

"That's right, one of his aunts married Marius and the other one married Sulla." Clodius looked pleased. "Well, he's some sort of cousin of mine, Marcus Silius, so that accounts for it."

"Accounts for what?"

"His bravery and the fact you liked him!"

"Did like him too. Was sorry when he went back to Rome with Thermus and the Asian soldiers."

"And the poor old Fimbriani had to stay behind as

always,'' said Clodius softly. ''Well, be of good cheer! I'm writing to everyone I know in Rome to get that senatorial decree lifted!''

''You,'' said Silius, his eyes filling with tears, ''are the Soldiers' Friend, Publius Clodius. We won't forget.''

Clodius looked thrilled. ''The Soldiers' Friend? Is that what you call me?''

''That's what we call you.''

''I won't forget either, Marcus Silius.''

Halfway through March a frostbitten and exhausted messenger arrived from Pontus to inform Lucullus that the Cilician legions had refused to move from Zela. Sornatius and Fabius Hadrianus had done everything they could think of, but the Cilicians would not budge, even after Governor Dolabella sent a stern warning. Nor was that the only unsettling news from Zela. Somehow, wrote Sornatius, the troops of the two Cilician legions had been led to believe that Lucullus had cheated them of their fair share in all booty divided since Lucullus had returned to the East six years earlier. It was undoubtedly the prospect of the heat along the Tigris had caused the mutiny, but the myth that Lucullus was a cheat and a liar had not helped.

The window at which Lucullus sat looked out across the city in the direction of Mesopotamia; Lucullus stared blindly toward the distant horizon of low mountains and tried to cope with the dissolution of what had become a possible, tangible dream. The fools, the idiots! He, a Licinius Lucullus, to exact petty sums from men under his command? He, a Licinius Lucullus, to descend to the level of those grasping get-rich-quick *publicani* in Rome? Who had done that? Who had spread a rumor like that? And why hadn't they been able to see for themselves that it was untrue? A few simple calculations, that was all it would have taken.

His dream of conquering the Kingdom of the Parthians was over. To take fewer than four legions into absolutely flat country would be suicide, and Lucullus was not suicidal. Sighing, he rose to his feet, went to find Sextilius

and Fannius, the most senior legates with him in Tigranocerta.

"What will you do, then?" asked Sextilius, stunned.

"I'll do what lies in my power with the forces I
have," said Lucullus, the stiffness growing in every moment. "I'll go north after Tigranes and Mithridates. I'll
force them to retreat ahead of me, pen them into Artaxata,
and break them into little pieces."

"It's too early in the year to go so far north," said
Lucius Fannius, looking worried. "We won't be able to
leave until—oh, Sextilis by the calendar. Then all we'll
have is four months. They say there's no land under five
thousand feet, and the growing season lasts a bare summer.
Nor will we be able to take much with us in supplies—I
believe the terrain is solid mountain. But you will go west
of Lake Thospitis, of course."

"No, I will go east of Lake Thospitis," Lucullus answered, now fully encased in his icy campaigning shell.
"If four months is all we have, we can't afford to detour
two hundred miles just because the going is a trifle easier."

His legates looked upset, but neither argued. Long
accustomed to that look on Lucullus's face, they didn't
think any argument would sway him. "In the meantime
what will you do?" asked Fannius.

"Leave the Fimbriani here to wallow," said Lucullus
with contempt. "They'll be pleased enough at that news!"

Thus it was that early in the month of Sextilis the
army of Lucullus finally left Tigranocerta, but not to
march south into the heat. This new direction (as Clodius
learned from Silius and Cornificius) did not precisely
please the Fimbriani, who would have preferred to loiter
in Tigranocerta pretending to be on garrison duty. But at
least the weather would be bearable, and there wasn't a
mountain in all of Asia could daunt a Fimbrianus! They
had climbed them all, said Silius complacently. Besides
which, four months meant a nice short campaign. They'd
be back in snug Tigranocerta by winter.

Lucullus himself led the march in stony silence, for

he had discovered on a visit to Antioch that he was removed from his governorship of Cilicia; the province was to be given to Quintus Marcius Rex, senior consul of the year, and Rex was anxious to leave for the East during his consulship. With, Lucullus was outraged to hear, three brand-new legions accompanying him! Yet he, Lucullus, couldn't prise a legion out of Rome when his very life had depended on it!

"All right for me," said Publius Clodius smugly. "Rex is my brother-in-law too, don't forget. I'm just like a cat—land on my feet every time! If you don't want me, Lucullus, I'll take myself off to join Rex in Tarsus."

"Don't hurry!" snarled Lucullus. "What I failed to tell you is that Rex can't start for the East as early as he planned. The junior consul died, then the suffect consul died; Rex is glued to Rome until his consulship is over."

"Oh!" said Clodius, and took himself off.

Once the march began it had become impossible for Clodius to seek out Silius or Cornificius without being noticed; during this initial stage he lay low among the military tribunes, said and did nothing. He had a feeling that as time went on opportunity would arrive, for his bones said Lucullus had lost his luck. Nor was he alone in thinking this; the tribunes and even the legates were also beginning to mutter about Lucullus's bad luck.

His guides had advised that he march up the Canirites, the branch of the Tigris which ran close to Tigranocerta and rose in the massif southeast of Lake Thospitis. But his guides were all Arabs from the lowlands; search as he would, Lucullus had found no one in the region of Tigranocerta who hailed from that massif southeast of Lake Thospitis. Which should have told him something about the country he was venturing into, but didn't because his spirit was so bruised by the failure of the Cilician legions that he wasn't capable of detachment. He did, however, retain enough coolness of mind to send some of his Galatian horsemen ahead. They returned within a market interval to inform him that the Canirites had a short course which ended in a sheer wall of alp no army could possibly cross, even on foot.

"We did see one nomad shepherd," said the leader of the patrol, "and he suggested we march for the Lycus, the next big Tigris tributary south. Its course is long, and winds between the same mountain wall. He thinks its source is kinder, that we should be able to cross to some of the lower land around Lake Thospitis. And from there, he says, the going will be easier."

Lucullus frowned direfully at the delay, and sent his Arabs packing. When he asked to see the shepherd with a view to making him the guide, his Galatians informed him sadly that the rascal had slipped away with his sheep and could not be found.

"Very well, we march for the Lycus," said the General.

"We've lost eighteen days," said Sextilius timidly.

"I am aware of that."

And so, having found the Lycus, the Fimbriani and the cavalry began to follow it into ever-increasing heights, an ever-decreasing valley. None of them had been with Pompey when he blazed a new route across the western Alps, but if one had been, he could have told the rest that Pompey's path was infant's work compared to this. And the army was climbing, struggling between great boulders thrown out by the river, now a roaring torrent impossible to ford, growing narrower, deeper, wilder.

They rounded a corner and emerged onto a fairly grassy shoulder which sat like a park, not quite a bowl but at least offering some grazing for the horses, growing thin and hungry. But it couldn't cheer them, for its far end— it was apparently the watershed—was appalling. Nor would Lucullus permit them to tarry longer than three days; they had been over a month on their way, and were actually very little further north than Tigranocerta.

The mountain on their right as they started out into this frightful wilderness was a sixteen-thousand-foot giant, and they were ten thousand feet up its side, gasping at the weight of their packs, wondering why their heads ached, why they could never seem to fill their chests with precious air. A new little stream was their only way out, and the walls rose on either side of it so sheer even snow could not find a foothold. Sometimes it took a whole day to negotiate less than a mile, scrambling up and over rocks, clinging to the edge of the boiling cataract they followed, trying desperately not to fall in to be bashed and mashed to pulp.

No one saw the beauty; the going was too dreadful. And it never seemed to grow less dreadful as the days dragged on and the cataract never calmed, just widened and deepened. At night it was perishing, though full summer was here, and during the day they never felt the sun, so enormous were the mountain walls which hemmed them in. Nothing could be worse, nothing.

Until they saw the bloodstained snow, just when the gorge they had been traversing started to widen a trifle, and the horses managed to nibble at a little grass. Less vertical now, if almost as tall, the mountains held sheets and rivers of snow in their crevices. Snow which looked exactly as snow did on a battlefield after the slaughter was over, brownish pink with blood.

Clodius bolted for Cornificius, whose legion preceded the senior legion under Silius.

"What does it mean?" cried Clodius, terrified.

"It means we're going to certain death," said Cornificius.

"Have you never seen it before?"

"How could we have seen it before, when it's here as an omen for the lot of us?"

"We must turn back!" shivered Clodius.

"Too late for that," said Cornificius.

So they struggled on, a little more easily now because the river had managed to carve two verges for itself, and the altitude was decreasing. But Lucullus announced they were too far east, so the army, still staring at the bloodstained snow all around them on the heights, turned to climb once more. Nowhere had they found evidence of life, though everyone had been ordered to capture any nomad who might appear. How could anyone live looking at bloodstained snow?

Twice they climbed up to ten and eleven thousand feet, twice they stumbled downward, but the second pass was more welcome, for the bloodstained snow disappeared, became ordinary beautiful white snow, and on top of the second pass they looked across the distance to see Lake Thospitis dreaming exquisitely blue in the sun.

Weak at the knees, the army descended to what seemed the Elysian Fields, though the altitude still lay at five thousand feet and of harvest there was none, for no one lived to plough soil which remained frozen until summer, and froze again with the first breath of autumn wind. Of trees there were none, but grass grew; the horses fattened if the men didn't, and at least there was wild asparagus again.

Lucullus pressed on, understanding that in two months he had not managed to get more than sixty miles north of Tigranocerta. Still, the worst was over; he could move faster now. Skirting the lake, he found a small village of nomads who had planted grain, and he took every ear of it to augment his shrinking supplies. Some few miles further on he found more grain, took that too, along with every sheep his army discovered. By this time the air didn't feel as thin—not because it wasn't as thin, but because everyone had grown used to the altitude.

The river which ran out of more snowcapped peaks to the north into the lake was a good one, fairly wide and placid, and it headed in the direction Lucullus wanted to go. The villagers, who spoke a distorted Median, had told him through his captive Median interpreter that there was only one more ridge of mountains left between him and the valley of the Araxes River, where Artaxata lay. Bad mountains? he asked. Not as bad as those from which this strange army had issued, was the reply.

Then as the Fimbriani left the river valley to climb into fairly rolling uplands, much happier at this terrain, a troop of cataphracts bore down on them. Since the Fimbriani felt like a good fight, they rolled the massive mailed men and horses into confusion without the help of the Galatians. After that it was the turn of the Galatians, who dealt capably with a second troop of cataphracts. And watched and waited for more.

More did not come. Within a day's march they un-

derstood why. The land was quite flat, but as far as the
eye could see in every direction it consisted of a new obstacle, something so weird and horrific they wondered
what gods they had offended, to curse them with such a
nightmare. And the bloodstains were back—not in snow
this time, but smeared across the landscape.

What they looked at were rocks. Razor-edged rocks
ten to fifty feet high, tumbled remorselessly without interruption on top of each other and against each other, leaning every way, no reason or logic or pattern to their
distribution.

Silius and Cornificius sought an interview with the
General.

"We can't cross those rocks," said Silius flatly.

"This army can cross anything, it's already proved
that," Lucullus answered, very displeased at their protest.

"There's no path," said Silius.

"Then we will make one," said Lucullus.

"Not through those rocks we won't," said Cornificius. "I know, because I had some of the men try. Whatever those rocks are made of is harder than our *dolabrae*."

"Then we will simply climb over them," said Lucullus.

He would not bend. The third month was drawing to
a finish; he *had* to reach Artaxata. So his little army entered the lava field fractured by an inland sea in some
remote past age. And shivered in fear because "those
rocks" were daubed with blood-red lichen. It was painfully slow work, ants toiling across a plain of broken pots.
Only men were not ants; "those rocks" cut, bruised, punished cruelly. Nor was there any way around them, for in
every direction more snowy mountains reared on the horizon, sometimes nearer, sometimes farther away, always
hemming them into this terrible travail.

Clodius had decided somewhere just to the north of
Lake Thospitis that he didn't care what Lucullus said or
did, he was going to travel with Silius. And when (learning
from Sextilius that Clodius had deserted to fraternize with
a centurion) the General ordered him back to the front of
the march, Clodius refused.

"Tell my brother-in-law," he said to the tribune dispatched to fetch him home, "that I am happy where I am. If he wants me up front, then he'll have to clap me in irons."

A reply which Lucullus deemed it wiser to ignore. In truth the staff was delighted to be rid of the whining, trouble-making Clodius. As yet no suspicion existed of Clodius's part in the mutiny of the Cilician legions, and as the Fimbriani had confined their protest about "those rocks" to an official one delivered by their head centurions, no suspicion existed of a Fimbriani mutiny.

Perhaps there never would have been a Fimbriani mutiny had it not been for Mount Ararat. For fifty miles the army suffered the fragmented lava field, then emerged from it onto grass again. Bliss! Except that from east to west across their path loomed a mountain the like of which no one had ever seen. Eighteen thousand feet of solid snow, the most beautiful and terrible mountain in the world, with another cone, smaller yet no less horrifying, on its eastern flank.

The Fimbriani lay down their shields and spears and looked. And wept.

This time it was Clodius who led the deputation to the General, and Clodius was not about to be cowed.

"We absolutely refuse to march another step," he said, Silius and Cornificius nodding behind him.

It was when Lucullus saw Bogitarus step into the tent that he knew himself beaten, for Bogitarus was the leader of his Galatian horsemen, a man whose loyalty he could not question.

"Are you of the same mind, Bogitarus?" Lucullus asked.

"I am, Lucius Licinius. My horses can't cross a mountain like that, not after the rocks. Their feet are bruised to the hocks, they've cast shoes faster than my smiths can cope with, and I'm running out of steel. Not to mention that we've had no charcoal since we left Tigranocerta, so I have no charcoal left either. We would follow you into Hades, Lucius Licinius, but we will not follow you onto that mountain," said Bogitarus.

"Thank you, Bogitarus," said Lucullus. "Go. You Fimbriani can go too. I want to speak to Publius Clodius."

"Does that mean we turn back?" asked Silius suspiciously.

"Not back, Marcus Silius, unless you want more rocks. We'll turn west to the Arsanias, and find grain."

Bogitarus had already gone; now the two Fimbriani centurions followed him, leaving Lucullus alone with Clodius.

"How much have you had to do with all this?" asked Lucullus.

Bright-eyed and gleeful, Clodius eyed the General up and down contemptuously. How worn he looked! Not hard to believe now that he was fifty. And the gaze had lost something, a cold fixity which had carried him through everything. What Clodius saw was a crust of weariness, and behind it a knowledge of defeat.

"What have I had to do with all this?" he asked, and laughed. "My dear Lucullus, I am its perpetrator! Do you really think any of those fellows have such foresight? Or the gall? All this is my doing, and nobody else's."

"The Cilician legions," said Lucullus slowly.

"Them too. My doing." Clodius bounced up and down on his toes. "You won't want me after this, so I'll go. By the time I get to Tarsus, my brother-in-law Rex ought to be there."

"You're going nowhere except back to mess with your Fimbriani minions," said Lucullus, and smiled dourly. "I am your commander, and I hold a proconsular imperium to fight Mithridates and Tigranes. I do not give you leave to go, and without it you cannot go. You will remain with me until the sight of you makes me vomit."

Not the answer Clodius wanted, or had expected. He threw Lucullus a furious glare, and stormed out.

The winds and snow began even as Lucullus turned west, for the campaigning season was over. He had used up his time of grace getting as far as Ararat, not more than two hundred miles from Tigranocerta as a bird would have flown. When he touched the course of the Arsanias, the

biggest of the northern tributaries of the Euphrates, he
found the grain already harvested and the sparse populace
fled to hide in their troglodyte houses dug out of tufa rock,
together with every morsel of any kind of food. Defeated
by his own troops Lucullus may have been, but adversity
was something he had come to know well, and he was not
about to stop here where Mithridates and Tigranes could
find him all too easily when spring arrived.

He headed for Tigranocerta, where there were supplies and friends, but if the Fimbriani had expected to winter there, they were soon disillusioned. The city was quiet
and seemed contented under the man he had left there to
govern, Lucius Fannius. Having picked up grain and other
foodstuffs, Lucullus marched south to besiege the city of
Nisibis, situated on the river Mygdonius, and in drier, flatter country.

Nisibis fell on a black and rainy night in November,
yielding much plunder as well as a wealth of good living.
Ecstatic, the Fimbriani settled down with Clodius as their
mascot, their good-luck charm, to spend a delightful winter beneath the snow line. And when Lucius Fannius
materialized not a month later to inform his commander
that Tigranocerta was once more in the hands of King
Tigranes, the Fimbriani carried an ivy-decked Clodius
shoulder-high around the Nisibis marketplace, attributing
their good fortune to him; here they were safe, spared a
siege at Tigranocerta.

In April, with winter nearing its end and the prospect
of a new campaign against Tigranes some comfort, Lucullus learned that he had been stripped of everything save
an empty title, commander in the war against the two
kings. The knights had used the Plebeian Assembly to take
away his last provinces, Bithynia and Pontus, and then
deprived him of all four of his legions. The Fimbriani were
to go home at last, and Manius Acilius Glabrio, the new
governor of Bithynia-Pontus, was to have the Cilician
troops. The commander in the war against the two kings
had no army with which to continue his fight. All he had
was his imperium.

Whereupon Lucullus resolved to keep the news of

their fully honorable discharge from the Fimbriani. What they didn't know couldn't bother them. But of course the Fimbriani knew they were free to go home; Clodius had intercepted the official letters and discovered their contents before they reached Lucullus. Hard on the heels of the letter from Rome came letters from Pontus informing him that King Mithridates had invaded. Glabrio wouldn't inherit the Cilician legions after all; they had been annihilated at Zela.

When orders went out to march for Pontus, Clodius came to see Lucullus. "The army refuses to move out of Nisibis," he announced.

"The army will march for Pontus, Publius Clodius, to rescue those of its compatriots left alive," said Lucullus.

"Ah, but it isn't your army to command anymore!" crowed the jubilant Clodius. "The Fimbriani have finished their service under the eagles, they're free to go home as soon as you produce their discharge papers. Which you'll do right here in Nisibis. That way, you can't cheat them when the spoils of Nisibis are divided."

At which moment Lucullus understood everything. His breath hissed, he bared his teeth and advanced on Clodius with murder in his eyes. Clodius dodged behind a table, and made sure he was closer to the door than Lucullus.

"Don't you lay a finger on me!" he shouted. "Touch me and they'll lynch you!"

Lucullus stopped. "Do they love you so much?" he asked, hardly able to believe that even ignoramuses like Silius and the rest of the Fimbriani centurions could be so gullible.

"They love me to death. *I* am the Soldiers' Friend."

"You're a trollop, Clodius, you'd sell yourself to the lowest scum on the face of this globe if that meant you'd be loved," said Lucullus, his contempt naked.

Why exactly it occurred to him at that moment, and in the midst of so much anger, Clodius never afterward understood. But it popped into his head, and he said it gleefully, spitefully: "*I'm* a trollop? Not as big a trollop as your wife, Lucullus! My darling little sister Clodilla, whom I love as much as I hate you! But she is a trollop, Lucullus. I think that's why I love her so desperately. Thought you had her first, didn't you, all of fifteen years old when she married you? Lucullus the pederast, despoiler of the little girls and little boys! Thought you got to Clodilla first, eh? Well, you didn't!'' screamed Clodius, so carried away that foam gathered at the corners of his mouth.

Lucullus was grey. ''What do you mean?'' he whispered.

''I mean that I had her first, high and mighty Lucius Licinius Lucullus! *I* had her first, and long before you! I had Clodia first too. We used to sleep together, but we did more than just sleep! We played a lot, Lucullus, and the play grew greater as *I* grew greater! I had them both, I had them hundreds of times, I paddled my fingers inside them and then I paddled something else inside them! I sucked on them, I nibbled at them, I did things you can't imagine with them! And guess what?'' he asked, laughing. ''Clodilla deems you a poor substitute for her *little* brother!''

There was a chair beside the table separating Clodius from Clodilla's husband; Lucullus seemed suddenly to lose all the life in him and fell against it, into it. He gagged audibly.

''I dismiss you from my service, Soldiers' Friend, because the time has come to vomit. I curse you! Go to Rex in Cilicia!''

After a tearful parting from Silius and Cornificius, Clodius went. Of course the Fimbriani centurions loaded their Friend down with gifts, some of them very precious, all useful. He jogged off on the back of an exquisite small horse, his retinue of servants equally well mounted, and with several dozen mules bearing the booty. Thinking himself headed in a direction minus danger, he declined Silius's offer of an escort.

All went well until he crossed the Euphrates at Zeugma, his destination Cilicia Pedia and then Tarsus. But

between him and Cilicia Pedia's flat and fertile river plains
lay the Amanus Mountains, a piddling coastal range after
the massifs Clodius had recently struggled across; he regarded them with contempt. Until a band of Arab brigands
waylaid him down a dry gulch and filched all his gifts, his
bags of money, his exquisite small horses. Clodius finished
his journey alone and on the back of a mule, though the
Arabs (who thought him terrifically funny) had given him
enough coins to complete his journey to Tarsus.

Where he found his brother-in-law Rex had not yet
arrived! Clodius usurped a suite in the governor's palace
and sat down to review his hate list: Catilina, Cicero, Fabia, Lucullus—and now Arabs. The Arabs would pay too.

It was the end of Quinctilis before Quintus Marcius
Rex and his three new legions arrived in Tarsus. He had
traveled with Glabrio to the Hellespont, then elected to
march down through Anatolia rather than sail a coast notorious for pirates. In Lycaonia, he was able to tell an avid
Clodius, he had received a plea of help from none other
than Lucullus, who had managed to get the Fimbriani
moving after the Soldiers' Friend departed, and set off for
Pontus. At Talaura, well on his way, Lucullus was attacked by a son-in-law of Tigranes named Mithradates,
and learned that the two kings were rapidly bearing down
on him.

"And would you believe he had the temerity to send
to *me* for help?" asked Rex.

"He's your brother-in-law too," said Clodius mischievously.

"He's *persona non grata* in Rome, so naturally I refused. He had also sent to Glabrio for help, I believe, but
I imagine he was refused in that quarter as well. The last
I heard, he was in retreat and intending to return to Nisibis."

"He never got there," said Clodius, better informed
about the end of Lucullus's march than about events in
Talaura. "When he reached the crossing at Samosata, the
Fimbriani baulked. The last we've heard in Tarsus is that
he's now marching for Cappadocia, and from there he intends to go to Pergamum."

Of course Clodius had discovered from reading Lucullus's mail that Pompey the Great was the recipient of an unlimited imperium to clear the pirates from the Middle Sea, so he left the subject of Lucullus and proceeded to the subject of Pompey.

"And what do you have to do to help the obnoxious Pompeius Magnus sweep up his pirates?" he asked.

Quintus Marcius Rex sniffed. "Nothing, it appears. Cilician waters are under the command of our mutual brother-in-law Celer's brother, your cousin Nepos, barely old enough to be in the Senate. *I* am to govern my province and keep out of the way."

"Hoity-toity!" gasped Clodius, seeing more mischief.

"Absolutely," said Rex stiffly.

"I haven't seen Nepos in Tarsus."

"You will. In time. The fleets are ready for him. Cilicia is the ultimate destination of Pompeius's campaign, it seems."

"Then I think," said Clodius, "that we ought to do a little good work in Cilician waters before Nepos gets here, don't you?"

"How?" asked Claudia's husband, who knew Clodius, but still lived in ignorance of Clodius's ability to wreak havoc. What flaws he saw in Clodius, Rex dismissed as youthful folly.

"I could take out a neat little fleet and go to war on the pirates in your name," said Clodius.

"Well . . ."

"Oh, go on!"

"I can't see any harm in it," said Rex, wavering.

"Let me, please!"

"All right then. But don't annoy anyone except pirates!"

"I won't, I promise I won't," said Clodius, who was seeing in his mind's eye enough pirate booty to replace what he had lost to those wretched Arab brigands in the Amanus.

* * *

Within a market interval of eight days, Clodius the
admiral set sail at the head of a flotilla rather than a fleet,
some ten well-manned and properly decked biremes which
neither Rex nor Clodius thought Metellus Nepos would
miss when he turned up in Tarsus.

What Clodius didn't take into account was the fact
that Pompey's broom had been sweeping so energetically
that the waters off Cyprus and Cilicia Tracheia (which was
the rugged western end of that province, wherein so many
pirates had their land bases) swarmed with refugee pirate
fleets of far larger size than ten biremes. He hadn't been
at sea for five days when one such fleet hove in sight,
surrounded his flotilla, and captured it. Together with Publius Clodius, a very short-lived admiral.

And off he was hied to a base in Cyprus that was not
very far from Paphos, its capital and the seat of its regent,
that Ptolemy known as the Cyprian. Of course Clodius had
heard the story of Caesar and his pirates, and at the time
had thought it brilliant. Well, if Caesar could do that sort
of thing, so too could Publius Clodius! He began by informing his captors in a lordly voice that his ransom was
to be set at ten talents rather than the two talents custom
and pirate scales said was the right ransom for a young
nobleman like Clodius. And the pirates, who knew more
of the Caesar story than Clodius did, solemnly agreed to
ask for a ransom of ten talents.

"Who is to ransom me?" asked Clodius grandly.

"In these waters, Ptolemy the Cyprian" was the answer.

He tried to play Caesar's role around the pirate base,
but he lacked Caesar's physical impressiveness; his loud
boasts and threats somehow came out ludicrously, and
while he knew Caesar's captors had also laughed, he was
quite acute enough to divine that this lot absolutely refused
to believe him even after the revenge Caesar had taken.
So he abandoned that tack, and began instead to do what
none did better: he went to work to win the humble folk
to his side, create trouble at home. And no doubt he would
have succeeded—had the pirate chieftains, all ten of them,
not heard what was going on. Their response was to throw

him into a cell and leave him with no audience beyond
the rats which tried to steal his bread and water.

He had been captured early in Sextilis, and wound
up in that cell not sixteen days later. And in that cell he
lived with his ratty companions for three months. When
finally he was released it was because the Pompeian broom
was so imminent that the settlement had no alternative
than to disband. And he also discovered that Ptolemy the
Cyprian, on hearing what ransom Clodius thought himself
worth, had laughed merrily and sent a mere two talents—
which was all, said Ptolemy the Cyprian, Publius Clodius
was really worth. And all he was prepared to pay.

Under ordinary circumstances the pirates would have
killed Clodius, but Pompey and Metellus Nepos were too
near to risk a death sentence: word had got out that capture
did not mean an automatic crucifixion, that Pompey preferred to be clement. So Publius Clodius was simply abandoned when the fleet and its horde of hangers-on departed.
Several days later one of Metellus Nepos's fleets swept
past; Publius Clodius was rescued, returned to Tarsus and
Quintus Marcius Rex.

The first thing he did once he'd had a bath and a
good meal was to review his hate list: Catilina, Cicero,
Fabia, Lucullus, Arabs, and now Ptolemy the Cyprian.
Sooner or later they'd all bite the dust—nor did it matter
when, how long he would have to wait. Revenge was such
a delicious prospect that the when of it hardly mattered.
The only important thing to Clodius was that it should
happen. Would happen.

He found Quintus Marcius Rex in an ill humor, but
not at his, Clodius's, failure. To Rex, the failure was his
own. Pompey and Metellus Nepos had utterly eclipsed
him, had commandeered his fleets and left him to twiddle
his thumbs in Tarsus. Now they were mopping up rather
than sweeping; the pirate war was over and all the pickings
had gone elsewhere.

"I understand," said Rex savagely to Clodius, "that
after he's made a grand tour of Asia Province he is to
come here to Cilicia and 'tour the dispositions,' was how
he put it."

"Pompeius or Metellus Nepos?" asked Clodius, bewildered.

"Pompeius, of course! And as his imperium outranks mine even in my own province, I'll have to follow him around with a sponge in one hand and a chamber pot in the other!"

"What a prospect," said Clodius clinically.

"It's a prospect I cannot abide!" snarled Rex. "Therefore Pompeius will not find me in Cilicia. Now that Tigranes is incapable of holding anywhere southwest of the Euphrates, I am going to invade Syria. It pleased Lucullus to set up a Lucullan puppet on the Syrian throne— Antiochus Asiaticus, he calls himself! Well, we shall see what we shall see. Syria belongs in the domain of the governor of Cilicia, so I shall make it my domain."

"May I come with you?" asked Clodius eagerly.

"I don't see why not." The governor smiled. "After all, Appius Claudius created a furor while he kicked his heels in Antioch waiting for Tigranes to give him an audience. I imagine that the advent of his little brother will be most welcome."

It wasn't until Quintus Marcius Rex arrived in Antioch that Clodius began to see one revenge was at hand. "Invasion" was the term Rex had employed, but of fighting there was none; Lucullus's puppet Antiochus Asiaticus fled, leaving Rex—King—to do his own kingmaking by installing one Philippus on the throne. Syria was in turmoil, not least because Lucullus had released many, many thousands of Greeks, all of whom had flocked home. But some came home to discover that their businesses and houses had been taken over by the Arabs whom Tigranes had winkled out of the desert, and to whom he had bequeathed the vacancies created by the Greeks he had kidnapped to Hellenize his Median Armenia. To Rex it mattered little who owned what in Antioch, in Zeugma, in Samosata, in Damascus. But to his brother-in-law Clodius it came to matter greatly. Arabs, he *hated* Arabs!

To work went Clodius, on the one hand by whispering in Rex's ear about the perfidies of the Arabs who had usurped Greek jobs and Greek houses, and on the other hand by visiting every single discontented and dispossessed Greek man of influence he could find. In Antioch, in Zeugma, in Samosata, in Damascus. Not an Arab ought to remain in civilized Syria, he declared. Let them go back to the desert and the desert trade routes, where they belonged!

It was a very successful campaign. Soon murdered Arabs began to appear in gutters from Antioch to Damascus, or floated down the broad Euphrates with their outlandish garb billowing about them. When a deputation of Arabs came to see Rex in Antioch, he rebuffed them curtly; Clodius's whispering campaign had succeeded.

"Blame King Tigranes," Rex said. "Syria has been inhabited by Greeks in all its fertile and settled parts for six hundred years. Before that, the people were Phoenician. You're Skenites from east of the Euphrates, you don't belong on the shores of Our Sea. King Tigranes has gone forever. In future Syria will be in the domain of Rome."

"We know," said the leader of this delegation, a young Skenite Arab who called himself Abgarus; what Rex failed to understand was that this was the hereditary title of the Skenite King. "All we ask is that Syria's new master should accord us what has become ours. We did not ask to be sent here, or to be toll collectors along the Euphrates, or inhabit Damascus. We too have been uprooted, and ours was a crueler fate than the Greeks'."

Quintus Marcius Rex looked haughty. "I fail to see how."

"Great governor, the Greeks went from one kindness to another. They were honored and paid well in Tigranocerta, in Nisibis, in Amida, in Singara, everywhere. But we came from a land so hard and harsh, so stung by sand and barren that the only way we could keep warm at night was between the bodies of our sheep or before the smoky fire given off by a wheel of dried dung. And all that happened twenty years ago. Now we have seen grass growing, we have consumed fine wheaten bread every day, we have drunk clear water, we have bathed in luxury, we have slept

in beds and we have learned to speak Greek. To send us
back to the desert is a needless cruelty. There is prosperity
enough for all to share here in Syria! Let us stay, that is
all we ask. And let those Greeks who persecute us know
that you, great governor, will not condone a barbarity unworthy of any man who calls himself Greek,'' said Abgarus with simple dignity.

''I really can't do anything to help you,'' said Rex,
unmoved. ''I'm not issuing orders to ship all of you back
to the desert, but I will have peace in Syria. I suggest you
find the worst of the Greek troublemakers and sit down
with them to parley.''

Abgarus and his fellow delegates took part of that
advice, though Abgarus himself never forgot Roman duplicity, Roman connivance at the murder of his people.
Rather than seek out the Greek ringleaders, the Skenite
Arabs first of all organized themselves into well-protected
groups, and then set about discovering the ultimate source
of growing discontent among the Greeks. For it was
bruited about that the real culprit was not Greek, but Roman.

Learning a name, Publius Clodius, they then found
out that this young man was the brother-in-law of the governor, came from one of Rome's oldest and most august
families, and was a cousin by marriage of the conqueror
of the pirates, Gnaeus Pompeius Magnus. Therefore he
could not be killed. Secrecy was possible in the desert
wastes, but not in Antioch; someone would sniff the plot
out and tell.

''We will not kill him,'' said Abgarus. ''We will
teach him a severe lesson.''

Further enquiries revealed that Publius Clodius was
a very strange Roman nobleman indeed. He lived, it turned
out, in an ordinary house among the slums of Antioch,
and he frequented the kind of places Roman noblemen
usually avoided. But that of course made him accessible.
Abgarus pounced.

Bound, gagged and blindfolded, Publius Clodius was
carried to a room without windows, a room without murals
or .decorations or differences from half a million such

rooms in Antioch. Nor was Publius Clodius allowed to see beyond a glimpse as the cloth over his eyes was removed along with his gag, for a sack was slipped over his head and secured around his throat. Bare walls, brown hands, they were all he managed to take in before a less complete blindness descended; he could distinguish vague shapes moving through the rough weave of the bag, but nothing more.

His heart tripped faster than the heart of a bird; the sweat rolled off him; his breath came short and shallow and gasping. Never in all his life had Clodius been so terrified, so sure he was going to die. But at whose hands? What had he *done*?

The voice when it came spoke Greek with an accent he now recognized as Arabic; Clodius knew then that he would indeed die.

"Publius Clodius of the great Claudius Pulcher family," said the voice, "we would dearly love to kill you, but we realize that is not possible. Unless, that is, after we free you, you seek vengeance for what will be done here tonight. If you do try to seek vengeance, we will understand that we have nothing to lose by killing you, and I swear by all our gods that we will kill you. Be wise, then, and quit Syria after we free you. Quit Syria, and never come back as long as you live."

"What—you—do?" Clodius managed to say, knowing that whatever it was could not be less than torture and flogging.

"Why, Publius Clodius," said the voice, unmistakably amused, "we are going to make you into one of us. We are going to turn you into an Arab."

Hands lifted the hem of his tunic (Clodius wore no toga in Antioch; it cramped his style too much) and removed the loincloth Romans wore when out and about the streets clad only in a tunic. He fought, not understanding, but many hands lifted him onto a flat hard surface, held his legs, his arms, his feet.

"Do not struggle, Publius Clodius," said the voice, still amused. "It isn't often our priest has something this large to work on, so the job will be easy. But if you move, he might cut off more than he intends to.''

Hands again, pulling at his penis, stretching it out— what was happening? At first Clodius thought of castration, wet himself and shit himself, all amid outright laughter from the other side of the bag depriving him of sight; after which he lay perfectly still and shrieked, screamed, babbled, begged, howled. Where was he, that they didn't need to gag him?

They didn't castrate him, though what they did was hideously painful, something to the tip of his penis.

''There!'' said the voice. ''What a good boy you are, Publius Clodius! One of us forever. You should heal very well if you don't dip your wick in anything noxious for a few days.''

On went the loincloth over the shit, on went the tunic, and then Clodius knew no more, though afterward he never knew whether his captors had knocked him out or whether he had fainted.

He woke up in his own house, in his own bed, with an aching head and something so sore between his legs that it was the pain registered first, before he remembered what had happened. Pain forgotten, he leaped from the bed and, gasping with terror that perhaps nothing remained, he put his hands beneath his penis and cradled it to see what was there, how much was left. All of it, it seemed, except that something odd glistened purply between crusted streaks of blood. Something he usually saw only when he was erect. Even then he didn't really understand, for though he had heard of it, he knew no people save for Jews and Egyptians who were said to do it, and he knew no Jews or Egyptians. The realization dawned very slowly, but when it did Publius Clodius wept. The Arabs did it too, for they had made him into one of them. They had circumcised him, cut off his foreskin.

Publius Clodius left on the next available ship for Tarsus, sailing serenely through waters free at last from pirates thanks to Pompey the Great. In Tarsus he took ship for Rhodus, and in Rhodus for Athens. By then he had

healed so beautifully that it was only when he held himself
to urinate that he remembered what the Arabs had done
to him. It was autumn, but he beat the gales across the
Aegaean Sea, landed in Athens. From there he rode to
Patrae, crossed to Tarentum, and faced the fact that he was
almost home. He, a circumcised Roman.

The journey up the Via Appia was the worst leg of
his trip, for he understood how brilliantly the Arabs had
dealt with him. As long as he lived, he could never let
anyone see his penis; if anyone did, the story would get
out and he would become a laughingstock, an object of
such ridicule and merriment that he would never be able
to brazen it out. Urinating and defaecating he could manage; he would just have to learn to control himself until
absolute privacy was at hand. But sexual solace? That was
a thing of the past. Never again could he frolic in some
woman's arms unless he bought her but didn't know her,
used her in the darkness and kicked her out lightless.

Early in February he arrived home, which was the
house big brother Appius Claudius owned on the Palatine,
thanks to his wife's money. When he walked in, big
brother Appius burst into tears at sight of him, so much
older and wearier did he seem; the littlest one of the family
had grown up, and clearly not without pain. Naturally Clodius wept too, so that some time went by before his tale
of misadventure and penury tumbled out. After three years
in the East, he returned more impoverished than when he
had left; to get home, he had had to borrow from Quintus
Marcius Rex, who had not been pleased, either at this summary, inexplicable desertion or at Clodius's insolvency.

"I had so much!" mourned Clodius. "Two hundred
thousand in cash, jewels, gold plate, horses I could have
sold in Rome for fifty thousand each—all gone! Snaffled
by a parcel of filthy, stinking Arabs!"

Big brother Appius patted Clodius's shoulder,
stunned at the amount of booty: *he* hadn't done half as
well out of Lucullus! But of course he didn't know of
Clodius's relationship with the Fimbriani centurions, or
that that was how most of Clodius's haul had been acquired. He himself was now in the Senate and thoroughly

at ease with his life, both domestically and politically. His term as quaestor for Brundisium and Tarentum had been officially commended, a great start to what he hoped would be a great career. And he was also the bearer of great news for Publius Clodius, news he revealed as soon as the emotion of meeting calmed down.

"There's no need to worry about being penniless, my dearest little brother," said Appius Claudius warmly. "You'll never be penniless again!"

"I won't? What do you mean?" asked Clodius, bewildered.

"I've been offered a marriage for you—*such* a marriage! In all my days I never dreamed of it, I wouldn't have looked in that direction without Apollo's appearing to me in my sleep—and Apollo didn't. Little Publius, it's wonderful! Incredible!"

When Clodius turned white at this marvelous news, Appius Claudius put the reaction down to happy shock, not terror.

"Who is it?" Clodius managed to say. Then, "Why me?"

"Fulvia!" big brother Appius trumpeted. "*Fulvia!* Heiress of the Gracchi and the Fulvii; daughter of Sempronia, the only child of Gaius Gracchus; great-granddaughter of Cornelia the Mother of the Gracchi; related to the Aemilii, the Cornelii Scipiones—"

"Fulvia? Do I know her?" asked Clodius, looking stupefied.

"Well, you may not have noticed her, but she's seen you," said Appius Claudius. "It was when you prosecuted the Vestals. She couldn't have been more than ten years old—she's eighteen now."

"Ye gods! Sempronia and Fulvius Bambalio are the most remote pair in Rome," said Clodius, dazed. "They can pick and choose from anyone. So why me?"

"You'll understand better when you meet Fulvia," said Appius Claudius, grinning. "She's not the granddaughter of Gaius Gracchus for nothing! Not all Rome's legions could make Fulvia do something Fulvia doesn't want to do. Fulvia picked you herself."

"Who inherits all the money?" asked Clodius, beginning to recover—and beginning to hope that he could
manage to talk this divine plum off the tree and into his
lap. His circumcised lap.

"Fulvia inherits. The fortune's bigger than Marcus
Crassus's."

"But the *lex Voconia*—she can't inherit!"

"My dear Publius, of course she can!" said Appius
Claudius. "Cornelia the Mother of the Gracchi procured
a senatorial exemption from the *lex Voconia* for Sempronia, and Sempronia and Fulvius Bambalio procured another one for Fulvia. Why do you think Gaius Cornelius,
the tribune of the plebs, tried so hard to strip the Senate
of the right to grant personal exemptions from laws? One
of his biggest grudges was against Sempronia and Fulvius
Bambalio for asking the Senate to allow Fulvia to inherit."

"Did he? Who?" asked Clodius, more and more bewildered.

"Oh, of course! You were in the East when it happened, and too busy to pay attention to Rome," said Appius Claudius, beaming fatuously. "It happened two years
ago."

"So Fulvia inherits the lot," said Clodius slowly.

"Fulvia inherits the lot. And you, dearest little
brother, are going to inherit Fulvia."

But was he going to inherit Fulvia? Dressing with
careful attention to the way his toga was draped and his
hair was combed, making sure his shave was perfect, Publius Clodius set off the next morning to the house of Sempronia and her husband, who was the last member of that
clan of Fulvii who had so ardently supported Gaius Sempronius Gracchus. It was, Clodius discovered as an aged
steward conducted him to the atrium, not a particularly
large or expensive or even beautiful house, nor was it located in the best part of the Carinae. The temple of Tellus
(a dingy old structure being let go to rack and ruin) excluded it from the view across the Palus Ceroliae toward
the mount of the Aventine, and the insulae of the Esquiline
reared not two streets away.

Marcus Fulvius Bambalio, the steward had informed him, was indisposed; the lady Sempronia would see him. Well aware of the adage that all women looked like their mothers, Clodius felt his heart sink at his first sight of the illustrious and elusive Sempronia. A typical Cornelian, plump and homely. Born not long before Gaius Sempronius Gracchus perished by his own hand, the only surviving child of that entire unlucky family had been given as a debt of honor to the only surviving child of Gaius Gracchus's Fulvian allies, for they had lost everything in the aftermath of that futile revolution. They were married during the fourth of Gaius Marius's consulships, and while Fulvius (who had preferred to assume a new cognomen, Bambalio) set out to make a new fortune, his wife set out to become invisible. She succeeded so well that even Juno Lucina had not been able to find her, for she was barren. Then in her thirty-ninth year she attended the Lupercalia, and was lucky enough to be struck by a piece of flayed goat skin as the priests of the College danced and ran naked through the city. This cure for infertility never failed, nor did it for Sempronia. Nine months later she bore her only child, Fulvia.

"Publius Clodius, welcome," she said, indicating a chair.

"Lady Sempronia, this is a great honor," said Clodius, on his very best behavior.

"I suppose Appius Claudius has informed you?" she asked, eyes assessing him, but face giving nothing away.

"Yes."

"And are you interested in marrying my daughter?"

"It is more than I could have hoped for."

"The money, or the alliance?"

"Both," he said, seeing no point in dissimulation; no one knew better than Sempronia that he had never seen her daughter.

She nodded, not displeased. "It is not the marriage I would have chosen for her, nor is Marcus Fulvius overjoyed." A sigh, a shrug. "However, Fulvia is not the grandchild of Gaius Gracchus for nothing. In me, none of the Gracchan spirit and fire ever dwelled. My husband too did not inherit the Fulvian spirit and fire. Which must have angered the gods. Fulvia took both our shares. I do not know why her fancy alighted on you, Publius Clodius, but it did, and a full eight years ago. Her determination to marry you and no one else began then, and has never faded. Neither Marcus Fulvius nor I can deal with her, she is too strong for us. If you will have her, she is yours.''

''Of course he'll have me!'' said a young voice from the open doorway to the peristyle garden.

And in came Fulvia, not walking but running; that was her character, a mad dash toward what she wanted, no time to ponder.

To Clodius's surprise, Sempronia got up immediately and left. No chaperon? How determined *was* Fulvia?

Speech was impossible for Clodius; he was too busy staring. Fulvia was beautiful! Her eyes were dark blue, her hair a funny streaky pale brown, her mouth well shaped, her nose perfectly aquiline, her height almost his own, and her figure quite voluptuous. Different, unusual, like no Famous Family in Rome. Where had she come from? He knew the story of Sempronia at the Lupercalia, of course, and thought now that Fulvia was a visitation.

''Well, what do you have to say?'' this extraordinary creature demanded, seating herself where her mother had been.

''Only that you leave me breathless.''

She liked that, and smiled to reveal beautiful teeth, big and white and fierce. ''That's good.''

''Why me, Fulvia?'' he asked, his mind now fixing itself on the chief difficulty, his circumcision.

''You're not an orthodox person,'' she said, ''and nor am I. You *feel*. So do I. Things matter to you the way they did to my grandfather, Gaius Gracchus. I *worship* my ancestry! And when I saw you in court struggling against insuperable odds, with Pupius Piso and Cicero and the rest sneering at you, I wanted to kill everyone who ground you down. I admit I was only ten years old, but I *knew* I had found my own Gaius Gracchus.''

Clodius had never considered himself in the light of either of the Brothers Gracchi, but Fulvia now planted an intriguing seed: what if he embarked on that sort of career—an aristocratic demagogue out to vindicate the underprivileged? Didn't it blend beautifully with his own career to date? And how easy it would be for him, who had a talent for getting on with the lowly that neither of the Gracchi had owned!

"For you, I will try," he said, and smiled delightfully.

Her breath caught, she gasped audibly. But what she said was strange. "I'm a very jealous person, Publius Clodius, and that will not make me an easy wife. If you so much as look at another woman, I'll tear your eyes out."

"I won't be able to look at another woman," he said soberly, switching from comedy to tragedy faster than an actor could change masks. "In fact, Fulvia, it may be that when you know my secret, you won't look at me either."

This didn't dismay her in the least; instead she looked fascinated, and leaned forward. "Your secret?"

"My secret. And it is a secret. I won't ask you to swear to keep it, because there are only two kinds of women. Those who would swear and then tell happily, and those who would keep a secret without swearing. Which kind are you, Fulvia?"

"It depends," she said, smiling a little. "I think I am both. So I won't swear. But, Publius Clodius, I am loyal. If your secret doesn't diminish you in my eyes, I will keep it. You are my chosen mate, and I am loyal. I would die for you."

"Don't die for me, Fulvia, live for me!" cried Clodius, who was falling in love more rapidly than a child's cork ball could tumble down a cataract.

"Tell me!" she said, growling the words ferociously.

"While I was with my brother-in-law Rex in Syria," Clodius began, "I was abducted by a group of Skenite Arabs. Do you know what they are?"

"No."

"They're a race out of the Asian desert, and they had usurped many of the positions and properties the Greeks of Syria had owned before Tigranes transported the Greeks to Armenia. When these Greeks returned after Tigranes fell, they found themselves destitute. The Skenite Arabs controlled everything. And I thought that was terrible, so I began to work to have the Greeks restored and the Skenite Arabs returned to the desert.''

"Of course," she said, nodding. "That is your nature, to fight for the dispossessed."

"My reward," said Clodius bitterly, "was to be abducted by these people of the desert, and subjected to something no Roman can abide—something so disgraceful and ludicrous that if it became known, I would never be able to live in Rome again."

All sorts of somethings chased through that intense dark blue gaze as Fulvia reviewed the alternatives. "What could they have done?" she asked in the end, absolutely bewildered. "Not rape, sodomy, bestiality. Those would be understood, forgiven."

"How do you know about sodomy and bestiality?"

She looked smug. "I know everything, Publius Clodius.''

"Well, it wasn't any of them. They circumcised me."

"*What* did they do?"

"You don't know everything after all."

"Not that word, anyway. What does it mean?"

"They cut off my foreskin."

"Your what?" she asked, revealing deeper layers of ignorance.

Clodius sighed. "It would be better for Roman virgins if the wall paintings didn't concentrate on Priapus," he said. "Men are not erect all the time."

"I know *that*!"

"What you don't seem to know is that when men are not erect, the bulb on the end of their penis is covered by a sheath called the foreskin," said Clodius, beads of sweat on his brow. "Some peoples cut it off, leaving the bulb on the end of the penis permanently exposed. That's called circumcision. The Jews and the Egyptians do it. So, it appears, do the Arabs. And that is what they did to me. They branded me an outcast, as un-Roman!"

Her face looked like a boiling sky, changing, turning. "Oh! Oh, my poor, poor Clodius!" she cried. Her tongue came out, wet her lips. "Let me look!" she said.

The very thought of that caused twitches and stirs; Clodius now discovered that circumcision did not produce impotence, a fate which permanent limpness since Antioch had seemed to promise. He also discovered that in some ways he was a prude. "No, you most definitely can't look!" he snapped.

But she was on her knees in front of his chair, and her hands were busy parting the folds of toga, pushing at his tunic. She looked up at him in mingled mischief, delight and disappointment, then waved at a bronze lamp of an impossibly enormous Priapus, the wick protruding from his erection. "You look like him," she said, and giggled. "I want to see you down, not up!"

Clodius leaped out of the chair and rearranged his clothing, panicked eyes on the door in case Sempronia came back. But she did not, nor it seemed had anyone else witnessed the daughter of the house inspecting what were to be her goods.

"To see me down, you'll have to marry me," he said.

"Oh, my darling Publius Clodius, of course I'll marry you!" she cried, getting to her feet. "Your secret is safe with me. If it really is such a disgrace, you'll never be able to look at another woman, will you?"

"I'm all yours," said Publius Clodius, dashing away his tears. "I adore you, Fulvia! I worship the ground you walk on!"

Clodius and Fulvia were married late in Quinctilis, after the last of the elections. They had been full of surprises, starting with Catilina's application to stand *in absentia* for next year's consulship. But though Catilina's return from his province was delayed, other men from Africa had made it their business to be in Rome well before the elections. It seemed beyond any doubt that Catilina's governorship of Africa was distinguished only for its corruption; the African farmers—tax and otherwise—who had come to Rome were making no secret of their intention to have Catilina prosecuted for extortion the moment he arrived home. So the supervising consul of the curule elections, Volcatius Tullus, had prudently declined to accept Catilina's *in absentia* candidacy on the grounds that he was under the shadow of prosecution.

Then a worse scandal broke. The successful candidates for next year's consulships, Publius Sulla and his dear friend Publius Autronius, were discovered to have bribed massively. Gaius Piso's *lex Calpurnia* dealing with bribery might be a leaky vessel, but the evidence against Publius Sulla and Autronius was so ironclad that not even slipshod legislation could save them. Whereupon the guilty pair promptly pleaded guilty and offered to conclude a deal with the existing consuls and the new consuls-elect, Lucius Cotta and Lucius Manlius Torquatus. The upshot of this shrewd move was that the charges were dropped in return for payment of huge fines and an oath sworn by both men that neither of them would ever again stand for public office; that they got away with it was thanks to Gaius Piso's bribery law, which provided for such solutions. Lucius Cotta, who wanted a trial, was livid when his three colleagues voted that the miscreants could keep both citizenship and residency as well as the major portions of their immense fortunes.

None of which really concerned Clodius, whose target was, as eight years earlier, Catilina. Mind running riot with dreams of revenge at last, Clodius prevailed upon the African plaintiffs to commission him to prosecute Catilina. Wonderful, wonderful! Catilina's comeuppance was at hand just when he, Clodius, had married the most exciting girl in the world! All his rewards had come at once, not least because Fulvia turned out to be an ardent partisan and helper, not at all the demure little stay-at-home bride other men than Clodius might perhaps have preferred.

At first Clodius worked in a frenzy to assemble his evidence and witnesses, but the Catilina case was one of those maddening affairs wherein nothing happened quickly enough, from finding the evidence to locating the witnesses. A trip to Utica or Hadrumetum took two months, and the job needed many such trips to Africa. Clodius fretted and chafed, but then, said Fulvia, ''Think a little, darling Publius. Why not drag the case out forever?

If it isn't concluded before next Quinctilis, then for the second year in a row, Catilina won't be allowed to run for the consulship, will he?''

Clodius saw the point of this advice immediately, and slowed down to the pace of an African snail. He would secure Catilina's conviction, but not for many moons to come. Brilliant!

He then had time to think about Lucullus, whose career was ending in disaster. Through the *lex Manilia,* Pompey had been dowered with Lucullus's command against Mithridates and Tigranes, and had proceeded to exercise his rights. He and Lucullus had met at Danala, a remote Galatian citadel, and quarreled so bitterly that Pompey (who had until then been reluctant to squash Lucullus under the weight of his *imperium maius*) formally issued a decree outlawing Lucullus's actions, then banished him from Asia. After which Pompey re-enlisted the Fimbriani; free though they were at last to go home, the Fimbriani couldn't face such a major dislocation after all. Service in the legions of Pompey the Great sounded good.

Banished in circumstances of awful humiliation, Lucullus went back to Rome at once, and sat himself down on the Campus Martius to await the triumph he was certain the Senate would grant him. But Pompey's tribune of the plebs, his nephew Gaius Memmius, told the House that if it tried to grant Lucullus a triumph, he would pass legislation in the Plebeian Assembly to deny Lucullus any triumph; the Senate, said Memmius, had no constitutional right to grant such boons. Catulus, Hortensius and the rest of the *boni* fought Memmius tooth and nail, but could not marshal sufficient support; most of the Senate was of the opinion that its right to grant triumphs was more important than Lucullus, so why allow concern for Lucullus to push Memmius into creating an unwelcome precedent?

Lucullus refused to give in. Every day the Senate met, he petitioned again for his triumph. His beloved brother, Varro Lucullus, was also in trouble with Memmius, who sought to convict him for peculations alleged to have occurred years and years before. From all of which it might safely be assumed that Pompey had become a nasty enemy

of the two Luculli—and of the *boni*. When he and Lucullus had met in Danala, Lucullus had accused him of
walking in to take all the credit for a campaign he, Lucullus, had actually won. A mortal insult to Pompey. As
for the *boni,* they were still adamantly against these special
commands for the Great Man.

It might have been expected that Lucullus's wife,
Clodilla, would visit him in his expensive villa on the
Pincian Hill outside the *pomerium,* but she didn't. At
twenty-five she was now a complete woman of the world,
had Lucullus's wealth at her disposal and no one save big
brother Appius to supervise her activities. Of lovers she
had many, of reputation none savory.

Two months after Lucullus's return, Publius Clodius
and Fulvia visited her, though not with the intention of
effecting a reconciliation. Instead (with Fulvia listening
avidly) Clodius told his youngest sister what he had told
Lucullus in Nisibis—that he, Clodia and Clodilla had done
more than just sleep together. Clodilla thought it a great
joke.

"Do you want him back?" asked Clodius.

"Who, Lucullus?" The great dark eyes widened,
flashed. "No, I do not want him back! He's an old man,
he was an old man when he married me ten years ago—
had to fill himself up with Spanish fly before he could get
a stir out of it!"

"Then why not go out to the Pincian and see him,
tell him you're divorcing him?" Clodius looked demure.
"If you fancy a little revenge, you could confirm what I
told him in Nisibis, though he might choose to make the
story public, and that could be hard for you. I'm willing
to take my share of the outrage, so is Clodia. But both of
us will understand if you're not."

"Willing?" squeaked Clodilla. "I'd love it! Let him
spread the story! All we have to do is deny it, with many
tears and protestations of innocence. People won't know
what to believe. Everyone is aware of the state of affairs
between you and Lucullus. Those on his side will believe
his version of events. Those in the middle will vacillate.

And those on our side, like brother Appius, will think us shockingly injured.''

''Just get in first and divorce him,'' said Clodius. ''That way, even if he also divorces you, he can't strip you of a hefty share in his wealth. You've no dowry to fall back on.''

''How clever,'' purred Clodilla.

''You could always marry again,'' said Fulvia.

The dark and bewitching face of her sister-in-law twisted, became vicious. ''Not I!'' she snarled. ''*One* husband was one too many! I want to manage my own destiny, thank you very much! It's been a joy to have Lucullus in the East, and I've salted away quite a snug little fortune at his expense. Though I do like the idea of getting in first with the divorce. Brother Appius can negotiate a settlement which will give me enough for the rest of my life.''

Fulvia giggled gleefully. ''It will set Rome by the ears!''

It did indeed set Rome by the ears. Though Clodilla divorced Lucullus, he then publicly divorced her by having one of his senior clients read out his proclamation from the rostra. His reasons, he said, were not merely because Clodilla had committed adultery with many men during his absence; she had also had incestuous relations with her brother Publius Clodius and her sister Clodia.

Naturally most people wanted to believe it, chiefly because it was so deliciously awful, but also because the Claudii/Clodii Pulchri were an outlandish lot, brilliant and unpredictable and erratic. Had been for generations! Patricians, say no more.

Poor Appius Claudius took it very hard, but had more sense than to be pugnacious about it; his best defense was to stalk around the Forum looking as if the last thing in the world he wanted to talk about was incest, and people took the hint. Rex had remained in the East as one of Pompey's senior legates, but Claudia, his wife, adopted the same attitude as big brother Appius. The middle one of the three brothers, Gaius Claudius, was rather intellectually dull for a Claudian, therefore not considered a worthy target by the Forum wits. Luckily Clodia's husband, Celer, was another absentee on duty in the East, as was his brother, Nepos; they would have been more awkward, asked some difficult questions. As it was, the three culprits went about looking both innocent and indignant, and rolled on the floor laughing when no outsiders were present. What a *gorgeous* scandal!

Cicero, however, had the last word. "Incest," he said gravely to a large crowd of Forum frequenters, "is a game the whole family can play."

Clodius was to rue his rashness when finally the trial of Catilina came on, for many of the jury looked at him askance, and allowed their doubts to color their verdict. It was a hard and bitter battle which Clodius for one fought valiantly; he had taken Cicero's advice about the nakedness of his prejudices and his malice seriously, and conducted his prosecution with skill. That he lost and Catilina was acquitted couldn't even be attributed to bribery, and he had learned enough not to imply bribery when the verdict of ABSOLVO came in. It was, he concluded, just the luck of the lots and the quality of the defense, which had been formidable.

"You did well, Clodius," said Caesar to him afterward. "It wasn't your fault you lost. Even the *tribuni aerarii* on that jury were so conservative they made Catulus look like a radical." He shrugged. "You couldn't win with Torquatus leading the defense, not after the rumor that Catilina planned to assassinate him last New Year's Day. To defend Catilina was Torquatus's way of saying he didn't choose to believe the rumor, and the jury was impressed. Even so, you did well. You presented a neat case."

Publius Clodius rather liked Caesar, recognizing in him another restless spirit, and envying him a kind of self-control Clodius was unhappily aware he didn't own. When the verdict came in, he had been tempted to scream and howl and weep. Then his eyes fell on Caesar and Cicero standing together to watch, and something in their faces gave him pause. He would have his revenge, but not today.

To behave like a bad loser could benefit no one save Catilina.

"At least it's too late for him to run for the consulship," said Clodius to Caesar, sighing, "and that's some sort of victory."

"Yes, he'll have to wait another year."

They walked up the Sacra Via toward the inn on the corner of the Clivus Orbius, with the imposing facade of Fabius Allobrogicus's arch across the Sacred Way filling their eyes. Caesar was on his way home, and Clodius heading for the inn itself, where his clients from Africa were lodging.

"I met a friend of yours in Tigranocerta," said Clodius.

"Ye gods, who could that have been?"

"A centurion by name of Marcus Silius."

"Silius? Silius from Mitylene? A Fimbrianus?"

"The very one. He admires you very much."

"It's mutual. A good man. At least now he can come home."

"It appears not, Caesar. I had a letter from him recently, written from Galatia. The Fimbriani have decided to enlist with Pompeius."

"I wondered. These old campaigners weep a lot about home, but when an interesting campaign crops up, somehow home loses its allure." Caesar extended his hand with a smile. "*Ave*, Publius Clodius. I intend to follow your career with interest."

Clodius stood outside the inn for some time, staring into nothing. When he finally entered, he looked as if he was prefect of his school—upright, honor-bound, incorruptible.

PART III

---

from JANUARY of 65 B.C.
until QUINCTILIS of 63 B.C.

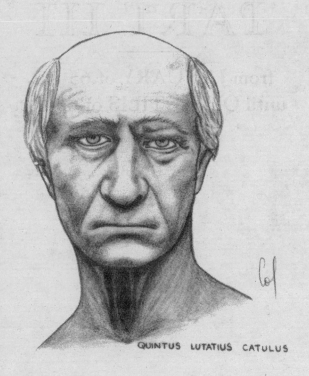

QUINTUS LUTATIUS CATULUS

MARCUS CALPURNIUS BIBULUS

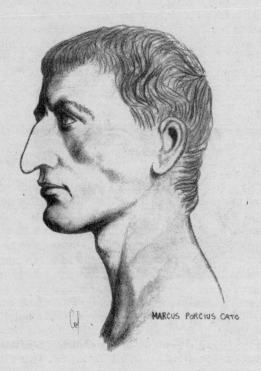

MARCUS PORCIUS CATO

Marcus Licinius Crassus was now so rich that he had begun to be called by a second cognomen, Dives, which just meant fabulously wealthy. And when together with Quintus Lutatius Catulus he was elected censor, nothing was missing from his career save a great and glorious military campaign. Oh, he had defeated Spartacus and earned an ovation for it, but six months in the field against a gladiator in whose army were many slaves rather took the gloss off his victory. What he hankered after was something more in the line of Pompey the Great—savior of his country, that kind of campaign. And that kind of reputation. It *hurt* to be eclipsed by an upstart!

Nor was Catulus an amicable colleague in the censorship, for reasons which escaped the bewildered Crassus. No Licinius Crassus had ever been apostrophized as a demagogue or any other sort of political radical, so what was Catulus prating about?

"It's your money," said Caesar, to whom he addressed this peevish question. "Catulus is *boni,* he doesn't condone commercial activities for senators. He'd dearly love to see himself in tandem with another censor and both of them busy investigating you. But since you're his colleague, he can't very well do that, can he?"

"He'd be wasting his time if he tried!" said Crassus indignantly. "I do nothing half the Senate doesn't do! I make my money from owning property, which is well within the province of every or any senator! I admit I have a few shares in companies, but I am not on a board of directors, I have no vote in how a company will conduct its business. I'm simply a source of capital. That's unimpeachable!"

"I realize all that," said Caesar patiently, "and so does our beloved Catulus. Let me repeat: it's your money. There's old Catulus toiling away to pay for the rebuilding of Jupiter Optimus Maximus, never managing to increase the family fortune because every spare sestertius has to go

227

into Jupiter Optimus Maximus. Whereas you just keep on
making money. He's jealous.''

"Then let him save his jealousy for men who deserve
it!" growled Crassus, unmollified.

Since stepping down from the consulship he had
shared with Pompey the Great, Crassus had gone into a
new kind of business, one pioneered forty years earlier by
a Servilius Caepio: namely, the manufacture of arms and
armaments for Rome's legions in a series of townships
north of the Padus River in Italian Gaul. It was his good
friend Lucius Calpurnius Piso, the armaments gatherer for
Rome during the Italian War, who had drawn Crassus's
attention to it. Lucius Piso had recognized the potential in
this new industry, and espoused it so wholeheartedly that
he succeeded in making a great deal of money out of it.
His ties of course were to Italian Gaul anyway, for his
mother had been a Calventia from Italian Gaul. And when
Lucius Piso died, his son, another Lucius Piso, continued
both in this activity and in the warm friendship with Crassus. Who had finally been brought to see the advantages
in owning whole towns devoted to the manufacture of
chain mail, swords, javelins, helmets, daggers; senatorially
proper too.

As censor Crassus was now in a position to help his
friend Lucius Piso as well as young Quintus Servilius Caepio Brutus, the heir to the Servilius Caepio manufactories
in Feltria, Cardianum, Bellunum. Italian Gaul on the far
side of the Padus had been Roman for so long by now
that its citizens, many of them Gauls but many more of
mixed stock due to intermarriage, had come to harbor
much resentment because they were still being denied the
citizenship. Only three years earlier there had been stir-
rings, quietened after the visit of Caesar returning from
Spain. And Crassus saw his duty very clearly once he became censor and had charge of the rolls of Roman citizens:
he would help his friends Lucius Piso and Caepio Brutus
and establish a huge clientele for himself by giving the
full Roman citizenship to everyone on the far side of the
Padus in Italian Gaul. Everyone south of the Padus had
the full citizenship—it didn't seem right to deny people

of exactly the same blood just because they were located on the wrong side of a river!

But when he announced his intention to enfranchise all of Italian Gaul, his fellow censor Catulus seemed to go mad. No, no, no! Never, never, never! Roman citizenship was for Romans, and Gauls were not Romans! There were already too many Gauls calling themselves Romans, like Pompey the Great and his Picentine minions.

"The old, old argument," said Caesar, disgusted. "The Roman citizenship must be for Romans only. Why can't these idiot *boni* see that all the peoples of Italia everywhere are Romans? That Rome herself is really Italia?"

"I agree with you," said Crassus, "but Catulus doesn't."

Crassus's other scheme was not favored either.

He wanted to annex Egypt, even if that meant going to war—with himself at the head of the army, of course. On the subject of Egypt, Crassus had become such an authority that he was encyclopaedic. And every single fact he learned only served to confirm what he had suspected, that Egypt was the wealthiest nation in the world.

"Imagine it!" he said to Caesar, face for once anything but bovine and impassive. "Pharaoh owns *everything*! There's no such thing as freehold land in Egypt— it's all leased from Pharaoh, who collects the rents. All the products of Egypt belong to him outright, from grain to gold to jewels to spices and ivory! Only linen is excluded. It belongs to the native Egyptian priests, but even then Pharaoh takes a third of it for himself. His private income is at least six thousand talents a year, and his income from the country another six thousand talents. Plus extra from Cyprus."

"I heard," said Caesar, for no other reason than that he wanted to bait the Crassus bull, "that the Ptolemies have been so inept they've run through every drachma Egypt possesses."

The Crassus bull did snort, but derisively rather than angrily. "Rubbish! Absolute rubbish! Not the most inept Ptolemy could spend a tenth of what he gets. His income

from the country keeps the country—pays for his army of
bureaucrats, his soldiers, his sailors, police, priests, even
his palaces. They haven't been to war in years except on
each other, and then the money simply goes to the victor,
not out of Egypt. His private income he puts away, and
all the treasures—the gold, the silver, the rubies and ivory
and sapphires, the turquoise and carnelian and lapis laz-
uli—he never even bothers to convert into cash, they all
get put away too. Except for what he gives to the artisans
and craftsmen to make into furniture or jewelry.''

''What about the theft of the golden sarcophagus of
Alexander the Great?'' asked Caesar provocatively. ''The
first Ptolemy called Alexander was so impoverished he
took it, melted it down into gold coins and replaced it with
the present rock-crystal sarcophagus.''

''And there you have it!'' said Crassus scornfully.
''Truly, all these ridiculous stories! That Ptolemy was in
Alexandria for about five days all told before he fled. And
do you mean to tell me that in the space of five days he
removed an object of solid gold weighing at least *four
thousand* talents, cut it into pieces small enough to fit into
a goldsmith's beaker-sized furnace, melted all those little
pieces down in however many furnaces, and then stamped
out what would have amounted to many millions of coins?
He couldn't have done it inside a year! Not only that, but
where's your common sense, Caesar? A transparent rock-
crystal sarcophagus big enough to contain a human
body—yes, yes, I am aware Alexander the Great was a
tiny fellow!—would cost a dozen times what a solid-gold
sarcophagus would cost. And take years to fashion once a
big enough piece was found. Logic says someone found
that big enough piece, and by coincidence the replacement
happened while Ptolemy Alexander was there. The priests
of the Sema wanted the people to actually *see* Alexander
the Great.''

''Ugh!'' said Caesar.

''No, no they preserved him perfectly. I believe he's
quite as beautiful today as he was in life,'' said Crassus,
thoroughly carried away.

''Leaving aside the questionable topic of how well

preserved Alexander the Great is, Marcus, there's never smoke without some fire. One is forever hearing tales of this or that Ptolemy down the centuries having to flee shirtless, without two sesterces to rub together. There cannot be nearly as much money and treasure as you say there is.''

"Aha!" cried Crassus triumphantly. "The tales are based on a false premise, Caesar. What people fail to understand is that the Ptolemaic treasures and the country's wealth are not kept in Alexandria. Alexandria is an artificial graft on the real Egyptian tree. The priests in Memphis are the custodians of the Egyptian treasury, which is located there. And when a Ptolemy—or a Cleopatra—needs to fly the coop, they don't head down the delta to Memphis, they sail out of the Cibotus Harbor at Alexandria and they head for Cyprus or Syria or Cos. Therefore they can't lay their hands on more funds than there are in Alexandria.''

Caesar looked terrifically solemn, sighed, leaned back in his chair and put his hands behind his head. "My dear Crassus, you have convinced me," he said.

It was only then that Crassus calmed down enough to see the ironic gleam in Caesar's eyes, and burst out laughing. "Wretch! You've been teasing me!"

"I agree with you about Egypt in every respect," said Caesar. "The only trouble is that you'll never manage to talk Catulus into this venture."

Nor did he talk Catulus into it, while Catulus talked the Senate out of it. The result was that after less than three months in office and long before they could revise the roll of the Ordo Equester, let alone take a census of the people, the censorship of Catulus and Crassus ceased to be. Crassus resigned publicly and with much to say about Catulus, none of it complimentary. So short a term had it been, in fact, that the Senate decided to have new censors elected in the following year.

Caesar acquitted himself as a good friend ought by speaking in the House in favor of both Crassus's proposals, enfranchisement of the Trans-Padane Gauls and the annexation of Egypt, but his chief interest that year lay elsewhere: he had been elected one of the two curule aediles, which meant that he was now permitted to sit in the ivory curule chair, and was preceded by two lictors bearing the *fasces*. It had happened ''in his year,'' an indication that he was exactly as far up the *cursus honorum* of public magistracies as he was supposed to be. Unfortunately his colleague (who polled far fewer votes) was Marcus Calpurnius Bibulus.

They had very different ideas as to what the curule aedileship consisted of, and that went for every aspect of the job. Together with the two plebeian aediles, they were responsible for the general upkeep of the city of Rome: the care of streets, squares, gardens, marketplaces, traffic, public buildings, law and order, the water supply including fountains and basins, land registers, building ordinances, drainage and sewers, statues displayed in public places, and temples. Duties were either carried out by all four together, or else amicably assigned to one or more among them.

Weights and measures fell to the lot of the curule aediles, who had their headquarters in the temple of Castor and Pollux, a very central location on the Vestal fringe of the lower Forum; the set of standard weights and measures was kept under the podium of this temple, always referred to simply as ''Castor's,'' Pollux being quite overlooked. The plebeian aediles were located much farther away, in the beautiful temple of Ceres at the foot of the Aventine, and perhaps because of this seemed to pay less attention to the duties involved in caring for Rome's public and political center.

One duty all four shared was most onerous of all: the grain supply in all its aspects, from the moment in which it was taken off the barges until it disappeared into an entitled citizen's sack to be carried home. They also were responsible for buying in grain, paying for it, tallying it on arrival, and collecting the money for it. They kept the list of citizens entitled to low-priced State grain, which meant they had a copy of the roll of Roman citizens. They issued the chits from their booth in the Porticus Metelli on the Campus Martius, but the grain itself was stored in huge silos lining the cliffs of the Aventine along the Vicus Portae Trigeminae at the Port of Rome.

The two plebeian aediles of that year were no competition for the curule aediles, with Cicero's younger brother, Quintus, the senior of the pair.

"Which means undistinguished games from them," said Caesar to Bibulus, and sighing as he said it. "It appears they're not going to do much about the city either."

Bibulus eyed his colleague with sour dislike. "You may disabuse yourself of any grand pretensions in the curule aediles as well, Caesar. I will contribute to good games, but not great games. My purse won't run to that any more than yours will. Nor do I intend to undertake any surveys of the sewers, or have the adjutages inspected along every branch of the water supply, or put a new coat of paint on Castor's, or go rushing around the markets checking every pair of scales."

"What do you intend to do?" asked Caesar, lifting his lip.

"I intend to do what is necessary, and nothing more."

"Don't you think checking scales is necessary?"

"I do not."

"Well," said Caesar, grinning nastily, "I think it's very appropriate that we're located in Castor's. If you want to be Pollux, go right ahead. But don't forget Pollux's fate—never to be remembered and never to be mentioned."

Which was not a good start. However, always too busy and too well organized to bother with those who declared themselves unwilling to co-operate, Caesar went about his duties as if he were the only aedile in Rome. He had the advantage of owning an excellent network of reporters of transgressions, for he enlisted Lucius Decumius and his crossroads brethren as informers, and cracked down very hard on merchants who weighed light or measured short, on builders who infringed boundaries or used poor materials, on landlords who had cheated the water companies by inserting bigger-bore adjutage pipes from the mains into their properties than the law prescribed. He fined ruthlessly, and fined heavily. No one escaped, even his friend Marcus Crassus.

"You're beginning to annoy me," said Crassus grumpily as February commenced. "So far you've cost me a fortune! Too little cement in some building mix, too few beams in that insula I'm putting up on the Viminal— and it does *not* encroach on public land, I don't care what you say! Fifty thousand sesterces in fines just because I tapped into the sewer and put private latrines into my new flats on the Carinae? That's *two talents,* Caesar!"

"Break the law and I'll get you for it," said Caesar, not at all contrite. "I need every sestertius I can put into my fine chest, and I'm not about to exempt my friends."

"If you continue like this, you won't have any friends."

"What you're saying, Marcus, is that you're a fine-weather friend," said Caesar, a little unfairly.

"No, I am not! But if you're after money to fund spectacular games, then borrow it, don't expect every businessman in Rome to foot the bill for your public extravaganzas!" cried Crassus, goaded. "I'll lend you the money, and I won't charge you interest."

"Thank you, but no," said Caesar firmly. "If I did that, I'd be the fine-weather friend. If I have to borrow, I'll go to a proper moneylender and borrow."

"You can't, you're in the Senate."

"I can, Senate or no. If I get thrown out of the Senate for borrowing from usurers, Crassus, it will go down to fifty members overnight," said Caesar. His eyes gleamed. "There is something you can do for me."

"What?"

"Put me in touch with some discreet pearl merchant who might want to pick up the finest pearls he's ever seen for less by far than he'll sell them for."

"Oho! I don't remember your declaring any pearls when you tabulated the pirate booty!"

"I didn't, nor did I declare the five hundred talents I kept. Which means my fate is in your hands, Marcus. All you have to do is lodge my name in the courts and I'm done for.''

"I won't do that, Caesar—*if* you stop fining me," said Crassus craftily.

"Then you'd better go down to the *praetor urbanus* this moment and lodge my name," said Caesar, laughing, "because you won't buy me that way!"

"Is that all you kept, five hundred talents and some pearls?"

"That's all."

"I don't understand you!"

"That's all right, nor does anyone else," said Caesar, and prepared to depart. "But look up that pearl merchant for me, like a good chap. I'd do it myself—if I knew whereabouts to start. You can have a pearl as your commission."

"Oh, keep your pearls!" said Crassus, disgusted.

Caesar did keep one pearl, the huge strawberry-shaped and strawberry-colored one, though why he didn't quite know, for it would probably have doubled the five hundred talents he got for all the others. Just some instinct, and that was even after the eager buyer had seen it.

"I'd get six or seven million sesterces for it," the man said wistfully.

"No," said Caesar, tossing it up and down in his hand, "I think I'll keep it. Fortune says I should."

Profligate spender though he was, Caesar was also capable of totting up the bill, and when by the end of February he had totted up the bill, his heart sank. The aedile's chest would probably yield five hundred talents; Bibulus had indicated that he would contribute one hundred talents toward their first games, the *ludi Megalenses* in April, and two hundred talents toward the big games, the *ludi Romani,* in September; and Caesar had close to a thousand talents of his own money—which represented all he had in the world aside from his precious land, and that he would not part with. That kept him in the Senate.

According to his reckoning, the *ludi Megalenses* would cost seven hundred talents, and the *ludi Romani* a

thousand talents. Seventeen hundred all told, just about
what he had. The trouble was that he intended to do more
than give two lots of games; every curule aedile had to
give the games, all the distinction a man could earn was
in their magnificence. Caesar wanted to stage funeral
games for his father in the Forum, and he expected them
to cost five hundred talents. He would have to borrow,
then offend everyone who voted for him by keeping on
fining for his aedile's chest. Not prudent! Marcus Crassus
tolerated it only because, despite his stinginess and his
rooted conviction that a man helped his friends even at
the expense of the State, he really did love Caesar.

"You can have what I got, Pavo," said Lucius Decumius, who was there to watch Caesar work over his
figures.

Though he looked tired and a little discouraged, out
flashed a special smile for this odd old man who was such
a huge part of his life. "Go on, dad! What you've got
wouldn't hire a single pair of gladiators."

"I got close to two hundred talents."

Caesar whistled. "I can see I'm in the wrong profession! Is that what you've salted away all these years guaranteeing peace and protection for the residents of the outer
Via Sacra and the Vicus Fabricii?"

"It mounts up," said Lucius Decumius, looking
humble.

"You keep it, dad, don't give it to me."

"Where you going to get the rest from, then?"

"I'll borrow it against what I make as propraetor in
a good province. I've written to Balbus in Gades, and he's
agreed to give me letters of reference to the right people
here in Rome."

"Can't you borrow it from him?"

"No, he's a friend. I can't borrow from my friends,
dad."

"Oh, you are a strange one!" said Lucius Decumius,
shaking his grizzled head. "That's what friends are for."

"Not to me, dad. If something happens and I can't
pay the money back, I'd rather owe strangers. I couldn't

bear the thought that my idiocies meant any of my friends were out of purse.''

"If you can't pay it back, Pavo, I'd say Rome was done.''

Some of the care lifted, Caesar drew a breath. "I agree, dad. I'll pay it back, have no fear. Therefore," he went on happily, "what am I worrying about? I'll borrow however much it takes to be the greatest curule aedile Rome has ever seen!''

This Caesar proceeded to do, though at the end of the year he was a thousand talents in debt rather than the five hundred he had estimated. Crassus helped by whispering in these obliging moneylending ears that Caesar was a good prospect, so ought not to be charged extortionate rates of interest, and Balbus helped by putting him in touch with men who were prepared to be discreet as well as not too greedy. Ten percent simple interest, which was the legal rate. The only difficulty was that he had to begin to pay the loan back within a year—otherwise the interest would go from simple to compound; he would be paying interest on the interest he owed as well as on the capital borrowed.

The *ludi Megalenses* were the first games of the year and religiously the most solemn, perhaps because they heralded the arrival of spring (in years when the calendar coincided with the seasons) and emerged out of the terrible second war Rome had fought against Carthage, when Hannibal marched up and down Italy. It was then that the worship of Magna Mater, the Great Asian Earth Mother, was introduced to Rome, and her temple was erected on the Palatine looking directly down on the Vallis Murcia, in which lay the Circus Maximus. In many ways it was an inappropriate cult for conservative Rome; Romans abhorred eunuchs, flagellatory rites, and what was considered religious barbarism. However, the deed was done in the moment the Vestal Virgin Claudia miraculously pulled the barge bearing Magna Mater's Navel Stone up the Tiber, and now Rome had to suffer the consequences as castrated priests bleeding from self-inflicted wounds screeched and trumpeted their way through the streets on the fourth day of April, towing the Great Mother's effigy and begging alms from all those who came to watch this introduction to the games.

The games themselves were more typically Roman, and lasted for six days, from the fourth to the tenth day of April. The first day consisted of the procession, then a ceremony at Magna Mater's temple, and finally some events in the Circus Maximus. The next four days were devoted to theatrical performances in a number of temporary wooden structures put up for the purpose, while the last day saw the procession of the Gods from the Capitol to the Circus, and many hours of chariot racing in the Circus.

As senior curule aedile, it was Caesar who officiated at the first day's events, and Caesar who offered the Great Mother an oddly bloodless sacrifice, considering that Kubaba Cybele was a bloodthirsty lady; the offering was a dish of herbs.

Some called these games the patrician games, for on the first evening patrician families feasted each other and kept their guest lists absolutely patrician; it was always thought an auspicious omen for the Patriciate when the curule aedile who made the sacrifice was a patrician, as was Caesar. Bibulus of course was plebeian in rank, and felt utterly ostracized on that opening day; Caesar had filled the special seating on the great wide steps of the temple with patricians, doing special honor to the Claudii Pulchri, so intimately connected to the presence of Magna Mater in Rome.

Though on this first day the celebrating aediles and the official party did not descend into the Circus Maximus, but rather watched from Magna Mater's temple steps, Caesar had elected to put on a pageant in the Circus instead of trying to entertain the crowd which had followed the Goddess's bloody procession with the usual fare of boxing matches and foot races. Time did not permit chariot racing. Caesar had tapped into the Tiber and channeled water across the Forum Boarium to create a river inside the Circus, with the *spina* doing duty as Tiber Island and separating this cunning stream. While the vast crowd oohed and aahed its total enchantment, Caesar depicted the Vestal Claudia's feat of strength. She towed the barge in from the Forum Boarium end where on the last day the starting gates for the chariots would be installed, took it once entirely around the *spina,* then brought it to rest at the Capena end of the stadium. The barge glittered with gilt and had billowing purple embroidered sails; all the eunuch priests were assembled on its deck around a glassy black ball representing the Navel Stone, while high on the poop stood Magna Mater's statue in her chariot drawn by a pair of lions, absolutely lifelike. Nor did Caesar employ a strongman dressed as a Vestal for Claudia; he used a slight and slender, beautiful woman of Claudia's type, and concealed the men who pushed the barge, shoulders bent to it in waist-deep water, with a gilded false hull.

The crowd went home ecstatic after this three-hour show. Caesar stood surrounded by delighted patricians, accepting their fulsome compliments for his taste and imagination. Bibulus took the hint and left in a huff because everyone ignored him.

There were no fewer than ten wooden theaters erected from the Campus Martius to the Capena Gate, the largest of which held ten thousand, the smallest five hundred. And instead of being content to have them look what they were, temporary, Caesar had insisted they be painted, decorated, gilded. Farces and mimes were staged in the bigger theaters, Terence and Plautus and Ennius in the smaller ones, and Sophocles and Aeschylus in the littlest, very Greek-looking auditorium; every thespian taste was catered for. From early in the morning until nearly dusk, all ten theaters played for four whole days, a feast. Literally a feast, as Caesar served free refreshments during the intervals.

On the last day the procession assembled on the Capitol and wended its way down through the Forum Romanum and the Via Triumphalis to the Circus Maximus, parading gilded statues of some Gods like Mars and Apollo—and Castor and Pollux. Since Caesar had paid for the gilding, it was perhaps not surprising that Pollux was much smaller in size than his twin, Castor. Such a laugh!

Though the games were supposed to be publicly funded and the chariot races were dearest to every spectator's heart, in actual fact there was never State money for the entertainments themselves. This hadn't stopped Caesar, who produced more chariot races on that last day of the *ludi Megalenses* than Rome had ever seen. It was his duty as senior curule aedile to start the races, each one comprising four chariots—Red, Blue, Green and White. The first race was for cars drawn by four horses poled up abreast, but other races saw two horses poled up abreast, or two or three horses harnessed in tandem one after the other; Caesar even put on races with unyoked horses ridden bareback by postilions.

The course of each race was five miles long, consisting of seven laps around the central division of the *spina,* a narrow and tall ridge adorned with many statues and showing at one end seven golden dolphins, at the other seven golden eggs perched in big chalices; as each lap ended one dolphin's nose was pulled down to bring its tail up, and one golden egg was taken from its chalice. If the twelve hours of day and the twelve hours of night were of equal length, then each race took one quarter of an hour to run, which meant the pace was fast and furious, a wild gallop. Spills when they happened usually occurred rounding the *metae,* where each driver, reins wound many times about his waist and a dagger tucked into them to free him if he crashed, fought with skill and courage to keep on the inside, a shorter course.

The crowd adored that day, for instead of long breaks after each race, Caesar kept them coming with hardly an interruption; the bookmakers scrambling through the excited spectators taking bets had to work in a frenzy to keep up. Not a single bleacher was vacant, and wives sat on husbands' laps to jam more in. No children, slaves or even freedmen were allowed, but women sat with men. At Caesar's games more than two hundred thousand free Romans jammed into the Circus Maximus, while thousands more watched from every vantage point on Palatine and Aventine.

"They're the best games Rome has ever seen," said

Crassus to Caesar at the end of the sixth day. "What a feat of engineering to do that to the Tiber, then remove it all and have dry ground again for the chariot races."

"These games are nothing," replied Caesar with a grin, "nor was it particularly difficult to use a Tiber swollen from the rains. Wait until you see the *ludi Romani* in September. Lucullus would be devastated if only he'd cross the *pomerium* to see."

But between the *ludi Megalenses* and the *ludi Romani* he did something else so unusual and spectacular that Rome talked about it for years. When the city was choked with vacationing rural citizens who had poured into town for the great games early in September, Caesar put on funeral games in memory of his father, and used the entire Forum Romanum. Of course it was hot and cloudless, so he tented the whole area over with purple sailcloth, hitching its edges to the buildings on either side if they were high enough; where there were no buildings to serve as supports, he propped up the massive fabric structure with great poles and guy ropes. An exercise in engineering he relished, both devising and supervising it himself.

But when all this incredible construction began, a wild rumor went round that Caesar intended to display a thousand pairs of gladiators. Catulus summoned the Senate into session.

"What are you really planning, Caesar?" demanded Catulus to a packed House. "I've always known you intended to undermine the Republic, but a thousand pairs of gladiators when there are no legions to defend our beloved city? This isn't secretly mining a tunnel, this is using a battering ram!"

"Well," drawled Caesar, rising to his feet on the curule dais, "it is true that I do own a mighty battering ram, and also true that I have secretly mined many a tunnel, but always the one with the other." He pulled the front neckline of his tunic away from his chest and put his head down to address the space thus created, and shouted, "Isn't that right, O battering ram?" His hand fell, his tunic flattened, and he looked up with his sweetest smile. "He says that's right."

Crassus emitted a sound somewhere between a mew and a howl, but before his laugh could gather force Cicero's bellow of mirth overtook it; the House dissolved in a gale of hilarity which left Catulus as speechless as his face was purple.

Whereupon Caesar proceeded to display the number he had always meant to display, three hundred and twenty pairs of gladiators gorgeously clad in silver.

But before the funeral games actually got under way, another sensation outraged Catulus and his colleagues. When the day dawned and the Forum appeared from the houses on the edge of the Germalus to look like Homer's gently heaving wine-dark sea, those who came early to get the best places discovered something else than a tent had been added to the Forum Romanum. During the night Caesar had restored every statue of Gaius Marius to its pedestal or plinth, and put Gaius Marius's trophies of war back inside the temple to Honor and Virtue he had built on the Capitol. But what could the arch-conservative senators actually do about it? The answer was, nothing. Rome had never forgotten—nor learned to stop loving—the magnificent Gaius Marius. Out of everything Caesar did during that memorable year when he was curule aedile, the restoration of Gaius Marius was deemed his greatest act.

Naturally Caesar didn't waste this opportunity to remind all the electors who and what he was; in every little arena wherein some of his three hundred and twenty pairs of sawdust soldiers clashed—at the bottom of the Comitia well, in the space between the tribunals, near the temple of Vesta, in front of the Porticus Margaritaria, on the Velia—he had his father's ancestry proclaimed, all the way back to Venus and to Romulus.

Two days after this, Caesar (and Bibulus) staged the *ludi Romani,* which at this time ran for twelve days. The parade from the Capitol through the Forum Romanum to the Circus Maximus took three hours to pass. The chief magistrates and the Senate led it off, with bands of beautifully mounted youths following, then all the chariots which were to race and the athletes who were to compete;

many hundreds of dancers and mummers and musicians; dwarves tricked out as satyrs and fauns; every prostitute in Rome clad in her flame-colored toga; slaves bearing hundreds of gorgeous silver or gold urns and vases; groups of mock warriors in bronze-belted scarlet tunics wearing fabulous crested helmets on their heads and brandishing swords and spears; the sacrificial animals; and then, in last and most honored place, all twelve major Gods and many other Gods and heroes riding on open litters of gold and purple, realistically painted, clad in exquisite clothes.

Caesar had decorated the whole of the Circus Maximus, and gone one better than for any of his other entertainments by using millions of fresh flowers. As Romans adored flowers, the vast audience was ravished almost to swooning point, drowned in the perfume of roses, violets, stocks, wallflowers. He served free refreshments, thought of novelties of all kinds from rope walkers to fire belchers to scantily clad women who seemed to be able almost to turn themselves inside out.

Each day of the games saw something else new and different, and the chariot races were superb.

Said Bibulus to any who remembered him enough to comment, "He told me I'd be Pollux to his Castor. How right he was! I may as well have saved my precious three hundred talents—they only served to pour food and wine down two hundred thousand greedy throats, while *he* took the credit for the rest."

Said Cicero to Caesar, "On the whole I dislike games, but I must confess yours were splendid. To have the most lavish in history is laudable enough in one way, but what I really liked about your games was that they weren't vulgar."

Said Titus Pomponius Atticus, knight plutocrat, to Marcus Licinius Crassus, senatorial plutocrat, "It was brilliant. He managed to give business to everybody. What a year the flower growers and wholesalers have had! They'll vote for him for the rest of his political career. Not to mention bakers, millers—oh, very, very clever!"

And said young Caepio Brutus to Julia, "Uncle Cato is really disgusted. Of course he is a great friend of Bibulus's. But why is it that your father always has to make such a splash?''

Cato loathed Caesar.

When he had finally returned to Rome at the time Caesar took up his duties as curule aedile, he executed his brother Caepio's will. This necessitated a visit to see Servilia and Brutus, who at almost eighteen years of age was well embarked on his Forum career, though he had undertaken no court case yet.

''I dislike the fact that you are now a patrician, Quintus Servilius,'' said Cato, punctilious in his use of the correct name, ''but as I was not willing to be anyone other than a Porcius Cato, I suppose I must approve.'' He leaned forward abruptly. ''What are you doing in the Forum? You should be in the field with someone's army, like your friend Gaius Cassius.''

''Brutus,'' said Servilia stiffly, emphasizing the name, ''has received an exemption.''

''No one ought to be exempt unless he's crippled.''

''His chest is weak,'' said Servilia.

''His chest would soon improve if he got out and did his legal duty, which is to serve in the legions. So would his skin.''

''Brutus will go when *I* consider him well enough.''

''Doesn't he have a tongue?'' Cato demanded, but not in the fierce way he would have before leaving for the East, though it still came out aggressively. ''Can't he speak for himself? You smother this boy, Servilia, and that is un-Roman.''

To all of which Brutus listened mumchance, and in a severe dilemma. On the one hand he longed to see his mother lose this—or any other—battle, but on the other hand he dreaded military duty. Cassius had gone off gladly, while Brutus developed a cough which kept getting worse. It hurt to see himself lessened in his Uncle Cato's eyes, but Uncle Cato didn't tolerate weakness or frailty of any kind, and Uncle Cato, winner of many decorations for valor in battle, would never understand people who didn't thrill when they picked up a sword. So now he began to

cough, a thick hacking sound which started at the base of
his chest and reverberated all the way to his throat. That
of course produced copious phlegm, which enabled him
to look wildly from his mother to his uncle, mumble an
excuse, and leave.

"See what you've done?" asked Servilia, teeth bared.

"He needs exercise and a bit of life in the open air.
I also suspect you're quacking his skin, it looks appalling."

"Brutus is not your responsibility!"

"Under the terms of Caepio's will, he most certainly
is."

"Uncle Mamercus has already been through everything with him, he doesn't need you. In fact, Cato, no one
needs you. Why don't you take yourself off and jump into
the Tiber?"

"Everyone needs me, so much is plain. When I left
for the East, your boy was starting to go to the Campus
Martius, and for a while it looked as if he might actually
learn to be a man. Now I find a mama's lapdog! What's
more, how could you let him contract himself in marriage
to a girl with no dowry to speak of, another wretched
patrician? What sort of weedy children will they have?"

"I would hope," said Servilia icily, "that they have
sons like Julia's father and daughters like me. Say what
you will about patricians and the old aristocracy, Cato, in
Julia's father you see everything a Roman ought to be,
from soldier to orator to politician. Brutus wanted the
match, actually, it wasn't my idea, but I wish I had thought
of it. Blood as good as his own—and that is far more
important than a dowry! However, for your information
her father has guaranteed a dowry of one hundred talents.
Nor does Brutus need a girl with a big dowry, now that
he's Caepio's heir."

"If he's prepared to wait years for a bride, he could
have waited a few more and married my Porcia," said
Cato. "That is an alliance I would have applauded wholeheartedly! My dear Caepio's money would have gone to
the children of both sides of his family."

"Oh, I see!" sneered Servilia. "The truth will out,

eh, Cato? Wouldn't change your name to get Caepio's money, but what a brilliant scheme to get it through the distaff side! *My* son marry the descendant of a slave? Over my dead body!''

''It might happen yet,'' said Cato complacently.

''If that happened, I'd feed the girl hot coals for supper!'' Servilia tensed, understanding that she was not doing as well against Cato as she used to—he was cooler, more detached, and more difficult to wound. She produced her nastiest barb. ''Aside from the fact that you, the descendant of a slave, are Porcia's father, there's her mother to think of too. And I can assure you that I will never let my son marry the child of a woman who can't wait for her husband to come home!''

In the old days he would have flown at her verbally, shouted and badgered. Today he stiffened, said nothing for a long moment.

''I think that statement needs elucidating,'' he said at last.

''I am happy to oblige. Atilia has been a very naughty girl.''

''Oh, Servilia, you are one of the best reasons why Rome needs a few laws on the books to oblige people to hold their tongues!''

Servilia smiled sweetly. ''Ask any of your friends if you doubt me. Ask Bibulus or Favonius or Ahenobarbus, they've been here to witness the carryings-on. It's no secret.''

His mouth drew in, lips disappearing. ''Who?'' he asked.

''Why, that Roman among Romans, of course! Caesar. And don't ask which Caesar—you know which Caesar has the reputation. My darling Brutus's prospective father-in-law.''

Cato rose without a word.

He went home immediately to his modest house in a modest lane at the viewless center of the Palatine, wherein he had installed his philosopher friend, Athenodorus Cordylion, in the only guest suite before he had remembered to greet his wife and children.

Reflection confirmed Servilia's malice. Atilia *was* different. For one thing, she smiled occasionally and presumed to speak before being spoken to; for another, her breasts had filled out, and that in some peculiar way revolted him. Though three days had elapsed since his arriving in Rome, he had not visited her sleeping cubicle (he preferred to occupy the master sleeping cubicle alone) to assuage what even his revered great-grandfather Cato the Censor had deemed a natural urge, not only permissible between man and wife (or slave and master), but really quite an admirable urge.

Oh, what dear kind benevolent God had prevented him? To have put himself inside his legal property not knowing that she had become someone else's illegal property—Cato shivered, had to force down his rising gorge. Caesar. Gaius Julius Caesar, the worst of a decayed and degenerate lot. What on earth had he seen in Atilia, whom Cato had chosen because she was the absolute opposite of round, dark, adorable Aemilia Lepida? Cato knew himself to be a little intellectually slow because it had been drummed into him from infancy that he was, but he didn't have to search very far for Caesar's reason. Patrician though he was, that man was going to be a demagogue, another Gaius Marius. How many wives of the stalwart traditionalists had he seduced? Rumor was rife. Yet here was he, Marcus Porcius Cato, not old enough yet to be in the Senate—but obviously deemed a future enemy of note. That was good! It said he, Marcus Porcius Cato, had the strength and will to be a great force in Forum and Senate. Caesar had cuckolded *him*! Not for one moment did it occur to him that Servilia was the cause, for he had no idea Servilia lived on intimate terms with Caesar.

Well, Atilia may have admitted Caesar into her bed and between her legs, but she hadn't admitted Cato since the day it happened. What Caepio's death had begun, Atilia's treachery finished. Never care! Never, never care! To care meant endless pain.

He did not interview Atilia. He simply summoned his steward to his study and instructed the man to pack her up and throw her out at once, send her back to her brother.

A few words scrawled on a sheet of paper, and the deed was done. She was divorced, and he would not give back one sestertius of an adultress's dowry. As he waited in his study he heard her voice in the distance, a wail, a sob, a frantic scream for her children, and all the time his steward's voice overriding hers, the noise of slaves falling over each other to do the master's bidding. Finally came the front door opening, closing. After which, his steward's knock.

"The lady Atilia is gone, *domine*."

"Send my children to me."

They came in not many moments later, bewildered at the fuss but unaware what had taken place. That both were his he could not deny, even now that doubt gnawed. Porcia was six years old, tall and thin and angular, with his chestnut hair in a thicker and curlier version, his grey and well-spaced eyes, his long neck, his nose in a smaller form. Cato Junior was two years younger, a skinny little boy who always reminded Cato of what he himself had been like in the days when that Marsian upstart Silo had held him out the window and threatened to drop him on sharp rocks; except that Cato Junior was timid rather than doughty, and tended to cry easily. And, alas, already it was apparent that Porcia was the clever one, the little orator and philosopher. Useless gifts in a girl.

"Children, I have divorced your mother for infidelity," said Cato in his normal harsh voice, and without expression. "She has been unchaste, and proven herself unfit to be wife or mother. I have forbidden her entry to this house, and I will not allow either of you to see her again."

The little boy hardly understood all these grown-up words, save that something awful had just happened, and that Mama was at the heart of it. His big grey eyes filled with tears; his lip wobbled. That he did not burst into howls was purely due to his sister's sudden grip on his arm, the signal that he must control himself. And she, small Stoic who would have died to please her father, stood straight and looked indomitable, no tear or wobble of the lip.

"Mama has gone into exile," she said.

"That is as good a way of putting it as any."

"Is she still a citizen?" asked Porcia in a voice very like her father's, no lilt or melody to it.

"I cannot deprive her of that, Porcia, nor would I want to. What I have deprived her of is any participation in our lives, for she does not deserve to participate. Your mother is a bad woman. A slut, a whore, a harlot, an adultress. She has been consorting with a man called Gaius Julius Caesar, and he is all that the Patriciate stands for— corrupt, immoral, outmoded."

"Will we truly never see Mama again?"

"Not while you live under my roof."

The intent behind the grown-up words had finally sunk in; four-year-old Cato Junior began to wail desolately. "I want my mama! I want my mama! I want my mama!"

"Tears are not a right act," said the father, "when they are shed for unworthy reasons. You will behave like a proper Stoic and stop this unmanly weeping. You cannot have your mother, and that is that. Porcia, take him away. The next time I see him I expect to see a man, not a silly runny-nosed baby."

"I will make him understand," she said, gazing at her father in blind adoration. "As long as we are with you, Pater, everything is all right. It is you we love most, not Mama."

Cato froze. "Never love!" he shouted. "Never, never love! A Stoic does not love! A Stoic does not want to be loved!"

"I didn't think Zeno forbade love, just wrong acts," said the daughter. "Is it not a right act to love all that is good? You are good, Pater. I must love you, Zeno says it is a right act."

How to answer that? "Then temper it with detachment and never let it rule you," he said. "Nothing which debases the mind must rule, and emotions debase the mind."

When the children had gone, Cato too left the room. Not far down the colonnade were Athenodorus Cordylion, a flagon of wine, some good books, and even better conversation. From this day on, wine and books and conversation must fill every void.

Ah, but it cost Cato dearly to meet the brilliant and feted curule aedile as he went about his duties so stunningly well, and with such a flair!

"He acts as if he's King of Rome," said Cato to Bibulus.

"I think he believes he's King of Rome, dispensing grain and circuses. Everything in the grand manner, from the easy way he has with ordinary people to his arrogance in the Senate."

"He is my avowed enemy."

"He's the enemy of every man who wants the proper *mos maiorum,* no man to stand one iota taller than any of his peers," said Bibulus. "I will fight him until I die!"

"He's Gaius Marius all over again," said Cato.

But Bibulus looked scornful. "*Marius?* No, Cato, no! Gaius Marius knew he could never be King of Rome—he was just a squire from Arpinum, like his equally bucolic cousin Cicero. Caesar is no Marius, take my word for it. Caesar is another Sulla, and that is far, far worse."

In July of that year Marcus Porcius Cato was elected one of the quaestors, and drew a lot for the senior of the three urban quaestors; his two colleagues were the great plebeian aristocrat Marcus Claudius Marcellus and a Lollius from that Picentine family Pompey the Great was happily thrusting into the heart of Roman dominance of Senate and Comitia.

With some months to go before he actually took office or was allowed to attend the Senate, Cato occupied his days in studying commerce and commercial law; he hired a retired Treasury bookkeeper to teach him how the *tribuni aerarii* who headed that domain did their accounting, and he ground away at what did not come at all naturally until he knew as much about State finances as Caesar knew, unaware that what cost him so much pain had been taken in almost instantly by his avowed enemy.

The quaestors took their duty lightly and never both-

ered to concern themselves overmuch with an actual po-
licing of what went on in the Treasury; the important part
of the job to the average urban quaestor was liaison with
the Senate, which debated and then deputed where the
State's moneys were to go. It was accepted practice to cast
a cursory eye over the books Treasury staff let them see
from time to time, and to accept Treasury figures when
the Senate considered Rome's finances. The quaestors also
did their friends and families favors if these people were
in debt to the State by turning a blind eye to the fact or
ordering their names erased from the official records. In
short, the quaestors located in Rome simply permitted the
permanent Treasury staff to go about their business and
get the work done. And certainly neither the permanent
Treasury staff nor Marcellus and Lollius, the two other
urban quaestors, had any idea that things were about to
change radically.

Cato had no intention of being lax. He intended to
be more thorough within the Treasury than Pompey the
Great within Our Sea. At dawn on the fifth day of December, the day he took office, he was there knocking at the
door in the side of the basement to the temple of Saturn,
not pleased to learn that the sun was well up before anyone
came to work.

"The workday begins at dawn," he said to the Treasury chief, Marcus Vibius, when that worthy arrived
breathless after a harried clerk had sent for him urgently.

"There is no rule to that effect," said Marcus Vibius
smoothly. "We work within a timetable we set for ourselves, and it's flexible."

"Rubbish!" said Cato scornfully. "I am the elected
custodian of these premises, and I intend to see that the
Senate and People of Rome get value for every sestertius
of their tax moneys. Their tax moneys pay you and all the
rest who work here, don't forget!"

Not a good beginning. From that point on, however,
things for Marcus Vibius just got worse and worse. He
had a zealot on his hands. When on the rare occasions in
the past he had found himself cursed with an obstreperous
quaestor, he had proceeded to put the fellow in his place

by withholding all specialized knowledge of the job; not having a Treasury background, quaestors could do only what they were allowed to do. Unfortunately that tack didn't stop Cato, who revealed that he knew quite as much about how the Treasury functioned as Marcus Vibius did. Possibly more.

With him Cato had brought several slaves whom he had seen trained in various aspects of Treasury pursuits, and every day he was there at dawn with his little retinue to drive Vibius and his underlings absolutely mad. What was this? Why was that? Where was so-and-so? When had such-and-such? How did whatever happen? And on and on and on. Cato was persistent to the point of insult, impossible to fob off with pat answers, and impervious to irony, sarcasm, abuse, flattery, excuses, fainting fits.

"I feel," gasped Marcus Vibius after two months of this, when he had gathered up his courage to seek solace and assistance from his patron, Catulus, "as if all the Furies are hounding me harder than ever they hounded Orestes! I don't care what you have to do to shut Cato up and ship him out, I just want it done! I have been your loyal and devoted client for over twenty years, I am a *tribunus aerarius* of the First Class, and now I find both my sanity and my position imperiled. Get rid of Cato!"

The first attempt failed miserably. Catulus proposed to the House that Cato be given a special task, checking army accounts, as he was so brilliant at checking accounts. But Cato simply stood his ground by recommending the names of four men who could be temporarily employed to do a job no elected quaestor should be asked to do. Thank you, he would stick to what he was there for.

After that Catulus thought of craftier ploys, none of which worked. While the broom sweeping out every corner of the Treasury never wore down or wore out. In March the heads began to roll. First one, then two, then three and four and five Treasury officials found Cato had terminated their tenure and emptied out their desks. Then in April the axe descended: Cato fired Marcus Vibius, and added insult to injury by having him prosecuted for fraud.

Neatly caught in the patron's trap, Catulus had no

alternative other than to defend Vibius personally in court. One day's airing of the evidence was enough to tell Catulus that he was going to lose. Time to appeal to Cato's sense of fitness, to the time-honored precepts of the client-and-patron system.

"My dear Cato, you must stop," said Catulus as the court broke up for the day. "I know poor Vibius hasn't been as careful as perhaps he ought, but he's *one of us*! Fire all the clerks and bookkeepers you like, but leave poor Vibius in his job, please! I give you my solemn word as a consular and an ex-censor that from now on Vibius will behave impeccably. Just drop this awful prosecution! Leave the man something!"

This had been said softly, but Cato had only one vocal volume, and that was top of his voice. His answer was shouted in his usual stentorian tones, and arrested all progress out of the area. Every face turned; every ear cocked to listen.

"Quintus Lutatius, you ought to be ashamed of yourself!" yelled Cato. "How could you be so blind to your own *dignitas* as to have the effrontery to remind me you're a consular and ex-censor, then try to wheedle me out of doing my sworn duty? Well, let me tell you that I will be ashamed if I have to summon the court's bailiffs to eject you for attempting to pervert the course of Roman justice! For that is what you're doing, perverting Roman justice!"

Whereupon he stalked off, leaving Catulus standing bereft of speech, so nonplussed that when the case resumed the following day he didn't appear for the defense at all. Instead, he tried to acquit himself of his patron's duty by talking the jury into a verdict of ABSOLVO even if Cato succeeded in producing more damning evidence than Cicero had to convict Verres. Bribe he would not; talk was both cheaper and more ethical. One of the jurors was Marcus Lollius, Cato's colleague in the quaestorship. And Lollius agreed to vote for acquittal. He was, however, extremely ill, so Catulus had him carried into court on a litter. When the verdict came in, it was ABSOLVO. Lollius's vote had tied the jury, and a tied jury meant acquittal.

Did that defeat Cato? No, it did not. When Vibius turned up at the Treasury, he found Cato barring his path. Nor would Cato consent to re-employ him. In the end even Catulus, summoned to preside over the unpleasantly public scene outside the door into the Treasury, had to give up. Vibius had lost his position, and that was going to be that. Then Cato refused to give Vibius the pay owing to him.

"You must!" cried Catulus.

"I must not!" cried Cato. "He cheated the State, he owes the State far more than his pay. Let it help to compensate Rome."

"Why, why, why?" Catulus demanded. "Vibius was acquitted!"

"I am not," shouted Cato, "going to take the vote of a sick man into account! He was out of his head with fever."

And so in the end it had to be left. Absolutely sure that Cato would lose, the survivors in the Treasury had been planning all kinds of celebrations. But after Catulus shepherded the weeping Vibius away, the survivors in the Treasury took the hint. As if by magic every account and every set of books settled into perfect order; debtors were made to rectify years of neglected repayments, and creditors were suddenly reimbursed sums outstanding for years. Marcellus, Lollius, Catulus and the rest of the Senate took the hint too. The Great Treasury War was over, and only one man stood on his feet: Marcus Porcius Cato. Whom all of Rome was praising, amazed that the Government of Rome had finally produced a man so incorruptible he couldn't be bought. Cato was famous.

"What I don't understand," said a shaken Catulus to his much loved brother-in-law Hortensius, "is what Cato intends to make of his life! Does he really think he can vote-catch by being utterly incorruptible? It will work in the tribal elections, perhaps, but if he continues as he's begun, he'll never win an election in the Centuries. No one in the First Class will vote for him."

Hortensius was inclined to temporize. "I understand what an invidious position he put you in, Quintus, but I must say I do rather admire him. Because you're right.

He'll never win a consular election in the Centuries. Imagine the kind of passion it needs to produce Cato's sort of integrity!''

''You,'' snarled Catulus, losing his temper, ''are a fish-fancying dilettante with more money than sense!''

But having won the Great Treasury War, Marcus Porcius Cato set out to find fresh fields of endeavor, and succeeded when he started perusing the financial records stored in Sulla's Tabularium. Out of date they might be, but one set of accounts, very well kept, suggested the theme of his next war. These were the records itemizing all those who during Sulla's dictatorship had been paid the sum of two talents for proscribing men as traitors to the State. In themselves they spoke no more than figures could, but Cato began to investigate each person on the list who had been paid two talents (and sometimes several lots of two talents) with a view to prosecuting those who turned out to have extracted it by violence. At the time it had been legal to kill a man once he was proscribed, but Sulla's day had gone, and Cato thought little of the legal chances these hated and reviled men would stand in today's courts—even if today's courts were Sulla's brainchild.

Sadly, one small canker ate at the righteous virtue of Cato's motives, for in this new project he saw an opportunity to make life very difficult for Gaius Julius Caesar. Having finished his year as curule aedile, Caesar had been given another job; he was appointed as the *iudex* of the Murder Court.

It never occurred to Cato that Caesar would be willing to co-operate with a member of the *boni* by trying those recipients of two talents who had murdered to get them; expecting the usual sort of obstructive tactics that court presidents used to wriggle out of trying people they didn't think ought to be on trial, Cato discovered to his chagrin that Caesar was not only willing, but even prepared to be helpful.

''You send them, I'll try them,'' said Caesar to Cato cheerfully.

Despite the fact that all of Rome had buzzed when Cato divorced Atilia and sent her back dowerless to her family, citing Caesar as her lover, it was not in Caesar's nature to feel at a disadvantage in these dealings with Cato. Nor was it in Caesar's nature to suffer qualms of conscience or pity at Atilia's fate; she had taken her chances, she could always have said no. Thus the president of the Murder Court and the incorruptible quaestor did well together.

Then Cato abandoned the small fish, the slaves, freedmen and centurions who had used those two-talent rewards to found fortunes. He decided to charge Catilina with the murder of Marcus Marius Gratidianus. It had happened after Sulla won the battle at the Colline Gate of Rome, and Marius Gratidianus had been Catilina's brother-in-law at the time. Later, Catilina inherited the estate.

"He's a bad man, and I'm going to get him," said Cato to Caesar. "If I don't, he'll be consul next year."

"What do you suspect he might do if he were consul?" Caesar asked, curious. "I agree that he's a bad man, but—"

"If he became consul, he'd set himself up as another Sulla."

"As Dictator? He couldn't."

These days Cato's eyes were full of pain, but they looked into Caesar's cold pale orbs sternly. "He's a Sergius; he has the oldest blood in Rome, even including yours, Caesar. If Sulla had not had the blood, he couldn't have succeeded. That's why I don't trust any of you antique aristocrats. You're descended from kings and you all want to be kings."

"You're wrong, Cato. At least about me. As to Catilina—well, his activities under Sulla were certainly abhorrent, so why not try? I just don't think you'll succeed."

"Oh, I'll succeed!" shouted Cato. "I have dozens of witnesses to swear they saw Catilina lop Gratidianus's head off."

"You'd do better to postpone the trial until just before the elections," Caesar said steadily. "My court is quick, I don't waste any time. If you arraign him now, the trial will be over before applications close for the curule elections. That means Catilina will be able to stand if he's acquitted. Whereas if you arraign him later, my cousin Lucius Caesar as supervisor would never permit the candidacy of a man facing a murder charge.''

"That," said Cato stubbornly, "only postpones the evil day. I want Catilina banished from Rome and any dream of being consul.''

"All right then, but be it on your own head!" said Caesar.

The truth was that Cato's head had been just a little turned and swollen by his victories to date. Sums of two talents were pouring into the Treasury now because Cato insisted on enforcing the law the consul/censor Lentulus Clodianus had put on the tablets some years before, requiring that all such moneys be paid back no matter how peacefully they had been collected. Cato could foresee no obstacles in the case of Lucius Sergius Catilina. As quaestor he didn't prosecute himself, but he spent much thought on choosing a prosecutor—Lucius Lucceius, close friend of Pompey's and an orator of great distinction. This, as Cato well knew, was a shrewd move; it proclaimed that Catilina's trial was not at the whim of the *boni,* but an affair all Roman men must take seriously, as one of Pompey's friends was collaborating with the *boni.* Caesar too!

When Catilina heard what was in the wind, he shut his teeth together and cursed. For two consular elections in a row he had seen himself denied the chance to stand because of a trial process; now here he was again, on trial. Time to see an end to them, these twisted persecutions aimed at the heart of the Patriciate by mushrooms like Cato, descended from a slave. For generations the Sergii had been excluded from the highest offices in Rome due to poverty—a fact that had been as true of the Julii Caesares until Gaius Marius permitted them to rise again. Well, Sulla had permitted the Sergii to rise again, and Lucius Sergius Catilina was going to put his clan back in the consul's ivory chair if he had to overthrow the whole of Rome to do so! He had, besides, a very ambitious wife in the beauteous Aurelia Orestilla; he loved her madly and he wanted to please her. That meant becoming consul.

It was when he understood that the trial would come on well before the elections that he decided on a course of action: this time he would be acquitted in time to stand—*if* he could ensure acquittal. So he went to see Marcus Crassus and struck a bargain with that senatorial plutocrat. In return for Crassus's support throughout the trial, he undertook when consul to push Crassus's two pet schemes through the Senate and the Popular Assembly. The Trans-Padane Gauls would be enfranchised, and Egypt formally annexed into the empire of Rome as Crassus's private fief.

Though his name was never bruited as one of Rome's outstanding advocates for technique, brilliance or oratorical skills, Crassus nonetheless had a formidable reputation in the courts because of his doggedness and his immense willingness to defend even the humblest of his clients to the top of his bent. He was also very much respected and cultivated in knight circles because so much Crassus capital underlay all kinds of business ventures. And these days all juries were tripartite, consisting of one third of senators, one third of knights belonging to the Eighteen, and one third of knights belonging to the more junior *tribuni aerarii* Centuries. It was therefore safe to say that Crassus had tremendous influence with at least two thirds of any jury, and that this influence extended to those senators who owed him money. All of which meant that Crassus didn't need to bribe a jury to secure the verdict he wanted; the jury was disposed to believe that whatever verdict he wanted was the right verdict to deliver.

Catilina's defense was simple. Yes, he had indeed lopped off the head of his brother-in-law, Marcus Marius Gratidianus; he did not deny the deed because he could not deny the deed. But at the time he had been one of Sulla's legates, and he had acted under Sulla's orders. Sulla had wanted Marius Gratidianus's head to fire into Praeneste as a missile aimed at convincing Young Marius that he couldn't succeed in defying Sulla any longer.

Caesar presided over a court which listened patiently to the prosecutor Lucius Lucceius and his team of supporting counsel, and realized very soon that it was a court which had no intention of convicting Catilina. Nor did it. The verdict came in ABSOLVO by a large majority, and even Cato afterward was unable to find hard evidence that Crassus had needed to bribe.

"I told you so," said Caesar to Cato.

"It isn't over yet!" barked Cato, and stalked off.

There were seven candidates for the consulship when the nominations closed, and the field was an interesting one. His acquittal meant Catilina had declared himself, and he had to be regarded as a virtual certainty for one of the two posts. As Cato had said, he had the blood. He was also the same charming and persuasive man he had been at the time he wooed the Vestal Virgin Fabia, so his following was very large. If too it consisted of too many men who skated perilously close to ruin, that did not negate its power. Besides which, it was now generally known that Marcus Crassus supported him, and Marcus Crassus commanded very many of the First Class of voters.

Servilia's husband Silanus was another candidate, though his health was not good; had he been hale and hearty, he would have had little trouble in gathering enough votes to be elected. But the fate of Quintus Marcius Rex, doomed to be sole consul by the deaths of his junior colleague and then the suffect replacement, intruded into everyone's mind. Silanus didn't look as if he would last out his year, and no one thought it wise to let Catilina hold the reins of Rome without a colleague, Crassus notwithstanding.

Another likely candidate was the vile Gaius Antonius Hybrida, whom Caesar had tried unsuccessfully to prosecute for the torture, maiming and murder of many Greek citizens during Sulla's Greek wars. Hybrida had eluded justice, but public opinion inside Rome had forced him to go into a voluntary exile on the island of Cephallenia; the discovery of some grave mounds had yielded him fabulous wealth, so when he returned to Rome to find himself expelled from the Senate, Hybrida simply started again. First he re-entered the Senate by becoming a tribune of the plebs; then in the following year he bribed his way into a praetorship, ardently supported by that ambitious and able New Man Cicero, who had cause to be grateful to him. Poor Cicero had found himself in a severe financial embarrassment brought about by his passion for collecting Greek statues and installing them in a plethora of country villas; it was Hybrida who lent him the money to extricate himself. Ever since then Cicero spoke up for him, and was doing so at the moment so strenuously that it could safely be deduced that he and Hybrida were planning to run as a team for the consulship, Cicero lending their campaign respectability and Hybrida putting up the money.

The man who might have offered Catilina the stiffest competition was undoubtedly Marcus Tullius Cicero, but the trouble was that Cicero had no ancestors; he was a *homo novus,* a New Man. Sheer legal and oratorical brilliance had pushed him steadily up the *cursus honorum,* but much of the First Class of the Centuries deemed him a presumptuous hayseed, as did the *boni.* Consuls ought to be men of proven Roman origins, and from illustrious families. Though everyone knew Cicero to be an honest man of high ability (and knew Catilina to be extremely shady), still and all the feeling in Rome was that Catilina deserved the consulship ahead of Cicero.

After Catilina was acquitted, Cato held a conference with Bibulus and Ahenobarbus, who had been quaestor two years before; all three were now in the Senate, which meant they were now fully entrenched within the ultraconservative rump, the *boni.*

"We *cannot* permit Catilina to be elected consul!" brayed Cato. "He's seduced the rapacious Marcus Crassus into supporting him."

"I agree," said Bibulus calmly. "Between the two of them, they'll wreak havoc on the *mos maiorum.* The Senate will be full of Gauls, and Rome will have another province to worry about."

"What do we do?" asked Ahenobarbus, a young man more famous for the quality of his temper than his intellect.

"We seek an interview with Catulus and Hortensius," Bibulus said, "and between us we work out a way to swing opinion in the First Class from the idea of Catilina as consul." He cleared his throat. "However, I suggest that we appoint Cato the leader of our deputation."

"I refuse to be a leader of any kind!" yelled Cato.

"Yes, I know that," Bibulus said patiently, "but the fact remains that ever since the Great Treasury War you've become a symbol to most of Rome. You may be the youngest of us, but you're also the most respected. Catulus and Hortensius are well aware of that. Therefore you will act as our spokesman."

"It ought to be you" from Cato, annoyed.

"The *boni* are against men thinking themselves better than their peers, and I am of the *boni,* Marcus. Whoever is the most suitable on a particular day is the spokesman. Today, that's you."

"What I don't understand," said Ahenobarbus, "is why *we* have to seek an audience at all. Catulus is our leader, he ought to be summoning us."

"He's not himself," Bibulus explained. "When Caesar humiliated him in the House over that battering-ram business, he lost clout." The cool silvery gaze transferred to Cato. "Nor were you very tactful, Marcus, when you humiliated him in public while Vibius was on trial for fraud. Caesar was self-evident, but a man loses huge amounts of clout when his own adherents upbraid him."

"He shouldn't have said what he did to me!"

Bibulus sighed. "Sometimes, Cato, you're more a liability than an asset!"

The note asking Catulus for an audience was under Cato's seal, and written by Cato. Catulus summoned his brother-in-law Hortensius (Catulus was married to Hortensius's sister, Hortensia, and Hortensius was married to Catulus's sister, Lutatia) feeling a small glow of pleasure; that Cato should seek his help was balm to his wounded pride.

"I agree that Catilina cannot be allowed the consulship," he said stiffly. "His deal with Marcus Crassus is now public property because the man can't resist an opportunity to boast, and at this stage he's convinced he can't lose. I've been thinking a lot about the problem, and I've come to the conclusion that we ought to use Catilina's boasting of his alliance with Marcus Crassus. There are many knights who esteem Crassus, but only because there are limitations to his power. I predict that droves of knights won't want to see Crassus's influence increased by an influx of clients from across the Padus, as well as from all that Egyptian money. If they thought Crassus would share Egypt with them, it would be different, but luckily everyone knows Crassus won't share. Though technically Egypt would belong to Rome, in actual fact it would become the private kingdom of Marcus Licinius Crassus to rape to his heart's content.''

"The trouble is,'' said Quintus Hortensius, "that the rest of the field is horribly unappealing. Silanus, yes—if he were a well man, which he's so obviously not. Besides which, he declined to take a province after his term as praetor on the grounds of ill health, and that won't impress the voters. Some of the candidates—Minucius Thermus, for example—are hopeless.''

"There's Antonius Hybrida,'' said Ahenobarbus.

Bibulus's lip curled. "If we take Hybrida—a bad man, but so monumentally inert that he won't do the State any harm—we also have to take that self-opinionated pimple Cicero.''

A gloomy silence fell, broken by Catulus.

"Then the real decision is, which one of two unpalatable men is the preferable alternative?'' he said slowly. "Do the *boni* want Catilina with Crassus triumphantly pulling his strings, or do we want a low-class braggart like Cicero lording it over us?''

"Cicero,'' said Hortensius.

"Cicero,'' said Bibulus.

"Cicero,'' said Ahenobarbus.

And, very reluctantly from Cato, "Cicero.''

"Very well,'' said Catulus, "Cicero it is. Ye Gods, I'll find it hard to hang on to my gorge in the House next year! A jumped-up New Man as one of Rome's consuls. Tchah!''

"Then I suggest,'' said Hortensius, pulling a face,

"that we all eat very sparingly before meetings of the Senate next year."

The group dispersed to go to work, and for a month they worked very hard indeed. Much to Catulus's chagrin it became obvious that Cato, barely thirty years old, was the one who had the most clout. The Great Treasury War and all those proscription rewards safely back in the State coffers had made a terrific impression on the First Class, who had been the ones to suffer most under Sulla's proscriptions. Cato was a hero to the Ordo Equester, and if Cato said to vote for Cicero and Hybrida, then that was whom every knight lower than the Eighteen would vote for!

The result was that the consuls-elect were Marcus Tullius Cicero in senior place and Gaius Antonius Hybrida as his junior colleague. Cicero was jubilant, never really understanding that he owed his victory to circumstances having nothing to do with merit or integrity or clout. Had Catilina not been a candidate, Cicero would never have been elected at all. But as no one told him this, he strutted around Forum Romanum and Senate in a daze of happiness liberally larded with conceit. Oh, what a year! Senior consul *in suo anno,* the proud father of a son at last, and his fourteen-year-old daughter, Tullia, formally betrothed to the wealthy and august Gaius Calpurnius Piso Frugi. Even Terentia was being nice to him!

When Lucius Decumius heard that the present consuls, Lucius Caesar and Marcius Figulus, proposed to legislate the crossroads colleges out of existence, he was thrown into a panic-stricken rage and horror, and ran immediately to see his patron, Caesar.

"This," he said wrathfully, "is just not fair! When has we ever done anything wrong? We minds our own business!"

A statement which threw Caesar into a dilemma, for he of course knew the circumstances leading to the proposed new law.

It all went back to the consulship of Gaius Piso three years earlier, and to the tribunate of the plebs of Pompey's

man, Gaius Manilius. It had been Aulus Gabinius's job to
secure the eradication of the pirates for Pompey; now it
became Gaius Manilius's job to secure the command
against the two kings for Pompey. In one way an easier
job, thanks to Pompey's brilliant handling of the pirates,
yet in another way a more difficult job, as those opposed
to special commands could see only too clearly that Pompey was a man of enormous ability who might just use
this new commission to make himself Dictator when he
returned victorious from the East. And with Gaius Piso as
sole consul, Manilius faced an adamant and irascible foe
in the Senate.

At first glance Manilius's initial bill seemed harmless
and irrelevant to Pompey's concerns: he merely asked the
Plebeian Assembly to distribute Rome's citizen freedmen
across the full gamut of the thirty-five tribes, instead of
keeping them confined to two urban tribes, Suburana and
Esquilina. But no one was fooled. Manilius's bill directly
affected senators and senior knights, as they were both the
major slave owners and those who had multitudes of freedmen in their clienteles.

A stranger to the way Rome worked might have been
pardoned for assuming that the law of numbers would ensure that any measure altering the status of Rome's freedmen would make no difference, for the definition of abject
poverty in Rome was a man's inability to own one slave—
and there were few indeed who did not own one slave.
Therefore on the surface any plebiscite distributing freedmen across all thirty-five tribes should have little effect on
the top end of society. But such was not the case.

The vast majority of slave owners in Rome kept no
more than that single slave, or perhaps two slaves. But
these were not male slaves; they were female. For two
reasons: the first, that her master could enjoy a female
slave's sexual favors, and the second, that a male slave
was a temptation to the master's wife, and the paternity
of his children suspect in consequence. After all, what
need had a poor man for a male slave? Servile duties were
domestic—washing, fetching water, preparing meals, assisting with the children, emptying chamber pots—and not

well done by men. Attitudes of mind didn't change just because a person was unlucky enough to be slave rather than free; men liked to do men's things, and despised the lot of women as drudgery.

Theoretically every slave was paid a *peculium* and got his or her keep besides; the little sum of money was hoarded to buy freedom. But practically, freedom was something only the well-to-do master could afford to bestow, especially since manumission carried a five percent tax. With the result that the bulk of Rome's female slaves were never freed while useful (and, fearing destitution more than unpaid labor, they contrived to remain useful even after they grew old). Nor could they afford to belong to a burial club enabling them to buy a funeral after death, together with decent interment. They wound up in the lime pits without so much as a grave marker to say they had ever existed.

Only those Romans with a relatively high income and a number of households to maintain owned many slaves. The higher a Roman's social and economic status, the more servants in his employ—and the more likely he was to have males among them. In these echelons manumission was common and a slave's service limited to between ten and fifteen years, after which he (it was usually he) became a freedman in the clientele of his previous master. He donned the Cap of Liberty and became a Roman citizen; if he had a wife and adult children, they too were freed.

His vote, however, was useless unless—as did happen from time to time—he made a large amount of money and bought himself membership in one of the thirty-one rural tribes, as well as being economically qualified to belong to a Class in the Centuries. But the great majority remained in the urban tribes of Suburana and Esquilina, which were the two most enormous tribes Rome owned, yet were able to deliver only two votes in the tribal Assemblies. This meant that a freedman's vote could not affect a tribal Assembly vote result.

Gaius Manilius's projected bill therefore had huge significance. Were Rome's freedmen to be distributed

across the thirty-five tribes, they might alter the outcome
of tribal elections and legislation, and this despite the fact
that they were not in a majority among the citizens of
Rome. The prospective danger lay in the fact that freedmen lived *inside* the city; were they to belong to rural
tribes, they could by voting in these rural tribes outnumber
the genuine rural tribe members present inside Rome during a vote. Not such a problem for the elections, held
during summer when many rural people were inside
Rome, but a serious peril for legislation. Legislation happened at any time of year, but was particularly prevalent
during December, January and February, the months
which saw the lawmaking pinnacle of the new tribunes of
the plebs—and months when rural citizens did not come
to Rome.

Manilius's bill went down to decisive defeat. The
freedmen remained in those two gigantic urban tribes. But
where it spelled trouble for men like Lucius Decimius lay
in the fact that Manilius had sought out Rome's freedmen
to drum up support for his bill. And where did Rome's
freedmen congregate? In crossroads colleges, as they were
convivial places as stuffed with slaves and freedmen as
they were with ordinary Roman lowly. Manilius had gone
from one crossroads college to another, talking to the men
his law would benefit, persuading them to go to the Forum
and support him. Knowing themselves possessed of worthless votes, many freedmen had obliged him. But when the
Senate and the senior knights of the Eighteen saw these
masses of freedmen descend on the Forum, all they could
think of was the danger. Anyplace where freedmen gathered ought to be outlawed. The crossroads colleges would
have to go.

A crossroads was a hotbed of spiritual activity, and
had to be guarded against evil forces. It was a place where
the Lares congregated, and the Lares were the myriad
wraiths which peopled the Underworld and found a natural
focus for their forces at a crossroads. Thus each crossroads
had a shrine to the Lares, and once a year around the start
of January a festival called the Compitalia was devoted to
the placation of the Lares of the crossroads. On the night

before the Compitalia every free resident of the district leading to a crossroads was obliged to hang up a woolen doll, and every slave a woolen ball; in Rome the shrines were so overwhelmed by dolls and balls that one of the duties of the crossroads colleges was to rig up lines to hold them. Dolls had heads, and a free person had a head counted by the censors; balls had no heads, for slaves were not counted. Slaves were, however, an important part of the festivities. As on the Saturnalia, they feasted as equals with the free men and women of Rome, and it was the duty of slaves (stripped of their servile insignia) to make the offering of a fattened pig to the Lares. All of which was under the authority of the crossroads colleges and the urban praetor, their supervisor.

Thus a crossroads college was a religious brotherhood. Each one had a custodian, the *vilicus,* who made sure that the men of his district gathered regularly in rent-free premises close to the crossroads and the Lares shrine; they kept the shrine and the crossroads neat, clean, unattractive to evil forces. Many of Rome's intersections did not have a shrine, as these were limited to the major junctions.

One such crossroads college lay in the ground-floor apex of Aurelia's insula under the care of Lucius Decumius. Until Aurelia had tamed him after she moved into her insula, Lucius Decumius had run an extremely profitable side business guaranteeing protection to the shop owners and factory proprietors in his district; when Aurelia exerted that formidable strength of hers and demonstrated to Lucius Decumius that she was not to be gainsaid, he solved his quandary by moving his protection business to the outer Sacra Via and the Vicus Fabricii, where the local colleges were lacking in such enterprise. Though his census was of the Fourth Class and his tribe urban Suburana, Lucius Decumius was definitely a power to be reckoned with.

Allied with his fellow custodians of Rome's other crossroads colleges, he had successfully fought Gaius Piso's attempt to close down all the crossroads colleges because Manilius had exploited them. Gaius Piso and the *boni* had therefore been forced to look elsewhere for a victim, and chose Manilius himself, who managed to survive a trial for extortion, then was convicted of treason and exiled for life, his fortune confiscated to the last sestertius.

Unfortunately the threat to the crossroads colleges did not go away after Gaius Piso left office. The Senate and the knights of the Eighteen had got it into their heads that the existence of crossroads colleges provided rent-free premises wherein political dissidents might gather and fraternize under religious auspices. Now Lucius Caesar and Marcius Figulus were going to ban them.

Which led to Lucius Decumius's wrathful appearance at Caesar's rooms on the Vicus Patricii.

"It isn't fair!" he repeated.

"I know, dad," said Caesar, sighing.

"Then what are you going to do about it?" the old man demanded.

"I'll try, dad, that goes without saying. However, I doubt there's anything I can do. I knew you'd come to see me, so I've already talked to my cousin Lucius, only to learn that he and Marcius Figulus are quite determined. With very few exceptions, they intend to outlaw every college, sodality and club in Rome."

"Who gets excepted?" Lucius Decumius barked, jaw set.

"Religious sodalities like the Jews. Legitimate burial clubs. The colleges of civil servants. Trade guilds. That's all."

"But we're religious!"

"According to my cousin Lucius Caesar, not religious enough. The Jews don't drink and gossip in their synagogues, and the Salii, the Luperci, the Arval Brethren and others rarely meet at all. Crossroads colleges have premises wherein all men are welcome, including slaves and freedmen. That makes them potentially very dangerous, it's being said."

"So who's going to care for the Lares and their shrines?"

"The urban praetor and the aediles."

"They're already too busy!"

"I agree, dad, I agree wholeheartedly," said Caesar. "I even tried to tell my cousin that, but he wouldn't listen."

"Can't you help us, Caesar? Honestly?"

"I'll be voting against it and I'll try to persuade as many others as I can to do the same. Oddly enough, quite a few of the *boni* oppose the law too—the crossroads colleges are a very old tradition, therefore to abolish them offends the *mos maiorum*. Cato is shouting about it loudly. However, it will go through, dad."

"We'll have to shut our doors."

"Oh, not necessarily," said Caesar, smiling.

"I knew you wouldn't let me down! What does we do?"

"You'll definitely lose your official standing, but that merely puts you at a financial disadvantage. I suggest you install a bar and call yourselves a tavern, with you as its proprietor."

"Can't do that, Caesar. Old Roscius next door would complain to the urban praetor in a trice—we've been buying our wine from him since I was a boy."

"Then offer Roscius the bar concession. If you close your doors, dad, he's severely out of purse."

"Could all the colleges do it?"

"Throughout Rome, you mean?"

"Yes."

"I don't see why not. However, due to certain activities I won't name, you're a wealthy college. The consuls are convinced the colleges will have to shut their doors because they'll have to pay ground-floor rents. As you will to my mother, dad. She's a businesswoman, she'll insist. In your case you might get a bit of a discount, but others?" Caesar shrugged. "I doubt the amount of wine consumed would cover expenses."

Brows knitted, Lucius Decumius thought hard. "Does the consuls know what we does for a real living, Caesar?"

"If *I* didn't tell them—and I didn't!—then I don't know who would."

''Then there's no problem!'' said Lucius Decumius cheerfully. ''We're most of us in the same protection business.'' He huffed with great content. ''And we'll go on caring for the crossroads too. Can't have the Lares running riot, can we? I'll call a meeting of us custodians—we'll beat 'em yet, Pavo!''

''That's the spirit, dad!''

And off went Lucius Decumius, beaming.

Autumn that year brought torrential rains to the Apennines, and the Tiber flooded its valley for two hundred miles. It had been some generations since the city of Rome had suffered so badly. Only the seven hills protruded out of the waters; the Forum Romanum, Velabrum, Circus Maximus, Forums Boarium and Holitorium, the whole of the Sacra Via out to the Servian Walls and the manufactories of the Vicus Fabricii drowned. The sewers backwashed; buildings with unsafe foundations crumbled; the sparsely settled heights of Quirinal, Viminal and Aventine became vast camps for refugees; and respiratory diseases raged. Miraculously the incredibly ancient Wooden Bridge survived, perhaps because it lay farthest downstream, whereas the Pons Fabricius between Tiber Island and the Circus Flaminius perished. As this happened too late in the year to stand for next year's tribunate of the plebs, Lucius Fabricius, who was the current promising member of his family, announced that he would stand next year for the tribunate of the plebs. Care of bridges and highways into Rome lay with the tribunes of the plebs, and Fabricius was not about to allow any other man to rebuild what was his family's bridge! The Pons Fabricius it was, and the Pons Fabricius it would remain.

And Caesar received a letter from Gnaeus Pompeius Magnus, conqueror of the East.

Well, Caesar, what a campaign. Both the kings rolled up and everything looking good. I can't understand why Lucullus took so long. Mind you, he couldn't control his troops, yet here I've got every man who served under him, with never a peep out of them. Marcus Silius sends his regards, by the way. A good man.

What a strange place Pontus is. I now see why King Mithridates always had to use mercenaries and northerners in his army. Some of his Pontic people are so primitive that they live in trees. They also brew some sort of foul liquor out of twigs, of all things, though how they manage to drink it and stay alive I don't know. Some of my men were marching through the forest in eastern Pontus and found big bowls of the stuff on the ground. You know soldiers! They guzzled the lot, had a fine time of it. Until they all fell over dead. Killed them!

The booty is unbelievable. I took all those so-called impregnable citadels he built all over Armenia Parva and eastern Pontus, of course. Not very hard to do. Oh, you mightn't know who I mean by "he." Mithridates. Yes, well, the treasures he'd managed to salt away filled every one of them—seventy-odd, all told—to the brim. It will take years to ship the lot back to Rome; I've got an army of clerks taking inventory. It's my reckoning that I'll double what's in the Treasury and then double Rome's income from tributes from now on.

I brought Mithridates to battle in a place in Pontus I renamed Nicopolis—already had a Pompeiopolis—and he went down badly. Escaped to Sinoria, where he grabbed six thousand talents of gold and bolted down the Euphrates to find Tigranes. Who wasn't having a good time of it either! Phraates of the Parthians invaded Armenia while I was tidying up Mithridates, and actually laid siege to Artaxata. Tigranes beat him off, and the Parthians went back home. But it finished Tigranes. He wasn't in a fit state to hold me off, I can tell you! So he sued for a separate peace, and wouldn't let Mithridates enter Armenia. Mithridates went north instead, headed for Cimmeria. What he didn't know was that I've been having some correspondence with the son he'd installed in Cimmeria as satrap—called Machares.

Anyway, I let Tigranes have Armenia, but tributary to Rome, and took everything west of the Euphrates off him along with Sophene and Corduene. Made him pay me the six thousand talents of gold Mithridates filched, and asked for two hundred and forty sesterces for each of my men.

What, wasn't I worried about Mithridates? The answer is no. Mithridates is well into his sixties. Well past it, Caesar. Fabian tactics. I just let the old boy run, couldn't see he was a danger anymore. And I did have Machares. So while Mithridates ran, I marched. For which blame Varro, who doesn't have a bone in his body isn't curious. He was dying to dabble his toes in the Caspian Sea, and I thought, well, why not? So off we went northeastward.

Not much booty and far too many snakes, huge vicious spiders, giant scorpions. Funny how our men will fight all manner of human foes without turning a hair, then scream like women over crawlies. They sent me a deputation begging me to turn back when the Caspian Sea was only miles away. I turned back. Had to. I scream at crawlies too. So does Varro, who by this was quite happy to keep his toes dry.

You probably know that Mithridates is dead, but I'll tell you how it actually happened. He got to Panticapaeum on the Cimmerian Bosporus, and began levying another army. He'd had the forethought to bring plenty of daughters with him, and used them as bait to draw Scythian levies—offered them to the Scythian kings and princes as brides.

You have to admire the old boy's persis-

tence, Caesar. Do you know what he intended to
do? Gather a quarter of a million men and march
on Italia and Rome the long way! He was going
to go right round the top end of the Euxine and
down through the lands of the Roxolani to the
mouth of the Danubius. Then he intended to
march up the Danubius gathering all the tribes
along the way into his forces—Dacians, Bessi,
Dardani, you name them. I hear Burebistas of
the Dacians was very keen. Then he was going
to cross to the Dravus and Savus, and march into
Italia across the Carnic Alps!

Oh, I forgot to say that when he got to Panticapaeum he forced Machares to commit suicide. Bloodthirsty for his own kin, can never
understand that in eastern kings. While he was
busy raising his army, Phanagoria (the town on
the other side of the Bosporus) revolted. The
leader was another son of his, Pharnaces. I'd
also been writing to him. Of course Mithridates
put the rebellion down, but he made one bad
mistake. He pardoned Pharnaces. Must have
been running out of sons. Pharnaces repaid him
by rounding up a fresh lot of revolutionaries and
storming the fortress in Panticapaeum. That was
the end, and Mithridates knew it. So he murdered however many daughters he had left, and
some wives and concubines and even a few sons
who were still children. Then he took an enormous dose of poison. But it wouldn't work; he'd
been too successful all those years of deliberately poisoning himself to become immune. The
deed was done by one of the Gauls in his bodyguard. Ran the old man through with a sword. I
buried him in Sinope.

In the meantime, I was marching into Syria,
getting it tidied up so Rome can inherit. No more
kings of Syria. I for one am tired of eastern potentates. Syria will become a Roman province,
much safer. I also like the idea of putting good

Roman troops against the Euphrates—ought to make the Parthians think a bit. I also settled the strife between the Greeks displaced by Tigranes and the Arabs displaced by Tigranes. The Arabs will be quite handy, I think, so I did send some of them back to the desert. But I made it worth their while. Abgarus—I hear he made life so hard in Antioch for young Publius Clodius that Clodius fled, though exactly what Abgarus did I can't find out—is the King of the Skenites, then I put someone with the terrific name of Sampsiceramus in charge of another lot, and so forth. This sort of thing is really enjoyable work, Caesar; it gives a lot of satisfaction. No one out here is very practical, and they squabble and quarrel with each other endlessly. Silly. It's such a rich place you'd think they'd learn to get on, but they don't. Still, I can't repine. It does mean that Gnaeus Pompeius from Picenum has kings in his clientele! I have earned that Magnus, I tell you.

The worst part of it all turns out to be the Jews. A very strange lot. They were fairly reasonable until the old Queen, Alexandra, died a couple of years ago. But she left two sons to fight out the succession, complicated by the fact that their religion is as important to them as their state. So one son has to be High Priest, as far as I can gather. The other one wanted to be King of the Jews, but the High Priest one, Hyrcanus, thought it would be nice to combine both offices. They had a bit of a war, and Hyrcanus was defeated by brother Aristobulus. Then along comes an Idumaean prince named Antipater, who whispered in Hyrcanus's ear and then persuaded Hyrcanus to ally himself with King Aretas of the Nabataeans. The deal was that Hyrcanus would hand over twelve Arab cities to Aretas that the Jews were ruling. They then laid siege to Aristobulus in Jerusalem, which is their name for Hierosolyma.

I sent my quaestor, young Scaurus, to sort the mess out. Ought to have known better. He picked Aristobulus as the one in the right, and ordered Aretas back to Nabataea. Then Aristobulus ambushed him at Papyron or some such place, and Aretas lost. I got to Antioch to find that Aristobulus was the King of the Jews, and Scaurus didn't know what to do. The next thing, I'm getting presents from both sides. You should see the present Aristobulus sent me—well, you will at my triumph. A magical thing, Caesar, a grapevine made of pure gold, with golden bunches of grapes all over it.

Anyway, I've ordered both camps to meet me in Damascus next spring. I believe Damascus has a lovely climate, so I think I'll winter there and finish sorting out the mess between Tigranes and the King of the Parthians. The one I'm interested to meet is the Idumaean, Antipater. Sounds like a clever sort of fellow. Probably circumcised. They almost all are, the Semites. Peculiar practice. I'm attached to my foreskin, literally as well as metaphorically. There! That came out quite well. That's because I've still got Varro with me, as well as Lenaeus and Theophanes of Mitylene. I hear Lucullus is crowing because he brought back this fabulous fruit called a cherry to Italia, but I'm bringing back all sorts of plants, including this sweet and succulent sort of lemon I found in Media—an orange lemon, isn't that strange? Ought to grow well in Italia, likes a dry summer, fruits in winter.

Well, enough prattle. Time to get down to business and tell you why I'm writing. You're a very subtle and clever chap, Caesar, and it hasn't escaped my notice that you always speak up for me in the Senate, and to good effect. No one else did over the pirates. I think I'll be another two years in the East, ought to fetch up at home about the time you'll be leaving office as praetor, if you're going to take advantage of Sulla's law letting patricians stand two years early.

But I'm making it my policy to have at least one tribune of the plebs in my Roman camp until after I get home. The next one is Titus Labienus, and I know you know him because you were both on Vatia Isauricus's staff in Cilicia ten or twelve years ago. He's a very good man, comes from Cingulum, right in the middle of my patch. Clever too. He tells me the pair of you got on well together. I know you won't be holding a magistracy, but it might be that you can lend Titus Labienus a hand occasionally. Or he might be able to lend you a hand—feel free. I've told him all this. The year after—the year of your praetorship, I imagine—my man will be Mucia's younger brother, Metellus Nepos. I ought to arrive home just after he finishes his term, though I can't be sure.

So what I'd like you to do, Caesar, is hold a watch for me and mine. You're going to go far, even if I haven't left you much of the world to conquer! I've never forgotten that it was you who showed me how to be consul, while corrupt old Philippus couldn't be bothered.

Your friend from Mitylene, Aulus Gabinius, sends you his warm regards.

Well, I might as well say it. *Do what you can to help me get land for my troops*. It's too early for Labienus to try, the job will go to Nepos. I'm sending him home in style well before next year's elections. A pity you can't be consul when the fight to get my land is on, a bit too early for you. Still, it might drag out until you're consul-elect, and then you can be a real help. It isn't going to be easy.

Caesar laid the long letter down and put his chin in his hand, having much to think about. Though he found it naïve, he enjoyed Pompey's bald prose and casual asides; they brought Magnus into the room in a way that the polished essays Varro wrote for Pompey's senatorial dispatches never did.

When he had first met Pompey on that memorable day Pompey had turned up to claim Mucia Tertia at Aunt Julia's, Caesar had detested him. And in some ways he probably never would warmly like the man. However, the years and exposure had somewhat softened his attitude, which now, he decided, contained more like than dislike. Oh, one had to deplore the conceit and the rustic in him, and his patent disregard for due process of the law. Nonetheless he was gifted and so eminently capable. He hadn't put a foot wrong very often, and the older he became, the more unerring his step. Crassus loathed him of course, which was a difficulty. That left him, Caesar, to steer a course between the two.

Titus Labienus. A cruel and barbarous man. Tall, muscular, curly-headed, hook-nosed, snapping black eyes. Absolutely at home on a horse. Quite what his remote ancestry was had flummoxed more Romans than merely Caesar; even Pompey had been heard to say that he thought Mormolyce had snatched the mother's newborn babe out of its cradle and substituted one of her own to be brought up as Titus Labienus's heir. Interesting that Labienus had informed Pompey how well he had gotten on with Caesar in the old days. And it was true enough. Two born riders, they had shared many a gallop through the countryside around Tarsus, and talked endlessly about cavalry tactics in battle. Yet Caesar couldn't warm to him, despite the man's undeniable brilliance. Labienus was someone to be used but never trusted.

Caesar quite understood why Pompey was concerned enough about Labienus's fate as a tribune of the plebs to enlist Caesar in a support role; the new College was a particularly weird mixture of independent individuals who would probably fly off in ten tangents and spend more time vetoing each other than anything else. Though in one respect Pompey had erred; if Caesar had been planning his assortment of tame tribunes of the plebs, then Labienus would have been saved for the year Pompey started to press for land for his veterans. What Caesar knew of Metellus Nepos indicated that he was too Caecilian; he wouldn't have the necessary steel. For that kind of work, a fiery Picentine without ancestors and nowhere to go save up yielded the best results.

Mucia Tertia. Widow of Young Marius, wife of Pompey the Great. Mother of Pompey's children, boy, girl, boy. Why had he never got round to her? Perhaps because he still felt about her the way he had about Bibulus's wife, Domitia: the prospect of cuckolding Pompey was so alluring he kept postponing the actual deed. Domitia (the cousin of Cato's brother-in-law, Ahenobarbus) was now an accomplished fact, though Bibulus hadn't heard about it yet. He would! What fun! Only—did Caesar really want to annoy Pompey in a way he understood Pompey particularly would loathe? He might need Pompey, just as Pompey might need him. What a pity. Of all the women on his list, Caesar fancied Mucia Tertia most. And that she fancied him he had known for years. Now . . . was it worth it? Probably not. Probably not. Conscious of a twinge of regret, Caesar mentally erased Mucia Tertia's name from his list.

Which turned out to be just as well. With the year drawing to its close, Labienus returned from his estates in Picenum and moved into the very modest house he had recently bought on the Palatium, which was the less settled and more unfashionable side of the Palatine. And the very next day hied himself off to see Caesar just sufficiently too late for anyone left in Aurelia's apartment to assume he was Caesar's client.

"But let's not talk here, Titus Labienus," said Caesar, and drew him back toward the door. "I have rooms down the street."

"This is very nice," said Labienus, ensconced in a comfortable chair and with weak watered wine at his elbow.

"Considerably quieter," said Caesar, sitting in another chair but not with the desk between them; he did not wish to give this man the impression that business was the order of the day. "I am interested to know," he said, sipping water, "why Pompeius didn't conserve you for the year after next."

"Because he didn't expect to be in the East for so long," said Labienus. "Until he decided he couldn't abandon Syria with the Jewish question unsettled, he really thought he'd be home by next spring. Didn't he tell you that in his letter?"

So Labienus knew all about the letter. Caesar grinned. "You know him at least as well as I do, Labienus. He did ask me to give you any assistance I could, and he also told me about the Jewish difficulties. What he neglected to mention was that he had planned to be home earlier than he said he was going to be."

The black eyes flashed, but not with laughter; Labienus had little sense of humor. "Well, that's it, that's the reason. So instead of a brilliant tribunate of the plebs, I'm going to have no more to do than legislate to allow Magnus to wear full triumphal regalia at the games."

"With or without *minim* all over his face?"

That did provoke a short laugh. "You know Magnus, Caesar! He wouldn't wear *minim* even during his triumph itself."

Caesar was beginning to understand the situation a little better. "Are you Magnus's client?" he asked.

"Oh, yes. What man from Picenum isn't?"

"Yet you didn't go east with him."

"He wouldn't even use Afranius and Petreius when he cleaned up the pirates, though he did manage to slip them in after some of the big names when he went to war against the kings. And Lollius Palicanus, Aulus Gabinius. Mind you, I didn't have a senatorial census, which is why I couldn't stand as quaestor. A poor man's only way into the Senate is to become tribune of the plebs and then hope he makes enough money before the next lot of censors to qualify to stay in the Senate," said Labienus harshly.

"I always thought Magnus was very open-handed. Hasn't he offered to assist you?"

"He saves his largesse for those in a position to do

great things for him. You might say that under his original plans, I was on a promise.''

''And it isn't a very big promise now that triumphal regalia is the most important thing on his tribunician schedule.''

''Exactly.''

Caesar sighed, stretched his legs out. ''I take it,'' he said, ''that you would like to leave a name behind you after your year in the College is over.''

''I would.''

''It's a long time since we were both junior military tribunes under Vatia Isauricus, and I'm sorry the years since haven't been kind to you. Unfortunately my own finances don't permit of a trifling loan, and I do understand that I can't function as your patron. However, Titus Labienus, in four years I will be consul, which means that in five years I will be going to a province. I do not intend to be a tame governor in a tame province. Wherever I go, there will be plenty of military work to do, and I will need some excellent people to work as my legates. In particular, I will need one legate who will have propraetorian status whom I can trust to campaign as well without me as with me. What I remember about you is your military sense. So I'll make a pact with you here and now. Number one, that I'll find something for you to do during your tribunate of the plebs that will make your year a memorable one. And number two, that when I go as proconsul to my province, I'll make sure you come with me as my chief legate with propraetorian status,'' said Caesar.

Labienus drew a breath. ''What I remember about you, Caesar, is your military sense. How odd! Mucia said you were worth watching. She spoke of you, I thought, with more respect than she ever does of Magnus.''

''Mucia?''

The black gaze was very level. ''That's right.''

''Well, well! How many people know?'' asked Caesar.

''None, I hope.''

''Doesn't he lock her up in his stronghold while he's away? That's what he used to do.''

"She's not a child anymore—if she ever was," said Titus Labienus, eyes flashing again. "She's like me, she's had a hard life. You learn from a hard life. We find ways."

"Next time you see her, tell her that the secret is safe with me," said Caesar, smiling. "If Magnus finds out, you'll get no help from that quarter. So are you interested in my proposition?"

"I most certainly am."

After Labienus departed Caesar continued to sit without moving. Mucia Tertia had a lover, and she hadn't needed to venture outside Picenum to find him. What an extraordinary choice! He couldn't think of three men more different from each other than Young Marius, Pompeius Magnus and Titus Labienus. That was a searching lady. Did Labienus please her more than the other two, or was he simply a diversion brought about by loneliness and lack of a wide field to choose from?

Nothing surer than that Pompey would find out. The lovers might delude themselves no one knew, but if the affair had been going on in Picenum, discovery was inevitable. Pompey's letter did not indicate anyone had tattled yet, but it was only a matter of time. And then Titus Labienus stood to lose everything Pompey might have given him, though clearly his hopes of Pompey's favor had already waned. Maybe his intriguing with Mucia Tertia had arisen out of disillusionment with Pompey? Very possible.

All of which scarcely mattered; what occupied Caesar's mind was how to make Labienus's year as a tribune of the plebs a memorable one. Difficult if not impossible in this present climate of political torpor and uninspiring curule magistrates. About the only thing capable of kindling a fire beneath the rear ends of these slugs was a fearsomely radical land bill suggesting that every last *iugerum* of Rome's *ager publicus* be given away to the poor, and that wouldn't please Pompey at all—Pompey needed Rome's public lands as a gift for his troops.

When the new tribunes of the plebs entered office on the tenth day of December, the diversity among its members became glaringly obvious. Caecilius Rufus actually had the temerity to propose that the disgraced ex–consuls-elect Publius Sulla and Publius Autronius be allowed to stand for the consulship in the future; that all nine of his colleagues vetoed Caecilius's bill came as no surprise. No surprise either was the response to Labienus's bill giving Pompey the right to wear full triumphal regalia at all public games; it swept into law.

The surprise came from Publius Servilius Rullus when he said that every last *iugerum* of Rome's *ager publicus* both in Italy and abroad be given away to the poor. Shades of the Gracchi! Rullus lit the fire turning senatorial slugs into ravening wolves.

"If Rullus succeeds, when Magnus comes home there'll be no State land left for his veterans," said Labienus to Caesar.

"Ah, but Rullus neglected to mention that fact," replied Caesar, unruffled. "As he chose to present his bill in the House before taking it to the Comitia, he really ought to have made mention of Magnus's soldiers."

"He didn't have to mention them. Everyone knows."

"True. But if there's one thing every man of substance detests, it's land bills. The *ager publicus* is sacred. Too many senatorial families of enormous influence rent it and make money out of it. Bad enough to propose giving some of it away to a victorious general's troops, but to demand that all of it be given away to Head Count vermin? Anathema! If Rullus had only come out and said directly that what Rome no longer owns cannot be awarded to Magnus's troops, he might have gained support from some very peculiar quarters. As it is, the bill will die."

"You'll oppose it?" asked Labienus.

"No, no, certainly not! I shall support it vociferously," said Caesar, smiling. "If I support it, quite a lot of the fence-sitters will jump down to oppose it, if for no other reason than that they don't like what I like. Cicero is an excellent example. What's his new name for men like Rullus? *Popularis*—for the People rather than for the Senate. That rather appeals to me. I shall endeavor to be labeled a Popularis."

"You'll annoy Magnus if you speak up for it."

"Not once he reads the covering letter I'll send him together with a copy of my speech. Magnus knows a ewe from a ram."

Labienus scowled. "All of this is going to take a lot of time, Caesar, yet none of it involves me. Where am I going?"

"You've passed your bill to award Magnus triumphal regalia at the games, so now you'll sit on your hands and whistle until the fuss over Rullus abates. It will! Remember that it's best to be the last man left on his feet."

"You have an idea."

"No," said Caesar.

"Oh, come!"

Caesar smiled. "Rest easy, Labienus. Something will occur to me. It always does."

When he went home Caesar sought out his mother. Her minute office was one room Pompeia never invaded; if nothing else about her mother-in-law frightened her, Aurelia's affinity for the lightning totting up of figures certainly did. Besides, it had been a clever idea to give his study over for Pompeia's use (Caesar had his other apartment in which to work). Tenure of the study and the master sleeping cubicle beyond it kept Pompeia out of the other parts of Aurelia's domain. Sounds of feminine laughter and chatter emanated from the study, but no one appeared from that direction to hinder Caesar's progress.

"Who's with her?" he asked, seating himself in the chair on the far side of Aurelia's desk.

The room was indeed so small that a stouter man than Caesar could not have squeezed into the space this chair occupied, but the hand of Aurelia was very evident in the economy and logic with which she had organized herself: shelves for scrolls and papers where she wouldn't hit her head on them as she rose from her own chair, tiered wooden trays on those parts of her desk not needed for her actual work, and leather book buckets relegated to the room's remote corners.

"Who's with her?" he repeated when she didn't answer.

Down went her pen. His mother looked up reluctantly, flexed her right hand, sighed. "A very silly lot," she said.

"That I do not need to be told. Silliness attracts more silliness. But who?"

"Both the Clodias. And Fulvia."

"Oh! Racy as well as vacant. Is Pompeia intriguing with men, Mater?"

"Definitely not. I don't permit her to entertain men here, and when she goes out I send Polyxena with her. Polyxena is my own woman, quite impossible to bribe or suborn. Of course Pompeia takes her own idiotic girl with her too, but both of them combined are no match for Polyxena, I assure you."

Caesar looked, his mother thought, very tired. His year as president of the Murder Court had been an extremely busy one, and acquitted with all the thoroughness and energy for which he was becoming famous. Other court presidents might dally and take protracted vacations, but not Caesar. Naturally she knew he was in debt—and for how much—though time had taught her that money was a subject sure to create tension between them. So while she burned to quiz him about money matters, she bit her tongue and managed not to say a word. It was true that he did not allow himself to become depressed over a debt now mounting rapidly because he could not afford to pay back the principal; that some inexplicable part of him genuinely believed the money would be found; yet she also knew that money could lie like a grey shadow at the back of the most sanguine and optimistic of minds. As it lay like a grey shadow at the back of his mind, she was certain.

And he was still heavily involved with Servilia. That was a relationship nothing seemed able to destroy. Besides which, Julia, menstruating regularly now that her thirteenth birthday was a month away, was displaying less and less enthusiasm for Brutus. Oh, nothing could provoke the girl into rudeness or even covert discourtesy, but instead of becoming more enamored of Brutus now that her womanhood was upon her, she was unmistakably cooling, the

child's affection and pity replaced by—boredom? Yes,
boredom. The one emotion no marriage could survive.

All these were problems which gnawed at Aurelia,
while others merely niggled. For instance, this apartment
had become far too small for a man of Caesar's status.
His clients could no longer gather all at once, and the
address was a bad one for a man who would be senior
consul within five years. Of that last fact Aurelia harbored
no doubts whatsoever. Between the name, the ancestry,
the manner, the looks, the charm, the ease and the intellectual ability, whatever election Caesar contested would
see him returned at the top of the poll. He had enemies
galore, but none capable of destroying his power base
among the First and the Second Classes, vital for success
in the Centuries. Not to mention that among the Classes
too low to count in the Centuries he stood high above all
his peers. Caesar moved among the Head Count as readily
as among the consulars. However, it was not possible to
broach the subject of a suitable house without money's
raising its ugly face. So would she, or would she not?
Ought she, or ought she not?

Aurelia drew a deep breath, folded her hands one
over the other on the table in front of her. "Caesar, next
year you will be standing for praetor," she said, "and I
foresee one very severe difficulty."

"My address," he said instantly.

Her smile was wry. "One thing I can never complain
about—your astuteness."

"Is this the prelude to another argument about
money?"

"No, it is not. Or perhaps it would be better to say,
I hope not. Over the years I have managed to save a fair
amount, and I could certainly borrow against this insula
comfortably. Between the two, I could give you enough
to purchase a good house on the Palatine or the Carinae."

His mouth went thin. "That is most generous of you,
Mater, but I will not accept money from you any more
than I will from my friends. Understood?"

Amazing to think she was in her sixty-second year.
Not one single wrinkle marred the skin of face or neck,

perhaps because she had plumped out a trifle; where age
showed at all was in the creases which ran down either
side of her nostrils to meet the corners of her mouth.

"I thought you'd say that," she said, composure intact. Then she remarked, apropos it seemed of nothing, "I
hear that Metellus Pius Pontifex Maximus is ailing."

That startled him. "Who told you so?"

"Clodia, for one. Her husband, Celer, says the whole
family is desperately worried. And Aemilia Lepida, for
another. Metellus Scipio is very cast down by the state of
his father's health. He hasn't been well since his wife
died."

"It's certainly true that the old boy hasn't been attending any meetings of late," said Caesar.

"Nor will he in the future. When I said he is ailing,
I really meant he is dying."

"And?" asked Caesar, for once baffled.

"When he dies, the College of Pontifices will have
to co-opt another Pontifex Maximus." The large and
lustrous eyes which were Aurelia's best feature gleamed
and narrowed. "If you were to be appointed Pontifex
Maximus, Caesar, it would solve several of your most
pressing problems. First and foremost, it would demonstrate to your creditors that you are going to be consul
beyond any doubt. That would mean your creditors would
be more willing to carry your debts beyond your praetorship if necessary. I mean, if you draw Sardinia or Africa
as your province in the praetor's lots, you won't be able
to recoup your losses as a praetor governor. Should that
happen, I would think your creditors will grow very restless indeed."

The ghost of a smile kindled his eyes, but he kept his
face straight. "Admirably summed up, Mater," he said.

She went on as if he hadn't spoken. "Secondly, Pontifex Maximus would endow you with a splendid residence
at the expense of the State, and as it is a lifetime position,
the Domus Publica would be yours for life. It is within
the Forum itself, very large and eminently suitable. So,"
his mother ended, her voice as level and unexcited as ever,

"I have begun to canvass on your behalf among the wives of your fellow priests."

Caesar sighed. "It's an admirable plan, Mater, but one which you cannot bring to fruition any more than I can. Between Catulus and Vatia Isauricus—not to mention at least half the others in the College!—I don't stand a chance. For one thing, the post normally goes to someone who has already been consul. For another, all the most conservative elements in the Senate adorn this College. They do not fancy me."

"Nevertheless I shall go to work," said Aurelia.

At which precise moment Caesar realized how it could be done. He threw his head back and roared with laughter. "Yes, Mater, by all means go to work!" he said, wiping away tears of mirth. "I know the answer—oh, what a furor it's bound to create!"

"And the answer is?"

"I came to see you about Titus Labienus, who is— as I'm sure you know—Pompeius Magnus's tame tribune of the plebs this year. Just to air my thoughts aloud. You're so clever that I find you a most useful wall for bouncing ideas off," he said.

One thin black brow flew up, the corners of her mouth quivered. "Why, thank you! Am I a better wall to bounce off than Servilia?"

Again he cried with laughter. It was rare for Aurelia to succumb to innuendo, but when she did she was as witty as Cicero. "Seriously," he said when he could, "I know how you feel about that liaison, but acquit me of stupidity, please. Servilia is politically acute. She is also in love with me. However, she is not of my family, nor is she entirely to be trusted. When I use her as a wall, I make very sure I'm in complete control of the balls."

"You ease my mind enormously," said Aurelia blandly. "What is this brilliant inspiration, then?"

"When Sulla nullified the *lex Domitia de sacerdotiis,* he went one step further than custom and tradition dictated by also removing the office of Pontifex Maximus from tribal election by the People. Until Sulla, the Pontifex Maximus had always been elected, he was never co-opted

by his fellow priests. I'll have Labienus legislate to return
the choice of priests and augurs to the People in their
tribes. Including the office of Pontifex Maximus. The People will love the idea.''

"They love anything which ablates a law of Sulla's.''

"Precisely. Then all I have to do,'' said Caesar, rising, "is get myself elected Pontifex Maximus.''

"Have Titus Labienus enact the law now, Caesar.
Don't put it off! No one can be sure how much longer
Metellus Pius has to live. He's lonely without his Licinia.''

Caesar took his mother's hand and raised it to his
lips. "Mater, I thank you. The matter will be expedited,
because it's a law can benefit Pompeius Magnus. He's
dying to be a priest or an augur, but he knows he'll never
be co-opted. Whereas at an election he'll bolt in.''

The volume of laughter and chatter from the study
had risen, Caesar noticed as he entered the reception room;
he had intended to leave immediately, but on the spur of
the moment decided to visit his wife instead.

Quite a gathering, he thought, standing unobserved in
the doorway from the dining room. Pompeia had completely redecorated the once-austere room, which was now
overfilled with couches mattressed in goose down, a plethora of purple cushions and coverlets, many precious yet
commonplace knick-knacks, paintings and statues. What
had been an equally austere sleeping cubicle, he noted gazing through its open door, now bore the same cloyingly
tasteless touch.

Pompeia was reclining on the best couch, though not
alone; Aurelia might forbid her to entertain men, but could
not prevent visits from Pompeia's full brother, Quintus
Pompeius Rufus Junior. Now in his early twenties, he was
a wild blade of increasingly unsavory reputation. No doubt
it was through his offices that she had come to know ladies
of the Claudian clan, for Pompeius Rufus was the best
friend of none other than Publius Clodius, three years
older but no less wild.

Aurelia's ban forbade the presence of Clodius himself, but not of his two younger sisters, Clodia and

Clodilla. A pity, thought Caesar clinically, that the undisciplined natures of these two young matrons were fueled by a considerable degree of good looks. Clodia, married to Metellus Celer (the elder of Mucia Tertia's two half brothers) was marginally more beautiful than her younger sister, Clodilla, now divorced from Lucullus amid shock waves of scandal. Like all the Claudii Pulchri they were very dark, with large and luminous black eyes, long and curling black lashes, a profusion of waving black hair, and faintly olive—but perfect—skins. Despite the fact that neither was tall, both had excellent figures and dress sense, moved with grace. And they were quite well read, again especially Clodia, who had a taste for poetry of high order. They sat side by side on a couch facing Pompeia and her brother, each with her robe falling away from gleaming shoulders to give more than a hint of deliciously shaped plump breasts.

Fulvia was not unlike them physically, though her coloring was paler and reminded Caesar of his mother's ice-brown hair, purplish eyes, dark brows and lashes. A very positive and dogmatic young lady, imbued with a lot of rather silly ideas stemming from her romantic attachment to the Brothers Gracchi—grandfather Gaius and great uncle Tiberius. Her marriage to Publius Clodius had not met with her parents' approval, Caesar knew. Which had not stopped Fulvia, determined to have her way. Since her marriage she had become intimate with Clodius's sisters, to the detriment of all three.

None of these young women, however, worried Caesar as much as the two ripe and shady ladies who together occupied a third couch: Sempronia Tuditani, wife of one Decimus Junius Brutus and mother of another (an odd choice of friend for Fulvia—the Sempronii Tuditani had been obdurate enemies of both the Gracchi, as had the family of Decimus Junius Brutus Callaicus, grandfather of Sempronia Tuditani's husband); and Palla, who had been wife to both the censor Philippus and the censor Poplicola, and had borne each of them a son. Sempronia Tuditani and Palla had to be fifty years old, though they employed every artifice known to the cosmetics industry to disguise the fact, from painted and powdered complexions to *stibium* around the eyes and carmine on their cheeks and mouths. Nor had they been content to allow the bodily subsidence of middle age; they starved themselves assiduously to be stick-thin, and wore flimsy, floating robes they fancied brought back their long-vanished youth. The result of all this tampering with the ageing process, reflected Caesar with an inward grin, was as unsuccessful as it was ludicrous. His own mother, the merciless onlooker decided, was far more attractive, though at least ten years their senior. Aurelia, however, did not court the company of men, whereas Sempronia Tuditani and Palla were aristocratic whores who never lacked for masculine attention because they were famous for giving by far the best fellatio in Rome, including that obtainable from professionals of both sexes.

Their presence meant, Caesar concluded, that Decimus Brutus and young Poplicola also frequented the vicinity of Pompeia. Of Decimus Brutus perhaps no more was to be said than that he was young, bored, high-spirited and up to the usual mischief, from too much wine and too many women to the dice box and the gaming table. But young Poplicola had seduced his stepmother and tried to murder his father the censor, and had been formally relegated to penury and obscurity. He would never be permitted to enter the Senate, but since Publius Clodius's marriage to Fulvia and Clodius's subsequent access to almost unlimited money, young Poplicola was starting to be seen again in high circles.

It was Clodia who noticed Caesar first. She sat up much straighter on her couch, thrust out her breasts and gave him an alluring smile.

"Caesar, how absolutely *divine* to see you!" she purred.

"I return the compliment, of course."

"Do come in!" said Clodia, patting her couch.

"I'd love to, but I'm afraid I'm on my way out."

And that, Caesar decided as he let himself out the front door, was a room full of trouble.

* * *

Labienus beckoned, but first he would have to see Servilia, who had probably been waiting in his apartment down the road for some time, he realized. Women! Today was a day of women, and mostly women with nuisance value. Except for Aurelia, of course. Now there was a woman! A pity, thought Caesar, bounding up the stairs to his apartment, that none other measures up to her.

Servilia was waiting, though she was far too sensible to reproach Caesar for his tardiness, and far too pragmatic to expect an apology. If the world belonged to men—and it did—then undoubtedly it was Caesar's oyster.

No word was exchanged between them for some time. First came several luxurious and languorous kisses, then a sighing subsidence into each other's arms on the bed, freed from clothing and care. She was so delicious, so intelligent and untrammeled in her ministrations, so inventive. And he was so perfect, so receptive and powerful in his attentions, so unerring. Thus, absolutely content with each other and fascinated by the fact that familiarity had bred not contempt but additional pleasure, Caesar and Servilia forgot their worlds until the level of water in the chronometer had dripped away quite a lot of time.

Of Labienus he would not speak; of Pompeia he would, so he said as they lay entwined, "My wife is keeping odd company."

The memory of those frenzied months of wasted jealousy had not yet faded from Servilia's mind, so she loved to hear any word from Caesar that indicated dissatisfaction. Oh, it was only scant moments after they were reconciled following the birth of Junia Tertia that Servilia understood Caesar's marriage was a sham. Still and all, the minx was delectable, and proximity was her ally; no woman of Servilia's age could rest in perfect surety when her rival was almost twenty years her junior.

"Odd company?" she asked, stroking voluptuously.

"The Clodias and Fulvia."

"That's to be expected, considering the circles Brother Pompeius moves in."

"Ah, but today there were additions to the menagerie!"

"Who?"

"Sempronia Tuditani and Palla."

"Oh!" Servilia sat up, the delight of Caesar's skin evaporating. She frowned, thought, then said, "Actually that shouldn't have surprised me."

"Nor me, considering who Publius Clodius's friends are."

"No, I didn't mean through that connection, Caesar. You know of course that my younger sister, Servililla, has been divorced by Drusus Nero for infidelity."

"I had heard."

"What you don't know is that she's going to marry Lucullus."

Caesar sat up too. "That's to exchange a dunderhead for an imbecile in the making! He conducts all manner of experiments with substances which distort reality, has done for years. I believe one of his freedmen has no duty other than to procure every kind of soporific and ecstatic for him—syrup of poppies, mushrooms, brews concocted from leaves, berries, roots."

"Servililla says he likes the effect of wine, but dislikes its aftereffects intensely. Those other substances apparently don't produce the same painful aftereffects." Servilia shrugged. "Anyway, it seems Servililla isn't complaining. She thinks she'll get to enjoy all that money and taste without a watchful husband to cramp her style."

"He divorced Clodilla for adultery—and incest."

"That was Clodius's doing."

"Well, I wish your sister the best of luck," said Caesar. "Lucullus is still stuck on the Campus Martius demanding the triumph the Senate keeps refusing him, so she won't see much of Rome from the inside of the walls."

"He'll get his triumph soon," said Servilia confidently. "My spies tell me that Pompeius Magnus doesn't want to have to share the Campus Martius with his old enemy when he comes home from the East positively covered in glory." She snorted. "Oh, what a poseur! Anyone with any sense can see that Lucullus did all the hard work! Magnus just had to harvest the results of that hard work."

"I agree, little though I care for Lucullus." Caesar cupped a hand around one breast. "It is not like you to digress, my love. What has this to do with Pompeia's friends?"

"They call it the Clodius Club," said Servilia, stretching. "Servililla told me all about it. Publius Clodius, of course, is its president. The chief—indeed, I suppose one would have to call it the only—aim of the Clodius Club is to shock our world. That's how the members entertain themselves. They're all bored, idle, averse to work, and possessed of far too much money. Drinking and wenching and gambling are tame. Shocks and scandals are the Club's sole purpose. Hence raffish women like Sempronia Tuditani and Palla, allegations of incest, and the cultivation of such peerless specimens as young Poplicola. The male members of the Club include some very young men who ought to know better—like Curio Junior and your cousin Marcus Antonius. I hear one of *their* favorite pastimes is to pretend they're lovers."

It was Caesar's turn to snort. "I'd believe almost anything of Marcus Antonius, but not that! How old is he now, nineteen or twenty? Yet he's got more bastards littered through every stratum of Roman society than anyone else I know."

"Conceded. But littering Rome with bastards isn't nearly shocking enough. A homosexual affair—particularly between the sons of such pillars of the conservative establishment!—adds a certain luster."

"So this is the institution to which my wife belongs!" Caesar sighed. "How am I to wean her away, I wonder?"

That was not an idea which appealed to Servilia, who got out of bed in a hurry. "I fail to see how you can, Caesar, without provoking exactly the kind of scandal the Clodius Club adores. Unless you divorce yourself by divorcing her."

But this suggestion offended his sense of fair play; he shook his head emphatically. "No, I'll not do that without more cause than idle friendships she can't turn into anything worse because my mother keeps too sharp an eye on her. I pity the poor girl. She hasn't a scrap of intelligence or sense."

The bath beckoned (Caesar had given in and installed a small furnace to provide hot water); Servilia decided to hold her peace on the subject of Pompeia.

Titus Labienus had to wait until the morrow, when he saw Caesar in Caesar's apartment.

"Two items," said Caesar, leaning back in his chair.

Labienus looked alert.

"The first is bound to win you considerable approval in knight circles, and will sit very well with Magnus."

"It is?"

"To legislate the return of selection of priests and augurs to the tribes in the Comitia."

"Including, no doubt," said Labienus smoothly, "election of the Pontifex Maximus."

"*Edepol,* you're quick!"

"I heard Metellus Pius is likely to qualify for a State funeral any time."

"Quite so. And it is true that I have a fancy to become Pontifex Maximus. However, I do not think my fellow priests want to see me at the head of their College. The electors, on the other hand, may not agree with them. Therefore, why not give the electors the chance to decide who the next Pontifex Maximus will be?"

"Why not, indeed?" Labienus watched Caesar closely. There was much about the man appealed to him strongly, yet that streak of levity which could rise to his surface on scant provocation was, in Labienus's opinion, a flaw. One never really knew just how serious Caesar was. Oh, the ambition was boundless, but like Cicero he could sometimes give off strong signals that his sense of the ridiculous might intervene. However, at the moment Caesar's face seemed serious enough, and Labienus knew as well as most that Caesar's debts were appalling. To be elected Pontifex Maximus would enhance his credit with the usurers. Labienus said, "I imagine you want a *lex Labiena de sacerdotiis* enacted as soon as possible."

"I do. If Metellus Pius should die before the law is

changed, the People might decide not to change it. We'll
have to be quick, Labienus.''

''Ampius will be glad to be of assistance. So will the
rest of the tribunician College, I predict. It's a law in absolute accord with the *mos maiorum,* a great advantage.''
The dark eyes flashed. ''What else do you have in mind?''

A frown came. ''Nothing earthshaking, unfortunately.
If Magnus came home it would be easy. The only thing I
can think of sure to create a stir within the Senate is to
propose a bill restoring the rights of the sons and grandsons of Sulla's proscribed. You won't get it through, but
the debates will be noisy and well attended.''

This idea obviously appealed; Labienus was grinning
broadly as he rose to his feet. ''I like it, Caesar. It's a
chance to pull Cicero's jauntily waving tail!''

''It isn't the tail matters in Cicero's anatomy,'' said
Caesar. ''The tongue is the appendage needs amputation.
Be warned, he'll make mincemeat of you. But if you introduce the two bills together, you'll divert attention from
the one you really want to get through. And if you prepare
yourself with great care, you might even be able to make
some political capital out of Cicero's tongue.''

The Piglet was dead. Quintus Caecilius
Metellus Pius Pontifex Maximus, loyal son to
Metellus Piggle-wiggle and loyal friend to
Sulla the Dictator, died peacefully in his sleep of a wasting
disorder which defied diagnosis. The acknowledged leading light of Roman medicine, Sulla's doctor Lucius Tuc-
cius, asked the Piglet's adopted son for permission to do
an autopsy.

But the adopted son was neither as intelligent nor as
reasonable as his father; the blood son of Scipio Nasica
and the elder of Crassus Orator's two Licinias (the
younger was his adoptive mother, wife of the Piglet), Metellus Scipio was chiefly famous for his hauteur and sense
of aristocratic fitness.

''No one will tamper with my father's body!'' he said

through his tears, and clutching his wife's hand convulsively. "He will go to the flames unmutilated!"

The funeral was, of course, conducted at State expense, and was as distinguished as its object. The eulogy was given from the rostra by Quintus Hortensius after Mamercus, father of Metellus Scipio's wife, Aemilia Lepida, declined that honor. Everyone was there, from Catulus to Caesar, from Caepio Brutus to Cato; it was not, however, a funeral which attracted a huge crowd.

And on the day after the Piglet was committed to the flames, Metellus Scipio held a meeting with Catulus, Hortensius, Vatia Isauricus, Cato, Caepio Brutus and the senior consul, Cicero.

"I heard a rumor," said the bereaved son, red-eyed but now tearless, "that Caesar intends to put himself up as a candidate for Pontifex Maximus."

"Well, that surely can't come as a surprise," said Cicero. "We all know who pulls Labienus's strings in Magnus's absence, though at this moment I'm uncertain as to whether Magnus even has any interest in who pulls Labienus's strings. Popular election to choose all priests and augurs can't benefit Magnus, whereas it gives Caesar a chance he could never have had when the College of Pontifices chose its own Pontifex Maximus."

"It never did choose its own Pontifex Maximus," said Cato to Metellus Scipio. "The only unelected Pontifex Maximus in history—your father—was personally chosen by Sulla, not the College."

Catulus had a different objection to make against what Cicero said. "How blind you can be about our dear heroic friend Pompeius Magnus!" he threw at Cicero. "No advantage to Magnus? Come, now! Magnus hankers to be a priest or augur himself. He'd get what he hankers after from a Popular election, but never from co-optation within either College."

"My brother-in-law is right, Cicero," said Hortensius. "The *lex Labiena de sacerdotiis* suits Pompeius Magnus very well."

"Rot the *lex Labiena*!" cried Metellus Scipio.

"Don't waste your emotions, Quintus Scipio," said

Cato in his harsh and toneless voice. "We're here to decide how to prevent Caesar's declaring his candidacy."

Brutus sat with his eyes traveling from one angry face to another, bewildered as to why he had been invited to such a senior gathering. He had assumed it was part of Uncle Cato's relentless war against Servilia for control of her son, a war which frightened yet attracted him, the more so as he got older. Of course it did occur to him to wonder if perhaps, thanks to his engagement to Caesar's daughter, they thought to have him there to quiz him about Caesar; but as the discussion proceeded and no one applied to him for information, he was forced eventually to conclude that his presence was indeed simply to annoy Servilia.

"We can ensure your election to the College as an ordinary pontifex easily," said Catulus to Metellus Scipio, "by persuading anyone tempted to stand against you not to stand."

"Well, that's something, I suppose," said Metellus Scipio.

"Who intends to stand against Caesar?" asked Cicero, another member of this group who didn't quite know why he had been invited. He presumed it was at Hortensius's instigation, and that his function might be to find a loophole which would prevent Caesar's candidacy. The trouble was he knew there was no loophole. The *lex Labiena de sacerdotiis* had not been drafted by Labienus, so much was certain. It bore all the stamps of Caesar's drafting skill. It was watertight.

"I'm standing," said Catulus.

"So am I," said Vatia Isauricus, quiet until now.

"Then, as only seventeen of the thirty-five tribes vote in religious elections," said Cicero, "we will have to rig the lots to ensure both of your tribes are chosen, but that Caesar's tribe is not. That increases your chances."

"I disapprove of bribery," said Cato, "but I think this is one time we have to bribe." He turned to his nephew. "Quintus Servilius, you're by far the richest man here. Would you be willing to put up money in such a good cause?"

Brutus broke out in a cold sweat. So this was why!

He wet his lips, looked hunted. "Uncle, I would love to help you," he said, voice trembling, "but I dare not! My mother controls my purse strings, not I."

Cato's splendid nose thinned, its nostrils turned to blisters. "At twenty years of age, Quintus Servilius?" he blared.

All eyes were upon him, amazed; Brutus shrank down in his chair. "Uncle, please try to understand!" he whimpered.

"Oh, I understand," said Cato contemptuously, and deliberately turned his back. "It seems then," he said to the rest, "that we will have to find the money to bribe from out of our own purses." He shrugged. "As you know, mine is not plump. However, I will donate twenty talents."

"I can't really afford anything," said Catulus, looking miserable, "because Jupiter Optimus Maximus takes every spare sestertius I have. But from somewhere I will find fifty talents."

"Fifty from me," said Vatia Isauricus curtly.

"Fifty from me," said Metellus Scipio.

"And fifty from me," said Hortensius.

Cicero now understood perfectly why he was there, and said, voice beautifully modulated, "The penurious state of my finances is too well known for me to think you expect anything more from me than an onslaught of speeches to the electors. A service I am extremely happy to provide."

"Then there only remains," said Hortensius, his voice quite as melodious as Cicero's, "to decide which of the two of you will finally stand against Caesar."

But here the meeting ran into an unexpected snag; neither Catulus nor Vatia Isauricus was willing to stand down in favor of the other, for each believed absolutely that he must be the next Pontifex Maximus.

"Utter stupidity!" barked Cato, furious. "You'll end in splitting the vote, and that means Caesar's chances improve. If one of you stands, it's a straight battle. Two of you, and it becomes a three-way battle."

"I'm standing," said Catulus, looking mulish.

"And so am I," said Vatia Isauricus, looking pugnacious.

On which unhappy note the congress broke up. Bruised and humiliated, Brutus wended his way from the sumptuous dwelling of Metellus Scipio to his betrothed's unpretentious apartment in the Subura. There was really nowhere else he wanted to go, as Uncle Cato had rushed off without so much as acknowledging his nephew's existence, and the thought of going home to his mother and poor Silanus held no appeal whatsoever. Servilia would prise all the details out of him as to where he had been and what he had done and who was there and what Uncle Cato was up to; and his stepfather would simply sit like a battered doll minus half its stuffing.

His love for Julia only increased with the passage of the years. He never ceased to marvel at her beauty, her tender consideration for his feelings, her kindness, her liveliness. And her understanding. Oh, how grateful he was for the last!

Thus it was to her that he poured out the story of the meeting at Metellus Scipio's, and she, dearest and sweetest pet, listened with tears in her eyes.

"Even Metellus Scipio suffered little parental supervision," she said at the end of the story, "while the others are far too old to remember what it was like when they lived at home with the *paterfamilias*."

"Silanus is all right," said Brutus gruffly, fighting tears himself, "but I am so terribly afraid of my mother! Uncle Cato isn't afraid of anyone, that's the trouble."

Neither of them had any idea of the relationship between her father and his mother—any more than, indeed, did Uncle Cato. So Julia felt no constraints about communicating her dislike of Servilia to Brutus, and said, "I do understand, Brutus dear." She shivered, turned pale. "She has no compassion, no comprehension of her strength or her power to dominate. I think she is strong enough to blunt the shears of Atropos."

"I agree with you," said Brutus, sighing.

Time to cheer him up, make him feel better about himself. Julia said, smiling and reaching out to stroke his shoulder-length black curls, "I think you handle her beautifully, Brutus. You stay out of her way and do nothing to annoy her. If Uncle Cato had to live with her, he might understand your situation."

"Uncle Cato did live with her," said Brutus dolefully.

"Yes, but when she was a girl," said Julia, stroking.

Her touch triggered an impulse to kiss her, but Brutus did not, contenting himself with caressing the back of her hand as she drew it away from his hair. She was not long turned thirteen, and though her womanhood was now manifested by two exquisite little pointed bumps inside the bosom of her dress, Brutus knew she was not yet ready for kisses. He was also imbued with a sense of honor that had come from all his reading of the conservative Latin writers like Cato the Censor, and he deemed it wrong to stimulate a physical response in her that would end in making life for both of them uncomfortable. Aurelia trusted them, never supervised their meetings. Therefore he could not take advantage of that trust.

Of course it would have been better for both of them had he done so, for then Julia's increasing sexual aversion to him would have surfaced at an early enough age to make the breaking of their engagement an easier business. But because he did not touch or kiss her, Julia could find no reasonable excuse for going to her father and begging to be released from what she knew would be a ghastly marriage, no matter how obedient a wife she forced herself to be.

The trouble was that Brutus had so much money! Bad enough at the time of the betrothal, but a hundred times worse now that he had inherited the fortune of his mother's family as well. Like everyone else in Rome, Julia knew the story of the Gold of Tolosa, and what it had bought for the Servilii Caepiones. Brutus's money would be such a help to her father, of that there could be no doubt. *Avia* said it was her duty as her father's only child to make his life in the Forum more prestigious, to increase his *dignitas*. And there was only one way in which a girl could do this: she had to marry as much money and clout

as she could. Brutus may not have been any girl's idea of
marital bliss, but in respect of money and clout he had no
rival. Therefore she would do her duty and marry someone
whom she just didn't want to make love to her. *Tata* was
more important.

Thus when Caesar came to visit later that afternoon,
Julia behaved as if Brutus were the fiancé of her dreams.

"You're growing up," said Caesar, whose presence
in his home was rare enough these days that he could see
her evolving.

"Only five years to go," she said solemnly.

"Is that all?"

"Yes," she said with a sigh, "that's all, *tata*."

He settled her into the crook of his arm and kissed
the top of her head, unaware that Julia belonged to that
type of girl who could dream of no more wonderful husband than one exactly like her father: mature, famous,
handsome, a shaper of events.

"Any news?" he asked.

"Brutus came."

He laughed. "That is not news, Julia!"

"Perhaps it is," she said demurely, and related what
she had been told about the meeting at the house of Metellus Scipio.

"The gall of Cato!" he exclaimed when she was
done, "to demand large amounts of money from a twenty-
year-old boy!"

"They didn't get anywhere, thanks to his mother."

"You don't like Servilia, do you?"

"I'm in Brutus's shoes, *tata*. She terrifies me."

"Why, exactly?"

This she found difficult to elucidate for the benefit of
one famous for his love of undeniable facts. "It's just a
sort of feeling. Whenever I see her, I think of an evil black
snake."

He shook with mirth. "Have you ever seen an evil
black snake, Julia?"

"No, but I've seen pictures of them. And of Me-
dusa." She closed her eyes and turned her face into his
shoulder. "Do you like her, *tata*?"

That he could answer with perfect truth. "No."

"Well then, there you are," said his daughter.

"You're quite right," said Caesar. "There indeed I am!"

Naturally Aurelia was fascinated when Caesar recounted the story to her a few moments later.

"Isn't it nice to think that even mutual detestation of you can't obliterate ambition in either Catulus or Vatia Isauricus?" she asked, smiling slightly.

"Cato's right, if they both stand they'll split the vote. And if I have learned nothing else, I now know they'll rig the lots. No Fabian voters in this particular election!"

"But both their tribes will vote."

"I can deal with that provided that they both stand. Some of their natural partisans will see the strength of an argument from me that they should preserve their impartiality by voting for neither."

"Oh, clever!"

"Electioneering," said Caesar pensively, "is not merely a matter of bribery, though none of those hidebound fools can see that. Bribery is not a tool I dare use, even if I had the wish or the money to go in for it. If I am a candidate for an election, there will be half a hundred senatorial wolves baying for my blood—no vote or record or official will go uninvestigated. But there are many other ploys than bribery."

"It's a pity that the seventeen tribes which will vote will not be chosen until immediately beforehand," said Aurelia. "If they were selected a few days in advance, you could import some rural voters. The name Julius Caesar means a great deal more to any rural voter than either Lutatius Catulus or Servilius Vatia."

"Nonetheless, Mater, something can be done along those lines. There's bound to be at least one urban tribe— Lucius Decimius will prove invaluable there. Crassus will enlist his tribe if it's chosen. So will Magnus. And I do have influence in other tribes than Fabia."

A small silence fell, during which Caesar's face became grim; if Aurelia had been tempted to speak, sight of that change in his expression would have deterred her. It meant he was debating within himself whether to broach a less palatable subject, and the chances of that happening were greater if she effaced herself as much as possible. What less palatable subject could there be than money? So Aurelia held her peace.

"Crassus came to see me this morning," said Caesar at last.

Still she said nothing.

"My creditors are restless."

No word from Aurelia.

"The bills are still coming in from the days of my curule aedileship. That means I haven't managed to pay back anything I took as a loan."

Her eyes dropped to look at the surface of the desk.

"That includes the interest on the interest. There's talk among them of impeaching me to the censors, and even with one of them my uncle, the censors would have to do what the law says they must. I would lose my seat in the Senate and all my goods would be sold up. That includes my lands."

"Has Crassus any suggestions?" she ventured to asked.

"That I get myself elected Pontifex Maximus."

"He wouldn't lend you money himself?"

"That," said Caesar, "is a last resort as far as I'm concerned. Crassus is a great friend, but he's not got hay on his horns for nothing. He lends without interest, but he expects to be paid the moment he calls a loan in. Pompeius Magnus will be back before I'm consul, and I need to keep Magnus on my side. But Crassus detests Magnus, has done ever since their joint consulship. I have to tread a line between the pair of them. Which means I dare not owe either of them money."

"I see that. Will Pontifex Maximus do it?"

"Apparently so, with opponents as prestigious as Catulus and Vatia Isauricus. Victory would tell my creditors I will be praetor, and I will be senior consul. And that when I go to my consular province I'll recoup my losses, if not before. They'll be paid in the end, if not in the beginning. Though compound interest is ghastly and ought to be outlawed, it does have one advantage: creditors charging compound interest stand to make huge profits when a debt is paid, even if only in part."

"Then you had better be elected Pontifex Maximus."

"So I think."

The election to choose a new Pontifex Maximus and a fresh face for the College of Pontifices was set for twenty-four days' time. Who would own the fresh face was no mystery; the only candidate was Metellus Scipio. Both Catulus and Vatia Isauricus declared themselves available for election as Pontifex Maximus.

Caesar threw himself into campaigning with as much relish as energy. Like Catilina, the name and ancestry were an enormous help, despite the fact that neither of the other two candidates was a New Man, or even one of the moderately prominent *boni*. The post normally went to a man who had already been consul, but this advantage both Catulus and Vatia Isauricus held was negated to some extent at least by their ages: Catulus was sixty-one and Vatia Isauricus sixty-eight. In Rome the pinnacle of a man's ability, skills and prowess was considered to be his forty-third year, the year in which he ought to become consul. After that he was inevitably something of a has-been, no matter how huge his *auctoritas* or *dignitas*. He might be censor, Princeps Senatus, even consul a second time ten years further along, but once he attained the age of sixty he was inarguably past his prime. Though Caesar had not yet been praetor, he had been in the Senate for many years, he had been a pontifex for over a decade, he had shown himself a curule aedile of magnificence, he wore the Civic Crown on all public occasions, and he was known by the voters to be not only one of Rome's highest aristocrats, but also a man of huge ability and potential. His work in the Murder Court and as an advocate had not gone unnoticed; nor had his scrupulous care of his clients. Caesar in short was the future. Catulus and Vatia Isauricus were definitely the past—and tainted, both of them, with the faint odium of having enjoyed Sulla's favor. The majority of the voters who would turn up were knights, and Sulla had mercilessly persecuted the Ordo Equester. To counteract the undeniable fact that Caesar was Sulla's nephew by marriage, Lucius Decumius was deputed to trot out the old stories of Caesar's defying Sulla by refusing to divorce Cinna's daughter, and almost dying from disease when in hiding from Sulla's agents.

Three days before the election Cato summoned Catulus, Vatia Isauricus and Hortensius to a meeting at his house. This time there were no mushrooms like Cicero or youths like Caepio Brutus present. Even Metellus Scipio would have been a liability.

"I told you," said Cato with his usual lack of tact, "that it was a mistake for both of you to stand. I'm asking now that one of you step down and throw his weight behind the other."

"No," said Catulus.

"No," said Vatia Isauricus.

"Why can't you understand that both of you split the vote?" cried Cato, pounding his fist on the dowdy table which served him as a desk. He looked gaunt and unwell, for last night had seen a heavy session with the wine flagon; ever since Caepio's death Cato had turned to wine for solace, if solace it could be called. Sleep evaded him, Caepio's shade haunted him, the occasional slave girl he used to assuage his sexual needs revolted him, and even talking to Athenodorus Cordylion, Munatius Rufus and Marcus Favonius could occupy his mind only for a short period at a time. He read and he read and he read, yet still his loneliness and unhappiness came between him and the words of Plato, Aristotle, even his own great-grandfather, Cato the Censor. Thus the wine flagon, and thus his shortness of temper as he glared at the two unyielding elderly noblemen who refused to see the mistake they were making.

"Cato is right," said Hortensius, huffing. He too was not very young anymore, but as an augur he could not stand for Pontifex Maximus. Ambition could not cloud his wits, though his high living was beginning to. "One of you might beat Caesar, but both of you halve the votes either man alone could get.''

"Then it's time to bribe," said Catulus.

"Bribe?" yelled Cato, pounding the table until it shook. "There's no point in even starting to bribe! Two hundred and twenty talents can't buy you enough votes to beat Caesar!''

"Then," said Catulus, "why don't we bribe Caesar?''

The others stared at him.

"Caesar is close to two thousand talents in debt, and the debt is mounting every day because he can't afford to pay back a sestertius," said Catulus. "You may take it from me that my figures are correct.''

"Then *I* suggest," said Cato, "that we report his situation to the censors and demand that they act immediately to remove Caesar from the Senate. That would get rid of him forever!''

His suggestion was greeted with gasps of horror.

"My dear Cato, we can't do that!" bleated Hortensius. "He may be a pestilence, but he's one of *us*!''

"No, no, no! He is not one of us! If he isn't stopped he will tear all of us down, so I promise you!" roared Cato, fist hammering the defenseless table again. "Turn him in! Turn him in to the censors!''

"Absolutely not," said Catulus.

"Absolutely not," said Vatia Isauricus.

"Absolutely not," said Hortensius.

"Then," said Cato, looking cunning, "prevail upon someone well outside the Senate to turn him in—one of his creditors.''

Hortensius closed his eyes. A stauncher pillar of the *boni* than Cato did not exist, but there were times when the Tusculan peasant and the Celtiberian slave in him succeeded in overcoming truly Roman thought. Caesar was a kinsman to all of them, even Cato, no matter how remote the blood link might be—though in Catulus it was very close, come to think of it.

"Forget anything like that, Cato," Hortensius said,

opening his eyes wearily. "It is un-Roman. There is no more to be said."

"We will deal with Caesar in the Roman way," said Catulus. "If you are willing to divert the money you were to contribute toward bribing the electorate into bribing Caesar, then I will go to Caesar myself and offer it to him. Two hundred and twenty talents will make a fine first payment to his creditors. I am confident Metellus Scipio will agree."

"Oh, so am I!" snarled Cato between his teeth. "However, you spineless lot of fools, you can count me out! I wouldn't contribute a lead forgery to Caesar's purse!"

Thus it was that Quintus Lutatius Catulus sought an interview with Gaius Julius Caesar in his rooms on the Vicus Patricii between the Fabricius dye works and the Suburan Baths. It took place on the day before the election, quite early in the morning. The subtle splendor of Caesar's office took Catulus aback; he hadn't heard that his first cousin once removed had a fine eye for furniture and superior taste, nor had he imagined a side like that to Caesar. Is there nothing the man hasn't been gifted with? he asked himself, sitting down on a couch before he could be bidden occupy the client's chair. In which assumption he did Caesar an injustice; no one of Catulus's rank would have been relegated to the client's chair.

"Well, tomorrow is the big day," said Caesar, smiling as he handed a rock-crystal goblet of watered wine to his guest.

"That's what I've come to see you about," said Catulus, and took a sip of what turned out to be an excellent vintage. "Good wine, but I don't know it," he said, sidetracked.

"I grow it myself, actually," said Caesar.

"Near Bovillae?"

"No, in a little vineyard I own in Campania."

"That accounts for it."

"What was it you wished to discuss, cousin?" asked Caesar, not about to be sidetracked into oenology.

Catulus drew a deep breath. "It has come to my attention, Caesar, that your financial affairs are in a state of acute embarrassment. I'm here to ask you not to stand for election as the Pontifex Maximus. In return for doing me that favor, I will undertake to give you two hundred silver talents." He reached into the sinus of his toga and withdrew a small rolled paper which he extended to Caesar.

Not so much as a glance did Caesar give it, nor did he make any attempt to take it. Instead, he sighed.

"You would have done better to use the money to bribe the electors," he said. "Two hundred talents would have helped."

"This seemed more efficient."

"But wasted, cousin. I don't want your money."

"You can't afford not to take it."

"That is true. But I refuse to take it nonetheless."

The little roll remained in Catulus's extended hand. "Do please reconsider," he said, two spots of crimson beginning to show in his cheeks.

"Put your money away, Quintus Lutatius. When the election is held tomorrow I will be there in my particolored toga to ask the voters to return me as Pontifex Maximus. No matter what."

"I beg you, Gaius Julius, one more time. *Take the money!*"

"I beg you, Quintus Lutatius, one more time. *Desist!*"

Whereupon Catulus threw the rock-crystal goblet down on the floor and walked out.

Caesar sat for a moment gazing at the starred pink puddle spreading across the minute checkerboard of mosaic tiles; then he rose, went to the service room for a rag, and wiped the mess up. The goblet fell into small crazed pieces the moment he put his hand upon it, so he carefully collected all the fragments into the rag, bunched it into a parcel, and threw it into the refuse container in the service room. Armed with a fresh rag, he then completed his cleaning.

*   *   *

"I was glad he threw the goblet down so hard," said Caesar to his mother the next morning at dawn when he called to receive her blessing.

"Oh, Caesar, how can you be glad? I know the thing well—and I know how much you paid for it."

"I bought it as perfect, yet it turned out to be flawed."

"Ask for your money back."

Which provoked an exclamation of annoyance. "Mater, Mater, when *will* you learn? The crux of the matter has nothing to do with buying the wretched thing! It was flawed. I want no flawed items in my possession."

Because she just didn't understand, Aurelia abandoned the subject. "Be successful, my dearest son," she said, kissing his brow. "I won't come to the Forum, I'll wait here for you."

"If I lose, Mater," he said with his most beautiful smile, "you'll wait for a long time! If I lose, I won't be able to come home at all."

And off he went, clad in his priest's toga of scarlet and purple stripes, with hundreds of clients and every Suburan man streaming after him down the Vicus Patricii, and a feminine head poking out of every window to wish him luck.

Faintly she heard him call to his windowed well-wishers: "One day Caesar's luck will be proverbial!"

After which Aurelia sat at her desk and totted up endless columns of figures on her ivory abacus, though she never wrote one answer down, nor remembered afterward that she had worked so diligently with nothing to show for it.

He didn't seem to be away very long, actually; later she learned it had been all of six springtime hours. And when she heard his voice issuing jubilantly from the reception room, she hadn't the strength to get up; he had to go to find her.

"You regard the new Pontifex Maximus!" he cried from the doorway, hands clasped above his head.

"Oh, Caesar!" she said, and wept.

Nothing else could have unmanned him, for in all his

life he could never remember her shedding a tear. He gulped, face collapsing, stumbled into the room and lifted her to her feet, his arms about her, her arms about him, both of them weeping.

"Not even for Cinnilla," he said when he was able.

"I did, but not in front of you."

He used his handkerchief to mop his face, then performed the same service for her. "We won, Mater, we won! I'm still in the arena, and I still have a sword in my hand."

Her smile was shaky, but it was a smile. "How many people are out in the reception room?" she asked.

"A terrible crush, that's all I know."

"Did you win by much?"

"In all seventeen tribes."

"Even in Catulus's? And Vatia's?"

"I polled more votes in their two tribes than they did put together, can you imagine it?"

"This is a sweet victory," she whispered, "but why?"

"One or the other of them ought to have stepped down. Two of them split their vote," said Caesar, beginning to feel that he could face a room jammed with people. "Besides which, I was Jupiter Optimus Maximus's own priest when I was young, and Sulla stripped me of it. The Pontifex Maximus belongs to the Great God too. My clients did a lot of talking in the Well of the Comitia before the vote was taken, and right up until the last tribe polled." He grinned. "I told you, Mater, that there is more to electioneering than mere bribery. Hardly a man who voted wasn't convinced I would be lucky for Rome because I have always belonged to Jupiter Optimus Maximus."

"It could as easily have gone against you. They might have concluded that a man who had been *flamen Dialis* would be unlucky for Rome."

"No! Men always wait for someone to tell them how they ought to feel about the Gods. I just made sure I got in before the opposition thought of that tack. Needless to say, they didn't."

* * *

Metellus Scipio had not lived in the Domus Publica of the Pontifex Maximus since his marriage to Aemilia Lepida some years before, and the Piglet's barren Licinia had died before him. The State residence of the Pontifex Maximus was vacant.

Naturally no one at the Piglet's funeral had thought it in good taste to remark on the fact that this one un-elected Pontifex Maximus had been inflicted upon Rome by Sulla as a wicked joke because Metellus Pius stammered dreadfully whenever he was under stress. This tendency to stammer had led to every ceremony's being fraught with the additional tension of wondering whether the Pontifex Maximus would get all the words out properly. For every ceremony had to be perfect, in word as well as in execution; were it not perfect, it had to begin all over again.

The new Pontifex Maximus was hardly likely to stumble over a word, the more so as it was well known that he drank no wine. Yet another of Caesar's little electoral ploys, to have that morsel of information well bruited about during the pontifical election. And to have comments made about old men like Vatia Isauricus and Catulus beginning to wander. After nearly twenty years of having to worry about stammers, Rome was delighted to see a Pontifex Maximus in office who would give none but flawless performances.

Hordes of clients and enthusiastic supporters came to offer their help in moving Caesar and his family to the Domus Publica in the Forum Romanum, though the Subura was desolate at the prospect of losing its most prestigious inhabitant. Especially old Lucius Decumius, who had worked indefatigably to see the thing done, yet knew his life would never be the same again with Caesar gone.

"You're always welcome, Lucius Decumius," said Aurelia.

"Won't be the same," said the old man gloomily. "I always knew you was here next door, that you was all right. But down there in the Forum among the temples and the *Vestals*? Ugh!"

"Cheer up, dear friend," said the lady in her sixties

with whom Lucius Decimius had fallen in love during her nineteenth year. "He doesn't intend to rent this apartment or give up his rooms down the Vicus Patricii. He says he still needs his bolt-holes."

That was the best news Lucius Decimius had heard in days! Off he went to tell his Crossroads Brethren that Caesar would still be a part of the Subura, skipping like a little boy.

It worried Caesar not a scrap that he now stood firmly and legally at the head of an institution filled mostly with men who detested him. His investiture in the temple of Jupiter Optimus Maximus concluded, he summoned the priests of his own College to a meeting which he held then and there. This he chaired with such efficiency and detachment that priests like Sextus Sulpicius Galba and Publius Mucius Scaevola breathed sighs of delighted relief, and wondered if perhaps the State religion would benefit from Caesar's elevation to Pontifex Maximus, obnoxious and all as he was politically. Uncle Mamercus, getting old and wheezy, just smiled; none knew better than he how good Caesar was at getting things done.

Each second year was supposed to see twenty extra days inserted into the calendar to keep it in step with the seasons, but a series of Pontifices Maximi like Ahenobarbus and Metellus Pius had neglected this duty, within the sphere of the College. In future these extra twenty days would be intercalated without fail, Caesar announced firmly. No excuses or religious quibbles would be tolerated. He then went on to say that he would promulgate a law in the Comitia which would intercalate an extra hundred days and finally bring the calendar and the seasons into perfect step. At the moment the season of summer was just beginning when the calendar said that autumn was just about over. This scheme caused mutters of outrage from some, but no violent opposition; all present (including Caesar) knew that he would have to wait until he was consul to have any chance of passing the law at all.

During a lull in the proceedings Caesar gazed about at the interior of Jupiter Optimus Maximus with a frown.

Catulus was still struggling to complete its rebuilding, and the work had fallen far behind schedule once the shell was up. The temple was habitable but uninspiring, and quite lacked the splendor of the old structure. Many of the walls were plastered and painted but not adorned with frescoes or suitably elaborate moldings, and clearly Catulus did not have the enterprise—or perhaps the turn of mind—to badger foreign states and princes into donating wonderful objects of art to Jupiter Optimus Maximus as a part of their homage to Rome. No solid or even skinned gold statues, no glorious Victories driving four-horsed chariots, no Zeuxis paintings—not even as yet an image of the Great God to replace the ancient terracotta giant sculpted by Vulca before Rome was more than an infant crawling onto the world stage. But for the moment Caesar held his peace. Pontifex Maximus was a lifetime job, and he was not yet thirty-seven years old.

After the meeting concluded with his announcement that he would hold his inaugural feast in the temple of the Domus Publica in eight days' time, he began the short downhill walk from the temple of Jupiter Optimus Maximus to the Domus Publica. Long used to the inevitable crowd of clients who accompanied him everywhere and thus able to shut out their chatter, he moved more slowly than his wont, deep in thought. That he did in truth belong to the Great God was inarguable, which meant he had won this election at the Great God's behest. Yes, he would have to administer a public kick to Catulus's backside, and bend his own mind to the urgent problem of how to fill the temple of Jupiter Optimus Maximus with beauty and treasures in a day and age wherein the best of everything went into private houses and peristyle gardens instead of into Rome's temples, and wherein the best artists and artisans obtained far greater incomes working in private employment than for the pittance the State was prepared to pay them for working on public buildings.

He had left the most important interview until last, deeming it better to establish his authority within the College of Pontifices before he saw the Vestal Virgins. All the priestly and augural Colleges were a part of his re-

sponsibility as titular and actual head of Roman religion,
but the College of Vestal Virgins enjoyed a unique relationship with the Pontifex Maximus. Not only was he their
paterfamilias; he also shared a house with them.

The Domus Publica was extremely old and had endured no fires. Generations of wealthy Pontifices Maximi
had poured money and care into it, even knowing that
whatever portable they gave, from chryselephantine tables
to inlaid Egyptian couches, could not later be removed for
the benefit of family heirs.

Like all the very early Republican Forum buildings,
the Domus Publica lay at an odd angle to the vertical axis
of the Forum itself, for in the days when it had been built
all sacred or public structures had to be oriented between
north and south; the Forum, a natural declivity, was oriented from northeast to southwest. Later buildings were
erected on the Forum line, which made for a tidier, more
attractive overall landscape. As one of the Forum's largest
edifices, the Domus Publica was also rather glaringly obvious to the eye, and did not gladden it. Partly obscured
by the Regia and the offices of the Pontifex Maximus, the
tall facade on its ground floor was built of unrendered tufa
blocks with rectangular windows; the top floor, added by
that quirky Pontifex Maximus Ahenobarbus, was *opus incertum* brickwork with arched windows. An unhappy combination which would—at least from the front aspect of
the Sacra Via—be vastly improved by the addition of a
proper and imposing temple portico and pediment. Or so
thought Caesar, deciding in that moment what his contribution to the Domus Publica would be. It was an inaugurated temple, therefore no law existed to prevent his
doing this.

In shape the building was more or less square, though
it had a jog on either side which widened it. Behind it was
the little thirty-foot-high cliff forming the lowest tier of
the Palatine. On top of that cliff was the Via Nova, a busy
street of taverns, shops and insulae; an alley ran behind
the Domus Publica and gave access to the substructure of
the Via Nova buildings. All these premises reared high
above the level of the cliff, so that their back windows

had a wonderful view of what went on inside the Domus Publica courtyards. They also completely blocked any afternoon sun the residence of the Pontifex Maximus and the Vestal Virgins might have received, which meant that the Domus Publica, already handicapped by its low-lying location, was sure to be a cold place to live in. The Porticus Margaritaria, a gigantic rectangular shopping arcade just uphill from it and oriented on the Forum axis, actually abutted onto its rear end, and sliced off a corner of it.

However, no Roman—even one as logical as Caesar—found anything odd in peculiarly shaped buildings, missing a corner here, sprouting an excrescence there; what could be built on a straight line was, and what had to go around adjacent structures already there, or boundaries so ancient the priests who had defined them had probably followed the track of a hopping bird, went around them. If one looked at the Domus Publica from that point of view, it really wasn't very irregular. Just huge and ugly and cold and damp.

His escort of clients hung back in awe when Caesar strode up to the main doors, which were of bronze cast in sculpted panels telling the story of Cloelia. Under normal circumstances they were not used, as both sides of the building had entrances. Today, however, was not a normal day. Today the new Pontifex Maximus took possession of his domain, and that was an act of great formality. Caesar pounded three times with the flat of his right hand upon the right-hand leaf of the door, which opened immediately. The Chief Vestal admitted him with a low reverence, then closed it upon the sighing, teary-eyed horde of clients, who now reconciled themselves to a long wait outside, and started thinking of snacks and gossip.

Perpennia and Fonteia had been retired for some years; the woman who was now the Chief Vestal was Licinia, close cousin of Murena and remoter cousin of Crassus.

"But," she said as she led Caesar up the curving central ramp of the vestibule to another set of beautiful bronze doors at its top, "I intend to retire as soon as possible. My cousin Murena is standing for consul this year, and begged me to remain Chief Vestal long enough to assist him in his canvassing.''

A plain and pleasant woman, Licinia, though not nearly strong enough to fill her position adequately, Caesar knew. As a pontifex he had had dealings with the adult Vestals over the years, and as a pontifex he had deplored their fate since the day Metellus Pius the Piglet had become their *paterfamilias*. First Metellus Pius had spent ten years fighting Sertorius in Spain, then he had returned aged beyond his years and in no mood to worry about the six female creatures whom he was supposed to care for, supervise, instruct, advise. Nor had his doleful, negative wife been of much help. And, in the way things usually did happen, none of the three women who had in turn become Chief Vestal could cope without firm guidance. As a consequence the College of Vestal Virgins was in decline. Oh, the sacred fire was rigorously tended and the various festivals and ceremonies conducted as was proper. But the scandal of Publius Clodius's accusations of unchastity still hung like a pall over the six women thought to be a personification of Rome's good luck, and none of them old enough to have been in the College when it had occurred had emerged from it without terrible scars.

Licinia struck the right-hand door three times with the flat of her right hand, and Fabia admitted them to the temple with a low reverence. Here within these hallowed portals the Vestal Virgins had assembled to greet their new *paterfamilias* on the only ground within the Domus Publica which was common to both lots of tenants.

So what did their new *paterfamilias* do? Why, he gave them a cheerful, unreligious smile and walked straight through their midst in the direction of a third set of double doors at the far end of the dimly lit hall!

''Outside, girls!'' he said over his shoulder.

In the chilly precinct of the peristyle garden he found a sheltered spot where three stone benches lay alongside each other in the colonnade, then—effortlessly, it seemed—he lifted one around to face the other two. He sat upon it in his gorgeous scarlet-and-purple-striped toga, now wearing the scarlet-and-purple-striped tunic of the

Pontifex Maximus beneath it, and with a casual flap of his hand indicated that they were to sit. A terrified silence fell, during which Caesar looked his new women over.

Object of the amorous intentions of both Catilina and Clodius, Fabia was held to be the prettiest Vestal Virgin in generations. Second in seniority, she would succeed Licinia when that lady retired soon. Not a very satisfactory prospect as Chief Vestal; had the College been inundated with candidates when she had been admitted to it, she would never have been admitted at all. But Scaevola, who had been Pontifex Maximus at the time, had no other alternative than to stifle his wish that a plain girl child would be offered, and take this ravishing scion of Rome's oldest (albeit now entirely adoptive) Famous Family, the Fabii. Odd. She and Cicero's wife, Terentia, shared the same mother. Yet Terentia possessed none of Fabia's beauty or sweetness of nature—though she was very much the more intelligent of the two. At the present moment Fabia was twenty-eight years old, which meant that the College would keep her for another eight to ten years.

Then there were two the same age, Popillia and Arruntia. Both charged with unchastity by Clodius, citing Catilina. Far plainer than Fabia, thanks the Gods! When they had stood trial the jury had found no difficulty in deeming them completely innocent, though they had been but seventeen. A worry! Three of these present six would retire within two years of each other, which left the new Pontifex Maximus with the job of finding three new little Vestals to replace them. However, that was ten years away. Popillia of course was a close cousin of Caesar's, whereas Arruntia, of a less august family, had almost no blood tie to him. Neither had ever recovered from the stigma of alleged unchastity, which meant they clung together and led very sequestered lives.

The two replacements for Perpennia and Fonteia were still children, again of much the same age, eleven.

One was a Junia, sister of Decimus Brutus, daughter of Sempronia Tuditani. Why she had been offered to the College at six years of age was no mystery: Sempronia Tuditani couldn't stomach a potential rival, and Decimus

Brutus was proving ruinously expensive. Most of the little girls came healthily provided for by their families, but Junia was dowerless. Not an insuperable problem, as the State was always willing to provide a dowry for those who lacked one from their families. She would be quite attractive once the pangs of puberty were done with—how *did* these poor creatures cope with that in such a restricted and motherless environment?

The other child was a patrician from an old though somewhat decayed family, a Quinctilia who was very fat. She too was dowerless. An indication, thought Caesar grimly, of the present College's reputation: no one who could dower a girl well enough to get her a reasonable husband was going to give her to the Vestals. Costly for the State, and bad luck as well. Of course they had been offered a Pompeia, a Lucceia, even an Afrania, a Lollia, a Petreia; Pompey the Great was desperate to entrench himself and his Picentine followers within Rome's most revered institutions. But old and sick though he had been, the Piglet was not about to accept any of *that* stock! Preferable by far to have the State dower children with the proper ancestors—or at least a father who had won the Grass Crown, like Fonteia.

The adult Vestals knew Caesar about as well as he knew them, a knowledge acquired mostly through attendance at the formal banquets and functions held within the priestly Colleges—not, therefore, a deep or even a particularly friendly knowledge. Some private feasts in Rome might degenerate into affairs of too much wine and too many personal confidences, but never the religious ones. The six faces turned in Caesar's direction held—what? It would take time to find out. Yet his breezy and cheerful manner had thrown them a little off balance. That was deliberate on his part; he didn't want them shutting him out or concealing things from him, and none of these Vestals had been born when there was last a young Pontifex Maximus in the person of the famous Ahenobarbus. Essential then to make them think that the new Pontifex Maximus would be a *paterfamilias* to whom they could turn with real security. Never a salacious glance from him,

never the familiarity of touch from him, never an innuendo
from him. Nor, on the other hand, any coldness, lack of
sympathy, off-putting formality, awkwardness.

Licinia coughed nervously, wet her lips, ventured to
speak. "When will you be moving in, *domine*?"

He was, of course, in truth their lord, and he had
already decided that it was fitting they should always address him as such. He could call them his girls, but they
would never have any excuse to call him their man.

"Perhaps the day after tomorrow," he said with a
smile, stretching his legs out and sighing.

"You will want to be shown over the whole building."

"Yes, and again tomorrow, when I bring my
mother."

They had not forgotten that he had a highly respected
mother, nor were they ignorant of all the aspects of his
family structure, from the engagement of his daughter and
Caepio Brutus to the dubious folk with whom his empty-
headed wife associated. His answer told them clearly what
the pecking order would be: mother first. That was a relief!

"And your wife?" asked Fabia, who privately
thought Pompeia very beautiful and alluring.

"My wife," said Caesar coolly, "is not important. I
doubt that you'll ever see her, she leads a busy social life.
Whereas my mother is bound to be interested in everything." He said the last with another of those wonderful
smiles, thought for a moment, and added, "Mater is a
pearl beyond price. Don't be afraid of her, and don't be
afraid to talk to her. Though I am your *paterfamilias,* there
are corners of your lives which you will prefer to discuss
with a woman. Until now you have had either to go outside this house or confine such discussions to yourselves.
Mater has a fount of experience and a mine of common
sense. Bathe in the one, and delve in the other. She never
gossips, even to me."

"We look forward to her advent," said Licinia formally.

"As for you two," said Caesar, addressing the children, "my daughter isn't much older than you, and she's

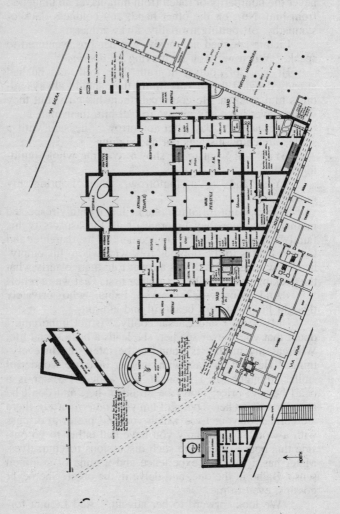

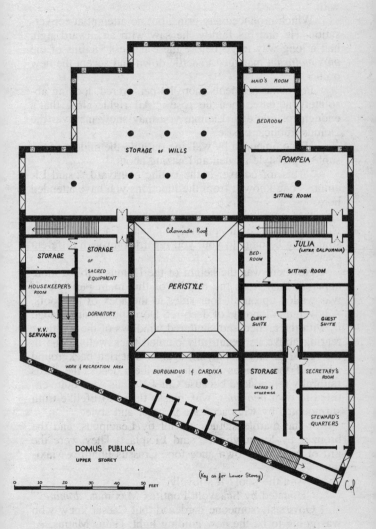

MAID'S ROOM

BEDROOM

POMPEIA

STORAGE of WILLS

SITTING ROOM

Colonnade Roof

STORAGE
OF
SACRED
EQUIPMENT

STORAGE

BED-
ROOM

JULIA
(LATER CALPURNIA)

SITTING ROOM

HOUSEKEEPER'S
ROOM

PERISTYLE

DORMITORY

GUEST
SUITE

GUEST
SUITE

V.V.
SERVANTS

WORK & RECREATION AREA

BURGUNDUS & CARDIXA

STORAGE

SACRED &
OTHERWISE

SECRETARY'S
ROOM

STEWARD'S
QUARTERS

DOMUS PUBLICA

UPPER STOREY

(Key as for Lower Storey)

0   10   20   30   40   50 FEET

Col

another pearl beyond price. You'll have a friend to play with.''

Which produced shy grins, but no attempt at conversation. He and his family, he saw with an inward sigh, had a long way to go before these hapless victims of the *mos maiorum* managed to settle down and accept the new order.

For some moments more he persevered, looking absolutely at ease, then he rose. ''All right, girls, that's enough for one day. Licinia, you may show me over the Domus Publica, please.''

He commenced by walking out into the middle of the sunless peristyle garden and gazing about.

''This, of course, is the public courtyard,'' said Licinia. ''You know it from the functions you have attended here.''

''At none of which I've ever had the leisure or the isolation to see it properly,'' said Caesar. ''When something belongs to you, you regard it through different eyes.''

Nowhere was the height of the Domus Publica more apparent than from the middle of this main peristyle; it was walled up on all four sides to the apex of the roofs. A covered colonnade of deep-red Doric pillars surrounded it, with the arched and shuttered windows of the top floor rearing above its beautifully painted back walls, done in the red style and displaying against that rich background some of the famous Vestals and their deeds, the faces faithfully reproduced because Chief Vestals were quite entitled to own *imagines,* wax masks tinted to lifelike truth surmounted by wigs accurate in color and style.

''The marble statues are all by Leucippus, and the bronzes by Strongylion,'' said Licinia. ''They were the gift of one of my own ancestors, Crassus Pontifex Maximus.''

''And the pool? It's lovely.''

''Donated by Scaevola Pontifex Maximus, *domine.*''

Obviously someone gardened, but Caesar knew who was going to be the new guiding light: Gaius Matius. At which moment he turned to observe the back wall, and

saw what seemed like hundreds of windows peering down
from the Via Nova, most of them filled with faces; everyone knew that today the new Pontifex Maximus underwent
inauguration, and was bound to call in to see his residence
and his charges, the Vestals.

"You have absolutely no privacy," he said, pointing.

"None, *domine,* from the main peristyle. Our own
peristyle was added by Ahenobarbus Pontifex Maximus,
and he built its walls so high we are invisible." She
sighed. "Alas, we get no sun."

They moved then into the only public room, the *cella*
between the building's two sides that constituted the temple. Though it contained no statues, it too was frescoed
and lavishly gilded; the light unfortunately was too dim to
appreciate the quality of the work the way it demanded.
Down either side, each on a precious stand, marched a
row of miniature temples, the cabinets in which lived the
imagines of the Chief Vestals since the order had been
started in the misty days of the earliest kings of Rome. No
use opening one to peer in at the color of Claudia's skin
or the way she had worn her hair; the light was too poor.

"We will have to see what we can do about that,"
said Caesar, proceeding back to the vestibule, the first
room he had entered.

Here, he realized now, the antiquity of the place
showed best, for it was so old Licinia could not tell him
exactly why it was the way that it was, or what the purpose
of its features might have been. The floor rose ten feet
from the outer doors to the temple doors in three separate
ramps tiled with a truly fabulous mosaic of what he
guessed might be glass or faience in convoluted but abstract patterns. Dividing the ramps from each other and
giving them their curving outline were two *amygdalae,*
almond-shaped wells paved with time-blackened blocks of
tufa, each one containing at its ritual middle a pedestal of
polished black stone upon which stood the halves of a
hollow spherical rock lined with garnet-colored crystals
glittering like beads of blood. On either side of the outer
doors lay another tufa-paved well, inner edge curved. The
walls and ceiling were much newer, a complex riot of

plaster flowers and lattices, painted in shades of green and picked out with gilt.

"The sacred car upon which we move our dead passes easily down either side ramp—Vestals use one, the Pontifex Maximus the other—but we do not know who used the central ramp, or what for. Perhaps the death car of the King, but I do not know. It is a mystery," said Licinia.

"There must be answers somewhere," said Caesar, fascinated. He gazed at the Chief Vestal with brows raised. "Where now?"

"Whichever side you prefer to see first, *domine.*"

"Then let it be your side."

The half of the Domus Publica which accommodated the Vestals also housed an industry, plain to see when Licinia ushered Caesar into an L-shaped room fifty feet long. What would have been the atrium or reception room of an ordinary *domus* was here the workplace of the Vestals, who were the formal custodians of Roman wills. It had been most intelligently converted to serve its purpose, with box shelves to the lofty ceiling for book buckets or unprotected scrolls, desks and chairs, ladders and stools, and a number of stands from which hung big sheets of Pergamum parchment made up of smaller rectangles carefully and minutely sewn together.

"We accept custody of the will through there," said the Chief Vestal, pointing toward the area closest to the outside doors through which entered those who wished to lodge their wills within the Atrium Vestae. "As you can see, it is walled off from the main part of the room. Would you like to look, *domine*?"

"Thank you, I know the spot well," said Caesar, executor of many wills.

"Today, of course, being *feriae,* the doors are closed and no one is on duty. Tomorrow we'll be busy."

"And this part of the room contains the wills."

"Oh, no!" gasped Licinia, horrified. "This is just our record room, *domine.*"

"Record room?"

"Yes. We keep a record of every will lodged with us

as well as the testament itself—name, tribe, address, age when lodged, and so forth. When the will is executed it leaves us. But the records never do. Nor do we ever discard them.''

"So all these book buckets and pigeonholes are stuffed with records, nothing but records?''

"Yes.''

"And these?'' he asked, walking across to one of the stands to count the number of parchment sheets suspended from it.

"Those are our master plans, an instruction manual for finding everything from which names belong to which tribes, to lists of *municipia,* towns all over the world, maps of our storage system. Some of them contain the full roll of Roman citizens.''

The stand held six parchment sheets two feet wide and five feet long, each of them written upon both sides, the script clear and fine and darkly delineated, quite the equal of any trained Greek scribe's writing that Caesar had ever known. His eyes roamed the room and counted thirty stands in all. "They list more than you've told me.''

"Yes, *domine.* We archive everything we can, it interests us to do so. The first Aemilia who was ever a Vestal was wise enough to know that the everyday tasks, tending the sacred fire and carrying all of our water from the well—it was the Fountain of Egeria in those days, admittedly a lot farther away than Juturna—were not enough to keep our minds busy and our intentions and our vows pure. We had been custodians of wills when all the Vestals were daughters of the King, but under Aemilia we expanded the work we did, and commenced to archive.''

"So here I see a veritable treasure-house of information.''

"Yes, *domine.*''

"How many wills do you have in your care?''

"About a million.''

"All listed here,'' he said, hand sweeping around the high, crammed walls.

"Yes and no. The current wills are confined to pigeonholes; we find it easier to consult a naked scroll than to struggle in and out of book buckets all the time. We keep things well dusted. The buckets contain the records of wills departed from our custody.''

"How far do your records go back, Licinia?''

"To the two youngest daughters of King Ancus Marcius, though not in the detail Aemilia instituted.''

"I begin to understand why that unorthodox fellow Ahenobarbus Pontifex Maximus installed your plumbing and reduced the taking of water from the Well of Juturna to a ritual daily pitcherful. You have more important work to do, though at the time Ahenobarbus did it, he created a furor.''

"We will never cease to be grateful to Ahenobarbus Pontifex Maximus,'' said Licinia, leading the way to a flight of stairs. "He added the second storey not only to make our lives healthier and more comfortable, but also to give us room to store the wills themselves. They used to be in the basement, we had nowhere else. Even so, storage is once again a problem. In earlier times wills were confined to Roman citizens, and mostly citizens who lived within Rome herself at that. These days we accept almost as many wills from citizens and non-citizens who live all over the world.'' She coughed and sniffled as she reached the top of the stairs and opened the door into a vast cavern lit from windows on one side only, that looking at the House of Vesta.

Caesar understood her sudden attack of respiratory distress; the place exuded a miasma of paper particles and bone-dry dust.

"Here we store the wills of Roman citizens, perhaps three quarters of a million,'' said Licinia. "Rome, there. Italia, here. The various provinces of Rome, there and there and there. Other countries, over here. And a new section for Italian Gaul, here. It became necessary after the Italian War, when all the communities south of the Padus River were enfranchised. We had to expand our section for Italia too.''

They were pigeonholed in rank after rank of wooden box shelves, each one tagged and labeled, perhaps fifty to one single box; he withdrew a specimen from Italian Gaul, then another and another. All different in size and thickness and the sort of paper, all sealed with wax and someone's insignia. This one hefty—a lot of property! That one slender and humble—perhaps a tiny cottage and a pig to bequeath.

"And where are the wills of non-citizens stored?" he asked as Licinia descended the stairs ahead of him.

"In the basement, *domine,* together with the records of all army wills and deaths on military service. We do not, of course, ever have custody of soldiers' wills themselves—they remain in the care of the legion clerks, and when a man finishes his time, they destroy his will. He then makes a new one and lodges it with us." She sighed mournfully. "There is still space down there, but I fear it won't be long before we have to shift some of the provincial citizen wills to the basement, which also has to house quite a lot of sacred equipment we and you need for ceremonies. So where," she enquired plaintively, "will we go when the whole of the basement is as full as it was for Ahenobarbus?"

"Luckily, Licinia, it won't be your worry," said Caesar, "though it will undoubtedly be mine. How extraordinary to think that feminine Roman efficiency and attention to detail has bred a repository the like of which the world has never known before! Everyone wants his will kept safe from prying eyes and tampering pens. Where else is that possible except in the Atrium Vestae?"

The largeness of this observation escaped her, she was too busy shocking herself at discovery of an omission. "*Domine,* I forgot to show you the section for women's wills!" she cried.

"Yes, women do make wills," he said, preserving gravity. "It is a great comfort to realize that you segregate the sexes, even in death." When this sailed somewhere miles above her head, he thought of something else. "It amazes me that so many people lodge their wills here in Rome, yet may dwell in places up to several months' journey away. I would have thought all the movable property and coin would have vanished by the time the will itself could be executed."

"I do not know, *domine,* because we never find out things like that. But if people do it, then surely they must feel secure in doing it. I imagine," she concluded simply, "that everyone fears Rome and Roman retribution. Look at the will of King Ptolemy Alexander! The present King of Egypt is terrified of Rome because he knows Egypt really belongs to Rome from that will."

"True," said Caesar solemnly.

From the workplace (where, he noticed, even the two child Vestals were now busy at some task, *feriae* notwithstanding) he was conducted to the living quarters. These were, he decided, very adequate compensation for a conventual existence. However, the dining room was country style, chairs round a table.

"You don't have men to dine?" he asked.

Licinia looked horrified. "Not in our own quarters, *domine*! You are the only man who will ever enter here."

"What about doctors and carpenters?"

"There are good women doctors, also women craftsmen of all kinds. Rome bears no prejudices against women in trades."

"So much I don't know, despite the fact that I've been a pontifex for over ten years," said Caesar, shaking his head.

"Well, you were not in Rome during our trials," said Licinia, her voice trembling. "Our private entertaining and living habits were publicly aired then. But under normal circumstances only the Pontifex Maximus among the priests concerns himself with how we live. And our relatives and friends, naturally."

"True. The last Julia in the College was Julia Strabo, and she died untimely. Do many of you die untimely, Licinia?"

"Very few these days, though I believe death here was common before we had water and plumbing laid on. Would you like to see the bathrooms and latrines? Ahenobarbus believed in hygiene for everyone, so he gave the servants baths and latrines too."

"A remarkable man," said Caesar. "How they reviled him for changing the law—and getting himself elected Pontifex Maximus at the same time! I remember Gaius Marius telling me there was an epidemic of marble-latrine-seat jokes after Ahenobarbus finished with the Domus Publica."

Though Caesar was reluctant, Licinia insisted that he should see the Vestal sleeping arrangements.

"Metellus Pius Pontifex Maximus thought of it after he came back from Spain. You see?" she asked, conducting him through a series of curtained archways leading off her own sleeping cubicle. "The only way out is through my room. We all used to have doors onto the passageway, but Metellus Pius Pontifex Maximus bricked them up. He said we must be protected from all allegations."

Lips tight, Caesar said nothing; they retraced their steps back to the Vestal workplace. There he returned to the subject of wills, which fascinated him.

"Your figures shocked me," he said, "but I realize they ought not. All my life has passed in the Subura, and how many times I have seen it for myself, that Head Count man owning a single slave solemnly parading down to the Atrium Vestae to lodge his will. Nothing to leave but a brooch, some chairs and a table, a prized haybox oven, and his slave. Tricked out in his citizen's toga and bearing his grain chit as proof of his Roman status, as proud as Tarquinius Superbus. He can't vote in the Centuries and his urban tribe makes his comitial vote worthless, but he can serve in our legions and he can lodge his will."

"You neglected to say, *domine,* how many times he arrives with you at his side as his patron," said Licinia. "It does not escape us which patrons find the time to do this, and which just send one of their freedmen."

"Who comes in person?" asked Caesar, curious.

"You and Marcus Crassus, always. Cato too, and the Domitii Ahenobarbi. Of the rest, hardly any."

"No surprise in those names!"

Time to change the subject while a loud voice would enable all the toiling white-clad figures to hear him. "You work very hard," he said. "I've lodged enough wills and demanded enough of them for probate, but it never oc-

curred to me what an enormous task it is to care for
Rome's last testaments. You are to be commended."

Thus it was a very pleased and happy Chief Vestal
who let him into the vestibule again, and handed him the
keys to his domain.

Wonderful!

The L-shaped reception room was a mirror-image
twin of the Vestal workplace, fifty feet on its long side.
No expense or luxury had been spared, from the glorious
frescoes to the gilding to the furniture and art objects littered everywhere. Mosaic floor, fabulous ceiling of plaster
roses and gold honeycomb, colored marble pilasters engaging the walls and colored marble sheaths on the sole
freestanding column.

A study and sleeping cubicle for the Pontifex Maximus, and a smaller suite for his wife. A dining room which
held a full six couches. A peristyle garden off to one side,
adjacent to the Porticus Margaritaria and on full view to
the windows of the Via Nova insulae. The kitchen could
feed thirty diners; though it was within the main structure,
most of the outside wall was missing, and the dangerous
cooking fires were in the yard. As was a cistern large
enough to wash the clothes and serve as a reservoir in case
of fire.

"Ahenobarbus Pontifex Maximus tapped into the
Cloaca Maxima, which made him very popular with the
Via Nova too," said Licinia, smiling because she was talk-
ing about her idol. "When he put the sewer down our back
alley, it enabled the insulae to use it, and the Porticus
Margaritaria as well."

"And the water?" asked Caesar.

"The Forum Romanum on this side abounds with
springs, *domine*. One feeds your cistern, another the cistern in our yard."

There were servants' quarters both upstairs and
downstairs, including a suite which would house Burgundus, Cardixa and their unmarried sons. And how ecstatic

Eutychus would be to have his own little nest!

However, it was the front section of the top storey which put the final touch on Caesar's gratitude for being dowered with the Domus Publica. The front stairs ascended between the reception room and his study, and conveniently divided the area into two. He would give all the rooms anterior to the stairs to Pompeia, which meant they need never see her or hear her from one market day clear through to the next! Julia could have the spacious suite behind the front stairs for her use, as there were two guest suites reached by the back stairs.

So whom did Caesar plan to install in the wife's suite downstairs? Why, his mother, naturally. Whom else?

"What do you think?" he asked his mother as they walked up the Clivus Orbius after their inspection on the following day.

"It is superb, Caesar." She frowned. "Only one aspect does worry me—Pompeia. Too easy for people to creep upstairs! The place is vast, no one will see who comes and goes."

"Oh, Mater, don't sentence me to keeping her downstairs right next door to me!" he cried.

"No, my son, I won't do that. However, we have to find a way to police Pompeia's comings and goings. In the apartment it was so easy to make sure Polyxena attended her the moment she ventured out the door, but here? We'd never know. Nor can she smuggle men into the apartment, whereas here? We'd never know."

"Well," said Caesar with a sigh, "my new position carries a good number of public slaves with it. On the whole they're lazy and irresponsible because they're not supervised and no one thinks to praise them if they do good work. That will most definitely change. Eutychus is getting old, but he's still a wonderful steward. Burgundus and Cardixa can come back from Bovillae with their four youngest. Their four oldest can caretake Bovillae. It will be your job to organize a new regimen and a better frame of mind among the servants, both those we bring with us and those already here. I won't have the time, so it must devolve upon you."

"I understand that," she said, "but it doesn't answer our problem with Pompeia."

"What that amounts to, Mater, is adequate supervision. We both know you can't put just one servant on door duty or any kind of watch. He goes to sleep, from boredom if not from weariness. Therefore we'll put two on permanent duty at the bottom of the front stairs. Day *and* night. And we set them some sort of task—folding linens without a crease, polishing knives and spoons, washing dishes, mending clothes—you know the duties better than I do. A certain amount must be done on each shift. Luckily there is a good-sized alcove between the beginning of the stairs and the end wall. I'll put a loudly creaking door on it to shut it from view of the reception room, and that means whoever uses the stairs has to open it first. If our sentries should doze off, that at least will alert them. When Pompeia appears at the bottom to go out, one of them will notify Polyxena immediately. As well for us that Pompeia hasn't got the gumption to run off before Polyxena can be found! If her friend Clodia tries to put her up to that, it will only happen once, I can assure you. For I shall inform Pompeia conduct of that kind is a good way to be divorced. I shall also instruct Eutychus to put servants on sentry duty who won't collude with each other to accept bribes."

"Oh, Caesar, I hate it!" cried Aurelia, striking her hands together. "Are we legionaries guarding the camp from attack?"

"Yes, Mater, I rather think we are. Her own silly fault. She's mixing in the wrong circles and refuses to abandon them."

"As the result of which we are obliged to imprison her."

"Not really. Be fair! I haven't forbidden her access to her women friends, either here or elsewhere. She and they can come and go as they please, including beauties like Sempronia Tuditani and Palla. And the appalling Pompeius Rufus. But Pompeia is now the wife of Caesar Pontifex Maximus, a social elevation of no mean order. Even for Sulla's granddaughter. I can't trust her good

sense, because she hasn't any. We all know the story of
Metella Dalmatica and how she managed despite Scaurus
Princeps Senatus to make Sulla's life a misery when he
was trying to be elected to the praetorship. Sulla spurned
her then—evidence of his instinct for self-preservation, if
nothing else. But can you see Clodius or Decimus Brutus
or young Poplicola behaving with Sulla's circumspection?
Hah! They'd whip Pompeia off in a trice.''

    ''Then,'' said Aurelia with decision, ''when you see
Pompeia to inform her of the new rules, I suggest you
have her mother there as well. Cornelia Sulla is a splendid
person. And she knows what a fool Pompeia is. Reinforce
your authority with the authority her mother wields. It is
no use bringing me into it, Pompeia detests me for chaining her to Polyxena.''

    No sooner decided upon than done. Though the move
to the Domus Publica took place the next day, Pompeia
had been fully acquainted with the new rules before she
and her handful of personal servants set eyes upon her
palatial suite upstairs. She had wept, of course, and protested the innocence of her intentions, but to no avail. Cornelia Sulla was sterner than Caesar, and adamant that in
the event of a fall from grace, her daughter would not be
welcome to return to Uncle Mamercus's house divorced
on grounds of adultery. Fortunately Pompeia was not the
type to nurse grudges, so by the time the move occurred
she was completely immersed in the transfer of her tasteless but expensive knickknacks, and planning shopping
trips to overfill those areas she considered denuded.

    Caesar had wondered how Aurelia would cope with
the change from landlady of a thriving insula to doyenne
of the closest thing Rome had to a palace. Would she insist
upon continuing to keep her books? Would she break the
ties of more than forty years in the Subura? But by the
time the afternoon of his inaugural feast came round, he
knew that he need not have worried about that truly remarkable lady. Though she would personally audit, she
said, the insula's accounts would now be done by a man
whom Lucius Decumius had found and vouched for. And
it turned out that most of the work she had done was not

on behalf of her own property; to fill in her days she had
acted as agent for more than a dozen other landlords. How
horrified her husband would have been if he had known
that! Caesar just chuckled.

In fact, he realized, his elevation to Pontifex Maximus had given Aurelia a new lease on life. She was absolutely everywhere on both sides of the building, had
established ascendancy over Licinia effortlessly and pain-
lessly, made herself liked by all six Vestals, and would
soon be, her son thought with silent laughter, absorbed in
improving the efficiency not only of the Domus Publica,
but also of its testamentary industry.

"Caesar, we ought to be charging a fee for this service," she said, looking determined. "So much work and
effort! Rome's purse should see a return."

But that he refused to countenance. "I agree that a
fee would increase the Treasury's profits, Mater, but it
would also deprive the lowly of one of their greatest pleasures. No. On the whole, Rome has no trouble with her
proletarii. Keep their bellies full and the games coming,
and they're content. If we begin to charge them for the
entitlements of their citizenship, we'll turn the Head Count
into a monster which would devour us."

As Crassus had predicted, Caesar's election as Pontifex Maximus quietened his creditors magically. The office besides gave him a considerable income from the
State, as was also true of the three major *flamines,* Dialis,
Martialis and Quirinalis. Their three State residences stood
on the opposite side of the Sacra Via from the Domus
Publica, though of course there was no *flamen Dialis,* had
not been since Sulla had let Caesar take off the helmet
and cape of Jupiter Optimus Maximus's special priest; that
had been the bargain, no new *flamen Dialis* until after
Caesar's death. No doubt his State house had been let go
to rack and ruin since it had lost Merula as tenant twenty-
five years ago. As it was in his province now, he would
have to see it, decide what needed to be done, and allocate
the funds for repairs from the unused salary Caesar would
have collected had he lived in it and practised as *flamen.*

After that, he'd rent it for a fortune to some aspiring knight dying to have a Forum Romanum address. Rome would see a return.

But first he had to deal with the Regia and the offices of the Pontifex Maximus.

The Regia was the oldest building in the Forum, for it was said to have been the house of Numa Pompilius, second King of Rome. No priests save the Pontifex Maximus and the Rex Sacrorum were permitted to enter it, though the Vestals served as the attendants of the Pontifex Maximus when he offered to Ops, and when the Rex Sacrorum sacrificed his ram on the *dies agonales* he employed the usual priestlings to help him and clean up afterward.

Thus when Caesar entered it he did so with flesh crawling and hair on end, so awesome an experience was it. Earthquakes had necessitated its rebuilding on at least two occasions during the Republic, but always on the same foundations, and always in the same unadorned tufa blocks. No, thought Caesar, gazing around, the Regia had never been a house. It was too small and it had no windows. The shape, he decided, was probably deliberate, too strange to have been anything other than a part of some ritual mystery. It was a quadrilateral of the kind the Greeks termed a trapezium, having no side parallel to any other. What religious meaning had it held for those people who had lived so long ago? It didn't even face in any particular direction, if to do so meant considering one of its four walls a front. And perhaps that was the reason. Face no compass point and offend no God. Yes, it had been a temple from its inception, he was sure. This was where King Numa Pompilius had celebrated the rites of infant Rome.

There was one shrine against the shortest wall; that of course was to Ops, a *numen* with no face and no substance and no sex (for convenience, Ops was spoken of as feminine) who directed the forces which kept Rome's Treasury replete and her people full-bellied. The roof at the far end contained a hole below which in a minute courtyard there grew two laurel trees, very slender and branchless until they poked out of the hole to drink up a little sun. This court was not walled off to the ceiling, the builder having contented himself with a waist-high tufa surround. And between the surround and the end wall there lay stacked neatly in four rows the twenty-four Shields of Mars, with the twenty-four Spears of Mars racked in the Sacra Via corner.

How fitting that it should be Caesar finally to come here as the servant of this place! He, a Julian descended from Mars. With an invocation to the God of War he carefully peeled off the covers of soft hide that hid one row of shields, and gazed down on them with breath suspended in awe. Twenty-three of them were replicas; one was the actual shield which had fallen from the sky at the behest of Jupiter to protect King Numa Pompilius from his foes. But the replicas were of the same age, and no one except King Numa Pompilius would ever know which was the genuine shield. He had done that on purpose, so the legend went, to confuse potential thieves; for only the real shield had the real magic. The only others like them were in wall paintings in Crete and the Peloponnese of Greece; they were almost man-high and shaped like two teardrops joined to form a slender waist, made from beautifully turned frames of hardwood upon which were stretched the hides of black-and-white cattle. That they were still in reasonably good condition was probably only because they were taken out for an airing every March and every October, when the patrician priests called Salii did their war dance through the streets to mark the opening and closing of the old campaign season. And here they were, *his* shields. *His* spears. He had never seen them at close quarters before, because at the age when he might have come to belong to the Salii, he had been *flamen Dialis* instead.

The place was dirty and dilapidated—he would have to speak to Lucius Claudius, the Rex Sacrorum, about smartening up his bevy of priestlings! A stench of old blood lay everywhere, despite the hole in the roof, and the floor was smothered in rat droppings. That the Sacred Shields had not suffered was truly a miracle. By rights the rats ought to have eaten every scrap of hide off them centuries ago. A haphazard collection of book buckets stacked against the longest wall had not been so lucky, but some dozen stone tablets ranged next to them would defeat the sharpest incisors. Well, no time like the present to start repairing the ravages of time and rodents!

"I suppose," he said to Aurelia over dinner that afternoon, "that I can't introduce a busy little dog or a couple of needy mother cats into the Regia, it might contravene our religious laws. So how can I get rid of the rats?"

"I would say their presence in the Regia contravened our religious laws quite as much as any dog or cat would," said Aurelia. "However, I do see what you mean. It is not a great difficulty, Caesar. The two old women who take care of the public latrine across the road from us in the Subura Minor can tell me the name of the man who makes their rat traps. Very clever! A sort of longish small box with a door on one end. The door is poised on a balance, and the balance is connected to a string, and the string is connected to a piece of cheese impaled on a hooked spike at the back of the box. When the rat tries to remove the cheese, the door falls down. The trick is to make sure that the fellow you depute to take the rats out of the box and kill them isn't afraid of them. If he is, they escape."

"Mater, you know everything! May I leave the acquisition of a few rat traps to you?"

"Certainly," she said, pleased with herself.

"There were never any rats in your insula."

"I should hope not! You know perfectly well that dear Lucius Decumius is never without a dog."

"And every one of them named Fido."

"*And* every one of them an excellent ratter."

"I notice that our Vestals prefer to keep cats."

"Very handy animals provided they are females." She looked mischievous. "One can of course understand why they keep no males, but it is the female cats which hunt, you know. Unlike dogs in that respect. Their litters are a nuisance, so Licinia tells me, but she is very firm, even with the children when they plead. The kittens are drowned at birth."

"And Junia and Quinctilia drown in tears."

"We must all," said Aurelia, "grow used to death. And to not getting the desire of our hearts."

As this was inarguable, Caesar changed the subject. "I was able to rescue some twenty book buckets and their contents, a little mangled but reasonably intact. It would seem that my predecessors did think to put the contents into new buckets whenever the old ones started to disintegrate from the rats, but it would have been more sensible, surely, to have eliminated the rats. For the time being I'll keep the documents here in my study—I want to read them and catalogue them."

"Archives, Caesar?"

"Yes, but not of the Republic. They date back to some of the earliest kings."

"Ah! I understand why they interest you so much. You've always had a passion for ancient laws and archives. But can you read them? Surely they're indecipherable."

"No, they're in good sound Latin of the kind written about three hundred years ago, and they're on Pergamum parchment. I imagine one of the Pontifices Maximi of that era deciphered the originals and made these copies." He leaned back on his couch. "I also found stone tablets, inscribed in the same writing as that on the stele in the well of the Lapis Niger. So archaic one can hardly recognize the language as Latin. A precursor of it, I suppose, like the song of the Salii. But I shall decipher them, never fear!"

His mother gazed at him fondly enough, yet with a little sternness too. "I hope, Caesar, that in the midst of all this religious and historical exploration you find the time to remember that you are standing for election as praetor this year. You must pay proper attention to the duties of the Pontifex Maximus, but you cannot neglect your career in the Forum."

He had not forgotten, nor did the vigor and pace of his election campaign suffer because the lamps in his study burned until very late each night while he worked his way

through what he had decided to call the Commentaries of
the Kings. And thank all the Gods for that unknown Pontifex Maximus who had deciphered and copied them onto
Pergamum parchment! Just where or what the originals
were, Caesar did not know. They were certainly not in the
Regia, nor were they similar to the stone tablets he had
found. Those, he decided from his preliminary work, were,
annalistic and dated from the earliest kings, perhaps even
from Numa Pompilius. *Or Romulus?* What a thought!
Chilling. Nothing on parchment or stone was a history of
the times, however. Both related to laws, rules, religious
rites, precepts, functions and functionaries. At some moment soon they would have to be published; all of Rome
must know what lay in the Regia. Varro would be ecstatic,
and Cicero fascinated. Caesar would plan a dinner party.

As if to cap what had been an extraordinary year of
ups and downs for Caesar, when the curule elections were
held early in Quinctilis, he came in at the top of the praetors' poll. Not one Century failed to name him, which
meant he was able to rest secure long before the last man
returned was sure he had been elected. Philippus, his
friend from Mitylene days, would be a colleague; so too
would Cicero's irascible younger brother, tiny Quintus
Cicero. But, alas, Bibulus was a praetor too.

When the lots were cast to decide which man should
have which job, Caesar's victory was complete. His name
was on the first ball out of the spout; he would be urban
praetor, the most senior man among the eight. That meant
Bibulus couldn't annoy him (he had received the Violence
Court)—but he could certainly annoy Bibulus!

Time to break Domitia's heart by discarding her. She
had turned out to be discreet, so as yet Bibulus had no
idea. But he would the moment she started weeping and
wailing. They all did. Except Servilia. Perhaps that was
why she alone had lasted.

PART IV

---

from JANUARY 1
until DECEMBER 5 of 63 B.C.

MARCUS TULLIUS CICERO

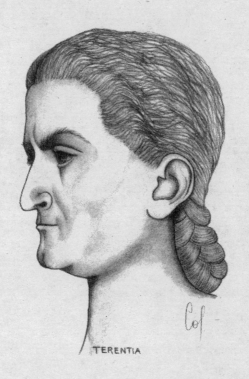

TERENTIA

It was Cicero's misfortune to enter upon his year as consul in the midst of a severe economic depression, and as economics was not his speciality, he faced his year of office in a rather gloomy mood. Not the sort of consulship he had hoped for! He wanted people to say of him after his year was over that he had given Rome the same kind of halcyon prosperity commonly attributed to the joint consulship of Pompey and Crassus seven years earlier. With Hybrida as his junior colleague, it was inevitable all the credit would go to him, which meant he wouldn't need to end on bad terms with Hybrida, as Pompey had with Crassus—and vice versa.

Rome's economic troubles emanated from the East, which had been closed to Roman businessmen for over twenty years. First King Mithridates had conquered it, then when Sulla wrested it off him, Sulla introduced praiseworthy financial regulations there and thus prevented the knight community of Rome from going back to the old days of milking the East dry. Added to which, the problem of piracy on the high seas did not encourage business ventures east of Macedonia and Greece. Consequently those who farmed taxes, lent money, or traded in goods and commodities like wheat, wine and wool kept their capital at home; a phenomenon which increased when the war against Quintus Sertorius broke out in Spain and a series of droughts diminished the harvest. Both ends of Our Sea became risky or impracticable areas for business endeavors.

All of these things had contrived to concentrate capital and investment within Rome and Italy for twenty years. No seductive overseas opportunities presented themselves to Rome's knight-businessmen, who as a result had little need to find large amounts of money. The borrowing interest rate was low, rents were low, inflation was high, and creditors were in no hurry to call in debts.

Cicero's misfortune was to be laid entirely at Pompey's door. First the Great Man had cleaned up the pirates,

then he chased Kings Mithridates and Tigranes out of
those areas which used to be a part of Rome's business
sphere. He also abolished Sulla's financial regulations,
though Lucullus had persisted in retaining them—the sole
reason why the knights had lobbied to remove Lucullus
and give his command to Pompey. And so just as Cicero
and Hybrida assumed office, a literal wealth of business
opportunities was opening up in the East. Where once had
been Asia Province and Cilicia were now four provinces;
Pompey had added the new provinces of Bithynia-Pontus
and Syria to the empire. He set them up the same way as
the other two by giving the great companies of *publicani*
based in Rome the right to farm their taxes, tithes and
tributes. Private contracts let out by the censors saved the
State the burden of gathering taxes and prevented the pro-
liferation of civil servants. Let the *publicani* have the
headaches! All the Treasury wanted was its stipulated
share of the profits.

Capital flowed out of Rome and Italy in obedience to
the new drive to obtain control of these eastern business
ventures. As a result the interest rate went up dramatically,
usurers suddenly called in old debts, and credit was hard
to come by. In the cities rents soared; in the country farmers were strapped by mortgage repayments. Inevitably the
price of grain—even that supplied by the State—increased. Huge amounts of money were pouring out of
Rome, and nobody in government knew how to control
the situation.

Informed by friends like the knight plutocrat Titus
Pomponius Atticus (who had no intention of letting Cicero
in on too many commercial secrets) that the money drain
was due to resident alien Jews in Rome sending the proceeds home, Cicero quickly brought in a law forbidding
the Jews to send any money home. Of course it had little
effect, but what else he could do the senior consul did not
know—nor was Atticus about to enlighten him.

It was not in Cicero's nature to turn his year as consul
into a mission he now saw would be as vain as it would
prove unpopular, so instead he turned his attention toward
matters he regarded as well within his sphere of excel-

lence; the economic situation would solve itself given
time, whereas laws required a personal touch. *His* year
meant that for once Rome had a legislating consul in office, so he would legislate.

First he attacked the law the consul Gaius Piso had
brought in four years earlier against electoral bribery in
the consular polls. Himself guilty of massive bribery, Piso
had been forced into legislating against it. Perhaps not il-
logically, what Piso passed leaked in all directions, but
after Cicero patched up the worst of the holes it began to
look quite presentable.

And where to from that? Ah! Ah yes, men returning
from a term governing a praetorian province who had ex-
torted in that province and intended to wriggle out of prosecution by getting elected consul *in absentia*! Praetors sent
out to govern provinces were more likely to extort than
consul-governors; there were eight of them and only two
consul-governors, which meant that the majority of them
knew their only chance to make a fortune governing a
province was as a praetor-governor. Yet how, after squeezing his province dry, was a returning praetor-governor to
avoid prosecution for extortion? If he was a strong con-
tender for the consulship, then the best way was to petition
the Senate to be allowed to stand for the consular elections
in absentia. No holder of imperium could be prosecuted.
Provided a returning praetor-governor did not cross the
sacred boundary into the city of Rome itself, he retained
the imperium Rome had given him to govern his province.
So he could sit on the Campus Martius just outside the
city, imperium intact, petition the Senate to stand for consul *in absentia*, conduct his campaign from the Campus
Martius, and then, if he was lucky enough to be elected
consul, he walked straight into a fresh imperium. This ploy
meant he managed to elude prosecution for two more
years, by which time the wrathful provincials who had
originally intended to prosecute him would have given up
and gone home. Well, thundered Cicero in the Senate and
Comitia, that sort of thing must cease! Therefore he and
his junior colleague, Hybrida, proposed to forbid any returning praetor-governor standing for consul *in absentia*.

Let him come inside Rome, take his chances with prosecution! And as the Senate and People deemed this excellent, the new law passed.

Now what else could he do? Cicero thought of this and that, all useful little laws which would enhance his reputation. Though not, alas, *make* his reputation. As consul rather than as legal luminary. What Cicero needed was a crisis, and not an economic one.

That the second half of his term as senior consul would give him that hungered-for crisis did not occur to Cicero even when the lots gave him the duty of presiding over the elections held in the month of Quinctilis. Nor did he at first fully appreciate the ramifications which were to emerge from his wife's invasion of his privacy not long before those elections.

Terentia marched into his study with her customary lack of ceremony, and oblivious to the sanctity of his thought processes.

"Cicero, stop that whatever-it-is you're doing!" she barked.

The pen went down immediately; he looked up without being foolish enough to betray his creative distress. "Yes, my dear, what is it?" he enquired mildly.

She dumped herself down in the client's chair, looking grim. However, as she always looked grim, he had no idea of the cause of this particular grimness; he just hoped devoutly that it was nothing *he* had done.

"I had a visitor this morning," she said.

It was on the tip of his tongue to ask whether having a visitor had tickled her fancy, but he kept that normally unruly organ silent; if no one else had the power to still it utterly, Terentia certainly did. So he merely assumed an air of interest and waited for her to go on.

"A visitor," she repeated. She then sniffed. "Not one of my circle, I do assure you, husband! Fulvia."

"Publius Clodius's wife?" he asked, astonished.

"No, no! Fulvia Nobilioris."

Which elucidation did not decrease his surprise, as the Fulvia she meant was distinctly shady. Of excellent family, but divorced in disgrace, lacking an income, and currently attached to that Quintus Curius who had been expelled from the Senate in the famous purge of Poplicola and Lentulus Clodianus seven years before. A most inappropriate visitor for Terentia to receive! Terentia was as renowned for her rectitude as she was for her sourness.

"Goodness gracious me! What on earth did *she* want?"

"I quite liked her, actually," said Terentia reflectively. "She is no more and no less than a Hapless Victim of Men."

And how was he expected to answer that? Cicero compromised with an inarticulate bleat.

"She came to see me because that is the correct procedure for a woman to adopt when she wishes to speak to a married man of your prominence."

And a man married to you, Cicero added silently.

"Naturally you will wish to see her for yourself, but I shall give you what information she gave me," said the lady whose glance could turn Cicero to stone. "It appears that her—her—her *protector*, Curius, has been behaving most oddly of late. Since his expulsion from the Senate his financial circumstances have been so embarrassed he can't even run for the tribunate of the plebs to get back into public life. Yet all of a sudden he's begun to talk wildly of coming into riches and a high position. This," Terentia went on in a voice of doom, "appears to stem from his conviction that Catilina and Lucius Cassius will be consuls next year."

"So that's the way Catilina's wind blows, is it? Consul with a fat and torpid fool like Lucius Cassius," said Cicero.

"Both of them will declare themselves candidates tomorrow when you open the election tribunal."

"All very well, my dear, but I fail to see how a joint consulship of Catilina and Lucius Cassius can promote Curius to sudden wealth and eminence."

"Curius is talking of a general cancellation of debts."

Cicero's jaw dropped. "They wouldn't be such idiots!"

"Why not?" asked Terentia, contemplating the matter coolly. "Only consider, Cicero! Catilina knows that if he doesn't get in this year, his chances are over. It looks like quite a battle if all the men who are thinking of standing do stand. Silanus is much improved in health and will definitely be running, so dear Servilia tells me. Murena is being backed by many influential people, and, so dear Fabia tells me, is using his Vestal connection through Licinia to the maximum. Then there's your friend Servius Sulpicius Rufus, highly favored by the Eighteen and the *tribuni aerarii,* which means he'll poll well in the First Class. What can Catilina and a running partner like Lucius Cassius offer against such an array of solid worth as Silanus, Murena and this Sulpicius? Only one of the consuls can be a patrician, which means the vote for a patrician will be split between Catilina and Sulpicius. If *I* had a vote, I'd be choosing Sulpicius ahead of Catilina."

Frowning, Cicero forgot his terror of his wife and spoke to her as he would have to a Forum colleague. "So Catilina's platform is a general cancellation of debts, is that what you're saying?"

"No, that's what Fulvia is saying."

"I must see her at once!" he cried, getting up.

"Leave it to me, I'll send for her," said Terentia.

Which meant, of course, that he would not be permitted to speak to Fulvia Nobilioris alone; Terentia intended to be there hanging on every word—and every look.

The trouble was that Fulvia Nobilioris volunteered very little more than Terentia had already told him, just couched her story in a highly emotional and scatterbrained way. Curius was up to his ears in debt, gambling heavily, drinking a great deal; he was always closeted with Catilina, Lucius Cassius and their cronies, and would return home from one of these sessions promising his mistress all kinds of future prosperity.

"Why are you telling me, Fulvia?" Cicero asked, as much at a loss as she appeared to be, for he couldn't work out why she was so terrified. A general cancellation of debt was bad news, but—

"You're the senior consul!" she whimpered, weeping and beating her breast. "I had to tell *someone!*"

"The trouble is, Fulvia, that you've given me not one iota of proof that Catilina plans a general cancellation of debt. I need a pamphlet, a reliable witness! All you've give me is a story, and I can't go to the Senate with nothing more tangible than a story told to me by a woman."

"But it is wrong, isn't it?" she asked, wiping her eyes.

"Yes, very wrong, and you've acted very correctly in coming to me. But I need proof," said Cicero.

"The best I can offer you are some names."

"Then tell me."

"Two men who used to be centurions of Sulla's—Gaius Manlius and Publius Furius. They own land in Etruria. And they've been telling people who plan to come to Rome for the elections that if Catilina and Cassius are made consuls, debt will cease to exist."

"And, how, Fulvia, am I to connect two ex-centurions from Sulla's legions with Catilina and Cassius?"

"I don't know!"

Sighing, Cicero rose to his feet. "Well, Fulvia, I do most sincerely thank you for coming to me," he said. "Keep on trying to find out exactly what's going on, and the moment you locate real evidence that the scent of the fish markets is stealing onto the Campus Martius at election time, tell me." He smiled at her, he hoped platonically. "Continue to work through my wife, she will keep me informed."

When Terentia ushered the visitor from the room, Cicero sat down again to ponder. Not that this luxury was allowed him for very long: Terentia bustled in moments later.

"What do you really think?" she asked.

"I wish I knew, my dear."

"Well," she said, leaning forward eagerly because she liked nothing better than to offer her husband political advice, "I'll tell you what I think! I think Catilina is plotting revolution."

Cicero gaped. "Revolution?" he squeaked.

"That's right, revolution."

"Terentia, it's a far cry from an electoral policy based in a general cancellation of debt to revolution!" he protested.

"No, it is not, Cicero. How can legally elected consuls initiate a revolutionary measure like a general cancellation of debt? You know well enough that is the ploy of men who overthrow the State. Saturninus. Sertorius. It means dictators and masters of the horse. How could legally elected consuls hope to legislate such a measure? Even if they brought it before the People in their tribes, at least one tribune of the plebs would veto it in *contio*, let alone in formal promulgation. And do you think those in favor of a general cancellation of debt do not understand all that? Of course they do! Anyone who would vote for consuls advocating such a policy is painting himself in the color of a revolutionary."

"Which," said Cicero heavily, "is red. The color of blood. Oh, Terentia, not during my consulship!"

"You must prevent Catilina's standing," said Terentia.

"I can't do that unless I have proof."

"Then we'll just have to find proof." She rose and headed for the door. "Who knows? Perhaps Fulvia and I between us will be able to persuade Quintus Curius to testify."

"That would be a help," said Cicero, a little dryly.

The seed was sown; Catilina was planning revolution, had to be planning revolution. And though the events of the coming months seemed to confirm this, Cicero was never to know in his heart of hearts whether the concept of revolution occurred to Lucius Sergius Catilina before or after those fateful elections.

The seed being sown, the senior consul went to work to unearth all the information he could. He sent agents to Etruria, and agents to that other traditional nucleus of revolution, Samnite Apulia. And sure enough, they all reported back that it was indeed being bruited about that if

Catilina and Lucius Cassius were elected the consuls, they would bring in a general cancellation of debt. As to more tangible evidence of revolution, like the amassing of arms or the covert recruitment of forces, none was forthcoming. However, Cicero told himself, he had enough to try.

The curule elections for consuls and praetors were to be held on the tenth day of Quinctilis; on the ninth day Cicero summarily postponed them until the eleventh, and summoned the Senate into session on the tenth.

The senatorial turnout was splendid, of course; curiosity piqued, all those not prostrated by illness or absent from Rome came early enough to see for themselves that the much-admired Cato really did sit there before a meeting with a bundle of scrolls at his feet and one spread out between his hands, reading slowly and intently.

"Conscript Fathers," said the senior consul after the rites were concluded and the rest of the formalities over, "I have summoned you here rather than to elections in the *saepta* to help me unravel a mystery. I apologize to those of you who are thereby inconvenienced, and can only hope that the result of our session enables the elections to proceed tomorrow."

They were avid for an explanation, so much was easy to see, but for once Cicero was in no mood to toy with his audience. What he hoped to do was to air the thing, make Catilina and Lucius Cassius see that their ploy was futile now that it was generally known, and nip in the bud any plans Catilina might be nourishing. Not for one moment did he truly think there was more to Terentia's vision of revolution than a lot of idle talk over too many flagons of wine, and some economic measures more usually associated with revolution than with law-abiding consuls. After Marius, Cinna, Carbo, Sulla, Sertorius and Lepidus, even Catilina must surely have learned that the Republic was not so easily destroyed. He was a bad man—everyone knew that—but until he was elected consul he held no magistracy, he was possessed neither of imperium nor a ready-made army, and he had nothing like the number of clients in Etruria of a Marius or a Lepidus. Therefore, what Catilina needed was a fright to bring him into line.

No one, the senior consul thought as his gaze roamed from tier to tier on both sides of the House, no one had any idea what was in the wind. Crassus was sitting impassively, Catulus looked a little old and his brother-in-law Hortensius a little the worse for wear, Cato had his hackles up like an aggressive dog, Caesar was patting the top of his head to make sure his definitely thinning hair did hide his scalp, Murena undoubtedly chafed at the delay, and Silanus was not as fit and spry as his electioneering agents were insisting he was. And there at last among the consulars sat the great Lucius Licinius Lucullus, triumphator. Cicero, Catulus and Hortensius had waxed eloquent enough to persuade the Senate that Lucullus must be allowed his triumph, which meant that the real conqueror of the East was free now to cross the *pomerium* and take his rightful place in Senate and Comitia.

"Lucius Sergius Catilina," said Cicero from the curule dais, "I would appreciate it if you would stand up."

At first Cicero had thought to accuse Lucius Cassius as well, but after deliberation he had decided it was better to focus entirely on Catilina. Who stood now looking the picture of bewildered concern. Such a handsome man! Tall and beautifully built, every inch the great patrician aristocrat. How Cicero loathed them, the Catilinas and the Caesars! What was the matter with his own eminently respectable birth, why did they dismiss him as a pernicious growth on the Roman body?

"I am standing, Marcus Tullius Cicero," said Catilina gently.

"Lucius Sergius Catilina, do you know two men named Gaius Manlius and Publius Furius?"

"I have two clients by those names."

"Do you know where they are at the moment?"

"In Rome, I hope! They should be on the Campus Martius right now voting for me. Instead, I imagine they're sitting somewhere in a tavern."

"Whereabouts were they recently?"

Catilina raised both black brows. "Marcus Tullius, I do not require that my clients report their every move to me! I know you're a nonentity, but do you have so few clients that you have no idea of the protocol governing the client-patron bond?''

Cicero went red. ''Would it surprise you to learn that Manlius and Furius have been seen recently in Faesulae, Volaterrae, Clusium, Saturnia, Larinum and Venusia?''

A blink from Catilina. ''How could it surprise me, Marcus Tullius? They both have land in Etruria, and Furius has land in Apulia as well.''

''Would it surprise you then to learn that both Manlius and Furius have been telling anyone important enough to have a vote which counts in the Centuriate elections that you and your named colleague, Lucius Cassius, intend legislating a general cancellation of debt once you assume office as consuls?''

That provoked an amazed laugh. When he sobered, Catilina stared at Cicero as if Cicero had suddenly gone mad. ''It does indeed surprise me!'' he said.

Beginning to stir the moment Cicero had pronounced that awful phrase, a general cancellation of debt, the House now broke into audible murmuring. Of course there were those present who desperately needed such a radical measure now that the moneylenders were pressing for full payment—including Caesar, the new Pontifex Maximus—but few who did not appreciate the horrific economic repercussions a general cancellation of debt entailed. Despite their problems generating a constant cash flow, the members of the Senate were innately conservative creatures when it came to radical change of any kind, including how money was structured. And for every financially distressed senator, there were three who stood to lose far more from a general cancellation of debt than they stood to gain, men like Crassus, Lucullus, the absent Pompeius Magnus. Therefore it was not astonishing that both Caesar and Crassus were now leaning forward like leashed hounds.

''I have been making full enquiries in both Etruria and Apulia, Lucius Sergius Catilina,'' said Cicero, ''and it grieves me to say that I believe these rumors are true. I believe you do intend to cancel debts.''

Catilina's response was to laugh and laugh and laugh. The tears poured down his face; he held his sides; he tried valiantly to control his mirth and lost the battle several times. Seated not far away, Lucius Cassius chose red-faced indignation as his reaction.

"Rubbish!" Catilina cried when he could, mopping his face with a fold of toga because he couldn't command himself enough to locate his handkerchief. "Rubbish, rubbish, rubbish!"

"Will you take an oath to that effect?" asked Cicero.

"No, I will not!" snapped Catilina, drawing himself up. "I, a patrician Sergius, to take an oath on the unfounded and malicious yammerings of an immigrant from Arpinum? Just who do you think you are, Cicero?"

"I am the senior consul of the Senate and People of Rome," said Cicero with painful dignity. "If you remember, I am the man who defeated you in last year's curule election! And as senior consul, I am the head of this State."

Another fit of laughter, then: "They say Rome has two bodies, Cicero! One is feeble and has a moron's head, the other is strong but has no head at all. What do you think that makes you, O head of this State?"

"No moron, Catilina, and that is sure! I am Rome's father and guardian in this year, and I intend to do my duty, even in situations as bizarre as this one! Do you absolutely deny that you plan to cancel all debts?"

"Of course I do!"

"But you will not take an oath to that effect."

"I most definitely will not." Catilina drew a breath. "No, I will not! However, O head of this State, your despicable conduct and unfounded accusations this morning would tempt many a man in my shoes to say that if Rome's strong but headless body were to find a head, it could do worse than to pick mine! At least mine is Roman! At least mine has ancestors! You are setting out to ruin me, Cicero, ruin my chances at what was yesterday a fair and unsullied election! I stand here defamed and impugned, the utterly innocent victim of a presumptuous upstart from the hills, neither Roman nor noble!"

It took a huge effort not to react to these taunts, but Cicero maintained his calm. Did he not, he would lose the encounter. Seeing, as he did from this moment on, that Fulvia Nobilioris was right. That Terentia was right. He could laugh, he could deny it, but Lucius Sergius Catilina was plotting revolution. An advocate who had faced down (and acted for) many a villain could not mistake the face and body language of a man brazening it out, adopting aggression and derision and wounded virtue as the best of all possible defenses. Catilina was guilty, Cicero knew it.

But did the rest of the House know it?

"May I have some comments, Conscript Fathers?"

"No, you may not!" shouted Catilina, leaping up from his place to assume a position in the middle of the black-and-white floor, where he stood and shook his fist at Cicero. Then he strode up the House to the great doors, turned there and faced the ranks of enthralled senators.

"Lucius Sergius Catilina, you are breaking this body's standing orders!" Cicero cried, suddenly aware that he was about to lose control of the meeting. "Return to your seat!"

"I will not! Nor will I remain here one moment longer to listen to this impudent mushroom with no ancestors accuse me of what I interpret to be treason! And, Conscript Fathers, I serve notice on this House that at dawn tomorrow I will be at the *saepta* to contest the curule election for consul! I sincerely hope that all of you come to your senses and direct the moronic head of this State to do the duty the lots gave him, and hold the elections! For I warn you, if the *saepta* is empty tomorrow morning, you had better come there with your lictors, Marcus Tullius Cicero, arrest me and charge me with *perduellio*! *Maiestas* will not do for one whose forefathers belonged to the hundred men who advised King Tullus Hostilius!"

Catilina turned to the doors, wrenched them open, disappeared.

"Well, Marcus Tullius Cicero, what do you intend to do now?" asked Caesar, leaning back with a yawn. "He's right, you know. On the slenderest of pretexts, you have virtually impeached him."

Vision blurred, Cicero sought a face which said its owner was on his side, its owner believed him. Catulus?

No. Hortensius? No. Cato? No. Crassus? No. Lucullus? No. Poplicola? No.

He squared his shoulders; he stood straight. "I will see a division of this House," he said, voice hard. "All those who think that the curule elections should be held tomorrow and that Lucius Sergius Catilina should be allowed to stand for office as consul, pass to my left. All those who think that the curule elections should be further postponed pending investigation of Lucius Sergius Catilina's candidacy, pass to my right."

It was a forlorn hope, despite Cicero's cunning in putting his motion with the result he wanted to his right; no senator was happy passing to the left, regarded as unpropitious. But for once prudence outweighed superstition. The House passed without a single exception to the left, thereby allowing the election to take place on the morrow, and Lucius Sergius Catilina to stand for the office of consul.

Cicero dismissed the meeting, wanting only to reach home before he broke down and wept.

Pride dictated that Cicero should not back down, so he presided over the curule elections with a cuirass beneath his toga after placing several hundreds of young men conspicuously around the vicinity of the *saepta* to prevent trouble's breaking out. Among them was Publius Clodius, whose hatred for Catilina was far stronger than the mild irritation Cicero provoked in him. And where Clodius was, naturally, so too were young Poplicola, young Curio, Decimus Brutus, and Mark Antony—all members of the now-thriving Clodius Club.

And, Cicero saw with huge relief, what the senators had not chosen to believe, the whole of the Ordo Equester definitely did. Nothing could be more appalling to a knight-businessman than the specter of a general cancellation of debt, even if he was in debt himself. One by one the Centuries voted solidly for Decimus Junius Silanus and Lucius Licinius Murena as consuls for the next year. Catilina lagged behind Servius Sulpicius, though he did get more votes than Lucius Cassius.

"You malicious slanderer!" snarled one of the present year's praetors, the patrician Lentulus Sura, as the Centuries broke up after a long day electing two consuls and eight praetors.

"What?" asked Cicero blankly, oppressed by the weight of that wretched cuirass he had chosen to wear, and dying to release a waist grown too thick for armored comfort.

"You heard me! It's your fault Catilina and Cassius didn't get in, you malicious slanderer! You deliberately frightened the voters away from them with your wild rumors about debt! Oh, very clever! Why prosecute them and thereby give them a chance to answer? You found the perfect weapon in the political arsenal, didn't you? The irrefutable allegation! Smear, slur, muddy! Catilina was right about you—you're an impudent mushroom with no ancestors! And it's high time peasants like you were put in their place!"

Cicero stood slack-jawed as Lentulus Sura strode away, feeling tears begin to form. He was right about Catilina, he was *right*! Catilina would end in destroying Rome and the Republic.

"If it's any consolation, Cicero," said a placid voice at his elbow, "I shall keep my eyes open and my nose well primed for the next few months. Upon reflection, I think you may well be correct about Catilina and Cassius. They are not pleased this day!"

He turned to see Crassus standing there, and lost his temper at last. "*You!*" he cried in a voice filled with loathing. "It's you responsible! You got Catilina off at his last trial! Bought the jury and gave him to understand that there are men inside Rome who'd love to see him title himself Dictator!"

"I didn't buy the jury," said Crassus, seeming unoffended.

"Tchah!" spat Cicero, and stormed off.

"What was all that about?" asked Crassus of Caesar.

"Oh, he thinks he has a crisis on his hands, and he cannot see why no one in the Senate agrees with him."

"But I was telling him I did agree with him!"

"Leave it, Marcus. Come and help me celebrate my electoral win at the Domus Publica of the Pontifex Maximus. Such a nice address! As for Cicero, the poor fellow has been dying to sit at the center of a sensation, and now that he thinks he's found one, he can't flog up a morsel of interest in it. He would adore to save the Republic," said Caesar, grinning.

"But I am not giving up!" cried Cicero to his wife. "I am not defeated! Terentia, keep in close touch with Fulvia, and do not let go! Even if she has to listen at doors, I want her to find out everything she can—who Curius sees, where he goes, what he does. And if, as you and I think, revolution is brewing, then she must persuade Curius that the best thing he can do is to work in with me."

"I will, never fear," she said, face quite animated. "The Senate will rue the day it chose to side with Catilina, Marcus. I've seen Fulvia, and I know you. In many ways you are an idiot, but not when it comes to sniffing out villains."

"How am I an idiot?" he asked indignantly.

"Writing rubbishy poetry, for one. For another, trying to earn a reputation as a connoisseur of art. Overspending, most especially on a parade of villas you'd never have time to live in even if you traveled constantly, which you don't. Spoiling Tullia atrociously. Sucking up to the likes of Pompeius Magnus."

"Enough!"

She desisted, watching him through eyes which never lit up with love. Which was a pity, for the truth was that she loved him very well. But she knew all of his many weaknesses, yet had none of her own. Though she had no ambition to be deemed the new Cornelia the Mother of the Gracchi, she owned all the virtues of the Roman matron, which made her extremely difficult to live with for a man of Cicero's character. Frugal, industrious, cool, hardheaded, uncompromising, outspoken, afraid of no one, and aware she was any man's equal in mental sinew. That was Terentia, who suffered no fool gladly, even her husband. She didn't begin to comprehend his insecurity and

sense of inferiority, for her own birth was impeccable and
her ancestry Roman through and through. To Terentia, he
would do best to relax and ride into the heart of Roman
society on her trailing skirts; instead, he kept pushing her
into domestic obscurity and flying off at a thousand tangents in search of an aristocracy he just couldn't claim.

"You ought to ask Quintus over," she said.

But Cicero and his younger brother were as incom-
patible as Cicero and Terentia, so the senior consul turned
down the corners of his mouth and shook his head. "Quintus is as bad as the rest of them, he thinks I'm making a
mountain out of a bucket of sand. Though I shall see Atticus tomorrow, he did believe. But then, he's a knight and
has common sense." He thought for a moment, said,
"Lentulus Sura was very rude to me today at the *saepta*.
I cannot begin to understand why. I know a lot of the
Senate blames me for ruining Catilina's chances, but there
was something so odd about Lentulus Sura. It seemed to—
to matter *too* much."

"Him and his Julia Antonia and those frightful lumps
of stepsons!" said Terentia scornfully. "A more shiftless
lot one would have to look hard to find. I don't know
which of them annoys me more, Lentulus or Julia Antonia
or her awful sons."

"Lentulus Sura's done well enough, considering the
censors expelled him seven years ago," said Cicero, tem-
porizing. "Got back into the Senate through the quaestorship and has done it all over again. He *was* consul before
his expulsion, Terentia. It must be a shocking comedown
to have to be praetor again at this time of life."

"Like his wife, he's feckless," said Terentia unsympathetically.

"Be that as it may, today was odd."

Terentia snorted. "In more ways than just Lentulus
Sura."

"Tomorrow I shall find out what Atticus knows, and
that is likely to be interesting," said Cicero, yawning until
his eyes began to water. "I'm tired, my dear. Might I ask
you to send our darling Tiro in? I'll give him dictation."

"You must be tired! Not like you to prefer someone

else doing the scribbling, even Tiro. I will send him in, but only for a little while. You need sleep.''

As she got up from her chair Cicero held out his hand to her impulsively, and smiled. ''Thank you, Terentia, for everything! What a difference it makes to have you on my side.''

She took the proffered hand, squeezed it hard, and gave him a rather shy grin, boyish and immature. ''Think nothing of it, husband,'' she said, then whisked herself off before the mood in the room could become emotionally sloppy.

Had someone asked Cicero whether he loved his wife and his brother, he would have answered instantly in the affirmative, and there would have been truth in that answer. But neither Terentia nor Quintus Cicero lay as close to his heart as several other people, only one of them his relation by blood. That of course was his daughter, Tullia, a warm and sparkling contrast to her mother. His son was still too young to have wormed his way into Cicero's strong affections; perhaps little Marcus never would, as he was more like brother Quintus in nature, impulsive, quick-tempered, strutting, and no prodigy.

Who then were the others?

The name which sprang first to Cicero's mind would have been Tiro. Tiro was his slave, but also literally a part of his family, as did happen in a society wherein slaves were not so much inferior beings as unfortunates subject to the laws of ownership and status. Because a Roman's domestic slaves lived in such close—indeed, almost intimate—proximity to the free persons of the household, it was in many ways an extended-family situation, and carried all the advantages and disadvantages of that state. The interweaving of personalities was complex, major and minor storms came and went, power bases existed on both free and servile sides, and it was a hard master who could remain impervious to servile pressures. In the Tullius household Terentia was the one a slave had to look out for, but even Terentia was unable to resist Tiro, who could calm little Marcus down as easily as he could persuade Tullia that her mother was right.

He had come to the Tullius household young, a Greek who had sold himself into bondage as an alternative preferable to stagnation in a poor and obscure Boeotian town. That he would take Cicero's fancy was inevitable, for he was as tender and kind as he was brilliant at his secretarial work, the sort of person one could not help but love. As Tiro was abidingly thoughtful and considerate, not even the nastiest and most selfish among his fellow slaves in the Tullius household could accuse him of currying favor with the master and mistress; his sweetness spilled over into his relations with his fellow slaves and made them love him too.

However, Cicero's affection for him outweighed all others. Not only were Tiro's Greek and Latin superlatively good, but so were his literary instincts, and when Tiro produced a faint look of disapproval at some phrase or choice of adjective, his master paused to reconsider the offending item. Tiro took flawless shorthand, transcribed into neat and lucid writing, and never presumed to alter one word.

At the time of the consulship, this most perfect of all servants had been in the bosom of the family for five years. He was of course already emancipated in Cicero's will, but in the normal scheme of things his service as a slave would continue for ten more years, after which he would pass into Cicero's clientele as a prosperous freedman; his wage was already high, and he was always the first to receive another raise in his *stips*. So what it boiled down to in the Tullius household was simply, how could it exist without Tiro? How could Cicero exist without Tiro?

Second on the list was Titus Pomponius Atticus. That was a friendship which went back many, many years. He and Cicero had met in the Forum when Cicero had been a youthful prodigy and Atticus training to take over his father's multiple businesses, and after the death of Sulla's eldest son (who had been Cicero's best friend), it was Atticus who took young Sulla's place, though Atticus was four years the older of the two. The family name of Pomponius had considerable distinction, for the Pomponii were in actual fact a branch of the Caecilii Metelli, and that meant they belonged at the very core of high Roman society. It also meant that, had Atticus wanted it, a career in the Senate and perhaps the consulship were not unattainable. But Atticus's father had hankered after senatorial distinction, and suffered for it as the factions which controlled Rome during those terrible years had come and gone. Firmly placed in the ranks of the Eighteen—the eighteen senior Centuries of the First Class—Atticus had abjured both Senate and public office. His inclinations went hand in hand with his desires, which were to make as much money as possible and pass into history as one of Rome's greatest plutocrats.

In those early days he had been, like his father before him, simple Titus Pomponius. No third name. Then in the troubled few years of Cinna's rule, Atticus and Crassus had formed a plan and a company to mine the taxes and goods of Asia Province, Sulla having wrested it back from King Mithridates. They had milked the necessary capital from a horde of investors, only to find that Sulla preferred to regulate Asia Province's administration in a way which prevented the Roman *publicani* from profiting. Both Crassus and Atticus were forced to flee their creditors, though Atticus managed to take his own personal fortune with him, and therefore had the wherewithal to live extremely comfortably while in exile. He settled in Athens, and liked it so well that it ever afterward held first place in his heart.

It was no real problem to establish himself with Sulla after that formidable man returned to Rome as its Dictator, and Atticus (now so called because of his preferences for the Athenian homeland, Attica) became free to live in Rome. Which he did for some of the time, though he never relinquished his house in Athens, and went there regularly. He also acquired huge tracts of land in Epirus, that part of Greece on the coast of the Adriatic Sea to the north of the Gulf of Corinth.

Atticus's predilection for young male lovers was well known, but remarkably free from taint in such a homo-

phobic place as Rome. That was because he indulged it
only when he traveled to Greece, wherein such preferences
were the norm, and actually added to a man's reputation.
When in Rome, he betrayed neither by word nor look that
he practised Greek love, and this rigid self-control enabled
his family, friends and social peers to pretend that there
was no different side to Titus Pomponius Atticus. Important too because Atticus had become enormously wealthy
and a great power in financial circles. Among the *publicani* (who were businessmen bidding for public contracts)
he was the most powerful and the most influential. Banker,
shipping magnate, merchant prince, Atticus mattered immensely. If he couldn't quite make a man consul, he could
certainly go a long way toward visibly assisting that man,
as he had Cicero during Cicero's campaign.

He was also Cicero's publisher, having decided that
money was a little boring, and literature a refreshing
change. Extremely well educated, he had a natural affinity
for men of letters, and admired Cicero's way with words
as few others could. It both amused and satisfied him to
become a patron of writers—and also enabled him to make
money out of them. The publishing house which he set up
on the Argiletum as a rival establishment to the Sosii
thrived. His connections provided him with an ever-
widening pool of new talent, and his copyists produced
highly prized manuscripts.

Tall, thin and austere looking, he might have passed
as the father of none other than Metellus Scipio, though
the blood links were not close, as Metellus Scipio was a
Caecilius Metellus only by virtue of adoption. The resemblance did mean, however, that all the members of the
Famous Families understood his bloodline was unimpeachable and of great antiquity.

He genuinely loved Cicero, but was proof against
Ciceronian weaknesses—in which he followed the example set by Terentia, also wealthy, also unwilling to help
Cicero out when his finances needed supplementing. On
the one occasion when Cicero had drummed up the courage to ask Atticus for a trifling loan, his friend had refused
so adamantly that Cicero never asked again. From time to

time he half-hoped Atticus would offer, but Atticus never did. Quite willing to procure statues and other works of art for Cicero during his extensive travels in Greece, Atticus also insisted on being paid for them—and for the cost of shipping them to Italy. What he didn't charge for, Cicero supposed, was his time in finding them. In the light of all this, was Atticus incurably stingy? Cicero didn't think so, for unlike Crassus he was a generous host and paid good wages to his slaves as well as to his free employees. It was more that money mattered to Atticus, that he saw it as a commodity meriting huge respect, and could not bear to bestow it gratuitously upon those who did not hold it in equal respect. Cicero was an arty fellow, a fritterer, a dilettante, a blower hot and cold. Therefore he did not—*could* not—esteem money as it deserved.

Third on the list was Publius Nigidius Figulus, of a family quite as old and venerated as Atticus's. Like Atticus, Nigidius Figulus (the nickname Figulus meant a worker in clay, a potter, though how the first Nigidius to bear it had earned it, the family did not know) had abjured public life. In Atticus's case, public life would have meant giving up all commercial activities not arising out of the ownership of land, and Atticus loved commerce more than he did politics. In Nigidius Figulus's case, public life would have eaten too voraciously into his greatest love, which was for the more esoteric aspects of religion. Acknowledged the chief expert on the art of divination as practised by the long-gone Etruscans, he knew more about the liver of a sheep than any butcher or veterinarian. He knew about the flight of birds, the patterns in lightning flashes, the sounds of thunder or earth movements, numbers, fireballs, shooting stars, eclipses, obelisks, standing stones, pylons, pyramids, spheres, tumuli, obsidian, flint, sky eggs, the shape and color of flames, sacred chickens, and all the convolutions an animal intestine could produce.

He was of course one of the custodians of Rome's prophetic books and a mine of information for the College of Augurs, no member of which was an authority on the subject of augury, as augurs were no more and no less than elected religious officials who were legally obliged to consult a chart before pronouncing the omens auspicious or inauspicious. It was Cicero's most ardent wish to be elected an augur (he was not fool enough to think he stood a chance of being elected a pontifex); when he was, he had vowed, he would know more about augury than any of the fellows who, whether elected or co-opted, calmly rode into religious office because their families were entitled.

Having first cultivated Nigidius Figulus because of his knowledge, Cicero soon succumbed to the charm of his nature, unruffled and sweet, humble and sensitive. No snob despite his social pre-eminence, he enjoyed quick wit and lively company, and thought it wonderful to spend an evening with Cicero, famous for wit and always lively company. Like Atticus, Nigidius Figulus was a bachelor, but unlike Atticus, he had chosen this state for religious reasons; he firmly believed that to introduce a woman into his household would destroy his mystical connections to the world of invisible forces and powers. Women were earth people. Nigidius Figulus was a sky person. And air and earth never mixed, never enhanced each other any more than they consumed each other. He also had a horror of blood save in a holy place, and women bled. Thus all his slaves were male, and he had put his mother to live with his sister and her husband.

Cicero had intended to see Atticus and Atticus only on the day following the curule elections, but family matters intruded. Brother Quintus had been elected a praetor. Naturally that called for a celebration, especially as Quintus had followed his older brother's example and got himself elected *in suo anno,* exactly the right age (he was thirty-nine). This second son of a humble squire from Arpinum lived in the house on the Carinae which the old man had bought when he first moved his family to Rome in order to give the prodigy Marcus all the advantages his intellect demanded. So it was that Cicero and his family trudged from the Palatine to the Carinae shortly before the dinner hour, though this fraternal obligation did not negate a talk with Atticus—he would be there because Quintus was married to Atticus's sister, Pomponia.

There was a strong likeness between Cicero and his brother, but Cicero himself was inarguably the more attractive of the two. For one thing, he was physically much taller and better built; Quintus was tiny and sticklike. For another, Cicero had kept his hair, whereas Quintus was very bald on top. Quintus's ears seemed to protrude more than Cicero's, though that was actually a visual illusion due to the massive size of Cicero's skull, which dwarfed these appendages. They were both brown-eyed and brown-haired, and had good brown skins.

In one other respect they had much in common: both men had married wealthy termagants whose near relations had despaired of ever giving them away in wedlock. Terentia had been justly famous for being impossible to please as well as such a difficult person that no one, however needy, could summon up the steel to ask for her in marriage even if she had been willing. It had been she who chose Cicero, rather than the other way around. As for Pomponia—well, Atticus had twice thrown up his hands in exasperation over her! She was ugly, she was fierce, she was rude, she was bitter, she was truculent, she was vengeful, and she could be cruel. His feet firmly on the commercial ladder thanks to Atticus's support, her first husband had divorced her the moment he could do without Atticus, leaving her back on Atticus's doorstep. Though the ground for divorce was barrenness, all of Rome assumed (correctly) that the real ground was lack of desire to cohabit. It was Cicero who suggested that brother Quintus might be prevailed upon to marry her, and he and Atticus between them had done the persuading. The union had taken place thirteen years before, the groom being considerably younger than the bride. Then ten years after the wedding Pomponia gave the lie to barrenness by producing a son, also Quintus.

They fought constantly, and were already using their poor little boy as ammunition in their never-ending struggle for psychic supremacy, pushing and pulling the hapless child from one side to the other and back again. It worried

Atticus (this son of his sister's was his heir) and it worried
Cicero, but neither man succeeded in convincing the an-
tagonists that the real sufferer was little Quintus. Had
brother Quintus only owned the sense to be a doormat like
Cicero, bent over backward to placate his wife and strive
never to draw her attention toward himself, the marriage
might have worked better than that of Cicero and Terentia,
for what Pomponia wanted was simple dominance,
whereas what Terentia wanted was political clout. But,
alas, brother Quintus was far more like their father than
Cicero was; he would be master in his own house no matter what.

The war was going well, so much was plain when
Cicero, Terentia, Tullia and two-year-old Marcus entered
the house. It was the steward bore Tullia and baby Marcus
off to the nursery; Pomponia was too busy screaming at
Quintus, and Quintus equally engrossed in shouting her
down.

"Just as well," roared Cicero in his loudest Forum
voice, "that the temple of Tellus is right next door! Otherwise there'd be yet more neighbors complaining."

Did that stop them? Not at all! They continued as if
the newcomers didn't exist, until Atticus too arrived. His
technique to terminate the battle was as direct as it was
elementary: he simply strode forward, grabbed his sister
by the shoulders and shook her until her teeth rattled.

"Go away, Pomponia!" he snapped. "Go on, take
Terentia somewhere and pour your troubles out in her
ear!"

"I shake her too," said brother Quintus plaintively,
"but it doesn't work. She just knees me in the you-know-
whats."

"If she kneed me," said Atticus grimly, "I'd kill
her."

"If *I* killed her, you'd see me tried for murder."

"True," said Atticus, grinning. "Poor Quintus! I'll
have another talk with her and see what I can do."

Cicero did not participate in this exchange, as he had
beaten a retreat before Atticus's advent, and emerged now

from the direction of the study with a scroll opened between his hands.

"Writing again, brother?" he asked, looking up.

"A tragedy in the style of Sophocles."

"You're improving, it's quite good."

"I hope I'm improving! You've usurped the family reputation for speeches and poetry, which leaves me to choose from history, comedy and tragedy. I haven't the time for the research history demands, and tragedy comes easier to me than comedy, given the kind of atmosphere I live in."

"I would have thought *that* called for farce," said Cicero demurely.

"Oh, shut up!"

"There are always philosophy and natural science."

"My philosophy is simple and natural science baffling, so it still comes down to history, comedy or tragedy."

Atticus had wandered off, and spoke now from the far end of the atrium. "What's this, Quintus?" he asked, a hint of laughter in his voice.

"Oh, bother, you found it before I could show it to you!" cried Quintus, hurrying to join him, Cicero in his wake. "Now I'm a praetor, it's permitted."

"Indeed it is," said Atticus gravely, only his eyes betraying his mirth.

Cicero shoved between them and stood at the proper distance to absorb its glory fully, face solemn. What he gazed at was a gigantic bust of Quintus, so much larger than life that it could never be displayed in a public place, for only the gods might exceed the actual stature of a man. Whoever had done it had worked in clay, then baked it before applying the colors, which made it both good and bad. Good because the likeness was speaking and the colors beautifully tinted, bad because clay-work was cheap and the chances of breakage into shards considerable. None knew better than Cicero and Atticus that Quintus's purse would not run to a bust in marble or bronze.

"Of course it isn't permanent," said Quintus, beaming, "but it will do until I can afford to use it as the mold

for a really splendid bronze. I had the man who is making
my *imago* do it—it always seems such a shame to have
one's wax likeness shut up in a cupboard for none to see.''
He glanced sideways at Cicero, still staring raptly. ''What
do you think, Marcus?'' he asked.

''I think,'' said Cicero deliberately, ''that this is the
first time in my life that I've ever seen the half manage to
be bigger than the whole.''

Too much for Atticus, who laughed until he had to
sit down on the floor, where Cicero joined him. Which left
poor Quintus with only two choices: fly into a monumental
huff or join the mockers in their amusement. Since he was
not Cicero's brother for nothing, he selected merriment.

After that it was time for dinner, which a mollified
Pomponia attended together with Terentia and the peacemaker Tullia, who dealt with her aunt-by-marriage better
than anyone else could.

''So when's the wedding?'' asked Atticus, who
hadn't seen Tullia in so long that her grown-up appearance
had come as quite a surprise. Such a pretty girl! Soft
brown hair, soft brown eyes, a great look of her father,
and a lot of his wit. She had been engaged to young Gaius
Calpurnius Piso Frugi for some years, and it was a good
match in more ways than merely money and clout; Piso
Frugi was by far the most appealing member of a clan
more famous for nastiness than niceness, hardness than
gentleness.

''Two more years,'' Tullia answered with a sigh.

''A long wait,'' said Atticus sympathetically.

''Too long,'' said Tullia, sighing again.

''Well, well,'' from Cicero jovially, ''we shall see,
Tullia. Perhaps we can move it forward a bit.''

Which reply sent all three ladies back to Pomponia's
sitting room in a fever of anticipation, already planning
the wedding.

''Nothing like nuptials to keep women happy,'' said
Cicero.

''She's in love, Marcus, and that's rare in arranged
unions. As I rather gather Piso Frugi feels the same way,
why not let them set up house together before Tullia turns

eighteen?'' Atticus asked, smiling. ''What is she now, sixteen?''

''Almost.

''Then let them marry at the end of this year.''

''I agree,'' said brother Quintus gruffly. ''It's nice to see them together. They get on so well that they're friends.''

Neither of his listeners commented on this remark, but to Cicero it represented the perfect opportunity to change the subject from marriage and women to Catilina—not only more interesting, but also easier to deal with.

''Do you believe that he intended to cancel debts?'' he asked Atticus anxiously.

''I'm not sure I believed it, Marcus, but I certainly could not afford to ignore it,'' said Atticus frankly. ''The accusation is enough to frighten most men in business, especially at the moment, with credit so hard to get and interest rates so high. Oh, there are plenty who would welcome it, but they're never in the majority, and they're rarely at the top of the business heap. A general cancellation of debt is most appealing to little men and men without enough liquid assets to maintain a good cash flow.''

''What you're saying is that the First Class turned away from Catilina and Lucius Cassius from prudence,'' said Cicero.

''Absolutely.''

''Then Caesar was right,'' Quintus butted in to say. ''You virtually impeached Catilina in the House on the slenderest of pretexts. In other words, you started a rumor.''

''No, I did not!'' Cicero yelled, pounding the bolster beneath his left elbow. ''I did not! I wouldn't be so irresponsible! Why are you being so dense, Quintus? That pair were planning to overthrow good government, whether they planned to do it as consuls or as revolutionaries! As Terentia correctly said, men do not plan a general cancellation of debt unless they're wooing the men of Classes lower than the First. It's the typical ploy of men who want to set up a dictatorship.''

"Sulla was Dictator, but he didn't cancel debts," said Quintus stubbornly.

"No, all he did was cancel the lives of two thousand knights!" cried Atticus. "The confiscation of their estates filled the Treasury, and enough newcomers got fat on the proceeds to make other economic measures unnecessary."

"He didn't proscribe you," said Quintus, bristling.

"I should hope not! Sulla was feral, but never a fool."

"Meaning I am?"

"Yes, Quintus, you are a fool," said Cicero, saving Atticus the trouble of finding a tactful answer. "Why do you always have to be so aggressive? No wonder you and Pomponia can't get on—you're as like as two peas in a pod!"

"Grrr!" snarled Quintus, subsiding.

"Well, Marcus, the damage is done," said Atticus pacifically, "and there's every chance that you were right to act before the elections. I think your source of information is suspect because I know the lady a little—but on the other hand, I'd be willing to bet that what she knows about economics could be easily written on the head of a pin. Pluck a phrase like a general cancellation of debt out of thin air? Impossible! No, insofar as it goes, I believe you had sufficient reason to act."

"Whatever you do," cried Cicero, suddenly aware that both his companions knew too much about Fulvia Nobilioris, "do not ever mention her name to anyone! Or even hint that I have a spy in Catilina's camp! I want to go on using her."

Even Quintus could see the sense in this appeal, and agreed to keep Fulvia Nobilioris to himself. As for Atticus, that eminently logical man was fully in favor of a continued watch on the activities of those around Catilina.

"It may be that Catilina himself isn't involved" was the last comment from Atticus, "but certainly his circle warrants our attention. Etruria and Samnium have been constantly boiling since the Italian War, and the fall of

Gaius Marius only exacerbated the situation. Not to mention Sulla's measures.''

Thus it was that Quintus Cicero escorted the various ladies of both households to the seaside with their offspring in Sextilis, while Marcus Cicero himself remained in Rome to monitor events; the Curius ménage did not have the money for vacations at Cumae or Misenum, so Fulvia Nobilioris had to suffer the summer heat. A burden for Cicero too, but one he suspected would be well worth it.

The Kalends of September came and went with no more than a perfunctory meeting of the Senate, traditionally bound to sit on this day. After which most of the senators went back to the seaside, as the calendar was so far ahead of the season that the hottest weather was yet to come. Caesar stayed in town; so did Nigidius Figulus and Varro, for an identical reason: the new Pontifex Maximus had announced the finding of what he called the Stone Annals and the Commentaries of the Kings. After convoking the College of Priests on the last day of Sextilis to inform them first and give them an opportunity to examine both the tablets and the manuscript, he then used the meeting of the Senate on the Kalends of September to display his discovery. Most people just yawned (even some of the priests), but Cicero, Varro and Nigidius Figulus were among those who thought it thrilling, and spent much of the first half of September poring over these antique documents.

Still mildly besotted with the spaciousness and luxury of his new house, Caesar gave a dinner party on the Ides of that month for Nigidius Figulus, Varro, Cicero and two of the men with whom he had messed as a junior military tribune before the walls of Mitylene, Philippus Junior and Gaius Octavius. Philippus was two years older than Caesar and would be a praetor next year too, but Octavius's age lay between them, which meant his first chance to become praetor would not fall until the year after; this of course because patrician Caesar could occupy curule office two years earlier than any plebeian.

Old Philippus, malign and amoral, famous chiefly for the number of times he had switched allegiances from one faction to another, was still alive and still occasionally attended meetings of the Senate, but his days as a force in that body were long past. Nor would his son ever replace him, thought Caesar, either for vice or power. ''Young'' Philippus was too much the Epicurean, too addicted to the exquisitely regulated pleasures of the dining couch and the gentler arts, happy to do his duty in the Senate and ascend the *cursus honorum* because it was his right, but never in a way likely to breed enmity in any political faction. He could get on with Cato as easily as he got on with Caesar, though he much preferred Caesar's company to Cato's. He had been married to a Gellia, and upon her death had chosen not to wed again, preferring not to inflict a stepmother upon his son and daughter.

Between Caesar and Gaius Octavius lay an extra incentive for friendship: after the death of Octavius's first wife (an Ancharia from the wealthy praetorian family) he had sued for the hand of Caesar's niece, Atia, daughter of Caesar's younger sister. Her father, Marcus Atius Balbus, had asked Caesar's opinion about the alliance because Gaius Octavius was not of a noble family, merely a hugely wealthy one, from Velitrae in the Latin homelands. Remembering Octavius's loyalty at Mitylene and aware that he loved the beautiful and delightful Atia madly, Caesar advocated the match. There was a stepdaughter, luckily a nice little girl with no malice in her, but no son of that first marriage to spoil the inheritance of any son Atia might have to Octavius. So the deed was done and Atia installed in one of Rome's loveliest houses, albeit peculiarly situated on the wrong side of the Palatium at the end of a lane called the Ox Heads. And in October of the year before last Atia had borne her first child—alas, a girl.

Naturally the conversation revolved around the Stone Annals and the Commentaries of the Kings, though in deference to Octavius and Philippus, Caesar made considerable efforts to deflect his three more scholarly guests from this marvel.

''Of course you are acknowledged the great authority

on ancient law,'' said Cicero, prepared to concede superiority in an area he thought of little moment in modern Rome.

''I thank you,'' said Caesar gravely.

''A pity there's not more information about the day-to-day activities of the King's court,'' said Varro, freshly returned from a long period in the East as Pompey's resident natural scientist and part-time biographer.

''Yes, but between the two documents we now have an absolutely clear picture of the trial procedure for *perduellio,* and that in itself is fascinating,'' said Nigidius Figulus, ''considering *maiestas.*''

''*Maiestas* was Saturninus's invention,'' said Caesar.

''He only invented *maiestas* because no one could get a conviction for treason in the old form,'' said Cicero quickly.

''A pity Saturninus didn't know of the existence of your finds then, Caesar,'' said Varro dreamily. ''Two judges and no jury makes a big difference to a trial outcome!''

''Rubbish!'' cried Cicero, sitting up straight. ''Neither the Senate nor Comitia would permit a criminal trial without a jury!''

''What I find most interesting,'' said Nigidius Figulus, ''is that there are only some four men alive today who could qualify as judges. You, Caesar. Your cousin Lucius Caesar. Fabius Sanga. And Catilina, oddly enough! All the other patrician families were not around when Horatius was tried for the murder of his sister.''

Philippus and Octavius were looking a little lost as well as rather bored, so Caesar made another effort to change the subject.

''When's the big day?'' he asked Octavius.

''About a market interval to go.''

''And will it be a boy or a girl?''

''We think a boy this time. A third girl between two wives would be a cruel disappointment,'' said Gaius Octavius with a sigh.

''I remember that before Tullia was born I was sure she was a boy,'' said Cicero, grinning. ''Terentia was sure too. As it was, we had to wait fourteen years for my son.''

"That long between tries, was it, Cicero?" asked Philippus.

To which Cicero vouchsafed no answer beyond a blush; like most ambitious social-climbing New Men, he was habitually prudish unless a witticism too stunning to resist sprang to mind. The entrenched aristocrats could afford a salty tongue; Cicero could not.

"The woman whose husband caretakes the Old Meeting Houses says it will be a boy," said Octavius. "She tied Atia's wedding ring to a thread and held it over Atia's belly. It rotated rapidly to the right—a sure sign, she says."

"Well, let's hope she's right," from Caesar. "My older sister threw boys, but girls do run in the family."

"I wonder," asked Varro, "how many men were actually tried for *perduellio* back in the days of Tullus Hostilius?"

Caesar stifled a sigh; to invite three scholars and only two Epicureans to a dinner clearly did not work. Luckily the wine was superlative and so were the Domus Publica cooks.

The news from Etruria came not many days after that dinner with the Pontifex Maximus, and was conveyed by Fulvia Nobilioris.

"Catilina has sent Gaius Manlius to Faesulae to recruit an army," she said to Cicero, perched on the edge of a couch and mopping a forehead dewed with sweat, "and Publius Furius is in Apulia doing the same."

"Proof?" asked Cicero sharply, his own brow suddenly moist.

"I have none, Marcus Tullius."

"Did Quintus Curius tell you?"

"No. I overheard him talking to Lucius Cassius last night after dinner. They thought I had gone to bed. Since the elections they've all been very quiet, even Quintus Curius. It was a blow to Catilina, and I think he's taken some time to recover. Last night was the first time I've heard a whisper of anything.''

"Do you know when Manlius and Furius began their operations?"

"No."

"So you have no idea how far advanced recruitment might be? Would it, for instance, be possible for me to get confirmation if I sent someone to Faesulae?"

"I don't know, Marcus Tullius. I wish I did!"

"What of Quintus Curius? Is he keen on outright revolution?"

"I'm not sure."

"Then try to find out, Fulvia," Cicero said, careful to keep the exasperation out of his voice and manner. "If we can persuade him to testify before the Senate, its members would have no choice but to believe me."

"Rest assured, husband, Fulvia will do her best," said Terentia, and ushered the visitor out.

Positive that all insurgent forces would be willing to recruit slaves, Cicero sent a very sharp and presentable fellow north to Faesulae with instructions to volunteer. Aware that many in the House deemed him gullible and overeager for a crisis to distinguish his consulship, Cicero borrowed this slave from Atticus; the fellow could therefore testify that he was not under obligation to Cicero personally. But, alas, when he returned he had little to offer. Something was definitely going on, and not only in Faesulae. The trouble was that slaves, he had been told when he started to fish for information, did not belong in Etruria, a place of free men owning sufficient free men to serve the interests of Etruria. Just what that answer meant was difficult to say, as of course Etruria was as liberally dowered with slaves as any other place inside or outside Italy. The whole world depended on slaves!

"If it is indeed an uprising, Marcus Tullius," Atticus's servant concluded, "then it is an uprising limited to free men."

"What next?" asked Terentia over dinner.

"I honestly don't know, my dear. The thing is, do I convene the Senate and try again, or do I wait until I can gather several free-man agents together and produce some hard evidence?"

"I have a feeling that hard evidence is going to be very difficult to find, husband. No one in northern Etruria trusts any outsider, free or servile. They're clannish and secretive."

"Well," said Cicero, sighing, "I shall summon the House into session the day after tomorrow. If it serves no other purpose, it will at least tell Catilina that my eye is still upon him."

It served no other purpose, exactly as Cicero had foreseen. Those senators not still at the seaside were skeptical at best and downright insulting at worst. Especially Catilina, who was present and vocal but remarkably cool for a man whose hopes for the consulship had been permanently dashed. This time he made no attempt to rant at Cicero or at adversity; he simply sat on his stool and answered patiently, calmly. A good tactic which impressed the skeptics and allowed the partisans to gloat. Little wonder then that what might otherwise have been a rowdy and heated debate gradually dwindled to an inertia leavened only by the sudden eruption of Gaius Octavius through the doors, whooping and dancing.

"I have a son! I have a son!"

Thankful for an excuse to close the meeting, Cicero dismissed his clerks and joined the crowd around Octavius.

"Is the horoscope auspicious?" asked Caesar. "Mind you, they are never not."

"More miraculous than auspicious, Caesar. If I am to believe what the astrologer fellow says, my son Gaius Octavius Junior will end in ruling the world." The proud father chuckled. "But I fell for it! Gave the astrologer a bonus as well as a fee."

"My natal horoscope just had lots to say about mysterious illnesses of the chest, if I am to believe my mother," said Caesar. "She never will show it to me."

"And mine said I would never make money," said Crassus.

"Fortune-telling keeps the women happy," said Philippus.

"Who intends to come with me to register the birth

with Juno Lucina?'' Octavius asked, still beaming.

"Who else than Uncle Caesar Pontifex Maximus?''
Caesar threw an arm about Octavius's shoulders. "And
after that, I demand to be shown my new nephew.''

Eighteen days of October had ground away without
significant information from either Etruria or Apulia, nor
a word from Fulvia Nobilioris. An occasional letter from
the agents both Cicero and Atticus had dispatched held
out little hope of hard evidence, though every one of these
missives vowed *something* was definitely going on. The
chief trouble seemed to lie in the fact that there was no
real nucleus, just stirs and shudders in this village, then in
that village, on some Sullan centurion's foundering farm
or in some Sullan veteran's low tavern. Yet the moment
a strange face showed itself, everyone walked about whistling innocently. Inside the walls of Faesulae, Arretium,
Volaterrae, Aesernia, Larinum and all the other urban settlements of Etruria and Apulia, nothing was visible save
economic depression and grinding poverty. There were
houses and farms for sale to cover hopeless debts everywhere, but of their erstwhile owners, not a sign.

And Cicero was tired, tired, tired. He *knew* it was
busily happening under his nose, yet he couldn't prove it
and he was now beginning to believe he never would until
the day of revolt arrived. Terentia too was in despair, a
state which surprisingly seemed to make her easier to live
with; though his fleshly urges were never strong, these
days Cicero found himself wanting to retire early and seek
a solace in her body which he found as mystifying as it
was incongruous.

Both of them were sunk into a deep sleep when Tiro
came to wake them shortly after the middle hour of night
on that eighteenth day of October.

"*Domine, domine!*'' the beloved slave whispered
from the door, his charmingly elfin face above the lamp
turned into a visage from the underworld. "*Domine,* you
have visitors!''

"What's the hour?'' Cicero managed, swinging his

legs off the bed on one side as Terentia stirred and opened
her eyes.

"Very late, *domine*."

"Visitors, did you say?"

"Yes, *domine*."

Terentia was struggling to sit up on her side of the
bed, but made no move to dress; well she knew that whatever was afoot would not include her, a woman! Nor could
she go back to sleep. She would just have to contain herself until Cicero could return to inform her what the trouble was.

"Who, Tiro?" asked Cicero, pushing his head into a
tunic.

"Marcus Licinius Crassus and two other noblemen,
domine."

"Ye gods!"

No time for ablutions or footwear; Cicero hurried out
to the atrium of the house he now felt was too small and
too humdrum for one who would from the end of this year
call himself a consular.

Sure enough, there was Crassus—accompanied by
Marcus Claudius Marcellus and Metellus Scipio, of all
people! The steward was busy kindling lamps, Tiro had
produced writing paper, pens and wax tablets just in case,
and noises from outside indicated that wine and refreshments would appear shortly.

"What's amiss?" asked Cicero, dispensing with ceremony.

"You were right, my friend," said Crassus, and held
out both hands. His right contained an open sheet of paper;
his left held several letters still folded and sealed. He
passed the open sheet across. "Read that and you'll know
what's amiss."

It was very short, but authored by someone well
schooled, and it was addressed to Crassus.

I am a patriot who has by mischance become
embroiled in an insurrection. That I send these
letters to you rather than to Marcus Cicero

arises out of your standing in Rome. No one has believed Marcus Cicero. I hope everyone will believe you. The letters are copies; I could not make off with the originals. Nor dare I tell you any names. What I can tell you is that fire and revolution are coming to Rome. Get out of Rome, Marcus Crassus, and take all who do not wish to be killed with you.

Though he couldn't compete with Caesar when it came to swift and silent reading, Cicero wasn't that far behind; in a shorter time than it had taken Crassus to read the note, Cicero looked up.

"Jupiter, Marcus Crassus! How did you come by this?"

Crassus sat down in a chair heavily, Metellus Scipio and Marcellus going together to a couch. When a servant offered him wine, Crassus waved it aside.

"We were having a late dinner at my place," he said, "and I'm afraid I got carried away. Marcus Marcellus and Quintus Scipio had a scheme in mind to increase their family fortunes, but they didn't want to break senatorial precedents, so they came to me for advice."

"True," said Marcellus warily; he didn't trust Cicero not to blab about unsenatorial business ventures.

But the last thing on Cicero's mind was the thin line between proper senatorial practices and illegal ones, so he said, "Yes, yes!" impatiently, and to Crassus, "Go on!"

"Someone hammered on the door about an hour ago, but when my steward went to answer it there was no one outside. At first he didn't notice the letters, which had been put on the step. It was the noise made by the pile falling over drew his attention to them. The one I've opened was addressed to me personally, as you can see for yourself, though I opened it more out of curiosity than from any presentiment of alarm—who would choose such an odd way to deliver mail, and at such an hour?" Crassus looked grim. "When I'd read it and shown it to Marcus and Quintus here, we decided the best thing to do was bring everything to you at once. You're the one who's been making all the fuss.''

Cicero took the five unopened packets and sat down with an elbow on the peacock-grained citrus-wood table he had paid half a million sesterces for, heedless of its depreciation should he scratch it. One by one he held the letters up to the light, examining the cheap wax closures.

"A wolf seal in ordinary red wax," he said, sighing. "You can buy them in any shop." His fingers slipped beneath the edge of the paper of the last in the pile, he tugged sharply and broke the little round wax emblem in half while Crassus and the other two watched eagerly. "I'll read it out," he said then, opening the single sheet of paper. "This one isn't signed, but I see it's addressed to Gaius Manlius." He began to pore over the squiggles.

> "You will start the revolution five days before the Kalends of November by forming up your troops and invading Faesulae. The town will come over to you in mass, so you have assured us. We believe you. Whatever else you do, make straight for the arsenal. At dawn of this same day your four colleagues will also move: Publius Furius against Volaterrae, Minucius against Arretium, Publicius against Saturnia, Aulus Fulvius against Clusium. By sunset we expect that all these towns will be in your hands, and our army much bigger. Not to mention better equipped from the arsenals.
>
> "On the fourth day before the Kalends, those of us in Rome will strike. An army is not necessary. Stealth will serve us better. We will kill both the consuls and all eight praetors. What happens to the consuls-elect and the praetors-elect depends on their good sense, but certain powers in the business sphere will have to die: Marcus Crassus, Servilius Caepio Brutus, Titus Atticus. Their fortunes will fund our enterprise with money to spare.

"We would have preferred to wait longer, build up our strength and our forces, but we cannot afford to wait until Pompeius Magnus is close enough to move against us before we are ready for him. His turn will come, but first things are first. May the Gods be with you."

Cicero put the letter down to gaze at Crassus in horror. "Jupiter, Marcus Crassus!" he cried, hands trembling. "It is upon us in nine days!"

The two younger men looked ashen in the flickering light, eyes passing from Cicero to Crassus and back again, minds obviously unable to assimilate anything beyond the word "kill."

"Open the others," said Crassus.

But these proved to be much the same as the first, addressed to each of the other four men mentioned by name in Gaius Manlius's.

"He's clever," said Cicero, shaking his head. "Nothing put down in the first person singular for me to level at Catilina, no word of who in Rome is involved. All I really have are the names of his military henchmen in Etruria, and as they're already committed to revolution, they can't matter. Clever!"

Metellus Scipio licked his lips and found his voice. "Who wrote the letter to Marcus Crassus, Cicero?" he asked.

"I would think Quintus Curius."

"*Curius?* That Curius who was thrown out of the Senate?"

"The same."

"Then can we get him to testify?" Marcellus asked.

It was Crassus who shook his head. "No, we daren't. All they'd have to do was kill him and we'd be right back where we are at the moment except that we'd lack an informer at all."

"We could put him in protective custody even before he testified," said Metellus Scipio.

"And shut his mouth?" asked Cicero. "Protective

custody at any stage is likely to shut his mouth. The most important thing is to push Catilina into declaring himself.''

Whereupon Marcellus said, frowning, ''What if the ringleader isn't Catilina?''

''That's a point,'' said Metellus Scipio.

''What do I have to do to get it through all your thick skulls that the only man it can be is Catilina?'' yelled Cicero, striking the precious surface of his table so hard that the gold and ivory pedestal beneath it shivered. ''It's Catilina! It's Catilina!''

''Proof, Marcus,'' said Crassus. ''You need proof.''

''One way or another I will get proof,'' said Cicero, ''but in the meantime we have a revolution in Etruria to put down. I will summon the Senate into session tomorrow at the fourth hour.''

''Good,'' said Crassus, lumbering to his feet. ''Then I'm for home and bed.''

''What about you?'' asked Cicero on the way to the door. ''Do you believe Catilina is responsible, Marcus Crassus?''

''Very probably, but not certainly'' was the answer.

''And isn't *that* typical?'' asked Terentia some moments later, sitting up straight. ''He wouldn't commit himself to an alliance with Jupiter Optimus Maximus!''

''Nor will many in the Senate, I predict,'' sighed Cicero. ''However, my dear, I think it's time you sought Fulvia out. We've heard nothing from her in many days.'' He lay down. ''Blow out the lamp, I must try to sleep.''

What Cicero hadn't counted on was the full degree of doubt in the Senate's mind as to Catilina's masterminding what certainly did appear to be a brewing insurrection. Skepticism he expected, but not outright opposition, yet outright opposition was what he got when he produced and read his letters. He had thought that bringing Crassus into the story would procure a *senatus consultum de re publica defendenda*—the decree proclaiming martial law—but the House denied him.

''You should have retained the letters unbroken until this body assembled,'' said Cato harshly. He was now a tribune of the plebs–elect, and entitled to speak.

"But I opened them in front of unimpeachable witnesses!"

"No matter," said Catulus. "You usurped the Senate's prerogative."

Through all of it Catilina had sat with exactly the right series of emotions reflected on face and in eyes— indignation, calm, innocence, mild exasperation, incredulity.

Tried beyond endurance, Cicero turned to face him. "Lucius Sergius Catilina, will you admit that you are the prime mover in these events?" he asked, voice ringing round the rafters.

"No, Marcus Tullius Cicero, I will not."

"Is there no man present who will support me?" the senior consul demanded, looking from Crassus to Caesar, Catulus to Cato.

"I suggest," said Crassus after a considerable silence, "that this House request the senior consul to further investigate all sides of this matter. It would not be surprising if Etruria revolted, I will give you that, Marcus Tullius. But when even your colleague in the consulship says the whole thing is a practical joke and then announces that he's going back to Cumae tomorrow, how can you expect the rest of us to fly into a panic?"

And so it was left. Cicero must find further evidence.

"It was Quintus Curius who got the letters to Marcus Crassus," said Fulvia Nobilioris early the following morning, "but he will not testify for you. He's too afraid."

"Have you and he talked?"

"Yes."

"Then can you give me any names, Fulvia?"

"I can only tell you the names of Quintus Curius's friends."

"Who are?"

"Lucius Cassius, as you know. Gaius Cornelius and Lucius Vargunteius, who were expelled from the Senate with my Curius."

Her words suddenly linked up with a fact buried at the back of Cicero's mind. "Is the praetor Lentulus Sura a friend?'' he asked, remembering that man's abuse of him at the elections. Yes, Lentulus Sura had been one of the seventy-odd men expelled by the censors Poplicola and Clodianus! Even though he had been consul.

But Fulvia knew nothing about Lentulus Sura. ''Though,'' she said, ''I have seen the younger Cethegus—Gaius Cethegus?—with Lucius Cassius from time to time. And Lucius Statilius and the Gabinius nicknamed Capito too. They are not *close* friends, mind you, so it's hard to say if they're in on the plot.''

''And what of the uprising in Etruria?''

''I only know that Quintus Curius says it will happen.''

''Quintus Curius says it will happen,'' Cicero repeated to Terentia when she returned from seeing Fulvia Nobilioris off the premises. ''Catilina is too clever for Rome, my dear. Have you ever in your life known a Roman who could keep a secret? Yet every way I turn, I'm baffled. How I wish I came from noble stock! If my name was Licinius or Fabius or Caecilius, Rome would be under martial law right now, and Catilina would be a public enemy. But because my name is Tullius and I hail from Arpinum—Marius country, that!—nothing I say carries any weight.''

''Conceded,'' said Terentia.

Which provoked a rueful glance from Cicero, but no comment. A moment later he slapped his hands upon his thighs and said, ''Well, then I just have to keep on trying!''

''You've sent enough men to Etruria to sniff something out.''

''One would think. But the letters indicate that rebellion isn't concentrated in the towns, that the towns are to be taken over from bases outside in the country.''

''The letters also indicate a shortage of armaments.''

''True. When Pompeius Magnus was consul and insisted there must be stocks of armaments north of Rome, many of us didn't like the idea. I admit that his arsenals are as hard to get into as Nola, but if the towns revolt— well . . .''

"The towns haven't revolted so far. They're too afraid."

"They're full of Etrurians, and Etrurians hate Rome."

"This revolt is the work of Sulla's veterans."

"Who don't live in the towns."

"Precisely."

"So shall I try again in the Senate?"

"Yes, husband. You have nothing to lose, so try again."

Which he did a day later, the twenty-first day of October. His meeting was thinly attended, yet one more indication what Rome's senators thought of the senior consul—an ambitious New Man out to make much from very little and find himself a cause serious enough to produce several speeches worth publishing for posterity. Cato, Crassus, Catulus, Caesar and Lucullus were there, but much of the space of the three tiers on either side of the floor was unoccupied. However, Catilina was flaunting himself, solidly hedged around by men who thought well of him, deemed him persecuted. Lucius Cassius, Publius Sulla the Dictator's nephew, his crony Autronius, Quintus Annius Chilo, both the sons of dead Cethegus, the two Sulla brothers who were not of the Dictator's clan but well connected nonetheless, the witty tribune of the plebs–elect Lucius Calpurnius Bestia, and Marcus Porcius Laeca. Are they all in on it? asked Cicero of himself. Am I looking at the new order in Rome? If so, I don't think much of it. All these men are villains.

He drew a deep breath and began. . . .

"I am tired of saying a mouthful like *senatus consultum de re publica defendenda*," he announced an hour of well-chosen words later, "so I am going to coin a new name for the Senate's ultimate decree, the only decree the Senate can issue as binding on all Comitia, government bodies, institutions and citizens. I am going to call it the Senatus Consultum Ultimum. And, Conscript Fathers, I want you to issue a Senatus Consultum Ultimum."

"Against me, Marcus Tullius?" Catilina asked, smiling.

"Against revolution, Lucius Sergius."

"But you have proven neither point, Marcus Tullius. Give us proof, not words!"

It was going to fail again.

"Perhaps, Marcus Tullius, we would be more prepared to take credence of rebellion in Etruria if you would cease this personal attack on Lucius Sergius," said Catulus. "Your accusations against him have absolutely no basis in fact, and that in turn casts huge shadows of doubt on any unusual state of unrest northwest of the Tiber. Etruria is old hat, and Lucius Sergius clearly a scapegoat. No, Marcus Tullius, we will not believe a word of it without far more concrete evidence than pretty speeches."

"I have the concrete evidence!" boomed a voice from the door, and in walked the ex-praetor Quintus Arrius.

Knees sagging, Cicero sat down abruptly on his ivory chair of office and gaped at Arrius, disheveled from the road and still clad in riding gear.

The House was murmuring and beginning to look at Catilina, who sat amid his friends seeming stunned.

"Come up on the dais, Quintus Arrius, and tell us."

"There is revolution in Etruria," said Arrius simply. "I have seen it for myself. Sulla's veterans are all off their farms and busy training volunteers, mostly men who have lost their homes or properties in these hard times. I found their camp some miles out of Faesulae."

"How many men under arms, Arrius?" asked Caesar.

"About two thousand."

That produced a sigh of relief, but faces soon fell again when Arrius went on to explain that there were similar camps at Arretium, Volaterrae and Saturnia, and that there was every chance Clusium also was involved.

"And what of me, Quintus Arrius?" asked Catilina loudly. "Am I their leader, though I sit here in Rome?"

"Their leader, as far as I can gather, Lucius Sergius, is a man called Gaius Manlius, who was one of Sulla's centurions. I did not hear your name, nor have I any evidence to incriminate you.''

Whereupon the men around Catilina began to cheer, and the rest of the House to look relieved. Swallowing his chagrin, the senior consul thanked Quintus Arrius and asked the House again to issue its Senatus Consultum Ultimum, permit him and his government to move against rebellious troops in Etruria.

''I will see a division,'' he said. ''All those who approve the issuance of a Senatus Consultum Ultimum to deal with rebellion in Etruria please pass to my right. All those opposed, please pass to my left.''

Everyone passed to the right, including Catilina and all his supporters, Catilina with a look which said, Now do your worst, you Arpinate upstart!

''However,'' said the praetor Lentulus Sura after everyone had returned to his place, ''troop concentrations do not necessarily mean an uprising is seriously intended, at least for the time being. Did you hear a date of any kind, Quintus Arrius—five days before the Kalends of November, for instance, that being the date in those famous letters sent to Marcus Crassus?''

''I heard no date,'' said Arrius.

''I ask,'' Lentulus Sura went on, ''because the Treasury is not in a position at the moment to find large sums of money for massive recruitment campaigns. May I suggest, Marcus Tullius, that for the present moment you exercise your—er—'Senatus Consultum Ultimum' in a restrained way?''

The faces staring at him approved, so much was easy to see; Cicero therefore contented himself with a measure expelling every professional gladiator from Rome.

''What, Marcus Tullius, no directive to issue arms to all this city's citizens registered to bear them in times of emergency?'' asked Catilina sweetly.

''No, Lucius Sergius, I do not intend to order that until I have proven you and yours public enemies!'' snapped Cicero. ''Why should I hand weapons to anyone I think will end in turning those weapons against all loyal citizens?''

"This person is pernicious!" cried Catilina, hands stretched out. "He has not one iota of proof, yet still he persists in a malicious persecution of me!"

But Catulus was remembering how he and Hortensius had felt the year before, when they had conspired to exclude Catilina from the chair in which they had virtually installed Cicero as the preferable alternative. *Was* it possible that Catilina was the prime mover? Gaius Manlius was his client. So was one of the other revolutionaries, Publius Furius. Perhaps it might be wise to discover whether Minucius, Publicius and Aulus Fulvius were also clients of his. After all, none of those who sat around Catilina was a pillar of rectitude! Lucius Cassius was a fat fool, and as for Publius Sulla and Publius Autronius— hadn't they been stripped of office as consuls before they could take office? And had there not been a wild rumor at the time that they were planning to assassinate Lucius Cotta and Torquatus, their replacements? Catulus decided to open his mouth.

"Leave Marcus Tullius alone, Lucius Sergius!" he commanded wearily. "We may be obliged to put up with a little private war between the pair of you, but we need not put up with a *privatus* trying to tell the legally elected senior consul how to implement his—er—'Senatus Consultum Ultimum.' I happen to agree with Marcus Tullius. From now on the troop concentrations in Etruria will be monitored closely. Therefore no one in this city needs to be issued arms at the moment."

"You're getting there, Cicero," said Caesar as the House disbanded. "Catulus is having second thoughts about Catilina."

"And what about you?"

"Oh, I think he's a genuine bad man. That's why I asked Quintus Arrius to do a little investigating in Etruria."

"*You* put Arrius up to it?"

"Well, you weren't managing, were you? I picked Arrius because he soldiered with Sulla, and Sulla's veterans love him dearly. There are few faces from Rome's upper echelons capable of lulling suspicion in those discontented veteran farmers, but Arrius's face is one of them," said Caesar.

"Then I am obliged to you."

"Think nothing of it. Like all my kind, I am reluctant to abandon a fellow patrician, but I'm not a fool, Cicero. I want no part of insurrection, nor can I afford to be identified with a fellow patrician who does. My star is still rising. A pity that Catilina's has set, but it *has* set. Therefore Catilina is a spent force in Roman politics." Caesar shrugged. "I can have no truck with spent forces. The same might be said for many of us, from Crassus to Catulus. As you now observe."

"I have men stationed in Etruria. If the uprising does take place five days before the Kalends, Rome will know within a day."

But Rome didn't know within a day. When the fourth day before the Kalends of November rolled round, nothing whatsoever happened. The consuls and praetors who according to the letters were to be killed went about their business unmolested, and no word of rebellion came from Etruria.

Cicero existed in a frenzy of doubt and expectation, his mood not helped by Catilina's constant derision, nor by the sudden coolness he felt emanating from Catulus and Crassus. What had happened? Why did no word come?

The Kalends of November arrived; still no word. Not that Cicero had been entirely idle during those awful days when he had to wait upon events. He hedged the city in with detachments of troops from Capua, posted a cohort at Ocriculum, another at Tibur, one at Ostia, one at Praeneste, and two at Veii; more than that he could not do because more troops ready enough to fight were just not available, even at Capua.

Then after noon on the Kalends everything happened at once. A frantic message for help came from Praeneste, which proclaimed itself under attack. And a frantic message finally arrived from Faesulae, also under attack. The uprising had indeed begun five days earlier, exactly as the letters had indicated. As the sun was setting further messages told of restless slaves in Capua and Apulia. Cicero summoned the Senate for dawn on the morrow.

Astonishing how convenient the process of triumphing could be! For fifty years the presence of a triumphator's army on the Campus Martius during a time of crisis for Rome had managed to extricate the city from peril. This present crisis was no different. Quintus Marcius Rex and Metellus Little Goat Creticus were both on the Campus Martius awaiting their triumphs. Of course neither man had more than a legion with him, but those legions were veteran. With the full agreement of the Senate, Cicero sent orders to the Campus Martius that Metellus Little Goat was to proceed south to Apulia and relieve Praeneste on the way, and that Marcius Rex was to proceed north to Faesulae.

Cicero had eight praetors at his disposal, though within his mind he had excluded Lentulus Sura; he instructed Quintus Pompeius Rufus to go to Capua and commence recruiting troops from among the many veterans settled on land in Campania. Now, who else? Gaius Pomptinus was a Military Man and a good friend besides, which meant he was best retained in Rome for serious duty. Cosconius was the son of a brilliant general, but not adequate in the field at all. Roscius Otho was a great friend of Cicero's, but more effective as a favor currier than a general or a recruiter. Though Sulpicius was not a patrician, he seemed nonetheless to sympathize a little with Catilina, and the patrician Valerius Flaccus was another Cicero could not quite bring himself to trust. Which left only the *praetor urbanus,* Metellus Celer. Pompey's man and utterly loyal.

"Quintus Caecilius Metellus Celer, I order you to go to Picenum and commence recruiting soldiers there," said Cicero.

Celer rose, frowning. "Naturally I am glad to do so, Marcus Tullius, but there is a problem. As urban praetor I cannot be out of Rome for more than ten days at a time."

"Under a Senatus Consultum Ultimum, you can do

anything the State instructs you to do without breaking law or tradition.''

''I wish I agreed with your interpretation,'' Caesar interrupted, ''but I do not, Marcus Tullius. The ultimate decree extends only to the crisis, it does not dislocate normal magisterial functions.''

''I need Celer to deal with the crisis!'' snapped Cicero.

''You have five other praetors as yet unused,'' said Caesar.

''I am the senior consul, I will send the praetor best suited!''

''Even if you act illegally?''

''I am *not* acting illegally! The Senatus Consultum Ultimum overrides all other considerations, including 'normal magisterial functions,' as you call Celer's duties!'' Face reddening, Cicero had begun to shout. ''Would you question the right of a formally appointed dictator to send Celer out of the city for more than ten days at a time?''

''No, I would not,'' said Caesar, very cool. ''Therefore, Marcus Tullius, why not do this thing the proper way? Rescind the toy you're playing with and ask this body to appoint a dictator and a master of the horse to go to war against Gaius Manlius.''

''What a brilliant idea!'' drawled Catilina, sitting in his customary place and surrounded by all the men who supported him.

''The last time Rome had a dictator, she ended up with his ruling her like a king!'' cried Cicero. ''The Senatus Consultum Ultimum was devised to deal with civil crises in a way which does not throw one man into absolute control!''

''What, are you not in control, Cicero?'' asked Catilina.

''I am the senior consul!''

''And making all the decisions, just as if you were dictator,'' gibed Catilina.

''I am the instrument of the Senatus Consultum Ultimum!''

''You're the instrument of magisterial chaos,'' said

Caesar. "In not much more than a month, the new tribunes of the plebs take office, and the few days before and after that event require that the urban praetor be present in Rome."

"There's no law on the tablets to that effect!"

"But there is a law to say that the urban praetor cannot be absent from Rome for more than ten days at a time."

"All right, all right!" Cicero yelled. "Have it your own way! Quintus Caecilius Metellus Celer, I order you to Picenum, but require that you return to Rome every eleventh day! You will also return to Rome six days before the new tribunes of the plebs enter office, and remain in Rome until six days after they enter office!"

At which moment a scribe handed the irate senior consul a note. Cicero read it, then laughed. "Well, Lucius Sergius!" he said to Catilina, "another little difficulty seems to be forming for you! Lucius Aemilius Paullus intends to prosecute you under the *lex Plautia de vi*, so he has just announced from the rostra." Cicero cleared his throat ostentatiously. "I am sure you know who Lucius Aemilius Paullus is! A fellow patrician, and a fellow revolutionary at that! Back in Rome after some years in exile and well behind his little brother Lepidus in terms of public life, but apparently desirous of showing that he no longer harbors a rebellious bone in his noble body. You would have it that only us jumped-up New Men are against you, but you cannot call an Aemilius jumped up, now can you?"

"Oh, oh, oh!" drawled Catilina, one brow raised. He put out his right hand and made it flutter and tremble. "See how I quake, Marcus Tullius! I am to be prosecuted on a charge of inciting public *violence*? Yet when have I done that?" He remained seated, but gazed around the tiers looking terribly wounded. "Perhaps I ought to offer myself into some nobleman's custody, eh, Marcus Tullius? Would that please you?" He stared at Mamercus. "Ho there, Mamercus Aemilius Lepidus Princeps Senatus, will you take me into your house as your prisoner?"

Head of the Aemilii Lepidi and therefore closely related to the returned exile Paullus, Mamercus simply shook his head, grinning. "I don't want you, Lucius Sergius," he said.

"Then how about you, senior consul?" Catilina asked Cicero.

"What, admit my potential murderer to my house? No, thank you!" said Cicero.

"What about you, *praetor urbanus*?"

"Can't be done," said Metellus Celer. "I'm off to Picenum in the morning."

"Then how about a plebeian Claudius? Will you volunteer, Marcus Claudius Marcellus? You were quick enough to follow your master Crassus's lead a few days ago!"

"I refuse," said Marcellus.

"I have a better idea, Lucius Sergius," said Cicero. "Why not take yourself out of Rome and openly join your insurrection?"

"I will not take myself out of Rome, and it is not my insurrection," said Catilina.

"In which case, I declare this meeting closed," said Cicero. "Rome is protected to the best of our abilities. All we can do now is wait and see what happens next. Sooner or later, Catilina, you will betray yourself."

"Though I do wish," he said to Terentia later, "that my pleasure-loving colleague Hybrida would return to Rome! Here it is an officially declared state of emergency, and where is Gaius Antonius Hybrida? Still lolling on his private beach at Cumae!"

"Can't you command him to return under the Senatus Consultum Ultimum?" asked Terentia.

"I suppose so."

"Then do it, Cicero! You may need him."

"He's pleading gout."

"The gout is in his head" was Terentia's verdict.

Some five hours before dawn of the seventh day of November, Tiro again woke Cicero and Terentia from a deep sleep.

"You have a visitor, *domina,*" said the beloved slave.

Famous for her rheumatism, the wife of the senior consul showed no sign of it as she leaped from her bed (decently clad in a nightgown, of course—no naked sleepers in Cicero's house!).

"It's Fulvia Nobilioris," she said, shaking Cicero. "Wake up, husband, wake up!" Oh, the joy of it! She was in on a war council at last!

"Quintus Curius sent me," Fulvia Nobilioris announced, her face old and bare because she had not had time to apply makeup.

"He's come around?" asked Cicero sharply.

"Yes." The visitor took the cup of unwatered wine Terentia gave her and sipped at it, shuddering. "They met at midnight in the house of Marcus Porcius Laeca."

"Who met?"

"Catilina, Lucius Cassius, my Quintus Curius, Gaius Cethegus, both the Sulla brothers, Gabinius Capito, Lucius Statilius, Lucius Vargunteius and Gaius Cornelius."

"Not Lentulus Sura?"

"No."

"Then it appears I was wrong about him." Cicero leaned forward. "Go on, woman, go on! What happened?"

"They met to plan the fall of Rome and further the rebellion," said Fulvia Nobilioris, a little color returning to her cheeks as the wine took effect. "Gaius Cethegus wanted to take Rome at once, but Catilina wants to wait until uprisings are under way in Apulia, Umbria and Bruttium. He suggested the night of the Saturnalia, and gave as his reason that it is the one night of the year when Rome is topsy-turvy, slaves ruling, free households serving, everyone drunk. And he thinks it will take that long to swell the revolt."

Nodding, Cicero saw the point of this: the Saturnalia was held on the seventeenth day of December, six market intervals from now. By which time all of Italy might be boiling. "So who won, Fulvia?" he asked.

"Catilina, though Cethegus did succeed in one respect."

"And that is?" the senior consul prompted gently when she stopped, began to shake.

"They agreed that you should be murdered immediately."

He had known since the letters that he was not intended to live, but to hear it now from the lips of this poor terrified woman gave it an edge and a horror Cicero felt for the first time. He was to be murdered immediately! *Immediately!* "How and when?" he asked. "Come, Fulvia, tell me! I'm not going to haul you into court, you've earned rewards, not punishment! Tell me!"

"Lucius Vargunteius and Gaius Cornelius will present themselves here at dawn with your clients," she said.

"But they're not my clients!" said Cicero blankly.

"I know. But it was decided that they would ask to become your clients in the hope that you would support their return to public life. Once inside, they are to ask for a private interview in your study to plead their case. Instead, they are to stab you to death and make their escape before your clients know what has happened," said Fulvia.

"Then that's simple," said Cicero, sighing with relief. "I will bar my doors, set a watch in the peristyle, and refuse to see my clients on grounds of illness. Nor will I stir outside all day. It's time for councils." He got up to pat Fulvia Nobilioris on the hand. "I thank you most sincerely, and tell Quintus Curius his intervention has earned him a full pardon. But tell him too that if he will testify to all this in the House the day after tomorrow, he will be a hero. I give him my word that I will not let a thing happen to him."

"I will tell him."

"What exactly does Catilina plan for the Saturnalia?"

"They have a large cache of arms somewhere— Quintus Curius does not know the place—and these will be distributed to all the partisans. Twelve separate fires are to be started throughout the city, including one on the Capitol, two on the Palatine, two on the Carinae, and one at either end of the Forum. Certain men are to go to the houses of all the magistrates and kill them."

"Except for me, dead already."

"Yes."

"You'd better go, Fulvia," said Cicero, nodding to his wife. "Vargunteius and Cornelius may arrive a little early, and we don't want them to set eyes on you. Did you bring an escort?"

"No," she whispered, white-faced again.

"Then I will send Tiro and four others with you."

"A pretty plot!" barked Terentia, marching into Cicero's study the moment she had organized the flight of Fulvia Nobilioris.

"My dear, without you I would have been dead before now."

"I am well aware of it," Terentia said, sitting down. "I have issued orders to the staff, who will bolt and bar everything the moment Tiro and the others return. Now print a notice I can have put on the front door that you are ill and won't receive."

Cicero printed obediently, handed it over and let his wife take care of the logistics. What a general of troops she would have made! Nothing forgotten, everything battened down.

"You will need to see Catulus, Crassus, Hortensius if he's returned from the seaside, Mamercus, and Caesar," she said after all the preparations were finished.

"Not until this afternoon," said Cicero feebly. "Let's make sure first that I'm out of danger."

Tiro was posted upstairs in a window which gave a good view of the front door, and was able to report an hour after dawn that Vargunteius and Cornelius had finally gone away, though not until they had tried several times to pick the lock of Cicero's stout front door.

"Oh, this is disgusting!" the senior consul cried. "I, the senior consul, barred into my own house? Send for all the consulars in Rome, Tiro! Tomorrow I'll have Catilina running."

Fifteen consulars turned up—Mamercus, Poplicola, Catulus, Torquatus, Crassus, Lucius Cotta, Vatia Isauricus,

Curio, Lucullus, Varro Lucullus, Volcatius Tullus, Gaius
Marcius Figulus, Glabrio, Lucius Caesar and Gaius Piso.
Neither of the consuls-elect nor the urban praetor–elect,
Caesar, was invited; Cicero had decided to keep the coun-
cil of war advisory only.

"Unfortunately," he said heavily when all the men
were accommodated in an atrium too small for comfort—
he would have to earn the money somehow to buy a bigger
house!—"I can't prevail upon Quintus Curius to testify,
and that means I have no solid case. Nor will Fulvia Nobilioris testify, even if the Senate was to agree to hear
evidence from a woman."

"For what it's worth, Cicero, I now believe you,"
said Catulus. "I don't think you could have conjured up
those names out of your imagination."

"Why, thank you, Quintus Lutatius!" snapped Cicero, eyes flashing. "Your approbation warms my heart,
but it doesn't help me decide what to say in the Senate
tomorrow!"

"Concentrate on Catilina and forget the rest of them"
was Crassus's advice. "Pull one of those terrific speeches
out of your magic box and aim it at Catilina. What you
have to do is push him into quitting Rome. The rest of his
gang can stay—but we'll keep a very good eye on them.
Chop off the head Catilina would graft on the neck of
Rome's strong but headless body."

"He won't leave if he hasn't already," said Cicero
gloomily.

"He might," said Lucius Cotta, "if we can manage
to persuade certain people to avoid his vicinity in the
House. I'll undertake to go and see Publius Sulla, and
Crassus can see Autronius, he knows him well. They're
by far the two biggest fish in the Catilina pool, and I'd be
willing to bet that if they were seen to shun him when
they enter the House, even those whose names we've
heard today would desert him. Self-preservation does tend
to undermine loyalty." He got up, grinning. "Shift your
arses, fellow consulars! Let's leave Cicero to write his
greatest speech."

That Cicero had labored to telling effect was evident

on the morrow, when he convened the Senate in the temple of Jupiter Stator on the corner of the Velia, a site difficult to attack and easy to defend. Guards were ostentatiously posted everywhere outside, and that of course drew a large and curious audience of professional Forum frequenters. Catilina came early, as Lucius Cotta had predicted he would, so the technique of ostracizing him was blatant. Only Lucius Cassius, Gaius Cethegus, the tribune of the plebs–elect Bestia and Marcus Porcius Laeca sat by him, glaring furiously at Publius Sulla and Autronius.

Then a visible change swept over Catilina. He turned first to Lucius Cassius, whispered in his ear, then whispered to each of the others. All four shook their heads violently, but Catilina prevailed. Silently they got up and left his vicinity.

Whereupon Cicero launched into his speech, the tale of a meeting at night to plan the fall of Rome, complete with all the names of the men present and the name of the man in whose house the meeting took place. Every so often Cicero demanded that Lucius Sergius Catilina quit Rome, rid the city of his evil presence.

Only once did Catilina interrupt.

"Do you want me to go into voluntary exile, Cicero?" he asked loudly because the doors were open and the crowd outside straining to hear every word. "Go on, Cicero, ask the House whether I should go into voluntary exile! If it says I must, then I will!"

To which Cicero made no answer, just swept on. Go away, leave, quit Rome, that was his theme.

And after all the uncertainty, it turned out to be easy. As Cicero finished Catilina rose and gathered majesty around him.

"I'm going, Cicero! I'm quitting Rome! I don't even want to stay here when Rome is being run by a lodger from Arpinum, a resident alien neither Roman nor Latin! You're a Samnite bumpkin, Cicero, a rough peasant from the hills without ancestors or clout! Do you think *you* have forced me to leave? Well, you haven't! It is Catulus, Mamercus, Cotta, Torquatus! I leave because they have deserted me, not because of anything you say! When a man's peers desert him, he is truly finished. That is why I go.''

There were confused sounds from outside as Catilina swept through the middle of the Forum frequenters, then silence.

Senators now got up to shift away from those Cicero had named in his speech, even a brother from a brother—Publius Cethegus had clearly decided to divorce himself from Gaius as well as from the conspiracy.

''I hope you're happy, Marcus Tullius,'' said Caesar.

It was a victory, of course it was a victory, and yet it seemed to fizzle, even after Cicero addressed the Forum crowd from the rostra the next day. Apparently stung by Catilina's concluding remarks, Catulus got up when the House met two days after that and read out a letter from Catilina which protested his innocence and consigned his wife, Aurelia Orestilla, to the care and custody of Catulus himself. Rumors began to circulate that Catilina was indeed going into voluntary exile, and had headed out of Rome on the Via Aurelia (the right direction) with only three companions of no note, including his childhood friend Tongilius. This completed the backlash; men now began to swing from believing Catilina guilty to thinking him victimized.

Life might have become steadily more intolerable for Cicero had it not been for independent news from Etruria only a few days later. Catilina had *not* proceeded into exile in Massilia; instead he had donned the *toga praetexta* and insignia of a consul, clad twelve men in scarlet tunics and given them *fasces* complete with the axes. He had been seen in Arretium with a sympathizer, Gaius Flaminius of that decayed patrician family, and he now sported a silver eagle he declared was the original one Gaius Marius had given to his legions. Always Marius's chief source of strength, Etruria was rallying to that eagle.

That of course terminated the disapproval of consulars like Catulus and Mamercus (Hortensius it seemed had decided that gout at Misenum was preferable to a headache in Rome, but the gout of Antonius Hybrida at Cumae was rapidly becoming an unseemly excuse for staying away from Rome and his duty as junior consul).

However, some of the senatorial smaller fry were still of the opinion that events had been Cicero's doing all along, that it was actually Cicero's tireless persecution had pushed Catilina over the edge. Among these was the younger brother of Celer, Metellus Nepos, soon to assume office as tribune of the plebs. Cato, who would also be a tribune of the plebs, commended Cicero—which only made Nepos scream louder, because he loathed Cato.

"Oh, when was an insurrection ever such a contentious and tenuous affair?" cried Cicero to Terentia. "At least Lepidus declared himself! Patricians, patricians! They can do no wrong! Here am I with a pack of villains on my hands and no way to convict them of tinkering with the water adjutages, let alone treason!"

"Cheer up, husband," said Terentia, who apparently enjoyed seeing Cicero grimmer than she usually was herself. "It has begun to happen, and it will go on happening, you just wait and see. Soon all the doubters from Metellus Nepos to Caesar will have to admit that you are right."

"Caesar could have helped me more than he has," said Cicero, very disgruntled.

"He did send Quintus Arrius," said Terentia, who approved of Caesar these days because her half sister, Fabia the Vestal, was full of praise for the new Pontifex Maximus.

"But he doesn't back me in the House, he keeps picking on me for the way I interpret the Senatus Consultum Ultimum. It seems to me he still thinks Catilina has been wronged."

"Catulus thinks that too, yet there's no love lost between Catulus and Caesar," said Terentia.

Two days later word came to Rome that Catilina and Manlius had finally joined forces, and that they had two full legions of good experienced troops plus some thousands more still in training. Faesulae hadn't crumbled, which meant its arsenal was intact, nor had any of the other major towns in Etruria consented to donating the

contents of their arsenals to Catilina's cause. An indication
that much of Etruria had no faith in Catilina.

The Popular Assembly ratified a senatorial decree and
declared both Catilina and Manlius public enemies; this
meant they were stripped of their citizenship and its per-
quisites, including trial for treason if they were apprehended. Gaius Antonius Hybrida having finally returned
to Rome—gouty toe and all—Cicero promptly instructed
him to take charge of the troops recruited in Capua and
Picenum—all veterans of earlier wars—and march to oppose Catilina and Manlius outside Faesulae. Just in case
the gouty toe continued to be a handicap, the senior consul
had the forethought to give Hybrida an excellent second-
in-command, the *vir militaris* Marcus Petreius. Cicero
himself took responsibility for organizing the defenses of
the city of Rome, and began now to dole out those armaments—though not to people he or Atticus or Crassus
or Catulus (now thoroughly converted) deemed suspect.
What Catilina was currently plotting no one knew, though
Manlius sent a letter to the triumphator Rex, still in the
field in Umbria; it came as a surprise that Manlius would
write so, but it could change nothing.

At which point, with Rome poised to repel an attack
from the north, and Pompeius Rufus in Capua and Metellus Little Goat in Apulia ready to deal with anything in
the south from a force of gladiators to a slave uprising,
Cato chose to upset Cicero's stratagems and imperil the
city's ability to cope after the coming changeover of consuls. November was drawing to an end when Cato got up
in the House and announced that he would institute proceedings against the junior consul–elect, Lucius Licinius
Murena, for gaining office through bribery. As tribune of
the plebs–elect, he shouted, he felt he could not spare the
time to run a criminal trial himself, so the defeated candidate Servius Sulpicius Rufus would prosecute, with his
son (barely a man) as second prosecutor, and the patrician
Gaius Postumius as third. The trial would take place in
the Bribery Court, as the prosecutors were all patrician and
therefore could not use Cato and the Plebeian Assembly.

"Marcus Porcius Cato, you can't!" cried Cicero,

aghast, and leaping to his feet. "The guilt or innocence of Lucius Murena is beside the point! We have rebellion on our heads! That means we cannot afford to enter the New Year minus one of the new consuls! If you intended to do this, why now, why so late in the year?"

"A man's duty is his duty," said Cato, unmoved. "The evidence has only just come to light, and I vowed months ago in this House that if it came to my attention that a consular candidate had bribed, I would personally make sure he was charged and prosecuted. It makes no difference to me *what* Rome's situation is at the New Year! Bribery is bribery. It must be eradicated at any cost."

"The cost is likely to be the fall of Rome! Postpone it!"

"Never!" yelled Cato. "I am not your or anyone else's puppet on strings! I see my duty and I do it!"

"No doubt you'll be doing your duty and arraigning some poor wretch while Rome sinks beneath the Tuscan Sea!"

"Until the moment the Tuscan Sea drowns me!"

"May the gods preserve us from any more like you, Cato!"

"Rome would be a better place if there were more like me!"

"Any more like you and Rome wouldn't work!" Cicero shouted, arms raised, hands clawing at the sky. "When wheels are so clean they squeak, Marcus Porcius Cato, they also seize up! Things run a great deal better with a little dirty grease!"

"And isn't that the truth," said Caesar, grinning.

"Postpone it, Cato," said Crassus wearily.

"The matter is now entirely out of my hands," said Cato smugly. "Servius Sulpicius is determined."

"And to think I once thought well of Servius Sulpicius!" said Cicero to Terentia that evening.

"Oh, Cato put him up to it, husband, nothing surer."

"What *does* Cato want? To see Rome fall all because justice must be done forthwith? Can't he see the danger in having only one consul take office on New Year's

Day—and a consul as sick as Silanus into the bargain?''
Cicero smacked his hands together in anguish. ''I am beginning to think that one hundred Catilinas do not represent the threat to Rome that one Cato does!''

''Well, then you'll just have to see that Sulpicius
doesn't convict Murena,'' said Terentia, ever practical.
''Defend Murena yourself, Cicero, and get Hortensius and
Crassus to back you.''

''Consuls in office do not normally defend consuls-
elect.''

''Then create a precedent. You're good at that. It's
also lucky for you, I've noticed it before.''

''Hortensius is still in Misenum with his big toe padded.''

''Then get him back, if you have to kidnap him.''

''And get the case over and done with. You're quite
right, Terentia. Valerius Flaccus is *iudex* in the Bribery
Court—a patrician, so we'll just have to hope that he has
the sense to see my side rather than Servius Sulpicius's.''

''He will,'' said Terentia, grinning savagely. ''It isn't
Sulpicius he'll blame. It's Cato, and no patrician really
esteems Cato unless he thinks himself cheated out of the
consulship, like Servius Sulpicius.''

A hopeful but cunning gleam entered Cicero's eyes.
''I wonder if Murena would be so grateful when I get him
off that he'd give me a splendid new house?''

''Don't you dare, Cicero! You need Murena, not the
other way around. Wait for someone considerably more
desperate before you demand fees of that kind.''

So Cicero refrained from hinting to Murena that he
needed a new house, and defended the consul-elect for no
greater reward than a nice little painting by a minor Greek
of two centuries ago. Grumbling and moaning, Hortensius
was dragged back from Misenum, and Crassus entered the
fray with all his thoroughness and patience. They were a
triumvirate of defense counsels too formidable for the cha-
grined Servius Sulpicius Rufus, and managed to get Murena acquitted without needing to bribe the jury—never a
consideration, with Cato standing there watching every
move.

What else could possibly happen after that? wondered Cicero as he trotted home from the Forum to see whether Murena had sent the painting round yet. What a good speech he had given! The last speech, of course, before the jury gave its verdict. One of Cicero's greatest assets was his ability to change the tenor of his address after he had gauged the mood of the jury—men he mostly knew well, naturally. Luckily Murena's jury consisted of fellows who loved wit and loved to laugh. Therefore he had couched his speech humorously, got huge fun out of deriding Cato's adherence to the (generally unpopular) Stoic philosophy founded by that awful old Greek nuisance, Zeno. The jury were absolutely thrilled, adored every word of it, every nuance—and especially his brilliant impersonation of Cato, from voice to stance to hand aping Cato's gigantic nose. As for when he managed to wriggle out of his tunic—the entire panel had fallen on the ground in mirth.

"What a comedian we have for senior consul!" said Cato loudly after the verdict came in ABSOLVO. Which only made the jury laugh more, and deem Cato a bad loser.

"Reminds me of the story I heard about Cato in Syria after his brother Caepio died," said Atticus over dinner that afternoon.

"What story?" asked Cicero dutifully; he really wasn't at all interested in hearing anything about Cato, but he had cause to be grateful to Atticus, foreman of the jury.

"Well, he was walking down the road like a beggar, three slaves plus Munatius Rufus and Athenodorus Cordylion, when the gates of Antioch loomed in the distance. And outside the city he saw a huge crowd approaching, cheering. 'See how my fame goes ahead of me?' he asked Munatius Rufus and Athenodorus Cordylion. 'The whole of Antioch has come out to do me homage because I am such a perfect example of what every Roman should be— humble, frugal, a credit to the *mos maiorum*!' Munatius Rufus—he told me the story when we ran into each other in Athens—said he rather doubted this, but old Athenodorus Cordylion believed every word, started bowing and scraping to Cato. Then the crowd arrived, hands full of garlands, maidens strewing rose petals. The *ethnarch* spoke: 'And which of you is the great Demetrius, freedman of the glorious Gnaeus Pompeius Magnus?' he asked. Whereupon Munatius Rufus and the three slaves fell on the road laughing, and even Athenodorus Cordylion found Cato's face so funny he joined in. But Cato was livid! Couldn't see the funny side of it at all, especially since Magnus's freedman Demetrius was such a perfumed ponce!''

It was a good story, and Cicero laughed sincerely.

''I hear Hortensius hobbled back to Misenum quick-smart.''

''It's his spiritual home—all those bumbling fish.''

''And no one has surrendered to take advantage of the Senate's amnesty, Marcus. So what will happen next?''

''I wish I knew, Titus, I wish I knew!''

That the next development should emerge from the presence in Rome of a deputation of Allobroges, Gallic tribesmen from far up the Rhodanus in Further Gaul, no one could have predicted. Led by one of their tribal elders known in Latin as Brogus, they had arrived to protest to the Senate against their treatment by a series of governors like Gaius Calpurnius Piso, and by certain moneylenders masquerading as bankers. Unaware of the *lex Gabinia* which now confined the hearing of such deputations to the month of February, they had not succeeded in getting a dispensation to speed up their petition. So it was either back to Further Gaul, or remain in Rome for two more months spending a fortune on inn charges and bribes to needy senators. They had therefore decided to go home, return at the beginning of February. Nor was the mood a happy one among them, from the meanest Gallic slave all the way up to Brogus. As he said to his best friend among the Romans, the freedman banker Publius Umbrenus, ''It seems a lost cause, Umbrenus, but we will return if I can persuade the tribes to be patient. There are those among us who talk of war.''

''Well, Brogus, there is a long Allobrogan tradition

of war on Rome," said Umbrenus, a brilliant idea beginning to blossom in his head. "Look at how you made Pompeius Magnus hop when he went to Spain to fight Sertorius."

"War with Rome is futile, I believe," said Brogus gloomily. "The legions are like the millstone, they grind on relentlessly. Kill them in a battle and tell yourself you've defeated them, and there they are the next season to do it all over again."

"What about," said Umbrenus softly, "if you had Rome's backing in a war?"

Brogus gasped. "I don't understand!"

"Rome isn't a cohesive whole, Brogus, it's split into many factions. Right at this moment as you know, there is a powerful faction led by some very clever men which has chosen to dispute the rule of the Senate and People of Rome as they exist."

"Catilina?"

"Catilina. What if I could secure a guarantee from Catilina that after he is Dictator in Rome, the Allobroges are awarded full possession of all the Rhodanus Valley north of, say, Valentia?"

Brogus looked thoughtful. "A tempting offer, Umbrenus."

"A genuine offer, I do assure you."

Brogus sighed, smiled. "The only trouble is, Publius, that we have no way of knowing how high you stand in the estimation of a man like the great aristocrat Catilina."

Under different circumstances Umbrenus might have taken exception to this assessment of his clout, but not now, not while that brilliant idea continued to grow. So he said, "Yes, I see what you mean, Brogus. Of course I see what you mean! Would it allay your fears if I were to arrange that you meet a praetor who is a patrician Cornelius, whose face you know well?"

"That would allay my fears," said Brogus.

"Sempronia Tuditani's house would be ideal—it's close and her husband is away. But I don't have time to guide you there, so it had better be behind the temple of

Salus on the Alta Semita two hours from now,'' said Umbrenus, and ran from the room.

How he managed to get the thing together in those two hours Publius Umbrenus couldn't recollect later, but get it together he did. It necessitated seeing the praetor Publius Cornelius Lentulus Sura, the senators Lucius Cassius and Gaius Cethegus, and the knights Publius Gabinius Capito and Marcus Caeparius. As the second hour ended, Umbrenus arrived in the alley behind the temple of Salus—a desolate spot—with Lentulus Sura and Gabinius Capito.

Lentulus Sura stayed only long enough to give Brogus a lordly greeting; he was clearly uneasy and very anxious to get away. It was therefore left to Umbrenus and Gabinius Capito to deal with Brogus, Capito acting as spokesman for the conspirators. The five Allobroges listened attentively, but when Capito finally finished the Gauls hedged, looking timid and wary.

''Well, I don't know . . .'' said Brogus.

''What would it take to convince you we mean what we say?'' asked Umbrenus.

''I'm not sure,'' Brogus said, looking confused. ''Let us think on it tonight, Umbrenus. Could we meet here at dawn tomorrow?''

And so it was agreed.

Back went the Allobroges to the inn on the Forum's edge, a curious coincidence, for just uphill from it on the Sacra Via was the triumphal arch erected by Quintus Fabius Maximus Allobrogicus, who had (temporarily) conquered this selfsame tribe of Gauls many decades ago, and taken their name to add to his own. Brogus and his fellow Allobroges therefore gazed at a structure which reminded them that they were in the clientele of Allobrogicus's descendants. Their present patron was Quintus Fabius Sanga, the great-grandson.

''It sounds attractive indeed,'' said Brogus to his companions as he stared at the arch. ''However, it could also mean disaster. If any of the hotbloods learn about this proposal, they won't stop to think, they'll go to war at once. Whereas my bones say no.''

As the deputation contained no hotbloods, the Allobroges decided to see their patron, Quintus Fabius Sanga.

A wise decision, as things turned out. Fabius Sanga went straight to Cicero.

"We have them at last, Quintus Fabius!" cried Cicero.

"In what way?" asked Sanga, who was not bright enough to seek higher office, and in consequence needed to have everything explained.

"Go back to the Allobroges and tell them that they must ask for letters from Lentulus Sura—I was right, I was right!—and from three other high-ranking conspirators as well. They must insist they be taken to see Catilina himself in Etruria—a logical request, considering what they're being asked to do. It also means a trip out of Rome, and the presence of a guide from among the conspirators."

"What's the importance of the guide?" asked Sanga, blinking.

"Only that having one of the conspirators with them will make it more prudent for the party to leave Rome by stealth and in the middle of the night," said Cicero patiently.

"Is it necessary that they leave by night?"

"Very necessary, Quintus Fabius, believe me! I'll post men at either end of the Mulvian Bridge, easier to do at night. When the Allobroges and their conspirator guide are on the bridge, my men will pounce. We'll have hard evidence at last—the letters."

"You don't intend to harm the Allobroges?" asked Sanga, quite alarmed at anyone's pouncing on anyone.

"Of course not! They'll be party to the plan, and make sure you instruct them not to offer any resistance. You might also tell Brogus to insist he keep the letters himself, and surround himself with his own tribesmen in case any conspirator who goes along tries to destroy my hard evidence." Cicero looked sternly at Fabius Sanga. "Is it all clear, Quintus Fabius? Can you remember all that without getting muddled?"

"Lead me through it again," said Sanga.

Sighing, Cicero did so.

And by the end of the following day Cicero heard
from Sanga that Brogus and his Allobroges had taken custody of three letters, one from Lentulus Sura, one from
Gaius Cethegus, and one from Lucius Statilius. When
asked to write, Lucius Cassius had refused and appeared
uneasy. Did Cicero think three letters would be enough?

Yes, yes! Cicero sped back by his fleetest servant.

And so in the second quarter of the night a little cavalcade started out of Rome on the Via Lata, which turned
into the great north road, the Via Flaminia, after it crossed
the Campus Martius on its way to the Mulvian Bridge.
With Brogus and the Allobroges traveled their guide, Titus
Volturcius of Croton, as well as one Lucius Tarquinius
and the knight Marcus Caeparius.

All went well until the party reached the Mulvian
Bridge about four hours before dawn, and hastened onto
its stone paving. As the last horse trotted onto the bridge
proper, the praetor Flaccus at the south end flashed his
lamp to the praetor Pomptinus at the north end; both praetors, each backed by a century of good volunteer city militia, moved swiftly to block the bridge. Marcus Caeparius
drew his sword and tried to fight, Volturcius gave in, and
Tarquinius, a strong swimmer, leaped off the bridge into
the darkness of the Tiber. The Allobroges stood obediently
in a huddle, the reins of their horses held as firmly as the
letters Brogus carried in a pouch at his waist.

Cicero was waiting when Pomptinus, Valerius Flaccus, the Allobroges, Volturcius and Caeparius arrived at
his house just before dawn. So too was Fabius Sanga waiting—not very bright, perhaps, but exquisitely conscious
of his patron's duty.

"Have you the letters, Brogus?" asked Fabius Sanga.

"Four of them," said Brogus, opening his pouch and
producing three slender scrolls plus one folded and sealed
single sheet.

"Four?" Cicero asked eagerly. "Did Lucius Cassius
change his mind?"

"No, Marcus Tullius. The folded one is a private

communication from the praetor Sura to Catilina, so I was told.''

"Pomptinus," said Cicero, standing straight and tall, "go to the houses of Publius Cornelius Lentulus Sura, Gaius Cornelius Cethegus, Publius Gabinius Capito and Lucius Statilius. Command them to come here to my house at once, but don't give them any idea why, is that understood? And take your militia with you.''

Pomptinus nodded solemnly; the events of that night seemed almost dreamlike, he hadn't yet realized what had actually happened when he apprehended the Allobroges on the Mulvian Bridge.

"Flaccus, I need you here as a witness," said Cicero to his other praetor, "but send your militia to take up station around the temple of Concord. I intend to summon the Senate into session there as soon as I've done a few things here.''

All eyes watched him, including, he noticed wryly, Terentia's from a dark corner. Well, why not? She had stuck by him through all of it; she had earned her backseat at the play. After some thought he sent the Allobroges (save Brogus) to the dining room for food and wine, and sat down with Brogus, Sanga and Valerius Flaccus to wait for Pomptinus and the men he had been ordered to summon. Volturcius was no danger—he huddled in the corner farthest from Terentia and wept—but Caeparius looked as if he might still have some fight left in him. Cicero ended in locking him into a cupboard, wishing he had sent him off under guard—if Rome had only possessed some secure place to put him, that is!

"The truth is," said Lucius Valerius Flaccus, swinging the cupboard key, "that your impromptu prison is undoubtedly more secure than the Lautumiae.''

Gaius Cethegus arrived first, looking wary and defiant; not very many moments later Statilius and Gabinius Capito came in together, with Pomptinus just behind them. The wait for Lentulus Sura was much longer, but eventually he too came through the door, face and body betraying nothing beyond annoyance.

"Really, Cicero, this is too much!" he cried before

he set eyes on the others. His start was minuscule, but Cicero saw it.

"Join your friends, Lentulus," said Cicero.

Someone began hammering on the outside door. Clad in armor because of their nocturnal mission, Pomptinus and Valerius Flaccus drew their swords.

"Open it, Tiro!" said Cicero.

But it was not danger or assassins in the street; in walked Catulus, Crassus, Curio, Mamercus and Servilius Vatia.

"When we were summoned to the temple of Concord by express command of the senior consul," said Catulus, "we decided it was better to seek out the senior consul first."

"You're very welcome indeed," said Cicero gratefully.

"What's going on?" asked Crassus, looking at the conspirators.

As Cicero explained there were more knocks on the door; more senators piled in, bursting with curiosity.

"How does the word get around so quickly?" Cicero demanded, unable to conceal his jubilation.

But finally, the room packed, the senior consul was able to get down to business, tell the story of the Allobroges and the capture at the Pons Mulvius, display the letters.

"Then," said Cicero very formally, "Publius Cornelius Lentulus Sura, Gaius Cornelius Cethegus, Publius Gabinius Capito and Lucius Statilius, I place you under arrest pending a full investigation of your part in the conspiracy of Lucius Sergius Catilina." He turned to Mamercus. "Princeps Senatus, I give these three scrolls into your custody and request that you do not break their seals until the entire Senate is assembled in the temple of Concord. It will then be your duty as Princeps Senatus to read them out." He held up the folded sheet for all to see. "This letter I will open here and now, under all your eyes. If it compromises its author, the praetor Lentulus Sura, then there is nothing to stop our going ahead with our investigation. If it is innocent, then we must decide what we do with the three scrolls before the Senate meets.''

"Go ahead, Marcus Tullius Cicero," said Mamercus, caught up in this nightmare moment, hardly able to believe that Lentulus Sura, once consul, twice praetor, could really be involved.

Oh, how good it was to be the center of all eyes in a drama as huge and portentous as this one! thought Cicero as, consummate actor that he was, he broke the wax seal everyone had identified as Lentulus Sura's with a hard, loud crack. It seemed to take him forever to unfold the sheet, glance at it, assimilate its contents before beginning to read it out.

> "Lucius Sergius, I beg you to change your mind. I know you do not wish to taint our enterprise with a slave army, but believe me when I say that if you do admit slaves into the ranks of your soldiers, you will have a landslide of men and victory within days. All Rome can send against you are four legions, one each from Marcius Rex and Metellus Creticus, and two under the command of that drone Hybrida.
>
> "It has been prophesied that three members of the *gens* Cornelia will rule Rome, and I know that I am the third of those three men named Cornelius. I understand that your name, Sergius, is much older than the name Cornelius, but you have already indicated that you would prefer to rule in Etruria than in Rome. In which case, reconsider your stand on slaves. I condone it. Please consent to it."

He ended in the midst of a silence so profound that it seemed not even a breath disturbed the air of that crowded room.

Then Catulus spoke, hard and angry. "Lentulus Sura, you're done for!" he snapped. "I piss on you!"

"I think," said Mamercus heavily, "that you should open the scrolls now, Marcus Tullius."

"What, and have Cato accuse me of tampering with State's evidence?" asked Cicero, opening his eyes wide and then crossing them. "No, Mamercus, they stay sealed. I wouldn't want to annoy our dear Cato, no matter how right an act opening them might be!"

The praetor Gaius Sulpicius was there, Cicero noted. Good! Give him a job too, let it not look as if he played favorites, let there be absolutely nothing for Cato to find fault with.

"Gaius Sulpicius, would you go to the houses of Lentulus Sura, Cethegus, Gabinius and Statilius, and see if they contain any arms? Take Pomptinus's militia with you, and have them continue the search to Porcius Laeca's residence—also Caeparius, Lucius Cassius, this Volturcius here, and one Lucius Tarquinius. I say let your men continue the search after you personally have inspected the houses of the senatorial conspirators because I will need you in the Senate as soon as possible. You can report your findings to me there."

No one was interested in eating or drinking, so Cicero let Caeparius out of the cupboard and summoned the Allobroges from the dining room. What fight Caeparius might have owned before being shut away had quite deserted him; Cicero's cupboard had proved to be almost airtight, and Caeparius came out of it gibbering.

A praetor holding office yet a traitor! And once a consul too. How to deal with it in a way which would reflect well upon that upstart New Man, that lodger, that resident alien from Arpinum? In the end Cicero crossed the room to Lentulus Sura's side and took the man's limp right hand in his own firm clasp.

"Come, Publius Cornelius," he said with great courtesy, "it is time to go to the temple of Concord."

"How odd!" said Lucius Cotta as the crocodile of men streamed across the lower Forum from the Vestal Stairs to the temple of Concord, separated from the Tullianum execution chamber by the Gemonian Steps.

"Odd? What's odd?" asked Cicero, still leading the nerveless Lentulus Sura by the hand.

"Right at this moment the contractors are putting the

new statue of Jupiter Optimus Maximus on its plinth inside
his temple. Long overdue! It's nearly three years since
Torquatus and I vowed it.'' Lucius Cotta shivered. ''All
those portents!''

''Hundreds of them in your year,'' said Cicero. ''I
was sorry to see the old Etruscan wolf lose her suckling
babe to lightning. I used to love the look on her face, so
doggy! Giving Romulus her milk, but not a bit concerned
about him.''

''I never understood why she didn't give suck to two
babes,'' said Cotta, then shrugged. ''Oh well, perhaps
among the Etrusci the legend only called for one child.
The statue certainly predates Romulus and Remus, and we
still have the wolf herself.''

''You're right,'' said Cicero as he helped Lentulus
Sura mount the three steps to the porch of the very low
temple, ''it is an omen. I hope orienting the Great God to
the east means good!'' At the door he came to an abrupt
halt. ''*Edepol,* what a crush!''

The word had flown. Concord was bursting at the
seams to contain every senator present in Rome, for the
sick came too. This choice of venue wasn't entirely capricious, though Cicero had a tic about concord among the
orders of Roman men; no meeting dealing with the consequences of treason was supposed to be held in the Curia
Hostilia, and as this treason ran the full gamut of the orders
of Roman men, Concord was a logical place to meet. Unfortunately the wooden tiers put inside temples like Jupiter
Stator when the Senate assembled there just did not fit
inside Concord. Everyone had to stand where he fetched
up, wishing for better ventilation.

Eventually Cicero managed to produce some kind of
crowded order by having the consulars and magistrates sit
on stools in front of the senators of *pedarius* or minor
rank. He sent the curule magistrates to the middle rear,
then between the two rows of stools facing each other he
put the Allobroges, Volturcius, Caeparius, Lentulus Sura,
Cethegus, Statilius, Gabinius Capito and Fabius Sanga.

''The arms were stored in the house of Gaius Cethegus!'' said the praetor Sulpicius, entering breathless.

"Hundreds and hundreds of swords and daggers. A few shields, no cuirasses."

"I am an ardent collector of weapons," said Cethegus, bored.

Frowning, Cicero pondered on another logistical problem this confined space had generated. "Gaius Cosconius," he said to that praetor, "I hear you're brilliant at shorthand. Candidly, I can see no room whatsoever in here for half a dozen scribes, so I'll dispense with the professionals. Choose three *pedarii* who are also capable of taking down the proceedings verbatim. That divides the task among four of you, and four will have to be enough. I doubt this will be a long meeting, so you'll have time after it to compare notes and get a draft together."

"Will you look at him and listen to him?" whispered Silanus to Caesar—an odd choice of confidant given the relationship between them, but probably, Caesar decided, there was no one else jammed near Silanus he deemed worth speaking to, including Murena. "In his glory at last!" Silanus made a noise Caesar interpreted as disgust. "Well, I for one find this business unspeakably sordid!"

"Even squires from Arpinum must have their day," said Caesar. "Gaius Marius started a tradition."

Finally and fussily Cicero opened his meeting with the prayers and the offerings, the auspices and the salutations. But his prior assessment was right; it was not a protracted affair. The guide Titus Volturcius listened to Fabius Sanga and Brogus testify, then wept and demanded to be allowed to tell all. Which he did, answering every question, incriminating Lentulus Sura and the other four more and more heavily. Lucius Cassius, he explained, had departed very suddenly for Further Gaul, Volturcius guessed on his way to Massilia and a voluntary exile. Others too had fled, including the senators Quintus Annius Chilo, the Brothers Sulla, and Publius Autronius. Name after name tumbled out, knights and bankers, minions, leeches. By the time Volturcius got to the end of his litany, there were some twenty-seven Roman men importantly involved, from Catilina all the way down to himself (and the Dictator's nephew, Publius Sulla—*not* named—was sweating profusely).

After which Mamercus Princeps Senatus broke the seals on the letters and read them out. Almost an anticlimax.

Looking forward to playing the role of great advocate in howling chase of the truth, Cicero questioned Gaius Cethegus first. But, alas, Cethegus broke down and confessed immediately.

Next came Statilius, with a similar result.

After that it was Lentulus Sura's turn, and he didn't even wait for the questioning to begin before he confessed.

Gabinius Capito fought back for some time, but confessed just as Cicero was getting into stride.

And finally came Marcus Caeparius, who erupted into frenzied weeping and seemed to confess between bouts of sobbing.

Though it came hard to Catulus, when the business was over he moved a vote of thanks to Rome's brilliant and vigilant senior consul, the words sticking a little, but emerging quite as clearly as Caeparius's confession.

"I hail you as *pater patriae*—father of our country!" was Cato's contribution.

"Is he serious or sarcastic?" asked Silanus of Caesar.

"With Cato, who knows?"

Cicero was then given the authority to issue warrants for the apprehension of the conspirators not present, after which it was time to farm out the five conspirators present to senatorial custody.

"I will take Lentulus Sura," said Lucius Caesar sadly. "He is my brother-in-law. By family he should go to another Lentulus, perhaps, but by right he falls to me."

"I'll take Gabinius Capito," said Crassus.

"And I Statilius," said Caesar.

"Give me young Cethegus," said Quintus Cornificius.

"And I'll have Caeparius," said old Gnaeus Terentius.

"What do we do with a treasonous praetor in office?'' asked Silanus, who looked very grey in that airless atmosphere.

''We command that he doff his insignia of office and dismiss his lictors,'' said Cicero.

''I don't believe that's legal,'' said Caesar, a little wearily. ''No one has the power to terminate the office of a curule magistrate before the last day of his year. Strictly, you can't arrest him.''

''We can under a Senatus Consultum Ultimum!'' snapped Cicero, nettled. Why was Caesar always picking fault? ''If you prefer, don't call it a termination! Just think of it as the removal of his curule trappings!''

Whereupon Crassus, fed up with the crush and dying to get out of Concord, interrupted this acrimonious exchange to move that a public thanksgiving be celebrated for the discovery of the plot without bloodshed within the city walls. But he didn't name Cicero.

''While you're about it, Crassus, why don't you vote our dear Marcus Tullius Cicero a Civic Crown?'' snarled Poplicola.

''Now *that*,'' said Silanus to Caesar, ''is definitely ironic.''

''Oh, the Gods be thanked, he's finally breaking the meeting up'' was Caesar's reply. ''Couldn't he have thought of a reason why we could meet in Jupiter Stator or Bellona?''

''Here tomorrow at the second hour of day!'' cried Cicero to a chorus of groans, then rushed from the temple to mount the rostra and deliver a reassuring speech to the large and expectant crowd.

''I don't know why he's in such a tearing hurry,'' said Crassus to Caesar as they stood flexing their muscles and breathing deeply of the sweet outside air. ''He can't go home tonight, his wife's hosting the Bona Dea.''

''Yes, of course,'' said Caesar, sighing. ''My wife and mother are off there, not to mention all my Vestals. And Julia too, I suppose. She's growing up.''

''I wish Cicero would.''

''Oh, come, Crassus, he's in his element at last! Let him have his little victory. It's not really a very big conspiracy, and it stood about as much chance of succeeding as Pan competing against Apollo. A tempest inside a bottle, no more.''

"Pan against Apollo? He won, didn't he?''

"Only because Midas was the judge, Marcus. For which he wore a pair of ass's ears ever after.''

"Midas always sits in judgement, Caesar.''

"The power of gold.''

"Exactly.''

They began to move up the Forum, not the least bit tempted to stop and hear Cicero's address to the People.

"You've family involved, of course,'' said Crassus when Caesar ignored the Via Sacra and headed toward the Palatine too.

"Indeed I have. One very silly cousin and her three strapping lout sons.''

"Will she be at Lucius Caesar's, do you think?''

"Definitely not. Lucius Caesar is too punctilious. He's got his sister's husband there in custody. So, with my mother at Cicero's house celebrating the Bona Dea, I thought I'd look in on Lucius and tell him I'll go straight over to see Julia Antonia.''

"I don't envy you,'' said Crassus, grinning.

"Believe me, I don't envy myself!''

He could hear Julia Antonia before he knocked on the door of Lentulus Sura's very nice house, and squared his shoulders. Why did it have to be the Bona Dea tonight? Julia Antonia's entire circle of friends would be at Cicero's house, and Bona Dea was not the sort of deity one ignored in favor of a distressed friend.

All three of Antonius Creticus's boys were ministering to their mother with a degree of patience and kindness Caesar found surprising—which didn't stop her leaping to her feet and throwing herself on Caesar's chest.

"Oh, cousin!'' she howled. "What am I to do? Where will I go? They'll confiscate all Sura's property! I won't even have a roof over my head!''

"Leave the man alone, Mama,'' said Mark Antony, her eldest, pulling her clutching fingers away and escorting her back to her chair. "Now sit there and keep your misery to yourself, it's not going to help us out of this predicament."

Perhaps because she had already worn herself into exhaustion, Julia Antonia obeyed; her youngest, Lucius, a rather fat and clumsy fellow, sat on the chair next to her, took her hands in his and began to make soothing noises.

"It's his turn," said Antony briefly, and drew his cousin outside into the peristyle, where the middle son, Gaius, joined them.

"It's a pity the Cornelii Lentuli comprise the majority of Cornelians in the Senate these days," said Caesar.

"And none of them will be a bit happy to claim a traitor in the bosom of the family," said Mark Antony grimly. "*Is* he a traitor?"

"Beyond any shadow of doubt, Antonius."

"You're sure?"

"I just said so! What's the matter? Worried that it will come out you're involved too?" asked Caesar, suddenly anxious.

Antony flushed darkly, but said nothing; it was Gaius who answered, stamping his foot.

"We're *not* involved! Why is it that everyone—including you!—always believes the worst of us?"

"It's called earning a reputation," said Caesar patiently. "All three of you have shocking reputations—gambling, wine, whores." He looked at Mark Antony ironically. "Even the occasional boyfriend."

"It isn't true about me and Curio," said Antony uncomfortably. "We only pretend to be lovers to annoy Curio's father."

"But it's all a part of earning a reputation, Antonius, as you and your brothers are about to find out. Every hound in the Senate is going to be sniffing around your arses, so I suggest that if you are involved, even remotely, you tell me so now."

All three of Creticus's sons had long ago concluded that this particular Caesar had the most disconcerting eyes of anyone they knew—piercing, cold, omniscient. It meant they didn't like him because those eyes put them on the defensive, made them feel less than they secretly believed they were. And he never bothered to condemn them for what they deemed minor failings; he came around only when things were really bad, as now. Thus his appearances were reminiscent of a harbinger of doom, tended to strip them of the ability to fight back, defend themselves.

So Mark Antony answered sulkily, "We're not even remotely involved. Clodius said Catilina was a loser."

"And whatever Clodius says is right, eh?"

"Usually."

"I agree," said Caesar unexpectedly. "He's shrewd."

"What will happen?" asked Gaius Antonius abruptly.

"Your stepfather will be tried for treason and convicted," Caesar said. "He's confessed, had to. Cicero's praetors caught the Allobroges with two incriminating letters of his, and they're not forgeries, I can assure you."

"Mama is right, then. She'll lose everything."

"I shall try to see that she doesn't, and there will be a good number of men who will agree with me. It's time Rome stopped punishing a man's family for his crimes. When I'm consul I shall try to put a law on the tablets to that effect." He began to move back toward the atrium. "There's nothing I can do for your mother personally, Antonius. She needs female company. As soon as my mother comes home from the Bona Dea, I'll send her over." In the atrium he gazed around. "A pity Sura didn't collect art, you might have had a few things to salt away before the State arrives to collect. Though I meant what I said, I will do my best to ensure that the little Sura has is not confiscated. I suppose that's why he joined the conspiracy, to increase his fortune."

"Oh, undoubtedly," said Antony, ushering Caesar to the door. "He was forever moaning about how badly expulsion from the Senate had ruined him—and that he'd done nothing to warrant it. He's always maintained that the censor Lentulus Clodianus had it in for him. Some family squabble going back to when Clodianus was adopted into the Lentuli."

"Do you like him?" asked Caesar, stepping across the threshold.

"Oh, yes! Sura is a splendid fellow, the best of men!"

And that was interesting, he thought, making his way back to the Forum and the Domus Publica. Not every step-father would have managed to make himself liked by *that* trio of young men! They were such typical Antonii. Heedless, passionate, impulsive, prone to indulge their lusts of whatever kind. No political heads on any of those broad shoulders! Massive brutes, all three of them, and ugly in a way that women seemed to find enormously attractive. What on earth would they do to the Senate when they were old enough to stand for quaestor? Provided, that is, that they had the money to stand. Creticus had suicided in disgrace, though no one had moved to indict him posthumously for crimes against the State; he had lacked sense and judgement, not loyalty to Rome. However, his estate was eroded when Julia Antonia married Lentulus Sura, a man without children of his own—but without a large fortune either. Lucius Caesar had a son and a daughter; the Antonii could hope for nothing there. Which meant that it would be up to him, Caesar, to try to improve the Antonian fortune. How he was going to do this he had no idea, but he would do it. Money always appeared when it was desperately needed.

The fugitive Lucius Tarquinius who had jumped off the Mulvian Bridge into the Tiber was apprehended on the road to Faesulae and brought to Cicero before the Senate met in Concord the day after the Bona Dea. His house being closed to him, Cicero had spent the night with Nigidius Figulus, who had most thoughtfully asked Atticus and Quintus Cicero to dinner. They had spent a pleasant evening made more pleasant when Terentia sent a message to say that after the fire on the altar to Bona Dea had gone out, a huge flare of flame suddenly roared up, which the Vestals had taken to mean that Cicero had saved his country.

What a delightful thought that was! Father of his

country. Savior of his country. He, the lodger from Arpinum.

He was not, however, entirely at ease. Despite his reassuring speech to the People from the rostra, this morning's clients who had managed to track him down to the house of Nigidius Figulus were edgy, anxious, even afraid. How many ordinary people inside Rome were in favor of a new order—and a general cancellation of debt? Many, it seemed; Catilina might well have been able to take the city from within on the night of the Saturnalia. All those hopes in all those financially distressed breasts were permanently dashed as of yesterday, and those who had harbored those hopes were today aware that there would be no respite. Rome seemed peaceful; yet Cicero's clients insisted there were violent undercurrents. So did Atticus. And here am I, thought Cicero, conscious of a tiny panic, responsible for arresting five men! Men with clout and clients, especially Lentulus Sura. But Statilius was from Apulia, and Gabinius Capito from southern Picenum—two places with a history of revolt or devotion to an Italian rather than a Roman cause. As for Gaius Cethegus—his father had been known as the King of the Backbenchers! Enormous wealth and clout there. And he, Cicero, the senior consul, was solely responsible for their arrest and detention. For producing the hard evidence which had caused all five to break down and confess. Therefore he would be responsible for their condemnation at trial, and that was going to be a long, drawn-out process during which violent undercurrents might boil to the surface. None of this year's praetors would want the duty of being president of a specially convened Treason Court—treason trials had been so thin on the ground of late that no praetor had been assigned to it in two years. Therefore his prisoners would continue to live under custody in Rome until well into the New Year, which also meant new tribunes of the plebs like Metellus Nepos yammering that Cicero had exceeded his authority, and other tribunes of the plebs like Cato hovering to pounce on any legal slip.

If only, thought Cicero, conducting his prisoner Tarquinius to the temple of Concord, those wretched men didn't have to stand trial! They were guilty; everyone knew that from their own mouths. They would be condemned; they could not be acquitted by the most lenient or corrupt jury. And eventually they would be—executed? But the courts couldn't execute! The best the courts could do was pronounce permanent exile and confiscate all property. Nor could a trial in the Popular Assembly produce a death sentence. To get that would necessitate trial in the Centuries under *perduellio,* and who was to say what verdict that might bring in, with phrases like "a general cancellation of debt" still passing from mouth to mouth? Sometimes, thought the Champion of the Courts as he plodded along, trials were a wretched nuisance.

Lucius Tarquinius had little new to offer when questioning began in the temple of Concord. Cicero retained the privilege of asking the questions himself, and took Tarquinius through the steps leading up to apprehension at the Mulvian Bridge. After which the senior consul threw questions open to the House, feeling that it might be prudent to allow someone else a little glory.

What he didn't expect was the answer Tarquinius gave to the first such question, put to him by Marcus Porcius Cato.

"Why were you with the Allobroges in the first place?" Cato asked in his loud, harsh voice.

"Eh?" from Tarquinius, a cheeky fellow with scant respect for his senatorial betters.

"The Allobroges had a guide in the person of Titus Volturcius. Marcus Caeparius said he was present to report the result of the meeting between the Allobroges and Lucius Sergius Catilina back to the conspirators in Rome. So why were you there, Tarquinius?"

"Oh, I really didn't have much to do with the Allobroges, Cato!" said Tarquinius cheerfully. "I just traveled with the party because it was safer and more amusing than going north on my own. No, I had different business with Catilina."

"Did you now? And what business was that?" asked Cato.

"I was carrying a message from Marcus Crassus to Catilina."

The crowded little temple fell absolutely silent.

"Say that again, Tarquinius."

"I was carrying a message from Marcus Crassus to Catilina."

A buzz of voices arose, growing in volume until Cicero had to have his chief lictor pound the *fasces* on the floor.

"Silence!" he roared.

"You were carrying a message from Marcus Crassus to Catilina," Cato repeated. "Then where is it, Tarquinius?"

"Oh, it wasn't written down!" chirped Tarquinius, seeming happy. "I had it inside my head."

"Do you still have it inside your head?" asked Cato, gazing now at Crassus, who sat on his stool looking stunned.

"Yes. Want to hear it?"

"Thank you."

Tarquinius went up on his toes and jigged. " 'Marcus Crassus says to be of good cheer, Lucius Catilina. Rome is not fully united against you, there are more and more important people coming over,' " chanted Tarquinius.

"He's as cunning as a sewer rat!" growled Crassus. "Accuse me, and that automatically means that in order to clear myself, I will have to spend a great deal of my fortune getting men like him acquitted!"

"Hear, hear!" cried Caesar.

"Well, Tarquinius, I won't do it!" said Crassus. "Pick on someone more vulnerable. Marcus Cicero knows well enough that *I* was the first person in this whole body of men to come to him with specific evidence. *And* accompanied by two unimpeachable witnesses, Marcus Marcellus and Quintus Metellus Scipio."

"That is absolutely so," said Cicero.

"It is so," said Marcellus.

"It is so," said Metellus Scipio.

"Then, Cato, do you wish to take this matter any further?" asked Crassus, who detested Cato.

"No, Marcus Crassus, I do not. It is clearly a fabrication."

"Does the House agree?" Crassus demanded.

A show of hands revealed that the House agreed.

"Which means," said Catulus, "that our dear Marcus Crassus is a big enough fish to spit out the hook without even tearing his mouth. But I have the same accusation to level at a much smaller fish! I accuse Gaius Julius Caesar of being party to the conspiracy of Catilina!"

"And I join with Quintus Lutatius Catulus in leveling that accusation!" roared Gaius Calpurnius Piso.

"Evidence?" asked Caesar, not even bothering to get up.

"Evidence will be forthcoming," said Catulus smugly.

"What does it consist of? Letters? Verbal messages? Sheer imagination?"

"Letters!" said Gaius Piso.

"Then where are these letters?" asked Caesar, unruffled. "To whom are they addressed, if I am supposed to have written them? Or are you having trouble forging my handwriting, Catulus?"

"It's correspondence between you and Catilina!" cried Catulus.

"I think I did write to him once," said Caesar pensively. "It would have been when he was propraetor in Africa Province. But I definitely haven't written to him since."

"You have, you have!" said Piso, grinning. "We've got you, Caesar, wriggle how you like! We've got you!"

"Actually," said Caesar, "you haven't, Piso. Ask Marcus Cicero what help *I* gave his case against Catilina."

"Don't bother, Piso," said Quintus Arrius. "I am happy to tell what Marcus Cicero can confirm. Caesar asked me to go to Etruria and talk to the Sullan veterans around Faesulae. He knew no one else of sufficient standing had their trust, which is why he asked me. I was happy to oblige him, though I kicked my own arse for not thinking of it for myself. I didn't think. It takes a man like

Caesar to see events clearly. If Caesar was a part of the conspiracy, he would never have acted.''

"Quintus Arrius speaks the truth," said Cicero.

"So sit down and shut up, the pair of you!" Caesar snapped. "If a better man beat you in the election for Pontifex Maximus, Catulus, then accept it! And, Piso, it must have cost you a large fortune to bribe your way out of conviction in my court! But why paint yourselves in shabby colors out of simple spite? This House knows you, this House knows what you're capable of!"

There might have been more to say on that subject, save that a messenger came sprinting to inform Cicero that a band of freedmen belonging to Cethegus and Lentulus Sura were recruiting through the city with some success, and that when they had sufficient men they intended to attack the houses of Lucius Caesar and Cornificius, rescue Lentulus Sura and Cethegus, set them up as consuls, then rescue the other prisoners and take over the city.

"This kind of thing," said Cicero, "is going to go on until the trials are over! Months of it, Conscript Fathers, months of it! Start thinking how we can reduce the time, I beg you!"

He dissolved the meeting and had his praetors call up the city militia; detachments were sent to all the houses of the custodians, every important public place was garrisoned, and a group of knights of the Eighteen, including Atticus, went to the Capitol to defend Jupiter Optimus Maximus.

"Oh, Terentia, I don't want my year as consul to end in uncertainty and possible failure, not after such a triumph!" cried Cicero to his wife when he got home.

"Because while ever those men are inside Rome and Catilina in Etruria with an·army, the whole thing still hangs in the balance," she said.

"Exactly, my dear."

"And you will end like Lucullus—do all the hard work, then see Silanus and Murena take the credit because they'll be the consuls when it's finally concluded."

Actually that hadn't occurred to him, but as his wife said it so succinctly, he shuddered. Yes, that was how it would turn out, all right! Cheated by time and tradition.

"Well," he said, squaring his shoulders, "if you will excuse my absence from the dining room, I think I must retire to my study and lock myself in until I can come up with an answer."

"You know the answer already, husband. However, I understand. What you need to do is screw up your courage. While you attempt that, keep it in your mind that the Bona Dea is on your side."

"Rot them, I say!" said Crassus to Caesar, quite violently for such a placid man. "At least half of those *fellatores* sat there hoping Tarquinius would make his charges stick! Lucky for me that it was my doorstep Quintus Curius chose for his batch of letters! Otherwise, today I would have been in serious trouble."

"My defense was more tenuous," said Caesar, "but happily so were the accusations. Stupid! Catulus and Piso only got the idea to accuse me when Tarquinius accused you. Had they thought of it last night, they could have forged some letters. Or else they should have said nothing until they managed to forge letters.

"One of the few things which always cheer me up, Marcus, is how *thick* one's enemies are! I find it a great consolation that I will never meet an adversary as clever as I am myself."

Though he was used to Caesar's making statements like that, Crassus nonetheless found himself staring at the younger man with fascination. Did he never doubt himself? If he did, Crassus had never seen a sign of it. Just as well he was a cool man, Caesar. Otherwise Rome might find herself wishing for a thousand Catilinas.

"I'm not attending tomorrow," said Crassus then.

"I wish you would! It promises to be interesting."

"I don't care if it's more riveting than two perfectly matched gladiators! Cicero can have his glory. *Pater patriae!* Tchah!" he snorted.

"Oh, Cato was being sarcastic, Marcus!"

"I know that, Caesar! What annoys me is that Cicero took him literally."

"Poor man. It must be awful always to have to stand on the outside looking in."

"Are you feeling all right, Caesar? Pity? *You?*"

"Oh, I have a streak of pity occasionally. That Cicero rouses it is no mystery. He's such a vulnerable target."

Despite his having to organize the militia and think of how to extract himself from the dilemma of time, Cicero had also given thought to turning the temple of Concord into a more acceptable venue for the Senate to occupy. Thus when the senators turned up at dawn on the following day, the fifth one of December, they found that carpenters had toiled to some effect. There were three tiers on either side, taller but narrower, and a dais at the end for the curule magistrates, with a bench in front of it for the tribunes of the plebs.

"You won't be able to sit on your stools, the tiers are too narrow, but you can use the tiers themselves as seats," said the senior consul. He pointed to the top of the side and end walls. "I've also installed plenty of ventilators."

Perhaps three hundred men had come, a few less than on the earlier days; after a short interval of settling like hens in a roost, the Senate indicated it was ready for the day's business.

"Conscript Fathers," said Cicero solemnly, "I have convened this body yet again to discuss something we dare not put off, nor turn away from. Namely, what to do with our five prisoners.

"In many ways the situation resembles the one which existed thirty-seven years ago, after Saturninus and his rebel confederates surrendered their occupation of the Capitol. No one knew what to do with them! No one was willing to take custody of such desperate fellows when the city of Rome was known to harbor many sympathizers— the house of a man agreeing to take custody might burn to the ground, he himself die, his prisoner be freed. So in the end the traitor Saturninus and his fourteen senior henchmen were locked up in our beloved Senate House, the Curia Hostilia. No windows, solid bronze doors. Impregnable. Then a group of slaves led by one Scaeva mounted the roof, tore off the tiles and used them to kill the men inside. A deplorable deed—but a great relief too! Once Saturninus was dead, Rome calmed down and the trouble went away. I admit the presence of Catilina in Etruria is an additional complication, but first and foremost we need to calm the city of Rome!''

Cicero paused, knowing perfectly well that some of the men who listened were among the band Sulla had urged up onto the Curia Hostilia roof, and that no slaves had been among them. The owner of the slave Scaeva had been there, Quintus—Croton?—and after the tumult had died down enough to be deemed well and truly over, Croton had freed Scaeva with lavish public praise for his deed—and thereby shifted the blame. A story Sulla never denied, most especially after he became Dictator. Slaves were so handy!

''Conscript Fathers,'' said Cicero sternly, ''we are sitting on a volcano! Five men lie under arrest in various houses, five men who in front of you and inside this House broke down and freely confessed to all their crimes. Confessed to high treason! Yes, they convicted themselves out of their own mouths after seeing proof so concrete its mere existence damned them! And as they confessed they also damned other men, men now under warrants for capture whenever and wherever they might be found. Consider then what will happen when they are found. We will have anything up to twenty men in custody in ordinary Roman houses until they have undergone the full and atrociously slow trial process.

''Yesterday we saw one of the evils arising from this awful situation. A group of men banded together and managed to recruit more men so that our self-confessed traitors might be freed from custody, the consuls murdered, and them installed as consuls instead! In other words, the revolution is going to go on while ever self-confessed traitors remain inside Rome and the army of Catilina remains inside Italia. By quick action, I averted yesterday's attempt. But I will remain consul for less than another month. Yes, Conscript Fathers, the annual upheaval is almost upon us, and we are not in fit condition to deal with a change in magistrates.

"My chief ambition is to depart from office with the city's end of this catastrophe properly tidied up, thereby spelling to Catilina the very clear message that he has no allies inside Rome with power enough to help him. And there is a way. . . ."

The senior consul stopped for that to sink in, wishing that his old enemy and friend Hortensius was in the House. Hortensius would see the beauty of the argument, whereas most of the others would see only the expedience. As for Caesar, well . . . Cicero wasn't even sure he cared to receive Caesar's approbation, as lawyer or man. Crassus hadn't bothered to come, and he was the last of the men Cicero cared to impress with his legal reasoning.

"Until Catilina and Manlius are defeated or surrender, Rome continues to exist under the martial law of a Senatus Consultum Ultimum. Just as Rome still lay under a Senatus Consultum Ultimum when Saturninus and his minions perished in the Curia Hostilia. It meant that no one could be held accountable for taking matters to their inevitable end and executing those rebels. The Senatus Consultum Ultimum extended indemnity to all who participated in the throwing of the tiles, slaves though they were, for a slave's master is accountable at law for his slave's actions, therefore all the men who owned those slaves could have faced prosecution for murder. Except for the Senatus Consultum Ultimum. The blanket decree which in a state of emergency the Senate of Rome is authorized to issue in order to preserve the well-being of the State, no matter what it takes to preserve that well-being.

"Consider our self-confessed traitors here in Rome, plus the other traitors we are looking for because they fled before they could be apprehended. All guilty out of the mouths of the five men we have in custody, not to mention the testimony you have heard from Quintus Curius, Titus Volturcius, Lucius Tarquinius and Brogus of the Allobroges. Under the conditions of an existing Senatus Consultum Ultimum, these self-confessed traitors do not have to be tried. Because at present we are in the midst of a

dire emergency, this august body of men, the Senate of
Rome, has been empowered to do whatever is necessary
to preserve the well-being of Rome. To keep these men in
custody pending a trial process and then have to air them
in the public Forum during that trial is tantamount to stirring up a fresh rebellion! Especially if Catilina and Manlius, formally declared public enemies, are still at liberty
in Italia with an army. That army could even descend on
our city in an attempt to free the traitors during their trials!''

Did he have them? Yes, decided Cicero. Until he
looked at Caesar, who was sitting very straight on the bottom step, mouth thin, two spots of scarlet burning in his
pale cheeks. He would meet opposition from Caesar, a
very great speaker. Urban praetor–elect, which meant he
would speak early unless the order changed.

He had to ram his point home before Caesar spoke!
But how? Cicero's eyes wandered along the back tier behind Caesar until they lighted upon little old Gaius Rabirius, in the Senate for forty years without ever once
standing for a magistracy, which meant he was still a *pedarius*. The quintessential backbencher. Not that Rabirius
was the sum of all manly virtues! Thanks to many shady
deals and immoralities, Rabirius was little loved by most
of Rome. He was also one of that band of noblemen who
had sneaked onto the Curia Hostilia roof, torn off the tiles,
shelled Saturninus. . . .

"If this body were to decide the fate of the five men
in our custody and of those men who fled, its members
would be as free from legal blame as—as—why, trying
to arraign dear Gaius Rabirius on charges that he murdered
Saturninus! Manifestly ridiculous, Conscript Fathers. The
Senatus Consultum Ultimum covers all, and allows all too.
I am going to advocate that in full debate this House
should reach a decision today on the fate of our five self-
confessed prisoners, guilty out of their own mouths. To
hold them for trial would, in my opinion, be to imperil
Rome. Let us debate here today and decide what to do
with them under the existing blanket protection of the Senatus Consultum Ultimum! Under that decree we can order

them executed. Or we can order them into a permanent exile, confiscate their property, forbid them fire and water within Italia for the rest of their lives."

He drew a breath, wondering about Cato, also sure to oppose it. Yes, Cato sat rigid and glaring. But as a tribune of the plebs–elect, he was very far down the speaking hierarchy indeed.

"Conscript Fathers, it is not my business to make a decision on this matter. I have done my duty in outlining the legalities of the situation to you, and in informing you what you can do under a Senatus Consultum Ultimum. Personally I am in favor of a decision here today, not a trial process. But I refuse to indicate exactly what this body should do with the guilty men. That is better from some other man than I."

A pause, a challenging look at Caesar, another at Cato. "I direct that the order of speaking be not in elected magistracy, but in age and wisdom and experience. Therefore I will ask the senior consul–elect to speak first, then the junior consul–elect, after which I will ask an opinion from every consular present here today. Fourteen all told, by my count. After which the praetors-elect will speak, beginning with the urban praetor–elect, Gaius Julius Caesar. Following the praetors-elect, the praetors will speak, then aediles-elect and aediles, plebeian ahead of curule. After which it will be the turn of the tribunes of the plebs–elect, and finally the current tribunes of the plebs. I pend a decision on ex-praetors, as I have already enumerated *sixty* speakers, though three current praetors are in the field against Catilina and Manlius. Therefore I make it fifty-seven speakers without calling on ex-praetors."

"Fifty-eight, Marcus Tullius."

How could he have overlooked Metellus Celer, urban praetor?

"Ought you not to be in Picenum with an army?"

"If you recollect, Marcus Tullius, you yourself deputed me to Picenum on the condition that I returned to Rome every eleventh day, and for twelve days around the tribunician changeover."

"So I did. Fifty-eight speakers, then. That means no one has the time at his disposal to make a reputation as a dazzling orator, is that understood? This debate *must* finish today! I want to see a division before the sun sets. Therefore I give you fair warning, Conscript Fathers, that I will cut you short if you start to orate." Cicero looked at Silanus, senior consul–elect.

"Decimus Junius, begin the debate."

"Mindful of your caution about time, Marcus Tullius, I will be brief," said Silanus, sounding a little helpless; the man who spoke first was supposed to set the tenor and carry all succeeding speakers his way. Cicero could do it, always. But Silanus wasn't sure he could, especially because he had no idea which way the House would go on this issue.

Cicero had made it as plain as he dared that he was advocating the death penalty—but what did everybody else want? So in the end Silanus compromised by advocating "the extreme penalty," which everybody assumed was death. He managed not to mention a trial process in any way whatsoever, which everybody took to mean that there should be no trial process.

Then came Murena's turn; he too favored "the extreme penalty."

Cicero of course didn't speak, and Gaius Antonius Hybrida was in the field. Thus the next in line was the Leader of the House, Mamercus Princeps Senatus, senior among the consulars. Uncomfortably he elected "the extreme penalty." Then the consulars who had been censors—Gellius Poplicola, Catulus, Vatia Isauricus, a worried Lucius Cotta—"the extreme penalty." After which came consulars who had not been censors, in order of seniority—Curio, the two Luculli, Piso, Glabrio, Volcatius Tullus, Torquatus, Marcius Figulus. "The extreme penalty." Very properly, Lucius Caesar abstained.

So far so good. Now it was Caesar's turn, and since few knew his views as well as Cicero did, what he had to say came as a surprise to many. Including, it was plain to see, Cato, who had not looked for such a disconcerting, unwelcome ally.

"The Senate and People of Rome, who together constitute the Republic of Rome, do not make any allowances
for the punishment of full citizens without trial," said Caesar in that high, clear, carrying voice. "Fifteen people have
just advocated the death penalty, yet not one has mentioned the trial process. It is clear that the members of this
body have decided to abrogate the Republic in order to go
much further back in Rome's history for a verdict on the
fate of some twenty-one citizens of the Republic, including
a man who has been consul once and praetor twice, and
who actually is still a legally elected praetor at this moment. Therefore I will not waste this House's time in praising the Republic or the trial and appeal processes every
citizen of the Republic is entitled to undergo before his
peers can enforce a sentence of any kind. Instead, since
my ancestors the Julii were Fathers during the reign of
King Tullus Hostilius, I will confine my remarks to the
situation as it was during the reign of the kings."

The House was sitting up straighter now. Caesar went
on. "Confession or no, a sentence of death is not the Roman way. It was not the Roman way under the kings,
though the kings put many men to death even as we do
today—by murder during public violence. King Tullus
Hostilius, warlike though he was, hesitated to approve a
formal sentence of death. It looked bad, he could see that
so clearly that it was he who advised Horatius to appeal
when the *duumviri* damned him for the murder of his sister, Horatia. The hundred Fathers—ancestors of our Republican Senate—were not inclined to be merciful, but
they took the royal hint, thereby establishing a precedent
that the Senate of Rome has no business doing Romans to
death. When Romans are done to death by men in government—who does not remember Marius and Sulla?—it
means that good government has perished, that the State
is degenerate.

"Conscript Fathers, I have little time, so I will just
say this: let us not go back to the time of the kings if that
means execution! Execution is no fitting punishment. Execution is death, and death is merely an eternal sleep. *Any*
man must suffer more if he is sentenced to a living exile

than if he dies! Every day he must think of his reduction to non-citizen, poverty, contempt, obscurity. His public statues come tumbling down; his *imago* cannot be worn in any family funeral procession, nor displayed anywhere. He is an outcast, disgraced and ignoble. His sons and grandsons must always hang their heads in shame, his wife and daughters weep. And all of this he knows, for he is still alive, he is still a man, with all a man's feelings and weaknesses. And all a man's strengths, now of little use to him save as torment. Living death is infinitely worse than real death. I do not fear death, so long as it be sudden. What I fear is some political situation which could result in permanent exile, the loss of my *dignitas*. And if I am nothing else, I am a Roman to the tiniest bone, the most minute scrap of tissue. Venus made me, and Venus made Rome.''

Silanus was looking confused, Cicero angry, everyone else very thoughtful, even Cato.

''I appreciate what the learned senior consul has had to say about what he insists on calling the Senatus Consultum Ultimum—that under its shelter all normal laws and procedures are suspended. I understand that the learned senior consul's chief concern is the present welfare of Rome, and that he considers the continued residence of these self-confessed traitors within our city walls to be a peril. He wants the business concluded as quickly as is possible. Well, so do I! But not with a death sentence, if we must go back to the time of the kings. I do not worry about our learned senior consul, or any of the fourteen brilliant men sitting here who have already been consul. I do not worry about next year's consuls, or this year's praetors, or next year's praetors, or all the men sitting here who have already been praetor and may still hope to be consul.''

Caesar paused, looked extremely grave. ''What worries me is some consul of the future, ten or twenty years down the road of time. What kind of precedent will he see in what we do here today? Indeed, what kind of precedent is our learned senior consul taking when he cites Saturninus? On the day when we-all-really-know-who illegally executed Roman citizens without a trial, those self-appointed executioners desecrated an inaugurated temple, for that is what the Curia Hostilia is! Rome herself was profaned. My, my, *what* an example! But it is not our learned senior consul worries me! It is some less scrupulous and less learned consul of the future.

"Let us keep a cool head and look at this business with our eyes open and our thinking apparatus detached. There are other punishments than death. Other punishments than exile in a luxurious place like Athens or Massilia. How about Corfinium or Sulmo or some other formidably fortified Italian hill town? That's where we've put our captured kings and princes for centuries. So why not Roman enemies of the State too? Confiscate their property to pay such a town extremely well for the trouble, and simultaneously make sure they cannot escape. Make them suffer, yes! *But do not kill them!*"

When Caesar sat down no one spoke, even Cicero. Then the senior consul–elect, Silanus, got to his feet, looking sheepish.

"Gaius Julius, I think you mistake what I meant by saying 'the extreme penalty,' and I think everyone else made the same mistake. I did not mean death! Death is un-Roman. No, I meant much what you mean, actually. Life imprisonment in a house in an impregnable Italian hill town, paid for by property confiscation."

And so it went, everyone now advocating a stringent confinement paid for by confiscation of property.

When the praetors were finished, Cicero held up his hand. "There are just too many ex-praetors present here to allow everyone to speak, and I did not count ex-praetors in that total of fifty-eight men. Those who wish to contribute nothing new to the debate, please hold up your hands in response to the two questions I will put to you now: those in favor of a death sentence?"

None, as it turned out. Cicero flushed.

"Those in favor of strict custody in an Italian town and complete confiscation of property?"

All save one, as it turned out.

"Tiberius Claudius Nero, what do you have to say?"

"Only that the absence of the word 'trial' from all these speeches today disturbs me greatly. Every Roman man, self-confessed traitor or not, is entitled to a trial, and these men must be tried. But I do not think they should be tried before Catilina is either defeated or surrenders. Let the chief perpetrator stand trial first of all."

"Catilina," said Cicero gently, "is no longer a Roman citizen! Catilina is not entitled to trial under *any* law of the Republic."

"He should be tried too," said Claudius Nero stubbornly, and sat down.

Metellus Nepos, president of the new College of Tribunes of the Plebs to go into office in five days' time, spoke first. He was tired, he was ravenous; eight hours had gone by, which really wasn't bad considering the importance of the subject and the number of men who had already spoken. But what he dreaded was Cato, who would follow him—when was Cato not long-winded, prolix, awkward and utterly boring? So he rattled off his speech supporting Caesar, and sat down with a glare for Cato.

It never occurred to Metellus Nepos that the only reason Cato stood in the House today a tribune of the plebs–elect was due entirely to him, Metellus Nepos. When Nepos had returned from the East after a delightful campaign as one of Pompey the Great's senior legates, he traveled in some style. Naturally. He was one of the most important Caecilii Metelli, he was extremely rich and had managed to enrich himself even more since going east, and he was Pompey's brother-in-law into the bargain. So he had journeyed up the Via Appia at his leisure, well before the elections and well before the summer's heat. Men in a hurry rode or drove, but Nepos had had enough of hurrying; his choice of locomotion was a huge litter borne by no less than twelve men. In this fabulous equipage he lolled on a down mattress covered in Tyrian purple, and had a servant crouched in one corner to minister to him with food and drink, a chamber pot, reading materials.

As he never stuck his head between the litter's curtains, he never noticed the humble pedestrians his cavalcade frequently encountered, so of course he never noticed a group of six extremely humble pedestrians headed in the opposite direction. Three of the six were slaves. The other three were Munatius Rufus, Athenodorus Cordylion, and Marcus Porcius Cato, on their way to Cato's estate in Lucania for a summer of studying and freedom from children.

For a long time Cato simply stood on the side of the road watching the parade amble by, counting the number of people, counting the number of vehicles. Slaves, dancing girls, concubines, guards, loot, cook-wagons, libraries on wheels and wine cellars on wheels.

"Ho, soldier, who travels like Sampsiceramus the potentate?" Cato cried to a guard when the parade had nearly passed.

"Quintus Caecilius Metellus Nepos, brother-in-law of Magnus!" called the soldier.

"He's in a terrific hurry," said Cato sarcastically.

But the soldier took the remark seriously. "Yes, he is, pilgrim! He's running for the tribunate of the plebs in Rome!"

Cato walked on a little way south, but before the sun was halfway down the western sky, he turned around.

"What's the matter?" asked Munatius Rufus.

"I must return to Rome and stand for the tribunate of the plebs," said Cato through clenched teeth. "There must be someone in that buffoon's College to make life difficult for him—and for his all-powerful master, Pompeius *Magnus*!"

Nor had Cato done badly in the elections; he had come in second to Metellus Nepos. Which meant that when Metellus Nepos sat down, Cato got up.

"Death is the only penalty!" he shouted.

The room froze, every eye turned upon Cato in wonder. He was such a stickler for the *mos maiorum* that it had occurred to no one to doubt that his speech would follow along the line either of Caesar's or Tiberius Claudius Nero's.

"Death is the only penalty, I say! What is all this rubbish about law and the Republic? When has the Republic sheltered the likes of self-confessed traitors under her skirts? No law is ever made for self-confessed traitors. Laws are made for lesser beings. Laws are made for men who may transgress them, but do so with no harm intended to their country, the place which bred them and made them what they are.

"Look at Decimus Junius Silanus, weak and vacillating fool! When he thinks Marcus Tullius wants a death sentence, he suggests 'the extreme penalty'! Then when Caesar speaks, he changes his mind—what he meant was what Caesar said! How could he ever offend his beloved Caesar? And what of this Caesar, this overbred and effeminate fop who boasts he is descended from Gods and then proceeds to defaecate all over mere men? Caesar, Conscript Fathers, is the real prime mover in this business! Catilina? Lentulus Sura? Marcus Crassus? No, no, no! *Caesar!* It's Caesar's plot! Wasn't it Caesar who tried to have his uncle Lucius Cotta and his colleague Lucius Torquatus assassinated on their first day in office as consuls three years ago? Yes, Caesar preferred Publius Sulla and Autronius to his own blood uncle! Caesar, Caesar, always and ever Caesar! Look at him, senators! Better than all the rest of us put together! Descended from Gods, born to rule, eager to manipulate events, happy to push other men into the furnace while he skulks in the shade! *Caesar!* I spit on you, Caesar! *I spit!*"

And he actually tried to do so. Most of the senators sat with their jaws sagging, so amazing was this hate-filled diatribe. Everyone knew Cato and Caesar disliked each other; most knew Caesar had cuckolded Cato. But this blistering torrent of farfetched abuse? This implication of treason? What on earth had gotten into Cato?

"We have five guilty men in our custody who have confessed to their crimes and to the crimes of sixteen other men not in our custody. Where is the need for a trial? A trial is a waste of time and good State money! And, Conscript Fathers, wherever there is a trial, is also the possibility of bribery. Other juries in other cases quite as serious as this have acquitted in the face of manifest guilt! Other juries have reached out greedy hands to take vast fortunes from the likes of Marcus Crassus, Caesar's friend and financial backer! Is Catilina to rule Rome? No! Caesar is to rule, with Catilina as his master of the horse and Crassus free to do as he likes in the Treasury!''

"I hope you have proof of all this," said Caesar mildly; he was well aware that calm drove Cato to distraction.

"I will get proof, never fear!" Cato shouted. "Where there is wrongdoing, one can always find proof! Look at the proof which found five men traitors! They saw it, they heard it, and they all confessed. Now that is proof! And I will find proof of Caesar's implication in this conspiracy and in the one of three years ago! No trial for the guilty five, I say! No trial for any of them! Nor ought they escape from death! Caesar argues for clemency on philosophical grounds. Death, he says, is merely an eternal sleep. But do we know that for certain? No, we do not! No one has ever come back from death to tell us what happens after we die! Death is cheaper. And death is final. Let the five die today!''

Caesar spoke again, still mildly. "Unless the treason be *perduellio,* Cato, death is not a legal penalty. And if you do not intend to try these men, how can you decide whether they committed *perduellio* or *maiestas*? You seem to argue *perduellio,* but are you?''

"This is not the time or the place for legal quibbling, even if you had no other reason behind your drive for clemency, Caesar!" blared Cato. "They must die, and they must die today!''

On he went, oblivious to the passage of time. Cato was in stride, the harangue would continue until he saw to his satisfaction that his sheer grinding monotony had worn everyone down. The House flinched; Cicero almost wept. Cato was going to rant on until the sun set, and the vote would not be taken today.

It wanted an hour before sunset was due when a servant sidled into the chamber and unobtrusively handed Caesar a folded note.

Cato pounced. "Ah! The traitor is revealed!" he roared. "He sits receiving treasonous notes under our very eyes—that is the extent of his arrogance, his contempt for this House! I say you are a traitor, Caesar! I say that note contains proof!''

While Cato thundered, Caesar read. When he looked up his face bore a most peculiar expression—mild anguish? Or *amusement*?

"Read it out, Caesar, read it out!" screamed Cato.

But Caesar shook his head. He folded the note, got up from his seat, crossed the floor to where Cato sat on the middle tier of the other side, and handed him the note with a smile. "I think you might prefer to keep its contents to yourself," he said.

Cato was not a good reader. The endless squiggles unseparated save into columns (and sometimes a word would be continued onto the line below, an additional confusion) took a long time to decipher. And while he mumbled and puzzled, the senators sat in some gratitude for this relative silence, dreading Cato's resumption (and dreading that indeed the note would be construed as treasonous).

A shriek erupted from Cato's throat; everybody jumped. Then he screwed the piece of paper up and threw it at Caesar.

"Keep it, you disgusting philanderer!"

But Caesar didn't get the note. When it fell well short of where he sat, Philippus snatched it up—and immediately opened it. A better reader than Cato, he was guffawing within moments; as soon as he finished he handed it on down the line of praetors-elect in the direction of Silanus and the curule dais.

Cato realized he had lost his audience, busy laughing, reading, or dying of curiosity. "It is typical of this body that something so contemptible and petty should prove more fascinating than the fate of traitors!" he cried. "Senior consul, I demand that the House instruct you under the terms of the existing Senatus Consultum Ultimum to execute the five men in our custody at once, and to pass a death sentence on four more men—Lucius Cassius Longinus, Quintus Annius Chilo, Publius Umbrenus and Publius Furius—to become effective the moment any or all of them are captured.''

Of course Cicero was as eager to read Caesar's note as any other man present, but he saw his chance, and took it.

''Thank you, Marcus Porcius Cato. I will see a division on your motion that the five men in our custody be executed at once, and that the four other men so named be executed immediately after they are apprehended. All those favoring a death sentence, pass to my right. Those not in favor, pass to my left.''

The senior consul–elect, Decimus Junius Silanus, husband of Servilia, got the note just before Cicero put his motion. It said:

> Brutus has just rushed in to tell me that my low-life half brother Cato has accused you of treason in the House, even admitting he has absolutely no proof! My most precious and darling man, take no notice. It's spite because you stole Atilia and put horns upon his head—not to mention that I know she told him he was *pipinna* compared to you. A fact that I am well able to vouch for myself. The rest of Rome is *pipinna* compared to you.
>
> Remember that Cato is not so much as the dirt beneath a patrician's feet, that he is no more than the descendant of a slave and a cantankerous old peasant who sucked up to patricians enough to get himself made censor—whereupon he deliberately ruined as many patricians as he could. This Cato would love to do the same. He loathes all patricians, but you in particular. And did he know what lies between us, Caesar, he would loathe you more.
>
> Keep up your courage, ignore the pernicious weed and all his minions. Rome is better served by one Caesar than half a hundred Catos and Bibuluses. As their wives could all testify!

Silanus looked at Caesar with grey dignity and no
other emotion. Caesar's face was sad, but not contrite.
Then Silanus rose and passed to Cicero's right; he would
not vote for Caesar.

Nor did many vote for Caesar, though not everyone
passed to the right. Metellus Celer, Metellus Nepos, Lucius Caesar, several of the tribunes of the plebs including
Labienus, Philippus, Gaius Octavius, both Luculli, Tiberius Claudius Nero, Lucius Cotta, and Torquatus stood to
Cicero's left, together with some thirty of the *pedarii* from
the back bench. And Mamercus Princeps Senatus.

"I note that Publius Cethegus is among those voting
for his brother's execution," said Cicero, "and that Gaius
Cassius is among those voting for his cousin's execution.
The vote is near enough to unanimous."

"The bastard! He always exaggerates!" growled Labienus.

"Why not?" asked Caesar, shrugging. "Memories
are short and verbatim reports prone to reflect statements
like that, as Gaius Cosconius and his scribes are not likely
to want to record names."

"Where's the note?" asked Labienus, avid to see it.

"Cicero's got it now."

"Not for long!" said Labienus, turned, walked up to
the senior consul pugnaciously, and wrested it from him.
"Here, it belongs to you," he said, holding it out to Caesar.

"Oh, do read it first, Labienus!" said Caesar, laughing. "I fail to see why you shouldn't know what everyone
else knows, even the lady's husband."

Men were returning to their seats, but Caesar stood
until Cicero recognized him.

"Conscript Fathers, you have indicated that nine men
must die," said Caesar without emotion. "That is, according to the argument put forward by Marcus Porcius Cato,
infinitely the worst punishment the State can decree. In
which case, it should be enough. I would like to move that
nothing more is done. That no property should be confiscated. The wives and children of the condemned men will
never again set eyes on their faces. Therefore that too is

punishment enough for haboring a traitor in their bosoms. They should at least continue to have the wherewithal to live.''

''Well, we all know why you're advocating mercy!'' howled Cato. ''You don't want to have to support gutter-dirt like the three Antonii and their trollop of a mother!''

Lucius Caesar, brother of the trollop and uncle of the gutter-dirt, launched himself at Cato from one side, and Mamercus Princeps Senatus from the other. Which brought Bibulus, Catulus, Gaius Piso and Ahenobarbus to Cato's defense, fists swinging. Metellus Celer and Metellus Nepos joined the fray, while Caesar stood grinning.

''I think,'' he said to Labienus, ''that I ought to ask for tribunician protection!''

''As a patrician, Caesar, you're not entitled to tribunician protection,'' Labienus said solemnly.

Finding the fight impossible to break up, Cicero decided to break the meeting up instead; he grabbed Caesar by the arm and hustled him out of the temple of Concord.

''For Jupiter's sake, Caesar, go home!'' he begged. ''What a problem you can be!''

''That cuts both ways,'' said Caesar, glance contemptuous, and made a move to re-enter the temple.

''Go home, please!''

''Not unless you give me your word that there will be no confiscation of property.''

''I give you my word gladly! Just go!''

''I'm going. But don't think I won't hold you to your word.''

He had won, but that speech of Caesar's swirled remorselessly through Cicero's mind as he plodded with his lictors and a good party of militia to the house of Lucius Caesar, where Lentulus Sura still lodged. He had sent four of his praetors to fetch Gaius Cethegus, Statilius, Gabinius Capito and Caeparius, but felt he must collect Lentulus Sura himself; the man had been consul.

Was the price too high? No! The moment these traitors were dead Rome would quieten magically; any thought of insurrection would vanish from all men's imaginations. Nothing deterred like execution. If Rome executed more often, crime would diminish. As for the trial process, Cato was right on both counts. They were guilty out of their own mouths, so to try them was a waste of State money. And the trouble with the trial process was that it could so easily and deftly be tampered with, provided someone was prepared to put up enough cash to meet the jury's price. Tarquinius had accused Crassus, and though logic said Crassus could not be involved in any way—it had been he, after all, who gave Cicero the first concrete evidence—the seed was sown in Cicero's mind. What if Crassus *had* been involved, then thought better of it, and craftily engineered those letters?

Catulus and Gaius Piso had accused Caesar. So had Cato. None of them with one iota of proof, and all of them Caesar's implacable enemies. But the seed was sown. What about that item Cato produced about Caesar's conspiring to assassinate Lucius Cotta and Torquatus nearly three years before? There had been a wild rumor about an assassination plot at the time, though the culprit at the time had been said to be Catilina. Then Lucius Manlius Torquatus had shown his disbelief of the rumor by defending Catilina at his extortion trial. No hint of Caesar's name then. And Lucius Cotta was Caesar's uncle. Yet . . . Other Roman patricians had conspired to kill close relatives, including Catilina, who had murdered his own son. Yes, patricians were different. Patricians obeyed no laws save those they respected. Look at Sulla, Rome's first true dictator—and a patrician. Better than the rest. Certainly better than a Cicero, a lodger from Arpinum, a mere resident alien, a despised New Man.

He would have to watch Crassus, decided Cicero. But he would have to watch Caesar even more closely. Look at Caesar's debts—who stood to gain more than Caesar by a general cancellation of debt? Wasn't that reason enough to back Catilina? How else could he hope to extricate himself from an otherwise inevitable ruin? He would need to conquer vast tracts as yet untouched by Rome, and Cicero for one deemed that impossible. Caesar was no Pompey; he had never commanded armies. Nor would Rome be tempted to endow *him* with special commissions! In fact, the more Cicero thought about Caesar, the more convinced he became that Caesar had been a part of the Catilinarian conspiracy, if only because victory for Catilina meant that his burden of debt would be removed.

Then as he was returning to the Forum with Lentulus Sura (whom again he led by the hand like a child), another Caesar intruded. Neither as gifted nor as dangerous as Gaius, Lucius Caesar was still a formidable man: consul the year before, an augur, and likely to be elected censor at some time in the future. He and Gaius were close cousins, and they liked each other.

But Lucius Caesar had stopped in his tracks, incredulity written on his face as his eyes took in the sight of Cicero leading Lentulus Sura by the hand.

"Now?" he asked Cicero.

"Now," said Cicero firmly.

"Without preparation? Without mercy? Without a bath, clean clothes, the right frame of mind? Are we barbarians?"

"It has to be now," Cicero said miserably, "before the sun sets. Don't try to obstruct me, please."

Lucius Caesar stepped out of the way ostentatiously. "Oh, the Gods preserve me from obstructing Roman justice!" he said, sneering. "Have you broken the news to my sister that her husband is to die without a bath, without clean clothes?"

"I haven't the time!" cried Cicero for something to say. Oh, this was awful! He was only doing his duty! But he couldn't say that to Lucius Caesar, could he? What *could* he say?

"Then I had better go to her house while it's still in Sura's name!" Lucius Caesar snapped. "No doubt you'll be convening the Senate tomorrow to dispose of all the property."

"No, no!" Cicero said, almost weeping. "I've given your cousin Gaius my solemn word that there will be no confiscation of property."

"Big of you," said Lucius Caesar. He looked at his brother-in-law Lentulus Sura, lips parted as if to say

something; then he shut them firmly, shook his head, and
turned away. Nothing could help, nor did he think Lentulus Sura capable of hearing. Shock had parted him from
his wits.

Trembling from that encounter, Cicero proceeded
down the Vestal Steps into the lower Forum, which was
jammed with people—and not all of them professional Forum frequenters, either. As his lictors pushed a path
through those masses of people, Cicero fancied he caught
glimpses of faces he knew. Was that young Decimus Brutus Albinus? Surely that wasn't Publius Clodius! Gellius
Poplicola's outcast son? Why would any of them be mingling cheek by jowl with the ordinary folk of Rome's back
streets?

There was a feeling in the air, and its nature frightened the already shaken Cicero. People were growling,
their eyes were dark, their faces sullen, their bodies hard
to move aside for Rome's senior consul and the victim he
led by the hand. A frisson of terror flashed up Cicero's
spine, almost caused him to turn about and run. But he
couldn't. This was *his* doing. He had to see it through now.
He was the father of his country; he had single-handedly
saved Rome from a nest of patricians.

On the far side of the Gemonian Steps, which led up
onto the Arx of the Capitol, lay Rome's ramshackle, tum-
bledown (and only) prison, the Lautumiae; its first and
most ancient building was the Tullianum, a tiny, three-
sided relic of the days of the kings. In the wall facing onto
the Clivus Argentarius and the Basilica Porcia was its only
door, a thick wooden ugliness always kept closed and
locked.

But this evening it stood wide open, its aperture filled
by half-naked men, six of them. Rome's public executioners. They were slaves, of course, and lived in barracks on
the Via Recta outside the *pomerium* together with Rome's
other public slaves. Where their lot differed from the other
tenants of that barracks lay in the fact that Rome's public
executioners did not cross the *pomerium* into the city except to perform their duty. A duty normally confined to

putting their big, brawny hands around foreign necks only, snapping them; a duty normally occurring only once or twice in any year, during a triumphal parade. It was a very long time since the necks they would break had belonged to Romans. Sulla had killed many Romans, but never officially inside the Tullianum. Marius had killed many Romans, but never officially inside the Tullianum.

Luckily the physical location of the execution chamber did not permit the entire front of that crowd to witness what happened, and by the time Cicero had assembled his five wretched condemned and placed a solid wall of lictors and militia between them and the masses, there was little indeed to see.

When Cicero mounted the few steps to stand outside the door, the smell hit him. Fierce, foetid, an overwhelming stench of decay. For no one ever cleaned out the execution chamber. A man went in; he approached a hole in the middle of the floor, and descended into the depths below. There some feet down his executioners waited to break his neck. After which his body simply lay there and rotted. The next time the chamber was needed, the executioners shoved the moldering remains into an open conduit which joined the sewers.

Gorge rising, Cicero stood ashen-faced as the five men filed inside, Lentulus Sura first, Caeparius last. None of them so much as spared him a glance, for which he was very grateful. The inertia of shock held them fast.

It took no more than a few moments. One of the executioners emerged from the door and nodded to him. I can leave now, thought Cicero, and walked behind his lictors and militia to the rostra.

From its top he gazed down on the crowd stretching away to the limit of his vision, and wet his lips. He was within the *pomerium,* Rome's sacred boundary, and that meant he could not use the word "dead" as part of an official pronunciation.

What could he say instead of "dead"? After a pause he threw his arms wide and shouted, *"Vivere!"* "They have lived!" Past perfect, over and done with, finished.

No one cheered. No one booed. Cicero climbed down

and began to walk in the direction of the Palatine while
the crowd dispersed mostly toward the Esquiline, the Subura, the Viminal. When he reached the little round House
of Vesta a large group of knights of the Eighteen led by
Atticus appeared, torches kindled because it was growing
quite dark. And they hailed him as the savior of his country, as *pater patriae,* as a hero straight out of myth. Balm
to his *animus*! The conspiracy of Lucius Sergius Catilina
was no more, and he alone had exposed it, killed it.

PART V

---

from DECEMBER 5 of 63 B.C.
until MARCH of 61 B.C.

POMPEIA SULLA

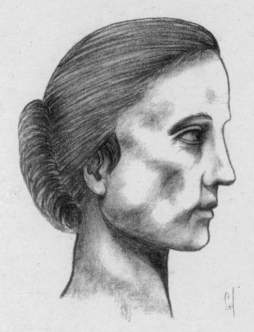

AURELIA

Caesar stalked home to the Domus Publica in a towering rage, Titus Labienus almost running to keep up with him. A peremptory jerk of Caesar's head had summoned Pompey's tame tribune of the plebs to accompany him, for what reason Labienus didn't know; he went because in Pompey's absence Caesar was his controller.

The invitation to help himself to liquid refreshments was given by another jerk of Caesar's head; Labienus poured wine, sat down, and watched Caesar pace the confines of his study.

Finally Caesar spoke. "I will make Cicero wish he had never been born! How dared he presume to interpret Roman law! And how did we ever elect such a *swan* senior consul?"

"What, didn't you vote for him?"

"Neither for him nor for Hybrida."

"You voted for Catilina?" Labienus asked, surprised.

"And Silanus. Candidly, there was no one I really wanted to vote for, but one can't not vote, that's to avoid the issue." The red spots still burned in Caesar's cheeks, and the eyes were, thought Labienus with unusual imagination, frozen yet on fire.

"Sit down, man, do! I know you don't touch wine, but tonight is exceptional. A drink will do you good."

"A drink never does any good," Caesar said emphatically; he did, however, sit down. "If I am not in error, Titus, your uncle Quintus Labienus perished under a tile in the Curia Hostilia thirty-seven years ago."

"Together with Saturninus, Lucius Equitius and the rest, yes."

"And how do you feel about that?"

"How else than that it was as unforgivable as unconstitutional? They were Roman citizens, and they had not been tried."

"True. However, they were not officially executed. They were murdered to avoid keeping them alive to undergo a trial process neither Marius nor Scaurus could be

457

sure would not cause far worse violence. Naturally it was
Sulla who solved the dilemma by murder. He was Marius's right hand in those days—very quick, very clever,
very ruthless. So fifteen men died, there were no incendiary treason trials, the grain fleet arrived, Marius distributed it dirt-cheap, Rome settled down full-bellied, and later
on Scaeva the slave got all the credit for murdering those
fifteen men.''

Labienus frowned, added more water to his wine. ''I
wish I knew where you're going.''

''I know where, Labienus, which is what matters,''
said Caesar, smiling to reveal clenched teeth. ''Consider
if you will that dubious piece of relatively recent Republican expedience, the *senatus consultum de re publica defendenda*—or, as Cicero so cutely renamed it, the Senatus
Consultum Ultimum. Invented by the Senate when no one
wanted a dictator appointed to make the decisions. And it
did serve the Senate's purpose in the aftermath of Gaius
Gracchus, not to mention Saturninus, Lepidus and some
others.''

''I still don't know where you're going,'' said Labienus.

Caesar drew a breath. ''Now here is the Senatus Consultum Ultimum again, Labienus. But look what's happened to it! In Cicero's mind for one it has become
respectable, inevitable, and highly convenient. Seduce the
Senate into passing it, and then beneath its shelter proceed
to flout both constitution and *mos maiorum*! Without altering it at law in any way, Cicero has employed his Senatus Consultum Ultimum to crush Roman windpipes and
snap Roman necks without trial—without ceremony—
without even common decency! Those men went to their
deaths faster than soldiers are cut down in a lost battle!
Not unofficially beneath a rain of tiles from a roof, *but
with the full sanction of the Senate of Rome*! Which at
Cicero's urging took upon itself the functions of judge and
jury! How do you think it must have looked to that crowd
in the Forum this evening, Labienus? I will tell you how
it looked. As if from this day forward, no Roman citizen
can ever again be sure that he will be accorded his abso-

lutely inalienable right to a trial before any condemnation. And that so-called brilliant man, that conceited and feckless fool Cicero, actually thinks he has extricated the Senate from a very difficult situation in the best and most suitable way! I will grant him that for the Senate it was the easy way. But for the vast majority of Roman citizens of every kind from the First Class to the Head Count, what Cicero engineered today spells the death of an inalienable right should the Senate decide under a future Senatus Consultum Ultimum that Roman men must die without a trial, without due process of the law! What's to stop its happening again, Labienus? Tell me what?''

Suddenly short of breath, Labienus managed to put his goblet down on the desk without spilling its contents, then stared at Caesar as if he had never seen him before. Why did Caesar see so many ramifications when no one else had? Why hadn't he, Titus Labienus, understood better what Cicero was actually doing? Ye gods, *Cicero* hadn't understood! Only Caesar had. Those who voted against execution had done so because their hearts could not approve, or else had groped after the truth like blind men debating the nature of an elephant.

''When I spoke this morning I made a terrible mistake,'' Caesar went on angrily. ''I chose to be ironic, I didn't think it right to inflame feelings. I decided to be clever, to point out the insanity of Cicero's proposal by talking of the time of the kings and saying that Cicero was abrogating the Republic by dragging us back to the time of the kings. It wasn't simple enough. I ought to have been down on a child's level, slowly spelling out manifest truths. But I deemed them grown and educated men of some little intelligence, so I chose to be ironic. Never realizing that they wouldn't fully follow where my argument was going, why I was taking that tack. I ought to have been blunter then than I am now to you, but I didn't want to set their backs up because I thought *rage* would blind them! They were already blind, I had nothing to lose! I don't often make mistakes, but I made one this morning, Labienus. Look at Cato! The one man I felt sure would support me, little though he likes me. What he said made

absolutely no sense. But they chose to follow him like a
lot of eunuchs after Magna Mater.''

"Cato is a yapping dog.''

"No, Labienus, he's just the worst kind of fool there
is. He thinks he's not a fool.''

"That's true of most of us.''

Up went Caesar's brows. "*I* am not a fool, Titus.''

Then Titus was to soften it, of course. "Granted.''
Why was it that when one was in the company of a man
who did not drink wine, wine lost its allure? Labienus
poured himself water. "No point in going over lost ground
now, Caesar. I believe you when you say you'll make
Cicero wish he'd never been born, but how?''

"Simple. I will ram his Senatus Consultum Ultimum
somewhere down around his golden tonsils,'' said Caesar
dreamily, his smile not reaching his eyes.

"But how? How, how, how?''

"You have four days left of your year as a tribune
of the plebs, Labienus, and they are just enough if we act
quickly. We can allow tomorrow to organize ourselves and
refine our roles. The day after will see the first phase. The
two days following that are for the final phase. The business won't have finished by then, but it will have gone far
enough. And you, my dear Titus Labienus, will quit your
tribunate in an absolute blaze of glory! If nothing else
recommends your name to posterity, I promise you that
the events of the next four days surely will!''

"What do I have to do?''

"Nothing this evening, except perhaps—do you have
access to—no, you wouldn't. I'll frame it differently. Can
you manage to get hold of a bust or a statue of Saturninus?
Or of your uncle Quintus Labienus?''

"I can go one better than that,'' said Labienus
promptly. "I know where there's an *imago* of Saturninus.''

"An *imago*? But he was never praetor!''

"True,'' said Labienus, grinning. "The trouble with
being a great nobleman, Caesar, is that you can have no
idea how our minds work, we ambitious up-and-coming
Picentines, Samnites, New Men from Arpinum and the

like. We just can't wait to see our features exquisitely formed and tinted like life in beeswax, with real hair of exactly the right color and style! So as soon as we have the money in our purses we sneak off to one of the craftsmen in the Velabrum, and we commission an *imago*. I know men who will never even belong to the Senate who have *imagines*. How else do you think Magius of the Velabrum got so rich?''

''Well, in this situation I'm very pleased you up-and-coming men of Picenum commission *imagines*,'' Caesar said briskly. ''Get Saturninus's likeness, and find an actor to wear it to good effect.''

''Uncle Quintus had an *imago* too, so I'll hire an actor to wear his. I can also get busts of both men.''

''In which case I have nothing further for you until dawn tomorrow, Labienus. Then I promise I'll work you remorselessly until the time comes to depart your tribunate.''

''Is it to be just you and me?''

''No, there will be four of us,'' said Caesar, rising to escort Labienus to the front door. ''What I plan needs you, me, Metellus Celer and my cousin Lucius Caesar.''

Which didn't help elucidate matters for Titus Labienus, who left the Domus Publica intrigued, baffled, and wondering how his curiosity and excitement were ever going to let him sleep.

Caesar had abandoned all idea of sleep. He returned to his study so immersed in thought that Eutychus, his steward, had to clear his throat several times in the doorway before his presence was noticed.

''Ah, excellent!'' said the Pontifex Maximus. ''I am at home to no one, Eutychus, even my mother. Is that understood?''

''*Edepol!*'' cried the steward, plump hands going to plumper face. ''*Domine,* Julia is most anxious to speak to you at once.''

''Tell her I know what she wants to speak to me about, and that I will be happy to see her for as long as she likes on the first day of the new tribunate of the plebs. But not a moment before.''

"Caesar, that's five days off! Truly, I don't think the poor little girl can wait five days!''

"If I say she must wait twenty years, Eutychus, then she must wait twenty years,'' was Caesar's reply, coldly given. "Five days are not twenty years. All family and domestic matters must wait for five days. Julia has a grandmother, she is not dependent upon me. Is that absolutely clear?''

"Yes, *domine,*'' whispered the steward, carefully shutting the door and creeping away down the passage to where Julia stood, face pale, hands locked in each other. "I'm sorry, Julia, he says he will see no one until the day the new tribunes of the plebs enter office.''

"Eutychus, he didn't!''

"He did. He refuses to see even the lady Aurelia.''

Who appeared at that moment from the direction of the Atrium Vestae, eyes hard, mouth thin. "Come,'' she said to Julia, drawing her into the suite belonging to the mother of the Pontifex Maximus.

"You've heard,'' said Aurelia, pushing Julia into a chair.

"I don't know quite what I've heard,'' said Julia distractedly. "I asked to speak to *tata,* and he said no!''

That gave Aurelia pause. "Did he? How odd! It is not like Caesar to refuse to face facts or people.''

"Eutychus says he won't see anyone, even you, until five days from now, *avia*. He was quite specific, we must all wait until the day the new tribunes of the plebs enter office.''

Frowning, Aurelia began to pace the room; nor did she answer for some time. Eyes misted but tears held back resolutely, Julia watched her grandmother. The trouble is, she thought, that the three of us are so dauntingly different from each other!

Julia's mother had died when she was barely seven years old, which meant Aurelia had been mother as well as grandmother for most of her formative years. Not very approachable, perpetually busy, strict and unsparing, Aurelia had nonetheless given Julia what all children need most, an unshakable sense of security and belonging. Though she laughed but little, she had an acute wit which could pop out at the most disconcerting moments, and she thought no less of Julia because Julia loved to laugh. Every care had been lavished upon the child's upbringing, from guidance in such matters as tasteful dress to merciless training in good manners. Not to mention the unsentimental and unvarnished way Aurelia had taught Julia to accept her lot—and to accept it gracefully, with pride, without developing a sense of injury or resentment.

"There is no point in wishing for a different or a better world" was Aurelia's perpetual moral. "For whatever reason, this world is the only one we have, and we must live in it as happily and pleasantly as we can. We cannot fight Fortune or Fate, Julia."

Caesar was not at all like his mother except in his steel, nor was Julia unaware of the friction which could scratch into being between them on sometimes scant provocation. But for his daughter he was the beginning and the end of that world Aurelia had disciplined her into accepting: not a god, but definitely a hero. To Julia, no one was as perfect as her father, as brilliant, as educated, as witty, as handsome, as ideal, as *Roman*. Oh, she was well acquainted with his failings (though he never visited them upon her), from that terrifying temper to what she thought of as his besetting sin, which was to play with people the way a cat played with a mouse in every sense—pitiless and cool, a smile of sheer pleasure on his face.

"There is a compelling reason for Caesar's withdrawal from us," said Aurelia suddenly, ceasing to pace. "It is not that he is afraid to confront us, of that I am now absolutely sure. I can only assume that his motives have nothing to do with us."

"Nor probably," said Julia, enlightened, "anything to do with what is preying on our minds."

Aurelia's beautiful smile flashed. "You grow more perceptive every day, Julia. Quite so, quite so."

"Then, *avia*, until he has time to see us, I will have

to talk to you. Is it true, what I heard in the Porticus Margaritaria?''

''About your father and Servilia?''

''Is *that* it? Oh!''

''What did you think it was, Julia?''

''I couldn't catch it all, because as soon as people saw me they stopped talking. What I gathered was that *tata* is involved in some great scandal with a woman, and that it all came out in the Senate today.''

Aurelia grunted. ''It certainly did.'' And without mincing matters she told Julia of the events in the temple of Concord.

''My father and Brutus's mother,'' said Julia slowly. ''What a muddle!'' She laughed. ''But how close he is, *avia*! All this time, and neither Brutus nor I has ever suspected. What on earth does he see in her?''

''You've never liked her.''

''No, indeed!''

''Well, that's understandable. You're so much on Brutus's side you couldn't like her.''

''Do you?''

''For what she is, I like her very well.''

''Yet *tata* told me he didn't like her, and he doesn't lie.''

''He definitely does not like her. I have no idea— nor, frankly, do I want to have any idea!—what holds him to her, except that it is very strong.''

''I imagine she's excellent in bed.''

''*Julia!*''

''I'm not a child anymore,'' said Julia with a chuckle. ''And I do have ears.''

''For what's bruited about the shops of the Porticus Margaritaria?''

''No, for what's said in my stepmother's rooms.''

Aurelia stiffened dangerously. ''I'll soon put a stop to that!''

''Don't *avia,* please!'' cried Julia, putting her hand on her grandmother's arm. ''You mustn't blame poor Pompeia, and it isn't her, anyway. It's her friends. I know I'm not grown up yet, but I always think of myself as much older and wiser than Pompeia. She's like a pretty puppy, she sits there wagging her tail and grinning all over her face as the conversation wafts far above her head, so terribly anxious to please and belong. They torment her dreadfully, the Clodias and Fulvia, and she never can see how cruel they are.'' Julia looked thoughtful. ''I love *tata* to death and I'll hear no word against him, but he's cruel to her too. Oh, I know why! She's far too stupid for him. They ought never to have married, you know.''

''*I* was responsible for that marriage.''

''And for the best of reasons, I'm sure,'' said Julia warmly. Then she sighed. ''Oh, but I do wish you'd picked someone a great deal cleverer than Pompeia Sulla!''

''I picked her,'' said Aurelia grimly, ''because she was offered to me as a bride for Caesar, and because I thought the only way I could make sure Caesar didn't marry Servilia was to get in first.''

After comparing notes in later days, a goodly number of the members of the Senate discovered that they had preferred not to linger in the lower Forum to witness the execution of Lentulus Sura and the others.

One such was the senior consul–elect, Decimus Junius Silanus; another was the tribune of the plebs–elect, Marcus Porcius Cato.

Silanus reached his house some time ahead of Cato, whose progress was retarded by people wishful of congratulating him for his speech and his stand against Caesar's blandishments.

The fact that he was obliged to let himself in the front door prepared Silanus for what he found inside: a deserted atrium with nary a servant in sight or sound. Which meant everyone servile already knew what had happened during the debate. But did Servilia? Did Brutus? Face drawn because the pain in his gut was gnawing and griping, Silanus forced his legs to hold him up and went immediately to his wife's sitting room.

She was there, poring over some of Brutus's accounts, and looked up with an expression of simple irritation.

"Yes, yes, what is it?" she growled.

"Then you don't know," he said.

"Don't know what?"

"That your message to Caesar fell into the wrong hands."

Her eyes widened. "What do you mean?"

"The precious fellow you so love to have run your errands because he sucks up to you so cleverly isn't clever enough," said Silanus with more iron in his voice than Servilia had ever heard. "He came prancing into Concord and didn't have the sense to wait. So he handed your note to Caesar at the worst possible moment, which was the moment your esteemed half brother Cato had reserved to accuse Caesar of masterminding Catilina's conspiracy. And when in the midst of this drama Cato saw that Caesar was anxious to read the piece of paper he had been handed, Cato demanded that Caesar read it out to the whole House. He assumed it contained evidence of Caesar's treason, you see."

"And Caesar read it out," said Servilia tonelessly.

"Come, come, my dear, is that all you know about Caesar after so much intimacy with the man?" asked Silanus, lip curling. "He's not so unsubtle, nor so little in command of himself. No, if anyone came out of the affair looking the victor, it was Caesar. Of course it was Caesar! He simply smiled at Cato and said that he rather thought Cato would prefer that the contents of the note remain private. He got up and gave Cato the note so courteously, so pleasantly—oh, it was well done!"

"Then how was I exposed?" whispered Servilia.

"Cato just couldn't believe what his eyes saw. It took him ages to decipher those few words, while we all waited with bated breath. Then he crushed your message into a ball and threw it at Caesar like a missile. But of course the distance was too great. Philippus grabbed it from the floor and read it. Then he passed it along the praetors-elect until it reached the curule dais."

''And they roared with laughter,'' said Servilia between her teeth. ''Oh, they would!''

''*Pipinna*,'' he mocked.

Another woman would have flinched, but not Servilia, who snarled. ''Fools!''

''The hilarity made it hard for Cicero to make himself heard when he demanded a division.''

Even in the midst of her travail her avidity for politics showed. ''A division? For what?''

''To decide the fate of our captive conspirators, poor souls. Execution or exile. I voted to execute, that's what your note forced me to do. Caesar had advocated exile, and had the House on his side until Cato spoke up for execution. Cato swung everyone around. The division went for execution. Thanks to you, Servilia. If your note hadn't silenced Cato he would have filibustered until sunset, and the vote wouldn't have been taken until tomorrow. My feeling is that by tomorrow the House would have seen the sense of Caesar's argument. If I were Caesar, my dear, I'd cut you up and feed you to the wolves.''

That disconcerted her, but her contempt for Silanus eventually made her dismiss this opinion. ''When are the executions to take place?''

''They're taking place right at this moment. I deemed it best to come home and warn you before Cato could arrive.''

She leaped to her feet. ''Brutus!''

But Silanus, not without satisfaction, had cocked his ear in the direction of the atrium, and now smiled sourly. ''Too late, my dear, far too late. Cato is upon us.''

Still Servilia made a move toward the door, only to stop short of it when Cato erupted through it, the first finger and thumb of his right hand pincered agonizingly into Brutus's earlobe.

''Get in here and look at her, your strumpet of a mother!'' bellowed Cato, releasing Brutus's ear and pushing him so hard in the small of the back that he staggered and would have fallen were it not for Silanus, who steadied him. The lad looked so appalled and bewildered that he probably had not even begun to understand what was happening, thought Silanus as he moved away.

Why do I feel so strange? then asked Silanus of himself. Why am I in some secret corner so delighted by this, so vindicated? Today my world has learned that I am a cuckold, and yet I find that of much less moment than I find this delicious retribution, my wife's hugely deserved comeuppance. I hardly find it in me to blame Caesar. It was her, I know it was her. He doesn't bother with the wives of men who haven't irritated him politically, and until today I have never irritated him politically. It was her, I know it was her. She wanted him, she went after him. That's why she gave Brutus to his daughter! To keep Caesar in the family. He wouldn't marry her, so she beggared her pride. Quite a feat for Servilia, that! And now Cato, the man she loathes most in all the world, is privy to both her passions—Brutus *and* Caesar. Her days of peace and self-satisfaction are over. From now on there will be a hideous war, just as in her childhood. Oh, she'll win! But how many of them will live to see her triumph? I for one will not, for which I am profoundly glad. I pray I am the first to go.

"Look at her, your strumpet of a mother!" Cato bellowed again, slapping Brutus viciously about the head.

"Mama, Mama, what is it?" Brutus whimpered, ears ringing and eyes watering.

" 'Mama, Mama!' " Cato mimicked, sneering. " 'Mama, Mama!' What a dimwit you are, Brutus, what a lapdog, what an apology for a man! Brutus the baby, Brutus the booby! 'Mama, Mama!' " Slapping Brutus's head viciously.

Servilia moved with the speed and style of a striking snake, straight for Cato, and so suddenly that she was upon him before he could swing his attention away from Brutus. Between them she went with both hands up, fingers crooked into claws, took Cato's face in their embrace and dug her nails into his flesh until they sank like grapples. Had he not instinctively screwed his eyes shut she would have blinded him, but her talons raked him from brow to jawline on right side and on left side, gouged down to muscle and then kept on going along his neck and into his shoulders.

Even a warrior like Cato retreated, thin howls of terrible pain dying away as his opening eyes took in the sight of a Servilia more frightful than anything except dead Caepio's face, a Servilia whose lips were peeled back from her teeth and whose eyes blazed murder. Then under the distended gaze of her son, her husband and her half brother she lifted her dripping fingers to her mouth and luxuriously sucked Cato's flesh from them. Silanus gagged and fled. Brutus fainted. Which left Cato glaring at her between rivers of blood.

"Get out and don't ever come back," she said softly.

"I will end in owning your son, never doubt it!"

"If you so much as try, Cato, what I've done to you today will look like the kiss of a butterfly."

"You are monstrous!"

"Just get out, Cato."

Cato got out, holding folds of toga against his face and neck.

"Now why didn't I think to tell him that it was I sent Caepio to his death?" she wondered as she squatted down beside the inanimate form of her son. "Never mind," she went on, wiping Cato from her fingers before she began to minister to Brutus, "I have that little item saved for another time."

He came to full consciousness slowly, perhaps because inside his mind there now dwelled an absolute terror of his mother, who could eat Cato's flesh with relish. But eventually he had no other choice than to open his eyes and stare up at her.

"Get up and sit on the couch."

Brutus got up and sat on the couch.

"Do you know what all that was about?"

"No, Mama," he whispered.

"Not even when Cato called me a strumpet?"

"No, Mama," he whispered.

"I am not a strumpet, Brutus."

"No, Mama."

"However," said Servilia, disposing herself in a

chair from which she could move quickly to Brutus's side if she needed, "you are definitely old enough to understand the ways of the world, so it is time I enlightened you about certain matters anyway. What all that was about," she went on in conversational tones, "is the fact that for some years Julia's father has been my lover."

He leaned forward and dropped his head into his hands, quite unable to put two thoughts together, a hapless mass of misery and bewildered pain. First, all that in Concord while he stood at its doors listening—then, reporting to his mother—then, a blissful interval of wrestling with the writings of Fabius Pictor—then, Uncle Cato charging in and seizing his ear—then, Uncle Cato shouting at his mother—then, Mama attacking Uncle Cato, and—and— The full horror of what his mother had done after that struck Brutus afresh; he shivered and shuddered, wept desolately behind his hands.

Now this. Mama and Caesar were lovers, had been lovers for years. How did he feel about this? How was he *supposed* to feel about this? Brutus liked guidance; he hated the rudderless sensation of having to make a decision—especially a decision about emotions—without having first learned how people like Plato and Aristotle regarded these unruly, illogical and mystifying entities. Somehow he didn't seem able to feel anything about this. All that between Mama and Uncle Cato over *this*? But why? Mama was a law unto herself; surely Uncle Cato realized that. If Mama had a lover, there would be good reason. And if Caesar was Mama's lover, there would be good reason. Mama did nothing without good reason. Nothing!

Further than that he hadn't managed to get when Servilia, tired of his silent weeping, spoke. "Cato," she said, "is not all there, Brutus. He never was, even as a baby. Mormolyce got at him. He hasn't improved with the passage of time. He's thick, narrow, bigoted and unbelievably complacent. It is none of his business what I do with my life, any more than you are his business."

"I never realized how much you hate him," said Brutus, lifting his hands from his face to look at her. "Mama, you've scarred him for life! *For life!*"

"Good!" she said, looking genuinely pleased. Then her eyes fully assimilated the picture her son presented, and she winced. Because of the pimples he couldn't shave, had to content himself with a close clipping of his dense black beard; between the huge pimples and the snot smeared everywhere, he was more than merely ugly. He was ghastly. Her hand scrabbled behind her until it located a small soft cloth near the wine and water flagons; she tossed it to him. "Wipe your face and blow your nose, Brutus, please! I do not acknowledge Cato's criticisms of you, but there are certainly times when you disappoint me dreadfully."

"I know," he whispered, "I know."

"Oh well, never mind!" she said bracingly, got up and went to stand behind him, her arm about his bent shoulders. "You have birth, wealth, education and clout. And you are not yet twenty-one years old. Time is bound to improve you, my son, but time will not do the same for Cato. Nothing can improve Cato."

Her arm felt like a cylinder of hot lead, but he didn't dare shrug it off. He straightened a little. "May I go, Mama?"

"Yes, provided that you understand my position."

"I understand it, Mama."

"What I do is my affair, Brutus, nor am I about to offer you one single excuse for the relationship between Caesar and me. Silanus knows. He has known for a very long time. That Caesar, Silanus and I have preferred to keep our secret is logical."

Light broke on Brutus. "Tertia!" he gasped. "Tertia is Caesar's daughter, not Silanus's! She looks like Julia."

Servilia regarded her son with some admiration. "How very perspicacious of you, Brutus. Yes, Tertia belongs to Caesar."

"And Silanus knows."

"From the beginning."

"Poor Silanus!"

"Don't waste your pity on undeserving objects."

A tiny spark of courage crept into Brutus's breast. "And what of Caesar?" he asked. "Do you love him?"

"More than anyone in this world except for you."

"Oh, poor Caesar!" said Brutus, and escaped before she could say another word, his heart pounding at his temerity.

Silanus had made sure that this only male child had a large and comfortable suite of rooms for himself, with a pleasant outlook onto the peristyle. Here Brutus fled, but not for long. After washing his face, trimming his beard back to a minimal stubble, combing his hair and summoning his servant to assist him into his toga, he left Silanus's brooding house. He did not walk Rome's streets alone, however. As darkness had fallen, he went escorted by two slaves bearing torches.

"May I see Julia, Eutychus?" he asked at Caesar's door.

"It is very late, *domine,* but I will find out if she is up," said the steward respectfully, admitting him into the house.

Of course she would see him; Brutus trod up the stairs and knocked upon her door.

When she opened it she took him into her arms and just held him, her cheek against his hair. And the most exquisite feelings of utter peace and infinite warmth seeped through him from skin to bones; Brutus finally understood what some people meant when they said there was nothing lovelier than coming home. Home was Julia. His love for her welled up and up and up; the tears slid from beneath his lowered lids in healing bliss; he clung to her and inhaled the smell of her, delicate as all else about her. Julia, Julia, Julia . . .

Without conscious volition his hands slid around her back, he lifted his head from her shoulder and groped for her mouth with his own, so fumbling and inexpert that she did not understand his intention until it was too late to draw away without hurting his feelings. So Julia experienced her first kiss at least filled with pity for its giver, and found it not nearly as unpleasant as she had feared. His lips felt quite nice, soft and dry, and with her eyes closed she could not see his face. Nor did he attempt further intimacies. Two more of the same kind of kisses, then he released her.

"Oh, Julia, I love you so!"

What could she say except, "I love you too, Brutus"?

Then she drew him inside and seated him on a couch, though she very properly went to a chair some distance away, and left the door a little ajar.

Her sitting room was large and, at least in Brutus's eyes, especially beautiful. Her hand had been upon it, and her hand was not ordinary. The frescoes were of airy birds and frail flowers in pale clear colors, the furniture was slender and graceful, and there was not one touch of Tyrian purple to be seen, nor any gilt.

"Your mother and my father," she said.

"What does it mean?"

"For them, or for us?"

"For us. How can we know what it means for them?"

"I suppose," she said slowly, "it can do us no harm. There are no laws forbidding them love because of us, though I imagine it will be frowned upon."

"My mother's virtue is above reproach, and this doesn't change that!" snapped Brutus, sounding truculently defensive.

"Of course it doesn't change that. My father represents a unique circumstance in your mother's life. Servilia is no Palla or Sempronia Tuditani."

"Oh, Julia, it's so wonderful that you always understand!"

"Understanding them is easy, Brutus. My father can't be lumped in with other men, just as your mother is a singularity among women." She shrugged. "Who knows? Perhaps their relationship was inevitable, given the sort of people they are."

"You and I have a half sister in common," said Brutus abruptly. "Tertia is your father's, not Silanus's."

Julia stilled, then gasped, then laughed in delight. "Oh, I have a sister! How lovely!"

"Don't, Julia, please don't! Neither of us can ever admit to that, even within our families."

Her smile wobbled, faded. "Oh. Yes, of course you're right, Brutus." Tears gathered but did not fall. "I must never show it to her. All the same," she said more brightly, "*I* know."

"Though she does look like you, she's not a bit like you, Julia. In nature Tertia takes after my mother."

"Oh, rubbish! How can you tell at four years of age?"

"Easily," said Brutus grimly. "She's going to be betrothed to Gaius Cassius because his mother and my mother compared our horoscopes. Our lives are closely linked, apparently through Tertia."

"And Cassius must never know."

That provoked a derisive snort from Brutus. "Oh, come now, Julia! Do you think someone won't tell him? Though it can't matter to him. Caesar's blood is better than Silanus's."

And there, thought Julia, was his mother talking! She went back to the original subject. "About our parents," she said.

"You think what lies between them cannot affect us?"

"Oh, it must affect us. But I think we ought to ignore it."

"Then that," he said, rising to his feet, "is what we will do. I must go, it's very late." At her door he lifted her hand and kissed it. "In four more years we will be married. It's hard to wait, but Plato says the waiting will enhance our union."

"Does he?" asked Julia, looking blank. "I must have missed that bit."

"Well, I'm interpreting between the lines."

"Of course. Men have a superior ability to do that, I've noticed it quite often."

Night was just beginning to yield to day when Titus Labienus, Quintus Caecilius Metellus Celer and Lucius Julius Caesar arrived at the Domus Publica to find Caesar wide awake and apparently none the worse for lack of sleep. Water, mild sweet wine, new-baked bread, virgin oil and an excellent honey from Hymettos had been placed on a console table at the back of the room, and Caesar waited patiently until his guests had helped themselves. He himself sipped something steaming from a carved stone cup, though he ate nothing.

"What's that you're drinking?" asked Metellus Celer, curious.

"Very hot water with a little vinegar."

"Ye gods, how vile!"

"One gets used to it," said Caesar tranquilly.

"Why would one want to?"

"Two reasons. The first, that I believe it is good for my health, which I intend to keep in rude excellence until I am an old man, and the second, that it inures my palate to all manner of insults from rancid oil to sour bread."

"I'll grant you the first reason, but what's the virtue in the second unless you've espoused Stoicism? Why should you ever have to put up with poor food?"

"On campaign one often has to—at least, the way I campaign. Does Pompeius Magnus do you prouder, does he, Celer?"

"I should hope so! And every other general I've served under! Remind me not to campaign with you!"

"Well, in winter and spring the drink isn't quite so vile. I replace the vinegar with lemon juice."

Celer rolled his eyes; Labienus and Lucius Caesar laughed.

"All right, time to get down to business," said Caesar as he seated himself behind his desk. "Please forgive my patron's pose, but it seems more logical for me to sit where I can see all of you, and all of you can see me."

"You are forgiven," said Lucius Caesar gravely.

"Titus Labienus was here last night, so I have his reasons for voting with me yesterday," Caesar said, "and I understand completely why you voted with me, Lucius. However, I am not entirely privy to your motives, Celer. Tell me now."

The long-suffering husband of his own first cousin,

Clodia, Metellus Celer was also the brother-in-law of
Pompey the Great, as the mother of Celer and his younger
brother, Metellus Nepos, was also Mucia Tertia's mother.
Devoted to each other, Celer and Nepos were liked and
esteemed, for they were charming and convivial men.

To Caesar, Celer had never seemed particularly radical in his political leanings, until now respectably conservative. How he answered was critical to success; Caesar
could not hope to carry out what he planned unless Celer
was prepared to back him to the hilt.

Handsome face grim, Celer leaned forward, hands
clenched into fists. "To begin with, Caesar, I disapprove
of mushrooms like Cicero dictating policy to genuine Romans. Nor for one single moment will I condone the execution of Roman citizens without a trial! It does not
escape me that Cicero's ally turned out to be another
quasi-Roman, Cato of the Saloniani. What are we coming
to when those who presume to interpret our laws are descended from slaves or ancestorless bumpkins?''

An answer which—did Celer realize it?—also dismissed his relative by marriage Pompey the Great. However, provided no one was crass enough to mention this
fact, it might conveniently be ignored.

"What can you do, Gaius?" asked Lucius Caesar.

"Quite a lot. Labienus, you will excuse me if I re-
capitulate what I said to you last night. Namely, exactly
what it was Cicero did. The execution of citizens without
trial is not the crux of the issue, but rather a by-product
of it. The real crime lies in Cicero's interpretation of the
senatus consultum de re publica defendenda. I do not believe that this ultimate decree was ever intended as a blanket protection enabling the Senate or any other body of
Roman men to do precisely as it likes. That is Cicero's
own interpretation.

"The ultimate decree was invented to deal with a
civil disturbance of short duration, that of Gaius Gracchus.
The same can be said of its employment during the revolution of Saturninus, though its shortcomings were more
obvious then than when it was first used. It was invoked
by Carbo against Sulla when he landed in Italia, and

against Lepidus too. In the case of Lepidus, it was reinforced by Sulla's constitution, which gave the Senate full and clear powers in all matters relating to war, if not to civil disturbances. The Senate chose to call Lepidus a war.

"That is not so today," Caesar continued sternly. "The Senate is once more constrained by the three Comitia. Nor did any of the five men who were executed last night lead armed troops against Rome. In fact, none so much as picked up a weapon against any Roman, unless you count Caeparius's resisting what he might have thought a simple attack on the Mulvian Bridge in the middle of the night. They were not declared public enemies. And, no matter how many arguments are advanced to prove their treasonous intentions, even now they are dead their intentions remain just that—no more and no less than intentions. *Intentions,* not concrete deeds! The letters were letters of intent, written before the fact.

"Who can say what the arrival of Catilina outside Rome might have done to their intentions? And with Catilina gone from the city, what happened to their intention to kill the consuls and praetors? Two men—neither of them among last night's five dead men!—are said to have tried to enter Cicero's house to murder him. Yet our consuls and our praetors are hale and hearty to this day! There's not a scratch on them! Are we now to be executed without trial because of our intentions?"

"Oh, I wish you'd said that yesterday!" sighed Celer.

"So do I. However, I very much doubt that any argument had the power to move them once Cato got into stride. For all his fine words about keeping our speeches short, Cicero never even tried to stop his talking. I wish he'd continued until sunset."

"Blame Servilia that he didn't," said Lucius Caesar, mentioning the unmentionable.

"Don't worry, I do," said Caesar, tight-lipped.

"Well, if you plan to murder her, just make sure you don't tell her so in a letter," Celer contributed, grinning. "Intent is all you need these days."

"That is precisely my point. Cicero has converted the

Senatus Consultum Ultimum into a monster which can turn on any of us.''

''I fail to see what we can do in hindsight,'' said Labienus.

''We can turn the monster against Cicero, who undoubtedly at this moment is scheming to have the Senate ratify his claim to the title *pater patriae*,'' said Caesar, curling his lip. ''He says he's saved his country, whereas I maintain that his country is in no real danger, Catilina and his army notwithstanding. If ever a revolution was doomed to fail, this one is it. Lepidus was dismal enough. I'd call Catilina an outright joke, except that some good Roman soldiers will have to die putting him down.''

''What do you intend?'' asked Labienus. ''What can you?''

''I mean to cast the whole concept of the Senatus Consultum Ultimum into disrepute. You see, I intend to try someone for high treason who acted under its protection,'' Caesar said.

Lucius Caesar gasped. *''Cicero?''*

''Certainly not Cicero—or Cato, for that matter. It's far too soon to attempt retaliation against any of the men involved in this latest version. Were we to try, we'd find our own necks throttled. The time for that will come, cousin, but not yet. No, we'll go after someone well known to have acted criminally under a far earlier Senatus Consultum Ultimum. Cicero was thoughtful enough to name our quarry in the House. Gaius Rabirius.''

Three pairs of eyes widened, but no one spoke for some time.

''Murder, you mean, surely,'' said Celer eventually. ''Gaius Rabirius was inarguably one of those on the Curia Hostilia roof, but that wasn't treason. It was murder.''

''That's not what the law says, Celer. Think about it. Murder becomes treason when it is done to usurp the legal prerogatives of the State. Therefore the murder of a Roman citizen being held for trial on charges of high treason is itself treasonous.''

''I begin to see where you're going,'' said Labienus,

eyes glittering, "but you'd never succeed in getting into court."

"*Perduellio* is not a court offense, Labienus. It must be tried in the Centuriate Assembly," said Caesar.

"You'd never get it there either, even with Celer as urban praetor."

"I disagree. There is a way to get it before the Centuries. We begin with a trial process far older than the Republic, yet no less Roman law than any law of the Republic. It's all in the ancient documents, my friend. Even Cicero will not be able to contest the legality of what we do. He'll be able to counter it by sending it to the Centuries, is all."

"Enlighten me, Caesar, I'm no student of ancient law," said Celer, beginning to smile.

"You are renowned as an urban praetor who has scrupulously adhered to his edicts," said Caesar, choosing to keep his audience on tenterhooks a little longer. "One of your edicts says that you will agree to try any man if his *accusator* acts within the law. At dawn on the morrow Titus Labienus will appear at your tribunal and demand that Gaius Rabirius be tried *perduellionis* for the murders of Saturninus and Quintus Labienus in the form outlined during the reign of King Tullus Hostilius. You will inspect his case, and—how perspicacious of you!—you will just happen to have a copy of my dissertation on ancient procedures for high treason under your elbow. This will confirm that Labienus's application to charge Rabirius *perduellionis* for these two murders is within the letter of the law."

His audience sat fascinated; Caesar drained what was left of his water and vinegar, now tepid, and continued.

"The procedure for the only trial which has come down to us during the reign of Tullus Hostilius—that of Horatius for the murder of his sister—calls for a hearing before two judges only. Now there are only four men in today's Rome who qualify as judges because they come from families installed among the Fathers at the time the trial took place. I am one and you are another, Lucius. The third is Catilina, officially a public enemy. And the fourth is Fabius Sanga, at present well on his way to the lands of the Allobroges in the company of his clients. You, Celer, will therefore appoint me and Lucius as the judges, and direct that the trial take place immediately on the Campus Martius.''

''Are you sure about your facts?'' asked Celer, brow wrinkling. ''The Valerii are attested at that time, and certainly the Servilii and Quinctilii came from Alba Longa after its destruction, just as the Julii did.''

Lucius Caesar chose to answer. ''The trial of Horatius took place well before Alba Longa was sacked, Celer, which disqualifies the Servilii and the Quinctilii. The Julii emigrated to Rome when Numa Pompilius was still on the throne. They were banished from Alba by Cluilius, who usurped the Alban kingship from them. As for the Valerii''—Lucius Caesar shrugged—''they were Rome's military priests, which disqualifies them too.''

''I stand corrected,'' chuckled Celer, vastly diverted, ''but can only plead that I am, after all, a mere Caecilius!''

''Sometimes,'' said Caesar, acknowledging this hit, ''it pays to choose your ancestors, Quintus. Caesar's luck that no one from Cicero to Cato will be able to dispute your choice of judges.''

''It will provoke a furor,'' said Labienus with satisfaction.

''That it will, Titus.''

''And Rabirius will follow Horatius's example by appealing.''

''Of course. But first we'll put on a wonderful show with all the ancient trappings on full display—the cross fashioned out of an unlucky tree—the forked stake for the flogging—three lictors bearing the rods *and* axes to represent the original three Roman tribes—the veil for Rabirius's head and the ritual bindings for his wrists—superb theater! Spinther will die of envy.''

''But,'' said Labienus, reverting to gloom, ''they'll keep on finding excuses to delay Rabirius's appeal in the Centuries until public resentment dies down. Rabirius's case won't be heard while anyone remembers the fate of Lentulus Sura and the others.''

"They can't do that," said Caesar. "The ancient law prevails, so an appeal has to be held immediately, just as Horatius's appeal was held immediately."

"I take it that we damn Rabirius," said Lucius Caesar, "but I'm out of my depth, cousin. What's the point?"

"First of all, our trial is very different from a modern trial as set up by Glaucia. In modern eyes it will seem a farce. The judges decide what evidence they want to hear, and they also decide when they've heard enough. Which we will after Labienus has presented his case to us. We will decline to allow the accused to present any evidence in his own defense. It is vital that justice be seen *not* to be done! For what justice did those five men executed yesterday receive?"

"And secondly?" asked Lucius Caesar.

"Secondly, the appeal goes on straightaway, which means the Centuries will still be boiling. And Cicero is going to panic. If the Centuries damn Rabirius, his own neck is at risk. Cicero isn't stupid, you know, just a trifle obtuse when his conceit and his certainty that he's right get the better of his judgement. The moment he hears what we're doing, he'll understand exactly why we're doing it."

"In which case," said Celer, "if he has any sense he'll go straight to the Popular Assembly and procure a law invalidating the ancient procedure."

"Yes, I believe that's how he'll approach it." Caesar looked at Labienus. "I noted that Ampius and Rullus voted with us in Concord yesterday. Do you think they'd co-operate with us? I need a veto in the Popular Assembly, but you'll be busy on the Campus Martius with Rabirius. Would Ampius or Rullus be prepared to exercise his veto on our behalf?"

"Ampius certainly, because he's tied to me and we're both tied to Pompeius Magnus. But I think Rullus would co-operate too. He'd do anything he fancied might make Cicero and Cato suffer. He blames them for the death of his land bill."

"Rullus then, with Ampius in support. Cicero will ask the Popular Assembly for a *lex rogata plus quam perfecta* so that he can legally punish us for instituting the ancient procedure. I add that he'll have to invoke his precious Senatus Consultum Ultimum to hurry it into law at once—thereby focusing public attention on the ultimate decree just when he'll be wishing it burned and forgotten. Whereupon Rullus and Ampius will interpose their vetoes. After which I want Rullus to take Cicero to one side and propose a compromise. Our senior consul is such a timid soul that he'll grasp at any proposal likely to avoid violence in the Forum—provided it allows him to get half of what he's after.''

''You ought to hear Magnus on the subject of Cicero during the Italian War,'' said Labienus contemptuously. ''Our heroic senior consul fainted at the sight of a sword.''

''What's Rullus's deal to be?'' asked Lucius Caesar, frowning at Labienus, whom he deemed a necessary evil.

''First, that the law Cicero procures not render us liable for prosecution later. Secondly, that Rabirius's appeal to the Centuries take place the following day so that Labienus can continue as prosecutor while still a tribune of the plebs. Thirdly, that the appeal be conducted according to the rules of Glaucia. Fourthly, that the death sentence be replaced by exile and a fine.'' Caesar sighed luxuriously. ''And fifthly, that *I* am appointed the appeal judge in the Centuries, with Celer as my personal *custos*.''

Celer burst out laughing. ''Jupiter, Caesar, that's clever!''

''Why bother to change the sentence?'' asked Labienus, still disposed to be gloomy. ''The Centuries haven't convicted a man on a charge of *perduellio* since Romulus was a boy.''

''You're unduly pessimistic, Titus.'' Caesar folded his hands loosely together on the desk top. ''What we have to do is fan the feelings already simmering inside most of those who watched the Senate deny a Roman's inalienable right to trial. This is one issue wherein the First and Second Classes will not consent to follow the example of the Senate, even among the ranks of the Eighteen. The Senatus Consultum Ultimum gives the Senate too much power, and there's not a knight or a moderately affluent man out there who doesn't understand that. It's been war between the Orders since the Brothers Gracchi. Rabirius isn't at all liked, he's an old villain. Therefore his fate won't matter nearly as much to the Centuriate voters as their own threatened right to trial. I think there's a very good chance indeed that the Centuries will choose to damn Gaius Rabirius.''

"And send him into exile,'' said Celer a little unhappily. "I know he's an old villain, Caesar, but he *is* old. Exile would kill him.''

"Not if the verdict is never delivered,'' said Caesar.

"How can it not be delivered?''

"That rests entirely with you, Celer,'' Caesar said, smiling wickedly. "As urban praetor, you're in charge of protocol for meetings on the Campus Martius. Including keeping an eye on the red flag you have to hoist atop the Janiculum when the Centuries are outside the walls. Just in case invaders are sighted.''

Celer began to laugh again. "Caesar, no!''

"My dear fellow, we're under a Senatus Consultum Ultimum because Catilina is in Etruria *with an army*! The wretched decree wouldn't exist if Catilina didn't have an army, and five men would be alive today. Under more normal conditions no one even bothers to look at the Janiculum, least of all the urban praetor—he's quite busy down at ground level, not up on a tribunal. But with Catilina and an army expected to descend on Rome any day, the moment that red flag comes down panic will ensue. The Centuries will abandon the vote and flee home to arm against the invaders, just as in the days of the Etrusci and the Volsci. I suggest,'' Caesar went on demurely, "that you have someone on the Janiculum ready to lower the red flag, and arrange some sort of signal system—a fire, perhaps, if the sun isn't far enough west, or a flashing mirror if it is.''

"All very well,'' said Lucius Caesar, "but what will such a tortuous sequence of events accomplish if Rabirius is not to be convicted and the Senatus Consultum Ultimum continues to be in effect until Catilina and his army are defeated? What lesson do you really think to teach Cicero?

Cato is a lost cause, he's too thick to learn from anything.''

"About Cato you're right, Lucius. But Cicero is different. As I've already said, he's a timid soul. At present he's carried away by the floodwaters of success. He wanted a crisis during his term as consul, and he got one. It hasn't yet occurred to him that there's any possibility of personal disaster involved. But if we drive it home to him that the Centuries would have convicted Rabirius, he will understand the message, believe me.''

"But what exactly *is* the message, Gaius?"

"That no man who acts under the shelter of a Senatus Consultum Ultimum is safe from retribution at some time in the future. That no senior consul can hoodwink a body of men as important as the Senate of Rome into sanctioning the execution of Roman citizens without a trial, let alone an appeal. Cicero will get the message, Lucius. Every man in the Centuries who votes to damn Rabirius will be telling Cicero that he and the Senate are not the arbiters of a Roman's fate. They will also be telling him that in executing Lentulus Sura and the others without trial, he has lost their confidence as well as their admiration. And that last, to Cicero, will be worse by far than any other aspect of the whole business," said Caesar.

"He'll *hate* you for this!" cried Celer.

Up went both fair brows; Caesar looked haughty. "What can that be to me?" he asked.

The praetor Lucius Roscius Otho had been a tribune of the plebs in the service of Catulus and the *boni*, and had earned the dislike of nearly all Roman men by returning the fourteen rows of theater seats just behind the senatorial seats to the knights of the Eighteen. But his affection had been given to Cicero on the day when a theater full of people had whistled and booed him viciously for reserving those delectable seats at law, and Cicero had talked the angry crowd of lesser beings around.

Praetor responsible for foreign litigation, Otho was in the lower Forum when he saw that savage-looking fellow Titus Labienus stride up to Metellus Celer's tribunal and start talking very insistently. Curiosity piqued, Otho strolled over in time to hear the last part of Labienus's demand that Gaius Rabirius be tried for high treason according to the law during the reign of King Tullus Hostilius. When Celer produced Caesar's fat dissertation on ancient laws and started checking the validity of Labienus's contentions, Otho decided it was time he repaid a part of his debt to Cicero by informing him what was going on.

As it happened Cicero had slept late, for on the night after the execution of the conspirators he had not been able to sleep at all; then yesterday's day had been stuffed full of people calling round to compliment him, a kind of excitement more conducive to sleep by far.

Thus he had not emerged from his sleeping cubicle when Otho came banging on his front door, though he came quickly enough into the atrium when he heard the racket—such a small house!

"Otho, my dear fellow, I'm so sorry!" Cicero cried, beaming at the praetor while he ran his hands through his tousled hair to smooth it. "Blame the events of the past few days—last night I finally had a really good rest." His bubbling sense of well-being began to fade a little when he took in Otho's perturbed expression. "Is Catilina on his way? Has there been a battle? Have our armies been defeated?"

"No, no, nothing to do with Catilina," said Otho, shaking his head. "It's Titus Labienus."

"What about Titus Labienus?"

"He's down in the Forum at Metellus Celer's tribunal asking that he be allowed to prosecute old Gaius Rabirius *perduellionis* for the murders of Saturninus and Quintus Labienus."

"He's *what*?"

Otho repeated his statement.

Cicero's mouth went dry; he could feel the blood drain from his face, feel his heart begin to trip and stammer while his chest emptied of air. One hand went out, grasped Otho by the arm. "I don't believe it!"

"You had better, because it's happening, and Metellus Celer was looking as if he was going to approve the case. I wish I could say I understood what exactly was going on, but I didn't. Labienus kept quoting King Tullus Hostilius, something about an ancient trial process, and Metellus Celer got busy poring over a huge scroll he said was something to do with ancient laws. I don't quite know why my left thumb started to prick, but it did. That's terrible trouble coming! I thought I'd better run and tell you at once.''

But he ended talking to vacant space; Cicero had vanished shouting for his valet. Within no time he was back, clad in all the majesty of his purple-bordered toga.

"Did you see my lictors outside?"

"They're there, playing dice."

"Then we're off."

Normally Cicero liked to amble behind his twelve white-clad lictors; it enabled everybody to see him properly and admire. But this morning his escort was exhorted to move at the double, not merely once, but every time it slackened its pace. The distance to the lower Forum was not great, but to Cicero it seemed as far as Rome to Capua. He itched to abandon majesty and run, though he preserved enough sense not to do so. Well he remembered that it was he who had introduced the name Gaius Rabirius into his speech opening the debate in Concord; he also remembered that he had done so in order to illustrate any individual's immunity from the consequences of any actions performed while a Senatus Consultum Ultimum was in force. Now here was Titus Labienus—*Caesar's* tame tribune of the plebs, not Pompey's!—applying to prosecute Gaius Rabirius for the murders of Quintus Labienus and Saturninus! But not on a charge of murder. On an antique charge of *perduellio,* the same *perduellio* Caesar had described during his speech in Concord.

By the time Cicero's entourage streamed hastily across the space between Castor's temple and the urban praetor's tribunal, a small crowd had gathered about the tribunal to listen avidly. Not that anything important was being discussed as Cicero arrived; Labienus and Metellus Celer were speaking of some woman or other.

"What is it? What's going on?" demanded Cicero breathlessly.

Celer raised his brows in surprise. "The normal business of this tribunal, senior consul."

"Which is?"

"To adjudicate in civil disputes and decide whether criminal charges merit trial," said Celer, emphasizing the word "trial."

Cicero flushed. "Don't play games with me!" he said nastily. "I want to know what's going on!"

"My dear Cicero," drawled Celer, "I can assure you that you are the last person in the world I'd choose to play games with."

"WHAT IS GOING ON?"

"The good tribune of the plebs Titus Labienus here has brought a charge of *perduellio* against Gaius Rabirius for the murders of his uncle Quintus Labienus and Lucius Appuleius Saturninus thirty-seven years ago. He wishes to prosecute under the procedure in force during the reign of King Tullus Hostilius, and after perusing the relevant documents, I have decided according to my own edicts published at the beginning of my term as urban praetor that Gaius Rabirius may be so tried," said Celer without drawing a breath. "At the moment we are waiting for Gaius Rabirius to appear before me. As soon as he comes I will charge him and appoint the judges for his trial, which I will set in motion immediately."

"This is ridiculous! You can't!"

"Nothing in the relevant documents or my own edicts says I can't, Marcus Cicero."

"This is aimed at me!"

Celer's face registered stagy astonishment. "What, Cicero, were you on the Curia Hostilia roof pelting tiles thirty-seven years ago?"

"Will you stop being deliberately obtuse, Celer? You're acting as Caesar's puppet, and I had thought better of you than that you could be bought by the likes of Caesar!"

"Senior consul, if we had a law on our tablets which forbade baseless allegations under pain of a large fine, you'd be paying up right now!'' said Celer fiercely. ''I am urban praetor of the Senate and People of Rome, and I will do my job! Which is exactly what I was trying to do until you barged in telling me *how* to do my job!'' He turned to one of his four remaining lictors, listening to this exchange with grins on their faces because they esteemed Celer and enjoyed working for him.

''Lictor, pray summon Lucius Julius Caesar and Gaius Julius Caesar to this tribunal.''

At which moment his two missing lictors appeared from the direction of the Carinae. Between them shuffled a little man who looked ten years older than the seventy he acknowledged, wizened and unappealing of mien, scrawny of body. Ordinarily he wore an expression of sour and furtive satisfaction, but as he approached Celer's tribunal under official escort his face betrayed nothing beyond fuddled bewilderment. Not a nice man, Gaius Rabirius, but something of a Roman institution even so.

Shortly afterward the two Caesars appeared with suspicious promptness, looking so magnificent together that the growing crowd oohed its admiration. Both were tall, fair and handsome; both were dressed in the purple-and-scarlet-striped toga of the major religious Colleges; but whereas Gaius wore the purple-and-scarlet-striped tunic of the Pontifex Maximus, Lucius carried the *lituus* of an augur—a curved staff crowned by a curlicue. They looked sumptuous. And while Metellus Celer formally charged the stupefied Gaius Rabirius with the murders of Quintus Labienus and Saturninus under the *perduellio* of King Tullus Hostilius, the two Caesars stood to one side watching impassively.

''There are only four men who may act as judges in this trial,'' cried Celer in a ringing voice, ''and I will summon them in turn! Lucius Sergius Catilina, step forward!''

''Lucius Sergius Catilina is under interdiction,'' answered the urban praetor's chief lictor.

''Quintus Fabius Maximus Sanga, step forward!''

''Quintus Fabius Maximus Sanga is out of the country.''

''Lucius Julius Caesar, step forward!''

Lucius Caesar stepped forward.

"Gaius Julius Caesar, step forward!"

Caesar stepped forward.

"Fathers," said Celer solemnly, "you are hereby directed to try Gaius Rabirius for the murders of Lucius Appuleius Saturninus and Quintus Labienus according to the *lex regia de perduellionis* of King Tullus Hostilius. I further direct that the trial take place two hours from now on the Campus Martius in the grounds adjacent to the *saepta*.

"Lictor, I hereby direct that you summon from your College three of your colleagues to act as the representatives of the three original tribes of Roman men, one for Tities, one for Ramnes, and one for Luceres. I further direct that they shall attend the court as its servants."

Cicero tried again more sweetly. "Quintus Caecilius," he said very formally to Celer, "you cannot do this! A trial *perduellionis* this actual day? In two hours? The accused must have time to assemble his defense! He must choose his advocates and find the witnesses who will testify for him."

"Under the *lex regia de perduellionis* of King Tullus Hostilius there are no such provisions," said Celer. "I am merely the instrument of the law, Marcus Tullius, not its originator. All I am allowed to do is to follow procedure, and procedure in this case is clearly defined in the documents of the period."

Without a word Cicero turned on his heel and quit the vicinity of the urban praetor's tribunal, though whereabouts he was going from there he had absolutely no idea. They were serious! They intended to try that pathetic old man under an archaic law Rome typically had never expunged from the tablets! Oh, why was it that in Rome everything archaic was reverenced, nothing archaic tampered with? From rude thatched huts to laws dating back to the earliest kings to obstructing columns within the Basilica Porcia, it was ever the same: what had always been there must always be there.

Caesar was at back of it, of course. It had been he who had discovered the missing pieces which made sense not only of the trial of Horatius—the oldest known trial in Rome's history—but also of his appeal. And cited both in the House the day before yesterday. But what exactly did he hope to accomplish? And why was a man of the *boni* like Celer aiding and abetting him? Titus Labienus was understandable, so too Lucius Caesar. Metellus Celer was inexplicable.

His footsteps had taken him in the direction of Castor's, so he decided to go home, shut himself up and think, think, think. Normally the organ which produced Cicero's thought had no difficulty with the process, but now Cicero wished he knew exactly where that organ was—head, chest, belly? If he knew, he might be able to shock it into functioning by beating it, or fomenting it, or purging it. . . .

At which precise moment he almost collided with Catulus, Bibulus, Gaius Piso and Metellus Scipio, hastening down from the Palatine. He hadn't even noticed their approach! What *was* the matter with him?

While they climbed the endless steps to Catulus's house, the closest, Cicero told the other four his story, and when at last they were settled in Catulus's spacious study he did something he rarely did, drank off a whole beaker of unwatered wine. Eyes starting to focus then, he realized one person was missing.

"Where's Cato?"

The other four looked rather uncomfortable, then exchanged resigned glances which indicated to Cicero that he was about to be informed of something the rest would much rather have kept to themselves.

"I suppose you'd have to classify him as walking wounded," said Bibulus. "Someone scratched his face to ribbons."

"*Cato?*"

"It's not what you're thinking, Cicero."

"What is it, then?"

"He had an altercation with Servilia over Caesar, and she went for him like a lioness."

"Ye gods!"

"Don't gossip about it, Cicero," said Bibulus sternly. "It will be hard enough for the poor fellow when he does

appear in public without all of Rome knowing who and
why.''

"It's that bad?''

"It's worse.''

Catulus smacked his hand down on the desk so loudly
everyone jumped. ''We are not here to exchange news
about Cato!'' he snapped. ''What we're here for is to stop
Caesar.''

''That,'' said Metellus Scipio, ''is becoming a refrain.
Stop Caesar this, stop Caesar that—but we never do stop
him.''

''What's he after?'' asked Gaius Piso. ''I mean, why
try an old fellow under some antique law on a trumped-
up charge he won't have any trouble refuting?''

''It's Caesar's way of getting Rabirius before the
Centuries,'' said Cicero. ''Caesar and his cousin will damn
Rabirius, and he'll appeal to the Centuries.''

''I don't see the point of any of it,'' said Metellus
Scipio.

''They're charging Rabirius with high treason because he was one of the men who killed Saturninus and
his confederates and was indemnified from the consequences under the Senatus Consultum Ultimum of that
time,'' said Cicero patiently. ''In other words, Caesar is
attempting to show the People that a man isn't safe from
any action he took under a Senatus Consultum Ultimum,
even after thirty-seven years. It's his way to tell me that
one day he'll prosecute me for the murder of Lentulus
Sura and the others.''

That produced a silence which hung so heavily Catulus broke it by getting up from his chair and beginning
to pace.

''He'll never succeed.''

''In the Centuries, I agree. But it will produce a lot
of interest, Rabirius's appeal will be crowded,'' said Cicero, looking miserable. ''Oh, I wish Hortensius was in
Rome!''

''He's on his way back, as a matter of fact,'' said
Catulus. ''Someone in Misenum started a rumor that there
was going to be a slave uprising in Campania, so he

packed up two days ago. I'll send a messenger to find him on the road and tell him to hurry.''

"Then he'll be with me to defend Rabirius when he appeals.''

"We'll just have to stall the appeal,'' said Piso.

Cicero's superior knowledge of the ancient documents provoked him into throwing Piso a contemptuous glare. "We can't postpone anything!'' he growled. "It has to be held immediately after the trial before the two Caesars is finished.''

"Well, it all sounds like a tempest in a bottle to me,'' said Metellus Scipio, whose ancestry was far greater than his intellect.

"It's far from that,'' said Bibulus soberly. "I know you generally don't see anything even when it's rammed under your snooty nose, Scipio, but surely you've noticed the mood of the People since we executed the conspirators? They don't like it! We're senators, we're on the inside, we understand all the nuances of situations like Catilina. But even a lot of the knights of the Eighteen are grumbling that the Senate has usurped powers that the courts and the Assemblies no longer have. This trumped-up trial of Caesar's gives the People the opportunity to congregate in a public place and voice their displeasure very loudly.''

"By damning Rabirius at appeal?'' asked Lutatius Catulus, a little blankly. "Bibulus, they'd never do that! The two Caesars can—and no doubt will—pronounce a death sentence on Rabirius, but the Centuries absolutely refuse to damn, always have. Yes, they'll grumble, perhaps, but the thing *will* die a natural death. Caesar won't succeed in the Centuries.''

"I agree he shouldn't,'' said Cicero unhappily, "yet why am I haunted by a feeling that he will? He's got another trick in the sinus of his toga, and I can't work out what it is.''

"Die a natural death or not, Quintus Catulus, are you inferring that we just have to sit tamely on the side of the battlefield and watch Caesar stir up trouble?'' asked Metellus Scipio.

Cicero answered. "Of course not!" he said testily; Metellus Scipio really was thick! "I agree with Bibulus that the People aren't happy at the moment. Therefore we can't allow Rabirius's appeal to proceed immediately. The only way to prevent that is to nullify the *lex regia de perduellionis* of King Tullus Hostilius. So this morning I'll call the Senate together and ask for a decree directing the Popular Assembly to nullify. It won't take long to procure the decree, I'll make sure of that. Then I'll convoke the Popular Assembly at once." He closed his eyes, shivered. "I am afraid, however, that I'll have to use the Senatus Consultum Ultimum in order to bypass the Didian Law. We just can't wait seventeen days for ratification. Nor can we allow *contiones*."

Bibulus frowned. "I don't pretend to have your knowledge of the law, Cicero, but surely the Senatus Consultum Ultimum doesn't extend to the Popular Assembly unless the Popular Assembly is meeting to do something about Catilina. I mean, *we* know the trial of Rabirius is all to do with Catilina, but the only Popular Assembly voters who share our knowledge are senators, and there won't be enough of them in the Comitia to carry the vote."

"The Senatus Consultum Ultimum functions in the same way as a dictator," said Cicero firmly. "It replaces all normal comitial and public activities."

"The tribunes of the plebs will veto you," said Bibulus.

Cicero looked smug. "Under a Senatus Consultum Ultimum, they can't veto."

"What do you mean, Marcus Tullius, I can't veto?" asked Publius Servilius Rullus three hours later in the Popular Assembly.

"My dear Publius Servilius, Rome lies under a Senatus Consultum Ultimum, which means the tribunician veto is suspended," said Cicero.

Attendance was mediocre, as many of the Forum frequenters had preferred to rush out to the Campus Martius to see what the Caesars were doing to Gaius Rabirius. But those who had remained within the *pomerium* to see how

Cicero was going to handle the Caesar attack were not limited to senators and the clients of Catulus's faction. Perhaps more than half of the gathering, seven hundred strong, belonged to the opposing side. And among them, Cicero noted, were the likes of Mark Antony and his hulking brothers, young Poplicola, Decimus Brutus, and none other than Publius Clodius. Very busy talking to anyone prepared to listen. Restlessness followed in their wake, and darkling looks, and audible growls.

"Now just a moment, Cicero," said Rullus, dropping formality, "what's all this about a Senatus Consultum Ultimum? There is one, yes, but it is purely concerned with revolt in Etruria and the activities of Catilina. It is not meant to obstruct the normal functioning of the Popular Assembly! We are here to consider the passing of a law to nullify the *lex regia de perduellionis* of King Tullus Hostilius—a matter having nothing to do with revolt in Etruria or with Catilina! First you inform us that you intend to invoke your Senatus Consultum Ultimum to overturn normal comitial procedure! You want to waive *contiones,* you want to bypass the Didian Law. And now you inform us that legally elected tribunes of the plebs cannot exercise their power of veto!"

"Precisely," said Cicero, chin up.

From the floor of the Comitia well the rostra was an imposing edifice rising some ten feet above the level of the Forum. Its top was large enough to accommodate forty standing men, and this morning the space was occupied by Cicero and his twelve lictors, by the urban praetor Metellus Celer and his six lictors, by the praetors Otho and Cosconius and their twelve lictors, and by three tribunes of the plebs—Rullus, Ampius and one man from the Catulus faction, Lucius Caecilius Rufus.

One of those cold winds confined to the Forum was blowing, which might have accounted for the fact that Cicero looked quite small huddled inside the massive folds of his purple-bordered toga; though he was held the greatest orator Rome had ever produced, the rostra didn't suit his style nearly as well as the more intimate theaters of Senate chamber and court, and he was miserably aware of it. The florid and exhibitionistic style of Hortensius suited the rostra far better, but Cicero could not be comfortable in widening his performance to a Hortensian scale. Nor was there time to orate properly. He would just have to battle on.

"*Praetor urbanus,*" cried Rullus to Metellus Celer, "do you agree with the senior consul's interpretation of the Senatus Consultum Ultimum at present in force to deal with revolt in Etruria and conspiracy in Rome?"

"No, tribune, I do not," said Celer with weighty conviction.

"Why?"

"I cannot agree with *anything* that prevents a tribune of the plebs from exercising the rights given to him by the Roman Plebs!"

When Celer said this, Caesar's supporters roared approval.

"Then, *praetor urbanus,*" Rullus went on, "is it your opinion that the Senatus Consultum Ultimum at present in force cannot forbid a tribunician veto in this Assembly on this morning?"

"Yes, that is my opinion!" Celer cried.

As the crowd's restlessness increased, Otho came closer to Rullus and Metellus Celer. "It's Marcus Cicero who is right!" he shouted. "Marcus Cicero is the greatest lawyer of our day!"

"Marcus Cicero is a turd!" someone called.

"Dictator Turd!" called someone else. "Dictator Turd!"

"Cicero's a tur-urd! Cicero's a tur-urd! Cicero's a tur-urd!"

"Order! I will have order!" yelled Cicero, beginning to be afraid of the crowd.

"Cicero's a tur-urd, Cicero's a tur-urd, Dic-a-tator Tur-urd!"

"Order! Order!"

"Order," cried Rullus, "will be restored when the tribunes of the plebs are allowed to exercise their rights without interference from the senior consul!" He walked to the edge of the rostra and looked down into the well. "*Quirites,* I hereby propose that we enact a law to investigate the nature of the Senatus Consultum Ultimum our senior consul has used to such telling effect for the last few days! Men have *died* because of it! Now we are told that tribunes of the plebs are not allowed to veto because of it! Now we are told that tribunes of the plebs are once again the ciphers they were under Sulla's constitution! Is today's debacle the prelude to another Sulla in the person of this spouter and touter of the Senatus Consultum Ultimum? He flourishes it like a magic wand! Whoosh! and impediments vanish into nothing! Bring in a Senatus Consultum Ultimum—chain and gag the men you haven't done to death—end the right of Romans to assemble in their tribes to enact laws or veto them—and forbid the trial process entirely! Five men have died without a trial, another man is on trial at the Campus Martius right now, and our Dictator Turd the senior consul is using his putrefied Senatus Consultum Ultimum to subvert justice and turn all of us into slaves! *We* rule the world, but Dictator Turd is out to rule us! It is my right to exercise the veto I was given by a true congress of Roman men, but Dictator Turd says I can't!'' He swung round on Cicero viciously. ''What's your next move, Dictator Turd? Am I to be sent to the Tullianum to have my neck squashed to pulp without a trial? Without a trial, without a trial, without a trial, WITHOUT A TRIAL!''

Someone in the Comitia well took the chant up, and before Cicero's appalled eyes even the Catulus faction joined in: ''Without a trial! Without a trial! Without a trial!'' over and over and over.

Yet there was no violence. Owning volatile tempers, Gaius Piso and Ahenobarbus ought by rights to have assaulted someone by now, but instead they stood transfixed. Quintus Lutatius Catulus looked at them and at Bibulus in sick horror, finally understanding the full extent of opposition to the execution of the conspirators. Hardly realizing that he did so, he put his right arm up to Cicero on the rostra in a mute command to cease, to back down immediately.

Cicero stepped forward so quickly he almost tripped, hands held with palms out to implore calm and quiet.

When the noise died enough for him to be heard, he visibly licked his lips and swallowed. "*Praetor urbanus,*" he cried, "I accede to your superior position as interpreter of law! Let your opinion be adopted! The Senatus Consultum Ultimum does not extend to the tribunician right to veto in a matter having nothing to do with revolt in Etruria or conspiracy in Rome!"

Though as long as he lived he would never cease to fight, in that moment Cicero knew he had lost.

Numbed and perished, he accepted the proposal Caesar had instructed Rullus to put forward, not sure why he was apparently being let off so lightly. Rullus even agreed to the waiving of preliminary discussions and the seventeen-day waiting period stipulated by the *lex Caecilia Didia*! But couldn't the idiots in the crowd see that if the Senatus Consultum Ultimum could not forbid the tribunician veto, it also could not waive *contiones* or the waiting period of the Didian Law? Oh yes, of course the hand of Caesar was in it—why else was Caesar to be the judge at Rabirius's appeal? But what exactly was Caesar after?

"Not everyone is against you, Marcus," said Atticus as they walked up the Alta Semita to Atticus's magnificent house right on top of the Quirinal heights.

"But too many are," said Cicero miserably. "Oh, Titus, we *had* to get rid of those wretched conspirators!"

"I know." Atticus stopped at a place where a large expanse of vacant ground permitted a wonderful view of the Campus Martius, the sinuous curve of the Tiber, the Vatican plain and hill beyond. "If Rabirius's trial is still on, we'll see it from here."

But the grassy space adjacent to the *saepta* was quite deserted; whatever old Rabirius's fate, it was already decided.

"Who did you send to hear the two Caesars?" asked Atticus.

"Tiro in a toga."

"Risky for Tiro."

"Yes, but I can trust him to give me an exact account, and I can't say that of anyone else other than you. You, I needed in the Popular Assembly." Cicero gave a grunt of what might have been laughter or pain. "The Popular Assembly! What a travesty."

"You have to admit Caesar's clever."

"I do that! But what makes you say it now, Titus?"

"His condition that the penalty in the Centuries be altered from death to exile and a fine. Now that they don't have to see Rabirius flogged and beheaded, I think the Centuries will vote to convict him."

It was Cicero's turn to stop. "They wouldn't!"

"They will. Trial, Marcus, *trial*! Men outside the Senate don't possess real political forethought, they see politics as it affects their own hides. So they have no idea how dangerous it would have been for Rome to keep those men alive to undergo trial in the full glare of the Forum. All they see is how their own hides are threatened when citizens are executed—even self-confessed traitors!— without benefit of trial or appeal."

"My actions saved Rome! I saved my *country*!"

"And there are plenty who agree with you, Marcus, believe me. Wait until feelings die down and you'll see. At the moment those feelings are being worked on by some genuine experts, from Caesar to Publius Clodius."

"Publius Clodius?"

"Oh yes, very much so. He's collecting quite a following, didn't you know it? Of course he specializes in attracting the lowly, but he also has quite a bit of influence among the more minor businessmen. Entertains them lavishly and gives them a lot of custom—presents for the lowly, for instance," said Atticus.

"But he's not even in the Senate yet!"

"He will be in twelve months."

"Fulvia's money must be a help."

"It is."

"How do you know so much about Publius Clodius? Through your friendship with Clodia? And why are you friends with Clodia?"

"Clodia," said Atticus deliberately, "is one of those women I like to call professional virgins. They pant and palpitate and pout at every man they meet, but let a man try to assault their virtue and they run screaming, usually to a besotted husband. So they prefer to mix intimately with men who are no danger to their virtue—homosexuals like me.''

Cicero swallowed, tried vainly not to blush, didn't know where to look. This was the first time he had ever heard Atticus speak that word, let alone admit it applied to him.

''Don't be embarrassed, Marcus,'' said Atticus with a laugh. ''Today isn't an ordinary day, is all. Forget I said it.''

Terentia did not mince matters, but the words she used were all of a variety permitted to women of her quality.

''You saved your country,'' she said harshly at the end of it.

''Not until Catilina is defeated in the field.''

''How can you think he won't be?''

''Well, my armies certainly don't seem to be doing much at the moment! Hybrida's gout is still the chief thing on his mind, Rex has found a comfortable billet in Umbria, the Gods only know what Metellus Creticus is doing in Apulia, and Metellus Celer is intent on fueling Caesar's fire here in Rome.''

''It will be finished by the New Year, wait and see.''

What Cicero most wanted to do was to pillow his head on his wife's very nice breast and weep until his eyes were sore, but that, he understood, would not be permitted. So he stilled his wobbling lip and drew a long breath, unable to look at Terentia for fear she'd comment on the glisten of tears.

''Tiro has reported?'' she asked.

''Oh, yes. The two Caesars pronounced a sentence of death on Rabirius after the most disgraceful display of partisan bigotry in the history of Rome. Labienus was allowed to run rampant—he even had actors there wearing the masks of Saturninus and Uncle Quintus, who came out of it looking like Vestals rather than the traitors they were. And he had Quintus's two sons—both over forty!—there weeping like little children because Gaius Rabirius deprived them of their *tata*! The audience howled in sympathy and threw flowers. Not surprising, it was a scintillating performance. The two Caesars had the cant down pat—'Go, lictor, tie his hands! Go, lictor, attach him to the stake and scourge him! Go, lictor, transfix him on a barren tree!' Tchah!''

"But Rabirius appealed."

"Of course."

"And it is to be tomorrow in the Centuries. According to Glaucia, I hear, but limited to one hearing only because of the lack of witnesses and evidence." Terentia snorted. "If that in itself can't tell the jury what a lot of nonsense the charge is, then I despair of Roman intellect!"

"I despaired of it some time ago," said Cicero wryly. He got to his feet, feeling very old. "If you'll excuse me, my dear, I won't eat. I'm not hungry. It's getting toward sunset, so I'd better go and see Gaius Rabirius. I'll be defending him."

"With Hortensius?"

"And Lucius Cotta, I hope. He makes a useful first man up, and he works particularly well with Hortensius."

"You'll speak last, naturally."

"Naturally. An hour and a half should be ample, if Lucius Cotta and Hortensius will agree to less than an hour each."

But when Cicero saw the condemned man at his very luxurious and fortresslike residence on the Carinae, he discovered that Gaius Rabirius had other ideas for his defense.

The day had taken it out of the old man; he shook and blinked rheumily as he settled Cicero in a comfortable chair in his big and dazzling atrium. The senior consul gazed about like a rustic on his first visit to Rome, wondering whether he would be able to afford to adopt this kind of decor in his new house when he found the money to buy one; the room cried out to be copied in a consular's residence, though perhaps not so ostentatiously. Its ceiling was awash with glittering gem-studded golden stars, its walls had been sheeted in real gold, its pillars had been gold-sheathed too, and even the long shallow *impluvium* pool was tiled with gold squares.

"Like my atrium, eh?" asked Gaius Rabirius, looking lizardlike.

"Very much," said Cicero.

"Pity I don't entertain, eh?"

"A great pity. Though I see why you live in a fortress."

"Waste of money, entertaining. I put my fortune on my walls, safer than a bank if you live in a fortress."

"Don't the slaves try to peel it off?"

"Only if they fancy crucifixion."

"Yes, that would deter them."

The old man clenched both hands around the lion's head ends on the gilded arms of his gilded chair. "I love gold," he said. "Such a pretty color."

"Yes, it is."

"So you want to lead my defense, eh?"

"Yes, I do."

"And how much are you going to cost me?"

It was on the tip of Cicero's tongue to say a sheet of gold ten by ten would do nicely, thank you, but he smiled instead. "I regard your case as so important for the future of the Republic, Gaius Rabirius, that I will defend you for nothing."

"So you should, too."

And thus much for gratitude at obtaining the services of Rome's greatest advocate free of charge. Cicero swallowed. "Like all my fellow senators, Gaius Rabirius, I've known you for years, but I don't *know* a great deal about you aside from"—he cleared his throat—"er, what might be called common gossip. I shall need to ask you some questions now in order to prepare my speech."

"Won't give you any answers, so save your breath. Make it up."

"Out of common gossip?"

"Like my being in on Oppianicus's activities in Larinum, you mean? You did defend Cluentius."

"But never mentioned you, Gaius Rabirius."

"Good thing you didn't. Oppianicus died long before

Cluentius was tried, how would anyone know the true story? You did a lovely bit of embroidering lies, Cicero, which is why I don't mind your leading my defense. No, no, don't mind at all! You managed to imply that Oppianicus murdered more of his relations than rumor says Catilina has. All for gain! Yet Oppianicus didn't have walls of gold in his house. Interesting, eh?''

"I wouldn't know," said Cicero feebly. "I never saw his house."

"I own half of Apulia and I'm a hard man, but I don't deserve to be sent into exile for something Sulla put me and fifty other fellows up to. Lots of more important fish than me were on the Curia Hostilia roof. Lots of names like Servilius Caepio and Caecilius Metellus. Front bench most of them were, or would be in the future."

"Yes, I realize that."

"You want to go last before the jury votes."

"I always do. I thought Lucius Cotta first, then Quintus Hortensius, with me last."

But the old horror reared back, outraged. "Only *three*?" he gasped. "Oh no you don't! Want to grab all the glory, eh? I'm having seven of you. Seven's my lucky number."

"The judge in your case," said Cicero slowly and clearly, "will be Gaius Caesar, and the Glaucian format one *actio* only—no witnesses are willing to come forward to testify, so there's no point in two *actiones,* Gaius Caesar says. Caesar will allow the prosecution two hours, and the defense three hours. But if seven defense advocates are to speak, each of us will hardly get into stride before it's time to stop!"

"More likely less time will sharpen your presentation," said Gaius Rabirius adamantly. "That's the trouble with all you would-be-if-you-could-be fellows! Love to hear the sound of your voice. Two thirds of the words you dribble would be better not uttered at all—and that goes for you too, Marcus Cicero. Waffle, waffle."

I want to get out of here! thought Cicero wildly. I want to spit in his eye and tell him to go hire Apollo! Why did I ever ever ever put the idea into Caesar's head by using this awful old *mentula* as my example?

"Gaius Rabirius, *please* reconsider!"

"Won't. Absolutely won't, so there! I'm going to have Lucius Lucceius and the boy Curio, Aemilius Paullus, Publius Clodius, Lucius Cotta, Quintus Hortensius *and* you. Like it or lump it, Marcus Cicero, that is how it's going to be. Seven is my lucky number. Everyone says I'll go down, but *I* know I won't if I have seven on my team." He snorted with laughter. "Even better if each of you only spoke for one seventh of an hour! Hee hee!"

Cicero got up and left without another word.

But seven was indeed his lucky number. It suited Caesar to be the perfect *iudex,* scrupulous to a fault in accommodating the defense in all agreed Glaucian respects. They got their three hours to speak, Lucceius and young Curio nobly sacrificing enough of their time to permit both Hortensius and Cicero a full half hour each. But on the first day the trial commenced late and then ended early, which left Hortensius and Cicero to conclude Gaius Rabirius's defense on the ninth day of that awful December, the last day of Titus Labienus's tribunate of the plebs.

Meetings in the Centuries were at the mercy of the weather, as there was no kind of roofed structure to protect the *Quirites* from sun or rain or wind. Sun was by far the least tolerable, but in December, summer though the season actually was, a fine day might be bearable. Postponement was at the discretion of the presiding magistrate; some insisted upon holding elections (trials in the Centuries were extremely rare) no matter how hard the rain was pelting down, which may have been why Sulla had transferred the election month from November, more likely to be rainy, to July and the full heat of summer, traditionally dry.

Both days of Gaius Rabirius's trial turned out to be perfect: a clear sunny sky and a slightly chill breeze. Which ought to have predisposed the jury, four thousand strong, toward charity. Especially since the appellant was such a pitiful object as he stood huddled inside his toga producing a wonderful imitation of a tremulous palsy, both clawlike hands fastened around a support one of the lictors had rigged up for him. But the mood of the jury was ominous from the beginning, and Titus Labienus brilliant as he single-handedly ran his case for the allocated two hours, complete with actors wearing the masks of Saturninus and Quintus Labienus, and his two cousins sitting on full view weeping loudly throughout. There were also many voices whispering through the crush, perpetually reminding the First and Second Classes that their right to trial was at peril, that the conviction of Rabirius would teach men like Cicero and Cato to tread warily in future, and teach bodies like the Senate to stick to finance, wrangling and foreign affairs.

The defense fought hard, but had no trouble in seeing that the jury was not prepared to listen, let alone weep at the sight of poor little old Gaius Rabirius clinging to his perch. When the second day's proceedings commenced on time, Hortensius and Cicero knew they would have to be at the top of their form if Rabirius was to be exonerated. Unfortunately neither man was. The gout, which plagued a great many of those fish-fancying individuals addicted to the pleasures of the dining couch and the wine flagon, refused to leave Hortensius alone; he had besides been forced to complete his journey from Misenum at a pace not beneficial to the well-being of an exquisitely painful big toe. He spoke for his half hour glued to the same spot and leaning heavily on a stick, which didn't suit his oratory at all. After which Cicero delivered one of the limpest speeches of his career, constrained by the time limit and his consciousness that some at least of what he said would have to defend his own reputation rather than Rabirius's— in a carefully engineered way, of course.

Thus most of the day was still in reserve when Caesar cast the lots to see which Century of Juniors in the First Class would take the prerogative and vote first; only the thirty-one rural tribes could participate in this draw, and whichever tribe drew the lot was called upon to vote before the normal routine began. All activity was suspended then until the votes of this Century having *praerogativa* were counted and the result announced to the waiting Assembly. Tradition had it that whichever way the Juniors of the chosen rural tribe voted would reflect the outcome of the election. Or the trial. Therefore much depended upon which tribe drew the lot and set the precedent. Were it Cicero's tribe of Cornelia or Cato's tribe of Papiria, trouble was afoot.

"*Clustumina iuniorum!*" The Juniors of the *tribus Clustumina*.

The tribe of Pompey the Great—a good omen, thought Caesar as he left his tribunal to proceed inside the *saepta* and take his stand at the end of the right-hand bridge connecting voters with the baskets wherein their little wax-coated wooden tablets were deposited.

Nicknamed the Sheepfold because it bore a strong resemblance to the structure farmers used for culling and sorting their sheep, the *saepta* were a roofless maze of portable wooden palisades and corridors moved to suit the functions of a particular Assembly. The Centuries always voted in the *saepta* and sometimes the tribes held their elections there too, if the presiding magistrate felt that the Well of the Comitia was too small to handle the number of voters, and disliked using Castor's temple instead.

And here I approach my fate, thought Caesar soberly as he drew near the entrance of the odd-looking compound; the verdict will go whichever way the Clustumina Juniors poll, I know it in my very bones. LIBERO for acquittal, DAMNO for conviction. DAMNO, it *must* be DAMNO!

At which portentous moment he encountered Crassus lingering alongside the entrance looking less impassive than usual. Good! If this business did not move the immovable Crassus, then it would surely fail in its purpose. But he was moved, clearly moved.

"One day," said Crassus as Caesar paused, "I expect some yokel shepherd with a dye-stick in his hand to daub a spot of vermilion on my toga and tell me I can't go in to vote a second time when I try. They mark sheep, why not Romans?"

"Is *that* what you were just thinking?"

A tiny spasm passed across the Crassus face, an indication of surprise. "Yes. But then I decided marking us wasn't Roman."

"You're quite right," said Caesar, needing to exert every ounce of will he owned in order not to laugh, "though it might prevent the tribes from trotting through several times, especially those rascally urbanites from Esquilina and Suburana."

"What difference does it make?" asked Crassus, bored. "Sheep, Caesar, sheep. Voters are sheep. Baaaa!"

Caesar rushed inside still dying to laugh; that would teach him to believe men—even close friends like Crassus—appreciated the solemnity of this occasion!

The verdict of the Clustumina Juniors was DAMNO, and tradition indicated they were right as two by two the Centuries filed through the palisaded corridors, up over the two bridges, to deposit tablets bearing the letter D. Caesar's associate in the scrutineering was his *custos,* Metellus Celer; when both men were sure that the eventual verdict would indeed be DAMNO, Celer relinquished his bridge to Cosconius and left.

There followed a dangerously long wait—had Celer forgotten his mirror, had the sun gone behind a cloud, was his accomplice on the Janiculan Hill dozing? *Come on, Celer, hurry up!*

"ARM! ARM! INVADERS ARE UPON US! ARM! ARM! INVADERS ARE UPON US! ARM! ARM!"

Barely in the nick of time.

Thus ended the trial and appeal of old Gaius Rabirius, in a mad scramble of fleeing voters back behind the safety of the Servian Walls, there to arm and disperse in military Centuries to the places where the duty roster put them.

But Catilina and his army never came.

If Cicero plodded rather than ran back to the Palatine, he had every excuse. Hortensius had departed the moment his speech was done, carried moaning to his litter, but pride forbade the less secure and far less wellborn Cicero that luxury. Face sternly composed, he waited for his Century to vote, his tablet firmly marked with an L for LIBERO—not too many Ls among the voters on this terrible day! Not even in his own Century could he persuade its members to vote for acquittal. And was forced, face sternly composed, to witness the opinion of the men of the First Class: that thirty-seven years were not long enough to prevent damnation.

The clarion call to arms had burst upon him as a miracle, though like everyone else he half-expected Catilina to bypass the armies in the field against him, swoop on Rome. Despite which, he plodded. Death seemed suddenly preferable to the fate he now understood Caesar had in store for him. One day when Caesar or some tribune of the plebs minion deemed the time right, Marcus Tullius Cicero would stand where Gaius Rabirius stood, accused of treason; the most he could hope for was that it would be *maiestas,* not *perduellio.* Exile and the confiscation of all his property, the removal of his name from the roll of Roman citizens, his son and daughter branded as of a tarnished family. He had lost more than a battle; he had lost the war. He was Carbo, not Sulla.

But, he said to himself as finally he climbed those endless steps up to the Palatine, I must never admit it. I must never allow Caesar or anyone else to believe that I am a broken man. I saved my country, and I will maintain that until I die! Life goes on. I will behave as if nothing whatsoever threatens me, even in my mind.

Thus he greeted Catulus in the Forum the next day cheerfully; they were there to see the first performance of the new tribunes of the plebs. "I thank all the Gods for Celer!" he said, smiling.

"I wonder," said Catulus, "whether Celer lowered the red flag on his own initiative, or whether Caesar ordered it?"

"*Caesar* ordered it?" asked Cicero blankly.

"Grow up, Cicero! It can't have been any part of Caesar's intentions to convict Rabirius, that would have spoiled a sweet victory." Face pinched and drawn, Catulus looked very ill and very old. "I am so terribly afraid! He's like Ulysses, his life strand is so strong that it frays all those it rubs against. I am losing my *auctoritas,* and when

it's finally gone I'll have nowhere to go except into
death."

"Rubbish!" Cicero exclaimed warmly.

"Not rubbish, just unpalatable fact. You know, I
think I could forgive the man if only he wasn't so sure of
himself, so arrogant, so insufferably confident! My father
was a full Caesar, and there are echoes of him in this one.
But only echoes." He shivered. "This one has a far better
mind, and no brakes. No brakes at all. I am afraid."

"A pity Cato won't be here today," said Cicero to
change the subject. "Metellus Nepos will have no competition on the rostra. Odd how those brothers have suddenly espoused Popularist ideas."

"Blame Pompeius Magnus," said Catulus contemptuously.

As he had cherished a soft spot for Pompey ever since
their joint service under Pompey Strabo during the Italian
War, Cicero might have taken up cudgels in the absent
conqueror's defense; instead, he gasped in shock.
"Look!"

Catulus turned to see Marcus Porcius Cato marching
across the open space between the Pool of Curtius and the
Well of the Comitia, wearing a tunic beneath his toga.
Everyone who had noticed him was gaping, and not because of the tunic. From the top of his brow to where his
neck merged into his shoulders, there ran on right and left
sides ragged crimson stripes, puckered and oozing.

"Jupiter!" squawked Cicero.

"Oh, how I love him!" cried Catulus, almost running
to meet Cato, and taking his right hand. "Cato, Cato, why
did you come?"

"Because I am a tribune of the plebs and today is the
first day of my term," said Cato in his normal stentorian
tones.

"But your face!" Cicero protested.

"Faces mend, wrong acts don't. Were I not on the
rostra to contend with Nepos, he'd run riot." And to the
sound of applause he ascended the rostra to take his place
with the other nine men about to enter office. Not that he

acknowledged the acclamation; he was too busy glaring at
Metellus Nepos. Pompey's man. Scum!

Because the whole People (patricians as well as plebeians) did not elect the tribunes of the plebs and because
they served only the interests of the plebeian part, meetings of the Plebeian Assembly were not ''official'' in the
same way as meetings of the Popular or the Centuriate
Assembly. Therefore they began and ended with scant ceremony; the auspices were not taken, nor the ritual prayers
said. These omissions added considerably to the popularity
of the Plebeian Assembly. Things got off to a rousing start,
no boring litanies and clucking augurs to put up with.

Today's convocation of the Plebeian Assembly was
extremely well attended, between the festering sore of executions without trial and the balm of knowing sparks
were going to fly. The old tribunes of the plebs exited
quite gracefully, Labienus and Rullus getting all the
cheers. After which the meeting proper began.

Metellus Nepos got in first, which surprised no one;
Cato was a retaliator rather than an initiator. Nepos's subject was juicy—the execution of citizens without trial—
and his presentation of it splendid from irony to metaphor
to hyperbole.

''Therefore I propose a plebiscite so gentle, so merciful, so unobtrusive that no man present can possibly do
other than agree to vote it into law!'' Nepos said at the
end of a long speech which had reduced its audience now
to tears, now to laughter, now to deep thought. ''No death
sentences, no exile, no fines. Fellow members of the Plebs,
all I propose is that any man who has executed Roman
citizens without trial be forbidden ever to speak in public
again! Isn't that sweet justice? A voice forever stilled, a
power to move masses rendered impotent! Will you join
me? Will you muzzle megalomaniacs and monsters?''

It was Mark Antony who led the cheering, which
rolled down upon Cicero and Catulus like an avalanche.
Only Cato's voice could have surmounted it; only Cato's
voice did.

''I interpose my veto!'' he howled.

''To protect your own neck!'' said Nepos scornfully

as the roar died away so everyone could hear what followed. He looked Cato up and down with ostentatious
surprise. "Not that there's too much left of your neck,
Cato! What happened? Did you forget to pay the whore
before you left, or did you need her to do that to you
before anything happened below your navel?"

"How can you call yourself a noble Caecilius Metellus?" Cato asked. "Go home, Nepos, go home and
wash the excrement from your mouth! Why should we be
forced to listen to putrid innuendo in a holy assemblage
of Roman men?"

"Why should we be forced to lie down under a flimsy
senatorial decree which gives the men in power the right
to execute men more Roman by far than they are themselves? I never heard that Lentulus Sura had a slave for a
great-grandam, or that Gaius Cethegus's father still had
pig shit behind his ears!"

"I refuse to engage in a slanging match, Nepos, and
that is that! You can rant and rave from here until next
December, and it won't make a scrap of difference!" bellowed Cato, the stripes on his face standing out like dark
red ropes. "I interpose my veto, and there is nothing you
can say will alter that!"

"Of course you interpose your veto! If you neglect
to, Cato, you'll never speak in public again! It was you
and no one else who talked the Senate of Rome around
from clemency to barbarism! Not terribly surprising, really. Your great-grandam was a moist barbarian morsel,
so they say. Very tasty for a silly old man from Tusculum
who ought to have stayed in Tusculum and tickled his
pigs, not gone to Rome to tickle a barbarian piggy-
wiggy!"

And if that can't cause a fight, thought Nepos, nothing on earth can! If I were he, I'd be insisting on daggers
at close quarters. The Plebs are lapping the insults up as
dogs do vomit, and that means I'm winning. Hit me, Cato,
punch me in the eye!

Cato did nothing of the kind. With an heroically Stoic
effort only he knew the cost of, he turned and retreated to
the back of the rostra. For a moment the crowd was

tempted to boo this craven act, but Ahenobarbus got in before Mark Antony and began to cheer madly at this magnificent display of self-control and contempt.

Lucius Calpurnius Bestia saved the day and the victory for Nepos by beginning to attack Cicero and his Senatus Consultum Ultimum in the most savagely witty way. The Plebs sighed ecstatically, and the meeting proceeded with plenty of vim and vigor.

When Nepos thought the audience had had enough of citizen execution, he changed his tack.

"Speaking of a certain Lucius Sergius Catilina," said he in a conversational tone, "it has not escaped my attention that absolutely nothing is happening on the war front. There they are scattered around Etruria, Apulia and Picenum, beautifully separated by many lusciously safe miles, Catilina and his so-called adversaries. Who have we got, now?" he asked, and held up his right hand with fingers splayed wide. "Well, there's Hybrida and his throbbing toe." He tucked one finger away. "There's the second Man of Chalk, Metellus of the goaty branch." Away with another finger. "And there's a King up there, Rex the doughty foe of—who? *Who?* Oh, petunias, I can't seem to remember!" The only digits left were thumb and little finger. At which point he abandoned his count and used the hand to slap his forehead loudly. "Oh! Oh! How could I forget my own big brother? He's supposed to be there, but he came to Rome to participate in a right act! I daresay I will just have to forgive him, the naughty fellow."

This sally brought Quintus Minucius Thermus forward. "Where are you going, Nepos?" he asked. "What's the mischief this time?"

"Mischief? *I?*" Nepos recoiled theatrically. "Thermus, Thermus, don't let the fire under your big arse bring you to the boil, please! With a name like that, tepid *suits* you, my darling one!" he fluted, fluttering his eyelashes at Thermus outrageously while the Plebs howled with laughter. "No, sweetheart, I was just trying to remind our excellent fellow plebeians here that we *do* have some armies in the field to fight Catilina—when they find him, that is. The north of our peninsula is a big place, easy to get lost in. Especially considering the morning fog on Father Tiber—makes it hard for them to find a place to empty their porphyry chamber pots!''

"Do you have any suggestions?'' asked Thermus dangerously. He was striving valiantly to follow Cato's example, but Nepos was now blowing him kisses, and the crowd was hysterical.

"Well, piggykins, as a matter of fact I do!'' said Nepos brightly. "I was just standing watching the patterns on Cato's face—*pipinna, pipinna!*—when another face swam before my eyes—no, dear one, not yours! See over there? That soldierly man on the plinth fourth from the end among the busts of the consuls? Lovely face, I always think! So fair, such *beautiful* blue eyes! Not as gorgeous as yours, of course, but not bad all the same.'' Nepos cupped his hands around his mouth and hollered. "Ho there, *Quiris*—yes, you, right at the back near the busts of the consuls! Can you read the name on that one? Yes, that's right, the one with the gold hair and the big blue eyes! What's that? Pompeius? Which Pompeius? Manus, did you say? Magus, is it? Oh, *Magnus*! Thank you, *Quiris,* thank you! The name is Pompeius Magnus!''

Thermus clenched his fists. "Don't you dare!'' he snarled.

"Dare what?'' asked Nepos innocently. "Though I do admit that Pompeius Magnus dares anything. Does he have any peers on a battlefield? I think not. And he's over in Syria getting ready to come home, all his battles finished. The East is conquered, and Gnaeus Pompeius Magnus did the conquering. Which is more than you can say for the goaty Metellus and the kingly Rex! I wish I had gone to war with either of them rather than with Pompeius Magnus! What piddling foes they must have encountered to qualify for triumphs! I could have been a genuine hero if I'd gone to war with them, I could have been like Gaius Caesar and hidden my thinning hair with a chaplet of oak leaves!''

Nepos paused to salute Caesar, standing on the Curia Hostilia steps wearing his chaplet of oak leaves.

"I suggest, *Quirites,* that we bring in a small plebiscite to fetch Pompeius Magnus home, and give him a special command to crush the reason why we're still enduring a never-ending Senatus Consultum Ultimum! I say, bring Pompeius Magnus home to finish what the gouty one can't even begin—Catilina!"

And the cheering started again until Cato, Thermus, Fabricius and Lucius Marius interposed their vetoes.

President of the College and therefore convener of the meeting, Metellus Nepos decided enough had been done. He closed it well satisfied with what he had accomplished, and went off arm in arm with his brother, Celer, cheerfully acknowledging the plaudits of the overjoyed Plebs.

"How would you," said Caesar as he joined them, "like to be going bald when your cognomen means a fine thick head of hair?"

"Your *tata* shouldn't have married an Aurelia Cottae," said Nepos unrepentantly. "Never met an Aurelius Cotta yet who didn't look like an egg on top by the time he was forty."

"You know, Nepos, until today I never realized that you had such a talent for demagoguery. Up there on the rostra you had *style*. They ate out of your hand. And *I* loved your performance so much I have forgiven you for the slap at my hair."

"I thoroughly enjoyed myself, I must confess. However, I'll never get a thing done with Cato bawling out his veto."

"I agree. You'll have an utterly frustrating year of it. But at least when it comes time to stand for higher office, the electors will remember you with great affection. I might even give you my vote."

The Brothers Metelli were going to the Palatine, but strolled the short distance up the Via Sacra to the Domus Publica to keep Caesar company.

"I take it you're returning to the fray in Etruria?" Caesar asked Celer.

"Off tomorrow at the crack of dawn. I'd like to think I'll get a chance to fight Catilina, but our commander-in-chief Hybrida wants me to maintain a holding action on the borders of Picenum. Too far for Catilina to march without stumbling over someone else first.'' Celer squeezed his brother's wrist fondly. "The bit about morning fog on Father Tiber was wonderful, Nepos.''

"Are you serious about bringing Pompeius home?'' asked Caesar.

"In practical terms there's not much sense in it,'' said Nepos seriously, "and I'm prepared to admit to you that I mostly said it to watch the rump react. However, if he left his army behind and came home alone he could make the trip in a month or two, depending upon how quickly he got the summons.''

"In two months even Hybrida will have brought Catilina to battle,'' Caesar said.

"You're right, of course. But after listening to Cato today, I'm not sure I want to spend a whole year in Rome being vetoed. You summed it up when you said I'd have an utterly frustrating time of it.'' Nepos sighed. "One cannot reason with Cato! He won't be talked round to anyone else's point of view no matter how much sense it makes, and no one can intimidate him either.''

"They say,'' from Celer, "that he even had good training for the day when his fellow tribunes of the plebs get so incensed with him that they hold him out over the end of the Tarpeian Rock. When Cato was two years old the Marsian leader Silo used to hold him out over a cluster of sharp rocks and threaten to drop him, but the little monster just hung there and defied him.''

"Yes, that's Cato,'' said Caesar grinning. "It's a true story, so Servilia vows. Now back to your tribunate, Nepos. Do I read you alright? Are you thinking of resigning?''

"More of creating a terrific fuss, forcing the Senate to invoke the Senatus Consultum Ultimum against me.''

"By harping on bringing Pompeius home.''

"Oh, I don't think *that* would boot Catulus's rump over the edge, Caesar!''

"Exactly.''

"However,'' said Nepos demurely, "if I were to propose a bill to the full People to fire Hybrida for incompetence and bring our Magnus home with the same imperium and dispositions as he's had in the East, that would start them rumbling. Then if I added a little extra to the bill—say that Magnus be permitted to keep his imperium and his armies in Etruria and stand for the consulship next year *in absentia*—do you think that would be enough to cause a major eruption?''

Caesar began to laugh. ''I'd say the whole of Italia would be covered in fiery clouds!''

''You're known as a meticulous lawyer, Pontifex Maximus. Would you be willing to help me work out the details?''

''I might.''

''Let's keep it in mind just in case January rolls round to find Hybrida still unable to close with Catilina. I'd love to exit from the tribunician stage under interdiction!''

''You'll stink worse than the inside of a legionary's helmet, Nepos, but only to people like Catulus and Metellus Scipio.''

''Bear in mind too, Caesar, that it will have to be the whole People, which means I can't convoke the meeting. I'll need at least a praetor for that.''

''I wonder,'' Caesar asked Celer, ''which praetor your brother could be thinking of?''

''No idea,'' said Celer solemnly.

''And after you're forced to flee under interdiction, Nepos, you'll go east to join Pompeius Magnus.''

''East to join Pompeius Magnus,'' Nepos agreed. ''That way they won't have the courage to enforce the interdiction when I come home with the selfsame Pompeius Magnus.''

The Brothers Metelli saluted Caesar affectionately and went their way, leaving Caesar staring after them. Excellent allies! The trouble was, he thought with a sigh as he let himself inside his front door, that one never knew when things might change. The allies of this month could turn out to be the enemies of next month. One never knew.

*   *   *

Julia was easy. When Caesar sent for her, she hurled herself at him and hugged him.

"*Tata,* I understand everything, even why you couldn't see me for five days. How brilliant you are! You've put Cicero in his place for good and all."

"Do you think so? I find most people don't know their place well enough to find it when someone like me puts them in it."

"Oh," said Julia doubtfully.

"And what about Servilia?"

She sat on his lap and began to kiss his white fans. "What is there to say, *tata*? Speaking of places, it isn't *my* place to stand in judgement on you, and I at least do know where my place is. Brutus feels as I do. We intend to go on as if nothing has changed." She shrugged. "Really, nothing has."

"What a wise little bird I have in my nest!" Caesar's arms tightened; he squeezed her so hard she had to gasp for breath. "Julia, no father could ever have asked for such a daughter! I am blessed. I wouldn't accept Minerva and Venus rolled in one as a replacement for you."

In all her life she had never been as happy as she was at that moment, but was a wise enough little bird not to weep. Men disliked women who wept; men liked women who laughed and made them laugh. To be a man was so very difficult—all that public strife, forced to fight tooth and nail for everything, enemies lurking everywhere. A woman who gave the men in her life more joy than anguish would never lack for love, and Julia knew now that she would never lack for love. She was not Caesar's daughter for nothing; some things Aurelia could not teach her, but they were things she had learned for herself.

"I take it then," said Caesar, cheek on her hair, "that our Brutus won't punch me in the eye when we next meet?"

"Of course he won't! If Brutus thought the worse of you for it, he would have to think the worse of his mother."

"Very true."

"Have you seen Servilia during the past five days, *tata*?"

"No."

A little silence fell; Julia stirred, screwed up her courage to speak.

"Junia Tertia is your daughter."

"I believe so."

"I wish I could know her!"

"It isn't possible, Julia. *I* don't know her."

"Brutus says she's like her mother in nature."

"If that is the case," said Caesar, tipping Julia off his lap and getting to his feet, "it's better that you don't know her."

"How can you be together with someone you dislike?"

"Servilia?"

"Yes."

His wonderful smile bloomed for her, his eyes creased up at their corners and obliterated those white fans. "If I knew that, little bird, I would be as good a father as you are a daughter. Who knows? I don't. Sometimes I think even the Gods don't begin to understand. It may be that all of us search for some kind of emotional completion in another person, though I believe we never find it. And our bodies make demands at loggerheads with our minds, just to complicate things. As for Servilia"—he shrugged wryly—"she's my disease."

And he was gone. Julia stood for a moment very still, her heart full. Today she had crossed a bridge, the bridge between girlhood and adulthood. Caesar had held out his hand to her, and helped her to his side of it. He had opened his innermost self to her, and somehow she knew he had never done that with anyone before, even with her mother. When she did move she danced, and was still dancing when she reached the hall outside Aurelia's rooms.

"Julia! Dancing is vulgar!"

And that, thought Julia, was *avia*. Suddenly she felt so sorry for her grandmother that she flung both arms about Aurelia's stiffening form and kissed her smackingly on both cheeks. Poor, poor *avia*! How much in life she must have missed, and no wonder she and *tata* quarreled with such regularity!

"It would be more convenient for me if you came to my house in future," said Servilia to Caesar as she marched into his rooms on the lower Vicus Patricii.

"It isn't your house, Servilia, it's Silanus's, and the poor wretch has enough trouble looming without having to watch me invade his house to copulate with his wife!" snapped Caesar. "I enjoyed doing that to Cato, but I won't do it to Silanus. For a great patrician lady, you sometimes have the ethics of a brat from the Suburan gutter!"

"Have it your own way," said Servilia, sitting down.

To Caesar this reaction was significant; dislike Servilia he might, but by now he knew her very well, and the fact that she chose to sit fully clad rather than automatically stood to disrobe herself told him she was not nearly as sure of her ground as her attitude suggested. So he sat down too, in a chair from which he could watch her and in which she could see him from head to toe. His pose was graceful and curule, left foot back, right extended, left arm draped along the chair back, right hand lying in his lap, head level but chin up.

"By rights I ought to strangle you," he said after a pause.

"Silanus thought you'd chop me into pieces and feed me to the wolves."

"Did he now? That's interesting."

"Oh, he was all on your side! How you men do stick together! He actually had the temerity to be angry with *me* because—though I fail to see why!—my letter to you forced him to vote to execute the conspirators. A nonsense if ever I heard one!"

"You fancy yourself a political expert, my dear, but the truth is that you're a political ignoramus. You can never watch senatorial politics in action, and there's a vast difference between senatorial politics and comitial politics. I suppose men go about their public life armed with the knowledge that sooner or later they'll wear a pair of horns, but no man expects to have to don his horns in the Senate during a critical debate,'' said Caesar harshly. ''Of course you forced him to vote for execution! Had he voted with me, the whole House would have assumed that he was my pander. Silanus is not a well man, but he is a proud one. Why else do you think he kept silent after he was informed what was occurring between us? A note read by half the Senate, and that the important half? You really did rub his nose in it, didn't you?''

''I see you're on his side as much as he's on yours.''

He gave an explosive sigh and rolled his eyes ceilingward. ''The only side I'm on, Servilia, is my own.''

''You would be!''

A silence fell; he broke it.

''Our children surpass us for maturity. They've taken it very well, and very sensibly.''

''Have they?'' she asked indifferently.

''You've not spoken to Brutus about it?''

''Not since the day it happened and Cato arrived to inform Brutus that his mother is a slut. 'Strumpet' is the word he used, actually.'' She smiled reminiscently. ''I made mincemeat of his face.''

''Ah, so that's the answer! Next time I see Cato I must tell him that I feel for him. I too have sampled your claws.''

''Only where the marks are not on public display.''

''I see I must be thankful for small mercies.''

She leaned forward eagerly. ''Did he look frightful? Did I scar him badly?''

''Shockingly. He looked as if a harpy had been at him.'' A grin came. ''Come to think of it, 'harpy' is a better word for you than 'slut' or 'strumpet.' However, don't congratulate yourself too much. Cato has good skin, so in time the marks will disappear.''

''You don't scar easily either.''

''Because Cato and I have the same kind of skin. War experience teaches a man what will stay and what will go.'' Another explosive sigh. ''What am I going to do with you, Servilia?''

''Perhaps to ask that question is putting your left shoe

on your right foot, Caesar. The initiative might belong to
me, not to you.''

That provoked a chuckle. ''Rubbish,'' he said gently.

She went pale. ''You mean I love you more than you
love me.''

''I don't love you at all.''

''Then why are we together?''

''You please me in bed, which is rare in women of
your class. I like the combination. And you have more
between your ears than most women, even though you're
a harpy.''

''Is that where you think it is?'' she asked, desperate
to get him away from her failings.

''What?''

''Our thinking apparatus.''

''Ask any army surgeon or soldier and he'll tell you.
It's blows to the head damage our thinking apparatus. *Cerebrum,* the brain. What all the philosophers argue about
isn't *cerebrum,* it's *animus.* The animating spirit, the soul.
The part which can conceive ideas bearing no relation to
our senses, from music to geometry. The part which soars.
That's in a place we do not know. Head, chest, belly . . .''
He smiled. ''It might even live in our big toes. Logical,
when you think of how gout can destroy Hortensius.''

''I believe you have answered my question. I now
know why we are together.''

''Why?''

''Because of that. I am your hone. You sharpen your
wits on me, Caesar.''

She got out of the chair and began to remove her
clothing. Suddenly Caesar wanted her badly, but not to
cradle her or treat her tenderly. One didn't tame a harpy
by kindness. A harpy was a grotesque one took on the
floor with teeth in her neck and her claws locked behind
her back, then took again, and again.

Rough usage always did tame her; she became soft
and slightly kittenish after he transferred her from the floor
to the bed.

''Have you ever loved any woman?'' she asked then.

"Cinnilla," he said abruptly, and closed his eyes on tears.

"Why?" asked the harpy. "There was nothing special about her, she wasn't witty or intelligent. Though she was patrician."

In answer he turned on his side away from her, and pretended to nap. Talk to Servilia about Cinnilla? Never!

Why did I love her so, if that is what it was I felt? Cinnilla was mine *from the time I took her hand and led her home from the house of Gaius Marius in the days when he had become a demented shadow of himself. How old was I, thirteen? And she was all of seven, the adorable little thing. So dark and plump and sweet . . . The way her upper lip folded under when she smiled, and she smiled a lot. Gentleness personified. No cause of her own, unless her cause was I. Did I love her so much because we were children together first? Or was it that in chaining me to a priesthood and marrying me to a child he didn't know, old Gaius Marius gifted me with something so precious I will never meet it again?*

He sat up convulsively and slapped Servilia so hard on the behind that she wore the mark for the rest of the day.

"Time to go," he said. "Go on, Servilia, go! Go now!"

She went without a word, and she hurried, something in his face filling her with the same kind of terror she inspired in Brutus. As soon as she had gone Caesar turned his head into the pillow and wept as he had not wept since Cinnilla died.

The Senate didn't meet again that year. Not an unusual state of affairs, as no formal schedule of meetings existed; they were called by a magistrate, and usually by the consul with the *fasces* for that month. It being December, Antonius Hybrida was supposed to be in the chair, but Cicero was filling in for him, and Cicero had had his fill. Nor was there any news from Etruria worth ferreting the senators out of their burrows. The craven lot! Besides, the senior consul just couldn't be sure what else Caesar

might do if given half a chance. Every comitial day Metellus Nepos kept trying to fire Hybrida, and Cato kept
vetoing him. Atticus and Cicero's other knightly adherents
in the Eighteen were working hard to bring people around
to the Senate's point of view, yet there were many dark
faces and darker looks on all sides.

The one factor Cicero had not counted on was the
young men; deprived of their beloved stepfather, the Antonii had enlisted the members of the Clodius Club. Under
normal circumstances no one of Cicero's age and standing
would have noticed them, but the conspiracy of Catilina
and its outcome had pushed them out of the shadows their
youth created. And what huge clout they had! Oh, not
among the First Class, but at all levels below that, certainly.

Young Curio was a case in point. Wild to a fault, he
had even been imprisoned in his room by the elder Curio,
at his wits' end to cope with the consequences of Curio's
drinking, gambling and sexual exploits. That hadn't
worked. Mark Antony had broken him out and the two of
them had been seen in a low tavern losing at dice, drinking, and kissing voluptuously. Now young Curio had a
cause, and suddenly he displayed a side not associated
with idle vice. Young Curio was cleverer by far than his
father, and a brilliant orator. Every day he was in the Forum making trouble.

Then there was Decimus Junius Brutus Albinus, son
and heir of a family bound by tradition to oppose every
Popularist cause; Decimus Brutus Callaicus had been one
of the most obdurate enemies of the Brothers Gracchi, allied to the non-Gracchan branch of the clan Sempronius,
cognominated Tuditanus. *Amicitia* persisted from one generation to the next, which meant that young Decimus Brutus should have been supporting men like Catulus, not
destructive agitators like Gaius Caesar. Instead, there was
Decimus Brutus in the Forum egging Metellus Nepos on,
cheering Caesar when he appeared, and making himself
absolutely charming to all sorts of people from freedmen
to the Fourth Class. Another extremely intelligent and capable young man who apparently was lost to the principles

upheld by the *boni*—and kept low company!

As for Publius Clodius—well . . . Since the trial of the Vestals a full ten years earlier, everyone had known Clodius to be Catilina's most vocal enemy. Yet here he was, complete with hordes and hordes of clients (how did he come to have more clients than his oldest brother, Appius Claudius?), stirring up trouble for Catilina's enemies! Usually squiring his wretched wife on his arm, in itself a colossal affront! Women didn't frequent the Forum; women didn't listen to comitial meetings from a prominent place; women didn't raise their voices to shout encouragement and bawdy abuse. Fulvia did all of those—and the crowd apparently loved it, if for no other reason than that she was the granddaughter of Gaius Gracchus, who had left no male progeny.

Until the execution of their stepfather, no one had ever taken the Antonii seriously. Or was it that men looked no further than the scandals trailing in their wake? None of the three owned the ability or brilliance of young Curio or Decimus Brutus or Clodius, but they had something in its way more appealing to the crowd, the same fascination exerted by outstanding gladiators or charioteers: sheer physical power, a dominance arising out of brute strength. Mark Antony was in the habit of appearing clad only in a tunic, which garb allowed people to see the massive calves and biceps, the width of the shoulders, the flatness of the belly, the vault of the chest, the forearms like oak; he also pulled that tunic very tightly across his front, thereby displaying the outline of his penis so revealingly that the whole world knew it was not looking at padding. Women sighed and swooned; men swallowed miserably and wished they were dead. He was very ugly in the face, with a big beaky nose which strove to meet a huge and aggressive chin across a small but thick-lipped mouth; his eyes were too close together and his cheeks fleshy. But the auburn hair was thick, crisp and curling, and women joked that it was terrific fun to find his mouth for a kiss without being turtle-nipped by his nose and chin. In short, Mark Antony (and his brothers, though to a lesser extent) didn't have to be a great orator or a courtroom eel; he simply rolled along like the awesome monster he was.

Several very good reasons why Cicero chose not to convene the Senate for the rest of his year—had Caesar himself not been sufficient cause to lie low.

However, on the last day of December as the sun neared its rest, the senior consul went to meet the People in the Popular Assembly and lay down his insignia of office. He had worked long and hard on his valediction, intending to exit from the consular stage with a speech the like of which Rome had never heard. His honor demanded it; so did his self-esteem. Even if Antonius Hybrida had been in Rome he would have presented no competition, but as it was, Cicero had the stage to himself. How lovely!

"*Quirites,*" he began in his most mellifluous voice, "this has been a momentous year for Rome—"

"Veto, veto!" shouted Metellus Nepos from the Comitia well. "I veto any speeches, Cicero! No man who executed Roman citizen men without a trial can be allowed the opportunity to justify what he did! Shut your mouth, Cicero! Take the oath and get off the rostra!"

For a long moment there was absolute silence. Of course the senior consul had hoped that the turnout would be large enough to warrant transferring the venue from the Well of the Comitia to the rostra of Castor's temple, but it was not. Atticus had worked to some effect; all those knightly supporters of Cicero were present, and looked to outnumber the opposition. But that Metellus Nepos would veto something as traditional as the outgoing consul's right to speak had not occurred to Cicero. And there could be no way around it, numbers or not. For the second time in a short period, Cicero wished with all his heart that Sulla's law forbidding the tribunician veto was still in effect. But it was not. How then could he say something? Anything? *Everything!*

In the end he began to swear his oath according to the age-old formula, then as it concluded: "I also swear that by my single-handed efforts I saved my country, that I, Marcus Tullius Cicero, consul of the Senate and People of Rome, have ensured the maintenance of legal government and preserved Rome from her enemies!"

Whereupon Atticus began to cheer, and his followers

took it up resoundingly. Nor were the young men present
to boo and bay; it was New Year's Eve, apparently they
had better things to do than watch Cicero relinquish office.
Some sort of win, thought Marcus Tullius Cicero as he
descended the rostral steps and held out his arms to Atticus. The next thing he was shoulder-high, a wreath of
laurel sat on his head, and the crowd chaired him all the
way to the Ringmakers' Stairs. A pity Caesar wasn't there
to witness it. But, like all the incoming magistrates, Caesar
could not attend. Tomorrow was his day, when he and the
new magistrates would be sworn into office in the temple
of Jupiter Optimus Maximus and begin what (in Caesar's
case, anyway) Cicero very much feared would be a calam-
itous year for the *boni*.

The morrow confirmed that foreboding. No sooner
was the formal swearing-in ceremony concluded and the
calendar adjusted than the new *praetor urbanus,* Gaius Julius Caesar, left that first meeting of the Senate to hurry
to the Well of the Comitia and call the Popular Assembly
into session. That it was prearranged was obvious; only
those of Popularist view were waiting for him, from the
young men to his senatorial adherents and the inevitable
throng of men little better than Head Count, relics of all
those years in the Subura—skullcapped Jews with the citizenship who with Caesar's connivance had managed to
get themselves enrolled in a rural tribe, freedmen, a multitude of small tradesmen and businessmen also inserted
into rural tribes, and on the fringes wives and sisters and
daughters and aunts.

The naturally deep voice vanished; Caesar adopted
that high, clear tenor tone which carried so well as far as
the crowd extended. ''People of Rome, I have called you
here today to witness my protest against an insult to Rome
of such magnitude that the Gods are weeping! Over twenty
years ago the temple of Jupiter Optimus Maximus burned
down. In my youth I was *flamen Dialis,* the special priest
of Jupiter Optimus Maximus, and now in my prime I am
the Pontifex Maximus, dedicated to the service of the
Great God once again. Today I have had to swear my oath
of office inside the new premises Lucius Cornelius Sulla

Felix commissioned Quintus Lutatius Catulus to build eighteen years ago. And, People of Rome, I was ashamed! Ashamed! I abased myself before the Great God, I wept beneath the shelter of my *toga praetexta,* I could not look up at the face of the Great God's exquisite new statue— commissioned *and paid for* by my uncle Lucius Aurelius Cotta and his colleague in the consulship, Lucius Manlius Torquatus! Yes, until scant days ago the temple of Jupiter Optimus Maximus even lacked its effigy of the Great God!''

Never insignificant even in the midst of the largest crush of people, Caesar now that he was urban praetor seemed nonetheless to have grown both in stature and magnificence; the sheer force which lived within him poured out of him, caught hold of every listener, dominated, enthralled.

''How can this be?'' he asked the crowd. ''Why is the guiding spirit of Rome so neglected, so insulted, so *denigrated*? Why are the temple walls devoid of the greatest art our times can offer? Why are there no gorgeous gifts from foreign kings and princes? Why do Minerva and Juno exist as air, as *numina,* as nothings? No statue of either one, even in cheap baked clay! Where is the gilt? Where are the golden chariots? Where the glorious moldings, the fabulous floors?''

He paused, drew a breath, looked like thunder. ''I can tell you, *Quirites*! The money for them resides in Catulus's purse! All the millions of sesterces the Treasury of Rome has supplied to Quintus Lutatius Catulus have never left his personal bank account! I have been to the Treasury and asked for the records, and there are none! None, that is, describing the fate of the many, many sums paid out to Catulus over the years! Sacrilege! That is what it amounts to! The man entrusted with re-creating the house of Jupiter Optimus Maximus in greater beauty and glory than ever before has scuttled off with the funds!''

The diatribe went on while the audience grew more indignant; what Caesar said was true, hadn't everyone seen it for himself?

Down from the Capitol came Quintus Lutatius Catulus at a run, followed by Cato, Bibulus and the rest of the *boni*.

"There he is!" shouted Caesar, pointing. "Look at him! Oh, the gall! The temerity of the man! However, *Quirites,* you have to grant him courage, don't you? Look at the barefaced swindler run! How can he move so fast with all that State money dragging him down? Quintus Lutatius Peculatus the embezzler! Embezzler!"

"What is the meaning of this, *praetor urbanus*?" Catulus demanded, breathless. "Today is *feriae,* you can't call a meeting!"

"As Pontifex Maximus I am at perfect liberty to convene the People to discuss a religious topic at any time on any day! And this is definitely a religious topic. I am explaining to the People why Jupiter Optimus Maximus lacks a fit home, Catulus."

Catulus had heard that derisive "Embezzler!" and needed no further information to draw the correct conclusions. "Caesar, I will have your skin for this!" he cried, shaking a fist.

"Oh!" gasped Caesar, shrinking back in mock alarm. "Do you hear him, *Quirites*? I expose him as a sacrilegious wolfer-down of Rome's public moneys, and he threatens to flay me! Come, Catulus, why not admit what everyone in Rome knows for a fact? The proof is there for all the world to see—more proof by far than you had to offer when you accused me of treason in the House! All any man has to do is look at the walls, the floors, the empty plinths and the absence of gifts to see what humiliation you have inflicted on Jupiter Optimus Maximus!"

Catulus stood bereft of words, for in truth he had no idea how in an angry public meeting he could possibly explain his position—the position *Sulla* had put him in! People never had any real concept of the horrifying expense involved in building an edifice as huge and eternal as the temple of Jupiter Optimus Maximus. Whatever he tried to say in his own defense would come out sounding like a tissue of laughably feeble lies.

"People of Rome," said Caesar to the glowering crowd, "I move that we take up in *contio* the consideration of two laws, one to impeach Quintus Lutatius Catulus for the embezzlement of State funds, and another to try him for sacrilege!''

''I veto any discussion of either matter!'' roared Cato.

Whereupon Caesar shrugged, held out his hands in a gesture which clearly asked what any man could do once Cato started to veto, and cried loudly, ''I dismiss this meeting! Go home, *Quirites,* and offer sacrifices to the Great God—pray that he allows Rome to continue standing when men steal his funds and break the sacred contracts!''

He came down from the rostra lightly, gave the *boni* a happy grin, and walked away up the Sacra Via surrounded by hundreds of indignant people, all obviously pleading with him not to close the matter, to go ahead and prosecute Catulus.

Bibulus became aware that Catulus was breathing jerkily and in great gasps, and moved to support him. ''Quickly!'' he snapped to Cato and Ahenobarbus, shrugging himself out of his toga. The three of them made a stretcher of it, forced the protesting Catulus to lie down, and with Metellus Scipio on the fourth corner carried Catulus home. His face was more grey than blue, a good sign perhaps, but it was with relief that they got the leader of the *boni* home and into his bed, wife Hortensia fluttering distractedly. He would be all right—this time.

''But how much more can poor Quintus Catulus take?'' Bibulus asked as they emerged into the Clivus Victoriae.

''Somehow,'' said Ahenobarbus between his teeth, ''we have to shut that *irrumator* Caesar up for good! If there's no other way, then let it be murder!''

''Don't you mean *fellator*?'' asked Gaius Piso, so afraid of the look on Ahenobarbus's face that he groped for anything to lighten the atmosphere. Not normally a prudent man, he sensed disaster now, and had a thought for his own fate.

''Caesar on the giving end?'' asked Bibulus scornfully. ''Not he! Uncrowned kings don't give, they take!''

''Here we go again,'' sighed Metellus Scipio. ''Stop

Caesar this, and stop Caesar that. But we never do.''

"We can, and we will," said silvery, diminutive Bibulus. "A little bird told me that very shortly Metellus Nepos is going to propose that we bring Pompeius back from the East to deal with Catilina—and that he should be given *imperium maius*. Imagine that, if you can! A general inside Italia owning a degree of imperium never before given to anyone save a dictator!"

"How does that help us with Caesar?" asked Metellus Scipio.

"Nepos can't bring a bill like that before the Plebs, he'll have to go to the People. Do you think for a moment that Silanus or Murena would consent to convoke a meeting designed to award Pompeius an *imperium maius*? No, it will be Caesar."

"So?"

"So we'll make sure the meeting is a violent one. Then, as Caesar will be responsible at law for any violence, we'll charge him under the *lex Plautia de vi*. In case you've forgotten, Scipio, *I* am the praetor in charge of the Violence Court! Not only am I willing to pervert justice in any way I can to get Caesar sent down, I'd even walk up to Cerberus and give each head a pat!"

"Bibulus, that's brilliant!" said Gaius Piso.

"And for once," said Cato, "there will be no protestations from me that justice is not being done. If Caesar is convicted, justice *will* be done!"

"Catulus is dying," said Cicero abruptly. He had hung on the outskirts of the group, painfully aware that no member of it considered him of sufficient moment to include him in their plotting. He, the lodger from Arpinum. Savior of his country, yet forgotten the day after leaving office.

The rest turned to look at him, startled.

"Rubbish!" barked Cato. "He'll recover."

"I daresay he will this time. But he's dying," maintained Cicero stubbornly. "Not long ago he said to me that Caesar was fraying his life strand like tough string a gossamer thread."

"Then we *must* get rid of Caesar!" cried Ahenobarbus. "The higher he goes, the more insufferable he becomes."

"The higher he goes, the further he has to fall," said Cato. "For as long as I am alive and he is alive, I will be shoving at my lever to bring about that fall, and so I solemnly swear it by all our Gods."

Oblivious to this massive amount of ill will the *boni* were directing at his person, Caesar went home to a dinner party. Licinia had given up her vows, and Fabia was now the Chief Vestal. The changeover had been marked by ceremonies and an official banquet for all the priestly colleges, but on this New Year's Day the Pontifex Maximus was giving a much smaller dinner: just the five Vestals; Aurelia; Julia; and Fabia's half sister, Cicero's wife, Terentia. Cicero had been invited, but declined. So too did Pompeia Sulla decline; like Cicero, she pleaded a prior commitment. The Clodius Club was celebrating. However, Caesar had good reason to know that she could not imperil her good name. Polyxena *and* Cardixa were stuck to her more firmly than burrs to an ox.

My little harem, thought Caesar in some amusement, though his mind quailed when his eyes rested on the sour, forbidding Terentia. Impossible to think of Terentia in that context, whimsy or no!

Enough time had gone by for the Vestals to have lost their shyness. This was especially true of the two children, Quinctilia and Junia, who obviously worshiped him. He teased them, laughed and joked with them, was never on his dignity with them, and seemed to understand a great deal of what went on in their girlish minds. Even the two dour ones, Popillia and Arruntia, now had good cause to know that with Gaius Caesar in the other half of the Domus Publica, there would be no lawsuits alleging unchastity.

Astonishing, thought Terentia as the meal progressed merrily, that a man with such a shocking reputation for philandering could handle this clutch of extremely vulnerable women so deftly. On the one hand he was approachable, even affectionate; on the other hand he gave them absolutely no hope. They would all spend the rest of their lives in love with him, no doubt, but not in a tortured sense. He gave them absolutely no hope. And interesting that not even Bibulus had produced a canard about Caesar and his clutch of Vestal women. Not in more than a century had there been a Pontifex Maximus so punctilious, so devoted to the job; he had enjoyed the position for less than a year so far, but already his reputation in it was unassailable. Including his reputation anent Rome's most precious possession, her consecrated virgins.

Naturally Terentia's chief loyalty was to Cicero, and no one had suffered for him more through the Catilina business than his wife. Since the night of the fifth day of December she had woken to listen to his mumbling nightmares, heard him repeat Caesar's name over and over, and never without anger or pain. It was Caesar and no one else who had ruined Cicero's triumph; it was Caesar who had fanned the smoldering resentment of the People. Metellus Nepos was a gnat grown fangs because of Caesar. And yet from Fabia came another view of Caesar, and Terentia was too cool a woman not to appreciate its justice, its authenticity. Cicero was a far nicer man, a more worthy man. Ardent and sincere, he brought boundless enthusiasm and energy into everything he did, and no one could impugn his honesty. However, Terentia decided with a sigh, not even a mind as huge as Cicero's could outthink a mind like Caesar's. Why was it that these incredibly old families could still throw up a Sulla or a Caesar? They ought to have been worn out centuries ago.

Terentia came out of her reverie when Caesar ordered the two little girls to bed.

"It's up with the sparrows in the morning, no more holidays." He nodded to the hovering Eutychus. "See the ladies safely home, and make sure the servants are awake to take charge of them at the Atrium Vestae door."

Off they went, lissome Junia several feet in front of the waddling Quinctilia. Aurelia watched them go with a mental sigh: that child ought to be put on a diet! But when she had issued instructions to this effect some months earlier, Caesar had grown angry and forbidden it.

"Let her be, Mater. You are not Quinctilia, and Quinctilia is not you. If the poor little puppy is happy eating, then she shall eat. For she *is* happy! There are no husbands waiting in the wings, and I would have her continue to like being a Vestal."

"She'll die of overeating!"

"Then so be it. I will only approve when Quinctilia herself elects to starve."

What could one do with a man like that? Aurelia had shut her mouth tightly and desisted.

"No doubt," she said now with a touch of acid in her voice, "you are going to choose Minucia from among the candidates to fill Licinia's place."

The fair brows rose. "What leads you to that conclusion?"

"You seem to have a soft spot for fat children."

Which didn't have the desired effect; Caesar laughed. "I have a soft spot for children, Mater. Tall, short, thin, fat—it makes little difference. However, since you've brought the subject up, I'm pleased to say that the Vestal slough is over. So far I've had five offers of very suitable children, all of the right blood, and all furnished with excellent dowries."

"Five?" Aurelia blinked. "I had thought there were three."

"Are we permitted to know their names?" asked Fabia.

"I don't see why not. The choice is mine, but I don't move in a feminine world, and I certainly don't pretend to know everything about the domestic situations within families. Two of them, however, don't matter; I'm not seriously considering them. And one of them is Minucia, as it happens," said Caesar, quizzing his mother wickedly.

"Then who are you considering?"

"An Octavia of the branch using Gnaeus as a *praenomen*."

"That would be the grandchild of the consul who died in the Janiculan fortress when Marius and Cinna besieged Rome."

"Yes. Does anyone have any information to offer?"

No one did. Caesar produced the next name, a Postumia.

Aurelia frowned; so did Fabia and Terentia.

"Ah! What's wrong with Postumia?"

"It's a patrician family," said Terentia, "but am I correct in assuming this girl is of the Albinus branch, last consul over forty years ago?"

"Yes."

"And she is turned eight?"

"Yes."

"Then don't take her. It's a household much addicted to the wine flagon, and all the children—far too many of them! I really can't think what the mother was about!— are allowed to lap unwatered wine from the time they're weaned. This girl has already drunk herself senseless on several occasions."

"Dear me!"

"So who's left, *tata*?" asked Julia, smiling.

"Cornelia Merula, the great-granddaughter of the *flamen Dialis* Lucius Cornelius Merula," said Caesar solemnly.

Every pair of eyes looked at him accusingly, but it was Julia who answered.

"You've been teasing us!" she chuckled. "I thought you were!"

"Oh?" asked Caesar, lips twitching.

"Why would you look any further, *tata*?"

"Excellent, excellent!" said Aurelia, beaming. "The great-grandmother still rules that family, and every generation has been brought up in the most religious way. Cornelia Merula will come willingly, and adorn the College."

"So I think, Mater," said Caesar.

Whereupon Julia rose. "I thank you for your hospitality, Pontifex Maximus," she said gravely, "but I ask your leave to go."

"Brutus coming round?"

She blushed. "Not at this hour, *tata*!"

"Julia," said Aurelia when she had gone, "will be fourteen in five days' time."

"Pearls," said Caesar promptly. "At fourteen she can wear pearls, Mater, is that right?"

"Provided they're small."

He looked wry. "Small is all they can be." Sighing, he got up. "Ladies, thank you for your company. There's no need to go, but I must. I have work to do."

"Well! A Cornelia Merula for the College!" Terentia was saying as Caesar shut the door.

Outside in the corridor he leaned against the wall and for several moments laughed silently. What a tiny world they lived in! Was that good or bad? At least they were a pleasant group, even if Mater was growing a little curmudgeonly, and Terentia always had been. But thank the Gods he didn't have to do that often! More fun by far to engineer Metellus Nepos's move to get himself banished than to make small talk with women.

Though when Caesar convened the Popular Assembly early in the morning of the fourth day of January, he had no idea that Bibulus and Cato intended to use the meeting to bring about a worse fall from grace than Metellus Nepos's: his own fall.

Even when he and his lictors arrived in the lower Forum very early, it was evident that the Well of the Comitia was not going to hold the crowd; Caesar turned immediately in the direction of the temple of Castor and Pollux and issued orders to the small group of public slaves who waited nearby in case they were needed.

Many thought Castor's the most imposing temple in the Forum, for it had been rebuilt less than sixty years ago by Metellus Dalmaticus Pontifex Maximus, and he had built in the grand style. Large enough inside for the full Senate to hold a meeting there very comfortably, the floor of its single chamber stood twenty-five feet above the ground, and within its podium lay a warren of rooms. A stone tribunal had once stood in front of the original temple, but when Metellus Dalmaticus tore it down and started again he incorporated this structure into the whole, thus creating a platform almost as large as the rostra some ten feet off the ground. Instead of bringing the wonderful flight of shallow marble steps all the way from the entrance to the temple itself to the level of the Forum, he had stopped them at the platform. Access from the Forum to the platform was via two narrow sets of steps, one on either side. This allowed the platform to serve as a rostrum, and Castor's to serve as a voting place; the assembled People or Plebs stood below in the Forum and looked up.

The temple itself was completely surrounded by fluted stone columns painted red, each surmounted by an Ionic capital painted in shades of rich blue with gilded edges to the volutes. Nor had Metellus Dalmaticus enclosed the chamber by walls within the columns; one could look straight through Castor's, it soared airy and free as the two young Gods to whom it was dedicated.

As Caesar stood watching the public slaves deposit the big, heavy tribunician bench on the platform, someone touched his arm.

"A word to the wise," said Publius Clodius, dark eyes very bright. "There's going to be trouble."

Caesar's own eyes had already absorbed the fact that there were many in the idling crowd whose faces were not familiar save in one way: they belonged to Rome's multitude of bully-boys, the ex-gladiators who upon being liberated drifted from places like Capua to find seedy employment in Rome as bouncers, bailiffs, bodyguards.

"They're not my men," said Clodius.

"Whose, then?"

"I'm not sure because they're too cagey to say. But they all have suspicious bulges beneath their togas—cudgels, most likely. If I were you, Caesar, I'd have someone call out the militia in a hurry. Don't hold your meeting until it's guarded."

"Many thanks, Publius Clodius," said Caesar, and turned away to speak to his chief lictor.

Not long afterward the new consuls appeared. Silanus's lictors bore the *fasces,* whereas Murena's dozen walked with left shoulders unburdened. Neither man was happy, for this meeting, the second of the year, was also the second one called into being by a mere praetor; Caesar had got in before the consuls, a great insult, and Silanus had not yet had an opportunity to address the People in his laudatory *contio*. Even Cicero had fared better! Thus both waited stony-faced as far from Caesar as they could, while their servants placed their slender ivory chairs to one side of the platform's center, occupied by the curule chair belonging to Caesar and—ominous presence!—the tribunician bench.

One by one the other magistrates trickled in and found a spot to sit. Metellus Nepos when he came perched on the very end of the tribunician bench adjacent to Caesar's chair, winking at Caesar and flourishing the scroll containing his bill to summon Pompey home. Eyes everywhere, the urban praetor told off the clotting groups in the crowd, now three or four thousand strong. Though the very front area was reserved for senators, those just behind and to either side were ex-gladiators. Elsewhere were groups he thought belonged to Clodius, including the three Antonii and the rest of the young blades who belonged to the Clodius Club. Also Fulvia.

His chief lictor approached and bent down to Caesar's chair. "The militia are beginning to arrive, Caesar. As you directed, I've put them out of sight behind the temple."

"Good. Use your own initiative, don't wait for my command."

"It's all right, Caesar!" said Metellus Nepos cheerfully. "I heard that the crowd was full of strange tough faces, so I've got a few tough faces of my own out there."

"I don't think, Nepos," said Caesar, sighing, "that's a very clever idea. The last thing I want is another war in the Forum."

"Isn't it high time?" asked Nepos, unimpressed. "We haven't had a good brawl in more years than I've been out of diapers."

"You're just determined to go out of office with a roar."

"That I am! Though I would love to wallop Cato before I go!"

Last to arrive, Cato and Thermus ascended the steps

on the side where Pollux sat his painted marble horse, picked their way between the praetors with a grin for Bibulus, and attained the bench. Before Metellus Nepos knew what had happened, the two newcomers had each lifted him beneath an elbow and whisked him to the middle of the bench. They then sat down between him and Caesar, with Cato next to Caesar and Thermus next to Nepos. When Bestia tried to flank Nepos on his other side, Lucius Marius shoved his way between them. Metellus Nepos thus sat alone amid his enemies, as did Caesar when Bibulus suddenly shifted his ivory seat to Caesar's side of a startled Philippus.

Alarm was spreading; the two consuls were looking uneasy, and the uninvolved praetors were clearly wishing the platform stood three times farther off the ground than it did.

But the meeting got under way at last with the prayers and auguries. All was in order. Caesar spoke briefly to the effect that the tribune of the plebs Quintus Caecilius Metellus Nepos wished to present a bill for discussion by the People.

Metellus Nepos rose, pulling the ends of his scroll apart. "*Quirites,* it is the fourth day of January in the year of the consulship of Decimus Junius Silanus and Lucius Licinius Murena! To the north of Rome lies the great district of Etruria, where the outlaw Catilina struts with an army of rebels! In the field against him is Gaius Antonius Hybrida, commander-in-chief of a force at least twice the size of Catilina's! But nothing happens! It is now almost two months since Hybrida left Rome to deal with this pathetic collection of veteran soldiers so old their knees creak, but nothing has happened! Rome continues to exist under a Senatus Consultum Ultimum while the ex-consul in charge of her legions bandages his toe!"

The scroll came into play, but seriously; Nepos was not foolish enough to think that this assemblage would appreciate a clown. He cleared his throat and launched immediately into the details. "I hereby propose that the People of Rome relieve Gaius Antonius Hybrida of his imperium and his command! I hereby ask the People of

Rome to install Gnaeus Pompeius Magnus in his place as commander-in-chief of the armies! I hereby direct that the People of Rome endow Gnaeus Pompeius Magnus with an *imperium maius* effective within all Italia except the city of Rome herself! I further direct that Gnaeus Pompeius be· given whatever moneys, troops, equipment and legates he requires, and that his special command together with his *imperium maius* not be terminated until he thinks the time right to lay them down!''

Cato and Thermus were on their feet as the last word left Nepos's mouth. ''Veto! Veto! I interpose my veto!'' cried both men in unison.

A rain of stones came out of nowhere, whizzing viciously at the assembled magistrates, and the bully-boys charged through the ranks of the senators in the direction of both sets of steps. Curule chairs overturned as consuls, praetors and aediles fled up the broad marble stairs into the temple, with all the tribunes of the plebs except for Cato and Metellus Nepos after them. Clubs and cudgels were out; Caesar wrapped his toga about his right arm and retreated between his lictors, dragging Nepos with him.

But Cato hung on longer, it seemed miraculously preserved, still shouting that he vetoed with every higher step he took until Murena dashed out from among the columns and pulled him forcibly inside. The militia waded into the fray with shields round and staves thudding, and gradually those louts who had attained the platform were driven down again. Senators now scurried up the two flights of steps, making for the shelter of the temple. And below in the Forum a full-scale riot broke out as a whooping Mark Antony and his boon companion Curio fell together on some twenty opponents, their friends piling in after them.

''Well, this is a good start to the year!'' said Caesar as he walked into the center of the light-filled temple, carefully redraping his toga.

''It is a disgraceful start to the year!'' snapped Silanus, his blood coursing fast enough through his veins to banish belly pain. ''Lictor, I command you to quell the riot!''

''Oh, rubbish!'' said Caesar wearily. ''I have the mi-

litia here, I marshaled them when I saw some of the faces
in the crowd. The trouble won't amount to much now
we're off the rostra.''

"This is your doing, Caesar!" snarled Bibulus.

"To hear you talk, Flea, it's always my doing.''

"Will you please come to order?" Silanus shouted.
"I have summoned the Senate into session, and I will have
order!"

"Hadn't you better invoke the Senatus Consultum
Ultimum, Silanus?" asked Nepos, looking down to find
that he still held his scroll. "Better still, as soon as the
fuss dies down outside, let me finish my proper business
before the People.''

"Silence!" Silanus tried to roar; it came out more
like a bleat. "The Senatus Consultum Ultimum empowers
me as the consul with the *fasces* to take all the measures
I deem necessary to protect the Res Publica of Rome!"
He gulped, suddenly needing his chair. But it lay on the
platform below, he had to send a servant to fetch it. When
someone unfolded it and set it down for him, he collapsed
into it, grey and sweating.

"Conscript Fathers, I will see an end to this appalling
affair at once!" he said then. "Marcus Calpurnius Bibulus,
you have the floor. Kindly explain the remark you made
to Gaius Julius Caesar.''

"I don't have to explain it, Decimus Silanus, it's
manifest," said Bibulus, pointing to a darkening swelling
on his left cheek. "I accuse Gaius Caesar and Quintus
Metellus Nepos of public violence! Who else stands to
gain from rioting in the Forum? Who else would want to
see chaos? Whose ends does it serve except theirs?''

"Bibulus is right!" yelled Cato, so elated by the brief
crisis that for once he forgot the protocol of names. "Who
else stood to gain? Who else needs a Forum running with
blood? It's back to the good old days of Gaius Gracchus,
Livius Drusus, that filthy demagogue Saturninus! You're
both Pompeius's minions!"

Growls and rumbles came from all sides, for there
were none among the hundred-odd senators inside the temple who had voted with Caesar during that fateful division

on the fifth day of December when five men were condemned to death without trial.

"Neither the tribune of the plebs Nepos nor I as urban praetor had anything to gain from violence," said Caesar, "nor were those who threw the stones known to us." He looked derisively at Marcus Bibulus. "Had the meeting I convoked progressed peacefully, Flea, the outcome would have been a resounding victory for Nepos. Do you genuinely think the serious voters who came today would want a dolt like Hybrida in charge of their legions if they were offered Pompeius Magnus? The violence began when Cato and Thermus vetoed, not before. To use the power of the tribunician veto to prevent the People from discussing laws in *contio* or registering their votes is in absolute violation of everything Rome stands for! I don't blame the People for starting to shell us! It's months since they've been acknowledged to have any rights at all!"

"Speaking of rights, every tribune of the plebs has the right to exercise his veto at his discretion!" bellowed Cato.

"What a *fool* you are, Cato!" cried Caesar. "Why do you think Sulla took the veto off the likes of you? Because the veto was never intended to serve the interests of a few men who control the Senate! Every time you yap another veto, you insult the intelligence of all those thousands out there in the Forum cheated by you of their right to listen—calmly!—to laws presented to them— calmly!—then to vote—calmly!—one way or the other!"

"Calm? *Calm?* It wasn't my veto disturbed the calm, Caesar, it was your bully-boys!"

"I wouldn't soil my hands on such rabble!"

"You didn't have to! All you had to do was issue orders."

"Cato, the People are sovereign," said Caesar, striving to be more patient, "not the Senate's rump and its few tribunician mouthpieces. You don't serve the interests of the People, you serve the interests of a handful of senators who think they own and rule an empire of millions! You strip the People of their rights and this city of her *dignitas*!

You shame me, Cato! You shame Rome! You shame the People! You even shame your *boni* masters, who use your naïveté and sneer at your ancestry behind your back! You call me a minion of Pompeius Magnus? I am not! But you, Cato, are no more and no less than a minion of the *boni*!''

"Caesar," said Cato, striding to stand with his face only inches from Caesar's, "you are a cancer in the body of Roman men! You are everything I abominate!" He turned to the stunned group of senators and held out his hands to them, the healing stripes on his face giving him in that filtered light the savagery of a fierce cat. "Conscript Fathers, this Caesar will ruin us all! He will destroy the Republic, I know it in my bones! Don't listen to him prate of the People and the People's rights! Instead, listen to me! Drive him and his catamite Nepos out of Rome, forbid them fire and water within the bounds of Italia! I will see Caesar and Nepos charged with violent crime, I will see them outlawed!''

"Listening to you, Cato," said Metellus Nepos, "only reminds me that *any* violence in the Forum is better than letting you run rampant vetoing every single meeting, every single proposal, every single *word*!''

And for the second time in a month someone took Cato off-guard to do things to his face. Metellus Nepos simply walked up to him, threw every ounce of himself into his hand, and slapped Cato so hard that Servilia's scratches burst and bled anew.

"I don't care what you do to me with your precious piddling Senatus Consultum Ultimum!" Nepos yelled at Silanus. "It's worth dying in the Tullianum to know I've walloped Cato!''

"Get out of Rome, go to your master Pompeius!" panted Silanus, helpless to control the meeting, his own feelings, or the pain.

"Oh, I intend to!" said Nepos scornfully, turned on his heel and walked out. "You'll see me again!" he called as he clattered down the steps. "I'll be back with brother-in-law Pompeius at my side! Who knows? It might be

Catilina ruling Rome by then, and you'll all be deservedly dead, you shit-arsed sheep!''

Even Cato was silenced, another of his scant supply of togas rapidly bloodying beyond redemption.

"Do you need me further, senior consul?" asked Caesar of Silanus in conversational tones. "The sounds of strife appear to be dying away outside, and there's nothing more to be said here, is there?" He smiled coldly. "Too much has been said already."

"You are under suspicion of inciting public violence, Caesar," said Silanus faintly. "While ever the Senatus Consultum Ultimum remains in effect, you are disbarred from all meetings and all magisterial business." He looked at Bibulus. "I suggest, Marcus Bibulus, that you start preparing your case to prosecute this man *de vi* today."

Which set Caesar laughing. "Silanus, Silanus, get your facts correct! How can this flea prosecute me in his own court? He'll have to get Cato to do his dirty work for him. And do you know something, Cato?" asked Caesar softly of the furious grey eyes glaring at him between folds of toga. "You don't stand a chance. I have more intelligence in my battering ram than you do in your citadel!" He pulled his tunic away from his chest and bent his head to address the space created. "Isn't that right, O battering ram?" A sweet smile for the assembled refugees, then: "He says that's right. Conscript Fathers, good day."

"That," said Publius Clodius, who had been eavesdropping just outside, "was a stunning performance, Caesar! I had no idea you could get so angry."

"Wait until you enter the Senate next year, Clodius, and you will see more. Between Cato and Bibulus, I may never be whole of temper again." He stood on the platform amid a shambles of broken ivory chairs and gazed across the Forum, almost deserted. "I see the villains have all gone home."

"Once the militia entered the scene, they lost most of their enthusiasm." Clodius led the way down the side steps beneath the equestrian statue of Castor. "I did find out one thing. They'd been hired by Bibulus. He's a rank amateur at it too.''

''The news doesn't surprise me.''

''He planned it to compromise you and Nepos. You'll go down in Bibulus's court for inciting public violence, wait and see,'' said Clodius, waving at Mark Antony and Fulvia, who were sitting together on the bottom tier of Gaius Marius's plinth, Fulvia busy patting Antony's right knuckles with her handkerchief.

''Oh, wasn't that terrific?'' asked Antony, one eye puffed up so badly he couldn't see out of it.

''No, Antonius, it wasn't terrific!'' said Caesar tartly.

''Bibulus intends to have Caesar prosecuted under the *lex Plautia de vi*—his own court, no less,'' said Clodius. ''Caesar and Nepos got the blame.'' He grinned. ''No surprise, really, with Silanus holding the *fasces*. I don't imagine you're very popular in that quarter, all considered.'' And he began to hum a well-known ditty about a wronged and broken-hearted husband.

''Oh, come home with me, the lot of you!'' Caesar chuckled, slapping at Antony's knuckles and Fulvia's hand. ''You can't sit here like alley thieves until the militia sweep you up, and any moment now those heroes still drifting around the inside of Castor's are going to poke their noses out to sniff the air. I'm already accused of fraternizing with ruffians, but if they see me with you, they'll send me packing immediately. Not being Pompeius's brother-in-law, I'll have to join Catilina.''

And of course during the short walk to the residence of the Pontifex Maximus—a matter of moments only—Caesar's equilibrium returned. By the time he had ushered his raffish guests into a part of the Domus Publica Fulvia didn't know nearly as well as she did Pompeia's suite upstairs, he was ready to deal with disaster and upset all Bibulus's plans.

The next morning at dawn the new *praetor urbanus* took up position on his tribunal, his six lictors (who already thought him the best and most generous of magistrates) standing off to one side with *fasces* grounded like spears, his table and curule chair arranged to his liking, and a small staff of scribes and messengers waiting for orders. Since the urban praetor dealt with the preliminaries of all civil litigation as well as heard applications for prosecutions on criminal charges, a number of potential litigants and advocates were already clustered about the tribunal; the moment Caesar indicated he was open for business, a dozen people surged forward to do battle for first served, Rome not being a place where people lined up in an orderly fashion and were content to take their turn. Nor did Caesar try to regulate the insistent clamor. He selected the loudest voice, beckoned, and prepared to listen.

Before more than a few words had tumbled out, the consular lictors appeared with the *fasces* but without the consul.

"Gaius Julius Caesar," said the chief of Silanus's lictors as his eleven companions shoved the little crowd away from the vicinity of the tribunal, "you have been disbarred under the Senatus Consultum Ultimum still in effect. Please desist this moment from all praetorian business."

"What do you mean?" asked the advocate who had been about to lay his case before Caesar—not a prominent lawyer, simply one of the hundreds who haunted the lower Forum touting for business. "I need the urban praetor!"

"The senior consul has deputed Quintus Tullius Cicero to take over the urban praetor's duties," said the lictor, not pleased at this interruption.

"But I don't want Quintus Cicero, I want Gaius Caesar! He's urban praetor, and he doesn't dally and dither the way most of Rome's praetors do! I want my case sorted out this morning, not next month or next year!"

The cluster about the tribunal was growing now in leaps and bounds, the Forum frequenters attracted by the sudden presence of so many lictors and an angry individual protesting.

Without a word Caesar rose from his chair, signed to his personal servant to fold it and pick it up, and turned to the six lictors he called his own. Smiling, he went to each of them in turn and dropped a handful of denarii into each right palm.

"Pick up your *fasces,* my friends, and take them to the temple of Venus Libitina. Lie them where they belong when the man who should be preceded by them is deprived of his office by death or disbarment. I'm sorry our time together has been so short, and I thank you most sincerely for your kind attentions."

From his lictors he proceeded to his scribes and messengers, giving each man a sum of money and a word of thanks.

After which he drew the folds of his purple-bordered *toga praetexta* off his left arm and shoulder, rolling the vast garment into a loose ball as he stripped it away; not as much as one corner of it touched the ground, so handily was the disrobing done. The servant holding the chair received the bundle; Caesar nodded to him to go.

"Your pardon," he said then to the swelling throng, "it seems I am not to be permitted to perform the duties I was elected by you to do." The knife went in: "You must content yourselves with half a praetor, Quintus Cicero."

Lurking some distance away with his own lictors, Quintus Cicero gasped in outrage.

"What's the meaning of this?" shouted Publius Clodius from the rear of the crowd, pushing his way to the front as Caesar prepared to leave his tribunal.

"I am disbarred, Publius Clodius."

"For what?"

"Being under suspicion of inciting violence during a meeting of the People *I* had convened."

"They can't do that!" cried Clodius theatrically. "First you have to be tried, and then you have to be convicted!"

"There is a Senatus Consultum Ultimum in effect."

"What's that got to do with yesterday's meeting?"

"It came in handy," said Caesar, leaving his tribunal.

And as he walked in his tunic in the direction of the Domus Publica, the entire gathering turned to escort him. Quintus Cicero took his place on the urban praetor's tribunal to find he had no customers; nor did he all day.

But all day the crowd in the Forum grew, and as it grew became ugly. This time there were no ex-gladiators to be seen, just many respectable inhabitants of the city liberally interspersed with men like Clodius, the Antonii, Curio, Decimus Brutus—and Lucius Decumius and his crossroads brethren of all walks from the Second Class to the Head Count. Two praetors beginning to try criminal cases looked across a sea of faces and decided the omens were not auspicious; Quintus Cicero packed up and went home early.

Most unnerving of all, no one left the Forum during the night, which was lit by many little fires to keep out the chill; from the houses on the Germalus of the Palatine the effect was eerily reminiscent of a camping army, and for the first time since the empty-bellied masses had filled the Forum during the days which led to the rebellion of Saturninus, those in power understood how many ordinary people there were in Rome—and how few the men in power were by comparison.

At dawn Silanus, Murena, Cicero, Bibulus and Lucius Ahenobarbus clustered at the top of the Vestal Steps and gazed at what looked like fifteen thousand people. Then someone below in that horrifying gathering saw them, shouted, pointed; the whole ocean of people turned as if beginning the first great encirclement of a whirlpool, and the little group of men stepped back instinctively, realizing that what they saw was a potential dance of death. Then as every face fixed on them, every right arm went up to shake a fist at them, seaweed oscillating in the swell.

"All that for *Caesar*?" whispered Silanus, shivering.

"No," said the praetor Philippus, joining them. "All that for the Senatus Consultum Ultimum and the execution of citizens without trial. Caesar's just the final blow." He gave Bibulus a scorching glare. "What fools you are! Don't you know who Caesar is? I'm his friend, *I* know! Caesar is the one person in Rome you daren't attempt to destroy publicly! All your lives you've spent up here on the heights looking down on Rome like gods on a seething pestilence, but all his life he's spent among them and been thought of as one of them. There's hardly a person in this enormous city that man doesn't know—or maybe it would be better to say that everyone in this enormous city thinks Caesar knows them. It's a smile and a wave and a cheerful greeting wherever he goes—and to the whole world, not merely to valuable voters. They *love* him! Caesar's not a demagogue—he doesn't *need* to be a demagogue! In Libya they tie men down and let ants kill them. Yet you're stupid enough to stir up Rome's ants! Rest assured, it's not Caesar they'll kill!''

"I'll order out the militia," said Silanus.

"Oh, rubbish, Silanus! The militia are down there with the carpenters and bricklayers!"

"Then what do we do? Bring the army home from Etruria?"

"By all means, if you want Catilina in hot pursuit!"

"What *can* we do?"

"Go home and bar your doors, Conscript Fathers," Philippus said, turning away. "That at least is what I intend to do."

But before anyone could find the strength to take this advice, a huge roar went up; the faces and fists aimed at the top of the Vestal stairs swung away.

"Look!" squeaked Murena. "It's Caesar!"

The crowd was somehow compressing itself to create an empty corridor which began at the Domus Publica and opened before Caesar as he walked clad in a plain white toga in the direction of the rostra. He made no acknowledgment of the deafening ovation, nor looked to either side, and when he reached the top of the speaker's platform he made no movement of the body nor gesture of the hand which the watchers on the Palatine could classify as encouragement to the masses now turned to see him.

When he began to speak the noise died utterly away, though what he said was inaudible to Silanus and the rest, now standing with twenty magistrates and at least a hundred senators. He talked for perhaps an hour, and as he talked the crowd seemed to grow ever calmer. Then he dismissed them with a wave of his hand and a smile so wide his teeth flashed. Limp with relief and amazement, the audience at the top of the Vestal Steps watched that enormous crowd begin to disperse, to stream into the Argiletum and the area around the Markets, up the Via Sacra to the Velia and those parts of Rome beyond. Everyone obviously discussing Caesar's speech, but no one angry anymore.

"As Princeps Senatus," said Mamercus stiffly, "I hereby call the Senate into session in the temple of Jupiter Stator. An appropriate location, for what Caesar has done is to stay open revolt. At once!" he snapped, rounding on a shrinking Silanus. "Senior consul, send your lictors to fetch Gaius Caesar, since you sent them to strip him of his office."

When Caesar entered the temple of Jupiter Stator, Gaius Octavius and Lucius Caesar began to applaud; one by one others joined in, until even Bibulus and Ahenobarbus had at least to pretend they were clapping. Of Cato there was no sign.

Silanus rose from his seat. "Gaius Julius Caesar, on behalf of this House I wish to thank you for ending a most dangerous situation. You have acted with perfect correctness, and you are to be commended."

"What a bore you are, Silanus!" cried Gaius Octavius. "Ask the man how he did it, or we'll all die of curiosity!"

"The House wishes to know what you said, Gaius Caesar."

Still in his plain white toga, Caesar shrugged. "I simply told them to go home and be about their business. Did they want to be deemed disloyal? Uncontrollable? Who did they think they were, to gather in such numbers all because of a mere praetor who had been disciplined? I told them that Rome is well governed, and everything would turn out to their satisfaction if they had a little patience."

"And there," whispered Bibulus to Ahenobarbus, "is the threat beneath the fair words!"

"Gaius Julius Caesar," said Silanus very formally, "assume your *toga praetexta* and return to your tribunal as *praetor urbanus*. It is clear to this House that you have acted in all ways as you ought, and that you did so at the meeting of the People the day before yesterday by noting the malcontents in that assembly and having the militia ready to act. There will be no trial under the *lex Plautia de vi* for the events of that day.''

Nor did one voice in the temple of Jupiter Stator raise itself to protest.

"What did I tell you?'' said Metellus Scipio to Bibulus as they left the senatorial session. "He beat us again! All we did was spend a lot of money hiring ex-gladiators!''

Cato rushed up, breathless and looking very much the worse for wear. "What is it? What happened?'' he asked.

"What happened to you?'' asked Metellus Scipio.

"I was ill,'' said Cato briefly, which Bibulus and Metellus Scipio interpreted correctly as a long night with Athenodorus Cordylion and the wine flagon.

"Caesar beat us as usual,'' said Metellus Scipio. "He sent the crowd home and Silanus has reinstated him. There will be no trial in Bibulus's court.''

Cato literally screamed, so loudly that the last of the senators flinched, turned to one of the pillars outside Jupiter Stator and punched it until the others managed to hold his arm down and pull him away.

"I will not rest, I will not rest, I will not rest,'' he kept saying as they led him up the Clivus Palatinus and through the lichen-whiskered Porta Mugonia. "If I have to die to do it, I will ruin him!''

"He's like the phoenix,'' said Ahenobarbus gloomily. "Rises out of the ashes of every funeral pyre we put him on.''

"One day he won't rise again. I'm with Cato, I'll never rest until he's ruined,'' vowed Bibulus.

"You know,'' said Metellus Scipio thoughtfully, eyeing Cato's swelling hand and freshly opened face, "at this stage you must bear more wounds due to Caesar than to Spartacus.''

"And you, Scipio,'' said Gaius Piso savagely, "are asking for a drubbing!''

* * *

January was almost done when word came at last from the north. Since early December Catilina had been moving steadily into the Apennines, only to discover that Metellus Celer and Marcius Rex lay between him and the Adriatic coast. There was no escape from Italy, he would have to stand and fight—or surrender. Surrender was inconceivable, so he staked his all on a single battle within a narrow valley near the town of Pistoria. But Gaius Antonius Hybrida did not take the field against him; that honor was reserved for the Military Man, Marcus Petreius. Oh, the pain in his toe! Hybrida never left the safety of his cozy command tent. Catilina's soldiers fought desperately, over three thousand of them electing to die where they stood. As did Catilina, killed holding the silver eagle which had once belonged to Gaius Marius. Men said that when he was found among the bodies he wore the same glittering smile he had turned on everyone from Catulus to Cicero.

No more excuses: the Senatus Consultum Ultimum was finally lifted. Not even Cicero could summon up the courage to advocate that it be kept in force until the rest of the conspirators were dealt with. Some of the praetors were sent to mop up pockets of resistance, including Bibulus to the lands of the Paeligni in mountainous Samnium, and Quintus Cicero to equally craggy Bruttium.

Then in February the trials began. This time there would be no executions, nor any men condemned to exile out of hand; the Senate decided to set up a special court.

An ex-aedile, Lucius Novius Niger, was appointed its president after no one else could be found willing to take the job; those praetors remaining in Rome gleefully pleaded huge loads of work in their own courts, from Caesar to Philippus. That Novius Niger was willing lay in his nature and his circumstances, for he was one of those irritating creatures possessed of far more ambition than talent, and he saw the job as a certain way to attain the consulship. His edicts when he published them were most imposing: no one would be uninspected, no one would be cosseted, no one would buy his way out with bribery, the jury roster would smell sweeter than a bank of violets in

Campania. His last edict did not find as much favor. He announced that he would pay a two-talent reward for information leading to a conviction—the reward to be paid out of the fine and property confiscation, of course. No cost to the Treasury! But, most people thought, this was too uncomfortably close to the techniques of Sulla's proscriptions. Thus when the president of the special court opened it, the professional Forum frequenters tended to think poorly of him.

Five men went on trial first, all certain to be condemned: the Brothers Sulla, Marcus Porcius Laeca, and the two who had tried to assassinate Cicero, Gaius Cornelius and Lucius Vargunteius. To assist the court, the Senate went into session with Quintus Curius, Cicero's secret agent, timing their cross-examination of Curius to coincide with Novius Niger's opening his hearings. Naturally Novius Niger attracted a far larger congregation, as he set himself up in the largest area of vacant Forum space.

One Lucius Vettius was the first—and last—informer. A minor knight of bare *tribunus aerarius* status, he went to Novius Niger and announced that he had more than enough information to earn that tidy fifty thousand sesterces of reward money. Testifying before the court, he confessed that in the early stages of the conspiracy he had toyed with the idea of joining it, but, "I knew where my allegiance belonged," he said, sighing. "I am a Roman, I couldn't harm Rome. Rome means too much to me."

After a great deal more of the same, he dictated a list of men he swore had been involved beyond a shadow of a doubt.

Novius Niger sighed too. "Lucius Vettius, not one of these names is very inspiring! It seems to me that this court's chances of securing sufficient evidence to start proceedings are slim. Is there no one against whom you can produce really concrete evidence? Like a letter, or unimpeachable witnesses other than yourself?"

"Well . . ." said Vettius slowly, then suddenly shivered and shook his head emphatically. "No, no one!" he said loudly.

"Come now, you're under the full protection of my

court,'' said Novius Niger, scenting prey. ''Nothing can happen to you, Lucius Vettius, I give you my word! If you do know of any concrete evidence, you *must* tell me!''

''Big, big fish,'' muttered Lucius Vettius.

''No fish is too big for me and my court.''

''Well . . .''

''Lucius Vettius, spit it out!''

''I do have a letter.''

''From whom?''

''From Gaius Caesar.''

The jury sat up straight, the onlookers began to buzz.

''From Gaius Caesar, but to whom?''

''Catilina. It's in Gaius Caesar's own handwriting.''

Whereupon a small group of Catulus's clients in the crowd began to cheer, only to be drowned by boos, jeers, invective. Some time elapsed before the court's lictors could establish order and allow Novius Niger to resume his cross-examination.

''Why have we heard nothing of this before, Lucius Vettius?''

''Because I'm afraid, that's why!'' the informer snapped. ''I don't fancy the thought of being responsible for incriminating a big fish like Gaius Caesar.''

''In this court, Lucius Vettius, *I* am the big fish, not Gaius Caesar,'' said Novius Niger, ''and you *have* incriminated Gaius Caesar. You are in no danger. Please go on.''

''With what?'' asked Vettius. ''I said I had a letter.''

''Then you must produce it before this court.''

''He'll say it's a forgery.''

''Only the court can say that. Produce the letter.''

''Well . . .''

By now almost everybody in the lower Forum was either around Novius Niger's court or hurrying to it; the word was flying that as usual Caesar was in trouble.

''Lucius Vettius, I command you to produce that letter!'' said Novius Niger in a goaded voice; he then went on to say something extremely foolish. ''Do you think that men like Gaius Caesar are above the power of this court because they have an ancestry a thousand years old and multitudes of clients? Well, they are not! If Gaius Caesar wrote a letter to Catilina in his own hand, I will try him in this court and convict him!''

''Then I'll go home and get it,'' said Lucius Vettius, convinced.

While Vettius went on his errand, Novius Niger declared a recess. Everyone not busy talking excitedly (Caesar watching was becoming the best entertainment in years) rushed off to buy a little something to eat or drink, the jury sat at ease being waited on by the court servants, and Novius Niger strolled over to chat with the jury foreman, tremendously pleased with his idea to pay for information.

Publius Clodius was somewhat more purposeful. He hied himself across the Forum to the Curia Hostilia, where the Senate was sitting, and talked his way inside. Not a very difficult business for one who next year would be strolling through its portals as of right.

Just inside the doors he paused, discovering that Vettius's alto in court was keeping perfect harmony with Curius's baritone in the Senate.

''I tell you I heard it from Catilina's own lips!'' Curius was saying to Cato. ''Gaius Caesar was a central figure in the whole conspiracy, from its beginning right up to its end!''

Seated on the curule dais to one side of the presiding consul, Silanus, and slightly behind him, Caesar rose to his feet.

''You're lying, Curius,'' he said very calmly. ''We all know which men in this revered body will stop at nothing to see me permanently ejected from it. But, Conscript Fathers, I give leave to tell you that I never was and never would have been a part of such a hole-in-the-corner, appallingly bungled affair! Anyone who credits this pathetic fool's story is a bigger fool than he is! I, Gaius Julius Caesar, willingly to consort with a raggle-taggle lot of wine bibbers and gossips? I, so scrupulous in my attention to duty and to my own *dignitas,* to stoop to plotting with the likes of Curius here? I, the Pontifex Maximus, to connive at handing Rome to *Catilina*? I, a Julian descended from the founders of Rome, to consent to Rome's being

governed by worms like Curius and tarts like Fulvia Nobilioris?''

The words came out with the crack of a whip, and
no one tried to interrupt.

''I am well used to the mud-slinging of politics,'' he
went on, still in that calm but punishing voice, ''but I am
not going to stand idly by while someone pays the likes
of Curius to bandy *my* name about in connection with a
business I wouldn't be caught dead participating in! For
someone is paying him! And when I find out who, senators, they will pay *me*! Here you all sit, as brilliant and
wondrous as a collection of hens in a roost listening to the
sordid details of a so-called conspiracy, while there are
some hens here conspiring far more viciously to destroy
me and my good name! To destroy my *dignitas*!'' He drew
a breath. ''Without my *dignitas,* I am nothing. And I give
every last one of you a solemn warning—do not tamper
with my *dignitas*! To defend it, I would tear this venerable
chamber down around your ears! I would pile Pelion on
top of Ossa and steal Zeus's thunder to strike every last
one of you dead! Don't try my patience, Conscript Fathers,
for I tell you now that I am no Catilina! If I conspired to
unseat you, down you'd go!''

He turned to Cicero. ''Marcus Tullius Cicero, this is
the last time I will ask this question: did I or did I not
furnish you with assistance in the uncovering of this conspiracy?''

Cicero swallowed; the House sat in absolute silence.
No one had ever seen or heard anything quite like that
speech, and no one wanted to draw attention to himself.
Even Cato.

''Yes, Gaius Julius, you did assist me,'' said Cicero.

''Then,'' said Caesar in a less steely voice, ''I demand that this House forthwith refuse to pay Quintus Curius one sestertius of the reward money he was promised.
Quintus Curius has lied. He deserves no consideration.''

And such was the fear inside every senator that the
House agreed unanimously not to pay Quintus Curius one
sestertius of the promised reward.

Clodius stepped forward. ''Noble Fathers,'' he said

in a loud voice, "I crave your pardon for intruding, but I must ask the noble Gaius Julius to accompany me to the court of Lucius Novius Niger as soon as he can do so."

About to seat himself, Caesar looked instead at a dumbstruck Silanus. "Senior consul, it seems I am wanted elsewhere, I suspect on the same kind of business. In which case, remember what I have said. *Remember every word!* Pray excuse me."

"You are excused," whispered Silanus, "and so are you all."

Thus it was that when Caesar left the Curia Hostilia with Clodius trotting alongside him, the entire company of senators streamed in their wake.

"That," said Clodius, panting a little, "was absolutely the *best* wigging I have ever heard! There must be shit all over the Senate House floor."

"Don't talk nonsense, Clodius, tell me what's happening in Niger's court," said Caesar curtly.

Clodius obliged. Caesar stopped walking.

"Lictor Fabius!" he called to his chief lictor, hurrying his five companions to keep ahead of Caesar in the mood for war.

The three pairs of men stopped, received orders.

Then down on Novius Niger's court Caesar descended, scattering the onlookers in every direction, straight through the ranks of the jury to where Lucius Vettius stood with a letter in his hand.

"Lictors, arrest this man!"

Letter and all, Lucius Vettius was taken into custody and marched out of Novius Niger's court in the direction of the urban praetor's tribunal.

Novius Niger got to his feet so quickly that his much-prized ivory chair fell over. "What is the meaning of this?" he shrilled.

"WHO DO YOU THINK YOU ARE?" roared Caesar.

Everyone backed away; the jury shifted uneasily, shivered.

"Who do you think are?" Caesar repeated more softly, but in a voice which could be heard halfway across

the Forum. "How *dare* you, a magistrate of mere aedilician rank, admit evidence into your court concerning your
senior in the hierarchy? Evidence, what is more, from the
mouth of a paid informer? Who do you think you are? If
you don't know, Novius, then I will tell you. You are a
legal ignoramus who has no more right to preside over a
Roman court than the dirtiest trollop hawking her fork
outside Venus Erucina's! Don't you understand that it is
absolutely unheard of for a junior magistrate to act in a
way which could result in the trial of his senior? What
you were stupid enough to say to that piece of sewer refuse
Vettius deserves impeachment! That you, a mere aedilician
magistrate, would attempt to convict me, the urban praetor,
in *your* court? Brave words, Novius, but impossible to
fulfill. If you have cause to believe that a magistrate senior
to yourself is criminally implicated in proceedings going
on in your court, then you suspend your court immediately
and you take the whole matter to that senior magistrate's
peers. And since I am the *praetor urbanus,* you go to the
consul with the *fasces.* This month, Lucius Licinius Murena; but today, Decimus Junius Silanus."

The avid crowd hung on every word while Novius
Niger stood, face ashen, his hopes for a future consulship
tumbling down about his incredulous ears.

"You take the whole matter to your senior's peers,
Novius, you do not *dare* to continue the business of your
court! You do not *dare* to continue to admit evidence
about your senior, grinning all over your face! You have
held me up before this body of men as if you have the
right to do so! You do not. Hear me? *You do not!* How
glorious a precedent you set! Is this what senior magistrates are to expect from their juniors in the future?"

One hand went out, pleading; Novius Niger wet his
lips and tried to speak.

"Tace, inepte!" cried Caesar. "Lucius Novius Niger,
in order to remind you and every other junior magistrate
of his place in Rome's scheme of public duties, I, Gaius
Julius Caesar, *praetor urbanus,* do hereby sentence you to
one market interval of eight days in the cells of the Lautumiae. That should prove long enough to think about

what is your rightful place, and to think of how you will manage to convince the Senate of Rome that you should be allowed to continue as *iudex* in this special court. You will not leave your cell for one moment. You will not be allowed to bring in food, or have your family visit you. You will not be let have reading or writing materials. And while I am aware that no cell in the Lautumiae has a door of any kind, let alone one which locks, you will do as you are told. When the lictors are not watching you, half of Rome will be.'' He nodded to the court lictors abruptly. ''Take your master to the Lautumiae, and put him in the most uncomfortable cell you can find. You will stay on guard until I send lictors to relieve you. Bread and water, nothing else, and no light after dark.''

Then without a backward glance it was across to the tribunal belonging to the urban praetor, where Lucius Vettius waited atop its platform, a lictor on either side. Caesar and the four lictors still attending him mounted the steps, now avidly trailed by all the members of Novius Niger's court, from the jury to the scribes to the accused. Oh, what fun! But what could Caesar do to Lucius Vettius save put him in the next cell to Novius Niger?

''Lictor,'' he said to Fabius, ''unbind your rods.''

And to Vettius, still clutching the letter, ''Lucius Vettius, you have conspired against me. Whose client are you?''

The crowd twittered and fluttered, amazed, awestruck, torn between watching Caesar deal with Vettius and watching Fabius the lictor squatting down to dismember the bundle of birch rods tied in a ritual crisscross pattern with red leather thongs. Thin and slightly whippy, thirty for the thirty Curiae lay within the neat circular bundle, for they had been trimmed and turned until each one was as round as the whole cylinder called the *fasces*.

Vettius's eyes had widened; he couldn't seem to tear them from Fabius and the rods.

''Whose client are you, Vettius?'' Caesar repeated sharply.

It came out in an agony of fear. ''Gaius Calpurnius Piso's.''

"Thank you, that is all I need to know." Caesar turned to face the men assembled below him, front ranks filled with senators and knights. "Fellow Romans," he said, pitching his voice high, "this man on my tribunal has borne false witness against me in the court of a judge who had no right to admit his evidence. Vettius is a *tribunus aerarius,* he knows the law. He knows he ought not to have done that, but he was hungry to put the sum of two talents in his bank account—plus whatever his patron Gaius Piso promised him in addition, of course. I do not see Gaius Piso here to answer, which is just as well for Gaius Piso. Were he here, he would join Lucius Novius in the Lautumiae. It is my right as the *praetor urbanus* to exercise the power of *coercitio* upon this Roman citizen Lucius Vettius. I hereby do so. He cannot be flogged with a lash, but he can be beaten with a rod. Lictor, are you ready?"

"Yes, *praetor urbanus,*" said Fabius, who in all his long career as one of the ten prefects of the College of Lictors had never before been called upon to untie his *fasces.*

"Choose your rod."

Because ravenous animalcules chewed through the rods no matter how carefully they were tended—and these were among the most revered objects Rome owned—the *fasces* were regularly retired amid great ceremony to be ritually burned, and were replaced by new bundles. Thus Fabius had no difficulty unlashing his rods, nor needed to sort through them to find one sturdier than the rest. He simply picked the one closest to his trembling hand, and stood up slowly.

"Hold him," said Caesar to two others, "and remove his toga."

"Where? How many?" whispered Fabius urgently.

Caesar ignored him. "Because this man is a Roman citizen, I will not diminish his standing by stripping away his tunic or baring his backside. Lictor, six strokes to his left calf, and six strokes to his right calf." His voice dropped to ape Fabius's whisper. "And make them hard or it'll be your turn, Fabius!" He twitched the letter from

Vettius's slack grasp, glanced briefly at its contents, then walked to the edge of the tribunal and held it out to Silanus, who was substituting this day for Murena (and wishing he too had had the sense to come down with a blinding headache). "Senior consul, I give this evidence to you for your perusal. The handwriting is not mine." Caesar looked contemptuous. "Nor is it written in my style—vastly inferior! It reminds me of Gaius Piso, who never could string four words together."

The beating was administered to yelps and skips from Vettius; the chief lictor Fabius had liked Caesar enormously from the days when he had served him as curule aedile and then as judge in the Murder Court. He had thought he knew Caesar. Today was a revelation, so Fabius hit hard.

While it went on Caesar strolled down from the tribunal and went into the back of the crowd, where those of humble origin stood enthralled. Anyone wearing a shabby or homespun toga to the number of twenty individuals he tapped on the right shoulder, then brought the group back to wait just below his platform.

The chastisement was over; Vettius stood dancing and sniffling from pain of two kinds, one for the bruises on his calves, the other for the bruises on his self-esteem. Quite a number of those who had witnessed his humiliation knew him, and had cheered Fabius on deliriously.

"I understand that Lucius Vettius is something of a furniture fancier!" Caesar said then. "To be beaten with a rod leaves no lasting memory of wrongdoing, and Lucius Vettius must be made to remember today for a long time to come! I therefore order that a part of his property be confiscated. Those twenty *Quirites* I touched on the shoulder are authorized to accompany Lucius Vettius back to his house, and there to select one item of furniture each. Nothing else is to be touched—not slaves nor plate nor gilding nor statuary. Lictors, escort this man to his house, and see that my orders are carried out."

Off went the hobbling and howling Vettius under guard, followed by twenty delighted beneficiaries, already chortling among themselves and dividing the spoils—who

needed a bed, who a couch, who a table, who a chair, who
had the room to fit in a desk?

One of the twenty turned back as Caesar came down
off his tribunal. "Do we get mattresses for the beds?" he
yelled.

"A bed's no use without a mattress, no one knows
that better than I, *Quiris*!" laughed Caesar. "Mattresses
go with beds and bolsters go with couches, but no cloths
to cover them, understand?"

Caesar went home, though only to attend to his person; it had been an eventful day, the time had gone nowhere, and he had an assignation with Servilia.

An ecstatic Servilia was an exhausting experience.
She licked and kissed and sucked in a frenzy, opened herself and tried to open him, drained him dry then demanded
more.

It was, thought Caesar as he lay flat on his back, mind
cooling into sleep, the best and only way to eliminate the
kind of driving tension days like today provoked.

But though temporarily sated, Servilia had no intention of letting Caesar sleep. Annoying that he had no pubic
hair to tweak; she pinched the loose skin of his scrotum
instead.

"That woke you up!"

"You're a barbarian, Servilia."

"I want to talk."

"I want to sleep."

"Later, later!"

Sighing, he rolled onto his side and threw his leg over
her to keep his spine straight. "Talk away."

"I think you've beaten them," she said, paused, then
added, "for the time being, anyway."

"For the time being is correct. They'll never let up."

"They would if you'd grant them room for their *dignitas* too."

"Why should I? They don't know the meaning of the
word. If they want to preserve their own *dignitas,* they
should leave mine alone." He made a noise both scornful
and exasperated. "It's one thing after another, and the

older I get, the faster I have to run. My temper is fraying too easily.''

''So I gather. Can you mend it?''

''I'm not sure I want to. My mother used to say that that and my lack of patience were my two worst faults. She was a merciless critic, and a strict disciplinarian. By the time I went to the East I thought I'd beaten both faults. But I hadn't met Bibulus or Cato then, though I did encounter Bibulus very quickly after. On his own I could deal with him. Allied to Cato, he's a thousand times more intolerable.''

''Cato needs killing.''

''Leaving me with no formidable enemies? My dear Servilia, I am not wishing either Cato or Bibulus dead! The more opposition a man has, the better his mind works. I like opposition. No, what worries me is inside myself. That temper.''

''I think,'' said Servilia, stroking his leg, ''that you have a very peculiar sort of temper, Caesar. Most men are blinded by rage, whereas you seem to think more lucidly. It's one of the reasons why I love you. I am the same.''

''Rubbish!'' he said, laughing. ''You're coldblooded, Servilia, but your emotions are strong. You think you're planning lucidly when your temper is provoked, but those emotions get in the way. One day you'll plot and plan and scheme to achieve some end or other, only to find that having attained it, the consequences are disastrous. The knack is in going exactly as far as is necessary, and not one fraction of an inch further. Make the whole world tremble in fear of you, then show it mercy as well as justice. A hard act for one's enemies to follow.''

''I wish you had been Brutus's father.''

''Had I been, he would not be Brutus.''

''That's what I mean.''

''Leave him alone, Servilia. Let go of him a little more. When you appear he palpitates like a rabbit, yet he's not all weakling, you know. Oh, there's no lion in him, but I think he has some wolf and some fox. Why see him as a rabbit because in your company he is a rabbit?''

"Julia is fourteen now," she said, going off at a tangent.

"True. I must send Brutus a note to thank him for his gift to her. She loved it, you know."

Servilia sat up, astonished. "A *Plato* manuscript?"

"What, you thought it an unsuitable present?" He grinned and pinched her as hard as she had pinched him. "I gave her pearls, and she liked them very well. But not as much as Brutus's Plato."

"Jealous?"

That made him laugh outright. "Jealousy," he said, sobering, "is a curse. It eats, it corrodes. No, Servilia, I am many, many things, but I am not jealous. I was delighted for her, and very grateful to him. Next year I'll give her a philosopher." His eyes quizzed her wickedly. "Much cheaper than pearls too."

"Brutus both fosters and harbors his fortune."

"An excellent thing in Rome's wealthiest young man," agreed Caesar gravely.

Marcus Crassus returned to Rome after a long absence overseeing his various business enterprises just after that memorable day in the Forum, and eyed Caesar with new respect.

"Though I can't say that I'm sorry I found good excuse to absent myself after Tarquinius accused me in the House," he said. "I agree it's been an interesting interlude, but my tactics are very different from yours, Caesar. You go for the throat. I prefer to amble off and plough my furrows like the ox I'm always said to resemble."

"Hay tied well in place."

"Naturally."

"Well, as a technique it certainly works. It's a fool tries to bring you down, Marcus."

"And a fool tries to bring *you* down, Gaius." Crassus coughed. "How far in debt are you?"

Caesar frowned. "If anyone other than my mother knows, you do. But if you insist upon hearing the figure aloud, about two thousand talents. That's fifty million sesterces."

"I know that you know that I know how many sesterces there are in two thousand talents," said Crassus with a grin.

"What are you getting at, Marcus?"

"You're going to need a really lucrative province next year, is what I'm getting at. They won't let you fix the lots, you're too controversial. Not to mention that Cato will be hovering like a vulture above your carcass." Crassus wrinkled his brow. "Quite frankly, Gaius, I can't see how you'll do it even if the lots are favorable. Everywhere is pacified! Magnus has cowed the East, Africa hasn't been a danger since—oh, Jugurtha. Both the Spains are still suffering from Sertorius. The Gauls have nothing much to offer either."

"And Sicily, Sardinia and Corsica aren't worth mentioning," said Caesar, eyes dancing.

"Absolutely."

"Have you heard I'm going to be dunned at law?"

"No. What I do hear is that Catulus—he's much better, so they say, he'll be back making a nuisance of himself in Senate and Comitia shortly—is organizing a campaign to prorogue all the current governors next year, leaving this year's praetors with no provinces at all."

"Oh, I see!" Caesar looked thoughtful. "Yes, I should have taken a move like that into consideration."

"It might go through."

"It might, though I doubt it. There are a few of my fellow praetors who wouldn't take at all kindly to being deprived of a province, particularly Philippus, who might be a bit of an indolent Epicurean, but knows his worth too. Not to mention me."

"Be warned, is all."

"I am, and I thank you."

"Which doesn't take away from your difficulties, Caesar. I don't see how you can begin to pay your debts from a province."

"I do. My luck will provide, Marcus," said Caesar tranquilly. "I want Further Spain because I was quaestor there, and I know it well. The Lusitani and the Callaici are all I need! Decimus Brutus Callaicus—how easily they award those empty titles!—barely touched the fringes of northwestern Iberia. And northwestern Iberia, in case you've forgotten—you shouldn't, you were in Spain—is where all the gold comes from. Salamantica has been stripped, but places like Brigantium haven't even seen a Roman yet. But they'll see this Roman, so much I promise!''

"So you'll stake your chances on your luck in the lots." Crassus shook his head. "What a strange fellow you are, Caesar! I don't believe in luck. In all my life I've never offered a gift to Goddess Fortuna. A man makes his own luck."

"I agree unconditionally. But I also believe that Goddess Fortuna has her favorites among Roman men. She loved Sulla. And she loves me. Some men, Marcus, have Goddess-given luck as well as what they make for themselves. But none have Caesar's luck."

"Does your luck include Servilia?"

"Come as a surprise, did it?"

"You hinted at it once. That's playing with a firebrand."

"Ah, Crassus, she's marvelous in bed!"

"Huh!" grunted Crassus. He propped his feet up on a nearby chair and scowled at Caesar. "I suppose one can expect nothing else from a man who publicly talks to his battering ram. Still and all, you'll have more latitude to exercise your battering ram in the months to come. I predict people like Bibulus, Cato, Gaius Piso and Catulus will be licking their wounds for a long time."

"That," said Caesar, eyes twinkling, "is what Servilia says."

Publius Vatinius was a Marsian from Alba Fucentia. His grandfather was a humble man who had made a very wise decision and emigrated from the lands of the Marsi well before the Italian War broke out. Which in turn meant that his son, a young man then, was not called upon to take up arms against Rome, and consequently upon the conclusion of hostilities could apply to the *praetor peregrinus* for the Roman citizenship. The grandfather died, and his son moved back to Alba Fucentia possessed of a citizenship so shabby it was hardly worth the paper it was written on. Then when Sulla became Dictator he distributed all these new citizens across the thirty-five tribes, and Vatinius Senior was admitted into the tribe Sergia, one of the very oldest. The family fortunes prospered mightily. What had been a small merchant business became a large landholding one, for the Marsian country around the Fucine Lake was rich and productive, and Rome close enough down the Via Valeria to provide a market for the fruits, vegetables and fat lambs the Vatinius properties produced. After which Vatinius Senior went in for growing grapes, and was shrewd enough to pay a huge sum for vine stock yielding a superb white wine. By the time Publius Vatinius was twenty, his father's lands were worth many millions of sesterces, and produced nothing save this famous Fucentine nectar.

Publius Vatinius was the only child, and Fortune did not seem to favor him. When he was a lad he succumbed to what was called the Summer Disease, and emerged from it with the muscles below the knees of both legs so wasted that the only way he could walk was to pinch his thighs together tightly and fling his lower legs to each side; the resulting gait was reminiscent of a duck's. He then developed swelling lumps in his neck which sometimes abscessed, burst, and left terrible scars. He was therefore not a pretty sight. However, what had been denied his physical appearance was given instead to his nature and his mind. The nature was truly delightful, for he was witty, joyous, and very hard to ruffle. The mind was so acute it had early perceived that his best defense was to draw attention to his unsightly diseases, so he made a joke of himself and allowed others to do the same.

Because Vatinius Senior was relatively young to have a grown son, Publius Vatinius was not really needed at home, nor would he ever be able to stride around the properties the way his father did; Vatinius Senior concentrated upon training more remote relatives to take over the business, and sent his son to Rome to become a gentleman.

The vast upheavals and dislocations which followed in the wake of the Italian War had created a before-and-after situation which saw these newly prosperous families—and there were many of them—patronless. Every enterprising senator and knight of the upper Eighteen was looking for clients, yet prospective clients aplenty went unnoticed. As had the Vatinius family. But not once Publius Vatinius, a little old at twenty-five, finally arrived in Rome. Having settled in and settled down in lodgings on the Palatine, he looked about for a patron. That his choice fell on Caesar said much about his inclinations and his intelligence. Lucius Caesar was actually the senior of the branch, but Publius Vatinius went to Gaius because his unerring nose said Gaius was going to be the one with the real clout.

Of course Caesar had liked him instantly, and admitted him as a client of great value, which meant Vatinius's Forum career got under way in a most satisfactory manner. The next thing was to find Publius Vatinius a bride, since, as Vatinius said, ''The legs don't work too well, but there's nothing wrong with what hangs between them.''

Caesar's choice fell on the eldest child of his cousin Julia Antonia, her only daughter, Antonia Cretica. Of dowry she had none, but by birth she could guarantee her husband public prominence and admission to the ranks of the Famous Families. Unfortunately she was not a very prepossessing female creature, nor was she bright of intellect; her mother always forgot she existed, so wrapped up was she in her three sons, and perhaps too Antonia Cretica's size and shape proved a maternal embarrassment. At six feet in height she had shoulders nearly as wide as her young brothers', and while Nature gave her a barrel for a chest, Nature forgot to add breasts. Her nose and chin fought to meet across her mouth, and her neck was as thick as a gladiator's.

Did any of this worry the crippled and diminutive Publius Vatinius? Not at all! He espoused Antonia Cretica with zest in the year of Caesar's curule aedileship, and proceeded to sire a son and a daughter. He also loved her, his massive and ugly bride, and bore with perpetual good humor the opportunities this bizarre alliance offered to the Forum wits.

"You're all green with envy," he would say, laughing. "How many of you climb into your beds knowing you're going to conquer Italia's highest mountain? I tell you, when I reach the peak, I am as filled with triumph as she is with me!"

In the year of Cicero's consulship he was elected a quaestor, and entered the Senate. Of the twenty successful candidates he had polled last, no surprise given his lack of ancestry, and drew the lot for duty supervising all the ports of Italy save for Ostia and Brundisium, which had their own quaestors. He had been sent to Puteoli to prevent the illegal export of gold and silver, and had acquitted himself very respectably. Thus the ex-praetor Gaius Cosconius, given Further Spain to govern, had personally asked for Publius Vatinius as his legate.

He was still in Rome waiting for Cosconius to leave for his province when Antonia Cretica was killed in a freak accident on the Via Valeria. She had taken the children to see their grandparents in Alba Fucentia, and was returning to Rome when her carriage ran off the road. Mules and vehicle rolled and tumbled down a steep slope, breaking everything.

"Try to see the good in it, Vatinius," said Caesar, helpless before such genuine grief. "The children were in another carriage, you still have them."

"But I don't have her!" Vatinius wept desolately. "Oh, Caesar, how can I live?"

"By going to Spain and keeping busy," said his patron. "It is Fate, Vatinius. I too went to Spain having lost my beloved wife, and it was the saving of me." He got up to pour Vatinius another goblet of wine. "What do you want done with the children? Would you rather they went to their grandparents in Alba Fucentia, or stayed here in Rome?"

"I'd prefer Rome," Vatinius said, mopping his eyes, "but they need to be cared for by a relative, and I have none in Rome."

"There's Julia Antonia, who is also their grand-mother. Not a very wise mother, perhaps, but adequate for such young charges. It would give her something to do."

"You advise it, then."

"I think so—for the time being, while you're in Fur-ther Spain. When you come home, I think you should marry again. No, no, I'm not insulting your grief, Vatinius. You won't ever replace this wife, it doesn't work that way. But your children need a mother, and it would be better for you to forge a new bond with a new wife by siring more. Luckily you can afford a large family."

"You didn't sire more with your second wife."

"True. However, I'm not uxorious, whereas you are. You like a home life, I've noticed it. You also have the happy ability to get on with a woman who is not your mental equal. Most men are built so. I am not, I suppose." Caesar patted Vatinius on the shoulder. "Go to Spain at once, and remain there until at least next winter. Fight a little war if you can—Cosconius isn't up to that, which is why he's taking a legate. And find out all you can about the situation in the northwest."

"As you wish," said Vatinius, hauling himself to his feet. "And you're right, of course, I must marry again. Will you look out for someone for me?"

"I most certainly will."

A letter came from Pompey, written after Metellus Nepos had arrived in the Pompeian fold.

Still having trouble with the Jews, Caesar! Last time I wrote to you I was planning to meet the old Queen's two sons in Damascus, which I did last spring. Hyrcanus impressed me as more suit-able than Aristobulus, but I didn't want them to know whom I favored until I'd dealt with that old villain, King Aretas of Nabataea. So I sent the brothers back to Judaea under strict orders to keep the peace until they heard my decision—

didn't want the losing brother intriguing in my rear while I marched on Petra.

But Aristobulus worked out the right answer, that I was going to give the lot to Hyrcanus, so he decided to prepare for war. Not very smart, but still, I suppose he didn't have my measure yet. I put the expedition against Petra off, and marched for Jerusalem. Went into camp all around the city, which is extremely well fortified and naturally well placed for defense—cliffy valleys around it and the like.

No sooner did Aristobulus see this terrific-looking Roman army camped on the hills around than he came running to offer surrender. Along with several asses loaded down with bags of gold coins. Very nice of him to offer them to me, I said, but didn't he understand that he'd ruined my campaigning plans and cost Rome a much bigger sum of money than he had in his bags? But I'd forgive all if he agreed to pay for the expense of moving so many legions to Jerusalem. That, I said, would mean I wouldn't have to sack the place to find the money to pay. He was only too happy to oblige.

I sent Aulus Gabinius to pick up the money and order the gates opened, but Aristobulus's followers decided to resist. They wouldn't open the gates to Gabinius, and did some pretty rude things on top of the walls as a way of saying they were going to defy me. I arrested Aristobulus, and moved the army up. That made the city surrender, but there's a part of the place where this massive temple stands—a citadel, you'd have to call it. A few thousand of the diehards barricaded themselves in and refused to come out. A hard place to take, and I never was enthusiastic about siege. However, they had to be shown, so I showed them. They held out for three months, then I got bored and took the place. Faustus Sulla was first over the walls—

nice in a son of Sulla's, eh? Good lad. I intend
to marry him to my daughter when we get home,
she'll be old enough by then. Fancy having Sulla's son as my son-in-law! I've moved up in the
world nicely.

The temple was an interesting place, not
like our temples at all. No statues or anything
like that, and it sort of growls at you when
you're inside. Raised my hackles, I can tell you!
Lenaeus and Theophanes (I miss Varro terribly)
wanted to go behind this curtain into what they
call their Holy of Holies. So did Gabinius and
some of the others. It was bound to be full of
gold, they said. Well, I thought about it, Caesar,
but in the end I said no. Never set foot inside,
wouldn't let anyone else either. I'd got their
measure by then, you see. Very strange people.
Like us the religion is a part of the State, but
it's also different from us. I'd call them religious
fanatics, really. So I issued orders that no one
was to offend them religiously, from the rankers
all the way up to my senior legates. Why stir up
a nest of hornets when what I want from one
end of Syria to the other is peace, good order,
and client kings obedient to Rome, without turning the local customs and traditions upside
down? Every place has a *mos maiorum*.

I put Hyrcanus in as both King and High
Priest, and took Aristobulus prisoner. That's because I met the Idumaean prince, Antipater, in
Damascus. Very interesting fellow. Hyrcanus
isn't impressive, but I rely on Antipater to manipulate him—in Rome's direction, of course.
Oh yes, I didn't neglect to inform Hyrcanus that
he's there not by the grace of his God but by
the grace of Rome, that he's Rome's puppet and
always under the thumb of the Governor of Syria. Antipater suggested that I sweeten this cup
of vinegar by telling Hyrcanus that he ought to
channel most of his energies into the High

Priesthood—clever Antipater! I wonder does he know I know how much civil power he's usurped without lifting a warring finger?

I didn't leave Judaea quite as big as it was before the two silly brothers focused my attention on such a piddling spot. Anywhere that Jews were in a minority I drafted into Syria as an official part of the Roman province—Samaria, the coastal cities from Joppa to Gaza, and the Greek cities of the Decapolis all got their autonomy and became Syrian.

I'm still tidying up, but it begins to near the end at last. I'll be home by the end of this year. Which leads me to the deplorable events of the last year and the beginning of this one. In Rome, I mean. Caesar, I can't thank you enough for your help with Nepos. You tried. But why did we have to have that sanctimonious fart Cato in office? Ruined everything. And as you know, I haven't got a tribune of the plebs left worth pissing on. Can't even find one for next year!

I am bringing home mountains of loot, the Treasury won't even begin to hold Rome's share. There were sixteen thousand talents given in bonuses to my troops alone. Therefore I absolutely refuse to do what I've always done in the past, give my soldiers tenure of my own land. This time Rome can give them land. They deserve it, and Rome owes it to them. So if I die trying, I'll see they get State land. I rely on you to do what you can, and if you happen to have a tribune of the plebs inclined to think your way, I would be happy to share the cost of his hire. Nepos says there's going to be a big fight over land, not that I didn't expect it. Too many powerful men leasing public land out for their *latifundia*. Very shortsighted of the Senate.

I heard a rumor, by the way, and wondered if you'd heard it too. That Mucia's being a naughty girl. I asked Nepos, and he flew so high

I wondered if he was ever going to come down
again. Well, brothers and sisters do tend to stick
together, so I suppose it's natural he didn't like
the question. Anyway, I'm making enquiries. If
there's any truth in it, it's bye-bye to Mucia.
She's been a good wife and mother, but I can't
say I've missed her much since I've been away.

"Oh, Pompeius," said Caesar as he put the letter
down, "you are in a league all of your own!"

He frowned, thinking of the last part of Pompey's
missive first. Titus Labienus had left Rome to return to
Picenum soon after he relinquished office, and presumably
had resumed his affair with Mucia Tertia. A pity. Ought
he perhaps to write and warn Labienus what was coming?
No. Letters were prone to be opened by the wrong people,
and there were some who were past masters of the art of
resealing them. If Mucia Tertia and Labienus were in danger, they would have to deal with it themselves. Pompey
the Great was more important; Caesar was beginning to
see all sorts of alluring possibilities after the Great Man
came home with his mountains of loot. The land wasn't
going to be forthcoming; his soldiers would go unre-
warded. But in less than three years' time, Gaius Julius
Caesar would be senior consul, and Publius Vatinius
would be his tribune of the plebs. What an excellent way
to put the Great Man in the debt of a far greater man!

Both Servilia and Marcus Crassus had been right; after that amazing day in the Forum, Caesar's year as urban
praetor became very peaceful. One by one the rest of Catilina's adherents were tried and convicted, though Lucius
Novius Niger was no longer the judge in the special court.
After some debate the Senate decided to transfer the trials
to Bibulus's court once the first five had been sentenced
to exile and confiscation of property.

And, as Caesar learned from Crassus, Cicero got his
new house. The biggest Catilinarian fish of all had never
been named by any of the informers—Publius Sulla. Most

people knew, however, that if Autronius had been involved, so had Publius Sulla. The nephew of the Dictator and husband of Pompey's sister, Publius Sulla had inherited enormous wealth, but not his uncle's political acumen and certainly not his uncle's sense of self-preservation. Unlike the rest, he had not entered the conspiracy to increase his fortune; it had been done to oblige his friends and alleviate his perpetual boredom.

"He's asked Cicero to defend," said Crassus, chuckling, "and that puts Cicero in a frightful predicament."

"Only if he intends to consent, surely," said Caesar.

"Oh, he's already consented, Gaius."

"How do you know all this?"

"Because our swan of an ex-consul has just been to see me. Suddenly he has the money to buy my house—or hopes he has."

"Ah! How much are you asking?"

"Five million."

Caesar leaned back in his chair, shaking his head dolefully. "You know, Marcus, you always remind me of a speculation builder. Every house you build for your wife and children you swear by all the Gods is going to stay theirs. Then along comes someone with more money than sense, offers you a fat profit, and—bang! Wife and children are homeless until the next house is built."

"I paid a long price for it," said Crassus defensively.

"Not nearly as long as five million!"

"Well, yes," said Crassus, then brightened. "Tertulla has taken a dislike to the place, as a matter of fact, so she isn't brokenhearted at the thought of moving. I'm going to buy on the Circus Maximus side of the Germalus this time—next door to that palace Hortensius maintains to house his fish ponds."

"Why has Tertulla taken a dislike to it after all these years?" Caesar asked skeptically.

"Well, it belonged to Marcus Livius Drusus."

"I know that. I also know he was murdered in its atrium."

"There's something there!" Crassus whispered.

"And it's welcome to gnaw at Cicero and Terentia,

eh?'' Caesar began to laugh. ''I told you at the time that it was a mistake to use black marble inside—too many dark corners. And, knowing how little you pay your servants, Marcus, I'd be willing to bet some of them have a fine old time of it moaning and sighing out of the shadows. I would also be willing to bet that when you move, your evil presences will go with you—unless you cough up some solid wage rises, that is.''

Crassus brought the subject back to Cicero and Publius Sulla. ''It appears,'' he said, ''that Publius Sulla is willing to 'lend' Cicero the entire sum if he defends.''

''*And* gets him off,'' said Caesar gently.

''Oh, he'll do that!'' This time Crassus laughed, an extremely rare event. ''You ought to have heard him! Busy rewriting the history of his consulship, no less. Do you remember all those meetings through September, October and November? When Publius Sulla sat beside Catilina supporting him loudly? Well, according to Cicero that wasn't Publius Sulla sitting there, it was Spinther wearing his *imago*!''

''I hope you're joking, Marcus.''

''Yes and no. Cicero now insists that Publius Sulla spent the bulk of those many *nundinae* looking after his interests in Pompeii! He was hardly in Rome, did you know that?''

''You're right, it must have been Spinther wearing his *imago*.''

''He'll convince the jury of it, anyway.''

At which moment Aurelia poked her head round the door. ''When you have the time, Caesar, I would like a word with you,'' she said.

Crassus rose. ''I'm off, I have some people to see. Speaking of houses,'' he said as he and Caesar walked to the front door, ''I must say the Domus Publica is the best address in Rome. On the way to and from everywhere. Nice to pop in knowing there's a friendly face and a good drop of wine.''

''You could afford the good drop of wine yourself, you old skinflint!''

''You know, I am getting old,'' said Crassus, ignoring the noun. ''What are you, thirty-seven?''

''Thirty-eight this year.''

''Brrr! I'll be fifty-four.'' He sighed wistfully. ''You know, I did want a big campaign before I retired! Something to rival Pompeius Magnus.''

''According to him, there are no worlds left to conquer.''

''What about the Parthians?''

''What about Dacia, Boiohaemum, all the lands of the Danubius?''

''Is that where you're going, is it, Caesar?''

''I've been thinking of it, yes.''

''The Parthians,'' said Crassus positively, stepping through the door. ''More gold that way than to the north.''

''Every race esteems gold most,'' said Caesar, ''so every race will yield gold.''

''You'll need it to pay your debts.''

''Yes, I will. But gold isn't the great lure, at least for me. In that respect Pompeius Magnus has things correct. The gold just appears. What's more important is the length of Rome's reach.''

Crassus's answer was a wave; he turned in the direction of the Palatine and disappeared.

There was never any point in trying to avoid Aurelia when she wanted a word, so Caesar went straight from the front door to her quarters, now thoroughly imprinted with her hand: none of the handsome decor was visible anymore, covered with pigeonholes, scrolls, papers, book buckets, and a loom in the corner. Suburan accounts no longer interested her; she was helping the Vestals in their archiving.

''What is it, Mater?'' he asked, standing in the doorway.

''It's our new Virgin,'' she said, indicating a chair.

He sat down, willing now to listen. ''Cornelia Merula?''

''The very same.''

''She's only seven, Mater. How much trouble can she make at that age? Unless she's wild, and I didn't think she was.''

"We have put a Cato in our midst," said his mother. "Oh!"

"Fabia can't deal with her, nor can any of the others. Junia and Quinctilia loathe her, and are beginning to pinch and scratch."

"Bring Fabia and Cornelia Merula to my office now, please."

Not many moments later Aurelia ushered the Chief Vestal and the new little Vestal into Caesar's office, an immaculate and most imposing setting glowing dully in crimson and purple.

There was a Cato look to Cornelia Merula, who reminded Caesar of that first time he had ever seen Cato, looking down from Marcus Livius Drusus's house onto the loggia of Ahenobarbus's house, where Sulla had been staying. A skinny, lonely little boy to whom he had waved sympathetically. She too was tall and thin; she too had that Catonian coloring, auburn hair and grey eyes. And she stood the way Cato always stood, legs apart, chin out, fists clenched.

"Mater, Fabia, you may sit down," said the Pontifex Maximus formally. One hand went out to the child. "You may stand here," he said, indicating a spot in front of his desk. "Now what's the trouble, Chief Vestal?" he asked.

"A great deal, it seems!" said Fabia tartly. "We live too luxuriously—we have too much spare time—we are more interested in wills than Vesta—we have no right to drink water which hasn't been fetched from the Well of Juturna—we don't prepare the *mola salsa* the way it was done during the reigns of the kings—we don't mince the October Horse's parts properly—and more besides!"

"And how do you know what happens to the October Horse's parts, little blackbird?" Caesar asked the child kindly, preferring to call her that (Merula meant a blackbird). "You haven't been in the Atrium Vestae long enough to have seen an October Horse's parts." Oh, how hard it was not to laugh! The parts of the October Horse which were rushed first to the Regia to allow some blood to drip onto the altar, then to Vesta's sacred hearth to allow the same, were the genitalia plus the tail complete with

anal sphincter. After the ceremonies all of these were cut
up, minced, mixed with the last of the blood, then burned;
the ashes were used during a Vestal feast in April, the
Parilia.

"My great-grandmother told me," said Cornelia
Merula in a voice which promised one day to be as loud
as Cato's.

"How does she know, since she isn't a Vestal?"

"You," said the little blackbird, "are in this house
under false pretenses. That means I don't have to answer
you."

"Do you want to be sent back to your great-
grandmother?"

"You can't do that, I'm a Vestal now."

"I can do it, and I will if you don't answer my questions."

She was not at all cowed; instead, she thought about
what he said carefully. "I can only be ejected from the
Order if I am prosecuted in a court and convicted."

"What a little lawyer! But you are wrong, Cornelia.
The law is sensible, so it always makes provision for the
occasional blackbird caged up with snow-white peahens.
You *can* be sent home." Caesar leaned forward, eyes
chilly. "Please don't try my patience, Cornelia! Just believe me. Your great-grandmother would not be amused if
you were declared unsuitable and sent home in disgrace."

"I don't believe you," Cornelia said stubbornly.

Caesar rose to his feet. "You'll believe me after I've
taken you home this very moment!" He turned to Fabia,
listening fascinated. "Fabia, pack her things, then send
them on."

Which was the difference between seven and twenty-
seven; Cornelia Merula gave in. "I'll answer your questions, Pontifex Maximus," she said heroically, eyes
shining with tears, but no tears falling.

By this time Caesar just wanted to squash her with
hugs and kisses, but of course one couldn't do that, even
were it not so important that she be, if not tamed, at least
made tractable. Seven or twenty-seven, she was a Vestal
Virgin and could not be squashed with hugs and kisses.

''You said I'm here under false pretenses, Cornelia. What did you mean by that?''

''Great-grandmother says so.''

''Is everything great-grandmother says true?''

The grey eyes widened in horror. ''Yes, of course!''

''Did great-grandmother tell you why I'm here under false pretenses, or was it simply a statement without facts to back it up?'' he asked sternly.

''She just said so.''

''I am not here under false pretenses, I am the legally elected Pontifex Maximus.''

''You are the *flamen Dialis*,'' Cornelia muttered.

''I was the *flamen Dialis*, but that was a very long time ago. I was appointed to take your great-grandfather's place. But then some irregularities in the inauguration ceremonies were discovered, and all the priests and augurs decided I could not continue to serve as *flamen Dialis*.''

''You are still the *flamen Dialis*!''

''*Domine*,'' he said gently. ''I am your lord, little blackbird, which means you behave politely and call me *domine*.''

''*Domine*, then.''

''I am not still the *flamen Dialis*.''

''Yes you are! *Domine*.''

''Why?''

''Because,'' said Cornelia Merula triumphantly, ''there isn't a *flamen Dialis*!''

''Another decision of the priestly and augural colleges, little blackbird. I am not the *flamen Dialis*, but it was decided not to appoint another man to the post until after my death. Just to make everything in our contract with the Great God absolutely legal.''

''Oh.''

''Come here, Cornelia.''

She came round the corner of his desk reluctantly, and stood where he pointed, two feet away from his chair.

''Hold out your hands.''

She flinched, paled; Caesar understood great-grandmother a great deal better when Cornelia Merula held out her hands as a child does to receive punishment.

His own hands went out, took hers in a firm warm clasp. "I think it's time you forgot great-grandmother as the authority in your life, little blackbird. You have espoused the Order of Rome's Vestal Virgins. You have passed out of great-grandmother's hands and into mine. Feel them, Cornelia. Feel my hands."

She did so, shyly and very timidly. How sad, he thought, that until her eighth year she has clearly never been hugged or kissed by the *paterfamilias,* and now her new *paterfamilias* is bound by solemn and sacred laws never to hug or kiss her, child that she is. Sometimes Rome is a cruel mistress.

"They're strong, aren't they?"

"Yes," she whispered.

"And much bigger than yours."

"Yes."

"Do you feel them shake or sweat?"

"No, *domine.*"

"Then there is no more to be said. You and your fate are in my hands, I am your father now. I will care for you as a father, the Great God and Vesta require it. But most of why I will care for you is because you are you, a little girl. You won't be slapped or spanked, you won't be shut in dark cupboards or sent to bed without your supper. That is not to say the Atrium Vestae is a place without punishment, only that punishments should be carefully thought out, and always made to fit the crime. If you break something, you will have to mend it. If you soil something, you will have to wash it. But the one crime for which there is no other punishment than being sent home as unsuitable is the crime of sitting in judgement on your seniors. It is not your place to say what the Order drinks, how that drink is obtained, nor which side of the cup is the side to sip from. It is not your place to define what exactly is Vestal tradition or custom. The *mos maiorum* is not a static thing, it doesn't stay as it was during the reigns of the kings. Like everything else in the world, it changes to suit the times. So no more criticisms, no more sitting in judgement. Is that understood?"

"Yes, *domine.*"

He let go her hands, never having put himself closer to her than those two feet. "You may go, Cornelia, but wait outside. I want to speak to Fabia."

"Thank you, Pontifex Maximus," sighed Fabia, beaming.

"Don't thank me, Chief Vestal, just cope with these ups and downs sensibly," said Caesar. "I think in future it might be wise if I take a more active part in the education of the three young girls. Classes once every eight days from an hour after dawn until noon. On, let us say, the third day after the *nundinus*."

The interview was clearly at an end; Fabia rose, made an obeisance, and left.

"You handled that extremely well, Caesar," said Aurelia.

"Poor little thing!"

"Too many spankings."

"What an old horror great-grandmother must be."

"Some people live to be too old, Caesar. I hope I do not."

"The important thing is, have I banished Cato?"

"Oh, I think so. Especially if you tutor her. That's an excellent idea. Not Fabia nor Arruntia nor Popillia has one grain of common sense, and I cannot interfere too much. I am a woman, not the *paterfamilias*."

"How odd, Mater! In all my life I have never been *paterfamilias* to a male!"

Aurelia got to her feet, smiling. "For which I am very glad, my son. Look at Young Marius, poor fellow. The women in your hand are grateful for your strength and authority. If you had a son, he would have to live under your shadow. For greatness skips not one but usually many generations in all families, Caesar. You would see him as yourself, and he would despair."

The Clodius Club was gathered in the big and beautiful house Fulvia's money had bought for Clodius right next door to the expensive insula of luxury apartments that represented his most lucrative investment. Everyone of genuine importance was there: the two Clodias, Fulvia,

Pompeia Sulla, Sempronia Tuditani, Palla, Decimus Brutus (Sempronia Tuditani's son), Curio, young Poplicola
(Palla's son), Clodius, and an aggrieved Mark Antony.

"I wish I were Cicero," he was saying gloomily,
"then I'd have no need to get married."

"That sounds like a non sequitur to me, Antonius,"
said Curio, smiling. "Cicero's married, and to a shrew at
that."

"Yes, but he's so well known to be able to get people
off at trial that they're even willing to 'lend' him five
million," Antony persisted. "If I could get people off at
trial, I'd have my five million without needing to marry."

"Oho!" said Clodius, sitting up straighter. "Who's
the lucky little bride, Antonius?"

"Uncle Lucius—he's *paterfamilias* now because Uncle Hybrida won't have anything to do with us—refuses
to pay my debts. My stepfather's estate is embarrassed,
and there's nothing left of what my father had. So I have
to marry some awful girl who smells of the shop."

"Who?" asked Clodius.

"Her name's Fadia."

"Fadia? I've never heard of a Fadia," said Clodilla,
a very contented divorcée these days. "Tell us more, Antonius, do!"

The massive shoulders lifted in a shrug. "That's it,
really. No one has ever heard of her."

"Getting information out of you, Antonius, is like
squeezing blood out of a stone," said Celer's wife, Clodia.
"Who is Fadia?"

"Her father's some filthy-rich merchant from Placen-
tia."

"You mean she's a *Gaul*?" gasped Clodius.

Another man might have bridled defensively; Mark
Antony merely grinned. "Uncle Lucius swears not. Im-
peccably Roman, he says. I suppose that means she is.
The Caesars are experts on bloodlines."

"Well, go on!" from Curio.

"There's not much more to tell you. Old man Titus
Fadius has a son and a daughter. He wants the son in the
Senate, and decided the best way he can do that is to find

a noble husband for the daughter. The son's ghastly, apparently, no one would have him. So I'm it.'' Antony flashed a smile at Curio, displaying surprisingly small but regular teeth. ''You were nearly it, but your father said he'd prostitute his daughter before he'd consent.''

Curio collapsed, shrieking. ''He should hope! Scribonia is so ugly only Appius Claudius the Blind would have been interested.''

''Oh, do shut up, Curio!'' said Pompeia. ''We all know about Scribonia, but we don't know about Fadia. Is she pretty, Marcus?''

''Her dowry's very pretty.''

''How much?'' asked Decimus Brutus.

''Three hundred talents are the going price for the grandson of Antonius Orator!''

Curio whistled. ''If Fadius asked my *tata* again, I'd be glad to sleep wearing a blindfold! That's half as much again as Cicero's five million! You'll even have a bit left over after you've paid all your debts.''

''I'm not quite Cousin Gaius, Curio!'' said Antony, chortling. ''I don't owe more than half a million.'' He sobered. ''Anyway, none of them are about to let me get my hands on ready cash. Uncle Lucius and Titus Fadius are drawing up the marriage agreements so that Fadia keeps control of her fortune.''

''Oh, Marcus, that's dreadful!'' cried Clodia.

''Yes, that's what I said straight after I refused to marry her on those terms,'' Antony said complacently.

''You refused?'' asked Palla, raddled cheeks working like a squirrel nibbling nuts.

''Yes.''

''And what happened then?''

''They backed down.''

''All the way?''

''Not all the way, but far enough. Titus Fadius agreed to pay my debts and give me a cash settlement of a million besides. So I'm getting married in ten days' time, though none of you has been asked to the wedding. Uncle Lucius wants me to look pure.''

''No gall, no Gaul!'' howled Curio.

Everyone fell about laughing.

The meeting proceeded merrily enough for some time, though nothing important was said. The only attendants in the room were poised behind the couch on which lay Pompeia together with Palla, and they both belonged to Pompeia. The younger was her own maid, Doris, and the elder was Aurelia's valued watchdog, Polyxena. Not one member of the Clodius Club was unaware that everything Polyxena heard would be reported faithfully to Aurelia once Pompeia returned to the Domus Publica, an annoyance of major proportions. In fact, there were many meetings held without Pompeia, either because the mischief being plotted was not for dissemination to the mother of the Pontifex Maximus, or because someone was proposing yet again that Pompeia be ejected. One good reason, however, had permitted Pompeia continued admission: there were times when it was useful to know that a rigid old pillar of society with a great deal of influence in that society was being fed information.

Today Publius Clodius reached the end of his tether. "Pompeia," he said, voice hard, "that old spy behind you is an abomination! There's nothing going on here all of Rome can't know, but I object to spies, and that means I have to object to you! Go home, and take your wretched spy with you!"

The luminous and amazingly green eyes filled with tears; Pompeia's lip trembled. "Oh, please, Publius Clodius! Please!"

Clodius turned his back. "Go home," he said.

An awkward silence fell while Pompeia bundled herself off her couch, into her shoes and out of the room, Polyxena following with her customary wooden expression, and Doris sniffling.

"That was unkind, Publius," said Clodia after they had gone.

"Kindness is not a virtue I esteem!" Clodius snapped.

"She's Sulla's granddaughter!"

"I don't care if she's Jupiter's granddaughter! I am sick to death of putting up with Polyxena!"

"Cousin Gaius," said Antony, "is not a fool. You'll gain no access to *his* wife without someone like Polyxena present, Clodius."

"I know that, Antonius!"

"He's had so much experience himself," Antony explained with a grin. "I doubt there's a trick he doesn't know when it comes to cuckolding husbands." He sighed happily. "He's the north wind, but he does adorn our stuffy family! More conquests than Apollo."

"I don't want to cuckold Caesar, I just want to be free of Polyxena!" snarled Clodius.

Suddenly Clodia began to giggle. "Well, now that the Eyes and Ears of Rome have departed, I can tell you what happened at Atticus's dinner party the other evening."

"That must have been exciting for you, Clodia dear," young Poplicola said. "Very prim and proper!"

"Oh, absolutely, especially with Terentia there."

"So what makes it worth mentioning?" Clodius asked grumpily, still incensed over Polyxena.

Clodia's voice dropped, became fraught with significance. "I was seated opposite Cicero!" she announced.

"How could you bear such ecstasy?" asked Sempronia Tuditani.

"How could *he* bear such ecstasy, you mean!"

All heads turned her way.

"Clodia, he didn't!" cried Fulvia.

"He certainly did," Clodia said smugly. "He fell for me as hard as an insula coming down in an earthquake."

"In front of Terentia?"

"Well, she was round the corner facing the *lectus imus,* so she had her back to us. Yes, thanks to my friend Atticus, Cicero slipped his leash."

"What happened?" asked Curio, helpless with laughter.

"I flirted with him from one end of the dinner to the other, that's what happened. I flirted *outrageously,* and he adored it! Not to mention me. Told me he didn't know there was a woman in Rome so well read. That was after

I quoted the new poet, Catullus." She turned to Curio. "Have you read him? Glorious!"

Curio wiped his eyes. "Haven't heard of him."

"Brand new—published by Atticus, of course. Comes from Italian Gaul across the Padus. Atticus says he's about to descend on Rome—I can't wait to meet him!"

"Back to Cicero," said Clodius, seeing Forum possibilities. "What's he like in the throes of love? I didn't think he had it in him, frankly."

"Oh, very silly and kittenish," said Clodia, sounding bored. She rolled over on her back and kicked her legs. "Everything about him changes. The *pater patriae* becomes a Plautus ponce. That was why it was so much fun. I just kept prodding him to make a bigger and bigger fool of himself."

"You're a wicked woman!" said Decimus Brutus.

"That's what Terentia thought too."

"Oho! So she did notice?"

"After a while the whole room noticed." Clodia wrinkled up her nose and looked adorable. "The harder he fell for me, the louder and sillier he became. Atticus was almost paralyzed with laughter." She shivered theatrically. "Terentia was almost paralyzed with rage. Poor old Cicero! Why do we think he's old, by the way? To repeat, poor old Cicero! I don't imagine they were more than a foot from Atticus's door before Terentia was gnawing on his neck."

"She wouldn't have been gnawing on anything else," purred Sempronia Tuditani.

The howl of mirth which went up made the servants in Fulvia's kitchen at the far end of the garden smile—such a happy house!

Suddenly Clodia's merriment changed tenor; she sat up very straight and looked gleefully at her brother. "Publius Clodius, are you game for some delicious mischief?"

"Is Caesar a Roman?"

The next morning Clodia presented herself at the Pontifex Maximus's front door accompanied by several other female members of the Clodius Club.

"Is Pompeia in?" she asked Eutychus.

"She is receiving, *domina,*" said the steward, bowing as he admitted them.

And off up the stairs the party went, while Eutychus hurried about his business. No need to summon Polyxena; young Quintus Pompeius Rufus was out of Rome, so there would be no men present.

It was evident that Pompeia had spent the night weeping; her eyes were puffed and reddened, her demeanor woebegone. When Clodia and the others bustled in, she leaped to her feet.

"Oh, Clodia, I was sure I'd never see you again!" she cried.

"My dear, I wouldn't do that to you! But you can't really blame my brother, now can you? Polyxena tells Aurelia everything."

"I know, I know! I'm so sorry, but what can I do?"

"Nothing, dear one, nothing." Clodia seated herself in the manner of a gorgeous bird settling, then smiled around the group she had brought with her: Fulvia, Clodilla, Sempronia Tuditani, Palla, and one other whom Pompeia didn't recognize.

"This," said Clodia demurely, "is my cousin Claudia from the country. She's down on a holiday."

"*Ave,* Claudia," said Pompeia Sulla, smiling with her usual vacancy, and thinking that if Claudia was a rustic, she was very much in the mold of Palla and Sempronia Tuditani—wherever she came from must deem her racy indeed, with all that paint and lush bleached hair. Pompeia tried to be polite. "I can see the family likeness," she said.

"I should hope so," said cousin Claudia, pulling off that fantastic head of bright gold tresses.

For a moment Pompeia looked as if she was about to faint: her mouth dropped open, she gasped for air.

All of which was too much for Clodia and the others. They screamed with laughter.

"*Sssssh!*" hissed Publius Clodius, striding in a most unfeminine way to the outer door and slamming its latch home. He then returned to his seat, pursed up his mouth and fluttered his lashes. "My dear, what a *divine* apartment!" he fluted.

"Oh, oh, oh!" squeaked Pompeia. "Oh, you *can't*!"

"I can, because here I am," said Clodius in his normal voice. "And you're right, Clodia. No Polyxena."

"Please, please don't stay!" said Pompeia in a whisper, face white, hands writhing. "My mother-in-law!"

"What, does she spy on you here too?"

"Not usually, but the Bona Dea is happening soon, and it's being held here. I'm supposed to be organizing it."

"You mean Aurelia's organizing it, surely," sneered Clodius.

"Well yes, of course she is! But she's very meticulous about pretending to consult me because I'm the official hostess, the wife of the praetor in whose house Bona Dea is being held. Oh, Clodius, *please* go! She's in and out all the time at the moment, and if she finds my door latched, she'll complain to Caesar."

"My poor baby!" crooned Clodius, enfolding Pompeia in a hug. "I'll go, I promise." He went to a magnificent polished silver mirror hanging on the wall, and with Fulvia's assistance twitched his wig into place.

"I can't say you're pretty, Publius," said his wife as she put the finishing touches to his coiffure, "but you make a passable woman"—she giggled—"if of somewhat dubious profession!"

"Come on, let's go," said Clodius to the rest of the visitors, "I only wanted to show Clodia that it could be done, and it can!"

The door latch flipped; the women went out in a cluster with Clodius in its middle.

Just in time. Aurelia appeared shortly thereafter, with her brows raised. "Who were they, hustling themselves off in a hurry?"

"Clodia and Clodilla and a few others," said Pompeia vaguely.

"You'd better know what sort of milk we're serving."

"Milk?" asked Pompeia, astonished.

"Oh, Pompeia, honestly!" Aurelia stood just looking at her daughter-in-law. "Is there *nothing* inside that head except trinkets and clothes?"

Whereupon Pompeia burst into tears. Aurelia emitted one of her extremely rare mild expletives (though in a muffled voice), and whisked herself away before she boxed Pompeia's ears.

Outside on the Via Sacra the five genuine articles plus Clodius scurried up the road rather than down it toward the lower Forum; safer than encountering someone male they knew very well. Clodius was delighted with himself, and pranced along attracting quite a lot of attention from the well-to-do lady shoppers who frequented the area of the Porticus Margaritaria and the upper Forum. It was therefore with considerable relief that the women managed to get him home without someone's penetrating his disguise.

"I'm going to be asked for days to come who was that strange creature with me this morning!" said Clodia wrathfully once the trappings were off and a washed, respectable Publius Clodius had disposed himself on a couch.

"It was all your idea!" he protested.

"Yes, but you didn't have to make a public spectacle of yourself! The understanding was that you'd wrap up well there and back, not simper and wiggle for all the world to wonder at!"

"Shut up, Clodia, I'm thinking!"

"About what?"

"A little matter of revenge."

Fulvia cuddled up to him, sensing the change. No one knew better than his wife that Clodius kept a list of victims inside his head, and no one was more prepared to help him than his wife. Of late the list had shrunk; Catilina was no more, and Arabs were probably permanently erased from it. So which one was it?

"Who?" she asked, sucking his earlobe.

"Aurelia," he said between his teeth. "It's high time someone cut her down to size."

"And just how do you plan to do that?" Palla asked.

"It won't do Fabia any good either," he said thoughtfully, "and she's another needing a lesson."

"What are you up to, Clodius?" asked Clodilla, looking wary.

"Mischief!" he caroled, grabbed for Fulvia and began to tickle her unmercifully.

Bona Dea was the Good Goddess, as old as Rome herself and therefore owning neither face nor form; she was *numen*. She did have a name, but it was never uttered, so holy was it. What she meant to Roman women no man could understand, nor why she was called Good. Her worship lay quite outside the official State religion, and though the Treasury did give her a little money, she answered to no man or group of men. The Vestal Virgins cared for her because she had no priestesses of her own; they employed the women who tended her sacred medicinal garden, and they had custody of Bona Dea's medicines, which were for Roman women only.

As she had no part in masculine Rome, her huge temple precinct lay outside the *pomerium* on the slope of the Aventine just beneath an outcropping rock, the Saxum Sacrum or sacred stone, and close to the Aventine water reservoir. No man dared come near, nor myrtle. A statue stood within the sanctuary, but it was not an effigy of Bona Dea, only something put there to trick the evil forces generated by men into thinking that was her. Nothing was what first it seemed in the world of Bona Dea, who loved women and snakes. Her precinct abounded in snakes. Men, it was said, were snakes. And owning so many snakes, what need had Bona Dea for men?

The medicines Bona Dea was famous for came from a garden all about the temple itself, beds of various herbs here, and elsewhere a sea of diseased rye planted each May Day and harvested under the supervision of the Vestals, who took its smutty ears of grain and made Bona Dea's elixir from them—while thousands of snakes dozed or rustled amid the stalks, ignored and ignoring.

On May Day the women of Rome woke their Good Goddess from her six-month winter sleep amid flowers and festivities held in and around her temple. Roman citizen women from all walks of life flocked to attend the mysteries, which began at dawn and were ended by dusk. The exquisitely balanced duality of the Good Goddess was manifest in May birth and rye death, in wine and milk. For wine was taboo, yet had to be consumed in vast quantities. It was called milk and kept in precious silver vessels called honeypots, yet one more ruse to confound male things. Tired women wended their way home replete with milk poured from honeypots, still tingling from the voluptuous dry slither of snakes and remembering the powerful surge of snake muscle, the kiss of a forked tongue, earth broken open to receive the seed, a crown of vine leaves, the eternal female cycle of birth and death. But no man knew or wanted to know what happened at Bona Dea on May Day.

Then at the beginning of December Bona Dea went back to sleep, but not publicly, not while there was a sun in the sky or one ordinary Roman woman abroad. Because what she dreamed in winter was her secret, the rites were open only to the highest born of Rome's women. All her daughters might witness her resurrection, but only the daughters of kings might watch her die. Death was sacred. Death was holy. Death was private.

That this year Bona Dea would be laid to rest in the house of the Pontifex Maximus was a foregone conclusion; the choice of venue was in the province of the Vestals, who were constrained by the fact that this venue had to be the house of an incumbent praetor or consul. Not since the time of Ahenobarbus Pontifex Maximus had there been an opportunity to celebrate the rites in the Domus Publica itself. This year there was. The urban praetor Caesar's house was selected, and his wife Pompeia Sulla would be the official hostess. The date was to be the third night of December, and on that night no man or male child was permitted to remain in the Domus Publica, including slaves.

Naturally Caesar was delighted at the choice of his house, and happy to sleep in his rooms on the lower Vicus Patricii; he might perhaps have preferred to use the old apartment in Aurelia's insula, except that it was at present occupied by Prince Masintha of Numidia, his client and the loser in a court case earlier in the year. That temper definitely frayed easier these days! At one stage he had become so incensed at the lies Prince Juba was busy telling that he had reached out and hauled Juba to his feet by seizing his beard. Not a citizen, Masintha faced flogging and strangling, but Caesar had whisked him away in the care of Lucius Decumius and was still hiding him. Perhaps, thought the Pontifex Maximus as he wandered uphill toward the Subura, just this night he could sample one of those deliciously earthy Suburan women time and the elevation of his fortunes had removed from his ken. Yes, what a terribly good idea! A meal with Lucius Decumius first, then a message to Gavia or Apronia or Scaptia . . .

Full darkness had fallen, but for once that part of the Via Sacra which meandered through the Forum Romanum was illuminated by torches; what seemed an endless parade of litters and lackeys converged on the main doors of the Domus Publica from all directions, and the smoky pall of light caught flashes of wondrously hued robes, sparks from fabulous jewelry, glimpses of eager faces. Cries of greeting, giggles, little snatches of conversation floated on the air as the women alighted and passed into the vestibule of the Domus Publica, shaking their trailing garments out, patting their hair, adjusting a brooch or an earring. Many a headache and many a temper tantrum had gone into the business of planning what to wear, for this was the best opportunity of the year to show one's peers how fashionably one could dress, how expensive the treasures in the jewel box were. Men never noticed! Women always did.

The guest list was unusually large because the premises were so spacious; Caesar had tented over the main peristyle garden to exclude prying eyes on the Via Nova, which meant the women could congregate there as well as in the atrium temple, the Pontifex Maximus's vast dining room, and his reception room. Lamps glimmered everywhere, tables were loaded with the most sumptuous and tasty food, the honeypots of milk were bottomless and the

milk itself was a superb vintage. Coveys of women musicians sat or walked about playing pipes and flutes and
lyres, little drums, castanets, tambourines, silvery rattles;
servants passed constantly from one cluster of guests to
another with plates of delicacies, more milk.

Before the solemn mysteries began the mood had to
be correct, which meant the party had to have passed beyond its food, milk and chatty stage. No one was in a
hurry; there was too much catching up to do as faces long
unseen were recognized and hailed, and warm friends
clumped to exchange the latest gossip.

Reptilian snakes had no part in putting the Bona Dea
to sleep; her winter soporific was the snakelike whip, a
wicked thing ending in a cluster of Medusa-like thongs
which would curl as lovingly about a woman's flesh as
any reptile. But the flagellation would be later, after Bona
Dea's winter altar was lit and enough milk had been drunk
to dull the pain, raise it instead to a special kind of ecstasy.
Bona Dea was a hard mistress.

Aurelia had insisted that Pompeia Sulla stand alongside Fabia to do door duty and welcome the guests, profoundly glad that the ladies of the Clodius Club were
among the last to arrive. Well, of course they would be!
It must have taken hours for middle-aged tarts like Sempronia Tuditani and Palla to paint that many layers on their
faces—though a mere sliver of time to insert their stringy
bodies into so little! The Clodias, she had to admit, were
both exquisite: lovely dresses, exactly the right jewelry
(and not too much of it), touches only of *stibium* and carmine. Fulvia as always was a law unto herself, from her
flame-colored gown to several ropes of blackish pearls;
there was a son about two years old, but Fulvia's figure
had certainly not suffered.

''Yes, yes, you can go now!'' her mother-in-law said
to Pompeia after Fulvia had gushed her greetings, and
smiled sourly to herself as Caesar's flighty wife skipped
off arm in arm with her friend, chattering happily.

Not long afterward Aurelia decided everyone was
present and left the vestibule. Her anxiety to make sure
things were going well would not let her rest, so she

moved constantly from place to place and room to room, eyes darting hither and thither, counting servants, assessing the volume of food, cataloguing the guests and whereabouts they had settled. Even in the midst of such a controlled chaos her abacus of a mind told off this and that, facts clicking into place. Yet something kept nagging at her—what *was* it? Who was missing? *Someone* was missing!

Two musicians strolled past her, refreshing themselves between numbers. Their pipes were threaded round their wrists, leaving their hands to cope with milk and honey-cakes.

"Chryse, this is the best Bona Dea ever," said the taller one.

"Isn't it just?" agreed the other, mumbling through a full mouth. "I wish all our engagements were half as good, Doris."

Doris! *Doris!* That's who was missing, Pompeia's maid Doris! The last time Aurelia had seen her was an hour ago. Where was she? What was she up to? Was she smuggling milk on the sly to the kitchen staff, or had she guzzled so much milk herself that she was somewhere in a corner sleeping or sicking up?

Off went Aurelia, oblivious to the greetings and invitations to join various groups, nose down on a trail only she could follow.

Not in the dining room, no. Nor anywhere in the peristyle. Definitely not in the atrium or the vestibule. Which left the reception room to search before starting into other territory.

Perhaps because Caesar's saffron tent above the peristyle was such a novelty, most of the guests had decided to gather there, and those who remained were ensconced in the dining room or the atrium, both opening directly onto the garden. Which meant that the reception room, enormous and difficult to light because of its shape, was quite deserted. The Domus Publica had proved once more that two hundred visitors and a hundred servants couldn't crowd it.

Aha! There was Doris! Standing at the Pontifex Maximus's front door in the act of admitting a woman musician. But what a musician! An outlandish creature clad in the most expensive gold-threaded silk from Cos, fabulous jewels around her neck and woven through her startling yellow hair. Tucked into the crook of her left arm was a superb lyre of tortoiseshell inlaid with amber, its pegs made of gold. Did Rome own a female musician able to afford a dress or jewels or an instrument like this woman's? Surely not, else she would have been famous!

Something was wrong with Doris too. The girl was posturing and simpering, covering her mouth with her hand and rolling her eyes at the musician, in an agony of conspiratorial glee. Making no sound, Aurelia inched her way toward the pair with her back to the wall where the shadows were thickest. And when she heard the musician speak in a man's voice, she pounced.

The intruder was a slight fellow of no more than medium height, but he had a man's strength and a young man's agility; shrugging off an elderly woman like Caesar's mother would be no difficulty. The old *cunnus*! This would teach her and Fabia to torment him! But this wasn't an elderly woman! This was Proteus! No matter how he twisted and turned, Aurelia hung on.

Her mouth was open and she was shouting: "Help, help! We are defiled! Help, help! The mysteries are profaned! Help, help!"

Women came running from everywhere, automatically moving to obey Caesar's mother as people had snapped to obey her all of her life. The musician's lyre fell jangling to the floor, both the musician's arms were pinioned, and sheer numbers defeated him. At which moment Aurelia let go, turned to face her audience.

"This," she said harshly, "is a man."

By now most of the guests were assembled to stand horror-struck as Aurelia pulled off the golden wig, ripped the flimsy and costly gown away to reveal a man's hairy chest. Publius Clodius.

Someone began to scream sacrilege. Wails and cries and shrieks swelled to such a pitch that the entire Via Nova was soon craning from every window; women fled in all directions howling that the rites of Bona Dea were polluted and profaned while the slaves bolted to their quarters, the musicians prostrated themselves tearing out hair and scratching breasts, and the three adult Vestal Virgins flung their veils over their devastated faces to keen their grief and terror away from all eyes save those belonging to Bona Dea.

By now Aurelia was scrubbing at Clodius's insanely laughing face with a part of her robe, smearing black and white and red into a streaky muddy brown.

"Witness this!" she roared in a voice she had never possessed. "I call upon all of you to bear witness that this male creature who violates the mysteries of Bona Dea is Publius Clodius!"

And suddenly it wasn't funny anymore. Clodius stopped his cackling, stared at the stony and beautiful face so close to his own, and knew a terrible fear. He was back inside that anonymous room in Antioch, only this time it wasn't his testicles he was afraid of losing; this time it was his life. Sacrilege was still punishable by death the old way, and not even an Olympus of every great advocate Rome had ever produced would get him off. Light broke on him in a paroxysm of horror: *Aurelia* was the Bona Dea!

He marshaled every vestige of strength he owned, tore free of the imprisoning arms, then bolted for the passageway which led between the Pontifex Maximus's suite of rooms and the *triclinium*. Beyond lay the private peristyle garden, freedom beckoning from the far side of a high brick wall. Like a cat he leaped for its top, scrabbled and clawed his way up, twisted his body to follow his arms, and fell over the wall onto the vacant ground below.

"Bring me Pompeia Sulla, Fulvia, Clodia and Clodilla!" snapped Aurelia. "They are suspect, and I will see them!" She bundled up the gold-tissue dress and the wig and handed them to Polyxena. "Put those away safely, they're evidence."

The gigantic Gallic freedwoman Cardixa stood silently waiting for orders, and was instructed to see the ladies off the premises as expeditiously as possible. The rites could not continue, and Rome was plunged into a religious crisis more serious than any in living memory.

"Where is Fabia?"

Terentia appeared, wearing a look Publius Clodius would not have cared to see. "Fabia is gathering her wits, she'll be better soon. Oh, Aurelia, Aurelia, this is shocking! What can we do?"

"We try to repair the damage, if not for our own sakes, for the sake of every Roman woman. Fabia is the Chief Vestal, the Good Goddess is in her hand. Kindly tell her to go to the Books and discover what we can do to avert disaster. How can we bury Bona Dea unless we expiate this sacrilege? And if Bona Dea is not buried, she will not rise again in May. The healing herbs will not come up, no babies will be born free of blemish, every snake creature will move away or die, the seed will perish, and black dogs will eat corpses in the gutters of this accursed city!"

This time the audience didn't scream. Moans and sighs rose and whispered away into the blacknesses behind pillars, inside corners, within every heart. The city was accursed.

A hundred hands pushed Pompeia, Fulvia, Clodia and Clodilla to the front of the dwindling crowd, where they stood weeping and staring about in confusion; none of them had been anywhere near when Clodius was discovered, they knew only that Bona Dea had been violated by a man.

The mother of the Pontifex Maximus looked them over, as just as she was merciless. Had they been a part of the conspiracy? But every pair of eyes was wide, frightened, utterly bewildered. No, Aurelia decided, they had not been in on it. No woman above a silly Greek slave like Doris would consent to something so monstrous, so inconceivable. And what had Clodius promised that idiotic girl of Pompeia's to obtain her co-operation?

Doris stood between Servilia and Cornelia Sulla, weeping so hard that nose and mouth ran faster than eyes. Her turn in a moment, but first the guests.

"Ladies, all of you except the four front rows please

go outside. This house is unholy, your presence here unlucky. Wait in the street for your conveyances, or walk home in groups. Those at the front I need to bear witness, for if this girl is not put to the test now, she will have to wait to be questioned by men, and men are foolish when they question young women.''

Doris's turn came.

''Wipe your face, girl!'' barked Aurelia. ''Go on, wipe your face and compose yourself! If you do not, I'll have you whipped right here!''

The girl's homespun gown came into play, the command obeyed because Aurelia's word was absolute law.

''Who put you up to this, Doris?''

''He promised me a bag of gold and my freedom, *domina*!''

''Publius Clodius?''

''Yes.''

''Was it only Publius Clodius, or was someone else involved?''

What could she say to lessen the coming punishment? How could she shrug off at least a part of the blame? Doris thought with the speed and cunning of one who had been sold into slavery after pirates had raided her Lycian fishing village; she had been twelve years old, ripe for rape and suitable for sale. Between that time and Pompeia Sulla she had endured two other mistresses, older and colder than the wife of the Pontifex Maximus. Life in service to Pompeia had turned out to be an Elysian Field, and the little chest beneath Doris's cot in her very own bedroom within Pompeia's quarters was full of presents; Pompeia was as generous as she was careless. But now nothing mattered to Doris except the prospect of the lash. If her skin was flayed off her, Astyanax would never look at her again! If men looked, they would shudder.

''There was one other, *domina*,'' she whispered.

''Speak up so you can be heard, girl! Who else is involved?''

''My mistress, *domina*. The lady Pompeia Sulla.''

''In what way?'' asked Aurelia, ignoring a gasp from Pompeia and a huge murmur from the witnesses.

"If there are men present, *domina,* you never let the lady Pompeia out of Polyxena's sight. I was to let Publius Clodius in and take him upstairs, where they could be alone together."

"It's not true!" wailed Pompeia. "Aurelia, I swear by all our Gods that it isn't true! I swear it by Bona Dea! I swear it, I swear it, I swear it!"

But the slave girl clung stubbornly to her story of assignation; she would not be budged.

An hour later Aurelia gave up. "The witnesses may go home. Wife and sisters of Publius Clodius, you too may go. Be prepared to answer questions tomorrow when one of us will see you. This is a women's affair; you will be dealt with by women."

Pompeia Sulla had collapsed to the ground long since, where she lay sobbing.

"Polyxena, take the wife of the Pontifex Maximus to her own rooms and do not leave her side for one instant."

"Mama!" cried Pompeia to Cornelia Sulla as Polyxena helped her to her feet. "Mama, help me! Please help me!"

Another beautiful but stony face. "No one can help you save Bona Dea. Go with Polyxena, Pompeia."

Cardixa had returned from her duty at the great bronze doors; she had let the tearful guests out, their creased and wilting robes whipping about their bodies in a bitter wind, unable to walk from shock yet doomed to wait a long time for vanished litters and escorts certain they wouldn't be needed until dawn. So they sat down on the verge of the Via Sacra and huddled together to keep out the cold, gazing through horrified eyes at a city accursed.

"Cardixa, lock Doris up."

"What will happen to me?" the girl cried as she was marched away. "*Domina,* what will happen to me?"

"You will answer to Bona Dea."

The hours of the night wore down toward the thin misery of cock-crow; there were left Aurelia, Servilia and Cornelia Sulla.

"Come to Caesar's office and sit. We'll drink some

wine''—a sad laugh—''but we won't call it milk.''

The wine, from Caesar's stock on a console table, helped a little; Aurelia passed a trembling hand across her eyes, pulled her shoulders back and looked at Cornelia Sulla.

''What do you think, *avia*?'' Pompeia's mother asked.

''I think the girl Doris was lying.''

''So do I,'' said Servilia.

''I've always known my poor daughter was very stupid, but I have never known her to be malicious or destructive. She just wouldn't have the courage to assist a man to violate the Bona Dea, she really wouldn't.''

''But that's not what Rome is going to think,'' said Servilia.

''You're right, Rome will believe in assignations during a most holy ceremony, and gossip. Oh, it is a nightmare! Poor Caesar, poor Caesar! To have *this* happen in his house, with his wife! Ye gods, what a feast for his enemies!'' cried Aurelia.

''The beast has two heads. The sacrilege is more terrifying, but the scandal may well prove more memorable,'' from Servilia.

''I agree.'' Cornelia Sulla shuddered. ''Can you imagine what's being said along the Via Nova this moment, between the uproar which went on here and the servants all dying to spread the tale as they hunt for litter bearers through the taverns? Aurelia, how can we show the Good Goddess that we love her?''

''I hope Fabia and Terentia—what an excellent and sensible woman she is!—are busy finding that out right now.''

''And Caesar? Does he know yet?'' asked Servilia, whose mind never strayed far from Caesar.

''Cardixa has gone to tell him. They speak Arvernian Gallic together if there's anyone else present.''

Cornelia Sulla rose to her feet, lifting her brows to Servilia in a signal that it was time to go. ''Aurelia, you look so tired. There's nothing more we can do. I'm going home to bed, and I hope you intend to do the same.''

* * *

Very correctly, Caesar did not return to the Domus Publica before dawn. He went instead first to the Regia, where he prayed and sacrificed upon the altar and lit a fire in the sacred hearth. After that he set himself up in the official domain of the Pontifex Maximus just behind the Regia, lit all the lamps, sent for the Regia priestlings, and made sure there were enough chairs for the pontifices at present in Rome. Then he summoned Aurelia, knowing she would be waiting for that summons.

She looked old! His mother, *old*?

"Oh, Mater, I am so sorry," he said, helping her into the most comfortable chair.

"Don't be sorry for me, Caesar. Be sorry for Rome. It is a terrible curse."

"Rome will mend, all her religious colleges will see to that. More importantly, you must mend. I know how much holding the Bona Dea meant to you. What a wretched, idiotic, bizarre business!"

"One might expect some rude fellow from the Sub-ura to climb a wall out of drunken curiosity during the Bona Dea, but I *cannot* understand Publius Clodius! Oh yes, I know he was brought up by that doting fool Appius Claudius—and I am aware Clodius is a mischief-maker. But to disguise himself as a woman to violate Bona Dea? Consciously to commit sacrilege? He must be mad!"

Caesar shrugged. "Perhaps he is, Mater. It's an old family, and much intermarried. The Claudii Pulchri do have their quirks! They've always been irreverent—look at the Claudius Pulcher who drowned the sacred chickens and then lost the battle of Drepana during our first war against Carthage—not to mention putting your daughter the Vestal in your illegal triumphal chariot! An odd lot, brilliant but unstable. As is Clodius, I think."

"To violate Bona Dea is far worse than violating a Vestal."

"Well, according to Fabia he tried to do that too. Then when he didn't succeed he accused Catilina." Caesar sighed, shrugged. "Unfortunately Clodius's lunacy is of the sane kind. We can't brand him a maniac and shut him up."

"He will be tried at law?"

"Since you unmasked him in front of the wives and daughters of consulars, Mater, he will have to be tried."

"And Pompeia?"

"Cardixa said you believed her innocent of complicity."

"I do. So do Servilia and her mother."

"Therefore it boils down to Pompeia's word against a slave girl's—unless, of course, Clodius too implicates her."

"He won't do that," said Aurelia grimly.

"Why?"

"He would then have no choice but to admit that he committed sacrilege. Clodius will deny everything."

"Too many of you saw him."

"Caked in face paint. I rubbed at it, and revealed Clodius. But I think a parcel of Rome's best advocates could make most of the witnesses doubt their eyes."

"What you are actually saying, I think, is that it would be better for Rome if Clodius were acquitted."

"Oh, yes. The Bona Dea belongs to women. She won't thank Rome's men for exacting punishment in her name."

"He can't be allowed to escape, Mater. Sacrilege is public."

"He will never escape, Caesar. Bona Dea will find him and take him in her own good time." Aurelia got up. "The pontifices will be arriving soon, I'll go. When you need me, send for me."

Catulus and Vatia Isauricus came in not long after, and Mamercus so quickly behind them that Caesar said nothing until all three were seated.

"I never cease to be amazed, Pontifex Maximus, at how much information you can fit into one sheet of paper," said Catulus, "and always so logically expressed, so easy to assimilate."

"But not," said Caesar, "a pleasure to read."

"No, not that, this time."

Others were stepping through the door: Silanus, Acilius Glabrio, Varro Lucullus, next year's consul Marcus Valerius Messala Niger, Metellus Scipio, and Lucius Claudius the Rex Sacrorum.

"There are no others at present in Rome. Do you agree we may start, Quintus Lutatius?" Caesar asked.

"We may start, Pontifex Maximus."

"You already have an outline of the crisis in my note, but I will have my mother tell you exactly what happened. I am aware it ought to be Fabia, but at the moment she and the other adult Vestals are searching the Books for the proper rituals of expiation."

"Aurelia will be satisfactory, Pontifex Maximus."

So Aurelia came and told her story, crisply, succinctly, with eminent good sense and great composure. Such a relief! Caesar, men like Catulus were suddenly realizing, took after his mother.

"You will be prepared to testify in court that the man was Publius Clodius?" asked Catulus.

"Yes, but under protest. Let Bona Dea have him."

They thanked her uneasily; Caesar dismissed her.

"Rex Sacrorum, I ask for your verdict first," said Caesar then.

"Publius Clodius *nefas esse*."

"Quintus Lutatius?"

"Nefas esse."

And so it went, every man declaring that Publius Clodius was guilty of sacrilege.

Today there were no undercurrents arising out of personal feuds or grudges. All the priests were absolutely united, and grateful for a firm hand like Caesar's. Politics demanded enmity, but a religious crisis did not. It affected everyone equally, needed union.

"I will direct the Fifteen Custodians to look at the Prophetic Books immediately," said Caesar, "and consult the College of Augurs for their opinion. The Senate will meet and ask us for an opinion, and we must be ready."

"Clodius will have to be tried," said Messala Niger, whose flesh crawled at the very thought of what Clodius had done.

"That will require a decree of recommendation from
the Senate and a special bill in the Popular Assembly. The
women are against it, but you're right, Niger. He must be
tried. However, the rest of this month will be expiatory,
not retaliatory, which means the consuls of next year will
inherit the business."

"And what of Pompeia?" asked Catulus when no
one else would.

"If Clodius does not implicate her—and my mother
seems to think he will not—then her part in the sacrilege
rests upon the testimony of a slave witness herself involved," Caesar answered, voice clinical. "That means
she cannot be publicly condemned."

"Do you feel she was implicated, Pontifex Maximus?"

"No, I do not. Nor does my mother, who was there.
The slave girl is anxious to save her skin, which is understandable. Bona Dea will demand her death—which
she has not yet realized—but that is not in our hands. It's
women's business."

"What of Clodius's wife and sisters?" asked Vatia
Isauricus.

"My mother says they're innocent."

"Your mother is right," said Catulus. "No Roman
woman would profane the mysteries of Bona Dea, even
Fulvia or Clodia."

"However, I still have something to do about Pompeia," said Caesar, beckoning to a priestling-scribe holding tablets. "Take this down: 'To Pompeia Sulla, wife of
Gaius Julius Caesar, Pontifex Maximus of Rome: I hereby
divorce you and send you home to your brother. I make
no claim on your dowry.' "

Nobody said a word, nor found the courage to speak
even after the terse document was presented to Caesar for
his seal.

Then as the bearer of the waxen note left to deliver
it at the Domus Publica, Mamercus spoke.

"My wife is her mother, but she will not have Pompeia."

"Nor should she be asked to," said Caesar coolly.

"That is why I have directed that she be sent to her elder brother, who is her *paterfamilias*. He's governing Africa Province, but his wife is here. Whether they want her or not, they must take her."

It was Silanus who finally asked the question everyone burned to. "Caesar, you say you believe Pompeia innocent of any complicity. Then why are you divorcing her?"

The fair brows rose; Caesar looked genuinely surprised. "Because Caesar's wife, like all Caesar's family, must be above suspicion," he said.

And some days later when the question was repeated in the House, he gave exactly the same answer.

Fulvia slapped Publius Clodius from one side of his face to the other until his lip split and his nose bled.

"Fool!" she growled with every blow. "Fool! Fool! Fool!"

He didn't attempt to fight back, nor to appeal to his sisters, who stood watching in anguished satisfaction.

"Why?" asked Clodia when Fulvia was done.

It was some time before he could answer, when the bleeding was staunched and the tears ceased to flow. Then he said, "I wanted to make Aurelia and Fabia suffer."

"Clodius, you've blighted Rome! We are accursed!" cried Fulvia.

"Oh, what's the matter with you?" he yelled. "A parcel of women getting rid of their resentment of men, what's the sense in that? I saw the whips! I know about the snakes! It's a lot of absolute nonsense!"

But that only made matters worse; all three women flew at him, Clodius was slapped and punched again.

"Bona Dea," said Clodilla between her teeth, "is not a pretty Greek statue! Bona Dea is as old as Rome, she is ours, she is the Good Goddess. Every woman who was there to be a part of your defilement and who is pregnant will have to take the medicine."

"And that," said Fulvia, beginning to weep, "includes me!"

"No!"

"Yes, yes, yes!" cried Clodia, administering a kick. "Oh, Clodius, why? There must be thousands of ways to revenge yourself on Aurelia and Fabia! Why commit sacrilege? You're doomed!"

"I didn't think, it seemed so perfect!" He tried to take Fulvia's hand. "Please don't harm our child!"

"Don't you understand yet?" she shrieked, wrenching away. "*You* harmed our child! It would be born deformed and monstrous, I must take the medicine! Clodius, you are accursed!"

"Get out!" Clodilla shouted. "On your belly like a snake!"

Clodius crawled away on his belly, snakelike.

"There will have to be another Bona Dea," said Terentia to Caesar when she, Fabia and Aurelia came to see him in his study. "The rites will be the same, though with the addition of a piacular sacrifice. The girl Doris will be punished in a certain way no woman can reveal, even to the Pontifex Maximus."

Thank all the Gods for that, thought Caesar, having no trouble in imagining who would constitute the piacular sacrifice. "So you need a law to make one of the coming comitial days *nefasti*, and you are asking the Pontifex Maximus to procure it from the Religious Assembly of seventeen tribes?"

"That is correct," said Fabia, thinking she must speak if Caesar were not to deem her dependent upon two women outside the Vestal College. "Bona Dea must be held on *dies nefasti*, and there are no more until February."

"You're right, Bona Dea can't remain awake until February. Shall I legislate for the sixth day before the Ides?"

"That would be excellent," said Terentia, sighing.

"Bona Dea will go happily to sleep," comforted Caesar. "I'm sorry that any woman at the feast who is newly pregnant will have to make a harder and a very special sacrifice. I say no more, it is women's business. Remember too that no Roman woman was guilty of sacrilege. Bona

Dea was profaned by a man and a non-Roman girl.''

"I hear,'' Terentia announced, rising, "that Publius Clodius likes revenge. But he will not like Bona Dea's revenge.''

Aurelia remained seated, though she did not speak until after the door had closed behind Terentia and Fabia.

"I've sent Pompeia packing,'' she said then.

"And all her possessions too, I hope?''

"That's being attended to this moment. Poor thing! She wept so, Caesar. Her sister-in-law doesn't want to take her, Cornelia Sulla refuses—it's so sad.''

"I know.''

" 'Caesar's wife, like all Caesar's family, must be above suspicion,' '' Aurelia quoted.

"Yes.''

"It seems wrong to me to punish her for something she knew nothing about, Caesar.''

"And wrong to me, Mater. Nevertheless, I had no choice.''

"I doubt your colleagues would have objected had you elected to keep her as your wife.''

"Probably not. But *I* objected.''

"You're a hard man.''

"A man who isn't hard, Mater, is under the thumb of some woman or other. Look at Cicero and Silanus.''

"They say,'' said Aurelia, expanding the subject, "that Silanus is failing fast.''

"I believe it, if the Silanus I saw this morning is anything to go by.''

"You may have cause to regret that you will be divorced at the same moment as Servilia is widowed.''

"The time to worry about that is when my ring goes on her wedding finger.''

"In some ways it would be a very good match,'' she said, dying to know what he really thought.

"In some ways,'' he agreed, smiling inscrutably.

"Can you do nothing for Pompeia beyond sending her dowry and possessions with her?''

"Why should I?''

"No valid reason, except that her punishment is undeserved, and she will never find another husband. What man would espouse a woman whose husband suspects she connived at sacrilege?''

''That's a slur on me, Mater.''

''No, Caesar, it is not! You know she isn't guilty, but in divorcing her you have not indicated that to the rest of Rome.''

''Mater, you are fast outwearing your welcome,'' he said gently.

She got up immediately. ''Nothing?'' she asked.

''I will find her another husband.''

''Who could be prevailed upon to marry her after this?''

''I imagine Publius Vatinius would be delighted to marry her. The granddaughter of Sulla is a great prize for one whose own grandparents were Italians.''

Aurelia turned this over in her mind, then nodded. ''That,'' she said, ''is an excellent idea, Caesar. Vatinius was such a doting husband to Antonia Cretica, and she was at least as stupid as poor Pompeia. Oh, splendid! He will be an Italian husband, keep her close. She'll be far too busy to have time for the Clodius Club.''

''Go away, Mater!'' said Caesar with a sigh.

The second Bona Dea festival passed off without a hitch, but it took a long time for feminine Rome to settle down, and there were many newly pregnant women throughout the city who followed the example of those present at the first ceremony; the Vestals dispensed the rye medicine until their stocks were very low. The number of male babies abandoned on the shards of the Mons Testaceus was unprecedented, and for the first time in memory no barren couples took them to keep and rear; every last one died unwanted. The city ran with tears and put on mourning until May Day, made worse because the seasons were so out of kilter with the calendar that the snakes would not awaken until later, so who would know whether the Good Goddess had forgiven?

Publius Clodius, the perpetrator of all this misery and panic, was shunned and spat upon. Time alone would heal the religious crisis, but the sight of Publius Clodius was a perpetual reminder. Nor would he do the sensible thing, quit the city; he brazened it out, protesting that he was innocent, that he had never been there.

It also took time for Fulvia to forgive him, though she did after the ordeal of aborting her pregnancy had faded, but only because she saw for herself that he was as grief stricken about it as she. *Then why?*

"I didn't think, I just didn't think!" he wept into her lap. "It seemed such a lark."

"You committed sacrilege!"

"I didn't think of it like that, I just didn't!" He lifted his head to gaze at her out of red-rimmed, swollen eyes. "I mean, it's only some silly old women's binge—everyone gets stinking drunk and makes love or masturbates or something—I just didn't think, Fulvia!"

"Clodius, the Bona Dea isn't like that. It's *sacred*! I can't tell you what exactly it is, I'd shrivel up and give birth to snakes for the rest of time if I did! Bona Dea is for *us*! All the other Gods of women are for men too, Juno Lucina and Juno Sospita and the rest, but Bona Dea is ours alone. She takes care of all those women's things men can't know, wouldn't want to know. If she doesn't go to sleep properly she can't wake properly, and Rome is more than men, Clodius! Rome is women too!"

"They'll try me and convict me, won't they?"

"So it seems, though none of us wants that. It means men are sneaking in where men do not belong, they are usurping Bona Dea's godhead." Fulvia shivered uncontrollably. "It isn't a trial at the hands of men terrifies me, Clodius. It's what Bona Dea will do to you, and that can't be bought off the way a jury can."

"There's not enough money in Rome to buy off this jury."

But Fulvia simply smiled. "There will be enough money when the time comes. We women don't want it. Perhaps if it can be averted, Bona Dea will forgive. What she won't forgive is the world of men taking over her prerogatives."

* * *

Just returned from his legateship in Spain, Publius Vatinius jumped at the chance to marry Pompeia.

"Caesar, I am very grateful," he said, smiling. "Naturally you couldn't keep her as your wife, I understand that. But I also know that you wouldn't offer her to me if you thought her a party to the sacrilege."

"Rome may not be so charitable, Vatinius. There are many who think I divorced her because she was intriguing with Clodius."

"Rome doesn't matter to me, your word does. My children will be Antonii *and* Cornelii! Only tell me how I can repay you."

"That," said Caesar, "will be easy, Vatinius. Next year I go to a province, and the year after I'll be standing for consul. I want you to stand for the tribunate of the plebs at the same elections." He sighed. "With Bibulus in my year, there is a strong possibility that I'll have him as my consular colleague. The only other nobleman of any consequence in our year is Philippus, and I believe that for the time being the Epicurean will outweigh the politician in his case. He hasn't enjoyed his praetorship. The men who have been praetor earlier are pathetic. Therefore I may well need a good tribune of the plebs, if Bibulus is to be consul too. And you, Vatinius," Caesar ended cheerfully, "will be an extremely able tribune of the plebs."

"A gnat versus a flea."

"The nice thing about fleas," said Caesar contentedly, "is that they crack when one applies a thumbnail. Gnats are far more elusive creatures."

"They say Pompeius is about to land in Brundisium."

"They do indeed."

"And looking for land for his soldiers."

"To no avail, I predict."

"Mightn't it be better if I ran for the tribunate of the plebs next year, Caesar? That way I could get land for Pompeius, and he would be very much in your debt. The only tribunes of the plebs he has this year are Aufidius Lurco and Cornelius Cornutus, neither of whom will prevail. One hears he'll have Lucius Flavius the year after, but that won't work either.''

''Oh no,'' Caesar said softly, ''let's not make things *too* easy for Pompeius. The longer he waits the more heartfelt his gratitude will be. You're my man *corpus animusque,* Vatinius, and I want our hero Magnus to understand that. He's been a long time in the East, he's used to sweating.''

The *boni* were sweating too, though they had a tribune of the plebs just entering office who was more satisfactory than Aufidius Lurco and Cornelius Cornutus. He was Quintus Fufius Calenus, who turned out to be more than a match for the other nine put together. At the start of his year, however, it was difficult to see that, which accounted for some of the despondency of the *boni*.

''Somehow we have to get Caesar,'' said Gaius Piso to Bibulus, Catulus and Cato.

''Difficult, considering the Bona Dea,'' said Catulus, shivering. ''He behaved absolutely as he ought, and all of Rome knows it. He divorced Pompeia without claiming her dowry, and that remark about Caesar's wife having to be above suspicion was so apt it's passed into Forum lore already. A brilliant move! It says he thinks she's innocent, yet protocol demands that she go. If you had a wife at home, Piso—or you, Bibulus!—you'd know there's not a woman in Rome will hear Caesar criticized. Hortensia dins in my ear as hard as Lutatia dins in Hortensius's. Quite why is beyond me, but the women don't want Clodius sent for public trial, and they all know Caesar agrees with them. Women,'' Catulus finished gloomily, ''are an underestimated force in the scheme of things.''

''I'll have another wife at home shortly,'' said Bibulus.

''Who?''

''Another Domitia. Cato has fixed me up.''

''More like you're fixing Caesar up,'' snarled Gaius Piso. ''If I were you, I'd stay single. That's what I'm going to do.''

To all of which Cato vouchsafed no comment, simply sat with his chin on his hand looking depressed.

The year had not turned out to be a wonderful success for Cato, who had been compelled to learn yet another lesson the hard way: that to exhaust one's competition early on left one with no adversaries to shine against. Once Metellus Nepos left to join Pompey the Great, Cato's term as a tribune of the plebs dwindled to insignificance. The only subsequent action he took was not a popular one, especially with his closest friends among the *boni;* when the new harvest saw grain prices soar to a record high, he legislated to give grain to the populace at ten sesterces the *modius*—at a cost of well over a thousand talents to the Treasury. And *Caesar* had voted for it in the House, where Cato had most correctly first proposed it. With a very graceful speech suggesting a huge change of heart in Cato, and *thanking* him for his foresight. How galling to know that men like Caesar understood perfectly that what he had proposed was both sensible and ahead of events, whereas men like Gaius Piso and Ahenobarbus had squealed louder than pigs. They had even accused him of trying to become a bigger demagogue than Saturninus by wooing the Head Count!

"We'll have to get Caesar attached for debt," said Bibulus.

"We can't do that with honor," said Catulus.

"We can if we don't have anything to do with it."

"Daydreams, Bibulus!" from Gaius Piso. "The only way is to prevent the praetors of this year from having provinces, and when we attempted to prorogue the present governors we were howled down."

"There is another way," said Bibulus.

Cato lifted his chin from his hand. "How?"

"The lots for praetorian provinces will be drawn on New Year's Day. I've spoken to Fufius Calenus, and he's happy to veto the drawing of the lots on the grounds that nothing official can be decided until the matter of the Bona Dea sacrilege is dealt with. And," said Bibulus contentedly, "since the women are nagging that no action be taken and at least half the Senate is highly susceptible to nagging women, that means Fufius Calenus can go on vetoing for months. All we have to do is whisper in a few moneylending ears that this year's praetors will never go to provinces.''

"There's one thing I have to say for Caesar," Cato barked, "and that is that he's sharpened your wits, Bibulus. In the old days you wouldn't have managed."

It was on the tip of Bibulus's tongue to say something rude to Cato, but he didn't; he just smiled sickly at Catulus.

Catulus reacted rather strangely. "I agree to the plan," he said, "on one condition—that we don't mention it to Metellus Scipio."

"Whyever not?" asked Cato blankly.

"Because I couldn't stand the eternal litany—destroy Caesar this and destroy Caesar that, but we never do!"

"This time," said Bibulus, "we can't possibly fail. Publius Clodius will never come to trial."

"That means he'll suffer too. He's a newly elected quaestor who won't get duties if the lots aren't drawn," said Gaius Piso.

The war in the Senate to try Publius Clodius broke out just after the New Year's Day fiasco in the temple of Jupiter Optimus Maximus (much improved inside since last year—Catulus had taken Caesar's warning seriously). Perhaps because business ground to a halt, it was decided to elect new censors; two conservatives in Gaius Scribonius Curio and Gaius Cassius Longinus were returned, which promised a fairly co-operative censorship—provided the tribunes of the plebs left them alone, which was not a foregone conclusion with Fufius Calenus in office.

The senior consul was a Piso Frugi adopted into the Pupius branch from the Calpurnius branch of the family, and he was one of those with a nagging wife. He therefore adamantly opposed any trial for Publius Clodius.

"The cult of Bona Dea is outside the province of the State," he said flatly, "and I question the legality of anything beyond what has already been done—a pronouncement by the College of Pontifices that Publius Clodius did commit sacrilege. But his crime is not in the statutes. He did not molest a Vestal Virgin, nor attempt to tamper with the persons or rites of any official Roman God. Nothing can take away from the enormity of what he did, but I am one of those who agree with the city's women—let Bona Dea exact retribution in her own way and her own time.''

A statement which did not sit at all well with his junior colleague, Messala Niger. ''I will not rest until Publius Clodius is tried!'' he declared, and sounded as if he meant it. ''If there is no law on the tablets, then I suggest we draft one! It isn't good enough to bleat that a guilty man can't be tried because our laws don't have a pigeon-hole to fit his crime! It's easy enough to make room for Publius Clodius, and I move that we do so now!''

Only Clodius, thought Caesar in wry amusement, could manage to sit on the back benches looking as if the subject concerned everyone save him, while the argument raged back and forth and Piso Frugi came close to blows with Messala Niger.

In the midst of which Pompey the Great took up residence on the Campus Martius, having disbanded his army because the Senate couldn't discuss his triumph until the problem of the Bona Dea was solved. His bill of divorcement had preceded him by many days, though no one had seen Mucia Tertia. And rumor said Caesar was the culprit! It therefore gave Caesar great pleasure to attend a special *contio* in the Circus Flaminius, a venue permitting Pompey to speak. Very poorly, as Cicero was heard to say tartly.

At the end of January, Piso Frugi began to retreat when the new censors joined the fray, and agreed to draft a bill to enable the prosecution of Publius Clodius for a new kind of sacrilege.

''It's a complete farce,'' Piso Frugi said, ''but farces are dear to every Roman heart, so I suppose it's fitting. You're fools, the lot of you! He'll get off, and that puts him in a far better position than if he continued to exist under a cloud.''

A good legal draftsman, Piso Frugi prepared the bill himself, which was a severe one if looked at from the point of view of the penalty—exile for life and full forfeiture of all wealth—but also contained a curious clause to the effect that the praetor chosen to preside over the special court had to hand-pick the jury himself—meaning that the court president held Clodius's fate in his hands. A pro-Clodian praetor meant a lenient jury. A pro-conviction praetor meant the harshest jury possible.

This put the *boni* in a cleft stick. On the one hand they didn't want Clodius tried at all, because the moment it was put in train the praetorian provinces would be drawn; on the other hand they didn't want Clodius convicted because Catulus thought the Bona Dea affair outside the realm of men and the State.

"Are Caesar's creditors at all worried?" asked Catulus.

"Oh yes," said Bibulus. "If we can manage to keep vetoing proceedings against Clodius until March, it will really look as if the lots won't be drawn. Then they'll act."

"Can we keep going another month?"

"Easily."

On the Kalends of February, Decimus Junius Silanus woke from a restless stupor vomiting blood. It was many moons since he had first put the little bronze bell beside his bed, though he used it so rarely that whenever it did ring the whole house woke.

"This is how Sulla died," he said wearily to Servilia.

"No, Silanus," she said in a bracing tone, "this is no more than an episode. Sulla's plight was far worse. You'll be all right. Who knows? It might be your body purging itself."

"It's my body disintegrating. I'm bleeding from the bowel as well, and soon there won't be enough blood left." He sighed, tried to smile. "At least I managed to be consul, my house has one more consular *imago*."

Perhaps so many years of marriage did count for something; though she felt no grief, Servilia was stirred enough to reach for Silanus's hand. "You were an excellent consul, Silanus."

"I think so. It wasn't an easy year, but I survived it." He squeezed the warm dry fingers. "It's you I didn't manage to survive, Servilia."

"You've been ill since before we married."

He fell silent, his absurdly long fair lashes fanned against sunken cheeks. How handsome he is, thought his wife, and how I liked that when I first met him. I am going to be a widow for the second time.

"Is Brutus here?" he asked some time later, lifting tired lids. "I should like to speak to him." And when Brutus came he looked beyond the dark unhappy face to Servilia. "Go outside, my dear, fetch the girls and wait. Brutus will bring you in."

How she detested being dismissed! But she went, and Silanus made sure she was gone before he turned his head to see her son.

"Sit down on the foot of my bed, Brutus."

Brutus obeyed, his black eyes in the flickering lamp-light shining with tears.

"Is it me you weep for?" Silanus asked.

"Yes."

"Weep for yourself, my son. When I'm gone she'll be harder to deal with."

"I don't think," said Brutus, suppressing a sob, "that that is possible, Father."

"She'll marry Caesar."

"Oh yes."

"Perhaps it will be good for her. He's the strongest man I have ever met."

"Then it will be war between them," said Brutus.

"And Julia? How will the two of you fare if they marry?"

"About the same as we do now. We manage."

Silanus plucked feebly at the bedclothes, seemed to shrink. "Oh, Brutus, my time is here!" he cried. "So much I had to say to you, but I've left it until too late. And isn't that the story of my life?"

Weeping, Brutus fled to fetch his mother and sisters. Silanus managed to smile at them, then closed his eyes and died.

The funeral, though not held at State expense, was a huge affair not without its titillating side: the lover of the widow presided over the obsequies of the husband and gave a fine eulogy from the rostra as if he had never in his life met the widow, yet knew the husband enormously well.

"Who was responsible for Caesar's giving the funeral oration?" asked Cicero of Catulus.

"Who do you think?"

"But it isn't Servilia's place!"

"Does Servilia have a place?"

"A pity Silanus had no sons."

"A blessing, more like."

They were trudging back from the Junius Silanus tomb, which lay to the south of the city alongside the Via Appia.

"Catulus, what are we going to do about Clodius's sacrilege?"

"How does your wife feel about it, Cicero?"

"Torn. We men ought never to have stuck our noses in, but as we have, then Publius Clodius must be condemned." Cicero stopped. "I must tell you, Quintus Lutatius, that I am placed in an extremely awkward and delicate situation."

Catulus stopped. "You, Cicero? How?"

"Terentia thinks I'm having a love affair with Clodia."

For a moment Catulus could do no more than gape; then he threw his head back and laughed until some of the other mourners stared at them curiously. They looked quite ridiculous, both in black mourning toga with the thin purple stripe of the knight on the right shoulder of the tunic, officially accoutred for a death; yet the one was howling with mirth, and the other stood in what was obviously furious indignation.

"And what's so funny?" asked Cicero dangerously.

"You! Terentia!" gasped Catulus, wiping his eyes. "Cicero, she doesn't—you—*Clodia*?"

"I'll have you know that Clodia has been making sheep's eyes at me for some time," said Cicero stiffly.

"That lady," Catulus said, resuming his walk, "is harder to get inside than Nola. Why do you think Celer puts up with her? *He* knows how she operates! Coos and giggles and flutters her eyelashes, makes a complete fool of some poor man, then retreats behind her walls and bolts the gates. Tell Terentia not to be so silly. Clodia is probably having fun at your expense.''

''*You* tell Terentia not to be so silly.''

''Thank you, Cicero, but no. Do your own dirty work. I have enough to contend with in Hortensia, I don't need to cross swords with Terentia.''

''Nor do I,'' said Cicero miserably. ''Celer wrote to me, you know. Well, he's been doing that ever since he went to govern Italian Gaul!''

''Accusing you of being Clodia's lover?'' asked Catulus.

''No, no! He wants me to help Pompeius get land for his men. It's very difficult.''

''It will be if you enlist in that cause, my friend!'' said Catulus grimly. ''I can tell you right now that Pompeius will get land for his men over my dead body!''

''I knew you'd say that.''

''Then what are you rambling about?''

Out went Cicero's arms; he ground his teeth. ''I am not in the habit of rambling! But doesn't Celer know that all of Rome is talking about Clodia and that new poet fellow, Catullus?''

''Well,'' said Catulus comfortably, ''if all of Rome is talking about Clodia and some poet fellow, then it can't take you and Clodia very seriously, can it? Tell Terentia that.''

''Grrr!'' grumped Cicero, and decided to walk in silence.

Very properly, Servilia left a space of some days between the death of Silanus and a note to Caesar asking for an interview—in the rooms on the Vicus Patricii.

The Caesar who went to meet her was not the usual Caesar; if the knowledge that this was likely to be a troubled confrontation had not been sufficient to cause a change, then the knowledge that his creditors were suddenly pressing certainly would have. The word was up and down the Clivus Argentarius that there would be no praetorian provinces this year, a state of affairs which turned

Caesar from a likely bet into an irretrievable loss. Catulus, Cato, Bibulus and the rest of the *boni,* of course. They had found a way to deny provinces to the praetors after all, and Fufius Calenus was a very good tribune of the plebs. And if matters could be made worse, the economic situation achieved that; when someone as conservative as Cato saw the need to lower the price of the grain dole, then Rome was in severe straits indeed. Luck, what had suddenly become of Caesar's luck? Or was Goddess Fortuna simply testing him?

But it seemed Servilia was not in the mood to sort out her status; she greeted him fully clad and rather soberly, then sat in a chair and asked for wine.

"Missing Silanus?" he asked.

"Perhaps I am." She began to turn the goblet between her hands, round and round. "Do you know anything about death, Caesar?"

"Only that it must come. I don't worry about it as long as it's quick. Were I to suffer Silanus's fate, I'd fall on my sword."

"Some of the Greeks say there is a life after it."

"Yes."

"Do you believe that?"

"Not in the conscious sense. Death is an eternal sleep, of that I'm sure. We don't float away disembodied yet continue to be ourselves. But no substance perishes, and there are worlds of forces we neither see nor understand. Our Gods belong in one such world, and they're tangible enough to conclude contracts and pacts with us. But we don't ever belong to it, in life or in death. We balance it. Without us, their world would not exist. So if the Greeks see anything, they see that. And who knows that the Gods are eternal? How long does a force last? Do new ones form when the old ones dwindle? What happens to a force when it is no more? Eternity is a dreamless sleep, even for the Gods. That I believe."

"And yet," said Servilia slowly, "when Silanus died something went out of the room. I didn't see it go, I didn't hear it. But it went, Caesar. The room was empty."

"I suppose what went was an idea."

"An idea?"

"Isn't that what all of us are, an idea?"

"To ourselves, or to others?"

"To both, though not necessarily the same idea."

"I don't know. I only know what I sensed. What made Silanus live went away."

"Drink your wine."

She drained the cup. "I feel very strange, but not the way I felt when I was a child and so many people died. Nor the way I felt when Pompeius Magnus sent me Brutus's ashes from Mutina."

"Your childhood was an abomination," he said, got up and crossed to her side. "As for your first husband, you neither loved him nor chose him. He was just the man who made your son."

She lifted her face for his kiss, never before so aware of what constituted Caesar's kiss because always before she had wanted it too badly to savor and dissect it. A perfect fusion of senses and spirit, she thought, and slid her arms about his neck. His skin was weathered, a little rough, and he smelled faintly of some sacrificial fire, ashes on a darkening hearth. Perhaps, her wondering mind went on through touch and taste, what I try to do is have something of his force with me forever, and the only way I can get it is this way, my body against his, him inside me, the two of us spared for some few moments all knowledge of other things, existing only in each other . . .

Neither of them spoke then until both of them had slipped in and out of a little sleep; and there was the world again, babies howling, women shrieking, men hawking and spitting, the rumble of carts on the cobbles, the dull clunk of some machine in a nearby factory, the faint tremble which was Vulcan in the depths below.

"Nothing," said Servilia, "lasts forever."

"Including us, as I was telling you."

"But we have our names, Caesar. If they are not forgotten, it is a kind of immortality."

"The only one I'm aiming for."

A sudden resentment filled her; she turned away from

him. "You're a man, you have a chance at that. But what about me?"

"What about you?" he asked, pulling her to face him.

"That," she said, "was not a philosophical question."

"No, it wasn't."

She sat up and linked her arms about her knees, the ridge of down along her spine hidden by a great mass of fallen black hair.

"How old are you, Servilia?"

"I'll soon be forty-three."

It was now or never; Caesar sat up too. "Do you want to marry again?" he asked.

"Oh, yes."

"Who?"

She turned wide eyes to stare at him. "Who else, Caesar?"

"I can't marry you, Servilia."

Her shock was perceptible; she cringed. "Why?"

"For one thing, there are our children. It isn't against the law for us to marry and for our children to marry each other. The degree of blood is permissible. But it would be too awkward, and I won't do it to them."

"That," she said tightly, "is a prevarication."

"No, it isn't. To me it's valid."

"And what else?"

"Haven't you heard what I said when I divorced Pompeia?" he asked. " 'Caesar's wife, like all Caesar's family, must be above suspicion.' "

"I am above suspicion."

"No, Servilia, you're not."

"Caesar, that's just not so! It's said of me that I am too proud to ally myself with Jupiter Optimus Maximus."

"But you weren't too proud to ally yourself with me."

"Of course not!"

He shrugged. "And there you have it."

"Have *what*?"

"You're not above suspicion. You're an unfaithful wife."

"I am not!"

"Rubbish! You've been unfaithful for years."

"But with you, Caesar, with you! Never before with anyone, and never since with anyone else, even Silanus!"

"It doesn't matter," said Caesar indifferently, "that it was with me. You are an unfaithful wife."

"Not to you!"

"How do I know that? You were unfaithful to Silanus. Why not later to me?"

It was a nightmare; Servilia drew a breath, fought to keep her mind on these incredible things he was saying. "Before you," she said, "all men were *insulsus*. And after you, all other men are *insulsus*."

"I won't marry you, Servilia. You're not above suspicion, and you're not above reproach."

"What I feel for you," she said, struggling on, "cannot be measured in terms of the right thing to do or the wrong thing to do. You are unique. Not for any other man—or for a god!—would I have beggared my pride or my good name. How can you use what I feel for you against me?"

"I'm not using anything against you, Servilia, I'm simply telling you the truth. Caesar's wife must be above suspicion."

"I am above suspicion!"

"No, you're not."

"Oh, I don't believe this!" she cried, shaking her head back and forth, hands wrung together. "You are unfair! Unjust!"

And clearly the interview was over; Caesar got off the bed. "You must see it that way, of course. But that doesn't change it, Servilia. Caesar's wife must be above suspicion."

Time went by; she could hear Caesar in the bath, apparently at peace with his world. And finally she dragged herself out of the bed, dressed.

"No bath?" he asked, actually smiling at her when she went through to the balcony service room.

"Today I'll go home to bathe."

"Am I forgiven?"

"Do you want to be?"

"I am honored to have you as my mistress."

"I believe you really do mean that!"

"I do," he said sincerely.

Her shoulders went back, she pressed her lips together. "I will think about it, Caesar."

"Good!"

Which she took to mean that he knew she'd be back.

And thank all the Gods for a long walk home. How did he manage to do that to me? So deftly, with such horrible civility! As if my feelings were of no moment—as if I, a patrician Servilia Caepionis, could not matter. He made me ask for marriage, then he threw it in my face like the contents of a chamber pot. He turned me down as if I had been the daughter of some rich hayseed from Gaul or Sicily. I reasoned! I begged! I lay down and let him wipe his feet on me! I, a patrician Servilia Caepionis! All these years I've held him in thrall when no other woman could—how then was I to know he would reject me? I genuinely thought he would marry me. And he knew I thought he would marry me. Oh, the pleasure he must have experienced while we played out that little farce! I thought I could be cold, but I am not cold the way he is cold. Why then do I love him so? Why in this very moment do I go on loving him? *Insulsus*. That is what he has done to me. After him all other men are utterly insipid. He's won. But I will never forgive him for it. Never!

Having Pompey the Great living in a hired mansion above the Campus Martius was a little like knowing that the only barrier between the lion and the Senate was a sheet of paper. Sooner or later someone would cut a finger and the smell of blood would provoke an exploratory paw. For that reason and no other it was decided to hold a *contio* of the Popular Assembly in the Circus Flaminius to discuss Piso Frugi's format for the prosecution of Publius Clodius. Bent on embarrassing Pompey because Pompey so clearly wanted no part of the Clodius scandal, Fufius

Calenus promptly asked him what he thought of the clause instructing the judge himself to hand-pick the jury. The *boni* beamed; anything which embarrassed Pompey served to diminish the Great Man!

But when Pompey stepped to the edge of the speaker's platform a huge cheer went up from thousands of throats; apart from the senators and a few senior knights of the Eighteen, everyone had come just to see Pompey the Great, Conqueror of the East. Who over the course of the next three hours managed so thoroughly to bore his audience that it went home.

"He could have said it all in a quarter of an hour," whispered Cicero to Catulus. "The Senate is right as always and the Senate must be upheld—that's all he actually said! Oh, so *interminably*!"

"He is one of the worst orators in Rome," said Catulus. "My feet hurt!"

But the torture wasn't done, though the senators could now sit down; Messala Niger called the Senate into session on the spot after Pompey concluded.

"Gnaeus Pompeius Magnus," said Messala Niger in ringing tones, "would you please give this House a candid opinion on the sacrilege of Publius Clodius and the bill of Marcus Pupius Piso Frugi?"

So strong was fear of the lion that no one groaned at this request. Pompey was seated among the consulars and next to Cicero, who swallowed hard and retreated into a daydream about his new city house and its decor. This time the speech took a mere hour; at its end Pompey sat down on his chair with a thump loud enough to wake Cicero with a start.

Tanned face gone crimson with the effort of trying to remember the techniques of rhetoric, the Great Man ground his teeth. "Oh, surely I've said enough on the subject!"

"You surely have said enough," Cicero answered, smiling sweetly.

The moment Crassus rose to speak, Pompey lost interest and began to quiz Cicero about the more gossipy events in Rome during his absence, but Crassus hadn't got into stride before Cicero was sitting bolt upright and paying absolutely no attention to Pompey. How wonderful! The bliss! Crassus was praising him to the skies! What a terrific job he'd done when consul to bring the Orders much closer together; knights and senators ought to be happily entwined. . . .

"What on earth made you do that?" Caesar asked Crassus as they walked along the Tiber towpath to avoid the vegetable vendors of the Forum Holitorium, clearing up at the end of a busy day.

"Extol Cicero's virtues, you mean?"

"I wouldn't have minded if you hadn't provoked him into such a long-winded reply about concord among the Orders. Though I do admit he's lovely to listen to after Pompeius."

"That's why I did it. I loathe the way everyone bows and scrapes to the odious Magnus. If he looks sideways at them, they cringe like dogs. And there was Cicero sitting next to our hero, utterly wilted. So I thought I'd annoy the Great Man."

"You did. You managed to avoid him in Asia, I gather."

"Assiduously."

"Which might be why some people have been heard to say that you packed yourself and Publius off in an easterly direction to avoid being in Rome when Magnus got here."

"People never cease to amaze me. I *was* in Rome when Magnus got here."

"People never cease to amaze *me*. Did you know that I'm the cause of the Pompeius divorce?"

"What, aren't you?"

"For once I am absolutely innocent. I haven't been to Picenum in years and Mucia Tertia hasn't been to Rome in years."

"I was teasing. Pompeius honored you with his widest grin." The Crassus throat produced a rumble, the signal that he was about to embark upon a touchy subject. "You're not doing too well with the loan wolves, are you?"

"I'm keeping them at bay."

"It's being said in money circles that this year's praetors will never go to provinces thanks to Clodius."

"Yes. But not thanks to Clodius, the idiot. Thanks to Cato, Catulus and the rest of the *boni* faction."

"You've sharpened their wits, I'll say that."

"Have no fear, I'll get my province," said Caesar serenely. "Fortune hasn't abandoned me yet."

"I believe you, Caesar. Which is why I'm now going to say something to you that I've never said to any other man. Other men have to ask me—but if you find you can't get out from under your creditors before that province comes along, apply to me for help, please. I'd be putting my money on a certain winner."

"Without charging interest? Come, come, Marcus! How could I repay you when you're powerful enough to obtain your own favors?"

"So you're too stiff-necked to ask."

"I am that."

"I'm aware how stiff a Julian neck is. Which is why I've offered, even said please. Other men fall on their knees to beg. You'd fall on your sword first, and that would be a shame. I won't mention it again, but do remember. You won't be asking, because I've offered with a please. There is a difference."

At the end of February, Piso Frugi convoked the Popular Assembly and put his bill outlining the prosecution of Clodius to the vote. With disastrous consequences. Young Curio spoke from the floor of the Well to such telling effect that the entire gathering cheered him. Then the voting bridges and gangways were erected, only to be stormed by several dozen ardent young members of the Clodius Club led by Mark Antony. They seized possession of them and defied the lictors and Assembly officials so courageously that a full-scale riot threatened. It was Cato who took matters into his own hands by mounting the rostra and abusing Piso Frugi for holding a disorderly meeting. Hortensius spoke up in support of Cato;

whereupon the senior consul dismissed the Assembly and called the Senate into session instead.

Inside the packed Curia Hostilia—every senator had turned up to vote—Quintus Hortensius proposed a compromise measure.

"From the censors to the junior consul, it's clear to me that there is a significant segment in this House determined to hie Publius Clodius before a court to answer for the Bona Dea," said Hortensius in his most reasonable and mellow tones. "Therefore those Conscript Fathers who do not favor trial for Publius Clodius ought to think again. We are about to conclude our second month without being able to do normal business, which is the best way I know to bring government down around our ears. All because of a mere quaestor and his band of youthful rowdies! It cannot be allowed to go on! There's nothing in our learned senior consul's law which can't be adjusted to suit every taste. So if this House will permit me, I will undertake to spend the next few days redrafting it, in conjunction with the two men most implacably opposed to its present form—our junior consul Marcus Valerius Messala Niger and the tribune of the plebs Quintus Fufius Calenus. The next comitial day is the fourth day before the Nones of March. I suggest that Quintus Fufius present the new bill to the People as a *lex Fufia*. And that this House accompany it with a stern command to the People—put it to the vote, no nonsense!"

"I am opposed!" shouted Piso Frugi, white-faced with fury.

"Oh, oh, oh, so am I!" came a high wail from the back tier; down stumbled Clodius to fall to his knees in the middle of the Curia Hostilia floor, hands clasped beseechingly in front of him, groveling and howling. So extraordinary was this performance that the entire jam-packed Senate sat stunned. Was he serious? Was he playacting? Were the tears mirth or grief? No one knew.

Messala Niger, who held the *fasces* for February, beckoned to his lictors. "Remove this creature," he said curtly.

Publius Clodius was carried out kicking and deposited in the Senate portico; what happened to him after that was a mystery, for the lictors shut the doors in his screaming face.

"Quintus Hortensius," said Messala Niger, "I would add one thing to your proposal. That when the People meet on the fourth day before the Nones of March to vote, we call out the militia. Now I will see a division."

There were four hundred and fifteen senators in the chamber. Four hundred voted for Hortensius's proposal; among the fifteen who voted against it were Piso Frugi and Caesar.

The Popular Assembly took the hint as well, and passed the *lex Fufia* into law during a meeting distinguished for its calm—and the number of militia distributed about the lower Forum.

"Well," said Gaius Piso as the meeting dispersed, "between Hortensius, Fufius Calenus and Messala Niger, Clodius shouldn't have a great deal of trouble getting off."

"They certainly took the iron out of the original bill," said Catulus, not without satisfaction.

"Did you notice how careworn Caesar's looking?" Bibulus asked.

"His creditors are dunning him unmercifully," said Cato with glee. "I heard from a broker in the Basilica Porcia that their bailiffs are banging on the Domus Publica door every day, and that our Pontifex Maximus can't go anywhere without them in attendance. We'll have him yet!"

"So far he's still a free man," said Gaius Piso, less optimistic.

"Yes, but we now have censors far less kindly disposed toward Caesar than Uncle Lucius Cotta," said Bibulus. "They're aware of what's going on, but they can't act before they have proof at law. That won't happen until Caesar's creditors march up to the urban praetor's tribunal and demand repayment. It can't be too far in the future."

Nor was it; unless the praetorian provinces were apportioned within the next few days, Caesar on the Nones of March saw his career in ruins. He said not a word to his mother, and assumed such a forbidding expression

whenever she was in his vicinity that poor Aurelia dared
say nothing which had not to do with Vestal Virgins, Julia
or the Domus Publica. How thin he was growing! The
weight seemed suddenly to melt away, those angular
cheekbones jutted as sharp as knives and the skin of his
neck sagged like an old man's. Day after day Caesar's
mother went to the precinct of Bona Dea to give saucers
of real milk to any insomniac snakes, weed the herb garden, leave offerings of eggs on the steps leading up to
Bona Dea's closed temple door. Not my son! Please, Good
Goddess, not my son! I am yours, take me! Bona Dea,
Bona Dea, be good to my son! Be good to my son!

The lots were cast.

Publius Clodius drew a quaestorship at Lilybaeum in
western Sicily, yet could not leave Rome to take up his
duties there until he had undergone trial.

It seemed at first as if Caesar's luck had not deserted
him after all. He drew Further Spain as his province,
which meant he was endowed with a proconsular imperium and answered to no one except the consuls of the
year.

With the new governor went his stipend, the sum of
money the Treasury had set aside for one year of State
disbursements to hold the province safe: to pay its legions
and civil servants, to keep up its roads, bridges, aqueducts,
drains and sewers, public buildings and facilities. The sum
for Further Spain amounted to five million sesterces, and
was given as a lump to the governor; it became his personal property as soon as it was paid over. Some men
chose to invest it in Rome before they left for their province, trusting that the province could be squeezed of
enough to fund itself while the stipend turned over nicely
in Rome.

At the meeting of the Senate which included the
drawing of the lots Piso Frugi, holding the *fasces* again,
asked Caesar if he would give a deposition to the House
concerning the events on the night of Bona Dea's first
festival.

"I would be happy to oblige you, senior consul, if I
had anything to tell. I do not," Caesar said firmly.

"Oh, come, Gaius Caesar!" Messala Niger snapped. "You're being asked very properly for a deposition because you'll be in your province by the time Publius Clodius is tried. If any man here knows what went on, you do."

"My dear junior consul, you just uttered the significant word—*man*! I wasn't at the Bona Dea. A deposition is a solemn statement made under oath. It must therefore contain the truth. And the truth is that I know absolutely nothing."

"If you know nothing, why did you divorce your wife?"

This time the whole House answered Messala Niger: " 'Caesar's wife, like all Caesar's family, must be above suspicion!' "

The day after the lots were drawn the thirty lictors of the Curiae met in their archaic assembly and passed the *leges Curiae* which endowed each of the new governors with imperium.

And on the same day during the afternoon dinner hour a small group of important-looking men appeared before the tribunal of the *praetor urbanus,* Lucius Calpurnius Piso, just in time to prevent his leaving for an overdue meal. With them were a larger number of far seedier individuals who fanned out around the tribunal and politely but firmly ushered the curious out of listening range. Thus ensured privacy, the spokesman of the group demanded that the five million sesterces granted to Gaius Julius Caesar be attached on their behalf as part payment of his debts.

This particular Calpurnius Piso was not cut from the same cloth as his cousin Gaius Piso; the grandson and son of two men who had made colossal fortunes out of armaments for Rome's legions, Lucius Piso was also a close relative of Caesar's. His mother and his wife were both Rutilias, and Caesar's mother's mother had been a Rutilia of the same family. Until now Lucius Piso's path had not crossed Caesar's very often, but they usually voted the same way in the House, and they liked each other very well.

So Lucius Piso, now urban praetor, frowned direfully at the little group of creditors and postponed a decision until he had looked carefully through every one of the huge bundle of papers presented to him. A Lucius Piso direful frown was not easy to cope with, for he was one of the tallest and swarthiest men in noble Roman circles, with enormous and bristling black brows; and when he followed that direful frown with a grimace displaying his teeth—some black, some dirty yellow—a witness's instinctive reaction was to back away in terror, as the urban praetor looked for all the world like a ferocious man-eating *something*.

Naturally the usuring creditors had expected a decision to garnish on the spot, but those among them whose mouths had opened to protest, even to insist that the urban praetor hustle himself because he was dealing with pretty influential men, now decided to say nothing and come back in two days' time, as directed.

Lucius Piso was also clever, so he didn't close his tribunal the moment the aggrieved plaintiffs went away; dinner would have to wait. He went on conducting business until the sun had set and his little staff was yawning. By this time there were hardly any people left in the lower Forum, but there were several rather suspicious characters lurking in the Comitia well with their noses poking above the top tier. Moneylenders' bailiffs? Definitely.

After a short conversation with his six lictors, off went Lucius Piso up the Via Sacra in the direction of the Velia, his ushers moving with unusual speed; when he passed the Domus Publica he spared it not a glance. Opposite the entrance to the Porticus Margaritaria he paused, bent down to do something to his shoe, and all six lictors clustered around him, apparently to help. Then he got to his feet and proceeded on his way, still well ahead of those suspicious characters, who had stopped when he did.

What they couldn't see from so far behind was that the tall figure in the purple-bordered toga was now preceded by five lictors only; Lucius Piso had changed togas with his loftiest lictor and nipped within the Porticus Margaritaria. There he located an exit in its Domus Publica side and emerged into the vacant ground which the shopkeepers used as a rubbish dump. The lictor's plain white toga he rolled up and tucked into an empty box; scaling the wall of Caesar's peristyle garden was not work suited to a toga.

"I hope," he said, strolling into Caesar's study clad only in a tunic, "that you keep some decent wine in that terrifically elegant flagon."

Few people ever saw an amazed Caesar, but Lucius Piso did.

"How did you get in?" Caesar asked, pouring wine.

"The same way rumor says Publius Clodius got out."

"Dodging irate husbands at your age, Piso? Shame on you!"

"No, moneylenders' bailiffs," said Piso, drinking thirstily.

"Ah!" Caesar sat down. "Help yourself, Piso, you've earned the entire contents of my cellar. What's happened?"

"Four hours ago I had some of your creditors—the less salubrious ones, I'd say—at my tribunal demanding to garnish your governor's stipend, and very furtive they were about it too. Their henchmen shooed everyone else away, and they proceeded to state their case in complete privacy. From which I deduced that they didn't want what they were doing to leak back to you—odd, to say the least." Piso got up and poured another goblet of wine. "I was watched for the rest of the day, even followed home. So I changed places with my tallest lictor and got in through the shops next door. The Domus Publica is under supervision, I saw that lot as I passed by up the hill."

"Then I go out the way you came in. I'll cross the *pomerium* tonight and assume my imperium. Once I have my imperium no one can touch me."

"Give me an authorization to withdraw your stipend first thing in the morning, and I'll bring it to you on the Campus Martius. It would be better to invest it here, but who knows what the *boni* might think of next? They really are out to get you, Caesar.''

''I'm well aware of it.''

''I don't suppose,'' said Piso, that direful frown back, ''that you could manage to pay the wretches something on account?''

''I'll see Marcus Crassus on the way out tonight.''

''Do you mean to say,'' asked Lucius Piso incredulously, ''you can go to Marcus Crassus? If you can, why haven't you done so months ago—years ago?''

''He's a friend, I couldn't ask.''

''Yes, I can see that, though I wouldn't be so stiff-necked myself. But then again, I'm not a Julian. Comes very hard for a Julian to be beholden, doesn't it?''

''That it does. However, he offered, which makes it easier.''

''Write out that authorization, Caesar. You can't send for food, and I'm famished. So it's home for me. Besides, Rutilia will be worried.''

''If you're hungry, Piso, I can feed you,'' said Caesar, already writing. ''My own staff are completely trustworthy.''

''No, you've a lot to do.''

The letter was finished, furled, joined with hot melted wax and sealed with Caesar's ring. ''There's no need to go out over a wall if you'd rather a more dignified exit. The Vestals will be in their own quarters, you can go out through their side door.''

''I can't,'' said Piso. ''I left my lictor's toga next door. You can give me a leg up.''

''I'm in your debt, Lucius,'' said Caesar as they entered the garden. ''Rest assured I won't forget this.''

Piso chuckled softly. ''Isn't it just as well people like moneylenders don't know the ins and outs of Roman nobility? We may fight like cocks between ourselves, but let an outsider try to pluck our feathers, and the ranks close up. As if I'd ever let a slimy lot like that get their hands on *my* cousin!''

* * *

Julia had gone to bed, so that was one fewer painful farewell Caesar had to make. His mother was difficult enough.

"We must be grateful to Lucius Piso," she said. "My uncle Publius Rutilius would approve, were he alive to tell."

"That he would, dear old man."

"You'll have to work terribly hard in Spain to clear yourself of debt, Caesar."

"I know how to do it, Mater, so don't worry. And in the meantime, you'll be safe in case abominations like Bibulus try to pass some law or other permitting creditors to collect from a man's relatives. I'm going to see Marcus Crassus tonight."

She stared. "I thought you wouldn't."

"He offered."

Oh, Bona Dea, Bona Dea, thank you! Your snakes will have eggs and milk all year round! But aloud all she said was "Then he is a true friend."

"Mamercus will be acting Pontifex Maximus. Keep an eye on Fabia, and make sure the little blackbird doesn't turn into Cato. Burgundus knows what to pack for me. I'll be at Pompeius's hired villa, he won't mind a little company now he's eating grass."

"So it wasn't you got at Mucia Tertia?"

"Mater! How many times have I been to Picenum? Look for a Picentine and you'll be nearer the mark."

"*Titus Labienus?* Ye gods!"

"You're quick!" He took her face between his hands and kissed her mouth. "Look after yourself, please."

He made lighter work of the wall than either Lucius Piso or Publius Clodius; Aurelia stood for quite a long time looking at it, then turned and went inside. It was cold.

Cold it was, but Marcus Licinius Crassus was exactly where Caesar thought he'd be: in his offices behind the Macellum Cuppedenis, toiling diligently away by the light of as few lamps as his fifty-four-year-old eyes would tolerate, a scarf round his neck and a shawl draped across his shoulders.

"You deserve every sestertius you make," said Caesar, coming into the vast room so soundlessly that Crassus jumped when he spoke.

"How did you get in?"

"Exactly the same question I asked Lucius Piso earlier this evening. *He* climbed over my peristyle wall. *I* picked the lock."

"Lucius Piso climbed your peristyle wall?"

"To avoid the bailiffs all around my house. That portion of my creditors who were not recommended either by you or by my Gadetanian friend Balbus went to Piso's tribunal and petitioned to attach my gubernatorial stipend."

Crassus leaned back in his chair and rubbed his eyes. "Your luck really is phenomenal, Gaius. You get the province you wanted, and your more dubious creditors petition your cousin. How much do you want?"

"I honestly don't know."

"You must know!"

"It was the one question I forgot to ask Piso."

"If that isn't typical! Were you anyone else, I'd toss you in the Tiber as the worst bet in the world. But somehow I know in my bones that you're going to be richer than Pompeius. No matter how far you fall, you land on your feet every time."

"It must be more than five million, because they asked for the whole sum."

"Twenty million," said Crassus instantly.

"Explain."

"A quarter of twenty million would see them make a worthwhile profit, since you've been on compound interest for at least three years. You probably borrowed three million all up."

"You and I, Marcus, are in the wrong profession!" said Caesar, laughing. "We have to sail or march halfway round the globe, wave our eagles and swords at savage barbarians, squeeze the local plutocrats harder than a child a puppy, make ourselves thoroughly obnoxious to people who ought to be prospering under us, and then answer to People, Senate and Treasury the moment we get home.

When all the time we could be making more right here in Rome.''

"I make plenty right here in Rome," said Crassus.

"But you don't lend money for interest."

"I'm a Licinius Crassus!"

"Precisely."

"You're dressed for the road. Does that mean you're off?''

"As far as the Campus Martius. Once I assume my imperium there's not a thing my creditors can do. Piso will collect my stipend tomorrow morning and get it to me.''

"When is he seeing your creditors again?"

"The day after tomorrow, at noon."

"Good. I'll be at his tribunal when the moneylenders arrive. And don't flog yourself too hard, Caesar. Very little of my money will go their way, if any at all. I'll go guarantor for whatever sum Piso arrives at. With Crassus behind you, they'll have to wait.''

"Then I'll leave you in peace. I'm very grateful."

"Think nothing of it. I may need you just as badly one day." Crassus got up and escorted Caesar all the way down to the door, holding a lamp. "How did you see to get up here?" he asked.

"There's always light, even in the darkest stairwell."

"That only makes it more difficult."

"What?"

"Well, you see," said the imperturbable one imperturbably, "I thought that the day you become consul for the second time I'd erect a statue to you in a very public place. I was going to have the sculptor make a beast with the parts of a lion, a wolf, an eel, a weasel and a phoenix. But between landing on your feet, seeing in the dark and tomcatting around Rome, I'll have to have the whole thing painted in tabby stripes.''

Since no one inside the Servian Walls kept a stable, Caesar walked out of Rome, though not by any route an enterprising usurer might have thought to watch. He ascended the Vicus Patricii to the Vicus ad Malum Punicum,

turned onto the Vicus Longus and left the city through the
Colline Gate. From there he struck off across the Pincian
summit where a collection of wild animals amused the
children in fine weather, and so came down to Pompey's
temporary dwelling place from above. It of course had
stables beneath its lofty loggia; rather than wake the sleeping soldier, he made a nest for himself in some clean straw
and lay wide awake until the sun came up.

His departures for provinces never seemed to be orthodox, he reflected with a slight smile. Further Spain the
last time had been a mist of grief for Aunt Julia and Cinnilla, and Further Spain this time was as fugitive. A fugitive with a proconsular imperium, no less. He had it
worked out in his mind already—Publius Vatinius had
proven an assiduous scout for information, and Lucius
Cornelius Balbus Major was waiting in Gades.

Balbus was bored, he had written to Caesar. Unlike
Crassus, he did not find the making of money fulfilling in
itself; Balbus hungered for some new challenge now that
he and his nephew were the two wealthiest men in Spain.
Let Balbus Minor mind the shop! Balbus Major was keen
to study military logistics. So Caesar had nominated Balbus as his *praefectus fabrum,* a choice which surprised
some in the Senate, though not those who knew Balbus
Major. This appointee was, at least in Caesar's eyes, far
more important than a senior legate (he had asked for
none), as the *praefectus fabrum* was a military commander's most trusted assistant, responsible for the equipping
and supplying of the army.

There were two legions in the further province, both
of Roman veterans who had preferred not to come home
when the war against Sertorius finally ended. They'd be
in their thirties now, and very eager for a good campaign.
However, two legions would not be quite enough; the first
thing Caesar intended to do when he reached his domain
was to enlist a full legion of auxiliaries—Spanish troops
who had fought with Sertorius. Once they had his measure
they'd fight for him just as happily as they had for Sertorius. And then it would be off into unexplored territory.
After all, it was ridiculous to think that Rome claimed all

of the Iberian Peninsula, yet hadn't subdued a good third of it. But Caesar would.

When Caesar appeared at the top of the steps leading from the stables he found Pompey the Great sitting on his loggia admiring the view across the Tiber toward the Vatican Hill and the Janiculum.

"Well, well!" Pompey cried, leaping to his feet and seizing the unexpected visitor's hand. "Riding?"

"No. I walked out too late to bother waking you, so it was a straw bed for me. It's possible that I'll have to borrow one or two horses from you when I leave, but only to take me to Ostia. Can you put me up for a few days, Magnus?"

"Delighted to, Caesar."

"So you don't believe I seduced Mucia?"

"I know who did that job," Pompey said grimly. "Labienus, the ingrate! He can whistle!" Caesar was waved to a comfortable chair. "Is that why you haven't been to see me? Or said no more than *ave* in the Circus Flaminius?"

"Magnus, I'm a mere ex-praetor! You're the hero of the age, one can't get any closer than consulars four deep."

"Yes, but at least I can *talk* to you, Caesar. You're a real soldier, not a couch commander. When the time comes you'll know how to die, face covered and thighs covered. Death will find nothing to expose in you that isn't beautiful."

"Homer. How well said, Magnus!"

"Did a lot of reading in the East, got to like it very much. Mind you, I had Theophanes of Mitylene with me."

"A great scholar."

"Yes, that was more important to me than the fact that he's richer than Croesus. I took him to Lesbos with me, made him a Roman citizen in the agora at Mitylene in front of all the people. Then I freed Mitylene from tribute to Rome in his name. Went down very well with the locals."

"As it ought. I believe Theophanes is a close relative of Lucius Balbus of Gades."

"Their mothers were sisters. Know Balbus, do you?"

"Very well. We met while I was quaestor in Further Spain."

"He served as my scout when I was fighting Sertorius. I gave *him* the citizenship—his nephew too—but there were so many I split them up between my legates so the Senate wouldn't think I was personally enfranchising half of the Spains. Balbus Major and Balbus Minor got a Cornelius—Lentulus, I think, though not the one they're calling Spinther these days." He laughed joyously. "I do love clever nicknames! Fancy being called after an actor famous for playing *second* leads! Says what the world feels about a man, doesn't it?"

"That it does. I've made Balbus Major my *praefectus fabrum.*"

The vivid blue eyes twinkled. "Astute!"

Caesar looked Pompey up and down blatantly. "You seem fit for an old man, Magnus," he said with a grin.

"Forty-four," said Pompey, patting his flat belly complacently.

He did indeed seem fit. The eastern sun had almost joined his freckles up and tried to bleach his mop of bright gold hair—as thick as ever, Caesar noted ruefully.

"You'll have to give me a full account of what's been going on in Rome while I've been away."

"I would have thought your ears were deaf from the din of that kind of news."

"What, from conceited squeakers like Cicero? Pah!"

"I thought you were good friends."

"A man in politics has no real friends," the Great Man said deliberately. "He cultivates what's expedient."

"Absolutely true," said Caesar, chuckling. "You heard what I did to Cicero with Rabirius, of course."

"I'm glad you stuck the knife in. Otherwise he'd be prating that banishing Catilina was more important than conquering the East! Mind you, Cicero has his uses. But he always seems to think that everyone else has as much time to write thousand-sheet letters as he does. He wrote to me last year, and I did manage to send him back a few lines in my own hand. So what does he do? Takes exception, accuses me of treating him coldly! He ought to go out to govern a province, then he'd learn how busy a man is. Instead, he lies comfortably on his couch in Rome and advises us military types how to conduct our business. After all, Caesar, what *did* he do? Gave a few speeches in the Senate and the Forum, and sent Marcus Petreius to crush Catilina.''

"Very succinctly put, Magnus.''

"Well, now that they've decided what to do with Clodius I should get a date for my triumph. At least this time I did the clever thing, and disbanded my army at Brundisium. They can't say I'm sitting on the Campus Martius trying to blackmail them.''

"Don't count on a date for your triumph.''

Pompey sat up straight. "Eh?''

"The *boni* are working against you, have been since they heard you were coming home. They intend to deny you everything—the ratification of your arrangements in the East, your awards of the citizenship, land for your veterans—and I suspect one of their tactics will be to keep you outside the *pomerium* for as long as possible. Once you can take your seat in the House you'll be able to counter their moves more effectively. They have a brilliant tribune of the plebs in Fufius Calenus, and I believe he's set to veto any proposals likely to please you.''

"Ye gods, they can't! Oh, Caesar, what's the matter with them? I've increased Rome's tributes from the eastern provinces—and turned two into four!—from eight thousand talents a year to *fourteen* thousand! And do you know what the Treasury's share of the booty is? *Twenty thousand talents!* It's going to take two days for my triumphal parade to pass, that's how much loot I've got, that's how many campaigns I have to show on pageant floats! With this Asian triumph, I will have celebrated triumphs over all three continents, and *no one* has ever done that before! There are dozens of towns named after me or my victories—towns *I* founded! I have *kings* in my clientele!''

Eyes swimming with tears, Pompey leaned forward in his chair until they fell, hardly able to believe that what he had achieved was not going to be appreciated. "I'm not asking to be made King of Rome!'' he said, dashing the tears away impatiently. ''What I'm asking for is dog's piss compared to what I'm giving!''

''Yes, I agree,'' said Caesar. ''The trouble is that they all know they couldn't do it themselves, but they hate to give credit where credit's due.''

''And I'm a Picentine.''

''That too.''

''So what *do* they want?''

''At the very least, Magnus, your balls,'' Caesar said gently.

''To put where they've none of their own.''

''Exactly.''

This was no Cicero, thought Caesar as he watched the ruddy face harden and set. This was a man who could swat the *boni* into pulp with one swipe of a paw. But he wouldn't do it. Not because he lacked the testicular endowments to do it. Time and time again he'd shown Rome that he'd dare—almost anything. But somewhere in a secret corner of his self there lurked an unacknowledged consciousness that he wasn't quite a Roman. All those alliances with Sulla's relatives said a lot, as did his patent pleasure in boasting of them. No, he wasn't a Cicero. But they did have things in common. And I, who *am* Rome, what would I do if the *boni* pushed me as hard as they're going to push Pompeius Magnus? Would I be Sulla or Magnus? What would stop me? Could anything?

On the Ides of March, Caesar finally left for Further Spain. Reduced to a few words and figures on a single sheet of parchment, his stipend came borne by Lucius Piso himself, and a merry visit ensued with Pompey, who was carefully brought by Caesar to see that Lucius Piso was worth cultivating. The faithful Burgundus, grizzled now, fetched the few belongings Caesar needed: a good sword, good armor, good boots, good wet-weather gear, good snow gear, good riding gear. Two sons of his old warhorse Toes, each with toes instead of uncloven hooves. Whetstones, razors, knives, tools, a shady hat like Sulla's for the southern Spanish sun. No, not much, really. Three medium-sized chests held it all. There would be luxuries enough in the governor's residences at Castulo and in Gades.

So with Burgundus, some valued servants and scribes, Fabius and eleven other lictors clad in crimson tunics and bearing the axes in their *fasces,* and Prince Masintha muffled inside a litter, Gaius Julius Caesar sailed from Ostia in a hired vessel large enough to accommodate the baggage, mules and horses his entourage made necessary. But this time he would encounter no pirates. Pompey the Great had swept them from the seas.

Pompey the Great . . . Caesar leaned on the stern rail between the two huge rudder oars and watched the coast of Italy slip below the horizon, his spirit soaring, his mind gradually letting the homeland and its people go. Pompey the Great. The time spent with him had proven useful and fruitful; liking for the man grew with the years, no doubt of that. Or was it Pompey had grown?

No, Caesar, don't be grudging. He doesn't deserve to be grudged anything. No matter how galling it might be to see a Pompey conquer far and wide, the fact remains that a Pompey *has* conquered far and wide. Give the man his due, admit that maybe it's you has done the growing. But the trouble with growing is that one leaves the rest behind, just like the coast of Italia. So few people grow. Their roots reach bedrock and they stay as they are, content. But under me lies nothing I cannot thrust aside, and over me is infinity. The long wait is over. I go to Spain to command an army legally at last; I will put my hands on a living machine which in the right hands—*my* hands— cannot be stopped, warped, dislocated, ground down. I have yearned for a supreme military command since I sat, a boy, at old Gaius Marius's knee and listened spellbound to a master of warfare telling stories. But until this moment I did not understand how passionately, how fiercely I have lusted for that military command.

I will lay my hands on a Roman army and conquer the world, for I believe in Rome, I believe in our Gods. And I believe in myself. I am the soul of a Roman army. I cannot be stopped, warped, dislocated, ground down.

PART VI

---

from MAY of 60 B.C.
until MARCH of 58 B.C.

POMPEY
THE GREAT

JULIA

To Gaius Julius Caesar, proconsul in Further Spain, from Gnaeus Pompeius Magnus, triumphator; written in Rome on the Ides of May in the consulship of Quintus Caecilius Metellus Celer and Lucius Afranius:

Well, Caesar, I am consigning this to the Gods and the winds in the hope that the first can endow the second with enough speed to give you a chance. Others are writing, but I am the only one prepared to outlay the money to hire the fastest ship I can find just to carry one letter.

The *boni* are in the saddle and our city is disintegrating. I could live with a *boni*-dominated government if it actually did anything, but a *boni* government is dedicated to only one end—do absolutely nothing, and block any other faction when it tries to alter that.

They managed to delay my triumph until the last two days in September, and they did it smoothly too. Announced that I'd done so much for Rome I deserved to triumph on my birthday! So I kicked my heels on the Campus Martius for nine months. Though the reason for their attitude baffles me, I gather their chief objection to me is that I've had so many special commands in my lifetime that I am conclusively proven to be a danger to the State. According to them, I'm aiming at being the King of Rome. That is total rubbish! However, the fact that they *know* it's total rubbish doesn't stop their saying it.

I scratch my head, Caesar; I can't work them out. If ever there was a pillar of the establishment, it's surely Marcus Crassus. I mean, I understand that they call me a Picentine upstart, the would-be King of Rome and all the rest of it, but Marcus Crassus? Why make him their tar-

get? He's no danger to the *boni;* he's next door
to being one himself. Terrifically well born, terrifically rich, and certainly no demagogue. Crassus is harmless! And I say that as a man who
doesn't like him, never did like him, never will
like him. Sharing a consulship with him was like
lying down in the same bed as Hannibal, Jugurtha and Mithridates. All he did was work to destroy my image in the people's eyes. Despite
which, Marcus Crassus is no threat to the State.

So what have the *boni* done to Marcus
Crassus to provoke me, of all men, into sticking
up for him? They've created a real crisis, that's
what. It started when the censors let out the contracts to farm the taxes of my four eastern provinces. Oh, a lot of the blame rests with the
publicani themselves! They looked at how much
loot I'd brought back from the East, totted up
the figures, and decided the East was better than
a gold mine. So they submitted tenders for these
contracts that were completely unrealistic. Promised the Treasury untold millions, and thought
they could so do as well as make a fat profit for
themselves. Naturally the censors accepted the
highest tenders. It's their duty to do so. But it
wasn't very long before Atticus and the other
publicani plutocrats realized that the sums they
had undertaken to pay the Treasury were not feasible. My four eastern provinces couldn't possibly pay what they were being asked to pay, no
matter how hard the *publicani* squeezed.

Anyway, Atticus, Oppius and some others
went to Marcus Crassus and asked him to petition the Senate to cancel the tax-gathering contracts for the East, then instruct the censors to
let out new contracts calling for two thirds of
the sums originally agreed on. Well, Crassus petitioned. Never so much as dreaming that the
boni would—or could!—persuade the whole
House to say a resounding NO. But that is what

happened. The Senate said a resounding NO.

At that stage I confess I chuckled; it was such a pleasure to see Marcus Crassus flattened—oh, he was flattened! All that hay wrapped round both horns, yet Crassus the ox stood there stunned and defeated. But then I saw what a stupid move it was on the part of the *boni,* and stopped chuckling. It seems they have decided it's high time the knights were shown for once and for all that the Senate is supreme, that the Senate runs Rome and the knights can't dictate to it. Well, the Senate may flatter itself that it runs Rome, but you and I know it doesn't. If Rome's businessmen are not allowed to do profitable business, then Rome is finished.

After the House said NO to Marcus Crassus, the *publicani* retaliated by refusing to pay the Treasury one sestertius. Oh, what a storm that caused! I daresay the knights hoped this would force the Senate to instruct the censors to cancel the contracts because they weren't being honored—and of course when new tenders were called, the sums tendered would have been much lower. Only the *boni* control the House, and the House in consequence won't cancel the contracts. It's an impasse.

The blow to Crassus's standing was colossal, both in the House and among the knights. He's been their spokesman for so long and with such success that it never occurred to him or them that he wouldn't get what he asked for. Particularly as his request to reduce the Asian contracts was so reasonable.

And who do you think the *boni* had managed to recruit as their chief spokesman in the House? Why, none other than my ex–brother-in-law, Metellus Celer! For years Celer and his little brother Nepos were my loyalest adherents. But ever since I divorced Mucia they've been my worst enemies. Honestly, Caesar, you'd think that Mucia was the only wife ever divorced in the history of Rome! I had every right to divorce her, didn't I? She was an adultress, spent the time I was away in conducting an affair with Titus Labienus, my own client! What was I supposed to do? Close my eyes and pretend I never heard about it because Mucia's mother is also the mother of Celer and Nepos? Well, I wasn't about to close my eyes. But the way Celer and Nepos carried on, you'd think it was *I* committed the adultery! Their precious sister divorced? Ye gods, what an intolerable insult!

They've been making trouble for me ever since. I don't know how they did it, but they've even managed to find another husband for Mucia of sufficiently exalted birth and rank to infer that *she* was the wronged party! My quaestor Scaurus, if you please. She's old enough to be his mother. Well, almost. He's thirty-four and she's forty-seven. What a match. Though I do think they suit for intelligence, as neither of them has any. I understand Labienus wanted to marry her, but the Brothers Metelli took terrible exception to that idea. So it's Marcus Aemilius Scaurus, who embroiled me in all that business with the Jews. Rumor has it that Mucia is pregnant, another slur on me. I hope she dies having the brat.

I have a theory as to why the *boni* have suddenly become so unbelievably obtuse and destructive. The death of Catulus. Once he was gone, the senatorial rump fell totally into the clutches of Bibulus and Cato. Fancy turning up your toes and dying because you weren't asked to speak first or second among the consulars during a House debate! But that's what Catulus did. Leaving his faction to Bibulus and Cato, who don't have his saving grace, namely the ability to distinguish between mere negativity and political suicide.

I also have a theory as to why Bibulus and

Cato turned on Crassus. Catulus left a priesthood vacant, and Cato's brother-in-law Lucius Ahenobarbus wanted it. But Crassus nipped in first and got it for his son, Marcus. A mortal insult to Ahenobarbus, as there isn't a Domitius Ahenobarbus in the College. How picayune. I, by the way, am now an augur. I'm tickled, I can tell you. But I didn't endear myself to Cato, Bibulus or Ahenobarbus in being elected an augur! It was the second election in a very short space of time that Ahenobarbus lost.

My own affairs—land for my veterans, ratification of my settlements in the East, and so forth—have foundered. It cost me millions to bribe Afranius into the junior consul's chair—money wasted, I can tell you! Afranius has turned out to be a better soldier than he is a politician, but Cicero goes around telling everyone he's a better dancer than he is a politician. This because Afranius got disgustingly drunk at his inauguration banquet on New Year's Day and pirouetted all over Jupiter Optimus Maximus. Embarrassing for me, as everyone knows I bought him the job in an attempt to control Metellus Celer, who as senior consul has walked over Afranius as if he didn't exist.

When Afranius did manage to have my affairs discussed in the House during February, Celer, Cato and Bibulus among them ruined it. They dragged Lucullus out of his retirement, almost imbecilic with mushrooms and the like, and used him to stall me. Oh, I could kill the lot of them! Every day I wish I hadn't done the right thing and disbanded my army, not to mention paid my troops their share of the spoils while we were still in Asia. Of course that's being criticized too. Cato said it wasn't my place to dole out the spoils minus the consent of the Treasury—that is, the Senate—and when I reminded him that I had an *imperium maius* empowering

me to do just about anything I wanted in Rome's
name, he said that my *imperium maius* had been
obtained illegally in the Plebeian Assembly, that
it hadn't been bestowed on me by the People.
Arrant nonsense, but the House applauded him!

Then in March the discussion of my affairs
ended. Cato put forward a division in the Senate
proposing that no business be discussed until the
tax-farming problem is solved—and the idiots
voted for it! *Knowing* that Cato was simultaneously blocking any solution to the tax-farming
problem! The result is that nothing whatsoever
has been discussed. The moment Crassus brings
up the tax-farming problem, Cato filibusters.
And the Conscript Fathers think Cato is terrific!

I can't work it out, Caesar, I just can't.
What has Cato ever done? He's only thirty-four
years old, he's held no senior magistracy, he's a
shocking speaker and a prig of the first order.
But somewhere along the way the Conscript Fathers have become convinced that he's utterly
incorruptible, and that makes him wonderful.
Why can't they see that incorruptibility is disastrous when it's allied to a mentality like Cato's? As for Bibulus—well, he's incorruptible
too, they say. And both never cease to prate that
they're the avowed enemies of all men who
stand one fraction of an inch higher than their
peers. A laudable objective. Except that *some*
men simply can't help standing higher than their
peers because they're better. If we were all
meant to be equal, we'd all be created exactly
the same. We're not, and that's a fact there's no
getting around.

Whichever way I turn, Caesar, I'm howled
at by a pack of enemies. Don't the fools understand that my army might be disbanded, yet its
members are right here in Italia? All I have to
do is stamp my foot for soldiers to spring up
eager to do my bidding. I can tell you, I am

sorely tempted. I conquered the East, I just about doubled Rome's income, and I did everything the right way. So *why* are they against me?

Anyway, enough of me and my troubles. This letter is really to warn you that you're in for trouble too.

It all started with those terrific reports you keep sending to the Senate—a perfect campaign against the Lusitani and the Callaici; heaps of gold and treasures; proper disposition of the province's resources and functions; the mines producing more silver, lead and iron than in half a century; relief for the towns Metellus Pius punished—the *boni* must have spent a fortune sending spies to Further Spain to catch you out. But they haven't caught you out, and rumor says they never will. Not a whiff of extortion or peculation anywhere near your vicinity, buckets of letters from grateful residents of Further Spain, the guilty punished and the innocent exonerated. Old Mamercus Princeps Senatus—he's failing badly, by the way—got up in the House and said that your conduct as governor had provided a manual of gubernatorial conduct, and the *boni* couldn't refute a word of what he said. How that hurt!

All of Rome knows you'll be senior consul. Even if we leave aside the fact that you always come in at the top of the polls, your popularity is growing in leaps and bounds. Marcus Crassus is going around telling every knight in the Eighteen that when you're senior consul the tax-farming business will soon be sorted out. From which I gather that he knows he's going to need your services—and knows he'll get them.

Well, I need your services too, Caesar. Far more than Marcus Crassus does! All he has at stake is his damaged clout, whereas I need land for my veterans and treaties ratifying my settlements in the East.

There's a good chance of course that you're already on your way home—Cicero certainly seems to think so—but my bones tell me you're like me, prone to stay until the very last moment so that every thread is woven into place and every tangle combed away.

The *boni* have just struck, Caesar, and extremely cunning they have been. All candidates for the consular elections have to declare themselves by the Nones of June at the latest, even though the elections will not take place until the usual five days before the Ides of Quinctilis. Egged on by Celer, Gaius Piso, Bibulus (a candidate himself, of course, but safely inside Rome because he's like Cicero, never wants to govern a province) and the rest of the *boni,* Cato succeeded in passing a *consultum* putting the closing date at the Nones of June. Over five *nundinae* before the elections instead of the three *nundinae* custom and tradition have laid down.

Someone must have whispered that you travel like the wind, because they then produced another ploy to frustrate you—this one in case you arrive in Rome before the Nones of June. Celer asked the House to set a date for your triumph. Very affable he was, full of praise for the splendid job you've done as governor. After which he suggested that the date of your triumph be set as the Ides of June! Everyone thought that a splendid idea, so the motion was carried. Yes, you are to triumph eight days *later* than the closing of the consular candidates' booth. Wonderful, eh?

So, Caesar, if you do manage to reach Rome before the Nones of June, you will have to petition the Senate to run for consul *in absentia.* You can't cross the *pomerium* into the city to lodge your candidacy in person without giving up your imperium and thereby your right to triumph. I add that Celer was very careful to

point out to the House that Cicero had passed a
law forbidding consular candidates to stand *in
absentia*. A gentle reminder I took to mean that
the *boni* intend to oppose your petition to run *in
absentia*. They have got you by the balls, just as
you said—with perfect truth!—they've got me.
I will be working to persuade our senatorial
sheep—*why* do they let themselves be led by a
mere handful of men who are not even anything
special?—to have you allowed to stand *in absentia*. So will Crassus, Mamercus Princeps Senatus and many others, I know.

The main thing is to get to Rome before the
Nones of June. Ye gods, can you, even if the
winds blow my hired ship to Gades in record
time? What I'm hoping is that you're already
well on your way down the Via Domitia. I've
sent a messenger to meet you if you are, just in
case you're dawdling.

You *have* to make it, Caesar! I need you
desperately, and I am not ashamed to say so.
You've hauled me out of boiling water before in
a way which preserved the legalities. All I can
say is that if you're not on hand to help me this
time, I might have to stamp my foot. I don't
want to do that. If I did, I'd go down in the
history books as no better than Sulla. Look how
everyone hates him. It's really uncomfortable to
be hated, though Sulla never seemed to mind.

Pompey's letter reached Gades on the twenty-first day
of May, a remarkably swift passage. And Caesar happened
to be in Gades to receive it.

"It's fifteen hundred miles by road from Gades to
Rome," he said to Lucius Cornelius Balbus Major,
"which means I can't get to Rome by the Nones of June
even if I average a hundred miles a day. Rot the *boni*!"

"No man can average a hundred miles a day," said
the little Gadetanian banker, looking anxious.

"I can in a fast gig harnessed to four good mules, provided I can change teams often enough," Caesar said calmly. "However, the road isn't feasible. It will have to be Rome by ship."

"The season is wrong. Magnus's letter proves that. Five days in front of a northeasterly gale."

"Ah, Balbus, but I have luck!"

Caesar did indeed have luck, Balbus reflected. No matter how badly matters appeared to have gone wrong, somehow that magical—and it *was* magical—luck came to his rescue. Though he seemed to manufacture it himself out of sheer willpower. As if, having made up his mind, he could compel natural and unnatural forces to obey him. The past year and more had been the most exhilarating, the most stimulating experience of Balbus's entire life, toiling and panting in Caesar's wake from one end of Spain to the other. Who could ever have thought he would sail before an Atlantic Ocean wind in pursuit of foes convinced they had eluded the reach of Rome? But they hadn't. Out came the ships from Olisippo, down came the legions. Then more voyages to remote Brigantium, untold treasures, a people feeling for the first time a wind of change, an influence from the Middle Sea that would never again go away. What did Caesar say? It wasn't the gold, it was the lengthening of Rome's reach. What did they have, that small race from a little city on the Italian salt route? Why was it they who swept all before them? Not like a gigantic wave, more like a millstone grinding patiently, patiently at whatever was thrown down as grist. They never gave up, the Romans.

"And what will Caesar's luck consist of this time?"

"To begin with, one *myoparo*. Two teams of the best oarsmen Gades can furnish. No baggage and no animals. As passengers, just you and me and Burgundus. And a strong sou'wester," said Caesar, grinning.

"A piddling order," said Balbus without answering that smile. He rarely smiled; Gadetanian bankers of impeccably Phoenician lineage were not prompted to take life or circumstances lightly. Balbus looked what he was, a subtle, placid man of extraordinary intelligence and ability.

Caesar was already halfway to the door. "I'm off to find the right *myoparo*. Your job is to find me a pilot capable of navigating out of sight of land. We're going the direct route—through the Pillars of Hercules, a stop for food and water at New Carthage, then Balearis Minor. From there we head directly for the strait between Sardinia and Corsica. We have a thousand miles of water to cover, and we can't hope for the kind of winds which blew Magnus's letter here in five days. We have twelve days."

"Something over eighty miles between sunrise and sunrise. Not so piddling," said Balbus, rising to his feet.

"But possible, provided there are no adverse winds. Trust to my luck and the Gods, Balbus! I shall make magnificent offerings to the Lares Permarini and Goddess Fortuna. They'll listen to me."

The Gods listened, though how Caesar managed to squeeze all that he did into five short hours before he set sail from Gades was more than Balbus could fathom. Caesar's quaestor was a most efficient young man who swung with enormous enthusiasm into organizing the shipping of the governor's possessions along the land route from Spain to Rome, the Via Domitia; the booty had long gone, accompanied by the single legion Caesar had chosen to march with him in his triumphal parade. Somewhat to his surprise, the Senate had acceded to his request for a triumph without a murmur from the *boni,* but that mystery was fully explained in Pompey's letter. No reason to refuse what they had every intention of making sure would be a dismal affair. Dismal it would be. His troops were due to arrive on the Campus Martius by the Ides of June—an ironic twist, given that Celer had assigned that day for the triumph. Were Caesar allowed to run for consul *in absentia* and the triumph went ahead, it would be a poor triumph indeed. Weary soldiers, no time to manufacture sumptuous floats and displays, booty thrown higgledy-piggledy into wagons. Not the sort of triumph Caesar had bargained for. However, getting to Rome before the Nones of June was the first problem. Pray for a stiff sou'wester!

And indeed the winds did blow out of the southwest, though they were gentle rather than stiff. A very slight following sea helped the oarsmen, as did a small push from the sail, but it was backbreaking work almost all the way. Caesar and Burgundus rowed a full shift of three hours four times in each sunrise to sunrise, which appealed to the professional oarsmen as much as Caesar's cheerful friendliness did. The bonus would be worth it, so they put their shoulders to the task and rowed while Balbus and the pilot busied themselves bearing *amphorae* of water weakly flavored with a good fortified Spanish wine to those who called for it.

When the pilot brought the *myoparo* into sight of the Italian coast and there in front of them was the mouth of the Tiber, the crew shouted themselves hoarse, then paired up on each oar and sprinted the trim little monoreme into Ostia Harbor; the voyage had taken twelve days, and the port attained two hours after dawn on the third day of June.

Leaving Balbus and Burgundus to reward the *myoparo* pilot and oarsmen, Caesar threw himself across a good hired horse and rode for Rome at the gallop. His journey would end on the Campus Martius, but not his travail; he would have to find someone to hurry into the city and locate Pompey. A conscious decision which would not please Crassus, yet the correct decision. Pompey was right. He needed Caesar more than Crassus did. Besides which, Crassus was an old friend; he would settle down once matters were explained.

The news that Caesar had arrived outside Rome reached Cato and Bibulus almost as quickly as it did Pompey, for all three were in the House enduring yet another session debating the fate of the Asian tax-farmers. The message was given to Pompey, who whooped so loudly that dozing backbenchers almost fell off their stools, then leaped to his feet.

"Pray excuse me, Lucius Afranius," he chortled, already on his way out. "Gaius Caesar is on the Campus

Martius, and I must be the first of us to welcome him in person!''

Which somehow left those remaining in the poorly attended meeting feeling as flat as an Asian *publicanus*. Afranius, who held the *fasces* for June, dismissed the assembly for the day.

"Tomorrow an hour after dawn," he said, well aware that he would have to hear Caesar's petition to stand *in absentia,* and that tomorrow was the last day before the Nones of June, when the electoral officer (Celer) would close his booth.

"I told you he'd do it," said Metellus Scipio. "He's like a piece of cork. No matter how you try to hold him under, up he pops again hardly wet.''

"Well, there was always a very good chance he'd turn up," said Bibulus, lips tight. "After all, we don't even know when he set out from Spain. Just because we heard he was planning to remain in Gades until the end of May doesn't mean he actually did. He can't know what's in store for him.''

"He will the moment Pompeius reaches the Campus Martius," Cato said harshly. "Why do you think the Dancer convened another meeting for tomorrow? Caesar will be petitioning to stand *in absentia,* nothing surer.''

"I miss Catulus," said Bibulus. "It's times like tomorrow his clout would be extremely useful. Caesar did better in Spain than any of us thought he would, so the sheep will be inclined to let the ingrate stand *in absentia.* Pompeius will urge it, so will Crassus. And Mamercus! I wish *he'd* die!''

Cato simply smiled and looked mysterious.

Whereas Pompey on the Campus Martius had nothing to smile about and no mysteries to contemplate. He found Caesar leaning against the rounded marble wall of Sulla's tomb, his horse's bridle over one arm; above his head was that famous epitaph: NO BETTER FRIEND • NO WORSE ENEMY. It might, thought Pompey, have been written as much for Caesar as for Sulla. Or for himself.

"What on earth are you doing here?" Pompey demanded.

"It seemed as good a place as any to wait."

"Haven't you heard of a villa on the Pincian?"

"I do not intend to be here long enough."

"There's an inn not far down the Via Lata, we'll go there. Minicius is a good fellow, and you have to put a roof over your head, Caesar, even if it is for a few days only."

"More important to find you before I thought about where to stay, I thought."

That melted Pompey's heart; he too had dismounted (since he had resumed his seat in the Senate he kept a small stable inside Rome), and now turned to stroll down the perfectly straight and wide road which actually was the commencement of the Via Flaminia.

"I suppose nine months of kicking your heels gave you plenty of time to find out where the inns are located," said Caesar.

"I found that out back before I was consul."

The inn was a fairly commodious and respectable establishment, its proprietor well used to the sight of famous Roman military men; he greeted Pompey like a long-lost friend, and indicated with some charm that he was aware who Caesar was. They were ushered into a comfortable private parlor where two braziers warmed the smoky air, and were served immediately with water and wine, together with such goodies as roast lamb, sausages, fresh crusty bread and an oil-laced salad.

"I'm ravenous!" Caesar exclaimed, surprised.

"Tuck in then. I confess I don't mind helping you. Minicius prides himself on his food."

Between mouthfuls Caesar managed to give Pompey a bald outline of his voyage.

"A sou'wester at this time of year!" said the Great Man.

"No, I don't think I'd call it a noble wind like that. But it was enough to give me a push in the right direction. I gather the *boni* didn't expect to see me so soon?"

"Cato and Bibulus got a nasty jolt, certainly. Whereas others like Cicero seem simply to have assumed you would be well on your way as a matter of course—

however, they didn't have spies in Further Spain to keep them informed of your intentions.'' Pompey scowled. ''Cicero! What a poseur that man is! Do you know he had the gall to stand up in the House and refer to his banishment of Catilina as an 'immortal glory'? Every speech he makes contains some sort of sermon on how he saved his country.''

''I heard you were thick with him,'' said Caesar, mopping up his salad oil with a piece of bread.

''*He* would have it so. He's frightened.''

''Of what?'' Caesar leaned back with a sigh of content.

''The change in Publius Clodius's status. The tribune of the plebs Herennius had the Plebeian Assembly transfer Clodius from the Patriciate to the Plebs. Now Clodius is saying he intends to run for the tribunate of the plebs and exile Cicero for good for the execution of Roman citizens without trial. It's Clodius's new purpose in life. And Cicero is white with fear.''

''Well, I can understand a man like Cicero being terrified of our Clodius. Clodius is a force of nature. Not quite mad, but not quite sane either. However, Herennius is wrong to use the Plebeian Assembly. A patrician can only become a plebeian by adoption.''

Minicius bustled in to remove the dishes, creating a pause in the conversation Caesar found welcome. Time to get down to business.

''Is the Senate still stalled among the tax-farmers?'' he asked.

''Eternally, thanks to Cato. But as soon as Celer closes his electoral booth I'm sending my tribune of the plebs Flavius back to the Plebs with my land bill. Emasculated, thanks to that officious fool Cicero! He managed to remove any *ager publicus* older than the tribunate of Tiberius Gracchus from it, then said that Sulla's veterans—the very ones who allied themselves with Catilina!—must be confirmed in their land grants, and that Volaterrae and Arretium must be allowed to keep their public lands. Most of the land for my veterans will therefore have to be purchased, and the money is to come out of the increased

tributes from the East. Which gave my ex–brother-in-law
Nepos a terrific idea. He suggested that all port duties and
taxes be removed from the whole of Italia, and the Senate
thought that was wonderful. So he got a *consultum* from
the Senate and passed his law in the Popular Assembly.''

"Clever!" said Caesar appreciatively. "That means
the State's income from Italia has gone down to two items
only—the five percent tax on manumission of slaves and
the rents from *ager publicus*."

"Makes me look good, doesn't it? The Treasury will
end in seeing not one extra sestertius from my work, between the loss of port revenues, loss of the *ager publicus*
when it's deeded to my veterans, and the cost of buying
in extra land as well."

"You know, Magnus," said Caesar, looking wry, "I
am always hoping that the day comes when these brilliant
men think more of their homeland than they do of getting
back at their enemies. Every political move they make is
aimed at some other fellow or done to protect the privileges of a very few, rather than for the sake of Rome and
her domains. You've exerted yourself mightily to extend
Rome's reach and plump out her public purse. Whereas
they extend themselves mightily to put you in your
place—at poor Rome's expense. You said in your letter
that you needed me. And here I am at your service."

"Minicius!" Pompey bellowed.

"Yes, Gnaeus Pompeius?" asked the innkeeper, appearing with great alacrity.

"Fetch us writing materials."

"However," said Caesar as he completed his short
letter, "I think it would be better if Marcus Crassus presented my petition to stand *in absentia* for the consulship.
I'll send this to him by messenger."

"Why can't I present your petition?" Pompey asked,
annoyed that Caesar preferred to use Crassus.

"Because I don't want the *boni* to realize that we've
come to any kind of agreement," said Caesar patiently.
"You will already have set them wondering by dashing
out of the House announcing that you were off to see me
on the Campus Martius. Don't underestimate them, Mag-

nus, please. They can tell a radish from a ruby. The bond
between you and me must be kept secret for some time to
come."

"Yes, I do see that," said Pompey, a little mollified.
"I just don't want you becoming more committed to Crassus than you are to me. I don't mind if you help him with
the tax-farmers and bribery laws aimed at the knights, but
it's far more important to get land for my soldiers and
ratify my settlement of the East."

"Quite so," said Caesar serenely. "Send Flavius to
the Plebs, Magnus. It will throw dust in many pairs of
eyes."

At which moment Balbus and Burgundus arrived.
Pompey greeted the Gadetanian banker with great joy,
while Caesar concentrated on a very tired looking Burgundus. His mother would say he had been inconsiderate,
expecting a man as old as Burgundus to labor at an oar
twelve hours a day for twelve days.

"I'll be off," said Pompey.

Caesar escorted the Great Man to the inn door. "Lie
low and make it look as if you're still fighting your own
war unaided."

"Crassus won't like it that you sent for me."

"He probably won't even know. Was he in the
House?"

"No," said Pompey, grinning. "He says it's too del-
eterious to his health. Listening to Cato gives him a headache."

When the Senate convened an hour after dawn on the
fourth day of June, Marcus Crassus applied to speak. Gracious consent was accorded him by Lucius Afranius, who
accepted Caesar's petition to stand for the consulship *in
absentia*.

"It's a very reasonable request," said Crassus at the
end of a workmanlike oration, "which this House ought
to approve. Every last one of you is well aware that not
the slightest hint of improper conduct in his province is
attached to Gaius Caesar, and improper conduct was the
cause of our consular Marcus Cicero's law. Here is a man

who did everything correctly, including solving a vexed problem Further Spain had suffered for years: Gaius Caesar brought in the best and fairest debt legislation I have ever seen, and not one individual, debtor or creditor, has complained.''

"Surely that doesn't surprise you, Marcus Crassus," Bibulus drawled. "If anyone knows how to deal with debt, it's Gaius Caesar. He probably owed money in Spain too.''

"Then you might well have to apply to him for information, Marcus Bibulus," said Crassus, unruffled as ever. "If you manage to get yourself elected consul, you'll be up to your eyebrows in debt from bribing the voters." He cleared his throat and waited for a reply; not receiving one, he continued. "I repeat, this is a very reasonable request which the House ought to approve.''

Afranius called for other consular speakers, who all indicated that they agreed with Crassus. Not many of the incumbent praetors fancied adding anything until Metellus Nepos rose.

"Why," he asked, "should this House accord any favors to a notorious homosexual? Has everyone forgotten how our gorgeous Gaius Caesar lost his virginity? Face down on a couch in the palace of King Nicomedes, a royal penis stuck up his arse! Do what you like, Conscript Fathers, but if you want to grant a pansy like Gaius Caesar the privilege of becoming consul without showing his pretty face inside Rome, you may count me out! I'll do no special favors to a man with a well-poked anus!''

The silence was complete; no one so much as drew a breath.

"Retract that, Quintus Nepos!" Afranius snapped.

"Shove it up your own arse, son of Aulus!" cried Nepos, and strode out of the Curia Hostilia.

"Scribes, you will delete Quintus Nepos's remarks," Afranius directed, red-faced at the insults thrown his way. "It has not escaped me that the manners and conduct of members of the Senate of Rome have undergone a marked deterioration over the years I've belonged to what used to be an august and respectable body. I hereby ban Quintus Nepos from attendance at meetings of the Senate while I hold the *fasces*. Now who else has anything to say?''

''I do, Lucius Afranius,'' said Cato.

''Then speak, Marcus Porcius Cato.''

It seemed to take Cato an eternity to get himself settled; he shifted, fiddled, cleared his respiratory passages with some deep-breathing exercises, smoothed his hair, adjusted his toga. Finally he opened his mouth to bark words.

''Conscript Fathers, the state of morals in Rome is a tragedy. We, the men who stand above all others because we are members of Rome's most senior governing body, are not fulfilling our duty as custodians of Roman morals. How many men here are guilty of adultery? How many wives of men here are guilty of adultery? How many children of men here are guilty of adultery? How many parents of men here are guilty of adultery? My great-grandfather the Censor—the best man Rome has ever produced—held absolute opinions on morality, as he did about everything. He never paid more than five thousand sesterces for a slave. He never pilfered the affections of a Roman woman, nor lay with her. After his wife Licinia died, he contented himself with the services of a slave, as is fitting for a man in his seventies. But when his own son and daughter-in-law complained that the slave had set herself up as queen of the household, he put the girl away and married again. But he would not choose a bride from among his peers, for he deemed himself too aged to be an adequate husband for a Roman noblewoman. So he married the daughter of his freedman Salonius. I am descended from that stock, and proud to say it. Cato the Censor was a moral man, an upright man, an adornment to this State. He used to love thunderstorms because his wife would cling to him in terror, and thus he could permit himself to embrace her in front of the servants and the free members of his household. Because, as we all know, a decent and moral Roman husband ought not to indulge his senses in places and at times not suited to private activities. I have modeled my own life and conduct on my great-grandfather, who when it came time to die forbade the expenditure of large sums of money on his obsequies. He went to a modest pyre and his ashes into a plain glazed

jar. His tomb is even plainer, yet it sits on the side of the
Via Appia always adorned with flowers brought by some
admiring citizen. But what if Cato the Censor were to walk
the streets of modern Rome? What would those clear eyes
see? What would those perceptive ears hear? What would
that formidable and lucid intellect think? I shudder to
speak of it, Conscript Fathers, but I fear I must. I do not
think he could bear to live in this cesspool we call Rome.
Women sit in the gutters so drunk they vomit. Men lurk
in alleyways to rob and murder. Children of both sexes
prostitute themselves outside Venus Erucina's. I have even
seen what appeared to be respectable men lift their tunics
and squat to defaecate in the street when a public latrine
is in full sight! Privacy for bodily functions and modesty
in conduct are deemed old-fashioned, ridiculous, laugh-
able. Cato the Censor would weep. Then he would go
home and hang himself. Oh, how often I have had to resist
the temptation to do the same!''

"Don't, Cato, don't resist it a moment longer!'' cried
Crassus.

Cato ground on without seeming to notice. "Rome is
a stew. But what else can one expect when the men sitting
in this House have plundered the wives of other men, or
think no more of the sanctity of their flesh than to yield
unmentionable orifices to unmentionable acts? Cato the
Censor would weep. And look at me, Conscript Fathers!
See how I weep? How can a state be strong, how can it
contemplate ruling the world, when the men who rule it
are degenerate, decadent, filthy running sores? We must
stop all this interest in extraneous irrelevancies like the
Asian *publicani* and devote one whole year to weeding
Rome's moral garden!—to putting decency back as our
highest priority!—to enacting laws which make it impossible for men to violate other men, for patrician delin-
quents to boast openly of incestuous relationships, for
governors of our provinces to sexually exploit children!
Women who commit adultery ought to be executed, as
they were in the old days. Women who drink wine ought
to be executed, as they were in the old days. Women who
appear at public meetings in the Forum to barrack and

shout coarse insults ought to be executed—though not as they were in the old days, because in the old days no woman would have dreamed of doing that! Women bear and mother children, they have no other use! But where are the laws we need to enforce a proper moral standard? They do not exist, Conscript Fathers! Yet if Rome is to survive they *must* come into existence!''

''You'd think,'' Cicero whispered to Pompey, ''that he was talking to the inhabitants of Plato's ideal Republic, not to men who have to wallow in Romulus's shit.''

''He's going to filibuster until after the sun sets,'' Pompey said grimly. ''What utter rubbish he's prating! Men are men and women are women. They got up to the same tricks under the first consuls that they do under Celer and Afranius today.''

''Mind you,'' roared Cato, ''the present scandalous conditions are a direct result of too much exposure to eastern laxity! Since we extended our reach down Our Sea to places like Anatolia and Syria, we Romans have fallen into disgustingly dirty habits imported from those sinks of iniquity! For every cherry or orange brought back to increase our beloved homeland's fruitfulness, there are ten thousand evils. It is a wrong act to conquer the world, and I make no bones about saying so. Let Rome continue to be what Rome always was in the old days, a contained and moral place filled with hardworking citizens who minded their own business and cared not a rush what happened in Campania or Etruria, let alone Anatolia or Syria! Every Roman then was happy and content. The change came when greedy and ambitious men lifted themselves above the level set for all men—we must control Campania, we must impose our rule on Etruria, every Italian must become Roman, and all roads must lead to Rome! The worm began to eat—enough money was no longer enough, and power was more intoxicating than wine. Look at the number of State-funded funerals we endure these days! How often in the old days did the State disburse its precious moneys to bury men well able to pay for their own funerals? How often does the State do so today? Sometimes it feels as if we endure one State funeral per *nundinum*! I was urban quaestor, I know how much public money is wasted on fribbles like funerals and feasts! Why should the State contribute to public banquets so that the Head Count can gorge itself on eels and oysters, take home the leftovers in a sack? I can tell you why! In order that some ambitious man can buy himself the consulship! 'Oh, but!' he cries. 'Oh, but the Head Count can't give me votes! I am a Roman patriot, I simply like to give pleasure to those who cannot afford pleasure!' No, the Head Count can't give him votes! But all the merchants who provide the food and drink can and do give him votes! Look at Gaius Caesar's flowers when he was curule aedile! Not to mention sufficient refreshments to fill two hundred thousand undeserving bellies! Try to add up, if you can, the number of fish and flower vendors who owe Gaius Caesar their first vote! But it is legal, our bribery laws cannot touch him. . . .''

At which point Pompey got up and walked out, starting a mass exodus of senators. When the sun went down only four men remained to listen to one of Cato's best filibusters: Bibulus, Gaius Piso, Ahenobarbus and the hapless consul with the *fasces*, Lucius Afranius.

Both Pompey and Crassus sent letters to Caesar on the Campus Martius, where he had taken up residence at the inn of Minicius. Very tired because—despite his massive size and strength—he was no longer young enough to row with impunity for days on end, Burgundus sat quietly in a corner of Caesar's private parlor watching his beloved master converse softly with Balbus, who had elected to keep him company rather than enter Rome without him.

The letters arrived carried by the same messenger, and took very little time to read. Caesar looked up at Balbus.

''Well, it seems I am not to stand for consul *in absentia*,'' he said calmly. ''The House appeared willing to grant me the favor, but Cato talked out any possibility of a vote. Crassus is on his way to see me now. Pompeius won't come. He thinks he's being watched, and he's probably right.''

''Oh, Caesar!'' Balbus's eyes filled, but what he might have said after this was never uttered; Crassus erupted into the room breathing fire.

''The sanctimonious, puffed-up prig! I detest Pompeius Magnus and I despise idiots like Cicero, but Cato I could kill! What a leader the rump has inherited in him! Catulus would imitate his father and suffocate from fresh plaster fumes if he knew! Who said incorruptibility and honesty are the virtues which matter most? I'd rather deal with the shiftiest, slimiest usurer in the world than piss in Cato's general direction! He's a bigger upstart than any New Man who ever strolled down the Via Flaminia sucking a straw! *Mentula! Verpa! Cunnus!* Pah!''

To all of this Caesar listened fascinated, a delighted smile spreading from ear to ear. ''My dear Marcus, I never thought I'd have to say it to you, but calm down! Why suffer a stroke over the likes of Cato? He won't win, for all his much-extolled integrity.''

''Caesar, he's already won! You can't be consul in the New Year now, and what's going to happen to Rome? If she doesn't get a consul strong enough to squash slugs like Cato and Bibulus, I despair! There won't *be* any Rome! And how am I going to protect my standing with the Eighteen if you're not senior consul?''

''It's all right, Marcus, truly. I'll be senior consul in the New Year, even if I'm saddled with Bibulus for my colleague.''

The rage vanished; Crassus stared at Caesar slack-jawed. *''You mean you'll give up your triumph?''* he squawked.

''Certainly I will.'' Caesar turned in his chair. ''Burgundus, it's time you saw Cardixa and your sons. Go to the Domus Publica and stay there. Give my mother two messages: that I'll be home tomorrow evening, and pack up my *toga candida* and send it to me here tonight. At dawn tomorrow I'll cross the *pomerium* into Rome.''

''Caesar, it's too great a sacrifice!'' moaned Crassus, on the verge of tears.

"Nonsense! What sacrifice? I'll have more triumphs—I do not intend to go to a tame province after my consulship, I assure you. You ought to know me by now, Marcus. If I went ahead and triumphed on the Ides, what sort of show would it be? Anything but worthy of me. There's some pretty stiff competition in Magnus, who took two days to parade. No, when I triumph, it will be at my leisure and without parallel. I am Gaius Julius Caesar, not Metellus Little Goat Creticus. Rome must talk about *my* parade for generations. I will never consent to being an also-ran."

"I don't believe I'm hearing this! To give up your triumph? Gaius, Gaius, that's the height of a man's glory! Look at me! All my life a triumph has eluded me, and it's the one thing I want before I die!"

"Then we'll have to make sure you triumph. Cheer up, Marcus, do. Sit down and drink a beaker of Minicius's best wine, then let's have some supper. Rowing twelve hours a day for twelve days gives a man a huge appetite, I've found."

"I could kill Cato!" said Crassus as he seated himself.

"As I keep saying to largely deaf ears, death is no fitting punishment, even for Cato. Death cheats one of the best victory, which is to spare one's enemies the sight of defeat. I love to pit myself against the Catos and Bibuluses. They'll never win."

"How can you be so sure?"

"Simple," said Caesar, surprised. "They don't want to win as badly as I do."

The rage was gone, but Crassus had not yet managed to put on his normal impassive mien when he said, a little uncomfortably, "I have something less important to tell you, but perhaps you'll not see it in that light."

"Oh?"

Whereupon Crassus actually quailed. "Later will do. Here we've been talking as if your friend over there doesn't exist."

"Ye gods! Balbus, forgive me!" cried Caesar. "Come here and meet a plutocrat more bloated by far than you. Lucius Cornelius Balbus Major, this is Marcus Licinius Crassus.''

And that, thought Caesar, is a handshake between equals if ever I saw one. I don't know what pleasure they get out of making money, but between them they could probably buy and sell the whole of the Iberian Peninsula. And how delighted they are finally to meet. Not so odd that they haven't met before. Crassus's days in Spain were finished while Balbus was still unknown there. And this is Balbus's first trip to Rome, where I very much hope he will take up residence.

The three men made a merry meal, for it seemed that once the imperturbable one was catapulted out of his imperturbability he found it difficult to regain that state of mind. Not until the dishes were removed and the lamps trimmed did Crassus refer again to his other news for Caesar.

''I have to tell you, Gaius, but you won't like it,'' he said.

''Like what?''

''Nepos made a short speech in the House about your petition.''

''Not in my favor.''

''Anything but.'' Crassus stopped.

''What did he say? Come, Marcus, it can't be that bad!''

''Worse.''

''Then you'd best tell me.''

''He said he wouldn't grant any kind of favor to a notorious homosexual like you. That was the polite bit. You know Nepos, very salty indeed. The rest was extremely graphic and concerned King Nicomedes of Bithynia.'' Crassus stopped again, but when Caesar said nothing he hurried on. ''Afranius ordered the scribes to strike the statement from the records, and forbade Nepos to attend any more meetings of the Senate if he's holding the *fasces*. He handled the situation quite well, really.''

Of course Caesar wasn't staring at either Crassus or Balbus, and the light was dim. He didn't move, there was no look on his face to cause alarm. Yet why did the temperature of the room seem suddenly so much colder?

The pause wasn't long enough to qualify as a silence before Caesar said, voice normal, "That was foolish of Nepos. He'd do the *boni* more good in the House than barred from it. He must be in on all the *boni* councils—and very thick with Bibulus. I've been waiting years for that canard to be remembered. Bibulus made much of it almost half a lifetime ago, then it seemed to die." His smile flashed, but there was no amusement in it. "My friends, I predict this is going to be a very dirty election."

"It didn't sit well with the House," said Crassus. "You could have heard a moth land on a toga. Nepos must have realized he'd harmed himself more than he'd managed to harm you, because when Afranius pronounced sentence he said something equally rude to Afranius—the old 'son of Aulus' jibe—and walked out."

"I'm disappointed in Nepos, I thought he had more finesse."

"Or perhaps he's cherishing a tendency that way himself," rumbled Crassus. "It was very funny at the time, but thinking about how he used to carry on during meetings of the Plebs when he was a tribune, he always made much of fluttering his eyelashes and blowing kisses at hulking lumps like Thermus."

"All of which," said Caesar, rising to his feet as Crassus did, "is beside the point. Nepos has eroded my *dignitas*. That means I'll have to erode Nepos."

When he returned to the parlor after ushering Crassus out, he found Balbus wiping away tears.

"Grief over something as trite as Nepos?" he asked.

"I know your pride, so I know how it hurts."

"Yes," said Caesar, sighing, "it does hurt, Balbus, though I'd not admit that to any Roman of my own class. One thing were it true, but it isn't. And in Rome an accusation of homosexuality is very damaging. *Dignitas* suffers."

"I think Rome is wrong," Balbus said gently.

"So do I, as a matter of fact. But it's irrelevant. What matters is the *mos maiorum,* our centuries of traditions and customs. For whatever reason—and I do not know the reason—homosexuality is not approved of. Never was approved of. Why do you think there was such resistance in Rome to things Greek two hundred years ago?''

''But it must be here in Rome too.''

''Wagonloads of it, Balbus, and not only among those who don't belong to the Senate. It was said of Scipio Africanus by Cato the Censor, and it was certainly true of Sulla. Never mind, never mind! If life were easy, how bored we'd be!''

Senior consul and electoral officer, Quintus Caecilius Metellus Celer had set up his booth in the lower Forum fairly close to the urban praetor's tribunal, and there presided to consider the many applications put to him by those desirous of standing for election as praetor or consul. His duties also embraced the other two sets of elections, held later in Quinctilis, which had provided the excuse for Cato to bring the closing date for curule men forward. That way, said Cato, the electoral officer could devote the proper care and consideration to his curule candidates before he needed to cope with the People and the Plebs.

The man putting himself up as a candidate for any magistracy donned the *toga candida,* a garment of blinding whiteness achieved by long days of bleaching in the sun and a final rubbing with chalk. In his train went all his clients and friends, the more important the better. Those of poor memory employed a *nomenclator,* whose duty it was to whisper the name of every man he met in the candidate's permanently cocked ear—more awkward these days, as *nomenclatores* had been officially outlawed.

The clever candidate mustered his last ounce of patience and prepared himself to listen to anyone and everyone who wanted to talk to him, no matter how long-winded or prolix. If he happened to find a mother and babe, he smiled at the mother and kissed the babe— no votes there, of course, but she might well persuade her husband to vote for him. He laughed loudly when it was called for, he wept copiously at tales of woe, he looked grave and serious when grave and serious subjects were broached; but he never looked bored or uninterested, and he made sure he didn't say the wrong thing to the wrong person. He shook so many hands that he had to soak his own right hand in cold water every evening. He persuaded his friends famous for their oratory to mount the rostra or Castor's platform and address the Forum frequenters about what a superb fellow he was, what a pillar of the establishment he was, how many generations of *imagines* crowded out his atrium—and what a dismal, reprehensible, dishonest, corrupt, unpatriotic, vile, sodomizing, faeces-eating, child-molesting, incestuous, bestial, depraved, fish-fancying, idle, gluttonous, alcoholic lot his opponents were. He promised everything to everybody, no matter how impossible it would prove to deliver those promises.

Many were the laws Rome had put on her tablets to constrain him: he wasn't supposed to hire that necessary *nomenclator,* he couldn't give gladiatorial shows, he was forbidden to entertain all save his most intimate friends and relatives, he couldn't hand out presents—and he certainly couldn't pay out bribe money. So what had happened was that some of the prohibited items (the *nomenclator,* for example) were winked at, and the ones like gladiatorial shows and banquets had gone by the board, the money they would have cost channeled instead into cash bribery.

The interesting thing about a Roman was that if he consented to be bought, he stayed bought. There was honor in it, and a man known to have reneged on a bribe was shunned. Hardly anyone below the level of a knight of the Eighteen was impervious to bribes, which provided a handy little sum of much-needed cash. The chief beneficiaries were men of the First Class below the level of the Eighteen senior Centuries, and to a lesser extent the men of the Second Class. The Third, Fourth and Fifth Classes were not worth the expenditure, as they were rarely called upon to vote in the centuriate elections. A man who carried every Century had no real need to bribe the Second Class, so heavily weighted were the Centuries in favor of First Class voters—who were also the richest, as the Centuries were classified on the basis of financial means.

Tribal elections were more difficult to influence by

bribes, but not impossible. No candidate for aedile or tribune of the plebs bothered bribing the members of the four
vast urban tribes; he concentrated instead on rural tribes
having few members inside Rome at polling time.

How much a man offered was up to him. It might be
a thousand sesterces to each of two thousand voters, or
fifty thousand to each of forty voters owning sufficient
clout to influence hordes of other men. Clients were
obliged to vote for their patrons, but a gift of cash helped
there too. A total outlay of two million sesterces was the
sum an extremely rich man might contemplate spending,
if that; some elections were equally famous for stingy brib-
ers, and spoken of scathingly by those who expected to be
bribed.

The bribes were mostly distributed before polling
day, though most candidates who had outlaid vast sums to
bribe made sure they had scrutineers as close to the baskets
as possible to check what a voter had inscribed on his little
tablet. And the danger lay in bribing the wrong person;
Cato was famous for rounding up a good number of men
to take bribes and then using them to testify in the Bribery
Court. This was not dishonorable, as the bribed man would
indeed vote the proper way, but then feel no pangs about
giving evidence at a prosecution because he had been recruited to do just that before he took the money. For which
reason most of the men prosecuted for electoral bribery
had succeeded in being elected, from Publius Sulla and
Autronius to Murena. Court time was not prone to be
wasted on failures.

Normally there were anything up to ten consular candidates, with six or seven the usual number, and at least
half of them from the Famous Families. The electorate
usually had a fairly rich and varied choice. But in the year
Caesar stood for consul Fortune favored Bibulus and the
boni. Most of the praetors in Caesar's year had been prorogued in their provinces, so were not in Rome to contest
an election so heavily weighted in one man's direction:
every political Roman knew Caesar couldn't lose. And that
fact reduced the chances of everyone else. Only one man
other than Caesar could become consul, and he would be

the junior consul at that. Caesar was certain to come in at
the top of the poll, which would make him senior consul.
Therefore many men aspiring to be consul decided not to
run in Caesar's year. A defeat was damaging.

In consequence, the *boni* decided to stake everything
on one man, Marcus Calpurnius Bibulus, and went round
persuading all the potential candidates of old or noble family not to run against Bibulus. He *had* to be the junior
consul! As junior consul, he would be in a position to
make Caesar's life as senior consul a very difficult and
frustrating one.

The result was that there were only four candidates,
only two of whom came from noble families—Caesar and
Bibulus. The two other candidates were both New Men,
and of those two, only one stood any chance at all—Lucius Lucceius, a famous court advocate and loyal adherent
of Pompey's. Naturally Lucceius would bribe, having
Pompey's wealth behind him as well as a considerable
fortune of his own. The amount of money tendered as
bribes gave Lucceius a chance, but it was an outside one
only. Bibulus was a Capurnius, he had the *boni* behind
him, and he too would undoubtedly bribe.

Caesar crossed the *pomerium* into Rome as dawn was
breaking.

Accompanied only by Balbus, he walked down the
Via Lata to the Hill of the Bankers, entered the city
through the Fontinalis Gate, and came down to the Forum
with the Lautumiae prison on his right hand and the Basilica Porcia to his left. He caught Metellus Celer neatly,
for the curule electoral officer was seated at his booth and
staring raptly at an eagle perched on Castor's roof, oblivious to any traffic from the direction of the prison.

"An interesting omen," Caesar said.

Celer gasped, choked, swept all his papers into a heap
and bounded to his feet. "You're too late, I'm closed!"
he cried.

"Come now, Celer, that unconstitutional you dare not
be. I am here to declare my candidacy for the consulship
by the Nones of June. Today you are open, the Senate has

decreed it. When I arrived before you, you were seated for business. You will therefore accept my candidacy. No impediment exists.''

Suddenly the lower Forum was crowded; all of Caesar's clients were there, and one man so important Celer knew he didn't dare close his booth. Marcus Crassus strode up to Caesar and ranged himself alongside the brilliantly white left shoulder.

''Is there any trouble, Caesar?'' he growled.

''None that I know of. Well, Quintus Celer?''

''You haven't tendered your province's accounts.''

''I have, Quintus Celer. They arrived at the Treasury yesterday morning, with instructions to review them immediately. Do you wish to stroll across to Saturn's with me now and find out if there are any discrepancies?''

''I accept your candidacy for the consulship,'' Celer said, and leaned forward. ''You fool!'' he snarled. ''You've abandoned your triumph, and for what? You'll have Bibulus to tie you hand and foot, so much I swear! You should have waited until next year.''

''By next year there wouldn't be a Rome if Bibulus were let ride rampant. No, that is not the correct phrase. If Bibulus were to do nothing and forbid everything. Yes, that's better.''

''He'll forbid everything with you as his senior!''

''A flea may try.''

Caesar turned away, threw an arm about Crassus's shoulder and walked into the midst of an ecstatic but weeping throng, as upset by the loss of Caesar's triumph as it was overjoyed at his appearance inside the city.

For a moment Celer watched this emotional reception, then gestured curtly to his attendants. ''This booth is closed,'' he said, and got to his feet. ''Lictors, the house of Marcus Calpurnius Bibulus—and be quick for once!''

It being the Nones and no meeting of the Senate scheduled, Bibulus was at home when Celer arrived.

''Guess who just declared himself a candidate?'' he said through his teeth as he burst into Bibulus's study.

The bony, bald-looking face confronting him went

even paler, something opinion said would be impossible.
"You're joking!"

"I am not joking," Celer said, throwing himself into
a chair with a disagreeable glance at the occupant of the
important chair, Metellus Scipio. Why did it have to be
that gloomy *mentula* here? "Caesar crossed the *pomerium*
and laid down his imperium."

"But he was to triumph!"

"I told you," said Metellus Scipio, "that he'd win.
And do you know why he wins all the time? Because he
doesn't stop to count the cost. He doesn't think like us.
None of us would have given up a triumph when the consulship is there every year."

"The man's mad" from a scowling Celer.

"Very mad or very sane, I'm never sure which,"
Bibulus said, and clapped his hands. When a servant ap-
peared he issued orders: "Send for Marcus Cato, Gaius
Piso and Lucius Ahenobarbus."

"A council of war?" asked Metellus Scipio, sighing
as if at the prospect of another lost cause.

"Yes, yes! Though I'm warning you, Scipio, not one
single word about Caesar's always winning! We don't
need a prophet of doom in our midst, and when it comes
to prophesying doom you're in Cassandra's league."

"Tiresias, thank you!" said Metellus Scipio stiffly.
"I am not a woman!"

"Well, *he* was for a while," giggled Celer. "Blind
too! Been seeing any copulating snakes lately, Scipio?"

By the time Caesar entered the Domus Publica it was
after noon. Everything possible had slowed his progress,
so many people had flocked to the Forum to detain him,
and he had Balbus to think of; Balbus had to be accorded
every distinguished attention, introduced to every prominent man Caesar encountered.

Then it took a little time to install Balbus in one of
the guest suites upstairs, and more time to greet his
mother, his daughter, the Vestals. But finally not long before dinner he was able to shut the door of his study on
the world and commune with himself.

The triumph was a thing of the past; he wasted no thought whatsoever upon it. More important by far was to decide what to do next—and to divine what the *boni* would do next. Celer's swift departure from the Forum had not escaped him, which meant no doubt that the *boni* were even now engaged upon a council of war.

A great pity about Celer and Nepos. They had been excellent allies. But why had they gone to the trouble of antagonizing him so mortally? Pompey was their avowed target, nor did they have any real evidence that Caesar once consul intended to be Pompey's puppet. Admittedly he had always spoken up for Pompey in the House, but they had never been intimate, nor were they related by blood. Pompey hadn't offered Caesar a legateship while he was conquering the East; no state of *amicitia* existed between them. Had the Brothers Metelli been obliged to take on all the enemies of the *boni* as the price of admission to the ranks? Highly unlikely, given the clout the Brothers Metelli owned. No need for them to woo the *boni*. The *boni* would have come crawling.

Most puzzling was that absolutely scurrilous attack of Nepos's in the House; it indicated colossal rancor, a very personal feud. Over what? Had they loathed him two years ago when they collaborated with him so splendidly? Definitely not. Caesar was no Pompey, he was not subject to the kind of insecurities which led Pompey to fret about whether people esteemed or despised him; his common sense informed him now that two years ago the feud had not existed. Then why had the Brothers Metelli turned on him to rend him? *Why?* Mucia Tertia? Yes, by all the Gods, Mucia Tertia! What had she said to her uterine brothers to justify her conduct during Pompey's absence? Yielding her noble body to the likes of Titus Labienus would not have endeared her to the two most influential Caecilii Metelli left alive, yet they had not only forgiven her, they had championed her against Pompey. Had she blamed Caesar, whom she had known since she married Young Marius twenty-six years before? Had she told them Caesar was her true seducer? The rumor had to have started somewhere. What better source than Mucia Tertia?

Very well then, the Brothers Metelli were now obdurate foes. Bibulus, Cato, Gaius Piso, Ahenobarbus and a multitude of lesser *boni* like Marcus Favonius and Munatius Rufus would do anything short of murder to bring him down. Which left Cicero. The world was amply provided with men who could never make up their minds, flirted with this group, flattered that group, and ended in having no allies, few friends. Such was Cicero. Whereabouts Cicero stood at the moment was anybody's guess; in all probability Cicero himself didn't know. One moment he adored his dearest Pompey, the next moment he hated everything Pompey was or stood for. What chance did that leave Caesar, who was friendly with Crassus? Yes, Caesar, abandon all hope of Cicero. . . .

The sensible thing was to form a political alliance with Lucius Lucceius. Caesar knew him well because they had done a great deal of court duty together, most of it with Caesar on the bench. A brilliant advocate, a splendid orator, and a clever man who deserved to ennoble himself and his family. Lucceius and Pompey could afford to bribe, no doubt would bribe. But would it answer? The more Caesar thought about that, the less confident he felt. If only the Great Man had supporters in the Senate and the Eighteen! The trouble was that he did not, particularly in the Senate, an amazing state of affairs that could be directly attributed to his old contempt for the Law and Rome's unwritten constitution. He had rubbed the Senate's nose in its own excrement in order to force it to allow him to run for consul without ever having been a senator. And they hadn't forgotten, any of the Conscript Fathers who had belonged to the Senate in those days. Days not so distant, really. A mere decade. Pompey's only loyal senatorial adherents were fellow Picentines like Petreius, Afranius, Gabinius, Lollius, Labienus, Lucceius, Herennius, and they just didn't matter. They couldn't summon a backbencher vote among them if the backbencher was not a Picentine. Money could buy some votes, but the logistics of distributing enough of it to enough voters would defeat Pompey and Lucceius if the *boni* also decided to bribe.

Therefore the *boni* would be bribing. Oh yes, definitely. And with Cato condoning the bribery, there was no chance of its being discovered unless Caesar himself adopted Cato's tactics. Which he wouldn't do. Not from principles, simply from lack of time and lack of knowledge of whom to approach to act as an informer. To Cato it was a perfected art; he'd been doing it for years. So gird your loins, Caesar, you are going to have Bibulus as your junior colleague, love it or loathe it. . . .

What else might they do? Manage to deny next year's consuls access to provinces afterward. They might well succeed. At the moment the two Gauls were the consular provinces, due to unrest in the further province among the Allobroges, the Aedui and the Sequani. The Gauls were usually worked in tandem, with Italian Gaul serving as a recruiting and supply base for Gaul-across-the-Alps, the one governor fighting, the other maintaining strengths. This year's consuls, Celer and Afranius, had been given the Gauls for next year, Celer to do the fighting across the Alps, Afranius backing him up from this side of the Alps. How easy it would be to prorogue them for a year or two. The pattern had been set already, as most of the present governors of provinces were in their second or even third year of tenure.

Provided the Allobroges had genuinely quietened down—and everyone seemed to think they had—then the strife in Further Gaul was intertribal rather than aimed in Rome's direction. Over a year earlier the Aedui had complained bitterly to the Senate that the Sequani and the Arverni were making inroads into Aedui territory; the Senate had not listened. Now it was the turn of the Sequani to complain. They had formed an alliance with a German tribe from across the Rhenus, the Suebi, and given King Ariovistus of the Suebi a third of their land. Unfortunately Ariovistus had not thought one third enough. He wanted two thirds. Then the Helvetii began to emerge out of the Alps looking for new homes in the Rhodanus Valley. None of which really interested Caesar, who was happy to let Celer have the responsibility for sorting out the shambles several powerful warring tribes of Gauls could create.

Caesar wanted Afranius's province, Italian Gaul. He knew where he was going: into Noricum, Moesia, Dacia, the lands around the river Danubius, all the way to the Euxine Sea. His conquests would link Italy to Pompey's conquests in Asia, and the fabulous riches of that enormous river would belong to Rome, give Rome a land route to Asia and the Caucasus. If old King Mithridates had thought he could do it moving from east to west, why not Caesar working from west to east?

The consular provinces were still allocated by the Senate according to a law brought in by Gaius Gracchus; it stipulated that the provinces to be given to the next year's consuls must be decided before the next year's consuls had been elected. In that way, the candidates for the next year's consulships knew which provinces they would be going to in advance.

Caesar deemed it an excellent law, designed as it was to prevent men's plotting to secure the province of their choice after they became consul and had consular powers. Under the present circumstances it was best to know as soon as possible which province would be his. If things didn't go the way he wanted them to go—if the consuls for next year were denied provinces, for example—then the law of Gaius Gracchus gave him at least seventeen months to maneuver, to think and plan how to end with the province he wanted. Italian Gaul, he *must* get Italian Gaul! Interesting that Afranius might prove to be a worse stumbling block than Metellus Celer. Would Pompey be willing to take a promised prize off Afranius in order to reward a helpful senior consul in Caesar?

During his time governing Further Spain, Caesar's thinking had changed a little. The actual experience of governing had been enlightening. So had the chance to be away from Rome herself. At that distance much fell into place that had eluded him until then, and other ideas underwent modification. His goals were unchanged: he would not only be the First Man in Rome, but the greatest of all Rome's First Men.

However, he could now see that these goals were impossible to attain in the old, simple way. Men like Scipio

Africanus and Gaius Marius had stepped with one stunning, giant stride from the consulship into a military command of such magnitude that it gave them the title, the clout, the enduring fame. Cato the Censor had broken Scipio Africanus after Scipio had become the undeniable First Man in Rome, and Gaius Marius had broken himself after his mind eroded thanks to those strokes. Neither man had been obliged to deal with an organized and massive opposition like the *boni*. The presence of the *boni* had radically altered the situation.

Caesar now understood that he couldn't get there alone, that he needed allies more powerful than the men of a faction created by himself for himself. His faction was coming along nicely, and it contained men like Balbus, Publius Vatinius (whose wealth and wit made him immensely valuable), the great Roman banker Gaius Oppius, Lucius Piso since Piso had saved him from the moneylenders, Aulus Gabinius, Gaius Octavius (the husband of his niece and an enormously wealthy man as well as a praetor).

He needed Marcus Licinius Crassus, for one. How extraordinary that his luck had thrown Crassus into his waiting arms; the tax-farming contracts constituted a development no one could have predicted. If as senior consul he solved matters for Crassus, he knew that ever after all the man's connections would be his.

But he also needed Pompey the Great. I need the man, I need Pompeius Magnus. But how am I going to bind him to me after I've secured his land and ratified his settlement of the East? He's neither a true Roman nor grateful by nature. Somehow, without subjecting myself to his rule, I *have* to keep him on my side!

At which point his mother invaded his privacy.

"Your timing is exactly right," he said, smiling at her and rising to assist her into a chair, a compliment he rarely paid her. "Mater, I know where I'm going."

"That doesn't surprise me, Caesar. To the stars."

"If not to the stars, certainly to the ends of the earth."

She frowned. "No doubt you've been told what Metellus Nepos said in the House?"

"Crassus, actually. Looking very upset."

"Well, it had to bubble to the surface again sooner or later. How will you deal with it?"

His turn to frown. "I'm not quite sure. Though I am very glad I wasn't there to hear him—I might have killed him, which wouldn't have been beneficial to my career at all. Ought I, for instance, to blow him lots of kisses and shift the suspicion from my shoulders to his? Crassus thinks him inclined that way."

"No," she said firmly. "Ignore it and him. There are more feminine corpses—well, metaphorically speaking!—strewn in your wake than there were behind Adonis. You have intrigued with no man, nor have your enemies been able to pluck a man's name out of the air for all their trying. They can do no better than poor old King Nicomedes. It remains the only allegation very nearly twenty-five years later. Time alone renders it thin, Caesar, if you consider it coolly. I realize that your temper is wearing down, but I beg you to hold it in whenever this subject arises. Ignore, ignore, ignore."

"Yes, you're right." He sighed. "Sulla used to say that no man ever had a harder road to the consulship nor a harder time of it when he finally was consul. But I fear I might eclipse him."

"That's good! He stood above all the rest, and he still does."

"Pompeius would hate to be hated the way men hate Sulla, but on thinking about it, Mater, I would rather be hated than sink into obscurity. One never knows what the future will bring. All one can do is be prepared for the worst."

"And act," said Aurelia.

"Always that. Is dinner ready? I'm still replacing whatever it was I used up rowing."

"I came to tell you dinner was ready, actually." She got up. "I like your Balbus. A terrific aristocrat, am I right?"

"Like me, he can trace his ancestry back a thousand

years. Punic. His real name is astonishing—Kinahu Hadasht Byblos.''

"Three names? Yes, he's a nobleman.''

They walked out into the corridor and turned toward the door of the dining room.

"No troubles among the Vestals?'' he asked.

"None at all.''

"And my little blackbird?''

"Blooming.''

At which moment Julia came from the direction of the stairs, and Caesar had the tranquillity of mind to see her properly. Oh, she had grown up so much in his absence! So beautiful! Or was that judgement a father's natural prejudice?

It really wasn't. Julia had inherited Caesar's bones, which he had inherited from Aurelia. She was still so fair that her skin shone transparent and her rich crop of hair had almost no color, a combination which endowed her with an exquisite fragility reflected in huge blue eyes set in faint violet shadows. As tall as the average man, her body was perhaps too slender and her breasts too small for masculine taste, but distance now showed her father that she did have her own allure, and would ravish many men. Would I have wanted her, had I not been her sire? I'm not sure about wanting, but I think I would have loved her. She is a true Julia, she will make her men happy.

"You'll be seventeen in January,'' he said, having put her chair opposite his own, and Aurelia's opposite Balbus, who occupied the *locus consularis* on their couch. "How's Brutus?''

She answered with complete composure, though her face, he noted, did not light up at mention of her betrothed's name. "He's well, *tata*.''

"Making a name for himself in the Forum?''

"More in publishing circles. His epitomes are prized.'' She smiled. "Actually I think he likes business best, so it's a shame his rank will be senatorial.''

"With Marcus Crassus as an example? The Senate won't restrict him if he's shrewd.''

"He's shrewd.'' Julia drew a deep breath. "He would

do much better in public life if only his mother left him alone.''

Caesar's smile held no trace of anger. "I agree with you wholeheartedly, daughter. I keep telling her not to make a rabbit of him, but, alas, Servilia is Servilia.''

The name caught Aurelia's attention. ''I knew there was something else I had to tell you, Caesar. Servilia wishes to see you.''

But it was Brutus he saw first; he arrived to visit Julia just as the four of them came out of the dining room.

Oh, dear! Time certainly hadn't improved poor Brutus. As hangdog as ever, he shook Caesar's hand limply and looked everywhere but into Caesar's eyes, a characteristic which had always irritated Caesar, who deemed it shifty. That awful acne actually seemed worse, though at twenty-three it should surely have been starting to clear up. If he hadn't been so dark the stubble spread untidily over his cheeks and chin and jawline might not have looked so villainous; no wonder he preferred to scribble rather than orate. Were it not for all that money and an impeccable family tree, who could ever have taken him seriously?

He was, however, obviously as deeply in love with Julia as he had been years ago. Kind, gentle, faithful, affectionate. His eyes as they rested on her were filled with warmth, and he held her hand as if it might break. No need to worry that her virtue had ever been subjected to siege! Brutus would wait until they were married. In fact, it occurred to Caesar now that Brutus *would* wait until they were married—that he had had no sort of sexual experience at all. In which case marriage might do much for him in all sorts of ways, including the skin and the spirit. Poor, poor Brutus. Fortune had not been kind to him when she gave him that harpy Servilia as mother. A reflection which led him to wonder how Julia would cope with Servilia as her mother-in-law. Would his daughter be another the harpy rended tooth and claw, cowed into perpetual obedience?

*   *   *

He met his harpy the next day toward evening in his rooms on the Vicus Patricii. Forty-five years old, though she didn't look it. The voluptuous figure hadn't spread, nor the wonderful breasts sagged; in fact, she looked magnificent.

Expecting a frenzy, instead she offered him a slow and erotic languorousness he found irresistible, a tangled web of the senses she wove in tortuous patterns which reduced him to a helpless ecstasy. When he had first known her, he had been able to sustain an erection for hours without succumbing to orgasm, but she had, he admitted, finally beaten him. The longer he knew her, the less able he was to resist her sexual spell. Which meant that his only defense was to conceal these facts from her. Never yield vital information to Servilia! She would chew on it until she sucked it dry.

"I hear that since you crossed the *pomerium* and declared your candidacy, the *boni* have declared an all-out war," she said as they lay together in the bath.

"You surely didn't expect anything else?"

"No, of course not. But the death of Catulus has released a brake. Bibulus and Cato are a terrible combination in that they have two assets they can now use without fear of criticism or disapproval—one is the ability to rationalize any atrocious action into virtue, and the other is a complete lack of foresight. Catulus was a vile man because he had a smallness of nature his father never had—that came of owning a Domitia for mother. His father's mother was a Popillia, much better stock. Yet Catulus did have some idea of what being a Roman nobleman is, and he could upon occasion see the outcome of certain *boni* tactics. So I warn you, Caesar, his death is a disaster for you."

"Magnus said something like that about Catulus too. I'm not asking for guidance, Servilia, but I am interested in your opinion. What would you have me do to counter the *boni*?"

"I think the time has come to admit that you can't win without some very strong allies, Caesar. Until now it's been a lone battle. From now it must be battle united with other forces. Your camp has been too small. Enlarge it."

"With what? Or perhaps that ought to be, with whom?"

"Marcus Crassus needs you to salvage his clout among the *publicani,* and Atticus is not fool enough to glue himself to Cicero blindly. He has a soft spot for Cicero, but a softer spot by far for his commercial activities. Money he doesn't need, but power he craves. Lucky perhaps that political power has never intrigued him, otherwise you'd have some competition. Gaius Oppius is the greatest of all Roman bankers. You already have Balbus, the greatest banker of them all, in your camp. Entice Oppius to your side as well. Brutus is definitely yours, thanks to Julia."

She lay with those gorgeous breasts floating gently on the surface of the water, her thick black hair pulled up in unplanned loops to keep it dry, and those big black eyes staring into the layers of her own mind, absolutely inward.

"And what about Pompeius Magnus?" he asked idly.

She stiffened; the eyes suddenly focused on him. "No, Caesar, no! Not the Picentine butcher! He doesn't understand how Rome works, he never did and he never will. There's a mine of natural ability there, a massive force for good or ill. But he isn't a Roman! Were he a Roman, he would never have done what he did to the Senate before he became consul. He has no subtle streak, no inner conviction of invincibility. Pompeius thinks rules and laws were meant to be broken for his personal benefit. Yet he hungers for approval and he is perpetually torn by conflicting desires. He wants to be the First Man in Rome for the rest of his life, but he really has no idea of the right way to do that."

"It's true that he didn't handle his divorce of Mucia Tertia very wisely."

"That," she said, "I put down to Mucia Tertia. One forgets who she is. Scaevola's daughter, Crassus Orator's loved niece. Only a Picentine oaf like Pompeius would have locked her up in a fortress two hundred miles from Rome for years on end. So when she cuckolded him, she did it with a peasant like Labienus. She would much rather have had you.''

"That I've always known.''

"So too her brothers. That's why they believed her.''

"Ah! I thought as much.''

"However, Scaurus suits her well enough.''

"So you think I should stay away from Pompeius.''

"A thousand times, yes! He can't play the game because he doesn't know the rules.''

"Sulla controlled him.''

"And he controlled Sulla. Never forget that, Caesar.''

"You're right, he did. Still and all, Sulla needed him.''

"More fool Sulla,'' said Servilia scornfully.

When Lucius Flavius took Pompey's land bill back to the Plebs any chance of its passing died. Celer was there in the Comitia to torment and harangue; so bitter was the confrontation with poor Flavius that he ended in invoking his right to conduct business unobstructed, and hied Celer off to the Lautumiae. From his cell Celer convoked a meeting of the Senate; then when Flavius barred its door with his own body, Celer ordered the wall pulled down and personally supervised its demolition. Nothing prevented his leaving the cell, the Lautumiae being what it was, but the senior consul preferred to show Lucius Flavius up by ostentatiously conducting his consular and senatorial business from that cell. Frustrated and very angry, Pompey had no choice other than to call his tribune of the plebs to order. With the result that Flavius authorized Celer's release, and went no more to meetings of the Plebeian Assembly. The land bill was impossible to promulgate.

In the meantime canvassing for the curule elections proceeded at a hectic pace, public interest stimulated enormously by the return of Caesar. Somehow when Caesar wasn't in Rome everything tended to be boring, whereas the presence of Caesar guaranteed that fur would fly. Young Curio was up on the rostra or Castor's platform every time one or the other became vacant, and seemed to have decided to replace Metellus Nepos as Caesar's most personal critic (Nepos had departed for Further Spain). The tale of King Nicomedes was retold with many witty embellishments—though, said Cicero to Pompey in complete exasperation, "It's young Curio I'd call effeminate. He was certainly Catilina's cub, if not something more to Catilina than that."

"I thought he belonged to Publius Clodius?" asked Pompey, who always found it difficult to keep track of the intricacies involved in political and social alliances.

Cicero could not suppress a shiver at mention of that name. "He belongs to himself first," he said.

"Are you doing your best to help Lucceius's candidacy?"

"Naturally!" Cicero said haughtily.

As indeed he was, though not without constant awkward chance encounters during escort duty in the Forum.

Thanks to Terentia, Publius Clodius had become a very bitter and dangerous enemy. Why was it that women made life so hard? If she had only left him alone, Cicero might have avoided testifying against Clodius when his trial for sacrilege finally came on a twelvemonth ago. For Clodius announced that at the time of the Bona Dea he had been in Interamna, and produced some respectable witnesses to confirm this. But Terentia knew better.

"He came around to see you on the day of the Bona Dea," she said sternly, "to tell you that he was going to western Sicily as quaestor, and wanted to do well. It was the day of Bona Dea, I know it was! You told me he'd come to ask for a few tips."

"My dear, you're mistaken!" Cicero had managed to gasp. "The provinces weren't even assigned until three months after that!"

"Rubbish, Cicero! You know as well as I do that the lots are fixed. Clodius *knew* where he was going! It's that trollop Clodia, isn't it? You won't testify because of *her*."

"I won't testify because I have an instinct that this is one sleeping beast I ought not to arouse, Terentia. Clodius has never cared overmuch for me since I helped to defend Fabia thirteen years ago! I disliked him then. I now find him detestable. But he's old enough to be in the Senate, and he's a patrician Claudius. His senior brother Appius is a great friend of mine and Nigidius Figulus's. *Amicitia* must be preserved."

"You're having an affair with his sister Clodia, and that's why you refuse to do your duty," said Terentia, looking mulish.

"I am not having an affair with Clodia! She's disgracing herself with that poet fellow, Catullus."

"Women," said Terentia with awful logic, "are not like men, husband. They don't have just so many arrows in their quivers to shoot. They can lie on their backs and accept an arsenal."

Cicero gave in and testified, thereby breaking Clodius's alibi. And though Fulvia's money bought the jury (which acquitted him by thirty-one to twenty-five votes), Clodius had neither forgiven nor forgotten. Added to which, when Clodius immediately afterward assumed his seat in the Senate and tried to be witty at Cicero's expense, Cicero's unruly tongue had covered him in glory and Clodius in ridicule—yet one more grudge Clodius harbored.

At the beginning of this year the tribune of the plebs Gaius Herennius—a Picentine, so was he acting on Pompey's orders?—had begun to make moves to have Clodius's status changed from patrician to plebeian through the medium of a special act in the Plebeian Assembly. Clodia's husband, Metellus Celer, had looked on in some amusement, and done nothing to countermand it. Now Clodius was heard everywhere saying that the moment Celer opened the booth for elections in the Plebs, he would be applying to stand as a tribune of the plebs. And that once he was in office he would see Cicero prosecuted for executing Roman citizens without a trial.

Cicero was terrified, and not ashamed to say so to Atticus, whom he begged to use his influence with Clodia and have her call her little brother off. Atticus had refused, saying simply that no one could control Publius Clodius when he was in the mood for one of his revenges. Cicero was his choice of the moment.

Despite all of which, those chance encounters happened. If a consular candidate was not allowed to give gladiatorial games in his own name and with his own money, there was nothing to stop someone else's giving a grand show in the Forum in honor of the candidate's *tata* or *avus,* provided that *tata* or *avus* was also an ancestor or relation of the games giver. Therefore none other than Metellus Celer the senior consul was giving gladiatorial games in honor of a mutual ancestor of his and Bibulus's.

Clodius and Cicero were both escorting Lucceius as he moved through the lower Forum canvassing mightily, and found themselves thrown together by movements among those immediately surrounding Caesar, canvassing nearby. And since there was nothing else for it than to put on a good face and behave nicely to each other, Cicero and Clodius proceeded to do so.

"I hear you gave gladiatorial games after you returned from Sicily," said Clodius to Cicero, his rather bewitching dark face transformed by a big smile, "is that right, Marcus Tullius?"

"Yes, as a matter of fact I did," Cicero said brightly.

"And did you reserve places on the special seating for your Sicilian clients?"

"Er—no," said Cicero, flushing; how to explain that they had been extremely modest games and the seating not adequate for his Roman clients?

"Well, I intend to seat my Sicilian clients. The only trouble is that my brother-in-law Celer isn't co-operating."

"Then why not apply to your sister Clodia? She must have plenty of seats at her disposal, surely. She's the consul's wife."

"*Clodia?*" Her brother reared up, his voice becoming loud enough to attract the attention of those in the vicinity who were not already listening to these two avowed enemies being terribly nice to each other. "*Clodia?* She wouldn't give me an inch!"

Cicero giggled. "Well, why should she give you an inch when I hear that you give her six of your inches regularly?"

Oh, he'd done it this time! Why was his tongue such a traitor? The whole lower Forum suddenly lay down on the ground in helpless paroxysms of laughter, Caesar leading, while Clodius stood turned to stone and Cicero succumbed to the deliciousness of his own wit even in the midst of a bowel-watering panic.

"You'll pay for that!" Clodius whispered, gathered what he could of dignity about him and stalked off with Fulvia on his arm, her face a study in rage.

"Yes!" she shrieked. "You'll pay for that, Cicero! I'll make a rattle out of your tongue one day!"

An unbearable humiliation for Clodius, who was to find that June was not his lucky month. When his brother-in-law Celer threw open his booth to plebeian candidates and Clodius lodged his name as a candidate for the tribunate of the plebs, Celer refused him.

"You're a patrician, Publius Clodius."

"I am not a patrician!" said Clodius, hands clenched into fists. "Gaius Herennius procured a special enactment in the Plebs removing my patrician status."

"Gaius Herennius wouldn't know the law if he fell over it," Celer said coolly. "How can the Plebs strip you of patrician status? It isn't the prerogative of the Plebs to say anything about the Patriciate. Now go away, Clodius, you're wasting my time. If you want to be a plebeian, do it the proper way—get yourself adopted by a plebeian."

Off went Clodius, fuming. Oh, that list was growing! Now Celer had earned a prominent place on it.

But revenge could wait. First he had to find a plebeian willing to adopt him, if that was the only way to do it.

He asked Mark Antony to be his father, but all Antony did was roar with laughter. "I don't need the million I'd have to charge you, Clodius, not now I'm married to Fadia and her *tata* has an Antonian grandchild on the way."

Curio looked offended. "Rubbish, Clodius! If you think I'm going to go around calling you my son, you've got another think coming! I'd look sillier than I'm making Caesar look."

"Why *are* you making Caesar look silly?" Clodius asked, curiosity aroused. "I'd much rather the Clodius Club supported him to the last member."

"I'm bored," Curio said curtly, "and I'd really like to see him lose his temper—they say it's awesome."

Nor was Decimus Brutus about to oblige. "My mother would kill me if my father didn't," he said. "Sorry, Clodius."

And even Poplicola baulked. "Have you calling me *tata*? No, Clodius, no!"

Which of course was why Clodius had preferred to pay Herennius some of Fulvia's limitless supply of money to procure that act. He hadn't fancied being adopted; it was too ridiculous.

Then Fulvia became inspired. "Stop looking among your peers for help," she said. "Memories in the Forum are long, and they all know it. They won't do something that might see them laughed at later on. So find a fool."

Well, there were any number of those available! Clodius sat down to think, and found the ideal face swimming in front of his gaze. Publius Fonteius! Dying to get into the Clodius Club but constantly rebuffed. Rich, yes; deserving, no. Nineteen years old, no *paterfamilias* to hamper him, and clever as a bit of wood.

"Oh, Publius Clodius, what an honor!" breathed Fonteius when approached. "Yes, please!"

"Of course you understand that I can't acknowledge you as my *paterfamilias,* which means that as soon as the adoption is over you'll have to release me from your authority. It's very important to me that I keep my own name, you see."

"Of course, of course! I'll do whatever you want."

Off went Clodius to see Caesar Pontifex Maximus.

"I've found someone willing to adopt me into the Plebs," he announced without preamble, "so I need the permission of the priests and augurs to procure a *lex Curiata*. Can you get it for me?"

The handsome face considerably above Clodius's own did not change its mildly enquiring expression, nor was there a shadow of doubt or disapproval in the pale, dark-ringed, piercing eyes. The humorous mouth didn't twitch. Yet for a long moment Caesar said nothing. Finally, "Yes, Publius Clodius, I can get it for you, but not in time for this year's elections, I'm afraid.''

Clodius went white. "Why not? It's simple enough!"

"Have you forgotten that your brother-in-law Celer is an augur? He did refuse your application to stand for the tribunate.''

"Oh."

"Be of good cheer, it will happen eventually. The matter can wait until he goes to his province.''

"But I wanted to be tribune of the plebs *this* year!"

"I appreciate that. However, it isn't possible." Caesar paused. "There is a fee, Clodius," he added gently.

"What?" Clodius asked warily.

"Persuade young Curio to stop prating about me.''

Clodius stuck his hand out immediately. "Done!" he said.

"Excellent!''

"Are you sure there's nothing else you want, Caesar?''

"Only gratitude, Clodius. I think you'll make a splendid tribune of the plebs because you're enough of a villain to be aware of the power in Law.'' And Caesar turned away with a smile.

Naturally Fulvia was waiting nearby.

"Not until Celer goes to his province," Clodius said to her.

She put her arms about his waist and kissed him lasciviously, scandalizing several bystanders. "He's right," she said. "I do like Caesar, Publius Clodius! He always reminds me of a wild beast pretending to be tamed. What a demagogue he'd make!''

Clodius experienced a twinge of jealousy. "Forget Caesar, woman!" he snarled. "Remember me, the man you're married to? *I* am the one who'll be the great demagogue!''

On the Kalends of Quinctilis, nine days before the curule elections, Metellus Celer called the Senate into session to debate the allocation of the consular provinces.

"Marcus Calpurnius Bibulus has a statement to

make,'' he said to a crowded House, ''so I will give him the floor.''

Surrounded by *boni,* Bibulus rose looking as majestic and noble as his diminutive size allowed. ''Thank you, senior consul. My esteemed colleagues of the Senate of Rome, I want to tell you a story concerning my good friend the knight Publius Servilius, who is not of the patrician branch of that great family, but shares the ancestry of the noble Publius Servilius Vatia Isauricus. Now Publius Servilius has the four-hundred-thousand-sesterces census, yet relies entirely for this income upon a rather small vineyard in the Ager Falernus. A vineyard, Conscript Fathers, which is so famous for the quality of the wine it produces that Publius Servilius lays it down for years before selling it for a fabulous price to buyers from all over the world. It is said that both King Tigranes and King Mithridates bought it, while King Phraates of the Parthians still does. Perhaps King Tigranes still does too, given that Gnaeus Pompeius mistakenly called Magnus took it upon his own authority to absolve that royal personage of his transgressions—in Rome's name!—and even let him keep the bulk of his income.''

Bibulus paused to gaze about. The senators were very quiet, and no one on the back tier was napping. Catullus was right—tell them a story and they'd all stay awake to listen like children to a nursery maid. Caesar sat as always very straight on his seat, face wearing a look of studious interest, a trick he did better than anyone else, telling those who saw him that secretly he was absolutely bored, but too well mannered to let it show.

''Very good, we have Publius Servilius the respected knight in possession of one small yet extremely valuable vineyard. Yesterday able to qualify for the four-hundred-thousand-sesterces census of a full knight. Today a poor man. But how can that possibly be? How can a man so suddenly lose his income? Was Publius Servilius in debt? No, not at all. Did he die? No, not at all. Was there a war in Campania nobody told us about? No, not at all. A fire, then? No, not at all. A slave uprising? No, not at all. Perhaps a neglectful vigneron? No, not at all.''

He had them now, except for Caesar. Bibulus lifted himself upon his toes and raised his voice.

"I can tell you how my friend Publius Servilius lost his sole income, my fellow senators! The answer lies in a large herd of cattle which were being driven from Lucania to—oh, what *is* that noisome place on the Adriatic coast at the top of the Via Flaminia? Licenum? Ficenum? Pic . . . Pic . . . It's coming, it's coming! Picenum! Yes, that's it, Picenum! The cattle were being driven from the vast estates Gnaeus Pompeius mistakenly called Magnus inherited from the Lucilii to the even vaster estates he inherited from his father, the Butcher, in Picenum. Now cattle are useless creatures, really, unless one is in the armaments business or makes shoes and book buckets for a living. No one *eats* them! No one drinks their milk or makes cheese from it, though I do believe the northern barbarians of Gaul and Germania make something called butter from it, which they smear with equal liberality upon their coarse dark bread and their squeaky wagon axles. Well, they don't know any better, and they live in lands too chill and inclement to nurture our beautiful olive. But we in this warm and fertile peninsula grow the olive as well as the vine, the two best gifts the Gods gave to men. Why should anyone need to keep cattle in Italy, let alone to drive them hundreds of miles from one pasture to another? Only an armaments king or a cobbler! Which one do you suppose Gnaeus Pompeius mistakenly called Magnus is? Does he make war or shoes? Then again, perhaps he makes war and military boots! He could be both armaments king *and* cobbler!"

How fascinating, thought Caesar, maintaining that look of studious interest. Is it me he's after, or is it Magnus? Or is he killing two birds with the same stone? How utterly miserable the Great Man appears! If he could do it without being noticed, he'd get up right now and leave. But somehow this doesn't sound like our Bibulus. I wonder who's writing his speeches these days?

"The enormous herd of cattle blundered on into Campania, tended by a few scallywag shepherds, if those who escort cattle can be termed shepherds," said Bibulus

in a storytelling manner. "As you all know, Conscript Fathers, every *municipium* in Italy has its special routes and
trails reserved for the movement of livestock from one
place to another. Even the forests have trails demarcated
for livestock—for moving pigs to the acorns in oak woods
during winter—for moving the sheep from high to low
grazing as the seasons change—and most of all for driving
beasts to the greatest market in Italy, the yards of the Vallis Camenarum outside the Servian Walls of Rome. These
routes and trails and tracks are public land, and livestock
using them are not allowed to stray onto privately owned
lands to destroy privately owned grass, or crops, or . . .
vines."

The pause was very long. "Unfortunately," said Bibulus with a doleful sigh, "the scallywag shepherds who
tended the herd of cattle didn't quite know whereabouts
the proper trail was—though, I add, it is always a good
mile wide! The cattle found succulent vines to eat. Yes,
my dear friends, those vile and useless beasts belonging
to Gnaeus Pompeius mistakenly called Magnus invaded
the precious vineyard belonging to Publius Servilius. What
they did not eat, they trampled into the ground. And, in
case you are not aware of the habits and characteristics of
cattle, I will now tell you one more fact about them: their
saliva kills foliage, or else, if the plants are young, prevents regrowth for as long as two years. But the vines of
Publius Servilius were very, very old. So they died. And
my friend the knight Publius Servilius is a broken man. I
even find it in me to weep for King Phraates of the Parthians, who will never again drink that noble wine."

Oh, Bibulus, can you possibly be going where I think
you are going? asked Caesar silently, his face and posture
unchanged.

"Naturally Publius Servilius complained to the men
who manage the vast holdings and possessions of Gnaeus
Pompeius mistakenly called Magnus," Bibulus went on
with a sob, "only to be told that there was no possibility
of compensation being paid for the loss of the world's
finest vineyard. Because—because, Conscript Fathers, the
route along which those cattle were being driven had last

been surveyed so long before that the boundary markers had vanished! The scallywag shepherds hadn't erred, because they had no idea where they were supposed to be! Surely not in a vineyard, I hear you say. Quite so. But how easily can any of this be proven in a court of law or before the urban praetor's tribunal? Does anyone in each *municipium* even know where the maps are showing the routes and tracks and trails reserved for traveling livestock? And what of the fact that about thirty years ago Rome absorbed the whole of peninsular Italy into her own domains, giving in exchange the full citizenship? Does that make it Rome's duty to delineate the stock routes and trails and tracks from one end of Italy to the other? *I* think it does!''

Cato was leaning forward like a hound on a leash, Gaius Piso had succumbed to silent laughter, Ahenobarbus was snarling; the *boni* were obviously preparing for a victory.

''Senior consul, members of this House, I am a peaceful man who has acquitted himself faithfully of his military duty. I have no desire in my prime to march off to a province and make war on hapless barbarians to enrich my own coffers far more than Rome's. But I am a patriot. If the Senate and People of Rome say I must take up provincial duty after my consulship is over—for I *will* be consul!—then I will obey. But let it be a truly useful duty! Let it be a quiet and self-effacing duty! Let it be memorable not for the number of floats which roll along in a triumphal parade, but for a desperately needed job finally well done! I ask that this House apportion to next year's consuls exactly one year of proconsular duty afterward, surveying and properly demarcating the public routes, trails and paths for Italy's traveling livestock. I cannot restore Publius Servilius's murdered vines to him, nor hope to heal his rage. But if I can persuade all of you to see that there can be more to proconsular duty than making war in foreign parts, then in some small way I will have made a kind of reparation to my friend the knight Publius Servilius.''

Bibulus stopped, but did not sit down, apparently

thinking of something to add. "I have never asked this body for much during my years as a senator. Grant me this one boon and I will never ask for anything more. You have the word of a Calpurnius Bibulus."

The applause was enthusiastic and widespread; Caesar too applauded heartily, but not for Bibulus's proposal. It had been beautifully done. Far more effective than declining a province in advance. Take on a dolorous, thankless task voluntarily and make anyone who objects look small.

Pompey continued to sit unhappily while many men gazed on him and wondered that so wealthy and powerful a man could have treated poor Publius Servilius the knight so atrociously; it was Lucius Lucceius who answered Bibulus very strongly and loudly, protesting at anything so ridiculous as a task better suited to professional surveyors contracted out by the censors. Others spoke, but always in praise of Bibulus's proposal.

"Gaius Julius Caesar, you're a highly favored candidate for these elections," said Celer sweetly. "Do you have anything to add before I call for a division?"

"Not a thing, Quintus Caecilius," said Caesar, smiling.

Which rather took the wind out of the *boni* sails. But the motion to assign Italy's woodland and pasture trails and paths to next year's consuls passed overwhelmingly. Even Caesar voted for it, apparently perfectly content. What was he up to? Why hadn't he come roaring out of his cage?

"Magnus, don't look so down in the mouth," said Caesar to Pompey, who had remained in the House after the mass exodus.

"No one ever told me about this Publius Servilius!" he cried. "Just wait until I get my hands on my stewards!"

"Magnus, Magnus, don't be ridiculous! There is no Publius Servilius! Bibulus made him up."

Pompey stopped short, eyes as round as his face. *"Made him up?"* he squeaked. "Oh, that settles it! I'll kill the *cunnus*!"

"You'll do no such thing," said Caesar. "Stroll

home with me and drink a cup of better wine than Publius Servilius ever made. Remind me to send a pamphlet to King Phraates of the Parthians, would you? I think he'll love the wine I make. It might be a less wearing way to make money than governing Rome's provinces—or surveying her traveling stock routes."

This lighthearted attitude did much to mend Pompey's spirits; he laughed, cuffed Caesar on the arm and strolled as bidden.

"Time we had a talk," said Caesar, dispensing refreshments.

"I confess I've wondered when we were going to get together."

"The Domus Publica is a sumptuous residence, Magnus, but it does have some disadvantages. Everyone sees it—and who goes in and out. The same thing happens at your place, you're so famous there are always tourists and spies lurking." A sly smile lit Caesar's eyes. "So famous are you, in fact, that when I was going to see Marcus Crassus the other day, I noticed whole stalls in the markets selling little busts of you. Are you getting a good royalty? These miniature Pompeiuses were being snapped up faster than the vendors could put them out."

"Really?" asked Pompey, eyes sparkling. "Well, well! I'll have to look. Fancy that! Little busts of *me*?"

"Little busts of you."

"Who was buying them?"

"Young girls, mostly," Caesar said gravely. "Oh, there were quite a few older customers of both sexes, but in the main they were young girls."

"An old fellow like me?"

"Magnus, you're a hero. The mere mention of your name makes every feminine heart beat faster. Besides," he added, grinning, "they're not great works of art. Someone's made a mold and pops out plaster Pompeii as rapidly as a bitch pops pups. He's got a team of painters who slap some color on your skin and drench your hair with gaudy yellow, then put in two big blue eyes—you are not quite as you actually look."

Give Pompey his due, he could also laugh at himself

once he understood that he was being teased without malice. So he leaned back in his chair and laughed until he cried because he knew he could afford to. Caesar didn't lie. Therefore those busts were selling. He was a hero, and half of Rome's adolescent female population was in love with him.

"You see what you miss by not visiting Marcus Crassus?"

That sobered Pompey. He eased upright, looked grim. "I can't stand the man!"

"Who says you have to like each other?"

"Who says I have to ally myself with him?"

"I do, Magnus."

"Ah!" Down went the beautiful goblet Caesar had given him, up came two very shrewd blue eyes to stare into Caesar's paler and less comforting orbs. "Can't you and I do it alone?"

"Possibly, but not probably. This city, country, place, idea—call it what you will—is foundering because it's run by a timocracy dedicated to depressing the aims and ambitions of any man who wants to stand higher than the rest. In some ways that's admirable, but in other ways it's fatal. As it will be to Rome unless something is done. There ought to be room for outstanding men to do what they do best, as well as for many other men who are less gifted but nonetheless have something to offer in terms of public duty. Mediocrities can't govern, that's the problem. If they could govern, they'd see that putting all their strength into the kind of ludicrous exercise Celer and Bibulus ran in the Senate today accomplishes nothing. Here am I, Magnus, a very gifted and capable man, deprived of the chance to make Rome more than she already is. I am to become a surveyor tramping up and down the peninsula watching teams of men use their *gromae* to mark out the routes where traveling stock can legally eat with one end and shit with the other. And why am I to become a minor official doing a much-needed job which could be done, as Lucceius said, more efficiently by men contracted at the censors' booth? Because, Magnus, like you I dream of greater things and know I have the ability to carry them through.''

''Jealousy. Envy.''

''Is it? Perhaps some is jealousy, but it's more complicated than that. People don't like being outclassed, and that includes people whose birth and status should render them immune. Who and what are Bibulus and Cato? The one is an aristocrat whom Fortune made too small in every way, and the other is a rigid, intolerant hypocrite who prosecutes men for electoral bribery but approves of electoral bribery when it meets his own needs. Ahenobarbus is a wild boar, and Gaius Piso a totally corrupt bumbler. Celer is infinitely more gifted, yet falls down in that same area—he would rather channel his energies into trying to bring you crashing than forget personal differences and think of Rome.''

''Are you trying to say that they genuinely can't see their inadequacies? That they really believe themselves as capable as us? That conceited they couldn't be!''

''Why not? Magnus, a man has only one instrument whereby to measure intelligence—his own mind. So he measures everyone by the greatest intellect he knows of. His own. When you sweep Our Sea clear of pirates in the space of one short summer, all you're actually doing is showing him that it can be done. Ergo, he too could have done it. But you didn't let him. You denied him the opportunity. You forced him to stand by and watch you do it by enacting a special law. The fact that all he's been doing for years is talk is beside the point. You showed him it can be done. If he admits he couldn't do it the way you did, then he's telling himself he's worthless, and that he won't do. It isn't pure conceit. It's a built-in blindness coupled to misgivings he dare not acknowledge. I call him the revenge of the Gods on men who are genuinely superior.''

But Pompey was growing restless. Though he was quite capable of assimilating abstract concepts, he just didn't find the exercise a useful one.

''All well and good, Caesar, but it doesn't get us

anywhere to speculate. Why do we have to bring Crassus in?''

A logical and practical question. A pity then that in asking it Pompey rejected an offer of what might have become a deep and enduring friendship. What Caesar had been doing was reaching out to him, one superior sort of man to another. A pity then that Pompey was not the right superior man. His talents and interests lay elsewhere. Caesar's impulse died.

''We have to bring Crassus in because neither you nor I has anything like his clout among the Eighteen,'' Caesar said patiently, ''nor do we know one-thousandth the number of lesser knights Crassus does. Yes, both of us know many knights, senior and junior, so don't bother to say it. But we're not in Crassus's league! He's a force to be reckoned with, Magnus. I know you're probably far richer than he is, but you didn't make your money the way he does to this day. He's an entirely commercial creature, he can't help it. Everyone owes Crassus a favor. That is why we need him! At heart all Romans are businessmen. If they're not, why did Rome rise to dominate the world?''

''Because of her soldiers and her generals,'' Pompey said instantly—and defensively.

''Yes, that too. Which is where you and I come in. However, war is a temporary condition. Wars can also be more pointless and more costly to a country than any number of bad business ventures. Think of how much richer Rome would be today if she hadn't had to fight a series of civil wars for the last thirty years. It took your conquest of the East to put Rome back on her financial feet. But the conquering is done. From now on it's business as usual. Your contribution to Rome in relation to the East is finished. Whereas Crassus's is only just beginning. That's where his power comes from. What conquests win, commerce keeps. You win empires for Crassus to preserve and Romanize.''

''All right, you've convinced me,'' said Pompey, picking up his goblet. ''Let's say the three of us unite, form a triumvirate. What exactly will that do?''

''It endows us with the clout to defeat the *boni* because it gives us the numbers we need to enact laws in the Assemblies. We won't get approval from the Senate, basically a body designed to be dominated by ultraconservatives. The Assemblies are the tools of change. What you have to understand is that the *boni* have learned since Gabinius and Manilius legislated your special commands, Magnus. Look at Manilius. We'll never get him home, so he stands as an example to would-be tribunes of the plebs of what can happen when a tribune of the plebs defies the *boni* too much. Celer broke Lucius Flavius, which is why your land bill went down—not to defeat in a vote, it never even got that far. It died because Celer broke you and Flavius. You tried the old way. But these days the *boni* can't be bluffed. From now on, Magnus, brute strength is all-important. Three of us have to be better than two of us, simply because three are stronger than two. We can all do things for each other if we're united, and with me as senior consul we have the most powerful legislator the Republic owns. Don't underestimate consular power just because consuls don't usually legislate. I intend to be a legislating consul, and I have a very good man for my tribune of the plebs—Publius Vatinius.''

Eyes fixed on Pompey's face, Caesar paused to assess the effect of his argument. Yes, it was sinking in. Pompey was no fool, for all his need to be loved.

''Consider how long you and Crassus have been struggling to no avail. Has Crassus managed after almost a year of trying to get the Asian tax-farming contracts amended? No. Have you after a year and a half got your settlement of the East ratified or land for your veterans? No. Each of you has tried with all your individual power and strength to move the *boni* mountain, and each of you has failed. United, you might have succeeded. But Pompeius Magnus, Marcus Crassus and Gaius Caesar united can move the world.''

''I admit you're right,'' Pompey said gruffly. ''It has always amazed me how clearly you see, Caesar, even back in the days when I thought Philippus would be the one to get me what I wanted. He didn't. You did. Are you a politician, a mathematician, or a magician?''

"My best quality is common sense," laughed Caesar. "Then we approach Crassus."

"No, *I* approach Crassus," Caesar said gently. "After the drubbing both of us took in the House today, it won't come as any surprise that we're drowning our sorrows together at this moment. We're not known as natural allies, so let's keep it that way. Marcus Crassus and I have been friends for years, it will look logical that I form an alliance with him. Nor will the *boni* be terribly alarmed at that prospect. It's three of us can win. From now until the end of the year your participation in our triumvirate—I like that word!—is a secret known only among the three of us. Let the *boni* think they've won."

"I hope I can keep my temper when I have to mix with Crassus all the time," sighed Pompey.

"But you don't actually have to mix with him at all, Magnus. That's the beauty of three. I'm there to go between, I'm the link which obviates the need for you and Crassus to see each other much. You're not colleagues in the consulship, you're *privati*."

"All right, we know what I want. We know what Crassus wants. But what do you want out of this triumvirate, Caesar?"

"I want Italian Gaul and Illyricum."

"Afranius knows today that he's prorogued."

"He won't be prorogued, Magnus. That has to be understood."

"He's my client."

"Playing second lead to Celer."

Pompey frowned. "Italian Gaul and Illyricum for one year?"

"Oh, no. For five years."

The vivid blue eyes suddenly looked away; the basking lion felt the sun go behind a cloud. "What are you after?"

"A great command, Magnus. Do you grudge it to me?"

What Pompey knew of Caesar went under lightning assessment: some story about winning a battle near Tralles years ago—a Civic Crown for bravery—a good but peace-

ful quaestorship—a brilliant campaign in northwestern
Iberia just finished, but nothing really out of the common
way. Where was he going? Into the Danubius Basin, presumably. Dacia? Moesia? The lands of the Roxolani? Yes,
that would be a great campaign, but not like the conquest
of the East. Gnaeus Pompeius Magnus had done battle
with formidable *kings,* not barbarians in war paint and
tattoos. Gnaeus Pompeius Magnus had been on the march
at the head of armies since the age of twenty-two. Where
was the danger? There couldn't be any.

The chill rolled off the lion's fur; Pompey smiled
broadly. "No, Caesar, I don't grudge it to you at all. I
wish you luck."

Past the stalls displaying those crude busts of Pompey
the Great went Gaius Julius Caesar, into the Macellum
Cuppedenis, up the five flights of narrow stairs to see Marcus Crassus, who had not been in the Senate this day,
rarely bothered to attend. His pride was injured, his dilemma unsolved. Financial ruin was never a consideration,
but here he was with all that clout and utterly unable to
deliver what was actually a trifle. His position as the
brightest and biggest star in Rome's business firmament
was in jeopardy, his reputation in ruins. Every day important knights came asking him why he hadn't managed
to have the tax-farming contracts amended, and every day
he had to try to explain that a small group of men were
leading the Senate of Rome like a bull with a ring through
its nose. Ye gods, *he* was supposed to be the bull! And
more than *dignitas* was dwindling; many of the knights
now suspected he was up to something, that he was deliberately stalling renegotiation of those wretched contracts.
And his hair was falling out like a cat's in spring!

"Don't come near me!" he growled to Caesar.

"Whyever not?" asked Caesar, grinning as he sat
down on the corner of the Crassus desk.

"I have the mange."

"You're depressed. Well, cheer up, I have good
news."

"Too many people here, but I'm too tired to move."

He opened his mouth and bellowed at the crowded room: "Go home, the lot of you! Go on, go home! I won't even dock your pay, so go, go!"

They went, fleeing delightedly; Crassus insisted everyone put in every moment of the daylight hours, and they were lengthening into summer, still a long way off. Of course every eighth day was a holiday, so were the Saturnalia, the Compitalia and the major games, but not with pay. You didn't work, Crassus didn't pay you.

"You and I," said Caesar, "are going into partnership."

"It won't answer," said Crassus, shaking his head.

"It will if we're a triumvirate."

The big shoulders tensed, though the face remained impassive. "Not with Magnus!"

"Yes, with Magnus."

"I won't, and that's that."

"Then say goodbye to the work of years, Marcus. Unless you and I form an alliance with Pompeius Magnus, your reputation as patron of the First Class is utterly destroyed."

"Rubbish! Once you're consul you'll succeed in having the Asian contracts reduced."

"Today, my friend, I received my province. Bibulus and I are to survey and demarcate the traveling livestock routes of Italy."

Crassus gaped. "That's worse than not getting a province! It's laughingstock material! A Julian—and a Calpurnian for that matter!—forced to do the work of minor officials?"

"I note you said Calpurnian. So you think it will be Bibulus too. But yes, he's even willing to diminish his *dignitas* just to foil me. It was his idea, Marcus, and doesn't that tell you how serious the situation is? The *boni* will lie down to be slaughtered if that means I'm slaughtered too. Not to mention you and Magnus. We're taller than the field of poppies, it's Tarquinius Superbus all over again."

"Then you're right. We form an alliance with Magnus."

And it was as simple as that. No need to delve into the realm of philosophy when dealing with Crassus. Just shove facts under his nose and he'd come round. He even began to look happy about the projected triumvirate when he realized that, as both he and Pompey were *privati,* he wouldn't have to make any public appearances hand in hand with the man he detested most in all of Rome. With Caesar acting as go-between, the decencies would be preserved and the three-way partnership would work.

''I'd better start canvassing for Lucceius,'' said Crassus as Caesar removed himself from his perch.

''Don't spend too much, Marcus, that horse won't gallop. Magnus has been bribing heavily for two months, but after Afranius no one will look at his men. Magnus isn't a politician, he never makes the right moves at the right time. Labienus ought to have been where he put Flavius, and Lucceius ought to have been his first attempt to secure a tame consul.'' A cheerful pat for Crassus's naked pate, and Caesar was off. ''It will be Bibulus and I for sure.''

A prediction the Centuries confirmed five days before the Ides of Quinctilis: Caesar swept into the senior consulship by carrying literally every Century; Bibulus had to wait much longer, as the contest for the junior post was a close one. The praetors were disappointing for the triumvirs, though they could be sure of the support of Saturninus's nephew after the trial of Gaius Rabirius, and none other than Quintus Fufius Calenus was making overtures, as his debts were beginning to embarrass him badly. The new College of Tribunes of the Plebs was a difficulty, for Metellus Scipio had decided to stand, which gave the *boni* no less than four staunch allies—Metellus Scipio, Quintus Ancharius, Gnaeus Domitius Calvinus and Gaius Fannius. On the brighter side, the triumvirs definitely had Publius Vatinius and Gaius Alfius Flavus. Two good strong tribunes of the plebs would be enough.

There then occurred the long and exasperating wait for the New Year, not helped by the fact that Pompey had to lie low while Cato and Bibulus strutted, promising everyone who was prepared to listen that Caesar would get nothing done. Their opposition had become public knowledge through every Class of citizen, though few below the First Class understood exactly what was happening. Distant political thunder rumbled, was all.

Unruffled, it seemed, Caesar attended the House on all meeting days as senior consul–elect to give his opinion about very little; otherwise his time was devoted almost exclusively to drafting a new land bill for Pompey's veterans. In November he could see no reason why it should be a secret any longer—let the rump wonder what he and Pompey were to each other, it was time to apply a small amount of pressure. So in December he sent Balbus to see Cicero, his purpose to enlist Cicero's support for the land bill. If apprising Cicero what was in the wind didn't send the news far and wide, nothing would.

Uncle Mamercus died, a personal sorrow for Caesar and the cause of a vacancy in the College of Pontifices.

"Which," said Caesar to Crassus after the funeral, "can be of some use to us. I hear Lentulus Spinther desperately wants to be a pontifex."

"And might become one if he's prepared to be a good boy?"

"Precisely. He's got clout, he'll be consul sooner or later, and Nearer Spain lacks a governor. I hear he's smarting that he didn't get a province after his praetorship, so we might be able to help him into Nearer Spain on New Year's Day. Especially if he's a pontifex by then."

"How will you do it, Caesar? There's a big list of hopefuls."

"Rig the lots, of course. I'm surprised you asked. This is where being a triumvirate comes in very handy. Cornelia, Fabia, Velina, Clustumina, Teretina—five tribes already without moving out of our own ranks. Of course Spinther will have to wait until after the land bill is passed before he can go to his province, but I don't think he'll object to that. The poor fellow is still playing second leads, the *boni* sniff with contempt because they're riding for a fall. It doesn't pay to overlook important men you might need. But they've overlooked Spinther, more fool they."

"I saw Celer in the Forum yesterday," said Crassus, huffing contentedly, "and I thought he looked shockingly ill."

That provoked a laugh from Caesar. "It's not physical, Marcus. His little Nola of a wife has opened every gate she owns as wide as she can for Catullus, the poet fellow from Verona. He, by the way, seems to be flirting with the *boni*. I have it on good evidence that he invented the story of Publius Servilius's vineyard for Bibulus. That makes sense, Bibulus being permanently fused to the cobbles of the city of Rome. It takes a rustic to know all about cattle and vines."

"So Clodia's in love at last."

"Badly enough to worry Celer!"

"He'd do best to terminate Pomptinus and go to his province early. For a Military Man, Pomptinus hasn't acquitted himself very well in Further Gaul."

"Unfortunately Celer loves his wife, Marcus, so he doesn't want to go to his province at all."

"They deserve each other" was Crassus's verdict.

If anyone thought it significant that Caesar chose to ask Pompey to act as his augur during the night watch at the *auguraculum* on the Capitol before New Year's Day dawned, no one was publicly heard to comment. From the middle dark hour until the first light pearled the eastern sky, Caesar and Pompey in their scarlet-and-purple-striped togas stood together but back to back, eyes fixed upon the heavens. Caesar's luck that the New Year was four months in front of the seasonal year, for it meant that the shooting stars in the constellation Perseus were still tracing their dribbling sparkles down the black vault; of omens and auspices there were many, including a flash of lightning in a cloud off to the left. By rights Bibulus and his augural helper ought to have been present too, but even in that Bibulus took care to demonstrate that he would not co-operate with Caesar. Instead he took the auspices at his home—quite correct, yet not usual.

After which the senior consul and his friend repaired to their respective houses, there to don the day's garments. For Pompey, triumphal regalia, this now being permitted him on all festive occasions rather than merely at the games; for Caesar, a newly woven and very white *toga praetexta,* its border not Tyrian purple but the same ordinary purple it had been in the early days of the Republic, when the Julii had been as prominent as they now were again five hundred years later. For Pompey it had to be a gold senatorial ring, but for Caesar the ring was iron, as it had been for the Julii in the old days. He wore his crown of oak leaves, and the scarlet-and-purple-striped tunic of the Pontifex Maximus.

No pleasure in walking up the Clivus Capitolinus side by side with Bibulus, who never stopped muttering under his breath that Caesar would get nothing done, that if he died for it he would see Caesar's consulship a milestone for inactivity and mundanity. No pleasure either in having to seat himself on his ivory chair with Bibulus alongside while the crowd of senators and knights, family and friends hailed them and praised them. Caesar's luck that his flawless white bull went consenting to the sacrifice, while Bibulus's bull fell clumsily, tried to get to its feet and splattered the junior consul's toga with blood. A bad omen.

In the temple of Jupiter Optimus Maximus afterward it was Caesar as senior consul who called the Senate into session, Caesar as senior consul who fixed the *feriae Latinae,* and Caesar as senior consul who cast the lots for the praetors' provinces. No surprise perhaps that Lentulus Spinther received Nearer Spain.

"There are some other changes," the senior consul said in his normal deep voice, as the *cella* where the statue of Jupiter Optimus Maximus stood (facing to the east) was acoustically good enough for any kind of voice to carry. "This year I will return to the custom practised at the beginning of the Republic, and order my lictors to follow me rather than precede me during the months when I do not possess the *fasces*."

A murmur of approval went up, transformed into a gasp of shocked disapproval when Bibulus said, snarling, "Do what you want, Caesar, I don't care! Just don't expect me to reciprocate!"

"I don't, Marcus Calpurnius!" laughed Caesar, thus throwing the discourtesy of Bibulus's use of his cognomen into prominence.

"Anything else?" Bibulus asked, hating his lack of height.

"Not directly concerning you, Marcus Calpurnius. I have had a very long career in this House, both Senate and service to Jupiter Optimus Maximus, in whose house this House is meeting at this very moment. As *flamen Dialis* I joined it in my sixteenth year, then after a gap of less than two years I returned to it because I won the *corona civica*. Do you remember those months before Mitylene, Marcus Calpurnius? You were there too, though you didn't win a *corona civica*. Now at forty years of age I am senior consul. Which gives me a total of over twenty-three years as a member of the Senate of Rome."

His tones became brisk and businesslike. "Throughout those twenty-three years, Conscript Fathers, I have seen some changes for the better in senatorial procedure, particularly the habit we now have of a permanent verbatim record of our proceedings. Not all of us make use of these records, but certainly I do, and so do other serious politicians. However, they disappear into the archives. I have also known occasions upon which they bore little resemblance to what was actually said."

He stopped to look into the serried rows of faces; no one bothered with special wooden tiers for Jupiter Optimus Maximus on New Year's Day because the meeting was always a short one, comments confined to the senior consul.

"Consider too the People. Most of our meetings are held with doors wide open, enabling a small number of interested persons gathered outside to listen to us. What happens is inevitable. He who hears best relays what he has heard to those who can't hear, and as the ripple spreads outward on the Forum pond its accuracy declines. Annoying for the People, but also annoying for us.

"I now ask you to make two amendments to our records of the proceedings of this House. The first covers both kinds of session, open doors or closed doors. Namely that the scribes transpose their notes to paper, that both consuls and all praetors—if present at the meeting concerned, of course—peruse the written record, then sign it as correct. The second covers only those sessions held with open doors. Namely that the record of the proceedings be posted at a special bulletin area in the Forum Romanum, sheltered from inclement weather. My reasons are founded in concern for all of us, no matter which side of the political or factional fence we might happen to graze. It is as necessary for Marcus Calpurnius as it is for Gaius Julius. It is as necessary for Marcus Porcius as it is for Gnaeus Pompeius."

"In fact," said none other than Metellus Celer, "it is a very good idea, senior consul. I doubt I'll back your laws, but I will back this, and I suggest the House look favorably upon the senior consul's proposal."

With the result that everyone present save Bibulus and Cato passed to the right when the division came. A little thing, yes, but the first thing, and it had succeeded.

"So did the banquet afterward," said Caesar to his mother at the end of a very long day.

She was bursting with pride in him, naturally. All those years had been worth it. Here he was, seven months away from his forty-first birthday, and senior consul of the Senate and People of Rome. The Res Publica. The specter of debt had vanished when he came home from Further Spain with enough in his share to allow a settlement with his creditors which absolved him from future ruin. That dear little man Balbus had trotted from one office to another armed with buckets of papers and negotiated Caesar out of debt. How extraordinary. It had never occurred to Aurelia for a moment that Caesar wouldn't have to pay back every last sestertius of years of accumulated compound interest, but Balbus knew how to strike a bargain.

There was nothing left over to ward off another attack of Caesar's profligate spending, but at least he owed no money from past spending. And he did have a respectable income from the State, plus a wonderful house.

She rarely thought of her husband, dead for twenty-five years. Praetor, but never consul. That crown had gone in his generation to his older brother and to the other branch. Who could ever have known the danger in bending over to lace up a boot? Nor the shock of some messenger at the door thrusting a horrible little jar at her—his ashes. And she had not even known him dead. But perhaps if he had lived he would have equipped Caesar with brakes, though she had always been aware her son had none in his nature. Gaius Julius, dearly loved husband, our son is senior consul today, and he will make a mark for the Julii Caesares no other Julius Caesar ever has. And Sulla, what would Sulla have thought? The other man in her life, though they had come no closer to indiscretion than a kiss across a bowl of grapes. How I suffered for him, poor tormented man! I miss them both. Yet how good life has been to me. Two daughters well married, grandchildren, and this—this *god* for my son.

How lonely he is. Once I hoped that Gaius Matius in the other ground-floor apartment of my insula would be the friend and confidant he lacks. But Caesar moved on too far too fast. Will he always do that? Is there no one to whom he can turn as an equal? How I pray that one day he'll find a true friend. Not in a wife, alas. We women don't have the breadth of vision nor the experience of public life he needs in a true friend. Yet that slur on him about King Nicomedes has meant that he will admit no man as an intimate, he's too aware of what people would say. In all these years, no other rumor. You'd think that would prove it. But the Forum always has a Bibulus in it. And he has Sulla there as a warning. No old age like Sulla's for Caesar!

I understand at last that he'll never marry Servilia. That he never would have at any time. She suffers, but she has Brutus to vent her frustrations upon. Poor Brutus. I wish Julia loved him, but she doesn't. How can that

marriage work? A thought which clicked a bead into place
inside the abacus of her mind.

But all she said was "Did Bibulus attend the banquet?"

"Oh yes, he was there. So was Cato, so was Gaius
Piso and the rest of the *boni*. But Jupiter Optimus Maximus is a big place, and they arranged themselves on
couches as far from mine as they could. Cato's dear friend
Marcus Favonius was the center of the group, having got
in as quaestor at last." Caesar chuckled. "Cicero informed
me that Favonius is now known around the Forum as Cato's Ape, a delicious double pun. He apes Cato in every
way he can, including going bare beneath his toga, but
he's also such a dullard that he shambles along like an
ape. Nice, eh?"

"Apt, certainly. Did Cicero coin it?"

"I imagine so, but he was suffering from an attack
of modesty today, probably due to the fact that Pompeius
made him swear to be polite and friendly to me, and he
hates it after Rabirius."

"You sound desolate," she said with some irony.

"I'd really rather have Cicero on my side, but
somehow I can't see that happening, Mater. So I'm prepared."

"For what?"

"The day he decides to join his little faction to the
boni."

"Would he go that far? Pompeius Magnus wouldn't
like it."

"I doubt he'd ever become an ardent member of the
boni, they dislike his conceit as much as they dislike mine.
But you know Cicero. He's a grasshopper with an undisciplined tongue, if there is such an animal. Here, there,
everywhere, and all the time busy talking himself into
trouble. Witness Publius Clodius and the six inches. Terribly funny, but not to Clodius or Fulvia."

"How will you deal with Cicero if he becomes an
adversary?"

"Well, I haven't told Publius Clodius, but I secured

permission from the priestly Colleges to allow Clodius to become a plebeian.''

"Didn't Celer object? He refused to let Clodius stand as a tribune of the plebs.''

"Correctly so. Celer is an excellent lawyer. But as to the actuality of Clodius's status, he doesn't care one way or the other. Why should he? The only object of Clodius's nasty streak at the moment is Cicero, who has absolutely no clout with Celer or among the priestly colleges. It's not frowned on for a patrician to want to become a plebeian. The tribunate of the plebs appeals to men with a streak of the demagogue in them, like Clodius.''

"Why haven't you told Clodius you've secured permission?''

"I'm not sure I ever will. He's unstable. However, if I have to deal with Cicero, I'll slip Clodius's leash.'' Caesar yawned and stretched. "Oh, I'm tired! Is Julia here?''

"No, she's at a girls' dinner party, and as it's being held at Servilia's, I said she could stay the night. Girls of that age can spend days talking and giggling.''

"She's seventeen on the Nones. Oh, Mater, how times flies! Her mother has been dead for ten years.''

"But not forgotten,'' Aurelia said gruffly.

"No, never that.''

A silence fell, peaceful and warm. With no money troubles to worry her, Aurelia was a pleasure, reflected her son.

Suddenly she coughed, looked at him with a peculiar gleam in her eyes. "Caesar, the other day I had need to go to Julia's room to look among her clothes. At seventeen, birthday presents should be clothes. You can give her jewelry—I suggest earrings and necklace in plain gold. But I'll give her clothes. I know she ought to be weaving the fabric and making them herself—I did at her age— but unfortunately she's bookish, she'd rather read than weave. I gave up trying to make her weave years ago, it wasn't worth the energy. What she produced was disgraceful.''

"Mater, where are you going? I really don't give a fig what Julia does provided it isn't beneath a Julia.''

In answer Aurelia got up. "Wait here," she ordered, and left Caesar's study.

He could hear her mount the stairs to the upper storey, then nothing, then the sound of her footsteps descending again. In she came, both hands behind her back. Highly amused, Caesar tried to stare her out of countenance without success. Then she whipped her hands around and put something on his desk.

Fascinated, he found himself looking at a little bust of none other than Pompey. This one was considerably better made than the ones he had seen in the markets, but it was still mass-produced in that it was of plaster cast in a mold; the likeness was a more speaking one, and the paint quite delicately applied.

"I found it tucked among her children's clothes in a chest she probably never thought anyone would invade. I confess I wouldn't have myself, had it not occurred to me that there are any number of little girls in the Subura who would get so much wear out of things Julia has long grown out of. We've always kept her unspoiled in that she's had to make do with old clothes when girls like Junia parade in something new every day, but we've never allowed her to look *shabby*. Anyway, I thought I'd empty the chest and send Cardixa off to the Subura with the contents. After finding that, I left well alone."

"How much money does she get, Mater?" Caesar asked, picking up Pompey and turning him round between his hands, a smile tugging at the corner of his mouth; he was thinking of all those young girls clustered around the stalls in the market, sighing and cooing over Pompey.

"Very little, as we both agreed when she came of an age to need some money in her purse."

"How much do you think this would cost, Mater?"

"A hundred sesterces at least."

"Yes, I'd say that was about right. So she saved her precious money to buy this."

"She must have done."

"And what do you deduce from it?"

"That she has a crush on Pompeius, like almost every other girl in her circle. I imagine right at this moment there are a dozen girls clustered around a similar likeness of the same person, Julia included, moaning and carrying on, while Servilia tries to sleep and Brutus toils away over the latest epitome.''

"For someone who has never in her entire life been indiscreet, Mater, your knowledge of human behavior is astonishing.''

"Just because I've always been too sensible to be silly myself, Caesar, does not mean that I am incapable of detecting silliness in others," Aurelia said austerely.

"Why are you bothering to show me this?''

"Well," said Aurelia, sitting down again, "on the whole I'd have to say that Julia is not silly. After all, I am her grandmother! When I found *that*''—pointing at Pompey—"I started to think about Julia in a way I hadn't done before. We tend to forget that they're almost grown up, Caesar, and that's a fact. Next year at this time Julia will be eighteen, and marrying Brutus. However, the older she gets and the closer that wedding comes, the more misgivings I have about it.''

"Why?''

"She doesn't love him.''

"Love isn't a part of the contract, Mater," Caesar said gently.

"I know that, nor am I prone to be sentimental. I am not being sentimental now. Your knowledge of Julia is superficial because it has to be superficial. You see her often enough, but with you she presents a different face than she does to me. She adores you, she really does. If you asked her to plunge a dagger into her breast, she probably would.''

He shifted uncomfortably. "Mater, truly!''

"No, I mean it. As far as Julia is concerned, if you asked her to do that, she would assume that it was necessary for your future welfare. She's Iphigenia at Aulis. If her death could make the winds blow and fill the sails of your life, she'd go to it without counting the cost to herself. And such," Aurelia said deliberately, "is her attitude to marrying Brutus, I am convinced of it. She will do it to please you, and be a perfect wife to him for fifty years if he lives that long. But she won't ever be happy married to Brutus.''

''Oh, I couldn't bear that!'' he cried, and put the bust down.

''I didn't think you could.''

''She's never said a word to me.''

''Nor will she. Brutus is the head of a fabulously rich and ancient family. Marrying him will bring that family into your fold, she knows it well.''

''I'll talk to her tomorrow,'' he said with decision.

''No, Caesar, don't do that. She'll only assume you've seen her reluctance, and protest that you're wrong.''

''Then what *do* I do?''

An expression of feline satisfaction came over Aurelia's face; she smiled and purred in the back of her throat. ''If I were you, my son, I'd invite poor lonely Pompeius Magnus to a nice little family dinner.''

Between the dropped jaw and the smile fighting to close it, Caesar looked as he had when a boy. Then the smile won, turned into a roar of laughter. ''Mater, Mater,'' he said when he was able, ''what would I do without you? Julia and Magnus? Do you think it's possible? I've racked myself hollow trying to find a way to bind him to me, but this is one way never crossed my mind! You're right, we don't see them grown up. I thought I did when I came home. But Brutus was there—I just took them for granted.''

''It will work if it's a love match, but not otherwise,'' said Aurelia, ''so don't be hasty and don't betray by word or look to either of them what hangs upon their meeting.''

''I won't, of course I won't. When do you suggest?''

''Wait until the land bill is settled, whichever way it goes. And don't push him, even after they meet.''

''She's beautiful, she's young, she's a Julia. Magnus will be asking the moment dinner's over.''

But Aurelia shook her head. ''Magnus won't ask at all.''

''Why not?''

''Something Sulla told me once. That Pompeius was

always afraid to ask for the hand of a princess. For that is what Julia is, my son, a princess. The highest born in Rome. A foreign queen would not be her equal in Pompeius's eyes. So he won't ask because he is too afraid of being refused. That's what Sulla said—Pompeius would rather remain a bachelor than risk the injury to his *dignitas* a refusal would mean. So he's waiting for someone with a princess for a daughter to ask him. It's you will have to do the asking, Caesar, not Pompeius. Let him grow very hungry first. He knows she's engaged to Brutus. We will see what happens when they meet, but don't allow them to meet too soon." She rose and plucked the bust of Pompey from the desk. "I'll put this back."

"No, put it on a shelf near her bed and do what you intended to do. Give her clothes away," said Caesar, leaning back and closing his eyes in content.

"She'll be mortified that I've discovered her secret."

"Not if you scold her for accepting presents from Junia, who has too much money. That way she can continue to gaze on Pompeius Magnus without losing her pride."

"Go to bed," said Aurelia at the door.

"I intend to. And thanks to you, I am going to sleep as soundly as a siren-struck sailor."

"That, Caesar, is carrying alliteration too far."

On the second day of January Caesar presented his land bill to the House for its consideration, and the House shuddered at the sight of almost thirty large book buckets distributed around the senior consul's feet. What had been the normal length of a bill was now seen to be minute by comparison; the *lex Iulia agraria* ran to well over a hundred chapters.

As the chamber of the Curia Hostilia was not an acoustically satisfactory place, the senior consul pitched his voice high and proceeded to give the Senate of Rome an admirably concise and yet comprehensive dissection of this massive document bearing his name, and his name alone. A pity Bibulus was unco-operative; otherwise it might have been a *lex Iulia Calpurnia agraria*.

"My scribes have prepared three hundred copies of the bill; time prohibited more," he said. "However, there are enough for a copy between every two senators, plus fifty for the People. I will set up a booth outside the Basilica Aemilia with a legal secretary and an assistant in attendance so that those members of the People who wish to peruse it or query it may do so. Attached to each copy is a summary equipped with useful references to pertinent clauses or chapters in case some readers or enquirers are more interested in some provisions than in others."

"You've got to be joking!" sneered Bibulus. "No one will bother reading anything half that long!"

"I sincerely hope everyone reads it," said Caesar, lifting his brows. "I want criticism, I want helpful suggestions, I want to know what's wrong with it." He looked stern. "Brevity may be the core of wit, but brevity in laws requiring length means bad laws. Every contingency must be examined, explored, explained. Watertight legislation is long legislation. You will see few nice short bills from me, Conscript Fathers. But every bill I intend to present to you will have been personally drafted according to a formula designed to cover every foreseeable possibility."

He paused to allow comment, but nobody volunteered. "Italia is Rome, make no mistake about that. The public lands of Italia's cities, towns, municipalities and shires belong to Rome, and thanks to wars and migrations there are many districts up and down this peninsula that have become as underused and underpopulated as any part of modern Greece. Whereas Rome the city has become overpopulated. The grain dole is a burden larger than the Treasury ought to be expected to bear, and in saying this I am not criticizing the law of Marcus Porcius Cato. In my opinion his was an excellent measure. Without it, we would have seen riots and general unrest. But the fact remains that instead of funding an ever-increasing grain dole, we ought to be relieving overpopulation within the city of Rome by offering Rome's poor more than a chance to join the army.

"We also have some fifty thousand veteran soldiers wandering up and down the country—including inside this

city!—without the wherewithal to settle down in middle
age and become peaceful, productive citizens able to pro-
create legitimately and provide Rome with the soldiers of
the future, rather than with fatherless brats hanging on the
skirts of indigent women. If our conquests have taught us
nothing else, they have surely taught us that it is *Romans*
who fight best, *Romans* who give generals their victories,
Romans who can look with equanimity upon the prospect
of a siege ten years long, *Romans* who can pick up after
their losses and begin to fight all over again.

  "What I propose is a law which will distribute every
iugerum of public land in this peninsula, save for the two
hundred square miles of the Ager Campanus and the fifty
square miles of public land attached to the city of Capua,
our main training ground for the legions. It therefore includes the public lands attached to places like Volaterrae
and Arretium. When I go to fix my boundary stones along
Italia's traveling stock routes, I want to know that they
comprise the bulk of public land left in the peninsula outside of Campania. Why not the Campanian lands too?
Simply because they have been under lease for a very long
time, and it would be highly repugnant to those who lease
them to have to do without them. That of course includes
the maltreated knight Publius Servilius, who I hope by
now has replanted his vines and applied as much manure
as those delicate plants can tolerate."

  Not even that provoked a remark! Because Bibulus's
curule chair was actually a little behind his own, Caesar
couldn't see his face, but found it interesting that he remained silent. Silent too was Cato, back to wearing no
tunic beneath his toga since his Ape, Favonius, had entered
the House to imitate him. An urban quaestor, the Ape was
able to attend every sitting of the Senate.

  "Without dispossessing any person at present occupying our *ager publicus* under the terms of an earlier *lex
agraria,* I have estimated that the available public lands
will provide allotments of ten *iugera* each to perhaps thirty
thousand eligible citizens. Which leaves us with the task
of finding sufficient land at present privately owned for
another fifty thousand beneficiaries. I am counting on ac-

commodating fifty thousand veteran soldiers plus thirty thousand of Rome's urban poor. Not including however many veterans are inside the city of Rome, thirty thousand urban poor removed to productive allotments in rural areas will provide relief for the Treasury of seven hundred and twenty talents per year of grain dole moneys. Add the twenty thousand–odd veterans in the city, and the relief approximates the additional burden Marcus Porcius Cato's law put on public funds.

"But even accounting for the purchase of so much privately owned land, the Treasury can supply the finance necessary because of enormously increased revenues from the eastern provinces—even if, for example, the tax-farming contracts were to be reduced by, let us say, a third. I do not expect the twenty thousand talents of outright profit Gnaeus Pompeius Magnus added to the Treasury to stretch to buying land because of Quintus Metellus Nepos's relaxation of duties and tariffs, a munificent gesture which has deprived Rome of revenue she actually needs badly."

Did that get a response? No, it didn't. Nepos himself was still governing Further Spain, though Celer sat among the consulars. Time he took himself to govern his province, Further Gaul.

"When you examine my *lex agraria,* you will find that it is not arrogant. No pressure of any kind can be exerted upon present owners of land to sell to the State, nor is there a built-in reduction in land prices. Land bought by the State must be paid for at the value put upon it by our esteemed censors Gaius Scribonius Curio and Gaius Cassius Longinus. Existing deeds of ownership will be accepted as completely legal, with no recourse at law to challenge them. In other words, if a man has shifted his boundary stones and no one has yet quarreled with his action, then they define the extent of his property at sale.

"No recipient of a grant of land will be able to sell it or move off it for twenty years.

"And finally, Conscript Fathers, the law proposes that the acquisition and allocation of land reside with a commission of twenty senior knights and senators. If this

House gives me a *consultum* to take to the People, then this House will have the privilege of choosing the twenty knights and senators. If it does not give me a *consultum*, then the privilege goes to the People. There will also be a committee of five consulars to supervise the work of the commissioners. I, however, have no part in any of it. Neither commission nor committee. There must be no suspicion that Gaius Julius Caesar is out to enrich himself, or become the patron of those the *lex Iulia agraria* resettles."

Caesar sighed, smiled, lifted his hands. "Enough for today, honored members of this House. I give you twelve days to read the bill and prepare for debate, which means that the next session to deal with the *lex Iulia agraria* will occur sixteen days before the Kalends of February. The House will, however, sit again five days from now, which is the seventh day before the Ides of January." He looked mischievous. "As I would not like to think any of you is overburdened, I have arranged for the delivery of two hundred and fifty copies of my law to the houses of the two hundred and fifty most senior members of this body. Please don't forget the more junior senators! Those of you who read swiftly, send your copy on when you've finished. Otherwise, may I suggest the junior men approach their seniors and ask to share?"

Whereupon he dismissed the meeting and went off in the company of Crassus; passing Pompey, he acknowledged the Great Man with a grave inclination of the head, nothing more.

Cato had more to say as he and Bibulus walked out together than he had during the meeting.

"I intend to read every line of every one of those innumerable scrolls looking for the catches," he announced, "and I suggest you do the same, Bibulus, even if you do hate reading law. In fact, we must all read."

"He hasn't left much room to criticize the actual law if it's as respectable as he makes out. There won't be any catches."

"Are you saying you're in favor of it?" roared Cato.

"Of course I'm not!" Bibulus snapped. "What I'm

saying is that our blocking it will look spiteful rather than constructive.''

Cato looked blank. ''Do you care?''

''Not really, but I was hoping for a reworked version of Sulpicius or Rullus—something we could pick at. There's no point in making ourselves more odious to the People than necessary.''

''He's too good for us,'' said Metellus Scipio gloomily.

''No, he isn't!'' yelled Bibulus. ''He won't win, he won't!''

When the House met five days later the subject bruited was the Asian *publicani;* this time there were no buckets full of chapters, merely a single scroll Caesar held in his hand.

''This matter has been stalled for well over a year, during which a group of desperate tax-farming men has been destroying good Roman government in four eastern provinces—Asia, Cilicia, Syria and Bithynia-Pontus,'' said Caesar, voice hard. ''The sums the censors accepted on behalf of the Treasury have not been met even so. Every day this disgraceful state of affairs continues is one more day during which our friends the *socii* of the eastern provinces are squeezed remorselessly, one more day during which our friends the *socii* of the eastern provinces curse the name of Rome. The governors of these provinces spend their time on the one hand placating deputations of irate *socii* and on the other having to supply lictors and troops to assist the tax-farmers in squeezing.

''We have to cut our losses, Conscript Fathers. That simple. I have here a bill to present to the Popular Assembly asking it to reduce the tax revenues from the eastern provinces by one third. Give me a *consultum* today. Two thirds of something is infinitely preferable to three thirds of nothing.''

But of course Caesar didn't get his *consultum.* Cato talked the meeting out with a discussion of the philosophy of Zeno and the adaptations Roman society had forced upon it.

Shortly after dawn the next day Caesar convoked the Popular Assembly, filled it with Crassus's knights, and put the matter to the vote.

"For," he said, "if seventeen months of *contiones* on this subject are not enough, then seventeen years of *contiones* will not suffice! Today we vote, and that means that release for the *publicani* need be no further away than seventeen days from now!"

One look at the faces filling the Well of the Comitia told the *boni* that opposition would be as perilous as fruitless; when Cato tried to speak he was booed, and when Bibulus tried to speak the fists came up. In one of the quickest votes on record, the Treasury's revenues from the eastern provinces were reduced by one third, and the crowd of knights cheered Caesar and Marcus Crassus until they were hoarse.

"Oh, what a relief!" said Crassus, actually beaming.

"I wish they were all that easy," said Caesar, sighing. "If I could act as quickly with the *lex agraria* it would be over before the *boni* could organize themselves. Yours was the only one I didn't need to call *contiones* about. The silly *boni* didn't understand that I'd just—do it!"

"One thing puzzles me, Caesar."

"What's that?"

"Well, the tribunes of the plebs have been in office for a month, yet you haven't used Vatinius at all. Now here you are promulgating your own laws. I know Vatinius. A good client I'm sure, but you'll be charged for every service."

"*We'll* be charged, Marcus," Caesar said gently.

"The whole Forum is confused. A month of tribunes of the plebs without a single law or fuss."

"I have plenty of work for Vatinius and Alfius, but not yet. I'm the real lawyer, Marcus, and I love it. Legislating consuls are rare. Why should I let Cicero have all the glory? No, I'll wait until I'm having real trouble with the *lex agraria,* then I'll unleash Vatinius and Alfius. Just to confuse the issue."

"Do I really have to read all that paper?" asked Crassus.

"It would be good because you might have some bright ideas. There's nothing wrong with it from your point of view, of course."

"You can't trick me, Gaius. There is just no way in the world that you can settle eighty thousand people on ten *iugera* each without using both the Ager Campanus and the Capuan land."

"I never thought I would trick you. But I have no intention of pulling the curtain away from that beast's cage yet."

"Then I'm glad I got out of *latifundia* farming."

"Why did you?"

"Too much trouble, not enough profit. All those *iugera* with some sheep and some shepherds, a lot of strife chaining up the work gangs—the men in it are fribbles, Gaius. Look at Atticus. Much and all as I detest the man, he's too clever to graze half a million *iugera* in Italy. They like to say they graze half a million *iugera,* and that's about what it amounts to. Lucullus is a perfect example. More money than sense. Or taste, though he'd dispute it. You'll get no opposition from me, nor from the knights. Grazing the public land under lease from the State is a recreation for senators, not a business for knights. It might give a senator his million-sesterces census, but what are a million sesterces, Caesar? A piddling forty talents! I can make that in a day on"—he grinned, shrugged—"best not say. You might tell the censors."

Caesar picked up the folds of his toga and started to run across the lower Forum in the direction of the Velabrum. "Gaius Curio! Gaius Cassius! Don't go home, go to your censors' booth! I have something to report!"

Under the fascinated gaze of several hundred knights and Forum frequenters, Crassus gathered the folds of his toga about him and set off in pursuit, shouting: "Don't! Don't!"

Then Caesar stopped, let Crassus catch up, and the two of them howled with laughter before setting off in the direction of the Domus Publica. How extraordinary! Two of the most famous men in Rome running all over the place? And the moon wasn't even waxing, let alone full!

*   *   *

All through January the duel between Caesar and the *boni* over the land bill continued unabated. At every meeting set aside in the Senate to discuss it, Cato filibustered. Interested to see whether the technique could still work at all, Caesar finally had his lictors haul Cato out of his place and march him off to the Lautumiae, the *boni* following in his wake applauding, Cato with his head up and the look of a martyr on his horselike face. No, it wasn't going to work. Caesar called off his lictors, Cato returned to his place, and the filibuster went on.

Nothing else for it than to take the matter to the People without that elusive senatorial decree. He would now have to run it in *contio* right through the month of February, when Bibulus had the *fasces* and could more legally oppose the consul without them. So would the vote be in February, or March? No one really knew.

"If you're so against the law, Marcus Bibulus," cried Caesar at that first *contio* in the Popular Assembly, "then tell me why! It isn't enough to stand there baying that you'll oppose it, you must tell this lawful assemblage of Roman People what is wrong with it! Here am I offering a chance to people without a chance, doing so without bankrupting the State and without cheating or coercing those who already own land! Yet all you can do is say you oppose, you oppose, you oppose! Tell us why!"

"I oppose because you're promulgating it, Caesar, for no other reason! Whatever you do is cursed, unholy, evil!"

"You're speaking in riddles, Marcus Bibulus! Be specific, not emotional; tell us why you oppose this absolutely necessary piece of legislation! Give us your criticisms, please!"

"I have no criticisms to make, yet still I oppose!"

Considering that several thousand men had packed into the Comitia well, noise from the crowd was minimal. There were new faces in it, it was not composed entirely of knights, nor of young men belonging to Clodius, nor of professional Forum frequenters; Pompey was bringing his veterans into Rome in preparation for a vote or a fight, no one knew which. These were hand-picked men, evenly numbered across the thirty-one rural tribes and therefore immensely valuable as voters. But also handy in a fight.

Caesar turned to Bibulus and held out his hands, pleading. "Marcus Bibulus, why do you obstruct a very good and very much needed law? Can't you find it in yourself to help the People rather than hinder them? Can't you see from all these men's faces that this isn't a law the People will refuse? It's a law that the whole of Rome wants! Are you going to punish Rome because you don't like me, one single man named Gaius Julius Caesar? Is that worthy of a consul? Is that worthy of a Calpurnius Bibulus?"

"Yes, it's worthy of a Calpurnius Bibulus!" the junior consul cried from the rostra. "I am an augur, I know evil when I see it! You are evil, and everything you do is evil! No good can come of any law you pass! For that reason, I hereby declare that every comitial day for the rest of this year is *feriae,* a holiday, and that therefore no meeting of People or Plebs can be held for the rest of the year!" He drew himself up onto his toes, fists clenched by his sides, the massive pleats of toga upon his left arm beginning to unravel because his elbow was not crooked. "I do this because I know I am right to take recourse in religious prohibitions! For I tell you now, Gaius Julius Caesar, that I don't care if every single benighted soul in the whole of Italia wants this law! They will not get it in my year as consul!"

The hatred was so palpable that those not politically attached to either of the consuls shivered, furtively tucked thumb under middle and ring finger to let index and little fingers stick up in two horns—the sign to ward off the Evil Eye.

"Rub around him like servile animals!" Bibulus screamed to the crowd. "Kiss him, pollute him, offer yourselves to him! If that's how much you want this law, then go ahead and do it! But you will not get it in my year as consul! Never, never, never!"

The boos began, jeers, shouts, curses, catcalls, a rising wave of vocal violence so enormous and terrifying that Bibulus pulled what he could of his toga onto his left arm,

turned and left the rostra. Though only far enough away
to be safe; he and his lictors stood on the Curia Hostilia
steps to listen.

Then magically the abuse changed to cheers which
could be heard as far away as the Forum Holitorium; Caesar produced Pompey the Great and led him to the front
of the rostra.

The Great Man was angry, and anger lent him words
as well as power delivering them. What he said didn't
please Bibulus, nor Cato, now standing with him.

"Gnaeus Pompeius Magnus, will you lend me your
support against the opponents of this law?" cried Caesar.

"Let any man dare draw his sword against your law,
Gaius Julius Caesar, and I will take up my shield!" Pompey bellowed.

Then Crassus was there on the rostra too. "I, Marcus
Licinius Crassus, declare that this is the best land law
Rome has ever seen!" he shouted. "To those of you as-
sembled here who might be concerned over your property,
I give you my word that no man's property is in danger,
and that all men interested can expect to see a profit!"

Shaken, Cato turned to Bibulus. "Ye gods, Marcus
Bibulus, do you see what I see?" he breathed.

"The three of them together!"

"It isn't Caesar at all, it's Pompeius! We've been
going for the wrong man!"

"No, Cato, not that. Caesar is the personification of
evil. But I do see what you see. Pompeius is the prime
mover. Of course he is! What does Caesar stand to gain
except money? He's working for Pompeius, he's been
working for Pompeius all along. Crassus is in it too. The
three of them, with Pompeius the prime mover. Well, it's
his veterans stand to benefit, we knew that. But Caesar
threw dust in our eyes with his urban poor—shades of the
Gracchi and Sulpicius!"

The cheering was deafening; Bibulus drew Cato
away, walked down the Curia Hostilia steps and into the
Argiletum.

"We change our tactics a little, Cato," he said as

distance made it easier to hear. "From now on we aim
first for Pompeius."

"He's easier to break than Caesar," said Cato between his teeth.

"Anyone is easier to break than Caesar. But don't
worry, Cato. If we break Pompeius, we break up the co-
alition. Once Caesar has to fight alone, we'll get him too."

"That was a clever trick, to declare the rest of the
year's comitial days *feriae,* Marcus Bibulus."

"I borrowed it from Sulla. But I intend to go a great
deal further than Sulla, I assure you. If I can't stop their
passing laws, I can render those laws illegal," said Bibulus.

"I begin to think Bibulus a little demented," said
Caesar to Servilia later that day. "This sudden talk of evil
is quite hair-raising. Hatred is one thing, but this is
something more. There's no reason in it, no logic." The
pale eyes looked washed out: Sulla's eyes. "The People
felt it too, and they didn't like it. Political smears are one
thing, Servilia, we all have to cope with them. But the sort
of things Bibulus came out with today put the differences
between us on an inhuman plane. As if we were two
forces, I for evil, he for good. Exactly how it came out
that way is a puzzle to me, except that perhaps total lack
of reason and logic must appear to the onlooker as a man-
ifestation of good. Men assume evil needs to be reasonable, logical. So without realizing what he did, I believe
Bibulus put me at a disadvantage. The fanatic must be a
force for good; the thinking man, being detached, seems
evil by comparison. Is this all just too preposterous?"

"No," she said, standing over him as he lay upon
the bed, her hands moving strongly and rhythmically over
his back. "I do see what you mean, Caesar. Emotion is
very powerful, and it lacks all logic. As if it existed in a
separate compartment from reason. Bibulus wouldn't bend
when by all the rules of conduct he should have been
embarrassed, disadvantaged, humiliated, forced to bend.
He couldn't tell anyone there why he opposed your bill.
Yet he persisted in opposing it, and with such zeal, such

strength! I think things are going to get worse for you.''

''Thank you for that,'' he said, turning his head to look at her, and smiling.

''You'll get no comfort from me if truth gets in the way.'' She ceased, sat down on the edge of the bed until he moved over and made room for her to lie down beside him. Then she said, ''Caesar, I realize that this land bill is partly to gratify our dear Pompeius—even a blind man can see that. But today when the three of you were standing side by side, it looked like much more than a disinterested attempt to solve one of Rome's most persistent dilemmas—what to do with discharged veteran troops.''

He lifted his head. ''You were there,'' he said.

''I was. I have a very nice hiding place between the Curia Hostilia and the Basilica Porcia, so I don't emulate Fulvia.''

''What did you think was going on, then? Among the three of us, I mean.''

Her chin felt a trifle hairy; she must begin to pluck it. That resolution tucked away, she turned her attention to Caesar's question. ''Perhaps when you produced Pompeius it wasn't anything more than a shrewd political move. But Crassus made me stand up straight, I assure you. It reminded me of when he and Pompeius were consuls together, except that they arranged themselves one on either side of *you*. Without glaring at each other, without a flicker of discomfort. The three of you looked like three pieces of the same mountain. Very impressive! The crowd promptly forgot Bibulus, and that was a good thing. I confess I wondered. Caesar, you haven't made a pact with Pompeius Magnus, have you?''

''Definitely not,'' he said firmly. ''My pact is with Crassus and a cohort of bankers. But Magnus isn't a fool, even you admit that. He needs me to get land for his veterans and ratify his settlement of the East. On the other hand, my chief concern is to sort out the financial shambles his conquest of the East has brought to pass. In many ways Magnus has hindered Rome, not helped her. Everyone is spending too much and granting too many concessions to the voters. My policy for this year, Servilia, is to get enough poor out of Rome and the grain dole line to ease the Treasury's grain burden, and put an end to the impasse over the tax-farming contracts. Both purely fiscal, I assure you. I also intend to go a lot further than Sulla in making it difficult for governors to run their provinces like private domains belonging to them rather than to Rome. All of which should make me a hero to the knights.''

She was somewhat mollified, for that answer made sense. Yet as Servilia walked home she was conscious still of unease. He was crafty, Caesar. And ruthless. If he thought it politic, he would lie to her. He was probably the most brilliant man Rome had ever produced; she had watched him over the months when he had drafted his *lex agraria,* and couldn't believe the clarity of his perception. He had installed a hundred scribes upstairs in the Domus Publica, kept them toiling to make copies of what he dictated without faltering to a room full of them scribbling onto wax tablets. A law weighing a talent, not half a pound. So organized, so decisive.

Well, she loved him. Even the hideous insult of his rejection had not kept her away. Was there anything could? It was therefore necessary that she think him more brilliant, more gifted, more capable than any other man Rome had produced; to think that was to salve her pride. She, a Servilia Caepionis, to come crawling back to a man who wasn't the best man Rome had ever produced? Impossible! No, a Caesar wouldn't ally himself with an upstart Pompeius from Picenum! Particularly when Caesar's daughter was betrothed to the son of a man Pompeius had murdered.

Brutus was waiting for her.

As she wasn't in a mood for dealing with her son, formerly she would have dismissed him curtly. These days she bore him with more patience, not because Caesar had told her she was too hard on him, but because Caesar's rejection of her had changed the situation in subtle ways. For once her reason (evil?) had not been able to dominate her emotions (good?), and when she had returned to her house from that awful interview she had let grief and rage and pain pour out of her. The household had been shaken to its bowels, servants fled, Brutus shut in his rooms. Listening. Then she had stormed into Brutus's study and told him what she thought of Gaius Julius Caesar, who wouldn't marry her because she had been an unfaithful wife.

"Unfaithful!" she screamed, hair torn out in clumps, face and chest above her gown scratched to ribbons from those terrible nails. "Unfaithful! With him, only with him! But that isn't good enough for a Julius Caesar, whose *wife* must be above suspicion! Do you believe that? *I* am not good enough!"

The outburst had been a mistake, it didn't take her long to discover that. For one thing, it put Brutus's betrothal to Julia on a firmer footing, no danger now that society would frown at the union of the betrothed couple's parents—a technical incest for all that no close blood links were involved. Rome's laws were vague about the degree of consanguinity permissible to a married pair, and were—as so often—more a matter of the *mos maiorum* than a specific law on the tablets. Therefore a sister might not marry a brother. But when it came to a child marrying an aunt or uncle, only custom and tradition and social disapproval prevented it. First cousins married all the time. Thus no one could have legally or religiously condemned the marriage of Caesar and Servilia on the one hand and of Brutus and Julia on the other. But no doubt whatsoever that it would have been frowned upon! And Brutus was his mother's son. He liked society to approve of what he did. An unofficial union of his mother and Julia's father did not carry nearly the same degree of odium; Romans were pragmatic about such things because they happened.

The outburst had also made Brutus look at his mother as an ordinary woman rather than a personification of power. And implanted a tiny nucleus of contempt for her. He wasn't shriven of his fear, but he could bear it with more equanimity.

So now she smiled at him, sat down and prepared to chat. Oh, if only his skin would clear up a little! The scars beneath that unsightly stubble must be frightful, and they at least would never go away even if the pustules eventually did.

"What is it, Brutus?" she asked nicely.

"Would you have any objection to my asking Caesar if Julia and I could marry next month?"

She blinked. "What's brought this on?"

"Nothing, except that we've been engaged for so many years, and Julia is seventeen now. Lots of girls marry at seventeen."

"That's true. Cicero let Tullia marry at sixteen—not that he's any great example. However, seventeen is acceptable to true members of the nobility. Neither of you has wavered." She smiled and blew him a kiss. "Why not?"

The old dominance asserted itself. "Would you prefer to ask, Mama, or ought it be me?"

"You, definitely," she said. "How delightful! A wedding next month. Who knows? Caesar and I might be grandparents soon."

Off went Brutus to see his Julia.

"I asked my mother if she would object to us marrying next month," he said, having kissed Julia tenderly and ushered her to a couch where they could sit side by side. "She thinks it will be delightful. So I'm going to ask your father at the first chance."

Julia swallowed. Oh, she had so much counted on another year of freedom! But it was not to be. And, thinking about it, wasn't it better the way he suggested? The more time went by, the more she would grow to hate the idea. Get it over and done with! So she said, voice soft, "That sounds wonderful, Brutus."

"Do you think your father would see us now?" he asked eagerly.

"Well, it's grown dark, but he never sleeps anyway. The law distributing land is finished, but he's working on some other huge undertaking. The hundred scribes are still in residence. I wonder what Pompeia would say if she knew her old rooms have been turned into offices?"

"Isn't your father *ever* going to marry again?"

"It doesn't appear so. Mind you, I don't think he

wanted to marry Pompeia. He loved my mother.''

Brutus's poor besmirched brow wrinkled. ''It seems such a happy state to me, though I'm glad he didn't marry Mama. Was she so lovely, your mother?''

''I do remember her, but not vividly. She wasn't terribly pretty, and *tata* was away a lot. But I don't think *tata* truly thought of her the way most men think of their wives. Perhaps he never will esteem a wife because she's a wife. My mama was more his sister, I believe. They grew up together, it made a bond.'' She rose to her feet. ''Come, let's find *avia*. I always send her in first, she's not afraid to beard him.''

''Are you?''

''Oh, he'd never be rude to me, or even curt. But he's so desperately busy, and I love him so much, Brutus! My little concerns must seem a nuisance, I always feel.''

Well, that gentle, wise sensitivity to the feelings of others was one of the reasons why he loved her so enormously. He was beginning to deal with Mama, and after he was married to Julia he knew it would become easier and easier to deal with Mama.

But Aurelia had a cold and had gone to bed already; Julia knocked on her father's study door.

''*Tata,* can you see us?'' she asked through it.

He opened it himself, smiling, kissing her cheek, hand out to shake Brutus's hand. They entered the lamplit room blinking, it was filled with so many little flames, though Caesar used the very best oil and proper linen wicks, which meant no smoke and no overwhelming odor of burning oakum.

''This is a surprise,'' he said. ''Some wine?''

Brutus shook his head; Julia laughed.

''*Tata,*'' she said, ''I know how busy you are, so we won't take up much of your time. We'd like to marry next month.''

How did he manage to do that? Absolutely no change came over his face, yet a change had happened. The eyes looking at them remained exactly the same.

''What's provoked this?'' he asked Brutus.

Who found himself stammering. ''Well, Caesar,

we've been betrothed for almost nine years, and Julia is seventeen. We haven't changed our minds, and we love each other very much. A lot of girls marry at seventeen. Junia will, Mama says. And Junilla. Like Julia, they're betrothed to men, not boys.''

"Have you been indiscreet?" Caesar asked levelly.

Even in the ruddy lamplight Julia's blush was noticable. "Oh, *tata,* no, of course not!" she cried.

"Are you saying then that unless you marry you will succumb to indiscretion?" the advocate pressed.

"No, *tata,* no!" Julia wrung her hands, tears gathering. "It isn't like that!"

"No, it isn't like that," said Brutus, a little angrily. "I have come in all honor, Caesar. Why are you imputing dishonor?"

"I'm not," Caesar said, voice detached. "A father has to ask these things, Brutus. I've been a man a very long time, which is why most men are both protective and defensive about their girl children. I'm sorry if I've ruffled your feathers, I intended no insult. But it's a foolish father who won't ask."

"Yes, I see that," muttered Brutus.

"Then can we marry?" Julia persisted, anxious to have it fully settled, her fate decided.

"No," said Caesar.

A silence fell during which Julia began to look as if a huge burden had been lifted from her shoulders; Caesar had wasted no time in looking at Brutus, he watched his daughter closely.

"Why not?" from Brutus.

"I said eighteen, Brutus, and I meant eighteen. My poor little first wife was married at seven. It matters not that she and I were happy when we did become man and wife. I vowed that any daughter of mine would have the luxury of living out her years as a child *as* a child. Eighteen, Brutus. Eighteen, Julia.''

"We tried," she said when they were outside and the door was shut on Caesar. "Don't mind too much, Brutus dear.''

"I do mind!" he said, broke down and wept.

And having let the devastated Brutus out to mourn all the way home, Julia went back upstairs to her rooms. There she went into her sleeping cubicle—too spacious really for that term—and picked up the bust of Pompey the Great from the shelf where it resided near her bed. She held it cheek to cheek, danced it out into her sitting room, almost unbearably happy. She was still *his*.

By the time he reached Decimus Silanus's house on the Palatine, Brutus had composed himself.

"Thinking about it, I prefer your marriage this year to next," Servilia announced from her sitting room as he tried to tiptoe past it.

He turned in. "Why?" he asked.

"Well, your wedding next year would take some of the gloss off Junia and Vatia Isauricus," she said.

"Then prepare yourself for a disappointment, Mama. Caesar said no. Eighteen it must be."

Servilia stared, arrested. "What?"

"Caesar said no."

She frowned, pursed her lips. "How odd! Now why?"

"Something to do with his first wife. She was only seven, he said. Therefore Julia must be a full eighteen."

"What absolute rubbish!"

"He's Julia's *paterfamilias,* Mama, he can do as he wills."

"Ah yes, but this *paterfamilias* does nothing from caprice. What's he up to?"

"I believed what he said, Mama. Though at first he was quite unpleasant. He wanted to know if Julia and I had—had—"

"Did he?" The black eyes sparkled. "And have you?"

"No!"

"A yes would have knocked me off my chair, I admit it. You lack the gumption, Brutus. You ought to have said yes. Then he would have had no choice other than to let you marry now."

"A marriage without honor is beneath us!" Brutus snapped.

Servilia turned her back. "Sometimes, my son, you remind me of Cato. Go away!"

In one way Bibulus's declaration that every comitial day for the rest of the year was a holiday (holidays, however, did not forbid normal business, from market days to courts) was useful. Two years earlier the then consul Pupius Piso Frugi had passed a law, a *lex Pupia,* forbidding the Senate to meet on a comitial day. It had been done to reduce the power of the senior consul, enhanced by the law of Aulus Gabinius forbidding normal senatorial business during February, the junior consul's month; most of January was made up of comitial days, which meant the Senate now couldn't meet on them, thanks to Piso Frugi's law.

Caesar needed the Assemblies. Neither he nor Vatinius could legislate from the Senate, which recommended laws, but could not pass them. How then to get around this frustrating edict of Bibulus's making all comitial days holidays?

He called the College of Pontifices into session, and directed the *quindecimviri sacris faciundis* to search the sacred prophetic Books for evidence that this year warranted its comitial days' being changed to holidays. At the same time the Chief Augur, Messala Rufus, called the College of Augurs into session. The result of all this was that Bibulus was deemed to have overstepped his authority as an augur; the comitial days could not be religiously abolished on one man's say-so.

While *contiones* on the land bill progressed, Caesar decided to broach the matter of Pompey's settlement of the East. By a neat bit of maneuvering he summoned the Senate to meet on a comitial day toward the end of January, perfectly legal unless an Assembly was meeting. When the four tribunes of the plebs belonging to the *boni* rushed to summon the Plebeian Assembly to foil Caesar's ploy, they found themselves detained by members of the Clodius Club; Clodius was happy to oblige the man who had the power to plebeianize him.

"It is imperative that we ratify the settlements and

agreements entered into by Gnaeus Pompeius Magnus in the East,'' Caesar said. ''If tribute is to flow, it has to be sanctioned by the Roman Senate or one of the Roman Assemblies. Foreign affairs have never been the province of the Assemblies, which understand neither them nor how they are conducted. The Treasury has been severely inconvenienced by the two years of Senate inertia that I am now determined to end. Provincial tributes were set too high by the *publicani,* who contributed nothing in protest against having to contribute too much. That is now over and done with, but these revenues are by no means the only ones in question. There are kings and potentates all over Rome's new territories or client states who have agreed to pay large sums to Rome in return for her protection. Take the tetrarch Deiotarus of Galatia, who concluded a treaty with Gnaeus Pompeius that when ratified will bring five hundred talents a year into the Treasury. In other words, by neglecting to ratify this agreement, Rome has so far lost a thousand talents of tribute money from Galatia alone. Then we have others: Sampsiceramus, Abgarus, Hyrcanus, Pharnaces, Tigranes, Ariobarzanes Philopator, plus a host of minor princelings up and down the Euphrates. All committed to large tributes as yet uncollected because the treaties concluded with them have not been ratified. Rome is very rich, but Rome ought to be much richer! In order to pacify and settle Italia alone, Rome needs more than Rome has. I have called you together to ask that we sit on this subject until all the treaties have been examined and the objections thrashed out.''

He drew a breath and looked straight at Cato. ''A word of warning. If this House refuses to deal with the ratification of the East, I will see that the Plebs does so immediately. Nor will I, a patrician, interfere or offer any guidance to the Plebs! This is your only chance, Conscript Fathers. Either do the job now or watch the Plebs reduce it to a shambles. I don't care either way, for one of these two ways *will* be implemented!''

''No!'' shouted Lucullus from among the consulars. ''No, no, no! What about my arrangements in the East? Pompeius didn't do the conquering, I did! All the vile

Pompeius did was collect the glory! It was I who subjugated the East, and I had my own settlement ready to implement! I tell you plain, Gaius Caesar, that I will not allow this House to ratify any kind of treaty concluded in the name of Rome by an ancestorless bumpkin from Picenum! Lording it over us like a king! Prancing round Rome in fancy dress! No, no, no!''

The temper snapped. ''Lucius Licinius Lucullus, come here!'' Caesar roared. ''Stand before this dais!''

They had never liked each other, though they ought: both great aristocrats, both committed to Sulla. And perhaps that had been the cause of it, jealousy on the part of Lucullus for the younger man, who was Sulla's nephew by marriage. It was Lucullus who had first implied that Caesar was the catamite of old King Nicomedes, Lucullus who had broadcast it for toads like Bibulus to pick up.

In those days Lucullus had been a spare, trim, extremely capable and efficient governor and general, but time and a passion for ecstatic and soporific substances—not to mention wine and exotic foods—had wreaked a terrible havoc which showed in the paunchy slack body, the bloated face, the almost blind-looking grey eyes. The old Lucullus would never have responded to that bellowed command; this Lucullus tottered across the tessellated floor to stand looking up at Caesar, mouth agape.

''Lucius Licinius Lucullus,'' said Caesar in a softer voice, though not a kinder, ''I give you fair warning. Retract your words or I will have the Plebs do to you what the Plebs did to Servilius Caepio! I will have you arraigned on charges of failing in your commission from the Senate and People of Rome to subjugate the East and see an end of the two kings. I will have you arraigned, and I will see you sent into permanent exile on the meanest and most desolate dropping of land Our Sea possesses, without the wherewithal to so much as put a new tunic on your back! Is that clear? Do you understand? Don't try me, Lucullus, because I mean what I say!''

The House was absolutely still. Neither Bibulus nor Cato moved. Somehow when Caesar looked like that it didn't seem worth the risk. Though this Caesar pointed the

way to what Caesar might become if he wasn't stopped.
More than an autocrat. A king. But a king needed armies.
Therefore Caesar must never be given the opportunity to
have armies. Neither Bibulus nor Cato was quite old
enough to have participated in political life under Sulla,
though Bibulus remembered him; it was easy these days
to see him in Caesar, or what they believed he had been.
Pompey was a nothing, he didn't have the blood. Ye gods,
but Caesar did!

Lucullus crumpled to the ground and wept, dribbling
and drooling, begging forgiveness as a vassal might have
begged King Mithridates or King Tigranes, while the Senate of Rome looked on the drama, appalled. It wasn't appropriate; it was a humiliation for every senator present.

"Lictors, take him home," said Caesar.

Still no one spoke; two of the senior consul's lictors
took Lucullus gently by the arms, lifted him to his feet,
and assisted him, weeping and moaning, from the chamber.

"Very well," said Caesar then, "what is it to be?
Does this body wish to ratify the eastern settlement, or do
I take it to the Plebs as *leges Vatiniae*?"

"Take it to the Plebs!" cried Bibulus.

"Take it to the Plebs!" howled Cato.

When Caesar called for a division, hardly anyone
passed to the right; the Senate had decided that any alternative was preferable to giving Caesar his way. Let it go
to the Plebs, where it would be shown up for what it was:
one piece of arrogance authored by Pompey and another
piece of arrogance to be laid at Caesar's door. No one
liked being ruled, and Caesar's attitude that day smacked
of sovereignty. Better to die than live under another dictator.

"They didn't like that, and Pompeius is extremely
unhappy," said Crassus after what turned out to be a very
short meeting.

"What choice do they give me, Marcus? What ought
I to do? *Nothing?*" Caesar demanded, exasperated.

"Actually, yes," said the good friend, in no expectation that his words would be heeded. "They know you

love to work, they know you love to get things done. Your
year is going to degenerate into a duel of wills. They hate
being pushed. They hate being told they're a lot of
dithering old women. They hate any kind of strength that
smacks of excessive authority. It's not your fault you're a
born autocrat, Gaius, but what's gradually happening is
similar to two rams in a field butting head to head. The
boni are your natural enemies. But somehow you're turning the entire House into enemies. I was watching the
faces while Lucullus groveled at your feet. He didn't mean
to set an example, he's too far gone to be so cunning, but
an example he was nevertheless. They were all seeing
themselves down there begging your forgiveness, while
you stood like a monarch.''

"That's absolute rubbish!''

"To you, yes. To them, no. If you want my advice,
Caesar, then do nothing for the rest of the year. Drop the
ratification of the East, and drop the land bill. Sit back and
smile, agree with them and lick their arses. Then they
might forgive you.''

"I would rather," said Caesar, teeth clenched, "join
Lucullus on that dropping in Our Sea than lick their arses!''

Crassus sighed. "That's what I thought you'd say. In
which case, Caesar, be it on your own head.''

"Do you mean to desert me?''

"No, I'm too good a businessman for that. You mean
profits for the business world, which is why you'll get
whatever you want from the Assemblies. But you'd better
keep an eye on Pompeius, he's more insecure than I am.
He wants so badly to belong.''

Thus it was that Publius Vatinius took the ratification
of the East to the Plebeian Assembly in a series of laws
emerging from an initial general one which consented to
Pompey's settlement. The trouble was that the Plebs found
this endless legislation very boring after the excitement
wore off, and forced Vatinius to be quick. Nor, lacking
direction from Caesar (as good as his word—he refused
to offer any kind of guidance to Vatinius), did the son of

a new Roman citizen from Alba Fucentia understand anything about setting tributes or defining the boundaries of
kingdoms. So the Plebs blundered through act after act,
consistently setting the tributes too low and defining the
boundaries too cloudily. And for their part the *boni* allowed it all to happen by failing to veto one single aspect
of Vatinius's month-long activity. What they wanted was
to complain loud and long after it was finished, and use it
as an example of what happened when senatorial prerogatives were usurped by the legislating bodies.

But "Don't come crying to me!" was what Caesar
said. "You had your chance, you refused to take it. Complain to the Plebs. Or better still, having resigned from
your proper duties, teach the Plebs how to frame treaties
and set tributes. It seems they'll be doing it from now on.
The precedent has been set."

All of which paled before the prospect of the vote in
the Popular Assembly about Caesar's land bill. Sufficient
time and *contiones* having elapsed, Caesar convoked the
voting meeting of the Popular Assembly on the eighteenth
day of February, despite the fact that this meant Bibulus
held the *fasces*.

By now Pompey's hand-picked veterans had all arrived to vote, giving the *lex Iulia agraria* the support it
would need to pass. So great was the crowd which assembled that Caesar made no attempt to hold the vote in the
Well of the Comitia; he set himself up on the platform
attached to the temple of Castor and Pollux, and wasted
no time on the preliminaries. With Pompey acting as augur
and himself conducting the prayers, he called for the casting of lots to see the order in which the tribes would vote
not long after the sun had risen above the Esquiline.

The moment the men of Cornelia were called to vote
first, the *boni* struck. His *fasces*-bearing lictors preceding
him, Bibulus forced his way through the mass of men
around the platform with Cato, Ahenobarbus, Gaius Piso,
Favonius and the four tribunes of the plebs he controlled
surrounding him, Metellus Scipio in the lead. At the foot
of the steps on Pollux's side his lictors stopped; Bibulus
pushed past them and stood on the bottom step.

"Gaius Julius Caesar, you do not possess the *fasces*!" he screamed. "This meeting is invalid because I, the officiating consul this month, did not consent to its being held! Disband it or I will have you prosecuted!"

The last word had scarcely left his mouth when the crowd bellowed and surged forward, too quickly for any of the four tribunes of the plebs to interpose a veto, or perhaps too loudly for a veto to be heard. A perfect target, Bibulus was pelted with filth, and when his lictors moved to protect him their sacred persons were seized; bruised and beaten, they had to watch as their *fasces* were smashed to pieces by a hundred pairs of bare and brawny hands. The same hands then turned to rend Bibulus, slapping rather than punching, with Cato coming in for the same treatment, and the rest retreating. After which someone emptied a huge basket of ordure on top of Bibulus's head, though some was spared for Cato. While the mob howled with laughter, Bibulus, Cato and the lictors withdrew.

The *lex Iulia agraria* passed into law so positively that the first eighteen tribes all voted their assent, and the meeting then turned its attention to voting for the men Pompey suggested should fill the commission and the committee. An impeccable collection: among the commissioners were Varro, Caesar's brother-in-law Marcus Atius Balbus, and that great authority on pig breeding Gnaeus Tremellius Scrofa; the five consular committeemen were Pompey, Crassus, Messala Niger, Lucius Caesar and Gaius Cosconius (who was not a consular, but needed to be thanked for his services).

Convinced they could win after this shocking demonstration of public violence during an illegally convoked meeting, the *boni* tried the following day to bring Caesar down. Bibulus called the Senate into a closed session and displayed his injuries to the House, together with the bruises and bandages his lictors and Cato sported as they walked slowly up and down the floor to let everyone see what had happened to them.

"I make no attempt to have Gaius Julius Caesar charged in the Violence Court for conducting a lawless assemblage!" cried Bibulus to the packed gathering. "To do so would be pointless, no one would convict him. What I ask is better and stronger! I want a Senatus Consultum Ultimum! But not in the form invented to deal with Gaius Gracchus! I want a state of emergency declared immediately, with myself appointed Dictator until public violence has been driven from our beloved Forum Romanum, and this mad dog Caesar driven out of Italia forever! I'll have none of a half measure like the one we endured while Catilina occupied Etruria! I want it done the right way, the proper way! Myself as legally elected Dictator, with Marcus Porcius Cato as my master of the horse! Whatever steps are taken then fall to me—no one in this House can be accused of treason, nor can the Dictator be made to answer for what he does or his master of the horse deems necessary. I will see a division!''

''No doubt you will, Marcus Bibulus,'' said Caesar, ''though I wish you wouldn't. Why embarrass yourself? The House won't give you that kind of mandate unless you manage to grow a few inches. You wouldn't be able to see over the heads of your military escort, though I suppose you could draft dwarves. The only violence which erupted *you* caused. Nor did a riot develop. The moment the People showed you what they thought of your trying to disrupt their legally convened proceedings, the meeting returned to normal and the vote was taken. You were manhandled, but not maimed. The chief insult was a basket of ordure, and that was treatment you richly deserved. The Senate is not sovereign, Marcus Bibulus. The People are sovereign. You tried to destroy that sovereignty in the name of less than five hundred men, most of whom are sitting here today. Most of whom I hope have the sense to deny you your request because it is an unreasonable and baseless request. Rome stands in no danger of civil unrest. Revolution isn't even above the edge of the farthest horizon one can see from the top of the Capitol. You're a spoiled and vindictive little man who wants your own way and can't bear to be gainsaid. As for Marcus Cato, he's a bigger fool than he is a prig. I noted that your other adherents didn't linger yesterday to give you more excuse than this slender pretext on which you demand to be cre-

ated Dictator. Dictator Bibulus! Ye gods, what a joke! I
remember you from Mitylene far too well to blanch at the
thought of Dictator Bibulus. You couldn't organize an
orgy in Venus Erucina's or a brawl in a tavern. You're an
incompetent, vainglorious little maggot! Go ahead, take
your division! In fact, I'll move it for you!''

The eyes so like Sulla's passed from face to face,
lingered on Cicero with the ghost of a menace in them not
only Cicero felt. What a power the man had! It radiated
out of him, and hardly any senator there didn't suddenly
understand that what would work on anyone else, even
Pompey, would never stop Caesar. If they called his bluff,
they all knew it would turn out to be no bluff. He was
more than merely dangerous. He was disaster.

When the division was called, only Cato stood to Bibulus's right; Metellus Scipio and the rest gave in.

Whereupon Caesar went back to the People and demanded one additional clause for his *lex agraria:* that
every senator be compelled to swear an oath to uphold it
the moment it was ratified after the seventeen days' wait
was done. There were precedents, including the famous
refusal of Metellus Numidicus which had resulted in an
exile some years in duration.

But times had changed and the People were angry;
the Senate was seen as deliberately obstructive, and Pompey's veterans wanted their land badly. At first a number
of senators refused to swear, but Caesar remained determined, and one by one they swore. Except for Metellus
Celer, Cato and Bibulus. After Bibulus crumbled it went
down to Celer and Cato, who would not, would not, would
not.

"I suggest," Caesar said to Cicero, "that you persuade that pair to take the oath." He smiled sweetly. "I
have permission from the priests and augurs to procure a
lex Curiata allowing Publius Clodius to be adopted into
the Plebs. So far I haven't implemented it. I hope I never
have to. But in the long run, Cicero, it depends on you."

Terrified, Cicero went to work. "I've seen the Great
Man," he said to Celer and Cato, without realizing that
he had applied that ironic term to someone other than

Pompey, "and he's out to skin you alive if you don't swear."

"I'd look quite good hanging in the Forum flayed," said Celer.

"Celer, he'll take everything off you! I mean it! If you don't swear, it means political ruin. There's no punishment attached for refusing to swear, he's not so stupid. No one can say you've done anything particularly admirable in refusing, it won't mean a fine or exile. What it will mean is such odium in the Forum that you won't ever be able to show your face again. If you don't swear, the People will damn you as obstructive for the sake of obstruction. They'll take it personally, not as an insult to Caesar. Bibulus should never have shrieked to an entire meeting of the People that they'd never get the law no matter how badly they wanted it. They interpreted that as spite and malice. It put the *boni* in a very bad light. Don't you understand that the knights are for it, that it isn't simply Magnus's soldiers?"

Celer was looking uncertain. "I can't see why the knights are for it," he said sulkily.

"Because they're busy going round Italia buying up land to sell for a fat profit to the commissioners!" snapped Cicero.

"They're disgusting!" Cato shouted, speaking for the first time. "I'm the great-grandson of Cato the Censor, I won't bow down to one of these overbred aristocrats! Even if he does have the knights on his side! Rot the knights!"

Knowing that his dream of concord between the Orders was a thing of the past, Cicero sighed, held out both hands. "Cato, my dear fellow, swear! I see what you mean about the knights, I really do! They want everything their way, and they exert utterly unscrupulous pressures on us. But what can we do? We have to live with them because we can't do without them. How many men are there in the Senate? Certainly not enough to stick one's *medicus* up in a knightly direction, and that's what refusal means. You'd be offering anal insult to the Ordo Equester, which is far too powerful to tolerate that."

"I'd rather ride out the storm," said Celer.

"So would I," said Cato.

"Grow up!" cried Cicero. "Ride out the storm? You'll sink to the bottom, both of you! Make up your minds to it. Swear and survive, or refuse to swear and accept political ruin." He saw no sign of yielding in either face, girded his loins and went on. "Celer, Cato, swear, I *beg* of you! After all, what's at stake if you look at it coldly? What's more important, to oblige the Great Man this once in something which doesn't affect you personally, or go down to permanent oblivion? If you kill yourselves politically, you won't be there to continue the fight, will you? Don't you see that it's more important to remain in the arena than get carried out on a shield looking gorgeous in death?"

And more, and more. Even after Celer came round, it took the beleaguered Cicero another two hours of argument to make the very stubborn Cato give in. But he did give in. Celer and Cato took the oath, and, having taken it, would not forswear it; Caesar had learned from Cinna, and made sure neither man held a stone in his fist to render the swearing void.

"Oh, what an awful year this is!" Cicero said to Terentia with genuine pain in his voice. "It's like watching a team of giants battering with hammers at a wall too thick to break! If only I wasn't here to see it!"

She actually patted his hand. "Husband, you look absolutely worn down. Why are you staying? If you do, you'll become ill. Why not set out with me for Antium and Formiae? We could make it a delightful vacation, not return until May or June. Think of the early roses! I know you love to be in Campania for the start of spring. And we could pop in at Arpinum, see how the cheeses and the wool are doing."

It loomed deliciously before his gaze, but he shook his head. "Oh, Terentia, I'd give anything to go! It just isn't possible. Hybrida is back from Macedonia, and half of Macedonia has come to Rome to accuse him of extortion. The poor fellow was a good colleague in my consulship, no matter what they say. Never gave me any real trouble. So I'm going to defend him. It's the least I can do.''

"Then promise me that the moment your verdict is in, you'll leave," she said. "I'll go on with Tullia and Piso Frugi—Tullia is keen to see the games in Antium. Besides, little Marcus isn't well—he complains so of growing pains that I dread his inheriting my rheumatism. We all need a holiday. Please!''

Such a novelty was it to hear a beseeching Terentia that Cicero agreed. The moment Hybrida's trial was done, he would join them.

The problem was that Caesar's forcing him to remonstrate with Celer and Cato was still at the forefront of Cicero's mind when he undertook the defense of Gaius Antonius Hybrida. To have acted as Caesar's lackey smarted; it sat ill with someone whose courage and resolution had saved his country.

Not therefore so inexplicable that when the moment came to deliver his final speech before the jury found for or against his colleague Hybrida, Cicero found it beyond his control to stick to the subject. He did his habitual good job, lauded Hybrida to the skies and made it clear to the jury that this shining example of the Roman nobility had never pulled the wings off a fly as a child or maimed a considerable number of Greek citizens as a young man, let alone committed any of the crimes alleged by half of the province of Macedonia.

"Oh," he sighed as he built up to his peroration, "how much I miss the days when Gaius Hybrida and I were consuls together! What a decent and honorable place Rome was! Yes, we had Catilina skulking in the background ready to demolish our fair city, but he and I coped with that, he and I saved our country! But for what, gentlemen of the jury? For what? I wish I knew! I wish I could tell you why Gaius Hybrida and I stuck by our posts and endured those shocking events! All for nothing, if one looks around Rome on this terrible day during the consulship of a man not fit to wear the *toga praetexta*! And no, I do not mean the great and good Marcus Bibulus! I mean that ravening wolf Caesar! He has destroyed the con-

cord among the Orders, he has made a mockery of the
Senate, he has polluted the consulship! He rubs our noses
in the filth which issues from the Cloaca Maxima, he
smears it from our tails to our toes, he dumps it on our
heads! As soon as this trial is ended I am leaving Rome,
and I do not intend to come back for a long time because
I just cannot bear to watch Caesar defaecating on Rome!
I am going to the seaside, then I am sailing away to see
places like Alexandria, haven of learning and good government. . . .''

The speech ended, the jury voted. CONDEMNO. Gaius Antonius Hybrida was off to exile in Cephallenia, a
place he knew well—and that knew him too well. As for
Cicero, he packed up and quit Rome that afternoon, Terentia having left already.

The trial had ended during the morning, and Caesar
had been inconspicuously at the back of the crowd to hear
Cicero. Before the jury had delivered its verdict he had
gone, sending messengers flying in several directions.

It had been an interesting trial for Caesar in a number
of ways, commencing with the fact that he himself had
once tried to bring Hybrida down on charges of murder
and maiming while the commander of a squadron of Sulla's cavalry at Lake Orchomenus, in Greece. Caesar had
also found himself fascinated by the young man prosecuting Hybrida this time, for he was a protégé of Cicero's
who now had the courage to face Cicero from the opposite
side of the legal fence. Marcus Caelius Rufus, a very handsome and well-set-up fellow who had put together a brilliant case and quite cast Cicero into the shadows.

Within moments of Cicero's opening his speech in
Hybrida's defense, Caesar knew Hybrida was done for.
Hybrida's reputation was just too well known for anyone
to believe he hadn't pulled the wings off flies when a boy.

Then came Cicero's digression.

Caesar's temper went completely. He sat in the study
at the Domus Publica and chewed his lips as he waited
for those he had summoned to appear. So Cicero thought
himself immune, did he? So Cicero thought he could say

precisely what he liked without fear of reprisal? Well, Marcus Tullius Cicero, you have another think coming! I am going to make life very difficult for you, and you deserve it. Every overture thrown in my face, even now your beloved Pompeius has indicated he would like you to support me. And the whole of Rome knows why you love Pompeius—he saved you from having to pick up a sword during the Italian War by throwing the mantle of his protection around you when you were both cadets serving under Pompeius's father, the Butcher. Not even for Pompeius will you put your trust in me. So I will make sure I use Pompeius to help haul you down. I showed you up with Rabirius, but more than that—in trying Rabirius, I showed you that your own hide isn't safe. Now you're about to find out how it feels to look exile in the face.

Why do they all seem to believe they can insult me with total impunity? Well, perhaps what I am about to do to Cicero will make them see they can't. I am not powerless to retaliate. The only reason I have not so far is that I fear I might not be able to stop.

Publius Clodius arrived first, agog with curiosity, took the goblet of wine Caesar handed him and sat down. He then sprang up, sat down again, wriggled.

"Can you never sit still, Clodius?" Caesar asked.

"Hate it."

"Try."

Sensing that some sort of good news was in the offing, Clodius tried, but when he managed to control the rest of his appendages, his goatee continued to wriggle as his chin worked at pushing his lower lip in and out. A sight which Caesar seemed to find intensely amusing, for he finally burst out laughing. The odd thing about Caesar and his merriment, however, was that it failed to annoy Clodius the way—for instance—Cicero's did.

"Why," asked Caesar when his mirth simmered down, "do you persist in wearing that ridiculous tuft?"

"We're all wearing them," said Clodius, as if that explained it.

"I had noticed. Except for my cousin Antonius, that is."

Clodius giggled. "It didn't work for poor old Antonius, quite broke his spirit. Instead of sticking out, his goatee stuck up and kept tickling the end of his nose."

"Am I allowed to guess why you are all growing hair on the ends of your faces?"

"Oh, I think you know, Caesar."

"To annoy the *boni*."

"And anyone else who's foolish enough to react."

"I insist that you shave it off, Clodius. Immediately."

"Give me one good reason why!" said Clodius aggressively.

"It might suit a patrician to be eccentric, but plebeians are not sufficiently antique. Plebeians have to obey the *mos maiorum*."

A huge smile of delight spread over Clodius's face. "You mean you've got the consent of the priests and augurs?"

"Oh, yes. Signed, sealed, and delivered."

"Even with Celer still here?"

"Celer behaved like a lamb."

Down went the wine, Clodius leaped to his feet. "I'd better find Publius Fonteius—my adoptive father."

"Sit down, Clodius! Your new father has been sent for."

"Oh, I can be a tribune of the plebs! The greatest one in the history of Rome, Caesar!"

A goateed Publius Fonteius arrived on the echo of Clodius's words, and grinned fatuously when informed that he, aged twenty, would become the father of a man aged thirty-two.

"Are you willing to release Publius Clodius from your paternal authority and will you shave off that thing?" asked Caesar of him.

"Anything, Gaius Julius, anything!"

"Excellent!" said Caesar heartily, and came round his desk to welcome Pompey.

"What's amiss?" asked Pompey a trifle anxiously, then stared at the other two men present. "What *is* amiss?"

"Not a thing, Magnus, I assure you," said Caesar,

seating himself once more. "I need the services of an augur, is all, and I thought you might like to oblige me."

"Anytime, Caesar. But for what?"

"Well, as I'm sure you know, Publius Clodius has been desirous of abrogating his patrician status for some time. This is his adoptive father, Publius Fonteius. I'd like to get the business done this afternoon, if you'd act as augur."

No, Pompey was not a fool. Caesar hadn't got it out before he understood the object of the exercise. He too had been in the Forum to listen to Cicero, and he had hurt more from it than Caesar had, for whatever insults were heaped on Caesar's head reflected on him. For years he'd put up with Cicero's vacillations; nor was he pleased with the way Cicero had shied on every occasion he had asked for help since his return from the East. Savior of his country indeed! Let the conceited nincompoop suffer a little for a change! Oh, how he'd cringe when he knew Clodius was on his tail!

"I'm happy to oblige," said Pompey.

"Then let's all meet in the Well of the Comitia in one hour's time," said Caesar. "I'll have the thirty lictors of the *curiae* present, and we'll get on with it. Minus the beards."

Clodius lingered at the door. "Does it happen immediately, Caesar, or do I have to wait for seventeen days?"

"Since the tribunician elections are not due for some months yet, Clodius, what does it matter?" asked Caesar, laughing. "But to make absolutely sure, we'll have another little ceremony after three *nundinae* have elapsed." He paused. "I presume you're *sui iuris,* not under the hand of Appius Claudius still?"

"No, he ceased to be my *paterfamilias* when I married."

"Then there is no impediment."

Nor was there. Few of the men who mattered in Rome were there to witness the proceedings of *adrogatio,* with their prayers, chants, sacrifices and archaic rituals. Publius Clodius, formerly a member of the patrician *gens*

Claudia, became a member of the plebeian *gens Fonteia* for a very few moments before assuming his own name again and continuing to be a member of the *gens Claudia*—but this time of a new plebeian branch, distinct from the Claudii Marcelli. He was, in effect, founding a new Famous Family. Unable to enter the religious circle, Fulvia watched from the closest spot she could, then joined Clodius afterward to whoop about the lower Forum telling everyone that Clodius was going to be a tribune of the plebs next year—and that Cicero's days as a Roman citizen were numbered.

Cicero learned of it in the little crossroads settlement of Tres Tabernae, on his way to Antium; there he met young Curio.

"My dear fellow," said Cicero warmly, drawing Curio into his private parlor at the best of the three inns, "the only thing which saddens me to meet you is that it means you haven't yet resumed your brilliant attacks on Caesar. What happened? Last year so vocal, this year so silent."

"I got bored," said Curio tersely; one of the penalties of flirting with the *boni* was that one had to put up with people like Cicero, who also flirted with the *boni*. He was certainly not about to tell Cicero now that he had stopped attacking Caesar because Clodius had helped him out of a financial embarrassment, and fixed as his price silence on the subject of Caesar. So, having a little venom of his own, he sat down companionably with Cicero and let the conversation flow wherever Cicero wished for some time. Then he asked, "How do you feel about Clodius's new plebeian status?"

The effect was all he could have hoped for. Cicero went white, grabbed the edge of the table and hung on for dear life.

"*What* did you say?" the savior of his country whispered.

"Clodius is a plebeian."

"When?"

"Not too many days ago—you will travel by litter, Cicero; you move at the pace of a snail. I didn't see it myself, but I heard all about it from Clodius, very elated. He's standing for the tribunate of the plebs, he tells me, though I'm not quite sure why aside from settling his score with you. One moment he was praising Caesar like a god because Caesar had procured him his *lex Curiata,* the next moment he was saying that as soon as he entered office he'd invalidate all Caesar's laws. But that's Clodius!''

The color now flooded into Cicero's face, reddening it to the point whereat Curio wondered if he was about to have a stroke. ''Caesar made him a plebeian?''

''On the same day you let your tongue run away with you at the trial of Hybrida. At noon all was peace and quiet, three hours later there was Clodius screaming his new plebeian status from the rooftops. And that he'd be prosecuting you.''

''Free speech is dead!'' groaned Cicero.

''You're only just finding *that* out?'' Curio asked, grinning.

''But if Caesar made him a plebeian, why is he threatening to invalidate all Caesar's laws?''

''Oh, not because he's vexed with Caesar,'' Curio said. ''It's Pompeius he loathes. Caesar's laws are designed to benefit Magnus, that simple. Clodius deems Magnus a tumor in Rome's bowels.''

''Sometimes I agree with him,'' Cicero muttered.

Which didn't prevent his greeting Pompey with joy when he reached Antium to find the Great Man staying there on his way back to Rome after a quick trip to Campania as a land committeeman.

''Have you heard that Clodius is now a plebeian?'' he asked as soon as he considered it polite to terminate the courtesies.

''I didn't hear it, Cicero, I was a part of it,'' said Pompey, bright blue eyes twinkling. ''I took the auspices, and very fine they were too. The clearest liver! Classical.''

''Oh, what's going to happen to me now?'' moaned Cicero, his hands writhing.

''Nothing, Cicero, nothing!'' said Pompey heartily. ''Clodius is all talk, believe me. Neither Caesar nor I will let him harm a hair of your venerable head.''

"Venerable?" squawked Cicero. "You and I, Pompeius, are the same age!"

"Who said I wasn't venerable too?"

"Oh, I'm doomed!"

"Nonsense!" said Pompey, reaching over to pat Cicero's back between his huddled shoulders. "Give you my word he won't harm you, truly!"

A promise Cicero wanted desperately to cling to; but could anyone keep Clodius in check once he had a target in sight?

"How do you know he won't harm me?" he asked.

"Because I told him not to at the adoption ceremony. Time someone told him! He reminds me of a really bumptious and cocky junior military tribune who mistakes a little talent for a lot. Well, I'm used to dealing with those! He just needed smartening up by the man with the real talent—the general."

That was it. Curio's puzzle answered. Didn't Pompey begin to understand? A man of respectable birth from rural parts didn't presume to tell a patrician Roman how to behave. If Clodius had not already decided he loathed Pompey, to be treated like a junior military tribune by the likes of Pompeius Magnus at the very moment of his victory would surely have done it.

Rome during March buzzed, some of it arising from politics and some from the sensational death of Metellus Celer. Still dallying in Rome and leaving his province of Further Gaul to the ministrations of his legate Gaius Pomptinus, Celer seemed not to know what to do for the best. It had been bad enough when Clodia blazed a trail across Rome's social sky in the throes of her wild affair with Catullus, but that was finished. The poet from Verona was crazed with grief; his howls and sobs could be heard from the Carinae to the Palatine—and his wonderful poems read from the same to the same. Erotic, passionate, heartfelt, luminous—if Catullus had searched forever for a suitable object of a great love, he could not have found a better than his adored Lesbia, Clodia. Her perfidy, cunning, heartlessness and rapacity coaxed words out of him he hadn't known himself capable of producing.

She terminated Catullus when she discovered Caelius, about to commence his prosecution of Gaius Antonius Hybrida. What had attracted her to Catullus was present to some extent in Caelius, but in a more Roman mold; the poet was too intense, too volatile, too prone to gloomy depression. Whereas Caelius was sophisticated, witty, innately joyous. He came from good stock and had a rich father who was anxious that his brilliant son should snatch nobility for the Caelius family by attaining the consulship. Caelius was a New Man, yes, but not of the more obnoxious kind. The striking and stormy good looks of Catullus had ravished her, but the powerful thews and equally handsome face belonging to Caelius pleased Clodia more; it could become quite an ordeal to be a poet's mistress.

In short, Catullus began to bore Clodia at precisely the moment she spied Caelius. So it was off with the old and on with the new. And how did a husband fit into this frenzied activity? The answer was, not very well. Clodia's passion for Celer had lasted until she neared thirty, but that was the end of it. Time and increasing self-assurance had weaned her away from her first cousin and childhood companion, prompted her to seek whatever it was she looked for with Catullus, her second essay in illicit love— at least of a glaringly public kind. The incest scandal she, Clodius and Clodilla had provoked had whetted an appetite eventually grown too great not to be indulged. Clodia also found that she adored being despised by all the people she herself despised. Poor Celer was reduced to the role of helpless onlooker.

She was twelve years older than the twenty-three-year-old Marcus Caelius Rufus when she spied him, not that he had just arrived in Rome; Caelius had flitted in and out since he had come to study under Cicero three years before the consulship. He had flirted with Catilina, been sent in disgrace to assist the governor of Africa Province until the fuss died down because Caelius Senior happened to own a great deal of the wheatlands of the Bagradas River in that province. Recently Caelius had come home to start his Forum career in earnest, and with as much splash as possible. Thus he elected to prosecute the man even Gaius Caesar hadn't been able to convict, Gaius Antonius Hybrida.

For Celer the misery just kept on waxing at the same rate as Clodia's interest in him waned. And then, on top of being shown that he had no choice other than to swear the oath to uphold Caesar's land bill, he learned that Clodia had a new lover, Marcus Caelius Rufus. The inhabitants of the houses around Celer's residence had no trouble hearing the frightful quarrels which erupted out of Celer's peristyle at all hours of day and night. Husband and wife specialized in shouting threats of murder at each other, and there were sounds of blows struck, missiles landing, breaking pottery or glass, frightened servants' voices, shrieks which froze the blood. It couldn't last, all the neighbors knew it, and speculated how it would eventually end.

But who could have predicted such an end? Unconscious, brain herniating out of the splintered depths of a shocking head wound, Celer was hauled naked from his bath by servants while Clodia stood screaming, robe soaked because she had climbed into the bath in an attempt to get him out herself, covered in blood because she had held his head out of the water. When the horrified Metellus Nepos was joined by Appius Claudius and Publius Clodius, she was able to tell them what had happened. Celer had been very drunk, she explained, but insisted on a bath after he vomited—who could ever reason with a drunken man or persuade him not to do what he was determined to do? Repeatedly telling him that he was too drunk to bathe, Clodia accompanied him to the bathroom, and continued to plead with him as he undressed. Then, poised on the top step and about to descend into the tepid water, her husband fell and struck his head on the rear parapet of the tub—sharp, projecting, lethal.

Sure enough, when the three men went to the bathroom to inspect the scene of the accident, there on the rear parapet were blood, bone, brain. The physicians and surgeons tenderly inserted a comatose Metellus Celer into his bed, and a weeping Clodia refused to leave his side for any reason.

Two days later he died, never having regained consciousness. Clodia was a widow, and Rome plunged into
mourning for Quintus Caecilius Metellus Celer. His
brother, Nepos, was his principal heir, but Clodia had been
left extremely comfortably off, and no agnate relative of
Celer's was about to invoke the *lex Voconia*.

Busy preparing his case for the defense of Hybrida,
Cicero had listened fascinated when Publius Nigidius Figulus told him and Atticus (in Rome for the winter) the
details Appius Claudius had told him in confidence.

When the story was done the thought popped into
Cicero's mind; he giggled. ''Clytemnestra!'' he said.

To which the other two said not one word, though
they seemed distinctly uneasy. Nothing could be proved,
there had been no witnesses aside from Clodia. But certainly Metellus Celer had borne the same kind of wound
as King Agamemnon had after his wife, Queen Clytemnestra, had plied an axe to murder him in his bath so that
she could continue her liaison with Aegisthus.

So who spread the new nickname of Clytemnestra?
That was never established either. But from that time on
Clodia was also known as Clytemnestra, and many people
implicitly believed that she had murdered her husband in
his bath.

The sensation did not die down after Celer's funeral,
for he left a vacancy in the College of Augurs, and every
aspiring man in Rome wanted to contest the election. In
the old days when men had been co-opted into the priestly
colleges, the new augur would have been Metellus Nepos,
the dead man's brother. Nowadays, who knew? The *boni*
had very vocal supporters, but they were not in the majority. Perhaps aware of this, Nepos was heard saying that
he would probably not nominate himself, as he was so
brokenhearted he intended to travel abroad for several
years.

The squabbles over the augurship may not have attained the height of those frightful altercations heard from
the house of Celer before he died, but they enlivened the
Forum mightily. When the tribune of the plebs Publius
Vatinius announced that he would stand, Bibulus and the

Chief Augur, Messala Rufus, blocked his candidacy very simply. Vatinius had a disfiguring tumor on his forehead; he wasn't perfect.

"At least," Vatinius was heard to say loudly, though it seemed with great good humor, "my wen is where everyone can see it! Now Bibulus's wen is on his arse, though Messala Rufus goes one better—he has *two* wens where his balls used to be. I am going to move in the Plebs that all future candidates for an augurship should be required to strip naked and parade up and down the Forum."

In April the junior consul Bibulus could enjoy true possession of the *fasces* for the first time, given February's foreign affairs. He entered his month well aware that all was not going well with the execution of the *lex Iulia agraria:* the commissioners were unusually zealous and the five committeemen enormously helpful, but every organized settlement in Italy still retaining public lands was being obstructive, and sale of private lands was tardy because even knightly acquisition of land for resale to the State took time. Oh, the act was so beautifully thought out that things would sort themselves out eventually! The trouble was that Pompey needed to settle more of his veterans at once than could be done.

"They have to see action," said Bibulus to Cato, Gaius Piso, Ahenobarbus and Metellus Scipio, "but action isn't on the horizon as yet. What they need is a very large tract of public land already surveyed and apportioned out in ten-*iugera* lots by some previous land legislator who didn't live long enough to implement his law."

Cato's huge nose contracted, his eyes blazed. "They would never dare!" he said.

"Dare what?" asked Metellus Scipio.

"They will dare," Bibulus insisted.

"Dare what?"

"Bring in a second land bill to use the Ager Campanus and the Capuan public lands. Two hundred and fifty square miles of land parceled up by almost everyone since Tiberius Gracchus, ready for seizure and settlement."

"It will pass," said Gaius Piso, lips peeled away from teeth.

"I agree," said Bibulus, "it will pass."

"But we have to stop it," from Ahenobarbus.

"Yes, we have to stop it."

"How?" asked Metellus Scipio.

"I had hoped," said the junior consul, "that my ploy to make all comitial days *feriae* would answer, though I should have known that Caesar would use his authority as Pontifex Maximus. However, there is one religious ploy neither he nor the Colleges can counter. I may have exceeded my authority as a lone augur in the *feriae* business, but I will not exceed my authority as both augur and consul if I approach the problem in both roles."

They were all leaning forward eagerly. Perhaps Cato was the most publicly prominent one among them, but there could be no doubt that Bibulus's heroism in choosing to suggest a menial and very belittling proconsulship had given him the edge over Cato in all private meetings of the leaders of the *boni*. Nor did Cato resent this; Cato had no aspirations to lead.

"I intend to retire to my house to watch the skies until the end of my year as consul."

No one spoke.

"Did you hear me?" asked Bibulus, smiling.

"We heard, Marcus Bibulus," said Cato, "but will it work? How can it work?"

"It's been done before, and it's firmly established as a part of the *mos maiorum*. Besides which, I organized a secret little search of the Sacred Books, and found a prophecy which could easily be interpreted as meaning that this year the sky is going to produce an omen of extreme significance. Just what the sign is the prophecy didn't say, and that's what makes the whole ploy possible. Now when the consul retires to his house to watch the skies, all public business must be suspended until he emerges to take up his *fasces* again. Which I have no intention of doing!"

"It won't be popular," said Gaius Piso, looking worried.

"At first perhaps not, but we're all going to have to

work hard to make it look more popular than it actually will be. I intend to use Catullus—he's so good at lampooning, and now that Clodia's finished with him he can't do enough to make her or her little brother unhappy. I just wish I could get Curio again, but he won't oblige. However, we're not going to concentrate on Caesar, he's immune. We're going to set Pompeius Magnus up as our chief target, and for the rest of the year we make absolutely sure that not a day goes by without as many of our adherents in the Forum as we can marshal. Numbers don't actually mean much. Noise and numbers *in the Forum* are what count. The bulk of city and country want Caesar's laws, but they're hardly ever in the Forum unless there's a vote or a vital *contio*.''

Bibulus looked at Cato. ''You have a special job, Cato. On every possible occasion I want you to make yourself so obnoxious that Caesar loses his temper and orders you off to the Lautumiae. For some reason, he loses it more easily if it's you or Cicero doing the agitating. One must assume both of you have the ability to get under his saddle like burrs. Whenever possible we'll prearrange things so that we can have the Forum packed with people ready to support you and condemn the opposition. Pompeius is the weak link. Whatever we do has to be designed to make him feel vulnerable.''

''When do you intend to retire to your house?'' Ahenobarbus asked.

''The second day before the Ides, the only day between the Megalesia and the Ceriala, when Rome will be full of people and the Forum full of sightseers. There's no point in doing it without the biggest possible audience.''

''And do you think that all public business will cease when you retire to your house?'' asked Metellus Scipio.

Bibulus raised his brows. ''I sincerely hope not! The whole object of the ploy is to force Caesar and Vatinius to legislate in contraindication of the omens. It means that as soon as they're out of office we can invalidate their laws. Not to mention have them prosecuted for *maiestas*. Doesn't a conviction for treason sound wonderful?''

''What if Clodius becomes a tribune of the plebs?''

"I can't see how that can change anything. Clodius has—why I don't know!—conceived a dislike for Pompeius Magnus. He'll be our ally next year if he's elected, not our enemy."

"He's after Cicero too."

"Again, what is that to us? Cicero isn't *boni,* he's an ulcer. Ye gods, I'd vote for any law which could shut him up when he begins to prate about how he saved his country! Anyone would think Catilina worse than a combination of Hannibal and Mithridates."

"But if Clodius goes after Cicero he'll also go after you, Cato," said Gaius Piso.

"How can he?" Cato asked. "I merely gave my opinion in the House. I certainly wasn't the senior consul, I hadn't even gone into office as a tribune of the plebs. Free speech is becoming more perilous, but there's no law on the tablets yet forbidding a man to say what he thinks during a meeting of the Senate."

It was Ahenobarbus who thought of the major difficulty. "I see *how* we can invalidate any laws Caesar or Vatinius pass between now and the end of the year," he said, "but first we have to get the numbers in the House. That means it will have to be our men sitting in the curule chairs next year. But whom can we succeed in getting elected as consuls, not to mention *praetor urbanus*? I understand Metellus Nepos intends to leave Rome to heal his grief, so he's out. I'll be praetor, and so will Gaius Memmius, who hates Uncle Pompeius Magnus terrifically. But who for consul? Philippus sits in Caesar's lap. So does Gaius Octavius, married to Caesar's niece. Lentulus Niger wouldn't get in. Nor would Cicero's little brother Quintus. And anyone who was praetor earlier than that lot can't succeed either."

"You're right, Lucius, we have to get our own consuls in," said Bibulus, frowning. "Aulus Gabinius will run, so will Lucius Piso. Both with a foot in the Popularist camp, and both with much electoral clout. We'll just have to persuade Nepos to stay in Rome, run for augur and then for consul. And our other candidate had better be Messala Rufus. If we don't have sympathetic curule magistrates next year, we won't invalidate Caesar's laws.''

"What about Arrius, who's very annoyed with Caesar, I hear, because Caesar won't back him as a consular candidate?'' from Cato.

"Too old and not enough clout'' was the scornful reply.

"I heard something else,'' said Ahenobarbus, not pleased; no one had mentioned *his* name in connection with the augural vacancy.

"What?'' asked Gaius Piso.

"That Caesar and Magnus are thinking of asking Cicero to take Cosconius's place on the Committee of Five. Convenient that he dropped dead! Cicero would suit them better.''

"Cicero's too big a fool to accept,'' said Bibulus, sniffing.

"Not even if his darling Pompeius implores?''

"At the moment I hear Pompeius isn't his darling,'' said Gaius Piso, laughing. "He's heard who auspicated at the adoption of Publius Clodius!''

"You'd think that would tell Cicero something about his actual importance in the scheme of things,'' sneered Ahenobarbus.

"Well, there's a rumor emanating from Atticus that Cicero says Rome is sick of him!''

"He isn't wrong,'' said Bibulus, sighing theatrically.

The meeting broke up with great hilarity; the *boni* were happy.

Though Marcus Calpurnius Bibulus made his speech announcing that he was retiring to his house to watch the skies publicly from the rostra, and to a large crowd of people mostly gathered in Rome for the spring Games, Caesar chose not to reply publicly. He called the Senate into session and conducted the meeting with doors firmly closed.

"Marcus Bibulus has most correctly sent his *fasces* to the temple of Venus Libitina, and there they will reside until the Kalends of May, when I will assume them as is my right. However, this cannot be allowed to descend into one of those years wherein all public business founders. It is my duty to Rome's electors to fulfill the mandate they gave me—and Marcus Bibulus!—to *govern*. Therefore I intend to govern. The prophecy Marcus Bibulus quoted from the rostra is one I know, and I have two arguments as to Marcus Bibulus's interpretation of it: the first, that the actual year is unclear; and the second, that it can be interpreted in at least four ways. So while the *quindecim-viri sacris faciundis* examine the situation and conduct the proper enquiries, I must assume that Marcus Bibulus's action is invalid. Once again he has taken it upon himself to interpret Rome's religious *mos maiorum* to suit his own political ends. Like the Jews, we conduct our religion as a part of the State, and believe that the State cannot prosper if religious laws and customs are profaned. However, we are unique in having legal contracts with our Gods, with whom we retain bargaining power and dicker for concessions. What is important is that we keep divine forces properly channeled, and the best way to do that is to keep to our end of the bargain by doing what lies in our power to maintain Rome's prosperity and well-being. Marcus Bibulus's action accomplishes the opposite, and the Gods will not thank him. He will die away from Rome and in cold comfort.''

Oh, if only Pompey looked more at ease! After a career as long and glorious as his, you'd think he would know things don't always go smoothly! Yet there's still a lot of the spoiled baby in him. He wants everything to be perfect. He expects to get what he wants and have approval too.

''It is up to this House to decide what course I now adopt,'' the senior consul went on. ''I will call for a vote. Those who feel that all business must cease forthwith because the junior consul has retired to his house to watch the skies, please form on my left. Those who feel that, at least until the verdict of the Fifteen is in, government should continue as normal, please form on my right. I make no further plea for good sense and love of Rome. Conscript Fathers, divide the House.''

It was a calculated gamble which instinct told Caesar

he ought not to postpone; the longer the senatorial sheep pondered Bibulus's action, the more likely they were to become afraid of defying it. Strike now, and there was a chance.

But the results surprised everyone; almost the entire Senate passed to Caesar's right, an indication of the anger men felt at Bibulus's wanton determination to defeat Caesar, even at the cost of ruining Rome. The few *boni* on the left stood there stunned.

"I lodge a strong protest, Gaius Caesar!" Cato shouted as the senators returned to their places.

Pompey, mood soaring at this resounding victory for good sense and love of Rome, turned on Cato with claws out. "Sit down and shut up, you sanctimonious prig!" he roared. "Who do you think you are, to set yourself up as judge and jury? You're nothing but an ex–tribune of the plebs who'll never even make praetor!"

"Oh! Oh! Oh!" hollered Cato, staggering like a bad actor pierced by a paper dagger. "Listen to the great Pompeius, who was consul before he so much as qualified to stand as a mere tribune of the plebs! Who do you think *you* are? What, you don't even know? Then allow me to tell you! An unconstitutional, unprincipled, un-Roman lump of arrogance and fancy, that's *what* you are! As to *who*—you're a Gaul who thinks like a Gaul—a butcher who is the son of a butcher—a pander who sucks up to patricians to be let negotiate marriages far above him—a ponce who adores to dress up prettily to hear the crowd goo and gush—an eastern potentate who loves to live in palaces—a king who queens it—an orator who could send a rutting ram to sleep—a politician who has to employ competent politicians—a radical worse than the Brothers Gracchi—a general who hasn't fought a battle in twenty years without at least twice as many troops as the enemy—a general who prances in and picks up the laurels after other and better men have done all the real work—a consul who had to have a book of instructions to know how to act—AND A MAN WHO EXECUTED ROMAN CITIZENS WITHOUT TRIAL, WITNESS MARCUS JUNIUS BRUTUS!"

The House just couldn't help itself. It erupted into cheers, screeches, whistles, cries of joy; feet pounded the floor until the rafters shook, hands crashed together like drums. Only Caesar knew how hard he had to work to sit impassive, hands down at his sides and feet primly together. Oh, what a glorious diatribe! Oh, masterly! Oh, to have lived to hear it was a privilege!

Then he saw Pompey, and his heart sank. Ye gods, the foolish man was taking the hysterical applause personally! Didn't he yet understand? No one there would have cared who the target was, or what the subject of the tirade was. It was just the best piece of extemporaneous invective in years! The Senate of Rome would applaud a Tingitanian ape excoriating a donkey if it did it half that well! But there sat Pompey looking more crushed than he must have looked after Quintus Sertorius ran rings round him in Spain. Defeated! Conquered by a tongue of brass. Not until that moment did Caesar realize the extent of the insecurity and hunger to be approved of inside Pompey the Great.

Time to act. After he dismissed the meeting he stood on the curule dais as the ecstatic senators rushed away talking together excitedly, most of them clustered about Cato patting him on the back, pouring praise on his head. The worst of it was that Pompey sitting on his chair with his head down meant he, Caesar, couldn't do what he knew was the proper thing to do—congratulate Cato as warmly as if he had been a loyal political ally. Instead he had to look indifferent in case Pompey saw him.

"Did you see Crassus?" Pompey demanded when they were alone. "Did you *see* him?" His voice had risen to a squeak. "Lauding Cato to the skies! Which side is the man on?"

"Our side, Pompeius. You're too thin-skinned, my friend, if you take the House's reaction to Cato as a personal criticism. The applause was for a terrific little speech, nothing else. He is usually such a crashing bore, filibustering eternally. But that was so good of its kind."

"It was aimed at me! *Me!*"

"I wish it had been aimed at me," said Caesar, holding on to his temper. "Your mistake was not to join in the cheering. Then you could have come out of it looking a thoroughly good sport. Never show a weakness in politics, Magnus, no matter how you feel inside. He got beneath your armor, and you let everyone know it."

"You're on their team too!"

"No, Magnus, I'm not, any more than Crassus is. Let's just say that while you were out winning victories for Rome, Crassus and I were serving our apprenticeships in the political arena." He bent, put a hand beneath Pompey's elbow, and hauled him to his feet with a strength Pompey had not expected from such a slender fellow. "Come, they'll have gone."

"I can't show my face in the House ever again!"

"Rubbish. You'll be there at the next meeting looking your usual sunny self, and you'll go up to Cato and shake him by the hand and congratulate him. Just as I will."

"No, no, I can't do it!"

"Well, I won't convene the Senate for several days. By the time you need to, you'll be prepared. Come home with me now and share my dinner. Otherwise you're going to go back to that huge empty house on the Carinae with no better company than three or four philosophers. You really ought to marry again, Magnus."

"I'd quite like to, but I haven't seen anyone I fancy. It's not so urgent once a man has a brace of sons and a girl to round the family off. Besides, you're a fine one to talk! No wife in the Domus Publica either, and you don't even have a son."

"A son would be nice, but not necessary. I'm lucky in my one chick, my daughter. I wouldn't exchange her for Minerva and Venus rolled in one, and I do not mean that sacrilegiously."

"Engaged to young Caepio Brutus, isn't she?"

"Yes."

When they entered the Domus Publica his host saw Pompey put into the best chair in the study with wine at his fingertips, and excused himself to find his mother.

"We have a guest for dinner," Caesar said, poking

his head round Aurelia's door. "Pompeius. Can you and Julia join us in the dining room?"

Not a flicker of emotion crossed Aurelia's face. She nodded and got up from her desk. "Certainly, Caesar."

"Will you let us know when dinner's ready?"

"Of course," she said, and pattered away toward the stairs.

Julia was reading, and didn't hear her grandmother enter; on principle Aurelia never knocked, as she belonged to that school of parent who considered young persons ought to have some training in continuing to do the proper thing even when they thought themselves alone. It taught self-discipline and caution. The world could be a cruel place; a child was best off when prepared for it.

"No Brutus today?"

Julia looked up, smiled, sighed. "No, *avia,* not today. He has some sort of meeting with his business managers, and I believe the three of them are to dine at Servilia's afterward. She likes to know what's going on, even now she's allowed Brutus to take over his own affairs."

"Well, that will please your father."

"Oh? Why? I thought he liked Brutus."

"He likes Brutus very well, but he has his own guest to eat with us today, and they may want to converse privately. We are banished as soon as the food is taken out, but they couldn't do that to Brutus, now could they?"

"Who is it?" Julia asked, not really interested.

"I don't really know, he didn't say." Hmm, this is difficult! thought Aurelia. How do I get her into her most flattering robe without giving the plot away? She cleared her throat. "Julia, has *tata* seen you in your new birthday dress?"

"No, I don't think he has."

"Then why not put it on now? And his silver jewelry? How clever he was to get you silver rather than gold! I have no idea who's with him, but it's someone important, so he'll be pleased if we look our best."

Apparently all of that didn't sound too forced; Julia simply smiled and nodded. "How long before dinner?"

"Half an hour."

*   *   *

"What exactly does Bibulus's retiring to his house to watch the skies mean to us, Caesar?" Pompey asked. "For instance, could our laws be invalidated next year?"

"Not the ones which were ratified before today, Magnus, so you and Crassus are safe enough. It's my province will be at greatest peril, since I'll have to use Vatinius and the Plebs—though the Plebs are not religiously constrained, so I very much doubt that Bibulus's watching the skies can make plebiscites and the activities of tribunes of the plebs look sacrilegious. However, we'd have to fight it in court, and depend upon the urban praetor."

The wine, Caesar's very best (and strongest), was beginning to restore Pompey's equilibrium, even if his spirits were still low. The Domus Publica suited Caesar, he reflected, all rich dark colors and sumptuous gilt. We fair men look best against such backgrounds.

"You know of course that we'll have to legislate another land bill," Pompey said abruptly. "I'm in and out of Rome constantly, so I've seen for myself what it's like for the commissioners. We need the Ager Campanus."

"And the Capuan public lands. Yes, I know."

"But Bibulus makes it invalid."

"Perhaps not, Magnus," Caesar said tranquilly. "If I draft it as a supplementary bill attached to the original act, it's less vulnerable. The commissioners and committeemen wouldn't change, but that's not a problem. It will mean that twenty thousand of your veterans can be accommodated there well within the year, plus five thousand Roman Head Count to leaven the new settler bread. We should be able to put twenty thousand more veterans on other lands almost as quickly. Which leaves us with sufficient time to prise places like Arretium free of their lands, and puts far less pressure on the Treasury to buy private land. That's our argument for taking the Campanian *ager publicus,* the fact that it's already in State ownership."

"But the rents will cease," said Pompey.

"True. Though you and I both know that the rents

are not as lucrative as they ought to be. Senators are reluctant to pay up.''

"So are senators' wives with fortunes of their own,'' Pompey said with a grin.

"Oh?''

"Terentia. Won't pay a sestertius in rent, though she leases whole forests, oak for pigs. Very profitable. Hard as marble, that woman! Ye gods, I feel sorry for Cicero!''

"How does she get away with it?''

"Reckons there's a sacred grove in it somewhere.''

"Clever fowl!'' laughed Caesar.

"That's all right, the Treasury isn't being nice to brother Quintus now he's returning from Asia Province.''

"In what way?''

"Insists on paying him his last stipend in *cistophori*.''

"What's wrong with that? They're good silver, and worth four denarii each.''

"Provided you can get anyone to accept them,'' Pompey chuckled. "I brought back bags and bags and bags of the things, but I never intended them to be given to people in payment. You know how suspicious people are of foreign coins! I suggested the Treasury melt them down and turn them into bullion.''

"That means the Treasury doesn't like Quintus Cicero.''

"I wonder why.''

At which point Eutychus knocked to say that dinner was being served, and the two men walked the short distance to the dining room. Unless employed to accommodate a larger party, five of the couches were pushed out of the way; the remaining couch, with two chairs facing its length across a long and narrow table of knee height, sat in the prettiest part of the room, looking out at the colonnade and main peristyle.

When Caesar and Pompey entered two servants helped them remove their togas, so huge and clumsy that it was quite impossible to recline in them. These were carefully folded and put aside while the men walked to the back edge of the couch, sat upon it, took off their senatorial shoes with the consular crescent buckles, and let the same two servants wash their feet. Pompey of course occupied the *locus consularis* end of the couch, this being the place of honor. They lay half on their stomachs and half on their left hips, with the left arm and elbow supported by a round bolster. As their feet were at the back edge of the couch, their faces hovered near the table, whatever was upon it well within reach. Bowls were presented for them to wash their hands, cloths to dry them.

Pompey was feeling much better, didn't hurt the way he had. He gazed approvingly at the peristyle outside, with its fabulous frescoes of Vestal Virgins and magnificent marble pool and fountains. A pity it didn't get more sun. Then he began to track the frescoes adorning the dining room walls, which unfolded the story of the battle at Lake Regillus when Castor and Pollux saved Rome.

And just as he took in the doorway, the Goddess Diana came into the room. She had to be Diana! Goddess of the moonlit night, half not there, moving with such grace and silver beauty that she made no sound. The maiden Goddess unknown by men, who looked upon her and pined away, so chaste and indifferent was she. But this Diana, now halfway across the room, saw him staring and stumbled slightly, blue eyes widening.

"Magnus, this is my daughter, Julia." Caesar indicated the chair opposite Pompey's end of the couch. "Sit there, Julia, and keep our guest company. Ah, here's my mother!"

Aurelia seated herself opposite Caesar, while some of the servants began to bring food in, and others set down goblets, poured wine and water. The women, Pompey noted, drank water only.

How beautiful she was! How delicious, how delightful! And after that little stumble she behaved as a dream creature might, pointing out the dishes their cooks did best, suggesting that he try this or that with a smile containing no hint of shyness, but not sensuously inviting either. He ventured a question about what she did with her days (who cared about her days—what did she do with her nights when the moon rode high and her chariot took her to the stars?) and she answered that she read books or went for

walks or visited the Vestals or her friends, an answer given
in a deep soft voice like black wings against a luminous
sky. When she leaned forward he could see how tender
and delicate her chest was, though sight of her breasts
eluded him. Her arms were frail yet round, with a tiny
dimple in each elbow, and her eyes were set in skin faintly
shadowed with violet, a sheen of the moon's silver on each
eyelid. Such long, transparent lashes! And brows so fair
they could scarcely be seen. She wore no paint, and her
pale pink mouth drove him mad to kiss it, so full and
folded was it, with creases at the corners promising laughter.

        For all that either of them noticed, Caesar and Aurelia
might not have existed. They spoke of Homer and Hesiod,
Xenophon and Pindar, and of his travels in the East; she
hung on his words as if his tongue was as gifted as Cicero's, and plied him with all kinds of questions about
everything from the Albanians to the crawlies near the
Caspian Sea. Had he seen Ararat? What was the Jewish
temple like? Did people really walk on the waters of the
Palus Asphaltites? Had he ever seen a black person? What
did King Tigranes look like? Was it true that the Amazons
had once lived in Pontus at the mouth of the river Ther-
modon? Had he ever seen an Amazon? Alexander the
Great was supposed to have met their Queen somewhere
along the river Jaxartes. Oh, what wonderful names they
were, Oxus and Araxes and Jaxartes—how did human
tongues manage to invent such alien sounds?

        And terse pragmatic Pompey with his laconic style
and his scant education was profoundly glad that life in
the East and Theophanes had introduced him to reading;
he produced words he hadn't realized his mind had absorbed, and thoughts he hadn't understood he could think.
He would have died rather than disappoint this exquisite
young thing watching his face as if it was the fount of all
knowledge and the most wonderful sight she had ever beheld.

        The food stayed on the table much longer than busy
impatient Caesar usually tolerated, but as day began to
turn to night outside in the peristyle he nodded impercep-

tibly to Eutychus, and the servants reappeared. Aurelia got up.

"Julia, it's time we went," she said.

Deep in a conversation about Aeschylus, Julia jumped, came back to reality.

"Oh, *avia,* is it?" she asked. "Where did the time go?"

But, noted Pompey, neither by word nor look did she convey any impression that she was unwilling to leave, or resented her grandmother's termination of what she had told him was a special treat; when her father had guests she was not usually allowed to be in the dining room, as she was not yet eighteen.

She rose to her feet and held out her hand to Pompey in a friendly way, expecting him to shake it. But though Pompey was not prone to do such things, he took the hand as if it might fall to fragments, raised it to his lips and lightly kissed it.

"Thank you for your company, Julia," he said, smiling into her eyes. "Brutus is a very lucky fellow." And to Caesar after the women had gone, "Brutus really is a very lucky fellow."

"I think so," said Caesar, smiling at a thought of his own.

"I've never met anyone like her!"

"Julia is a pearl beyond price."

After which there didn't seem to be very much left to say. Pompey took his leave.

"Come again soon, Magnus," said Caesar at the door.

"Tomorrow if you like! I have to go to Campania the day after, and I'll be away a market interval at least. You were right. It's not a satisfactory way to live, just three or four philosophers for company. Why do you suppose we house them at all?"

"For intelligent masculine company not likely to appeal to the women of the house as lovers. And to keep our Greek pure, though I hear Lucullus was careful to pop a few grammatical solecisms in the Greek version of his memoirs to satisfy the Greek *literati* who will not believe any Roman speaks and writes perfect Greek. For myself, the habit of housing philosophers is not one I've ever been tempted to adopt. They're such parasites.''

"Rubbish! You don't house them because you're a forest cat. You prefer to live and hunt alone."

"Oh no," said Caesar softly. "I don't live alone. I am one of the most fortunate men in Rome, I live with a Julia."

Who went up to her rooms exalted and exhausted, her hand alive with the feel of his kiss. There on the shelf was the bust of Pompey; she walked across to it, took it off the shelf and dropped it into the refuse jar which lived in a corner. The statue was nothing, unneeded now she had seen and met and talked to the real man. Not as tall as *tata,* yet quite tall enough. Very broad-shouldered and muscular, and when he lay on the couch his belly stayed taut, no middle-aged spread to spoil him. A wonderful face, with the bluest eyes she had ever seen. And that hair! Pure gold, masses of it. The way it stood up from his brow in a quiff. So handsome! Not like *tata,* who was classically Roman, but more interesting because more unusual. As Julia liked small noses, she found nothing to criticize in that organ. He had nice legs too!

The next stop was her mirror, a gift from *tata* that *avia* did not approve of, for it was mounted on a pivoted stand and its highly polished silver surface reflected the viewer from head to foot. She took off all her clothes and considered herself. Too thin! Hardly any breasts! No dimples! Whereupon she burst into tears, cast herself upon her bed and wept herself to sleep, the hand he had kissed tucked against her cheek.

"She threw Pompeius's bust out," said Aurelia to Caesar the next morning.

"*Edepol!* I really thought she liked him."

"Nonsense, Caesar, it's an excellent sign! She is no longer satisfied with a replica, she wants the real man."

"You relieve me." Caesar picked up his beaker of hot water and lemon juice, sipped it with what looked like enjoyment. "He's coming to dinner again today, used a trip to Campania tomorrow as an excuse for coming back so soon.''

"Today will complete the conquest," said Aurelia.

Caesar grinned. "I think the conquest was complete the moment she walked into the dining room. I've known Pompeius for years, and he's hooked so thoroughly he hasn't even felt the barb. Don't you remember the day he arrived at Aunt Julia's to claim Mucia?''

"Yes, I do. Vividly. Reeking of attar of roses and as silly as a foal in a field. He wasn't at all like that yesterday.''

"He's grown up a bit. Mucia was older than he. The attraction isn't the same. Julia is seventeen, he's now forty-six." Caesar shuddered. "Mater, that's nearly thirty years' difference in ages! Am I being too coldblooded? I wouldn't have her unhappy.''

"She won't be. Pompeius seems to have the knack of pleasing his wives as long as he remains in love with them. He'll never fall out of love with Julia, she's his vanished youth." Aurelia cleared her throat, went a little red. "I am sure you are a splendid lover, Caesar, but living with a woman not of your own family bores you. Pompeius enjoys married life—provided the woman is suitable for his ambitions. He can look no higher than a Julia.''

He didn't seem to want to look any higher than a Julia. If anything saved Pompey's reputation after Cato's attack, it was the daze Julia induced in him as he went round the Forum that morning, having quite forgotten that he had resolved never to appear in public again. As it was, he drifted here and there to talk to anyone who appeared, and was so transparently unconcerned about the Cato diatribe that many decided yesterday's reaction had been pure shock. Today there was no resentment and no embarrassment.

She filled the inside of his eyes; her image transposed itself on every face he looked at. Child and woman all at one. Goddess too. So feminine, so beautifully mannered, so unaffected! Had she liked him? She seemed to, yet nothing in her behavior could he interpret as a signal, a lure. But she was betrothed. To *Brutus*. Not only callow, but downright ugly. How could a creature so pure and untainted bear all those disgusting pimples? Of course they'd been contracted for years, so the match wasn't of her asking. In social and political terms it was an excellent union. There were also the fruits of the Gold of Tolosa.

And after dinner in the Domus Publica that afternoon it was on the tip of Pompey's tongue to ask for her, Brutus notwithstanding. What held him back? That old dread of lowering himself in the eyes of a nobleman as patrician as Gaius Julius Caesar. Who could give his daughter to anyone in Rome. Had given her to an aristocrat of clout and wealth and ancestry. Men like Caesar didn't stop to think how the girl might feel, or consider her wishes. Any more, he supposed, than he did himself. His own daughter was promised to Faustus Sulla for one reason only: Faustus Sulla was the product of a union between a patrician Cornelius Sulla—the greatest ever of his family—and the granddaughter of Metellus Calvus the Bald, daughter of Metellus Dalmaticus—who had first been wife to Scaurus Princeps Senatus.

No, Caesar would have no wish to break off a legal contract with a Junius Brutus adopted into the Servilii Caepiones in order to give his only child to a Pompeius from Picenum! Dying to ask, Pompey would never ask. So oceans deep in love and unable to banish this goddess from the forefront of his mind, Pompey went off to Campania on land committee business and accomplished almost nothing. He burned for her; he wanted her as he had never wanted in his life before. And went back to the Domus Publica for yet another dinner the day after he returned to Rome.

Yes, she *was* glad to see him! By this third meeting they had reached a stage whereat she held out her hand expecting him to kiss it lightly, and plunged immediately into a conversation which excluded Caesar and his mother, left to avoid each other's eyes in case they fell about laughing. The meal proceeded to its end.

''When do you marry Brutus?'' Pompey asked her then, low-voiced.

''In January or February of next year. Brutus wanted

to marry this year, but *tata* said no. I must be eighteen.''

''And when are you eighteen?''

''On the Nones of January.''

''It's the beginning of May, so that's eight months off.''

Her face changed, a look of distress crept into her eyes. Yet she answered with absolute composure. ''Not very long.''

''Do you love Brutus?''

That question provoked a tiny inward panic, it reflected itself in her gaze, for she would not—could not?—look away. ''He and I have been friends since I was little. I will learn to love him.''

''What if you fall in love with someone else?''

She blinked away what looked suspiciously like moisture. ''I can't let that happen, Gnaeus Pompeius.''

''Don't you think it might happen in spite of resolutions?''

''Yes, I think it might,'' she said gravely.

''What would you do then?''

''Endeavor to forget.''

He smiled. ''That seems a shame.''

''It would not be honorable, Gnaeus Pompeius, so I would have to forget. If love can grow, it can also die.''

He looked very sad. ''I've seen a lot of death in my time, Julia. Battlefields, my mother, my poor father, my first wife. But it's never something I can view with dispassion. At least,'' he added honestly, ''not from where I stand now. I'd hate to see anything that grew in you have to die.''

The tears were too close, she would have to leave. ''Will you excuse me, *tata*?'' she asked of her father.

''Are you feeling well, Julia?'' Caesar asked.

''A little headache, that's all.''

''I think you must excuse me as well, Caesar,'' said Aurelia, rising. ''If she has a headache, she'll need some syrup of poppies.''

Which left Caesar and Pompey alone. An inclination of the head, and Eutychus supervised the clearing away of the dishes. Caesar poured Pompey unwatered wine.

"You and Julia get on well together," he said.

"It would be a stupid man who didn't get on well with her," Pompey said gruffly. "She's unique."

"I like her too." Caesar smiled. "In all her little life she's never caused a trouble, never given me an argument, never committed a *peccatum*."

"She doesn't love that awkward, shambling fellow Brutus."

"I am aware of it," Caesar said tranquilly.

"Then how can you let her marry him?" Pompey demanded, irate.

"How can you let Pompeia marry Faustus Sulla?"

"That's different."

"In what way?"

"Pompeia and Faustus Sulla are in love!"

"Were they not, would you break the engagement off?"

"Of course not!"

"Then there you are." Caesar refilled the goblet.

"Still," Pompey said after a pause, gazing into the rosy depths of his wine, "it seems a special shame with Julia. My Pompeia is a lusty, strapping girl, always roaring round the house. She'll be able to look after herself. Whereas Julia's so frail."

"An illusion," said Caesar. "Julia's actually very strong."

"Oh yes, that she is. But every bruise will show."

Startled, Caesar turned his head to look into Pompey's eyes. "That was a very perceptive remark, Magnus. It's out of character."

"Maybe I just see her more clearly than I do other people."

"Why should you do that?"

"Oh, I don't know. . . ."

"Are you in love with her, Magnus?"

Pompey looked away. "What man wouldn't be?" he muttered.

"Would you like to marry her?"

The stem of the goblet, solid silver, snapped; wine went on the table and floor, but Pompey never even noticed. He shuddered, threw the bowl of the vessel down. "I would give everything I am and have to marry her!"

"Well then," Caesar said placidly, "I had better get moving."

Two enormous eyes fixed themselves on Caesar's face; Pompey drew a deep breath. "You mean you'd give her to *me*?"

"It would be an honor."

"Oh!" gasped Pompey, flung himself backward on the couch and nearly fell off it. "Oh, Caesar!—whatever you want, whenever you want it—I'll take care of her, you'll never regret it, she'll be better treated than the Queen of Egypt!"

"I sincerely hope so!" said Caesar, laughing. "One hears that the Queen of Egypt has been supplanted by her husband's half sister from an Idumaean concubine."

But all and any answers were wasted on Pompey, who continued to lie gazing ecstatically at the ceiling. Then he rolled over. "May I see her?" he asked.

"I think not, Magnus. Go home like a good fellow and leave me to disentangle the threads this day has woven. The Servilius Caepio cum Junius Silanus household will be in an uproar."

"I'll pay her dowry to Brutus," Pompey said instantly.

"You will not," said Caesar, holding out his hand. "Get up, man, get up!" He grinned. "I confess I never thought to have a son-in-law six years older than I am!"

"Am I too old for her? I mean, in ten years' time—"

"Women," said Caesar as he guided Pompey in the direction of the door, "are very strange, Magnus. I have often noticed that they don't seem prone to look elsewhere if they're happy at home."

"Mucia, you're hinting."

"You left her alone for so long, that was the trouble. Don't do it to my daughter, who wouldn't betray you if you stayed away for twenty years, but would definitely not thrive."

"My military days are done," said Pompey. He

stopped, wet his lips nervously. "When can we marry? She said you wouldn't let her marry Brutus until she turned eighteen."

"What's suitable for Brutus and suitable for Pompeius Magnus are two different things. May is unlucky for weddings, but if it's within the next three days the omens aren't too bad. Two days hence, then."

"I'll come round tomorrow."

"You won't come round again until the wedding day—and don't chatter about it to anyone, even your philosophers," said Caesar, shutting the door firmly in Pompey's face.

"Mater! Mater!" the prospective father-in-law shouted from the bottom of the front stairs.

Down came his mother at a clip not appropriate for a respected Roman matron of her years. *"Is it?"* she asked, hands clasped about his right forearm, her eyes shining.

"It is. We've done it, Mater, we've done it! He's gone home somewhere up in the *aether,* and looking like a schoolboy."

"Oh, Caesar! He's yours now no matter what!"

"And that is no exaggeration. How about Julia?"

"She'll leave us for the moon when she knows. I've been upstairs listening patiently to a weepy jumble of apologies for falling in love with Pompeius Magnus and protests at having to marry a dreary bore like Brutus. It all came out because Pompeius pressed his suit over dinner." Aurelia sighed through the midst of a huge smile. "How lovely, my son! We've succeeded in getting what we want, yet we've also made two other people extremely happy. A good day's work!"

"A better day's work than tomorrow will bring."

Aurelia's face fell. "Servilia."

"I was going to say, Brutus."

"Oh yes, poor young man! But it isn't Brutus who'll plunge the dagger in. I'd watch Servilia."

Eutychus coughed delicately, slyly concealing his pleasure; trust the senior servants of a household to know which way the wind blew!

"What is it?" Caesar asked.

"Gnaeus Pompeius Magnus is at the outside door, Caesar, but he refuses to come in. He said he'd like a quick word with you."

"I've had a brilliant idea!" cried Pompey, feverishly wringing Caesar's hand.

"No more visits today, Magnus, please! What idea?"

"Tell Brutus I'd be delighted to give him Pompeia in exchange for Julia. I'll dower her with whatever he asks—five hundred, a thousand—makes no difference to me. More important to keep him happy than oblige Faustus Sulla, eh?"

By an Herculean effort Caesar kept his face straight. "Why, thank you, Magnus. I'll relay the offer, but don't do anything rash. Brutus mightn't feel like marrying anyone for a while."

Off went Pompey for the second time, waving cheerfully.

"What was all that about?" asked Aurelia.

"He wants to give Brutus his own daughter in exchange for Julia. Faustus Sulla can't compete with the Gold of Tolosa, it seems. Still, it's good to see Magnus back in character. I was beginning to wonder at his newfound sensitivity and perception."

"You surely won't mention his offer to Brutus and Servilia?"

"I'll have to. But at least I have time to compose a tactful reply to deliver to my future son-in-law. Mind you, it's as well he lives on the Carinae. Any closer to the Palatine and he'd hear what Servilia said for himself."

"When is the wedding to be? May and June are so unlucky!"

"Two days from now. Make offerings, Mater. So will I. I'd rather it was an accomplished thing before Rome gets to know." He bent to kiss his mother's cheek. "Now, if you'll excuse me, I must be off to see Marcus Crassus."

As she knew perfectly well why he was seeking Crassus without needing to ask, Caesar's mother went off to swear Eutychus to silence and plan the wedding feast. What a pity secrecy meant no guests. Still, Cardixa and

Burgundus could act as witnesses, and the Vestal Virgins help the Pontifex Maximus officiate.

"Burning the midnight oil as usual?" Caesar asked.

Crassus jumped, splattering ink across his neat rows of *M*s, *C*s, *L*s and *X*s. "Will you *please* stop picking the lock on my door?"

"You don't leave me an alternative, though if you like I'll rig up a bell and cord for you. I'm quite deedy at that sort of thing," said Caesar, strolling up the room.

"I wish you would, it costs money to repair locks."

"Consider it done. I'll be round with a hammer, a bell, some cord and staples tomorrow. You can boast that you have the only Pontifex Maximus–installed bell in Rome." Caesar pulled a chair around and sat down with a sigh of sheer content.

"You look like the cat that snatched the dinner quail for his own dinner, Gaius."

"Oh, I snatched more than a quail. I made off with a whole peacock."

"I'm consumed with curiosity."

"Will you lend me two hundred talents, payable as soon as I make my province payable?"

"Now you're being sensible! Yes, of course."

"Don't you want to know why?"

"I told you, I'm consumed with curiosity."

Suddenly Caesar frowned. "Actually you mightn't approve."

"If I don't, I'll tell you. But I can't until I know."

"I need one hundred talents to pay Brutus for breaking his engagement to Julia, and another hundred talents to give Magnus as Julia's dowry."

Crassus put his pen down slowly and precisely, no expression on his face. The shrewd grey eyes looked sideways at a lamp flame, then turned to rest on Caesar's face. "I have always believed," the plutocrat said, "that one's children are an investment only fully realized if they can bring their father what he cannot have otherwise. I am sorry for you, Gaius, because I know you would prefer that Julia marry someone of better blood. But I applaud

your courage and your foresight. Little though I like the
man, Pompeius is necessary for both of us. If I had a
daughter, I might have done the same thing. Brutus is a
little too young to serve your ends, nor will his mother let
him fulfill his potential. If Pompeius is married to your
Julia, we can have no doubt of him, no matter how the
boni prey upon his nerves.'' Crassus grunted. ''She is,
besides, a treasure. She'll make the Great Man idyllically
happy. In fact, were I younger, I'd envy him.''

''Tertulla would murder you,'' Caesar chuckled. He
looked at Crassus inquisitively. ''What of your sons? Have
you decided who will have them yet?''

''Publius is going to Metellus Scipio's daughter, Cornelia Metella, so he has to wait a few more years. Not a
bad little thing considering *tata*'s stupidity. Scipio's
mother was Crassus Orator's elder daughter, so it's very
suitable. As for Marcus, I've been thinking of Metellus
Creticus's daughter.''

''A foot in the camp of the *boni* is a foot well
placed,'' said Caesar sententiously.

''So I believe. I'm getting too old for all this fighting.''

''Keep the wedding to yourself, Marcus,'' said Caesar, rising.

''On one condition.''

''Which is?''

''That I'm there when Cato finds out.''

''A pity we won't see Bibulus's face.''

''No, but we could always send him a flask of hem-
lock. He's going to feel quite suicidal.''

Having very correctly sent a message ahead to make
sure he was expected, Caesar walked early the next morning up to the Palatine to the house of the late Decimus
Junius Silanus.

''An unusual pleasure, Caesar,'' purred Servilia, inclining her cheek to receive a kiss.

Watching this, Brutus said nothing, did not smile.
Since the day after Bibulus had retired to his house to
watch the skies, Brutus had sensed something wrong. For

one thing, he had succeeded in seeing Julia only twice between then and now, and on each occasion she hadn't really been there at all. For another, he was used to dining at the Domus Publica regularly several times in a market interval, yet of late when he had suggested it, he had been put off on the excuse of important confidential dinner guests. And Julia had looked radiant, so beautiful, so aloof; not exactly uninterested, more as if her interest lay elsewhere, a region inside her mind she had never opened to him. Oh, she had pretended to listen! Yet she hadn't heard a single word, just gazed into space with a sweet and secret half smile. Nor would she let him kiss her. On the first visit, it had been a headache. On the second, she hadn't felt like a kiss. Caring and apologetic, but no kiss was no kiss. Had he not known better, he would have thought someone else was kissing her.

Now here was her father on a formal embassage, heralded by a messenger, and clad in the regalia of the Pontifex Maximus. Had he ruined things by asking to marry Julia a year earlier than arranged? Oh, why did he feel this was all to do with Julia? And why didn't he look like Caesar? No flaw in that face. No flaw in that body. If there had been, Mama would have lost interest in Caesar long ago.

The Pontifex Maximus didn't sit down, but nor did he pace, or seem discomposed.

"Brutus," he said, "I know of no way to give bad news that can soften the blow, so I'll be blunt. I'm breaking your contract of betrothal to Julia." A slender scroll was placed on the table. "This is a draft on my bankers for the sum of one hundred talents, in accordance with the agreement. I am very sorry."

Shock sent Brutus sagging into a chair, where he sat with his poor mouth agape on no word of protest, his large and haunting eyes fixed on Caesar's face with the same expression in them an old dog has when it realizes that its beloved master is going to have it killed because it is no longer useful. His mouth closed, worked upon speech, but no word emerged. Then the light in his eyes went out as clearly and quickly as a snuffed candle.

"I am very sorry," Caesar said again, more emotionally.

Shock had brought Servilia to her feet, nor for long moments could she find speech either. Her eyes went to Brutus in time to witness the dying of his light, but she had no idea what was really happening to him, for she was as far from Brutus in temperament as Antioch was from Olisippo.

Thus it was Caesar felt Brutus's pain, not Servilia. Never conquered by a woman as Julia had conquered Brutus, he could yet understand exactly what Julia had meant to Brutus, and he found himself wondering whether if he had known he would have had the courage to kill like this. But yes, Caesar, you would have. You've killed before and you'll kill again. Yet rarely eye to eye, as now. The poor, poor fellow! He won't recover. He first wanted my daughter when he was fourteen years old, and he has never changed or wavered. I have killed him—or at least killed what his mother has left alive. How awful to be the rag doll between two savages like Servilia and me. Silanus also, but not as terribly as Brutus. Yes, we've killed him. From now on he's one of the *lemures*.

"*Why?*" rasped Servilia, beginning to pant.

"I'm afraid I need Julia to form another alliance."

"A better alliance than a Caepio Brutus? There's isn't one!"

"Not in terms of eligibility, that's true. Nor in terms of niceness, tenderness, honor, integrity. It's been a privilege to have your son in my family for so many years. But the fact remains that I need Julia to form another alliance."

"Do you mean you'd sacrifice *my* son to feather your own political nest, Caesar?" she asked, teeth bared.

"Yes. Just as you'd sacrifice my daughter to serve your ends, Servilia. We produce children to inherit the fame and enhancement we bring the family, and the price our children pay is to be there to serve our needs and the needs of our families. They never know want. They never know hardship. They never lack literacy and numeracy. But it is a foolish parent who does not bring a child up to understand the price for high birth, ease, wealth and education. The Head Count can love and spoil their children freely. But our children are the servants of the family, and in their turn they will expect from their children what we expect from them. The family is perpetual. We and our children are but a small part of it. Romans create their own Gods, Servilia, and all the truly Roman Gods are Gods of the family. Hearth, storage cupboards, the household, ancestors, parents and children. My daughter understands her function as a part of the Julian family. Just as I did.''

''I refuse to believe there's anyone in Rome could offer you more politically than Brutus!''

''That might be true ten years from now. In twenty years, definitely. But I need additional political clout at this very moment. If Brutus's father were alive, things would be different. But the head of your family is twenty-four years old, and that applies to Servilius Caepio as much as to Junius Brutus. I need the help of a man in my own age group.''

Brutus hadn't moved, nor closed his eyes, nor wept. He even heard all the words exchanged between Caesar and his mother, though he didn't actually feel them. They were just there, and they meant things he understood. He would remember them. Only why wasn't his mother angrier?

In fact Servilia was furiously angry, but time had taught her that Caesar could best her in every encounter if she pitted herself directly against him. After all, nothing he could say could make her angrier. Be controlled, be ready to find the chink, be ready to slip inside and strike.

''Which man?'' she asked, chin up, eyes watchful.

Caesar, there's something wrong with you. You're actually enjoying this. Or you would be if it were not for that poor broken young man over there. In the amount of time it will take you to speak the name, you will see a better sight than the day you told her you wouldn't marry her. Blighted love can't kill Servilia. But the insult I'm going to offer her just might. . . .

''Gnaeus Pompeius Magnus,'' he said.

"Who?"

"You heard me."

"You wouldn't!" Her head shook. "You wouldn't!" Her eyes protruded. "You wouldn't!" Her legs gave way, she tottered to a chair as far from Brutus as she could get. "You wouldn't!"

"Why not?" he asked coolly. "Tell me a better political ally than Magnus, and I'll break the engagement between him and Julia just as readily as I've broken this one."

"He's an—an—an upstart! A nobody! An ignoramus!"

"As to the first, I agree with you. As to the second and third descriptions, I can't. Magnus is far from a nobody. He's the First Man in Rome. Nor is he an ignoramus. Whether we like it or not, Servilia, Kid Butcher from Picenum has carved a wider path through Rome's forest than Sulla managed to. His wealth is astronomical, and his power greater. We should thank our luck that he'd never go as far as Sulla because he doesn't dare. All he really wants is to be accepted as one of us."

"He'll *never* be one of us!" she cried, fists clenched.

"Marrying a Julia is a step in the right direction."

"You ought to be flogged, Caesar! There's thirty years of age between them—he's an old man and she's hardly a woman yet!"

"Oh, shut up!" he said wearily. "I can tolerate you in most of your moods, *domina,* but not in righteous indignation. Here."

He tossed a small object into her lap, then walked over to Brutus. "I really am very sorry, lad," he said, gently touching the still-hunched shoulder. Brutus didn't shrug him off; his eyes lifted to Caesar's face, but the light was gone.

Ought he to say what he had fully intended to say, that Julia was in love with Pompeius? No. That would be too cruel. There wasn't enough of Servilia in him to make it worth the pain. Then he thought of saying Brutus would find someone else. But no.

There was a swirl of scarlet and purple; the door closed behind the Pontifex Maximus.

The thing in Servilia's lap was a large strawberry-pink pebble. In the act of pitching it through the open window into the garden, she saw the light catch it alluringly, and stopped. No, not a pebble. Its plump heart shape was not unlike the strawberry of its color, but it was luminous, brilliant, sheened as subtly as a pearl. *A pearl?* Yes, a pearl! The thing Caesar had tossed in her lap was a pearl as big as the biggest strawberry in any Campanian glade, a wonder of the world.

Servilia liked jewelry very much, loved ocean pearls most of all. Her rage trickled away as if the rich pink-red pearl sucked it up and fed on it. How sensational it felt! Smooth, cool, voluptuous.

A sound intruded; Servilia looked up. Brutus had fallen to the floor, unconscious.

After a semisenseless and wandering Brutus was put into his bed and briskly dosed with a soporific herbal potion, Servilia put on a cloak and went to visit Fabricius the pearl merchant in the Porticus Margaritaria. Who remembered the pearl well, knew exactly where it had come from, secretly marveled at a man who could give this beauty away to a woman neither outstandingly lovely nor even young. He valued it at six million sesterces, and agreed to set it for her in a cage of finest gold wire attached to a heavy gold chain. Neither Fabricius nor Servilia wanted to pierce the dimple at its top; a wonder of the world should be unmarred.

From the Porticus Margaritaria it was only a step or two to the Domus Publica, where Servilia asked to see Aurelia.

"Of course you're on his side!" she said aggressively to Caesar's mother.

Aurelia's finely feathered black brows rose, which made her look very much like her son. "Naturally," she said calmly.

"*But Pompeius Magnus?* Caesar's a traitor to his own class!"

"Come now, Servilia, you know Caesar better than

that! Caesar will cut his losses, not cut off his nose to spite his face. He does what he wants to do because what he wants to do is what he ought to do. If custom and tradition suffer, too bad. He needs Pompeius, you're politically acute enough to see that. And politically acute enough to see how perilous it would be to depend on Pompeius without tethering him by an anchor so firm no storm can pry him loose." Aurelia grimaced. "Breaking the engagement cost Caesar dearly, from what he said when he came home after telling Brutus. Your son's plight moved him deeply."

It hadn't occurred to Servilia to think of Brutus's plight because she viewed him as a mortally insulted possession, not as a person. She loved Brutus as much as she loved Caesar, but she saw her son inside her own skin, assumed he felt what she felt, yet could never work out why his behavior over the years was not her behavior. Fancy falling over in a fainting fit!

"Poor Julia!" she said, mind on her pearl.

That provoked a laugh from Julia's grandmother. "Poor Julia, nothing! She's absolutely ecstatic."

The blood drained from Servilia's face, the pearl vanished. "You surely don't mean—?"

"What, didn't Caesar tell you? He must have felt sorry for Brutus! It's a love match, Servilia."

"It can't be!"

"I assure you it is. Julia and Pompeius are in love."

"But she loves Brutus!"

"No, she never loved Brutus, that's the tragedy of it for him. She was marrying him because her father said she must. Because we all wanted it, and she's a dear, obedient child."

"She's searching for her father," Servilia said flatly.

"Perhaps so."

"But Pompeius isn't Caesar in any way. She'll rue it."

"I believe she'll be very happy. She understands that Pompeius is very different from Caesar, but the similarities are also there. They're both soldiers, both brave, both heroic. Julia has never been particularly conscious of her status, she doesn't worship the Patriciate. What you would find utterly repugnant in Pompeius will not dismay Julia in the least. I imagine she'll refine him a little, but she's actually well satisfied with him the way he is.''

''I'm disappointed in her,'' Servilia muttered.

''Then be glad for Brutus, that he's free.'' Aurelia got up because Eutychus himself brought the sweet wine and little cakes. ''Fluid finds its own level, don't you think?'' she asked, pouring wine and water into precious vessels. ''If Pompeius pleases Julia—and he does!—then Brutus would not have pleased her. And that is no slur upon Brutus. Look on the business positively, Servilia, and persuade Brutus to do the same. He'll find someone else.''

The marriage between Pompey the Great and Caesar's daughter took place the next day in the temple atrium of the Domus Publica. Because it was an unlucky time for weddings Caesar offered for his daughter everywhere he could think might help her, while his mother had gone the rounds of female deities making offerings too. Though it had long gone out of fashion to marry *confarreatio,* even among patricians, when Caesar suggested to Pompey that this union be *confarreatio,* Pompey agreed eagerly.

''I don't insist, Magnus, but I would like it.''

''Oh, so would I! This is the last time for me, Caesar.''

''I hope so. Divorce from a *confarreatio* marriage is well-nigh impossible.''

''There won't be any divorce,'' Pompey said confidently.

Julia wore the wedding clothes her grandmother had woven herself for her own wedding forty-six years before, and thought them finer and softer than anything to be bought in the Street of the Weavers. Her hair—thick, fine, straight and so long she could sit on it—was divided into six locks and pinned up beneath a tiara identical to those worn by the Vestal Virgins, of seven rolled woolen sausages. The gown was saffron, the shoes and fine veil of vivid flame.

Both bride and groom had to produce ten witnesses, a difficulty when the ceremony was supposed to be secret.

Pompey solved his dilemma by enlisting ten Picentine clients visiting the city, and Caesar by drafting Cardixa, Burgundus, Eutychus (all Roman citizens for many years), and
the six Vestal Virgins. Because the rite was *confarreatio*
a special seat had to be made by joining two separate
chairs and covering them with a sheepskin; both the *flamen
Dialis* and the Pontifex Maximus had to be present, not a
trouble because Caesar was Pontifex Maximus and had
been *flamen Dialis* (none other could exist until after his
death). Aurelia, who was Caesar's tenth witness, acted as
the *pronuba,* the matron of honor.

When Pompey arrived dressed in his gold-
embroidered purple triumphal toga, the palm-embroidered
triumphal tunic beneath it, the little group sighed
sentimentally and escorted him to the sheepskin seat,
where Julia already sat, face hidden by her veil. Ensconced
beside her, Pompey suffered the folds of an enormous
flame-colored veil now draped by Caesar and Aurelia
across both their heads; Aurelia took their right hands and
bound them together with a flame-colored leather strap,
which was the actual joining. From that moment they were
married. But one of the sacred cakes made from spelt had
to be broken, eaten half by bride and half by groom, while
the witnesses solemnly testified that all was in order, they
were now man and wife.

After which Caesar sacrificed a pig on the altar and
dedicated all of its succulent parts to Jupiter Farreus, who
was that aspect of Jupiter responsible for the fruitful
growth of the oldest wheat, emmer, and thereby, since the
marriage cake of spelt had been made from emmer, also
that aspect of Jupiter responsible for fruitful marriages. To
offer all of the beast would please the God, take away the
bad luck of marrying in May. Never had priest or father
worked as hard as Caesar did to dispel the omens of marriage in May.

The feast was merry, the little group of guests happy
because the happiness of bride and groom was so obvious;
Pompey beamed, wouldn't let his Julia's hand go. Then
they walked from the Domus Publica to Pompey's vast
and dazzling house on the Carinae, Pompey hurrying

ahead to make all ready while three small boys escorted Julia and the wedding guests. And there was Pompey waiting on the threshold to carry his new wife across it; inside were the pans of fire and water to which he led her, watched as she passed her right hand through the flames, then through the water, and was unharmed. She was now the mistress of the house, commander of its fire and water. Aurelia and Cardixa, each married only once, took her to the bedchamber, undressed her and put her into the bed.

After the two old women left, the room was very quiet; Julia sat up in the bed and linked her hands around her knees, a curtain of hair falling forward to hide either side of her face. This was no sleeping cubicle! It was bigger than the Domus Publica dining room. And so very grand! Hardly a surface was untouched by gilt, the color scheme was red and black, the wall paintings a series of panels depicting various Gods and heroes in sexual mode. There was Hercules (who needed to be strong to carry the weight of his erect penis) with Queen Omphale; Theseus with Queen Hippolyta of the Amazons (though she had two breasts); Peleus with the sea goddess Thetis (he was making love to a female bottom half topped by a cuttle-fish); Zeus assaulting a distressed-looking cow (Io); Venus and Mars colliding like warships; Apollo about to enter a tree with a knot resembling female parts (Daphne?).

Aurelia was too strict to have permitted such pictorial activity in her house, but Julia, a young woman of Rome, was neither unfamiliar with nor dismayed by this erotic decor. In some of the houses she visited, erotica was by no means limited to bedrooms. As a child it used to make her giggle, then later it became quite impossible to relate in any way to her and Brutus; being virgin, such art interested and intrigued her without having genuine reality.

Pompey entered the room in *tunica palmata,* his feet bare.

"How are you?" he asked anxiously, approaching the bed as warily as a dog a cat.

"Very well," Julia said gravely.

"Um—is everything all right?"

"Oh, yes. I was just admiring the pictures."

He blushed, waved his hands about. "Didn't have time to do anything about it. Sorry," he muttered.

"I don't honestly mind."

"Mucia liked them." He sat down on his side of the bed.

"Do you have to redecorate your bedroom every time you change wives?" she asked, smiling.

That seemed to reassure him, for he smiled back. "It's wise. Women like to put their own touch on things."

"So shall I." She reached out her hand. "Don't be nervous, Gnaeus—do I call you Gnaeus?"

The hand was clasped tightly. "I like Magnus better."

Her fingers moved in his. "I like it too." She turned a little toward him. "Why are you nervous?"

"Because everyone else was just a woman," he said, pushing the other hand through his hair. "You're a goddess."

To which she made no reply, too filled with first awareness of power; she had just married a very great and famous Roman, and he was afraid of her. That was very reassuring. And very nice. Anticipation began to work in her deliciously, so she lay back upon the pillows and did nothing more than look at him.

Which meant he had to do *something*. Oh, this was so important! Caesar's daughter, directly descended from Venus. How had King Anchises managed when Love manifested herself before him and said she pleased her? Had he trembled like a leaf too? Had he wondered if he was up to the task? But then he remembered Diana walking into the room, and forgot about Venus. Still trembling, he leaned over and pulled the tapestry cover back, the linen sheet below it. And looked at her, white as marble faintly veined with blue, slender limbs and hips, little waist. How beautiful!

"I love you, Magnus," she said in that husky voice he found so attractive, "but I'm too thin! I'll disappoint you."

"Disappoint?" Pompey stared now at her face, his own terror of disappointing her vanishing. So vulnerable.

So young! Well, she would see the quality of his disappointment.

The outside of one thigh was nearest; he put his lips to it, felt her skin leap and shudder, the touch of her hand in his hair. Eyes closed, he laid his cheek against her flank and inched himself fully onto the bed. A goddess, a goddess . . . He would kiss every bit of her with reverence, with a delight almost unbearable, this unstained flower, this perfect jewel. The silver tresses were everywhere, hiding her breasts. Tendril by tendril he picked them off, lay them down around her and gazed, ravished, at smooth little nipples so pale a pink that they fused into her skin.

"Oh, Julia, Julia, I love you!" he cried. "My goddess, Diana of the moon, Diana of the night!"

Time enough to deal with virginity. Today she should know nothing save pleasure. Yes, pleasure first, all the pleasure he could give her from lips and mouth and tongue, from hands and his own skin. Let her know what marriage to Pompey the Great would always bring her, pleasure and pleasure and pleasure.

"We have passed a milestone," said Cato to Bibulus that night in the peristyle garden of Bibulus's house, where the junior consul sat gazing at the sky. "Not only have they divided up Campania and Italia like eastern potentates, now they seal their unholy bonds with virgin daughters."

"Shooting star, left lower quadrant!" rapped Bibulus to the scribe who sat some distance away, patiently waiting to write down the stellar phenomena his master saw, the light of his tiny lamp focused on his wax tablet. Then Bibulus rose, said the prayers which concluded a session of watching the skies, and led Cato inside.

"Why are you surprised that Caesar should sell his daughter?" he asked, not bothering to ascertain of one of the hardest drinkers in Rome whether he wanted water in his wine. "I had wondered how he'd manage to bind Pompeius. I knew he would! But this is the best and cleverest way. One hears she's absolutely exquisite."

"You've not seen her either?"

"No one has, though no doubt that will change. Pompeius will parade her like a prize ewe. What is she, all of sixteen?"

"Seventeen."

"Servilia can't have been pleased."

"Oh, he dealt with her very cleverly too," said Cato, getting up to replenish his goblet. "He gave her a pearl worth six million sesterces—and paid Brutus the girl's hundred-talent dowry."

"Where did you hear all this?"

"From Brutus when he came to see me today. At least that's one good turn Caesar has done the *boni*. From now on we have Brutus firmly in our camp. He's even announcing that in future he'll not be known as Caepio Brutus, simply as Brutus."

"Brutus won't be nearly as much use to us as a marital alliance will be to Caesar," Bibulus said grimly.

"For the moment, no. But I have hopes for Brutus now he's worked free of his mother. The pity of it is that he won't hear a word against the girl. I offered him my Porcia once she's of an age to marry, but he declined. Says he's never going to marry." Down went the rest of his wine; Cato swung about, hands clenched around the goblet. "Marcus, I could vomit! This is the most coldblooded, loathsome piece of political maneuvering I've ever heard of! Ever since Brutus came to see me I've been trying to keep a level head, trying to talk in a rational manner—I can't one moment longer! Nothing we've ever done equals this! And it will work for Caesar, that's the worst of it!"

"Sit down, Cato, please! I've already said it will work for Caesar. *Be calm!* We won't beat him by ranting, or by showing our disgust at this marriage. Continue as you started, rationally."

Cato did sit down, but not before he poured himself more wine. Bibulus frowned. Why *did* Cato drink so much? Not that it ever seemed to impair him; perhaps it was his way to maintain strength.

"Do you remember Lucius Vettius?" Bibulus asked.

"The knight Caesar had beaten with the rods, then gave away his furniture to scum?"

"The very one. He came to see me yesterday."

"And?"

"He loathes Caesar," Bibulus said contemplatively.

"I'm not surprised. The incident made him a laughingstock."

"He offered me his services."

"That doesn't surprise me either. But how can you use him?"

"To drive a wedge between Caesar and his new son-in-law."

Cato stared. "Impossible."

"I agree the marriage makes it harder, but it's not impossible. Pompeius is so suspicious of everybody, including Caesar. Julia notwithstanding," said Bibulus. "After all, the girl is far too young to be dangerous in herself. She'll tire the Great Man out, between her physical demands and the tantrums immature females can never resist throwing. Particularly if we can encourage Pompeius to mistrust his father-in-law."

"The only way to do that," said Cato, refilling his goblet, "is to make Pompeius think that Caesar intends to assassinate him."

It was Bibulus's turn to stare. "That we'd never do! I had political rivalry in mind."

"We could, you know," said Cato, nodding. "Pompeius's sons aren't old enough to succeed to his position, but Caesar is. With Caesar's daughter married to him, a great many of Pompeius's clients and adherents would gravitate to Caesar once Pompeius died."

"Yes, they probably would. But how do you propose to put the thought into Pompeius's mind?"

"Through Vettius," Cato said, sipping more slowly; the wine was beginning to do its work, he was thinking lucidly. "And you."

"I don't know where you're going," said the junior consul.

"Before Pompeius and his new bride leave town, I suggest you send for him and warn him that there's a plot afoot to kill him."

"I can do that, yes. But why? To frighten him?"

"No, to divert suspicion from you when the plot comes out," said Cato, smiling savagely. "A warning won't frighten Pompeius, but it will predispose him to believe that there's a plot."

"Enlighten me, Cato. I like the sound of this," said Bibulus.

An idyllically happy Pompey proposed to take Julia to Antium for the rest of May and part of June.

"She's busy with the decorators right at this moment," he said to Caesar, beaming fatuously. "While we're away they'll transform my house on the Carinae." He sighed explosively. "What taste she has, Caesar! All light and airy, she says, no vulgar Tyrian purple and a lot less gilt. Birds, flowers and butterflies. I can't work out why I didn't think of it for myself! Though I'm insisting that our bedroom be done like a moonlit forest."

How to keep a straight face? Caesar managed, though it took considerable effort. "When are you off?" he asked.

"Tomorrow."

"Then we need to have a council of war today."

"That's what I'm here for."

"With Marcus Crassus."

Pompey's face fell. "Oh, do we have to have him?"

"We do. Come back after dinner."

By which time Caesar had managed to prevail upon Crassus to leave a series of important meetings to his inferiors.

They sat outside in the main peristyle, for it was a warm day and this location prevented anyone's overhearing what was said.

"The second land bill will go through, despite Cato's tactics and Bibulus's sky watch," Caesar announced.

"With you as patron of Capua, I note," said Pompey, nuptial bliss evaporated now there was some hard talking to do.

"Only in that the bill is a *lex Iulia,* and I as its author am giving Capua full Roman-citizen status. However, Magnus, it's you will be down there handing out the deeds to the lucky recipients, and you parading round the town.

Capua will consider itself in your clientele, not in mine.''

"And I'll be in the eastern parts of the Ager Campanus, which will regard me as patron,'' said Crassus contentedly.

"What we have to discuss today isn't the second land bill,'' said Caesar. "My province for next year needs some talk, as I do not intend to be a proconsular surveyor. Also, we have to own next year's senior magistrates. If we don't, a lot of what I've passed into law this year will be invalidated next year.''

"Aulus Gabinius,'' said Pompey instantly.

"I agree. The voters like him because his tribunate of the plebs produced some very useful measures, not to mention enabled you to clean up Our Sea. If all three of us work to that end, we ought to get him in as senior consul. But who for junior?''

"What about your cousin, Caesar? Lucius Piso,'' said Crassus.

"We'd have to buy him,'' from Pompey. "He's a businessman.''

"Good provinces for both of them, then,'' said Caesar. "Syria and Macedonia.''

"But for longer than a year,'' Pompey advised. "Gabinius would be happy with that, I know.''

"I'm not so sure about Lucius Piso,'' said Crassus, frowning.

"Why are Epicureans so expensive?'' Pompey demanded.

"Because they dine on gold and off gold,'' said Crassus.

Caesar grinned. "How about a marriage? Cousin Lucius has a daughter almost eighteen, but she's not highly sought. No dowry.''

"Pretty girl, as I remember,'' said Pompey. "No sign of Piso's eyebrows or teeth. Don't understand the lack of a dowry, though.''

"At the moment Piso's suffering,'' Crassus contributed. "No wars worth speaking of, and all his money's tied up in armaments. He had to use Calpurnia's dowry to keep himself afloat. However, Caesar, I refuse to give up either of my sons.''

''And if Brutus is to marry my girl, I can't afford to give up either of my boys!'' cried Pompey, bristling.

Caesar caught his breath, almost choked. Ye gods, he'd been so upset he hadn't remembered to mention that alliance to Brutus!

''*Is* Brutus to marry your girl?'' asked Crassus skeptically.

''Probably not,'' Caesar interjected coolly. ''Brutus wasn't in a fit state for questions or offers, so don't count on it, Magnus.''

''All right, I won't. But who can marry Calpurnia?''

''Why not me?'' asked Caesar, brows raised.

Both men stared at him, delighted smiles dawning.

''That,'' said Crassus, ''would answer perfectly.''

''Very well then, Lucius Piso is our other consul.'' Caesar sighed. ''We won't do as well among the praetors, alas.''

''With both consuls we don't need praetors,'' said Pompey. ''The best thing about Lucius Piso and Gabinius is that they're strong men. The *boni* won't intimidate them—or bluff them.''

''There remains,'' said Caesar pensively, ''the matter of getting me the province I want. Italian Gaul and Illyricum.''

''You'll have Vatinius legislate it in the Plebeian Assembly,'' said Pompey. ''The *boni* never dreamed they'd be standing against the three of us when they gave you Italy's traveling stock routes, did they?'' He grinned. ''You're right, Caesar. With the three of us united, we can get anything we want from the Assemblies!''

''Don't forget Bibulus is watching the skies,'' growled Crassus. ''Whatever acts you pass are bound to be challenged, even if years from now. Besides, Magnus, your man Afranius has been prorogued in Italian Gaul. It won't look good to your clients if you connive to take it off him and give it to Caesar.''

Skin a dull red, Pompey glared at Crassus. ''Very beautifully put, Crassus!'' he snapped. ''Afranius will do as he's told, he'll step aside for Caesar voluntarily. It cost me millions to buy him the junior consulship, and he knows he didn't give value for money! Don't worry about Afranius, you might have a stroke!''

''You wish,'' said Crassus with a broad smile.

''I'm going to ask more of you than that, Magnus,'' said Caesar, butting in. ''I want Italian Gaul from the moment Vatinius's law is ratified, not from next New Year's Day. There are things I have to do there, the sooner the better.''

The lion felt no chill on his hide, too warm from the attentions of Caesar's daughter; Pompey merely nodded and smiled, never even thought to enquire what things Caesar wanted to do. ''Eager to start, eh? I don't see why not, Caesar.'' He began to shift on his seat. ''Is that all? I really should get home to Julia, don't want her thinking I've got a girlfriend!'' And off he went, chuckling at his own joke.

''There's no fool like an old fool,'' said Crassus.

''Be kind, Marcus! He's in love.''

''With himself.'' Crassus turned his mind from Pompey to Caesar. ''What are you up to, Gaius? Why do you need Italian Gaul at once?''

''I need to enlist more legions, among other things.''

''Does Magnus have any idea that you're determined to supplant him as Rome's greatest conqueror?''

''No, I've managed to conceal that very nicely.''

''Well, you do certainly have luck, I admit it. Another man's daughter would have looked and sounded like Terentia, but yours is as lovely inside as she is out. She'll keep him in thrall for years. And one day he's going to wake up to find you've eclipsed him.''

''That he will,'' said Caesar, no doubt in his voice.

''Julia or no, he'll turn into your enemy then.''

''I'll deal with that when it happens, Marcus.''

Crassus emitted a snort. ''So you say! But I know you, Gaius. True, you don't attempt to leap hurdles before they appear. However, there are no contingencies you haven't thought about years ahead of their happening. You're canny, crafty, creative and courageous.''

"Very nicely put!" said Caesar, eyes twinkling.

"I understand what you plan when you're proconsul," Crassus said. "You'll conquer all the lands and
tribes to the north and east of Italia by marching all the
way down the Danubius to the Euxine Sea. However, the
Senate controls the public purse! Vatinius can have the
Plebeian Assembly grant you Italian Gaul together with
Illyricum, but you still have to go to the Senate for funds.
It won't be disposed to give them to you, Caesar. Even if
the *boni* didn't scream in outrage, the Senate traditionally
refuses to pay for aggressive wars. That's where Magnus
was unimpeachable. His wars have all been fought against
official Roman enemies—Carbo, Brutus, Sertorius, the pirates, the two kings. Whereas you're proposing to strike
first, be the aggressor. The Senate won't condone it, including many of your own adherents. Wars cost money.
The Senate owns the money. And you won't get it."

"You're not telling me anything I don't already
know, Marcus. I don't plan to apply to the Senate for
funds. I'll find my own."

"Out of your campaigns? Very risky!"

Caesar's reply was odd. "Are you still determined to
annex Egypt?" he asked. "I'm curious."

Crassus blinked at the change of subject. "I'd love
to, but I can't. The *boni* would die to the last man before
they'd let me."

"Good! Then I have my funds," said Caesar, smiling.

"I'm mystified."

"All will be revealed in due time."

When Caesar called to see Brutus the next morning
he found only Servilia, who glowered at him more, he was
quick to note, because she felt it called for than because
her feelings were permanently injured. Around her neck
was a thick gold chain, and depending from it in a cage
of gold was the huge strawberry-pink pearl. Her dress was
slightly paler, but of the same hue.

"Where's Brutus?" he asked, having kissed her.

"Around at his Uncle Cato's," she said. "You did me no good turn there, Caesar."

"According to Julia, the attraction has always been present," he said, sitting down. "Your pearl looks magnificent."

"I'm the envy of every woman in Rome. And how is Julia?" she asked sweetly.

"Well, I haven't seen her, but if Pompeius is anything to go by, she's very pleased with herself. Count yourself and Brutus lucky to be out of it, Servilia. My daughter has found her niche, which means a marriage to Brutus wouldn't have lasted."

"That's what Aurelia said. Oh, I could kill you, Caesar, but Julia was always his idea, not mine. After you and I became lovers I saw their betrothal as a way to keep you, but it was also quite uncomfortable once the news of us got out. Technical incest is not my ambition." She pulled a face. "Belittling."

"Things do tend to happen for the best."

"Platitudes," she said, "do not suit you, Caesar."

"They don't suit anyone."

"What brings you here so soon? A prudent man would have stayed away for some time."

"I forgot to relay a message from Pompeius," he said, eyes twinkling wickedly.

"What message?"

"That if Brutus liked, Pompeius would be happy to give him his daughter in exchange for my daughter. He was quite sincere."

She reared up like an Egyptian asp. "Sincere!" she hissed. "Sincere? You may tell him that Brutus would open his veins first! *My son* marry the daughter of the man who executed his father?"

"I shall relay your answer, but somewhat more tactfully, as he is my son-in-law." He extended his arm to her, a look in his eyes which informed her he was in a mood for dalliance.

Servilia rose to her feet. "It's quite humid for this time of year," she said.

"Yes, it is. Less clothes would help."

"At least with Brutus not here the house is ours," she said, lying with him in the bed she had not shared with Silanus.

"You have the loveliest flower," he remarked idly.

"Do I? I've never seen it," she said. "Besides, one needs a standard of comparison. Though I am flattered. You must have sniffed at most of Rome's in your time."

"I have gathered many posies," he said gravely, fingers busy. "But yours is the best, not to mention the most sniffable. So dark it's almost Tyrian purple, with the same ability to change as the light shifts. And your black fur is so soft. I don't like you as a person, but I adore your flower."

She spread her legs wider and pushed his head down. "Then worship it, Caesar, worship it!" she cried. "*Ecastor*, but you're wonderful!"

Ptolemy XI Theos Philopator Philadelphus, nicknamed Auletes the Flautist, had ascended the throne of Egypt during the dictatorship of Sulla, not long after the irate citizens of Alexandria had literally torn the previous King of nineteen days limb from limb; this was their retaliation for his murder of their beloved Queen, his wife of nineteen days.

With the death of this King, Ptolemy Alexander II, there had ended the legitimate line of the Ptolemies. Complicated by the fact that Sulla had held Ptolemy Alexander II hostage for some years, taken him to Rome, and forced him to make a will leaving Egypt to Rome in the event that he died without issue. A tongue-in-cheek testament, as Sulla was well aware that Ptolemy Alexander II was so effeminate he would never sire children. Rome would inherit Egypt, the richest country in the world.

But the tyranny of distance had defeated Sulla. When Ptolemy Alexander II parted company from himself in the agora at Alexandria, the palace cabal knew how long it would take for the news of his death to reach Rome and Sulla. The palace cabal also knew of two possible heirs to

the throne living much closer to Alexandria than Rome.
These were the two illegitimate sons of the old King, Ptolemy Lathyrus. They had been brought up first in Syria,
then were sent to the island of Cos, where they had fallen
into the hands of King Mithridates of Pontus. Who spirited
them off to Pontus and in time married them to two of his
many daughters, Auletes to Cleopatra Tryphaena, and the
younger Ptolemy to Mithridatidis Nyssa. It was from Pontus that Ptolemy Alexander II had escaped and fled to
Sulla; but the two illegitimate Ptolemies had preferred
Pontus to Rome, and stayed on at the court of Mithridates.
Then when King Tigranes conquered Syria, Mithridates
sent the two young men and their wives south to Syria
and Uncle Tigranes. He also apprised the palace cabal in
Alexandria of the whereabouts of the two last-ever Ptolemies.

　　Immediately after the death of Ptolemy Alexander II,
word was hurried to King Tigranes in Antioch, who gladly
obliged by sending both Ptolemies to Alexandria with their
wives. There the elder, Auletes, was made King of Egypt,
and the younger (henceforth known as Ptolemy the Cyprian) was dispatched to be regent of the island of Cyprus,
an Egyptian possession. As their queens were his own
daughters, the ageing King Mithridates of Pontus could
congratulate himself that eventually Egypt would be ruled
by his descendants.

　　The name Auletes meant a flautist or piper, but Ptolemy called Auletes had not received the sobriquet because
of his undeniable musicality; his voice happened to be
very high and fluting. Luckily, however, he was not as
effeminate as his younger brother, the Cyprian, who never
managed to sire any children: Auletes and Cleopatra Tryphaena confidently expected to give Egypt heirs. But an
un-Egyptian and unorthodox upbringing had not
inculcated in Auletes a true respect for the native Egyptian
priests who administered the religion of that strange country, a strip no more than two or three miles wide that
followed the course of the river Nilus all the way from the
Delta to the islands of the First Cataract and beyond to the
border of Nubia. For it was not enough to be King of

Egypt; the ruler of Egypt had also to be Pharaoh, and that
he could not be without the agreement of the native Egyptian priests. Failing to understand, Auletes had made no
attempt to conciliate them. If they were so important in
the scheme of things, why were they living down in Memphis at the junction of the Delta with the river, rather than
in the capital, Alexandria? For he never did come to realize that to the native Egyptians, Alexandria was a foreign
place having no ties of blood or history to Egypt.

Extremely exasperating to learn then that all Pharaoh's wealth was deposited in Memphis under the care of
the native Egyptian priests! Oh, as King, Auletes had control of the public income, which was enormous. But only
as Pharaoh could he run his fingers through the vast bins
of jewels, build pylons out of gold bricks, slide down veritable mountains of silver.

Queen Cleopatra Tryphaena, the daughter of Mithridates, was far cleverer than her husband, who suffered
from the intellectual disadvantages so much breeding of
sister with brother and uncle with niece brought in its train.
Knowing that they could not produce any offspring until
Auletes was at least crowned King of Egypt, Cleopatra
Tryphaena set to work to woo the priests. The result was
that four years after they had arrived in Alexandria, Ptolemy Auletes was officially crowned. Unfortunately only
as King, not as Pharaoh. Thus the ceremonies had been
conducted in Alexandria rather than in Memphis. They
were followed by the birth of the first child, a daughter
named Berenice.

Then in the same year which had seen the death of
old Queen Alexandra of the Jews, another daughter was
born; her name was Cleopatra. The year of her birth was
ominous, for it saw the beginning of the end for Mithridates and Tigranes, exhausted after the campaigns of
Lucullus, and it saw renewed interest from Rome in the
annexation of Egypt as a province of the burgeoning empire. The ex-consul, Marcus Crassus, was prowling in the
shadows. When little Cleopatra was only four and Crassus
became censor, he tried to secure the annexation of Egypt
in the Senate. Ptolemy Auletes shivered in fear, paid huge

sums to Roman senators to make sure the move failed. Successful bribes. The threat of Rome diminished.

But with the arrival of Pompey the Great in the East to terminate the careers of Mithridates and Tigranes, Auletes saw his allies to the north vanish. Egypt was worse than alone; her new neighbor on each side was now Rome, ruling both Cyrenaica and Syria. Though this change in the balance of power did solve one problem for Auletes. He had been desirous of divorcing Cleopatra Tryphaena for some time, as his own half sister by the old King, Ptolemy Lathyrus, was now of an age to marry. The death of King Mithridates enabled him to do so. Not that Cleopatra Tryphaena lacked Ptolemaic blood. She had several dollops from her father and her mother. Just not enough of it. When the time came for Isis to endow him with sons, Auletes knew that both Egyptians and Alexandrians would approve of these sons far more if they were of almost pure Ptolemaic blood. And he might at last be created Pharaoh, get his hands on so much treasure that he could afford to buy Rome off permanently.

So Auletes finally divorced Cleopatra Tryphaena and married his own half sister. Their son, who in time would rule as Ptolemy XII, was born in the year of the consulship of Metellus Celer and Lucius Afranius; his half sister Berenice was then fifteen, and his half sister Cleopatra eight. Not that Cleopatra Tryphaena was murdered, or even banished. She remained in the palace at Alexandria with her two daughters and contrived to stay on good terms with the new Queen of Egypt. It took more than divorce to devastate a child of Mithridates, and she was, besides, maneuvering to secure a marriage between the baby male heir to the throne and her younger girl, Cleopatra. That way the line of King Mithridates in Egypt would not die out.

Unfortunately Auletes mishandled his negotiations with the native Egyptian priests following the birth of his son; twenty years after arriving in Alexandria he found himself as far from being Pharaoh as he had been when he arrived. He built temples up and down the Nilus; he made offerings to every deity from Isis to Horus to Serapis; he did everything he could think of except the right thing.

Time then to dicker with Rome.

Thus it was that at the beginning of February in the year of Caesar's consulship, a deputation of one hundred Alexandrian citizens came to Rome to petition the Senate to confirm the King of Egypt's tenure of the throne.

The petition was duly presented during February, but an answer was not forthcoming. Frustrated and miserable, the deputation—under orders from Auletes to do whatever was necessary, and stay as long as might be needed—settled down to the grinding task of interviewing dozens of senators and trying to persuade them to help rather than hinder. Naturally the only thing the senators were interested in was money. If enough of it changed hands, enough votes might be secured.

The leader of the deputation was one Aristarchus, who was also the King's chancellor and leader of the current palace cabal. Egypt was so riddled with bureaucracy that she had been enervated by it for two or three thousand years; it was a habit the new Macedonian aristocracy imported by the first Ptolemy had not been able to break. Instead, the bureaucracy stratified itself in new ways, with the Macedonian stock at the top, those of mixed Egyptian and Macedonian blood in the middle, and the native Egyptians (save for the priests) at the bottom. Further complicated by the fact that the army was Jewish. A wily and subtle man, Aristarchus was the direct descendant of one of the more famous librarians at the Alexandrian Museum, and had been a senior civil servant for long enough to understand how Egypt worked. Since it was no part of the aims of the Egyptian priests to have the country end up being owned by Rome, he had managed to persuade them to augment that portion of Auletes's income left over from paying to run Egypt, so he had vast resources at his fingertips. Vaster, indeed, than he had given Auletes to understand.

By the time he had been in Rome for a month he divined that seeking votes among the *pedarii* and senators who would never rise higher than praetor was not the way

to get Auletes his decree. He needed some of the consulars—but not the *boni*. He needed Marcus Crassus, Pompey the Great and Gaius Caesar. But as he arrived at this
decision before the existence of the triumvirate was generally known, he failed to go to the right man among those
three. He chose Pompey, who was so wealthy he didn't
need a few thousand talents of Egyptian gold. So Pompey
had simply listened with no expression on his face, and
concluded the interview with a vague promise that he
would think about it.

Approaching Crassus was not likely to do any good,
even if Crassus's attraction to gold was fabled. It was
Crassus who had wanted to annex, and as far as Aristarchus knew he might still want to annex. Which left Gaius
Caesar. Whom the Alexandrian decided to approach in the
midst of the turmoil over the second agrarian law, and just
before Julia married Pompey.

Caesar was well aware that a Vatinian law passed by
the Plebs could endow him with a province, but could not
grant him funds to meet any of his expenses. The Senate
would dole him out a stipend reduced to bare bones in
retaliation for going to the Plebs, and make sure that it
was delayed in the Treasury for as long as possible. Not
what Caesar wanted at all. Italian Gaul owned a garrison
of two legions, and two legions were not enough to do
what Caesar fully intended to do. He needed four at least,
each up to full strength and properly equipped. But that
cost money—money he would never get from the Senate,
especially as he couldn't plead a defensive war. Caesar
intended to be the aggressor, and that was not Roman or
senatorial policy. It was delightful to have fresh provinces
incorporated into the empire, but it could happen only as
the result of a defensive war like the one Pompey had
fought in the East against the kings.

He had known whereabouts the money to equip his
legions was going to come from as soon as the Alexandrian delegation arrived in Rome, but he bided his time.
And made his plans, which included the Gadetanian
banker Balbus, fully in his confidence.

When Aristarchus came to see him at the beginning

of May, he received the man with great courtesy in the Domus Publica, and conducted him through the more public parts of the building before settling him in the study. Of course Aristarchus admired, but it was not difficult to see that the Domus Publica did not impress the chancellor of Egypt. Small, dark and mundane: the reaction was written all over him despite his charm. Caesar was interested.

"I can be as obtuse and roundabout as you wish," he said to Aristarchus, "but I imagine that after being in Rome for three months without accomplishing anything, you might appreciate a more direct approach."

"It is true that I would like to return to Alexandria as soon as possible, Gaius Caesar," said the obviously pure Macedonian Aristarchus, who was fair and blue-eyed. "However, I cannot leave Rome without bearing positive news for the King."

"Positive news you can have if you agree to my terms," Caesar said crisply. "Would senatorial confirmation of the King's tenure of his throne plus a decree making him Friend and Ally of the Roman People be satisfactory?"

"I had hoped for no more than the first," said Aristarchus, bracing himself. "To have King Ptolemy Philopator Philadelphus made a Friend and Ally as well is beyond my wildest dreams."

"Then expand the horizon of your dreams a little, Aristarchus! It can be done."

"At a price."

"Of course."

"What is the price, Gaius Caesar?"

"For the first decree confirming tenure of the throne, six thousand gold talents, two thirds of which must be paid before the decree is procured, and the final third one year from now. For the Friend and Ally decree, a further two thousand gold talents payable in a lump sum beforehand," said Caesar, eyes bright and piercing. "The offer is not negotiable. Take it or leave it."

"You have aspirations to be the richest man in Rome," said Aristarchus, curiously disappointed; he had not read Caesar as a leech.

"On six thousand talents?" Caesar laughed. "Believe me, chancellor, they wouldn't make me the richest man in Rome! No, some of it will have to go to *my* friends and allies, Marcus Crassus and Gnaeus Pompeius Magnus. I can obtain the decrees, but not without their support. And one doesn't expect favors from Romans extended to foreigners without hefty recompense. What I do with my share is my business, but I will tell you that I have no desire to settle down in Rome and live the life of Lucullus."

"Will the decrees be watertight?"

"Oh, yes. I'll draft them myself."

"The total price then is eight thousand gold talents, six thousand of which must be paid in advance, two thousand a year from now," said Aristarchus, shrugging. "Very well then, Gaius Caesar, so be it. I agree to your price."

"All the money is to be paid directly to the bank of Lucius Cornelius Balbus in Gades, in his name," Caesar said, lifting one brow. "He will distribute it in ways I would prefer to keep to myself. I must protect myself, you understand, so no moneys will be paid in my name, or the names of my colleagues."

"I understand."

"Very well then, Aristarchus. When Balbus informs me that the transaction is complete, you will have your decrees, and King Ptolemy can forget at last that the previous King of Egypt ever made a will leaving Egypt to Rome."

"Ye gods!" said Crassus when Caesar informed him of these events some days later. "How much do I get?"

"A thousand talents."

"Silver, or gold?"

"Gold."

"And Magnus?"

"The same."

"Leaving four for you, and two more to come next year?"

Caesar threw back his head and laughed. "Abandon

all hope of the two thousand payable next year, Marcus!
Once Aristarchus gets back to Alexandria, that's the end
of it. How can we collect without going to war? No, I
thought six thousand was a fair price for Auletes to pay
for security, and Aristarchus knows it.''

"Four thousand gold talents will equip ten legions.''

"Especially with Balbus doing the equipping. I intend to make him my *praefectus fabrum* again. As soon
as word comes from Gades that the Egyptian money has
been deposited there, he'll start for Italian Gaul. Both Lucius Piso and Marcus Crassus—not to mention poor Brutus—will suddenly be earning money from armaments.''

"But *ten* legions, Gaius?''

"No, no, only two extra to begin with. I'll invest the
bulk of the money. This will be a self-funding exercise
from start to finish, Marcus. It has to be. He who controls
the purse strings controls the enterprise. My time has
come, and do you think for one moment that anyone other
than I will control this enterprise? *The Senate?*''

Caesar got to his feet and lifted his arms toward the
ceiling, fists clenched; Crassus suddenly saw how thick
the muscles were in those deceptively slender limbs, and
felt the hair rise on the back of his neck. The power in
the man!

"The Senate is a nothing! The *boni* are nothing!
Pompeius Magnus is nothing! I am going to go as far as
I have to go to become the First Man in Rome for as long
as I live! And after I die, I will be called the greatest
Roman who ever lived! Nothing and no one will stop me!
I swear it by my ancestors, all the way back to Goddess
Venus!''

The arms came down, the fire and the power died.
Caesar sat in his chair and looked at his old friend ruefully.
"Oh, Marcus,'' he said, "all I have to do is get through
the rest of this year!''

His mouth was dry. Crassus swallowed. "You will,''
he said.

Publius Vatinius convoked the Plebeian Assembly
and announced to the Plebs that he would legislate to re-

move the slur of being a surveyor from Gaius Julius Caesar.

"Why are we wasting a man like Gaius Caesar on a job which might be suited to the talents of our stargazer Bibulus, but is infinitely beneath a governor and general of Gaius Caesar's caliber? He showed us in Spain what he can do, but that is minute. I want to see him given the chance to sink his teeth into a task worthy of his metal! There's more to governing than making war, and more to generaling than sitting in a command tent. Italian Gaul has not received a decent governor in a decade and more, with the result that the Delmatae, the Liburni, the Iapudes and all the other tribes of Illyricum have made eastern Italian Gaul a very dangerous place for Romans to live in. Not to mention that the administration of Italian Gaul is a disgrace. The assizes are not held on time if they're held at all, and the Latin Rights colonies across the Padus are foundering.

"I am asking you to give Gaius Caesar the province of Italian Gaul together with Illyricum as of the moment this bill becomes ratified!" cried Vatinius, shrunken legs hidden by his toga, face so ruddy that the tumor on his forehead disappeared. "I further ask that Gaius Caesar be confirmed by this body as proconsul in Italian Gaul and Illyricum until March five years hence! And that the Senate be stripped of any authority to alter one single disposition we make in this Assembly! The Senate has abrogated its right to dole out proconsular provinces because it can find no better job for a man like Gaius Caesar than to survey Italia's traveling livestock routes! Let the stargazer survey mounds of manure, but let Gaius Caesar survey a better prospect!"

Vatinius's bill had gone before the Plebs and it stayed with the Plebs, *contio* after *contio;* Pompey spoke in favor, Crassus spoke in favor, Lucius Cotta spoke in favor—and Lucius Piso spoke in favor.

"I can't manage to persuade one of our craven tribunes to interpose a veto," said Cato to Bibulus, trembling with anger. "Not even Metellus Scipio, do you believe that? All they answer is that they like living! *Like living!*

Oh, if only I was still a tribune of the plebs! I'd show them!''

''And you'd be dead, Marcus. The people want it, why I don't know. Except that I think he's their long-odds bet. Pompeius was a proven quantity. Caesar is a gamble. The knights think he's lucky, the superstitious lot!''

''The worst of it is that you're still stuck with the traveling stock routes. Vatinius was very careful to point out that one of you would be doing that necessary job.''

''And I *will* do it,'' Bibulus said loftily.

''We have to stop him somehow! Is Vettius progressing?''

Bibulus sighed. ''Not as well as I'd hoped. I wish you were more of a natural schemer, Cato, but you aren't. It was a good idea, but Vettius isn't the most promising material to work with.''

''I'll talk to him tomorrow.''

''No, don't!'' cried Bibulus, alarmed. ''Leave him to me.''

''Pompeius is to speak in the House, I note. Advocating that the House give Caesar everything he wants. Pah!''

''He won't get the extra legion he wants, so much is sure.''

''Why do I think he will?''

Bibulus smiled sourly. ''Caesar's luck?'' he asked.

''Yes, I don't like that attitude. It makes him look blessed.''

Pompey did speak in favor of Vatinius's bills to give Caesar a magnificent proconsular command, but only to increase the endowment.

''It has been drawn to my attention,'' said the Great Man to the senators, ''that due to the death of our esteemed consular Quintus Metellus Celer, the province of Gaul-across-the-Alps has not been given a new governor. Gaius Pomptinus continues to hold it in this body's name, apparently to the satisfaction of this body, though not with the approval of Gaius Caesar, or me, or any other proven commander of troops. It pleased you to award a thanksgiving to Pomptinus over our protests, but I say to you

now that Pomptinus is not competent to govern Further
Gaul. Gaius Caesar is a man of enormous energy and efficiency, as his governorship of Further Spain showed you.
What would be a task too big for most men is not big
enough for him, any more than it would be for me. I move
that this House award Gaius Caesar the governorship of
the further Gallic province as well as the nearer, together
with its legion. There are many advantages. One governor
for these two provinces will be able to move his troops
around as they are needed, without his being obliged to
distinguish between forces in the two provinces. For three
years Further Gaul has been in a state of unrest, and one
legion to control those turbulent tribes is ridiculous. But
by combining the two provinces under the one governor,
Rome will be spared the cost of more legions.''

Cato's hand was waving; Caesar, in the chair, smiled
broadly and acknowledged him. "Marcus Porcius Cato,
you have the floor."

"Is that how confident you are, Caesar?" roared
Cato. "That you think you can invite me to speak with
impunity? Well, it may be so, but at least my protest
against this carving up of an empire will go down on our
permanent record! How loyally and splendidly the new
son-in-law speaks up for his new father-in-law! Is this
what Rome has been reduced to, the buying and selling
of daughters? Is this how we are to align ourselves politically, by buying or selling a daughter? The father-in-law
in this infamous alliance has already used his minion with
the wen to secure for himself a proconsulship I and the
rest of Rome's true patriots strove with might and main
to deny him! Now the son-in-law wants to contribute another province to *tata*! One man, one province! That is
what the *mos maiorum* says. Conscript Fathers, don't you
see the danger? Don't you understand that if you accede
to Pompeius's request, you are putting the tyrant in his
citadel with your own hands? Don't do it! Don't do it!''

Pompey had listened looking bored, Caesar with that
annoying expression of mild amusement.

"It makes no difference to me," Pompey said. "I put
forward the suggestion for the best of motives. If the Sen-

ate of Rome is to retain its traditional right to distribute our provinces to their governors, then it had better do so. You can ignore me, Conscript Fathers. Feel free! But if you do, Publius Vatinius will take the matter to the Plebs, and the Plebs will award Further Gaul to Gaius Caesar. All I'm saying is that you do the job rather than let the Plebs do it. If you award Further Gaul to Gaius Caesar, then you control the award. You can renew the commission each New Year's Day or not, as you please. But if the matter goes to the Plebs, Gaius Caesar's command of Further Gaul will be for five years. Is that what you want? Every time the People or the Plebs passes a law in what used to be the sphere of the Senate, another bit of senatorial power has been nibbled away. I don't care! *You* decide.''

This was the sort of speech Pompey gave best, plain and unvarnished and the better for being so. The House thought about what he had said, and admitted the truth of it by voting to award the senior consul the province of Further Gaul for one year, from next New Year's Day to the following one, to be renewed or not at the Senate's pleasure.

''You fools!'' Cato shrieked after the division was over. ''You unmitigated fools! A few moments ago he had three legions, now you've given him four! Four legions, three of which are veteran! And what is this Caesar villain going to do with them? Use them to pacify his provinces in the plural? No! He'll use them to march on Italia, to march on Rome, to make himself King of Rome!''

It was not an unexpected speech, nor for Cato a particularly wounding one; no man present, even among the ranks of the *boni,* actually believed Cato.

But Caesar lost his temper, an indication of the tremendous tensions he had been living under for months, released now because he had what he needed.

He rose to his feet, face flinty, nostrils distended, eyes flashing. ''You can yell all you like, Cato!'' he thundered. ''You can yell until the sky falls in and Rome disappears beneath the waters! Yes, all of you can squeal, bleat, yell, whine, grizzle, criticize, carp, complain! But I don't care!

I have what I wanted, and I got it in your teeth! Now sit down and shut up, all of you pathetic little men! I have what I wanted. And if you make me, I will use it to crush your heads!''

They sat down and they shut up, simmering.

Whether that protest against what Caesar saw as injustice was the cause, or whether the cause was an accumulation of many insults including a marriage, from that day onward the popularity of the senior consul and his allies began to wane. Public opinion, angry enough at Bibulus's watching the skies to have given Caesar the two Gauls, now swung away until it hovered approvingly before Cato and Bibulus, who were quick to seize the advantage.

They also managed to buy young Curio, who had been released from his promise to Clodius and thirsted to make life difficult for Caesar. At every opportunity he was back on the rostra or on Castor's platform, satirizing Caesar and his suspect past unmercifully—and in an irresistibly entertaining way. Bibulus too entered the fray by posting witty anecdotes, epigrams, notes and edicts upon (thus adding insult to injury) Caesar's bulletin board in the lower Forum.

The laws went through nonetheless; the second land act, the various acts which together made up the *leges Vatiniae* endowing Caesar with his provinces, and many more inconspicuous but useful measures Caesar had been itching for years to implement. King Ptolemy XI Theos Philopator Philadelphus called Auletes was confirmed in his tenure of the Egyptian throne, and made Friend and Ally of the Roman People. Four thousand talents remained in Balbus's bank in Gades, Pompey and Crassus having been paid, and Balbus, together with Titus Labienus, hurried north to Italian Gaul to commence work. Balbus would procure armaments and equipment (where possible from Lucius Piso and Marcus Crassus), while Labienus started to enlist the third legion for Italian Gaul.

His sights set upon a war to the northeast and along the basin of the Danubius, Caesar regarded Further Gaul

as a nuisance. He had not recalled Pomptinus, though he
detested the man, preferring to deal with troubles along
the Rhodanus River by diplomatic means. King Ariovistus
of the German Suebi was a new force in Further Gaul; he
now held complete sway over the area between Lake Lemanna and the banks of the Rhenus River, which divided
Further Gaul from Germania. The Sequani had originally
invited Ariovistus to cross into their territory with the
promise that he would receive one third of Sequani land.
But the Suebi kept pouring across the great river in such
numbers that Ariovistus was soon demanding two thirds
of the Sequani lands. The domino effect had spread the
disturbances to the Aedui, who had been titled Friend and
Ally of the Roman People for years. Then the Helvetii, a
sept of the great tribe Tigurini, began to issue out of their
mountain fastnesses to seek more clement living at a lower
altitude in Further Gaul itself.

War threatened, so much so that Pomptinus established a more or less permanent camp not far from Lake
Lemanna, and settled down with his one legion to watch
events.

Caesar's discerning eye picked Ariovistus as the key
to the situation, so in the name of the Senate he began to
parley with the German King's representatives, his object
a treaty which would keep what was Rome's Rome's, contain Ariovistus, and calm the huge Gallic tribes the
German incursion was provoking. That in doing so he was
infringing the treaties Rome already had with the Aedui
worried him not one bit. More important to establish a
status quo spelling the least danger possible to Rome.

The result was a senatorial decree calling King Ariovistus a Friend and Ally of the Roman People; it was accompanied by lavish gifts from Caesar personally to the
leader of the Suebi, and it had the desired effect. Tacitly
confirmed in his present position, Ariovistus could sit back
with a sigh of relief, his Gallic outpost a fact acknowledged by the Senate of Rome.

Neither of the Friend and Ally decrees had proven
difficult for Caesar to procure; innately conservative and
against the huge expense of war, the Senate was quick to

see that confirming Ptolemy Auletes meant men like Crassus couldn't try to snaffle Egypt, and that confirming
Ariovistus meant war in Further Gaul had been averted. It
was hardly even necessary to have Pompey speak.

In the midst of all this waning popularity, Caesar acquired his third wife, Calpurnia, the daughter of Lucius
Calpurnius Piso. Just eighteen, she turned out to be exactly
the kind of wife he needed at this time in his career. Like
her father she was tall and dark, a very attractive girl owning an innate calm and dignity which rather reminded Caesar of his mother, who was the first cousin of Calpurnia's
grandmother, a Rutilia. Intelligent and well read, unfail-
ingly pleasant, never demanding, she fitted into life in the
Domus Publica so easily that she might always have been
there. Much the same age as Julia, she was some compensation for having lost Julia. Particularly to Caesar.

He had of course handled her expertly. One of the
great disadvantages of arranged marriages, particularly
those of rapid genesis, was the effect on the new wife. She
came to her husband a stranger, and if like Calpurnia she
was a self-contained person, shyness and awkwardness
built a wall. Understanding this, Caesar proceeded to demolish it. He treated her much as he had treated Julia, with
the difference that she was wife, not daughter. His lovemaking was tender, considerate, and lighthearted; his other
contacts with her were also tender, considerate, and lighthearted.

When she had learned from her delighted father that
she was to marry the senior consul and Pontifex Maximus,
she had quailed. How would she ever manage? But he was
so nice, so thoughtful! Every day he gave her some sort
of little present, a bracelet or a scarf, a pair of earrings,
some pretty sandals he had seen glitter on a stall in the
marketplace. Once in passing he dropped something in her
lap (though she was not to know how practised he was at
that). The something moved and then mewed a tiny
squeak—oh, he had given her a kitten! How did he know
she adored cats? How did he know her mother hated them,
would never let her have one?

Dark eyes shining, she held the ball of orange fur against her face and beamed at her husband.

"He's a little young yet, but give him to me at the New Year and I'll castrate him for you," said Caesar, finding himself quite absurdly pleased at the look of joy on her very appealing face.

"I shall call him Felix," she said, still smiling.

Her husband laughed. "Lucky because he's fruitful? In the New Year that will be a contradiction in terms, Calpurnia. If he isn't castrated he'll never stay at home to keep you company, and I will have yet one more tom to throw my boot at in the middle of the night. Call him Spado, it's more appropriate."

Still holding the kitten, she got up and put one arm about Caesar's neck, kissed him on the cheek. "No, he's Felix."

Caesar turned his head until the kiss fell on his mouth. "I am a fortunate man," he said afterward.

"Where did he come from?" she asked, unconsciously imitating Julia by kissing one white fan at the corner of his eye.

Blinking away tears, Caesar put both arms about her. "I am moved to make love to you, wife, so put Felix down and come with me. You make it easier."

A thought he echoed to his mother somewhat later. "She makes it easier to live without Julia."

"Yes, she does. A young person in the house is necessary, at least for me. I'm glad it's so for you too."

"They're not alike."

"Not at all, which is good."

"She liked the kitten better than the pearls."

"An excellent sign." Aurelia frowned. "It will be difficult for her, Caesar. In six months you'll be gone, and she won't see you for years."

"Caesar's wife?" he asked.

"If she liked the kitten better than the pearls, I doubt her fidelity will waver. It would be best if you quicken her before you go—a baby would keep her occupied. However, these things cannot be predicted, and I haven't noticed that your devotion to Servilia has waned. A man only has so much to go round, Caesar, even you. Sleep with Calpurnia more often, and with Servilia less often. You seem to throw girls, so I worry less about a son.''

"Mater, you're a hard woman! Sensible advice which I have no intention of taking.''

She changed the subject. "I hear that Pompeius went to Marcus Cicero and begged him to persuade young Curio to cease his attacks in the Forum.''

"Stupid!'' Caesar exclaimed, frowning. "I told him it would only give Cicero a false idea of his own importance. The savior of his country is bitten by the *boni* these days, it gives him exquisite pleasure to decline any offer we make him. He wouldn't be a committeeman, he wouldn't be a legate in Gaul next year, he wouldn't even accept my offer to send him on a trip at State expense. Now what does Magnus do? Offers him money!''

"He refused the money, of course,'' said Aurelia.

"Despite his mounting debts. I never saw a man so obsessed with owning villas!''

"Does this mean you will unleash Clodius next year?''

The eyes Caesar turned on his mother were very cold. "I will definitely unleash Clodius.''

"What on earth did Cicero say to Pompeius to make you so angry?''

"The same kind of thing he said during the trial of Hybrida. But unfortunately Magnus displayed sufficient doubt of me to let Cicero think he stood a chance to wean Magnus away from me.''

"I doubt *that,* Caesar. It's not logical. Julia reigns.''

"Yes, I suppose you're right. Magnus plays both ends against the middle, he wouldn't want Cicero knowing all his thoughts.''

"I'd worry more about Cato, if I were you. Bibulus is the more organized of the pair, but Cato has the clout,'' said Aurelia. "It's a pity Clodius couldn't eliminate Cato as well as Cicero.''

"That would certainly guard my back in my absence, Mater! Unfortunately I can't see how it can be done.''

"Think about it. If you could eliminate Cato, you'd

draw all the teeth fixed in your neck. He's the fountain-
head.''

The curule elections were held a little later in Quinctilis than usual, and the favored candidates were definitely
Aulus Gabinius and Lucius Calpurnius Piso. They can-
vassed strenuously, but were too canny to give Cato any
opportunity to cry bribery. Capricious public opinion
swung away from the *boni* again; it promised to be a good
election result for the triumvirs.

At which point, scant days before the curule elections, Lucius Vettius crawled out from beneath his stone.
He approached young Curio, whose Forum speeches were
directed mostly in Pompey's direction these days, and told
him that he knew of a plan to assassinate Pompey. Then
he followed this up by asking young Curio if he would
join the conspiracy. Curio listened intently and pretended
to be interested. After which he told his father, for he had
not the kidney of a conspirator or an assassin. The elder
Curio and his son were always at loggerheads, but their
differences went no further than wine, sexual frolics and
debt; when danger threatened, the Scribonius Curio ranks
closed up.

The elder Curio notified Pompey at once, and Pompey called the Senate into session. Within moments Vettius was summoned to testify. At first the disgraced knight
denied everything, then broke down and gave some
names: the son of the future consular candidate Lentulus
Spinther, Lucius Aemilius Paullus, and Marcus Junius
Brutus, hitherto known as Caepio Brutus. These names
were so bizarre no one could believe them; young Spinther
was neither a member of the Clodius Club nor famed for
his indiscretions, Lepidus's son had an old history of rebellion but had done nothing untoward since his return
from exile, and the very idea of Brutus as an assassin was
ludicrous. Whereupon Vettius announced that a scribe belonging to Bibulus had brought him a dagger sent by the
housebound junior consul. Afterward Cicero was heard to
say that it was a shame Vettius had no other source of a
dagger, but in the House everyone understood the signif-

icance of the gesture: it was Bibulus's way of saying that the projected crime had his support.

"Rubbish!" cried Pompey, sure of one thing. "Marcus Bibulus himself took the trouble to warn me back in May that there was a plot afoot to assassinate me. Bibulus can't be involved."

Young Curio was called in. He reminded everyone that Paullus was in Macedonia, and apostrophized the whole business as a tissue of lies. The Senate was inclined to agree, but felt it wise to detain Vettius for further questioning. There were too many echoes of Catilina; no one wanted the odium of executing any Roman, even Vettius, without trial, so this plot was not going to be allowed to escalate out of senatorial control. Obedient to the Senate's wishes, Caesar as senior consul ordered his lictors to take Lucius Vettius to the Lautumiae and chain him to the wall of his cell, as this was the only preventative for escape from that rickety prison.

Though on the surface the affair seemed utterly incongruous, Caesar felt a stirring of disquiet; this was one occasion, self-preservation told him, when every effort ought to be made to keep the People apprised of developments. Matters should not be confined to the interior of the Senate chamber. So after he had dismissed the Conscript Fathers he called the People together and informed them what had happened. And on the following day he had Vettius brought to the rostra for public questioning.

This time Vettius's list of conspirators was quite different. No, Brutus had not been involved. Yes, he had forgotten that Paullus was in Macedonia. Well, he might have been wrong about Spinther's son, it could have been Marcellinus's son—after all, both Spinther and Marcellinus were Cornelii Lentuli, and both were future consular candidates. He proceeded to trot out new names: Lucullus, Gaius Fannius, Lucius Ahenobarbus, and Cicero. All *boni* or *boni* flirts. Disgusted, Caesar sent Vettius back to the Lautumiae.

However, Vatinius felt Vettius needed sterner handling, so he hied Vettius back to the rostra and subjected him to a merciless inquisition. This time Vettius insisted he had the names correct, though he did add two more: none other than that thoroughly respectable pillar of the establishment, Cicero's son-in-law Piso Frugi; and the senator Iuventius, renowned for his vagueness. The meeting broke up after Vatinius proposed to introduce a bill in the Plebeian Assembly to conduct a formal enquiry into what was rapidly becoming known as the Vettius Affair.

By this time none of it made any sense beyond an inference that the *boni* were sufficiently fed up with Pompey to conspire to assassinate him. However, not even the most perceptive analyst of public life could disentangle the confusion of threads Vettius had—woven? No, tied up in knots.

Pompey himself now believed there was a plot in existence, but could not be brought to believe that the *boni* were responsible. Hadn't Bibulus warned him? But if the *boni* were not the culprits, who was? So he ended like Cicero, convinced that once Vatinius got his enquiry into the Vettius Affair under way, the truth would out.

Something else gnawed at Caesar, whose left thumb pricked. If he knew nothing more, he knew that Vettius loathed him, Caesar. So where exactly was the Vettius Affair going to go? Was it in some tortuous way aimed at him? Or at driving a wedge between him and Pompey? Therefore Caesar decided not to wait the month or more until the official enquiry would begin. He would put Vettius back on the rostra for another public interrogation. Instinct told him that it was vital to do so quickly. Maybe then the name of Gaius Julius Caesar would not creep into the proceedings.

It was not to be. When Caesar's lictors appeared from the direction of the Lautumiae, they came alone, and hurrying white-faced. Lucius Vettius had been chained to the wall in his cell, but he was dead. Around his neck were the marks of big strong hands, around his feet the marks of a desperate struggle to hang on to life. Because he had been chained it had not occurred to anyone to set a guard on him; whoever had come in the night to silence Lucius Vettius had come and gone unseen.

* * *

Standing by in a mood of pleasant expectation, Cato felt the blood drain from his face, and was profoundly glad the attention of the throng around the rostra was focused upon the angry Caesar, snapping instructions to his lictors to make enquiries of those in the vicinity of the prison. By the time those around him might have turned to him for an opinion as to what was going on, Cato was gone. Running too fast for Favonius to keep up.

He burst into Bibulus's house to find that worthy sitting in his peristyle, one eye upon the cloudless sky, the other upon his visitors, Metellus Scipio, Lucius Ahenobarbus and Gaius Piso.

"How dare you, Bibulus?" Cato roared.

The four men turned as one, jaws slack.

"How dare I what?" asked Bibulus, plainly astonished.

"Murder Vettius!"

"*What?*"

"Caesar just sent to the Lautumiae to fetch Vettius to the rostra, and found him dead. Strangled, Bibulus! Why? Oh, why did you do that? I would never have consented, and you knew I would never have consented! Political trickery is one thing, especially when it's aimed at a dog like Caesar, but murder is despicable!"

Bibulus had listened to this looking as if he might faint; as Cato finished he rose unsteadily to his feet, hand outstretched. "Cato, Cato! Do you know me so little? Why would I murder a wretch like Vettius? If I haven't murdered Caesar, why would I murder *anyone*?"

The rage in the grey eyes died; Cato looked uncertain, then held his own hand out. "It wasn't you?"

"It wasn't me. I agree with you, I always have and I always will. Murder is despicable."

The other three were recovering from their shock; Metellus Scipio and Ahenobarbus gathered round Cato and Bibulus, while Gaius Piso leaned back in his chair and closed his eyes.

"Vettius is really dead?" Metellus Scipio asked.

"So Caesar's lictors said. I believed them."

"Who?" asked Ahenobarbus. "*Why?*"

Cato moved to where a flagon of wine and some beakers stood on a table, and poured himself a drink. "I really thought it was you, Marcus Calpurnius," he said, and tipped the beaker up. "I'm sorry. I ought to have known better."

"Well, we know it wasn't us," said Ahenobarbus, "so who?"

"It has to be Caesar," said Bibulus, helping himself to wine.

"What did he have to gain?" asked Metellus Scipio, frowning.

"Even I can't tell you that, Scipio," said Bibulus. At which moment his gaze rested on Gaius Piso, the only one still sitting. An awful fear filled him; he drew in his breath audibly. "Piso!" he cried suddenly. "Piso, you didn't!"

The bloodshot eyes, sunk into Gaius Piso's fleshy face, blazed scorn. "Oh, grow up, Bibulus!" he said wearily. "How else was this idiocy to succeed? Did you and Cato really think Vettius had the gall and the guts to carry your scheme through? He hated Caesar, yes, but he was terrified of the man too. You're such amateurs! Full of nobility and high ideals, weaving plots you've neither the talent nor the cunning to push to fruition—sometimes you make me sick, the pair of you!"

"The feeling goes both ways!" Cato shouted, fists doubled.

Bibulus put his hand on Cato's arm. "Don't make it worse, Cato," he said, the skin of his face gone grey. "Our honor is dead along with Vettius, all thanks to this ingrate." He drew himself up. "Get out of my house, Piso, and never come back."

The chair was overturned; Gaius Piso looked from one face to the next, then deliberately spat upon the flagstones at Cato's feet. "Vettius was my client," he said, "and I was good enough to use to coach him in his role! But not good enough to give advice. Well, fight your own fights from now on! And don't try to incriminate me, either, hear me? Breathe one word, and I'll testify against the lot of you!"

Cato dropped to sit on the stone coping around the

fountain. playing in the sun, droplets flashing a myriad rainbows; he covered his face with his hands and rocked back and forth, weeping.

"Next time I see Piso, I'll flatten him!" said Ahenobarbus fiercely. "The cur!"

"Next time you see Piso, Lucius, you'll be very polite," said Bibulus, wiping away his tears. "Oh, our honor is dead! We can't even make Piso pay. If we do, we're looking at exile."

The sensation surrounding the death of Lucius Vettius was all the worse because of its mystery; the brutal murder lent a ring of truth to what might otherwise have been dismissed as a fabrication. *Someone* had plotted to assassinate Pompey the Great, Lucius Vettius had known who that someone was, and now Lucius Vettius was silenced. Terrified because Vettius had said his name (and also the name of his loyal and loving son-in-law), Cicero shifted the blame to Caesar, and many of the minor *boni* followed his example. Bibulus and Cato declined to comment, and Pompey blundered from one bewilderment to another. Logic said very loudly and clearly that the Vettius Affair had no meaning or basis in fact, but those involved were not disposed to think logically.

Public opinion veered away from the triumvirs yet again, and seemed likely to remain adverse. Rumors about Caesar proliferated. His praetor Fufius Calenus was booed at the theater during the *ludi Apollinares;* gossip had it that Caesar through Fufius Calenus intended to cancel the right of the Eighteen to the bank of reserved seats just behind the senators. Gladiatorial games funded by Aulus Gabinius were the scene of more unpleasantness.

Convinced now that his religious tactics were the best way, Bibulus struck. He postponed the curule and Popular elections until the eighteenth day of October, publishing this as an edict on the rostra, the platform of Castor's and the bulletin board for public notices. Not only was there a stench in the lower Forum arising from the body of Lucius Vettius, said Bibulus, but he had also seen a huge shooting star in the wrong part of the sky.

Pompey panicked. His tame tribune of the plebs was bidden summon the Plebs into meeting, and there the Great Man spoke at length about the irresponsibility Bibulus was displaying more blatantly than any shooting star could display itself in the night skies. As an augur himself, he informed the despondent crowd, he would swear that there was nothing wrong with the omens. Bibulus was making everything up in order to bring Rome down. The Great Man then talked Caesar into convoking the People and speaking against Bibulus, but Caesar could not summon up the enthusiasm to put his usual fire into his speech, and failed to carry the crowd. What ought to have been an impassioned plea that the People should follow him to Bibulus's house and there beg that Bibulus put an end to all this nonsense emerged without any passion whatsoever. The People preferred to go to their own homes.

"Which simply demonstrates their good sense," Caesar said to Pompey over dinner in the Domus Publica. "We're approaching this in the wrong way, Magnus."

Very depressed, Pompey lay with his chin on his left hand and shrugged. "The wrong way?" he asked gloomily. "There just isn't a right way, is the trouble."

"There is, you know."

One blue eye turned Caesar's way, though the look accompanying it was skeptical. "Tell me this right way, Caesar."

"It's Quinctilis and election time, correct? The games are on, and half of Italia is here to enjoy itself. Hardly anyone in the Forum crowd at the present moment is a regular. How do they know what's been happening? They hear of omens, junior consuls watching the skies, men murdered in prison, and terrific strife between factions in office as Rome's magistrates. They look at you and me, and they see one side. Then they look at Cato and hear of Bibulus, and they see another side. It must seem stranger than a Pisidian ritual."

"Huh!" said Pompey, chin back on his hand. "Gabinius and Lucius Piso are going to lose, that's all I know."

"You're undoubtedly right, but only if the elections

were to be held now," said Caesar, brisk and energetic
once more. "Bibulus has made a mistake, Magnus. He
should have left the elections alone, let them be held now.
Were they held now, both the consuls would be solidly
boni. By postponing them, he's given us time and the
chance to retrieve our position."

"We can't retrieve our position."

"If we agitate against this latest edict, I agree. But
we stop agitating against it. We accept the postponement
as legitimate, as if we wholeheartedly condone Bibulus's
edict. Then we work to recover our clout with the electorate. By October we'll be back in favor again, Magnus,
wait and see. And in October we'll have the consuls of
our faction, Gabinius and Lucius Piso."

"Do you really think so?"

"I am absolutely sure of it. Go back to your Alban
villa and Julia, Magnus, please! Stop worrying about politics in Rome. I shall skulk until I give the House my
legislation to stop governors of provinces fleecing their
flocks, which won't be for another two months. We lie
low, do nothing and say nothing. That gives Bibulus and
Cato nothing to scream about. It will also silence young
Curio. Interest dies when nothing happens."

Pompey tittered. "I heard that young Curio really
rammed his fist up your arse the other day."

"By referring to events during the consulship of Julius and Caesar, rather than Caesar and Bibulus?" asked
Caesar, grinning.

"In the consulship of Julius and Caesar is really very
good."

"Oh, very witty! I laughed when I heard it too. But
even that can work in our favor, Magnus. It says
something young Curio should have paused to think about
before he said it—that Bibulus is not a consul, that I have
had to be both consuls. By October that will be very apparent to the electors."

"You cheer me enormously, Caesar," said Pompey
with a sigh. He thought of something else. "By the way,
Cato seems to have had a severe falling out with Gaius

Piso. Metellus Scipio and Lucius Ahenobarbus are siding
with Cato. Cicero told me.''

"It was bound to happen," said Caesar gravely, "as
soon as Cato found out that Gaius Piso had Vettius murdered. Bibulus and Cato are fools, but they're honorable
fools when it comes to murder.''

Pompey was gaping. "Gaius Piso did it?''

"Certainly. And he was right to do it. Vettius alive
was no threat to us. Vettius dead can be laid at my door.
Didn't Cicero try to persuade you of that, Magnus?''

"Well . . .'' muttered Pompey, going red.

"Precisely! The Vettius Affair happened in order to
make you doubt me. Then when I began publicly questioning Vettius, and kept on publicly questioning him, Gaius Piso saw that the ploy was going to fail. Hence
Vettius's death, which prevented all conclusions save
those founded in sheer speculation.''

"I did doubt you," said Pompey gruffly.

"And very naturally. However, Magnus, do remember that you are of far more use to me alive than dead!
It's true that did you die, I'd inherit a great many of your
people. But do you live, your people are bound to support
me to the last man. I am no advocate of death.''

Because the Plebs and the plebeian magistrates did
not function under the auspices, Bibulus's edict could not
prevent the election of plebeian aediles or tribunes of the
plebs. Those went to the polls at the end of Quinctilis as
scheduled, and Publius Clodius was returned as president
of the new College of Tribunes of the Plebs. No surprise
in that; the Plebs were very prone to admire a patrician
who cared so much about the tribunate of the plebs that
he would abrogate his status in order to espouse it. Clodius
had besides a wealth of clients and followers due to his
generosity, and his marriage to Gaius Gracchus's granddaughter brought him many thousands more. In him, the
Plebs saw someone who would support the People against
the Senate; did he support the Senate, he would never have
abrogated his patrician status.

Of course the *boni* succeeded in having three tribunes

of the plebs elected, and Cicero was so afraid that Clodius would succeed in trying him for the murder of Roman citizens without trial that he had spent lavishly to secure the election of his devoted admirer Quintus Terentius Culleo.

"Not," said Clodius to Caesar, breathless with excitement, "that I'm very worried by any of them. I'll sweep them into the Tiber!"

"I'm sure you will, Clodius."

The dark and slightly mad-looking eyes flashed. "Do *you* think you own me, Caesar?" Clodius asked abruptly.

Which question provoked a laugh. "No, Publius Clodius, no! I wouldn't insult you by dreaming of it, let alone thinking it. A Claudian—even a plebeian one!—belongs to no one save himself."

"In the Forum they're saying that you own me."

"Do you care what they're saying in the Forum?"

"I suppose not, provided that it doesn't damage me." Clodius uncoiled with a sudden leap, sprang to his feet. "Well, I just wanted to ascertain that you didn't think you owned me, so I'll be off now."

"Oh, don't deprive me of your company quite yet," Caesar said gently. "Sit down again, do."

"What for?"

"Two reasons. The first is that I'd like to know what you plan for your year. The second is that I'd like to offer you any help you might need."

"Is this a ploy?"

"No, it's simply genuine interest. I also hope, Clodius, that you have sufficient sense to realize that help from me might make all the difference to the legality of your laws."

Clodius thought about this in silence, then nodded. "I can see that," he said, "and there is one area in which you can help."

"Name it."

"I need to establish better contact with real Romans. I mean the little fellows, the herd. How can we patricians know what they want if we don't know any of them? Which is where you're so different from the rest, Caesar.

You know everyone from the highest to the lowest. How did you do that? Teach me," said Clodius.

"I know everyone because I was born and brought up in the Subura. Every day I rubbed shoulders with the little fellows, as you call them. At least I detect no shade of patronage in you. But why do you want to get to know the little fellows? They're of no use to you, Clodius. They don't have votes which matter."

"They have numbers," said Clodius.

What was he after? Apparently interested only as a matter of courtesy, Caesar sat back in his chair and studied Publius Clodius. Saturninus? No, not the same type. Mischief? Certainly. What *could* he do? A question to which Caesar confessed he could find no answer. Clodius was an innovator, a completely unorthodox person who would perhaps go where no one had been before. Yet what could he do? Did he expect to draw thousands upon thousands of little fellows to the Forum to intimidate the Senate and the First Class into doing whatever it was that the little fellows wanted? But that would happen only if their bellies were empty, and though grain prices were high at the moment, Cato's law prevented the price's being handed down to the little fellows. Saturninus had seen a crowd of gigantic proportions and been inspired to use it to further his own end, which was to rule Rome. Yet when he summoned it to do his bidding, it never came. So Saturninus died. If Clodius tried to imitate Saturninus, death would be his fate too. Long acquaintance with the little fellows— what an extraordinary way to describe them!—gave Caesar insight none of his own big fellows could hope to have. Including Publius Clodius, born and brought up on the Palatine. Well, perhaps Clodius wanted to be Saturninus, but if so, all he would discover was that the little fellows could not be massed together destructively. They were just not politically inclined.

"I met someone you know in the Forum the other day," Clodius remarked some time later. "When you were trying to persuade the crowd to follow you to Bibulus's house."

Caesar grimaced. "A stupidity on my part," he said.

''That's what Lucius Decimius said.''

The impassive face lit up. ''Lucius Decimius? Now there's a fascinating little fellow! If you want to know about the little fellows, Clodius, then go to him.''

''What does he do?''

''He's a *vilicus,* the custodian of the crossroads college my mother has housed since before I was born. A little depressed these days because he and his college have no official standing.''

''Your mother's house?'' asked Clodius, brow wrinkling.

''Her insula. Where the Vicus Patricii meets the Subura Minor. These days the college is a tavern, but they still meet there.''

''I shall look Lucius Decimius up,'' said Clodius, sounding well satisfied.

''I wish you'd tell me what you plan to do as a tribune of the plebs,'' said Caesar.

''I'll start by making changes to the *lex Aelia* and the *lex Fufia,* that's certain. To permit consuls like Bibulus the use of religious laws as a political ploy is lunatic. After I get through with them, the *lex Aelia* and the *lex Fufia* will hold no attraction for the likes of Bibulus.''

''I applaud that! But do come to me for help in drafting.''

Clodius grinned wickedly. ''Want me to make it a retroactive law, eh? Illegal to watch the skies backward as well as forward?''

''To shore up my own legislation?'' Caesar looked haughty. ''I will manage, Clodius, without a retroactive law. What else?''

''Condemn Cicero for executing Roman citizens without trial, and send him into permanent exile.''

''Excellent.''

''I also plan to restore the crossroads colleges and other sorts of brotherhoods outlawed by your cousin Lucius Caesar.''

''Which is why you want to visit Lucius Decimius. And?''

''Make the censors conform.''

"An interesting one."

"Forbid the Treasury clerks to engage in private commerce."

"Well overdue."

"And give the People completely free grain."

The breath hissed between Caesar's teeth. "Oho! Admirable, Clodius, but the *boni* will never let you get away with it."

"The *boni* will have no choice," said Clodius, face grim.

"How will you pay for a free grain dole? The cost would be prohibitive."

"By legislating to annex the island of Cyprus. Don't forget that Egypt and all its possessions—chiefly Cyprus—were left to Rome in King Ptolemy Alexander's will. You reversed Egypt by getting the Senate to award Ptolemy Auletes tenure of the Egyptian throne, but you didn't extend your decree to cover his brother of Cyprus. That means Cyprus still belongs to Rome under that old will. We've never exercised it, but I intend to. After all, there are no kings in Syria any more, and Egypt can't go to war alone. There must be thousands and thousands of talents lying around in the palace at Paphos just waiting for Rome to pick them up."

It came out sounding quite virtuous, which pleased Clodius immensely. Caesar was a very sharp fellow; he'd be the first to smell duplicity. But Caesar didn't know about the old grudge Clodius bore Ptolemy the Cyprian. When pirates had captured Clodius, he had made them ask Ptolemy the Cyprian for a ten-talent ransom, trying to emulate Caesar's conduct with his pirates. Ptolemy the Cyprian had simply laughed, then refused to pay more than two talents for the hide of Admiral Publius Clodius, saying that was all he was worth. A mortal insult. Well, Ptolemy the Cyprian was about to pay considerably more than two talents to satisfy Clodius's thirst for revenge. The price would be everything he owned, from his regency to the last golden nail in a door.

Had Caesar known this story, he wouldn't have cared; he was too busy thinking of a different revenge. "What a

splendid idea!'' he said affably. ''I have just the person to
entrust with a delicate mission like the annexation of Cyprus. You can't send someone with sticky fingers or Rome
will end with less than half of what's there, and the grain
dole will suffer. Nor can you go yourself. You'll have to
legislate a special commission to annex Cyprus, and I have
just the person for the job.''

''You do?'' asked Clodius, taken aback at a kindred
malice.

''Give it to Cato.''

·''*Cato?*''

''Absolutely. It must be Cato! He'll ferret out every
stray drachma from the darkest corner, he'll keep immaculate accounts, he'll number off every jewel, every golden
cup, every statue and painting—the Treasury will get the
lot,'' said Caesar, smiling like the cat about to break the
mouse's neck. ''You must, Clodius! Rome needs a Cato
to do this job! *You* need a Cato to do this job! Commission
Cato, and you'll have the money to pay for a free grain
dole.''

Clodius went whooping away, leaving Caesar to reflect that he had just managed to do the most personally
satisfying piece of work in years. The opponent of all special commissions, Cato would find himself hemmed into
a corner with Clodius aiming a spear at him from every
direction. That was the beauty of the Beauty, as Cicero
was prone to refer to Clodius, punning on his nickname.
Yes, Clodius was very clever. He had seen the nuances of
commissioning Cato immediately. Another man might offer Cato a loophole, but Clodius wouldn't. Cato would
have no choice other than to obey the Plebs, and he would
be away for two or three years. Cato, who loathed being
out of Rome these days for fear his enemies would take
advantage of his absence. The Gods only knew what havoc
Clodius was planning for next year, but if he did nothing
more to oblige Caesar than eliminate Cicero and Cato,
then Caesar for one would not complain.

''I'm going to force Cato to annex Cyprus!'' said
Clodius to Fulvia when he got home. His face changed,

he scowled. "I ought to have thought of it for myself, but it's Caesar's idea."

By now Fulvia knew exactly how to deal with Clodius's more mercurial mood swings. "Oh, Clodius, how truly brilliant you are!" she cooed, worshiping him with her eyes. "Caesar is accustomed to use other people, now here you are using him! I think you ought to go right on using Caesar."

Which interpretation sat very well with Clodius, who beamed and started congratulating himself on his perception. "And I *will* use him, Fulvia. He can draft some of my laws for me."

"The religious ones, definitely."

"Do you think I ought to oblige him with a favor or two?"

"No," said Fulvia coolly. "Caesar's not fool enough to expect a fellow patrician to oblige him—and by birth you're a patrician, it's in your bones."

She got up a little clumsily to stretch her legs; her new pregnancy was beginning to hamper her, and she found that a nuisance. Just when Clodius would be at the height of his tribunate, she would be waddling. Not that she intended baby woes to interfere with her presence in the Forum. In fact, the thought of scandalizing Rome afresh by appearing publicly at eight and nine months was delectable. Nor would the birth ordeal keep her away for more than a day or two. Fulvia was one of the lucky ones: she found carrying and bearing children easy. Having stretched her aching legs, she lay down again beside Clodius in time to smile at Decimus Brutus when he came in, looking jubilant because of Clodius's victory at the polls.

"I have a name—Lucius Decumius," said Clodius.

"For your source of information about the little fellows, you mean?" asked Decimus Brutus, lying down on the couch opposite.

"I mean."

"Who is he?" Decimus Brutus began to pick at a plate of food.

"The custodian of a crossroads college in the Subura. And a great friend of Caesar's, according to Lucius Decumius, who swears he changed Caesar's diapers and got up to all sorts of mischief with him when Caesar was a boy.''

"So?" asked Decimus Brutus, sounding skeptical.

"So I met Lucius Decimius and I liked him. He also liked me. And," said Clodius, his voice sinking to a conspiratorial whisper, "I've found my way into the ranks of the lowly at last—or at least that segment of the lowly which can be of use to us."

The other two leaned forward, food forgotten.

"If Bibulus has demonstrated nothing else this year," Clodius went on, "he's shown what a mockery constitutionality can be. In the name of Law he's put the triumvirs outside it. The whole of Rome is aware that what he's really done is to use a religious trick, but it's worked. Caesar's laws are in jeopardy. Well, I'll soon make that sort of trick illegal! And once I do, there will be no impediment to prevent my passing *my* laws legally."

"Except persuading the Plebs to pass them in the first place," sneered Decimus Brutus. "I can name a dozen tribunes of the plebs foiled by that factor! Not to mention the veto. There are at least four other men in your College who will adore to veto you."

"Which is where Lucius Decimius is going to come in extremely handy!" cried Clodius, his excitement obvious. "We are going to build a following among the lowly which will intimidate our Forum and senatorial opponents to the point whereat no one will have the courage to interpose a veto! No law I care to promulgate will not be passed!"

"Saturninus tried that and failed," said Decimus Brutus.

"Saturninus thought of the lowly as a crowd, he never knew any names or shared drinks with them," Clodius explained patiently. "He failed to do what a really successful demagogue must do—be selective. I don't want or need huge crowds of lowly. All I want are several groups of real rascals. Now I took one look at Lucius Decimius and knew I'd found a real rascal. We went off to a tavern on the Via Nova and talked. Chiefly about his resentment at being disqualified as a religious college. He claimed to have been an assassin in his younger days, and I believed him. But, more germane to me, he let it slip that his and quite a few of the other crossroads colleges have been running a protection ploy for—oh, centuries!''

"Protection ploy?'' asked Fulvia, looking blank.

"They sell protection from robbery and assault to shopkeepers and manufacturers.''

"Protection from whom?''

"Themselves, of course!'' said Clodius, laughing. "Fail to pay up, and you're beaten up. Fail to pay up, and your goods are stolen. Fail to pay up, and your machinery is destroyed. It's perfect.''

"I'm fascinated,'' drawled Decimus Brutus.

"It's simple, Decimus. We will use the crossroads brethren as our troops. There's no need to fill the Forum with vast crowds. All we need are enough at any one time. Two or three hundred at the most, I think. That's why we have to find out how they're gathered, where they're gathered, when they're gathered. Then we have to organize them like a little army—rosters, everything.''

"How will we pay them?'' Decimus Brutus asked. He was a shrewd and extremely capable young man, despite his appearance of mindless vice; the thought of work which would make life difficult for the *boni* and all others of boringly conservative inclination he found immensely appealing.

"We pay them by buying their wine out of our own purses. One thing I've learned is that uneducated men will do anything for you if you pay for their drinks.''

"Not enough,'' said Decimus Brutus emphatically.

"I'm well aware of that,'' said Clodius. "I'll also pay them with two pieces of legislation. One: legalize all of Rome's colleges, sodalities, clubs and fraternities again. Two: bring in a free grain dole.'' He kissed Fulvia and got up. "We are now venturing into the Subura, Decimus, where we will see old Lucius Decumius and start laying our plans for when I enter office on the tenth day of December.''

* * *

Caesar promulgated his law to prevent governors' extorting in their provinces during the month of Sextilis, sufficiently after the events of the month before to have allowed tempers to cool down. Including his own.

"I am not acting in a spirit of altruism," he said to the half-filled chamber, "nor do I object to a capable governor's enriching himself in acceptable ways. What this *lex Iulia* does is to prevent a governor's cheating the Treasury, and protect the people of his province against rapacity. For over a hundred years government of the provinces in the provinces has been a disgrace. Citizenships are sold. Exemptions from taxes, tithes and tributes are sold. The governor takes half a thousand parasites with him to drain provincial resources even further. Wars are fought for no better reason than to ensure a triumph upon the governor's return to Rome. If they refuse to yield a daughter or a field of grain, those who are not Roman citizens are subjected to the barbed lash, and sometimes decapitated. Payment for military supplies and equipment isn't made. Prices are fixed to benefit the governor or his bankers or his minions. The practice of extortionate moneylending is encouraged. Need I go further?"

Caesar shrugged. "Marcus Cato says my laws are not legal due to the activities of my consular colleague in watching the skies. I have not let Marcus Bibulus stand in my way. I will not let him stand in the way of this bill either. However, if this body refuses to give it a *consultum* of approval, I will not take it to the People. As you see from the number of buckets around my feet, it is an enormous body of law. Only the Senate has the fortitude to plough through it, only the Senate appreciates Rome's predicament anent her governors. This is a senatorial law, it must have senatorial approval." He smiled in Cato's direction. "You might say I am handing the Senate a gift—refuse it, and it will die."

Perhaps Quinctilis had acted as a catharsis, or perhaps the degree of rancor and rage had been such that the sheer intensity of emotion could not be maintained a moment longer; whatever the reason might have been, Caesar's extortion law met with universal approval in the Senate.

"It is magnificent," said Cicero.

"I have no quarrel with the smallest subclause," said Cato.

"You are to be congratulated," said Hortensius.

"It's so exhaustive it will last forever," said Vatia Isauricus.

Thus the *lex Iulia repetundarum* went to the Popular Assembly accompanied by a *senatus consultum* of consent, and passed into law halfway through September.

"I'm pleased," said Caesar to Crassus amid the turmoil of the Macellum Cuppedenis, filled to overflowing with country visitors in town for the *ludi Romani*.

"You ought to be, Gaius. When the *boni* can't find anything wrong, you should demand a new kind of triumph awarded only for the pefect law."

"The *boni* could find absolutely nothing wrong with my land laws either, but that didn't stop their opposing me," said Caesar.

"Land laws are different. There are too many rents and leases at stake. Extortion by governors in their provinces shrinks the Treasury's revenues. It strikes me, however, that you ought not to have limited your law against extortion to the senatorial class only. Knights extort in the provinces too," said Crassus.

"Only with gubernatorial consent. However, when I'm consul for the second time, I'll bring in a second extortion law aimed at the knights. It's too long a process drafting extortion laws to permit more than one per consulship."

"So you intend to be consul a second time?"

"Definitely. Don't you?"

"I wouldn't mind, actually," said Crassus thoughtfully. "I'd still love to go to war against the Parthians, earn myself a triumph at last. I can't do that unless I'm consul again."

"You will be."

Crassus changed the subject. "Have you settled on your full list of legates and tribunes for Gaul yet?" he asked.

"More or less, though not firmly."

"Then would you take my Publius with you? I'd like him to learn the art of war under you."

"I'd be delighted to put his name down."

"Your choice of legate with magisterial status rather stunned me—Titus Labienus? He's never done a thing."

"Except be my tribune of the plebs, you're inferring," said Caesar, eyes twinkling. "Acquit me of that kind of stupidity, my dear Marcus! I knew Labienus in Cilicia when Vatia Isauricus was governor. He likes horses, rare in a Roman. I need a really able cavalry commander because so many of the tribes where I'm going are horsed. Labienus will be a very good cavalry commander."

"Still planning on marching down the Danubius to the Euxine?"

"By the time I'm finished, Marcus, the provinces of Rome will marry Egypt. If you win against the Parthians when you're consul for the second time, Rome will own the world from the Atlantic Ocean to the Indus River." He sighed. "I suppose that means I'll also have to subdue Further Gaul somewhere along the way."

Crassus looked thunderstruck. "Gaius, what you're talking about would take ten years, not five!"

"I know."

"The Senate *and* the People would crucify you! Pursue a war of aggression for ten years? No one has!"

While they stood talking the crowd swirled around them in an ever-changing mass, quite a few among it with cheery greetings for Caesar, who answered with a smile and sometimes asked a question about a member of the family, or a job, or a marriage. That had never ceased to fascinate Crassus: how many people in Rome *did* Caesar know? Nor were they always Romans. Liberty-capped freedmen, skullcapped Jews, turbaned Phrygians, longhaired Gauls, shaven Syrians. If they had votes, Caesar would never go out of office. Yet Caesar always worked within the traditional forms. Do the *boni* know how much of Rome lies in the palm of Caesar's hand? No, they do not have the slightest idea. If they did, it wouldn't have been a sky watch. That dagger Bibulus sent to Vettius would have been used. Caesar would be dead. Pompeius Magnus? Never!

"I've had enough of Rome!" Caesar cried. "For almost ten years I've been incarcerated here—I can't wait to get away! Ten years in the field? Oh, Marcus, what a glorious prospect that is! Doing something which comes more naturally to me than anything else, reaping a harvest for Rome, enhancing my *dignitas,* and never having to suffer the *boni* carping and criticizing. In the field I'm the man with the authority, no one can gainsay me. Wonderful!"

Crassus chuckled. "What an autocrat you are."

"So are you."

"Yes, but the difference is that I don't want to run the whole world, just the financial side of it. Figures are so concrete and exact that men shy away from them unless they have a genuine talent for them. Whereas politics and war are vague. Every man thinks if he has luck he can be the best at them. I don't upset the *mos maiorum* and two thirds of the Senate with my brand of autocracy, it's as simple as that."

Pompey and Julia returned more or less permanently to Rome in time to help Aulus Gabinius and Lucius Calpurnius Piso campaign for the curule elections on the eighteenth day of October. Not having set eyes on his daughter since her marriage, Caesar found himself a little shocked. This was a confident, vital, sparkling and witty young matron, not the sweet and gentle adolescent of his imagination. Her rapport with Pompey was astonishing, though who was responsible for it he could not tell. The old Pompey had vanished; the new Pompey was well read, entranced by literature, spoke learnedly of this painter or that sculptor, and displayed absolutely no interest in quizzing Caesar about his military aims for the next five years. On top of which, Julia ruled! Apparently totally unembarrassed, Pompey had yielded himself to feminine domination. No imprisonment in frowning Picentine bastions for Julia! If Pompey went somewhere, Julia went too. Shades of Fulvia and Clodius!

"I'm going to build a stone theater for Rome," the Great Man said, "on land I bought out between the *saepta* and the chariot stables. This business of erecting temporary wooden theaters five or six times a year whenever there are major games is absolute insanity, Caesar. I don't care if the *mos maiorum* says theater is decadent and immoral, the fact remains that Rome falls over itself to attend the plays, and the ruder, the better. Julia says that the best memorial of my conquests I could leave Rome would be a huge stone theater with a lovely peristyle and colonnade attached, and a chamber big enough to house the Senate on its far end. That way, she says, I can get around the *mos maiorum*—an inaugurated temple for the Senate at one end, and right up the top of the auditorium a delicious little temple to Venus Victrix. Well, it has to be Venus, as Julia is directly descended from Venus, but she suggested we make her Victorious Venus to honor my conquests. Clever chicken!" Pompey ended lovingly, stroking the fashionably arranged mass of hair belonging to his wife. Who looked, thought a tickled Caesar, insufferably smug.

"Sounds ideal," said Caesar, sure they wouldn't listen.

Nor did they. Julia spoke. "We've struck a bargain, my lion and I," she said, smiling at Pompey as if they shared many thousands of secrets. "I am to have the choice of materials and decorations for the theater, and my lion has the peristyle, the colonnade and the new Curia."

"And we're going to build a modest little villa behind it, alongside the four temples," Pompey contributed, "just in case I ever get stranded on the Campus Martius again for nine months. I'm thinking of standing for consul a second time one of these days."

"Great minds think alike," said Caesar.

"Eh?"

"Nothing."

"Oh, *tata,* you should see my lion's Alban palace!" cried Julia, hand tucked in Pompey's. "It's truly amazing, just like the summer residence of the King of the Parthians, he says." She turned to her grandmother. "*Avia,* when are you going to come and stay with us there? You never leave Rome!''

''Her lion, if you please!'' snorted Aurelia to Caesar after the blissful couple had departed for the newly decorated palace on the Carinae. ''She flatters him shamelessly!''

''Her technique,'' Caesar said gravely, ''is certainly not like yours, Mater. I doubt I ever heard you address my father by any name other than his proper one, Gaius Julius. Not even Caesar.''

''Love talk is silly.''

''I'm tempted to nickname her Leo Domitrix.''

''The lion tamer.'' That brought a smile at last. ''Well, she is obviously wielding the whip and the chair!''

''Very lightly, Mater. There's Caesar in her, her blatancy is actually quite subtle. He's enslaved.''

''That was a good day's work when we introduced them. He'll guard your back well while you're away on campaign.''

''So I hope. I also hope he manages to convince the electors that Lucius Piso and Gabinius ought to be consuls next year.''

The electors were convinced; Aulus Gabinius was returned as senior consul, and Lucius Calpurnius Piso as his junior colleague. The *boni* had worked desperately to avert disaster, but Caesar had been right. So firmly *boni* in Quinctilis, public opinion was now on the side of the triumvirs. Not all the canards in the world about marriages of virgin daughters to men old enough to be their grandfathers could sway the voters, who preferred triumviral consuls to bribes, probably because Rome was empty of rural voters, who tended to rely on bribes for extra spending money at the games.

Even lacking hard evidence, Cato decided to prosecute Aulus Gabinius for electoral corruption. This time, however, he did not succeed; though he approached every praetor sympathetic to his cause, not one would agree to try the case. Metellus Scipio suggested that he should take it directly to the Plebs, and convened an Assembly to procure a law charging Gabinius with bribery.

"As no court or praetor is willing to charge Aulus Gabinius, it becomes the duty of the Comitia to do so!" shouted Metellus Scipio to the crowd clustered in the Comitia well.

Perhaps because the day was chill and drizzling rain, it was a small turnout, but what neither Metellus Scipio nor Cato realized was that Publius Clodius intended to use this meeting as a tryout for his rapidly fruiting organization of the crossroads colleges into Clodian troops. The plan was to use only those members who had that day off work, and to limit their number to less than two hundred. A decision which meant that Clodius and Decimus Brutus had needed to avail themselves of two colleges only, the one tended by Lucius Decumius and the one tended by his closest affiliate.

When Cato stepped forward to address the Assembly, Clodius yawned and stretched out his arms, a gesture which those who noticed him at all took to mean that Clodius was reveling in the fact that he was now a member of the Plebs and could stand in the Comitia well during a meeting of the Plebs.

It meant nothing of the kind. As soon as Clodius had finished yawning, some one hundred and eighty men leaped for the rostra and tore Cato from it, dragged him down into the well and began to beat him unmercifully. The rest of the seven hundred Plebs took the hint and disappeared, leaving an appalled Metellus Scipio on the rostra with the three other tribunes of the plebs dedicated to the cause of the *boni*. No tribune of the plebs possessed lictors or any other kind of official bodyguard; horrified and helpless, the four of them could only watch.

The orders were to punish Cato but leave him in one piece, and orders were obeyed. The men vanished into the soft rain, job well done; Cato lay unconscious and bleeding, but unbroken.

"Ye gods, I thought you were done for!" said Metellus Scipio when he and Ancharius managed to bring Cato round.

"What did I do?" asked Cato, head ringing.

"You challenged Gabinius and the triumvirs without

owning our tribunician inviolability. There's a message in
it, Cato—leave the triumvirs and their puppets alone,"
said Ancharius grimly.

A message which Cicero received too. The closer the
time came to Clodius's stepping into office, the more terrified Cicero grew. Clodius's constant threats to prosecute
were regularly reported to him, but all his appeals to Pompey met with nothing more than absent assurances that
Clodius wasn't serious. Deprived of Atticus (who had
gone to Epirus and Greece), Cicero could find no one interested enough to help. So when Cato was attacked in the
Well of the Comitia and word got out that Clodius was
responsible, poor Cicero despaired.

"The Beauty is going to have me, and Sampsiceramus doesn't even care!" he moaned to Terentia, whose
patience was wearing so thin that she was tempted to pick
up the nearest heavy object and crown him with it. "I
don't begin to understand Sampsiceramus! Whenever I
talk to him privately he tells me how depressed he is—
then I see him in the Forum with his child bride hanging
on his arm, and he's wreathed in smiles!"

"Why don't you try calling him Pompeius Magnus
instead of that ridiculous name?" Terentia demanded.
"Keep it up, and with that tongue in your mouth, you're
bound to slip."

"What can it matter? I'm done for, Terentia, done
for! The Beauty will send me into exile!"

"I'm surprised you haven't gone down on your knees
to kiss that trollop Clodia's feet."

"I had Atticus do it for me, to no avail. Clodia says
she has no power over her little brother."

"She'd prefer you to kiss her feet, that's why."

"Terentia, I am not and never have been engaged in
an affair with the Medea of the Palatine! You're usually
so sensible—why do you persist in carrying on about a
nonsense? Look at her boyfriends! All young enough to
be her sons—my dearest Caelius! The nicest lad! Now he
moons and drools over Clodia the way half of female
Rome moons and drools over Caesar! Caesar! Another patrician ingrate!"

"He probably has more influence with Clodius than Pompeius does," she offered. "Why not appeal to him?"

The savior of his country drew himself up. "I would rather," he said between his teeth, "spend the rest of my life in exile!"

When Publius Clodius entered office on the tenth day of December, the whole of Rome waited with bated breath. So too did the members of the inner circle of the Clodius Club, particularly Decimus Brutus, who was Clodius's general of crossroads college troops. The Well of the Comitia was too small to contain the huge crowd which assembled in the Forum on that first day to see what Clodius was going to do, so he transferred the meeting to Castor's platform and announced that he would legislate to provide every male Roman citizen with five *modii* of free wheat per month. Only that part of the crowd—a minute part— belonging to the crossroads colleges Clodius had enlisted knew what was coming; the news broke on most of the listening ears as an utter surprise.

The roar which went up was heard as far away as the Colline and Capena Gates, deafened those senators standing on the steps of the Curia Hostilia even as their eyes took in the extraordinary sight of thousands of objects shooting into the air—Caps of Liberty, shoes, belts, bits of food, anything people could toss up in exultation. And the cheering went on and on and on, never seemed likely to stop. From somewhere flowers appeared in every hand; Clodius and his nine dazed fellow tribunes of the plebs stood on Castor's platform smothered in them, Clodius beaming and clasping his hands together over his head. Suddenly he bent and began to throw the flowers back at the crowd, laughing wildly.

Still bearing the marks of his brutal beating, Cato wept. "It is the beginning of the end," he said through his tears. "We can't afford to pay for all that wheat! Rome will be bankrupt."

"Bibulus is watching the skies," said Ahenobarbus. "This new grain law of Clodius's will be as invalid as everything else passed this year."

"Oh, learn sense!" said Caesar, standing close enough to hear. "Clodius isn't one-tenth as stupid as you are, Lucius Domitius. He'll keep everything in *contio* until New Year's Day. Nothing will go to the vote until December is over. Besides, I still have my doubts about Bibulus's tactics in relation to the Plebs. Their meetings are not held under the auspices."

"I'll oppose it," said Cato, wiping his eyes.

"If you do, Cato, you'll be dead very quickly," said Gabinius. "Perhaps for the first time in her history, Rome has a tribune of the plebs without the scruples which caused the fall of the Brothers Gracchi, or the loneliness which led to the death of Sulpicius. I don't think anyone or anything can cow Clodius."

"What next will he think of?" asked Lucius Caesar, face white.

Next came a bill to restore full legality to Rome's colleges, sodalities, fraternities and clubs. Though it was not as popular with the crowd as the free grain, it was so well received that after this meeting Clodius was chaired on the shoulders of crossroads brethren, shouting themselves hoarse.

And after that Clodius announced that he would make it utterly impossible for a Marcus Calpurnius Bibulus to disrupt government ever again. The Aelian and Fufian laws were to be amended to permit meetings of People and Plebs and the passing of laws when a consul stayed home to watch the skies; to invalidate them, the consul would have to prove the occurrence of an unpropitious omen within the day on which the meeting took place. Business could not be suspended due to postponed elections. None of the changes were retroactive, nor did they protect the Senate and its deliberations, nor did they affect the courts.

"He's strengthening the Assemblies at the entire expense of the Senate," said Cato drearily.

"Yes, but at least he hasn't helped Caesar," said Ahenobarbus. "I'll bet that's a disappointment for the triumvirs!"

"Disappointment, nothing!" snapped Hortensius.

"Don't you recognize the Caesar stamp on legislation by now? It goes just far enough, but not further than custom and tradition allow. He's much smarter than Sulla, is Caesar. There are no impediments to a consul's staying home to watch the skies, simply ways around it when he does. And what does Caesar care about the supremacy of the Senate? The Senate isn't where Caesar's power lies, it never was and it never will be!"

"Where's Cicero?" demanded Metellus Scipio out of the blue. "I haven't seen him in the Forum since Clodius entered office."

"Nor will you, I suspect," said Lucius Caesar. "He's quite convinced he'll hear himself interdicted."

"Which he well may be," said Pompey.

"Do you condone his interdiction, Pompeius?" asked young Curio.

"I won't lift my shield to prevent it, be sure of that."

"Why aren't you down there cheering, Curio?" asked Appius Claudius. "I thought you were very thick with my little brother."

Curio sighed. "I think I must be growing up," he said.

"You're likely to sprout like a bean very soon," said Appius Claudius with a sour grin.

A remark which Curio understood at Clodius's next meeting when Clodius announced that he would modify the conditions under which Rome's censors functioned— Curio's father was censor.

No censor, said Clodius, would be able to strike a member of the Senate or a member of the First Class off the rolls without a full and proper hearing and the written consent of both censors. The example Clodius used was ominous for Cicero: he asserted that Mark Antony's stepfather, Lentulus Sura (who he took considerable trouble to point out had been illegally executed by Marcus Tullius Cicero with the consent of the Senate), had been struck off the senatorial rolls by the censor Lentulus Clodianus for reasons based in personal vengeance. There would be no more senatorial and equestrian purges! cried Clodius.

With four different laws under discussion throughout

December, Clodius left his legislative program at that—
and left Cicero on the brink of terror, tottering. Would he,
or wouldn't he indict Cicero? Nobody knew, and Clodius
wouldn't say.

Not since April had the city of Rome set eyes on the
junior consul, Marcus Calpurnius Bibulus. But on the last
day of December as the sun slid toward its little death, he
emerged from his house and went to resign the office
which had scarcely seen him either.

Caesar watched him and his escort of *boni* approach,
his twelve lictors carrying the *fasces* for the first time in
over eight months. How he had changed! Always a tiny
fellow, he seemed to have shrunk and crabbed, walked as
if something chewed at his bones. The face, pallid and
sharp, bore no expression save a look of cold contempt in
the silvery eyes as they rested momentarily on the senior
consul, and widened; it was more than eight months since
Bibulus had seen Caesar, and what he saw quite obviously
dismayed him. He had shrunk. Caesar had grown.

"Everything Gaius Julius Caesar has done this year
is null and void!" he cried to the gathering in the Comitia
well, only to find its members staring at him in stony disapproval. He shuddered and said nothing more.

After the prayers and sacrifices Caesar stepped forward and swore the oath that he had acquitted himself of
his duties as the senior consul to the best of his knowledge
and abilities. He then gave his valediction, about which he
had thought for days yet not known what to say. So let it
be short and let it have nothing to do with this terrible
consulship now ending.

"I am a patrician Roman of the *gens Iulia,* and my
forefathers have served Rome since the time of King
Numa Pompilius. I in my turn have served Rome: as *flamen Dialis,* as soldier, as pontifex, as tribune of the soldiers, as quaestor, as curule aedile, as judge, as Pontifex
Maximus, as *praetor urbanus,* as proconsul in Further
Spain, and as senior consul. Everything *in suo anno.* I
have sat in the Senate of Rome for just over twenty-four
years, and watched its power wane as inevitably as does

the life force in an old, old man. For the Senate is an old, old man.

"The harvest comes and goes. Plenty one year, famine the next. So I have seen Rome's granaries full, and I have seen them empty. I have seen Rome's first true dictatorship. I have seen the tribunes of the plebs reduced to ciphers, and I have seen them run rampant. I have seen the Forum Romanum under a still cold moon, blanched and silent as the tomb. I have seen the Forum Romanum awash with blood. I have seen the rostra bristling with men's heads. I have seen the house of Jupiter Optimus Maximus fall in blazing ruins, I have seen it rise again. And I have seen the emergence of a new power, the landless, unendowed and impoverished troops who upon retirement must beseech their country for a pension, and all too often I have seen them denied that pension.

"I have lived in momentous times, for since I was born forty-one years ago Rome has undergone frightful upheavals. The provinces of Cilicia, Cyrenaica, Bithynia-Pontus and Syria have been added to her empire, and the provinces she already owned have been modified beyond recognition. In my time the Middle Sea has become Our Sea. Our Sea from end to end.

"Civil war has stalked up and down Italia, not once, but seven times. In my lifetime a Roman first led his troops against the city of Rome, his homeland, though Lucius Cornelius Sulla was not the last man so to march. Yet in my lifetime no foreign foe has set foot on Italian soil. A mighty king who fought Rome for twenty-five years went down to defeat and death. He cost Rome the lives of over one hundred thousand citizens. Even so, he did not cost Rome as many lives as her civil wars have. In my lifetime.

"I have seen men die bravely, I have seen them die gibbering, I have seen them die decimated, I have seen them die crucified. But ever and always I am most moved by the plight of excellent men and the blight of mediocre men.

"What Rome has been, is, and will be depends upon us who are Romans. Beloved of the Gods, we are the only people in the history of the world to understand that a force extends two ways—forward and backward, up and down, right and left. Thus Romans have enjoyed a kind of equality with their Gods no other people has. Because no other people understands. We must strive then to understand ourselves. To understand what our position in the world demands of us. To understand that internecine strife and faces turned obdurately to the past will bring us down.

"Today I pass from the summit of my life, the year of my consulship, into other things. Different heights, for nothing ever remains the same. I am Roman back to the beginning of Rome, and before I am done the world will know this Roman. I pray to Rome. I pray for Rome. I am a Roman."

He twitched the edge of his purple-bordered toga over his head. "O almighty Jupiter Optimus Maximus—if you wish to be addressed by this name, otherwise I hail you by whatever name it is you wish to hear—you who are of whichever sex you prefer—you who are the spirit of Rome—I pray that you continue to fill Rome and all Romans with your vital forces, I pray that you and Rome become mightier yet, I pray that we always honor the terms of our contractual agreements with you, and I beg you in all legal ways to honor these same treaties. Long live Rome!"

No one moved. No one spoke. The faces were impassive.

Caesar stepped to the back of the rostra and graciously inclined his head to Bibulus.

"I do swear before Jupiter Optimus Maximus, Jupiter Feretrius, Sol Indiges, Tellus and Janus Clusivius that I, Marcus Calpurnius Bibulus, did my duty as junior consul of Rome by retiring to my house as the Sacred Books directed and there did watch the skies. I do swear that my colleague in the consulship, Gaius Julius Caesar, is *nefas* because he violated my edict—"

"Veto! Veto!" cried Clodius. "That is not the oath!"

"Then I will speak my piece unsworn!" Bibulus shouted.

"I veto your piece, Marcus Calpurnius Bibulus!"

roared Clodius. "I veto you out of office without according you the opportunity to justify a whole year of utter inertia! Go home, Marcus Calpurnius Bibulus, and watch the skies! The sun has just set on the worst consul in the history of the Republic! And thank your stars that I do not legislate to strike your name from the *fasti* and replace it with the consulship of Julius and Caesar!"

Shabby, dismal, sour, thought Caesar, sickened, and turned to walk away without waiting for anyone to catch him up. Outside the Domus Publica he paid his lictors with extreme generosity, thanked them for their year of loyal service, then asked Fabius if he and the others would be willing to accompany him to Italian Gaul for his proconsulship. Fabius accepted on behalf of everyone.

Chance threw Pompey and Crassus together not so very far behind the tall figure of Caesar disappearing into the gloom of a low and misty dusk.

"Well, Marcus, we did better together when we were consuls than Caesar and Bibulus have, little though we liked each other," said Pompey.

"He's been unlucky, inheriting Bibulus as colleague through every senior magistracy. You're right, we did do better, despite our differences. At least we ended our year amicably, neither of us altered as men. Whereas this year has changed Caesar greatly. He's less tolerant. More ruthless. Colder, and I hate to see that."

"Who can blame him? Some were determined to tear him down." Pompey strolled in silence for a little distance, then spoke again. "Did you understand his speech, Crassus?"

"I think so. On the surface, at any rate. Underneath, who knows? He layers everything to contain many meanings."

"I confess I didn't understand it. It sounded—*dark*. As if he was warning us. And what was that about showing the world?"

Crassus turned his head and produced an astonishingly large and generous smile. "I have a peculiar feeling, Magnus, that one day you will find out."

* * *

On the Ides of March the ladies of the Domus Publica held an afternoon dinner party. The six Vestal Virgins, Aurelia, Servilia, Calpurnia and Julia gathered in the dining room prepared to have a very pleasant time.

Acting as the hostess (Calpurnia would never have dreamed of usurping that role), Aurelia served every kind of delicacy she thought might appeal, including treats sticky with honey and laden with nuts for the children. After the meal was over Quinctilia, Junia and Cornelia Merula were sent outside to play in the peristyle, while the ladies drew their chairs together cozily and relaxed now that there were no avid little ears listening.

"Caesar has been on the Campus Martius now for over two months," said Fabia, who looked tired and careworn.

"More importantly, Fabia, how is Terentia bearing up?" asked Servilia. "It's been several days since Cicero fled."

"Oh well, she's sensible as always, though I do think she suffers more than she lets on."

"Cicero was wrong to go," said Julia. "I know Clodius passed the nonspecific law prohibiting the execution of Roman citizens without a trial, but my li— Magnus says it was a mistake for Cicero to go into exile voluntarily. He thinks that if Cicero had only stayed, Clodius wouldn't have drummed up the courage to pass a specific law naming Cicero. But with Cicero not there, it was easy. Magnus couldn't manage to talk Clodius out of it."

Aurelia looked skeptical, but said nothing; Julia's opinion of Pompey and her own were rather too different to bear inspection by a besotted young woman.

"Fancy looting and burning his beautiful house!" said Arruntia.

"That's Clodius, especially with all those peculiar people he seems to have running after him these days," said Popillia. "He's so—so *crazy*!"

Servilia spoke. "I hear Clodius is going to erect a temple in the spot where Cicero's house used to be."

"With Clodius as High Priest, no doubt! Pah!" spat Fabia.

"Cicero's exile can't last," said Julia positively. "Magnus is working for his pardon already."

Stifling a sigh, Servilia let her gaze meet Aurelia's. They looked at each other in complete understanding, though neither of them was imprudent enough to smile the smile she wore inside.

"Why *is* Caesar still on the Campus Martius?" asked Popillia, easing the great tiara of wool off her brow and revealing that its pressure left a red mark on fragile skin.

"He'll be there for quite some time yet," Aurelia answered. "He has to make sure his laws stay on the tablets."

"*Tata* says Ahenobarbus and Memmius are flattened," Calpurnia contributed, smoothing Felix's orange fur as he lay snoozing in her lap. She was remembering how kind Caesar had been, asking her to stay with him on the Campus Martius regularly. Though she was too well brought up and too aware what sort of man her husband was to be jealous, it still pleased her enormously that he had not invited Servilia to the Campus Martius once. All he had given Servilia was a silly pearl. Whereas Felix was alive; Felix could love back.

Perfectly aware what Calpurnia was thinking, Servilia made sure her own face remained enigmatic. I am far older and far wiser, I know the pain in parting. My farewells are said. I won't see him for years. But that poor little sow will never matter to him the way I do. Oh, Caesar, why? Does *dignitas* mean so much?

Cardixa marched in unceremoniously. "He's gone," she said baldly, huge fists on huge hips.

The room stilled.

"Why?" asked Calpurnia, paling.

"Word from Further Gaul. The Helvetii are emigrating. He's off to Genava with Burgundus, and traveling like the wind."

"I didn't say goodbye!" cried Julia, tears spilling over. "He will be away so long! What if I never see him again? The danger!"

"Caesar," said Aurelia, poking one misshapen finger into fat Felix's side, "is like *him*. A hundred lives."

Fabia turned her head to where the three little white-clad girls giggled and chased each other outside. "He promised to let them come and say farewell. Oh, they'll cry so!"

"Why shouldn't they cry?" asked Servilia. "Like us, they're Caesar's women. Doomed to stay behind and wait for our lord and master to come home."

"Yes, that is the way of things," said Aurelia steadily, and rose to lift the flagon of sweet wine. "As the senior among Caesar's women, I propose that tomorrow we all go to dig in Bona Dea's garden."

AUTHOR'S NOTE

Caesar's Women marks the arrival of copious documentation from the ancient sources, which means that I am now writing about a period very much better known to non-scholars than the periods covered by the earlier books in this series.

Only the richness of the ancient sources has permitted me to dwell more fully in this volume upon the role of Roman women in noble Roman life, as most of the memorable events of the 60s B.C. took place inside the city of Rome. This is therefore a novel about women as well as politics and war, and I am grateful for the opportunity to say more about women than in the other books, particularly because the books yet to come must return to men's doings in far-flung places. Even so, little is really known about Rome's noblewomen, though the assumptions I have made all rest upon thorough research. Many of the actual incidents are attested, including Servilia's pearl and her love letter to Caesar on that fateful December 5 in the Senate—though all we know about the contents of the letter is that they disgusted Cato when he read it.

Some readers may be disappointed in my depiction of Cicero, but I am glued to the period rather than to modern assessments of Cicero's worth; the fact remains that in his own time the attitude of his contemporaries was not nearly as flattering to him as later attitudes have been.

It has not been my habit to use this Note as a forum for scholarly dissertation, nor to defend my interpretation of events. However, I have committed one cardinal sin which does necessitate some little discussion here: namely, the fact that I have chosen to place the trial of Gaius Rabirius *after* December 5 of 63 B.C. And this despite the personal testimony of Cicero in a letter to Atticus (II-I) written from Rome in June of 60 B.C. There Cicero lists the speeches he made while consul, as Atticus has asked for them (presumably to publish them).

Cicero lists his speech in defense of Gaius Rabirius as the fourth of the year, seemingly well before the conspiracy of Catilina came to light. And on that evidence, apparently, the later historians and biographers—Plutarch, Suetonius, Cassius Dio *et alii*—all put Rabirius before Catilina, a placement which reduces the Rabirius affair to a trite, silly sort of thing. The only near contemporary, Sallust, makes absolutely no mention of Rabirius. Did we have some letters of Cicero's spontaneously written during his consulship, that would be the clincher. But we do not. The reference in Atticus II-I is almost three years later, and written when it looked as if Caesar would arrive in time to stand for election as consul. Also written when Publius Clodius was badgering Cicero with threats of prosecution for the execution of Roman citizens without trial.

I wish I could say I always believe Cicero, but I do not. Particularly when he's writing in reflection on events which affected him (and his *dignitas*) very nearly. Like all politicians and lawyers since the world began—and presumably until it ends—he was a past master at the art of manipulating the facts to make himself look good. No matter how many times one reads the *pro Rabirio perduellionis,* it is impossible to pinpoint concrete evidence as to what was happening, let alone when. This is further complicated by two facts: the first, that there are lacunae in the surviving speech, and the second, that it is quite unclear how many hearings did actually occur.

Nor, despite Cicero's protests elsewhere, was the *pro Rabirio* a great speech; if read after the Catilinarian orations, it suffers badly. For Cicero to have ended the year's collection of consular speeches with the *pro Rabirio* would have reminded all of Rome that the trial of Rabirius was, for Cicero, a hideous hint that no man who had executed citizens without trial was safe from retribution at law. When the letter to Atticus was written in June of 60 B.C., Cicero was beginning to live in fear of Publius Clodius and prosecution. The speeches of Cicero's year in office would look far better if they ended with the four orations delivered against Catilina. Memories were short. No one knew that more surely than Cicero, who banked on it every time he defended a villain. All his writings after his year as consul show a man determined to demonstrate that his actions against Catilina had saved the Republic, that he was indeed *pater patriae*. Thus I do not find it impossible to think that Cicero "rearranged" the speeches of 63 B.C. to bury Rabirius in relative obscurity and thereby attempt to ensure that Rabirius did not mar the brilliance of his fight against Catilina, nor highlight the executions which took place on December 5.

There are those who despise the "novelization of history," but as a technique of historical exploration and deduction it has something to recommend it—provided that the writer is thoroughly steeped in the history of the period concerned. I cannot possibly lay claim to the in-depth knowledge of a Greenidge on Roman law of Cicero's time, nor a Lily Ross Taylor on Roman Republican voting Assemblies, nor many other modern authorities on this or that aspect of the late Roman Republic. However, I have done my research: thirteen years of it before I began *The First Man in Rome,* and continually since (which sometimes leads to my wishing I could rewrite the earlier books!). I work in the correct way, from the ancient sources to the modern scholars, and I make up my own mind from my own work whilst not dismissing opinion and advice from modern Academe.

The novelist works entirely from a simple premise: to have the story make sense to its readers. This is by no means as easy as it sounds. The characters, all historical, have to be true both to history and psychology. Caesar, for example, does not come across in any of the ancient sources as a creature of whim, despite his flaunting borders on his long sleeves as a young man. He comes across as

a man who always had very good reason for his actions.
To place the trial of Rabirius before Catilina smacks of, if
not caprice, at least pure naughtiness on Caesar's part. It
also endows him with clairvoyance if, as many modern
scholars argue, he "ran" the trial of Rabirius to warn Cicero whereabouts a Senatus Consultum Ultimum might take
him and the Senate. Caesar was a genius, yes, but not
endowed with that kind of prescience. He waited on
events, then he acted.

The trouble with looking back on history is that we
do so with the advantage of hindsight. Our interpretations
of historical events tend to become warped by our knowledge of what happens next—a knowledge that the people
inside the moment cannot possibly have owned. Modern
politics indicates that those engaged in it blunder blindly
from one decision to another, even after copious advice
and some soul-searching. Great statesmen are capable of
forethought, but not even the greatest is capable of seeing
the future in the way that a clairvoyant purports to. Indeed,
the average politician sees no further than the next election, and that must have been particularly true of politicians during the late Roman Republic. They lived in an
action-packed atmosphere, they had only one short year in
which to make their magisterial mark, they were subject
to reprisals out of the blue from political enemies, and the
absence of political parties or anything resembling a cau-
cus mechanism predicated against even short-term planning. Individuals tried to plan, but often their own
adherents were averse to what was seen as usurpation of
other men's rights and ideas.

It was the lowering of the red flag on the Janiculum
first chewed at me. This was followed closely by the fact
that there are strong indications in the ancient sources that
Rabirius's trial (or, as I believe it was, appeal) before the
Centuries was going to result in damnation, despite his
pathetic appearance and reverenced old age. *Why* should
the lowering of the red flag have caused the Assembly to
break up so very precipitately, and *why* would the Centuries damn a broken old man for something which had

happened thirty-seven years earlier? Why, why, why? And how was I going to make the trial believable for a readership which extends from formidable Roman scholars all the way to those who know absolutely nothing about Republican Rome?

The red flag incident haunted me. For instance, the ancient sources say that Metellus Celer journeyed to the top of the Janiculum and personally ordered the red flag lowered. One of the things I do is time things—pace them out or travel them out. Even in a taxi in modern Rome it's quite a hike from the vicinity of the Piazza del Popoli to a spot beyond the Hilton Hotel! Celer would either have had to avail himself of a ferry ride, or cut back within the Servian Walls to the Pons Aemilia (the Pons Fabricius was still being rebuilt), take the Via Aurelia and then the branch road to the fortress atop the Janiculum. One imagines it was a journey he could not have made in less than two hours, even well horsed. This is the kind of logistical problem I am faced with all the time in writing an historical novel, and it's astonishing whereabouts such problems can lead me. If the lowering of the red flag was all Celer's idea, did he then have to return to the *saepta* before sounding the alarm, or could he legally depute someone else to watch for the moment in which the red flag came down? How easy would it have been to see the red flag at all if the sun was sliding into the western sky? Did Celer simply pretend the red flag had come down? Or if the ploy was prearranged between him and Caesar, why should he have needed to make the journey at all? Why not have rigged up a signal system to someone on the lookout from the Janiculum? And, since red flags have been associated with danger from time immemorial, why didn't the Romans *raise* a red flag whenever danger threatened? Why lower it?

All of which pales into insignificance when one considers the result of lowering that red flag. The vote, apparently so close to a conclusion, was abandoned immediately; the Centuries fled home to arm against the invader. Now *mos maiorum* notwithstanding, Republican Romans seem to have been a very independent-minded lot.

Tempers flared and fists flew readily, but panic was not a common reaction even when things became very violent. Prior to October 21, the entire populace (save for Cicero) believed Italy was at peace, and it was well into November before most men could be prevailed upon to take real credence in an armed uprising to the north of Rome.

There is one solution which answers these vexed questions about the red flag with a minimum of illogicality: that its descent provoked instantaneous panic because at the time of the trial of Rabirius, Catilina was known to be in Etruria with an army. A good proportion of those at the *saepta* depositing their votes would have well remembered Lepidus and the battle beneath the Quirinal, if not the advent of Sulla in 82 B.C. Many must surely have been expecting Catilina to attempt an assault on Rome. Though there were armies in the field against him, he seems generally to have been accepted as a superior military tactician to commanders like Antonius Hybrida. It has never been a great difficulty for one army to slip past another and attack the most vulnerable target. Due to the absence of legions inside the home territory, Rome herself was always very vulnerable. And those who lived in Rome were well aware of it.

If one accepts that the red flag was lowered because of the presence of Catilina in Etruria with an army, then time telescopes. The trial of Rabirius must have occurred after Catilina joined Manlius and the Sullan rebels, presumably near Faesulae. Of course one might argue that Manlius alone represented sufficient threat, though with Catilina still in Rome (he left on or after November 8) it requires an assumption that Manlius had the clout to march without Catilina. A debatable assumption, to say the least. The date on which Catilina joined Manlius would have been about November 14 to November 18 (the latter being the postulated date Catilina and Manlius were declared public enemies).

The emphasis now shifts from Celer and the red flag to Caesar and Labienus. The other end of the telescoped time scale is December 9, the last day of Labienus's tribunate of the plebs. There are approximately sixteen days intervening between the middle of November and the apprehension of the Allobroges on the Mulvian Bridge. These were days during which the Senatus Consultum Ultimum was in force, Catilina and Manlius were officially outlawed, and Rome existed in something of a dilemma as to who exactly within the city was on Catilina's side. Names were bruited, but no proof was available; the conspirators inside Rome were sitting it out. Possibly the trial of Rabirius happened during those sixteen-odd days rather than after December 5 and the execution of the five conspirators.

That I have preferred December 6 to December 9— four days altogether—lies in my interpretation of Caesar's character. On December 5 he had spoken in the House to telling effect, advocating a very harsh brand of clemency for the conspirators. One of them was his relative by marriage, the husband of Lucius Caesar's sister. *Amicitia* therefore existed, despite the fact that some years earlier Caesar had sued the brother of Julia Antonia's first husband; that had been a civil suit, not a criminal charge. In the case of Lentulus Sura, Caesar could not have done anything else than advocate clemency (and though all the ancient sources say every consular recommended the death penalty, one cannot suppose Lucius Caesar did aught else than abstain). It was Cato who turned the tide, and Cato was chief among a mere handful of men (who included Cicero!) able to provoke Caesar into losing his temper. We have examples of how swiftly and with what devastating consequences Caesar could exercise his temper. We also know that Caesar could act with a speed which left his contemporaries breathless. Four days may not have been enough for others, but was that true of Caesar?

Finally, if one looks at the *pro Rabirio perduellionis* from the standpoint that it all happened between December 6 and December 9, the only impressive objection is the ponderous pace of Roman litigation. But if the format described in Livy for the trial of Horatius be accepted, then the trial itself before the two judges would have been a very brief affair, and Rabirius's appeal to the Centuries would have gone on immediately after.

We do know that there was a huge backlash among the People, even in the First Class, because Roman citizens had been officially executed by the Senate without standing trial and without being proclaimed at law as public enemies. Would not the time immediately after those executions have been the only time the Centuries (traditionally adamantly against damning men they were trying for *perduellio*) might have been moved to damn an old man for killing Romans without a trial thirty-seven years before? To me, the fact that the Centuries were prepared to damn Rabirius is the clinching argument that the trial occurred just after the summary execution of the five conspirators.

On the one hand, the trial of Rabirius as it is reported in the ancient sources seems trite and capricious; so much so that ancient and modern scholars scratch their heads as they try to give it the significance it apparently did have. On the other hand, shift its occurrence to the days immediately after December 5, and it makes perfect sense.

It is also difficult to believe that nothing more than the threats of Publius Clodius had happened to throw Cicero into such a lather of fear about the consequences of those executions. The Clodius of the tribunate of the plebs, the street gangs and Forum violence was still to come; nor in 60 B.C. was it certain Clodius would ever be able to implement his threats, as his attempts to convert from patrician to plebeian status had thus far failed. Apparently they couldn't succeed without Caesar's connivance. I believe something earlier and much nastier predisposed Cicero to fear the threats of Clodius—or anyone else. Put Rabirius after December 5, and Cicero's terror is far more reasonable. It is also from the time of his consulship that Cicero's hatred of Caesar stemmed. Would a speech advocating clemency have been sufficient to provoke a hatred which lasted until Cicero's death? Would the trial of Rabirius have been sufficient had it come on before the conspiracy of Catilina?

That Cicero is very quiet about the trial of Rabirius in his later writings is perhaps not surprising, as he does tend to skirt matters dimming his luster. As late as 58 B.C.

there were still many in Rome who deplored the execution of citizens without trial, and attributed the bulk of the blame to Cicero rather than to Cato. Hence Cicero's flight into exile before he could be impeached by the Plebs.

And there you have it. Attractive though my hypothesis is in terms of the logic of events and the psychology of the people involved, I am not foolish enough to insist that I am right. All I will say is that within the sphere of what I am trying to do, the trial of Rabirius as I have depicted it makes perfect sense. What it boils down to is whether or not one is prepared to accept Cicero's chronology in that letter to Atticus of June, 60 B.C. His consular speeches were published in the sequence he outlined, I assume, because all the later ancient writers follow it. But was it the correct sequence, or did Cicero prefer to bury Rabirius and thus make sure the Catilinarian orations crowned his career as consul and *pater patriae*?

For the Latin purists, my apologies for using the word *boni* as an adjective and an adverb as well as as a noun. To keep it a noun would have added immensely to the clumsiness of an English prose style. For the same reason, there may be other infringements of Latin grammar.

Of necessity there are a few minor chronological and identity discrepancies, such as the exchange between Cicero and Clodius while escorting an electoral candidate.

Now for a word on the drawings.

I have managed to scrape up five drawings of women, but none of them are authenticated. During the Republic, women were not hallowed by portrait busts; those few who were cannot be identified because no coin profiles nor descriptions in the ancient sources have come down to us. Aurelia and Julia are both taken from the full-length statue of a crone in the grounds of the Villa Albani; I have used it because the bone structure of the skull so strikingly resembles that of Caesar. I freely confess that I would not have bothered with Julia were it not that some of my more romantic readers will be dying to see what she looked

like—and I would prefer that she be properly Roman as
to nose, mouth and hairstyle. Pompeia Sulla is drawn from
a wonderfully vacant-looking bust possibly of early
Empire in date. Terentia is a bust of a Roman matron in
the Ny Carlsberg Glypotek, Copenhagen. The most curious one is Servilia. Brutus's busts all reveal a slight right
facial muscle weakness; the bust I used for Servilia has an
identical right facial weakness.

Caesar is becoming easier, as I can now insert some
of the lines in the mature face. An authenticated likeness,
of course. The young Brutus is taken from a bust in the
Naples Museum which is so like the authenticated bust of
the mature Brutus in Madrid that there can be little doubt
as to who the youth is. Publius Clodius is a "youthened"
version of a bust said to be a Claudian of the late Republic.
Both Catulus and Bibulus were drawn from unidentified
portrait busts of Republican times. Cato is an authenticated
likeness, but taken from the marble bust at Castel Gan-
dolfo rather than from the famous bronze found in North
Africa; bronze is extremely difficult to draw from. I used
the bust of Cicero in the Capitol Museum because it looks
like Cicero the fat cat at the height of his fame, and serves
as a marvelous contrast to another bust of Cicero I shall
use in a later volume. The Pompey is also of the right age,
and is a more attractive portrait than the famous one in
Copenhagen.

Two further comments.

I have not tried to depict the hair of any of these
people in a realistic manner. Instead, I have formalized it
so that the nature, cut and style are easily discerned.

The second comment concerns necks. Very few of
the extant busts still own necks. Like most people who
draw well, I can really draw well only from life. If the
neck isn't there, I have terrible trouble. So my apologies
for some of the awful necks.

Finally, some thank-yous. To my classical editor, Dr.
Alanna Nobbs of Macquarie University, Sydney, and to
her husband, Dr. Raymond Nobbs. To my friends at Macquarie University. To Joseph Merlino, who found me my

very own English-language Mommsen. To Pam Crisp, Kaye Pendleton, Ria Howell, Yvonne Buffett, Fran Johnston and the rest of the "Out Yenna" staff, with a special vote of thanks to Joe Nobbs, who keeps me going with everything from chair arms to typewriters. My thanks to Dr. Kevin Coorey, who keeps me going when my bones start crumbling. And, last but by no means least, my thanks to my greatest fan, my beloved husband, Ric Robinson.

The next book in the series is tentatively called *Let the Dice Fly.*

GLOSSARY

ABSOLVO The term employed by a jury when voting for the acquittal of the accused. It was used in the courts, not in the Assemblies.

actio Plural, *actiones*. In the sense used in this book, a complete segment of a trial in a court of law. There were usually two *actiones, prima* and *secunda,* separated by a period of some days (the exact duration of this intermission was at the discretion of the court president, the *iudex*).

adamas Diamond.

adjutage The connection between a water main and the water pipes leading from the main into a building, either publicly or privately owned. The size or bore of the adjutage was strictly regulated by law, and under the authority of the aediles. Romans understood the behavior of water as a volume, but not water pressure. They did, however, appreciate gravity feed, and located their city reservoirs on the highest ground.

adrogatio The legal act of adoption, in which the *adrogatus* was formally and legally adopted by the *adrogator*. At least when the adopted person's status changed from patrician to plebeian or plebeian to patrician, the ceremony of *adrogatio* had to take place in the *comitia curiata,* where the thirty lictors representing the thirty Roman *curiae* witnessed the adoption and passed a *lex curiata* of consent to the adoption.

advocate The term generally used by modern scholars to describe a man active in the Roman law courts. "Lawyer" is considered too modern.

aedile There were four Roman magistrates called aediles; two were plebeian aediles, two were curule aediles. Their duties were confined to the city of Rome. The plebeian aediles were created first (in 493 B.C.) to assist the tribunes of the plebs in their duties, but more particularly to guard the rights of the Plebs to their headquarters, the temple of Ceres in the Forum Boarium. The plebeian aediles soon inherited supervision of the city's buildings as a whole, as well as archival custody of all plebiscites passed in the Plebeian Assembly, together with any senatorial decrees (*consulta*) directing the passage of plebiscites. They were elected by the Plebeian Assembly. Then in 367 B.C. two curule aediles were created to give the patricians a share in custody of public buildings and archives; they were elected by the Assembly of the People. Very soon, however, the curule aediles were as likely to be plebeians by status as patricians. From the third century B.C. downward, all four were responsible for the care of Rome's streets, water supply, drains and sewers, traffic, public buildings, monuments and facilities, markets, weights and measures (standard sets of these were housed in the basement of the temple of Castor and. Pollux), games, and the public grain supply. They had the power to fine citizens and noncitizens alike for infringements of any regulation appertaining to any of the above, and deposited the moneys in their coffers to help fund the games. Aedile—plebeian or curule—was not a part of the *cursus honorum,* but because of its association with the games was a valuable magistracy for a man to hold before he stood for office as praetor. As the plebeian aediles were elected by the Plebeian Assembly, I have come to believe they did not hold imperium, and therefore were not entitled to sit in the curule chair or have lictors.

Aeneas Prince of Dardania, in the Troad. He was the son of King Anchises and the Goddess Aphrodite (Venus to the Romans). When Troy (Ilium to the Romans) fell to the forces of Agamemnon, Aeneas fled the burning city with his aged father perched upon his shoulder and the Palladium under one arm. After many adventures, he arrived in Latium and founded the race from whom true Romans implicitly believed they were descended. His son, variously called Ascanius or Iulus, was the direct ancestor of the Julian family; therefore the identity of Iulus's mother is of some import. Virgil says Iulus was actually Ascanius, the son of Aeneas by his Trojan wife, Creusa, and had accompanied Aeneas on all his travels. On the other hand, Livy says Iulus was the son of Aeneas by his Latin wife, Lavinia. What the Julian family of Caesar's day believed is not known. I shall go with Livy, who on the whole seems a more reliable source than Virgil; Virgil was very much under the influence of Augustus.

aether   That part of the upper atmosphere permeated by godly forces, or the air immediately around a god. It also meant the sky, particularly the blue sky of daylight.

ager publicus   Land vested in Roman public ownership. Most of it was acquired by right of conquest or confiscated from its original owners as a punishment for disloyalty. This latter was particularly common within Italy itself. Roman *ager publicus* existed in every overseas province, in Italian Gaul, and inside the Italian Peninsula. Responsibility for its disposal (usually in the form of large leaseholds) lay in the purlieu of the censors, though much of the foreign *ager publicus* was unused.

agora   The open space, usually surrounded by colonnades or some kind of public buildings, which served any Greek or Hellenic city as its public meeting place and civic center. The Roman equivalent was a forum.

Alba Longa   The city of the Alban Mount supposed to have been founded by Iulus or Ascanius, the son of Aeneas. In the time of King Tullus Hostilius it was attacked by Rome, defeated and razed to the ground. Some of its most prominent citizen families had already migrated to Rome; others were compelled to do so then at the command of King Tullus Hostilius.

Albanians   The members of a tribe occupying the lands between the high Caucasus and the Caspian Sea.

amanuensis   One who takes down in writing the words dictated by another.

amicitia   A condition of formal friendship between families (or states) of equal status; when status was unequal, the bond was more likely to be a client-patron one. *Ami-*

citia was traditional and passed on from one generation of a family to the next.

amphora Plural, amphorae. A pottery vessel, bulbous in shape, with a narrow neck and two large handles on the upper part, and a pointed or conical bottom which prevented its being stood upright on level ground. It was used for the bulk (usually maritime) transport of wine or wheat, its pointed bottom enabling it to be fitted easily into the sawdust which filled the ship's hold or cart's interior. It then sat upright during the journey, cushioned and protected. The pointed bottom enabled it to be dragged across level ground by a handler with considerable ease in loading and unloading. The usual size of amphora held about 6 American gallons (25 liters).

amygdala Plural, *amygdalae*. Something almond-shaped.

Anatolia Roughly, modern Asian Turkey. It extended from the south coast of the Black Sea (the Euxine) through to the Mediterranean, and from the Aegean Sea in the west to modern Armenia, Iran and Syria in the east and south. The Taurus and Antitaurus Mountains made its interior and much of its coastline very rugged. Its climate was continental.

animus *The Oxford Latin Dictionary* has the best definition, so I will quote it: "The mind as opposed to the body, the mind or soul as constituting with the body the whole person." There are further definitions, but this one is pertinent to the way *animus* is used herein. One must be careful, however, not to attribute belief in the immortality of the soul to Romans.

apex A close-fitting priest's helmet made of ivory. It covered all the hair but left the ears free, and was surmounted by a wooden spike on which was impaled a disc of wool.

Arausio In this book, used to mean the battle fought on October 6 of 105 B.C. near the town of Arausio in Further Gaul. A vast mass of migrating German tribes was moving down the east bank of the Rhodanus River (the Rhône) and was opposed by two Roman armies which the Senate had ordered to amalgamate under the authority of the con-

sul of the year, the New Man Gnaeus Mallius Maximus.
But the proconsul Quintus Servilius Caepio, a patrician,
refused to co-operate with Mallius Maximus because of
his low birth, and insisted on keeping his army separate.
The result was a defeat for Rome worse than the defeat at
Cannae; the number of Roman soldiers killed was said to
be over eighty thousand.

Armenia Magna In ancient times, Armenia Magna extended from the southern Caucasus to the Araxes River,
east to the corner of the Caspian Sea, and west to the
sources of the Euphrates. It was immensely mountainous
and very cold.

Armenia Parva Though called Little Armenia, this
small land occupying the rugged and mountainous regions
of the upper Euphrates and Arsanias rivers was not a part
of the Kingdom of Armenia. Until taken over by the sixth
King Mithridates of Pontus, it was ruled by its own royal
house, but always owed allegiance to Pontus rather than
to Armenia proper.

armillae The wide bracelets of gold or of silver awarded
as prizes for valor to Roman legionaries, centurions, cadets
and military tribunes of more junior rank.

Assembly (*comitia*) Any gathering of the Roman People
convoked to deal with governmental, legislative, judicial,
or electoral matters. In the time of Caesar there were three
true Assemblies—the Centuries, the People, and the Plebs.

The **Centuriate Assembly (*comitia centuriata*)** marshaled the People, patrician and plebeian, in their Classes,
which were filled by a means test and were economic in
nature. As this was originally a military assemblage, each
Class gathered in the form of Centuries. The **Eighteen**
(q.v.) numbered only one hundred men each, whereas the
other Centuries held many more than a hundred men. The
Centuriate Assembly met to elect consuls, praetors, and
(every five years, usually) censors. It also met to hear
charges of major treason (*perduellio*) and could pass laws.
Because of its originally military nature, the Centuriate
Assembly was obliged to meet outside the *pomerium,* and
normally did so on the Campus Martius at a place called

the *saepta*. It was not usually convoked to pass laws or conduct trials.

The **Assembly of the People** or **Popular Assembly** (*comitia populi tributa*) allowed the full participation of patricians, and was tribal in nature. It was convoked in the thirty-five tribes into which all Roman citizens were placed. Called together by a consul or praetor, it normally met in the Well of the Comitia. It elected the curule aediles, the quaestors, and the tribunes of the soldiers. It could formulate and pass laws; until Sulla established his standing courts, many trials were held in it.

The **Plebeian Assembly** (*comitia plebis tributa* or *concilium plebis*) met in the thirty-five tribes, but did not allow the participation of patricians. Because it contained a part only of the People, the Plebeian Assembly was not "official" in the same way as the Centuriate and Popular Assemblies. The auspices were not taken nor prayers said. The only magistrate empowered to convoke it was the tribune of the plebs. It had the right to enact laws (strictly, plebiscites) and conduct trials, though the latter were far less common after Sulla established his standing courts. Its members elected the plebeian aediles and the tribunes of the plebs. The normal place for its assemblage was in the Well of the Comitia. See also **voting** and **tribe**.

atrium   The main reception room of a Roman *domus,* or private house. It mostly contained an opening in the roof (the *compluvium*) above a pool (the *impluvium*) originally intended as a water reservoir for domestic use. By the time of the late Republic, the pool had become ornamental only.

auctoritas   A very difficult Latin term to translate, as it meant far more than the English word "authority" implies. It carried nuances of pre-eminence, clout, public importance and—above all—the ability to influence events through public office. All the magistracies possessed *auctoritas* as an intrinsic part of their nature, but *auctoritas* was not confined to those who held magistracies; the Princeps Senatus, Pontifex Maximus, other priests and augurs, consulars, and even some private individuals outside the ranks of the Senate also owned *auctoritas*.

augur   A priest whose duties concerned divination. He

and his fellow augurs comprised the College of Augurs, an official State body which had numbered twelve members (usually six patricians and six plebeians) until in 81 B.C. Sulla increased it to fifteen members; thereafter it usually contained at least one more plebeian than patrician. Originally augurs were co-opted by their fellow augurs, but in 104 B.C. Gnaeus Domitius Ahenobarbus brought in a law compelling election of future augurs by an Assembly of seventeen tribes chosen from the thirty-five by lot. Sulla removed election in 81 B.C., going back to co-optation, but in 63 B.C. the tribune of the plebs Titus Labienus restored election. The augur did not predict the future, nor did he pursue his auguries at his own whim; he inspected the proper objects or signs to ascertain whether or not the projected undertaking was one meeting with the approval of the Gods, be the undertaking a *contio* (q.v.), a war, a new law, or any other State business, including elections. There was a standard manual of interpretation to which the augur referred; augurs "went by the book." The augur wore the *toga trabea* (q.v.) and carried a staff called the *lituus* (q.v.).

auguraculum   A station on the Capitol whereat the new consuls stood their night watch to observe the skies before they were inaugurated.

avia   Grandmother.

avus   Grandfather.

bailiff   Not a word truly applicable to Roman Republican times, but one I have used to describe men deputed to keep law and order if lictors were not employed, and also to describe men employed by moneylenders to harass a debtor and prevent his absconding.

bireme   A ship constructed for use in naval warfare, and intended to be rowed rather than sailed (though it was equipped with a mast and sail, usually left ashore if action was likely). Some biremes were decked or partially decked, but most were open. It seems likely that the oarsmen sat in two levels at two banks of oars, the upper bank and its oarsmen accommodated in an outrigger, and the lower bank's oars poking through ports in the galley's sides. Built of fir or another lightweight pine, the bireme could be manned only in fair weather, and fight battles only in very calm seas. It was much longer than it was wide in the beam (the ratio was about 7:1), and probably averaged about 100 feet (30 meters) in length. Of oarsmen it carried upward of one hundred. A bronze-reinforced beak (*rostrum*) made of oak projected forward of the bow just below the waterline, and was used for ramming and sinking other vessels. The bireme was not designed to carry marines or grapple to engage other vessels in land-style combat. Throughout Greek and Republican Roman times, the ship was rowed by professional oarsmen, never by slaves.

boni Literally, "the good men." It was used of those men who belonged to an ultraconservative faction within and without the Senate of Rome. I have sometimes mis-used it in its Latin grammatical form because it is so clumsy in English always to use it as a noun; hence I have used it as an adjective or adverb from time to time.

Brothers Gracchi See **Gracchi.**

Campus Martius The Field of Mars. Situated north of the Servian Walls, the Campus Martius was bounded by the Capitol on its south and the Pincian Hill on its east; the rest of it was enclosed by a huge bend in the Tiber River. In Republican times it was not inhabited as a sub-urb, but was the place where triumphing armies bivou-acked, the young were trained in military exercises, horses engaged in chariot racing were stabled and trained, public slaves had their barracks, the Centuriate Assembly met, and market gardening vied with parklands. At the apex of the river bend lay the public swimming holes called the Trigarium, and just to the north of the Trigarium were medicinal hot springs called the Tarentum. The Via Lata (Via Flaminia) crossed the Campus Martius on its way to the Mulvian Bridge, and the Via Recta bisected it at right angles to the Via Lata.

Carinae One of Rome's more exclusive addresses. In-corporating the Fagutal, the Carinae was the northern tip of the Oppian Mount on its western side; it extended be-tween the Velia and the Clivus Pullius. Its outlook was southwestern, across the swamps of the Palus Ceroliae toward the Aventine.

Castor The never-forgotten Heavenly Twin. Though the imposing temple in the Forum Romanum was properly the temple of Castor and Pollux (also called the Dioscuri), it was always referred to by Romans as Castor's. This led to many jokes about dual enterprises in which one of the two prime movers was consistently overlooked. Religiously, Castor and Pollux were among the principal deities worshiped by Romans, perhaps because, like Romulus and Remus, they were twins.

catamite A youth used for homosexual purposes.

Celtiberian The general term covering the tribes inhabiting northern and north-central Spain. As the name suggests, racially they were an admixture of migratory Celts from Gaul and the more ancient indigenous Iberian stock. Their towns were almost all erected upon easily fortified crags, hills or rocky outcrops, and they were past masters at guerrilla warfare.

censor The censor was the most august of all Roman magistrates, though he lacked imperium and was therefore not entitled to be escorted by lictors. Two censors were elected by the Centuriate Assembly to serve for a period of five years (called a *lustrum*); censorial activity was, however, mostly limited to the first eighteen months of the *lustrum,* which was ushered in by a special sacrifice, the *suovetaurilia,* of pig, sheep and ox. No man could stand for censor unless he had been consul first, and usually only those consulars of notable *auctoritas* and *dignitas* bothered to stand. The censors inspected and regulated membership in the Senate and the Ordo Equester, and conducted a general census of Roman citizens throughout the Roman world. They had the power to transfer a citizen from one tribe to another as well as one Class to another. They applied the means test. The letting of State contracts for everything from the farming of taxes to public works was also their responsibility. In 81 B.C. Sulla abolished the office, but the consuls Pompey and Crassus restored it in 70 B.C. The censor wore a solid purple toga, the *toga purpurea.*

Centuriate Assembly See **Assembly**.

centurion The regular professional officer of both Roman citizen and auxiliary infantry legions. It is a mistake to equate him with the modern non-commissioned officer; centurions enjoyed a relatively exalted status uncomplicated by modern social distinctions. A defeated Roman general hardly turned a hair if he lost even senior military tribunes, but tore his hair out in clumps if he lost centurions. Centurion rank was graduated; the most junior commanded an ordinary century of eighty legionaries and twenty noncombatant assistants, but exactly how he progressed in what was apparently a complex chain of progressive seniority is not known. In the Republican army as reorganized by Gaius Marius, each cohort had six *centuriones* (singular, *centurio*), with the most senior man, the *pilus prior,* commanding the senior century of his cohort as well as the entire cohort. The ten men commanding the ten cohorts which made up a full legion were also ranked in seniority, with the legion's most senior centurion, the *primus pilus* (this term was later reduced to *primipilus*), answering only to his legion's commander (either one of the elected tribunes of the soldiers or one of the general's legates). During Republican times promotion to centurion was up from the ranks. The centurion had certain easily recognizable badges of office: he wore greaves on his shins, a shirt of scales rather than chain links, and a helmet crest projecting sideways rather than front-to-back; he carried a stout knobkerrie of vine wood. He also wore many decorations.

chryselephantine A work of art fashioned in a combination of gold and ivory.

Circus Flaminius The circus situated on the Campus Martius not far from the Tiber and the Forum Holitorium. Built in 221 B.C., it sometimes served as a place for a comitial meeting, when the Plebs or the People had to meet outside the *pomerium*. It seems to have been well used as a venue for the games, but for events pulling in smaller attendances than the Circus Maximus, as it could accommodate no more than fifty thousand spectators.

Circus Maximus The old circus built by King Tarquinius Priscus before the Republic began. It filled the whole of the Vallis Murcia, a declivity between the Palatine and Aventine mounts. Even though its capacity was at least 150,000 spectators, there is ample evidence that during Republican times freedman citizens were classified as slaves when it came to admission to the Circus Maximus, and were thus denied. Just too many people wanted to go to the circus games. Women were permitted to sit with men.

citizenship For the purposes of this series of books, the Roman citizenship. Possession of it entitled a man to vote in his tribe and his Class (if he was economically qualified to belong to a Class) in all Roman elections. He could not be flogged, he was entitled to the Roman trial process, and he had the right of appeal. The male citizen became liable for military service on his seventeenth birthday. After the *lex Minicia* of 91 B.C., the child of a union between a Roman citizen of either sex and a non-Roman was forced to assume the citizenship of the non-Roman parent.

Classes These were five in number, and represented the economic divisions of property-owning or steady-income-earning Roman citizens. The members of the First Class were the richest, the members of the Fifth Class the poorest. Those Roman citizens who belonged to the *capite censi* or Head Count were too poor to qualify for a Class status, and so could not vote in the Centuriate Assembly. In actual fact, it was rare for the Third Class to be called upon to vote in the Centuriate Assembly, let alone members of the Fourth or Fifth Class!

client In Latin, *cliens*. The term denoted a man of free or freed status (he did not have to be a Roman citizen) who pledged himself to a man he called his patron. In the most solemn and binding way, the client undertook to serve the interests and obey the wishes of his patron. In return he received certain favors—usually gifts of money, or a job, or legal assistance. The freed slave was automatically the client of his ex-master until discharged of this obligation—if he ever was. A kind of honor system governed the client's conduct in relation to his patron, and was adhered to with remarkable consistency. To be a client did not necessarily mean that a man could not also be a patron; more that he could not be an ultimate patron, as technically his own clients were also the clients of his patron. During the Republic there were no formal laws concerning the client-patron relationship because they were not necessary—no man, client *or* patron, could hope to succeed in life were he known as dishonorable in this vital function. However, there were laws regulating the foreign client-patron relationship: foreign states or client-kings acknowledging Rome as patron were legally obliged to find the ransom for any Roman citizen kidnapped in their territories, a fact that pirates relied on heavily for an additional source of income. Thus, not only individuals could become clients; whole towns and even countries often were.

clivus A hilly street.

coercitio The right of a curule magistrate to exact obedience to his directives by punitive measures. A citizen could not appeal against a magistrate invoking *coercitio* unless he was a plebeian and appealed to all ten tribunes of the plebs to rescue him. The customary measures were fines or confiscation of property; for a magistrate to physically chastise was extremely rare.

cognomen The last name of a Roman male anxious to distinguish himself from all his fellows possessed of identical first (*praenomen*) and family (*nomen*) names. He might adopt one for himself, as did Pompey with the *cognomen* Magnus, or simply continue to bear a *cognomen* which had been in the family for generations, as did the Julians cognominated Caesar. In some families it became necessary to have more than one *cognomen:* for example, Quintus Caecilius Metellus Pius Cornelianus Scipio Nasica, who was the adopted son of Metellus Pius the Piglet. Quintus was his first name (*praenomen*), Caecilius was his family name (*nomen*); Metellus Pius were *cognomina* belonging to his adoptive father; Cornelianus indicated that he was by blood a Cornelian; and Scipio Nasica were the *cognomina* of his blood father. As things turned out, he was always known as Metellus Scipio, a neat compromise to both blood and adoptive family.

The *cognomen* often pointed up some physical characteristic or idiosyncrasy—jug ears, flat feet, humpback, swollen legs—or else commemorated some great feat—as in the Caecilii Metelli who were cognominated Dalmaticus, Balearicus, Macedonicus, Numidicus, these being related to a country each man had conquered. The best *cognomina* were heavily sarcastic—Lepidus, meaning a thoroughly nice fellow, attached to a right bastard—or extremely witty—as with the already multiple-cognominated Gaius Julius Caesar Strabo Vopiscus, who earned an additional name, Sesquiculus, meaning he was more than just an arsehole, he was an arsehole and a half.

cohort   The tactical unit of the legion. It comprised six centuries, and each legion owned ten cohorts. When discussing troop movements, it was more customary for the general to speak of his army in terms of cohorts than legions—which perhaps indicates that, at least until the time of Caesar, the general deployed or peeled off cohorts in battle. The maniple, formed of two centuries (there were three maniples to the cohort), ceased to have any tactical significance from the time of Marius.

college   A body or society of men having something in common. Rome owned priestly colleges (such as the College of Pontifices), political colleges (as the College of Tribunes of the Plebs), civil colleges (as the College of Lictors), and trade colleges (for example, the Guild of Undertakers). Certain groups of men from all walks of life, including slaves, banded together in what were called crossroads colleges to look after the city of Rome's major crossroads and conduct the annual feast of the crossroads, the Compitalia.

comitia   See **Assembly.**

Comitia   The large round well in which meetings for the *comitia* were held. It was located in the lower Forum Romanum adjacent to the steps of the Senate House and the Basilica Aemilia, and proceeded below ground level in a series of steps, forming tiers upon which men stood; comitial meetings were never conducted seated. When packed, the well could hold perhaps two or three thousand

men. The rostra, or speaker's platform, was grafted into
one side.

CONDEMNO The word employed by a jury to deliver
a verdict of "guilty." It was a term confined to the courts;
both courts and Assemblies had their own vocabularies.

confarreatio The oldest and strictest of the three forms
of Roman marriage. By the time of Caesar, the practice of
confarreatio was confined to patricians, and then was not
mandatory. One of the chief reasons why *confarreatio* lost
much popularity lay in the fact that the *confarreatio* bride
passed from the hand of her father to the hand of her
husband, and thus had far lèss freedom than women married in the usual way; she could not control her dowry nor
conduct business. The other main reason for the unpopu-
larity of *confarreatio* lay in the extreme difficulty of dis-
solving it; divorce (*diffareatio*) was so legally and
religiously arduous that it was more trouble than it was
worth unless the circumstances left no alternative.

Conscript Fathers When it was established by the kings
of Rome (traditionally by Romulus himself), the Senate
consisted of one hundred patricians entitled *patres*—"fathers." Then when plebeian senators were added during
the first years of the Republic, they were said to be *conscripti*—"chosen without a choice." Together, the patrician and plebeian members were said to be *patres et
conscripti;* gradually the once-distinguishing terms were
run together, and all members of the Senate were simply
the Conscript Fathers.

consul The consul was the most senior Roman magistrate owning imperium, and the consulship (modern scholars do not refer to it as the "consulate" because a
consulate is a modern diplomatic institution) was the top
rung on the *cursus honorum.* Two consuls were elected
each year by the Centuriate Assembly, and served for one
year. They entered office on New Year's Day (January 1).
One was senior to the other; he was the one who had
polled his requisite number of Centuries first. The senior
consul held the *fasces* (q.v.) for the month of January,
which meant his junior colleague looked on. In February
the junior consul held the *fasces,* and they alternated

month by month throughout the year. Both consuls were
escorted by twelve lictors, but only the lictors of the consul
holding the *fasces* that month shouldered the actual *fasces*
as they preceded him wherever he went. By the last century of the Republic, a patrician or a plebeian could be
consul, though never two patricians together. The proper
age for a consul was forty-two, twelve years after entering
the Senate at thirty, though there is convincing evidence
that Sulla in 81 B.C. accorded patrician senators the privilege of standing for consul two years ahead of any plebeian, which meant the patrician could be consul at forty
years of age. A consul's *imperium* knew no bounds; it
operated not only in Rome and Italy, but throughout the
provinces as well, and overrode the imperium of a proconsular governor. The consul could command any army.

consular The name given to a man after he had been
consul. He was held in special esteem by the rest of the
Senate, and until Sulla became Dictator was always asked
to speak or give his opinion in the House ahead of the
praetors, consuls-elect, etc. Sulla changed that, preferring
to exalt magistrates in office and those elected to coming
office. The consular, however, might at any time be sent
to govern a province should the Senate require the duty
of him. He might also be asked to take on other duties,
like caring for the grain supply.

consultum The term for a senatorial decree, though it
was expressed more properly as a *senatus consultum*. It
did not have the force of law. In order to become law, a
consultum had to be presented by the Senate to any of the
Assemblies, tribal or centuriate, which then voted it into
law—*if* the members of the Assembly requested felt like
voting it into law. However, many senatorial *consulta*
(plural) were never submitted to any Assembly, therefore
were never voted into law, yet were accepted as laws by
all of Rome; among these *consulta* were decisions about
provincial governors, the declaration and conduct of wars,
and all to do with foreign affairs. Sulla in 81 B.C. gave
these particular senatorial decrees the formal status of
laws.

contio Plural, *contiones*. This was a preliminary meeting

of a comitial Assembly in order to discuss the promulgation of a projected law, or any other comitial business. All
three Assemblies were required to debate a measure in
contio, which, though no voting took place, had nonetheless to be convoked by the magistrate empowered.

contubernalis A military cadet: a subaltern of lowest
rank and age in the hierarchy of Roman military officers,
but excluding the centurions. No centurion was ever a cadet; he was an experienced soldier.

corona civica Rome's second-highest military decora-
tion. A crown or chaplet made of oak leaves, it was
awarded to a man who had saved the lives of fellow soldiers and held the ground on which he did this for the rest
of the duration of a battle. It could not be awarded unless
the saved soldiers swore a formal oath before their general
that they spoke the truth about the circumstances. L. R.
Taylor argues that among Sulla's constitutional reforms
was one relating to the winners of major military crowns;
that, following the tradition of Marcus Fabius Buteo, he
promoted these men to membership in the Senate, which
answers the vexed question of Caesar's senatorial status
(complicated as it was by the fact that, while *flamen Dialis,*
he had been a member of the Senate from the time he put
on the *toga virilis*). Gelzer agreed with her—but, alas,
only in a footnote.

corpus animusque Body and soul.

cuirass Armor encasing a man's upper body without
having the form of a shirt. It consisted of two plates of
bronze, steel, or hardened leather, the front one protecting
thorax and abdomen, the other the back from shoulder to
lumbar spine. The plates were held together by straps or
hinges at the shoulders and along each side under the arms.
Some cuirasses were exquisitely tailored to the contours
of an individual's torso, while others fitted any man of a
particular size and physique. The men of highest rank—
generals and legates—wore cuirasses tooled in high relief
and silver-plated (sometimes, though rarely, gold-plated).
Presumably as an indication of imperium, the general and
perhaps the most senior of his legates wore a thin red sash
around the cuirass about halfway between the nipples and

waist; the sash was ritually knotted and looped.

cunnus An extremely offensive Latin profanity—
"cunt."

Cuppedenis Markets Latin: *macellum Cuppedenis*.
Specialized markets lying behind the upper Forum Romanum on its eastern side, between the Clivus Orbius and
the Carinae/Fagutal. In it were vended luxury items like
pepper, spices, incense, ointments and unguents and
balms; it also served as the flower market, where a Roman
(all Romans loved flowers) could buy anything from a
bouquet to a garland to go round the neck or a wreath to
go on the head. Until sold to finance Sulla's campaign
against King Mithridates, the actual land belonged to the
State. It was flanked on its Esquiline side by *horrea pi-
perata*—warehouses storing spices and aromatics.

Curia Hostilia The Senate House. It was thought to
have been built by the shadowy third King of Rome, Tullus Hostilius, hence its name: "the meeting-house of Hostilius."

cursus honorum See **magistrates**.

curule chair The *sella curulis* was the ivory chair reserved exclusively for magistrates owning imperium.
Beautifully carved in ivory, the chair itself had curved legs
crossing in a broad X, so that it could be folded up. It was
equipped with low arms, but had no back.

curule magistrate A magistrate owning imperium and
therefore entitled to sit upon a curule chair.

custos An official delegated to supervise during a voting
procedure in one of the *comitia*.

Dacia A large area of land consisting of Hungary east
of the Tisa River, western Rumania and Transylvania. The
racial origins of the earliest peoples are cloudy, but by the
time Rome of the last century B.C. came to know anything
about Dacia its peoples were Celtic, at least in culture and
skill in mining and refining metals. Dacians were organized into tribes, lived in a settled way, and practised agriculture. After the rise of King Burebistas during the 60s
B.C., Dacian tribes began incursions into Roman-
dominated areas of northern Macedonia and Illyricum, and
became something of a concern to Rome.

DAMNO The word employed by a comitial Assembly to indicate a verdict of "guilty." It was not used in the courts.

Danubius River Also called the Danuvius by the Romans; to the Greeks it was the Ister, though the Greeks never knew its sources or course until the river approached its outflow into the Euxine (Black) Sea. Romans of Caesar's time knew vaguely that it was a very great and very long river, and that it flowed through Pannonia, the south of Dacia and the north of Moesia. It is variously known today as the Danube, Donau, Duna, Dunav, Dunarea and Dunay.

demagogue Originally a Greek concept, the demagogue was a politician whose chief appeal was to the crowds. The Roman demagogue (almost inevitably a tribune of the plebs) preferred the arena of the Comitia well to the Senate House, but it was no part of his policy to "liberate the masses," nor on the whole were those who flocked to listen to him composed of the very lowly. The term simply indicated a crowd-pleaser.

denarius Plural, denarii. Save for a very rare issue or two of gold coins, the denarius was the largest denomination of coin under the Republic. Of pure silver, it contained about 3.5 grams of the metal, and was about the size of a dime—very small. There were 6,250 denarii to 1 silver talent. Of actual coins in circulation, the majority were probably denarii.

diadem This was not a crown or a tiara, but simply a thick white ribbon about 1 inch (25 millimeters) wide, each end embroidered and often finished with a fringe. It was the symbol of the Hellenic sovereign; only the King and/or Queen could wear it. The coins show that it was worn either across the forehead or behind the hairline, and was knotted at the back below the occiput; the two ends trailed down onto the shoulders.

Didian Law See *lex Caecilia Didia*.

dies agonales There were four *dies agonales* in the Republican calendar: January 9, March 17, May 21 and December 11. The exact meaning of *agonalis* (plural, *agonales*) is disputed, but what can be established is that

on all four *dies agonales* the Rex Sacrorum sacrificed a
ram in the Regia. The gods involved seem to have been
Jupiter, Janus, Mars, Vediovis and Sol Indiges.

dies nefasti   Some fifty-eight days of the Republican calendar were marked *nefasti*. On them, citizens could not
initiate a lawsuit in the urban praetor's court or jurisdic-
tion, nor could voting meetings of the *comitia* be held.
However, the Senate could meet on *dies nefasti,* lawsuits
in the standing courts could proceed, and *contiones* could
take place in the *comitia.*

dies religiosi   Unlucky and ill-omened days. There were
several kinds, which included the three days of the year
on which the *mundus* (q.v.) was opened to allow the dead
to wander; the days when Vesta's shrine was open in June;
and the rites of the **Salii** (q.v.), priests of Mars. On *dies
religiosi* it was wrong or unlucky to do anything deemed
unnecessary, from beginning a marriage or a journey to
recruiting soldiers or holding meetings of the *comitia.*
Three of these days each month (the days after the Kalends, the Nones and the Ides) were considered so ill-
omened they had a special name, *dies atri,* or black days.

dignitas   Like *auctoritas* (q.v.), the Latin *dignitas* has
connotations not conveyed by the English word derived
from it, ''dignity.'' It was a man's personal clout in the
Roman world rather than his public standing, though his
public standing was enormously enhanced by great *dignitas.* It gave the sum total of his integrity, pride, family
and ancestors, word, intelligence, deeds, ability, knowledge, and worth as a man. Of all the assets a Roman nobleman possessed, *dignitas* was likely to be the one he
was most touchy about and protective of. I have elected
to leave the term untranslated in my text.

dolabra   Plural, *dolabrae.* This was the legionary's digging tool, a composite instrument which looked a little like
a pick at one end and a mattock at the other. Unless deputed to carry some other kind of tool, each soldier carried
one in his pack.

Doric   One of the three Greek architectural orders. The
capital of a Doric column (which might be plain or fluted)

was the plainest, and looked a little like the underside of a saucer.

drachma The name I have elected to use when speaking of Hellenic currency rather than Roman, because the drachma most closely approximated the denarius in weight at around 4 grams. Rome, however, was winning the currency race because of the central and uniform nature of Roman coins; during the late Republic, the world was beginning to prefer to use Roman coins rather than Hellenic.

duumviri Literally, "two men." It usually referred to two men of equal magisterial rank who were deputed as judges or elected as the senior magistrates of a *municipium* (q.v.).

Ecastor! Edepol! The most genteel and inoffensive of Roman exclamations of surprise or amazement, roughly akin to "Gee!" or "Wow!" Women used "Ecastor!" and men "Edepol!" The roots suggest they invoked Castor and Pollux.

edicta Singular, *edictum*. These were the rules whereby an elected magistrate outlined the way in which he was going to go about and discharge his magisterial duties. They were published by each magistrate at the beginning of his tenure of office, and he was supposed to abide by them throughout his term. That he often did not led to legislation compelling him to do so.

Eighteen In this book, used to refer to the eighteen senior Centuries of the First Class. See also **knights**.

Elymais A very fertile, large tract of land to the east of the lower Tigris River. It extended from the **Mare Erythraeum** (q.v.) to the hills around Susa, and lay in the domains of the King of the Parthians.

Epicurean Pertaining to the philosophical system of the Greek Epicurus. Originally Epicurus had advocated a kind of hedonism so exquisitely refined that it approached asceticism on its left hand, so to speak: a man's pleasures were best sampled one at a time, and strung out with such relish that any excess defeated the exercise. Public life or any other stressful work was forbidden. These tenets underwent considerable modification in Rome, so that a Roman nobleman could call himself an Epicurean yet still

espouse his public career. By the late Republic, the chief
pleasures of an Epicurean were food and wine.

epitome A synopsis or abridgment of a longer work
which concentrated more on packing a maximum amount
of information into a minimum wordage than on literary
style or literary excellence. The object of the epitome was
to enable an individual to gather encyclopaedic knowledge
without needing to plough through an entire work. Brutus
was very well known as an epitomizer.

equestrian Pertaining to the knights.

ethnarch The general Greek word for a city or town
magistrate. There were other and more specific names in
use, but I do not think it necessary to compound confusion
in readers by employing a more varied terminology.

Euxine Sea The modern Black Sea. Because of the enormous number of major rivers which flowed into it (especially in times before water volume was regulated by
dams), the Euxine Sea contained less salt than other seas;
the current through the Thracian Bosporus and Hellespont
always flowed from the Euxine toward the Mediterranean
(the Aegean)—which made it easy to quit the Euxine, but
hard to enter it.

faction The following of a Roman politician is best described as a faction; in no way could a man's followers
be described as a political party in the modern sense. A
faction formed around a man owning *auctoritas* and *dignitas,* and was purely evidence of that individual's ability
to attract and hold followers. Political ideologies did not
exist, nor did party lines.

fasces The *fasces* were bundles of thirty (one rod for
each *curia*) birch rods ritually tied together in a crisscross
pattern by red leather thongs. Originally an emblem of the
Etruscan kings, they passed into the customs of the emerging Rome, persisted in Roman life throughout the Republic, and on into the Empire. Carried by men called lictors,
the *fasces* preceded the curule magistrate (and the propraetor and proconsul as well) as the outward symbol of
his imperium. Within the *pomerium* only the rods went
into the bundles, to signify that the curule magistrate had
the power to chastise, but not to execute; outside the *pom-*

erium axes were inserted into the bundles, to signify that the curule magistrate or promagistrate did have the power to execute. The only man permitted to insert the axes into the midst of the rods inside the *pomerium* was the Dictator. The number of *fasces* indicated the degree of imperium: a Dictator had twenty-four; a consul or proconsul twelve; a master of the horse, praetor or propraetor six; and the curule aediles two. Sulla, incidentally, was the first Dictator to be preceded by twenty-four lictors bearing twenty-four *fasces;* until then, dictators had used the same number as consuls, twelve. See also **lictor.**

fasti The *fasti* were originally days on which business could be transacted, but the term came to mean other things as well: the calendar, lists relating to holidays and festivals, and the list of consuls (this last probably because Romans preferred to reckon up their years by remembering who had been the consuls in any given year). The entry in the glossary to *The First Man in Rome* contains a fuller explanation of the calendar than space permits me here— under *fasti,* of course.

fellator Plural, *fellatores*. The person sucking the penis.

feriae Holidays. Though attendance at public ceremonies on such holidays was not obligatory, *feriae* traditionally demanded that business, labor and lawsuits not be pursued, and that quarrels, even private ones, should be avoided. The rest from normal labors on *feriae* extended to slaves and also some animals, including oxen but excluding equines of all varieties.

feriae Latinae The annual festival on the Alban Mount, the Latin Festival. It was a movable feast, the date of which was fixed by the incoming consuls of New Year's Day during the meeting of the Senate called in the temple of Jupiter Optimus Maximus. The god was Jupiter Latiarus.

filibuster A modern word for a political activity at least as old as the Senate of Rome. It consisted, then as now, of "talking a motion out": the filibusterer droned on and on about everything from his childhood to his funeral plans, thus preventing other men from speaking until the political danger had passed. And preventing the taking of a vote!

flamen   Plural, *flamines*. These men were probably the oldest of Rome's priests in time, dating back at least as far as the kings. There were fifteen *flamines,* three major and twelve minor. The three major flaminates were *Dialis* (Jupiter Optimus Maximus), *Martialis* (Mars), and *Quirinalis* (Quirinus). Save for the poor *flamen Dialis,* none of the *flamines* seemed terribly hedged about with prohibitions or taboos, but all three major *flamines* qualified for a public salary, a State house, and membership in the Senate. The wife of the *flamen* was known as the *flaminica.* The *flamen* and *flaminica Dialis* had to be patrician in status, though I have not yet discovered whether this was true of the other *flamines,* major or minor. To be on the safe side, I have elected to stay with patrician appointments. The *flamen* was appointed for life.

Fortuna   One of Rome's most worshiped and important deities. Generally thought to be a female force, Fortuna had many different guises; Roman godhead was usually highly specific. Fortuna Primigenia was Jupiter's firstborn, Fors Fortuna was of particular importance to the lowly, Fortuna Virilis helped women conceal their physical imperfections from men, Fortuna Virgo was worshiped by brides, Fortuna Equestris looked after the knights, and Fortuna Huiusque Diei ("the fortune of the present day") was the special object of worship by military commanders and prominent politicians having military backgrounds. There were yet other Fortunae. The Romans believed implicitly in luck, though they did not regard luck quite as we do; a man *made* his luck, but was—even in the case of men as formidably intelligent as Sulla and Caesar—very careful about offending Fortuna, not to mention superstitious. To be favored by Fortuna was considered a vindication of all a man stood for.

forum   The Roman meeting place, an open area surrounded by buildings, many of which were of a public nature.

Forum Romanum   This long open space was the center of Roman public life, and was largely devoted, as were the buildings around it, to politics, the law, business, and religion. I do not believe that the free space of the Forum Romanum was choked with a permanent array of booths, stalls and barrows; the many descriptions of constant legal and political business in the lower half of the Forum would leave little room for such apparatus. There were two very large market areas on the Esquiline side of the Forum Romanum, just removed from the Forum itself by one barrier of buildings, and in these, no doubt, most freestanding stalls and booths were situated. Lower than the surrounding districts, the Forum was rather damp, cold, sunless— but very much alive in terms of public human activity. See map on page 37.

freedman A manumitted slave. Though technically a free man (and, if his former master was a Roman citizen, himself a Roman citizen), the freedman remained in the patronage of his former master, who had first call on his time and services. He had little chance to exercise his vote in either of the two tribal Assemblies, as he was invariably placed into one of the two vast urban tribes, Suburana or Esquilina. Some slaves of surpassing ability or ruthlessness, however, did amass great fortunes and power as freedmen, and could therefore be sure of a vote in the Centuriate Assembly; such freedmen usually managed to have themselves transferred into rural tribes as well, and thus exercised the complete franchise.

free man A man born free and never sold into outright slavery, though he could be sold as a *nexus* or debt slave. The latter was rare, however, inside Italy during the late Republic.

games In Latin, *ludi*. Games were a Roman institution and pastime which went back at least as far as the early Republic, and probably a lot further. At first they were celebrated only when a general triumphed, but in 336 B.C. the *ludi Romani* became an annual event, and were joined later by an ever-increasing number of other games throughout the year. All games tended to become longer in duration as well. At first games consisted mostly of chariot races, then gradually came to incorporate animal hunts, and plays performed in specially erected temporary

theaters. Every set of games commenced on the first day
with a solemn but spectacular religious procession through
the Circus, after which came a chariot race or two, and
then some boxing and wrestling, limited to this first day.
The succeeding days were taken up with theatricals; comedy was more popular than tragedy, and eventually the
freewheeling Atellan mimes and farces most popular of
all. As the games drew to a close, chariot racing reigned
supreme, with animal hunts to vary the program. Gladiatorial combats did *not* form a part of Republican games
(they were put on by private individuals, usually in connection with a dead relative, in the Forum Romanum
rather than in the Circus). Games were put on at the expense of the State, though men ambitious to make a name
for themselves dug deeply into their private purses while
serving as aediles to make ''their'' games more spectacular than the State-allocated funds permitted. Most of the
big games were held in the Circus Maximus, some of the
smaller ones in the Circus Flaminius. Free Roman citizen
men and women were permitted to attend (there was no
admission charge), with women segregated in the theater
but not in the Circus; neither slaves nor freedmen were
allowed admission, no doubt because even the Circus
Maximus, which held at least 150,000 people, was not
large enough to contain freedmen as well as free men.

Gaul, Gauls   A Roman rarely if ever referred to a Celt
as a Celt; he called a Celt a Gaul. Those parts of the world
wherein Gauls lived were known as some kind of Gaul,
even when the land was in Anatolia (Galatia). Before Caesar's conquests, Further Gaul—that is, Gaul on the western, French side of the Alps—was roughly divided into
Gallia Comata or Long-haired Gaul (neither Hellenized
nor Romanized), a Mediterranean coastal strip with a bulg-
ing extension up the valley of the Rhodanus River (both
Hellenized and Romanized) called The Province, and an
area around the port city of Narbo called Narbonese Gaul
(though it was not so officially called until the Principate
of Augustus). I refer to Further Gaul as Further Gaul or
Gaul-across-the-Alps, but it was more properly Transalpine Gaul. The Gaul more properly known as Cisalpine

Gaul because it lay on the Italian side of the Alps I have
elected to call Italian Gaul. Italian Gaul was divided into
two parts by the Padus River (the Po). There is no doubt
that the Gauls were closely akin to the Romans racially,
for their languages were of similar kind and so were many
of their technologies, particularly in metalworking. What
had enriched the Roman at the ultimate expense of the
Gaul was his centuries-long exposure to other Mediterranean cultures.

gens A man's clan or extended family. It was indicated
by his *nomen,* such as Cornelius or Julius, but was feminine in gender, hence they were the *gens Cornelia* and the
gens Iulia.

gladiator A soldier of the sawdust, a professional military athlete who fought in a ring before an audience to
celebrate funeral games in honor of the dead. During Republican times there were only two kinds of gladiator, the
Gaul and the Thracian; these were styles of combat, not
nationalities. Under the Republic, gladiatorial bouts were
not fought to the death. Gladiators then were not State
owned; few of them were slaves. They were owned by
private investors, and cost a great deal of money to acquire, train and maintain—far too much money, indeed,
to want to see them dead. The thumbs-up, thumbs-down
brutality of the Empire did not exist. A gladiator was recruited young, and fought between five and six bouts a
year to a total of thirty bouts maximum. After this he was
free to retire (though not automatically endowed with the
Roman citizenship) and usually drifted to a big city, where
he hired himself out as a bouncer, a bodyguard or a bully-
boy. During the Republic almost all gladiators were racially Roman, mostly deserters or mutineers from the
legions; occasionally a free man took up the profession for
the sheer pleasure of it (he was not compelled to give up
his citizenship if he did).

Gold of Tolosa Perhaps several years after 278 B.C., a
segment of the tribe Volcae Tectosages returned from
Macedonia to their homeland around Aquitanian Tolosa
(modern Toulouse) bearing the accumulated spoils from
many sacked temples. These were melted down and stored

in the artificial lakes which dotted the precincts of Tolosa's temples; the gold was left lying undisturbed beneath the water, whereas the silver was regularly hauled out—it had been formed into gigantic millstones which were used to grind the wheat. In 106 B.C. the consul Quintus Servilius Caepio was ordered during his consulship to make war against migrating Germans who had taken up residence around Tolosa. When he arrived in the area he found the Germans gone, for they had quarreled with their hosts, the Volcae Tectosages, and been ordered away. Instead of fighting a battle, Caepio the Consul found a vast amount of gold and silver in the sacred lakes of Tolosa. The silver amounted to 10,000 talents (250 imperial tons) including the millstones, and the gold to 15,000 talents (370 imperial tons). The silver was transported to the port of Narbo and shipped to Rome, whereupon the wagons returned to Tolosa and were loaded with the gold; the wagon train was escorted by one cohort of Roman legionaries, some 520 men. Near the fortress of Carcasso the wagon train of gold was attacked by brigands, the soldier escort was slaughtered, and the wagon train disappeared, together with its precious cargo. It was never seen again.

At the time no suspicion attached to Caepio the Consul, but after the odium he incurred over his conduct at the battle of Arausio a year later, it began to be rumored that Caepio the Consul had organized the attack on the wagon train and deposited the gold in Smyrna in his own name. Though he was never tried for the Great Wagon Train Robbery, he was tried for the loss of his army, convicted, and sent into exile. He chose to spend his exile in Smyrna, where he died in 100 B.C. The story of the Gold of Tolosa is told in the ancient sources, which do not state categorically that Caepio the Consul stole it. However, it seems logical. And there is no doubt that the Servilii Caepiones who succeeded Caepio the Consul down to the time of Brutus (the last heir) were fabulously wealthy. Nor is there much doubt that most of Rome thought Caepio the Consul responsible for the disappearance of more gold than Rome had in the Treasury.

governor A very useful English term to describe the

promagistrate—proconsul or propraetor—sent to direct,
command and manage one of Rome's provinces. His term
was set at one year, but very often it was prorogued,
sometimes (as in the case of Metellus Pius in Further
Spain) for many years.

Gracchi The Brothers Gracchi, Tiberius Sempronius
Gracchus and his younger brother, Gaius Sempronius
Gracchus. The sons of Cornelia (daughter of Scipio Africanus and Aemilia Paulla) and Tiberius Sempronius Gracchus (consul in 177 and 163 B.C., censor in 169 B.C.), they
had the consulship, high military command and the censorship as their birthright. Neither man advanced beyond
the tribunate of the plebs, due to a peculiar combination
of high ideals, iconoclastic thinking, and a tremendous
sense of duty to Rome. Tiberius Gracchus, a tribune of
the plebs in 133 B.C., set out to right the wrongs he saw
in the way the Roman State was administering its *ager
publicus;* his aim was to give these lands to the civilian
poor of Rome, thus encouraging them by dowering them
with land to breed sons and work hard. When the end of
the year saw his work still undone, Tiberius Gracchus
flouted custom by attempting to run for the tribunate of
the plebs a second time. He was clubbed to death on the
Capitol.

Gaius Gracchus, ten years Tiberius's junior, was elected
a tribune of the plebs in 123 B.C. More able than his
brother, he had also profited from Tiberius's mistakes, and
bade fair to alter the whole direction of the ultraconservative Rome of his time. His reforms were much wider
than Tiberius's, and embraced not only the *ager publicus*
but also cheap grain for the populace (a measure not exclusively aimed at the poor, for he adopted no means test),
regulation of service in the army, the founding of Roman
citizen colonies abroad, public works throughout Italy, removal of the courts from the Senate, a new system to farm
the taxes of Asia Province, and an enhancement of citizen
status for Latins and Italians. When his year as a tribune
of the plebs finished, Gaius Gracchus emulated his brother
and ran for a second term. Instead of being killed for his
presumption, he got in. At the end of his second term he

determined to run yet again, but was defeated in the elections. Helpless to intervene, he had to see all his laws and reforms begin to topple. Prevented from availing himself of peaceful means, Gaius Gracchus resorted to violence. Many of his partisans were killed when the Senate passed its first-ever "ultimate decree" (q.v. *senatus consultum de re publica defendenda*) but Gaius Gracchus himself chose to commit suicide before he could be apprehended.

The glossary attached to *The Grass Crown* contains a much a fuller article on the Gracchi.

groma Plural, *gromae*. An instrument used in surveying.

harpy A mythical Greek monster. If Virgil is to be believed, Romans thought harpies were birds with the heads of women, though the Greeks thought of them as women with wings and talons. They stole people and food, and left their faeces behind as an insult.

Head Count The *capite censi* or *proletarii:* the lowly of Rome. Called the Head Count because at a census all the censors did was to "count heads." Too poor to belong to a Class, the urban Head Count usually belonged to an urban tribe, and therefore owned no worthwhile tribal votes either. This rendered them politically useless beyond ensuring that they were fed and entertained enough not to riot. Rural Head Count, though usually owning a valuable tribal vote, rarely could afford to come to Rome at election time. Head Count were neither politically aware nor interested in the way Rome was governed, nor were they oppressed in an Industrial Revolution context. I have sedulously avoided the terms "the masses" and "the proletariat" because of post-Marxist preconceptions not applicable to the ancient lowly. In fact, they seem to have been busy, happy, rather impudent and not at all servile people who had an excellent idea of their own worth and scant respect for the Roman great. However, they had their public heroes; chief among them seems to have been Gaius Marius—until the advent of Caesar, whom they adored. This in turn might suggest that they were not proof against military might and the concept of Rome as The Greatest.

Hellenic, Hellenized Terms relating to the spread of Greek culture and customs after the time of Alexander the

Great. It involved life-style, architecture, dress, industry, government, commercial practices and the Greek language.

horse, Nesaean The largest kind of horse known to the ancients. How large it was is not known, but it seems to have been at least as large as the mediaeval beast which carried an armored knight, as the kings of Armenia and the Parthians both relied on Nesaeans to carry their cataphracts (cavalry clad in chain mail from head to foot, as were the horses). Its natural home was to the south and west of the Caspian Sea, in Media, but by the time of the late Republic there were some Nesaean horses in most part of the ancient world.

Horse, October On the Ides of October (this was about the time the old campaigning season finished), the best war-horses of that year were picked out and harnessed in pairs to chariots. They then raced on the sward of the Campus Martius, rather than in one of the Circuses. The right-hand horse of the winning team was sacrificed to Mars on a specially erected altar adjacent to the course of the race. The animal was killed with a spear, after which its head was severed and piled over with little cakes, while its tail and genitalia were rushed to the Regia in the Forum Romanum, and the blood dripped onto the altar inside the Regia. Once the ceremonies over the horse's cake-heaped head were concluded, it was thrown at two competing crowds of people, one comprising residents of the Subura, the other residents of the Via Sacra. The purpose was to have the two crowds fight for possession of the head. If the Via Sacra won, the head was nailed to the outside wall of the Regia; if the Subura won, the head was nailed to the outside wall of the Turris Mamilia (the most conspicuous building in the Subura). What was the reason behind all this is not known; the Romans of the late Republic may well not have known themselves, save that it was in some way connected with the close of the campaigning season. We are not told whether the war-horses were Public Horses or not, but we might be pardoned for presuming they were Public Horses.

Horse, Public A horse which belonged to the State—to

the Senate and People of Rome. Going all the way back
to the kings of Rome, it had been governmental policy to
provide the eighteen hundred knights of the eighteen most
senior Centuries with a horse to ride into battle—bearing
in mind the fact that the Centuriate Assembly had originally been a military gathering, and the senior Centuries
cavalrymen. The right of these senior knights to a Public
Horse was highly regarded and defended. That a member
of the Senate automatically lost his right to a Public Horse
is highly debatable.

Ides The third of the three named days of the month
which represented the fixed points of the month. Dates
were reckoned backward from each of these points—Kalends, Nones, Ides. The Ides occurred on the fifteenth day
of the long months (March, May, July and October), and
on the thirteenth day of the other months. The Ides were
sacred to Jupiter Optimus Maximus, and were marked by
the sacrifice of a sheep on the Arx of the Capitol by the
flamen Dialis.

Illyricum The wild and mountainous lands bordering the
Adriatic Sea on its eastern side. The native peoples belonged to an Indo-European race called Illyrians, were tri-
balized, and detested first Greek and then Roman coastal
incursions. Republican Rome bothered little about Illyricum unless boiling tribes began to threaten eastern Italian
Gaul, when the Senate would send an army to chasten
them.

imago Plural, *imagines.* An *imago* was a beautifully
tinted mask made of refined beeswax, outfitted with a wig,
and startlingly lifelike (anyone who has visited a
waxworks museum will understand how lifelike wax images can be made, and there is no reason to think a Roman
imago was inferior to a Victorian wax face). When a Roman nobleman reached a certain level of public distinction,
he acquired the *ius imaginis,* which was the right to have
a wax image made of himself. Some modern authorities
say the *ius imaginis* was bestowed upon a man once he
attained curule office, which would mean curule aedile.
Others plump for praetor, still others for consul. I plump
for praetor, also the Grass or Civic Crown, a major flam-

inate, and Pontifex Maximus. All the *imagines* belonging
to a family were kept in painstakingly wrought miniature
temples in the atrium of the house, and were regularly
sacrificed to. When a prominent man or woman of a family
owning the *ius imaginis* died, the wax masks were brought
out and worn by actors selected because they bore a physical resemblance in height and build to the men the masks
represented. Women of course were not entitled to the *ius
imaginis*—even Cornelia the Mother of the Gracchi. The
Chief Vestal Virgin, however, was so entitled.

imperium Imperium was the degree of authority vested
in a curule magistrate or promagistrate. It meant that a man
owned the authority of his office, and could not be gainsaid provided he was acting within the limits of his particular level of imperium and within the laws governing
his conduct. Imperium was conferred by a *lex curiata,* and
lasted for one year only. Extensions for prorogued governors had to be ratified by the Senate and/or People. Lictors shouldering *fasces* indicated a man's imperium; the
more lictors, the higher the imperium.

imperium maius A degree of imperium so high that the
holder of it outranked even the consuls of the year.

in absentia In the context used in these books, describes
a candidacy for office approved of by the Senate (and People, if necessary) and an election conducted in the absence
of the candidate himself. The candidate *in absentia* may
have been waiting on the Campus Martius because imperium prevented his crossing the *pomerium,* as with Pompey and Crassus in 70 B.C., or he may have been absent
on military service in a province, as with Gaius Memmius
when elected quaestor.

inepte An incompetent fool.

Insubres One of the Gallic tribes of Italian Gaul, concentrated at its western end around Mediolanum and the
river Ticinus. Their lands were to the north of the Padus
River (the Po), and they did not receive the full Roman
citizenship until 49 B.C., when Caesar enfranchised the
whole of Italian Gaul.

insula An island. Because it was surrounded on all sides
by streets, lanes or alleyways, an apartment building was

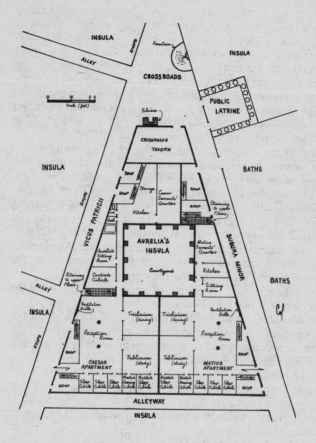

known as an insula. Roman insulae were very tall (up to 100 feet—30 meters—in height) and most were large enough to incorporate an internal light well; many were so large they contained multiple light wells. The insulae to be seen today at Ostia are not a real indication of the height insulae attained within Rome; we know that Augustus tried fruitlessly to limit the height of Roman city insulae to 100 feet. See illustration above.

insulsus Tasteless, unappetizing, utterly boring.

in suo anno   Literally, "in his year." The phrase was used of men who attained curule office at the exact age the law and custom prescribed for a man holding that office. To be praetor and consul *in suo anno* was a great distinction, for it meant that a man gained election at his first time of trying—many consuls and not a few praetors had to stand several times before they were successful, while others were prevented by circumstances from seeking office at this youngest possible age. Those who bent the law to attain office at an age younger than that prescribed were not accorded the distinction of being *in suo anno* either.

Ionic   One of the three Greek architectural orders. The capital of an Ionic column (it might be plain or fluted) looked like two partially unrolled scrolls (called volutes).

irrumator   Plural, *irrumatores*. A man having his penis sucked.

Italian Gaul   See **Gaul**

iudex   A judge at law.

iugerum   Plural, *iugera*. The Roman unit of land measurement. In modern terms the *iugerum* consisted of 0.623 (five eighths) of an acre, or 0.252 (one quarter) of a hectare. The modern reader used to acres will get close enough by dividing the number of *iugera* in two; if more accustomed to hectares, divide the number of *iugera* by four.

iuniores   Juniors.

ius   In the sense used in this book, an inalienable right or entitlement at law or under the *mos maiorum*.

Jupiter Stator   That aspect of Jupiter devoted to halting soldiers who were fleeing the field of battle. It was a military cult of generals. The chief temple to Jupiter Stator was on the corner of the Velia where the Via Sacra turned at right angles to run down the slope toward the Palus Ceroliae; it was large enough to be used for meetings by the Senate.

Kalends   The first of the three named days of each month which represented the fixed points of the month. Dates were reckoned backward from each of these points—Kalends, Nones, Ides. The Kalends always occurred on the

first day of the month. They were sacred to Juno, and
originally had been timed to coincide with the appearance
of the New Moon.

knights   The *equites,* the members of what Gaius Gracchus named the Ordo Equester. Under the kings of Rome,
the *equites* had formed the cavalry segment of the Roman
army; at this time horses were both scarce and expensive,
with the result that the eighteen original Centuries comprising the knights were dowered with the Public Horse
by the State. As the Republic came into being and grew,
the importance of Roman knight cavalry diminished, yet
the number of knight centuries in the First Class increased.
By the second century B.C. Rome no longer fielded horse
of her own, and the knights became a social and economic
group having little to do with military matters. The knights
were now defined by the censors in economic terms alone,
though the State continued to provide a Public Horse for
each of the eighteen hundred most senior *equites.* The
original eighteen Centuries were kept at one hundred men
each, but the rest of the ninety-one equestrian Centuries
(that is, the First Class) swelled within themselves to contain many more than one hundred men apiece. These seventy-three swollen Centuries were organized differently
than the Eighteen; seventy of them were tribal in nature,
a Century of Seniors and a Century of Juniors for each
tribe. In voting, one of the Eighteen was never given the
praerogativa; this went to one of the tribal Centuries of
Juniors.

Until 123 B.C. all senators were knights as well, but in
that year Gaius Gracchus split the Senate off as a separate
body of three hundred men. It was at best an artificial kind
of process; all non-senatorial members of senatorial families were still classified as knights, while the senators
themselves were not put into three senator-only Centuries,
but left for voting purposes in whatever Centuries they had
always occupied.

The insoluble puzzle is: who were the *tribuni aerarii?*
A knight's census was 400,000 sesterces, presumably income, whereas the *tribunus aerarius* had a census of
300,000 sesterces. At first I thought they were possibly

senior public servants—Treasury supervisors and the like—but I have swung round to thinking that Mommsen was right. He suggested that there were at least two echelons of knights of the First Class: those with a census of 400,000 sesterces, and those with a census of 300,000 sesterces; and that the lesser-incomed knights were the *tribuni aerarii*. Does that mean only the eighteen hundred knights owning the Public Horse possessed a census of 400,000 sesterces or more? I would doubt that too. There were many thousands of very rich men in Rome, and no census could so neatly divide one income group from another at a round-figure cutoff point. Perhaps it went more that a senior knight dowered with the Public Horse *had* to have at least 400,000 sesterces' income for census purposes. Whereas the other seventy-three Centuries of the First Class contained a mixture of full knights and *tribuni aerarii*. The Centuries of Juniors, one imagines, contained more census-rated *tribuni aerarii* than the Centuries of Seniors. But no one knows for certain!

There was nothing to stop a knight who qualified for the (entirely unofficial) senatorial means test of one million sesterces from becoming a senator under the old system, wherein the censors filled vacancies in the Senate; that by and large knights did not aspire to the Senate was purely because of the knightly love of trade and commerce—forbidden fruit for senators, who could only dabble in land and property.

laena A cape rather like a Mexican poncho, cut on the circle and containing a hole through which the head emerged. It was usually made from greasy Ligurian wool, and was therefore fairly waterproof. In this form it was standard issue to the legions (though called the *sagum*). Doubly thick and particolored, the *laena* was worn by the *flamen Dialis* (see **flamen**).

Lar Plural, Lares. These were among the most Roman of all gods, having no form, shape, sex, number, or mythology. They were *numina*. There were many different kinds of Lares, who might function as the protective spirits or forces of a locality (as with crossroads and boundaries), a social group (as with the family's private Lar, the Lar

Familiaris), sea voyages (the Lares Permarini), or a whole nation (Rome had public Lares, the Lares Praestites). By the late Republic, however, people had come to think of the Lares as two young men accompanied by a dog; they were depicted in this way in statues. It is doubtful, however, whether a Roman actually believed that there were only two of them, or that they owned this form and sex; more perhaps that the increasing complexity of life made it convenient to tag them.

latifundia   Large tracts of public land leased by one person and run as a single unit in the manner of a modern ranch. The activity was pastoral rather than agricultural. *Latifundia* were usually staffed by slaves who tended to be chained up in gangs and locked at night into barracks called *ergastula*. Running *latifundia* was a senatorial occupation rather than an equestrian one.

Latin Rights   An intermediate citizen status between the nadir of the Italian Allies and the zenith of the Roman citizenship. Those having the Latin Rights shared many privileges in common with Roman citizens: booty was divided equally, contracts with full citizens could be entered into and legal protection sought for these contracts, marriage was allowed with full citizens, and there was the right to appeal against capital convictions. However, there was no *suffragium*—no right to vote in any Roman election—nor the right to sit on a Roman jury. After the revolt of Fregellae in 125 B.C., the magistrates of Latin Rights towns and districts were entitled to assume the full Roman citizenship for themselves and their direct descendants.

legate   A *legatus*. The most senior members of a Roman general's staff were his legates. All men classified as legates were members of the Senate; they answered only to the general, and were senior to all types of military tribune. Not every legate was a young man, however. Some were consulars who apparently volunteered for some interesting war because they hankered after a spell of army life, or were friends of the general.

legion   *Legio*. The legion was the smallest Roman military unit capable of fighting a war on its own, though it was rarely called upon to do so. It was complete within itself in terms of manpower, equipment, facilities to make war. Between two and six legions clubbed together constituted an army; the times when an army contained more than six legions were unusual. The total number of men in a full-strength legion was about six thousand, of whom perhaps five thousand were actually soldiers, and the rest were classified as noncombatants. The internal organization of a legion consisted of ten cohorts of six centuries each; under normal circumstances there was a modest cavalry unit attached to each legion, though from the time of Sulla downward the cavalry tended more to be grouped together as a whole body separate from the infantry. Each legion was in charge of some pieces of artillery, though artillery was not employed on the field of battle; its use was limited to siege operations. If a legion was one of the consuls' legions it was commanded by up to six elected tribunes of the soldiers, who spelled each other. If a legion belonged to a general not currently a consul, it was commanded by one of the general's legates, or else by the general himself. Its regular officers were the centurions, of whom it possessed some sixty. Though the troops belonging to a legion camped together, they did not live together en masse; they were divided into units of eight men who tented and messed together. See also **cohort**.

legionary   This is the correct English word to describe an ordinary soldier (*miles gregarius*) in a Roman legion. "Legionnaire," which I have sometimes seen used, is more properly applied to a soldier in the French Foreign Legion, or to a veteran of the American Legion.

lemures   The ghosts or spirits of the dead, who dwelled in the underworld.

lex   Plural, *leges*. A law or laws. The word *lex* also came to be applied to the plebiscite (*plebiscitum*), passed by the Plebeian Assembly. A *lex* was not considered valid until it had been inscribed on bronze or stone and deposited in the vaults below the temple of Saturn. However, residence therein must have been brief, as space was limited and the temple of Saturn also housed the Treasury. After Sulla's new Tabularium was finished, laws were deposited there instead of (probably) all over the city. A law was named after the man or men who promulgated it and then succeeded in having it ratified, but always (since *lex* is feminine gender) with the feminine ending to his name or their names. This was then followed by a general description of what the law was about. Laws could be—and sometimes were—subject to repeal at a later date.

lex Caecilia Didia There were actually two laws by this name, but only one is of relevance to this volume. Passed by the consuls of 98 B.C., the relevant one stipulated that three *nundinae* or market days had to elapse between the vote of the Assembly that it become law and its actual ratification. There is some debate as to whether the waiting period consisted of twenty-four or seventeen days; I have elected seventeen.

lex Domitia de sacerdotiis Passed in 104 B.C. by Gnaeus Domitius Ahenobarbus, later Pontifex Maximus. It specified that new pontifices and augurs must be elected by a tribal Assembly comprising seventeen of the thirty-five tribes chosen by lot. Until this law, pontifices and augurs were co-opted by the College members. Sulla, once Dictator, repealed it, but the tribune of the plebs Titus Labienus re-enacted it in 63 B.C.

lex frumentaria The general term for a grain law. There were many such, commencing with Gaius Gracchus. All grain laws pertained to the public grain supply—that is, the grain bought by the State and distributed by the aediles. Most such laws provided cheap grain, but some took cheap grain away.

lex regia A law passed by one of the kings of Rome, therefore older than any Republican law. Most *leges regiae* were still perfectly valid at the end of the Republic, as it was not usual for Romans to repeal laws.

lex rogata A law promulgated in an Assembly by direct co-operation between the presiding magistrate and the members of the Assembly. In other words, the law was not presented to the Assembly in a cut-and-dried, fully drafted state, but was drafted during *contio* in the Assembly.

lex rogata plus quam perfecta A law drafted in an Assembly by the convoking magistrate that not only invalidated an act or previous law, but provided that those responsible for doing the act or using the law should be punished.

lex sumptuaria Any law regulating the purchase and consumption of luxuries. They were popular laws among magistrates who deplored luxury-loving tendencies, but rarely worked in practice. The most common articles legislated against were spices, peppers, perfumes, incenses, imported wines, and genuine Tyrian purple.

lex Voconia de mulierum hereditatibus Passed in 169 B.C., this law severely curtailed the right of a woman to inherit from a will. Under no circumstances could she be designated the principal heir, even if she was the only child of her father; his nearest agnate relatives (that is, on the father's side) superseded her. Cicero quotes a case wherein it was argued that the *lex Voconia* did not apply because the dead man's property had not been assessed at a census; but the praetor (Gaius Verres) overruled the argument and refused to allow the girl in question to inherit. The law was certainly got around—for we know of several great heiresses—by securing a Senatorial *consultum* waiving the *lex Voconia;* or by dying intestate, in which case the old law prevailed and children inherited irrespective of sex or close agnate relatives. Until Sulla as Dictator established permanent *quaestiones*, there does not appear to have been a court to hear testamentary disputes, which meant the urban praetor must have had the final say.

LIBERO The word used in Assembly trials to register a verdict of acquittal.

licker-fish A freshwater bass of the Tiber River. The creature was to be found only between the Wooden Bridge and the Pons Aemilius, where it lurked around the outflows of the great sewers and fed upon what they disgorged. Apparently it was so well fed that it was notoriously hard to catch. This may have been why it was so prized as a delicacy by Rome's Epicureans.

lictor The man who formally attended a curule magistrate as he went about his official business by preceding him in single or double file to clear a way, or by being on hand as he conducted his business in case he needed to employ restraint or chastise. The lictor had to be a Roman citizen and was a State employee, though he does not seem to have been of high social status; he was probably so poorly paid that he relied upon his magistrate's generosity with gratuities. On his left shoulder he bore the bundle of rods called *fasces* (q.v.). Within the city of Rome he wore a plain white toga, changing to a black toga for funerals; outside Rome he wore a scarlet tunic cinched by a broad black leather belt bossed in brass, and inserted the axes in his rods.

There was a College of Lictors, though the site of lictorial headquarters is not known. A tiny *collegium* existed attached to the front of the Basilica Aemilia, for what purpose is not known; I have made it a waiting station for lictors. Their headquarters I have placed behind the temple of the Lares Praestites on the eastern side of the Forum Romanum, adjacent to the great inn on the corner of the Clivus Orbius, but there is no factual evidence of any kind to support this location. Within the College the lictors (there must have been at least three hundred of them, possibly many more) were organized into decuries of ten men, each headed by a prefect, and the decuries were collectively supervised by several College presidents.

literatus   Plural, *literati*. A man of letters.

litter   A covered cubicle equipped with legs upon which it rested when lowered to the ground. A horizontal pole on each corner projected forward and behind the conveyance; it was carried by four to eight men who picked it up by means of these poles. The litter was a slow form of transport, but it was by far the most comfortable known in the ancient world. I imagine it was considerably more comfortable than most modern transport!

lituus   The staff carried by an augur. It was perhaps three or four feet (about 1 meter) long, curved in shape, and ended in a curlique.

ludi   The **games** (q.v.).

macellum   A market. See also **Cuppedenis Markets**.

magistrates   The elected representatives of the Senate and People of Rome. They embodied the executive arm of government, and with the exception of the tribunes of

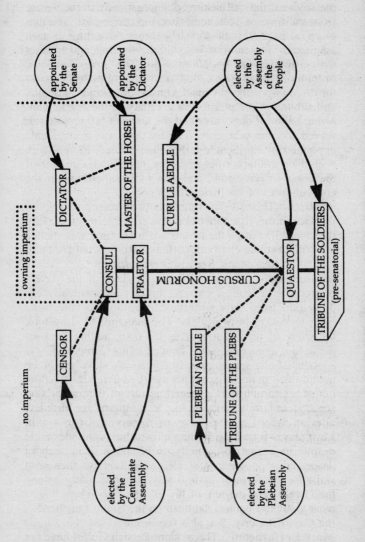

Roman Magistrates

the soldiers, they all belonged automatically to the Senate from the time of Sulla's dictatorship downward. The diagram on page 911 most clearly shows the nature of each magistracy: its seniority, who did the electing, and whether a magistrate owned imperium or not. The *cursus honorum,* or Path of Offices, proceeded in a straight line from quaestor through praetor to consul; censor, both kinds of aedile, and tribune of the plebs were ancillary to the *cursus honorum.* Save for the censor and the Dictator, all magistrates served for one year only. The Dictator was a magistrate appointed by the Senate rather than elected, to deal with a civil or military emergency; he appointed a master of the horse to serve him, and was indemnified against the consequences of his dictatorial actions.

maiestas   Treason. The refinements of treason introduced by **Saturninus** (q.v.) in 103 B.C. were largely canceled by the law Sulla put on the tablets when Dictator; this spelled out with absolute clarity the offenses Rome would hitherto find to be treasonous. See also *perduellio.*

manumission   The act of freeing a slave. If the slave's master was a Roman citizen, this act automatically endowed the freed slave with the citizenship. His vote, however, tended to be worthless. The manumitted slave took the name of his old master as his own, adding his own name to it as a *cognomen*—hence Lucius Cornelius Chrysogonus, Sulla's infamous freedman. A slave might be manumitted in one of several ways: by buying his freedom out of his earnings, as a special gesture of the master's on some great family occasion like a coming-of-age birthday, after an agreed number of years in service, or in a will. Most slaves found the Roman citizenship highly desirable despite its limitations, chiefly on behalf of their freeborn descendants. It was not at all uncommon for men with skills to sell themselves into slavery, particularly among the Greeks. For the rest of his life the freed slave had to wear a slightly conical skullcap on the back of his head— the Cap of Liberty. See also **freedman.**

Mare Erythraeum   The modern Persian Gulf. I have not translated it as the Red Sea because what we know today as the Red Sea was known to the Romans as the Sinus Arabicus.

measures and weights   Most measurements were based upon body parts, hence the foot, the hand, the pace. The Roman foot at 296 millimeters was just slightly short of 12 modern inches, and it was divided into 12 inches. Five feet made up a pace, and the Roman mile at 1,000 paces was about 285 feet short of the English mile, thus there were 20 Roman miles for every 19 English—too small a difference to make it necessary in my text to specify miles (or feet) as Roman.

Area was measured in *iugera* (see *iugerum*).

Grains such as wheat were dry-measured rather than weighed, as they poured like fluids; the dry measures were the *medimnus* and the *modius* (q.v.).

The bulk container was the **amphora** (q.v.), which held about 6 American gallons (25 liters) and was the volume of a Roman cubic foot. Ship's cargoes were always expressed in amphorae.

The Roman pound, or *libra,* weighed about seven tenths of an English pound at 327 grams, and was divided into 12 ounces (*unciae*). Heavy weights were measured in the **talent** (q.v.).

medicus   The middle finger.

medimnus   Plural, *medimni*. A dry measure for grains and other pourable solids. It equaled 5 *modii* and occupied a volume of 10 U.S. gallons (40 liters), and weighed about 65 Roman pounds (47.5 English pounds or about 23 kilograms). This provided sufficient grain for two 1-Roman-pound loaves of bread per day for about thirty days, given that the waste husked off the grain in grinding was replaced by water and other ingredients. The ordinary Roman who lived in one or two rooms in an insula did not normally grind his flour and bake his bread at home; he came to an arrangement with his local baker (as indeed was done in many parts of Europe until relatively recently), who took a cut of the grain ration as his price. Perhaps the final result was that one *medimnus* of wheat provided the ordinary Roman with one large loaf per day for thirty days?

mentula   A choice Latin obscenity for the penis.

metae   The pillars or obelisks at each end of the central dividing strip, the *spina,* of a circus course.

Middle Sea   The name I have used for the Mediterranean Sea. My observant readers will notice a new term now creeping into the narrative: Our Sea. *Mare Nostrum* (Our Sea) is what it came to be called as the Republic neared its end.

Military Man   The *vir militaris*. What might be called a "career officer." His whole life revolved around the army, and he continued to serve in the army after his obligatory number of years or campaigns had expired. If he entered the Roman political arena he relied upon his military reputation to catch votes, but many Military Men never bothered to enter the political arena at all. However, if a Military Man wanted to general an army, he had no choice other than to attain the praetorship, which was the lowest magistracy carrying command of an army with it. Gaius Marius, Quintus Sertorius, Titus Didius, Gaius Pomptinus and Publius Ventidius were all Military Men; but Caesar the Dictator, the greatest military man of them all, was never a Military Man.

minim   A bright vermilion pigment made from cinnabar (mercuric sulfide) which the triumphing general painted on his face, apparently to ape the terracotta face of the statue of Jupiter Optimus Maximus in his temple on the Capitol.

modius   Plural, *modii*. The customary measure of grain. A *modius* occupied 2 U.S. gallons or 8 liters, and weighed about 13 (presumably Roman) pounds (approximately 4 kilograms). The public grain was doled out in increments of 5 *modii* per month, this equaling 1 *medimnus* (see this entry also for information about bread).

Moesia   The lands now occupied by Serbia and north-western Bulgaria. Its peoples were Thracian, tribally organized and living in settlements. They farmed as well as grazed. The Dardani and the Triballi, two of the major tribes, constantly raided the borderlands of Roman Macedonia.

mola salsa   A holy cake made from spelt (the fine white

flour of emmer wheat) mixed with salt and water, and not leavened. To make it was the duty of the Vestal Virgins. They had to grow and harvest the emmer themselves, evaporate and make the salt themselves, and fetch the water personally from the well of Juturna.

monoreme A ship having one bank of oars.

Mormolyce A nursery bogey.

mos maiorum The established order of things; used to describe the habits and customs of government and public institutions. Perhaps the best definition is to say that the *mos maiorum* was Rome's unwritten constitution. *Mos* meant established custom; and in this context *maiores* meant ancestors or forebears. To sum up, the *mos maiorum* was how things had always been done—and how they should always be done in the future too!

mundus A beehive-shaped pit which was divided into two parts and normally kept covered. Its exact purpose is a mystery, but it seems to have been believed in late Republican times to be an entranceway to the Underworld. The lid was removed thrice in the year on *dies religiosi* (q.v.) in order to allow the shades of the dead to walk the city. A beehive-shaped pit still exists on the Palatine.

municipium Plural, *municipia*. Originally these were districts within Italy which were allies of Rome but did not possess the Roman citizenship. After the citizenship was made universal for all the peoples of the Italian Peninsula, a *municipium* principally meant a town and its district which had retained some of its self-governing powers, and still owned its public lands. A *municipium* elected its own magistrates and had its own records and archives and sources of income, though it was liable to inspection by prefects sent from Rome, presumably by the Senate.

myoparo Plural, *myoparones*. A small war galley much favored by pirates before they began to band together in much larger ships to sail as properly admiraled fleets capable of attacking and beating professional navies. The *myoparo* is somewhat mysterious as to its size and type, but it seems to have been an improvement upon the *hemiolia* and preferred to the *hemiolia*. The only drawing of it is not informative, though it does seem to indicate that the *myoparo* had only one bank of oars rowed over the top of the gunwale rather than through ports, and also possessed mast and sail.

nefas esse "Found to be sacrilegious."

Nesaean horse See **horse, Nesaean.**

Nola An extremely well fortified city of southern Campania. The first language spoken therein was Oscan, and Nola was always sympathetic to the Samnite cause. When war broke out between the Italian Allies and Rome in 91 B.C., Nola sided with Italia. The name of Nola became synonymous with perpetual resistance to attack, for it continued to resist siege by various Roman generals for over ten years, and was the last place to surrender. Sulla won his Grass Crown outside the walls of Nola. One of the canards about Clodia (sister of Publius Clodius, wife of Metellus Celer, mistress of Catullus and Caelius) was that she was a "Nola in the bedroom"—that is, impossible to take.

nomen The family, clan, or gentilicial name—the name of the *gens* in (for men) masculine form. Cornelius, Julius, Domitius, Licinius were all *nomina* (plural).

Nones The second of the three named days of the month which represented the fixed points of the month. Dates were reckoned backward from each of these points—Kalends, Nones, Ides. The Nones occurred on the seventh day of the long months (March, May, July and October) and on the fifth day of the other months. The Nones were sacred to Juno.

Noricum What might today be called the eastern Tyrol and the Yugoslavian Alps. Its people were called the Taurisci, and were Celts. The main settlement was Noreia.

nundinae The market days, occurring every eighth day; the singular, *nundinus,* was less used than the plural, *nundinae.* Under normal circumstances the courts were open on *nundinae,* but the Assemblies were not.

nundinum The interval between one market day and the next; the eight-day Roman week. Save for the Kalends, Nones and Ides, the days of the Roman calendar were not named; on the calendars themselves they are allocated a letter between A and H, with A (presumably) being the market day. When the Kalends of January coincided with the market day the whole year was considered to be unlucky, but this did not happen regularly because of intercalations and the fact that the eight-day round of letters was continued on without an interruption between last day of the old year and first (Kalends) day of the new year.

oakum A crudely tamped-together collection of fibers, in ancient times gathered from woolly seeds, maple ''cotton,'' or the coarsest fibers of the flax plant. It was occasionally used for caulking, but its main use was for lampwicks.

October Horse See **Horse, October.**

opus incertum The oldest of several ways in which the Romans built composite walls. A facing of irregular small stones mortared together was constructed with a hollow interior or cavity; this was filled with a mortar composed of black pozzolana and lime mixed through an aggregate of rubble and small stones (*caementa*). Even in the time of Sulla, *opus incertum* was still the most popular way to build a wall. It was probably also cheaper than brick.

Ordo Equester The name given to the **knights** (q.v.) by Gaius Gracchus.

orichalcum Brass.

Pannonia A very rich and fertile land occupying modern eastern Austria and Hungary as far east as the Tisa River. Its peoples were Illyrian by race, and organized into tribes which lived in settlements and farmed as well as grazed. The modern Drava and Danube were its principal rivers.

paterfamilias The head of the family unit. His right to do as he pleased with the various members of his family was rigidly protected at law.

pater patriae Father of his country.

patrician, Patriciate The Patriciate was the original Roman aristocracy. To an ancestor-revering, birth-conscious people like the Romans, the importance of belonging to patrician stock can hardly be overestimated. The older among the patrician families were aristocrats before the kings of Rome, the youngest among them (the Claudii) apparently emerging at the very beginning of the Republic. All through the Republic they kept the title of patrician, as well as a prestige unattainable by any plebeian—and this in spite of the nobility, the "new aristocracy" ennobled above mere plebeian status by having consuls in the family. However, by the last century of the Republic a patrician owned little distinction beyond his blood; the wealth and energy of the great plebeian families had steadily eroded original patrician rights. Sulla, a patrician himself, seems to have tried in small ways to elevate the patrician above his plebeian brothers, but did not dare legislate major privileges. Yet entitlement and privilege under the constitution mattered not a scrap to most Romans: they knew the patrician was better. During the last century of the Republic, the following patrician families were still producing senators, and some praetors and consuls: Aemilius, Claudius, Cornelius, Fabius (but through adoption only), Julius, Manlius, Pinarius, Postumius, Sergius, Servilius, Sulpicius, and Valerius.

patron, patronage Republican Roman society was organized into a system of patronage and clientship (see also **client**). Though perhaps the smallest businessmen and the lowly of Rome were not always participants in the system, it was nevertheless prevalent at all levels in society, and not all patrons were from the upper echelons of society. The patron undertook to offer protection and favors to those who acknowledged themselves his clients. Freed slaves were in the patronage of their ex-masters. No woman could be a patron. Many patrons were clients of patrons more powerful than themselves, which technically made their clients also the clients of their patrons. The patron might do nothing for years to obtain help or support from a client, but one day the client would be called upon to do his patron a favor—vote for him, or lobby for him, or perform some special task. It was customary for the patron to see his clients at dawn in his house on "business" days in the calendar; at these matinees the clients would ask for help or favor, or merely attend to offer respect, or offer services. A rich or generous patron often bestowed gifts of money upon his clients when they assembled at such times. If a man became the client of another man whom in earlier days he had hated to the point of implacable enmity, that client would thereafter serve his erstwhile enemy, now his patron, with complete fidelity and even to death (*vide* Caesar the Dictator and Curio the Younger).

Pavo A peacock. Gaius Matius called Caesar "Pavo."

peccatum A minor sin.

Peculatus An embezzler. Caesar cognominated Catulus this when he alleged Catulus had embezzled funds meant to build Jupiter's new temple.

peculium An amount of money paid as a wage or on a regular basis to a person not legally able to own it—a slave, for example, or an underage child earning interest or dividends. The *peculium* was therefore held by the legal guardian or owner for the person earning it until he was free to manage it for himself.

pedarius A senatorial backbencher (see **Senate**).

People of Rome This term embraced every single Roman who was not a member of the Senate; it applied to patricians as well as plebeians, and to the Head Count as well as to the First Class. However, I have sometimes used it to refer to those whose votes had value.

perduellio High treason. Until first Saturninus and then Sulla redefined treason and passed new treason laws, *perduellio* was the only form treason had in Roman law. Old enough to have existed under the kings of Rome, it required a trial or appeal process in the Centuriate Assembly, a most cumbersome affair.

peristyle An enclosed garden or courtyard which was surrounded by a colonnade and formed the outdoor area of a house.

phalerae Round, chased, ornamented silver or gold discs about 3 to 4 inches (75 to 100 millimeters) in diameter. Originally they were worn as insignia by Roman knights, and also formed a part of the trappings of a knight's horse. Gradually they came to be military decorations awarded for exceptional bravery in battle. Normally they were given in sets of nine (three rows of three each) mounted upon a decorated leather harness of straps designed to be worn over the mail shirt or cuirass.

Picenum That part of the eastern Italian Peninsula

roughly occupying the area of the Italian leg's calf muscle.
Its western boundary formed the crest of the Apennines;
Umbria lay to the north, and Samnium to the south. The
original inhabitants were of Italiote and Illyrian stock, but
there was a tradition that Sabines had migrated east of the
Apennine crest and settled in Picenum, bringing with them
as their tutelary god Picus, the woodpecker, from which
the region got its name. A tribe of Gauls called the Sen-
ones also settled in the area at the time Italy was invaded
by the first King Brennus in 390 B.C. Politically Picenum
fell into two parts: northern Picenum, closely allied to
southern Umbria, was under the sway of the great family
called Pompeius; and Picenum south of the Flosis or Flus-
sor River was under the sway of peoples allied to the Samnites.

piggy, piggykins, piggle-wiggle, etc. Latin: *porcella*.
Used derisively or affectionately, and pertaining to female
genitalia.

pilus prior   See **centurion.**

pipinna   A little boy's penis.

Pisidia, Pisidian   This region lay to the south of Phrygia,
and was even wilder and more backward. Extremely
mountainous and filled with lakes, it was held to have a
very healthy climate. Little industry or populous settlement existed; the countryside was heavily forested with
magnificent pines. Its people apparently were an ancient
and indigenous strain allied to the Thracians, and its language was unique. Those few Pisidians who came to the
notice of Rome and Romans were famous for their bizarre
religious beliefs.

plebeian, Plebs   All Roman citizens who were not patricians were plebeians; that is, they belonged to the Plebs
(the *e* is short, so that "Plebs" rhymes with "webs," not
"glebes"). At the beginning of the Republic no plebeian
could be a priest, a magistrate, or even a senator. This
situation lasted only a very short while; one by one the
exclusively patrician institutions crumbled before the onslaught of the Plebs, who far outnumbered the patricians—
and several times threatened to secede. By the late
Republic there was very little if any advantage to being a

patrician—except that everyone knew patrician was better.

Plebeian Assembly See **Assembly.**

plebiscite The correct name for a law passed in the Plebeian Assembly.

podex An impolite word for the posterior fundamental orifice: an arsehole rather than an anus.

Pollux The ever-forgotten Heavenly Twin. See **Castor.**

pomerium The sacred boundary enclosing the city of Rome. Marked by white stones called *cippi*, it was reputedly inaugurated by King Servius Tullius, and remained without change until Sulla's dictatorship. The *pomerium* did not exactly follow the Servian Walls, one good reason why it is doubtful that the Servian Walls were built by King Servius Tullius—who would certainly have caused his walls to follow the same line as his *pomerium*. The whole of the ancient Palatine city of Romulus was enclosed within the *pomerium,* whereas the Aventine lay outside it. So too did the Capitol. Tradition held that the *pomerium* might be enlarged, but only by a man who significantly increased the size of Roman territory. In religious terms, Rome herself existed only inside the *pomerium;* all outside it was merely Roman territory.

pontifex Plural, *pontifices.* Many Latin etymologists think that in very early times the pontifex was a maker of bridges (*pons:* bridge), and that the making of bridges was considered a mystical art putting the maker in close touch with the Gods. Be that as it may, by the time the Republic came along the pontifex was a priest. Incorporated into a special college, he served as an adviser to Rome's magistrates and *comitia* in all religious matters—and would inevitably himself become a magistrate. At first all pontifices had to be patrician, but a *lex Ogulnia* of 300 B.C. stipulated that half the College of Pontifices had to be plebeian. During periods when the pontifices (and augurs) were co-opted into the College by other members, new appointees tended to be well under senatorial age; the early twenties was common. Thus the appointment of Caesar at twenty-six years of age was not at all unusual or remarkable. The pontifex served for life.

Pontifex Maximus The head of Rome's State-administered religion, and most senior of all priests. He seems to have been an invention of the infant Republic, a typically masterly Roman way of getting round an obstacle without demolishing it and ruffling feelings. In the time of the kings of Rome, the Rex Sacrorum had been the chief priest, this being a title held by the King himself. Apparently considering it unwise to abolish the Rex Sacrorum, the anti-monarchical rulers of the new Republic of Rome simply created a new priest whose role and status were superior to the Rex Sacrorum. This new priest was given the title of Pontifex Maximus. To reinforce his statesmanlike position, it was laid down that he should be elected, not co-opted (the other priests were all co-opted). At first he was probably required to be a patrician, but soon could as easily be a plebeian. He supervised all the members of the various priestly Colleges—and the Vestal Virgins. The State gave him its most imposing house as his residence, but in Republican times he shared this residence with the Vestal Virgins, apparently on a half-and-half basis. His official headquarters had the status of an inaugurated temple: the little old Regia in the Forum Romanum just outside his State house. Pontifex Maximus was a lifetime appointment.

Popular Assembly   See **Assembly.**

Popularis   A term used by Cicero (and later) writers to describe the men of that faction of Senate and People which was, for want of a better description, more liberal in its political views than the faction of the *boni,* the ultraconservatives. I have attributed its genesis to Cicero, but cannot swear he did coin the term.

population of Rome   A vexed question upon which much ink has been expended by modern scholars. I think there is a tendency to underestimate the number of people who actually dwelled inside Rome herself, few if any of the scholars admitting to a number as great as one million. The general consensus seems to be half a million. However, we do know the dimensions of the Republican city inside the Servian Walls: in width, one-plus kilometers, in length, two-plus kilometers. Then as now, Rome was a city of apartment dwellers, and that is a strong clue to the actual population. Of Roman citizens—that is, males on the census rolls—there were perhaps a quarter of a million, plus wives and children, and plus slaves. It was an absolutely penurious household which did not have at least one slave in service; the Head Count seem to have owned slaves too. Then there were the non-citizens, of whom Rome had hordes: Jews, Syrians, Greeks, Gauls, all sorts. With wives, children, and slaves. Rome teemed with people; its insulae were multitudinous. Non-citizens, wives, children and slaves must have pushed that quarter million well above a million. Otherwise the insulae would have been half empty and the city smothered in parks. I think two million is closer to the mark.

portico The word I have chosen to indicate a large covered porch forming an entrance to a building or temple.

porticus Not a porch, but a whole building incorporating some sort of large central courtyard. The actual building was usually longer than wide, and constructed on a colonnade principle. The Porticus Margaritaria in the upper Forum Romanum housed Rome's most expensive shops. The Porticus Aemilia in the Port of Rome was a very long building which housed firms and agents dealing with shipping, import and export.

praefectus fabrum One of the most important men in a Roman army, technically the *praefectus fabrum* was not even a part of it; he was a civilian appointed to the post by the general. The *praefectus fabrum* was responsible for equipping and supplying the army in all respects, from its animals and their fodder to its men and their food. Because he let out contracts to businessmen and manufacturers for equipment and supplies, he was a very powerful figure— and, unless he was a man of superior integrity, in a perfect position to enrich himself. The evidence of Caesar's *praefectus fabrum,* the Gadetanian banker Lucius Cornelius Balbus, indicates just how important and powerful these suppliers of armies were.

praenomen A Roman man's first name. There were very few *praenomina* (plural) in use, perhaps twenty, and half of them were not common, or else were confined to the men of one particular *gens,* as with Mamercus, confined to the Aemilii Lepidi. Each *gens* or clan favored certain *praenomina* only, perhaps two or three out of the twenty. A modern scholar can often tell from a man's *praenomen* whether he was a genuine member of the *gens:* the Julii, for instance, favored Sextus, Gaius and Lucius only, with the result that a man called Marcus Julius is highly suspect. The Licinii favored Publius, Marcus and Lucius; the Pompeii favored Gnaeus, Sextus and Quintus; the Cornelii favored Publius, Lucius and Gnaeus; the Servilii of the patrician *gens* favored Quintus and Gnaeus. Appius belonged exclusively to the Claudii. One of the great puzzles for modern scholars concerns that Lucius Claudius who was Rex Sacrorum during the late Republic; Lucius was not a patrician Claudian *praenomen,* yet the Rex Sacrorum was certainly a patrician Claudius. I have postulated that there was a certain branch of the Claudii bearing the *praenomen* Lucius which always traditionally provided Rome with her Rex Sacrorum. The whole subject of *praenomina* has me in stitches whenever I watch one of those Hollywood Roman epics; they always get it wrong!

praerogativa   The right to go first.

praetor   This magistracy ranked second in the hierarchy of Roman magistrates. At the very beginning of the Republic, the two highest magistrates of all were known as praetors. By the end of the fourth century B.C., however, the term consul had come into being for the highest magistrates, and praetors were relegated to second best. One praetor was the sole representative of this position for many decades thereafter; he was obviously the *praetor urbanus,* as his duties were confined to the city of Rome, thus freeing up the two consuls for duties as war leaders outside the city. In 242 B.C. a second praetor, the *praetor peregrinus,* was created to cope with matters relating to foreign nationals and Italy rather than Rome. As Rome acquired her overseas provinces more praetors were created to govern them, going out to do so in their year of office rather than afterward as propraetors. By the last century of the Republic there were six praetors elected in most years but eight in some, depending upon the State's needs. Sulla brought the number of praetors up to eight during his dictatorship, and limited duty during their year in actual office to his law courts.

praetor peregrinus I have chosen to translate this as "the foreign praetor" because he dealt with non-citizens. By the time of Sulla his duties were confined to litigation and the dispensation of legal decisions; he traveled all over Italy as well as hearing cases involving non-citizens within Rome herself.

praetor urbanus The urban praetor, whose duties by the late Republic were almost all to do with litigation; Sulla further refined this by confining the urban praetor to civil rather than criminal suits. His imperium did not extend beyond the fifth milestone from Rome, and he was not allowed to leave Rome for longer than ten days at a time. If both the consuls were absent from Rome he was Rome's senior magistrate, therefore empowered to summon the Senate, make decisions about execution of government policies, even organize the defenses of the city under threat of attack.

primus pilus See **centurion.**

Princeps Senatus The Leader of the House. He was appointed by the censors according to the rules of the *mos maiorum:* he had to be a patrician, the leader of his decury, an *interrex* more times than anyone else, of unimpeachable morals and integrity, and have the most *auctoritas* and *dignitas.* The title Princeps Senatus was not given for life, but was subject to review by each new pair of censors. Sulla stripped the Leader of the House of a considerable amount of his *auctoritas,* but he continued to be prestigious.

privatus Plural, *privati.* Used within the pages of this book to describe a man who was a senator not currently serving as a magistrate.

proconsul One serving the State with the imperium of a consul but not in office as consul. Proconsular imperium was normally bestowed upon a man after he finished his year as consul and went to govern a province *proconsule.* A man's tenure of a proconsulship was usually for one year only, but it was very commonly prorogued (see **prorogue**), sometimes for several years; Metellus Pius was proconsul in Further Spain from 79 to 71 B.C. Proconsular imperium was limited to the proconsul's province or command, and was lost the moment he stepped across the *pomerium* into Rome.

proletarii Those Roman citizens who were too poor to give the State anything by way of taxes, duties, or service. The only thing they could give the State was *proles*—children. See **Head Count**.

promagistrate One serving the State in a magisterial role without actually being a magistrate. The offices of quaestor, praetor and consul (the three magistracies of the formal *cursus honorum*) were the only three relevant.

pronuba The matron of honor at a wedding. She had to be a woman who had been married only once.

propraetor One serving the State with the imperium of a praetor but not in office as a praetor. Propraetorian imperium was normally bestowed upon a man after he had finished his year as praetor and went to govern a province *propraetore*. Tenure of a propraetorship was usually for one year, but could be prorogued.

proquaestor One serving the State as a quaestor but not in office as a quaestor. The office did not carry imperium, but under normal circumstances a man elected to the quaestorship would, if asked for personally by a governor who ended in staying in his province for more than one year, remain in the province as proquaestor until his superior went home.

prorogue This meant to extend a man's tenure of promagisterial office beyond its normal time span of one year. It affected proconsuls and propraetors, but also quaestors. I include the word in this glossary because I have discovered that modern English-language dictionaries of small or even medium size neglect to give this meaning in treating the word "prorogue."

province Originally this meant the sphere of duty of a magistrate or promagistrate holding imperium, and therefore applied as much to consuls and praetors in office inside Rome as it did to those abroad. Then the word came to mean the place where the imperium was exercised by its holder, and finally was applied to that place as simply meaning it was in the ownership (or province) of Rome.

publicani   Tax-farmers, or contracted collectors of Rome's public revenues. Such contracts were let by the censors about every five years. *Publicani* formed themselves into companies, and were usually powerful senior knights.

Public Horse   See **Horse, Public**.

pulex   A flea.

Punic   Pertaining to Carthage and the Carthaginians. It derives from the original homeland of the Carthaginians—Phoenicia.

quaestor   The lowest rung on the senatorial *cursus honorum*. It was always an elected office, but until Sulla laid down during his dictatorship that in future the quaestorship would be the only way a man could enter the Senate, it was not necessary for a man to be quaestor in order to be a senator. Sulla increased the number of quaestors from perhaps twelve to twenty, and laid down that a man could not be quaestor until he was thirty years of age. The chief duties of a quaestor were fiscal. He might be (chosen by the lots) seconded to Treasury duty within Rome, or to collecting customs, port dues and rents elsewhere in Italy, or serve as the manager of a provincial governor's moneys. A man going to govern a province could ask for a quaestor by name. The quaestor's year in office began on the fifth day of December.

Quinctilis   Originally the fifth month when the Roman New Year had begun in March, it retained the name after January New Year made it the seventh month. We know it, of course, as July; so did the Romans—after the death of the great Julius.

Quiris   A Roman citizen.

Quirites   Roman citizens. The term was apparently reserved for civilians; it was not applied to soldiers.

Republic   The word was originally two words—*res publica*—meaning the things which constitute the people as a whole; that is, the government.

Rex Sacrorum   During the Republic, he was the second-ranking member of the College of Pontifices. A relic of the days of the kings of Rome, the Rex Sacrorum had to be a patrician, and was hedged around with as many taboos as the *flamen Dialis*.

Rhenus River The modern Rhine. In ancient times, it was the natural boundary between Germania and its German tribes, and Gallia and its Gallic tribes. So wide and deep and strong was it that it was considered impossible to bridge.

rhetoric The art of oratory, something the Greeks and Romans turned into a science. An orator was required to speak according to carefully laid-out rules and conventions which extended far beyond mere words; body language and movements were an intrinsic part of it. There were different styles of rhetoric; the Asianic was florid and dramatic, the Attic more restrained and intellectual in approach. It must always be remembered that the audience which gathered to listen to public oration—be it concerned with politics or with the law courts—was composed of connoisseurs of rhetoric. The men who watched and listened did so in an extremely critical way; they had learned all the rules and techniques themselves, and were not easy to please.

Rhodanus River The modern Rhône. Its large and fertile valley, inhabited by Celtic tribes of Gauls, came early under Roman influence; after the campaigns of Gnaeus Domitius Ahenobarbus in 122 and 121 B.C., the Rhône Valley up as far as the lands of the Aedui and Ambarri became a part of the Roman province of Transalpine Gaul—that is, of Gaul-across-the-Alps, or Further Gaul.

Roma The proper title in Latin of Rome. It is feminine.

Romulus and Remus The twin sons of Rhea Silvia, daughter of the King of Alba Longa, and the god Mars. Her uncle Amulius, who had usurped the throne, put the twins in a basket made of rushes and set it adrift on the Tiber (shades of Moses?). They were washed up beneath a fig tree at the base of the Palatine Mount, found by a she-wolf, and suckled by her in a cave nearby. Faustulus and his wife Acca Larentia rescued them and raised them to manhood. After deposing Amulius and putting their grandfather back on his throne, the twins founded a settlement on the Palatine. Once its walls were built and solemnly blessed, Remus jumped over them—apparently an act of horrific sacrilege. Romulus put him to death. Having no people to inhabit his Palatine town, Romulus then set out to find them, which he did by establishing an asylum in the depression between the two humps of the Capitol. This asylum attracted criminals and escaped slaves— which says something about the original Romans! However, he still had no women. These were obtained by tricking the Sabines of the Quirinal into bringing their women to a feast; Romulus and his desperadoes kidnapped them. Romulus ruled for a long time. Then one day he went hunting in the Goat Swamps of the Campus Martius and was caught in a terrible storm; when he didn't come home, it was believed he had been taken by the Gods and made immortal.

rostra   A *rostrum* (singular) was the reinforced oak beak of a war galley used to ram other ships. When in 338 B.C. the consul Gaius Maenius attacked the Volscian fleet in Antium Harbor, he defeated it completely. To mark the end of the Volsci as a rival power to Rome, Maenius removed the beaks of the ships he had sent to the bottom or captured and fixed them to the Forum wall of the speaker's platform, which was tucked into the side of the Well of the Comitia. Ever after, the speaker's platform was known as the rostra—the ships' beaks. Other victorious admirals followed Maenius's example, but when no more beaks could be put on the wall of the rostra, they were fixed to tall columns erected around the rostra.

Roxolani   A people inhabiting part of the modern Ukraine and Rumania, and a sept of the Sarmatae. Organized into tribes, they were horse people who tended to a nomadic way of life except where coastal Greek colonies of the sixth and fifth centuries B.C. impinged upon them sufficiently to initiate them into agriculture. All the peoples who lived around the Mediterranean despised them as barbarians, but after he conquered the lands around the Euxine Sea, King Mithridates VI used them as troops, mostly cavalry.

saepta   "The sheepfold." The word was plural, and referred to the wooden partitions which were used to transform the open space of the Campus Martius wherein the Centuries or tribes met to vote into a maze of corridors.

Salii Colleges of priests in service to Mars; the name meant "leaping dancers." There were twenty-four of them in two Colleges of twelve. They had to be patrician.

satrap The title given by the kings of Persia to their provincial or territorial governors. Alexander the Great seized upon the term and employed it, as did the later Arsacid kings of the Parthians and the kings of Armenia. The region administered by a satrap was called a satrapy.

Saturninus Lucius Appuleius Saturninus, tribune of the plebs in 103, 100 and 99 B.C. His early career was marred by an alleged grain swindle while he was quaestor of the grain supply at Ostia, and the slur remained with him throughout the rest of his life. During his first term as a tribune of the plebs he allied himself with Gaius Marius and succeeded in securing lands in Africa for resettlement of Marius's veteran troops. He also defined a new kind of treason, *maiestas minuta* or "little treason," and set up a special court to try cases of it. His second term as a tribune of the plebs in 100 B.C. was also in alliance with Marius, for whom he obtained more land for veterans from the German campaign. But eventually Saturninus became more of an embarrassment to Marius than a help, so Marius repudiated him publicly; Saturninus then turned against Marius.

Toward the end of 100 B.C. Saturninus began to woo the Head Count; there was a famine at the time, the Head Count were restless. He passed a grain law which he could not implement, as there was no grain to be had. When the elections were held for the tribunate of the plebs for 99 B.C., Saturninus ran again, successfully. Stirred by the famine and Saturninus's oratory, the Forum crowds became dangerous enough to force Marius and Scaurus Princeps Senatus into an alliance which resulted in the passing of the Senate's Ultimate Decree. Apprehended after the water supply to the Capitol was cut off, Saturninus and his friends were imprisoned in the Senate House until they could be tried. But before the trials could take place, they were killed by a rain of tiles from the Senate House roof.

All of Saturninus's laws were then annulled. It was said
ever after that Saturninus had aimed at becoming the King
of Rome. His daughter, Appuleia, was married to the patrician Marcus Aemilius Lepidus.

For a fuller narration of the career of Saturninus, see
the entry in the glossary of *The Grass Crown*.

Seleucid The adjective of lineage attached to the royal
house of Syria, whose sovereigns were descended from
Seleucus Nicator, one of Alexander the Great's companions, though not one of his known generals. After Alexander's death he cemented a kingdom which eventually
extended from Syria and Cilicia to Media and Babylonia,
and had two capitals, Antioch and Seleuceia-on-Tigris, and
two wives, the Macedonian Stratonice and the Bactrian
Apama. By the last century B.C the Kingdom of the Parthians had usurped the eastern lands, and Rome most of
Cilicia; the kingdom of the Seleucids dwindled to Syria
alone. Pompey then made Syria a Roman province, which
left the last of the Seleucids to occupy the throne of Com-
magene.

Senate Properly, *senatus*. Originally a patricians-only
body which first contained one hundred members and then
three hundred. Because of its antiquity, legal definition of
its rights, powers and duties was nonexistent. Membership
in the Senate was for life (unless a man was expelled by
the censors for inappropriate behavior or impoverishment),
which predisposed it to the oligarchical form it acquired.
Throughout its history its members fought strenuously to
preserve their pre-eminence in government. Until Sulla
prevented access to the Senate save by the quaestorship,
appointment was in the purlieu of the censors, though from
the middle Republic down the quaestorship if held before
admission to the Senate was soon followed by admission
to the Senate; the *lex Atinia* provided that tribunes of the
plebs should automatically enter the Senate upon election.
There was a means test of entirely unofficial nature; a senator was supposed to enjoy an income of a million sesterces.

Senators alone were entitled to wear the *latus clavus* on
their tunics; this was a broad purple stripe down the right

shoulder. They wore closed shoes of maroon leather and a ring which had originally been made of iron, but later came to be gold. Senatorial mourning consisted of wearing the knight's narrow stripe on the tunic. Only men who had held a curule magistracy wore a purple-bordered toga; ordinary senators wore plain white.

Meetings of the Senate had to be held in properly inaugurated premises; the Senate had its own *curia* or meeting-house, the Curia Hostilia, but was prone also to meet elsewhere at the whim of the man convening the meeting—presumably he always had well-founded reasons for choosing a venue other than the Senate House, such as a necessity to meet outside the *pomerium*. The ceremonies and meeting and feast on New Year's Day were always held in the temple of Jupiter Optimus Maximus. Sessions could go on only between sunrise and sunset and could not take place on days when any of the Assemblies met, though they were permissible on comitial days if no Assembly did meet.

Until Sulla reorganized this as he did so much else, the rigid hierarchy of who spoke in what turn had always placed the Princeps Senatus and consulars ahead of men already elected to office but not yet in office, whereas after Sulla consuls-elect and praetors-elect spoke ahead of these men; under both systems a patrician always preceded a plebeian of exactly equal rank in the speaking hierarchy. Not all members of the House were accorded the privilege of speaking. The *senatores pedarii* (I have used a British parliamentary term, backbenchers, to describe them, as they sat behind the men allowed to speak) could vote, but were not called upon in debate. No restrictions were placed upon the time limit or content of a man's speech, so filibustering was common. If an issue was unimportant or everyone was obviously in favor of it, voting might be by voice or a show of hands, but a formal vote took place by a division of the House, meaning that the senators left their stations and grouped themselves to either side of the curule dais according to their yea or nay, and were then physically counted. Always an advisory rather than a true legislating body, the Senate issued its *consulta* or decrees as requests to the various Assemblies. If the issue was serious, a quorum had to be present before a vote could be taken, though we do not know what precise number constituted a quorum. Certainly most meetings were not heavily attended, as there was no rule which said a man appointed to the Senate had to attend meetings, even on an irregular basis.

In some areas the Senate reigned supreme, despite its lack of legislating power: the *fiscus* was controlled by the Senate, as it controlled the Treasury; foreign affairs were left to the Senate; and the appointment of provincial governors, the regulation of provincial affairs, and the conduct of wars were left for the sole attention of the Senate.

senatus consultum See **consultum**.

senatus consultum de re publica defendenda The Senate's Ultimate Decree, so known until Cicero shortened its proper title to Senatus Consultum Ultimum. Dating from 121 B.C., when Gaius Gracchus resorted to violence to prevent the overthrow of his laws, the Ultimate Decree meant that in civil emergencies the Senate could override all other governmental bodies by passing it. This Ultimate Decree proclaimed the Senate's sovereignty and established what was, in effect, martial law. It was really a way to sidestep appointing a dictator.

Senatus Consultum Ultimum The name more usually given in this book's times to the *senatus consultum de re publica defendenda*. It was certainly used by Cicero, to whom I have attributed its genesis, though this is mere guesswork.

sestertius Plural, *sestertii,* more generally expressed in English as *sesterces*. Though the denarius was a more common coin in circulation than the sestertius, Roman accounting procedures were always expressed in sesterces. In Latin texts it is abbreviated as HS. A tiny silver coin weighing less than a gram (of silver, at any rate), the sestertius was worth a quarter of a denarius.

Sextilis Originally the sixth month when the Roman New Year had begun in March, it kept its name after January New Year made it the eighth month. We know it, of

course, as August; so too did the Romans—but not until
the reign of Augustus.

socius   Plural, *socii*. A *socius* was a man of a citizenship
having allied status with Rome.

Sol Indiges   One of the most ancient Italian gods, apparently (as the Sun) the husband of Tellus (the Earth).
Though little is known of his cult, he was apparently enormously reverenced. Oaths sworn by him were very serious
affairs.

spelt   A very fine, soft white flour used for making cakes,
never bread. It was ground from the variety of wheat now
known as *Triticum spelta* (emmer).

spina   The central dividing strip of a circus course or
arena.

Spinther   An actor in Roman theater famous for playing
second leads. To call upon his name was to deride the
efficacy of a person or deed.

stibium   The ancient version of mascara. A black anti-
mony-based powder soluble in water, *stibium* was used to
darken the brows and/or lashes, or to draw a line around
the perimeter of the eye. It would be interesting to know
just how recently a more benign substance than *stibium*
replaced it, but, alas, no work of reference tells me.

stips   A small payment for services rendered.

Stoic   An adherent of the school of philosophy founded
by the Phoenician Cypriot Zeno in the third century B.C.
Stoicism as a philosophical system of thought did not particularly appeal to the Romans. The basic tenet was concerned with nothing beyond virtue (strength of character)
and its opposite, weakness of character. Virtue was the
only good, weakness of character the only evil. Money,
pain, death, and the other things which plague Man were
not considered important, for the virtuous man is an essentially good man, and therefore by definition must be a
happy and contented man—even if impoverished, in perpetual pain, and under sentence of death. As with everything Greek they espoused, the Romans did not so much
modify this philosophy as evade its unpalatable concom-
itants by some very nice—if specious—reasoning.

strigilis   Sometimes Anglicized to strigil. It was a blunt, rather knifelike instrument with a curved blade, and was used to scrape sweat and dirt off the skin during a hot bath.

Subura   The poorest and most densely populated part of the city of Rome. It lay to the east of the Forum Romanum in the declivity between the Oppian spur of the Esquiline Mount and the Viminal Hill. Its people were notoriously polyglot and independent of mind; many Jews lived in the Subura, which at the time of Sulla contained Rome's only synagogue. Suetonius says Caesar the Dictator lived in the Subura.

sui iuris   In his own hand, or in control of his own destiny. As distinct from existing under the authority of a *paterfamilias* (q.v.) or other legal guardian.

Tace!   Plural, *tacete*. Shut up!

Tace inepte!   Shut up, you fool!

talent   This was the load a man could carry. Bullion and very large sums of money were expressed in talents, but the term was not confined to precious metals and money. In modern terms the talent weighed about 50 to 55 pounds (25 kilograms). A talent of gold weighed the same as a talent of silver, but was far more valuable, of course.

Taprobane   The island of Sri Lanka (Ceylon).

Tarpeian Rock   Its precise location is still hotly debated, but we do know that it was quite visible from the lower Forum Romanum, as people being thrown off it could be seen from the rostra. Presumably it was an overhang at the top of the Capitoline cliffs, but since the drop was not much more than 80 feet, the Tarpeian Rock must have been located directly over some sort of jagged outcrop— we have no evidence that anyone ever survived the fall. It was the traditional place of execution for Roman citizen traitors and murderers, who were either thrown from it or forced to jump from it. The tribunes of the plebs were particularly fond of threatening to throw obstructive senators from the Tarpeian Rock. I have located it on a line from the temple of Ops.

Tarquinius Superbus   Tarquin the Proud, the seventh and last King of Rome. He finished and dedicated the temple of Jupiter Optimus Maximus, but had more of a reputation as a warmaker than a builder. His accession to the throne was a lurid tale of murder and a woman (Tullia, daughter of King Servius Tullius), and his deposition was much the same kind of tale. An uprising of patricians led by Lucius Junius Brutus led to his flight from Rome, and the establishment of the Republic. Tarquin the Proud sought refuge with several local anti-Roman leaders in turn, and eventually died at Cumae. A curious story is told of how Tarquin the Proud finished his war against the city of Gabii: when asked what he wanted done with Gabii's prominent men, he said not a word; instead, he went into his garden, drew his sword, and lopped the head off every poppy taller than the rest; his son in Gabii interpreted the message correctly, and beheaded every Gabian man of outstanding merit. Few people today know the origins of the so-called Tall Poppy Syndrome, though the phrase is used metaphorically to describe the character assassination of men and women of superior ability or prominence.

tata The Latin diminutive for "father"—akin to our "daddy." I have, by the way, elected to use the almost universal "mama" as the diminutive for "mother," but the actual Latin was *mamma*.

terra incognita Unknown land.

tetrarch The chief of a fourth section of any state or territory. The three tribes of Galatia—Tolistobogii, Trocmi, and Volcae Tectosages—were each divided into four parts, and each of the four parts was headed by a *tetrarch*.

Tingitanian ape The Barbary ape, a macaque, terrestrial and tailless. Monkeys and primates were not common around the Mediterranean, but the macaque still found on Gibraltar was always present in North Africa.

tirocinium fori A youth's rhetorical and legal apprenticeship in the Forum.

toga The garment only a full citizen of Rome was entitled to wear. Made of lightweight wool, it had a peculiar shape (which is why the togate "Romans" in Hollywood movies never look right). After exhaustive and brilliant experimentation, Dr. Lillian Wilson of Johns Hopkins worked out a size and shape which produced a perfect-looking toga. To fit a man 5 feet 9 inches (175 centimeters) tall having a waist of 36 inches (89.5 centimeters), the toga was about 15 feet (4.6 meters) wide, and 7 feet 6 inches (2.25 meters) long. The length measurement is draped on the man's height axis and the much bigger width measurement is wrapped around him. However, the shape was far from being a simple rectangle! It looked like this:

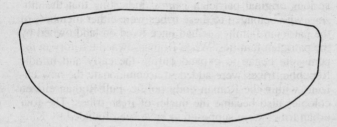

Unless the toga is cut as illustrated, it will absolutely refuse to drape the way it does on the togate men of the ancient statues. The Republican toga of the last century B.C. was very large (the size varied considerably during the thousand years it was the customary garb of the Roman). And a man draped in his toga could *not* have worn a loincloth or other undergarment!

toga candida The specially whitened toga worn by those seeking office as an elected magistrate. Its stark whiteness was achieved by bleaching the garment in the sun for many days, then working finely powdered chalk through it.

toga praetexta The purple-bordered toga of the curule magistrate. It continued to be worn by these men after their term in office was over. It was also the toga worn by children of both sexes.

togate The correct English-language term to describe a man clad in his toga.

toga trabea Cicero's "particolored toga." It was the striped toga of the augur, and very likely of the pontifex also. Like the *toga praetexta,* it had a purple border run-

ning all the way around it, but it was also striped in broad
bands of alternating red and purple down its length.

toga virilis The plain white toga of a Roman male. It
was also called the *toga alba* or the *toga pura*.

tribe *Tribus*. By the beginning of the Republic, *tribus* to
a Roman was not an ethnic grouping of his people, but a
political grouping of service only to the State. There were
thirty-five tribes altogether; thirty-one were rural, only four
urban. The sixteen really old tribes bore the names of the
various original patrician *gentes*, indicating that the citizens who belonged to these tribes were either members of
the patrician families or had once lived on land owned by
the patrician families. When Roman-owned territory in the
peninsula began to expand during the early and middle
Republic, tribes were added to accommodate the new citizens within the Roman body politic. Full Roman citizen
colonies also became the nuclei of fresh tribes. The four
urban tribes were supposed to have been founded by King
Servius Tullius, though they probably originated
somewhat later. The last tribe of the thirty-five was created
in 241 B.C. Every member of a tribe was entitled to register
one vote in a tribal Assembly, but his vote counted only
in helping to determine which way the tribe as a whole
voted, for a tribe delivered just one vote, that of the majority of its members. This meant that in no tribal Assembly could the huge number of citizens enrolled in the four
urban tribes sway the vote, as the urban tribes delivered
only four of the thirty-five ultimate votes. Members of
rural tribes were not disbarred from living in Rome, nor
were their progeny obliged to be enrolled in an urban tribe.
Most senators and knights of the First Class belonged to
rural tribes. It was a mark of distinction.

tribune, military Those on the general's staff who were
not elected tribunes of the soldiers but who ranked above
cadets and below legates were called military tribunes. If
the general was not a consul in office, military tribunes
might command legions. Otherwise they did staff duties
for the general. Military tribunes also served as cavalry
commanders, called prefects.

tribune of the plebs These magistrates came into being

early in the history of the Republic, when the Plebs was at complete loggerheads with the Patriciate. Elected by the tribal body of plebeians formed as the *concilium plebis* or *comitia plebis tributa* (the Plebeian Assembly), they took an oath to defend the lives and property of members of the Plebs, and to rescue a member of the Plebs from the clutches of a (patrician in those days) magistrate. By 450 B.C. there were ten tribunes of the plebs. A *lex Atinia de tribunis plebis in senatum legendis* in 149 B.C. provided that a man elected to the tribunate of the plebs automatically entered the Senate. Because they were not elected by the People (that is, by the patricians as well as by the plebeians), they had no power under Rome's unwritten constitution and were not magistrates in the same way as tribunes of the soldiers, quaestors, curule aediles, praetors, consuls, and censors; their magistracies were of the Plebs and their power in office resided in the oath the whole Plebs took to defend the sacrosanctity—the inviolability— of its elected tribunes. The power of the office also lay in the right of its officers to interpose a veto against almost any aspect of government: a tribune of the plebs could veto the actions or laws of his nine fellow tribunes, or any—or all!—other magistrates, including consuls and censors; he could veto the holding of an election; he could veto the passing of any law; and he could veto any decrees of the Senate, even those dealing with war and foreign affairs. Only a dictator (and perhaps an *interrex*) was not subject to the tribunician veto. Within his own Plebeian Assembly, the tribune of the plebs could even exercise the death penalty if his right to proceed about his duties was denied him.

The tribune of the plebs had no imperium, and the authority vested in the office did not extend beyond the first milestone outside the city of Rome. Custom dictated that a man should serve only one term as a tribune of the plebs, but Gaius Gracchus put an end to that; even so, it was not usual for a man to stand more than once. As the real power of the office was vested in negative action—the veto (it was called *intercessio*)—tribunician contribution to government tended to be more obstructive than constructive.

The conservative elements in the Senate loathed the tribunes of the plebs, though they always employed a few.

The College of Tribunes of the Plebs entered office on
the tenth day of December each year, and had its headquarters in the Basilica Porcia. Sulla as Dictator in 81 B.C.
stripped the tribunate of the plebs of all its powers save
the right to rescue a member of the Plebs from the clutches
of a magistrate, but the consuls Pompey and Crassus restored all the powers of the office in 70 B.C. It was too
important to do without. See also **plebeian.**

tribune of the soldiers Two dozen young men aged between twenty-five and twenty-nine years of age were
elected each year by the Assembly of the People to serve
as the *tribuni militum,* or tribunes of the soldiers. They
were true magistrates, the only ones too young to belong
to the Senate, and were the governmental representatives
of the consuls' legions (the four legions which belonged
to the consuls in office). Six tribunes of the soldiers were
allocated to each of the four legions, and normally commanded them. The command was shared in such a way
that there was always a tribune of the soldiers on duty as
commander, but apparently one of the six (probably by lot
or by his number of votes) was senior to the others.

tribuni aerarii Singular, *tribunus aerarius.* See **knights.**

triclinium The dining room. See illustration on facing
page. For additional information, see the glossary of any
of my earlier Roman books.

troglodytes In ancient times, people who lived not so
much in caves as in dwellings they carved out of soft
rocks. The Egyptian side of the Sinus Arabicus (now the
Red Sea) was reputed to have troglodytes, and the soft
tufa stone of the Cappadocian gorges provided homes for
the local peoples from times before recorded history.

Tullus Hostilius The third King of Rome, and a very
shadowy figure. A warlike man, he attacked, captured, and
destroyed Alba Longa, then brought its people into Rome
and added them to the populace; Alba Longa's ruling class
became a part of Rome's patriciate. Tullus Hostilius also
built the Senate House, called the Curia Hostilia in his
honor.

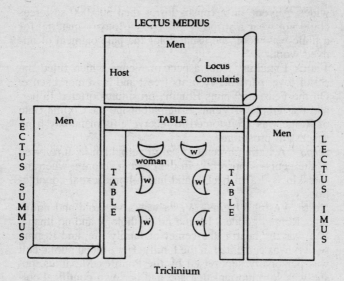

LECTUS MEDIUS

Men

Host

Locus
Consularis

LECTUS SUMMUS

Men

TABLE

Men

LECTUS IMUS

TABLE

woman

w

TABLE

w

w

w

w

Triclinium

tunic The ubiquitous article of clothing for all the ancient Mediterranean peoples, including the Greeks and the
Romans; trousers were considered the garb of a barbarian.
A Roman tunic tended to be rather loose and shapeless,
made without darts to give it a waisted look; it covered
the body from the shoulders and upper arms to the knees.
Sleeves were probably set in (the ancients knew how to
sew, cut cloth, and make clothing comfortable), and
sometimes long. The tunic was usually belted with a cord
or with buckled leather, and the Romans wore theirs
longer at the front than at the back by about 3 inches.
Upper-class Roman men were probably togate if outside
the doors of their own homes, but there is little doubt that
men of the lower classes wore their togas only on special
occasions, such as the games or elections. If the weather
was wet, a cloak of some kind was preferred to a toga.
The knight wore a narrow purple stripe down the right
(bared to show the tunic) shoulder called the *angustus clavus;* the senator's purple stripe, the *latus clavus,* was

wider. Anyone on a census lower than 300,000 sesterces
could not wear a stripe at all. The customary material for
a tunic was wool, the usual color the pale oatmeal of un-
dyed wool.

Venus Erucina That aspect of Venus which ruled the
act of love, particularly in its freest and least moral sense.
On the Feast of Venus Erucina prostitutes offered to her,
and the temple of Venus Erucina outside the Colline Gate
of Rome was accustomed to receive gifts of money from
successful prostitutes.

verpa A Latin obscenity used in verbal abuse. It referred
to the penis—apparently in the erect state only, when the
foreskin is drawn back—and had a homosexual connota-
tion.

Vesta, Vestal Virgins Vesta was a very old and numi-
nous Roman goddess having no mythology and no image.
She was the hearth, the center of family life, and Roman
society was cemented in the family. Her official public cult
was personally supervised by the Pontifex Maximus, but
she was so important that she had her own pontifical college, the six Vestal Virgins. The Vestal Virgin was in-
ducted at about seven or eight years of age, took vows of
complete chastity, and served for thirty years, after which
she was released from her vows and sent back into the
general community still of an age to bear children. Few
retired Vestals ever did marry; it was thought unlucky to
do so. The chastity of the Vestal Virgins was Rome's public luck: a chaste college was favored by Fortune. When
a Vestal was accused of unchastity she was formally
brought to trial in a specially convened court; her alleged
lover or lovers were tried in a separate court. If convicted,
she was cast into an underground chamber dug for the
purpose; it was sealed over, and she was left there to die.
In Republican times the Vestal Virgins shared the same
residence as the Pontifex Maximus, though sequestered
from him and his family. The House (Aedes)—it was not
an inaugurated temple—of Vesta was near this house, and
was small, round, and very old. It was adjacent to the
Regia of the Pontifex Maximus and to the well of Juturna,
which supplied the Vestals with water they had to draw

from the well each day in person; by the late Republic this ritual was a ritual only. A fire burned permanently inside Vesta's house to symbolize the hearth; it was tended by the Vestals, and could not be allowed to go out for any reason.

via A main thoroughfare or highway.

vicus A good-sized street.

vilicus An overseer. Used in this book to describe the custodian of a crossroads college.

vir militaris See **Military Man**.

voting Roman voting was timocratic in that the power of the vote was powerfully influenced by economic status, and in that voting was not "one man, one vote" style. Whether an individual was voting in the Centuries or in the tribes, his own personal vote could influence only the verdict of the Century or tribe in which he polled. Election outcomes were determined by the number of Centuriate or tribal votes going a particular way: thus in the Centuries of the First Class there were only ninety-one votes all told, the number of Centuries the First Class contained, and in the tribal Assemblies only thirty-five votes all told, the number of tribes. Juridical voting was different. A juror's vote did have a direct bearing on the outcome of a trial, as the jury was supposed to have an odd number of men comprising it and the decision was a majority one, not a unanimous one. If for some reason the jury was even in number and the vote was tied, the verdict had to be adjudged as for acquittal. Jury voting was timocratic also, however, in that a man without high economic status had no chance to sit on a jury.

Zeno The Greek who founded Stoic philosophy.